A Cosmic Legacy: From Earth to the Stars

Author – Matthew J. Opdyke
Publisher – Matthew J. Opdyke
Copyright © Matthew J. Opdyke, 2019, 2022
All Rights Reserved
Paperback Edition
ISBN – 978-1-7333131-1-7
Library of Congress Control Number:
2019909638

Disclaimers

This is a work of science fiction and utopian fantasy. The names, characters, businesses, places, incidents, locales, and events are either the products of the author's imagination or used in a fictitious way and with the utmost of respect toward all parties.

Reading this text and enjoying it may take you on a journey that is enjoyable while increasing your reading comprehension level as well as your philosophical, emotional, intuitive, and creative literacy. If there are any blatant errors or constructive suggestions, please advise the author through email, at:

mjopublications@gmail.com

Table of Contents

Preface by Author

With the joys of being a new author in the field of writing, I've taken the time over the last year to proof and reproof my published books many times over. I'm sure I'll find more to improve as time goes by, but my hope is that you'll enjoy the overall message in the *Pathway to the Stars* series, now combined in this text. Now, *A Cosmic Legacy: From Earth to the Stars*, will allow us to learn of a wonderful journey ultimately made possible by a young leader of leaders, named Eliza Williams.

In the words of a friend, *"She leads a bold innovative political and technological vision."*

Eliza grows her organization alongside many allies, with Yesha Alevtina and James Cooper close at her side, and we meet many more intriguing characters that are essential to this journey from Earth and into the Solar System. Eliza plans all with hopes of traveling throughout our Galaxy and eventually throughout the Universe.

In this fictional effort, inspired by science fiction books, space operas, and personal fantasies, I the author, will attempt to inspire and provide broad insights on many sciences in an effort to help everyone worldwide to reach a moment in life where our energies can be directed toward the kind of pursuits that will allow humanity to rise and bring a legacy to many civilizations throughout the Universe with a goal of preserving the Universe itself.

I was lucky enough to breathe life into amazing innovations, environments, and characters with genius minds, philosophical depth, and creative spirits, so I hope you are fortunate enough to enjoy their journeys!

Very Respectfully,

Matthew J. Opdyke
info@mjopublications.com
https://www.mjopublications.com
https://smile.amazon.com/author/matthewopdyke

Epigraph

"Heal, don't harm. Yet, be strong with clearness of mind, be very capable, and be properly prepared if healing does not work and as such, if lives are at risk, do what needs to be done to protect life, longevity, and an environment conducive to innovation and preservation of a noble and mighty legacy."

~ Vesha Celeste

"There is more strength in gentleness, more bravery in kindness, and more intellect and promise in studies and innovations founded from intent for well-being, an increase in the quality of life and the tenants espoused by the UP's Universal Ethics, founded by none other than my esteemed running mate, Eliza Williams, than by any others means."

~ Yesha Alevtina

"Nature and humanity can be amazing, but likewise, it can be brutal. Brutality, as far too many know it, is unnecessary if we consider and implement one thing, innovation with purpose—a good purpose is brutality's ideal replacement, and it comes minus unnecessary misery. It's starting to become clear to me now what it is that we can do and how we can do it."

- Eliza Williams

"Brutality has never been strength, it has always been myopia and cowardice, it has never led to lasting success and never will, it has always been a failure to raise the bar for humanity, and it has never given us the seeds of hope, because brutality is akin to uncontrolled chaos and as a result it is a failure to give humanity a legacy worthy of preserving."

~ Yesha Alevtina

"It's amazing how much the Earth needs to do. On the one hand, the things it does could result in the death of so many, but in so many ironic ways, in the very same instance and system of processes, it also engages in that which allows for life to be possible. Without these processes, life on Earth would cease to exist."

- Eliza Williams

"So long as we go forward with the well-being of others as well as ourselves in mind, we'll create a legacy that can be and will be worthy of preservation indefinitely."

~ Eliza Williams

"The young and innocent, the kind and those that care should never know sorrows so deep as those they have known through centuries of mistreatment, inherited disease, or an environment that breaks them down."

- Eliza Williams

Chapter 01: A Memorial

Database Moon Archive, Celestial-Sol Entry Date: 2018 December 25. The following is an excerpt from a private speech and presentation about Vesha Celeste preceding implementation of a new advancement inside Pathway's covert campus. Database Moon Archive input made by Yesha Alevtina, President of Pathway Industries, from 2015-2022.

"Notwithstanding her dedication to her craft, Vesha Celeste loved, taught, mentored, and raised her children in an enriching environment. She nurtured them until they, just as she, expressed their own genius and doctoral interests. Throughout her life there seemed to be beautiful dreams filled with amazing journeys, dreams that Vesha had hoped would eventually spring into reality. In the real world, she maintained firm footing in topics she found intriguing and honorable. She raised her children to demonstrate their beauty of expertise so that they could leave behind them a history replete with their own legacies. She wrote books for the masses about galaxies, our Universe, and dark matter. She wrote to her grandchildren about how their grandmother was an astronomer and a dreamer. What hadn't dawned on her was the fact that she had so much more potential than she had ever realized in the almost nine decades that she lived. Whether she had untold potential or had reached that state of self-actualization, her contributions were more than could be asked of anyone. Vesha shared her love of the Universe with many. She wrote to edify not only those closest to her but people all over the world. She wrote to enlighten and help us to understand and gain an interest in the many wonders yet to be found and understood throughout our grand Universe. She inspired many to pursue their dreams and to do so with purpose in their lives while living with confidence. She taught people to never shy away from the truth as evidenced in science, or from faith as this too had tempered her passions in life. No matter her journeys, her compassion for others continuously grew."

Yesha Alevtina, President of Pathway, was sharing her thoughts regarding her dear friend, Vesha. In so doing, she stood proudly deliberating before those in attendance at the Pathway Convention Center, two years after her passing. Yesha continued.

"It was the evening of December 25th, 2016, when Vesha's spirit left this world, but many visions stood before her, yet to be realized. Some of those dreams will begin today, and some will not be recognized for many years to come. Soon we will watch as a miracle of genius occurs and moves the blessings of the sands of time to a reality allowing us to connect to and save even more lives.

"Much has been said, and much may yet be told regarding her work and her journey. I, Yesha, am merely a young friend who loves her dearly. As I relay her story, I am doing so with the advantages of neuroscience and the ability to see what many may not. Vesha's never-ending struggle for education, her clarity about understanding our Universe, and her tenacity to thrive in a professional field despite being turned away in her youth are examples of her resilience. Even in her later years, due to our shared and unfortunate mortality, she was denied the opportunity of becoming a Nobel Laureate. Her vast impact on science and each one of us will not go unnoticed by any of us here today. She was inspiring to so many, including to myself. She is a testament that we should never betray humanity by silencing more than half of our human potential. We should never dare to silence anyone for that matter. We reveal our purpose and our character with the love emanating from our words and resultant actions. We should never find ourselves dismissing the staggering breadth of our shared mental capacity, nor should we alienate so many great individuals who would otherwise be extraordinary, if given the opportunity to fully blossom. This will be our opportunity to grant a fuller potential that will bless each of our lives in remarkable ways.

"Vesha was dedicated to her craft while respecting her personal beliefs. She balanced her respect for the truths found in science and her love of her children and grandchildren. Her virtues drew me in to honor her within the story I will share with each of you. I will share with you how a series of dynamic events has brought us all where we are now. Perhaps one day this story will be shared with many generations on many planets throughout the Universe and beyond. This journey and how it began may take us on an enjoyable and a promising pathway to the stars. With enough hope, vision, and action we will enjoy many potentially amazing voyages throughout the cosmos. Today, I will, in the most respectful way, cast Vesha in the favorable light she deserves. This hard-to-believe perspective was recorded from her mind during the last hour before she passed.

"Filled with fantasy and speculation to some who come upon this story in a different reality, you know now that without her we would not be where we are today. Today we are on the precipice of human history, longevity sciences, and readying to span the cosmos.

"Please journey with me on this presentation of her life, beginning just two years prior."

The Ebb of Life

It was late in the evening of December 25, 2016. After keying up music from Gabriel Yared's score for the movie, "Message in a Bottle," Vesha fluffed her pillow. She yearned to meet the angel who had accompanied her during her dreams throughout life. As she and her dream angel healed hearts and minds, they forged the bond of understanding between many, no matter where they went. Vesha turned the covers to lay propped up on her bed and drifted to thoughts of the beautiful day spent with her family. Having gazed upon photos of her daughter, Jillian Yenn, and her husband, Ralston Rayna, she thought of each of her family members while placing her smartphone on her dresser.

She contemplated on her own life and how, from her perspective, the time had been pretty good to her. As she did, Vesha felt overwhelmed by the beauty and wonder of it all. Vesha's final moments would pass soon, she knew that. Soon, she would embrace a sweet new reality. Perhaps this time she would journey with her life's fanciful dream angel, but first, she felt the need to think of her past and present, a habit she picked up from a much younger, but dear friend when she first talked about it twenty-two years ago. When Vesha would reflect on her experiences, she would consider her real-life happenings, what she could learn or appreciate from them, and then ponder upon her visions, before she would submit to the future. It had been a couple of prolonged and somewhat challenging years since her lovely daughter, Jillian, had passed away. Several years before Jillian's passing, her honorable, knowledgeable, supporting, and loving husband, Ralston, had gone on his journey to the afterlife as well.

"*Oh, how I miss them both.*" She paused.

"I wish they were here now," she thought as she felt her emotions loom and swell.

"Perhaps there will be plenty of time for exploration and discovery with those I love in the next part of my reality. Perhaps there is more to all that we know than we understand now. Yes, we're only beginning to comprehend the complexity of it all. There is certainly room for a fuller understanding of our Universe. It would be nice to hold on to this reality and find a day we can share a heartwarming existence with other civilizations throughout the cosmos. We'll see..." Vesha certainly had a hope of something more significant.

Pondering upon that which brought her peace of mind, Vesha felt comfortable with the contributions she had made to the world. She had brought clarity to the understanding of dark matter achievements in science, but she was more intrigued by the delightful people who had been a unique part of her life. No matter her grasp of the seemingly sane, she admired this beautiful angel who graced each stage of her life and who glowed with iridescent colors imperceptible to many. She had been there in benevolence within her dreams throughout her eighty-eight years in her own unique, somewhat extraordinary and sometimes normal-seeming, and yet unusual journey. She had met many brilliant people. Still, she wished she could reach many more, but life as she understood it came with a beginning and an end. Her two dear and young friends, Eliza and Yesha, had assured her that science within Pathway Industries had come with an opportunity to continue on. She could continue life in a healed and optimized state, as an immortal. Knowing those truths, she decided to lend herself to science and let them do their best, but only as she went to her rest first, as her God had planned. If her God saw fit to bring her back to this mortal realm, she would accept that.

A night-light had been installed, so when she looked up at her ceiling, a giant mural of the Andromeda Galaxy lay above her within her field of view. It seemed to glow after she reached behind her nightstand to turn the light switch to the off position. Again, she repositioned herself, this time settling on her back to lay to rest. As she put her head on her pillow, she sighed.

She had taken residency within the Princeton Assisted Living Facility, due to suffering from various stages of dementia. Luckily, the facility and her family gifted her with the ability to look up at the Andromeda Galaxy mural on her ceiling each night. Doing so brought her a sense of normalcy. Vesha marveled at the blessings of her own life with pause and gratitude. She embraced the rich complexities of love and reflected upon the miracles of experience. She contemplated upon her pursuits of happiness and the gifts her faith had given her as it tempered her fervor toward the complexities of science. She felt as though truth lay somewhere within both, or quite possibly between the two. Perhaps science and faith were merely portions of the truth. Maybe the answers to everything were scattered and hidden in places yet to be discovered.

The tug of the Universe beckoned.

She began to drift and think about the intricate details of her life – this day had been perfect. The visit had gone as planned; the weather outside had been clear; the evening had been perfect for viewing the nighttime sky. Quite warm for winter, it had been 49° Fahrenheit and had turned into an evening of delight shared with clear skies, a very slight crescent Moon, and lovely company. With one last gaze of the Universe and one final and fascinating view of the stars, nebula, and galaxies using her Orion SkyQuest XT10 Classic Dobsonian Telescope, installed on the balcony outside the sliding door of her living quarters, she found herself endlessly impressed as she scanned in the directions of Cassiopeia, Orion, and back to Andromeda. It had been given to Vesha for her eighty-fifth birthday by her daughter, who had discovered a month after Vesha's birthday that she had terminal cancer, and sadly passed away just six months later. Enjoying this gift from her sweet and thoughtful daughter, Vesha knew there was yet so much for humanity to understand, and so much further that civilization could go. *"Maybe she is flying in Heaven with my dream angel. Maybe she is with Ralston, playing a game of golf in some other Universe."*

Returning to what she knew was reality and contemplating the mechanics of such a fine and modern instrument, Vesha had used many powerful telescopes before, observed deep into the Universe, and made many scientific journal entries, but this one was special, it was not only a gift from Jillian, but it had demonstrated to her how far science had advanced. In her younger days, it took buildings the size of a home to see what she could see with this small telescope, just about as tall as she, with its capabilities—abilities that were similar to those she had found in professional observatories from her younger years. She was glad that now this was available to so many young and aspiring astronomers today. *"Maybe they will develop something that can be shared with the public that will afford everyone the opportunity to see with more clarity and detail the planets of our Galaxy, and within the galaxies just this side of the cosmic microwave background. Perhaps, they'll be able to derive the full complexity of our Universe, someday."*

Vesha had made an effort to stargaze every clear night, since the doctors had told her that due to her condition, stargazing would help her to stay grounded, triggering memories of critical experiences and influential people and ideas in her life.

Family and friends had visited Vesha where she was staying for the Christmas and Hanukkah holiday festivities in Princeton, New Jersey. Missing among those that attended were her daughter and husband; for them, the beautiful flicker of light had faded away—gone the way of the wind leaving behind them the wispy smoke of distant memories and unforgettable greatness of their lives. Her children, Daniel, Chris, and Avery, her five grandchildren, including Jillian's daughter, Lara, and her great-granddaughter had gathered with her friends, Eliza, Yesha, Najem, Jasmine, James, Amber, and Erin to celebrate the festivities together and this visit had been one of the most wonderfully charming parts of the season. Despite minor frustrations and lapses in memory, Vesha recalled quite pleasantly the holiday greetings exchanged, the stories told, and the smiles shared. To her, life had been lived to its fullest, and she felt that her pursuit of happiness had been blessed with a pleasant bookend; this was home. Her family had sung songs, they had exchanged gifts, and everyone had reminisced upon life's adventurous journeys and fondest memories—her domicile was still decorated for both Christmas and Hanukkah, and the scent of pine, holiday spices, and the smoke of blown out candles lingered in the air. Vesha had given and received goodbye hugs and kisses from those who she felt closest to throughout life.

Her Early Days

As Vesha Celeste continued to contemplate, she began to find herself drifting away from the affairs of the day to the very beginning of her life. Her Father, Lukas, had emigrated from Lithuania to the United States and had changed his last name from Petrauskas to Celeste more than a century ago. Life in that part of the world was difficult and still ravaged by the existence of various civil wars. Her Mother, born Irena Cara, had been an American immigrant from what is now known as Moldova, in the early 1900s, since antisemitism was on the rise in that region, with stories of murders within the newspapers of the day, and all-too-often. Lukas and Irena were both Jewish immigrants in those early days and despite all, they shared a fascination for science. As life took its course, they both found each other and fell in love in Philadelphia while working together at Bell Telephone, until their marriage shortly after.

Her father continued to work at Bell as an electrical engineer, yet because of specific workplace rules that existed in the US during those days, only one family member could work there at a time. Luckily, with the Celeste's first child on her way, Irena did her best to prepare for their newborn, and had more time to do so with reduced stress. Vesha's older sister, Evelina Celeste, came into this world first, and just as it would be for Vesha in the years that followed, Evelina was raised well. Later on, in Evelina's life, she rose above the social and gender politics of the day and became an Administrative Judge for the US Department of Defense—an honor deserving of its own story.

On a lovely day in Philadelphia, Pennsylvania, July 23, in the year of 1928, Vesha Florence Celeste came into this world. Her parents had shared with her many times how beautiful that summer day was, which had made the experience an unforgettably pleasant memory—they never failed to remind Vesha of how adorable she was as a little baby girl.

"You were beautiful, smiling, and a saint if I ever saw one," both of her parents told her, as she grew older and was filled with questions.

While she couldn't remember more than vicarious details about that experience, she wistfully and fleetingly recalled the memories of her journeys with her beautiful dream angel in those younger years, as well as the Celeste's move to Washington, DC, when she was ten years old.

Washington, DC in 1938 had an air of hope; it was teaming with genius minds, the arts and entertainment industries were in full bloom, and Vesha had become entranced by astronomy. The home base of a bustling and free country, full of vim and vigor, had added to how much it was that she fancied the breaks she would take from her studies during each day. During these breaks she would contemplate her dreams of the stars and ponder on what was out there so far away and just beyond our abilities to see. Vesha had looked forward to each night for years and became ensconced for hours merely gazing upon the stars as they sped by. Her mother would catch her doing so quite routinely, but she knew she did it to stay awake while doing her studies.

Nevertheless, Mrs. Celeste would tell Vesha, "Don't stay up all night hanging out by the window."

When Vesha was done with her lessons, she would rest and go on more journeys of love and honor, with her friend of deep-thought, an angel she named Sky. No matter her dreams, she kept them private and carried herself embracing the reality of each day.

Her father, Lukas, continued to cultivate his daughter's love for the cosmos and began to take her to science and astronomy conventions regularly. These conventions, in the heart of DC, was where she, in 1940 and only thirteen years old, met Najem Grace for the first time, who was fifteen years old. Najem had moved to Baltimore with her family, and shortly thereafter she wasted no time and put together another one of her many astronomy clubs. If there were one or two people who frequented her clubs, that was fine with Najem; it was nice to be in the company of other curious minds.

When they first met each other, Vesha's new friend, Najem, had traveled to Washington, DC to enjoy some of the university conventions. The world of physics in all its forms was expanding and understanding how the mechanisms that governed the Universe and how it worked was exciting to an increasing segment of society, as well as to both of these two young and beautiful friends.

Since Vesha and Najem were both young ladies, the two youngest members of the audience, and had so much in common they quickly warmed up to each other's love of all things related to space and the future and became pen-pals for life. Together, they spent many hours with each other every couple of weeks for more than two years during their visits, talking about the stars and how to improve the quality of life. After Najem finished high school, however, they rarely had an opportunity to see each other. Even though life kept them apart, they still wrote letters and eagerly sent them in the mail. They looked forward to their correspondence with each other, hoped for return letters, and were never disappointed.

Two years after moving to DC, in 1942, Mr. Celeste, who had mentored, taught, and inspired her—proud of her love of science, helped her build her first telescope to peer out into the heavens. Vesha wasted no time that first and glorious evening, taking her telescope out to the small backyard and peering up into the sky. *"Fitting,"* she thought, *"no wonder I named my angel, Sky."* She pondered a moment and then continued to gaze into the sky again.

Vesha was tickled silly, since the night was clear. She happened to peer north to see Cassiopeia and Andromeda, with Sagittarius in view to the southeast, with its bright glow of stars climbing up high and into the sky at a sixty-degree angle, where it met the Orion Spur and the Perseus Arm. She contemplated the position of the Earth's revolution around the Sun, compared to our point and place within our newly-understood galaxy, the Milky Way, and knew that by looking through the bright arms of stars, she was looking into the galactic disc. Looking over at the teapot asterism of Sagittarius also gave her reference to the galactic north and south poles. She enjoyed having clarity on those details, and she had her parents, Najem, one schoolteacher, and Sky to thank for it.

While her home environment was supportive, a couple of years later, as high school was reaching its finality for Vesha, life became somewhat dynamic. Her parents had reinforced her efforts throughout her life. However, when her professors asked what she planned to do following her graduation, giving an honest and sincere answer about her interest in studying science, she was rebuked. She remembered how she had confided with one professor about her plans to study astronomy in college and how she had planned on pursuing that as a profession. Her science teacher, despite hearing as she confidently shared her hopes, her intentions, and her dreams, and having full knowledge of her incredible work ethic, as well as the dedication demonstrated through her studies, scholastics, and award-winning academic achievements, dismissively responded, "You'll do alright so long as you stay away from science."

She remembered that day how she came home a bit taken back, a bit perplexed, and a little out of sorts. *"Was this how things were going to be for women in science? Would more than half our human potential be silenced in the name of societal norms?"* she thought.

Both of her parents picked up on her emotional cues and asked her what had happened, listened to her, and then lovingly reminded her that she could do anything that she put her mind to. "You should never let another individual destroy your hopes, your dreams, or your resolve," her mother told her. Her parents encouraged her to write to her friend, Najem, who was studying astronomy in college at the time, and let her know what had happened. Perhaps Vesha wasn't alone in the duplicities of society. She had talked to her parents during many dinner meals about how Najem had struggled to be able to study science as a young woman too. Mr. and Mrs. Celeste shared with Vesha that they felt it honorable from their point of view that she desired to continue putting her hopes in the starry night sky, and that she should not allow her spirits to dampen.

Her parents loved and supported Vesha through her studies because that was her wish, that was what she wanted to do, that was what inspired her, and they trusted and loved her decisions for her future, no matter her choices. Vesha had demonstrated and proved to them on many occasions and for many years that she could excel in and would be an asset to the science community or any field of study that she put her mind to.

That night, before falling asleep, she had thought about what her parents had said and had appreciated them for their support, their kindness, and their love. As she drifted into her dreams, there was Sky, her dream angel, heralding her along, engaging in heroic acts of daring-do, and letting her know, *"Your dreams are yours to pursue, they are beautiful, and you can't let anyone slow you down."*

As her years in high school drew to a close, Lukas and Irena continued to mentor Vesha on setting personal goals, developing her own code of ethics, and being driven from within by her own guiding standards. They had motivated her intrigues for many years, by providing an enriching environment that would cause her curiosity in the sciences to blossom; she had been in a setting that had balanced her spiritual life with her ambitions for a career, which in turn fomented her dedication toward understanding the beauty and complexities of her Universe. Her father had reminded her that when he signed her up for membership in that advanced science program for youth almost four years ago, the place where she had met Najem, she would come home and share the exciting developments and discoveries as revealed by the professors, the faculty, and the scientists. He assured her that he had taken her to these meetings regularly, because he had great hope in her and in her potential for a positive impact on life, on science, and on society. He told her that she would burn bright no matter the challenge.

The struggles for equality for women in science were rampant in the US in those days, as were similar unfortunate circumstances throughout the world. In addition to the bustle of society that brought her joy through her younger years, the world was significantly impacted by surrounding droughts and economic shortfalls. Adding to that era, were the events of the 1930s and the 1940s—the tragedies and the toll of the effects of the great depression, wars, and the toxicity prevalent in the minds of those who sought to harm others for no reason that could suitably justify the sacrifice of their lives. Notwithstanding, Vesha focused her energies on meaningful conquests by scraping together beat up old materials from 19th-century telescopes—much like her friend, Najem would have done, and occupy her time repairing them. She would challenge herself to defy her school counselors by focusing on astronomy with that field of study driving her sites in college.

Vesha graduated from high school in 1944 and never wavered in her pursuit of a career in science; *"No one can take my dreams away if I stay focused and dedicated,"* she recalled.

Love & Intellect

Through her studies, Vesha had built a collection of many favorite contemporaries. One of her favorites, Maria Mitchell, had been the first female astronomy professor in US history at Vassar College for Women, in 1865. Maria had also been the first American to be recognized worldwide as an astronomer. This brazen and profoundly-smart lady had, following years of research and dedication, discovered a comet in the nighttime skies above the US in the 1800s. Vesha had chosen to attend this college, and she too spent many hours combing the cosmos with her shrewd telescope at home, as well as the more robust telescopes on campus. The comparisons ran thick, and it inspired Vesha. As the only astronomy major in her graduating class, she persisted in her studies as she combed over physics, math, and her other core curriculum. A deeper understanding of her lessons and perseverance led to Vesha's graduation with an induction to Phi Beta Kappa—the oldest-known honor society for the liberal arts and sciences in the US.

After Vassar, Vesha was in full spirits and anxiously applied for the graduate astrophysics program at Princeton University. Again, she found controversy. Contemplating on the state of the day, Vesha opined.

"With the expectations that existed, I knew how things were, and I was aware of the social norms, but I valued astronomy, my goals, and an excellent education—my parents raised me well by supporting me and my life-enriching choices. Still, it's just as important to stay strong and step forward with hope and might," Vesha recalled, speaking to her angel, named Sky, in a quiet conversation within her mind.

Princeton, which happened to be one of the first colleges of the original thirteen colonies of the US, and was now a university, did not send her a graduate catalog in time for enrollment that year and they wouldn't mail one soon enough or any time within the foreseeable future.

"They were caught up in the sentiments and cultural norms of the time, but fortunately many years later they came around," she recalled and graciously forgave them. At that time in history, Princeton women were not allowed in science programs, at least not until 1975.

"Just as well," she thought to herself, as she reflected on the events that ensued shortly after. The first day, following her bus ride to campus, after being accepted to study at Cornell University, in Ithaca, NY, something wonderful happened. "Good things came because of it," Vesha pondered. She met her life-long love, Ralston Rayna.

Ralston had been sent to Cornell by the United States Navy to study chemical engineering. Vesha had enrolled there as well in both physics and astrophysics. She recalled her discussions later on, following her studies through the days, the weeks, and the months that followed, with him, and how they shared an affinity for science.

To Vesha, their discussions were intriguing and surprising. She recalled what Ralston said on their first trip to the local park, following a very philosophical conversation, "Perhaps the efforts of great scientists to understand humanity and the Universe will help solve more problems that plague the well-being of so many throughout the world than the currently accepted status quo."

As it would happen for any individual with at least a tender attachment to their personal nature, young love was not uncommon in those days. Vesha remembered how, not too long after she and Ralston met, their sentiments toward each other had brewed to an intense boil, "It was the good kind of boiling, Sky, you know, the kind that when making confectionary treats for fun, sweet caramel and chocolatey desserts are the result. Yes, it was quite the blessing meeting Ralston."

Vesha even recalled blissfully how little time it took for them to confide in each other the reality of how attracted they were and for more reasons than physical appeal alone. Although, there was that too.

Having grown into a lovely young lady with dark hair, kind blue eyes, and a cheerful and intellectual disposition, she was soon acutely aware that hers was also a disposition very striking to Ralston, "He let me know in so many ways throughout my life how much joy I brought to him. His feelings were reciprocated in kind since he brought so much joy to my life; I saw in him a tall, handsome, charismatic, and very considerate and knowledgeable young man."

Reminiscing back a pace to the first day she met Ralston on her way to her classes with a wave and a smile, and then again, shortly after her first day of school when her last class had ended, she recalled getting ready to walk alone on her way home. She hadn't gotten too far down the stairs of the middle-exit at the Department of Science and Technology Studies, before she had caught Ralston's charm out of the corner of her eye, and as he was going down the north stairs after exiting the same building and had smiled. He looked toward her, waived to her enthusiastically from a distance, and then noticed how she was struggling with the books in her hands. Without hesitation, he rushed over the lawn toward her, all too late to help her carry them. Vesha had stumbled, and her books had slipped from her grasp. Ralston then helped her pick them up, while at the same time offering her a ride home.

From that point on, Ralston J. Rayna picked Vesha up every day and became her life-long chauffeur. *"I never had to drive a car a day in my life,"* Vesha reminisced and looked at her angelic friend with a smile.

Vesha remembered the days that followed, the conversations they shared, and when they fell in love, describing her memories quietly to the angel in her mind, as if in an interview with some unseen persona, *"It must have been at some point during the many blissful, intriguing, and intellectual moments we shared. He had a depth of character I scant saw in any other man. He had an innocent charm, a love for knowledge and humanity, and he respected me through my spit, vim, and vinegar. I was in bliss in my own way, even though it was true that I was a stubborn one. I had my goals, I had shared them with Ralston, and he agreed to respect them—respect them he did,"* she recalled.

Both Vesha and Ralston attended courses under the guidance of the already renowned theoretical physicist, Dr. Philip Morrison. As with many scientists of the day, many danced close with the large budgets and goals of the US military. Dr. Morrison had been instrumental in helping with the Manhattan Project, yet after visiting the sites of the bombings of Hiroshima and Nagasaki, he founded organizations advocating the disarmament of nuclear weapons, and became a strong advocate of nuclear nonproliferation. By the time he had met Vesha and Ralston, he had changed his focus from nuclear physics to astrophysics and from there, he became well-versed in gamma-ray physics.

Vesha thought about those times, and how despite the sadness, her professor had changed his energies toward constructive pursuits.

After classes, she would find Ralston. *"Together we shared so many memories of conversations, afternoons filled with birds singing and nesting, blossoms blowing in the breeze during springtime, and leaves turning bristled colors of yellow, orange, and red through autumn. We would sip our cups of tea, only to get up scrambling, catching our papers during short gusts of wind, and chat for hours, making sense of those tenuous points in history where the stains of war seemed to result in little to show for it, other than misery and untold suffering. We would reach peace about what had happened within our minds, declare to each other that we would do what we could to never contribute to such devastation, and still get our homework done. Oh, Ralston's clarity and charm in explanation of Dr. Morrison's delivery of gamma-ray physics! I found Ralston's comprehension of each subject we discussed quite stimulating intellectually. This certainly amplified my understanding of chemistry and the Universe so much more."*

While going through their master's programs, Vesha and Ralston worked with each other, studying, and for hours on end, doing research, bouncing ideas off of each other, and it wasn't very long before they found they were growing quite a bit closer to each other. *"We would take breaks from everything at times and walk the twenty minutes it took to head northwest to Cayuga Lake, sit in the gazebo to read, and step to the shoreline to look up into the nighttime sky to see if we could spot the various constellations of the season. We would, on occasion, walk another twenty minutes to watch a play put on by the university's local comedy troupe or drama club.*

"Oh, Sky, I miss those times. Ralston was very level-headed, brilliant, enjoyed culture, and he was a gentleman with a keen sense for the arts, the sciences, and pleasantries. I felt at peace with him."

Both Vesha and Ralston had an affinity for good causes and preferred reduction in suffering and an open mind to bring an end the divisiveness throughout the world. *"We had a lot of confidence in the fact that the more we understood, the more the plight of the various cultures of humanity could be addressed. It seemed to us that at times culture, societal norms, laws that didn't protect kind and productive people but instead nitpicked the small things, and even religion if extreme toward brutality, could become an issue toward the realization of a beautiful future, especially, if we failed to step back from time-to-time and ask a few simple questions of ourselves, including the reasons why we act as we do, or do what we do. There is a micro and macro view with goals.*

"*If only people could step back in life, no matter nation, creed, religion, or anything else, and engage their focus, their energies, and their efforts toward the beauty of the world we live in, if only they could focus toward the beauty of the skies, the answers laying hidden within our Universe and the Heavens, maybe misery, irrational behavior, and needless violence could be reduced.*" Vesha thought deeply about all this, even during her young, love-filled, studious, marvelous life.

Vesha recalled, reflecting upon her past with her dream-angel, Sky, how she and Ralston had agreed that only, "*If people could be more constructive, productive, and helpful, humanity would become so much more evolved.*" She knew that if we all did, "*We as people, perhaps down the road and into the future, would grow to progress toward a better reality, where we could preserve life rather than watch in shame as it was stripped away.*"

Vesha knew she was surrounded by amazing people when she realized how burdened her professors had been by what had happened surrounding World War II, and the actions they took to prevent this from happening at any moment in the future.

Through Dr. Morrison's mentorship, notwithstanding his grief toward what had happened in the past, he resonated with clarity, and Vesha had begun to understand gamma-ray physics, quantum theory, and the more precise details of how large clusters of galaxies worked.

Following her first year at Cornell, Ralston asked her father, Lukas, for her hand in marriage. Ralston had told her father that they had agreed she would keep her last name, so she could carry her parents' legacy, and even help to bring in a more modern era—one of respect and of dignity. He had considered the resilience she demonstrated by doing all she needed to do, to become a scientist. Her father saw and appreciated the humanity within Ralston, was honored to consider him a son and he approved. Vesha Celeste and Ralston Rayna were married in 1948.

Throughout their lives, Ralston confided in her father how much it was that he respected her plans for a career, and he let him know that he would do all within his power to ensure that both their relationship and her career were respected.

"*Family life and career goals will be seamless, respect the rigor of scientific endeavor, and complement each other,*" Vesha overheard Ralston telling Lukas on several occasions. Their wedding was simple, yet it was also a graceful and memorable celebration.

As they stood at the banks of Cayuga Lake, Ralston wearing his shorts, blazer, white shirt, and tie, and Vesha wearing a knee-length skirt, white blouse, and gall cross-over tie, they watched as both of their parents attended, and throughout the ceremony, they observed both of Ralston's parents and her mother and father glowing with excitement. No matter her nerves, she would look toward Ralston, and he was an endless source of stability, joy, and peace.

As time went by and they pursued their studies further, both Ralston Rayna and Vesha Celeste found that they continuously and often shared professors. "*Dr. Richard Feynman took bits and pieces of ideas and notions of matter and energy in the 1940's and shaped them into the tools that ordinary physicists could understand and calculate with. He was such an honor to work with. His mannerisms made him quite a comic in his own right, making us laugh through class, while learning in a fun way and in a manner that was fulfilling,*" Vesha recalled.

Contemplating upon one of her other professors, she began to talk to her dream angel, Sky, again, *"Dr. Hans Bethe's dedication to his work and his understanding of nucleosynthesis was extraordinary. Studying with Feynman and Bethe, sharing ideas with Ralston and working with him, my clarity of understanding grew in spades! Several of our professors became Nobel Prize winners in the '60's!"*

As time went by, Vesha recalled how in 1950, she and Ralston welcomed a handsome baby boy into the world and named him Daniel. She remembered how he, at such a young age, seemed thrilled with the funny things her husband would bring home. *"Ralston would bring home science books, mathematic models, and even an abacus for Daniel when he was a young child; he seemed so intrigued by how they worked. My mom and dad were involved too. They were present and helped me out regularly and faithfully. This way, Daniel had proper parenting, while I was working on my studies and my thesis; family was a nice break from it all. Although I had to immerse myself in my studies, I still found time for him. Daniel had a loving environment."*

Vesha Celeste finished her graduate thesis in 1951, the same year her husband received his Ph.D. in chemistry. Following his graduation, Dr. Ralston J. Rayna was awarded a senior staff position at the Johns Hopkins Applied Physics Laboratory in Washington, DC.

Vesha pondered through her history, *"Ralston followed through on his promise to me, he arranged his work in DC, so I could further my education at Georgetown University for my doctoral studies. He always did the little things; he brought flowers home with a note I could see—and every bouquet looked and smelled so lovely! On so many occasions, he did things in a nuanced and quiet manner to help me out, or to make the pains of the day seem to drift away. His choices in career management enabled me to travel abroad all over the Americas, from Texas to Chile, and on to California and back, so I could gather the information necessary to write up the analysis for my thesis.*

"During my travels and studies at that time, I was able to examine the possibility of a bulk rotation in the Universe by researching the apparent expansion and how it affected or didn't affect all the galaxies. As similar as these rotations seemed, abiding by laws of physics, each region of space is unique to a fault, which adds to the complexed beauty of it all."

While at Georgetown, Vesha delivered speeches, gave seminars to professors, and pored over countless books and journals and became immersed in her studies. *"Meanwhile, Ralston juggled his private life sweetly and lovingly with me, in his professional life with brilliance, ease, responsibility, and as a father of patience and charm.*

"He became quite accomplished in his own right, and even took time for sports, engaged in community affairs and service projects, and wrote books. No matter how much was going on, he never let it slow any of us down. We also never lost our romantic spark." She loved him.

Full-bore and throughout her doctoral studies, Vesha had been paired up with many amazing professors. *"It was Ralston who had introduced me to Dr. George Gamow, who became my doctoral advisor."* She appreciated the fact that even though he was a professor working long hours at George Washington University, *"He had chosen to take time out of his schedule to spend many mind-expanding moments with me throughout my studies, providing advice and insight on nucleocosmogenesis, as I was going to Georgetown. At that time, it was the only school that had a doctoral program in astronomy."* Previously, in his career, Dr. Gamow had solved the theory of alpha decay of a nucleus via tunneling and had subsequently defected from the USSR, leading to the point in which he advised her on cosmology and quantum physics.

Vesha recalled examining the possibility of a bulk rotation in the Universe, *"In 1951, by searching for non-Hubble flow I made one of the first observations of deviations from the Hubble flow in the motions of galaxies, identifying a faster speed, a unique glow around groupings of galaxies, and a clear argument for dark matter."*

She recalled how, while completing her thesis she had argued with Dr. Gamow, *"Galaxies might be rotating around unknown centers, rather than simply moving outwards, as suggested by the Big Bang Theory. He agreed with me shortly thereafter. However, the established scientific community saw things differently. Oh, the presentation of these ideas was not well received, and my journalistic entries were rejected by both the astronomical and the astrophysical journals, but I knew better. I needed to provide further proof, and old habits die hard. Whenever it is that skeptics seem to prevail, it is ours to search deeper and enlighten ourselves and others with concrete evidence."*

Through it all, Vesha's parents had taught her humility so at this point in her life she realized that her data did not provide the clarity that she would have liked it to have. She knew despite all, there was something of value in her findings and argued that her thesis was significant in relation to Gérard de Vaucouleurs' claim of evidence for a "Local Supercluster."

On the home front, she gave birth to her daughter, Jillian, in 1952. As before, Vesha's parents, Lukas and Irena Celeste, eagerly helped Vesha and Ralston with their children.

Vesha recalled overhearing her parents one day talking to a reporter in an interview many years later, and Vesha had felt very much the same way about their daughter, *"We love dear sweet Jillian very much; she had been such a lovely girl, and she grew up to be interested in astronomy, just like her mother. She worked hard and earned a Ph.D. in cosmic-ray physics."*

Vesha appreciated the friend she made at the science conventions during her youth, and the earlier years of high school, as she recollected other moments shared later, *"Najem came to DC that year, in 1952, with a presentation during a science exposition that I attended. She had been working in Chicago on a study of AG Draconis and had, by a stroke of luck, discovered that its emission spectrum had completely changed since earlier observations. This was a big deal since this was one of the first observations of such a rare event documented in modern history. I also enjoyed spending time with her afterward as we talked about Andromeda and many other aspects relating to science and our personal lives for several hours."*

"It was nice rekindling our friendship after so many years of study, dedication, and she had come so far," thought Vesha.

A couple of years after her daughter Jillian's birth, Vesha completed her studies and was awarded her doctorate. Vesha reflected, *"My dissertation under Gamow, completed in 1954, made it clear that galaxies were clumped together rather than being distributed randomly throughout the Universe. This idea was not pursued by others for a couple of decades. However, I charged ahead of the pack as I dutifully completed my studies above expectations making observations well in advance of my peers. The award of Ph.D. in Astronomy was an honor."*

After receiving her doctorate, Vesha began working as a professor of mathematics and physics at the Montgomery County Community College and stayed there for a year. *"I enjoyed teaching the younger generation, and as always, there were among them some of the most brilliant people I could have ever imagined meeting. After working there for a year, I started doing what I had dreamed of doing for the longest time, which was working as a research astronomer in 1955, at Georgetown University,"* she recalled.

"In 1956 our adorable baby boy, Chris, was born," Vesha reminisced with fondness. *"He later grew up to earn his doctorate in mathematics. He was a smart*

young man who took after his father. I could never be prouder of his dedication, his intellect, and his attentiveness to his own family when he grew up. He seemed to understand how mathematics was essential to engineering and the application of our knowledge to mechanisms that raised the quality of life.

"My youngest, Avery, was born in 1960 and was quite a wonderful young man as well, who loved being in the outdoors, going on hiking trips, on camping trips, and spending time near mountains, hills, lakes, rivers, and streams, even as a child. That may have been where he garnered an interest in geology. He had a theory that naturally occurring ripples in the terrain shared a calculated depth of layers related to our Earth's core layers. Manmade mountains only had dirt mixed with rock and whatever else.

"Brilliant," she chuckled quietly to herself.

She recalled carrying Avery on her hip while delivering speeches to the board, *"I gave dissertations to professors and university leaders with Avery on my hip, so someone else wouldn't provide the presentation and take sole credit for the work I had spent hours on. I juggled family life, my personal interests, and my career at the same time. They were each important to me."*

Rising in Life

In 1962, Vesha ran into her childhood friend, Najem, again. They took advantage of their free time and talked while they went on a hike through town to catch up on the last ten years or so of their lives.

"It was exciting because, at this time in Najem's career, she had just accepted an administrative position at NASA. This was a first in a couple of ways—for women and for her new program, and I was very impressed. She was planning the beginning stages of travel to the Moon, involved with placing satellites in space to observe the Earth and the Universe, and two satellites, Voyager 1 and Voyager 2, were set to travel to the distant regions of our solar system. This was exciting stuff! We had to celebrate a little bit together." Arm in arm is how she recalled spending the evening going over life, their ideas on astrophysics, and their past, and they continued later, over a couple of simple martinis.

As Vesha Celeste continued to traipse through her moments in life, she never forgot that she was always close to and appreciated her parent's religious heritage, reminiscing and remembering graciously, *"There was never a conflict for me between science and religion."*

She mused over something she was quoted as saying during an interview when a particularly vindictive reporter asked her about this apparent conflict, *"In my own life, my science and my religion are always separate. My religion suggests that I am Jewish, but religion to me is like a moral code and a sort of history. I try to do my science morally, by not developing things to hurt people, but to help people, and I believe that ideally science should be looked upon as something that helps us to understand our role in the Universe."*

Vesha reflected on her first meeting with Jasmine Belle, eleven years later. Jasmine happened to be thirty at that time, on a worker's visa from the United Kingdom in the DC area, in 1973. She was working in one of Najem's NASA teams in preparation of several of the satellites that would be placed into outer space. *"It was an exciting time; it was a new space age, and she was brilliant!"*

Humanity's mission to the Moon, the 'space race' was on, work on the Mariner program was in full-bore, and work on the Hubble Space Telescope was filled with its challenges and ups and downs. At that same time, Vesha had been introduced by Najem to Jasmine Grace. They walked through town, but this time with Jasmine alongside them. They caught up on sciences and talked with each other more over root beer floats at the local A&W. They added Jasmine to their little circle, as they went over dark matter, astrophysics, and the future of space exploration.

Vesha then drifted, thinking about how she spent her time in the 1980s, 1990s, and 2000s. *"These decades came with some successes as well as the loss of heroes who gave their lives to science and were all-in during some of the tragedies of early pioneering space missions."* She whispered in her mind, toward her mental image of Sky hovering in the air above her, as she lay in bed.

"Oh, the people I have met; the young women, Eliza and Yesha, James, Amber and Erin, they were each an inspiration to me. Eliza and Yesha showed up to one of my conferences instead of going to their prom, in 1994, and that is some original thought, spunk, and tenacity. I admire those girls. Our subsequent discussions and meetings from time to time over the last almost two decades were always so vibrant, full of life, meaning, and intellectuality. I remember talking with them about the usual, and Eliza seemed especially intrigued. Hah, those two sweet young ladies, they certainly have great potential. They burn from within to do great things. I am pleased with Eliza, proud of her for finally running for office, with a successful bid at that, to represent her state in the United States Congress. I am also proud of Yesha, for the support and wisdom she has shown through the years too. It can be difficult to muddle through life alone, but it's worse getting by feeling lonely. I've been alone for a few years, but they've had each other's back since day one."

Vesha reflected on the meetings with the Pathway science teams. *"What a time for science, although it was a covert set of operations, Eliza and Yesha and James, Amber, and Erin, wow! They have done so much in the last eight years with little praise to show for it. So many lives have been blessed because of their care and their efforts."* Sky was smiling quietly, proud of Vesha.

Vesha also recalled when she spent time with Najem and Jasmine in the new Pathway facilities. Her encounters with young Amber, James, and little Erin were all so sweet and endearing. She thought of all that had passed through her gaze in life despite her advancing years and the contributions she had made, the many brilliant people who had brought her in—if for anything out of admiration of her efforts in science and her love for humanity.

She admired both Eliza and Yesha, as they grew to be very competent scientists, adults, and leaders, multiplying their ingenuity and compounding upon it at every turn. She applauded them for their self-motivation to improve things in the world and to make the core of well-being and quality of life the driving force for what they did. She also reflected on how she had spent a long life serving her world and humanity in her own way, in the search for wisdom, knowledge, and understanding of space and all its exhilarating intrigues.

She had written many scientific journal entries for the public audience, had made amazing discoveries that pushed physics into the palpable, with astronomical, quantum, and particle physics subjects and a more profound grasp of dark matter and the cosmic microwave background (CMB) both in public and private.

Early on, in 2000 is when she had begun to show signs of an increase of dementia, however, she did everything she could to delay its effects. *"Perhaps that's why Eliza and Yesha pleaded with me to join Pathway. They knew I wanted to live a natural life, they respected that, and they are allowing me to make a different decision in my own time. I can't recall all the details of what we did together, but I do know we met a lot of wonderful people who at one point were struggling and living in environments I would not wish on my worst enemy, and they too stepped up to the plate and helped so many more."*

Together with her late and beloved husband, Ralston, she had taught, mentored, and loved her children until they too had expressed their own doctoral expertise. Ralston had been an incredible tennis player, a mathematician, and a physicist in his own right, and had passed away at the age of eighty-one. *"Oh, how I miss him, and I'll never forget how heavy it was for me when he closed his eyes for the last time,"* she thought, with a tear running down her right cheek and a smile which was evidence of how proud of him she was and how much she loved him.

Vesha had provided instruction to countless fellows and many more students; she had been honored by the Washington Academy of Sciences, and together with Ralston she had taught their grandchildren about the many wonders of the Universe. *"Your grandmother was an astronomer, because the stars and the grand cosmos was always something that she loved deeply and cared so much about, and there is always so much to learn and appreciate about our Universe,"* Vesha thought, almost in a quiet conversation to her future generations. With dementia settling in, she did what she could to retain her memories, even if it required a conversation with her dream angel, Sky, who was hovering above her bed in an understanding posture with the mural of Andromeda behind her glowing back, resting on the ceiling above.

Generations of family Vesha would soon be leaving behind had visited that day, those she had missed would soon be standing before her, and her visitors left her there in pleasant solitude contemplating the time she spent with them and how she would soon be leaving them for the next great journey of the unknown. She hadn't thought of her dream angel for decades, until those years when her dementia seemed ready to abscond with another memory or two. *"Sky, you visited me when I needed you most. Lately, you have visited me even more. You reminded me that together we could succeed in life, that our dreams and goals are precious, with you and Ralston we successfully balanced our family and personal lives, even our magnificent careers, and while whispers of the Nobel Peace Prize were just that, whispers, we ought to be pleased with the notion of simply having helped people out."*

She looked up as her eyes adjusted to the darkness assisted by the dim flicker of the night light and slightly smiled as she faintly made out the seemingly glowing mural of Andromeda on her ceiling above. She closed her eyes to sleep that eternal sleep, as the tug of the Universe began to take its effect, to beckon, to call for her, as she gave way to this riptide of life, she let go allowing the waves to take her away. It was as if Sky was there with her all along, to help her on her next big journey, smiling, speaking to her mind the words of comfort, care, dignity, and love.

With knowledge solely of a beginning and an end to every turn and twist of fate, Vesha would soon become one with her Universe again, her memories, her particles, and her dreams would now be a part of that vital substance that would usher in new life, and perhaps a different life ripe with her own cognizance in the future.

Arpeggios of Harmony

After Vesha sighed, she felt at peace, and after closing her eyes, she blissfully lost herself in her dreams flying away with Sky on journeys of daring-do, of honor, of love, and shared understanding between one civilization or another, and then she began to feel young and vibrant, and with a unique and sudden clarity of mind. Vesha realized she could hear just as clearly as when she was ten; she no longer felt the need for sleep. Something was different about her surroundings, but she couldn't quite place what it was or where she was. Instead, Vesha started to enjoy everything she had contemplated as beautiful as if it were music that was playing in the air around her. *"Where am I?"*

She decided to lie there for a while. Vesha felt young again, and she imagined the sounds of arpeggios as if they were finely tuned pianos playing away harmoniously, a symphony of waves, the chiming of clocks, and the knocking of the door that had hummed synchronously as if a beautiful tune were permeating throughout her entire living space.

The door knocked again, as if to create a sense that grounded her and helped her to perceive a new reality.

The music seemed that it had quieted to lower decibels; her blissful errands seem to fade from reality, and her friendly and lovely dream angel began to disappear from before her, but somehow, she did so with an understanding farewell, the look of the wise, and a wave of her hand, and then she smiled before looking down and fading completely. It seemed as if the music were still playing within the background of her mind, but it too had begun to fade just as fast. And then Vesha realized that she had indeed heard another "tap" at the actual door.

"Oh my," she thought, as she slowly came to, from what seemed a deep slumber. *"I must be losing my mind. Do I have a visitor?"*

As soon as Vesha realized someone was at the door, she sprang from her covers like she did when she was in her youth, unaware that things had changed. There was a slight glow emanating from her skin, but she did not notice luminescent sparkles as she rushed to flick the light on. When it seemed to be the switch was in a different location, she stopped. *"That's odd."* She thought.

She saw her mural of Andromeda still on the ceiling above, her eyes had adjusted to the darkness, more quickly than she was used to, and then she saw her Van Gogh of "A Starry Night" on the wall near the doorway, but something was wildly different about the environment she was in and there was the switch.

"There is something up with and unusual about this," Vesha mumbled in her mind, and dismissed it as she gathered herself together, not wanting to keep her visitor waiting. She managed to find and place her fluffy warm slippers over the socks on her feet, and then recovered and wrapped her robe around her black and silky nightgown feeling a vibrancy she hadn't felt in decades. A tingling sensation reverberated throughout her body as if her skin were radiating a beautiful light accompanied by a more intense euphoria on her left side. Upon finding the light switch, she turned it on and headed toward the door.

"Vesha," she could hear a gentle and beautifully recognizable voice, followed by a softer tap at the door, and then a pause. The visitor was ever-so-patient and persistent.

Vesha called back through the hallway door toward the plausible entrance, from whence came the knocking, and noticed a younger timber to her own voice as she, in a kind and urgent manner, responded, "I'm coming! Sorry to make you wait. I seem to be a little confused, but I am on my way, and I'll be there in just a second!" After uttering those words, she knew something was indeed different about her own situation, and she could not yet figure out what it could be.

Vesha arrived at the door, looking into the security display above it of a video image of her visitor. On the other side of the entryway was an angelic face beset with a familiar, peaceful, and serene smile. On the porch was a most interesting, feminine, and exquisitely framed and beautifully dressed, nicely busted young lady, with medium-length hair in an up-do, a rainbow of highlights through her professionally groomed brunette locks. It donned on her that on the other side of the barrier was a recognizable young lady, and with no desire to keep her waiting any longer, she opened the door and greeted her lovely visitor.

"I'm Yesha Alevtina," said this entrancing, somewhat familiar emerald and hazel-eyed, beautiful brunette, who appeared to be a petite young lady, and with a mind-catching intellectual delivery of her speech. As she spoke, her words twisted like ageless and confectionery perfection in the air through her perfect and pouty lips. "I hope you recognize me. How are you doing? You're Vesha Celeste, correct? We met more than twenty years ago for the first time, and you visited us as an honorary member of Pathway several times. May I come in? There is so much to do, and we have a lot to discuss."

"Of course," said Vesha Celeste, making motions to enter her dwelling and wondering what there was so to do, and what it was they were going to chat about. At first, she thought that her dementia was confusing her perception of reality, but she let that concern dissipate as she opened the screen door further to politely let her come in. Yesha gently brushed by her, giving Vesha a gentle sensation as if life outside of her own had made contact and provided her a living reference point beyond her own mind. Directing Yesha to a comfortable couch, certain aspects of her reality and the setting she was in came to her all of a sudden. Her living facility resembled more of a home, the furniture was white and smooth and soft, and aside from other essential aspects of her main living quarters, things had changed rather drastically. She wasn't in a senior citizen's center anymore, that much was apparent; she was in an actual home, or so it seemed. Yesha was right, there might be a few things to do and a discussion beforehand might help—she was confused.

Vesha looked down and noticed that although her hands were slightly balmy and shivering, they were also glimmering and young. Gone were the wrinkles on the surfaces of the dermis visible to her, gone were the places where too much sun had kissed her skin for too long or too often, and before her, her hands and wrists were smooth, of pleasant scent, and silky—cleared away were the marks of age. She felt an unusual tingling sensation on her left shoulder, the left of her chest, breast, and on her left arm and down past her left hip, thigh, and down to her foot, and despite all, she ignored it.

She offered this dazzling beauty sitting on the couch before her some naturally sweetened and warmed herbal hydration—a favorite of hers—a dried hibiscus from Asia.

In a soft yet assertive, attractive, yet serenely excited voice, Yesha accepted, "Of course. I love the wonderful varieties of tea, and Asian hibiscus is among my favorites. They have so many natural and good qualities for our bodies. It's a shame that herbal teas are all-too-often overlooked and under-appreciated in many places throughout the world. Thank you, Vesha," and Yesha smiled as she sipped her tea.

"I've felt the same way for years as well," agreed Vesha.

After a few moments of quiet retreat, Yesha smiled with appreciation toward her pleasant agreement and continued, "I am so glad to see you. You can't imagine my excitement. First of all, it's been a while. I am curious, how do you feel? Do you know where you are? Have you seen yourself, yet? Because sitting here with you right now, you look amazing. Please humor me. We've sipped some tea, so could you please head past your kitchen, and then head just one room further than your bedroom to your bathroom on the right? Once you do, can you please take a look at yourself in the mirror? When you do, please tell me what you think?"

While Vesha appreciated the compliment, questions about where she thought she was and if she had seen herself in the mirror, seemed quite unique. There was no ridicule or sarcasm in her voice, yet she knew something was up. Vesha was pretty sure she was in a senior citizen's living facility, within her own domicile, and with her private balcony, at least that's where she had been earlier. Or so it seemed. Vesha hadn't looked at herself since the previous morning. She hadn't showered since the day before, or before the seasonal celebrations, and she still thought of herself as a finely-aged eighty-eight-year-old lady. Despite Yesha's sincere tone, she couldn't help but think that maybe she was just trying to be polite. Perhaps Yesha was pointing out that she was in all reality merely a mess. Vesha calmly rushed to the restroom to check. When she looked into the mirror, she couldn't believe what she beheld.

"Oh, my...!" Vesha exclaimed standing in her pajamas and robe, so used to the expressions and mannerisms of someone who had lived the eighty-eight years she had. The young person on the other side of the mirror gazed at her in disbelief. She liked what she saw; it reminded her of an amazingly artistic and spectacularly youthful, curvy, slender, and perky version of distant memories of something resembling herself. However, on this occasion for as much as she tried, she only distantly remembered each of her youthful features from so long ago. It was rare to consider, but Vesha was, in fact, beholding a reflection from her twenty-two-year-old days.

Acceptance

Yesha smiled as she sensed Vesha's excitement and well-given wonder and felt giddy inside for the first time in a long while, relatively speaking.

"I look... different! What exactly happened? Wait, you asked where I thought I was, and now I am at a loss; what is this place, and where am I?" Vesha had a thousand questions as she stood in baffled amazement, not used to her youthful yet wise and assertive voice, looking at the state-of-the-art technology in the bathroom. It hadn't sunk in that her environment had a glowing white aura, the sinks were spacious, and every item in the bathroom was as if it were one gigantic and carved out piece of glowing white marble, yet with sophisticated technology imbued into it, with every imaginable update provided, and all of it through-the-roof-awesome!

After taking in that bit of reality, she found herself momentarily at a state of disbelief at what she beheld looking back at her from the mirror. Instead of working herself into a baffled frenzy, she found herself even more excited by her newly perceived reality. Enchanted and in awe, she thought out loud, loud enough for Yesha to hear. "I won't lie, Yesha, I thought there was something odd about my living quarters, and I believed I was dying about twenty minutes ago. This bathroom is amazing, and this young lady on the other side of the mirror is beautiful!

"Putting the pieces together, I had some pretty deep and fleeting moments of memory as if my life were playing before my eyes, and a bit of a headache.

"Afterward, I started heading off into dreamland.

"The second I sighed, breathed out, and thought I wouldn't breathe in again, it was then and quite precisely when my pain was gone, I felt vibrant and like I could reach the stars! Yesha, it's starting to become clear now, and no, you're not just a familiar visitor, you're a long-time friend!" Her neural nanos were working hard, and she saw herself glow as her physiology and neurology were connecting all the sectors of cells and neurons in an optimal way, "But, I must have died, and you brought me back. How many years went by?"

Against every prudent aspect of the nature of personal expression that she was used to—one of humility and calm reserve, she began to ogle her reflection in the mirror divested of shame or narcissism, but filled with excitement and wonder, "Wow! I think I might like this! It dons on me now with quickened clarity that for years I was a bit more, how should I put it? I was too prudent during the last few decades of my life! However, to my credit, I was lost in noble pursuits, not to mention I'd been suffering from dementia. Oh my, I wonder what my friends and family would think if they saw me now. What about my surviving children, Daniel, Chris, Avery and their and Jillian's families, what would they think? How would they react?"

A subtle yet fleeting moment of terror passed through her as she thought about their reactions. Perhaps feelings of anger would surface and maybe even a sense of jealousy would boil through their blood, fester with their minds, and flow to freedom through their actions, but then her mind grew clear, and she realized how her family had always been kind and understanding.

The more her neural nanos created additional healthy links in her mind, the more Vesha realized how wonderful this entire experience was. It was clearer to her now, she had raised her children to respect noble pursuits, to love life, and appreciate the splendor of shared time. Vesha then thought how anyone of a healthy mind would be overjoyed and gracious, especially if they had been given this set of circumstances.

As more memories of her mortal life surfaced, she found herself thinking out loud, "I loved my family then, and I still do now. Nevertheless, I suppose this is my life and my reality now to choose whatever whim and detail I wish with reckless abandon and with no more doubt of self-expression; there's much ahead. Wow, Yesha!"

With an immediate sense of guilt that hung over from Vesha's previous life and her commitment to her values and doubts, it was as if pulsating waves of thoughts about her parents, her husband, and children had crept in and her concern arose again. This time she was worried that she was merely justifying her current reality, simply because she was happy with it. It took Vesha a moment to find a sense of clarity with this new wave of thoughts.

The constraints she put on herself were hers alone to deal with. They were not sourced in from any other direction. As the neural nanos cleared the areas of her mind that were capable of taking an outside view of experiential relativity, as if it were a game on the field, she shook it off, "I abided by the values my parents espoused throughout my life and I still appreciate everything I was taught, learned, and subsequently shared with my children. They grew up to be wonderful people. They were individuals who I still respect and love, no matter how they expressed themselves. It's now my turn to live and be free to express myself how I desire, and to be loved while living free and by my own whims," she voiced out loud.

As Vesha coached herself, she felt the freedom of her new reality sweep in and then she rejected her concerns and worries, because they were her very own critical views of herself, ones she had deemed the judgments of others, but they instead were perceptions she had of yesteryear, "Now is a new day. I have slept for some time, and I have no memories whatsoever of that timeless slumber. I can remember my life as clear as day now, before this moment that I am currently experiencing, and I can see who I am. I mean, I can't help it, look at me, there she is before me. My inner and outer beauty are connected and sharing the same message!

"Here I am now, and though I thought I had died, I'm quite alive, and, Wow! I feel more alive than ever, with potential oozing from every pore. My reflection tells me I'm ravishing! I can't stop looking, I'm so amazed! Who am I? Wait, I'm myself, but younger, yet with all my memories coming in as if they were yesterday, or a few minutes ago! What's the breadth of the changes? What can I do? What are my limits?"

"Fancy you asked," said Yesha, smiling and proud of Vesha's first responses. Yesha understood Vesha's reactions, because she had been in her shoes, at least to a certain degree before. Although she had never actually died, she remembered how it felt as every cell quivered into some sort of euphoria before releasing her inner will and finding the immensity of joy that comes with an optimized body and mind. On the day that she and Eliza had used the biopods for the first time, she too had had her mind racing with questions she never thought to ask before, and then like that, a surge of answers streamed in moments later with complete clarity. Fortunately, she was not alone in that experience, because both she and Eliza had pioneered the first biopod trial ever, and together.

Yesha was pleased with all aspects of Vesha's reactions to everything she beheld and felt.

Vesha showed depth in character, even signs that she indeed was the woman Yesha had grown to admire for more than two decades. She admired the fact that Vesha was embracing her new and wondrous reality so quickly.

Bringing Vesha Celeste back from the dead required a lot of science, a lot of care, and a lot of hard work, and as a result, Yesha Alevtina was glad that her heavy involvement in the full spectrum of results was reciprocated through Vesha's excitement.

"You are still the amazing you that you always were, Vesha. You are now a magnified and miraculous result of a collaborative effort of science, of love, and of dedication. You are a twenty-two-year-old version of you, with some extra, pleasant, and optimum aspects to your entire range of abilities and aesthetic, your physiology, and your physical and neural capacities.

"In theory, your limits are few, but your nature is benevolent to the core. I've seen you, known you, and appreciate everything about you. Since you are innately capable of benevolent actions and virtuous internal character, your abilities will multiply with little chance of losing them. Someone would practically have to hurl you into the Sun to harm you to any effect, and I'm sure you might even be able to endure that and come out okay.

"Vesha, you are remarkable in every way, you have tremendous and nearly unlimited potential, and what you choose to do with it lies within you alone.

"You will be able to learn anything, absorb so much more than before, pretty much everything you wish, travel anywhere, and do anything you put your mind to. My sweet friend, you will have the capacity to resolve some of the most rigorous issues known to mankind both in this world and throughout the Universe."

Vesha continued to look into the mirror and beheld herself with awe and a hearty side-dish of disbelief, but despite all, she beheld what she saw with an internal and increasing excitement, filled with gratitude.

"I suppose this is where it all starts. It all starts within each of us and goes out from there. What do you think of the tattoos and rainbow highlights in your hair?"

"I am impressed with your work, Yesha. This is unimaginable, yet so lovely! Who would have thought of this arrangement? Who would have guessed I would have been so amused? I am blown away by the aqua, the turquoise, the green, the rich purple, and the soft yellow highlights. I suppose I might never have imagined this in such a way, so many beautiful variations and shades that truly do complement my curly brunette angle-bobbed hair."

"Your right brain and its inventive processes are responsible for your look, and you are very creative," Yesha explained. "Look at the tattoo-like artwork on your left side, as it swirls and moves around. We didn't hire any artists for the intricate artwork, if we had, they would have made a viable fortune, it is your mind doing this.

"What do you think?"

Vesha thought about the question quickly and responded, "I'm still so amazed at my hair and my skin. I haven't seen anything resembling this face on myself in the mirror in decades, who would have thought that these extra details could bring so much wonder? The eye-catching colors—the locks of hair, I like how they match my eyes and everything else! I understand what you're saying about the regional and right-brain-controlled outward expressions of what I look like, in some cases my eyes, hair, and makeup seem to adjust every moment, like a large ship on a series of ocean waves, modifying smoothly and unnoticeably.

"I presume it was you and Eliza, who made most of this possible? If so, you guys did a wonderful job! I always knew you two had genius minds. I am impressed. Thank you to both of you!" In an excited sense of inquisitiveness, Vesha asked, "Is there a brief explanation as to how all this was possible? You asked about the tattoo-like artwork!? Oh, I haven't checked! Okay, sorry. I will look. Let's see."

Vesha paused as she untied and dropped her silk garments and beheld the fullness of splendor of her new physical and youthful attributes.

"Whatever it is that I had been feeling earlier—that tingling sensation on my left side when I got up to answer the door, it must be related to those, to these?" She paused again and began to realize that just as her body adjusted to its new system, as if in a complexed and harmonious symphony, something was optimizing and changing her internally impacting and adjusting her external artwork at every moment. The magnificence of it all hit her for a moment with inaudible gratitude. As the artwork adjusted, it was as if it were a series of scenes from a silent movie, and instead of causing pain, these changes filled her with euphoria and vibrancy. Vesha then glowed as she healed or adjusted.

"If that is the case now, if I am glowing because of the upgrades and adjustments now, the same could be true when my body is optimizing no matter where I might be, in private or public." It hit her, she might want to be discreet when in public and learn how to control it.

"Not only do the colors of my tattoo-like artistry intensify, but each shape and the intricate details on my physique change in form, almost continuously, like a picture-screen with sophisticated imagery in motion throughout various areas of my body, while leaving my skin aglow as I heal and upgrade."

In the bathroom, after she had shed her wardrobe to see the changes, Vesha graciously continued to talk to Yesha about her artwork, "Yesha? Wow! I haven't pictured myself like this in years! I was in the world for eighty-eight good ones, and aging took its toll, sagging, greying, and wrinkling, and I accepted its prettiness in my own way. Oh, I earned every bit of the wear and tear, but I would never have even imagined this was possible! Oh, wow, Yesha! My mind is blown!

"I remember when you told us about optimized physiology before I passed away, and I said I would live life out naturally. I arranged it so after my funeral, I would donate what was left to Pathway, for science. Knowing me, I am pretty sure that I wouldn't have approved of any of this, or its peculiarity. In a way, I suppose I was willing, since I donated my body for research with at least a little inkling of hope in you guys.

"I always believed, before seeing what I am seeing now, that aging in grace was gorgeousness in its own right; letting nature take its course was the moniker for dealing with senescence and death in the past. Death was a part of Nature's evolution with so many mixed results, but here I am, alive as can be, and with every result as desirable as my imagination allows it to be.

"My body was an empty tapestry just waiting for a masterpiece of self-expression before I passed away, and I took an almost quiet and condescending tone of minor judgment against those wearing artistry, but here I am, and here is the art, ornate, exquisite, and so expressive, and I like it. My apologies to all for not appreciating others as much as I ought to have for their self-expression before. This skin art is a part of me! Seeing what I see, knowing what I know, and feeling what I feel? It's magnificent!

"Wow, I can see my dream angel, Sky, moving around within my body-murals! Sky was such a lovely friend to me, during the worst of it all! I can tell you with full confidence that I approve of this and its oddities more than one-hundred percent, if that's possible, Yesha!"

Vesha was awash in enthusiasm and excitement. Deep down, she was thrilled and extremely impressed with the turn of events, courtesy of her friends. Vesha knew that it wasn't vanity to appreciate the merging of natural and humanity-driven evolution. The proof stood before her in the mirror and existed within the increasing clarity of her mind. She contemplated how, with speed, all she had ever learned and felt was multiplying in her mind and her body in both complexity and meaning. It became as clear as day to Vesha that she was now, everything she could have ever imagined being, feeling, and hoping for.

Vesha looked upon her renewed physical facial features, her pouty, full, and perfect lips, her slightly upturned nose and its soft point and was trying not to be smitten with herself. She couldn't help it though. Her smoothly-chiseled chin and high cheeks, her hair that was full in volume and color again, and her eyebrows perfectly trimmed without the need for effort, were any woman's dream. She gathered the courage to look upon her naked body, and with awe and disbelief, she could not take her eyes away from her newfound youth, her perfection, and all its splendor—her tight skin, her firm yet soft curves, her colors, and her perky faultlessness.

"I normally would not have found it within me to look at myself like this, or even ask, but I will now. What do you think, Yesha? Please look, I trust you; this is amazing! You've performed a scientific miracle!

"Thank you, Yesha!"

"How did you and Eliza do it?"

Yesha walked into the hallway from the living room and stood to the left of the bathroom entrance, with her back against one wall gazing across the hall opposite the doorway—mostly to maintain Vesha's sense of privacy for now, until she was sure Vesha was just a little more comfortable in her new skin.

Yesha then responded to Vesha's question, "It wasn't easy, we had your DNA, your full-on genetic code, and your entire neural network. It was recorded within our Twelve Database Moons, courtesy of the preservation transceivers placed into your system when you became an honorary member of Pathway, and then the notification alerted us from the app on your smartphone, that you had passed away. Luckily, the neural link between your mind and smartphone beamed everything we needed to the Twelve Database Moons and recorded everything about you, down to your last thoughts, before your final breath.

"Everything we needed to bring you back was available to work with, and it is clear now that we achieved as close to perfection as possible while retaining your will, your memories, your 'you-ness,' and here you are.

"So, yes, Vesha Celeste, you are still the amazing 'You' that you ever were and always have been; only now, your physiology has been optimized to near perfection in every possible and conceivable way. As you may have noticed, many will have difficulty not appreciating how beautiful you are, because your mind shows your inner and outer beauty.

"As you already noted, your artistic right-brain definitely has a say in your appearance to a certain degree, given all that was done—the hair, the colors, and the artwork. Seeing life pulsate through you again certainly brings my heart some peace and joy.

"Vesha, it indeed took a lot of work, a lot of study time, and again, even more work, but at last we did it. Eliza, James, Amber, Erin, Najem, Jasmine, and many of your friends at Pathway were involved. Despite all, I am so glad you approve. I'm impressed with you and your progress in such a short period of time!

"There is a lot about you that we updated in order to optimize your physiology and neurology, so I am sure you are aware we'll need to familiarize and train you on all of your upgrades, as well as show you what you can do. Eventually, you will learn how to 'normalize' the glow and the root of it. Your right brain will soon be able to take control of what you allow others to see of you more fully.

"Right now, we can't run around in public, either, while you're looking like a glow-in-the-dark person of the future. I mean, I can glow like you are if I choose, but, since your body and mind are making adjustments and enhancements and you are kind of going through a state of shock and glowing in a lesser controlled fashion, it is better that we wait. You'll have an opportunity to head out into the real world after training.

"Throughout our mentoring process there, we'll help you to learn to adjust your age as needed. Right now, you look like you did when you were twenty-two, with some extra aesthetic miracles of expression. If you'd like, you can adapt your age anytime to look anywhere between twenty and thirty-five years without looking too obviously out of the norm. There's no problem with personal expression or age, per say, we just need to be dialed down in our artistic appearance, when it comes to creative display, so we don't stand out in an obvious way. Looking youthful is a great idea, because fewer people will notice any oddities, especially since there is a great quantity of our youthful population that can be quite creative in their expressions anyway.

"Nonetheless, we will help you to learn how to create compartmentalized wardrobes and personalized facial and body imagery in your mind to avoid too much suspicion from anyone, outside of Pathway. Your unique facial construct and physique will always be you as if you were in the ideal condition, but certain aspects of artwork and imagery will still be yours to manipulate and hold in place. Right now, as you may have noticed, I've allowed my hair to express itself artistically, because we are at the Pathway Campus in Melrose, Massachusetts.

"I convey a conservative or professional vibe for my visual appearance in public, but from time to time, situation depending, I will let loose.

"In the coming years, we will all be able to allow ourselves to let go a little more in public, to be as creative as we wish to be, but only marginally. Once Eliza has convinced the Senate, and the associated powers-that-be, to allow physiological and neurological reanimation and optimization as an option, humanity will have all this available to them based on personal choice and consent.

"It's still an uphill battle right now, however, and for far too many reasons to explain at the moment. While somewhat frustrating, only in the purview of anyone of a sound mind would it seem that arguing against having optimized physiology and neurology is a sad way to expend one's energy. Seriously, doesn't it seem a waste of time on their part to discourage something so wonderful? I do believe that if chaos is their personal choice, so long as it doesn't hurt anyone, I can respect that.

"What do you think?"

Vesha understood the social dilemmas of so much progress so fast, and for a moment she got lost in thought. *"The perspectives of society are indeed limiting when it comes to personal expression and the sharing of each aspect of our attractiveness, whether internal or external. Although new to my present reality, I know that nothing expressed by anyone in Pathway suggests brutality or grotesqueness; still, people are unnerved by something that they don't understand, and it is unfortunate for so many, in the least helpful of ways.*

"There were many in my day that didn't let half the population become scientists; something as simple as that was considered taboo.

"Society could do so much more, though, if they didn't make rules that had nothing to do with the well-being of others. Instead, they seem to discourage things like this for all that they are worth.

"Society and governance would be better off if they didn't arbitrarily make rules, laws, and muddy the waters of ethics in ways that aren't very ethical, while

making enemies of others, engaging in witch-hunts and generalizing vast swaths of people—of innocent, unique, and beautiful people.”

Vesha knew that as a whole, society would be better off if they could focus on healing, optimizing, and preserving life. Vesha felt that doing so would lead to a beautiful reality. After contemplating for a brief moment, she thought about her friend, Eliza.

Without realizing she was doing so, for the first time Vesha had activated her neurological link and communicated to everyone who had been trained and optimized within Pathway, and then she did it again, thinking she was quietly whispering within her own mind.

“Thank you again, Eliza and Yesha, my friends, and thank you to all of our friends at Pathway. Each of you did an excellent job and this life standing before me right here is indeed a labor of love. This is amazing!

Vesha continued, but this time out loud, “So, Eliza, is in the Senate now. I am so happy she is there. I always knew she had a gift for leadership and decisions! I have no doubt she is winning over close colleagues, rubbing shoulders with the right leaders, and influencing people where it seems the big decisions are made. I wouldn’t mind visiting her at work to see how they keep our country functioning, sometime soon, if that is okay? She was always an inspiration. I am proud of her. No doubt she’s had some political battles along the way.

“Doing the guesswork, I presume it has been at least two years since I passed away?” asked Vesha.

“You are correct, Vesha. It has been two years.”

Vesha then thought about how her physiology would work, if she were to meet someone, special. “So, I have a question.” Vesha paused, “How does my body, um, work? I mean, if I do meet a wonderful person, will I be able to have family down the road, or maybe choose to hold off while on distant journeys to the great unknown throughout and beyond our massive Universe, while still having the splendor of a relationship with someone?”

Relieved she had asked this, Yesha explained. “This has been such a hot-button issue in society, and we have done everything we can within the development of our technologic advances to afford women their own choice when it comes to their bodies while avoiding issues that could potentially countermand the beliefs of those who might be religious regarding having children.”

Yesha had known why her team considered this for some time and continued to answer her inquisitive friend, “If you are ever in that special moment with someone, all you have to do is ask, are you ready for a family? Yes or no? If they aren’t ready, or you’re not ready, then enjoy that special moment. As a matter of fact, if someone is not ready, then the conception will never occur, and no matter the choice, the nanos in your body will add extra health, as well as glowing and colorful light, delightful sensations, and phenomenal pleasure. If you are ready, then you will have the option of childbirth in less than a week, and your child will receive all the nurture he or she will need to grow into an amazing, healthy, brilliant, and loving individual in a matter of weeks. They will become mature as soon as necessary with the Health and Education Matrices, available in the Virtual Universe, or a person can choose to rear their children organically.”

“That’s amazing, Yesha. What a weighty ordeal that has been for years! It has been lifted and enmity gone. Who would have known? This is a delightful day!”

Yesha smiled, “Yes, that ordeal has been resolved and those fears and worries are no longer necessary. Now, there is little need for people to feel compelled to go through with bringing more children into the world if they are not ready or if the resources surrounding them are meager at best. In the reverse, if they are at a time in their lives, they deem appropriate or right for that significant responsibility, they can go ahead with hope and joy.

"We have always sensed that people should not be deprived of intimacy and that it is a shared responsibility between two persons to enjoy their connections with each other, in a manner of consent. People should allow their inner love and desire for happiness, together, blossom in so many ways.

"We've always loved children, so it is nice to know that once they are born, at least in Pathway and the many Pathway tech cities, each child will be brought into an environment where they are loved, nurtured, and given everything needed to be successful within their own lives.

"Women, as a result, will have an opportunity to decide on whether or not this is a good time to have families from the very beginning, without fear, death, or controversy. Instead, their decisions will be made with love and the ability to provide the desired result, while still allowing them to be beholden to their faith if that is what drives them to be the wonderful people they are. Eliza has always promoted diversity."

"I don't believe it is possible to answer that question any more eloquently. You did good Yesha."

Realizing that Yesha was waiting outside the bathroom, she called her in and opened the door a little wider in order to allow Yesha the opportunity to appreciate her work, "Yesha, please come in, no worries."

Yesha turned to see Vesha and explained who had aided in her development and subsequent awakening, "Vesha, a lot has changed since you've passed away, as far as life is concerned. I must be fair, as far as your return to the world of the living is concerned, it wasn't just Eliza and me who helped to bring you back. Amber Blythe, Erin Carter, Najem Grace, and Jasmine Belle were in on much of this as well. Even James Cooper helped."

Yesha saw Vesha's right eyebrow raise into a peak, and trying not to laugh, knowing she was receptive to humor, she continued, "No worries; James helped with certain aspects of the scaffolding of your various organs and your skeletal structure.

"He took his panache for construction and multiplied it in spades to learn various other sciences, to include biotechnology, data processing, and neuroscience using the training capacities in the Virtual Universe.

"Besides, if he did see you, he was very respectful and dignified. The people in Pathway have an innocent mindset about all that. Vesha, we had quite a team working with us." said Yesha, and then she examined the perfection of her dear old friend's new look—she was impressed with the results, and the fact that Vesha was now very much alive again, and remarkably so. Yesha almost cried tears of joy seeing that Vesha was awake and aware and no longer laying lifeless in Pathway's labs.

Yesha continued, "Your body's artistry and your hair are all related and synced to your neural network and activity. As we have talked about, your right brain has now unleashed in certain harmless ways a beautiful set of expressions, kind of like a spiraling-kaleidoscope set of mandala patterns, galaxies, stars, flowers, an angel, and so much more. Your right brain, she certainly gets a say!

"It appears that Sky is quite deep with symbolism and artistic expression. I must note, I like how your mind's artistry wraps that beautifully frosted mandala pattern around your area, right there," Yesha pointed, but did not touch her, "And it dissipates in just the right places. It's something else, the beauty of the mind. Physically, every aspect of you is angelic and extremely gorgeous," Yesha said emotionally, with fascination for the beauty of life.

"You mentioned Sky? I suppose when my last thoughts were uploaded, perhaps you saw her?" Vesha was not sure at first whether to be embarrassed about this new revelation regarding her dream angel or not, but somehow Yesha had mentioned her, so she asked.

"I know about Sky. She is beautiful, with hair the color of icicles, with iridescent highlights throughout. There is nothing to be embarrassed about, Vesha. She is magnificent in every way. Please note, that from a view based in established science, different and significant regions of the brain identify themselves in diverse ways and at different times. Your right mind appears to express herself as a lovely, powerful, and very creative angel with nearly glowing white blonde hair, a rainbow of highlights, and soft pink and supple lips. Although she looks different than you do, Sky is having a big say on what you look like. Both of you look and are beautiful!

"Although you are a composite of your left and right mind, as well as your prefrontal cortex, among other regions of your awareness, your 'you-ness' is actually a summation of all that you are, linked via your corpus callosum, and as such, standing before me as we speak. It was mostly and purely by accident that we discovered these new artistic features and loved them, and with all that we know, there is something very special about her.

"Given all the rest of the benefits of indefinite lifespans, reawakening you from the dead, and optimized physiology and neurology, we brought you back as human as we could. Throughout your life, you both had a special connection. The additions you have to your gifted abilities include so much, but healing, resistance, strength, and survivability capabilities, even beyond our own is just the beginning of it all, and Sky was a part of that.

"We were very much pleased with the results, and I'm glad you are. In Pathway, those of us who have been fully read-in, we each have significant upgrades and the ability to do many of the things you do now. But Vesha, you are superior, you are unique, and you are currently the only one as powerful as you are, which I presume is all due to your alter ego, named Sky. Throughout your life, you harbored no aggression toward anyone and always demonstrated intrigue in the truths of our Universe as well as a desire for the well-being of those around you.

"Hence, you've been entrusted with so much more than many, and as such your abilities have grown in kind. As we improve ourselves, our mindsets, and more, and as we go along in life, we too will receive further updates, like yours. You are starting off nearly perfect and with the full spectrum of abilities available, many of which you can and will learn as you go along in life. There are many other capabilities we will all learn as they are conceived of and implemented, but we'll train you to learn how to control and use many of them as we enter the Virtual Universe. Step-by-step and easy does it, as they say; you'll learn and grasp so much more. Physiological optimizations tied-in with your right brain are only minor side-effects of all of this."

Vesha paused Yesha, thrilled with the idea that her lifelong dream friend was a part of her expressing herself beautifully and uniquely, while also respecting her own life-long sense of how she imagined herself. "I can't believe it! I don't understand. I mean I appreciate all of this," she waved her hands up and down her perfect body, "How do you know I named her Sky?"

Yesha grabbed a nearby portable mirror so Vesha could see. Just below her left breast was the angel, and right on the underside of her breast flowed the name, Sky. "Pretty obvious, don't you think?

"Your artistic artwork will change over time, but she kind of flies around a bit, and she does it ever-so artistically. Now, please understand, that there are many other aspects of your physiology and neurology integrated in a manner that affords you autonomously natural aspects that don't require conscious thought on your part, but you also have much more control with some of the most intriguing of things, such as manipulation of eyesight, healing, pain tolerance, and other adjustments.

"You're still a human and a biological miracle if you ask me, and you are not your right brain alone, but because of Sky, you have abilities that most would envy if they knew of them. To top that off, I don't think anyone can say they've seen anything or anyone more aesthetically pleasing as you, and soon we will both learn how your neurology works, now that you are awake.

"I'd imagine it will amaze us in much the same way as your physique." Yesha said as she motioned her hands—waving them over Vesha's entirely nude and exquisite frame, impressed with her, yet also so happy that everything turned out so well. "Our technology was something of diligence, but we grew to appreciate the beautiful set of enhancements that happened to appear automatically, through the artwork like a silent movie, and after much deliberation, we decided the mind's art was optimal too and left it free for expression.

"The artwork is not an arrangement of tattoos; it is a part of your cellular makeup as expressed by your mind. The highlights, your floral scent are all expressions of you, and whenever your body heals, you'll see iridescent sparkles all over your skin, kind of like shiny little diamonds glowing. When you blush, you'll glow a little bit as well."

"You're glowing a little bit, Yesha," said Vesha Celeste with a slight smile, but kidding around. She knew Yesha was being professional, was proud of her work, and she was grateful. Vesha didn't sense anything funny, the whole ambiance of it all was innocent and gracious.

"I know," said Yesha. "I'm just so happy that everything turned out so well. I mean, the lacy black and white sort of doily and mandala-like pattern with Sky's expressive artistry, all up and down your left shoulder and down to your left thigh and feet, combined with the colors of your eyes and your hair, are all in sync. The aesthetic of each feature complements the other. You are amazing in every way. You invoke beauty and charm, yet authority and loyalty, and I thank the stars. Do you know you used one of your new skills not too long ago?"

"I did? What did I do?"

"You talked about how society needs to appreciate the beauty of the human body, the wonder of evolution and the advancements we've achieved, to increase well-being and quality of life. You then thanked Eliza and everyone in Pathway for bringing you back so beautifully."

Vesha appreciated Yesha's genuine compliment, "Thank you and everyone for doing this for me. I suppose I owe some gratitude to Sky; she has been my kindred spirit for quite some time.

"So, it seems that we apparently have telepathic transceiver capabilities, too? I suppose in my state of dementia, there must have been a variety of upgrades, developments, and advancements that were brought about that I didn't retain or remember. My focus was mostly on recalling the memories of my family and friends, and all who had shown me love in my lifetime. I hope you don't mind, and I digress, I must say—and I don't want to sound too narcissistic or egotistical, but I do appreciate all of this. I could gaze at myself for hours since there is so much that is artistic and captivating, and right now I am overwhelmed and impressed; it is nice to share that with someone. Thank you so much for doing so well for me."

While gazing in the mirror at her fullness of beauty for just a little longer, Vesha asked, "You were saying I was out for two years and that there is more training to be had. I don't recall too much regarding the Virtual Universe since I was an honorary member at the time, but you hinted that we will need to go there for my more extensive training. When do we begin?"

"You were out for exactly two years, to the day. It is December 25th, 2018. Yes, you'll find out much more about everything in a more experiential sort of way, and in a little bit within the Virtual Universe. We can begin as soon as you'd like." Forgetting momentarily about the fact that Vesha was still undressed, because her nudity seemed unusually innocent and even normal in this particular environment, free of harsh or impure personalities or intentions, she beckoned, "Come. Let me show you the Virtual Universe. We'll be able to do some amazing training there and show you a robustly historic briefing when we interface with our biopods. At least, that's our first priority for now," said Yesha, with her typically calm demeanor and giddy intent.

"Like this?" Vesha fluttered her hands over her exposed and upgraded body. Vesha turned away from the mirror after looking one last time and then toward Yesha, who was impressed just a little more with the beauty and awesomeness of her gorgeous physical exterior.

Yesha, with a very approving smile, thought to herself for a fraction of a microsecond, *"I can't believe this is the first time we have revived someone who has passed away. We had a lot of healings and upgrades, but this is a full-on resurrection and a complete success! ...And, oh my, I'm speechlessly awestruck; she looks incredible!"*

Vesha picked up on something. It was as if Yesha had whispered to her. She recalled their conversation about telepathy, and then brushed it off knowing she would learn more about her powers soon.

As Vesha released her mind, knowing that Yesha had talked to her using telepathy, she saw a space-age-like outfit—a black, thick, rubbery, yet cloth-like material, with artistic colorations glimmering in streams of detailed and sewn-in embroidery, matching the colors of the highlights in her hair, her body's artwork, and the irises of her eyes. As she put it on, she noticed the embroidery was seamlessly sewn to the stretchy yet oddly comfortable contraption that was made-to-fit just for her.

It had been hanging at the level of her gaze, so she had gently pulled the uniform down off the garment fixture on the door and began to put it on. Vesha pulled her legs through, covered her perfect, gloriously perky, and ample bosoms, one at a time, hiding the artistic imagery, and thinking she'd need a little help with the back she asked, "Can you help me with this? This must be an outfit fitted just for me, since it fits me like a glove; it would seem that I may need you to get the zipper, or whatever it is back there, please?"

The bathroom door had been opened and Yesha had been observing her through the doorway, so she didn't need to reach too far to zip her up. Nonetheless, Yesha responded, "Your uniform does not have a zipper."

She motioned for her to turn her head so Vesha could see her back in the mirror, "It is made out of smart material and is designed to give you maximum comfort. Your smartsuit provides a mixture of just the right amount of moisture, flowery mind-controlled scent, and temperature control, as well as physical strength and dexterity. The sophisticated technology in your smartsuit augments your commanding yet easing appearance of beauty, respect, joy, and peace. The micro-nanos that are within it work with your mind, so you can seal it shut or adjust your wardrobe as desired.

"Both sealing and wardrobe mechanisms are triggered by your neural activity when you think, *'Seal my suit.'* In many cases, clothes already worn are converted to smartsuits via the biopod, but you are our first individual in the known history of humanity, and proven scientifically, to be resurrected, so for you, it's different.

"You'll only need one of these suits. This tech will allow you to encode it with compartmentalizations within your mind to give you any look you need at any moment. Plus, it is self-washing, providing you top-notch hygiene, no more need for waxing of unwanted hairs or needing a shower after something intense, because your nanos will kick in, and so will your smartsuit. Simply think of what you need done as far as wardrobe is concerned, and it will be done. All of that, while giving you the aromatic scent you prefer, given any situation.

"Although, all things considered, if you ask me, there never is something as amazing as slipping out of everything for a nice, large, warm bubble bath. But I digress;

sometimes, in the regular world, you'll want to look more professional, and at other times you'll want to wear a bikini for the beach.

"There are codes built into your clothing's neuro-ware that will allow it to take on the appearance you need, which can be activated merely on thought—eventually all of this will be second nature to you, and you'll want to ensure your appearance doesn't change right in front of John Q. Public. In the not-too-distant future, you may just want to look as creative as your heart desires."

As she spoke, Yesha's blouse and skirt turned into a revealing see-through dark negligée which accentuated her ample curves, and highlighted the natural colorings of her skin, eyes, and hair. Through the negligée, Vesha saw a hint of Yesha's tattoo-like artistry playing out before her, images circulating up and down her dermis as if it were a movie. This happened, but just for a few seconds, because like that her appearance returned to the professional yet attractive one, she'd had on before. "Just like that, and in a snap, you can change." Vesha had seen her uniform seal up just moments before as Yesha had explained everything, right after her telepathic command.

"That outfit you had on for a split second and your right-mind artistry, that was hot date material," Vesha laughed. "I didn't realize you would have artwork like that too. You also used your telepathy to seal up my uniform on command. I suppose you could peel it off if you wanted to as well. I'm kidding. I still can't get over how amazing all of this is!" Vesha said, she was good friends with Yesha, had been for years, and appreciated that she had a good sense of humor. She wanted to show off a bit longer, maybe if her husband from her previous life had been there, she would. She didn't mind Yesha being an observer since there was a lot of detail in the artwork and there seemed to be no rush. She was impressed that Yesha must have been affected by many of the same artwork benefits.

"These odd feelings I am having—why am I buzzing with intensity, and why does it feel so good? This is the bomb!" Vesha was starting to feel like one of the younger adults she had known and using the vocabulary she had heard them use seemed to come more naturally as the moments continued. *"I wonder what Yesha's artwork is like and I wonder if she has a unique alter-ego like I do, like Sky?"* Vesha was using one of her new gifts again, without realizing she had happened to be targeting Yesha for a very private conversation, but she knew in time, maybe if they went swimming on a beach somewhere, Yesha would show her. Vesha loved the new details, imaginative expressions, and being optimized.

"Oh? I'd show you more, but I won't for now. Maybe we can hit up a beach later on, but we don't have that on our list of things to do today," Yesha told Vesha through her mental link. She then climbed deeper into her mind and thoughts, trying to get back to task, *"We need to get you trained in the Virtual Universe,"* thought Yesha, as she smiled at Vesha. She had the innocent look of 'I know what you were thinking, and that's cool,' and then both seemed ready to get Vesha's training under way.

"I'm liking this telepathy we have. Goodbye cell phones!" Vesha laughed, and her skin blushed a little with a crystalline glow, as she realized her body was adjusting to allow her new gifted ability to set in for good. She then asked, "How much, exactly, has gone on since I put my head on my pillow? It seems to me like it was just a few hours ago that I hugged my family goodbye. Maybe my mind is still processing everything, but I honestly still have no idea what day it is or where I am, but," she paused, "I remember. Yeah, you said it is two years later. But where are we then? Oh, wait, you said we are in Massachusetts, at the Melrose Campus? Okay, I see you're looking at me funny. Go ahead and enlighten me, please?" Vesha was trying to remember all they'd talked about, but clearly her neuro nanos were working, and she was left just a little confused, temporarily. Yesha knew that.

"You are correct, Vesha. We are at the Pathway Campuses, but I didn't tell you that we are deep within the Earth, about fifty miles down, but as safe as can be. I also didn't tell you I am currently the leader and president of Pathway since Eliza is serving in the Senate. She is the leader of the Universal Party and is still connected with us via her neural link. She would visit us right now, but she is currently in deliberation at the Senate. Even though it is a holiday and two years exactly from the day you passed away. Eliza wanted to be here, but the Senate had some work that needed to be done, regardless, so her link is on but dampened right now. She honestly would have been here if she could have helped it, but I am here, plus I am sure you know by now that I, like she, was just as excited to see my dear and brilliant friend!

"We'd been working with your physiological and neurological aspects for a long time, to the point of which we had on multiple occasions triggered every possible and conceivable physiological response before waking you, and when all responses seemed to ensure perfection, we activated your mind. We also did so with you in a replica of your domicile at the Princeton Assisted Living center, with quite a few minor adjustments to get you thinking, which you did, and successfully I might add. As you began to awake, I started knocking on your door. Remember the neuro-transceivers and software applications we installed on all our phones at Pathway several years ago?"

"Oh, yes, I do recall that now. It's coming back to me. Since I'm new to the neuro nanos, my guess is that I get a little confused as they are running and linking my newly-discovered abilities and using them." Vesha then explained with the newfound clarity her gifted mind had bequeathed her with, "You were able to gather my final moments, all of my brain activity, and even capture my sense of self, using what Eliza's technology had been set up to do, with Pathway's crew of scientists?"

Impressed with Vesha's returning sense of short-term memory, navigating away from the signs of dementia that had taken her away from the world, and pleased with her increasing abilities toward critical thinking, as her nanos clearly indicated, Yesha continued for Vesha and went into more detail, "In fact we did.

"The moment you passed away we were all notified via our neural links, and at the same time your last moments of thought, as well as the rest of your physiological and neurological information, were backed up and automatically sent to Pathway's Twelve Database Moons. As this happened, the Twelve Database Moons essentially sounded off like an alarm in our minds, and we received all of your final and complete bits of information—your thoughts, your memories, your hopes, your dreams, your knowledge, your biological construct, your wisdom, and of course your moments with Sky.

"We then synced all of your information, including your actual consciousness, to a lifeless mold of you that we had synthesized based upon an optimized form of your own DNA, similar to the way in which we each had previously data-based our DNA when we began Pathway eight years ago.

"The body you are in now, not long ago, while we were working on you, had been imbued with nano-technology and was constantly checked, optimized, and improved upon in an anesthetized and 'off' state, save for the cells themselves which communicated their necessary functions. Just as we had previously agreed upon, we were able to complete every aspect of you in two years.

"Knowing how this is done now, we will now be able to do this for anyone else in a matter of a few minutes. Since you were the first to be reawakened after passing away, we took our time, ran every diagnostic, and did every check. We developed a systematic set of procedures for this same sort of resurrection in the future, depending on how all of this goes through.

"When everything was ready, we activated the opsin-nano-neural-links and turned you on. Thus far, everything has gone splendidly." Yesha smiled, noticing Vesha's mind was grasping all that she was explaining, *"I'm proud of you, Vesha. You are understanding and picking up everything quicker than the rest of us did,"* she continued, "You woke up with full control of your body. You also have naturally expected and automated responses, like breathing, which is no longer necessary, but we still use that function to keep the public from suspecting such, or getting creeped out, among other things. For you, a second had passed as if nothing had happened, for us it'd been exactly two years.

"Even though Eliza had just become a US Congressional Representative for our beloved state of Massachusetts, she, who had been very close, and I worked to optimize you and bring you back for quite some time. For a couple of years, to be exact, and together with Amber Blythe, Erin Carter, Najem Grace, Jasmine Belle, James Cooper, and other dear friends of Pathway, to include Eliza and me, we were able to optimize your DNA, and now you have these results, right before your eyes.

"Eliza would have been here too, today, but as you already know, she is currently dealing with pressing issues in the Senate, as well with the Press and the established scientific communities. Everything seems to be pretty well locked-down though. Everyone that can be here, who was involved with this entire process or any part of it, is here now, but out of view—since we didn't want to overwhelm you with too many changes or oddities at once. I was unanimously voted to awaken you, but of course, you know I already wanted to. Nevertheless, the Pathway community is observing our interactions and has been working closely with us tracking your progress intently and so far, you are doing phenomenally.

"This is your body, and as I have already suggested, and you seem to understand, you have both neuro and bio nanos roaming throughout your system. They are continually taking free radicals, bio-waste, dead cells, and harmful debris and converting them into useful proteins, cellular constructs, optimized organisms, max-capacity neurons, and providing the ideal fluctuation of energy for optimal use of your mind and body. They stand at the ready, should anything catastrophic ever occur, to heal you to complete and full health and memory.

"Your corpus callosum, prefrontal cortex, as well as all of your other cortices and deep brain regions, are interfaced by using your neuro-nanos to act as a transceiver. This allows your mind to send thoughts, ideas, dreams, memories, the whole gamut, wirelessly between every aspect of you and our Twelve Database Moons, enabling you to communicate and so much more with anyone you wish to link with, if they have been optimized and trained in the Virtual Universe.

"Since you recently reawakened, I currently have complete access to your neural activity, until you have completed your training for the sake of the safety and security of all involved including yourself. With so much going on, we didn't want to risk serious anomalies."

When Vesha heard this, she was slightly alarmed, yet she didn't feel too embarrassed. She examined the thoughts she had allowed to pass through her mind and sensed that all was okay with everyone and even Yesha.

"Don't worry, you're quite okay, and the feelings of gratitude are mutual in every sense. Get used to being flirted with though, since we'll both have an ultra-attractive effect on people for the foreseeable future, and it is a nice perk," Yesha continued, to put her at ease. Every word she said flourished with purity.

"Encrypted within your unique neural code is the ability to control what you share with others; it also serves to allow us to currently monitor you with your own unique identification since you were only recently revived. This also provides Pathway your vital signs, all while it protects your privacy. It gives you access to the locations within our organization and throughout the solar system using jump gates and teleportation, as well as to the different matrices within the Virtual Universe. It allows you to learn as much as you'd like, to gain associated experience and upgrade—as upgrades become available.

"When you're ready, we can sync up to the matrices and go to the Virtual Universe. From there we can share a journey through Eliza's life as well as the lives and experiences of a few other individuals critical to the growth of Pathway. We'll do this so you can have a more complete understanding of what it is that has happened while you were otherwise engaged and away. You'll learn what led to all of this in the first place, as well as what is planned for the future."

Vesha thought about all that Yesha had explained for a few brief seconds, and she approved of every aspect of her transition, had no problem if James or other scientists caught a glimpse during the process, and accepted her new reality. Vesha was excited to explore the Virtual Universe. First, however, she was curious about the possibilities of exploring the real world in her new body, "Would you be bothered if we went for a stroll out in the public, first? You know, to stretch the muscles and capture the sites and the sounds? Unless you have objections or other plans, I wouldn't mind showing off."

Yesha smiled, was proud of her newfound confidence, then stood, looked down, tapped her foot, and waited for Vesha's next response.

Vesha was willing to follow Yesha's guidance, and Yesha knew it. Vesha considered everything. Yesha was probably already well-versed on what was going on and had conveyed this in more ways than one.

The advancements, the legalities, the so-called ethical concerns prevalent in society and governance, which had nothing to do with ethics whatsoever, and well, she had essentially just resurrected her after all. It was most likely that all of this was still covert, but legitimate, so she was willing to press on with her request. Plus, she kind of looked at Yesha as sort of her own young and beautiful guardian angel with an additionally kindred spirit-like overtone. "I understand, Yesha. When can we go to the Virtual Universe for my training?"

"Follow me," said Yesha, with a pleasant sense of approval and happiness. Then Vesha felt something in her mind, and knew it was Yesha who seemed to say, "*Open.*"

Yesha led her down the hallway of her home to a door that she hadn't realized was there before—the corridor had pretty much been a dead end beyond her bedroom and bathroom, and then the door became unsealed and visible. Like that, it opened right before her eyes to reveal a very fascinating view of a room with a gentle white glow and another set of doors.

Okay," said Vesha, "I know that one of the additional optimizations we have is telepathy, I figured it out, you explained it when I forgot again, and then I recalled it all after my neuro nanos finished updating my capacities as it related to my upgrades, but it appears we also have telekinesis. I'm still trying to grasp the reality of it." Vesha thought for a second, felt the upgrade work its way through her system, and then continued, "Sweet deal! I suppose we only have telekinesis, for now, with things that are programmed to pick up our neural identification and then our telepathic orders. You and Eliza had a lot more figured out than I realized, I mean, look at you... you are mind-numbingly gorgeous and ultra-intelligent!"

"*Yes, Vesha, I was optimized, or we, I and Eliza, optimized ourselves the day we were one-hundred percent sure this technology was spot on. We didn't want to take the risk that would have come with the loss of the technology, nor did we want to be weak in the face of any of those who might suggest we do otherwise. She set hers ten years ago to maintain a static age of twenty-two, even though she is currently thirty-eight, but she did so in a way that wouldn't be obvious, and I have been a static age for quite a few years. People still haven't caught on to the fact that we're no spring chickens, per-say, but I still look like I did when I was twenty-five, and I'm forty-one.*" Yesha noticed that

Vesha was still kind of looking around with a bemused air of wonder, her eyes and neck cocked to pick up the audio transmission sent by voice, but she was catching on quickly, and she smiled.

Despite Vesha's disbelief, Yesha could tell that she was capable of perceiving what she was telling her mentally. That ability took many others quite a bit longer to practice and achieve. In many cases, a few hours of practice in the Virtual Universe was almost required, and Vesha hadn't even been there yet—she was actually pretty quick, all things considered.

"Were you able to hear me?" asked Yesha, "I know you were going to ask. I know there has been a lot loaded upon you all at once. Even with an optimized mind, things take practice, study, and more practice to perfect and retain. Yes, I can actually link up wirelessly to your mind as we stand or walk or even chat, and I can pick up on a few other things; as per our Pathway honorary member contract, once we've each been optimized, we can link up to each other and converse—as you say, telepathically. I was telling you that earlier. Do you believe me now?"

"Yes, of course, I believe you, Yesha. So, how do I talk to you like that?" asked Vesha.

"Well, you actually have on three occasions already, and I'm sure you'll recall that soon enough. But it will be easier to show you more clearly once we have entered the Virtual Universe or the matrices—and don't worry, Eliza had to show me in the Virtual Universe too.

"No one thus far has picked up on telepathy near as fast as you have. Everyone else found out how to, well after they were in the matrices, and we're just getting ready to go there. That said, it is okay that they took longer because it takes a while to consciously connect with those regions of the brain, but again, you are unique in a wonderful way," said Yesha.

"Okay," Yesha pointed down the hallway, "*Open*," and she continued through the other set of doors, after the final set opened before her, "This smart door, right here, activates when we issue the command 'open,' within our minds. It takes a while to be familiar with all the commands and how to control the different areas of the brain. In this case, we use the prefrontal cortex at a subconscious level, which is said to be virtually impossible. That's why we need to go into the Virtual Universe via the biopods, which are located in that room, for training.

"The reprogrammable matter technology within the infrastructure of the Pathway Melrose Campuses allows the doors to become visible as we interact with our neuro nanos. Our neural activity and the security system transceivers near the doors open when we issue the command, 'open.' We do that subconsciously while directing our thoughts to the door, which is designed with smart technology, and when we do, they will open upon instant neural identification recognition."

Yesha continued, "Through these doors are our biopods. This is your Earth domicile, and we each have several biopods in our homes. These biopods allow us to be in a sleep-like state, while we're synced-in with the matrices in the Virtual Universe. Having a few of them in our home affords a few friends to come along with us for a shared experience. A biopod gives any individual within them an added set of safety, security, and protection protocols while we are 'away' or 'out', and they also give our physiology a bit of a break.

"We can link to the Matrices standing, walking, or traveling in any manner as well, but it is safest to use the biopods, so we don't run into things or make spectacles of ourselves. Furthermore, our biopods interact with our nanos, stimulate our senses and tactile responses, and give us a real sense of doing what we do there and being where we are, virtually giving us muscle memory, all the while keeping us optimized both physiologically and neurologically. In a beautiful sense of difference to the surreal nature and residual forgetting of a dream before our neurological and physiological optimizations, now that we are enhanced, we will be able to remember everything."

Vesha finally grasped what she had been through during her awakening, began to understand in-depth what she was seeing, and quickly made sense of what she was hearing. Her neuro nanos were kicking into high gear with their seamless processes of optimizing her mind, and everything seemed to have a profound ability to make sense on so many levels.

Finally finding her mind give way to a new sense of clarity of her past, Vesha spoke, "I remember now like it was yesterday. Eliza talked about all of this when she was giving her first Pathway Industries convention speech in 2012, and she said something about how each of these technologies was involved in one way or another.

"I don't think that I was part of Pathway for very long after that before my dementia started kicking into high gear. But I do recall you were at my dear Jillian's funeral. You paid your respects and offered me consolation, so I thank you for that." Vesha paused in thought for a small moment, "All of those technologies were actually developed by you and Eliza. They were confirmed and improved through Pathway, and they are currently ready for proliferation worldwide yet remain on standby and only in use by Pathway members until legalities are right. These are the biopods, right here—each of which works as a secure Virtual Universe interface?"

Vesha looked at what she saw with awe and then continued, but this time she seemed to discover that it was easy to mentally flex her neural cortices and grasped how to telepathically speak to Yesha, *"I've got this Yesha. The two white beds with hard-shelled covers that are spacious enough to lie on, and have doors that can be brought down manually, or most likely using a mental command to enclose them, help to provide our physiology and neurology additional optimizations, safety, and security while our minds are interfaced elsewhere."*

"Oh yes, and so much more," Yesha responded, while quite impressed. "Here, take a seat and lay down. Once you are comfortably settled in and ready for the cover to enclose you, pull the cover down and think the words, *Link 1, 2, 3.*" Vesha heard Yesha's command as clear as day but in her mind. After issuing that command, the hardcover closed over her. She knew that Yesha had telepathically commanded her biopod cover to shut, and that had registered to her own mind from within Yesha's. Just as Yesha had explained before, she had temporary control over Vesha's neural links because she was in training. Vesha then concentrated, focused on her mind again, her mouth, her words, and felt them all unite.

"Can you hear me, Yesha?"

"Yes, I can," Yesha thought, with a smile of approval on her face, unseen by Vesha's physical eyes, but seen as plain as day within her mind, plus she could hear the assuring, gracious, giddy, and comforting tone of her mental voice. *"You're a quick learner, Vesha. No one has learned this fast, well, except Eliza. She showed me how to in the Matrices.*

"Are you ready? We can both trigger our biopods, now that we're settled in. Once we say, 'Link 1, 2, 3', we need to set it for real-world time and then Virtual Universe time. In our case, we'll be in there for five minutes of real-world time, and about twenty years or more, adjusting as needed while in there, of Virtual Universe time. We will be going on journeys and covering a lot of information. We will be experiencing life through our eyes, so you can see some of what Pathway has accomplished since you passed away. You will also be able to look through the eyes and minds of many others while learning so much more. We will train you on every type of

history you can imagine, on many more of the sciences, and on more of your new abilities."

"For five minutes?" Vesha asked out loud and somewhat in disbelief, but it was because her neuro nanos were kicking in again, adjusting her telepathic powers. When she spoke, it was barely audible through both of their enclosed biopods, but with Yesha's optimized mind and hearing she understood every word she said. Vesha would soon learn that Yesha was linked to her and could hear her, even if she muttered something seemingly inaudible under her breath.

Yesha paused, "Yes, my renewed, gifted, and dear friend, five minutes. Say 'Link 1, 2, 3, 5, 20' in your mind. Many of the questions that you're pretty much already answering due to your optimized intuition, right now, will be so much easier to retain and understand there. Do you see your glow? Look at your hand. That is because both your physiology and neurology are working to make sense of so much at once, and you are receiving collective updates based on your comprehension.

"The upgrades that are currently available are being released to you in kind. Once we sync up, everything else will make sense to you more clearly, and both your comprehension and capabilities will compound exponentially. The processes of application, efficiency, clarity, raw knowledge and skill will be multiplied using time dilation, and you will gain experiential wisdom. Although you've been keen enough to figure a lot out already, there is so much more, so, *are you ready?"*

A New Journey

Vesha thought about the soon-to-begin journey throughout the Virtual Universe for a few milliseconds and then realized that with her new optimizations she wasn't currently hungry, and she didn't feel the need to use the restroom. Focusing again on the same three senses, she pushed out mentally and conversed with Yesha mind to mind, *"I am ready. Let's do this."* Vesha then continued, *"...Link 1, 2, 3, 5, 20"*

And just like that, Vesha felt every single sensory gland within her body contort, almost convulse, and then everything began to relax and buzz with an almost euphoric sense of ecstasy. A few moments passed, and she felt completely normalized, in control again, yet within a whole new environment. She then felt a very amplified and spectacular sense that her understanding of all that she had perceived and was now receiving into her mind was growing and becoming increasingly clear in a very exponential manner, just as Yesha had promised.

As she let this altogether new reality take its hold, Vesha looked around with her eyes. She felt as though she was peering out at what was before her in a very rational and stable manner, and then she saw a pond with a little waterfall teeming with coy fish. Surrounding the pool of water was a series of flowering and aroma-giving plants and at the top of the waterfall in the center of the big bath of water stood a beautiful statue of an angel overlooking its surroundings. Vesha was amazed at the sense of peace and solitude that she felt, and then suddenly wondered if she was alone. Looking around, she saw Yesha to her right and to her astonishment Sky was to her left.

"This is beautiful, Yesha and Sky. Where are we?" Sky hovered slightly above both of them in silence and turned her gaze from Yesha to Vesha. Apparently, Vesha's dream angel, Sky, already knew where they were, but she listened intently to hear Yesha's response anyway.

"We're in the area of Eliza's property just behind her estate home, or a virtual and realistic replica of it, in every sense, down to single particles, within the quantum computers and the Twelve Database Moon Virtual Matrix Mainframes. When we go

that way, we will see the Virtual Universe depiction of Eliza's house," she briefly paused. Then, pointing toward a large white-stoned building surrounded with beautiful columns, while looking more enigmatic than ever, *"This is her home and her meditating moments as she experienced them the day Agent Epstein called her, in 2010. This was when she received the okay to start a relationship with the US Government and build Pathway's Federal Liaison Office, in Washington DC, based on the details of her authored and published book, 'Pathway to the Stars.'*

"We'll learn about that very soon.

"Eliza is sitting inside and meditating, and if you would like to experience her moments of reflection, follow me," Yesha said. Vesha and Sky followed her willingly. They walked away from the pond and toward the back entrance of Eliza's home. Leading to it was a stone pathway, encompassed by flowers. Vesha saw Yesha as she vanished like a ghost through the door, and then Sky followed Vesha, not too far behind. She then passed through the door in the same way, without needing to open it. Vesha looked around and noticed that when they entered the home, they were inside a spacious and beautifully decorated living room. She drifted her gaze around the beautiful internal aspects of this historical structure, and then she saw Eliza.

To her recollection, of all the people she had ever met or known, Eliza was the most beautiful being that she had ever beheld. Her nearly white and golden hair, with pink weaves throughout her mid-length hair, glowed, in some ways like her dream angel's, Sky. Her eyes were shut, and she was clearly meditating. Vesha then heard a beautiful compilation of music. She asked Yesha what it was, who then told her that it was from Jens Gad's "Glass House." The music played in the air as if floating, pulsating, and moving magic through the soul. Meanwhile, Tyson, her brindle Boxador dog, lay there beside her curled up in a cuddly fifty-pound ball as Eliza was lost in thought. Sky looked at Vesha, then Yesha, and then demurely toward Eliza.

Vesha spoke up, *"Will Eliza be able to see or hear us? Will she know that we are here? I see she is meditating, but wait, as you said, this is in her past. How can this be? Why is it that I get the sense that somehow, I may already know or have access to all of the answers to my questions?"*

"You are connected to the Twelve Database Moons, the Multi-Matrix Mainframe, and you are connected mentally to me, Sky, and anyone else within the Virtual Universe who has granted you access to their thoughts. You'll be surprised at how much clarity on everything you'll have as we move forward, observe, and listen— learning in fullness will come to the surface so much easier here." Yesha's eyes were closed in peaceful enjoyment of the ambiance, as she spoke. She had settled next to Eliza and Tyson and seemed to begin a thoughtful meditation process too.

It was as if a thick amalgamation of memories swirled in the air before Vesha. Clearly, there was a deep connection between Yesha, Eliza, Tyson, and this entire location—from the pond outside, to the couch in the living room, and beyond.

Yesha then opened her now bright and glowing eyes and continued, *"This simulation of Eliza is from her mind both three and eight years ago. In all actuality, Eliza and her current mental reality will sync with the latest updates of and to her mind, and she will know we were here and have complete awareness of everything we do and say in here, soon enough. She will be able to interact with us if we wish. At any point, you can choose to compartmentalize or privatize your thoughts, dreams, actions, and we can leave the Virtual Universe if you feel uncomfortable. We are here to learn and train, and if you are okay with it, we will continue."*

"I am fine. I am rather enjoying all of this and taking it all in. This is amazing."

"Well, let's continue. We can talk to Eliza now if you wish, or we can talk to her later. No matter when we choose to speak with her, right now she is, in physical form, on the Senate Floor. So, even though she can feel our emotions, which we will play out

for her as if they are briefly-correlated images of thoughts and waves in her mind that are encoded in a unique mental flavor to let her know they aren't her own thoughts through her neural link, she will soon be updated in near real-time. Even though she has muted most everything for the purpose of focus there, she will catch up with us after the deliberation. Right now, I will answer a few questions, maybe show you a few things, and then we'll follow her through her self-reflection.

"There is a lot of important nuance to what she has experienced in life, and it will help if I can give you sufficient historical context, as well as the proper updates to your cognitive framework, and the training you will need. Ultimately, it can change a life if a person can experience another's within their own mind—and in particular within her mind since she is the highest-level genius, healer, and empath in the world, and quite possibly within our known Universe. Our minds will meld together with hers and doing so will help us all to understand each other completely," Yesha said, with a Virtual Universe smile.

"Forgive me for this, and I've meant to ask you, Vesha, both you and Eliza have been through quite a few tragic events. Would you mind sharing that with me?" asked Vesha, in the most understanding of inquisitive tones possible. Vesha then noticed Yesha's smile and the peaceful and friendly understanding of her innocent intentions, and then Yesha looked down. As she did, her expressions began to take a more somber tone.

"We are close friends and have been ever since she was born, and a lot has happened that has led us to where we are now." Yesha then looked up at Sky, smiled, and then toward Vesha. Vesha saw Yesha's glowing, loving, and wise eyes—accentuating the beauty of the mixture of hazels, beiges, and greens radiating from her irises framed within thick black limbal rings, which suggested wisdom and youth. Yesha then continued, *"We've been through a lot together, have accomplished a lot together—much of which has yet to be revealed to the rest of the world. However, I had just turned three when I looked upon Eliza for the first time and saw as she opened her eyes not more than two minutes after she came to life. Even as a newborn she saw me in the room as if I were the only one there, looked toward me, and smiled. Those adorable big blue crystalline eyes were compelling, and I could tell, even with my three-year-old perceptions at the time with the clarity of that moment as if it took place yesterday, and by the immediate richness to her character, that right away she was destined for greatness. I also knew then that we were going to be kindred spirits, close to each other throughout life—we were going to be besties. Neither of us is currently in a relationship, and you'll understand why, soon enough—I can tell you now, but to experience it all is so much more profound. It won't always be that we are alone, but for now, our priorities are a big factor, and we have so much to do."*

Sobered by Yesha's pause, Vesha knew something had happened, that even Yesha had private memories, and perhaps there was more she would learn or be willing to share later. Despite their neural connection, she wasn't quite sure what it was she was withholding. Yet, she sensed a well of respect growing within herself for the provision and evidence of privacy despite the openness of her mind. Something about the ability to share what one was willing to share increased her trust in all that she was experiencing, learning, and beholding.

While she was in the Virtual Universe and interfaced through her biopod, the nanos, no matter where she went, would heal any damage she might incur and carry out or repurpose any debris. She could feel her optimizations and the abilities of her updates and upgrades increasing as her mind released more synaptic and neural pathways to an increase in vibrant clarity and forged new and even stronger ones on any given subject.

Pondering on how all this technology increasingly made sense, like that all of it began to unfold its internal mechanisms and purpose before her. Vesha realized the beauty of Eliza's and Yesha's internal discipline, their collective knowledge and wisdom, the intensity of their minds, and their sense of duty and responsibility. She also felt their pain and knew that they must have experienced a myriad of occasions where emotions ran very deep. They had both been through profound romance and pain in their lives. Vesha began to sense a willingness to share with Yesha the loss of her own husband and daughter, accompanied with an onslaught of dementia, each of which had caused her deep emotional pain. What helped her to get through it all with peace within had been the fact that Sky had helped her in her younger and later years. As far as Eliza and Yesha were concerned, Vesha still wasn't clear what it could be that left those yet-unhealed scars, but she sensed that the pursuit of their goals and their potential conclusions would mend them, and she found comfort in their determination to make right what was wrong in the world. She appreciated the fact that they shared an extraordinary set of experiences leading to a deep connection. Furthermore, Vesha could feel the beauty of what they shared beyond the ability to describe in words.

What Yesha and Eliza had was a unique bond, a genuine relationship, one of sisterhood, one of innocence, yet one of sadness and sorrow. In contrast, they shared a determination of joy and hope. She decided, for the time being, to shift the energy around them in a different direction, as she sensed a shared, yet belabored pain and a story of healing that went with it. However, she would only do that for a short period of time, because something about where they had been, the things they had done, and the visions they had seen intrigued her. *"I know you've both been through suffering, and I would imagine that despite your neurological healing capacities, there are still pains of loss and tragedy that will always be a part of us. Please only share what you can, when you feel the time is right. I know you are both wonderful young women and I can completely understand your need to hold back, especially when there are lessons to be learned when shared in the right context. That said, you mentioned something about a Virtual Universe Multi-Matrix Mainframe. What or where is that exactly?"*

Yesha responded reservedly, shifting her demeanor, and with almost a sense of happiness for the change in subject, she continued, *"Thank you, Vesha. I will share that with both you and Sky, but within an entirely different setting and context. You'll experience it in due time. In the meantime, since we're in here, I can show you the Mainframe, or better yet, one of the Twelve Database Moons. And, again, please don't worry, I'll share you the details of our history soon enough, but at the appropriate time."* Without warning, they started to rise up, through the roof of the house, and up into the nighttime sky.

Magnificent View

The breeze of movement passed through Vesha's hair as if she were flying in the real world, living in a real environment, and with clouds breezing by. The brisk winds and the density of the particles of the atmosphere seemed to pass through her system as if to remind her that the Universe, if possible, still recognized her existence. She felt as if she was a form of radiation encoded with information, yet moving along unaffected, similar to quantum particles, such as neutrinos or other exotic and yet-to-be-discovered quanta—the types that Eliza had already discovered, and her mind was only beginning to conceive of and grasp. As she climbed through the stratosphere with Yesha at the lead and Sky at her side, it was more comfortable than sleeping in bed and within a wonderful dream. Arriving to and passing beyond microgravity, or the Virtual-Universe-simulation of it, Sky looked as though she was right at home. Like that, Sky had been up, up, and up through the clouds, and into the starry night, and Vesha was thrilled with this new and seemingly surreal reality, which wasn't so surreal after all. This was an experience she was truly going through.

Vesha looked out and began toying around with some newly-acquired abilities she had found. Discovering that if she adjusted her sight to mitigate the brilliance of the Sun, she could see so much more and ever-so clearly. Even though it had been several years since the use of her more complexed conscious brain activity, due to her mortal battles with dementia, now her brain was so robustly operational that she was beside herself. As she looked to Sky, she thought of the phrase, "beside herself," and chuckled. After sharing the thoughts of her mind with the other two, they all shared a laugh as they continued through the vacuum of space with subtle reminders of their reality.

Vesha was fixated upon one star with her eyes. She began to use that star to carry out the astrophysical calculations in her mind of where every other stellar and deep space object was, as well as where they happened to be, relative to Earth, along with each constellation asterism. Vesha knew what time of year it was, based on the Earth's orbit around the Sun and the geophysical aspects of the shadows upon the various mountains and landmass shapes, and then where the Andromeda Galaxy would be in open space. Vesha knew her observable Universe well, based on the stars seen and instantaneous triangulation of the northern and southern poles of the galactic disc and a host of other astrophysics formulas processing subconsciously and even numerically before her. The formulas she processed quickly opened her vision and she peered deeper than she had ever before.

In fact, as she looked around at each object, Vesha noticed a three-dimensional data display with all of the essential information of anything she focused on intentionally, and all, such that she could clearly see the object of concentration accompanied simultaneously and strategically placed for clarity with a detailed readout of the information her mind had requested. Vesha was suddenly breath-taken by the fact that she could navigate her vision around the icebergs and ice planets in the Oort Cloud and see Andromeda more clearly now than she had ever before seen it with the naked eye or with any of the most advanced telescopes available to her when she worked in the real world as an astrophysicist.

Vesha knew there were things she would continue to learn or even discover later, when it came to her focus on the different sensory systems and areas of her brain. With just one of her new capabilities, she could tune out the light, and with appropriately-coordinated cellular and nano overlays, correctly placed around the lenses of her eyes, factoring in bend, crystallization-manipulation, photon decoding and a variety of algorithms and physics formulas, she could see beautiful arrays of colors everywhere, from nebulae to star-forming regions, to rogue planets racing through space in the dark, and decipher their molecular and chemical makeup.

It donned on Vesha that the Virtual Universe itself was beckoning for her to try looking deeper. So, she did. With a more-focused concentration in other areas of deep space she saw supernovae, globular clusters of stars, elliptical galaxies, spiral galaxies, galactic superclusters, the dark matter holding them all together—the substance she had studied much of her life as an astrophysicist, and so much more. After looking out into the dark ever-so-deeply, she was able to see anywhere, from everywhere.

As Vesha focused within each neural-region of her mind, she dove deep into her occipital lobe and its associated areas of the brain, as well as several other helpful cortices, and for the first time ever, she saw galaxies of types that had never been named or documented throughout all of history, and then she experienced vision omnidirectionally and processed it all as if it were the norm. Her digital displays factored in gravitational lensing, triangulation, the Doppler Effect, and so much more in mere moments, and she had a full scope of the Universe around her in all its complexities, relative to Earth. The colors out there were brilliant, and it was obvious that life existed out there, farther than humanity had ever been, through technology or any other means!

"Wow, Yesha and Sky, this is better than a dream! Instead of fleeting thoughts jumping around, it's as though there is this tied-in stability of the environment, yet I can focus wherever I would like, see farther than I ever have before, the nebulae, the galaxies, the supernovae, the rogue planets, all of the beautiful colors, and so much more, and it is amazing! I won't forget this or anything, because, unlike a dream, my environment isn't changing in an unstable manner, and my prefrontal cortex is as though it has expanded making sense of it all.

"To a certain extent, I see things differently, absorbing all of this information while accessing regions of my brain I never realized existed, but now I clearly realize these various regions do indeed exist and I can use them to hone the vast new options and capacities of my vision.

"Here we are; it's as if we are floating in space. I am here with you and Sky, and I can see any object I focus on clearer than I did while using the most advanced telescopes on Earth. I can see Lira, Cassiopeia, Orion, Perseus, Sagittarius, Pisces, and Pavo. I can zoom in on each star of each asterism, and deduce first, second, and third generation planetary systems. I am out in the near-absolute-zero temperature of space, and I'm not freezing. I'm not forgetting what I'm seeing, and I can see so much more.

"I'm looking around, yet I don't need to; I can see it all, and it is breathtakingly gorgeous. Seeing these locations in context, well, they make me curious to look even further. To add to this, the radiation and meteoroids don't have any negative effect on me, or us, whatsoever! It's wonderful being up here with you, Yesha, and my sweet dream angel, Sky; moments like these are beyond fantastic, especially when shared," Vesha and Sky looked around with her, while smiling and feeling a sweet release of freedom, and when they did, they all laughed in exhilaration and excitement.

"This is beautiful, Vesha and Yesha!" Said Sky.

Yesha smiled, allowing Vesha the time to enjoy what she saw for a few more marvelous and timeless moments, and then she responded. *"True and very astute on all accounts, both Vesha and Sky. There is a lot we can do, and I guarantee you, you have barely scratched the surface. As you learn something and use it, you will not forget it, so there is a lot of wisdom in your observations. I am proud of you and your rapid progress!*

"Now, I will also let you know, that when it comes to the fleeting thoughts we share, the more people we relate to and connect with, due to our neural links, the more rapidly we will learn and hone our new abilities. Interesting though, as we channel our skills, everything we can do will become mind-blowing in scope and awe, and as they say, the more of us linking just as we are now, the merrier we become. Among my favorite skills in the Virtual Universe or even when we wake up and practice them within the real world are telescopic vision, microscopic vision, omnivision, and buffeting the dangers of space with little effect upon our physiology.

"Still, there is more."

Advances Abound

Yesha continued speaking after shifting her gaze, *"There are so many stunning and spectacular aspects about what we can see so far away, but sometimes it is just as beautiful and awesome to bring our focus in and see that which is nearby. Did you know, we can essentially fly to any location in the Universe that has ever been digitized or triangulated by these Twelve Database Moons that revolve around the Earth like satellites, and we can see and go pretty much everywhere, anywhere, and anytime? Our minds are synced with these large moon-like data centers using the most robust and state-of-the-art equipment. The sensory and protective transceiving systems and high-tech quantum computers are the most advanced of any others that have ever been built in the history of humanity. Together, they act as faster-than-light transceivers, using a variety of exotic quantum factors to jump instantly between the biopods, our neural transmissions between each other, and our bio and neuro-nanos for thought, shared-experiences, healing, learning, excitement, you name it—and they are synced to every place like this...*" As Yesha pointed, Vesha and Sky saw Earth's Moon, and then they saw another moon.

It was much smaller, but it was still magnificent, huge, gargantuan, and full of intrigue and luminosity, and it appeared to be three-hundred miles in diameter, based on Vesha's digital display!

"*We are orbiting just on the outside of the gravitational pull of our Moon, or what we sometimes call Selene, so, between Selene, and what are called, LaGrange Points 1 and 2,*" said Yesha. "*This small moon and about eleven others like it are orbiting our Earth in a sophisticated array and tangent and are for all sakes and purposes more advanced than any construct made by humanity in the real world and are cloaked to the public eye, and thus are practically invisible. People cannot see them by just looking up at the sky or scanning with conventional radars, sensory systems, or telescopic technologies. These satellites, which have more capacity and capability than all the other satellites combined, have the latest in high-invisibility cloaking.*

"*Japanese scientists had been working on this technology for years, and they were doing a remarkable job. It was Eliza, however, who cracked the invisibility code a couple of years before the formation of Pathway and applied it as Pathway grew to every vulnerable and covert advancement she came up with. She did this to maximize our ability to protect humanity from the malicious use of any of the tech. Eliza ensured safety mechanisms were in place before the brewers of uncontrolled chaos or overmuch quantities of greed, selfishness, hatred, toxicity, and prejudice had an opportunity to grasp, understand, manipulate and use them for means that have nothing to do with the preservation of life, its longevity, or the well-being of humanity or life itself. It's a simple combination of undetectable multi-spectrum laser sensors, cameras, and digital pixilations, and particles that the established sciences have yet to discover. Look over there!*"

Yesha pointed toward several magnificent and gleaming cities sprawling the dark side of the Moon. "*These cities are but a few of many. They span the solar system with a total of twenty-thousand cities that can provide high-quality living for at least ten-million families, with capacity for growth, and can only be seen by those who have been optimized and interfaced for further training within the Virtual Universe. The designs for these high-tech cities, with self-sustaining, well, everything, had already existed in some lesser form of one kind or another throughout the world. We gathered them all together, picked the best aspects of each, reinvented every detail quite a bit, and improved upon their features in spades. Then, Eliza encoded large clouds of nanos to build them, while the rest of us worked with James Cooper and his crew in the building of the infrastructure of our then-new company, Pathway LLC, on Earth, before the formation of Pathway Industries. You were there, Vesha, but those memories may have faded, due to the dementia you were suffering from at the time. You now know or are relearning it all, but in quantities that are several orders of magnitude greater and in fractions-upon-fractions of a single second in time, and based upon our time dilation ratio, yet amenable to updates if we would wish to stay longer.*

That said, we finally dropped the reference to "LLC" or "Industries" and called our organization, Pathway. Everything you see was initially designed by Eliza and me. James helped us improve upon them, and together he and his crew helped us to make all of this happen. Believe me, Eliza thinks of everything. I helped a little bit, but you'd be amazed at how she thinks. We briefed every single one of Pathway's current population of more than two-billion citizens, fully, as soon as they were read-in, much like you now. Look over there."

Vesha suddenly felt her occipital lobe engage again, integrate with her vision, her hippocampus, her prefrontal cortex, and then connect from the corpus callosum. Vesha then discovered again that she now possessed what would be called, shared-thought, vision, and scope, and in this case, it was with Sky and Yesha, as she was now connected more deeply to their minds.

Vesha realized that her dominant and active cranial regions were coupled through each individual's corpus callosum to their dominant areas. Her visual ability multiplied exponentially zooming in to see extravagantly intricate details, down to the particles, then it scoped out again and she saw the fullness of the dark side of the Moon. It hovered within clear view, yet still gave way to the revelation of every finite detail.

Vesha and Sky were in fact seeing what Yesha was seeing. What left her even more impressed, were the waterfalls, the atmosphere that had an air of nature, calm, beauty, and a welcoming ambiance. Surrounding and within the tech cities, was cleanliness, colorful arrays of trees, forests, jungles, flowers, vegetation, morels, spices, and herbs of every kind. There were streams, and lakes, self-sustaining systems, and a unique melding of each aspect of nature with every single bit of the architecture of every building.

Vesha noticed how, although each building was unique, and in a magnificently beautiful way, they seemed to complement and integrate with each other and the nearby terrain with pristine quality and impenetrable durability. Each of the cities she beheld was connected in a variety of intuitive ways, beautiful to witness, and in its own intriguing manner—from the sky view of the city to the city's view of the sky and then the cosmos, itself.

Vesha drifted away, turned around and took advantage of the protection from the sunlight by the dark side of the Moon, to look at more of the constellations from the location she was at—she couldn't help herself, since she had done that as a professional all of her life.

There was Andromeda, the Milky Way's nearest major spiral galaxy, almost as clear as day. *"I can see her still there, coming closer, and she is beautiful. I can see better or more clearly than I ever did before, even with our country's most advanced telescopes. The stars, the constellations there, I can triangulate, and the physics that I know and am learning as I speak tell me there are quite a few fascinating planets that would be very nice to see soon. I'm hoping that 'someday' will be very shortly. Does this mean I am physiologically and neurologically upgraded with so much more than mere telescopic vision of a very cutting-edge variety?"*

"Yes, you are, and you can see her, Vesha. In every way, you are correct, it is due to telescopic vision, but that is one of the most advanced abilities along with one of the most difficult to learn, but you have learned it already, and I am proud of you. Your occipital lobe has been re-optimized, as well as your hippocampus, prefrontal cortex, corpus callosum, and the cornea, irises, pupils, and lenses of your physiological eyes. In the future, just like now, you will be able to engage these abilities as well as others you will be trained on, both inside and outside the Virtual Universe. Your hypothalamus and amygdala have been enhanced to maximize how your hippocampus processes

everything and retain it, also adding to the enjoyment and appreciation of it all, as well as your ability to recall each of your memories as clearly and as soon as you need them. Andromeda is beautiful though, isn't she?"

Then Yesha turned slightly to her right, to continue her training and pointed as she spoke, *"What do you think of this?"*

Vesha turned and looked where Yesha was pointing and realized that she had again sent a mental image of what she was leading at from Yesha's viewpoint and location. Before her, on the conveniently located digital display, was all the essential information.

Vesha then felt her mind fill with clarity and explained to Yesha's satisfaction what she saw, *"Just like a moment ago, I can see what you see right now, as if I were you, and I can study the intricate details of the Twelve Database Moons, but I've focused closer and can see their insignias and their ornate complexity, as well as the aesthetics of it all. Wow! Now I'm in awe of what they can do and what they hold within them. I am in fact receiving robust and phenomenal updates quickly. The speedy comprehension-levels, the clarity of the visual aspects of understanding, and the ability to derive and surmise so much based on just a few pages of what is available within my mind, courtesy of these Twelve Database Moons, has me in awe. I can fully understand the meaning for each symbol, all of which seems to be flooding into my mind as soon as I see it! You two were way ahead of many when it comes to robotics, nanos, and artificial intelligence!"* As the purpose behind each symbol became clear, so much more made complete sense, and then she was moved with emotion. *"Yesha, you should know that you, yourself, certainly deserve credit for lighting a fire under Eliza's innovative prowess. You have complemented her brilliance in every possible way. The closest friends I have, aside from my family that do that for me are Sky, Najem, and Jasmine.*

"Here I am, integrated with your and Eliza's minds, with Sky actually accompanying both of us as her own living entity, and this experience is through the roof—I'm trying not to cry! These symbols have quite a history to them! It's as if they represent in visual form, a bit of artistry, the desire for peace among civilizations, and communication of the Universe. I can understand so much more, to include the breadth of the physical properties and abilities of these database moons. I can see where and when these images and symbols were communicated by the ancients of every dominant religion and civilization of Earth's latest historical inhabitants. I can see somehow that each of these was received through frequencies and other radiated communications and put into play as intended. Who would have known these symbols had a higher value of purpose than what we had initially appreciated or took them for? They integrate, as if cracking some long-lost and encrypted code. Everything symbolic is there, and it is all so elegant and so majestic. I can see cryptograms, including those of the ancient Egyptians, the Assyrians, the Muslims, the Norse Pagans, and each of the Asian and Hindu Religions. Oh, Christian faiths of all genres, Jewish faiths of each type, and intriguing religions I had no idea about before. I can see the Navajo, Cherokee, Aztec, Mayan, Pomo, Pygmy, Aborigine, and Eskimo faith symbols, and so many more, and the list goes on, are all woven in from all over our world. Wow! They seem to tie into the radiation reflective-absorption balance and defensive capabilities of the Database Moons themselves. I'm quite taken aback by the artistry and sophistication here. This is truly amazing, Yesha. Really! This is awesome. Who would have known?

"Wow!

"This is beautiful.

"I am actually quite impressed.

"How did you guys pull this off?" Vesha then saw the gigantic shield-like massive constructs protecting the Earth, Selene, and the database moons. It had never donned on her how much Eliza and Yesha had planned and then through James and his crew, they had carried out ever-so-brilliantly. She felt peace in her heart at the safety and security the people on Earth could move forward with, if only they knew. She saw how each shield around each planet throughout the solar system provided just the right amount of energy and light in intervals to each spherical surface, so as to protect them all, and in a unique way. The Moon, for example, was given the kind of protection necessary to afford it a beautiful, yet cozy atmosphere, and she saw where the terrain was teeming with rivers, lakes, mountains, cliffs, waterfalls, islands, seas, and life. However, if viewed from outside the Virtual Universe, no one would ever know this existed at all or at least in that way.

Yesha then explained, *"Eliza thought about all of this, a way to preserve our minds, a way to preserve our solar system, a way to preserve our home world, and even a way to connect from one being to another. Since the creation of these shields and database moons, as well as the creation of Pathway, we have melded minds with people from all over the world, and so many more forms of life than I will list at this time.*

"Vesha, there is a lot of purpose behind each symbol; simply put, these symbols have everything to do with the proper balance of absorption and deflection of radiation of every single kind of particle, to include both baryonic and non-baryonic material, and all as your mind has revealed to you and you have noted."

Yesha then pointed toward another location on what she now understood as an ancient planetary spheroid they occasionally called Selene, and Vesha saw, again, it was the Moon. There it was, the Moon, beautiful Selene, and she was teeming with wildlife, with spacious running areas for stampedes of buffalo, deer, elephants, lions, leopards, bears, tigers, and giraffe; every single animal a person could imagine was right there, together, healthy, happy, safe, full of life, and no longer wild, but tame, domesticated, and sentient. They were all out for a stroll, linking mind-to-mind, and they were looking out for one another with an intriguing sense of politeness. Gone was any reason for predation, and in its place was a collective-sense of well-being, with plenty of locations filled with viable food in a beautiful home they all shared.

There were mountains, rivers, streams, forests, oceans, islands, and even continents filled with beautiful, artistic, and futuristic tech cities that were beyond description in their beauty and usefulness. Spaceports were everywhere, with a wide variety of transportation options, and each with a vast array of purposes.

"Just like you see on Selene, the same is true on Mars, its moons, Ceres and other spherical asteroids or small planets, the moons and planetoids of the giant gas planets, Pluto and the dwarf planets of the Edgeworth-Kuiper Belt, and further out to the Oort Cloud and each of their moons, and any spherical planetoid throughout our solar system.

"As we rescue the refugees, those reared in abusive homes, victims of malevolence, tragedies, or natural disasters, and each person willing, once pre-trained at Pathway Campuses, they are then optimized physiologically and neurologically, and they enter the Virtual Universe, and are encouraged to share their wisdom. From there, they are given safe domicile in any of the tech cities you see, with resplendent luxuries and views that are breathtaking year-around!

"With all that I have shared with you, the more we collectively learn and train each other and with each other, the more the entire process of mastering our new abilities become more comfortable to control. When that happens, you will find that fewer advanced-control-mechanisms and maintenance algorithms by our space nanos are needed. This is due to the fact that our bodies will, through this due diligence, emulate those abilities and adapt them to our own biological construct. In many ways this helps to preserve our humanity.

"Right now, as I have shared with you and Sky before, the total population of the tech cities is at two-billion citizens, and growing, so you can imagine that the collective wisdom in Pathway, via the Twelve Database Moons, shared by everyone here through the Virtual Universe, and continuously growing through our neural links, is exponential. No matter how connected we are, no matter how much we share, or how alike our overall goals may be, we still have, and always will have, our individuality and all the beauty that comes with it.

"Now, you haven't asked, but many do, and there is something that it is important for you to know, and that is how all of this was financed. So, I will put this briefly, because of Eliza's designs, her creation of the nano cloud systems for each individual and each area of any determinate size throughout our solar system, and her innate ability to reinvest, while providing what is needed to increase the quality of life for everyone within Pathway, economically, Eliza's financial worth is in the one-hundred-Octodecillions as valued by the US Dollar.

"There is much more to explore, but we need to return soon to Eliza. We saw the tech cities, we've seen the sprawling landscape, but have you seen the extent of the Moon Base?" Yesha, beckoned her mentally to follow her gaze, and there it was, another beautiful location with a seemingly infinite series of high tech, tall, and arching domes, also teeming with luscious forests, life, industry, productivity, and portals full of activity, with spacecraft entering and exiting the large spaceport. *"The science of all of this is quite exhilarating to consider, and all that you see is part of an advanced system protecting the life of our Sun for trillions of years and more. It is also still covert to the public eye. The people on Earth will be quite surprised when all of this is revealed, don't you think?"*

With that question, Vesha was again moved emotionally at how profound Eliza, Yesha, James, and all of Pathway had thought and prepared for countless possibilities that concerned so many. Considering how it was that humanity would no longer have need to worry about so many future events, other than the preservation of the local stellar region, the Milky Way, as well as all the galaxies and the Universe itself, she agreed. *"With everything going on here, Yesha, I have no doubt the public and all of humanity will be quite surprised."*

Just like that, Vesha, Sky, and Yesha had returned and were instantly back on the couch, sitting beside Eliza, with her dog, Tyson, cuddled beside her as she listened to her music and meditated.

All of a sudden, Vesha felt as though her mind was linked to Eliza's, to all of her emotions, her dreams, her experiences, her knowledge, her wisdom—it all came flooding in. Unexpectedly, she could no longer speak.

It was as though Vesha was suddenly, a drifter, peering out, observing, feeling, and experiencing the life of Eliza Amber Williams—it was as if she was Eliza.

It felt new, it felt refreshing, inspiring, and more unique than anything she had ever felt before. The complexity of it all, the sweet flavor of individual thought and experience and perspective, was mesmerizing.

This was more surreal, yet real and delicious, to her mind than she had ever had the capacity to experience at any point within her mortal life. The same was true of her understanding, and she knew she would never be able to express what she was feeling in words once she returned to the real world.

Vesha began to grasp with complete clarity why it was that she needed to be trained within the Virtual Universe. This was the most beautiful treat of all, to link minds, and while she had linked minds in other beautiful and indescribable ways with Yesha, and while she had always been linked to Sky, who had been with her all of her life and still was, her own thoughts began to drift away, and she released the perceptions of her own mind, tearing away the misconceptions of perceived reality and she let go...

Chapter 02: Visions & Miracles

Database Moon Archive, Celestial-Sol Entry Date: 2018 December 25. Yesha Alevtina trains Vesha Celeste. In this crucial part of her training, after her awakening, they explore the biography of Eliza Amber Williams, the most pivotal influence on a promising and long-lasting future, as if they were Eliza. These journeys are re-experienced within the Virtual Universe. Vesha and Yesha are interfaced via biopod within the Pathway Melrose Campus. Input by: Yesha Alevtina, President of Pathway Industries, 2015-2022.

Vesha Celeste and Yesha Alevtina looked at each other, and then Vesha felt an intriguing and new sense of reality changing all around her. As interesting as the experiences were, when looking upon Andromeda and all of Eliza's creations, Vesha and Yesha were, for all sakes and purposes, looking into Eliza's past as though they were Eliza. As they did, Vesha was floored at how beautiful, how delicate, yet how empowering this felt, and then she began to forget herself and all her own emotions for thirty-five years within the Virtual Universe. While drifting into a completely different reality, Vesha began embracing the experience of life as viewed from the beautiful mind of Eliza, and memories and experiences sophisticatedly infused with Yesha's.

"Oh, the surge of wisdom!" Vesha's last thought...

Experiential Cognitive Frameworking

Thirty-five years ago, Eliza opened her eyes for the very first time, but as circumstances were, here she was now in the year 2015, thirty-five years later, looking back. Her years throughout life had been no easy chore, but she felt that she had been the lucky benefactor all-the-same, no matter where she went or what choices she had made.

Eliza genuinely felt that she had been surrounded by lovely and extraordinary people, and somehow where she was now, the wondrous things she had done, it was all because of so much more than she would ever give herself credit for. She didn't consume herself in the negative for too much time. Instead, maintaining a careful balance in her quest for learning, built upon experiences absorbed and shared by others, was part of what drove her.

Now, Eliza sat with the peaceful sense of companionship that existed when near a being whose primary goal in life seemed to be companionship, loyalty, and unconditional love. She felt the rewarding sagacity of accomplishment as she readied herself for meditation on her soft sofa, as her brindle boxador dog, Tyson, was alive again and filled with love curled up beside her.

Soothing music played in the background, and her past played out in her mind. By this time in Eliza's life, she had accomplished many things more in comparison to many, but comparison and harsh judgments never moved her—she merely aimed to be a reasonable and good individual wherever she was, and in all of her pursuits, nothing more and nothing less.

Convictions and dreams of hope for not one's self alone, but for others as well, were essential to her internal locus and external focus. Regardless, most of what she had done was undetectable and unnoticed by anyone, save by her friends and teammates at Pathway.

In 2007, Eliza and Yesha had built three devices that would change the world forever. Early in 2008, they found James Cooper, who helped them begin building the infrastructure for Pathway LLC. Just two years later she was given the go-ahead to go to whatever ends she could dream of, with the approval of the US Government. It was then that she, Yesha, and James had officially formed the Universal Party, and proliferated ever-so-carefully tech devices, medical remedies, and services in such a way in which it seemed to the public as though Pathway were merely a small yet admirable venture. In that same year of 2010, they established a government-sanctioned science liaison branch within their quite large and covert company and were owners of other publicly unreleased, yet remarkable, advancements. Pathway and all its subsidiaries would in due time be recognized as the major economic titans that they were.

Throughout 2010, although still hidden in plain sight, they were already more powerful than any industry within the history of all of mankind. Pathway would slowly shift the energy of humanity from that of greed, lust for power, and visions of dystopian realities, toward the development and acceptance of innovations that led to the preservation of life and multi-planetary existence. This reality was not as foreseeable by many in the public arena at that time, but it would soon be what drove many.

Eliza thought about the growth of Pathway and the realities that existed in the public realm often. It was saddening to her, for only brief moments, that too many supposed that kindness, benevolence, innovation toward a better future, and adventures throughout the cosmos and deep space, where we could bridge our diplomatic communications with distant civilizations in a shared goal to preserve life and our Universe, were dull pursuits to others, although they were invigorating to her.

It seemed to Eliza that far too many people preferred tearing others down and making cynical jokes with passive-aggressive puns designed to put people in their place, with little to show for it but a chance to walk around feeling mighty. The place they assumed others ought to be in, when these arrogant fiends had their way, was one of misery and brutality. They saw cruelty and a mediocre reality as exciting; they saw death, destruction, and chaos as the glorified way of life, and all of it, something to celebrate. Eliza didn't see it that way; she knew that neither did anyone who was of a healthy mind.

The innovations of Pathway had been briefed to each new member of Eliza's cadre, her teams and allies, during their read-in, or biopod optimizations and their subsequent training in the Virtual Universe. Through this training, each member of Pathway was able to gain a full-scope-understanding of life from another's standpoint, an increased capacity to make sense of and retain everything they had learned, and tap into an ever-increasing vastness of collective wisdom, history and physical attributes that led to youth, health, and longevity, with the ability for increased power contingent upon consistency in virtues requisite of someone deemed healthy of mind, or driven toward compassion, empathy, consent, and innovation.

For the purposes of legalities and the well-being of society, products from Pathway that Eliza and her delegates deemed ready for public distribution were placed under official review by the US Government after all safety and anti-hacking mechanisms were in place, before they were made available worldwide.

Eliza's developments in their initial stages were private and happened seamlessly having been given the critical blind-eye of public personas that had any inkling of what might be going on. This was due in part, to the overnight successes of the age and death-defying medical breakthroughs and advances that were proliferated. There was so much more developed, the which combed the globe, and no matter the advancements, all of

Eliza's technologies brought acceptance, understanding, and excitement for the future, and all of this was a result of her published and released book five years and a month ago.

Eliza thought about those moments in 2010, and as she did, she was grateful Pathway had been given the blessing by the ANSSI. This was a covert federal organization, called the US Government Advanced Science and Spatial Development Agency. Due to her keen sense of ethics and humanity, the agent she had dealt with had given Eliza and her company, Pathway LLC, permission to engage in unmonitored activities and studies in any manner she chose. With these permissions, as provided by this high-level governmental organization, Pathway was given the go-ahead to operate, and to do as she pleased, and all of it with the benefit of officially sanctioned shielding from the scrutiny of the public or by any other prying or uninformed agency or entity.

Unlike other government contractors, everything that Pathway produced and was subsequently proliferated worldwide, had been pro-bono to the government and cost nothing to the taxpayer. These protections benefitted the other agencies or entities working with them.

Sanctioning Pathway's covert activities resulted in reduced overall costs to any of the industrial sectors that had agreed to sign on to increase the quality of life, for all living beings, and not solely themselves. This idea had been presented by Pathway and agreed upon by the government for many reasons having to do with the innate nature of everyone in Pathway.

Every delegate, member, and representative of this growing industrial complex was interested in guiding humanity to a more promising future. Proper guidance required a unique balance of protection and transparency for the sake of protecting the advancement of civilization, its well-being, and its longevity and legacy.

Eliza's robust novel, "Pathway to the Stars," had turned into a worldwide phenomenon in just a month, and University and Science journals were now filled with her writings, and those of many scientists working with her. Newspapers, blogs, and even television stations, all of which had put in requests to Eliza, Yesha, and James for countless interviews over a short period of time, filled the internet and newsstands of every street.

Talk shows and ideologues had been abuzz about Eliza's recently released quasi-political, utopian, and scientific masterpiece. It was a careful balance at that time to share with the masses only what they were ready for while protecting humanity from the malicious minds that pursued destruction, unbalanced and uncontrolled forms of chaos through improper use of technology, and both physical and emotional brutality—she ended this quickly.

Eliza desired to share every detail that ought to be released to the public sooner to save lives, but she also knew it was important to protect humanity from others with deviant minds, and not just any deviant mind, but those with aims toward cruelty and brutality, and from something much worse should these powerful tools fall into those wrong hands without proper and protective mechanisms in place.

Eliza and Yesha shared many ideas with each other growing up. Following Yesha's admonition and moral support began considering putting pen to paper. Following the shared efforts of James and his crew with the build-up and expansion of Pathway, Eliza followed Yesha's and James' advice to write a novel.

Within the first quarter of 2010, Eliza released her ideas of requirements for a successful civilization for the entire world to see. With the quick success of her masterpiece soon after its release, she had gained acclaim worldwide and a renewed hope that humanity just might be ready to take this opportunity to begin moving forward in science, and travel through space with a noble purpose.

Enthusiasm for science had begun to wane in the public eye, prior to the release of her thick and detailed novel, but her novel gave humanity a gentle nudge and something miraculous occurred and the eyes of the public had begun a full-on three-sixty turn-around as innovative spirits were on the rise and the fruits of their efforts ripened in a sweet and delicious manner. The words and admonitions in Eliza's novel had caught on like wildfire and all of this because people yearned for something that would provide substance to their minds, of hope, and of ideas that would give meaning toward vigorous focus, and all with a special insight that would imbue into them a renewed sense of depth and purpose, based in science.

The end of her time as Pathway's President was coming by all too quickly, to Eliza. She knew, however, that it was time to pass the torch on to another highly trusted leader of many. During her five years, after being sanctioned by the ANSSI, she continued to lead covert, public, and economic advances with very astounding success. Eliza was ready for her next role of influence and leadership. She prepared for the political arena. It was essential to her and as such the rest of humanity's future.

By 2015, Pathway LLC had grown to be one of the most beloved and influential employers throughout the world. Her pursuits had quickly matured into Pathway Industries, and shortly after that, it became a mighty titan of influence, commerce, and advancement as Pathway.

Eliza had built a mega-employment and a socio-politically-motivated, solar-system-spanning, covert, and societally advancing powerhouse which included every one of the major industries throughout the world. Amidst so much, she had developed some of the most advanced medical help-aids. Eliza had brought to reality lush living quarters that cost nothing to anyone but herself. She built these retreats for refugees, societal victims, and read-in members of Pathway. She also built beautiful getaways for those who were not read-in. The quarters at Pathway were at a quality-of-life-level that was just as lush as the most beautiful places throughout the world, yet affordable by way of Pathway's public safe homes, all of which were available within many communities worldwide.

Eliza had also upgraded, improved upon, and created an endless and vast array of enriching educational opportunities and capacities while enabling anyone who wished to attend school an affordable opportunity to do so. She had increased the utility, longevity, and safety of Pathway-based entertainment products and gadgets, and she had even developed environmental scrubbers for healthy air and healing mechanisms for the ground, water, air, and all of life. Her inventions and ideas were released with proper safeguards in place to improve the quality of life while protecting the most vulnerable.

Each item and service under Eliza's purview, once developed initially, was tested and perfected in every possible way. When ready, Pathway released them with permission from the US Government, courtesy of humane leaders and Pathway's political liaison wing.

Currently, late in 2015, Eliza was getting ready to step down and hand operations over to someone she had always looked at, and always would, as her dear friend, confidant, and fellow genius, Yesha Alevtina. Many years before, Eliza had had the gifted foresight to see the need for a newly established political party that would allow her to bring a positive influence on the Legislative Branch of the United States as well as inside many other positions of leadership throughout the world through her party's other delegates and representatives. She had known she would eventually need to run for political office and that it would become a long political career.

No matter the task, Eliza would be dedicated to a good cause and would see it through. For now, after beginning her official bid for Congress, Eliza settled into her family's estate, which she had inherited from the trust her parents had ever so wisely developed many years ago. Eliza had since become patient-zero, pioneering and testing on herself, along with Yesha at her side, her many upgrades, internal in so many advanced and useful ways.

After taking care of some miscellaneous duties on this day, much like any other, she watched the news as the countless personalities talked about her bid for Congress for a few hours, as well as the detailed formation and mission of her recently publicized Universal Party. She listened to a variety of interviews from people who she had known while growing up, testimonials from political refugees seeking asylum from violence and corruption, workers rescued from toxic places of employment who had been struggling to provide the basics for their families, and a multitude of others, all of whom she and her friends had helped.

Eliza also listened to the praise and critiques from pundits, politicians, lobbyists, and demagogues. All of this took her about twenty minutes in the real world, using the advantages of time-dilation through her neural link to the Virtual Universe. She did this, reviewing every detail and view absorbed by the Twelve Database Moons each day. Once she was sure she had a full grasp of the pulse of society in her state and worldwide, she disconnected from the Virtual Universe and began to meditate.

Eliza had meditated with Tyson by her side each day for the last five years. She did it before he was back in her life, by herself. No matter those blessed, yet subtle differences, when she meditated, she did so, thinking of the series of events that led to the rise of Pathway LLC, Tyson's return, the development of Pathway Industries, and its growth and maturity into Pathway. Eliza also thought of the voluntary optimizations and heroic acts of so many of the amazing people she had worked with and met along the way and considered what it all meant.

Ready to dig deeper, Eliza allowed her thoughts to drift back to May of 2010, five years prior.

Yesha was her best and dearest friend, her scientific confidant and cohort, her lifelong kindred spirit and extended family member who lived with Eliza on her estate and had worked with her for the last four and a half years post-doc to build Pathway LLC and all of its mysteries from the ground up, and in every way that mattered. Together, they had instructed at Harvard and MIT full time from 2006 to 2008 and then had moonlighted from 2008 to 2010 as part-time Senior Professors—Eliza, in the departments of biotechnology, quantum physics, and law, and Yesha, in the departments of neurology and psychology, while engaging in other projects that would lead to the building of Pathway LLC's infrastructure.

James Cooper had joined them in 2008 and after some beautiful moments, he became the third member of their professional collaboration, the following day both his crew and their families were on board as well. Tyson came back into her life earlier in 2010, always protecting her estate and enjoying the company of Yesenia, Yesha's mom— who resided in Eliza's estate as a close and extended family member, entertaining any visitors.

Eliza was at home and on a break meditating with Tyson lying beside her, while Yesha was going over her students' paperwork in her office at Harvard. They had at this time paused shortly from their activities within Pathway LLC. With Eliza's optimized mind, with wisdom that had been compounding since December of 2007 and her neural links, she could hear every word of the news about her new book while, simultaneously, her music played on in the background.

Yesha could likewise link with Eliza mentally, and even she rather enjoyed going back and forth using her that ability with Eliza, James, and any of the other twenty-million members of Pathway at that time. However, for some reason, they both found an appreciation for the shrewd technology of cell phones and the excitement of the latest public advances that went with it.

Yesha frowned upon the current lack of longevity, adaptability, and upgradability of these tech gadgets, however, but she didn't dwell on that for too long, at least not without making plans for improvements. It appeared that these, among many other devices and tools, were built by many for the sake of monetary gain alone, while allegedly using up and depleting the natural resources of Earth to drive up costs. At least it was clear from the public purview and spread worldwide that those motives for advancement were commonplace among the economic titans of the day. Nevertheless, Pathway had developed cold fusion and implemented it quietly, and only for the sake of safety from the hands of those with the direst of ends toward others on Earth or anywhere that life existed.

With resources no longer an escalating question of concern, Yesha saw a definite purpose in any form of technology. She saw opportunities to adapt genius-level thinking and residual production to ends that resulted in benevolence. She saw the ability to fuse great minds and ideas together to come up with greater solutions. Thus, she texted Eliza using a smartphone from time to time. Eliza felt likewise and decided to take a break from her meditation to read her texts:

"Congratulations, Eliza! Your book is a hit!

"Everyone at school is talking about it!

"I wanted to pass this on to you. I had a visit from a government official earlier today asking about you—apparently, they're going to read us in for a clearance of some sort. They want to establish an 'arrangement' to form an internal liaison arm or branch between Pathway LLC and the US Government.

"Have you heard from anyone yet?

"A lot of people throughout the world have shown quite an interest in what you wrote. It's good to have your influence within their grasp. I can't wait to see how everything plays out, because conducting leadership and governance with common sense, kindness, and care, should help to reduce the potential for malicious activities while providing a technologic boost to the medical industry, other industries, and our economy as a whole. An air of intellectual progress, a desire for well-being-oriented innovation, a pathway of getting out to space, and colonization where we can setup up safe areas, study these locations, and then adapt to the environments we find ourselves in, is among many in the arsenal of tools our leaders could use.

"These ideas all seem to resonate with the masses, Eliza."

Eliza's phone rang...

Ignoring the ringing of her cell, Eliza typed back fast, "I've heard lots of 'buzz.' There is so much going on, I went through quite a bit of it and watched many of the broadcasts in the Virtual Universe. Yesha, it looks like someone is calling. At any rate, we can only hope that our lifelong efforts, dreams, and ideas will reach the right minds.

"Everyone has an opportunity to play a significant role with their unique talents and their integration with the long-overdue effort in the upcoming years. Let's hope that those who can influence the changes necessary and who are brilliant enough to make good things happen are voted in, receptive, and productive.

"Just a second, Yesha, the phone is ringing."

The phone rang, again... and Eliza linked to Yesha and James, so they could hear.

"Hello, may I ask who is calling?" asked Eliza.

Agent Epstein

"This is Agent Epstein from the A. N. S. S. I. or 'an-see.' May I speak to Doctor Eliza Amber Williams?" inquired the Agent. She had worked with many gifted minds before. When the government was looking for hackers but wanted them on their team to fight terrorism and protect US citizens and allies from the brutality and machinations of dubious regimes and tyrants, she was put to task. When a young scientist came up with solutions that could improve both the economy and life, she was again put to task. Such was the case here, and on so many levels; daring not ask, she wouldn't now over the phone.

"Yes, this is she, how may I be of assistance?" Eliza asked, hoping it wasn't someone pretending to be who they said they were, while she quickly combed over her databases through her neural link to the Internet and the Virtual Universe. After doing so in a microsecond, she was pretty sure the individual she was talking to was someone who was legitimate. They were good with encryption, so little was found; what was found seemed safe enough. Eliza and Yesha had fielded a host of calls over the last month. It was usually a hassle since none of the callers were linked, which meant scrubbing and combing over the Virtual Universe to double check.

Agent Epstein, who picked up on Eliza's cautious tone, thought quickly, which was a gift of hers, and had been noted by the powers that be when she was much younger and finishing her graduate degree in national security. She responded, "Doctor Williams, I am sure you have received a lot of calls from those with less than an honorable agenda, but I assure you, I am very confident you will be satisfied once we have met. Plus, I won't be a bug in your ear for too long. I represent a more covert Federal agency, and we're very interested in meeting with you to support you in all the ways that matter in your endeavors. We would like to meet at a location and at a time of your choosing, at your earliest convenience to go over some important matters, if that is okay with you? Do you have any questions?" With much more to do and several briefs to give, Agent Angela Epstein had decided to cut to the chase and sate Eliza's need for clarity and answer any questions proposed, in the most precise and quickest manner possible. She had done this, many times before, and she could pick up on the wise and astute right away. Eliza was definitely one of those, and in ways only her organization knew, at least outside of Pathway.

Angela's organization had picked up on a number of odd, magnetic, and radiologic anomalies, through satellites and in various areas around the world, and they seemed to center around Eliza's estate in Cambridge and in some forestation just inside Melrose County, and both of them inside Massachusetts. These anomalies had provided a very positive impact for the US and its allies, so her bosses thought it best to bring Eliza under their wing, so they too could share in this amazing reality taking place. Furthermore, Eliza's novel had been rich in technology and advances that would benefit the globe.

"It does sound interesting, Agent Epstein, but can you please enlighten me? You are correct; the phone has been ringing quite a bit, and of course, I need to make sure this call is legitimate. I am aware of the ANSSI and that they invest in technologies in the interest of space travel, health, and human advancement; however, I don't know too much other than that. So, if I may, I'd like to ask you what it is that you need. And, can you deliberate on the ANSSI a little bit more?"

In truth, within these few brief moments, Eliza knew everything possible and available through every digital source about the ANSSI, yet she also knew that this visit and agreement was necessary. Eliza was brilliant enough to know that this meeting would put Pathway in safe footing when it came to legal matters. She also knew it was best to be reasonable and somewhat wise to play the fool.

"Sorry, of course, Ma'am. I work with the US Agency, called the Advanced National Science & Space Initiative or ANSSI, pronounced "An – See," as it seems you've already picked up on. I hope you don't mind, but your novel was so brilliant and popular that all our agents and subject matter experts have combed over each page of your book several times. With that knowledge, they have seen and paralleled with your writings, some of the technologies you have proliferated through the FDA.

"After much deliberation, we believe you might be able to assist us concerning matters related to medical care, neurological health, national welfare, our crumbling economy, global security, and advanced developmental science—among many others, all related to proper preparation for deep space exploration.

"This is an item of a sensitive nature, however, so we would very much prefer it if you could withhold from talking about our conversation with anyone else, except your friend, Dr. Yesha Alevtina and perhaps Mr. James Cooper, until we've had a chance to meet with and talk to you in a more private setting. We've already met with Yesha today, so, we'd like both of you and James to be there for the next visit." Angela was hoping she had been effective. She viewed her organization as stellar, and with an agenda that was noble and purely about human advancement thru science and preservation of humanity.

"That should be fine, Angela. I appreciate the fact that you took the time to reach me. I thank you for the time you and your team members have taken to read and examine what I wrote and what our organization has already done. What you're saying sounds intriguing, so I believe we would be happy to listen and potentially work with you. To make sure you are who you say you are, for security reasons, I'd like for us to meet first in the visitor's lobby, at Harvard University. I'm sure you'll understand our need to check your organizational badges and scan your personal identification before we can proceed to my office. Is tomorrow at fifteen-hundred hours okay with you?"

"Yes, Dr. Williams, that time will work for us, thank you. I also appreciate your keen emphasis on security. We'll gladly show you our badges and IDs before we get started." Angela was quite impressed with Eliza's response. She had been observing her activities in secret for the last three years or so, ever since she had been rebuked by the authorities for her development of the 'biopod.' Angela had disagreed with their stance, so when the moment was right, and the correct changes were made through voting-in a new administration with a big agenda on the socio-economic, welfare, and healthcare of the nation, she knew when she had pored over Eliza's book, and her cohorts had done likewise, that now was the right time to set the country up for success and popular footing in the eyes of the rest of the world. She had hoped to let the world know, indirectly of course, that the US did care about well-being beyond its borders, and within. Eliza was brilliant, and the exact vehicle that was needed.

"That sounds good. Oh, you don't have to 'ma'am' or 'doctor' me. Please, in the future just call me Eliza. If you have any questions, or if you can't get ahold of me for any reason, please contact Yesha or James. They'll be able to get ahold of me and relay any details." Eliza didn't mind being 'doctored,' but she preferred a sense of levity, the kind that first names provided. This type of freedom also lifted the mind to greater heights in innovation, hence.

Agent Epstein knew that as much as she wanted to be informal, she too was being monitored, and she didn't want to give away too much, at least in any way that might have suggested to her superiors that she was becoming complacent and letting her guard down. So, despite Eliza's request, she responded formally, "Copy all, Dr. Williams. We're looking forward to meeting with you."

"We'll see you then at fifteen hundred tomorrow," replied Eliza. *"Again with 'doctor,'"* she thought, as both ended their call. Eliza thought about it, and she knew her title was written in the introduction of her book, "Pathway to the Stars." Besides, Angela was obviously trained that way, and Eliza understood governmental protocol and

A Cosmic Legacy: From Earth to the Stars

professionalism. Eliza had written draft policy for her state and federal representatives on a regular basis for several years. *"It seems that some people have a better sense as to when to let rigid obedience go for the sake of fluid communication,"* Eliza thought. *"Still, the Agent had called, and clearly, this arrangement was going to be non-standard, so perhaps she was acting overly professional as a sort of cover."* With that thought in mind, Eliza was excited to meet with Agent Epstein but kept her excitement between herself, Yesha, and James.

After the call, Agent Epstein was content. She was looking forward to meeting this enigmatic character and couldn't wait for their meeting. She was pretty sure Eliza would be thrilled as well.

After the conversation between Angela and Eliza was complete, Eliza dispensed with texting and talked with Yesha and James using her neural link, *"Did you catch all of that? It looks like we need to meet together at the visitor's center at work, tomorrow at three in the afternoon. Will you be able to make it?"*

"Of course, and yes, I will, Eliza, and I'll be home in a few hours, so we can relax, watch the news, and chit-chat!" Yesha responded. She and James smiled, and Eliza picked up on it mentally.

James then responded, *"That sounds fair enough to me. Thank you for the heads-up!"*

Eliza's lifelong friend, Yesha, had encouraged her on numerous occasions to write and publish her ideas so she could inform others about what ought to be done to bridge the gaps between opportunity, survival, beautiful pursuits and personal discipline. Preservation and quality of life, optimizations of physiology and neurology and the clarity and capacity of body and mind were outstanding concerns as well. The enhancement of understanding and the successes afforded through true diplomacy were fundamental. The advancement of science and the nobility of exploration, the need for discovery, and the necessity for deep space colonization were other pursuits that Eliza had held dear for so long.

With Yesha's gentle push, Eliza had chosen to face her fears like the lion—and she wrote her ideas and published them. James had admonished her to do so over the last two years, as well, ever since they'd begun working together. After writing and publishing her book, the results took off on a path of their own. After considering the upcoming appointment with Agent Epstein, Eliza took some time, breathed in and out, and played some of the music she had compiled for moments like these to give her clarity, peace of mind, and inspiration to move forward. She did this to further optimize her mind, to process everything quickly and make sense of it all. Doing so augmented her unique and amplified features even more.

Reminiscing & Wisdom

Meditating with Tyson by her side and listening to her favorite music seemed to work wonders, especially when perfecting and enhancing her ever-developing physiological and neurological capabilities. Tyson, who was now curled up beside her had all the nuances, gestures, actions, reactions, and beloved qualities that were unique to him before he had passed away twenty years ago, in 1990.

Eliza had brought him back earlier that year, after the suggestion had been made by James to do so, using a lock of Tyson's hair she had preserved within a bookmark from her childhood. This dog was Tyson in every way he could be, and Eliza had brought him back using technology developed in her laboratories at Pathway LLC. It had been as if she had cracked a specific code perfecting stem cells using a perfected gene-editing tool that was introduced to the public as an acronym for clustered-regularly-interspaced-short-palindromic-repeats, or CRISPR, and she had developed the necessary genetic delivery system technologies.

Eliza's recently compiled playlist was in flow with her surroundings and floating beautifully through the air in shuffle mode. Music from a chill variety of new age, new wave, movie scores, and female vocal trance played from her Android, linked to an extremely advanced version of a Bose System. This allowed her favorite music to drift throughout her living room and home in a way that suited her meditation process.

Eliza had closed her eyes and put her hand gently on Tyson's head, as he lay beside her curled up. Gently massaging him behind his ears, he looked up at her, stretched his neck, licked her a few times on the face, and settled down again with his head in her lap. He was a peaceful spirit and a warm and loving companion. This was his way of telling Eliza that her love was reciprocated.

Eliza then engaged in some self-reflection. She had learned from her parents many years ago that it was essential to consider often all that had brought her to each critical point in life. Additionally, they had taught her that doing so with gratitude would increase her positive cognitive framework, expand upon her wisdom, and augment her ability to take the noble virtues of intellect, experience, gentleness, and kindness and meld them all together for increased intuition.

She meditated regularly to reflect on her past to stay well-grounded. This was Eliza's form of spirituality, this was her belief and her religion—being someone who was pensive, listening to her thoughts and the thoughts of others who were kind, as well as the kind of music that allowed her to both think and appreciate the beauty of this world. These rituals were all part of her unique nature.

Eliza felt that it helped her to become even more compassionate, considerate, and gentle, and those were traits that were important to her. As she would meditate in this way, it seemed she could pursue amazing goals as someone of a clear conscience. Settling down and taking time to ponder upon the highlights of life, reflecting on the parts of the past that were fundamental in bringing her to where she was now, were both important for her to stay well-grounded and not get lost in the chaotic shuffle of life. For Eliza, self-reflection aided the evolution of details necessary for forecasting the critical aspects of a beautiful future. As much as she might have seemed like an open book to many, throughout her life she had plenty of ideas that were bottled up or shared only with Yesha or James. Anyone else who became read-in to Pathway would experience these moments in the Virtual Universe but absorb these experiences in their own way.

Eliza hummed the tune to her favorite musical artist, Depeche Mode, as their song, "Precious," was playing through the air. With the rhythm gently pulsating through the ground below her, the irony struck her—the ideas written in her book seemed to her like precious and fragile things that were now out there for the whole world to see— *"There is so much to do, so much to share, and so much to say. Hopefully, I was effective in sharing my ideas with others using clarity; with any luck, I did not cast that which was of high value before those who would carelessly trample upon them without a second thought. I hope that the good people of the world will unite and heal rather than tear people down and harm each other; it would be nice for humanity to share in the journeys through the cosmos with a promising legacy soon..."* she coached herself.

She thought about the many stories accompanied by the reality that the population of Pathway LLC living within the tech cities had grown to twenty-million people in just two years. She thought about how together with each person they had helped, they had been subsequently involved with every design and aspect of infrastructure which was currently being maintained, beautified, and improved upon at every moment of every day. It was a smooth operating work of volunteerism that would inspire anyone who knew of what was going on.

Thinking back, Eliza, who was grateful that she had been raised well by parents who loved her dearly, was no stranger to somewhat harsh winters growing up in the northeast portion of the US yet came into this world on a mild summer day and in a relatively calm environment. She was raised by parents in much the fashion one would expect of a well-grounded university professor. *"I have written policy for congressional committees, both state and federal, that seem all-too-often watered down by bureaucrats with little or no compromise within them to meet the needs of the citizens. Instead, the clarity of principle I shared became filled with agendas that were unintended for many, yet very much intended for few. Great goals with common sense and clarity were replaced with changes that had nothing to do with the well-being of the people they were elected to serve,"* her thoughts continued. In a way, writing policy for congressional representatives, where noble intent was shared, yet fractured beyond repair by the whims of the powerful and unknown, was part of her parents' legacy. This was something Eliza felt she had in common.

A series of tragedies occurred throughout her life, some of which had been shared the world over, among them, there were three that hit closest to home for her. The loss that hit her hardest, it seemed, followed her tenth birthday, when she lost her dog, Tyson, whom she saw partly as a person in every way that mattered. Tragedy hit her again just as profoundly when both of her parents contracted acute leukemia and passed away following her freshman year of college. Then there was the loss of Charles and Eugene, Eliza's and Yesha's boyfriends, at the behest of terrorists at the Twin Towers.

Amidst all the tragedies, Eliza had saved a lock of Tyson's hair to help her meditate, even while young, during any spare moments as she would consider the most vital things in life. It had seemed to her that Tyson had been fixated on those things throughout his life, and he appeared to prove this through his demonstrations of companionship, kindness, and love.

Due to unpredictable circumstances surrounding both tragedies, and her geographic limitations at the time, Eliza hadn't saved a lock of her parents' hair, nor had she for Charles or Eugene because those circumstances had been unpredictable, and she had been too far away to do anything about it at the time. Moreover, Eliza had done as her parents had requested in their will, which was, "Please donate our organs for scientific research before our remains are cremated."

Technologies that would have brought that idea to mind had not been developed yet, or she would have thought to save some DNA and bring them back too, or raise them as her children, if needed. Eliza knew if she would have done something like that society would have scowled upon her for the thought alone, and the idea would be judged by too many to count, as unethical, to put it lightly. "Plus," She would reason with herself, "Would it be them?" As it was, many things reminded Eliza of her parents throughout her estate, and every now and then she would discover another sentimental item as if hidden by them on purpose for her to find later. *"Perhaps I'll find some DNA and try, someday,"* She would entertain certain thoughts to that extreme and quickly dismiss them.

As much of a double standard as it was, even then, at the age of twenty-nine and going on thirty that year, she could justify bringing Tyson back, but not her parents, or Charles, or Eugene. The human prefrontal cortex, left brain, right brain, hippocampus, and other related areas of the human brain, with her technology, could only allow her to bring back their physiology but not their neurology, at least not without a full mapping of the neural activity.

Her dog, on the other hand, based on DNA alone, seemed to exhibit every gesture, every mannerism, and every trait, all except the fact that now he had his full tale, and she had optimized him to where he no longer needed to use the restroom, but with the faculties to do so, when on walks, and for a sense of normalcy. Tyson was fully intact, verging on highly sentient, and aware of himself as he stared at himself with plenty of vanity in the mirror and a "doggy smile," from time-to-time, now that he had been reawakened. Eliza knew that it was just a matter of time before she would be able to bring back humanity, fully cognizant of their past, at least for those that wished it.

"I am so grateful for how meticulous, creative, and brilliant my parents were when they raised me," her mind wandered, *"yet I am so sad that they aren't here to share in the joy of so many of the efforts they put in to do so. I miss Charles and Eugene, and little Tyson, too; but I am glad that in a way I have him back."*

Eliza recalled moments spent even further back, sitting with her best friend, Yesha, and listening to her parents as they would read from a variety of science books. At the same time, Tyson, laying between her and Yesha, would nose her arm with his cute little black nose to play with her, or stand nearby to place his blue rubber ball in front of her to play catch. If he did, she or Yesha would squeak the rubber ball a few times, toss it for him, and he would bring it back as proud as he could be. They would jog around the furniture playing chase for a while and then go on a little walk with him. Then they would settle down, and he'd curl up right between them as they would listen to Eliza's parents and Yesha's mom, Yesenia, as they received their mentoring, teaching, and coaching.

Eliza reminisced upon how her parents would explain on various occasions the texts they read to her in a manner that a young child could understand and then upon the environment they provided that was conducive to learning. *"I miss how they would expound upon all of the subjects and texts that they read to me, I would listen, Yesha would listen, and even Tyson seemed to listen. I always have appreciated Tyson's unconditional love, and I have continuously appreciated Yesha's friendship from my first day in life to now. James has also inspired me since the day I met him. What a wonderful man. When I was so young, my parents, they were so good at answering my questions and helping me to understand,"* she thought. *"From neuroscience, to physics, to biology and zoology, to ornithology, to history, from psychology to law, and of course economics, these and many more were topics of the arts and sciences that my parents spent a great amount of time reading to me about, teaching me about, and breaking down for my very young mind at the time."* They had mentored both Eliza and her friend Yesha, ever since these young ladies opened their eyes.

She was told many times from early childhood through to her youth that she had shown a lot of promise. Eliza found herself eagerly sharing studies, discoveries, and ideas with her parents on many occasions and— *"Oh, the smiles of approval on their faces as I shared even the silliest of concepts—the proud looks on their faces were worth every moment,"* she often pondered.

Eliza's parents left this world so soon, yet with many accomplishments in physics and neuroscience. They handed down many critical aspects of these two sciences and more to future scientists for consideration and study, deep within textbooks, some of which were passed on to the ones Eliza studied from as she went through school. Nevertheless, Eliza understood, *"Most of the time my parents' names were rarely recognized by my peers, they did not brag, they did not believe it was right to do so, therefore, people did not know unless they were very astute or informed. I believe that I learned from them that being an open example of advanced evolutionary thought might inspire a standard that leads to further and continued innovation, kindness, empathy, and compassion. I suppose no one can know everything, at least in their natural state, or given our current technologies. If we did, I presume boredom for all-too-many might set in all too fast. Still, there is always so much to learn and so much to enjoy along the way."*

Her train of thought continued, *"Very well, then. The material they provided was the driving force behind advancement in so many ways. While accolades will serve to foster a sustained sense of innovation, and while it shows great character to applaud others for their wisdom and achievements, it is even more profoundly important to help others because it is the correct way to begin the preservation of humanity, our planet, our solar system, and our Universe. It is far greater to be self-governed by personal convictions related to well-being, quality of life, and the ability to properly control chaos, than to be recognized for greatness or to seek status or recognition us.*

"*Nevertheless, we need to internally pat ourselves on the back for a job well-done, from time to time, yet not try to seek it from others. Cheer others for their successes, and if they cheer us for a job well-done, we can be gracious and say, 'Thank you.' Whether others recognize the source of wisdom, or the wisdom shared, or they do not, we sometimes need to afford others an opportunity to go through life and become their better selves in their own time. Sometimes we must be gracious for their wisdom despite our current level of knowledge.*"

Much of what Eliza's parents had done, was far from any textbook and was more of experiential. They had a range in neuroscience and physics that would have been the envy of the world, had humanity known—most of which was handed down to Eliza and Yesha through their integrity of character, the likes of which had turned them both into the geniuses they became.

While much of what Eliza's parents had accomplished lay under the radar, her parents confided in her often, "*The most powerful legacy that we can leave behind for humanity is you, Eliza. Our greatest legacy is our daughter. In time you'll discover new things, more than we can expect to share or show you now. We have confidence that you will utilize the tools we have given you to benefit the lives of many others, as well as your own life. Now, now, don't shake your head and look up to us in innocent disbelief, it is you, Eliza Amber Williams, you who are our most precious treasure; you who are a pearl of happiness. Our gift of life was a simple one, yet our time spent with you and the quality of it, the knowledge, the which we have imparted to you and through you, is a gift that will change not just the world, but so much more.*" Her parents' belief in her added further fuel to the fire that burned ever-so brilliantly within, no matter which type of moment took its course.

Despite the plethora of harrowing experiences that would have caused many others to give up, Eliza had an internal drive not known to many—no matter the misfortune, she would never give up on humanity. She knew how to make her way through the world in the thickest of turmoil, but Eliza had always aimed to take the smartest, safest, and the most beautiful path to enable others to follow closely behind rather than finding themselves lost in confusion and self-doubt, no matter what she did. Her parents had raised her to love others, notwithstanding the folly of mankind. "*I know that deep within every person I will ever meet, there is some form of decency—it is my responsibility to find it, to bring it out, and to push wonderful people to a healthier day, if for no other reason than because they can't see it within themselves. It helps to have that extra boost on the toughest of days.*"

Those who knew Eliza knew she was not naïve to the injustices of this world, and although she handled most thoughts and mannerisms with a gentle and a suave demeanor, she still knew there were those that required a very stiff rebuke. "*Oh, the machinations of malicious dilatants, the cosmic clowns who seem to rule society or vile and brutal clans and gangs all too often without well-being in mind as the driving force. Oh, the people whether leading, or weathered from abuse, who speak as empty husks of themselves or who work in lazy servility feeding the bane of advancement, the destruction of our world, mired in bureaucracy of baseless naysayers and power seekers with zero vision beyond their own desire for power for the sake of power and the establishment of guile. For they are as poor frigid souls without any sign of fire burning within, except for their vapid lust for decay."*

To anyone who knew Eliza, there was no doubt, nor would there ever be, of her abilities, her drive toward purpose, and her vision of clarity toward the future, they also knew she did not suffer fools lightly—yet she was patient with them. Everyone she knew, to include her professors, her peers, her friends, and her family, saw the clarity of vision into the future obligatory of any great leader within her; she inspired them. They thought of her as perhaps the most phenomenal leader the world would ever know. Changing the perspectives of humanity and changing the world in beautifully and captivatingly unimaginable ways was second nature to Doctor Eliza Williams, *"or simply Eliza,"* as she thought to herself.

"No one should ever feel their personal character desecrated by the things we say. The thoughts we share, the ideas we converse about, or the actions that put power behind the words we speak are meant to inspire our best. Unless a person truly has malevolent intent, they should use that fire that burns within to change for the better for progress, even for life, for liberty, and the pursuit of happiness. If they feel possessed by malevolence, they can ask why or for what purpose they are doing what they do, and if the answers lay outside the well-being of others, their quality of life, and innovation for a better future, then it is possible and time to make the change. They should strive to be compassionate, yet fierce, kind, yet innovative, pragmatic, but benevolent, and all toward raising the bar for humanity and the quality of life for all, to include ourselves. That pursuit may seem elusive, but that is where joy is born, and with any issue affecting longevity and quality of life resolved, there are many more things we can pursue, always," Eliza, thought to herself.

Most people, who worked with her or knew her in any way, knew her intentions were genuine, her passions were real, her motivations were profound yet beautiful, and her internal will was unstoppable. Eliza's goals were set in stone and written deep within; she took it up as her duty to confront people with respect and dignity, no matter whom she was considered to be or what title she or anyone else had. If there were ever an occasion to fight with words or in any other way, it would be in defense of the meek, lowly, kind, and gentle people and in defiance of the hardened, brutal, surly, maliciously powerful, and unkind. She always found it within herself to look for the goodness in others, and notwithstanding, refine her own abilities even more as time would pass by—if anything, to reach out to more people, in a manner that was heart-to-heart, mind-to-mind, or to expand her influence of hope, optimism, and motivation to productivity with love.

In everything she did and in every moment as she grew, the idea of taking on tasks had an heir of benefitting the lives of all she knew, and love seemed no stranger to her. *"I must not succumb to lust for power but long for joy and love, nor should I thirst for wealth but have an appetite for intellect and compassion; I will not fall prey to greed or any sort of malice, yet I will boost those who are meek and seek praise for the innocent. If my perspectives are rooted in benevolence, I will look only to receive what is needed to get the job done. I will live as I want each person, I will ever meet to be able to live. I must not be a force for anything but that which brings ease, vigor, peace, passion, kindness, innovation, purpose and meaning."*

Despite her skepticism of the way the world was run, she still knew that the leaders could have done so much better and squandered so much less. Their mantra could have meant so much more if their source of influence hadn't been subjects of negligence to the sciences and art. If their focus had been toward the challenges of this world that led to the preservation of life, their results would have enabled long, and healthy lives filled with clarity of the mind and joy of the heart. If given more simplicity rather than unnecessary complications or given change with real purpose and meaning in conscious thought leading to a decrease in human suffering, rather than change merely for the sake of change alone, life would lose its toxicity and humanity would prevail over the long-term. She knew this could and had to be so.

In the face of the greed and lust for status that plagued the world, Eliza would eventually turn out to be the President of the US. She always believed that an inspired leader would, "*Shape the type of environment required in this world to enrich the lives of mankind and enable the development of capabilities that would send humanity into the cosmos. They would preserve life and diversify our history, our legacy, and do things right this time, rather than have a new civilization stricken with ignorance or shamed by leaders who are murderous tyrants and then subsequently suffer from plagues we already have learned to overcome. We can evolve, we can unite, and we can diversify our locations of existence throughout the stars and galaxies, but still keep in touch, and preserve life and abundance rather than leave desolation and devastation in our wake. In this way, we can go further than before with promise and surety.*"

At this time in her life, however, Eliza was not aware of her near-distant future, yet she contemplated on her internal ethics, what drove her, and to her the future was just a few steps away, "*Lives can be improved, suffering reduced, and through that, humanity has a promise of a future filled with joy and peaceful laughter. Ideas of seeking power cannot waste any time clouding my judgment. I am grateful that with my friends, or in other words all who work with me, we have already come a long, long way.*"

Eliza meditated on all she knew, upon each of her closest of friends, those who worked with her, and those who were motivated by the values she shared and held dear—they were her kindred spirits, they were those who reminded her of why it was she loved all of life and all of humanity. Eliza began to think more deeply about her experiences, the experiences that shaped who she was, the wisdom that helped her to grow, to invent, and to see so clearly what it was that was required to be done, and then she drifted to the very beginning...

Preparing the Way

Eliza was born on Wednesday, July 2nd of 1980.

Many years prior, Eliza's parents established their roots in the small and quaint colonial town of Cambridge within the state of Massachusetts, near several parks that were close enough to the coast, following a decently sized walk, and not too far northwest from Harvard and MIT. They had planned for and purchased a calming and pleasant brick and stone home with white columns and trim. Ivy covered some parts of the building architecture and most of the stone walls surrounding their ten-acre yard on the northwest end of Garden Street.

During their first summer at their acreage, Eliza's father and mother had built a small one-acre lake with a waterfall adorned with a human-sized feminine angelic statue atop the center of a tiny island that cycled the water. The pond was purified through the water pouring from the cupped hands of the marble figure, which was the source of replenished water as it fell upon the stones and small and colorful gravel creating mineralized water that was oxidized, before cycling calmly into the pond itself. The tiny lake was filled with healthy plants and organisms, providing a healthy ecosystem for the frogs and the coy fish within. As the water orbited around the statue, a small windmill picked up enough energy to cycle the water back through the statue, where the cycle would continue. The frogs and coy fish, in turn, helped to organically lessen the negative impact of too many mischievous bugs during the warmer summer months.

Surrounding the pond was beautiful, useful, full, and lush vegetation, with walkways like large spokes of a bicycle around the pond, dotted with steppingstones and lush, ground-combing vegetation that led to the center of a little island with the statue of an angel. Below each walkway were underwater portals with an underwater current light enough, allowing the fish and frogs to pass through unharmed, as the water completed its full cycle.

Along with the fragrant benefits of sage, mint, and the lightly scented flowers that surrounded the sandy shores of the pond, that kept unwanted insects away and added to the aromatic nature of the Williams' sanctuary of personal reflection, there were medicinal plants such as yarrow and Aloe vera in plenty supply available for any necessary purpose.

Surrounding the perimeter of the acreage, there were red and green leafed maple trees intermingled with cypress evergreens and several other variations of hardy, sturdy, and beautiful trees that brought shelter from the harsh winters and shade from too much sun to all who would partake of the peace, joy, and pleasant vibes that were found within.

Stone pathways hither and thither allowed for walking excursions from the house to the significant features of the yard, including the weather-proofed tool shed with electricity tied into solar arrays and several windmills and restroom facilities near the northeast perimeter. Flowers surrounded the stones, Tennessee blue grass filled the open spaces, flower beds, herbs, morels, and spices were in-between the many varieties of trees, along with the walkways, and on the grounds around the perimeter. A swing for two had been nestled between two white oak trees twenty yards from the pond. Stone benches were carefully placed around the tiny lake.

An ideal clearing for a view of the nighttime sky was located between the statue of an angel and their home. The Williams' terrain created the perfect environment for tenting and soaking in the ambiance. Their home was enviable to many, with an acreage that was a paradise of their own toil, thought, sweat, and love of life.

The Williams' choice of location and setting helped them to maximize their peace of mind and as such their focus toward their professions, their studies, and their eventual plans to raise a child or more with enough room and board for foreign exchange students or extended family available, if it were ever needed.

They waited years before having a child and spent their time-saving money, paying off their estate and creating the ideal situation for rearing children, investing their money strategically in the latest promising technologies and emerging industries, both in stocks and mutual funds, which they had vetted and believed in, and they had done so and continued to do so successfully.

Eliza's parents wanted to enable their children to attend the best universities the country had to offer, with instructors who taught with clarity, while motivating others' desires to learn, rather than suffer through the type of brutal instruction that sucked the life out of anyone's desire to absorb the wisdom of the ages through study, knowledge, and experience.

They did all of this because they wanted to raise any child in their home in a way that would grant them the best of all successes in life. They wanted them to have the opportunity to focus on constructive achievement in ways that had not been gifted to them when they were young. Diligent labor, wisdom, and struggle had helped their parents to achieve their hopes. Proper mentorship, instruction, coaching, teaching, love, joy, and nurture would help their children to attain the most benevolent dreams of humanity.

Drs. Janice Clarity Williams, Professor of Theoretical Physics at MIT, and James Gale Williams, Professor of Neurology at Harvard University, had both worked very hard, despite all. Every day of their careers they saved and invested money in promising enterprises and enjoyed their estate while improving upon it, rather than spending it on frivolity, keeping up with the mindless crowd, or going on lavish cruises or wild adventures unless they served a greater purpose.

They chose, as an alternative, to spend their free time beautifying their gardens, sharing ideas with each other, enjoying their ambiance while on walks along the beach nearby or around their community, and they waited until the time was right before they would bring new life into the world. Patience is almost always a virtue and little did they know that it would also bring about the right kinds of experiences at a point in history and time that would gift the world with a precious mind.

The environment for their child would be replete with the ideal influences, love for life, innovation, and ingenuity, as well as shared knowledge, and inspirational capacity for a gifted individual and a new generation to have the tools needed to help humanity to go even further than ever before.

Janice and Gale were not particularly religious; they were agnostic to the extent to which they had their own beliefs but appreciated the various religions if they taught kindness. They knew they had no idea about what came after death and were not afraid to admit the fact that they were pretty sure no one else honestly knew either way. They had their own sets of values and ethics, and only had hopes for some sort of progression no matter how eternity continued. Yet, they carried themselves with great respect toward anyone who was considerate of others and their well-being, regardless of their beliefs.

Eliza's parents worked together for many years, and because they approached life as a team, they were well-grounded and attracted friends whose beliefs were perceived through action, the sort of action that fomented dignity, kindness, respect, and compassion.

Her parents felt that *"People's spirituality is viable so long as people did not lose their way. Dictates that protect people from malevolence have a reasonable purpose. What a person believes is okay, so long as it is meant to drive them to be better people."*

They believed and would eventually teach Eliza, *"The environment a person chooses to surround oneself with will have a major effect on the health of the individual and the neurons in the brain and that will either help or hinder the genes expressed within an individual's DNA, which will, in turn, affect future generations. We ought to love everyone, but always seek to improve ourselves, while developing conveyances for others to improve and progress in life as well."*

While they didn't consign themselves to religion, they knew that generalizing anyone would be errant on their part, they also knew that there were terrific people of large varieties of faiths and belief systems, and they knew that they were beholden to their own set of values, as such, they led by example and not through ridicule or arrogance. They knew what 'good people' were and didn't feel the need to buy into someone else's definition of the "unknown" in order to help them to become the delightful human beings they believed in becoming, themselves.

In their own spiritual lives, they practiced and appreciated yoga regularly, they enjoyed physical fitness activities, listened to gentle and even modern music, took breaks with reflective meditation, and sought to enlarge their focus by studying the various sciences beyond those learned from their professions. On occasion, they engaged in silent prayer to whomever or whatever it might be that guided life and sentient beings, and sometimes they realized that kindness was truly their guide. That was as far as religion went for the Williams family, for they were both realists and visionaries.

"We believe in enabling a kinder world, where instead of the apparent way things are, decent people can and ought to be enabled to climb to positions of leadership and influence. Good people don't hurt others to get their way, nor do they murder,

maim, or reduce the quality of life of another. If the good lead, they will heal and raise the bar for humanity in so many promising ways that threaten the existence of no one."

She truly missed her parents. Both were wise and excellent in their professions as professors, and they were dedicated to science. They appreciated anyone who was understanding and compassionate, constructive and productive. They loved everyone yet respected deeply those who took pride in benevolent goals and actions.

It Takes a Team

As the big moment of Eliza's "day one" drew near, things began to fall into place rather well despite all. Due to the Williams' sterling nature and deep friendships among very resourceful, honorable, and intellectual persons, they were blessed to have the help of their family friend, Yesenia. Yesenia had learned English and had left what is known today as Estonia many years ago, during the time of the Union of the Soviet Socialist Republics, while on a foreign exchange diplomacy visa to attend MIT and work in the US.

After meeting Gale, who happened to be majoring in neuroscience at Harvard, he introduced Yesenia to Janice, his significant other, who was studying for her PhD in physics at MIT. That same day, Gale introduced Yesenia to his friend, Stewart, who was in the same classes as Gale. For these four new friends, many delightful dates and wonderful years lay ahead.

These two young couples, Janice and Gale, and Yesenia and Stewart, twenty-years-old, all, and in their second year of studies, had hit it off from the start. It was 1960, and all four began a long-term friendship that year that could have lasted a lifetime. Things seemed to fall into place ever-so-well. Yesenia was well into her studies and bravely taking on a triple major at MIT. Because of her brilliance, she was simultaneously earning doctorates in neurology, physiology, and psychology. With those three majors, she was also well-versed in neurological and physiological health and had a magnificent respect for education. This helped, especially since it pertained to those early childhood years. Together the two families would be able to raise their children as a sound team when ready.

After these two couples successfully finished their post-doctoral studies, Yesenia and Stewart, Janice and Gale, pursued their careers, and visited one another almost daily, providing validation and moral support along the way, excelling in their positions as professors and investing well, for their future families.

Sixteen years after meeting, they were ready, and as two couples they went to the Little White Wedding Chapel in Las Vegas, Nevada to elope. Janice and Gale Williams, and Yesenia and Stewart Alevtina were two happy couples, and together, they held their double wedding, taking their vows on September 11, 1976.

Emotions and hopes were high at that time in their lives since both couples considered each other family, friends, and part of one another's lifetime team. Together all four were witnesses to decisions made, successes shared, and they frequently reflected on their collective experiences. They also planned on worldwide journeys, fun activities, and cruises further into the future. While they'd maintained economic discipline, they knew that eventually they would take time for fun.

The four friends were delighted when Yesenia gave birth to their daughter, Yesha, on Friday, July 1st of 1977. The four had prepared ever so diligently. Yesenia and Stewart were overjoyed with their vibrant young girl—her greenish-hazel-beige eyes, her dark brown almost brunette hair, her beautiful soft skin and light tan complexion, and the most darling of smiles.

Stewart would fly his baby girl around like she was Supergirl, and both of her parents would take her on picnics, lay on their backs with her in between them, look up at the clouds, make shapes out of them, and describe what they saw to Yesha. Eventually, Yesha grew to explain and share what she saw within them as well.

Their bliss soon took a turn. Unfortunately, and heartbreakingly, after sharing numerous Thanksgivings together, on Friday evening, November 23, 1979, a day after the US celebration of Thanksgiving, this team of five experienced a tragedy that resulted in the first blow to this happy crew. After enjoying their meal and readying to settle down to read to Yesha, Stewart suffered a stroke and was carried by ambulance to the hospital.

The next day, he passed away, with the Williams, his wife, and his young daughter surrounding him, listening to see if he would speak again. They hoped, sat, paced back and forth, and took turns standing and watching to see if he would awake to their smiles and support. Instead, the heart monitor flat-lined. Doctors and nurses responded to the code blue to resuscitate him, but after all their efforts, his heart stopped. There was nothing else they could do. He left this world loved.

The Williams and Yesenia were crushed and devastated by the loss of Stewart. Yesha, only two years old, was still too young to fully understand. As Yesenia's visits began to diminish, Janice and Gale knew that they needed to do something. They realized that Yesenia's struggle was immense while simultaneously trying to raise Yesha alone. Yesenia was working to pay off the mortgage and costly hospital bills, while juggling care of the home, coordinating babysitters for Yesha, and providing for the funeral and her family. Janice and Gale helped as much as they could and agreed to have Yesenia and Yesha move in to live with them. Luckily, they had already prepared several additional living areas.

Eliza's parents went to great lengths to make sure Yesenia was comfortable, providing room and board and even gifting her generously the wherewithal to take care of the bills and her daughter, Yesha. Yesenia and Yesha moved in with the Williams on Christmas Day of 1979.

In early January 1980, Janice found out she was almost two months pregnant, and the Williams' first baby was healthy and on her way. In the face of her tragedy, Yesenia opened up and reciprocated the Williams' generosity by deciding to guide Janice throughout her pregnancy. She also recommended they adopt a young puppy and she, in-turn, would ensure that it was properly trained before their baby came into the world. Yesenia helped them to prepare their home for their new family member. She felt this was the best way to reset her focus and apply her skills. While this was a tough time, everyone was supportive one to the other, and with no harsh feelings had by anyone about Stewart's passing.

They all loved each other, understood the difficulty they were experiencing, and missed him dearly. Later on, they discovered that Stewart's family had a history of genetic disorders affecting the brain stem, resulting ultimately in strokes and death. At that time, apart from healthy routines, little was understood about preventative measures.

Yesenia appreciated having a place to live with friends, who understood, and who gave her the aid she needed while raising her own daughter, Yesha. Moral support among friends and family was something that came naturally to them but was likewise desired and shared in every possible way. Asking Yesenia to live with them was indeed one of the best decisions the Williams could have made given the circumstances they were facing. Yesenia agreed that in the years to come she would complement the efforts of the teachers and the Williams and give the young girls lessons, help them with their studies, take them on outings, and even take care of the Williams' new pitiable little puppy.

Tyson was a Humane Society rescue dog, born in Georgia and adopted in Massachusetts. Yesenia and the Williams were told that he was just two or three weeks old when the animal rescue society found him abandoned, bleeding from a broken stump of what was left of his tail, foraging through garbage cans, and eating whatever food his hungry tummy could digest. He was a Plott-Hound Boxer-Labrador mix, or a Boxador, with a lab face and a boxer build. They described his breed to others who would ask, in this way, to keep it brief. His fur had black, white, brown, and rusty brindle markings, he had white paws, and beautiful, tinted, golden, and brown flecked eyes.

With Yesenia's admonition, the Williams had adopted Tyson as soon as they found out about him and that their daughter, Eliza, was well on her way. They were ever-so-inquisitive, and the doctors were ever-so-glad to show her parents that they would be having a baby girl. She was healthy, strong, and coming along nicely.

Tyson had a timid, calm, loving, and curious demeanor. Companionship seemed to flow from his character like water as it passed through the hands of the angel overlooking the Williams' Pond. He loved his new and very affectionate family. Yesenia trained Tyson well through her amorous and caring treatment. Within the first few days he enjoyed being a part of their family and living in their home.

As he grew over the weeks, he enjoyed playing catch, being petted, being given treats, going on walks with the Williams, Yesenia, and Yesha, and curling up in a little ball, feeling at ease, as he slept beside anyone in his new pack. He seemed to pick up on the fact that Janice was full and getting closer to Eliza's birthday, because he seemed to be his calmest around her and rested beside her bed each night, waiting loyally until she woke up.

For Tyson, the carpets at the Williams' home were fluffier and less cumbersome than the jagged terrain he had been used to during his first couple of weeks of life, and life was less painful than he recalled from before. He seemed most especially delighted to live near the quaint town's boundaries—with walks to a dog park or a beach allowing him to see the sights and sounds of life. With his seeming joy and gratitude for his new home, he too was part of the Williams and Alevtina family team.

Less than a month after he came home with the Williams, it was apparent that Tyson enjoyed being called a good boy, since he learned to go to the bathroom outside and along the acreage perimeter. Smelling the flowers brought him bliss anyway, and he'd make sure the little rabbits only ate the weeds if he could help it.

Training him to not go to the restroom inside the house or on the walkways outside had involved creating a small zone in the house for him for a few hours with toys to play with, water to drink, and food to eat. If he did well, he was rewarded with affection and a treat that was good for his physiology and the health of his shiny coat and taken outside where he could relieve himself in bliss. Once finished, he would receive more rewards in the form of warmth, hugs, and petting, intermingled with more treats, and plenty of love. He was trained in each location throughout the house until he was thoroughly domesticated and well-disciplined. He also learned how to sit, stand, lie down, and stop barking on command followed by rewards for good behavior from Yesenia, Yesha, and the Williams.

Janice, Gale, and Yesenia had done everything imaginable to prepare for the Williams' child before and during Janice's pregnancy. They wanted to make sure that they peppered her with the best they could offer after she was born. They ensured that their home was a place of support, they had confidence in each other, and they were a successful team. They were prepared to enrich Yesha's, and Eliza's lives, to benefit them, and supplement healthy living. Considering and implementing childhood safety measures, as well as security and an inspiring ambiance, had been a top priority for them.

Intellectually engaging mathematical, artistic, and scientific models, all of which had the advantage of replicating positive technologies, books for many age-groups augmenting quick and intellectual advancement, and even mentally stimulating and engaging toys for children combed the walls of their home.

The Williams and Alevtinas had prepared their yard, so their daughter could harmlessly spend time out there, breathing in the fresh air on her infant swing, right beside Yesha's. Yesha was almost three, and even she helped and provided smiles, applause, and other forms of moral support.

This contraption which helped to increase fresh-air intake was placed near the pond with the angel statue, with its waterfall and sophisticated yet modest water cycling system. The frogs and coy fish her parents had given shelter to, so many years ago, had enjoyed the continuously maintained system in a way that even the living beings in the water sensed their contributions were meaningful to those who sat nearby finding the ambiance therapeutic.

Her parents had had a lifetime of commitment to living healthy and had encouraged physical fitness. They wanted their daughter to have a proper and well-rounded upbringing. The Williams prepared before Eliza was born, doing well by her when she came into this world, having saved as much as they could and invested their money well for her advanced education down the road. Eliza's parents had prepared in every way, with the help of Yesenia, for that first day of her life, to make this experience as seamless and smooth as possible.

Once all their arrangements were ready and this team had everything squared away for the big day, the Williams and Alevtinas were excited for what was to come. It just so happened, that the day after Yesha's third birthday would be a day that none of them would forget.

New Life

With great foresight, Eliza's parents and Yesenia had enlisted the aid of the best medical care teams available and had scheduled well in advance the when, the where, the why, and the how of each aspect, giving credibility to their knowledge of when their baby would be ready to grace the stage of life.

The day their daughter was born, both of Eliza's parents had taken the day off from work, and together Yesenia and Yesha had accompanied them as they walked to the hospital instead of going about their normal day-to-day business on that lovely balmy Wednesday.

The Williams and Yesenia, keen on physical fitness regimens and proper diets, with young Yesha now joining in, walked to the hospital as if it was a part of their routine. Walking into their Doctor's office was of little stress beyond that of carrying a precious package.

Both Eliza's parents and Yesenia had lived for balance in life, which included a healthy balance of veggies, proteins, exercise, achievements in education, a broad love of music and the arts, and an insatiable appreciation for civil and intellectual dialogue, yet they were not pretentious or condescending to anyone, they simply desired to live as good examples of humanity.

They talked for a couple of hours until Janice was ready, and when Eliza was on her way, all was as planned.

At 10 o'clock in the morning, Eliza was born.

Two hours later, the Williams brought their healthy and happy baby home—a child who had opened her eyes and smiled at each of them not more than two minutes after she was born. Young Yesha had noticed intently and felt an instant bond with her new friend.

Those precious first few moments intensified her parents' belief that their little girl was going to have a phenomenal future ahead of her. Since Janice was a theoretical physicist and Gale was a neuroscientist with friends at work and home who were into the latest of any of the biosciences, they had been quite a bit obsessive about providing the best to Eliza. With Yesenia by their side, thus far, they had been thoroughly rewarded.

As they walked into their home, with their new baby in Janice's arm, young Tyson stood waiting just beyond the door with a puppy smile, wagging his cropped tail and his little bootie.

Eliza and Tyson immediately hit it off. He licked her face, and she smiled silently with her hands waving about, almost as if to pet him. When she was in her crib sleeping, just as he had done for Janice, Tyson would lie down on the ground beside her, yawn, curl up in a cute little ball and be there for her when she woke up. When little Eliza awoke, he would wag his booty for her and lick her fingers as she silently poked them through her crib safety bars, until she would smile. Tyson would then go and nose Mom or Dad to let them know Eliza was up. Returning to her quickly, he would sit to watch her with kindness and care, and sometimes run-in circles to entertain her, until Mom and Dad arrived.

Throughout Eliza's first year, they began to take notice that young Eliza made very little noise, at least as was considered typical for infants her age. Sparked with concern, the Williams and Alevtinas did their research and inquired of their doctors. The responses they received gave them little comfort, but they were patient, played with her, and even read books aloud to her of every scientific and artistic sort. The doctors had told them that her hearing and ability for speech was healthy and normal, and that sometimes children observe and take in more of the world around them, even quicker than usual, in many similar cases. No matter their concerns, as the days, weeks, and months went by, Janice and Gale looked for ways to come home from work early to see their young girl as soon and as often as their careers would permit. Yesha would play with her often and get her to silently smile, and Yesenia would read to her when Eliza's parents were away. With Tyson there to provide further support, together, this team of five had been a beautiful part of ushering in new life.

Ups and Downs

Three-hundred-sixty-four days passed in Eliza's young and somewhat seemingly silent life, and the Williams and Yesenia celebrated Yesha's fourth birthday.

Over the last nine months, the Williams and Yesenia spent time reading to Yesha and Eliza. They learned from one particularly astute medical doctor, that given Eliza's condition, she would do well with variations of activities, reading sessions, and colors where possible. Her hearing and cognitive abilities were as they should be, if not heightened. As a matter of fact, despite not speaking Eliza was quite perceptive, aware, and capable.

The morning following Yesha's fourth birthday, was Eliza's first birthday. The Williams, Yesenia, and even young Yesha helped put together colorful streamers, a range of activities, and an array of coloring books with plenty of crayons and other fun yet mind-engaging games available for all who were present for Eliza's special day.

Eliza, while still quiet, smiled and made gestures for anything needed or desired. She had become very good with word and math puzzles, as well as jigsaw puzzles that were meant for six or seven-year-olds. The time for celebration began. With her birthday hat on ornament-like, blending in with her exquisite, Shirley-Temple-curled, and angelically blonde hair, partly piled upon her head, some of it down and aesthetically weaved, and some of it braided back and up to a bun, Eliza was angelic. Her cute little finger-painted blue birthday nose on her pale white skin, added extra character while she observed her audience pensively with her big round beautiful crystal blue eyes.

Although she never spoke, Eliza seemed wise beyond her years.

Despite the noticeable quietness about her, she came off as sophisticated and reserved. Eliza grew up well that year and flourished silently as she absorbed the world around her. Although she could communicate as the mute she was observed to be, she was an observant girl and began to talk that day, which surprised them all.

"Mom!" she called.

"Tyson!" she called.

"Bottle!" she called.

"Daddy!" she gushed, as Dr. Gale Williams came rushing into the room with a nutrient-dense, organic, yet tasty fruit and vegetable smoothie in a bottle, followed by a slice of a very finely designed birthday cake, both tasty and interestingly healthy, as well as people-and-pet-safe.

Looking down, just below Eliza's highchair, there was Tyson. Their adorable one-and-a-half-year-old dog who wagged his cute little kinked and stubbed tail along with his cute little behind. He would do this whenever he wanted to let the humans in the room know he was happy and expected a reward. On this occasion, he was standing on the earth-toned stone tile below eagerly awaiting whatever prize might come his way as Eliza was eating.

Eliza caught a glimpse of him out of the corner of her blue eyes and surprised all in the room, when she spoke more than a single-word sentence and asked, "Daddy, can you please give a piece to Tyson?" Amazed with what she had just uttered, her father shook his head, yes, he gave him a piece of cake, and Tyson wagged his bootie some more while licking the satin icing and buttercream from his chops and nose. On so many occasions he seemed to wear a doggy smile, and this was one of them. He also seemed to know that because of Eliza he was extra-spoiled but in a good way, for which he was grateful.

Janice and Gale, Yesenia and Yesha celebrated Eliza's first birthday, and all of them were pleasantly surprised that she was not just speaking her first words but assembling dialogue with full-on phrases. It was as if those first three words had opened up a treasure trove of highly logical and even sentimental expressions through vocal communication. It was as if she had kept everything bottled up that year, listening, absorbing, and making sense of everything, well-ahead of her time. She was in fact a genius from day one.

Eliza began walking around, obviously having taken in every move, every muscle, and every bend of a joint, such that it appeared she was a master of every aspect of her physiology. Speaking, expressions, and even training her dog became second nature to her, and as those abilities surfaced, in moments she trained Tyson how to shake his paw, saying, "handshake," and she had his utmost of love, loyalty, and trust, every day and night.

Puzzles meant for a six-to-seven-year-olds and sketching-in each object in her Scientific American Children's Coloring Book within the lines, was something new to her, but she picked up those skills like a champ. Upon finishing each work of art, she carefully removed her finished drawings and gifted a page to each person in the room. With medium length hair, side-swept spiral-curled bangs, her blonde and curled piggy tails, and an unforgettable smile, she looked enigmatically adorable. There was something special about that girl, and it was as clear as day. She was growing fast. Her parents, as well as Yesenia, Yesha, and even Tyson enjoyed spending every moment they could with her, and time flew.

A year later when she was two, Eliza was reading from books, magazines, and newspapers the level of a fourth grader, helped everyone with their chores all the time, and could sing the dictionary and be believable as an experienced professional. Nonetheless, her parents ensured she maintained her childhood within the scope that she wouldn't lose her private life, or with it the ability to think freely, and she did wonderfully in life, given the influences she already had. To that end, her parents allowed her to be a free spirit, and she was. At the end of almost every school day, her dear friend, Yesha, three years her senior and now in kindergarten, spent time with her. As dusk approached then passed, Eliza enjoyed sharing her time observing the Universe through their telescopes.

While taking Tyson on walks, when Yesha was away at school, Eliza would play ball with him, and he would protect her. Once he was tired, she would study and "get ahead." After Yesha came home for school, at times all three would play hide-and-go-seek together. Of course, Tyson would always find them, peeking over whatever bench or object they were hiding behind in an almost hilariously creepy but caring way, he would give away each of their locations with his wag of the behind and the drop of his ball, to play fetch just a little more.

Long ago, or at least it seemed that way to Eliza, since it had been a year, she trained him to shake hands. Tyson was very perceptive of quite a few human words and phrases, and his ears would perk up when Eliza told him, "I love you," and she asked, "Do you want to go on a walk?" or "do you want a hug?"

Although Yesha was about three years older, Eliza and Yesha considered each other as lifelong sisters and best friends. They spent a lot of time together, and some of it gliding down their slip and slide each summer. Typically, all three would end a hot day splashing around in their pond. Eliza, Yesha, and even Tyson, no matter their fun, were careful of the frogs and coy fish.

After feeding and singing to them, Eliza and Yesha would sit down by the outdoor kerosene heat lamp on small sitting stones to warm and dry up. Tyson would curl up in-between them, and on occasion get up to take turns putting his paw on each of their shoulders, as if giving them a hug of affection. He would often lay down on his back with his feet spread if he wanted to be petted on his tummy and chest. Together, Eliza and Yesha would take turns giving him affection as they sung the lyrics to their favorite tunes. On special occasions they would sing along to "I Just Can't Get Enough," by their favorite musical group, Depeche Mode.

As Yesha's first grade schoolyear approached and then began, Eliza missed her friend, but would spend her moments of solace with Tyson. Happily, back together, following Yesha's school day, they would settle down to read under the moonlit sky as time would go by. They always found it fulfilling to take time to look up at the stars while studying the constellations and looking for deep sky objects. They rarely spoiled themselves with indoor sleep-ins. Instead, they spent many nights slumbering in their sleeping bags in a tent in their backyard with Tyson nestled in-between them.

Sometimes they'd pull their sleeping bags out of the tent in such a way as to fall asleep watching the stars gaze down upon them, and Tyson would follow them wherever they went. As they did, they would talk about traveling out there someday. Tyson seemed to raise his ears at times as if he understood what they were talking about or as if he was a part of the conversation.

When Tyson got sleepy, he would snuggle between them—yawn with his cute little curled up little tongue, lick their faces, clean his feet until they smelt like popcorn, and finally rest. Meanwhile, Eliza and Yesha continued looking up at the stars, talking and singing, until they too fell asleep—all three side-by-side.

At the age of three, seeing that Eliza was a rapid learner, her parents enrolled her in a school for the young, gifted, and bright minds. With Yesha at the top of her class already, both academically and physically, and with Eliza thirsting for more knowledge at every moment, that year Eliza started kindergarten late, and skipped to and completed the first grade, still at the age of three alongside Yesha.

The following year, Eliza started the second grade and continued to be in school with Yesha. It seemed Yesha's presence motivated young Eliza to high achievement. Yesha, who until then had been at the top of her class, both scholastically and academically, was now neck and neck at the same level. While most children would have felt jealous at that time in their lives seeing their top spot in class nearly overtaken by someone younger, Yesha felt proud of Eliza.

Opportunities to hang out with each other even more, be productive, and enjoy their time in constructive pursuits were welcomed, and Yesha saw this as a blessing in her life. They typically completed their homework assignments and went over their finished products together, just to make sure they understood the subject matter—and always with Tyson nearby. They would occasionally throw the ball for him, run around with him, take him on walks, and then he would lay down watching them, his head on his front paws in peace and contentment.

In the third grade, Eliza and Yesha were enrolled in advanced courses in mathematics, English, art, history, and science and in each part of the school year they shined physically and academically.

In the fourth grade, Eliza and Yesha learned how to play the piano while singing together in a college choir. No matter how dedicated they were in their studies, they still found time to go outside with Tyson at the end of the day, feed the coy fish, and sing their favorite music to the frogs in the pond and the stars in the sky. In 1984, Depeche Mode had come out with the song, "People Are People," and this musical group by now was a family favorite. Without realizing it, Martin's lyrics and Dave's vocals had played an intriguing role in these two girls' young childhood development. Quite interestingly, this gave them a unique perspective of their world and helped them think more profoundly than their peers.

Now that it was 1986 and "People are People" had been released two years prior, it had been one of their favorites for a couple of years and would be for quite some time. They loved every song Depeche Mode produced, but this song, along with "A Question of Lust" and "But Not Tonight," were among their favorites. Not only were these young girls gifted and highly intelligent, they developed a character of persona that was evidenced in how they handled heavy obstacles in life, and in a very mature, impressively pensive, genuinely thoughtful, perceptively understanding, and even an enviably fun way.

Listening to each of their prized albums over and over again, they would mix in other favorite artists, while studying, asking philosophical questions, and enjoying their surroundings. Tears for Fears, O.M.D., The Pet Shop Boys, Duran-Duran, The Human League, Erasure, Bananarama, Icehouse, the Thompson Twins, and New Order typically accompanied their playlists. Eliza and Yesha listened while they pet Tyson, talked about what was yet to come in these grand plans of theirs, and sung to the frogs and coy fish in the pond and the stars in the sky. Maintaining all they could within a proper balance and perspective, time passed by quickly. For them life was second nature; they loved being outside, taking Tyson on walks, singing their favorite tunes, finding time to study the sciences together, reflecting upon their past, while embracing the present, along with their sweet and loyal dog, never falling asleep until they had planned their future.

Eliza could have easily finished schooling quickly, but she decided in the fourth grade, at the age of six, that she would appreciate getting more knowledge and social interaction and benefit from it by studying laterally with Yesha in more classes, rather than by speeding along and passing her up. Yesha could have hurried along beyond her peers as well, but they both had shared goals. Eliza's parents and her teachers agreed that she and Yesha were terrific for each other and to satisfy Eliza's need for more academics, they allowed her to engage in additional and advanced studies with Yesha while attending class for essential instruction with everyone else. Yesha and Eliza received the highest of grades at school. They also studied more subjects in depth and shared ideas with each other.

At this time in their lives, both Eliza and Yesha were already considered prodigies. Their teachers counseled with each other often and acknowledged both Eliza and Yesha as being phenomenally exceptional, while working with advanced professors on curriculum that would meet Eliza's and Yesha's academic capabilities and needs. The truth was that Eliza was actually known by the instructors as phenomenally more capable, but no one had the heart tell Yesha—she knew that for herself but loved Eliza all the more for it—she would support Eliza to the ends of the Earth if ever needed. It was as if Yesha was beyond brilliant, yet with a special gift of her own of selfless love; even still, Eliza was just as bright and loving.

It was an intriguing union of friendship because they genuinely complemented each other. Eliza and Yesha were extremely advanced with abilities to learn and grasp deep subjects quickly. They lived for demonstrating a concrete understanding of what they were taught and consistently explained it all in an in-depth manner as they shared their solutions to the world's most difficult problems.

Both Eliza and Yesha studied the typical classes but enrolled in multiple courses at the same time. Often sitting in the back of class they quietly worked on a variety of projects, studying their other courses, and participated with the other students by mentoring them and giving the teachers assistance as needed.

Their instructors were impressed with Eliza's and Yesha's abilities to process information and particularly amazed that despite Eliza's young age, she had a very mature manner of dealing with the world around her.

During their science hour in class, in 1986, both Eliza and Yesha watched, as did countless students in many other classrooms throughout the country, the news on television as the Space Shuttle Challenger was being prepared for takeoff. Since Christa McAuliffe, a schoolteacher, a payload specialist, and an astronaut, was heading out to space, their teacher was excited about this as well. Everyone in the classroom was excited to see this historical moment of scientific achievement.

Even though Valentina Tereshkova was the first woman in space, and Sally Ride was the first US woman with the same feat twenty years later, this was still another memorable moment. As the shuttle soared high in the sky, they felt a sense of pride.

However, all feelings of joy seemed to turn to concern and a new reality set in as they witnessed a series of flashes emanating from the fuel cells. A sense of horror crept in as the tragedy of the shuttle unfolded. Eliza had read up on the construction of the space shuttle, so she knew that the astronauts had no means to leave the fiery ball that developed around them—there were no escape pods or systems in place for that.

Their teacher stood frozen in shock, unable to move. Like everyone else, Eliza was stricken and shaken up too, but somehow, she gathered her thoughts, got up from her chair, and marched over to her teacher. She then stretched out her six-year-old arms and wrapped them around Miss Sumita knowing full well what shock was. Aware of what had just transpired and what it truly meant, from social and political impacts to psychological, Eliza understood that the astronauts had passed away before their eyes within the shuttle.

Feeling remorse for the loss of life, even though it meant a possible slowdown to the space program, was the most important and the gravest of lessons she learned. They had died for the cause of reaching self-actualization, yet the concept was slightly damaged that day for many nationwide.

Eliza saw her teacher, could read her expressions, mannerisms, and posture, and knew she was affected profoundly, while also worrying deeply about how this tragic state of events would affect her pupils' young minds. Knowing this and knowing that her teacher was seemingly left helpless as to what to do, Eliza hugged her, bringing her back to her senses.

Miss Sumita looked upon this young and wise six-year-old girl. There she was, with her darling blonde Shirley Temple curls and kind blue eyes, and she smiled with tears welling up in her own eyes. She was then able to put herself together, consult the other children, and the day passed more smoothly.

Shortly after class, Miss Sumita talked to and confided in Eliza about how she felt as the tragedy unfolded, her guilt for the shock she had let set in, and how she couldn't understand why. She apologized for not understanding what had caused her to freeze. Eliza, with a look of compassion, then responded to her teacher with calm, wisdom, and resolve, "Despite great tragedy, to have remorse for life is a wonderful thing. Tragedy affects us all in different ways. Please know that no matter the tragedy, I appreciate, and I love you, Miss Sumita." Miss Sumita was both calmed, filled with appreciation, and impressed.

Everyone was shocked by the events of that day and most of those who had witnessed the tragic moments unfold remembered where they were and what they were doing when it happened. Both Eliza and Yesha, after the school day had finished, walked home and found Tyson had somehow escaped the house, but there he was making his way down the sidewalk and wagging his booty upon seeing them. If one were to interpret his actions, it was as if somehow, he had sensed what was going on, and he too seemed to understand their emotions. After the sweet reunion, they then walked to a nearby park, sat down, and looked up at the sky. After releasing their emotions with tear-stained eyes, they hugged each other.

Tyson leaned into them as they embraced. When they sat on the park bench, with the trees and bushes to their back, Tyson took his place between them and curled up into a little ball between them. Once he was settled, he stretched his neck and licked both Eliza's and Yesha's faces, as they confided to each other the anguish they felt at the immensity of the tragedy and their sorrow at the tragic loss of life. He looked at each of the girls, stretched his paw toward their shoulders, and gave them both a doggy hug, as if to tell them, "It'll be okay." They smiled at Tyson, then at each other, were at peace with that healing affection, and continued to discuss their concerns over the possibility of a setback to science, exploration, and discovery, but these astronauts were heroes in their own right. They were pioneers in this new frontier for humanity and they had earned their respect and solace.

Together, Eliza and Yesha had shared a stinging moment in life, enriched by Tyson's limitless moral support as they went home, and were determined to understand their Universe more fully and change their world. They wouldn't allow anything or anyone to slow them down in their quest to reduce suffering. Together, they desired to cure this beautiful world of its many unfortunate diseases, lighten its burden on humanity, and enlighten society through scientific and other untold levels of achievement. Through their efforts, they would see that these pursuits would lend to the human need for exploration and discovery—pushing innovation so that humanity could travel into space with a much safer means to do so, and with less risk to life. They envisioned humankind spanning the Universe and solving each issue along the way.

Cancer Strikes

Throughout their schooling, as summer passed by while spending time together doing their routine and changing it up from time to time, throughout the fifth through the eighth grade, Eliza and Yesha completed countless sophisticated science projects together, won school science competitions, studied for numerous tests, and shared ideas of how to make this world better with each other. Time indeed flew by.

Secretly, Yesha appreciated her perception that Eliza had a much more advanced ability to soak in knowledge. She could translate it into concrete ideas and thoughts. This ironically gave Yesha a sense of security, and yet she would very rarely mention or hint at such. They were each unique and gifted in so many ways, and while it seemed Yesha could do three times what her peers could, and Eliza could do seven times what Yesha's peers could do, Yesha was still very remarkable. Instead of being lost in feelings of jealousy, she complemented Eliza in her efforts, her dreams, and her goals, and acknowledged her for every job well done. Together they would still find the time to go outside, lie on their backs with Tyson, snuggle with him in their sleeping bags, and listen to the latest albums of their favorite musicians.

Treasured Moments

It was 1990, Eliza was nine and Yesha twelve, and they had memorized the words to, "I Want to Know What You're Thinking," "Chorus," "Strangelove," "True Faith," "Policy of Truth," "World in My Eyes," and so much more. Amid songs, they talked about all the various sciences, the associated arithmetic, and their college and university plans. As they did, they cuddled with Tyson, who now had more gray hair and seemed to be getting a little older. Still thinking of him as the sweet little boy he was when he was a pup, Eliza and Yesha decided on what to do once they started High School and completed it.

One day, they found Tyson laying on his side, after calling for him and receiving no response. He seemed unable to move but was panting, breathing, and upon seeing Eliza and Yesha, he peered at them with his friendly and hopeful eyes just the same.

The Williams, Yesenia, Eliza, and Yesha took Tyson into the veterinarian clinic, and after a series of visits, the doctors diagnosed him with a rare form of acute leukemia, or cancer. His abdomen had been distended each time before bringing him in, and they found out that his system had developed a rare type of autoimmunity and that one of the results was that blood had gathered within his stomach region.

The veterinarian doctors wanted Eliza, Yesha, and their families to give Tyson about ten pills a day, but deep down they knew that doing so would get old quick. They did as the vet had instructed, but after going through every single treat, on a list of the tasty snacks to trick him with, so he would swallow them, he wouldn't have any of it.

Ultimately, Tyson was too smart and discovered the pills in his food. One by one, each treat on their list was no longer viable since he would no longer wish to eat the food used to trick him. Perhaps the pills made his stomachache and maybe, just maybe, he knew better than humans what he needed. In his world, time was short.

After trying to pry open his mouth on several occasions while trying to look with all the love in the world into his eyes to tell him it was okay and trying to put the pills in the back of his throat, and him spitting them out, Gale, Janice, Yesenia, Eliza, and Yesha decided they could no longer torture their boy any further. With a lot of tears, they decided to forgo the pills.

Instead, the families decided to give Tyson what they knew would perk him up— hugs, love, and his favorite dog jerky treats. Happy and as they had hoped, he ate them and seemed to spring back to life for a while.

However, Tyson had cancerous formations in his spleen and his liver. No matter the care, no matter the love, and no matter the time spent, Tyson's red blood cell counts were low, and his white blood cells seemed to be attacking everything. His platelet levels were bottomed out, and his lips and gums were turning pale—he was in pain and suffering.

No matter what it was Tyson was experiencing he was brazenly tough and never whimpered or complained. Rather than allow him to die of starvation in a desiccated version of himself, they spoiled him with his favorite foods, spent a lot of time with him, and soaked in his last moments the best they knew how.

Tyson lived strong even through those last few days. He passed away a week and four days following Yesha's thirteenth birthday and a week and three days after Eliza's tenth birthday on Friday, July 11, 1990.

The night before he passed away, they brought him to the best animal hospital they could find, but the doctors were determined to kennel him there out of fear that he might die.

At first, the Williams and Alevtina families went back to their house, heads down with remorse for life. However, after calmly talking together, they decided to return to the animal hospital to bring him home.

Tyson would have died in the worst way, alone, had they not taken him away from the hospital's kennel—where he would have been without love and by himself.

Instead, with the assistance of the Williams and Yesenia, they brought him back to their estate. For one last night, Eliza and Yesha snuggled close together with him in-between them in their sleeping bags outside.

Before taking him into the hospital one final time, they took him to his favorite park. It was a hot summer day, yet with a lake nearby he seemed to find enough strength to walk around and enjoy their company and the ambiance of his environment.

When Tyson passed, Eliza was torn severely and so was Yesha. Eliza had pleaded with her parents to give him another chance, but she knew better. He was suffering and the kindest way to let any living companion take that journey to the rainbow bridge, it seemed, was to bid them farewell, before they fell asleep. He looked into Eliza's eyes before closing his. Knowing he would never open them again, she hugged him—tears of a broken heart streamed down her face.

Hours went by, closure through this experience had begun to settle in. Considering what she could do to keep him with her, she developed a solution and raised a question that was thought to be quite odd. Eliza asked her parents and the veterinarian for a locket of Tyson's hair, to keep him close and remember him by, before leaving the clinic.

Thinking about the whole tragedy later, Eliza realized Tyson survived through her tenth birthday, and Yesha's thirteenth. So, even though they both believed he'd continue to be around for a long, long time, they realized that at least he had nobly muddled through it all to see them through their special days. Time was cruel, yet they embraced each other and cried countless tears. They loved him, they felt he was torn from their lives, seemingly all too soon, and unabashedly full of life. They remembered the many enjoyable, freeing, sweet and unforgettable moments Tyson had spent with them. Eliza and Yesha would never forget.

A Letter to Never Forget

The second night without him, to heal their spirits, Eliza and Yesha talked about all of the enlightening moments shared with Tyson with their parents, and then went on a walk together. Before going to bed, late that night, Eliza wrote Tyson a letter:

"*Dear Tyson, I will never forget how happy you were whenever any of us would come in through the door, every day of every year. You made each of us feel special; you made us feel loved and appreciated. You gave us caring companionship no matter what was going on, through thick or thin. As the end came near you may not have had the strength to go to the door anymore, but no matter, you would take what power you had and place yourself in locations where you knew we would be and lie there waiting for us, for me.*

"*Gazing into your beautiful brown and golden eyes, I knew you loved, you cared, and that I was your world; we were your world. You and Yesha are both the loves of my life. Never was there an awkward moment or a moment of shame with you around. No matter what we happened to be doing, you loved us just the same.*

"*I remember after your second set of trips to the hospital, having been stung several times with an IV, I was stung by a hornet. My parents took me to the clinical specialist, and you were there to keep me company. The doctor gave me a shot to make sure I didn't suffocate, and there you were, your paw extended. You reached out to me with your head nestled between your two front feet, and your eyes gazed up at mine as if you understood. You seemed to know what I was going through. We connected profoundly that day with a lovely shared and bonding experience.*

"*Those moments where I would look upon you for long periods of time, hoping that the image of your face, your nose, your kissy dog lips, and mouth would never leave my mind.*

"*I breathed you in, sniffing the fur just behind your eyes and by your neck so I would never forget your scent that I found to be so adorable. I did this on many occasions so that if I ever smelled that showered doggy perfume and natural aroma again, the pleasant smell that was only yours, I could think of you and imagine you were there with me, my friend.*

"*Your brindle coat, the white triangulated shape of hair from the bottom of your mouth to your chest and your tummy, the golden, brown, and black brindle colorings giving way to white and silver as you matured, all of your details are etched into my memories. Yesha and I would always pet you to let you know you were loved in much the same way you loved us—all these images and moments I will never forget.*

"*When I die, I hope I see you in Heaven, and I wish I could have you back. Perhaps not now, maybe not tomorrow, but someday, perchance that will be possible. I hope you can forgive me since I was a little rough with you when I was a little girl. I learned quickly, and so did you. I anticipate that you will be able to forgive me for being so enthusiastic with and engrossed in my studies on too many occasions when your cute wet nose would nudge my arm reminding me you were still there. You were dying from cancer, and we didn't know until it was too late. We didn't want you to suffer alone. We asked Mom and Dad to bring you home that last night to spend the time with you; I hope that the time we spent was as enjoyable for you as you made it for us.*

"*I hope you can forgive me for letting you go.*

"*Your life seemed rejuvenated when we took you to the lake—the small fight you gave to the doctor of death was as if you were saying, 'I love you, but keep me around for Heaven's sake!' But really, you were saying, 'I love you; I understand.' Now you're in*

Heaven if there is a Heaven, but to me, you deserve so much more—an abundantly longer life. Living in this world without you gets harder every moment that passes by. Those beautiful reminders of you are hidden away in every spot of our home, with spiritual images of you playing, and being there where you used to be, without even a thought that I would ever lose you.

"You were my sweet boy, and I could not let you face the indignity of a prolonged death, suffering and trying to be strong through it all. Instead, each of us gave you love, we took you to a happy place, and you showed us courage in the face of death. In the space of three seconds after the doctor put the needle in your arm, you went from looking into my eyes to an eternal sleep where I knew it was the last time, I would see you look up at me. I feared for the first time that I just may never get you back.

"I hope for a Heaven, a kind place without pain or suffering surrounded by you and all who were kind throughout the history of Earth. I miss you and love you and will do so until I can see you again.

"I will cry many tears yet try to be strong. My dear Tyson, Yesha was hurt dearly too. It has crushed her soul, so I will do my best to fill the void left behind with your passing. Unfortunately, I don't know if that will ever be possible.

"I went to school yesterday, just for personal study, and one of the teachers I had previously passed by me on my way to the library and asked me how I was doing. In-between tears I explained to him about you, Tyson, and how you blessed my life, how you were there for my family, and we were there for you. My teacher, amidst tears himself, shared with me a precious and even hopeful belief. He said that if we ever were to train another puppy that you would be there to help us.

"Everything you did was so perfect. The way you snuggled with Yesha and me, kissing us on our face as we sang our favorite songs to you, snuggling with us as we slept under the stars—you showed us how much you loved us. The way you would lie down in complete submission and obedience when I got down on my hands and my knees, you made me feel special. Occasionally when I was doing pushups or sit-ups you'd come and visit as if I was nuts, but sooth me in your own way. The way you helped clean any stray bits of food off the floor, the way you helped clean dishes, the last morsel of delicious food you enjoyed each time—I'll never forget. The way you sat at the door and watched for Mom when she would go get the mail, awaiting her return—I knew you truly cared while serving and protecting. The way you took after Dad and liked your feet to be clean, the only difference was that you would lick them until they smelled like popcorn and met your standard of cleanliness—I will always adore your obsessions. The way you appreciated our garden, our frogs, our fish, laying down in the sleeping bag or on our beds with us—without you here, it will always be... different.

"How cute it was when your ears would perk up, your right ear slightly more poised than your left, your big round eyes widening with interest as we would ask you if you wanted to go on a walk, or even when we would meow like a cat. The way you enjoyed your simple toys showed me how little materialism truly means—you loved what you had, took pride in the kindness shown, and you adored everything given, because it was a gift from someone you loved, no matter what it was. The way you would peer over the table a little creepy and funny like on the occasions that we would sit down and watch television—you were paying attention to us, watching us as we watched TV—how sweet! That last walk where you bravely went up to the fence of the mean German Shepherd who would always ravenously bark at you and scare you, you showed him you weren't scared and gave him a deep bark back—you were a hero! We saw him a day after you passed, and even he seemed to be apologetic and contrite despite all.

"All of these things are but a few of the priceless moments that were shared, acts you alone were selfless enough to pursue, and each thing you did was unique to you. You always seemed to carefully balance your affection between each person in the room. You would rest with Yesha, Mom, Dad, Yesenia, and me, and you would always wait until one of us would spoil you with treats as we came home, and you pawed the door to let us know when you needed to go outside. You would rest with me whenever I was deep in thought and concerned over the day.

"I may never get you back, at least that is my greatest fear, but when I breathe your scent in from the air, I will know you are near. I will never forget how your puppy face would slightly and cutely pucker up before you would bark, giving me enough time to hug you and tell you that all was okay. I loved you, I will always adore you, and I will never forget you.

"I hope you don't mind that I saved a lock of your hair to keep with me as I meditate and think things through. I miss you already. Goodbye, my dear and sweet friend.

"With Love, Eliza Amber Williams."

Pressing On

One year went by and then two years, and as she dedicated herself through high school, Eliza kept Tyson's lock of hair with her. After the first year, she crafted a bookmark with a Ziploc bag, a card-paper border with laminate, and a favorite picture enclosed within it and in an additional card-paper frame. Combining the pieces together artistically and smoothly, allowed her to keep him near without worrying about any questions as to why.

Eliza was proud of her parents, enjoyed spending time with Yesha, and knew she had to move on, at least from the pain of loss. She was strong and healthy, carrying him with her in her own way, and the bookmark reminded her to contemplate how to reduce the misery, the suffering, and the merciless indignity of things that hurt, wounded, and took away so many, so soon, and away from those that loved them all-too-often throughout life, and took them away to never allow them to return.

After some time, she breathed in and breathed out and felt good about all her treasured memories. Eliza decided to never let her dedication toward her studies slow down—she also promised she would never forget and vowed that one day she would bring Tyson back.

Nearly four years had gone by following Tyson's passing, and Eliza's and Yesha's focus began to change. Their senior prom came around, with schoolmates bustling and excited, planning, prepping, and deciding who was going with whom to that final social gathering before going off into their future as adults. It all seemed a façade of "keeping up with Joneses" and pretentious to Eliza and Yesha, since they saw too many wonderful and young people alienated and left out of very exclusive social networks, in the name of status, power, or one-up-ism.

In truth, they didn't have a problem with those that went, but freedom allowed them their own plans, and plan their own outing, they certainly did.

With that thought, they did something different, thought for themselves, and veered from the norm. A science convention in Washington, DC, was going on during that same evening, so they elected to go to that instead. With a sheer sense of duty, their parents desired that they ponder upon their choices and expressed their concern over their decision against spending this time with the other kids, their "friends."

Notwithstanding, they were still proud of them for making a less likely decision and approved of their excursion in the name of science.

These fine, outstanding, and brilliant young ladies were excited to see some of the greatest minds of the day as they climbed on board the bus. En route they shared their notes on the various Nobel Laureates, winners of such a high honor, recognized worldwide, and some who ought to have won, but hadn't, yet.

This was the first time Eliza and Yesha had the opportunity to meet Dr. Vesha Celeste, in person. This wonderful astronomer and astrophysicist happened to be in attendance at the event and provided a presentation. Although she was overdue for the Nobel Peace Prize for her work, her studies, and her discoveries in the name of astrophysics and various other related sciences, the girls had chosen her as a favorite.

Eliza's mom had talked to them about Dr. Celeste many times, and they studied her works in-depth, so naturally, they were excited to get to meet her. After the convention was over, Eliza and Yesha found themselves lucky as they approached and talked with her for a couple of hours. Once the meeting hall cleared, amidst their excitement, all three went to a nearby French Café, called La Madeleine to continue their conversations.

Dr. Celeste finally told them to call her Vesha.

"Wow! Our names are very much alike. I'm Yesha, and you're Vesha," Yesha had brought up at one point.

Vesha reciprocated, "We both have backgrounds from far eastern Europe, I would guess. So, it is a beautiful coincidence, my friend. I'm so proud of you and Eliza, and your love of science. You two are kindred spirits to me."

As the time went by, they grew more comfortable with each other and talked openly and enthusiastically, eating their scrumptious and savory meals, while sharing ideas about space, the stars, and how galaxies worked.

Before parting ways, Vesha complimented them for their pursuit of the sciences and their academic prowess, "Thank you so much for choosing to see me over going to that silly prom. Proms have their purpose, but so does science and freedom of choice. Plus, I am so pleased to have met you. I can see within you that you are both very vibrant youth, so willing to learn, and you should know that I have a good hunch that both of you have an amazing future ahead of you."

They were ecstatic about such a wonderful reflection that was expressed about their character, and from one of their favorite scientific icons. With all that Vesha knew, Eliza and Yesha felt she deserved so much more credit than she was ever given for the contributions she made to the scientific community.

They both felt she should have been duly awarded the honor of becoming a Nobel Laureate, and even more so upon hearing her speak. They also knew that there was a contingency of men that felt that only men should receive the Nobel Prize in Physics, because in their opinion it was a man that started physics. Were the truth known, however, many of those men were inspired by mothers who encouraged their creativity, their curiosity, and their scientific minds, and without these wonderful women in their lives, they would never have begged the questions to get them there in the first place.

Eliza and Yesha dismissed the thoughts of defeat, and agreed with Vesha as she told them, "Sooner or later, they'll come around. I am sure of it. No sense in squabbling over ego anyway, it's a notable honor, but the love of science is a worthier pursuit, to say the least!"

On their way to the bus stop, Eliza and Yesha talked with each other, as the early summer breeze blew through the landscaped brush and the carpool parking lot. When they arrived, they discovered Vesha was waiting for the bus as well. They were both there, and it would be a while. So, Vesha decided to spend what time she could with them while waiting to head back to Princeton. Since the bus was on a delay, Eliza, Yesha, and Vesha talked for hours about dark matter, dark energy, and the quanta of physics.

They also discussed how these particles, all smaller than atoms, played a significant role in keeping galaxies together, as well as how they affected the expansion of the Universe. What stayed with Eliza most was when Vesha mentioned, "There is a possibility, someday, that we will be able to harness some of these quantum energies for use in space travel and so many other wondrous possibilities.

"The trick, I believe, is creating or obtaining mechanisms to direct those particles, baryonic and non-baryonic, anti-particles, exotic particles, and the energies they produce in a manner that will stabilize and allow us to manipulate them. Once we do, they will help us to explore the Cosmos at speeds faster than light and we will be able to get them to express themselves in any manner of our choosing, creating machines that will move from one point to another in a matter of seconds, with all associated and connected baryonic materials intact."

As their final high school year came to a close, in 1994, Eliza soon to be fourteen and Yesha soon to be seventeen, both turned down being the valedictorian as high school graduates despite the requests of their scholastic advisors. Both were the most accomplished and highest academic achievers of their class, one after the other and no one else came even close. Still, they felt it was only fair to afford others the opportunity for that honor since universities were already offering them full-on scholarships and the best schools were already knocking on their door.

They had their educational plans worked out, and very much in advance. First, they planned to begin their studies in New York to pursue their associate degrees, next they would go to New Jersey for their bachelor's degrees, and finally they would return to Massachusetts for their masters and doctorate degrees.

Having done exceptionally well on their SATs, the ACTs, and entrance exams, they enrolled to study at City University of New York, Princeton, MIT, and Harvard. They were quickly accepted by each school long before their high school graduation. Just as they had hoped for and planned, their higher education goals were beginning to pan out. In truth, any university would have been proud to have them, so the schools accepting them interestingly approved of their proposed collegiate schedules and timelines from their associate degrees to their PhDs.

College Begins

Both very attractive young ladies, slender, pleasantly curvy, fit and healthy, with medium-length hair and still wearing it for love of the fashion with Shirley Temple curls, maturing into A-Frame medium length wavy bobs, sometimes pulled their hair back in darling up-dos. Eliza with blonde hair, crystal blue eyes, and a soft complexion, and Yesha with brunette hair, green and hazel eyes, and a light tan complexion, found it was very easy to have dates with the boys at any time they wished. Therefore, during their first year of college, they had decided together to fend off any potential suitors for a while. They had goals.

Furthermore, as easy as it would be to date, Eliza was going to be turning fifteen the following summer after their first year in college, and there was too much potential for an awkward situation. Yesha didn't want to date if Eliza couldn't, so they chose to be more focused on their studies rather than go out with boys, men, or anything related to romance. Having the right start with their minds focused on their academics was crucial to their goals. Together with Yesha, they both decided it would be best to wait, at least until Eliza was eighteen.

To blow off steam and stay focused on and alerted to their priorities, both Eliza and Yesha went on jogs every day, took breaks viewing Broadway shows, and concentrated on their schoolwork. Romance or parenting in a premature manner would not get in the way of their studies nor their goals, at least unless it was in the shows or the movies. Neither Eliza nor Yesha thought dating was incompatible in any way with achievement or success, but they knew where their attentions lay for the time being. Both were serious about what they hoped to achieve in life, from increasing longevity and quality of life to raising the bar for humanity. They yearned to nurture the world into a safer place to live and use their ingenuity make exploration a safer and more enriching objective with successful and prosperous results.

It was at the end of their first year of college, studying for their associate degrees at City University of New York, and shortly after Eliza's fifteenth birthday when Eliza found out that her parents had been stricken by acute leukemia and passed away. This struck Eliza to the core and sent her into a sort of hysteria, tears streaming down her cheeks. She was crushed, again.

Yesha too was torn, but took her for a walk and listened to her, "How is it that my parents were so strong, so intelligent, living such healthy lives, and then this? Ugh, I can't stand it!" Eliza said, pausing and continuing.

"This isn't right! Nature is playing a brutal game. Much of what it does is random and has led to so much beautiful evolution, but with all that is going on and the suffering prevalent, I am going to figure out just what the pieces of that game are and make all the right moves! We'll never get anywhere letting Nature take its course alone. So then, I dare to say we are going to change that game, so life doesn't have to be so miserable and so short! It has never had to be, so why do we let it be?"

While Eliza knew there was much more to her question than she let on, and that perhaps it was time for humanity to take over its own destiny and give Nature a break, both Eliza and Yesha were sorry for the loss of the two people they considered two among the most precious in their lives. They stayed with Yesenia, who was also just as wonderful, grieving together in her parents' home that summer.

Eliza, Yesha, and Yesenia attended the Williams' funeral, the proceedings, and the burial service, and they went home in somber spirits. It was summer break, and as time went by, Yesenia, who missed her two dear friends so much, shared with them wonderful stories. As she did, Yesenia tried to move their focus of sadness toward an emphasis on the positives. By all intents and purposes, she had a doctorate in psychology and years of real-world experience dealing with loss, so she also helped them to move on through honesty and matter-of-factness.

She let Eliza know that her parents had established a very large trust for her. Yesenia helped both Eliza and Yesha through their grieving process all the while helping them psychologically with their cognitive frame-working. Since Yesha was very close to Eliza's Father, both had an interest in neuroscience, and she too was torn apart.

Despite the emotional dilemma, at age fifteen and as an emancipated minor, Eliza analyzed the financial details and realized a vast estate and a financial trust were in her name—large enough to fund several lifetimes of laziness. She crunched the numbers further and realized that she could ensure Yesenia had enough money to maintain the family estate for a very long time while also giving her sufficient funds to take breaks, hire maids, go on cruises, and enjoy the world.

Eliza's trust was big enough to fund a broad, high-end education for a thousand students or more. Her parents, even in death, had gifted her beyond measure, and now she would never be able to repay them.

The only way she could possibly reciprocate their generosity and wisdom was to become who they saw in her. So, Eliza began by funding her and Yesha's academic studies, and then reinvesting much of the rest in some of the latest, promising, and even somewhat risky emerging tech companies, diversifying it all in stocks, bonds, mutual funds, real estate, and more, while taking care of forthcoming bills for the foreseeable future.

After the funeral services were carried out and the duties of managing the estate were fulfilled, Yesenia gave Eliza a letter from her parents:

"Both of us, Janice and Gale, are writing this together for you, dear Eliza. We are sorry to leave you so soon, but there is no doubt in our minds that we have imparted a gift to the world, through you.

"Science has not yet caught up to a cure for cancer, or sadly enough, it may be possible that our society or the powers-that-be cannot yet see fit to do what is necessary to relieve the suffering and misery rampant throughout our mortal lives due to diseases that could, in fact, be resolvable. Perhaps, our dear sweet daughter, we can go on through those that live, and you must go on.

"We all have great hopes for you, our beloved and fearsome daughter. We have a profound love for you, and if possible, even thru death. What comes after this mortal coil has released us from this journey of life is the endless question, we all have, the answer to which I am sure we both, your father and I are about to discover.

"We very much would like to have gone on this grand journey of life with you, Eliza and our wonderful friends Yesenia and Yesha, but at last, it just wasn't ours to grace the stage of life or travel on these temporal roads any longer.

"While we'd wish to traverse the Universe with you in endless mortality, it seems that as unfortunate as this new reality may be for us, mankind has become a-wash in mediocrity and lust for misery and death. They choose to squander their time away in the pursuit of societal norms, status, and in un-purposeful pursuits, rather than concern themselves with science, cures for disease, and pursuit of overcoming natural or man-made disasters. Instead, all-too-many choose to dedicate every waking hour of theirs entrenched in establishments of baseless naysayers, their thirst for power for the sake of power alone, and overgrown bureaucracies rather than transcend those mockeries of breakthroughs to carry humanity's legacy to the farthest reaches of the Universe and beyond.

"Now, we'll be going to the place that no honest man or woman knows exists or does not exist; yet, no matter where we go, our hope is to see you again, whether it is in trillions of years or in a grouping of decades. May your love for humanity stay within your heart, may the peace within that comes from gentleness, love, empathy, consideration for the consent of others, or in other words, a well-grounded character, that basks in the ethics of well-being stay within your mind and your soul, and may the promise of your efforts lead to knowledge, discovery, innovation, peace, love, and kind laughter, accompanying your days forward.

"Much love to you, Eliza, our lovely daughter, and to our dearest friends, Yesenia and Yesha. X's and O's... and, don't forget to feed the coy fish and frogs, while you sing to them and the stars! "With love, your Mother and your Father and both of us a friend to the very end."

After everything was taken care of, hugs and tears shared, Eliza and Yesha returned to New York to finish their associate degrees, and life continued. They both progressed forward with their life-long journeys and their quests of personal development. They had many other experiences in store for them, beyond what they could fathom or imagine at that time in their lives. Despite her grief, Eliza dedicated herself to researching and understanding what had caused this ill state of affairs yet was already well-versed on how to overcome it. She just needed the right tools. Something could be done, and she was sure of it.

Eliza would listen to those who inspired her and lifted her spirits, who educated her mind, and who spoke to her heart. She would not give up on life to negativity nor on the evangelization of society's increasing quantity of preachers of doom and political or theatrical titans of destiny. She would not become vulnerable to superstitions that would remove her ability to have the necessary control over her future, nor the fear-mongering or hatred of those, who despite all, she still loved. Instead, Eliza would fight for those who preached love, kindness, compassion, consent, and empathy. She would battle for the dreamers and the disadvantaged and do everything and anything necessary by conceiving of and creating an opportunity for life in a Universe of hope rather than of despair. It didn't matter to her, that she was only fifteen years old, her mind was from particles that were billions of years old, and she had no intention of allowing her mind to waste away.

To Eliza, there was so much to live for. There were so many lost in their paths of life and so many who had lost to the unfortunate circumstances that led to death, yet she was going to do everything within her power to do something to reign in the sadness and bring in the hope. Humanity needed hope, and she would do anything and everything to bring that to this Earth. She would do this to not only bring it in droves but to ensure it was most certainly the kind of hope that would not be in vain.

Chapter 03: Driven from Within

Database Moon Archive, Celestial-Sol Entry Date: 2018 December 25. Yesha Alevtina trains Vesha Celeste. Eliza continues with her academic goals, meets more tragedy, yet persists to continue on, burning from within to bring hope. Vesha and Yesha are interfaced via biopod within the Pathway Melrose Campus. Input by: Yesha Alevtina, President of Pathway Industries, 2015-2022.

Eliza had already enrolled in physics as her major but following the passing of her parents she realized she was only human, and she too thirsted to take her suffering and lay it to rest. She would hold on to the wonders of her parents lives that brought joy, and those delights were found in study and understanding her Universe.

For Eliza, burying her suffering seemed easier by additionally enrolling in two more majors. She added neuroscience and biotechnology to her plate for a triple-wham focus on the understanding of disease and neurological disorders. The type of complications that suggested that pain, suffering, misery, and death, either through negligence or design, were factors that were necessary for life, were half-truths to her.

This was a time for her to meditate, and from the moments she took to think deeply, she came away with the knowledge and the burning thoughts in her mind that, *"We can learn from our challenges, and we know that no matter the scene or state we find ourselves in, we can overcome the desire to give up and embrace the desire to love, to live, and to thrive. Joy can be had through diligence. Challenges will present themselves without humanity increasing that suffering of their own accord."*

All the while, Yesha was at her side, working with her, studying with her, listening to her, and even studying her own major in neurology, now coupled with psychology. Yesha had admired Eliza's father, because he had been a good man, and she too felt that both Eliza's parents had shared so much and been so wonderful to her mother and her. She also felt that Eliza's parents had so much in common with them when it came to personal values and ethics. She too wanted to understand the physical and socially experiential mental nuances.

Through all the challenges that lay before her, Yesha knew that Eliza was more than one of many and in fact her parents' greatest accomplishment, just as their letter had suggested.

Yesha was grateful for their unique relationship, and she knew that due to their friendship as well as Janice's, Gale's, and Yesenia's phenomenal parenting, mentoring, and training, Eliza was truly growing to be a mighty character and the amazing and powerful human being they had always known she would become. Yesha also saw in her friend, that Eliza had no lust for power, and because of that, she wanted to protect her in every way possible.

Yesha was indeed brilliant, and bless her soul, for she was a genuine and amazing friend, and in every way that a friend could be. She knew that just like she did, Eliza too, at this tough time in her life needed social, emotional, and moral support. Yesha looked to Eliza many times, as a little sister and much more. She happened to see Eliza as vulnerable at times, even though they were the best of friends. Yesha noticed of late that Eliza had buried herself in her studies quite a bit more than usual, so she decided to confront her about it. Perhaps her pursuits were noble, but she had seemed to lose interest in the ideal balance of life her parents had always taught.

"You know, studying what you are studying is an amazing ability at your age. You're only fifteen, yet you're taking on three different majors. I'll go down in the history books as telling you that that is quite impressive." Yesha paused, "Do you mind if we go for a walk, enjoy a play, and then get back to these tasks at hand? I think we both need fresh air. What do you say?"

Eliza loved her friend greatly for being there for her, through thick and thin. They'd spent their entire lives together and were more sisterly to each other than most who were born from the same parents. They had even developed their own sisterhood, and one of honesty, gentleness, kindness, and sincerity.

Eliza had confided in Yesha throughout so many occasions, and on this occasion, she told her, "I don't look at any of this as burying myself in my studies; instead, I view it as taking the initiative and having the drive to push toward a better understanding of things, so we can overcome the worst, and I am sure you would like to do so as well. I am looking for the keys that can lead us to connect the dots of neuroscience, physics, and biology so we can evolve beyond the current misery, suffering, and devastation prevalent today, and into a brighter and more hopeful future. I know there is something that can be done and that more ought to be done to prevent the loss of so many great hearts, lives, and minds."

Yesha was moved by what Eliza had said and understood what it was that she was doing. She too did wish to end suffering, misery, and devastation, all of which caused the loss of so much untold potential. So, she allowed Eliza to continue what she was doing for now and studied too. There was much to do, so they pressed on.

Eliza was very impressed when the President at the time had announced the Human Genome Project. She was, however, slightly appalled at humanity's consistent lack of progress and the obstacles humanity created for itself through irrational thinking, apathy, unfounded and sometimes reasonable fears. Nevertheless, she smiled with a quiet and internal celebration as the visionaries and scientists moved through all their frustrations and made each discovery and breakthrough possible.

Eliza maintained vigilance of each advance since the idea of gene therapy had taken off. When she was seventeen, she meditated to find herself again, through the ups and downs of progress and the ideas of power and strength through the efforts of achieving well-being. She meditated and drifted for a moment:

"All-too-often it seems scientists have missed grand swaths of micro-information considering the fact that in so many cases mutations of genes lead to leukemia. When they finally discover this, there will be an unfortunate and unhealthy moratorium on this type of research. This is sad, because they will be setting rejuvenation science research back by a minimum of two decades. I can see the writing on the wall, but I am determined to see through each study. I can see through to the truth of it all—cell-to-cell, gene-to-gene, and neuron-to-neuron communication and the proper introduction into the flow-of-traffic of red and white blood cells are at its core. I understand now, how cells communicate to each other their various complementary assignments and there is a way to encourage and augment their healing processes!"

By 1999, Eliza, nineteen, and Yesha, twenty-two, had spent countless hours in the labs of Princeton, visiting Vesha and her family regularly, and they finished their bachelor's degrees in stellar form. They barreled through their master's degrees in much the same way at MIT, through lab time, study time, and extensive verification of their results, while immersed in academic achievements.

Amazing Friends

During the summer just before the last year of their graduate studies, Eliza and Yesha both had begun dating. Eliza met her boyfriend, Charles—a tall, dark-skinned, golden-eyed, clean-cut, and handsome "metro-casual" man from Ohio, when Yesha hosted her eighteenth birthday party at her estate home in Massachusetts.

Eliza and Charles began to go on double dates with Yesha, regularly, when she had been introduced to her boyfriend, Eugene, who was a clean-cut young man with heritage from the inhabitants of the Americas long before modern expansion by western civilization. Eugene had moved to Massachusetts from Cheyenne, Wyoming.

Charles and Eugene became well-acquainted years before they met Eliza and Yesha and were friends and study partners going over their curriculum in Cambridge. It was by chance that they had met since the two young men were set to complete their doctorates in 2001. In their private lives as well as their pursuits, each of them understood the other quite well. Together, Eliza, Charles, Yesha, and Eugene were tightly-knit, helped each other with studies, and made life enjoyable and purposeful.

No matter how they enjoyed their time together, they were still firm with their emphasis on studies. Charles and Eugene were mature enough to appreciate vision, drive, and intellect in anyone, and they too saw the same in Eliza and Yesha. Each of the four had similar ideas of a better world—a world where kindness, compassion, drive, and innovation for well-being ruled the day.

Because Charles and Eugene were compassionate, dedicated, and gentlemanly, Eliza and Yesha knew that they would complement their own team very well, and quite possibly make a wonderful addition for the long-haul. These two young ladies knew that at some point they had to be a little more social anyway, to get out and into the world, enjoy the arts, and have some fullness in the balance of life. Their rhythm in academics was solid, they were now ready to embrace emotional connections.

By 2000, both Eliza and Yesha had finished their master's degrees at MIT. They did well, celebrated, and began their Doctoral studies at Harvard.

Together, Eliza and Yesha, along with Charles and Eugene, decided to move to a joint apartment with shared expenses in every way. No matter their dedication to their future, these four young and brilliant pre-doctorates took the time from everything on occasion to go on trips to the city, county, state and national parks for camping. They were resourceful and found other inexpensive forms of exploring and enjoying their world as well. They pinched their pennies often and visited the water slides for thrills and fun, danced at the Raves in Miami to let loose, and went on a cruise to breathe in the ocean mist and drink in the starry nights. This team of four did all of this during their weekends and winter, spring, and summer breaks.

As time continued and their studies intensified, Eliza and Yesha grew to be particularly impressed with Charles and Eugene, especially when they realized that they too balanced their lives by spending time studying while camping, bringing their telescopes, mapping the stars, gazing at deep sky objects, and even singing some of their favorites from Depeche Mode and other artists.

One of Eliza's fondest memories, looking back, was when, together with Charles, Yesha, and Eugene, they hopped aboard a bus and went to Princeton, in New Jersey. There were a lot of reasons to go, and they enjoyed the sights and sounds, but the most important reason of all was to visit Vesha, her husband, Ralston, her daughter, Jillian, and some of their friends. Together they caught up for the sake of old times and introduced their fairly new boyfriends. Eliza and Yesha relished their extensive and sophisticated conversations, valued Ralston's wit, adored Jillian's sweet charm, and were swept away with Vesha's spunk, humor, and tenacity about life's intrigues.

Vesha had had quite a life and quite a journey even though through her younger years she had confronted the sentiment in society that women weren't supposed to be scientists. She had always been of the mind to quip, "Oh yeah, watch it happen, because you aren't going to stop me." She could then embrace the world around her and share, "Oh, look at that, isn't it so beautiful?" Overall, their favorite astronomer and astrophysicist was a genius.

What was bittersweet, for Eliza, Yesha, Charles, and Eugene, however, was when she told them both, "I'm not getting any younger, but it is nice to have a certain sense of independence. Soon, I may be moving into Princeton Senior Citizen's center. I believe I am beginning to suffer from the pre-stages of Alzheimer's or Dementia. Oh, I do exercises to remember key moments, but I lose things fairly quick as well. Yesha, you remind me so much of my daughter, Jillian. Eliza, you are mighty and driven. All four of you are so sweet. Thank you for visiting an aging lady like myself, her handsome husband, and some of her family and friends, with these two handsome gentlemen."

Bittersweet

Early on, in the summer of 2001, Charles and Eugene finished their doctoral studies in Finance and Economics and found out about a great opportunity in New York. Both had, after much research and discussion, accepted the opportunity offered and were hired by a firm at the World Trade Center. They were anxious to begin saving for homes in Massachusetts, not too far from where Eliza and Yesha had grown up and had spent a lot of time together, were very close, had a strong and shared history now, and Cambridge was their "happy place."

Eliza had told Charles about her dreams earlier that year. She remembered as he gleamed with love, care, understanding, empathy, compassion, and joy when she told him about her goals.

One day Eliza voiced to Charles, "Someday, I would like to engage in a very large project. It isn't your typical project either. Through the years I have confronted one obstacle after another, but notwithstanding everything that has happened, I have dreamt of forming a company incorporating biotech, neuroscience, and physics with the goal of optimizing physiological and neurological health. I would like to work on space travel itself and find a way to navigate out to space and through the deep in a manner that is, for one, possible, and most importantly safer and more secure than it is now.

"I would like us all to be involved with cleaning up the debris that is gathering around the Earth, as well as controlling the movement of asteroids and other objects en tangent to Earth. We could begin by taking all these materials to the Moon, establishing bases using the regolith and other resources out there to build bases that are underground, above ground, and roaming.

"We can create space travel launch and landing centers, where we can be involved in the process of developing asteroid mining facilities that lead to making humanity interplanetary. We can be involved in other very robust projects that will take us surprisingly further and into the future.

"All of these bases and facilities can be established congruent with the mining that can be done in space with nanorobotics and artificial intelligence technologies.

"We as a team can be intimately involved with this. The ultimate reason I have for all these pursuits is that through these initiatives we will eventually be able to sculpt healthier, happier, and mind-expanding lives. Not to mention, it sure would be nice to have a safer space exploration take-off point and pay off our country's debts as well as the debts of each individual while developing robust health care, economic, educational, correctional, and technologically advanced innovation systems."

Charles knew she had big goals, and together they all did, but the goals that he had heard from Eliza were much greater than life itself and more genuine and powerful than he had ever heard from anyone else. He shared in her enthusiasm and had a hunch they would need to succeed in their current professions first, so they could stockpile and invest in their future venture company—a company that Charles had dubbed, "Pathway Industries." He finally worked up the courage to open up to Eliza about how much he cared for her and why he would need to leave.

Following Yesha's birthday party, on the first of July, Charles pulled Eliza aside and talked to her. "I want you to know that I love you very much, Eliza.

"Someday, and hopefully soon, I would like to see us be married. However, I want each of us, in our little team of four, to have a chance to finish our studies and become established professionals in our fields of expertise, first.

"This is primarily because I don't want something to happen that would jeopardize your dreams. Your dreams, Eliza, are worth everything to me, every moment spent, waiting, saving up, and making them possible.

"When we reach your primary goals and ideals, perhaps we can take our relationship further and get married. We could work as a team to make all of this happen. Maybe we can raise a family on distant planets even further down the road, once your current dreams and any subsequent visions you have playing within that great mind of yours have been realized to where you have achieved a good portion of what you wish to set out to do.

"Like you, Eliza, I believe we can have a future where our civilization has finally come together and spanned the Cosmos. We can do so much more throughout this world than we have ever done before. Oh, we've had our fun, we've kept our lives balanced, and now it is time for us to work to gain a more profound focus on the steps we need to take to make your dreams possible.

"What do you think?"

Eliza blushed as her pride in Charles' love of her goals emanated from his speech and his mannerisms. With tears welling up in her eyes, she looked up at her kind, large-minded, visionary, and handsome gentleman and said, "I know it will be tough for a while, yet as much as I would hate to admit it, it is a tough reality we all have to cope with, to face—being apart so we can achieve our full potential may be the next crucial step for us."

Looking into the silver lining, Eliza continued, "Hey, we'll have vacation times, where we can visit, I imagine. We can pinch pennies. We'll have moments where we can save by simply meeting up in a central location, maybe visit Vesha in Princeton, and we can go on hikes and look up at the stars. Charles? You know? I'm going to miss you, I love you very much, and, I think you are amazing, too! We'll be alright. I support you in your endeavors."

With a pause, Charles held her in his arms, hugged her and then told her with a bit of a swagger, in an effort to swing the mood in a lighter direction, "Thank you, Eliza. No matter what happens we'll be in each other's hearts."

They sighed and stared out at the horizon together in silence for a few moments. "Eugene and I have had offers sent to us, and by accepting this, we can begin our careers as investors at the World Trade Center, where we'll be part of a financial team that investigates potential clients for technological advancement and investment.

"We accepted that contract, wherein we were offered high-end six-figure incomes. We'll be involved in global trade, we'll be able to develop a network of friends who are savvy with all forms of investments, to include venture capitalism. While there are those driven by greed, we'll forge relationships with those who understand what true ethics are, we will work with and even help people from all over the world, and we'll be able to do all of that as we save up, so we can get you your dream, Eliza."

As Charles was having his private moments with the beautiful and highly intelligent young woman in his life, Eugene, likewise, was going over his details and listening to another beautiful woman, both inside and out, as he engaged in a similar sobering conversation with Yesha.

Both ladies were very keen on what needed to happen next, but this would be tough. While Eliza and Yesha wanted to be around their boyfriends and would rather they didn't have the distance, they also knew that they couldn't get where they needed to by stagnating and limiting themselves, nor could their gentlemen. It was essential to zero in on the big game ahead and get through their studies. There was a lot to get done, and right now, for all four, success in life called for separation, a time to realize their potential through education and experience.

After roasting marshmallows over a fire, finding the Andromeda Galaxy and the constellations of Cassiopeia to the northwest, Sagittarius to the southeast, and Lyra overhead, along with a few other nebulae, star clusters, and galaxies with their telescopes, they sipped herbal teas while nestled in lawn chairs. Eliza found an appropriate way to channel her emotions and she opened up to their whole team of four. "As much as I'd hate to admit it, you are right, Charles. Perhaps this will give us each more time to dedicate to our studies and our professions, with fewer distractions. We all seem to understand what we need to do so we can realize a bigger dream, one that is greater than each of us, and something wonderful for everyone.

"Yesha, I know you love Eugene; Charles, I love you, and you both love us. However, to follow through with our goals, we have to do what we know ought to be done. While you know within your hearts that we'll miss you both, please know our hearts will always be with you. We'll keep our contact limited, and our focus heightened, but that is only for now."

Both men and women saw eye-to-eye and shared each other's views and appreciated them. Charles then opened up, "While this is a somber moment, we know we have to spend more time dedicated to our future and not let our dreams fade away. Both Eugene and I have talked about this a lot. We want you to know that we agree that it is important that we each begin and become established in our careers, as one of many steps in the long journey ahead. We need to do this long before proposing our hands in marriage. It is no secret among us since we talk about these things often.

"Both Eugene and I should begin this next stage of life, so we can give you two a fair amount of time to focus on your doctoral studies and careers. When you are ready, perhaps we can have a simple marriage to keep costs low.

"Marriage is a commitment of shared excellence and as you've shared with me, Eliza, it makes more sense to invest our means into research, development, and further improvements to realize an even greater dream than pompous and pious circumstance."

When Charles said this, they laughed together in the spirit of humor about what he had said, gathered their senses about the reality of the changes that were about to begin, and then he continued, "I believe we will be able to chase our dreams with more vigor as we take this opportunity to gain enough experience and influence in New York. There is a lot for us to achieve and do there, and once we have, we can then set up our shared limited liability company in Massachusetts.

"We can grow this, together, into an industry, and then into something even greater and more influential, and not too far from here, our home, Eliza's home."

Eugene followed Charles' perspective, and told the group, "No matter where we go, no matter what happens in the future, no matter what life gives us or takes away from us, each of you, within and without, you will in your fullness and your all, always, be in my heart. Our friendship is one that I would never have dreamt possible. I truly appreciate every moment we have spent together.

"Let's look to the future, dream big, and stay strong!"

Eliza's twenty-first birthday came the following day, and together they shared her very first wine spritzer, made of homemade lemonade, sprite, and red wine.

Not long after, the day of departure came.

All four teammates stood at a juncture in their lives, where they wouldn't see each other, it seemed, for a long, long, time. They had planned their next shared moments to be the very next Thanksgiving, but this was another bittersweet moment in Eliza's and Yesha's lives.

Following big bear hugs and with tear-stained eyes, they both waved goodbye as Charles and Eugene climbed into their car to begin their two-month road-trip to their parents' homes. From there, the two young men would proceed forward to New York.

Love was no stranger among them, and it was tough on each of their spirits. Yet, they knew it was necessary, because affording Charles and Eugene these moments together, and with their families, before settling into the next chapter of their lives was the right thing to do. They waved as Charles and Eugene drove away, down the road, and far and into the distance. Once they were no longer in view, Eliza and Yesha turned to each other, and gave each other a hug, saying in unison, "We're going to miss them."

They then felt their emotions swell and they stopped by Eliza's estate home, spent a little time catching up with Yesenia, and went outside to the pond where the coy fish and the frogs congregated and swam about unaware of the great plans that lay ahead.

Eliza held her bookmark of Tyson in her right hand, brought it up, and held it to her heart. As she did, she looked toward Yesha, and together they looked up to the stars and sang "Shine" by Depeche Mode.

Evening set in as dusk grew to night-time, they donned their running shoes after that shared moment and embraced their emotions meticulously by going out on a good long night jog around town, while talking, before heading back to their apartment.

The end of their previous semester lingered in the air from the past, and their next semester was soon to be in full force. Even though their young men were away, they had a lot of productivity, studies, and life to focus on and goals to bring to the negotiating table.

Eliza's and Yesha's jog had been good for their spirits, the goodbyes to their boyfriends had been bitter but sweet, and they slept well in their own beds that first night with Charles and Eugene gone, but for no reason other than they were physically drained. No matter, each day following they would wake up ready for the world. Motivation and hard-core dedication set on achieving their dreams are what their sights were set on now.

Two months later, Eliza and Yesha received a call from Charles and Eugene. Eliza and Yesha had moved out of the apartment they were sharing with them before they left, and had moved back into Eliza's family estate, with Yesenia mostly quiet and doing her own thing. From time to time they would chat over muffins and tea, but most of the time they were busy and hyper-focused on their studies, such that time would simply speed by.

Eliza's estate was close enough to school, and with a good walk each morning, neither of them saw any sense in spending additional funds on an extra living space, when the estate was more than enough. Besides, its ambiance was perfect for studying and peace of mind.

Great Commitments

Eliza and Yesha had recently purchased two new Nokia radio-cellular phones, and Eliza had recently bought a new digital-messaging phone for their family estate home and had put it on speaker mode so that she and Yesha could listen as Charles and Eugene shared their journeys and excitement in a four-way conversation.

It was the second day on the job for Charles and Eugene, and they were giddy about how everything had unfolded the day prior. Settling down and into their small New York apartment was reasonably easy, only because they had very little to move.

They had gone for a minimalistic approach, and thus had sleeping bags, a small suitcase of clothes, a microwave and plenty of Ramen noodles.

On their first day, Charles and Eugene had finally settled down and were obliged to meet with the company President. It was inspiring. They both, in excitement, relayed to Eliza and Yesha how well it had gone, that the President had given them travel reimbursements, showed them the gym and other facilities, and he had even given them meal cards courtesy of the company.

This essentially afforded them excellent meals morning, noon, and night, along with healthy snacks. They wouldn't need a fridge or any of the other typical appliances, nor would they need the electricity consumed while working for the company. Everything was designed to reduce the carbon footprint, and the win-win was that it increased their ability to save on money overall.

Charles and Eugene were set up well in a genuinely top-notch work environment, in every way. After sharing all their enthusiasm for the way everything was setup, their sense of joy concerning this new and healthy work environment, and before the conversation came to a close, they told the young ladies how much they loved them.

Before heading to bed that night for their second day of work, they told Eliza and Yesha, "We can't wait to see you! We'll see you soon! Thanksgiving will be amazing this year! We'll head there then, but you'll have to visit!"

After exchanging pleasantries, they closed their conversations, "We love you, and we'll call you briefly in the morning." Fortunately, they did call, as planned, and then said their goodbyes early that following morning.

Charles and Eugene went into the World Trade Center, on Tuesday morning, September 11, 2001, anxious to begin their duties for their new company in New York City, NY. They enjoyed the elevator ride, as it took them high and into the sky. This would be a big day!

Eliza and Yesha were both anxiously awaiting to visit Charles and Eugene in New York, happy with their conversations, and appreciated how both of them had wished Yesha and her well, before going into work that day. An hour had gone by since their phone conversation. Eliza was studying at her estate, and she could never forget as Yesha rushed in after break had begun in one of her classes. This time, there had been a deathly scared and frightened look on her face, as she tried to not stumble over her words, "Eliza, you have to turn on the television!"

Eliza, curious, found the remote, pointed it toward the TV, changed it to a random news station, and with horror, watched the footage play, after play, after replay of the first jet crashing into one of the twin towers.

Together, Eliza and Yesha hoped that somehow their boyfriends were okay. They weren't sure, so they called the phone numbers to their office. Silence can say so much, especially when there is no answer to the dial tone.

They called their boyfriends' bosses' phone number with no success. Finally, they called the emergency hotline at the World Trade Center in New York City. There was no reprieve from the horror that was playing out before their eyes and in their minds, only the unsettling voice of an automated operator, "We're sorry, the number you are calling is currently unavailable. If you would like to make a call, please hang up and try again."

The television was still playing when Eliza and Yesha, with hands over their mouths, tears spilling from their eyes, lumps swelling within their throats, sitting on their knees on their couch, listened in silence and disbelief as they heard the news anchor with skepticism and anguish in his eyes, state, "Oh my," he paused in obvious surprise, horror, and disbelief at what he had to report.

"Oh my. I can't believe what I am seeing here. This is a drastic reality playing before us, a tough and horrendous day, the likes of which I never thought I would ever be forced to bear witness to. I can't imagine what it is like for each of you, the people inside, the horror, the terror. People are jumping trying to get away from the intense heat, but... what is that? It appears there is another jet... Oh, my. It appears that another jet has crashed into the second tower..." The broadcaster's words carried on.

Eliza and Yesha sat in a state of shock as their glands began to swell, and they no longer could hear the news anchor reporting. They were numb and almost paralyzed for a few brief moments that seemed like an eternity. They did not leave their couch, and at this moment, they could not move a muscle. Their bodies betrayed them, and they were stuck sitting in disbelief and horror, with their hands draped over their mouths and tears pouring down.

Finally, after what seemed an eternity, they saw each other's anguish and wrapped comforting arms around each other, with tears staining their cheeks, and feelings of anger, frustration, trauma, and sadness sweeping in.

They could hardly speak; they were so overcome. In a complete sense of dread to do so, Eliza and Yesha could not pry their eyes away, as they witnessed the towers fall as if in two piles of dust and rubble. There were no phone calls from Charles or Eugene, the nation may have been shocked, but their spirits were crushed.

With the terror attacks on the Pentagon and the World Trade Center, this was a day that they would never forget. Later, Eliza and Yesha would confide in each other that to them, this was an attack on love, on freedom, on innovation, on respect and dignity. This was an attack on humanity itself. The horrors of hate, malice, and brutality of the greatest degree and its actions brought only misery to the lives of so many treasured and beloved souls. It was evident to Eliza and Yesha, the profound effect this had on so many throughout the nation, and on them as well.

As the scene continued to unfold, Eliza tried to get up from the couch; she needed to get something, so she could drink some water, but found herself instead stumbling, broken in the heart, in the mind, and the soul, so she turned to Yesha. With tears gushing down her face, they embraced a while longer and fell to their knees. "This was supposed to be a wonderful day, Charles' and Eugene's big day to begin bringing about their dreams, and now this."

After settling down, and still in shock, several hours had passed by. Eliza had by then gathered herself together just enough to ask through swollen glands and a healthy dose of tears, "How is it, that people can engage in such inhumanity, and bring about unspeakable horrors to such peaceful, kind, innovative, and loving people, the likes of whom they may never know?" She was thinking beyond her own tragedy and seeing a grander picture of it all.

"Apparently, this is an act of terrorism against our nation, by people who are from countries who have received an overall increase in prosperity, because of US industry, yet instead of sharing the wealth, the cronies absorbing the wealth indoctrinate those who struggle at their hands and blame the US for the disparity in their well-being. Now, they've taken out their misguided rage on so many wonderful people who do care.

"Here we are in a nation that is a superpower. While we should each take pride in our roots, and while we know as a whole our nation is not perfect, this tragic act of the most demonic aspects of humanity was grotesque and malicious beyond justification.

"This nation has given more to those suffering from famine, disease, meager resources, and greed than any other superpower nation in the history of mankind. Yet despite all, today we have received a day of sadness and of loss from the hands of those who have become insanely wealthy, courtesy of the US and its allies, who instead of sharing, peppered their cronies and reviled those who are struggling while blaming the US and its allies for all of their woes.

"The gratitude for the sacrifices of many throughout our nation, and many impacted throughout our beautiful world, both for and in their behalf, has been hit with such a striking and undeserved blow by those who, had they been properly educated and not treacherously or malevolently indoctrinated, would have thrown thank you parties, replete with music, smiles, and hugs instead."

Eliza paused for a moment, blew her nose, and then continued, but with even more bravado than before.

"Perhaps I am venting, and although vindication and mistrust is a form of social justice in cases like these, it may well be we have yet to learn the truth of it all, and we may never know anything about what has truly happened unless someone is honest, and I believe it is fair to say that someone who would do this would never come clean of it. We need to heal minds and remove this societal toxicity."

Life was slow for a while. Days passed in silence, TVs were turned off, and studies were suddenly difficult to make sense of.

For three weeks Eliza and Yesha stopped their studies, and they slept, they wept, they hugged, and they drank tea. Their professors gave all of their students, extra time and an extra break to gather themselves after these shocking events. Psychologists were on hand to provide counseling, and together, Eliza and Yesha went in to receive therapy themselves. Yesenia had tried to help, but she knew that this was beyond her experience level, and it was difficult to counsel someone when she was moved to tears herself. She too was choked up and sought help.

It took a while to overcome the loss of Charles and Eugene. Yesenia had always appreciated how they treated her two girls. They would glow when they talked about them and smile big smiles of joy, well, before all of this. She, Eliza, and Yesha knew they had lost Charles and Eugene, since their place of work had been on the level of the building that had been impacted by the very first jet. They had finally reached the authorities and had received a confirmed presence in the building that day, and no other detail could be confirmed due to all the rubble.

As painful as this was for Eliza and Yesha, there was a certain amount of closure in knowing where they had been, rather than having no idea whatsoever. Yet, there was lingering sadness knowing they would never return.

Eliza, several days later, at home with Yesha, had meditated deeply, and found the strength to share more with her, "I will never forget his demeanor, his attention to our dreams and whims, or how he and Eugene wished us well before going in that day. I will never forget the horror when looking at the TV as we knew they were in their work center, with no opportunity for escape. They were beginning their new careers, they wanted to help us reach our dreams, and now our future with them has been blown to smithereens."

She paused, "No matter the tragedy, no matter the pain, we have had our mourning, we have shed our tears, and the day has come for us to pick ourselves up and move forward. We cannot let the actions of a depraved element in society, dripping with the blood of innocence and systematic inhumanity, slow us down. We must do more than we have ever thought we could before. We cannot tolerate this sort of injustice any longer. I realize that these were the actions of neurologically imbalanced and misguided individuals who were given the appropriate title of "terrorist" wreaking terror upon so many beautiful people they do not know. This cannot, nor will it ever be a time to let these types of acts slow us down.

"Yesha, I have analyzed and have worked out our trust, and we have plenty of funds to allow for the future we were going to share and had planned with Charles and Eugene. Our finances are well enough, that I have also chosen to enroll into four additional majors. I will not only be majoring in neuroscience, biotechnology, and physics, but I am now enrolled in the majors of mathematics, sociology, psychology, and law.

"There is a lot that can be done to mend the minds that are too far gone for the technologies we have with us today. However, we can work for something better—both of us, by creating advanced systems that will heal those minds. In the process, we can help to reduce the suffering, cure the diseases, and ease the pains of those who suffer for no consequence of their own making. We can work together to bring longevity to the masses, reduce debt to nothing, optimize health and well-being, and have the power to stop this type of action caused by the type of environment that unleashes an unhealthy mind.

"We can do this, and we will. I know you, and if we as a civilization can realize our goals, we will, each and every last breathing one of us, win. There are few other choices, aside from mediocrity and a lost will, suggesting we have given up. Well, I haven't lost my will, and I will not lose my mind. We have got a lot to do, so let's stop groveling, let's stop crying, let's stop giving up, and let's stop being sad. It's time to be happy, it's time to burn with fire within, and it's time to fill these husks of sorrow with the flame of will, driving us to share the clarity of a better day with the world, and go further than we ever have gone before."

After preaching these moving words, Yesha, amidst tears, gathered herself together and hugged Eliza.

After pondering on what Eliza shared, she was finally able to speak, "Wow, young lady. You should write a book once we're done with our studies. You have inspired me, and I have no doubt you can inspire the world. So, thank you. Thank you, Eliza, for sharing these moments and these powerful ideas. Thank you for sharing this time with me, whether bitter or sweet, whether good or bad, you have given me the will to go on. Thank you, my dear friend and my forever sister in spirit, my kindred spirit."

Over the next five years, Eliza and Yesha dedicated themselves toward balance in their lives, with a heightened emphasis on their studies.

Helping each other along the way, they finished their additional master's degrees and PhDs by late 2005. Following which, they continued as full-time professors at Harvard for two years.

Eliza began writing legislative papers and reports for the congressional and senatorial representatives of her state, and with Yesha, their many achievements seemed minor and under the radar, but they were in truth, huge.

Chapter 04: A Thoughtful Walk

Database Moon Archive, Celestial-Sol Entry Date: 2018 December 25. Yesha Alevtina trains Vesha Celeste. Following their university achievements, Drs Eliza Williams and Yesha Alevtina serve as professors at Harvard and MIT. Eliza engages in many lab studies and innovative intrigues, and then discovers something she decides to share with Yesha. Vesha and Yesha are in their biopods within the Pathway Melrose Campus. Input: Yesha Alevtina, President of Pathway, 2015-2022.

After completing their post-doctoral studies, theses, and all other requirements in the late part of 2005, Eliza and Yesha graduated with academic achievements at the level of Summa Cum Laude. Eliza received honors for seven PhDs, and Yesha received honors for three.

In February of 2006, Eliza and Yesha worked as Professors at Harvard University, full time, and part-time as professors at MIT, until late December of 2007.

While teaching at Harvard and MIT, after having spent a lot of time in the labs at both schools with unique permissions and accesses requiring high levels of trust, aside from fulfilling their duties as professors, Eliza and Yesha conducted the kind of research together that led to the development of some remarkable advancements.

Both were incredible professors and often lauded by their students and the faculty who admired their clarity. They were, in a very short period, renown for the way they brought understanding to the minds of those they taught. Eliza and Yesha were recognized by both schools for the motivation they had fostered, grown, and multiplied within their students toward their learning.

Drs Williams and Alevtina had inspired their peers and superiors like none other, through their diligence and dedication. Not only were they exceptionally brilliant professors, but they were also phenomenal researchers, innovators, and developers in the laboratory and on other highly advanced and sophisticated technical systems.

Eliza had led the way, working with Yesha, as they helped Harvard and MIT produce numerous patents. They also took time to go over ideas and thoughts with each other, with some projects of their own, and all with the interest of attaining even higher goals.

Upon conducting private research, Eliza came upon a significant breakthrough for physiological and neurological health, which subsequently caused her to contemplate beginning her new limited liability company. She wanted to do this, as planned with Yesha, Charles, and Eugene, in the interest of research, development, and worldwide distribution to raise the bar for humanity.

In the spirit of transparency and getting the goods out, so to speak, in Eliza's words, "This will be done so lives can be saved, and toxicity of every sort reduced." She wanted to introduce her new inventions to Harvard and MIT first, but in wisdom, Eliza decided she would confide with Yesha before doing so.

It was early one summery Saturday, in 2006, when she came to Yesha to share her ideas. "Teaching is one of my many passions, you know that. However, the things that seem to pull at us, even more, are the creation of technologies that can preserve life, raise the quality of life for everyone interested, and all the while, realize the well-being of others as well as ourselves.

"You know that I sense the ability to create something that I call 'a legacy worthy of preserving for the long-haul' is essential. In large part, it is there already through the many heroes, historians, artists, romantics, scientists, and even some of our politicians, each of whom have graced the stage of Earth at many different times throughout many millennia.

"I believe, however, that we can compound upon these discoveries and augment our innovations with a kind and caring way of thinking, while maintaining our health and strength, and we can create an environment that will allow goals for longevity in life, rather than lust for death, to flourish. Once that happens, I believe we will be even more moved with promise, because then hope and meaningful purpose will be imbued into what we do and teach." Eliza paused for a bit.

Yesha sipped her tea and put it down. She was with Eliza, one-hundred percent of the way, and as Yesha sipped her tea, she thought about what Eliza had said as her words danced around in her mind. Wanting to talk about it all at length, she asked Eliza if she would like to chat while going on a walk. Suggesting they could do so while going on a seven-hour round-trip jaunt from their estate in Cambridge to a small park along the ocean by Grover's Cliff and back, Eliza agreed with the idea. There was a lot to discuss. So, they packed their bags with plenty of water and nutritious snacks and began their journey.

"I totally get you, Eliza. We aren't interested in a mediocre existence, living to barely get by until we die, or stranding society as it goes down the same road, where many who have fought against the true heroes of this world have gone. I mean, the true heroes are those who brought change in a good way to reduce misery, suffering, and toxicity in the way one person treated another. Many of those true heroes, unfortunately, lost their lives while doing so.

"Every individual who has ever worked in the past or continues on now is all-too-often forgotten in their noble quest to end slavery, murder, rape, disease, hunger, thirst, abuse, and so much more. In too many instances, many wonderful people from the past are judged harshly by the standards of today, due to the fact that they rose from their past and redeemed themselves through moving forward out of the path to nowhere and into a lovely trail of healthy pursuits.

"When society solely maintains its focus on the misdeeds of the past of someone who learned from the challenges they were presented and turned around to think beyond themselves and their current state of affairs, many extraordinarily wonderful icons are unfairly deemed more horrible than they were, given their times.

"I believe, a majority of remarkable people are the result of their environment, and in many circumstances, they are amazing despite it or their teachings, and in so many ways more opportunities for personal choice is a beautiful reflection of each of those things. It is nice that there are those who have fought through the years, or no matter their lot in life, they have even transcended their childhood for the rights of everyone else to have a provision of a higher quality of education or a higher quality of life.

"These types of high-level thinkers transcend society itself, imbuing motivation toward innovation into others. These heroes have pushed many members of society in a noble way, and in a brilliant manner that has allowed many more to increase our knowledge of humanity for the better, and in our understanding of every detail of our Universe. All of this, so we can work toward a more lovely and promising future.

"All that has been done, well, all of that progress can be stymied, reversed completely, or go the way of dust and decay. We must continuously rise above the fray ourselves, and only look back for the purposes of wisdom and love. So yes, Eliza, we certainly have to and can do more."

Eliza thought about what Yesha had said, and she was right. She knew Yesha had more to say, so she listened. As they talked, they took in the sights and the sounds of the buzzing city and the parks nearby, some of the industry that had grown in recent years, and some of the creativity and industry of the shops, that carried with them the seeming spirit of the revolution in those once colonial homes, and they were appreciative of so much that was now accessible and enjoyable.

Yesha continued, "For far too long people have lived for merely one shared goal, due to the daunting nature that life seems to bring. That goal may be a noble one, but it comes short of progression in and of itself and does not recognize the complexity of life and all its nuances.

"This goal is survival through natural evolution. To merely survive, no matter the means, as noble as it may seem at first, will lead to the end of life and the end of humanity, whether through natural events or mankind's apparent affinity toward death.

"It's as if far too many people worship the almighty 'mixed result' rather than raise the quality of and joy in life through logic, study, innovation, and common sense, by enjoying what it can bring to the table, which will ultimately result in desired results.

"Finding cures for disease, both physiological and neurological, and possessing the ingenuity to innovate technologies as well as a pathway for humanity to quicken their pace for developing them will lead to preserving our Earth, our solar system, perhaps our Universe, and with it, each individual and humanity itself, as we travel to and push the limits of the Universe and its sustainability, trusting ourselves as we do so."

"Exactly," Eliza turned to Yesha and smiled. They both understood each other and were already pretty much of one mind, but with two different angles that enriched their shared ideas. Eliza was grateful to have a friend such as Yesha in her life. She brought clarity and calm.

As they passed by a small university to their right, they saw a coffee shop and stopped there for a little break. While sipping their nicely-flavored, yet healthy beverage, Eliza expounded on what was on her mind.

Yesha listened intently. "We are both whole-heartedly dedicated toward creating mechanisms for physical and mental, or better said physiological and neurological well-being. Humanity has unfortunately suffered way too much from erred judgment and myopic thinking, or even from bureaucracies that were perhaps well-intended in their development at one time but have become mired in inefficiency and red tape, and for far too long. To mend the decay of human injustice and to bring hope requires healing rather than harming.

"The evidence is obvious of the results of brutality, no matter their source of delivery, and nothing gained through misery-sourced means will bring everlasting joy or peace within, nor will it secure an indeterminate existence. The fundamental sciences and technologies are already there to cure illness, disease, and reduce suffering in so many ways, yet there is a gargantuan amount of negligence toward significant progress in large part due to the build-up of entrenched bureaucracies, and perhaps enough misguided individuals who have no clue beyond their wallets or their lust for power. Don't get me wrong, perhaps these organizations were once intended for good, but iron-clad virtues, ethics, and a moral code lays in shared well-being and not in winning popularity contests.

"However, I believe that as a result and for no principally specific or horrible intent of any particular individual, true progress has been slowed down. Too many, including myself, feel as though we are wrapped up in such a convoluted set of conundrums that lead to nowhere. I mean, the results have benefitted and profited far too few, and good for them, right?

"But, the well-being of others has actually and unfortunately become a burden beyond the abilities of anyone in power to visualize how to do anything about it, much less to have the clarity to take the appropriate steps toward getting us anywhere.

"I write legislation for our state representatives, and due to their expectations of the wordy and drawn out script for the law, once simple and clear requests for the people they represent get ignored all-too-often due to the deluge of meaningless wordiness.

"The leaders, they have been too entrenched within the bureaucracies or have been indoctrinated so deeply in a negative sense that it is near impossible to bear witness to or even account for well-being.

"I mean if you read blogs, see the news, talk to the students, and even experience life, it's obvious that what is actually and indeed the most important is actually and unfortunately considered laughable.

"We need a change."

After sipping their coffee and taking care of personal hygiene, they continued their walk down the avenue toward their destination.

Eliza's and Yesha's conversations continued as well.

Eliza went on further, "It seems clear to me that we both know how much humanity needs a nudge in the right direction in order to have the vision necessary to find what will lead to the understanding of, the advancement of, and the preservation of the Earth, as well as of civilization, and life itself."

They walked on, listening to the cars pass by.

Yesha agreed. As they passed by a cross-fit building, they looked toward it and were pleased. Yesha then expounded on Eliza's sentiments. "Instead of giving up on humanity or feeling at a loss, we need to take whatever privilege we have been blessed with and use the knowledge we've gained through our fortunate and high-quality upbringing and education to change the game of life to something that results in a positive future for, well, everyone. Your parents were amazing, they did that for us, and I am grateful for what they did for myself and my Mom. We went through a lot of loss when we lost your parents, but they did a lot to make sure that their efforts were not in vain. I mean, look at you. You're intelligent, you are very capable, you are healthy, and you actually care about others as well as yourself."

Yesha let her words hang in the air for a bit, and then Eliza responded, "Wise counsel, my friend. And thank you, look at you. You are a fantastic person too, due in part to your efforts, as well as the efforts of both your Mom and my parents. You have been a wonderful friend throughout so many experiences, and I couldn't ask for better.

"We've been through a lot, we've experienced life in such a way that our compassion has been tempered with strength, yet we understand that there are many who have been through so much worse without the proper environment or the necessary support to allow for healthy cognitive frame-working, and as a result they are at a loss as to what priorities indeed will increase the quality of life, with the meaning and purpose that suggests doing what is necessary for preserving the life and legacy of humanity.

"During those moments of mistaken priorities, too many have become awash in the corruption that can be found in goals that exist around materialism, the kind of hedonism that neglects their responsibility for the consent of others, a desire to wave the mighty hand of power, and mere survival. Perhaps many may have ideas that are even loftier than the typical drivers of a mediocre life, but with meager resources and so many other factors, they are helpless to do anything about it.

"Nature and humanity can be amazing, but likewise, it can be brutal. Brutality, as far too many know it, is unnecessary if we can consider and implement one thing, innovation with purpose—a good purpose is brutality's ideal replacement, and it comes minus the all-too-often added moments of unnecessary misery.

"It's starting to become very clear to me now what it is that we can do and how we can do it. We need to examine my plans when we return home, develop what I call a 'biopod,' and this will lead to both physiological and neurological healing. This biopod will have the capacity to heal any and all who desire to be treated, and to the extent that in all senses, if any individual has volunteered and has become affected by it, they will become optimized in every desirably conceivable and inconceivable way.

"Now, I am pretty sure that if I asked you if you'd like to be a part of building this, improving upon it, and experimenting with it in every way with these biopods, you'd accept. Having been best friends for more than twenty-six years, you know I will ask you to help me, and I know you'd be willing to jump into the heart of this, just as you know that I will.

"I would never ask you to do anything I wouldn't. So, Yesha, will you join me in the building and testing of these biopods, as well as help me to cultivate a new multi-industrial and a promising way of life?"

Passing Union Square, Eliza paused, and then they continued onto and down Washington Street. The fragrance of the flowers in the air drifted into their noses from a flower shop nearby. Eliza, followed by Yesha, went into the shop and purchased a small bouquet of stargazer lilies mixed with jasmine and honeysuckle.

They continued as they handed the bouquet back and forth to each other, and it added to the pleasant nature of their shared experience.

"I would. While you wouldn't need to ask, I appreciate that you did. We're one team in this shared quest, my friend, and I'm with you for as far and as long as you wish," said Yesha, who smiled.

Eliza smiled back after breathing in the scent of the bouquet, passed the flowers back to Yesha, and continued, "Thank you, Yesha. Everything seems crystal clear. We know what to do, and we know how to do it. We need to start Pathway Industries, as Charles called it, beginning with Pathway LLC. This will be our organization or our foundation for research, innovation, development, and proliferation of that which will increase life, liberty, and the pursuit of happiness."

Eliza paused, and Yesha noticed as a light breeze picked up and blew Eliza's blonde locks into a perfect medium-length balayage bob. Yesha smiled, her hair was in an up-do with side-swept bangs that culminated in a braided ponytail that spiraled attractively around and to the back of her head. Eliza always enjoyed Yesha's smiles, they seemed to light up wherever they were in the world.

"So, let's do it," responded Yesha, as they walked by a steakhouse.

"I love your dedication, Yesha," Eliza smiled and laughed, proud of Yesha's sincerity. "I have no doubt that with amazing and heartfelt discoveries and innovations on our part, some of which we've already come upon through working together, investing in the supplies at home, and to some extent due to the availability of some of the highly advanced tools for research provided by Harvard and MIT, we'll do well and so will so many others. We've certainly found a game-changer."

Eliza and Yesha continued their walk and their conversations with turns, different views, and several stops along the way. They arrived at the park along the beach and enjoyed the light and breezy ocean air carried in with the sound of the wispy waves from the coast overlooking Broad Sound Bay before them and the Atlantic Ocean not too far off in the distance and to their right. They walked along the sand for a bit.

Eliza and Yesha could almost hear the sounds of a brewing revolution as if what had played out more than two centuries and three decades earlier, were playing out before them now. They looked to each other and knew that soon they would, coming from the same location in this world, have yet another rebellion. Only, this time, there would be no lives lost, except through choosing on their own accord to die of old age rather than live for an indeterminate period of time.

This revolution would be a peaceful one with nary a drop of blood spilled, if any at all. They talked for a while longer, before returning and arriving at their home address. Once inside, they went grabbed some red wine and talked over details of their plans for the future and how each thing could be done, step-by-step.

As was their tradition, weary from the activities of the day, and feeling the moment was right, they grabbed their sleeping bags and some blankets, and played some of their favorite music, which of course included Depeche Mode's "Suffer Well" and "Precious," from their 2005 album, "Playing the Angel," among other favorites from various groups throughout the decades.

As their singing tapered off, it graduated to listening. Eliza and Yesha laid on their backs, looked up toward the stars, and smiled again as they looked toward each other with a feeling of peace, contentment, and joy to be the type of friend they would wish for anyone, and they fell asleep.

Shortly after this conversation and continuing as professors, Eliza and Yesha worked together on different projects throughout the many evenings, and sometimes late through the night, both at home and at the universities to innovate the discovery which had within it a multitude of findings that they knew, in theory, could change the face of humanity for a very long time.

Building Biopods

After the walk and conversation on that day, the days, the weeks, and the months that followed sped by with Eliza's and Yesha's regular walks, talks, shared thought, and songs as they dedicated themselves both as professors and as innovators, collaborating their resources with each other and sharing what was on their minds to bring their ideas to life.

By the end of 2007, Eliza and Yesha perfected something they called the biopod, which looked like a glowing white tanning booth and could do quite a few things more than give someone a good tan. It was also far more comfortable to lay in, due to the fact that instead of laying on glass, a person within it would be laying on material very similar to memory foam.

Through Eliza's and Yesha's innovative efforts and their resultant biopods, they developed a technological tool that would provide the mechanism necessary to change the course of history. The fruits of their labors would bring about advancements and a reciprocated sense of hope, resilience, creativity, and innovation, all the while augmenting drive, meaning, and clarity of purpose and increasing the enjoyment of life worldwide.

Eliza's biopod, since it was hers by design and theory, with cellular, genetic, DNA, particle, and neural nano delivery systems, based on all their studies, research, ingenuity, and dedication could optimize anyone.

Optimization in this sense suggested that an individual would be infused with nanos that could cure them of any conceivable or even inconceivable disease or illness, and then configure cells, genes, DNA, and neurons to do likewise. The biopod could infuse and encode these nanos, allowing the repurposing of senescent cells and materials, and doing so much more, thereby rendering an individual human or any sentient and living being for that matter a self-sustaining life support system of their own.

These benefits could render anyone capable of withstanding some of the worst and most treacherous of environments known to mankind, all while enjoying their ambiance no matter how grueling it seemed. Likewise, it could clear a mind for ingenuity and innovations that could further increase the quality of life and preserve it substantially. This biopod could enable all the abilities necessary to allow life itself to traverse throughout the solar system and Universe speedily without submitting to the ill effects of the cosmos or space travel.

The biopod that Eliza designed, Yesha helped her to build and improve. Together, they built it with strong, efficient, and sophisticated computer language, quantum computing, and data management capacities, in order to maximize every conceivable capacity for reading activity down to individual molecules, atoms, and even particles, and then optimize DNA, genes, cells, and neurons.

For example, the abilities of the human eye had an upgrade that enabled microscopic, telescopic, heat, infrared, Gama ray, X-ray, and so many other different types of vision as needed and whenever desired. These nanos could also increase pain tolerance, allow the mind to communicate with nearby objects, allowing them to bend without harm to the mind's will, it could enable the body to absorb unlimited quantities of radiation, all while maximizing safety, security, and normality.

The biopod, with its nano-delivery system, could do so much more, and every day, once they had cracked a seemingly limitless list of bio-codes. Eliza and Yesha came up with physical and neuronal optimizations, to include enabling the body to immediately heal and levitate, along with many other upgrades as they were conceived.

Eliza worked with Yesha, and together they designed every aspect of their biopod and its nanotechnology delivery systems to include the ability to truly maximize each region of the brain while increasing specific aspects of the various processing centers. They built these abilities in such a way as to allow the recipient to fine-tune their minds like the strings of a guitar, the keys of a piano, or the various qualities like bass and treble on a state-of-the-art equalizer to augment clarity of perception. The result helped maximize the virtues and traits of an individual, such as empathy, kindness, compassion, gentleness, humor, ingenuity, creativity, respect for personal consent, and even eloquence, within a zone they would refer to as the neural identification of the mind, optimized for the benefit of humanity and all of sentient and living civilization, within the Virtual Universe.

These were a few of the many characteristics that they were keen to germinate, expand upon, and maintain, and all in an effort to eliminate the potential for destructive, violent, and abusive intentions, behavior, or the improper use of science and technology, while also safeguarding the need to factor in mechanisms to protect and empower anyone who had been optimized, and not impinge upon their free will and sense of self. They wanted to preserve humanity, not destroy it, and they would pull no stops to make sure their technologies were safeguarded, but highly capable and noninvasive.

Once they were sure this biopod technology met their expectations, and after scrutinizing it in every conceivable way, which in turn resulted in many more capabilities to enhance the human experience without losing humanity altogether, they created two more biopods, and with good reason. They found out that at least two people going through a biopod journey or experience together, while they were linked through a physiological and neurological experiential interface, would result in the provision of a higher level of physiological and neurological capacities with more enriching outcomes of optimizing the mind.

This would be more effective than would a single biopod by way of a singular experience. While a single biopod, if needed, could optimize a single mind, together, as robustly designed, they would tie-in with their data-linked and powerful ultra-tech computers and allow for multiple neurological centers from one or more people to link and share thoughts, wisdom, and understanding.

This biopod could exponentially increase more than virtue and cure disease. It would upgrade their capacity for understanding, their mental fluidity, their cognitive frameworking, and all in the most helpful of ways. It could compartmentalize the various regions of the brain or marry them up as necessary and as consented, so that a person could in fact simultaneously think of a multitude of items at one time and have the benefit of focus.

The breadth of the advancements could be listed in several libraries worth of books, but they all-in-all included social, artistic, and scientific genius-level growth options and capacities. All of this could boost mental and physical capacity by several orders of magnitude, allowing the recipients to live indeterminately while resolving more hyper-complexed issues in short order.

By design, Eliza and Yesha perfected their biopods as well as their nanotechnology delivery integration systems allowing them to enable anyone who used them to not only neurologically link with others who had also been treated with one, optimizing them in so many surprising ways, but their designs had led to the provision of the aforementioned individual neurological identification or neural identification.

The neural identification would allow anyone who was "optimized," or had used the biopod, to sustain their mental clarity, develop their newly acquired skills, and gain access to future organizational locations throughout the world, the solar system, and the Universe. With this a person could gain a shared-understanding and thought differentiation of each individual they spent time within the Virtual Universe or were linked with, mind-to-mind, following their optimizations. This allowed all who used the machine to have the ability to tell the difference between personal and shared-thought.

Yesha helped develop this feature, which served to calm Eliza's concerns, in the sense that it would prevent violation of a person's intended and individual rights to their own private thoughts, while allowing them to securely compartmentalize that which they were not yet comfortable with sharing. Eliza treasured the privacy of personal thought and had no desire to invade another's mind without consent, nor did she want her new system to even hint at such. Therefore, Yesha had brought up the solution to the issue, and together, they implemented it.

They had imagined a stark scenario, in which they viewed a tragic misuse of their tech, where someone with malicious intentions could imbue evidence of a crime into someone else's mind by using malevolently manipulated technology. Something like this would only be possible, by undoing the measures Eliza and Yesha had taken, and could lead to a dystopian reality that could mean that law enforcement and the judicial system might find the wrong person guilty, if the issue were not mitigated right off.

Eliza figured this out quickly, and just as fast she and Yesha labored diligently, implementing Yesha's solution, to render impenetrable neurological defenses by creating a neural identification to use or buffet against malicious use of the intended goals found in collaborative thought, experiential understanding, and learning. This would now, and in-turn help law enforcement, if ever needed, while allowing people to differentiate their thoughts from the thoughts of others through thought source identifications.

The ideal purpose of neurological connection and identification was to allow a more robust form of communication between friends, family members, lovers, politicians, diplomats, or anyone desiring to connect with another individual who was willing, and not to hurt them but instead, reach a greater understanding, one between the other. So, they protected this technology in every way they could fathom, while preparing to bring forth the power of a great tool to be used in a very healthy manner.

Now, in maximum confidence, both theoretically and through their well-tested science, by linking mind-to-mind to understand another individual or group of individuals using neural identifications, nations could resolve more issues than ever before, both worldwide and beyond. Thus, they would have effective and fair results considering the well-being of themselves as well as others, and most importantly, those they were entrusted to serve.

The Virtual Universe, the playfield of the mind, the landscape of the imagination, yet the location of the most wonderful of achievements, and abilities to manipulate individual particles using the benefits of time dilation, doing centuries of work within a small moment, with physiological and neurological optimizations, and the neural identification, was built to enable the receipt of rudimentary to high-level education, the training necessary for highly technical careers and integration of sciences and arts, optimized training for physically demanding activities and much more.

Unlike any Virtual Universe or anything else similar to it that had ever been dreamed up or created before, quite phenomenally, this one had the ability to actually and in a virtually realistic way allow an individual to manipulate single electrons, muons, fermions, and many other baryonic, non-baryonic, and exotic particles related to gravity, mass, speed, and so much more. While creating a real world and Virtual Universe interface and set of automated commands for systematic completion of a project, to influence what was necessary on either side, they did so, creating passive and active options. If their wish was solely passive, it was for future planning; if it were active, it was to allow systems set aside with a specific purpose to mend, build, or augment as needed.

Using the Virtual Universe would allow humanity and its friends to innovate further with more profound technological advances all the more quickly. Now that the science was there, the efforts had been made in droves, the machines created, and the miracles put together in every aspect, to include the aforesaid conveyances for a robust technology that allowed for time-dilation. All that was left to do was to figure out who it was that would test these biopods and the Virtual Universe, and when.

Eliza and Yesha decided they should test this first.

Before doing so, they checked every detail, every bit of information, and ran scenarios on every conceivable outcome and drew up plans based on intellectually-pre-conceived and optimal outcomes. Eliza and Yesha did this all, while running multiple miniature programs and programs within programs, and so much more. Even still, they studied and improved upon each encoded algorithm, matrix, macro, loop, and course to successful completion.

As time flew by, despite their dedication during their off-campus pursuits, Eliza and Yesha made sure they were adequately fed, rested, and got their exercise so they could go all-in even further. They never forgot to feed the coy fish and sing to the stars, with the angel overlooking the pond providing a beautiful addition to the ambiance.

As Eliza and Yesha did their research and perfected their innovations, they were mindful to program, encode, encrypt, and set up these biopods to mutually protect that which was private and to only share that which would be of unbreakable benefit to humanity. Furthermore, they would try to share this when the time was right.

They wished they could make each of their ideas transparent, no matter what they were, but they also realized that they could be vulnerable to malicious manipulation, and as such, they ought to be kept only in trustworthy locations and shared only with those who were properly vetted.

In this sense, only one such location seemed best for this. This location was within their highly encrypted, quantum-encoded, and virtually impenetrable mainframe, all safeguarded within Eliza's quaint estate home. She had plans for something or several somethings much greater and phenomenal, later, but for now, this would do. Plus, once they expanded, this would serve as a backup hub of exponential sorts.

Eliza and Yesha agreed that they would not make their biopod advancements public for the time being. Much to their chagrin, they would only share these advancements with people who had been properly vetted, were trustworthy, were loyal to the plight of humanity, and thus agreed to become fully read-in. Until ironclad safety mechanisms were in place, when it came to the vulnerability of theft or sabotage, or even gross manipulation, this entire effort would be covert.

Eventually, Eliza and Yesha would share each aspect of each detail with anyone and everyone throughout the world, but they would begin with those who would opt to be read-in and involved with their research, to raise the bar for humanity and advance Earth-based civilization and beyond, within the various technology teams, that Eliza and Yesha had discussed were soon to be formed.

The culmination of their efforts was the result of Eliza and Yesha having broken the limitations set by so many facets of society, of political organizations, of medical bylaws, and they countermanded the most entrenched and established systems and their perceptions of ethics. They had in effect, destroyed the limitations of everything that from their purview detracted from the very essence of well-being.

Eliza and Yesha had discovered and taken apart, reassigned, and put together again everything up to and including the codes of every one of the most basic through to the most complexed components of every gene. As they did, they discovered what it was that each one, and in any array, could do to improve the quality of life. They learned how these basic biological constructs could interact with each other on poly-genomic and mono-genomic levels. Furthermore, they discovered how to optimize the physiological and neurological aspects of any living being.

By using a series of gene editing tools based on the mechanisms of stem cells, neurons, RNA and DNA, and using processes even more powerful, precise, rapid, and effective than CRISPR-Cas9 or any stem cell research tool available, they were able to digitize, store, replicate, and reproduce an entire genome in moments. The biopod was a fully functional high throughput sequencing device with a series of scanning and tunneling microscopes equipped with precision laser delivery systems that ultimately optimized both body and mind in every sector at one time.

All three biopods were integrated into Eliza's powerful computer mainframe with algorithms, codes, sequences, and much more than fathomable by today's greatest experts. Each of these biopods, and the mainframe itself, could be updated for further upgrades, optimizations, and mind-expansion capabilities with the purpose of connecting any biopod user to the robustly capable set of matrices they had developed and called the Virtual Universe. With this in play, they could theoretically backup and bring back to life any potential user, in a twenty-two-year-old version of themselves.

Eliza and Yesha had developed a system that would be accessible by initially entering a biopod and becoming optimized, from whence they could end the sequence, or continue on to the Virtual Universe.

The biopod could deliver this optimized state by running their highly detailed and technical sets of macros, robust and intricate programs, data analytics, and highly specialized encryptions. When powered with a biopod and paired with a living being, this system could understand in a quick manner how each aspect of its physiology communicated their commands from the central nervous system to neurons attached to each micro hub of each tissue and organ on the most basic of levels to every other cell, depending on the region, organism, type of cell, neuron, nerve, or synapse.

It could then recreate existing as well as new and detailed codes using the appropriate quantities of electrons, neutrons, and protons, as well as other baryonic and non-baryonic particles, to form perfected proteins that would optimize every function of every organ and organism within the living body and even improve upon it. All of this delivered optimizations to the body using a series of light electrical pulses in a matter of nano-seconds.

Eliza's and Yesha's new biopods and the nanos paired to an individual's DNA and neural identification could now enable an individual's cells to immediately communicate and adjust form as requested by that individual, and as needed.

An individual's nanos could optimize helpful organisms or adjust the body to adapt to any environment they might be in. They could also provide tactile reference while in the Virtual Universe or while receiving any updates, to allow for muscle memory.

They discovered that once a batch of nanos is infused with DNA and a neural identification via the biopod's delivery system, they could serve to optimize both the body and mind at every moment. This would create a link to other benefactors who had been optimized. Anyone optimized could have access to the computer mainframe at any time and in any location, to allow for updates, upgrades, and neural links for telepathic communication.

Finally, they built within each biopod a series of condensed laboratory and nano-particle nodes that were integrated with every aspect of the physiological and neurological systems and transposed and delivered through the very light electrical pulses to afford integration with the Virtual Universe. Once an individual was to enter the biopod, they could, via verbal command enter this virtual location.

Based on their prescribed settings, or at any point determined while in it, they would be able to leave the Virtual Universe and then the biopod. Once they did, they would continue to have nanos working within their cells at every level and in every possible way to heal their physiology and neurology in every aspect, and answer to the mind's bidding, with clarity of purpose of preserving life, increasing the quality of life, and acting on the virtues of kindness, wisdom, excellence, and solution resolution.

It was time to test these biopods, but before entering the Virtual Universe, Eliza and Yesha decided that it would be wise to primarily use them on themselves, as the first part of a two-step process.

Initially, they would climb into their biopods without interfacing with the Virtual Universe but receive the delivery of an initial optimization of their physiology and neurology, in every possible way.

Following that, and while in the real world, they would one-hundred-percent everything about the Virtual Universe, so they could then explore it for all that it was worth. This way, no matter the political, physical, or societal fall-out, or the acceptance or rejection of their inventions, one thing would hold true, they would, in fact, be living examples of optimized and capable humans.

Doing all of this would give them the means to operate in the pace and the stride necessary and be intellectually capable of taking proper courses of action to prevent losing the technology, should it be rejected by the associated authorities.

Eliza and Yesha kept their biopods in a special and highly-secured room, within the basement of Eliza's estate home, located below their bedrooms, accessible via a stairway just outside their bedroom doors.

Patients-Zero

On Friday, December 14, 2007, a week before introducing their completed technology to Harvard, MIT, and appropriate governmental authorities, to include the FDA, they went on a winter walk with gloves, coats, scarves, thermal underclothes, and layered socks to discuss the final parameters of their last effort to program their initial entrance into the biopods. Following that, they would commence with their second entrance into their biopods for a Virtual Universe experience.

After walking, talking, returning home, and putting out a kerosene heater close enough to warm their feet yet far enough away for safety, they laid down their blankets, their sleeping bags, and climbed in them to warm up a little more.

These two young individuals who were awarded multiple PhDs, followed that up by getting up, grabbing more linen and piling on a few more blankets, which were nearby due to years of habit. After further discussion, they ended the night as they typically did, calming their nerves by singing along with Dave and Martin of Depeche Mode, playing on their outdoor garden entertainment system.

They did this, as usual, while looking at the statue of the angel overlooking their would-be frozen pond, warmed beneath for the benefit of the frogs and coy fish, and then they looked up at the stars, between their clouds of breath as the mist rose into the sky, then froze and dissipated. They then continued talking back and forth for a while, sometimes laughing, and sometimes reminiscing, but most certainly discussing the plans for the next day.

Prior to their first entry into their biopod, they agreed to build a programmed welcoming zone within a matrix of this universe they could use for neurological interfacing, bringing calm and an ideal initial ambiance. They agreed to create and provide an initial environment within which to begin once an individual's mind had linked to the experiential reality of the Virtual Universe. Talking about this for several hours, they finally fell asleep.

When Eliza and Yesha awoke the next morning, they immediately got to work on what they had discussed the night before. Eliza suggested that they could always adjust the entry program, improve upon it more, or integrate further ideas as time went by, as necessary, or as any other improvements came to mind, and both were one-hundred percent in favor of the plan.

They programmed the mainframe's biopod-interface to the Virtual Universe, solely for a preliminary design, set both their biopods for optimizations only, and no Virtual Universe trips, and connected the mainframe to their biopods. Eliza climbed into one and Yesha climbed into the other, the third biopod lay unused, but simultaneously they laid on their backs, pulled the biopod covers down, and closed their eyes.

"This should only take two seconds," Eliza said, muffled, and then she grew quiet.

Two seconds passed, and it was as if nothing had happened.

They opened their eyes thinking perhaps they forgot to flip a switch, or plug something in, and stepped out of their biopods. It wasn't until Eliza and Yesha saw each other as they morphed and glowed that they knew they had been successful in more ways than they had predicted. It was a magnificent sight.

Along with what they saw, Eliza and Yesha felt an almost euphoric sense within. It was as if every single cell, organism, and neuron tingled inside and in a way that caused their bodies to shake and quiver. As they realized this, something within them caused them to laugh.

Laughing at each other while they felt all their senses peek and everything from their hairstyles to their clothing, and musculature change, they learned quickly that they had to train themselves to control it all, but they continued to laugh anyway.

As their laughter subsided and their minds seemed to sober up, they realized that their sight, as well as how their bodies expressed what their right minds were thinking, in terms of artistic expression throughout, and in particular on the left side of their bodies, with tattoos that weren't tattoos, yet were a real, artistic, mural-like, and mandala-like kaleidoscope of patterns that swirled, changed colors, shapes, and sizes, and vacillated based on one thought or another. Despite their newfound wisdom to all of this, they couldn't help themselves and laughed again.

Their hair did crazy things until they learned how to control that too. Once they were able to harness the basic aspects of their new and not-so-basic powers as well as their neurological compartmentalization capabilities, it became clear that they had learned to stabilize their own appearance, allowing them to look normal, and even professional and beautiful, with phenomenally-designed hairstyles and make-up designs that complemented it all, and all while coaching each other every step of the way.

Once they learned the basics of their new abilities, they all suddenly felt sober again. With an advanced clarity of mind on every aspect of everything they had worked on, and even ideas of what they had worked on that might improve the whole process and make the experience less odd than their experience, they began to ponder upon what they never thought was possible before.

Eliza and Yesha loved embracing this new and shared sense of collective thought, and through that, they worked together to develop and encode commands that did just that. They also set their mainframe systems up so that once within their biopods, the interface would allow them to link their minds to the Virtual Universe with a fail-safe, such that the biopod would send a signal if necessary, to exit for any urgent reason. They made sure there was always an expression they could use to pull themselves out of the virtual environment if needed and their new keywords were simple, "Exit Link." They then, that same day, entered their biopods the second time.

The Virtual Universe

This time they climbed into their biopods after setting up a time-dilation sequence using a variety of new physics laws they developed during the brief moments after their initial optimization-run in the biopods.

The sequence would work in this way: if they issued the command, "Link 1, 2, 3. Five minutes, twenty years," or the preferred real world to Virtual Universe time dilation ratio, they would immediately be interfaced mind-to-mind-to-Virtual Universe for the time they had chosen.

With this command and time-setting ready, quite simply, in five minutes, they would experience twenty years' worth of life.

Through this experience, they would discover if, as planned, an individual could receive and transmit from multiregional connections within various cortices and lobes of the mind and within the Virtual Universe for sensory and muscle memory feedback leading to a real world-like experience.

Effectively, a person should be able to learn while in the Virtual Universe, travel the World or Universe, based on every bit of information ever digitized, program anything down to the particle level, passively and even actively, and retain the memories and learned abilities via an interface with the biopod.

They could also reread and transfer necessary data to and from the real-world computer interface to a mainframe partition that was accessible in both the Virtual Universe and the real world.

Each of their Virtual Universe experiences would be as if it were a real part of life. The only difference between the Virtual Universe and real-world experiences, was that Virtual Universe experiences were wrought with immense clarity and comprehension, as well as a unique flavor of thought that clearly differentiated their own thoughts from the thoughts of others.

With their physiology and neurology now optimized, Eliza and Yesha were on the threshold of a new revolution in science, and about to conceive of the inconceivable, which would be a future of wonder, and of amazement, and of promise, about to be born.

It would be within the Virtual Universe where together, Eliza and Yesha, best friends since Eliza was born and the first known humans on Earth to submit themselves to this new technology, would enter for the very first time, around noon, on December 15, 2007.

While in their biopods, they would do more than link their minds to the computer mainframe, their nanos would be infused yet again with more upgrades enabling them to carry out programming, digital planning, create intricate blueprints, and conduct individual as well as collective training based on shared memory.

During their first entry into their biopods, Eliza and Yesha had taken advantage of setting their physiological age parameters to twenty-two.

In this way, their physiological health was that of healthy, physically fit, and very attractive versions of their twenty-two-year-old selves.

The development of their minds in the Virtual Universe, however, would theoretically mean that as they spent time within that region of reality, their "wisdom age" would accrue based on virtual years spent within the interface multiplying and compounding exponentially.

To assist with this reality and outcome, they set up robust recall, backup, and immediate access functionality systems within the mainframe and within their neural construct to reduce any informational dissonance. They were aware that both of them would eventually and in all actuality have minds with trillions of years of experiences or more following a few years of use of their new and impressive technology, due to the factoring of all the experiences of all who would enter.

So, this in mind, they designed their neuro-nanos to help keep their knowledge accessible, clear, and available at any moment in time.

Together, they had arranged their entry ambiance to the Virtual Universe in such a way that an individual would find themselves in a location resembling a well-lit version of Eliza's estate backyard, with the statue of an angel overlooking the coy fish pond, and a lovely view of the stars under a nighttime sky.

Once they were sufficiently oriented as to their environment, an individual or group of individuals could theoretically develop a variety of other starting and returning points intended for later use and travel to any place they wished, based on the real Universe as received by powerful sensors.

"Are you ready for our second round?"

"I'm as ready as I'll ever be!" said Yesha.

A New Kind of Journey

In unison, and for the first time, telepathically, Eliza uttered, *"Link 1, 2, 3, 5 Minutes, 20 Years."* While Yesha did so out loud.

Like that, they felt every single one of their cells, their neurons, and their genetic fabric twist and contort, and then with a sense of euphoria, every bit of pain was released completely and changed into something so painless and altogether completely enjoyable that it was difficult to describe in words.

Eliza opened her eyes, and there she was, in her backyard, but a very realistic and quite heavenly-seeming version of it. She looked around, and everything was there, down to the atoms and molecules, and even the smallest particles. She zoomed out, looked up, and saw the Moon, so close that she could have easily assumed it was part of the backyard. She then pulled her mind back to where she seemed to be at that moment, which was within her estate, and she saw Yesha. She looked more beautifully extravagant than ever before, and she had indeed been quite extravagantly gorgeous quite regularly, but this was beyond description. She combed her mind and realized that she could suddenly perceive of thoughts and memories that were not her own. She was perceiving Yesha's memories, thoughts, knowledge, experiences, and so much more. *"Wow, Yesha! This is amazing! Your mind is so beautiful!"*

"Oh, thank you! Did you feel that Eliza? It felt like I was about to burst into trillions of atoms, and then like that, I felt at peace and euphoric. It was almost an ecstasy of sorts. This is beautiful, you're, oh my, you're so beautiful, Eliza! I wish I could show you what I am seeing! You look like an angel!"

"Thank you, and so do you!" Eliza responded.

They then took advantage of their Virtual Universe and began to consider all their possibilities at this juncture. They would only be in the biopod, at least as perceived in the real world, for five minutes but with the advantages of the Virtual Universe's time dilation ratio. In this way, at least in this instance, they would gain the experiences equivalent to those received after twenty years. *"We're going to be here for twenty years, Eliza! You know? Now that we're here, wow, that seems like quite a long time. The funniest part about that, though, is that I am not bothered by it anymore! There's so much to do, so much to learn, and so much to understand! So, we might as well make the most of it. We'll get better at it as we visit, and sooner if we do so often. This is amazing. Say, I heard and felt you in my mind, when we linked! How did you do that, Eliza?"*

Eliza then taught Yesha how to talk telepathically and navigate through the permissive environments of another's mind, engaging the correct regions and cortices of the brain and of every kind. After spending some time training on various other capabilities and skills that she had set up for access and training for, within the Virtual Universe, they took advantage of the added time to develop and use high-tech equipment that they could create within the estate, they developed blueprints and models of the infrastructure they wanted to build, and they gained much more control over their capabilities. Finally, they realized that they could in fact take control of individual particles, baryonic, non-baryonic, and exotic. They also realized that in this state, they could peer and even journey hundreds to thousands of miles below the Earth's surface.

Eliza looked to Yesha, and Yesha looked back at Eliza, and then they decided to let their virtual bodies flow with their thoughts. As they did, they dove as if they were dark and wingless angels in form-fitting and very attractive, black, and exquisite travel uniforms, below the Earth's crust. They could see and understand all the intricate and magnanimous details of the upper and lower mantle, the outer and inner core, the divergent, convergent, and transform boundaries, and even some of the areas of the Earth's previously unexplored layers engaged in subduction. As they traveled from the crust, where they examined each layer beneath it, all the way down to about three-thousand-nine-hundred-sixty miles from the surface of the Earth to the Earth's core, they witnessed, far from merely the effects of fusion, all of its splendor. There it was, right before them, the bright and glowing whites and yellows flowing as waves crashing to shore and pulled back. They witnessed all of this without suffering from the effects of heat, or noxious smells or fumes, or pressure due to their manner of travel, and they realized with glee that they finally and completely understood how fusion worked.

Prior to entering the Virtual Universe, they had encoded the possibilities of integrating holographic informational interfaces in front of their virtual eyes to allow them to see highly accurate digital readouts of anything they were to look at. In this case, they were able to see minerals and gases as they formed, their mass, their velocity of motion in every wavelength, how plasma from heat condensed due to massive gravitational pull, every aspect of its physics taking place before their very eyes, visualizing in vivid detail electromagnetic influence, and ions colliding with other particles resulting in formation of all of the various elements on the periodic table.

They understood and comprehended in depth everything to include the density, mass, motion, and tectonics of the Earth. They could see where every particle went, where fusion began in the Earth's core, and where fission would take over as these molten materials traveled from the center, and out like an advancing bubble, expanding, popping, bringing more material in until there was sufficient material and pressure to release this build-up of magma through new and old volcanoes that were readying to burst, and all with a very accurate estimate as to when. They could see new islands readying to be born and places awaiting devastation.

Understanding how fusion and fission worked, they knew that there was a lot they needed to consider and do something about soon, because one of their favorite parks, Yosemite, had limited amounts of time before it would blow, destroying every ecosystem on Earth's thin crust within a five-hundred-mile (or 805 kilometer) radius. Eliza looked to Yesha, and Yesha looked to Eliza, and Yesha then spoke up, *"We need to find a way to tame the churn of material lending to Earth's fusion and fission, so we can diffuse the dangers as needed, maintain the core's activity, Earth's life-sustaining integrity, cause very minimal to no damage, and while doing so provide humanity with the resources necessary to help raise the quality of life!"*

"You read my mind," exclaimed, Eliza.

"Yeah, your mind was the one that thought of it first!" chuckled Yesha, having seen her thoughts on display in a holographic image, like an automated eBook with scrolling text before her eyes.

Strategically placed to not interfere with the essential parts of her field of view, Yesha and Eliza were able to multiply their capacity to see more than one item at once. They took notes, drew up highly detailed plans for protecting the integrity of the Earth's necessary processes while ensuring fusion and fission could occur in a manner that was no longer devastating to life. After which, they soared up through the Earth's crust and climbed into the atmosphere. Their garments changed from dark to light, as if in flowing robes. Once there, they talked while looking at the Earth below and floating just below the stratosphere, peering out at the ground below and throughout the solar system.

"It's great to be linked," responded Eliza, laughing along with Yesha's wit, *"Seriously, it is. You have ways of seeing things that indicate to me that you are truly a visionary. You know me now, and I know you. You are of a beautiful mind, Yesha! Don't ever underestimate yourself.*

"It's amazing how much the Earth needs to do. On the one hand, the things it does could result in the death of so many, but in so many ironic ways, in the very same instance and system of processes, it also engages in that which allows for life to be possible. Without these processes, life on Earth would cease to exist.

"Many of these mechanisms are not existent in this way on any other sphere within our solar system." Eliza paused, *"I say that, but in other ways, that's not at all true. Every sphere in our solar system has a core. All that is required is a structure for fusion and fission to begin, and from there it is just a matter of providing the right balance of mass, life-giving material, or excited particles and more, and other mechanisms that will ignite their core to work appropriately to build each layer through to its crust to allow for life, through increasing the magnetosphere, setting the right balance for their existing orbit that will assist in providing the right kind of gravity and velocity, along with balanced quantities of radiation and so much more.*

"We could develop atmospheres, control weather patterns, tectonic shifting, and control other natural disasters, and from there we could create the right kind of shielding. Or perhaps shielding is how it can all begin. Let's pause momentarily to plan, draft, and build preliminary blueprints for each planetary spheroid in our solar system,

so we can review them and improve upon them as we continue our journeys. There is so much we can do, so much that can be done, but we can't blame anyone else anymore, since we know that until now all of this chaos seemed impossible to control, it was all a fear-based tactic of survival alone."

"We'll need to build a lot of infrastructure, so we can create what is necessary to enable life on moons and planets in a way that we can protect them. Of course, we will database every aspect of what we find as we find it, for historical and scientific research purposes, for there is an abundance of wisdom to be gained by doing so. We need to do this, so we can enjoy all of this together. No matter what we do, only together can we ever hope to preserve the world, protect the innocence of the children, provide sanctuary to humanity and our solar system, and traverse through the cosmos with promise!" Eliza didn't need to yell, but the hum of the Earth and its magnetosphere was so loud, even inside their minds.

All that they concentrated on and contemplated about, they shared and stored within their neural awareness, in various compartments of their minds. They made plans for infrastructure that would mitigate the negative effects of each uncontrolled and destructive process. These plans would make each process capable of being controlled while sustaining life with quality.

As they developed each detail, they backed it up, to include everything they brainstormed for later study, improvement, and implementation. They ensured they had access to exhaustive information available within the real world and the Virtual Universe.

With their digital readouts before them, when allowing their minds to traverse the solar system, and even to the Sun and into its core, every bit of information would translate to the real world for intuitive, logical, advanced infrastructural innovations, once they returned.

Yesha and Eliza looked at each other, shared with each other what was in their minds, saw what was playing out in the other's heads, were proud of their initial plans for our home world and ideas for our solar system, and together they decided to hold hands as they rose above the stratosphere of the Earth and into the darkness of space.

Once in microgravity, they explored the ghost yard-like array of debris of broken satellites, space junk, and functional space objects man had seen fit to station out there. They saw manmade debris flying recklessly through space toward other objects man had put out there, and realized the danger posed to astronauts if these issues weren't taken care of soon. They saw some debris re-entering Earth's atmosphere, and then burning up into chemical and molecular pollution that was destroying Earth's ozone and creating a different chemical barrier between the crust and space itself.

As Eliza and Yesha witnessed the safety barrier of biologically friendly particles protecting all of life from too much radiation for many millions of years beginning to dissipate, they uttered at the same time their shared thoughts and wisdom, *"Something has to be done."*

Eliza and Yesha knew what to do, and they archived their plans, with hopes of making amends soon.

Everything seemed to reflect the light from the Sun and the Earth, providing profound clarity of vision and spatial orientation. Meteorites, comets, and asteroids of every size, distance, and up, close and personal, that combed the vacuum of space on errant missions with god knows what end. Noticing this, these two young PhDs categorized and documented each of them, entering their compositions and other details into their mainframe-database.

Eliza and Yesha then journeyed to the Moon. As they left microgravity, they found that a spectacular reality was quite common no matter the location of their journeys in space. They realized that they were no longer bothered by the cold, the heat, or the varying pressures. They felt no pain and ceased to worry about breathing.

It was as if every breath filled their lungs with the perfect quantity and quality of air, the kind that brings peace to the mind and vibrancy to the energy of the soul. Everywhere they looked, their focus was all that was needed. Simply gazing in any direction or upon any object, they saw digital readouts of all they wished to learn, study, or ascertain.

"We certainly didn't leave anything out. Thank goodness for exhaustive access to any database, sensory system, or computer mainframe throughout any portion of known civilization. There are a lot of brilliant people, both of action and inaction. Let's change that.

"Yesha, we need to ensure any of the decent people in governmental positions throughout the world don't feel as though we are trying to pry in any way to harm humanity or their sovereign rights.

"We are not; our scopes are passive. I hope that if they knew what we are doing right now, they would be thankful we're only gatherers of information and proud of us, because we are doing this for the purpose of helping others. We have no malicious intentions toward them or anyone for that matter.

"If they knew what we were up to I wonder if they would be angry. In some ways, it may seem we are violating almost every law known to humanity when it comes to space, information gathering and processing, and what we plan on doing. Perhaps we are pushing certain limits, but seriously, if that is the case, I believe that some limitations are ignorantly irrational, and in and of themselves they are vehemently unethical, and as such, these limitations certainly need pushing!

"Information almost seems a personal right, so we can better assess resolutions to problems that affect ourselves and everyone else and overcome and mitigate them with this technology and our new capabilities.

"Truly, we're here to learn, make plans, gain clarity and gather our own information and diagnostics, all so we can put together more detailed and viable plans for infrastructure in space and throughout the cosmos that are intended to safeguard and advance civilization, and nothing to the contrary. We love life and the collective wisdom of the ages." Eliza paused.

Yesha shifted her telescopic vision toward the large spheroidal asteroid, Ceres, and imagined building quite a few tech cities and bases there, sharing her ideas while agreeing with Eliza. *"There shouldn't be a problem with any of what we're doing unless people seriously want the demise of civilization and all that the Earth has harbored through all of known time and everything we've grown to appreciate throughout the history of humanity.*

"I don't think even the greedy want to destroy themselves, they just can't seem to see through their indoctrinated delusions. They think oppression makes them powerful, when all it does is bring the same dismal future to all of humanity. Your ideas will create a better future, a future of hope, of beauty, and of wonder."

Eliza was glad to have Yesha's clarity with its enigmatically supportive nature. *"Thank you, Yesha. It makes sense that we may be neurologically optimized, but that certainly doesn't mean we can't have well-placed concerns from time to time. You see? That is why I need you, and others. I may come up with ideal plans and ways to bring them about, but I would be stymied from doing any of it, absent a proper sanity check.*

"We can have the greatest of intentions, but my guess is that if a person possesses a moral core, they will run those ideas by others first in order to answer to doubts, concerns, and make sure they are overcoming challenges, so they can understand further challenges and overcome them, rather than create the type of reality we're trying to prevent. We aren't searching to be harbingers of uncontrolled chaos,

misery, or decay, we're trying to preserve our solar system and increase its potential for life, near indefinitely."

Yesha understood Eliza's concerns, "You are right on the mark, Eliza. That is why I trust you so much. You care, you want to do great things, yet you understand the need to bring the best out in others, if for anything to have a more amplified view and resolution to any problem you are trying to overcome.

"If we want to traverse the cosmos, we will need to be bringers of life, beauty inside and out, abundance, and bridge understanding between multiple civilizations, so we can tackle even greater issues together.

"We need to understand how dark energy and dark matter work, find ways to slow down the expansion or cause the Universe to breathe just enough to protect itself and all of life along with it. We need everyone who is willing. You are right, Eliza. Your heart and your mind are in the right place and they always have been.

"Now, also, please remember to trust yourself and don't waiver from your vision. Perhaps others' answers are necessary for a broader concept of how to overcome challenges, but you, my friend, are benevolent to the core, and that is rare, as such are your ideas and ideals. So, no matter the advice and counsel you seek, your uniqueness will actually benefit everyone."

They returned to their explorations, discoveries, analyzations, and creation of robust and detailed plans to preserve and protect Earth's atmosphere, the solar system, and so much more.

This time, Eliza moved forward with peace in her heart. She was grateful for her dear friend Yesha's support and unparalleled wisdom.

Once more, ideas came flooding into their minds as to what they could do on Earth and in the numerous locations affecting the future of humanity throughout the solar system.

After they gazed back at Earth from the Moon, Eliza and Yesha explored the Moon in a little more detailed manner, bringing up the sites of interest on their holo-displays. Looking closely across the Moon's terrain, they saw all the locations, the tread marks from the vehicles, the landing sites, and debris that proved that NASA had actually landed their astronauts in the locations they had told humanity that they had.

Focusing as they did, they could see the equipment left behind on Mare Tranquillitatis, Oceanus Procellarum, Fra Mauro, Hadley-Apennines, Descartes, and Taurus-Littrow, and the longitudinal and latitudinal information on the readouts before them on their displays.

"I knew it! The proof is there right before us, Eliza!

"The Moon landings were never a hoax, and they weren't lying after all—oh, the damaged minds of those who try to debunk anything noble that is done by honorable and amazing people! You're right, we need to heal and not harm, and there are a number of minds that could use some healing, so people can dedicate their energies to positive, productive, and forward moving pursuits, preserving life and making it more enjoyable for all, rather than getting lost in the quagmire of skepticism and misinformation!" exclaimed, Yesha.

"How many times does someone do something amazing, something great, and something wonderful, only to find that all their efforts in the days and years, and many decades later were dismissed as fodder and thrown to the wolves? We cannot forget the good within our heroes of the past, nor in the present, and we can't fail to see the potential of rising leaders that will bring about an even better future!" Replied Eliza.

After exploring the side of the Moon facing the Earth, they moved toward its opposite or "dark side." Once they had determined where they would build their tech cities and bases on the "dark side" of Earth's spheroidal satellite, or the Moon, which they called Selene, the Greek goddess of the morning, they continued to brainstorm the many possibilities for what could be done to preserve the solar system. Eliza and Yesha talked about, observed, and considered the resources available on every surface of every object throughout the solar system to that end.

They then considered their understanding of fusion, and of molecular and biologic compositions in all of their forms both large and small, all of their aspects, and each of their options. They conceived of together where they would build the bases, the bio-domes, and the bio-environments, in ways that would allow their advances to germinate a protective atmosphere, filled with life and in a bio-environment much like Earth's.

For this project, first, they would begin on the south pole of the Moon. From there, they would build large and protective environmental areas, bio-domes, both on and under its surface, as well as in ancient volcanic canals. Together, they would design, build, and explore each spheroid with roving biological environments for crews of scientists to roam, study, and innovate even more.

They then looked back at Earth again, appreciated its beauty and warmth, its colors and atmosphere. As they scanned the globe, they knew that while Earth's equator would be an ideal location for a space elevator, the perfect place for them to put their first Space Elevator from the terrestrial ground to just outside of microgravity, was near the border of New York, just inside Ontario, Canada.

They drafted plans, considered the materials to build it, and they moved on.

Eliza and Yesha immediately identified the Lagrange Points, and then found a number of other pockets in space with similar orbital and stable gravity points and noted how they were perfect places to place satellites and space stations with little to no requirement for additional energy when it came to the maintaining of their orbits.

These pockets would make ideal locations for their secured and technologically robust database moons. They also saw and archived the information for thousands of asteroids flying between Venus and Mars.

They would use these asteroids along with manmade debris, dangerously circling the Earth's atmosphere, to build protective barriers, bases, and tech cities on each planet and on any associated moon or dwarf planet while leaving a few harmless asteroids behind, whose tangents were not dangerous, and all of this for humanity to use for future economic improvement purposes.

They analyzed and discussed where they would place gigantic and robust shields for the protection of Earth, Mercury, Venus, Mars, and Ceres, as well as the moons of the gas giants, Pluto, and all of the spherical planetoids and moons out to the furthest reaches of the solar system, which would enable life to exist upon each of them.

In the future, they would determine the perfect balance to siphon necessary gases from Jupiter, Saturn, Uranus, and Neptune, while safeguarding their mass and orbit, adding the necessary components in the orbital rings around the Sun, to enable life on their moons and the gas giants themselves to exist and protect life for an indeterminate amount of time.

As they were thinking and sharing ideas for how they would use these resources, they continuously reminded each other that taking biopsies of each asteroid and non-Earth major object and storing them for availability for historical use, when it came to the understanding of the beginnings of our solar system, would be a must. They would create and maintain scientific-historical centers in each of their tech cities that would do just that.

Once they were done setting up plans for the planets, their moons, and the asteroid belts between Mars and Jupiter, they looked further, and the Trojan Asteroid Clouds following and leading Jupiter in orbit looked like excellent resources for both scientific history and even more tech cities around the moons of Jupiter, Saturn, Uranus, and Neptune.

When they arrived at Pluto, they saw what they could do with the resources available on the Kuiper Belt and in the Oort Clouds—a spacious portion of the solar system.

All the while, they discussed the importance of and analyzed the mathematics and physics of maintaining a balanced orbit for solar system integrity and protecting the solar system itself with an invisible barrier that could thwart off hostilities and absorb any other resources needed to complement the solar system's function.

They created exhaustive plans that lent to the preservation of our home world's star, the Sun.

With plenty of resources to create a system that would provide an attractive and powerful electromagnetic mechanism to provide for resource extraction of the Sun's heavier elements while providing it the basic radiation and particle nutrients needed to provide appropriate fusion, they could maintain life in the solar system and on Earth for trillions of years to come.

This was when, precisely, they developed their plans for infrastructure-building and self-replicating nano clouds, within the digital realm.

Eliza had the plans, the specs, and the details. Together, with Yesha and other delegates they would recruit soon, they could speed up all infrastructural development in an extra-terrestrial sense. Building all that they needed would be much faster through use of these nano clouds, reprogrammable within the Virtual Universe, while augmenting all mining techniques in an exponential way to create more reprogrammable matter, and all their off-Earth infrastructures.

Eliza and Yesha discussed everything in detail and had decided that's what they would create and do.

From there, they touched Earth's aging satellites, Voyagers I and II, and discussed the importance of protecting our solar system from too much or too little radiation from interstellar space, as well as unknown possibilities of much more advanced and quite conceivably dangerous civilizations.

As they discussed this, Eliza and Yesha decided they didn't dare go further than the Oort cloud limits for now, at least until humanity was sufficiently prepared for what was outside of the solar system.

The comprehension of everything they beheld was beyond anything they thought possible before. Together, they viewed and reviewed everything they could to make all that they had learned and planned easily available for comprehension in the environment within their minds accessible to them in their real-world digital interface.

After all that they had done, only several years passed as Eliza and Yesha went through this journey.

Therefore, while still within the Virtual Universe, they studied everything again, and scoped Earth once more, but this time in an almost microscopic manner to understand every square inch, centimeter, or millimeter that lay before them.

To further enlighten themselves, it was necessary that they understand in every perspective and scope what it was that they needed to do in order to protect life and the balance of Earth's ability to provide life at a much higher quality, all while compounding upon its beauty and minimizing or eliminating any damage to its ecosystems.

Once they were satisfied with their plans, the where, the what, and the how, they studied scores of literature, university books, and completed untold certifications, masters degrees, PhDs, and even learned physical defense, martial arts, and countless sports activities, as well as each of the arts and their instruments.

After many more journeys together, twenty years passed, and they were ready to return to Earth. Finally, it was time to return to the real world to make it all happen, but in as careful a manner as possible.

After they returned to Earth, having linked minds for the very first time in the real world, they checked their watches and the news to verify five minutes had passed, so they could be sure that those twenty hours had indeed been five minutes. Many times, they linked, agreed upon, and established their initial starting point for future training. They did this for all of whom they would allow to enter their biopods and link with the Virtual Universe. They would afford each sojourner the wisdom gained from exponential learning through every single one of the collaborative minds, and each with its own beautifully savory flavor.

The Virtual Universe would be available to anyone of upstanding character, initially. In wisdom, unless they were optimized, their knowledge would be limited as to what they needed for their projects.

Protected were the abilities of those who would choose to become optimized as well as the whereabouts of each of the covert technological advancements.

Eliza's and Yesha's advancements, through their biopod and nano upgrades, were currently now more powerful than any of the machinations of those disposed to more malevolent outcomes. Notwithstanding, they had no desire to introduce this technology to those with horrible intentions. While the toxicity of character could be mended, in the earlier days of optimizations, the risks were too severe to cave-in to folly. They would help those in need, the meek, the lowly, and the honorable.

The Real World

No matter where they went, and no matter how much they studied or how many plans they designed to the extent of detail, at the end of the day, Eliza and Yesha discovered that they were no longer tired and that their nanos were constantly optimizing their physiology and neurology. These abilities were painless and helpful.

They also discovered that sleep in and of itself was an enjoyable sort of luxury while it was no longer a necessity.

Nonetheless, as always, they recalled the essential balances of life, enjoyed their old pastimes, and grabbed their blankets, sleeping bags, and kerosene heater during this winter month, laid down by the pond with the statue of an angel overlooking it, and sang their favorite tunes to the coy fish and the stars until they fell asleep.

Eliza's and Yesha's dreams were so realistic they found themselves navigating through and within some of the most creative of environments they had ever been in before. Only, this time they found that they could dream and go wherever they went, together and remember it all.

As they waited for December 21, 2007, to arrive, Eliza and Yesha continuously returned to the Virtual Universe to explore the Earth, the Moon, and every location visible by satellite, probe, or tech available, while fine-tuning their plans, details, and designs from their first visit.

The Presentation

Finally, Friday's presentation day came. Even though every aspect of what they had created was due to their own genius intellect, diligent study, research, development, and even cataclysmic financing—when it came to every single physical piece of their biopods and their capabilities, before proliferation of all of this to the public, it was highly recommended that they receive approval from Harvard, MIT, and the FDA. Both Eliza and Yesha had a sneaking suspicion that all would go well, provided access to the Virtual Universe was not mentioned.

They had visited their Virtual Universe every day that week, through that Friday, and had learned so much. They downloaded every single University Program available online in their entirety and into their minds and processed the information to the peak of understanding and concrete application.

Both Eliza and Yesha were able to not only have a depth of understanding beyond the grasp of anyone else in the world of every science, art, and every aspect of what they were planning on doing, they had also gained the ability to experience it and train their bodies to remember every inflection, through muscle memory and every sensory node. Life took on a whole new meaning. Eliza and Yesha were filled with a whole sense of new charm and purpose.

Going back and forth with one experiment after another, using various tools, some equipment, and one study after another in-between Professor duties, they rented a truck to carry one of the biopods to Harvard for their presentation. The meetings would be grueling.

First, the provost and federal representatives had to review it and approve it before it could be vetted and approved by the FDA. This was something that would cure the world of all disease, including aging itself. It would also reverse it and maximize neurological capacity—making way for peace and prosperity worldwide.

After enduring the provost's and representatives' deliberations, Eliza and Yesha were crushed, even despite their enhanced cognition. They knew they could only work with the willing, because regardless of the common sense of it all and despite all of their efforts when they finally sought approval, they were turned down.

"How could that be!" asked Yesha, in frustration, only when they were safely away from audibility by the judgmental and baseless naysayers. "The way they shut us down, I'm surprised they have enough neurological residue to tie their own shoes in the morning! I suppose we ought to be glad that at least they can no longer, conceivably hurt us, even if they wanted to."

"It's frustrating, for sure," Eliza sighed. "They are not ready for it yet, Yesha. It looks like we've learned too much, too soon, well, for them. Perhaps we were too evolved for our own good?

"I don't believe so, though. In my opinion, there is no such thing as 'too evolved,' and, again, in my estimation, humanity will never become 'too advanced,' although I can see it quite possible that they will never progress enough to maintain existence for another million years, and most especially if they keep their sights on nescient goals that have nothing to do with the future of humanity or life itself.

"Perhaps as helpful as medicine, science, and great intentions with wonderful results can be, if proliferated, the reverse is true. Therefore, I believe that if stymied by dilatants, we can simplify. Medicines as supplements, science as inspiration and creativity, and intentions with desirable results as actions and entertainment meant to educate, can all still help, and possibilities can still exist."

Let's Try it a Different Way

"We'll need to do this in a very different way, Yesha. We aren't about forcing the issue or forcing anyone, or anything on anyone. I am willing, and I know you are willing to do what is needed to create an environment conducive to human acceptance of that which will preserve the light and life within them. It's still legally pursuable, we'll just need to do it through an LLC."

Eliza and Yesha, despite their healthy cognitive framework and ability to process untold amounts of information simultaneously, were both initially taken back by the fact that the Provost, the Congressional Representative Eliza was working with, Congress itself, Harvard, MIT, and the FDA had each reproached them telling them they could not use campus facilities to proliferate nor teach of biopods or any related technology.

Moreover, they were told that they were turned down because in their view, the release of these biopods would upset the natural order of things, turn the economy upside down, and that there was no way to make sure that they were safeguarded to prevent their use by those who had malicious intent.

"We don't want to cause a pandemic," was what each of these influential individuals explained, after they had deliberated in private prior to denying Eliza's and Yesha's request to approve of and proliferate their biopods.

Since Eliza's and Yesha's medical technologies were turned down for further review or public proliferation, their findings were not published. Funding would have to come from their own accounts, but they were essentially told to bury their work regarding this or face serious consequences, at least if they were to engage in further parlay within either of the campuses.

Since Eliza and Yesha had the advantage of being physiologically and neurologically optimized already, they each had the foresight to be polite and kind. Aside from the necessary dialog, they told the authorities nothing about any of their further plans.

Instead, they brought their biopod home on the same rental truck they used to bring it there, to supposedly bury their technology. They even acted as though they were obliged to acquiesce to the wishes of the stewards of the campuses and requests of the Federal Government.

Of course, those who told Eliza and Yesha to bury these things were only too happy to bury it themselves. The untold sentiments of the authorities were most notably that these technologies would harm their current financial investments and agreements, and they could have none of that. So, Eliza and Yesha took it all home and kept everything low-key for now.

While they appreciated being honored "under the radar" for their ingenious contributions to biological, physiological, and neurological sciences and received awards as well as tenured positions at Harvard, going into January 2008, they settled for part-time positions affording them time to create their own company, and call it Pathway LLC. Thus, they were brilliant, and they had a lot going on behind the scenes, and nothing would slow them down. They learned a lot from their dear friend, Vesha Celeste that day, that when the going gets tough, the tough keep on going, no matter the challenge.

As Honorary Tenured Professors at Harvard and MIT, and while teaching part-time, Eliza and Yesha decided that although they would hide their Virtual Universe journeys and their abilities and observe the "status quo" in public, they would continue on in private.

As they each taught seven two-hour classes weekly, they would merely do so giving very little sign that they were even remotely interested in bringing about the technologies that were so firmly turned down.

They did this, in wisdom, to appear as though they wanted to avoid losing access to the labs that enhanced their understanding of biotechnology, but secretly they did so to bring clarity to the effects of the technologies they had applied to themselves, using legacy systems. Furthermore, they acted in the face of the authorities as though they had dismantled their biopods all-together.

However, Eliza and Yesha had set up all their plans and very soon they would have all of the infrastructure they needed, and much, much more, within Pathway LLC.

Both brilliant doctors would build their reputations at the most reputable schools in the country and their knowledge and wisdom would become more robust than any other established institution throughout the world, but they would also be cautious.

Initially, these two "young" PhDs would agree upon appearances at the universities to educate both younger and older minds alike who truly showed signs of interest in the advancement of civilization, as well as innocently teach of its preservation, all while building their dream machines, and bringing to reality all of their other plans.

Interestingly, this in-turn would serve as an optimal professional opportunity for any of the students they saw as dedicated and with clarity and vision toward a more advanced civilization. They would recruit those who were interested in compounding upon the abundant joys of life—but first they would build their infrastructure and go from there. There was a lot they would carry out in short order.

Ultimately, they kept a level of confidentiality around their personal project that was equivalent to the highest level of secrecy held by any powerful government agent, but they maintained a public personification of normalcy.

Furthermore, they had no desire to lose all of their technologies or breakthroughs by way of secret agents seeing through to confiscation of them and quite possibly to their own untimely demise—at least that is how they had heard things would go down if they were not careful.

They knew that they could not be killed by human means, they were in effect immortal, but they could not exactly tell that to the authorities, or life would become very annoying, and exasperatingly so, very fast. Although they did not believe the worst would happen, conspiracies of a similar sort were out there in social media and alternative news reports and they did not want to pose an undue risk to their intellectual capital nor their goals of preserving life and building a long-term legacy.

By the don of the new year of 2008, and because of a decade and more of due diligence with her family's estate, economically or any other manner of speaking, on her part, Eliza had grown such a vast resource of personal intellect, wisdom, and even wealth, that she could effectively finance every plan she had, while procuring investments way beyond the scope of any capacity for current human comprehension.

To begin with, here on Earth, through wise investments in all of the right start-ups throughout the nineties and the early time-frame of the 2000s, Eliza realized she had gained a gloriously substantial enough accumulation of wealth to invest in a company that could be both covert and public. From there, she could hire the most qualified personnel to build the infrastructure.

This, she and Yesha very much planned to do, in order to provide the infrastructure and tools necessary to build the basics and continue from there. First, she had to buy several acreages, and then she had to transition their designs from the Virtual Universe to the real world and fund the development of even more infrastructure so she and Yesha could go even further than before for even greater advancements—the kind they had in mind when they first journeyed throughout the solar system while in the Virtual Universe beyond the current reach of Earth.

During the first weekend of that year, with minds that were several millennia old and physiology and neurology more vibrant and youthful than anyone twenty-two-years-of-age, they arranged a secret meeting with a trustworthy real estate agent and purchased several large acreages, so they could have their labs, campuses, hyperloops, jump gates, and so much more built underground, with a few state-of-the-art and highly attractive buildings above ground for public business.

Eliza worked with Yesha on a lot of purchases, which the realtor was only too happy to oblige when it came to their confidentiality, for a multitude of monetary reasons.

Eliza Williams barely had to tap into her investments to finance each of their real estate purchases. Upon research and then visiting various locations, she decided that the central hub of Pathway LLC would be in a forested reserve of twenty-two-thousand-three-hundred-nine acres, which was located in Middlesex County, Massachusetts.

To drive there from her estate, it would take twenty minutes by car and two hours by foot, if they didn't use their new abilities for fast-paced running. Of course, they decided they would not for now, in order to avoid any particularly wordy explanations. Eliza and Yesha also chose not to be too obvious about their abilities—so they chose to hold off on running in the open using their extra speed, strength, or agility, or flexing their newly-found speed, strength, and durability in the annual marathons in Boston for that matter, for a while, until they could establish a similar set of sports for augmented humans.

That said, this is when and where they registered Pathway LLC, which was centrally located within Melrose, Massachusetts—a small two-member organization.

Eliza worked with Yesha extensively, they had journeyed together so far, and because she loved Yesha as a dear sister and as a best friend, Eliza officially hired her as her first formal employee.

"I may be the President of Pathway LLC, but you are the Vice President and my closest friend and confidant. Our limited liability corporation will grow into many industries that will do a lot to help billions of people today and tomorrow, and in the future perhaps trillions of people if not more. Just as the galaxies, the stars, and the worlds in the cosmos are countless, so too will be the possibility of our influence to provide promise and hope.

"You are and have always been my nearest, dearest, and best friend since birth, Yesha. We have named our company Pathway LLC, and we will eventually name it Pathway Industries. As time goes by, we give it the title of Pathway, in honor of our late friends, Charles and Eugene.

"I can't believe it's already been seven years, three months, and twenty-one days since both passed away. Although many tragedies to include the tragedy surrounding 9/11 require proper vindication, let's work together to heal minds rather than harm them. I know you are with me on this, but I will ask you anyway outside of the Virtual Universe. Are you with me, Yesha?"

"Of course! You've got me 121%, Eliza. You know that. Don't ever worry, I've got your back, we're together on this, no matter where we are or how far you want to go. I have no doubt in the least that you have my back too and the places we'll aim to go will be amazing!"

"Of course, and I am with you too, Yesha," smiled Eliza. Both were excited to begin this new venture.

Eliza and Yesha purchased their land in order to develop the infrastructure they designed in the Virtual Universe, which would make way for more advancements. In the future, it would be in the safety and secrecy of their subtle location, and in many cases, deep within the woods.

They wanted to keep this safe from the hands of those who did not wish well upon others, nor themselves. Too many in positions of influence in their world had been mired and indoctrinated in the thoughts and ways of the establishment. The minds of those with the power to make decisions had very little to no clarity at all when it came to long-term prosperity.

From their purview, the bureaucrats and baseless naysayers did not seem to understand that they were harming themselves with their myopia just as much if not more than they were harming those they were elected to serve. Many of the rich seemed to make their gains based on fear, rather than through love.

Eliza had begun all of what she had in the effort of reducing the unnecessary suffering prevalent throughout humanity, as evidenced in so many places throughout the world, and all because of love, and Yesha shared her ideals.

She and Yesha had done the research and purchased the land and all of their rights, and when they were ready, they went into the Virtual Universe again during the first week of 2008 to perfect and improve upon their plans and designs based on the layouts of the acreages.

They augmented their original ideas and created additional plans, including reforestation with enhanced and vibrant, lush and rich growth above and below ground. Within this large forest, a new standard and norm would be set of optimization and sentience of wildlife of every possible sort. The development of their many laboratories, facilities, factories, hyperloops, and much more would be built with no pollution whatsoever, due to their robust containment technologies, which included exotic capabilities such as particle repurposing and one-hundred percent reuse and recycling of all materials.

"Let's consider what we have learned by developing the repurposing capacity of these 'throw-away' or 'decaying objects,' items, and particles, by using Earth's fusion, underground, on the Sun, and in space, with ways to contain and prevent damage to life, and germinate their proper use and re-use," voiced Eliza, and she continued.

"A wonderful, quiet, and peaceful revolution is about to begin, Yesha." Yesha listened and looked over her and Eliza's plans, their intricacy, and she was impressed.

Break Time

Once they were ready, Eliza and Yesha began to relax, search for general contractors who were, by career choices and publicly lauded reputation, willing and able to build infrastructure for a lot of money and for a lot more confidentiality. In so many ways, secrecy was worth as much as gold. So, they would respond in kind.

Before the end of the first week, or Friday, January 4, 2008, they had a list of possible contractors, and they began hitting up the Virtual Universe quite consistently to study this individual, and quickly ascertain who else it might be that would fit the bill.

"Who would have the right personality? I mean, look at this, Yesha. There is this one gentleman, and his name keeps on resurfacing. He seems like the right kind of soul, the type of disposition we're looking for, and his building designs are creative, with high quality, and are eco-friendly, while increasing the quality of life of everyone affected within each community. He could be the third partner in our long-term venture, but there is only one way to truly know."

"I know," said Yesha with a thoughtful look on her face. Stepping in to look at him some more.

That night they talked until late, and then for old time's sake, they grabbed their sleeping bags, even though they didn't need to, and looked up at the stars with their favorite music playing in the background, singing some favorite tunes. The songs, "I Just Can't Get Enough," by Depeche Mode, and "Shakespeare's Garden," by Cause & Effect, played in the air around them. They sang these songs as loud as they could get away with to the coy fish in the pond and looked up at the stars and galaxies.

"It's breath-taking, Eliza, now that we can actually see Pluto with our naked eyes. Look at the Andromeda Galaxy. If you zoom in real close, you can see a system much like ours, but still quite peculiar."

"Oh my," said Eliza, as she tapped into Yesha's mind and then focused as well. "Beautiful. Great find, proud of you my friend. What would you like to call it?"

"Eto."

"Short, simple, and not too obscure—I love it!" chuckled Eliza. Yesha laughed with her, as they both were taken by the idea and the humor of what Eliza had just said. Tired of unnecessary over-complication and lengthy drudgery, this name was perfect.

Eliza continued, "You know? It's interesting, I'm twenty-seven and you're thirty, but our bodies can stay the physiological age of twenty-two or whatever we choose for centuries, while our minds will continue to collectively age. I mean think about it, our neurological capacity has been given many millennia of education, experience, and practical application equating to untold wisdom. Who would have known that we could exist in a world where no one noticed that our minds were many millennia old? It's nice that we've been able to get to this point with so many abilities and so many plans.

"We've created the designs, Yesha, now it's time to make them happen."

"One, two, or a bazillion steps at a time," Yesha responded with a pleasant sense of humor in her tone. She then picked up a tone of seriousness and looked down, "We've certainly waited long enough."

Looking up, and with a gentle tone, Yesha continued, "Humanity, more than ever, needs hope. Everywhere we look we see the fight for intellectuality dying, the search for peace caving to violence, and the desire to live for a long time fade away to hopes for demise for the sake of a reprieve from all of the stressors of the day."

They decided to let their minds relax, and when they were done looking at the stars, the galaxies, and the cosmic microwave background radiation, they looked at each other until they fell asleep, in the snow, without needing blankets, but using their blankets anyway out of habit and out of love for the time they'd spent with each other for so long in that same location, to rest following the sharing of so many plans for a better future. Again, their dreams were met with each other going on journeys never dreamt of before, together.

The next day would be big.

"When it comes to the bits and bobbles of LLC economics...," Yesha started up with conversation the next morning, holding a hibiscus and astragalus-root tea in her hand, while looking over the table at Eliza, who was enjoying a lab-grown clean meat egg with sharp cheddar cheese, sourdough toast, a spirulina shake, and a grapefruit juice. "I'd love to invest my money into Pathway LLC, but I recall our conversations in the Virtual Universe, where you insisted, I save my money. You then suggested that whatever would be yours to claim, would also be mine.

"Then you told me that ultimately, whatever you planned on doing had nothing to do with money in any way whatsoever. Money is just a means to an end, for now.

"I see what you are saying, it makes complete sense. Eventually, the current economic system will change, but of course, that can't happen until we can make a gradual shift of focus prevalent throughout the world."

Eliza continued to listen intently, "We agreed that for now, we have to have investments that are terrestrial for tax purposes and for the appearance of normalcy. We need to use our money on normal expenditures, the day-to-day, and invest in that which will bring in earnings, so we can demonstrate compliance with the demands of authority and the existing establishment."

Eliza smiled, then interrupted, but with a kind tone, "The money that you make will serve to cover traveling expenditures, as well as eating costs and bills incurred while traveling overseas, and that is investment enough.

"Eventually, when all of this is set up, we will need to travel the world to recruit people, and Yesha, you have a heart of gold, a capacity to reach the minds, the hearts, and even the souls of others that few have.

"Your very nature makes you ideal for visiting our friends in the eastern hemisphere. I love you as a sister, a dear friend, and a kindred spirit. So, I ask that you please trust that everything will be okay. When the time comes, we'll be able to visit each other in moments. Plus, we're both neurologically linked, and with our plans with jump gates, sensors, and small-moon-sized database satellites, we'll be able to connect no matter where we go.

"Everything we do is for you, me, humanity, and every living being. People are forced into thinking certain ways because of what life has exposed them to for far too long, and the thinking that teaches people a sense of greed will go away. The idea that we can't do something helpful because it is too costly, will disappear.

"Furthermore, many have this notion that because of their unbridled paranoia of the future that we are the most worthless human beings on the planet and that our vision is merely child's play. They seek to see us fall so they can go, I told you so, and laugh as we go down.

"That will not happen on our clock. It is more important to have civil discourse than to engage in toxic arguments which lead to nowhere. It's more important we help rather than harm others, shifting our focus and lifting our gaze. With our abilities, we will no longer need to spend money on anything, really. This estate is to house your mother, Yesenia, and to provide a place for us to continue our research. Eventually, this will also serve as a sort of entry point into our Pathway Campus in Melrose.

"You've seen my designs for the hyperloops, you've seen the jump gates, and well, you've helped me with the plans for the tech cities. Not a dime is needed to live on them but for crunching the numbers in terms of worldly numerical economic value, and I'd say that makes us richer than a one-hundred-million worlds put together, and our value will only increase.

"For that reason, I've done initial investments, but once our infrastructure has been built, it will take off even more from there. When we recruit people, they won't need to live in horrible or toxic environments, instead, they will have the opportunity, free of any cost, to live in a dwelling more safe, luxurious and beautiful than any they have ever known, and with everything they need. If they need anything else, all they will need to do is request it or ask. Finances are merely a short-term means to an end.

"Big hug?"

After that discussion, Yesha hugged Eliza as a sister, and insisted on calling everything Eliza's, even though Eliza preferred she didn't, but she didn't do it for any reason other than the fact that she had seen Eliza's mind, it was pure, she was genuine, and she fully trusted her.

Yesha knew that with Eliza, money wasn't a concern in any manner, and it would soon never need to be.

In another interesting way, Yesha, for simplicity's sake, viewed Eliza as the ideal role model and figurehead, yet she never felt like she was made to feel or be the quiet part in Eliza's team. Eliza would always remind her that the role that Yesha played was every bit as essential as her own role and that it was also vital in its very own way for her to participate and voice any concerns.

"There are no quiet team members since we're all in this together," Eliza would insist.

Eliza would give Yesha outstanding props from time to time because it left a wonderful sense of dignity to remind her that at no time would she ever be playing the follower. They had so much in common, she prized her constructive dialog, they had a shared understanding of every aspect of what they were doing, and given their neural link, they were now almost one of mind and goals.

They still had their unique aspects, Yesha was a slight bit more provocative, yet she liked to stay outside of the limelight if she could help it—although that desire was starting to give way to a desire to inspire, just like Eliza had inspired her on so many occasions, and Eliza, well she was profoundly wise in so many ways, with compassion oozing from the seams.

Yesha was also gentle and trusted Eliza in every possible way, and complemented humanity's need for a leader, both Yesha's and Eliza's priorities lay in life, longevity, well-being, compassion, kindness, love, health, intellect, wisdom, and joy, and not a soul could put a price-tag or a title on that.

Completely on Eliza's side with all that they had planned, a beautiful future at that, Yesha merely wanted to avoid any unnecessary complications. She loved Eliza as a sister, a friend, a confidant, and a companion, and from that day forward, Eliza was considered by Yesha to be a full-fledged leader of any of their endeavors, no matter where they would go.

"You have a beautiful future before you. I can see it now," Eliza would remind Yesha, and told her again that morning over a cup of Jo.

After their morning discussion and after purchasing the acreages they had researched, Eliza and Yesha continued to work in the offices within Eliza's estate home throughout noon and then into the afternoon. They drew up even more extensive plans and increased the development of their Virtual Universe interface, so they could enhance the building of their plans for each of their edifices, laboratories of every sort, infrastructures, and tech cities, so that once they'd brought the ideal contractor on board, they could pretty much automate the process for efficiency.

Grateful for their keenness to build their biopods, which served as an interface for anyone's physiological and neurological systems, they never underestimated how much it helped them to compound upon their own ability to find a resolution to so many more issues plaguing humanity and Mother Nature herself.

Once in this Virtual Universe, they would in a very small amount of real-world time spend vast amounts of Virtual Universe moments to completely develop and create every aspect of their infrastructural plans, with the goal of giving Mother Nature a nice little break, and soon.

Together, they were detail-oriented in every aspect, since their plans were to create a robust and safe set of deep underground campuses and advanced laboratories.

Eliza and Yesha designed an extensive underground hyperloop transportation set of systems to carry people, supplies, and finished goods as well as bulk materials for industries around and to the countries of the US, Canada, and even to Mexico, Puerto Rico, and Central and South America. Eventually, they would go worldwide, under the Atlantic and the Pacific to every population center on Earth, free of tariffs and raising the quality of life.

These hyperloops would run from lab-to-lab, to docking stations underground that would translate to trucking stations from within their forested acreages, to and from other production centers courtesy of other purchased acreages of Eliza's around the US and Canada.

They purchased the needed permissions and acquired the necessary documentation for building infrastructure both above and under the ground, as well as above, on, and below each great body of water. They bought up every aspect and access possible, to include all mineral, water, and forestation rights in all of their acreages, as well as for the location of Eliza's estate in Cambridge, MA.

In comparison to many other purchasers, Eliza and Yesha would make sure that indigenous communities were still provided access to their water and the forested lands they had grown up with for centuries, and free of any pollution whatsoever. They would be merely asking in turn that they tend to the needs of the sentient "wildlife" and the forests. If they wished they could become particle science chefs—this would allow for a nutritious and delicious food cycle that made way for the protection of life with clean meats and nutrients of every sort, removing the brutality of prey versus predator. If they would also need to ask for any structure or dwelling, food to eat, or water to drink, which was in abundance, and thus, all would be built and provided in a way that could exceed their needs and desires.

Eliza and Yesha built plans to connect new hyperloop systems to plausible distribution and reception centers nationwide and throughout the western hemisphere and they would begin with a distribution center in Michigan.

A complex series of hyperloops would travel deep underground between Melrose, MA, Lake Ontario, Lake Erie, and Lake Huron, all the way to Eliza's overt distribution center in Alpena County.

It was there that Eliza had purchased 1450 acres of land. Moving out from there, she and Yesha planned to create another hyperloop system with an entryway onto Highway 75, just south of Grayling, where she purchased another two-hundred-acre plot of forested land to have additional trucking depots built. In every location, there would be union representatives who would ensure the highest quality of living for every employee.

Eliza and Yesha would make sure that all manner of medical supplies with subtle advancement assists from Pathway LLC would be distributed to medical facilities throughout the US, Puerto Rico, and each US territory, upon FDA and associated state governmental approval, as well as throughout Canada, Mexico, and the countries of Central and South America, with their associated governmental approvals, and likewise throughout the rest of the world.

Ore and finished goods would be distributed to manufacturers around Wisconsin, Minnesota, Michigan, Ohio, Illinois, Indiana, Pennsylvania, and upstate New York—the manufacturing capitals of the US. Eliza and Yesha would have raw goods distributed throughout the US in many places, to include Silicon Valley.

Pathway LLC would sell its ore, developed through their new cold fusion process, at competitive rates, so they could drive the overall costs of manufacturing down, save billions of dollars to the taxpayer, the manufacturer, and the consumer, and help the economy to begin to flourish. Eliza's plan was to slowly move population centers from where they were to places that would have the maximum positive effect on both humanity and Mother Nature, through the central focus of well-being, preservation of life, health, and clarity of mind toward healthy pursuits.

To build her initial infrastructure, Eliza decided she would need to hire high-quality contractors willing to be sworn to secrecy but paid very well to build a number of facilities. They would build a lot of infrastructure, up to and including three baryonic, non-baryonic, and exotic matter colliders. In comparison to similar technologies, these would be retrofitted with material storage containers.

These systems would be twice as big as and many times more capable than the ITER. The ITER had been projected for completion in 2030, in France, and would be larger than CERN—the large hadron collider, or LHC, in Switzerland. Most of Pathway LLC's infrastructure would be initially built within their acreage in MA. For those facilities alone, they would need to hire scores of scientists to be read-in as full members of Pathway LLC.

While there were only two members now, Eliza could see her cadre growing to millions in just a couple of years.

Both Eliza and Yesha knew this wouldn't be easy; they wanted everything constructed in as prompt of time and with as high quality as possible, all while upholding their own strictest codes of ethics. They were on a mission and together they had a whole lot of plans, the specifics, and every detail. That included legal loop-holes as well as safety and security every step of the way.

They knew that every worker, inventor, investor, and professional working for Pathway LLC would merit a high quality of life, replete with plenty of vacation time and means to explore their world, visit their families, and perfect their innovations.

Eliza and Yesha had exhausted hours on end that day, both in the Virtual Universe and then back in the real world, as they pored over legal documents, architectural designs and data, engineering processes, and conducted all-encompassing background researches of potential contractors, while reading through endless biographies and mini-bios of experienced personnel on the computers in the offices of their shared estate home.

After Eliza and Yesha conducted extensive research on the results of numerous high-tech facilities throughout the US and throughout the world, it was among the most advanced and highest quality facilities and buildings constructed, each meeting their high standard, that they noticed something remained constant, James Cooper's name kept surfacing. Following a lot of research, they decided they needed to meet with him to bring him on board.

With all their work Eliza and Yesha agreed that for now, they merited a refresher from the day, and they found time to be at a pause. Even though their minds and their bodies were optimized, it was still nice to step away from things to clear the mind and take in the sites, tastes, smells, and sounds of life.

Simultaneously testing their new internal will and relaxing was what gave them a sense of balance. Yesha decided to go for a long jog and Eliza decided she wanted to taste the savory delights of real-world food at the Tyson Organic or the T.O.

With their research pretty much complete, they had a lot to ponder on anyway. Although there weren't a lot of typically physical things they were required to do when it came to everyday nuance, they found something special about doing typical activities despite their optimizations. Eating to enjoy the savory flavors of a well-cooked meal, jogging to take in the natural sights and sounds, sleeping to allow the mind a natural way of exploring all that it knew and had gained in understanding throughout the day, and bathing with Epsom salts, tea tree oils, lilac, peppermint and other Essential Oils were all among their favorites.

Oh, the time had flown over the last few hours as they reviewed the often-negative critiques of YY Construction Corp, which happened to employ James' crew, a subcontracting firm, called "the 97." As far as the corporation itself was concerned and as it was run currently, even though they had quite a lengthy history, Eliza and Yesha weren't particularly impressed.

James' name, however, seemed to always be involved in what appeared to be the best in the industry. Therefore, he was certainly at the top of their list.

"Kudos to anyone who carries on despite all, and still does the right thing notwithstanding their environment."

Eliza and Yesha confided that sentiment to each other many times that day. They reached a firm agreement; he would be the ideal addition to their venture, and they would have to get in touch with him soon.

While they used the Virtual Universe to understand science, history, and all the different subjects that revolved around the well-being of humanity and Earth itself, neither Eliza nor Yesha used their covert access to all of the systems to pry unnecessarily into the private lives or plans of others. They could do that in real life by contacting people the old-fashioned way—through cell phones, private messaging, chat, and text.

In this way, they would get to know people and come to agreements using good old-fashioned negotiation, and as such, no matter their method, wills were never forced. As a matter of a fact, one of the things Eliza and Yesha did, mostly to appear normal, was use their cell phones as many people seemed to. However, unlike what they perceived far too many people to be doing, burying their heads in gadgets, they instead tried to maintain a higher level of professionalism or standards than typical. They believed that the most important people in any room, wherever they might be, were in the room, and not on any electronic device or other form of distraction.

After their last bit of research, Yesha and Eliza took their individual evening breaks. Yesha went for a jog and Eliza went to go savor her favorite food. Little did they know that if Providence was involved at all, this day was about to be filled with one miracle after another. If science were involved, then it was due to astute observations, study, and effort that great achievements would be made soon. Either way, they both carried themselves with a gracious attitude toward the good things in life, kindness toward any passers-by, and love for those who were dedicated to raising the quality of life for others as well as themselves. *"Let's heal, not harm..."* Eliza thought.

Chapter 05: A Person of Integrity

Database Moon Archive, Celestial-Sol Entry Date: 2018 December 25 – Experiential biography, as taught to Vesha Celeste about James Cooper, and what it is that drives his efforts and results. Contained within are thoughts from Eliza Williams, Yesha Alevtina, and James Cooper. Training Given by Yesha Alevtina, President of Pathway Industries, 2015-2022.

James Cooper was a company man—the first to arrive at work and the last to go. Today, he was on vacation, so he slept in until 7:30 in the morning, and went on a morning jog. He passed through Boston many years ago on his cross-country trip to Maine, before finally settling in to live in Grayling, Michigan. When he'd been here before, he'd merely passed through Cambridge, and he kind of wondered why he hadn't spent a few days there at the time. He didn't let that get to him too much.

James loved pretty much everything about it. Maybe it was time for a move, but he had his crew with him, he cared for them greatly and they were together on vacation, so he decided to dispense with thoughts of moving for now. Plus, he loved Grayling, Michigan.

In some ways, over the last thirteen years, this was part of a typical vacation for James. They would visit a place where his crew's children planned on going to college, and check out the hotels, the nightlife, followed up with camping in the nearby County, State, or National Parks.

He, his crew, and their families would stay in one location for about a week, and then do similarly elsewhere, until their two-month vacation was up. Today, he'd be going around town with thirteen people, after the meeting at ten in the morning, with his whole crew at a grange he'd rented through the following Saturday.

After about thirty minutes on foot, on his morning jog, and with plenty of time to think about the current schedule, he turned around to run back and then showered up. He could do weights at the hotel gym later that day before going to bed.

His smaller party of fourteen, himself included, was going to visit the campuses of Harvard and then MIT today, and then stroll around town until it was time to crash out. So, he cleaned himself up, with no three-day stubble this time. He shaved his chiseled features and showered his six foot one and muscular physique.

The hair on the sides and back of his head was trimmed in a close and faded manner. Using his wet fingers to comb through his hair tended to leave it a little wavier, so that's what he did. Furthermore, he'd received several compliments on his choice of hairstyle from quite a few ladies, older and younger ladies, some who could have been models, and a few larger women who were comfortable in their own skin and a joy to be around.

With those reassurances he kept his styles simple, attractive, and low maintenance. After using his favorite deodorant, Dr. Organic Moroccan Argon Oil, to provide a pleasant scent if sweating, he dressed in a thin light blue pin-striped button-up shirt and a nicely woven navy-blue suit. He then tied his tie into a double-Windsor knot, around his muscular neck. His tie was themed with a dark blue background and evenly spaced flowers, each with various shades of purple, pink, navy, and white, and cinched the knot tight, and good, and firm.

All that he wore had an arrangement of colors that complemented his blue eyes, his dark hair, and his lightly tanned pale white skin, courtesy of the outdoor sun. Ready for the day, and with a little mist of Healing-Scents Men's Natural Cologne, by 9:30 he was walking to the grange to meet his entire crew and their families.

James' Routine

Back at home on routine days, he would get up at four in the morning, jog around town, tidy up, and savor a coffee or tea just a block away at the Thanks a Latte, while poring over the local newspaper.

At the end of the day, he would change out of his professional attire, into clean clothes for a local service project, and then get into his workout gear, use his home gym, and go kayaking along the nearby AuSable River.

He had an agreement there, with Borcher's Bed and Breakfast near the river just off of Maple Street. Many of his visitors came from out of town and would stay there. Since he was a respected local employer, they gave him his own key to their storage bay, for use of course whenever he was in town. He would retrieve his kayak and paddle up or down the river and back. Sometimes he would bring a coworker or two and he tipped the B&B handsomely and often, so their arrangement was ideal for both parties.

Moments of solitude to reflect on his day were something he treasured greatly. This was his venue for private thought, and how he would ponder on the people who worked for him or on any upcoming projects.

As a regional contractor and a contracted project manager for YY Construction Corp, an architectural organization established in the 1920's out of Bay City, Michigan, James managed large infrastructural projects that were contracted out to him and his crew, and he parsed the different aspects of the project to mature completion between the crewmembers.

He could do a lot of the preparatory planning while working out of his office in Grayling. On many occasions and quite regularly, he traveled the globe with his crew for projects everywhere, but this was his home base.

No matter where he was, James would greet each of his employees as he passed them with a genuine smile, a "hello," and a "thank you" for something of honor he had noticed as they worked together. He also gave what he surmised as due props to those who coordinated the various aspects of projects effectively or if he saw community involvement by any crew members in the local news, no matter where they were or what their projects happened to be.

Against any of the wishes of all corporate sellouts, James cared about those he supervised, so, whenever he could, he would send them home once their daily training, planning, checklists, and tasks were complete with a full day's pay, so he could finish all of the paperwork and they could be involved with their families and the local service projects, in population centers, wherever they were.

Despite being part of a construction firm, James Cooper understood the political aspects of leadership in the industry and each time he cleaned up and wore business professional attire for his corporate meetings in Bay City.

To James it was essential he looked the part, so he could help his crew out, win the fight, and come home.

When he was back at his office in Grayling and working with his crew there, he would throw on his construction gear and roll up his sleeves to plan upcoming projects and work with his crew.

Traveling worldwide and in some places where he had to have close oversight of each crewmember and their families for their safety, James was protective and fair, but respectful. He found his crew was safer that way. He knew that no matter where he and his crew travelled, if they were courteous, dignified, and respected the laws of the land, the locals usually had their backs.

The character of he and his crew may have been why it was, that whenever he was in locations the news reported as dangerous, he had discovered an entirely different reality and truth about the people of each country he was in. Thus far, for all of the sensationalized horror stories he'd heard, he was continuously a witness to beautiful people, inside and out, whether rich or poor. He found people the world over, from the Middle East, or China, India, or Russia to be unique, full of dreams, and both helpful and kind. He grew to believe that we see in others what we fear and love most about ourselves, so he was fearless and had a passion for living honorably.

Despite being in a construction environment, traveling the globe often, typically and overwhelmingly populated by men, his crew was divided equally between women and men. He hired based on character and a desire to work, and he had a unique ability to see to the core of an individual.

Ultimately, if he was hiring, he hired people who came in to request to do the job or be a part of his team, and he worried little about any other qualifications, except to mentor and train them after they were hired. He knew he didn't need to treat someone brashly, or in an otherwise despicable way, since he could motivate pretty much anyone and train them to do anything that they put their minds to, so long as they were willing to make the basic effort of reliability.

After he put his crew together, early on in his role as manager, in 1995, everyone grew close, because of a very unique management system he had implemented from day one. As it was, from 1995 to 2008, only four of his crewmembers had retired, and four more became trained and successfully integrated into his hospitable and supportive crew.

Five of his eight construction teams were led by women; most of them were quite striking, and so much so, they were often complimented and told they ought to pursue modeling. Of course, in certain regions overseas, the ladies observed the customs of the pervasive cultures in public, and James would do everything he could to secure their safety. He always ensured that when overseas or in a distant location, they traveled as a group, whenever they would head out to visit the local population to do service projects with those who struggled most.

A couple of the women leaders had personalities that were a little easier to chat with without all the tension seemingly existent with women that were jaw-droppingly gorgeous, but they were still fit and attractive.

The men in his crew were clean-cut, worked out often, and had been encouraged by James to be studious and artistic, and because of such, even the most prudent of the women swooned over them.

One of James' appointed leaders was as tough as iron, yet she was very effective and capable, still somewhat physically attractive despite her larger than average and muscular stature; her name was Anne. James had a soft spot for genuine people, and all of those who worked with him were just that. They were real, unique, and kind. His team leads were all great workers, as were those who worked with them, and they were of a demeanor that was of a great source of morale for each person in his crew, and as such their character translated into shared motivation, instruction, mentorship, and leadership.

James treated each person in the 97 as the unparalleled professionals they were, yet in many ways as if they were siblings, or best of friends, and honorably personal confidants. As a result, to him, his crew was like a family. No matter their background or their past, with James, they became highly capable and hardworking.

The 97 had each other's backs, loved their world, considered the well-being of all who were in the crew and their families, and they would never violate shared trust or personal integrity by throwing a fellow coworker, or anyone else for that matter, no matter the issue, under the theoretical or real-life bus.

Due to James' upbringing, he had his own deeply-entrenched set of values, as well as views on integrity. He was consistent and had his crew's back at all times; likewise, they had his back, worked both smarter and harder, and loved his management style.

James was only materialistic in a very minor sense, and despite his belief in self-marketing, he didn't do things for status or popularity, rather instead he did what was necessary and smart. At home, he would often go to the St Francis Thrift Shop for most of his belongings and even his clothes. He typically did an amazing job of looking around and selecting items; so, no one could tell that he was very spendthrift, unless they'd seen him in the store. James didn't need to spend a lot of money to be classy, because no matter what he had, he looked well-kept and well-dressed, making humility a popular thing. On occasion and as needed for the respect necessary to win the political charades at corporate, he would go to North Country Corner in order to purchase an occasional suit combination.

Often, James would try out recipes to test his chef skills, and if the results were delicious, he would treat his coworkers to his chef-like talents. Some of his favorite recipes came from friends he had made from all over the globe, but he'd always found a way to add his own touch with nutrient-dense spices and an occasional addition to the recipe here and there.

The Save-A-Lot and Family Fare grocery stores were on the east part of town, so he'd shop around between the two stores online. James would drive his silver 2002 Hyundai Elantra around for sundry needs, to include the healthy, organic, and nutrient-dense food and ingredients he needed for the swath of entrées he would prepare and share with his employees the following day.

While James appreciated flashy vehicles, he did his part to get only what he needed along with what would suffice to get any job done. He kept his car clean, washed, and waxed. From his point of view, he had a frequent drive to Bay City anyway, this car had great gas mileage, and he'd only upgrade if a car had forty miles-to-gallon minimum. He hadn't found one for the right price, and he wasn't in town long enough to justify an exotic, even if he had the money. *"If they ever make a vehicle, like a twenty-thousand-dollar Lamborghini Gallardo with 90 miles to the gallon, I will march right on over to the dealership and purchase one tomorrow. I would prefer to help build infrastructure and invest in my crew, anyway,"* James often thought. He would only get a rental truck if needed for personal purposes.

James and his crew were dubbed "the 97," shortly after he put his team together. The first time he'd ever heard the term was from his corporate bosses, when they badgered him about reducing his crewmember's pay for a bonus. Out of defiance, he had this nomenclature written on a sign above his office building in Grayling.

Even though the 97 became a new subsidiary of YY Construction Corp, and they had permitted him to do what he wished to do, so long as he finished the projects he agreed to complete, corporate was full of examples of lives destroyed, people fired, and subcontractors who had been sued to decimation.

Nevertheless, he would go to Bay City, into the YY Construction Corp Offices, and then return to Grayling to get his crew briefed on the latest projects and the nuances of the latest technologies. He and his crew would hone their skills, train each other up in every way, and then use their expertise to benefit more than corporate or consumer, as well as everyone walking by any building they built, and they would build the type of infrastructure that would help to make tomorrow a better future.

All of the infrastructure built by the 97 came with campuses that had free private parks, more than enough underground parking, beautified and wide sidewalks with accommodations for families with pets, separate lanes for those jogging or walking, and a couple of lanes in both directions for those on bicycles.

Within a reasonable distance from any point around any building, there were always recycling and trash receptacles with agreements for locally contracted service. The areas around the buildings they built were crafted into beautiful and peaceful environments loaded with flora and fauna, as well as eateries that were of the highest quality, but surprisingly less expensive. Together with his crew, he would ensure the details, the plans, and what was needed to bring a shared architectural vision into reality were clear. James communicated eloquently and delegated effectively.

His Dreams

Even though James was a single man, he didn't go to work to date, he simply believed, *"Everything we do and everything we say is marketing ourselves, so it is our responsibility to be at our best, or to simply be humble and kind, to appreciate this world and its beauty, and to stay motivated toward the quality and efficiency of the services we render."*

Even though he, himself, was single and with no children of his own, he was good with his crew's children, and many had grown up and gone to college during his thirteen years as their boss.

Beyond the phenomenal parenting of many of their crewmembers, much of their success was due to James' mentorship, his coaching, his gentle demeanor, his one-on-one monthly interviews, his training, and because of the battles he'd won before his corporate bosses, for and in behalf of his crew.

The ladies appreciated him for his sterling nature around the children, yet he rarely noticed, since his heart was in devotion to their safety, their well-being, as well as the sanctity of life and of purpose, and he seldom thought of himself, other than for his overall health and fitness.

Many felt James deserved to have a life-mate, a unique companion of his own, but they never pressed the issue much, beyond some encouragement, knowing that in time he would find a life partner, and all would be well.

Just as it was with his work, when it came to companionship, he wanted to spend his life with someone who shared larger goals beyond themselves, like he and his crew. He wanted her, whoever she might be, to be capable of loving and taking care of her home, just as he did, and loved herself through thick or thin. Just as he would expect from himself, he would expect honor, trust, love, and dignity from her, no matter where either would travel, from the furthest reaches of known life, to home itself, taking charge of her own dreams and goals freely, and enjoying her life throughout each of her pursuits, and all for a greater purpose.

Ultimately, no matter how busy things were, one day, things would slow down, he and his future life-companion would settle down, and then, yes, perhaps then, they would consider relaxing, taking a break, and analyzing what else they could do to make the future better still, and not just for themselves, but for others around them, young or old, as well.

Many would never have guessed that he had ever considered dating. He looked great to all the women he probably would have found interest in, but he was interested in more than looks. His biggest goal with regard to dating, despite all, was to find someone with a fired-up vision of what could be done to improve the world. He imagined in his own way that he would be able to work with her and his existing crew someday to do something amazing. Beauty to him was a full-package deal. If he were to date, it would be without drama, and loaded with dreams, hopes, and goals, as well as plans to help each other realize them.

Growing Up

Born on July 9, 1973, at the Stanford University Hospital, he opened his eyes for the first time to a mother and father who were both in college but were very much entrenched within the hippy and drug era. While some hippies were such for moralistic reasons, others were there for the reckless form of hedonism and drugs, that were used in an abusive and damaging way to the brain's processes, if not curbed or properly controlled.

As far as he knew, his biological parents were part of that movement purely to numb their minds from the abuses they'd suffered courtesy of the puritanical platitudes of their own parents growing up.

Due to their drug abuse, his biological mother and father had unfortunately neglected his crucial care at an early age, and so much so, that he was eventually taken from them by the California State Social Services when he was eighteen-months-old and placed into a variety of foster homes enduring various forms of abuse until he was six years old.

The parents who took him in, loved him, and were responsible with how they raised him. These two delightful people came into his life and took him in when he was six years old and they were fifty. They battled the court system for three years fostering him until they could adopt under their terms while living in San Jose.

When he was ten, the Coopers moved north of the Bay Area just outside a small town within Lake County, California, to give him a chance to start fresh. The school systems in this area were humble yet of a high quality. The teachers had a wonderful reputation for being excellent mentors and educators. Plus, it was a chance for a new network of peers who knew James only as a Cooper.

It was on a ten-acre area of land at the top of a hill just five miles from the main part of town, overlooking where Highways 29 and 75 intersected, near the base of an ancient and dormant volcano, that he lived. It was here that his father and mother taught him his work ethic and how to love and to trust again.

Mr. and Mrs. Cooper were delightful and very affectionate with each other despite their age. They laughed with one another and they even managed to bring out James' humor and wit on many occasions throughout his childhood. They also owned a vast home library of historical, cultural, scientific, political, management, and positive thinking literature books, and his parents openly shared their literature with him. Among his favorites of the science fiction and mystery genres to read in the fifth and sixth grades within his own small library in his room were the full Tom Swift, Tom Corbett, and Alfred Hitchcock and the Three Investigators series. He enjoyed reading them, because they were creative, yet clean, innocent, and fun. On occasion, his mother or father would read from marked selections of books from their large library and provide mentorship, theoretical environmental examples, and day-to-day experiences.

His father was a baker from his childhood on and became a real estate agent in California, in his forties, to pay the bills. Mr. Cooper was also a handyman born and raised in the late 1920s and throughout the '30s, in Colorado Springs, Colorado. His mother had been a homemaker who eventually went to college when she was fifty-eight and James was in Junior High. When his father went on disability, Mrs. Cooper became an activities coordinator at senior citizen's centers around the area, to pay the bills.

James' parents were both born in 1929 and had been together ever since they eloped in the forties. Regardless of their humble background, they were studious, thoughtful, and caring and taught him to be thoughtful, honorable, and considerate of others through example. Above all else, he learned to be well-balanced through their mentorship, and through it all, they reminded him often how unique and loved he was as a human being.

"Often, his parents would say, "Many are born into families with little choice in the matter themselves, or on who will come along, on the part of their parents. It doesn't lessen the sacrifice either way, but children are special, no matter how they come to this life. Every child ought to have a home where their parents love each other, and where they are loved enough to be raised to have the tools necessary to be good people and successful in their endeavors, knowing they'll do well at anything they put their minds to.

"Some people struggle, and perhaps they may not have the time, so the most important thing to remember, as far as time is concerned, quality is always superior to quantity, especially when it comes to attention shared with others. James, you were chosen to be a part of our family and you chose us. You are and always will be exceptional." His parents would say.

They were structured, disciplined, and frugal, and no matter his past or his background, his parents loved him as their own.

In this small town, from the age of ten through graduation from high school, he studied well, and placed well in academic testing. When James wasn't doing homework, he worked hard on the family acreage, clearing the area of fire-hazardous dry weeds, star thistle, dead shrubs and trees, and all while building rock terraces from the cinder rocks and obsidian that lie scattered about the property to make way for gardens and walkways on their own little hill-top acreage. He worked with his father to nurture seedlings into trees, growing fruit orchards of many kinds for canning and fresh enjoyment.

Searching for fallen trees along the perimeter or anywhere around the property not only provided an assist for warmth in the winter, but it helped to prevent forest fires, since he would clear away the dead leaves, weeds, and debris. He learned to break down the wood into many sizes, from kindling to overnight-warmth, with special skills in preparing long-burning oak and madrone. James placed all resultant firewood into their refurbished greenhouse allowing it to dry enough throughout the summer for use during the blustery and cold winter. He was a hard worker who aimed to please his parents. In his heart of hearts, he reciprocated their love through his diligence and by honoring his father's name.

It was during his high school years that he started to feel a connection toward drafting and architecture. By the time of his high school graduation, he had coordinated with his parents to allow for a small funding of assistance to travel the vast region of the United States in order to find himself. Once everything was planned and ready, he went on a trip across the country stopping at various locations to get to know each town he visited, quite well.

Across the US

It was a bright and sunny summer afternoon, when he hugged his parents and bid them farewell. Little did he know that this might be the last time that he would ever see them. Still, he had developed a plan and presented it to his parents, "Mom and Dad, would it be possible, and I have some of the details right here, for me to travel from town-to-town and city-to-city, to figure out what it is that I would like to do with the rest of my life? We all know I enjoy architecture, but I would really like to know if there is anything else that might pull at me. Ultimately, I plan on settling down somewhere and making you proud."

"Of course, that would be fine, Son," said Mr. Cooper. "If you ever need anything, all you need to do is ask. I trust you will do well no matter where you go, and it is a good idea to ask yourself some pretty tough questions. Always try to consider why it is you will be doing something, how it is that you will get it done, and then ask yourself what your plan is as the result of all your efforts. I assure you that if you do this, you will be able to look back on your life and be proud of the actions you chose and the various accomplishments that lay before you, no matter how rich or poor you may be."

Mrs. Cooper followed that up, "Always know that we love you, Son. We love you no matter your choices. We know you have great potential, and it is up to you to figure out exactly what that is. We will all have challenges in life, and it is ours to learn from them. We cannot let the actions of others ever bring us down, but instead, we need to try to see the good in our world and in others, no matter how the various effects of our setting might try to affect us."

Content with the advice of his parents and double checking the contents of his humble vehicle one last time, he made a mental note to stop at the gas station before heading east on his long-term journey.

His first stop, of course, was his state capital, "The City of Trees." His first location to visit was the Capitol Museum, which had such a rich variety of culture and artistry that he couldn't help but feel inspired. Throughout his one-week stay there, while camping in a nearby tent-city, he took the time to see the guided tours and museums and enjoy some of the delicious meals of a few of their highly touted restaurants, courtesy of the funds his parents had provided him, in part because of their love for him, and in part because he had worked so hard for them around their yard while growing up. He fully planned to pay them back.

Before leaving, he stopped at the Crocker Art Museum and was again blown away. This was one of the first of these cultural art centers within the US, built in 1885, yet the architecture, the various cultures from all over the world, and the art all represented such a rich blend of sophistication and imagery. Within his mind, he was filled with gratitude for having taken the time, before moving on to Reno, Nevada, where he stayed in Lubbock.

After settling into his camp area, he drove into Reno and found a large parking area, paid the fees, and made his way to the Pioneer Center, which was a non-profit location that sponsored ballet, philharmonic, and many other cultural and spectacular types of show. He enjoyed the ballet that played that night, and while he waited, he toured the building, admiring the architecture there. Built in 1968, this building was five years older than he was, it had a modern and creative vibe, the type he enjoyed most, and this dazzled him, as mid-century Populuxe designs always did. He knew his architecture well and never settled for the mundane.

In Salt Lake, while keeping up with the theme, he was amazed as he beheld the Salt Lake City Temple and the Tabernacle that was nearby. While there, he met a lovely young lady, named Amina, and every bit the Nubian Princess the history of her name indicated it was. Amina was a warrior who had been given the acclaim of setting up one of the first uniting governance systems in far-west Africa. Now, the young lady he was entranced by, was a kind, gentle, and friendly person. She invited him to a dance his one Saturday there, and then to go to church with him the very next day. The congregation was just as receptive, kind, and friendly, and they welcomed him with open arms, despite being the only attendee there of such a pasty white complexion. Regardless, he felt appreciated, and never forgot how, as an outsider, he was brought in with kindness, leaving behind it all, a sweet taste of each of his memories of the past.

Traveling south and then east to Denver, and then on a south-bound detour to Colorado Springs, he had called up and met with a number of architects for beautiful homes in the lovely city just below the red mountains, and not too far from the Garden of the Gods. Several of these architects had impressive designs that blended with the rocks, the trees, and the overall areas they were situated within. It impressed him that designs could be integrated so well with the Earth around them yet be so appealing.

While in Colorado, he visited the Olympic Training Center, and appreciated all the city's cultural nuance.

Upon arriving to Kansas City, James made sure to stop by the Kemper Museum, enjoying the large atrium and its articulated skylight. Building began two years prior and the building had just opened not too long before he visited. Again, he was taken back by the beauty of the minds of those who designed this edifice. All that he saw suggested calm and creativity, and he embraced the imagination that was on display from within.

No matter where he went, while viewing each stunning piece of architecture, James would often recall the words of one famous architect, in the US, Gyo Obata, who once stated, "Buildings should be designed around people, and for people: buildings can be and must be more than an economic and efficient functioning machine. We believe that buildings must be designed to provide qualities of beauty both inside and out: qualities that contribute to people's sense of well-being and happiness."

He shared the same views as Gyo and admired his panache and character.

Traveling through Missouri, he saw an Amish covered stagecoach, with a beautiful young lady selling bread and jam, stopped, purchased, chatted for a few minutes, and continued through to Illinois, where he traveled north to Chicago, to take in the James R. Thompson Center. Walking inside, he looked up and appreciated its unique qualities. It was as if he was peering up in the atrium seeing every floor, and each with its own internal balcony.

Continuing, he paid a few tolls, before getting onto Interstate 196 to Highway 131 and on to Grayling. No matter his love for architecture, there was something that caught his heart about this beautiful and small town. *"I've got to settle here for a while, for sure,"* he thought.

Passing through Bay City, on his trek east, he noticed an advertisement for architectural education and jobs related to it, for a corporation, called YY Construction Corp. For James, it was as if it were a sign from above, *"I'll start here, and I hope with all my heart that I can return to Grayling."*

After absorbing the sights and sounds of New York, James arrived in Boston, Massachusetts, and stopped at the Kennedy Presidential Library and Museum, enjoyed its qualities, pored through a few books on architecture, and then continued through Maine, with always something intriguing that captured his intrigue.

From California to Maine, James had visited many beautiful hot spots, yet through it all, and despite the fact that he loved every town he visited, he recalled his moments most fondly with his time spent in Michigan and returned to live there following his long trip with the intention of settling down.

Settling Down

His parents, proud of him for branching out, forging his own path, and exploring his country and professional whims, financed his training. While in school, in Bay City, courtesy of YY Construction Corp, and because of his love of all things to do with architecture, design, and having a unique belief in quality, efficiency, and detail that always accompanied his panache for artistry, he became well-versed in so much of the material covered in the curriculum and earned a large variety of certifications in several of the construction professions, in short order.

James took his qualifications, and as agreed, worked for this well-established high-technology architectural firm, based out of Bay City.

In those days, as long as you walked in filled out the hiring forms, and showed up eager to begin working for anyone, a person could be hired on a trial basis. With little experience or skill and on-the-job training, in many cases, they would send the new hire to get the proper qualifications and training, on their dime, if they were ambitious enough and showed enough creative spirit.

If the new employee met the company's goals and the company met the new hires goals, they could stay on for the long-haul with further opportunities for college advancement and a strong resume of certifications.

In those days, morale was high, people worked hard, employees began to soar intellectually, and businesses seemed to thrive.

James did just that. He dedicated his life to his pursuits in developing, building, and improving upon all manner of architectural buildings, laboratories, offices, and industrial complexes throughout the country, while developing his style of campuses and architecture. As time went by, he travelled the world, building in a manner benefiting the consumer and the company the best way he knew. He believed that if he built something, it ought to be made to last and with high quality.

Every edifice that he and his crew were involved with could last centuries in original form and stood the test of time, unless as time went by, they weren't properly maintained. In most cases, buildings constructed by James' crew endured regardless.

Starting young, five years in, by the age of twenty-two, he had demonstrated an uncanny knack for leadership and craftsmanship. James completed his Bachelor of Applied Science in Management during his free time, and because of his diligence, the corporation he worked for promoted him and assigned him to an office in Grayling.

James achieved his goal of settling in the location that he wished to settle in, at least for a time. While there, as he built his team, some of the employees were local, and others moved in.

Here, he was able to manage all projects sent his way by taking on tasks himself or delegating them to his crew as a regional architectural and construction manager.

Within his first year as manager, James engaged with and got to know all the people who were employed at his new office. He developed a fully-trained and closely-knit crew of ninety-seven personnel, in which he was the ninety-seventh.

James worked hard with them and together they helped him design iron-clad management systems and integrated a worker-leadership environment optimizing worker participation, capacity, and process flow, without fear of loss in wages or respect.

No stranger to reason, common sense, intellect, and emotional intelligence, was something that came natural to James, and he could see the writing on the wall, so-to-speak, when it came to corporate.

He had a keen eye with a fine balance of rational thought and intuition, so it was second-nature for him to know who would fit in well and where within his various teams. If the truth were told, everyone worked well with each other because James had routinely taken the time to interview them. He integrated them within the various teams, helped them to resolve their concerns and doubts, motivated them toward higher learning, and was deeply involved with anyone who struggled without thought for shame in any way, garnering even more loyalty.

His crew and their teams were the best in the construction industry because he would lead by example and manage with common sense while affording them the opportunity to shine and cross-coordinate between the various teams and their members. He helped build and foster goodwill from one worker or team lead to another, no matter the title. Wearing his rank on his sleeves was never his thing; he led well, he was kind, and he was loved.

Indeed, James' highly-rated and highly-valued crew of ninety-seven became appreciated, recognized for their phenomenal results worldwide, and were awarded and applauded regularly. James' influence on his crew extended even further, to include all the families in the community of Grayling or any community he and his crew happened to be in worldwide. Every Halloween, Memorial Day, Thanksgiving, Christmas, Easter, Fourth of July, and every other special day, he would host a community event to raise morale and encourage enjoyment of education.

James was loved, but it never went to his head. He knew that increasing the health of the home and the work environments reduced unhealthy forms of stress, which affected everything else, to include the community, in a cyclical manner. So, he worked in the manner his parents had taught him, and as a result, he found that he was overall increasing camaraderie, innovation, and loyalty. He safeguarded his crewmembers' employment, listened to them, and gave them proper and due acknowledgment.

As times changed throughout the years, many were affected by companies and corporations tied up in legal issues, an increasing need to cut costs to be more attractive to investors and shareholders, and YY Construction Corp was affected significantly. No matter the influence from the outside, James seemed to go to bat for his employees, and had gained the trust of the corporation he worked for.

James made sure that safety briefs were genuinely focused on the well-being aspect of his workers and all involved. He instructed them with clarity on the details of each mission, protected their benefits, and ensured they had two months of vacation every single year, even after retirement, all expenses paid.

Before each weekend James held briefs giving accolades to those who shined in production and participated in community efforts wherever they happened to be. He delivered small pep-talks to the whole crew about how each of their weekly efforts had impacted the mission of the company in a positive way. Keeping things real, he was kind and compassionate. Key points, statistics, and an early release with a full day's wages to his whole crew was an honored tradition with him, when daily and weekly goals were met.

More time went by, and along with it, more cuts were made. The revolving door was thick throughout the country, in many corporations struck with fewer resources to do the job and pay the bills, or even compensate its employees, and toxicity was on the rise throughout. Nevertheless, since James' team was the most productive and produced the highest quality and most efficient output of the entire corporation, YY Construction Corp left the 97 alone. His bosses left his crew on their own in so many other ways, but in certain ways, it was becoming increasingly clear that things might change soon, and in a way that he could see might affect his crew negatively.

For now, YY Construction Corp allowed him to manage his team and run his projects the way he saw fit. It may have seemed as though no one in the hierarchy had noticed or even cared, but to a certain extent they were mired in bureaucracy, and those who knew better actually did care in their own way. The 97 worked well and were a major source of positive-flowing revenue, but the big wigs thought that if James would stop continuously spoiling his crew, they could pad their wallets a little more, and they began find ways to break it to him, more obviously.

James was quite intelligent and perceptive, so when he heard corporate's tone when addressing other team leads in each brief, he could tell that what he saw was his bosses increasingly behaving ruthlessly to them.

Somehow, upper management knew James had a heart of gold and they noticed enough to realize that YY Construction Corp would become bankrupt without him. So, they left him and his crew to their own devices, mostly because he'd earned his current position anyway. It was enough for James, for now, to shield his ninety-six employees from the "titans" in corporate.

Their meetings were as adult meetings ought to be, where each of his crewmembers was present with open-minds, they were well-studied and had thoughtful and problem-solving mind-sets creating a positive and innovative collaboration for a smooth rhythm of events. An atmosphere of constructive behavior, clarity on what steps would be taken each day on the various projects, and appreciation for productivity that graced each meeting.

Because of the type of management style James chose of integrated experience, input, clarity, and common sense in the communication of ideas, the workers were all very closely-knit. If someone had questions, they wouldn't make fun, they would help and answer right away. Along with collaborative meetings, he would interview his workers individually at least once a month and ask each one 'how things honestly were,' what could be done to improve processes, increase productivity, the quality, morale, and the overall features of the buildings and facilities they put up.

He had a very organized way of spreading the wealth of responsibilities while integrating his teams with each other. Like a well-greased machine, everything operated smoothly and helped every project and mission move forward. Corporate left him alone, even when they carried out their annual budget-cutting, people firings, and its own uninspiring and saddening downward spiral, among the other unlucky crews, which was quite an exemplary representation of the behavior demonstrated by many companies throughout the country, and unfortunately this critically affected the overall economy, and quite possibly the future of YY Construction Corp.

From the vantage point of anyone who took pride in proper management, everything that corporate was doing wrong, he was doing right. His team was keeping the corporation afloat, and the corporates knew it. He knew that if money wasn't the overarching goal and instead well-being trumped all else, the company would stay strong, no matter the trends of the day. So, of all the things they did wrong, perhaps the one thing they did right was to leave him and his team alone. They knew that if James and his crew did what they did best, the corporation would never disintegrate into bankruptcy, but somehow, they couldn't see that past his team.

What they should have done long ago was promote him and his team members. He had mentored, trained, and coached each of them to be leaders in their own right, allowing him to continue to lead in his own way and have his management and leadership style influence the entire company, but the company didn't seem to see it that way, since they were increasingly far too influenced by powers beyond their ability to control.

Rather instead, YY Construction Corp continued to hire and fire other team leads, other project managers, and other regional representatives, and all in order to get the experienced personnel they were looking for, without any investment in the form of training on their part, and all to acquiesce the established status quo of mediocre management and one of many negative factors hindering an increase to a higher quality of life.

Other than James, the other leaders were merely intent on opportunistic promotions, pretentious status, money for the love of it, and wielding their power in a manner that resulted in a revolving door, affecting the rest of the corporation. They viewed people as chess pieces, and their foolish intrigues were a part of the game. They thought they had the macro view, but they failed to see that while caught up in greed and lust for power, they were stuck in myopia, forgetting the greater aspects and the untold wealth of resources in the minds of their own people and the unlimited wealth in and throughout the Universe itself.

It seemed to be that YY Construction Corp was awash in hiring merely to feed the toxic cycle. This they did because their primary focus was something other than the well-being of those who worked for them or their customers. For YY Construction Corp, it wasn't about the company, the products, or the customers, it was solely about pleasing and padding the wallets of the investors, the shareholders, and pulling the strings. It was about power without true or benevolent purpose. In summation, the rest of the company forgot to invest in the employees, the customer, and the company.

James saw everyone who worked for him as more than a pawn. They were real, and they were visceral. Just like the value he saw in himself and his efforts, he saw value in them, and he viewed each one of those under his purview as precious, unique, and pivotal within the team. Virtues such as these, deeply woven within his character and evidenced through his choice of management and leadership styles resulted in the highest-quality of outcomes that in-turn bred loyalty and innovation within his crew, and both worker and customer satisfaction.

On occasion, there would be a heartfelt retirement, where the closest crewmembers to the retiree would go out of their way and pool their resources to pay for a nice meal for their entire crew and their families, provide meaningful retirement gifts, talk about the retiree's contributions and highlight how their efforts led to significant improvements over time. They would even talk over nice beverages about the years ahead. Every year, even those who retired would join in on the large crew-wide vacation with James.

Because James' crew and each of his teams had high morale and motivation, they also had high levels of ingenuity and integrity as a team, exceeded safety standards, developed common-sense work ethics, and were like family members—always checking in on each other and aware of those who were struggling for whatever reason. They even made it a point to include those who had retired and passed thoughtfully-worded cards around for each members' special occasions, or sympathy cards, and meaningful gifts for any tough times.

When vacation time came around, since they all shared schedules, they would plan for a group event with their coworkers and families to go to lakes on houseboats, adorned with hikes and a myriad of exciting activities, to include backpacking to potholes or swim holes that were a result of waterfalls coming from snowy mountains forging peaks into the clouds above, and were only accessible after a sizeable journey.

With safety in numbers and associated high morale, everyone naturally carried their own weight, and these shared vacation trips would result in phenomenal successes providing the much-needed break from the rigorous routines at work. On weekends, they would go camping and look up at the stars with high-powered telescopes the crew had purchased collectively from personal funds, to gaze at deep sky objects, distant galaxies, and the details of planets and stars nearby.

They would often go to museums, zoos, engage in the healing art of passive ornithology, visit art centers, geology centers, or engage in anything educational and fun. They would do all of this together. Together, life was fun, the spouses, the children, those who had no children, or no spouse, or no date whatsoever, they all took part in the shared enjoyment.

Looking out for one another and helping each other out where help was needed and asked for, further bonded them as a cohesive unit. When someone asked for clarity on any item of concern, it was given freely without heckling or harsh judgment.

So often, they would spot each other for holidays, visit sick family members at home or in the hospital, or prepare the latest of healthy and delicious cuisines for coworkers and their families, as they were grieving or otherwise experiencing hardships.

All of his efforts, from protecting their benefits allowing for vacations, to work compensation, to higher education, to providing an inclusive environment for those who had retired, and for all family members and significant others, resulted in work output that was met with high quality and high efficiency.

His leadership, his virtues, his personal ethics, and his management and working styles proved to be successful, resulting in technologically advanced buildings with infrastructure built from the ground up for the customer and the community in top-notch condition.

James, his team leads, and every person in his crew made certain that each person that worked for him was properly taken care of, and he negotiated regularly with YY Construction Corp to safeguard their employment and their benefits. He also did everything he could to ensure that they could go home each day knowing they had done amazing work, they could be proud of their efforts, and that they were properly compensated, reducing any unnecessary form of stress, thus freeing up creativity and innovation.

While austere to some, the corporation seemed like an alright place for him to continue to make his mark. His biggest concern was for his team, protecting the 97, and that included everyone and everything special in their lives. Those who worked for him were his responsibility, he had their backs, and it was on him to protect them from the negative slope of chaos provided by his "superiors," and many other economic think tanks of the day.

Since he had no spouse, no children, or no dog waiting for him at home, he gave himself to those he worked with, if anything to ensure that those he knew had a wonderful and happy life of comfort, purpose, and meaning that would drive their future goals. Even though he was thirty-five, he was an old soul and a boss who his employees were proud of, both in public and in private.

Going Global

From day one, James hit the road running on building some of the most beautiful environments bathing some of the most magnificent of architecture. He seemed to be one and one with Nature and a desirable outcome. From libraries to laboratories to emission-free industrial centers, James and his crew, the 97, were in it to not only impress, but to inspire the masses. His management style had everyone working together in every aspect of cradle to grave operations, as it related to design, building, and adding the finishing details and touches.

In February of 1995 one of James' first projects during the economic boom of the newly freed Russia, was in the breath-taking and beautiful Ural Mountains near the town of Yuryaton, where they built a magnificent getaway hotel for the new business tycoons that grew financially in the upswing that existed due to free commerce and high morale. Despite the frigid temperatures of late winter, he and his team completed the project in two months, and the now deceased billionaires were at the time alive and grateful.

Unfortunately, politics there had taken a turn for the worst and disappearances became exceedingly common.

After traveling around the world, one project after another that year, his crew finished a project that November in China. The request had been to build a resort and hotel that would seamlessly integrate with the Jinshanling section of the Great Wall of China, about seventy-eight miles northeast of Beijing. The six-and-a-half-mile-long section he worked near was in Luanping County, Hebei Province, with mountains and rolling hills everywhere, covered in beautiful forestry. Perhaps his greatest pastime, besides building this exquisite resort, was the lack of light pollution, and the ability to view the nighttime sky, which always intrigued him and his crew.

The history of more than 2300 years of culture and whispers of the past seemed to hang in the air. As one of the Seven Wonders of the World, this section carried memories of obvious maintenance. Without it, it would have crumbled after the time of the Ming Dynasty.

Upon completion, the resort James and his crew built there was lavish, luxurious, and virtually hidden. For vacation, his entire crew booked an opportune excursion to the base of the mountains where Mount Everest was located and hiked to the peak without losing a single person. They then travelled east, and secured passage on a heavily armed cruise liner, for protection in the event of piracy, to the island of Bali.

The first project they completed in 1996, from February through March, was another luxurious resort, near Kuta Village, southeast of Denpasar, Bali's capital city, and on the edge of the Seminyak. His crew had already demonstrated a knack for procuring resources, and throughout the many islands in the archipelago of Indonesia, untapped resources were in plenty supply. Luckily, James and his crew had friends of a friend, no matter where they went, who knew the local languages and the lay of the land. This helped his planning teams to have all materials on hand before arriving to begin the project. Once they got started, it was like clockwork, and the construction teams would be done in six weeks, with some time to spare.

Meanwhile, the planning teams worked with James, who maintained contact with his iridium satellite phone, and they would coordinate for the upcoming project well and in advance. As the years flew by, he'd built resorts all over the world and in the US itself. He even upgraded the facilities with his team, in Grayling, Michigan.

One experience he recalled quite enthusiastically, if ever asked, was his experience in Albany, Australia, next to Perth, on the southern portion of the southwest edge of this island continent. Just like in northern California, this location had fire season. Shortly after they built the new eco-friendly manufacturing plant, replete with hotels, eateries with delicious and nutrient dense food, and parks for walking, jogging, and bicycling, in 2003, he and his crew helped to put out a nearby wildfire, before it crept west and into town. Growing up in California, he'd discovered a fire-retardant weed near his home that had stalled the fire that would have gone up the hill and burnt his home down. Knowing the areas near Perth likewise suffered from natural and manmade wildfires, he'd ordered, shipped, and dispersed thousands of acres of these weeds, with permission from the local governments, throughout the county. So, when the fires came, he and his crew, who worked as volunteers for the local fire department had those fires easily contained.

Finished with construction, and through proper instruction of land conservation to prevent forest fires, his team was able to relax and enjoy the nearby beaches.

In the breadth of thirteen years, with projects in the US and various other developments spread globally, to include in Riyadh, Abu Dhabi, Dubai, the UK, Japan, the Philippines, India, Israel, Estonia, Spain, France, Kenya, New Zealand, and Canada, all told, James and his crew completed sixty-five as the crew chief of the 97.

Each of the buildings and projects the 97 worked on were immense. For every project they completed, they won accolades, awards, and the envy of many other notable and famous designers and architects. Working for YY Construction Corp as the 97 leader, James Cooper was phenomenal, as were each of his employees.

One of the biggest agreements with corporate he made, the which he considered an immeasurable success, due to their extraordinary efforts, was the ability to take his crew, the 97, on two-month vacations, anywhere in the US or throughout the world, and that he did.

His crew had been to many places few could only dream of. They'd been ice fishing as close as they could get to the North Pole in Greenland. They'd enjoyed the Northern Lights and Igloo Resorts in Norway. They'd been on cruises from Alaska to Chile. And now, on this occasion and for this vacation trip, James, his crew, his retirees, any significant others, and their children had planned to go to a Massachusetts college town named Cambridge. It was thick with history and intellect.

Presently, they were in Cambridge to check out Harvard and MIT for three of the crew's children who were preparing to go there for higher education. As always, they included within their planning visits to a variety of hotspots in the surrounding area. Little did they know that things were about to get quite a bit more interesting.

Chapter 06: Vacation in Cambridge

Database Moon Archive, Celestial-Sol Entry Date: 2018 December 25 – Experiential biography, as taught to Vesha Celeste, about James Cooper, his crew, "The 97," and the infrastructural and principal foundations of Pathway, during her Virtual Universe training, within Pathway Covert Campus in Melrose, MA. Contained within are thoughts from Eliza Williams, Yesha Alevtina, and James Cooper. Training Given by Yesha Alevtina, President of Pathway Industries, 2015-2022.

With his entire crew early on in 2008, James travelled to Cambridge, Massachusetts, on a vacation that would change everything and much of it beyond their wildest of imaginations, and they had seen a lot. As was typical for James and his crew on vacation, every day, late in the morning, everyone would meet up for group check-ins at a rented grange which had been pre-arranged and paid for by him, since their projects paid them quite well.

While there and gathered together at the beginning of each day, his crew, his retirees, and all their guests and families shared stories over brunch and ensured everyone was well-fed.

After brunch, James would speak, then others would come up as agreed upon, and he would make sure everyone had the ability to keep in contact throughout the day and that they had a daily itinerary. As a crew, they wanted to ensure that no one was lost, the children were safe, and everyone had plans that were amenable to change so that no one was alone. In James' words, "No one should be left out." Notwithstanding their plans, everyone was allowed some "me time." The intent was to ensure no one was lonely or at risk for malevolent exploitation, and that could happen anywhere. Human trafficking was on the rise, and his party and even the children were very aware and well-versed on measures to take should someone approach them, and it just seemed awkward. The simplest step to take was to avoid being alone, at least without the team you were with, aware, and nearby.

On this day, after getting ready, sharing breakfast, directing his meeting at the grange, and spending time with his entire crew, he was with a small group of thirteen. This was big enough to protect them, and small enough to keep eyes on everyone. Everyone looked out for themselves and those in their team. They'd been through the drill before, successfully.

They'd visited the campuses of MIT and Harvard and walked around town to see some of the many sights and sounds. The events of the day had been edifying and delightful. It was just before dusk that his merry band of travelers found they were famished. Hoping for a nearby restaurant, they weren't disappointed in the least.

There it was, the T.O. This restaurant was on the street they happened to find themselves on, with a sign that suggested only the finest served. So, his group, which consisted of seven employees, three team leads and three crew members, one of whom was in training, a retiree, and six family members, to include a crew member's spouse and his eleven-year-old son, a team lead's wife and his thirteen-year-old son, and the retiree's seventeen-year-old granddaughter, were all mingled together.

"The T.O.," as it read in big blue and white artistic letters and a rustic cedar wood background, seemed a quaint yet eclectic restaurant, so they decided to venture inside for dinner. As they entered, it was grand and rather posh.

Upon seating and after gathering everyone's dinner requests, James stood in line to make the group order. It wasn't long before he engaged in a conversation with an intriguing young lady who happened to be standing in the line right in front of him. Something drew him in to talk to her, although he couldn't figure out what it could be, so he asked her if she had been to this restaurant before.

This very attractive young lady introduced herself. During their brief conversation, he discovered that she was there by herself, and he offered her a place at his table with him and his crew.

Before beginning the orders, he briefly introduced each of his guests. As he did, they stood up, not out of obligation, but because this enchanting young lady exuded a very respectable authority about her.

Starting at the far end going clockwise, he began, "This is Anne and her boyfriend, Ryan, to her left." Anne and Ryan, both of a rather large stature, blonde hair and blue eyes, and most likely of Scandinavian origins, nodded and smiled. She was dressed to impress and so was he. Her blonde locks were in a pristine up-do, and he was clean-cut, shaven, and his wavy hair was parted to the left. All the men kept their hair trimmed short on the sides and back, like James, and she could tell beyond their professional appearance that they were all very close, like a family. There was nothing odd, but it was surprisingly peculiar and pleasant to witness.

"Hi, Anne and Ryan, nice to meet you. You both look wonderful. I'm Eliza."

"It's nice to meet you too, Eliza." After introducing themselves, Anne and Ryan nodded again, smiled, and took their seats.

"Next and to our right is Ethel," said James. "She worked for us for many years and retired from YY Construction Corp about two years ago. She is here with her granddaughter, Crystal, to her left. Her husband couldn't make it yet on this trip. His place of employment couldn't grant him leave, at least not until Monday. He's on-call in Grayling right now." Ethel's hair was silver, but Eliza could tell that at one time it had been red. Around her green irises, her fading limbal rings, or the black rings around the irises of people's eyes, gave her away.

She must have been a freckled and ravishing beauty in her day. Her persona was fine, she had lived a full life, but she had a very big future ahead of her, the likes of which she would never have guessed, and in this room, one that only Eliza could have fathomed.

"Nice to meet you both, Ethel and Crystal. Beautiful names. I'm so sorry your husband, and," she paused, looking at Ethel, then toward Crystal, and continued, "Your grandfather couldn't make it." Crystal's eyes matched her name. She was an exquisite, blonde, and intellectual beauty.

"It's quite alright, he'll be here in a couple of days. Nice to meet you too, Eliza." Ethel and Crystal sat down, grabbed their napkins, and placed them on their laps.

"This is Tom, to Crystal's left."

"Hi, Tom," said Eliza. He too, was tall and very well built, had pale skin, dark hair, and blue eyes. He had a unique, yet attractive personality that suggested that he too might be a benevolent leader worked out often and worked hard.

Tom tried not to swoon in Eliza's presence, but he blushed as he spoke anyway, "Nice to meet you." Tom then did a minor curtsy, rather than a bow, considering the limited space between his chair and the table, he then smiled, trying not to look too embarrassed, and then he sat down.

"You each have wonderful manners. I suppose once we get to know each other we'll be able to be a little less formal. Nevertheless, I am impressed," said Eliza.

"Thank you, Eliza, and next to Tom is Joseph. His girlfriend couldn't make it today. She is a paralegal, and the legal office she works at could not let her go since it is just after the New Year and they are swamped. I had a chat with her boss, so they agreed to let her come to meet us in a few days. She and Joseph are a cute couple though." Joseph had brown hair and light brown eyes. He too was of large stature, very physically fit, and had a very benevolent personality.

"I'm sure both of you are a wonderful match! What a beautiful group you all make!" affirmed Eliza.

"Thank you, Eliza," Joseph said with an attitude of gratitude and kind sincerity, looking toward Eliza, then toward James at peace.

James continued, "We'll be sitting next to Joseph." Joseph nodded, smiled, and sat down.

"On the opposite side of the table and continuing clockwise, is Paul, with his wife, Holly, and their son, Jaimie." Jaimie was eleven and had just begun going through puberty, so he found he couldn't stop looking just below Eliza's neckline, she caught him, smiled, and then turned her gaze to Holly and then to Paul. Paul was a very handsome, clean-cut, tall and muscular man with black hair, glasses, and golden-brown eyes that contrasted well with his dark brown skin. His wife was elegant, graceful, and dignified like a Nubian princess, yet both exuded benevolence, charm, kindness, and each of them was dressed in their Sunday best.

"It's nice to meet you three. You have a handsome son." She turned to him and winked to let him know he was off the hook. He gathered himself together, looked into her eyes and smiled.

"Thank you," said Molly.

"It's an honor to meet you, and thank you," said Paul, sitting down with Molly and Jaimie, as those before them had, after their introductions.

"This is Mike, his wife, Heather, and son, Edward." Mike had blue eyes, brown hair, and just like the other men, he was tall, muscular, clean-cut and clean-shaven, and dressed to impress. Impress he did, his wife was impressed with his every move, and just like two youthful lovebirds they complemented each other quite well. She too had brown hair, blue eyes, and she was curvy yet physically fit in all the breath-taking ways one could imagine.

"Nice to meet you, Mike, Heather, and Edward." Just like Jaimie, Edward was in his teens, thirteen to be exact, and his jaw was agape, and like Jaime, he was caught by Eliza too. No one else had noticed. "Cute young man," she said to let him know he too was off the hook.

"Finally, this is Brandy," who, like Tom, had curtsied due to the space between table and chair. She smiled and stayed standing. Her green eyes, red hair, and freckles were pretty and her character in every way was breath-taking. James' crew was one of a kind. They were close and they were very polite. Eliza could tell they must have travelled the world and been great diplomats, all.

"It's an honor to meet you, Eliza."

"It's an honor to meet you too," she reciprocated. Then Brandy sat down.

His crew seemed very pleased to meet her. As they saw Eliza, they were taken back by how this beautiful, assertive, and gentle young lady was inviting, affable, and gracious. After introductions, Eliza glanced quickly at each order, made astute recommendations from the T.O. menu, and returned to the line with James. While James and Eliza were away, everyone at the table agreed the night with Eliza was bound to be unforgettable. His crew and their present guests were grateful to meet her and were especially happy that they had cleared a place for her to sit beside James.

It wasn't until later that they would discover that she had paid for their meals. In line, James and Eliza had some wonderful conversations, which later carried over to the large and quite eager dinner table. They sat and while waiting for food, they engaged in small talk. There seemed to be a harmonious chatter about everyone at the table.

Chuckles were shared, stories were heard, and tales of James and his leadership were told. There was never a moment of awkward silence, perhaps an occasion of peaceful quiet, right after dinner was served. It was then that Eliza began a back and forth conversation in order to get to know them a little more. She wanted to learn a little more about "the 97" and YY Construction Corp.

"Please, tell me a little about yourselves and anything you'd like. Perhaps we can start in the same order as we were introduced? Can we start with you two, Anne and Ryan?"

"Of course," said Anne, who had a deep tenor yet still very feminine voice, "I met Ryan about ten years ago while at the hardware store getting some tools, and he happened to be looking for the same item I was. We began talking about projects we were working on and we hit it off right away. That's when we decided to start going out, hanging out and having so much fun. Although, for us, going out involved working together on each other's homes engaging in do-it-yourself projects to up the value, in the event we were to sell.

"One day it donned on me, why not have one of us move in with the other? We could still both be employed, but it would be two incomes in one home instead of two. We realized after a couple of years though that only one of us needed to work, so the other could take care of the home, the garden, the cooking and other frequent tasks that are necessary for a healthy and happy environment. He sold his home and moved in with me. We both knew that since James had become the boss at my workplace and given his involvement in the community and his character, my work environment would be the healthier of the two and it paid the best.

"James has gone to bat for all of us at one time or another, or on multiple occasions, and for that reason, we're all together like this today. Plus, I was compensated for my hours at work much more than Ryan was, and in a better place compared to the toxic work environment he had been forced to endure, so naturally, we decided to have him move in and he became our ever-so-gorgeous homemaker.

"It has worked out excellent since then. Ryan is kind of my own personal chef. As an added benefit, during vacations every year, while camping, he's the happy guy at the grill, and everyone else seems to enjoy it too."

Ryan heard Anne's pause and saw her smile, suggesting it was his turn to speak up, "Ah, thank you, Anne. I agree, Anne never comes home stressed, and I have complete confidence that it is because of the way she is treated at work. Every member of the crew and their families have brought me in like one of their own, and I have never worked for YY Construction Corp or the 97.

"I'm proud of James, he's built a wonderful team. He's done a good job for all of us, even those of us who could be considered extended family. We all feel like we belong. As things are, I can be at home trying to bring her a little piece of heaven, or travel with everyone on projects all over the world. Ultimately, I'm happy when she is."

Eliza was intrigued and impressed with this unique couple. As she ate and listened, she discovered that Anne was forty-two-years-old, and Ryan was forty. Eliza also learned that Anne was James' Team 07 Lead. "Please, can you tell me a little about the 97, what these teams are, and what do they do? I'm quite intrigued."

James let Anne explain the details, "It has been thirteen years since James was promoted as Regional Architectural and Construction Manager. As far as his duties are concerned, he did pretty much the same then as he does now, and he has always done everything well.

"His title changed to Global Project Manager since the corporation is trying to keep up with the times. We operate using James' own management construction subcontracting firm, called "the 97," and it is quite different from YY Construction Corp.

"For each day, each week, and each year, he maintained a consistent cycle of integration, training, operations, responsibilities, and leadership opportunities to prevent our crew from growing bored or stale from the same sundry and monotonous details.

"Only four people have retired during his time in management, one of them is Ethel right here," Anne pointed to her left at Ethel and continued, "And she, as well as Sophie, Ted, and Julio were thus given honors and fond farewells. No matter, they are always considered a part of our family." She smiled at Ethel. "Since they are now gone from the workforce, four people were integrated into and properly trained to cycle through one of four specialized coordination teams and eventually to one of eight construction teams.

"Brandy, to my right, has been with us for a little more than two years now and will be back in Team 04 when we return from vacation, where the integration into our crew begins. Now, she's among the best in the industry." She then looked at Brandy, smiled, and continued.

"Each of James' twelve teams consist of eight personnel, all of whom will ultimately complete five major projects each year, or one project every two months. In this way, from each of the twelve personnel that belong to one of eight construction teams, four people are delegated and dispersed in a cyclical manner to one of four coordination teams.

"From there, teams are cycled in a constant two-month rotation. With ninety-six construction team members, beyond James, who considers himself the 97th, this means that for each project sixty-four are in construction teams while thirty-two are in coordination teams. With his ten-month work cycle, followed by two months of vacation, James ensures each of us is the corporation's most lucrative, productive, constructive, educated, motivated, and capable crew around.

"The first year he ran his operations using his cycle, we completed five major projects, and we completed at least that many projects each year, from that time forward, with award-winning results. With twelve teams in total, he organized our crew to allow an individual worker to go through an entire integration cycle after twelve projects. Essentially, an individual would work eight construction team-specific and four coordination team assignments in training and production cycles.

"Team 01 is the Daily Project Coordination Team. This and all teams have eight crewmembers or one from each construction team. Unique to this team, each of these crewmembers are the ones who are responsible for daily project communication, task coordination, and timely completion. They are the ultimate go-to personnel for the timeliness of accomplishment and details of any current project. Team 01, each of whom cycle in from Team 02 of the previous project, are in effect conducting daily coordination for the project they planned during the previous cycle they were in. As such, they see through with clarity to the completion of their project, and once their project is finished, they cycle back into one of eight construction teams for eight subsequent assignments.

"Team 02 is the Succeeding Project Design and Planning Team, whose eight members are responsible for designing, engineering, and planning the completion of the following project. They coordinate with Team 03 for all needed materials, supplies, tools, and storage. Once everything is lined up and squared away for the next project, they provide manning and support to the construction teams as needed until the next project is ready to begin. Once the next project begins, they become Team 01 and assume the duties of that team.

"Team 03 is the Materials and Supply Management Team, whose eight members order all supplies, materials, and storage in coordination with Team 02 for the next project, as well as additional coordination and support for materials, equipment, and supplies needed for the current project by Team 01. They coordinate all transport through Team 05, and once the current project is complete, they cycle into Team 02.

"Team 04 is the Quality Control and Safety Team; whose eight members ensure project quality expectations are met. They coordinate with all of the construction teams and the other coordination teams to ensure repairs or corrections are made in a high quality and safe manner. They advise and brief the entire crew on safety and quality concerns. If there are any new personnel, this was where they are cycled in for training and given exposure to all aspects of each project through the innate nature of quality control. Once the current project is complete, they cycle to Team 03. Brandy is our newest crew member. She has already completed twelve projects with us and will be on Team 04 when we return from our vacation.

"Team 05, or Tom's Team, is the Heavy Equipment Operations and Transportation Team whose eight members coordinate and carry out all aspects of heavy equipment operations alongside Team 01 for the current project, and Teams 02 and 03 for all transportation-related aspects for the next project. In many cases, they are ready for and amenable to any cross-team coordination that might be necessary throughout any of the open projects. As with all construction teams, when project requirements are met, four Team 05 members will be on call each week to ensure project continuity. The others are at liberty to help as needed, spend time with family, or be involved in the communities we visit, or in the community as they please.

"Team 06, or Mike's team, is the Concrete and Masonry Team whose eight members coordinate and carry out their project-related duties while coordinating with Team 01 and the other construction crews to ensure seamless installation of all aspects of laying, pouring, finishing, and completion of concrete projects from buildings to parking areas and underground thorough-fares. They also coordinate all masonry projects and integrate with each construction team to ensure optimum completion efficiency and quality, while meeting plans and specs requirements.

"Team 07, or my team, is the Columns, Beams, and Framing Team whose eight members coordinate primarily with Team 05, as well as with all of the other construction teams to carry out and ensure timely and seamless installation of walls, load-bearing support structures, and upkeep to all aspects of infrastructural integrity, to make a guarantee toward the strength, safety, and security of any finished project handed over to the customer.

"Team 08, or the team that Joseph is on, is the Electrical Team whose eight members install all electrical conduit, electrical wiring, physical and digital connectivity to electrical equipment, and coordinate with each team to ensure electrical integrity and safety of the in-progress and completed product, as per spec from the customer, are met or exceeded. They also coordinate with the other teams to ensure temporary electricity does not reduce workplace safety, slow down project completion, or diminish the project integrity of the infrastructure.

"Team 09, the team Paul is on, is the HVAC/CRAC and Plumbing Team, or, as written out, the Heating, Ventilation, and Air Conditioning slash Computer Room Air Conditioning and Plumbing Team, whose eight members coordinate and install all aspects of air conditioning, heating, ventilation, and all plumbing to include that which is related to potable and non-potable sources. They cross-coordinate with all teams for efficiency and project integrity.

"Team 10 is the Carpentry and Walling Team whose eight members coordinate with all teams to carry out and ensure installation of walls, soundproofing, fire safety, and waterproofing for the project they are currently on, in an efficient and high-quality manner. In many cases, they coordinate with Team 06 for fur out walls, firewalls, security walls, etc.

"Team 11 is the Full-Scope Special Sciences Team whose eight members coordinate with Team 01 and carry out all aspects for the timing of and timely completion of ceilings, dropped ceilings, roofing, flooring, and any newly and specially integrated sciences within the project. They oversee, brief, and execute every aspect of laboratory capabilities, security and safety mechanisms, and industrial facilities installations. They do all of this in a manner that ensures pollution containment, prevention, and repurposing, with technologically advanced aspects necessary for project completion. Much of this is heavily coordinated and verified through Team 04 and then, likewise, carried out. They also are responsible for working with Team 08 on networking, network cabling, and coordinating with Teams 02 and 03 for follow-on projects, and finally for completion of the flooring, raised or carpeted, or otherwise. Crystal has her eyes on this team, and that is why she is planning on going to Harvard, to study an important aspect, biosciences.

"Team 12 is the Detailing and Final Installation Team and these eight members coordinate with each team as is situationally dependent to do detail work, furniture and equipment installation, and they ensure the highest quality delivery and integrity of the project prior to and during the turnover of the project to the customer.

"Because of James' on-the-job and refresh-as-needed training programs, each worker is now well-versed on every aspect of construction, and each of us could effectively be general contractors and are fully-licensed in every aspect of any given project. In this way, we share duties and spend a lot of time helping each other out in areas that need more attention to ensure high quality, high efficiency, and customer satisfaction. As a result, all of our projects have been completed in award-winning fashion and corporate leaders have afforded James more management leeway.

"In total, our crew consists of ninety-six personnel, and he considers himself the ninety-seventh—even though we think of him as the first. Of course, when we hire Crystal, our crew will grow, but who's counting anyway? Eventually, we'll all form a new company with James as the president, but we are all trying to keep that under wraps for now. We'll get there."

Eliza had listened intently, and found it was quite impressive how well their team was in sync with each other. Anne was phenomenal. She was well-educated with a BS in Logistics, had served six years in the Army, was heavily decorated from her services during Desert Storm, and with YY Construction Corp and James she had received a wide variety of certifications. Some of her strongest skills were in carpentry, general contracting, masonry, heavy equipment, and of course, logistics.

Ethel carried the torch from there, and spoke up, "Back in James' early days, he asked me to work with him to build his revolving and coordination schedule. I helped, but he did most of the work. I was merely supportive and cheered him along the way.

"Two years after working for James, my son and daughter-in-law were killed by a drunk driver. James funded the funeral, helped us get by until we were emotionally back on our feet following the devastating news. The only silver lining I can find through that tragedy is that our beautiful granddaughter, Crystal, became a close member of our family in our home, and as a retiree, I had more time to spend with her.

"I was able to teach, mentor, coach, and simply be there for her during each important phase of her life. She was our granddaughter, but we raised her as our own daughter. She is a brilliant young woman, and now she's getting ready to go to Harvard to study biosciences. My husband will be here Monday, otherwise, I would have introduced you. I am sure he would have been excited to meet you. Tom had been hired on, so when I left, he was ready to fill my shoes."

Crystal, seventeen, smiled, hugged her sixty-six-year-old grandmother as if she were her mother, and then looked toward Tom as if to indicate she was still just a little too shy to speak. In some ways, Eliza could tell she crushed on Tom since he was a nice guy and had it together. She introduced him, "And, this is Tom, who is twenty-eight years old. He is James' youngest team lead, for Team 05. He has an associate degree in heavy equipment and logistics and started working at YY Construction Corp just out of high school. You should see some of his personal projects. He is quite the naturally-gifted architect."

"Thank you, Crystal." Tom at first off seemed bashful, but he was quite gracious, yet assertive, where it was necessary. He was also humble. "I was struggling in high school when James took me under his wing. It is because of him that I received my GED, my Associates of Applied Science in Heavy Equipment and Logistics, and certifications on all the typical heavy machinery, along with experience on every job we do, and I was appointed as Team 05 Lead. The crew was very patient with me."

James then sensed Tom's typical selflessness and he spoke up, "There are museums and other buildings all over the world that were designed by you, I might recall." Shifting his gaze toward Eliza, he continued, "Tom is one of my ninety-six best crew members, and Crystal might find herself as part of my Full-Scope Special Sciences Team once she feels ready. Knowing Ethel, I'm sure she'll wait until she has completed her BAS in Biosciences," he said with a friendly smile and an assuring wink toward Tom and Crystal.

There was an age gap, but it was obvious Crystal was awestruck with Tom, who was quite a handsome young man. She had grown up before his eyes, and he hadn't yet seen her as a young woman, rather as the sweet little girl she was when James' entire crew attended her parents' funeral. To him, she was like a little sister, and he'd always respected her in that way. It was a matter of time though, before the stars crossed, and everyone else could tell, but Tom.

After some small talk in Tom's direction, Eliza asked Joseph about his background and he opened up. "My girlfriend, Janine, and I are studying for a BS in Physics, but that is, of course, courtesy of James going to bat for our crew, and education is something that he treasures. Since Janine and I have been together for about thirteen years, he saw that if we were to study as we wished, stress would be reduced, and our lives would be better. He thinks beyond the job.

"I am glad that he found a way for Janine and me to study together with a little extra time each day and tuition assistance. She is currently working as a paralegal and because her place of employment is a bit of a stress-tank, unfortunately, she couldn't be here today. We purchased a home together and share the chores to keep our home in good shape.

"Yes, it is nice taking turns each week; she does some and I do some, and then the following week we switch. I started working with YY Construction Corp about a week before Tom and worked as a handyman making ends meet before signing on. During James' initial hiring phase for his crew, I was recruited to be on his team."

James then spoke up, "He was very gifted in all things electrical, and when I saw his work ethic, I knew I needed him." James smiled at Joseph, Tom, and then at Eliza. She could tell that everyone at the table had outstanding character, and James was an excellent role model.

Eliza enjoyed being able to meet Joseph and looked forward to meeting Janine next week, and from what Joseph shared, she could tell they were a wonderful couple.

Eliza had always appreciated a good education, and she was impressed with the fact that James valued a good education as well, and he even made conveyances for his crewmembers and their significant others or extended family members to reach their academic goals.

"That's amazing, Joseph. I am sorry that Janine couldn't make it. I am sure you look forward to seeing her on Monday. How about you and your family, Paul?"

"My wife and I are originally from the projects in Chicago, Illinois. However, after an escalation in violence, we decided to uproot and move to a quieter part of our country. I worked in Bay City with YY Construction Corp for years and right when James started, I could tell he was going to do very well, for the employee, the employer, and the customer. There was something special about him.

"I can tell you now, many campouts and travels later, that his parents raised him well. He, during his early years and on through to the present day, has had an honorable character, a stellar career, an excellent work ethic, and he cares deeply about all of us and others. When he finished his bachelor's degree in Management, I was up for promotion, but I didn't want it.

"Knowing James, I pushed him up for that position. I will tell you, Eliza, he has never, and to this day, ever let me down. I am glad I requested thirteen years ago to move my family when James did, to Grayling, when he set up the 97. It is because of James that my wife and I felt we saw enough hope again in our world that it would be okay to have and finally raise a child. We named Jaimie after James because he is such a good example to all of us. With James, we have no fear of the coming years, and we know Jaimie will also have a lot of promise as he matures into the man he will become in the not-too-distant future."

"I'm sure you, Molly, and Jaimie are excellent leaders and role models, even now. There will always be room for vast amounts of unique and beautiful potential within each of us to flourish more abundantly than it does, even now, and every day we awake there is more room for us to bring joy to others, by simply being kind and gentle in all that we do." Eliza responded knowing she was seeing a great part of the future sitting right there with her.

"Wise words, Eliza," said James, he smiled at Paul, then Molly, and then Jaimie, before looking at Mike.

"My wife, Heather, my son, Edward, and I have been on these outings ever since Edward was still in his mother's tummy. I met Heather more than thirteen years ago. Edward came into this world shortly after. Working with James has been a great help in so many ways. He fought for wage increases, helped us to stay ahead of inflation and found a way to work a small percentage of revenue for worker's pay based on the value of our efforts in our work. With ninety-seven of us working together, we've gotten a lot done, and I've been able to ensure Edward has a high-quality education." Mike wanted to say more, but he held back and looked toward Heather and Edward.

"Mike married me when I was eighteen and pregnant with Edward, I'll be honest. I had no idea what to do. It was because of the stability of Mike's job, that our morale increased, and the healthy environment of the 97 and James' leadership, that Mike found himself. Mike was able to find the courage to raise Edward as his own. Edward's birth father didn't want to have anything to do with me when he found out. I would imagine, it was because we were both young at the time, he wasn't yet suited for fatherhood, and his parents had very few kind words to say. Mike made me feel loved and valued again."

"I love my Dad," said Edward. "The guy who left my Mom high and dry, I feel sorry for him. He was lost, but I hope he grows up and finds his way someday. My Dad is Mike. He raised me and loves my Mom. With all these changes going on as I am getting older, he gives me perspective and he seems to understand. I'm human, I make mistakes, but he loves me anyway."

"He's a good young man," affirmed Mike. "No matter what, I love him as my own. I love Heather very much, and I couldn't ask to work with a better crew. All of our words carry weight with James. He listens, he watches, and he truly cares."

"Thank you, each of you. You are too kind," responded James, blushing in disbelief. "Our youngest member of this crew is Brandy. She has worked with us for just over a couple of years now and has been a phenomenal asset to our team."

Brandy took over for James, following his introduction, fearlessly, without the need for anxiety. "My father is a carpenter, I watched him and then worked with him between studies, as I was growing up. I used to help my Dad with his business before corporate bought him out. Luckily, it was enough for him to retire. I'd heard about YY Construction Corp and I didn't think much of it until I saw the pristine quality of two of the edifices in Bay City.

"Both of these buildings were everything a person could appreciate, and most especially someone with my background. I started doing web searches to find out who the architects and builders were, and it was the 97. When I asked around, I found out that there was a job opening in Grayling, so naturally, I applied. After my interview with James, I got a good vibe. He'd taken me on a tour around the Grayling facility, with its parks, its waterfalls, and the beauty of the architecture, all riddled with purpose. He introduced me to the team, and everyone was professional, upbeat, and they each told me how wonderful of a place it was to work.

"Needless to say, I accepted, began with Team 04 and the rest is history. Every team I've been in has been a gem of its own, the projects have been amazing as well, and I have been able to finish my associate degree in Carpentry along with quite a few other certifications. Soon, I will go for a big juggle of studies as I am learning scientific infrastructure. I plan to finish my BS in Biotechnology Infrastructure, and then we'll see where I'll go from there."

"She's ambitious," said James, "I am proud of her."

Everyone was so polite and courteous, but it was due to their reciprocal love for James that they were loyal to him. They would follow him to the ends of the Earth if asked. Eliza was impressed, and she knew he was the guy for her and Yesha's gargantuan undertaking.

James had the right kind of character, experience, perspective, demeanor, creativity, and wisdom necessary for the technologies they were going to reveal.

"So, James, if you had to name two architects who are at the top of your list and are favorites, aside from your own designs of course, who would you choose?"

"Hands down? Zaha Hadid. I am enthused with her designs that lay throughout our world, from London to the Middle East, to even the US. She is phenomenal. Just the creativity, the smoothness of every curve, the brilliant qualities of the tones of colors she chose, they provide that perfect contrast of nature flowing with the desired effects of human-made architecture.

"I have yet to find another architect that comes even close. Although that might not be fair to say, since there are so many wonderful artisans of edifices out there, but I would say that Thomas Wright from the UK would be a shared second, especially his Burj Al Arab in Dubai, along with Santiago Calatrava from Spain, and his Santa Cruz de Tenerife Auditorium. I love architecture with that kind of flow. How about you?" James was intrigued and felt an untapped connection.

"We must be reading minds, James," Eliza had studied architecture for quite some time, especially since she was interested in the designs that Zaha Hadid had come up with for years but wanted to help a struggling crew to have a chance to flourish in a similar field.

Eliza had seen his buildings, as well as Zaha's, and somehow despite his humble nature, he had imbued all of his architecture with those same artistic qualities yet had somehow been inspired to create utility in every space of any building he built. Not a single square inch was space that didn't serve a purpose, and like Zaha, his buildings were beyond utility alone. She continued, "You hit the nail on the head. Those are my favorites as well. Could you imagine flora and fauna flowing through a city with architecture woven in and out ever so elegantly? Take any other design or historical monument and apply those artistic traits, and you will find yourself gushing in awe!

"Another question. Who is your favorite musical artist of the 80's, the 90's, and this first decade of the 2000's?"

James thought for a second and returned his response with an answer that seemed to please Eliza quite a bit, he knew it was just a simple question of curiosity and nothing meant to judge, since she smiled and seemed to glow as she asked.

"Depeche Mode, in the 80's through today, of course, hmm, Erasure, New Order, and OMD, through the 90's, and have you heard of Above & Beyond, Balligomingo, or Delerium? They are trance and new age groups with some amazing arpeggios of harmony, vocals that soar, and heavenly pads that sweep you off your feet. I know, you would think I'd name some country musicians or some folk bands, but as much as I appreciate that music and the people that love it, for some reason I must be moved in a different way. They seem to get me."

"Oh, no worries. We're more alike than you would think. We have the same taste in music. I think we're batting at a hundred!" Eliza was not trying to sound like she was impressed, but he had named her favorite bands and he'd never even met her before or knew who she was.

They talked for an hour, each person at the table, including the children, conversing as free as can be about the various styles, interior options, and joys of architectural design and building with quality in mind.

Eliza, James, and his guests continued just a little longer talking about some of their favorite music, and one thing seemed to remain constant, they were all futurists and cared deeply about this world.

When it came to architecture and design, which was their world, in an addition to aesthetic that was unique and inspiring, they talked about forestry, jungles, and the varieties of nature that were pleasing to behold.

At a certain point in the evening, Eliza began to talk to her audience about a new company she called Pathway LLC. She also got James to talk about YY Construction Corp, from his vantage point. Everything went well. With the crew, their families, and James, she had hit it off.

He and his friends had each expressed their desire to move on from YY Construction Corp eventually. They had mentioned on many occasions that it was a good deal for each one of them for a myriad of reasons, all of which stemmed from James' leadership style.

However, aside from the situation experienced by their own crew, the toxicity within the corporation itself was something they deemed unethical, unhealthy, with the capability of spreading like a plague, and the likes of which, if any humanity prevailed at all might lead to the company's undoing.

James explained how YY Construction Corp used to be a wonderful employer, and while he protected the 97, it was painful to see other crews being torn to shreds with little to show for it.

The rest of the corporation was steeped in non-agile management, creative and helpful ideas from other crew members were scoffed at or increasingly ignored, and in many cases, people were let go, on-the-job-training was non-existent, the revolving door was greased with the blood and sweat of its employees, and every penny of every dividend or investment seemed to go to the investors and shareholders.

The conversations carried on blissfully, time flew, and it was quite refreshing to vent to and be understood by this fascinating young lady. They excused Eliza, as she requested a few moments to "freshen up," and conversations churned around the table. It seemed that everyone at the table looked at him like he needed to do whatever he could, "She could be his once in a lifetime, and you better not let her slip away."

James graciously agreed. Before dessert, Eliza's friend arrived, and both of them sought approval from James' crew to take him away and talk business with him for a while at their estate. Things were going well for James, his crew, and their families, and he had a good feeling about how the night had gone.

A Meeting by Chance

For a moment, within her training in the Virtual Universe, Vesha Celeste could feel a shift from mind-to-mind. Yesha Alevtina whispered through their link, before they both drifted back into Eliza's, Yesha's, and James' shared memories, and it was as if Vesha were in a passive yet up-close observation.

"James' experience during this dinner setting, Vesha, was well documented within the archives of Pathway History, and so is this experience as shared from the minds of Eliza, me, and James. Going back to earlier that evening, please enjoy our shared perspective and then the amazing, beautiful, and promising results."

Details from Another Angle

While Yesha went for a jog, Eliza had decided to go to the T.O.; which was her favorite eatery, and after a few moments of waiting in line, the line behind her began to grow. She looked back, and then kind of felt herself blush or even glow a little. Eliza was still somewhat adapting to the latest updates to her optimizations and was trying to keep her glowing under control. How could it be? Perhaps all that work, research, learning, and more kept her nanos fired up full-bore almost too consistently?

It seemed as though it were a chronic condition, nonetheless, she kept her fears compartmentalized. Luckily, thus far there had been no devastating side effects, only a few quirky ones, with the worst being the potential for awkward moments. Plus, she knew she'd only had these new abilities for about three weeks and the average mind constantly works and tries to create normalcy out of anything that is bizarrely different or inconceivable, so in most cases, no one noticed the glow.

On top of that, this break might help. Food, that's all she needed, or at least that is what she enjoyed, and that tended to reduce the glow a little, because it brought peace to her mind.

The man standing behind her looked like the man in the pictures she'd seen while doing her research on James Cooper, who also happened to be a very handsome man.

Upon seeing him, she momentarily forgot everything else, was instantly smitten and had to take special actions to pull herself together and engage in an unplanned, non-practiced, much studied, very opportune conversation, which also happened to be very necessary. Luckily, her mind was optimized.

"Okay, Eliza," she coached herself mentally, in less than a second, *"You have seven real world Ph.Ds.; so, you know you can do this with ease. You have been neurologically optimized and have dealt with far greater challenges and have literally millions of years of knowledge in that mind of yours. Plus, your plans are to help*

everyone Universe-wide. So, you've got to do this, because this is where it all begins!" Her mind tapered off, as she focused on the task at hand. This was different from what she had planned, however, and something she hadn't considered.

It was as if some unseen force had seen fit that Eliza meet James that very day. To top that off, the last time she was drawn to anything remotely close to something that would be considered flirting or talking to someone who she wouldn't mind dating, it had ended tragically.

Considering all that was going on, Eliza hadn't considered physical or any other sort of attraction ever since. For all of her robust neurological networks, synaptic pathways and strengths, and the quantity of time she had invested into science, she hadn't thought of how she would deal with meeting an individual she might actually be fascinated with and in more ways than purely a professional sense.

Just like any of her other somewhat new abilities, this would take time and, *"Practice makes perfect."* She very lightly gazed around the room and then in his direction, in doing so, she felt her neuro nanos kick in helping her return to her typically alert, intellectual, friendly, and engaging self. *"Talk to me, James."* She tested her ability to influence him through her unique ability for thought persuasion.

Eliza began to think, *"Talk to me, James,"* and to her surprise...

"Have you ever eaten here before, Ma'am?"

"Did he just call me Ma'am? Oh well. Now is as good a time as any to make this happen and throw on the charm brigade so we can honorably convince him to work with us in building Pathway's infrastructure. This is how it all starts." Thought Eliza, caught again, just a little off-guard, *"It actually worked!* Yes?" She turned around again as she spoke, making the most of the situation.

Although Eliza didn't realize it outright, James was kind of struck by her professional allure and there was something magnificent, yet altogether captivating, about her demeanor, not to mention he found her quite stunning in a physical sense as well. James still tried to be respectful, just as he would have been for any person he talked to. The line seemed long anyway, so he thought he might as well get her attention; his friends had given him their food orders, so he was waiting like the others in the line to make the orders, pay for them, and then return to the table until the meals were brought out.

Since the line was rather long, he considered all of the reviews on this particular eatery, which were all very good, and although they never made plans they couldn't change, it was quite fortunate, at least in his mind at this moment, that they had decided to eat here.

Thinking about the order of things in the restaurant he thought that the setup here must have been the norm. He also thought he might as well take the time in waiting to get to know someone he hadn't met before. His crew would have chided him if he hadn't tried to speak to the young lady right next to or in front of him, since they were adamant that he ought to reach out to women and date with romance and honorable goals in mind every once in a while—he appreciated their intentions, since he knew they didn't want him to be single forever.

Most of his employees admired him as a kind, charming, and an exemplary older brother, and some saw him as a charming younger brother, and as such, they felt like he deserved the joys of a good relationship.

While he appreciated the honorable intentions of his crew members, pushing himself on others wasn't his way of going about things. He had no desire to cave to the natural evolution of mixed results, and he had specific criteria for the types of interests and standards that would draw him into dating. Notwithstanding, he thought there were much greater ideals to pursue in life.

Still, she seemed like an outstandingly pleasant individual, so he made his best effort to start the conversation and keep it going. As such, he was merely trying to be polite and seek some advice.

"I'm visiting from out of town with my friends over there," he pointed at the three table booths lined up, with ten adults and three teenagers, and continued, "I was wondering if you've been here before... maybe you know of some recommended entrées?"

He put Eliza at ease with his calm and non-overbearing demeanor, and she obliged an answer to his question, "This is my go-to restaurant. I come here all the time, so I have quite a few favorites, do you have anything in in mind?"

"Here is the list, it's for me and the people over there," he said as he nervously pointed a second time toward his crewmembers and their family members. He then handed his ordering list toward her, trying not to seem so nervous, or at least as nervous as he was, he didn't want to seem to be too awkward and as a result, blow his chances of maybe getting to know her a little better.

Eliza perused through James' meal ordering list, with the second-natured skill of someone who realized they'd been there often, while considering with the clarity of an optimized mind the menu items, and then some of the obviously unacquainted options made by James and his friends.

After looking their menu options over fairly quickly, she knew that this certainly wouldn't do, and with a natural, "Oh my," she turned back toward James and made some quick recommendations based on flavor, nutrition combination optimization, and other drink, appetizer, and dessert recipe matchups, which looked to leave him confused, with too much info all at once.

"There are quite a few orders, James. Could you introduce me to your table, and do you mind if I talk to your friends to offer more ideal suggestions? Oh, we'll lose our spot in line, but it will die down soon, and I assure you, your friends will be grateful if we took our time, and it will be worth it."

"Oh, of course, I am sure they will be." Then, with consideration for her, and not wanting to ruin her plans in any way, he politely asked, "Did you come here with someone, by chance?"

Eliza was impressed with how charming he was, the fact that he was trying to be polite, and the awkward truth his question revealed; and she answered, "I am a professor at Harvard, but I was doing some extra-curricular research with a friend earlier, I found myself famished, and I decided to come here. This happens to be my favorite restaurant to eat at. I'm Eliza, party of one." She said with a pleasant smile that was flirtatious and confident, yet it donned on her that it may have been interestingly and nervously wordy.

"I'm James Cooper. I'm sorry, I must have left my manners at the door," and they both chuckled and felt naturally at ease with each other throughout the rest of the night. After a brief pause, he asked: "I suppose we can step out of the line, for now, I can introduce you, and you can make recommendations to my friends?"

"Sure, that works for me. You know? You seem like a pretty cool guy. I wouldn't mind getting to meet them," Eliza looked up at James, who was a well-chiseled six feet and one inch tall, based on the digital readouts before her on her neural-optical display, and after some more small talk, she smiled again, before both made their way to the tables and booths occupied by James' crew members.

"These wonderful people are my co-workers," James said as they arrived at where they were seated. He had insisted on submitting and paying for the order. The restaurant was unique in some ways, at least to him. A person or party of people would look at the menu after sitting down, then make selections by checking the boxes next to the menu items, using the supplied markers, and write down the quantity of servings they wished to have served on a dry-erase book of cards provided at each seat. The party representative would then proceed to the line with the requests in hand to make and pay for their orders. The restaurant staff would bring the food out when it was ready, and in a manner that allowed each course to be enjoyed—fresh.

James introduced Eliza to his crew and their family members and guests who were present. Unanimously, they moved over to make space for Eliza and James to sit next to each other.

If James' crewmembers, their families, and present guests or significant others were amazed by Eliza's overwhelming and breath-taking presence, aura, and lovely scent which permeated through the air and filled them with ease and admiration, they hid it well. They were kind and very attentive nonetheless, and the two young men sitting with their parents couldn't stop staring at Eliza and her superb physique in awe. She understood and didn't mind. After all, if you are the beautiful flower in a room, is it a problem being appreciated, noticed, or even adored? She was about the health of it all, and these boys grasped that.

"James is actually our boss, and we're all here on vacation together. The rest of the crew is otherwise engaged and are in various locations throughout town at the moment. We meet up late in the mornings for brunch, daily, and then split up into smaller groups," said one of the women of remarkably large stature and a brusque yet friendly voice, who looked at her with approval. "My name is Anne," she said, affirming James' introduction.

Eliza pored over their requested menu items, listened to each individual, and one by one made suggestions for appetizers, entrees, wines, spirits, and desserts—she paired up each order for texture, flavor, nutrition, and aroma. If she had anything to do with it, everyone with James that evening would have the best meal they'd ever had. This was the first time she had witnessed such a close-knit crew, and James was at the helm.

Eliza's neural optimizations kicked into high gear. "*No wonder he received so many awards and has kept YY Construction Corp afloat,*" she thought. If what she was witnessing in the relationship between James and his crew and their harmony with each other equated in any way toward their demeanor and toward each other at work, they were most assuredly a phenomenal team. "*Because of James, each member of his crew is a phenomenal leader themselves,*" Eliza noted to herself.

"*If James and his people were ever to leave their company, the way YY Construction Corp treats the other crews, it would tank rather quickly or continue their toxic charade, thinking that is how to achieve success. No wonder why they at least had the presence of mind to leave him and his crew alone.*

"*I don't want the company to go bottom up though. We'll figure something out to help the situation improve. However, it is necessary, and perhaps without James, YY Construction Corp will wake up.*"

Eliza pondered some more, coaching herself quietly, as she listened at the same time, intently, "*Businesses who create toxic work environments need to learn there is a better way, learn their lessons, or stumble until they do.*

"*We need James and his crew for something greater than money, status, or power, and if needs are, our gloves are off.*

"*Hopefully, I can convince James and his crew to partner with Yesha and me. Our goals, missions, and purposes behind the creation of Pathway can then begin. James has the depth of character I admire. Plus, I think he's a pretty cool guy, maybe there's a future for us, but I'll just relax where emotions are concerned and let time take its course for now.*"

Once the dinner orders were finally taken down, Eliza nodded toward James, and as if they'd known each other for years, they got up and got back into the line to have their meal requests prepared for service and delivery.

After chatting, laughing, smiling, and flirting with each other quietly in line, and making their orders, they returned to the table. Each of James' crew and family members observed Eliza throughout their interactions and each viewed her as a respectful, extremely intelligent, gracious, and charmingly attentive individual to everyone there. She asked them to tell her a little about themselves, and as introduced, they started with Anne and went around the table counter-clockwise all the way to Brandy.

Eliza listened and responded to each one of James' guests objectively as they exchanged questions about work, family, and life.

To Eliza, James had played a positive and prominent role in their lives, and there seemed to be an unexplainable bond between James and his crew.

No matter where the conversations began, as they spoke, laughed, and chuckled with that comfortable and genuine air of peace and contentment, the crew and their family members all seemed to drift back to James, his background, limitless stories of shared moments, and how wonderful he as a boss was to them.

James called his crew and himself, "the 97," and together, based on all of the news articles, economist journal publications, and interviews about his buildings, he had kept YY Construction Corp solvent and made the most of everything in every possible way. Not a single member of his team lived in fear of losing their jobs, because he was iron-clad in all he did, including protecting their well-being. As a result, they seemed to love him, were loyal to him, and were part of the best construction team, hands-down, and worldwide.

James, meanwhile, was gracious and humble about any compliments sent his way and would quickly direct the conversation back to his workers and their families, their ingenuity, and on occasion, he would lead the conversation back to Eliza—which intensified Eliza's attraction to his innate character even more.

Although Eliza fought to think of her fascination toward James as something that was related to a desire for a professional partnership and nothing more, she also felt and tried to squelch the fact that there might be an attraction in a romantic sense.

James and his crew talked, laughed, and enjoyed their meals as they brought Eliza in. Once done with their entrées they showered her with compliments.

At one point, before their dessert and the final bottles of wine were served, Eliza politely dismissed herself from the table to "freshen up," so in truth she could text or link with, Yesha. While she was away, the people at James' table were still enjoying the last bit of their dinner prior to dessert, while occasionally conversing, exchanging glances, and imagining, as well as chiding James about wedding bells, gowns, and tuxedos.

They admonished James that while it was too soon to tell, and while they were in many ways kidding around with him, that he should most certainly consider maintaining contact with Eliza.

"James, Eliza is a winner and a one-of-a-kind person. We've never met someone so astute, so observant, so calm, so collected, and so beautiful in every way. You two would make a wonderful team, professionally, following the dreams you always talk about, and I'd imagine you two would quite amazingly make a wonderful team, even in a romantic sense," said the large-statured, attractive, and brusque-voiced Nordic woman, named Anne.

"Yesha, you won't believe who is in Massachusetts tonight!" Eliza was texting quickly, hoping Yesha would see her phone, *"Do you remember that one gentleman, the gorgeous and brilliant one we talked about earlier today? He is the award-winning architect and engineer we studied about from YY Construction Corp. He's here at the T.O. tonight, and with his crew on vacation!"*

Yesha had finished her jog and showered up—her towel was wrapped around her, with another towel wrapped around her head as if in a beehive hairstyle when she saw her phone light up. She typically kept it in silent mode since telemarketers would persistently call, and she had too much heart to say no, so instead she ignored the calls completely.

Telemarketers always seemed to have a knack for calling at the most inopportune of times. If it was important, they could leave a message. Still, texts from certain individuals were set up with a distinct vibrating sound, so she decided to see who it was.

She checked her phone and realized Eliza had texted, rather than neurologically linking. As she walked to reach for her phone on the nightstand next to her bed, her towel fell off exposing her optimized physiological aspects to only herself. She quickly forgot about her towel, saw herself in her mirror, and realized how perfect her perky aspects were. She then grabbed her phone and sat on her bed. She didn't mind sitting there on display, and she knew that no one else would have if they had seen her, or so it was that she had imagined, but they wouldn't see her since no one else was home.

The only one that would return home at the moment would be her mother, Yesenia, and she always was cool and down-to-Earth, anyway.

Yesha was a woman of increased confidence and she had grown to know that there was nothing indecent about the human form. As a matter of a fact, she knew it was quite unhealthy for the human mind and by association the physical health of anyone to not appreciate the beauty surrounding someone.

Whether it was of Nature or of optimized physiology or simply due to their prized aspects, the splendor to the eyes, the heart, and the peace to the soul they brought, she viewed it as inhumane or ungodly to ignore or shun it. It was inhumane because it was bad for their health to constantly wander around in disgust, jealousy, anger, and frustration when it was so unnecessary," Just *breathe*," Yesha would often think.

Texting back to Eliza, Yesha wrote, *"I just got your last text. I can't believe you just happened to run into James! What are the odds? Well, hmm... have you had a chance to talk to him about Pathway or the LLC we'd like to form, build, put together, or have the infrastructure to make happen and improve upon, especially when it comes to our capabilities?"*

Eliza returned with a texted response, *"I talked to him and his crew a little about it, but not much. I'm with seven in his crew and six of their family members. They've had some interesting stories and have a lot of good things to say about him. I can tell they all love him. Apparently, his entire crew and their families are in Cambridge right now, but only a handful of them are here with James at the T.O.*

"Three daughters from members of his crew are planning on going to Harvard next season, so they all visited Cambridge and Boston to check it out; one of their daughters is with us tonight. His crew is closely-knit, but they don't want to bombard one establishment with 97 people, four retirees, and their families, so James is here with thirteen people.

"I need to get back, though. I told them I had to 'freshen up' and I don't want to be gone for too long and send off a bad impression."

Yesha texted back, *"I completely understand. How about this, Eliza? If you can keep them entertained, I'll pick things up around the estate and head that direction. Sound good?"*

"That sounds perfect."

Yesha, just after cleaning up, and just before heading out, remembered just in time that she needed to get dressed. *"That could have been an awkward introduction,"* she thought, *"for them. Well, maybe not, but too much too soon takes away all the fun, and I don't want to end up in jail for public 'indecency,' with a bad stigma attached to my name. Society has its rules."*

She grabbed her smart suit, put it on, and put it in professional yet metro-casual mode. Once she was ready, she headed to the T.O. using her optimized physiology to arrive quickly.

When she arrived at her destination, she dampened her glow, made sure no one bore witness to her capabilities, and then Yesha saw Eliza from the window.

"That young lady is one enigmatic and beautifully artistic masterpiece of Mother Nature combined with the gorgeous ingenuity of the human mind," Yesha played out the thoughts of how it all happened three weeks ago within her mind, and when she entered, she saw James.

He was much more stunning in real life and James looked good in his pictures, *"Nature did right by him, oh my! James is a treasure, and in every way!"* Her glow started to kick in again. Eliza turned to Yesha, having picked up Yesha's neural link in her mind and her amazing curves out of the corner of her eye. It took a lot of work to optimize the physiology, and both were very happy with the results of their efforts.

Looking directly toward Yesha, Eliza looked angelic with her prize-winning smile, teeming with purpose, and genuine ferocity. She could understand Yesha's reaction completely.

"You're glowing, Yesha. Don't worry. I was too." Like that Yesha's glow dimmed before anyone else seemed to notice. Eliza and Yesha were close friends and kidded around with each other a lot without others knowing it.

James saw them both and his heart was moved, yet he knew not why, but he respected both young ladies for a host of untold reasons rather quickly. Experts on all sciences, and in this case, those that related to his gestures, the words he spoke, his timing, and the devoted nature to him of all who were around his table, Yesha and Eliza picked up on his intuition right away; in reciprocation, they were likewise absolutely charmed by him.

"James is a kindred spirit, genuine, and brilliant, you don't fall easily, Eliza, and I can see why," she told Eliza through their link.

"Maybe this was meant to be," Yesha continued to converse with Eliza, mind-to-mind.

"Oh, I am smitten, I can't believe we just happened to run into each other at random; regardless, we've chatted a bit and worked away some of the awkwardness.

"I am trying to think of this as an informal, professionally promising, and a chance meeting. I'd like to believe that energy can have a benevolent purpose, and given all that we are about to do, we were given a little assist by the Universe itself. He'll make the third member of our little venture, and as such, he will be one of the three leaders, alongside you and me.

"Each of his crew members is a leader in their own right, so all told, there are 213 people with him in Cambridge, and more are on their way. He's a true gentleman and has a heart of gold." Eliza continued to talk to her through their neural link. All that James crew saw was Eliza wave Yesha over to the table with a brightened countenance, and this glow they saw, they thought it was all in their heads.

After introductions, Yesha appreciated the warm reception, the experiences shared, and the ease with which they made space for her, sitting on the far end across from Anne, and to Eliza's left. James introduced himself to her, and she noticed that Eliza looked as though she'd known James for years.

Yesha listened to the crew and responded to them, while also trying to stay on task, *"He is handsome, you are right, yet there is so much more to him; I can see it already,"* she told Eliza through her link.

Eliza sent a neural experiential package to her mind, so she understood immediately all of the details of the night's conversations, *"We have a lot to do, and so, no matter how all of this plays out, we can't let each other lose focus for too long, thank goodness your neuro nanos kicked in and you've blazed a substantial trail with regard to the 97 and James. Something's running wild in you, Eliza, and we have got to let our spirits fly so we can get back on track—I have an idea.*

"*I know what we can do.*"

As she looked around listening to each person, she noticed as the two teenage boys in the group were obviously dazed looking in a smitten fashion toward her direction, *"Cute kids,"* she thought, and then spoke up. "Do you guys and gals mind if Eliza and I steal James for the night? I promise we'll return him to you in one piece and in mint condition tomorrow."

Strangely enough, as optimized as her neural nanos were, the unspoken yet thick double-entendre of what she had just said seemed to hang in the air.

After gazing at her briefly and sternly, they laughed to put her at ease. The rather attractive lady with a brusque voice at the far end of the table from Yesha, named Anne, answered, "Of course we don't mind. He's lovely to have around, but I suppose we can let him go for a short period of time. And, James, please give us a call if you need anything? I am sure I'm not the only one who picks up a good vibe from these two, so have fun!" She looked around the table and everyone else nodded in the affirmative. Anne was clearly in charge when James was absent, so Eliza knew they were in good hands.

With that, Eliza, Yesha, and James bid the rest of his crew in attendance at the T.O. a farewell until they would meet again the next day at the grange at ten in the morning, and the three new friends headed toward Eliza's estate home.

Indefinite Longevity

When they arrived at Eliza's estate home, James was rather impressed with the architecture, its white columns, burnt brick and ivy, high windows, and landscaping. Yesenia, Yesha's mom, had returned from her daily activities, still beautiful no matter her age, she was sixty-seven, but she looked no older than forty-five, and she had arrived in time to greet them at the door.

"Well aren't you three a splendid trio!" They all smiled, followed Yesenia into the living room. While Eliza and James sat down on the sofa, obviously ensconced with each other, Yesenia took note and went to get some hot ginger-mint and clove tea. Yesha did likewise and disappeared to retrieve their extensive and drafted real-world copy of the Pathway LLC infrastructural plans from her laptop but got lost for a few moments as she pored over them, making sure everything read according to standard, especially for someone well-versed in architecture for more than a decade, like James.

When Yesha returned, laptop in hand, Yesenia had served the tea, but having sensed a budding romance building between the two, she made her way upstairs to take care of some personal business and retired for the night. Yesha noticed this and appreciated that Eliza was explaining everything quite well. She maintained her professionalism, eloquence, and had a peculiar sense of charm about her as she gushed to James the details of the last week and twenty-four-hours.

After telling James about her search for an architect and team, and how she accidentally found him, he asked, "I'm glad we met. How did you two decide to do this?"

"Thank you, James. We worked for almost two years simultaneously as full-time professors and on side projects that would have a bottomless list of benefits to humanity, and even after receiving top honors at MIT and Harvard we received little to no reciprocation for our efforts. When all was said and done, they and even the government, when requesting their approval and open support, turned us down flat when it came to distribution of our latest breakthrough, the biopod.

"As a matter of a fact, the tone of our last meeting pertaining to our three new prototype devices suggested that trying to build more and distribute them would turn the economy upside down, and the unfortunate side effect could result in the medical and pharmaceutical career professionals finding themselves jobless.

"They wanted nothing to do with it, since the risks in their way of seeing it were too high, and hinted at compliance for now, stating no campus resources could be used for this project or else we should be prepared to face the consequences. We didn't want people to be without their jobs, and we had no desire to turn the economy into oblivion, or even let the technology go to waste. The subtle threats...? Come on, now... Don't they know we know better, and besides, by shutting us down they were playing God with peoples' lives, and were betraying humanity? Oh, they must comply to their bylaws, etc, so there was little they could do. We understood and don't blame them. They're fine institutions, so we had to find a different way."

James seemed to understand everything with clarity, yet he was intent on understanding everything even more fully, "And that is what led you to study who it would be that could help you two to build a quiet company, so you could grow it to a point to where you could safely leverage a better way, while not threatening anyone's way of life?"

"Exactly, James... Yesha and I took part-time tenured positions in return for supposedly sweeping our findings under the carpet. We took our biopods home—and have safeguarded and further improved upon them. To prepare for our new organization over the last week, we purchased several acreages, including the rights to everything above the surface, in the water, and deep underground.

"We have put together exhaustive plans for public and private arms of Pathway LLC. There will be an arm intended to vet advancements to allow them to become government-sanctioned for proliferation in productive and healthy increments to the public.

"There will be a very covert arm that will allow us to produce some of the highest technology advancements and breakthroughs not yet known to even the most tech-savvy professionals throughout the world, to prevent them from falling into the wrong hands."

"That makes sense. So, how would you like me to help?" In truth, Eliza could have built every last bit of infrastructure herself, even without Yesha, but her belief was that she needed to get all of humanity on board and involved, within reason and of their own free will, but she also knew her biopods were more successful in the long-run with people of upstanding character, like the 97.

"Well, James, we have researched how we will begin, have built exhaustive plans for infrastructure, and this is where you will come in. We would like to team up with you and hire a very capable team, your team, the 97 and perhaps their families and guests, for the building of our infrastructure, our labs, hyperloops, docking and truck stations, and underground campuses.

"You should note that we have fully vetted the prototype biopods that I talked about earlier. You, your crew, and anyone else you trust will see technologies that no one else knows about, are more advanced than anything released into the public at this time, and perhaps will not be released for quite some time yet. You'll also understand soon why I would like to invite family members and significant others to come along and help. It'll be like a volunteer project, but with huge dividends.

"With these biopods, a person's physiology and neurology can be extensively optimized while leaving with them a lovely cadre of physiological and neurological healing nanos that can continuously optimize every aspect of their physique and cognition. These nanos will work in-turn to drastically increase ingenuity, innovation, clarity of mind for task completion, and the physical capacity to allow any recipient to endure harsh labor and environments while healing and enjoying everything throughout the process.

"To be clear and honest with you, James, both Yesha and I tested everything on ourselves, to see how it works before trying it on anyone else. We knew we had to protect ourselves from the more austere parts of whatever seems to pull humanity's strings at the moment, and from sudden and mysterious disappearances. You know, the conspiracies? We also needed to protect the technology that we worked so hard to develop, so we can help advance civilization and decrease the unnecessary suffering had by far too many.

"Our connected intranet and highly sophisticated software algorithms and programming can keep us neurologically linked, in communication with the highly detailed and latest bits of information, all while keeping us up-to-date on further advancements and abilities.

"This basically allows our bodies to be healthy and to look as perfect as our minds allow them to. For example, we can set our appearance in static mode while changing our clothes using smart suits and compartmentalized regions of our minds dedicated to fashion expertise of every sort. We can also heal from pretty much anything—well, with the exception of a dive into the Sun or a fall beyond the abyss of the event horizon of a black hole—but, perhaps we'll figure out how to mitigate that later; an idea is already coming to mind! I digress, or progress, beyond the current topic," Eliza laughed.

"We can also look like we're twenty-five or twenty-two or any age of our choosing, indefinitely, or adjust as needed, and have minds free of insanity that can incur an accumulation of many millennia of wisdom and so much more, while making sense of it all, without damage.

"Neurologically what it does enhance is our clarity; it maximizes our introverted and extroverted tendencies. It helps us to have photographic memories with the ability to converge a plethora of sciences together for greater results quickly, so we can put things together and build things that physicists, biotechnology professionals, neuroscientists, and big data would merely only dream of, if that and by today's standards, they are very brilliant.

"In a few years, Yesha's mom will do the same. She has been a recipient of good health; hence she looks forty-five even though she'll be turning sixty-eight in October, but for all else, neither of us wanted it to be too obvious until she was ready, or until we've had a couple of years to get everything running full-bore and protected from the hands of those who might not have humanity's best interests at heart. This is intended to heal and not harm.

"We've built in encodings and algorithms, standard, quantum, and quite a bit more exotic, to ensure this technology stays the course as benevolent toward the advancement of civilization, with reduction of violence to zero, while controlling chaos to bring what is needed for life without the typical destruction or death and mayhem found in chaos that isn't controlled and increasing the clarity of benefactors as problems are solved contributing to the well-being of life.

"That said," Eliza paused with a slight look of concern and an observable glow as she looked toward James with sincerity, "We've done this to help and protect those whom we love, whether distant or nearby."

Eliza then looked up again, and smiled at both James and Yesha, before looking serenely down again. She was talking about genuine love.

Yesha, who was holding a laptop with a simplified copy of their infrastructural plans, smiled and walked to the other side of the sofa from James, smelling of roses and something rich and amazing, and pivoted the laptop so all three could see.

Eliza then continued, "Here they are. Thank you, Yesha. As you can see, these plans are just the beginning of all that it will take to help humanity to build a legacy that is worthy of preserving. We want people to have the option and availability of everything related to well-being, longevity, health, intellect, sanity, compassion, wisdom, joy, entertainment, and even fun. We will build first, and the rest will follow, as we coach society into realizing the untold potential that it indeed has."

James seemed pretty intrigued and not at all apprehensive, Yesha was sure of herself, Eliza was quietly confident, and after examining the details on Yesha's laptop, James spoke up, "I am impressed. Am I right in assuming that you would like for me, my crew and their families to build the infrastructure on these plans for you? You have noble goals, for sure. The goals you've shared are those which I can only dream of. But, I'm in. However, I'll have to ask my crew in the morning. You do realize that some of these plans, in my current state, and in my crew's current state, may be more complicated than we are capable of working with and if we could, this would cost a fortune."

"I assure you, James, we have every single one of those details figured out. Financially, speaking, my parents saved and invested for years in stocks, bonds, mutual funds, and all manner of diversified capital, all of which matured, and when they passed away, they left their trust to me. I left all but enough for Yesha's and my college tuition, our estate management funds, and regular living expenses compounding in interest in the most successful investments and continue to do so. As start-ups of the modern era began, I reinvested in them, and when the already rather large financial estate grew by a stroke of luck, after other strokes of luck, and at a rate of more than a hundred thousand-fold, we knew we had all the funding we needed to finance this.

"Believe me, this is an investment that will grow astronomically in value as we go along and continue to compound once we're done. Doing the math, once all is said and done, we'll be able to pay off every national debt, every hospital bill, every tuition debt, and afford everyone a luxurious lifestyle, many million times over. That is everyone in – the – world," Eliza made a point to enunciate this to James, to make it clear to him that her plans were so dynamic that everyone would have the option of being alive, healthy, and happy in trillions of years, if that were their wish, and they were simply kind.

"We have to build this because I don't want humanity to become a lost civilization, one that is completely decimated, or a civilization with nothing to show for all of our history, our sciences, our art, our romances, or our music. I want to do this, because I love humanity, and I want to set something up that will protect our people as well as life itself, yet we will still need to be patient as they learn to collaborate in their own way, with one mini-push after another, until they are ready for the big reveal."

Eliza paused, seeing James' ideas seem to percolate.

"Wow, Eliza. This is inspiring, the designs, the details, and everything. This is amazing, you didn't miss a thing! You and Yesha, I am impressed. You are both brilliant. I don't even know how to respond. Here I am, look at me, sitting in-between both of you, and you two are absolutely lovely, brilliant, gifted, and wonderful people. I'm not even worthy. How could I be so lucky to be sitting here with you two lovely archetypes of the future? Forgive me for saying this, but you two are in my humble opinion more dream-like and creative than the most beautiful angels and geniuses I could have ever aspired to meet—you two are amazing human beings!

"My crew and I have done a lot for our employer, YY Construction Corp, I admit. We are currently on a two-month 'vacation', but I believe with all of this already drawn up, I can brief my crew and we could get this all started right away, and our part, if we pass through the biopod experience and are optimized, might actually be pretty easy.

"YY Construction Corp has been kind to me and my crew, I'll give them that. I have no bone to pick with them, but it is mostly because we've kept them afloat for the last ten years. I am not naïve with regard to how they treat all of the other teams, however, and I believe our exodus could teach them a very valuable lesson, which is to be kind, fair, and concerned for the well-being of one's company as well as all of one's employees and their customers." James paused for a moment as he navigated through each page of Eliza's and Yesha's plans. His head nodded in the affirmative at each turn of a digital page.

"It looks like if we build these two labs first, you will be able to build a cloud of self-replicating and reprogrammable nanobots, and they will give us a mega assist with the rest. I'd say we could build all of this within a year or two!

"What do you think, Eliza?"

"It sounds like a plan! I must say, that I too am impressed with you, James. We aren't even neurologically linked, yet the way we connect; it's as if we've known each other for years. Do you have any other questions you would like to ask? Is there anything else you would like to know or see?" responded Eliza, with a glowing aura.

James just then noticed Eliza's glow and felt quite enticed by her appeal. "What does it mean to be linked? You said you were optimized both physiologically and neurologically, and I see neurologically it has panned out perfectly. You've thought of everything..."

As music seemed to drift in from another room... something soothing, something romantic, the arpeggios were familiar, yet the music soared beautifully with an almost orchestral feel, an angelic vocal crescendo permeated through the room. James suddenly seemed aware, the night was heading in a new direction, and then Yesha spoke up, "Follow Eliza and me; we'll show you what physiological optimization feels like."

James was all too gentlemanly to assume anything but decided that whatever they were up to, he was willing to go along with it and see where it led. As they entered a white and glowing room, Eliza and Yesha showed him the three white and glowing objects that looked like tanning beds. *"This is interesting,"* he thought. *"I'll follow along here, wherever this leads."*

"These are the three biopods I talked about earlier," said Eliza.

"Would you like to try one out?" asked Yesha. "There is one for each of us," she continued.

"If we each climb into one and pull down the lid, we can show you much more," said Eliza. She snapped her fingers, and in a comic manner, as if with perfect timing, Depeche Mode's song, "World in My Eyes," started playing. They chuckled at the humor of the timing, and then they danced a little. James smiled at Eliza and Yesha, and they both smiled back.

Yesha lay in her biopod first, lid up. Eliza then laid in hers. They both looked at James and then motioned with their hands and silent lips toward the third biopod and in unison said, "Common, James!"

James thought about it for a second, *"What am I getting myself into?"* He finally decided he might as well, and as he made his way to and then climbed into the third biopod, he thought in his mind, *"What's the worst that could happen?"*

Yesha then instructed James, "When you secure the cover or pull it down, say within your mind the words, 'Link, 1, 2, 3.' Once you say that, say, '5 minutes, 20 years.' Understood?"

"Twenty years?"

"We'll be in there for five minutes of real-world time, but truly gain twenty years of real life-like experience, knowledge, and wisdom in the Virtual Universe. All of which we can retain as if it truly happened, and with complete and immediate recall," Eliza responded.

"Yes. Okay, let's do this then, Eliza and Yesha," and James thought about what could happen within the space of twenty years, and then fearlessly reached up to the lid of the biopod he was laying in.

They pulled their biopod covers down. Eliza, said, "Okay guys. Ready when you are."

In unison, they said within their minds, *"Link, 1, 2, 3, 5 minutes, 20 years..."*

Time Dilation

Like that, James felt every nerve, every cell, and every neuron stand on end and then when he thought he could bear it no longer, he felt a larger sense of euphoria take its place, a pleasant feeling he'd never felt before. Once he came to, he looked around and noticed he was standing in a garden near a pond with an angelic statue that was looking down at its hands. He noticed her hands acting as a waterfall of recycling oxygenated water for the coy fish and frogs in the water surrounded by a small beach of sand, and equally spaced areas of shore where the water abutted to small brick walls, and above them there were sage, mint, and beautifully scented flowers—only, everything had a white and iridescent glow.

The gardens and pathways glowed and appeared like magic playing out before his eyes, and details of everything he looked at played out in a series of holo-images before him as he conjured them up and would fade if he didn't. No matter where he looked, he noticed a pleasing aura, until he beheld what led to something he recognized, based on the architecture, Eliza's estate home, with tall white glowing columns, and brilliant, yet burnt red bricks that were partially covered in glowing green ivy.

Above him, he saw the stars much more clearly, with the details of each one playing out as he conjured up the imagery using his mind, and then he looked back down toward the land and noticed that it was bordered by a mixture of glowing maple and other brilliantly colored and flowering ornamental trees, with a beautiful and glowing quartz crystal stone wall fence. He then looked to his right and saw Eliza glowing like the most beautiful angel he'd ever imagined or could ever have dreamt of. He looked to his left, he saw Yesha with an iridescence and splendor he had never imagined before as well.

"We're here, but we aren't, are we? What is this place? It's more beautiful than a dream and more tangible and sweeter than real life."

Eliza and Yesha, almost in unison and in the surround-sound voice of feminine angels started off, *"We're in the computer mainframe, with access to the shared collective minds of Eliza and Yesha synced with whatever you will bring to it, James. What do you think?"* Then they looked at each other, and James could read their minds for the first time in their lives, and he liked what played out before him. They were both pure. They were both innocent. They were both genuine. They were also wise, they loved, they had experienced tragedy and loss unimaginable, yet they had forged on and developed all of this, just so they could reduce the suffering existent in humanity.

They wanted to protect the Earth, yet they also wanted to cultivate the ecosphere to enable chaos to be more controlled, and where needed, for the preservation of humanity and abundance of beauty, quality of life, and joy. They had millions of ideas running through their minds at once, they truly had minds with many millennia of knowledge, experience, and wisdom, and then as if this symphony of thought translated into a visual masterpiece and a smorgasbord of emotions before him and what he beheld couldn't seem any more spectacular, he found a new clarity, a new vision, and a new and meaningful answer to all things, *"So long as we go forward with the well-being of others as well as ourselves in mind, we'll create a legacy that can be and will be worthy of preservation indefinitely.*

"If we are to contribute to the compassion, the kindness, and the awesomeness of well-being toward others as well as ourselves, we will each be true friends. We will also have unique potential that can be realized in its fullest form, each one of us, and as such I know what I will do. I will lead large numbers of people through training, development, and clarity when it comes to infrastructure throughout the solar system, the maintenance of it, governance of humanity, of many refugees of toxic environments at home or abroad, and clarity toward the future when it comes to the primary missions that lead me and others on a successful and enjoyable path of longevity, experience, and wisdom."

Eliza beckoned James to follow her, and he realized he was flying high enough in the sky to see everywhere, and to help him realize he had the ability to zoom in on anything and in any direction. *"How is this possible?"* he asked.

Yesha then flying to his left pointed at a forested area, and he saw their entire planned infrastructure as she had shown him on her laptop, where it lay as opposed to the rest of the geography surrounding the country and world. He saw how it would all lay out underneath the forest, with many magnificent portals for entrances, ventilation, and emergency exits. Eliza then took James by the hand, and together all three traversed through the designs as if they were already realized, and he could see the safety control mechanisms, the unbreakable, very thick, and spacious shell of the laboratories, and each detail filled with mechanical and digital redundancies, backups, and failsafes. He saw the fusion accelerators, the air scrubbers and HVAC systems, the electrical systems, the fiber optics, the copper cabling, the hallways that made it all accessible to maintenance crews, the spacious rooms and extremely large hadron colliders, the two ITERs and so much more. Although these maintenance crews might never be needed, accessibility was infused throughout each level of infrastructure to allow for ease of care, just in case.

He looked some more and saw deep underground dining facilities, campuses, living quarters, galleries, music labs, and entertainment, development, and enjoyment centers, all with redundant air and resource safety mechanisms. They left nothing out.

They had antimatter chambers with electromagnetic systems strong enough to safely contain millions of kilograms of antimatter and every other particle, both baryonic or non-baryonic, exotic or otherwise, in a manner that provided stability to each element, particle, and antiparticle as well as containment and the ability to move it all around, combine it, and divide it all in whichever way was necessary without decay. Eliza and Yesha were brilliant, and suddenly it was all as clear as day to him. It was as if Eliza's and Yesha's minds were converging with his, but he could differentiate between his thoughts and theirs. He enjoyed the sweet and enigmatic flavor of both of their unique thoughts.

"This is beyond amazing, you two. It's as if all of what you have learned is now a part of my own mind as well," said James, pondering with a display of it all in the clouds just above him.

"It's because that is precisely what is happening. You can see why Yesha and I keep this under wraps. This can be beautiful, but others with not so kind of demeanor or intentions might not see it this way. While some may say it is because malevolent intended individuals might try to influence our thoughts, they are errant, because that is not the case and won't be possible.

"We've taken every precaution and built safety mechanisms to protect our thoughts, as well as your free will and ours. We can share what we are ready to share, and all else is protected, according to the established US laws of consent. The only reason for secrecy with this technology is because humanity isn't yet ready to accept it; those that would decay the minds of others hold too much power over the hearts of men

and women, and they have even built laws to prevent advancements such as these to take place and be proliferated.

"This technology, if in the wrong hands, could theoretically be used for all sorts of malicious purposes, thus the fears. The truth is, we've scanned every system, every satellite, and every software program, and we have created safeguards that make malevolent intentions impossible. There are special algorithms and encodings for every single one of the many aspects of the mind, and as people volunteer to be read-in and thus are neurologically optimized, compassion, empathy, and the ability of the recipient to have the gift of persuasion through the understanding of others toward kindness, longevity, quality of life, and the advancement of civilization are in turn amplified and optimized."

Eliza sensed some concern and looked at James with serenity in her aura.

"You said people would have free will. Won't those 'optimizations' take that away?" asked James.

Eliza then brought a pause to his worries and rendered peace to his mind when she spoke, "These optimizations won't take away free will, and here is why, death is the opposite of free will of any kind, because, with death, all of your abilities to experience reality are gone, all of your potential that has been built up and improved upon for years is no longer available to you or the rest of humanity, and thus choice is no longer an option, your free will is gone. Life equates to free will since this allows you to experience this reality in a much more fulfilling and purposeful way as we develop a bridge between the realities we understand and the realities we have yet to know.

"Therefore, anything that leads to longevity, preservation, and the well-being of life is within the scope of free will. Optimizing our physiology relates to free will because doing so preserves life as well as the quality of it. Optimizing our neurology also relates to free will because it allows us the clarity of mind to develop and improve upon all of the necessary advancements that in turn increase longevity, preserves and protects life on this planet, throughout our solar system, and anywhere we go. Compassion, kindness, and love are essential components of free will—which are the preservation and protection of life. It can be said then, that anything that takes away from that takes away from free will, leads to uncontrolled chaos, and will eventually lead to the death of all life as we know it.

"Optimizing ourselves affords us the ability to compound upon our potential, rather than bury it with death. With our system, free will cannot be taken away, nor will it ever be, instead it will amplify immensely."

The brilliance of Eliza's mind, both in the abstract and in reality, knew no bounds, "So, I take it, that both of you, Eliza and Yesha, and now I, have a higher level of free will than many. The clarity of what can be done to take us on the pathway of indefinite lifespans is what constitutes free will in its purest form. Choosing how we'll contribute to the mission of humanity and its indefinite legacy is freedom. To shun advancements is to counter free will and to worship death, essentially.

"It's amazing how simple true freedom can be. It's so sad that there are so many lost and hopeless in life, so lost they are willing to cause others to lose that potential as well."

Yesha agreed with him with a polite, "Mm, hmm," and a smile, and then she responded, "You are correct, and interestingly enough, given your free will, here you are thinking in a collective mindset, and we can all see eye to eye, as one, but with different ideas, thoughts, and clarity of missions throughout the rest of life as we know it. We are unique and special in so many ways, and all of this while we're alike in understanding with clarity what free will is. We don't ever need to condemn anyone;

they do that to themselves. All we do is point people in the right direction. Now, there will be those that have the delusion that this would be considered in a sense submission, but they could not be further from the truth, and it is sad how lost their minds have become, yet that can change.

"Nevertheless, many get caught up in the philosophies of those whose minds were truly lost in fear, yet they can still learn that life and the unique contributions we each can individually make toward its healthy preservation is synonymous to free will. As they do, they'll realize how spectacular our realities can be."

"Listening, thinking, wow, this is the best I think I have ever felt in my life," said James.

"Wait until we return to the real world. While there is so much, we can still learn so well, and with clarity here, when we return, you'll find a unique awe in and savor of life, and you'll experience learning and living like you've never been able to before. When we awake, you will be fully optimized, both physiologically and neurologically, and you are now. Are you ready for the next part of our journey? Or do you have any other questions? Keep in mind, there are certain chores, activities, and things we no longer need to do once we leave, but to a certain extent doing those things can be profoundly more enjoyable.

"Still, as we do them, we want to keep in mind that one of the many purposes of these optimizations is to reduce our consumption of resources as much as we can. Soon, there will be no such thing as finite resources, since we have gained the ability to use cold-fusion in its fullest and most splendid form, constantly recycling, reusing, and rebuilding what already exists, so, as far as exemplary behavior is concerned, we'll use resources sparingly until humanity has been read-in, following proper approvals and legality, providing everyone their own choice to optimize.

"Ultimately, with our optimizations, we don't need to sleep, eat food, take showers, or even use our cell phones, because we are optimized, always updating, upgrading, and linked to each other, the mainframe, and we can control individual accesses to our personal links with our neural identifications.

"For example, instead of going to a regular bed, you can choose to spend that time doing more research and making more discoveries in the real world or in the Virtual Universe. If you're doing private things that no one else needs to know about, you can turn off your link, or compartmentalize your thoughts, which will be encrypted in a way that will back you up should something devastating occur and we need to bring you back, but these particular thoughts will only be available for that purpose and un-viewable by others unless you will them to be shared.

"Again, right now, there is nothing known to humanity that could cause something that devastating to happen to our technologies and infrastructure once they are built, because Eliza and I are about redundancies and proper preparation, no matter the outcome.

"We'd recommend that once we leave the Virtual Universe, you and anyone, who through you becomes read-in, take some time and explore the world, the Virtual Universe, and much more, as many times as needed. Please know, that it is still important to eat, sleep, shower, etc., when we are working with people who are not read-in, from time to time.

"Do this, if anything, because this is a free world, and, in some ways, it will keep you grounded. We'll teach you a lot more about all of your newly inherited abilities here, and again, and some the new nuances of it all, once we return to the real world. Remember, your nanos are constantly healing you, giving you clarity, and optimizing your capacities in every possible way."

"Keep in mind, James, it's great to be linked," responded Eliza, *"Seriously, it is. We each have ways of seeing things that others don't, even when linked we may*

understand things more fully than we ever have before. You know me now, Yesha knows me, and I know both of you. You both have beautiful minds, Yesha and James! No matter how many times you hear this, please don't ever underestimate yourselves.

"*So, as Yesha asked, are you ready to return to the real world? Or would you prefer to see a few more interesting things?*

"*Yes, and yes,*" said James, and they all laughed since they could see the clarity of each other's minds.

Eliza took Yesha and James by the hand and showed them everything that she and Yesha had already seen throughout the Earth and the rest of the solar system. She then showed Yesha and James her updated plans, based on what she and Yesha had talked about before, but with the full scope of details as to what they had planned on doing outside the gravity well of Earth.

For James, this was quite a journey, and even still at this time there was much more to show him.

James was exceedingly impressed with all of the details and everything seemed clear, with digital readouts laid out before him all the way down to explanations of how fusion worked and how to manipulate individual particles to allow them in the Virtual Universe to navigate around as non-baryonic matter, and materialize in light form, or as something lighter and faster, to essentially create autonomous, programmable, and reprogrammable systems with unlimited potential for compounding upon getting things done in several orders of magnitude with more efficiency and quality in the real world. She called the result, mainframe-linked nanos, or simply nanos.

Eliza showed him the magnitude of the space-based infrastructure that she and Yesha had planned on putting together, while he was engaged in the building of infrastructure on Earth. He was amazed. "*You'll quality check and improve upon what we build in space, once you are finished on Earth. You'll essentially govern the tech cities we build throughout the solar system and in essence be the employment manager.*

"*We'll in-turn do much of the same on Earth, once you are done here. We'll be able to freely come and go and help each other wherever and whenever needed, and we'll be able to start any projects we deem necessary wherever we need to start them with little to no fuss and no public repudiation.*

"*We have perfected our invisibility and cloaking technologies, which was really quite simple. We will apply them to our infrastructure throughout the solar system and Earth, so those who are not read-in will see things as they would be had we never been there, taking into account their safety and the well-being and beauty of the surrounding environment.*"

After training and further conversation, Eliza showed him everything he wished to see, and then they helped him learn every science, every art, every sport, and every martial art, just as they had, with extensive amounts of depth, perspective, experiential and muscle memory, all while accumulating extremely clear and concrete knowledge and compounded wisdom as to how and when to use it all, and then he was filled with so much anticipation, that they each hugged each other and closed their eyes.

Then like that, he woke up, feeling healthier, more vibrant, clear-minded, and awake than he had ever felt before. He remembered every bit of his twenty-year journey with complete clarity on each detail, and with a positive cognitive framework on every aspect he called to the front of his memory, yet he also could tell it had only been five minutes.

As he contemplated everything that he thought he knew before going into the Virtual Universe, his purpose in life seemed to shatter into a million pieces before him, making way for a new and beautiful clarity toward the purpose of indefinite longevity. He raised the lid to his biopod and saw Eliza and Yesha glowing brightly like angels, as they stood up from their biopods. They then looked at him and said, "Look at your own hands, the nanos in your body are optimizing you at every level." He looked, and he noticed that he was glowing too.

Chapter 07: Many New Gifts

Database Moon Archive, Celestial-Sol Entry Date: 2018 December 25 – Experiential biography, as taught to Vesha Celeste, about James Cooper, following his first journey through the Virtual Universe, experiencing some of the joys of his new gifts, during her Virtual Universe training, within Pathway Covert Campus in Melrose, MA. Contained within are thoughts from Eliza Williams, Yesha Alevtina, and James Cooper. Training Given by Yesha Alevtina, President of Pathway, 2015-2022.

As James contemplated his new reality, his new sense of undying vibrance and love for life, with its endless and joyful freedoms, Eliza and Yesha let him ponder for these small moments to allow his cognition to make sense of it all. They were linked, and they understood what he was going through, because the same had happened to them, amidst a lot of shared laughter, three weeks prior.

Together, these two amazing women taught him how to control his new abilities, and he learned that he was now neurally linked to both Eliza and Yesha. They showed him how his suit and tie, and all of his clothing had been kept the same, just as it was before he went into the biopod, but now it was merely a program transmitting what he wanted others to see, via his own smart suit.

They began thinking and sharing thoughts back and forth, and they felt a bond they had never felt before. With James there, he shared his strengths with them, and they shared their strengths with him, and they realized that as their team grew, every single person involved would become thus, exponentially more powerful, wise, involved in something greater than themselves alone, and kindness would soon be the most powerful influence above all else, combined with the power of genuine love.

Together, they left the room with the biopods and entered another room in Eliza's estate.

"How long has it been since you grabbed a sleeping bag, lay on your back, and looked up at the stars?" asked Eliza, in James' mind.

"About a year ago, my crew and friends went camping in Yosemite. We brought our telescopes and gazed at Cassiopeia, then Andromeda, and then Orion," replied James. *"All three were out around this time of night at this time of year and in our hemisphere. I've been out with my crew at night gazing at stars since then, but something tells me this will be quite different. Since you ask, I'd imagine that if we were to head outside right now, we could see the stars of those very same constellations overhead, but without telescopes."*

"In fact, you are right, James. You won't need a telescope anymore. Would you like to borrow one of our sleeping bags—and, sidenote, you don't need them either, but they're nice to have, just in case? Oh, new trick, your clothes have received an upgrade too. Since they are now part of your smart suit, you'll be able to simply think, 'pajamas' and the style you'd like to wear will become what you are actually wearing." Yesha, neurally linked, coached him. Like that, suddenly James was wearing some very stylish pajamas with navies, blues, purples and whites nicely arranged in a subdued, yet

embroidered and silken pattern, silken pants that matched, with cuffs at the ankles, and slippers of warming material that matched his smoker's robe, and all of his attire complemented his frame and aesthetic.

"It's pretty neat being able to communicate through the link, seeing what the other sees, while keeping multi-visual balance and not running into things, and having mental clarity on whatever it is you're coaching me on," said James, as Eliza handed James one of her sleeping bags, and then led them through the back door and into the backyard.

"You bet it is," smiled Eliza, as they began to settle down, with James' sleeping bag situated in-between both Eliza's and Yesha's, at their request.

Just to make sure he could still speak out loud, he spoke up, "Eliza, I noticed something was weighing on you while we were in the Virtual Universe. Although I couldn't quite understand what that would be. You are so well composed, are very well put together, and you love humanity so much. Yet, you are holding back quite a bit. Do you mind if I ask who Tyson is?" asked James. Somehow, he had been able to perceive a name and the associated pain while sharing those sweet moments with her and Yesha and sensed that there could be a lot gained when training others in the Virtual Universe, by sharing that experience. He knew it to be an insight on empathy.

"He was a very sweet boy. Before I was born, when my parents found out that I was on the way, Yesha's Mom recommended that they get a dog. They rescued Tyson, who lived with us, gave us so much joy in life, and then he passed away due to cancer when I was ten. He was one of the sweetest and most wonderful beings I know of.

"I'll take you on that journey, the next time we go into the Virtual Universe together, and I can tell by your thoughts that I'll need to add that to the training regimen in the Virtual Universe for the added neural benefit of others. Wow, yes, it helps teach empathy and love that is unconditional. For now, James and Yesha, let's enjoy the moment?" responded Eliza.

"Eliza, being torn away from another special and irreplaceable being can be traumatic. I firmly believe that remembering the wonderful moments and even shedding a tear or two or many helps to build our compassion and propensity for the love of others. Big heart my friend."

"Thank you, James." Eliza smiled, and then laid her head on her pillow slightly positioned closer to his and continued to gaze up at the stars.

They then drifted from the heavy conversation and into looking deep into the cosmos and sharing what they were watching with each other. *"Can you see Orion?"* inquired Eliza.

"Yes. There's his belt, and there's Rigel, and there's Betelgeuse, oh wow, and if I focus it's as if I can see as clear as day all of the colors and breadth of details of the Orion Nebula, oh wow, and the exoplanets circling the stars within it!" exclaimed James in surprise and awe toward his newly gifted abilities. He had sensed that it was time to drift with Eliza and Yesha into other topics of conversation, but he didn't want to press any matters further than they were willing.

They had shared so many amazing journeys that day, so he would take certain journeys with Eliza at another time. The colors of the various nebulae blossomed with clarity in detail and in every wavelength.

"You didn't need much coaching from us," Yesha said with a chuckle, putting her head slightly closer to James as well. He was a decent man, and a wonderful friend.

"It was just an idea I had, encoding our nanos to communicate on a cellular level the ability of our eyes to compress the cornea and lenses in such a way that we can see better than any telescope or even microscope if we, well, if we simply will that to happen," explained Eliza, using her real voice. She continued, "Now, check this out. If we link minds engaging the corpus callosum and occipital lobe, then we can see what the other is seeing and add a multidimensional aspect to the object we're looking at, and even extrapolate the data.

"Okay, I'm looking at the Apollo 11 landing on the Moon, zoomed in much more clearly and in real time than the LRO. If you link with me, I'll show you proof that NASA was not hoaxing the lunar landing after all."

James linked with Eliza, and he was impressed, first she zoomed out to show the sphere of the Moon, then she zoomed in to the sea of moon dust, then the remains of the lunar landing module, the burn marks in the dust, and right there, following the astronaut's footprints was the US flag. While he was linked visually, he spoke and shared his intrigue with audible voice, "Woah, hahaha, it's lying down and pretty faded! But there it is. And to think that the conspiracy theorists almost had me convinced! Why are people skeptical to a fault? It's one thing to want to make double sure something we invent doesn't hurt someone, but it's quite a pox on our character if we can't find it within us to trust the character of someone who has given us no reason to mistrust them, especially if there is no harm in doing so. I think I am with you both, Eliza and Yesha, when I scan your minds, there is a saying you've both shared, 'It's our responsibility to find the good in others. If we become critical of someone instead, without any constructive feedback which will properly inform them, then we will in no way help them to have the clarity for a better method, process, or day, so let's find the good and inspire people through noble character on our part, the kind of character that will inspire others to be their best as well.' Every person has amazing potential and it is our responsibility to see it, to applaud it, and to enlighten as necessary, but with kindness."

"You hit the nail on the head," Yesha laughed.

James could physically sense Eliza and Yesha lying on both sides of him in peace and contentment. He too was at peace, with contentment, and could feel the magic of them approving of him simply being happy laying there between these two beautiful angels and wise geniuses, and he could sense they were happy too, because he had approved of them. No matter our strengths, genuine validation always boosts the spirits.

While lying there in peace, Eliza and Yesha began to hum some of their favorite Depeche Mode tunes, looked up at Spica, Lyra, Cassiopeia and a few other constellation asterisms with exceptional clarity and linked with James, humming the lyrics of the tune inside James' mind. As James linked, he too knew the song inside and out. It was from Depeche Mode's Black Celebration album and sung by Martin Gore, an angel of a man in his own right. They continued to hum and share more tunes with their linked minds, including Red Flag's song, "The Things We Say," from their Lighthouse album, and James drifted with them for a close-up of the Andromeda Galaxy. Yesha nudged his link so he was able to gaze toward Eto, as she and Eliza had named it, located in the equivalent sector of that galaxy as our own Sun was located within ours.

"Wow! Look at all of those crystalline mountains and plum-colored seas!"

"Yesha saw it first. It's beautiful. The plum color, that's wine! Seas of wine! I don't yet know how, but we'll find out for real, hopefully, sooner than later, whether it's truly wine or simply a trick of perception. The stats are there, and they do indicate wine. It does appear to be quite beautiful," said Eliza.

They then drifted more into a quadrant of the Milky Way, very similar to the one the Sun belonged to, and there it was, another solar system very much like our own, with nine exoplanets, one of them just like Earth. However, as they zoomed in more, they could see the terrain, and they saw an asteroid pummel it. The large creatures on the planet had all been decimated right before their very eyes, save for a few large flying reptiles, which flew and flew until they found a cooler region of their planet. James understood then why chaos needed to be controlled if for any other reason, to protect life, guide it to sentience, and help it to evolve to have similar features to humans, like deposable thumbs, and arms that could reach and hold things, similar to embracing someone in a hug. He also saw this as important, so that they too could construct spacecraft and help humanity to preserve their star system's planets, and the Universe. He grew tired, as did Eliza and Yesha, and they willed themselves to sleep. James peered just a little more, and as these large reptilian birds nestled to slumber in their safe region of that planet, so too did James, Eliza, and Yesha, within their sleeping bags, nestled side by side, giving comfort to each other, and making way for shared dreams, unlike anything James had ever experienced before.

For James, shared dreams with these two were an adventure of emotion, love, intellect, joy, fun, raging hormones, and paradise he could never have fathomed before all that he had born witness to throughout the last few hours of the day. He was at peace, and to him this was heaven, and he wanted to hold onto this moment forever.

When they awoke, they all smiled at each other. They understood each other's dreams and shared experiences more than anyone else who had not been optimized could have imagined dreaming, and understanding one another and their thoughts, hopes, and dreams.

"That was absolutely breath-taking, Eliza, and James," said Yesha. "That dream where you showed us those buildings you constructed in Dubai? That was awesome! That dive in Paraguay from the top of a waterfall and plunging into the lake below, amazing! The music we made with our minds, beautiful!"

Yesha was happy they had met James and looked forward to the days ahead.

"When we build our tech cities, we want creativity similar to that, but we'll have the added advantage of a technology that allows our minds to link to the beauty of the city and the flora and fauna yearning to be beautified and seen. Every city will be a collaborated and shared vision brought to reality by all who live within it and will almost have a life of its own. Yes, our cities will be as beautiful as Dubai, but we'll be building them for the hungry, the poor, the down-trodden, and anyone seeking asylum, as well as any individual wanting to navigate through life with meaning, purpose, and most importantly, with love," said Eliza.

"I'm all for that," smiled James.

"So, you know," said Yesha, "link with me and Eliza for a second."

James linked.

"*Remember how Eliza told you in the Virtual Universe that you don't need to shower anymore? Hahaha, I know, that sounds weird, right?*" Yesha was amused by James' facial expressions but continued. "*The nanos communicate sort of a cold fusion and algorithmic encoding in sync with our right brains and amongst our cells, and any debris, unused food, anything our bodies no longer need will be converted into what our bodies do need, and as a consequence, any pleasant fragrances you conjure up in your mind will bathe you, optimize your skin, and you will look and smell incredible. Another reason we have to keep all of this on the 'down-low' is that it would put more industries out of business, but there are businesses to be built in the Virtual Universe, especially for those who are very creative. To be quite frank, that's not the purpose; the purpose is to reduce resource consumption. Instead of producing more objects at the cost of Nature, we can hire people to artistically design wardrobes, hairstyles, and the whole gamut to allow for download into the mind, an area compartmentalized just for that. These industries will then continue to breed ingenuity and they will allow people to be productive while taking care of themselves and their families. Nonetheless, in the meantime, we don't need to bathe any longer, although that is still enjoyable, and I recommend we do that now. Remember last night when I smelt like roses?*" Yesha paused.

"*I do,*" said James.

"Well, that's due to my mind and our optimizations."

The conversation continued, while their nanos took care of each of them. As they conversed, Eliza and Yesha trained James each step of the way. They climbed into the rather large shower and spent many wonderful moments together, along with a little sponge war and laughs. When they were done, they dressed and readied themselves for the real world. He then asked if they could accompany him to his next destination, and they agreed.

Because they were linked, they rehearsed and practiced how they would present their offer to become optimized, share the plans, and build the Pathway LLC infrastructure to James' crew.

As they walked to their destination, they also taught him how to control his glow. After the necessary time spent training James, merely assuring that the already formulating clarity was going from germination to healthy growth, all three knew they were on a straight path to the advancements of humanity, life, longevity, and joy, and they could clearly see how they would go about each step. As they continued to walk to their destination an interesting aura about them seemed to melt the hearts of each passerby, in so many ways that they could see, and they appreciated the double-take, the smile, the wave, and the added spring in the step of every person who saw them. They controlled their personal expressions and auras enough to impress onlookers yet conceal their true abilities and explorations they had shared the night before and earlier that morning. All three felt like they were walking in heaven and anxious to share this with others.

They eventually arrived at their desired meeting place and met with James' ninety-six crew members, wherein he was the ninety-seventh, as well as the four retirees and all of the family members and significant others of those who had them who were able to make it. About fifty percent of his crew was married, about fifty percent of those who were married had children of every age, and everyone else was either married or single without children. James had prearranged a grange to meet in each day at ten in the morning, so everyone could talk about the previous day's experiences, eat, and plan for the upcoming day's activities and events.

Sometimes, as inspired, he would get up on a pulpit that had been constructed of shining and clearly-waxed red cedar, to talk to the children, the men, and the women about something that concerned them all, captured their interest, or that he felt would inspire them toward continued excellence. So many subjects had been covered over the years, from investments and mortgages to emergency management in the home and healthy living, to educational opportunities and the next vacation, maybe on the Moon, or Selene, or Titan, or Enceladus, or further out and into the Oort Clouds. Today, it would be about a new set of projects and how everyone would have a chance to participate and benefit from them.

James waved at co-workers, shook the hands of those nearby, introduced Eliza and Yesha to those who hadn't met them at the T.O., and then walked up to the podium, cordially taking the microphone and proceeding. "I have a proposition and request for each of you." He then perceptively and eloquently explained to the crowd everything that he, Eliza, and Yesha had rehearsed.

Every person in the room was attentive, including the children. Everyone was sitting at the edge of their seats, and one-hundred percent of his audience was in with the plans that James had agreed to the night before. He continued as he finished sharing the plans and the offer, "You are free to take it, or you are free to leave it, but I have a strong sense that each one of you will find this better than any vacation..." He then introduced Eliza who explained more details, with the help of Yesha, who put up a slideshow with the plans on the projector screen, using her link to anything digital to conjure up the best display she could imagine.

After explaining everything, everyone agreed to back James, Eliza, and Yesha. James' crew, the four retirees, and one-hundred-twenty-nine family members present all called home to the seventy significant others who weren't there to speed up and finalize their plans to arrive in Cambridge from Grayling by Monday. They also made arrangements with their property managers and decided to take a few days of visits to Eliza's estate in reasonable numbers to visit the three biopods and go on Virtual Universe journeys. With one sojourner going through the Virtual Universe every five minutes, and this same process going on for eight hours on Sunday, Monday, when the rest of the significant others of his crew arrived, and through noon on Tuesday, this was finished in fewer than three days.

Yesha and Eliza had built one more biopod that Sunday morning, and shortly after, James was able to lead the way for each of his crewmembers and their families. Eliza and Yesha accompanied him.

All two-hundred-eighty-three crewmembers, family members, and significant others had agreed to become neurologically and physiologically optimized, the children included, and by Tuesday, they were all involved in building the various types of infrastructure.

Before heading arms-deep into building, they organized how everything would be completed and commenced on Tuesday at noon. Pathway LLC had grown from three to two-hundred-eighty-three in three days.

Every crew member, man, woman, and child had a unique and beautiful experience in the Virtual Universe, from Sunday morning through Tuesday at noon. The children's minds were protected from a perspective of consent, yet they too experienced many millennia of wisdom and journeys, and their minds were extraordinarily mature.

They too wanted to help in the mission with Pathway. Once everything was set up, however long that would take, with homeschooling and other legal arrangements made for the children, the men, women, and children of Pathway would return to the so-called normal life, possibly live in their homes in Grayling, the children would go back to school like normal, and everyone would recruit people across the globe to join Pathway, for a few hours each day.

Together, they would find those suffering most, befriend them, their families, maybe even rescue them, and give them an opportunity to make life a beautiful experience with more promise. First, they needed to build the entire layout of the infrastructure. All two-hundred-eighty-three Pathway LLC members, with Eliza, Yesha, and James at the helm, were eager and ready to begin.

Awesome Infrastructure

After the meetings with James and his crew, and during free moments in off hours while getting his crew moved out of their hotels and into Eliza's large estate, with room enough for more than three-hundred under a canopy, camping style, with all of the necessities and luxuries one could ask for, Eliza, Yesha, and James spent a lot of dilated time together in the Virtual Universe to further integrate their specific plans to the environment of the properties Eliza had purchased the Friday before, with sustainable design and protection of the ecosystems of each location. They developed private shipping and transportation abilities that would be equally as viable, both during and after construction. Hyperloops and jump gates, like the private hub at Eliza's estate, would carry personnel, equipment, and material to their desired locations quickly and effectively. This included to James' and his crewmembers' hometown, Grayling, where the shipping and receiving depot would be located.

James, with Eliza and Yesha worked in the Virtual Universe to ensure each building was more thoroughly designed to improve energy efficiency, with carbon dioxide and other molecular and chemical scrubbers in optimal locations, all designed with utility, comfort, and aesthetics in mind to provide pollution-free and decay-scrubbed bio-environments, clean energy, and higher productivity to the environment and their facilities. Safety redundancies for non-optimized individuals were imbued in every manner. They made conveyances for these capacities to benefit each local community by creating energy interfaces that could connect to each electrical grid, removing emissions concerns and dependence upon other sources of energy, ever-so-gently and in a way that would not contaminate the environment or break the wallets of struggling families.

Working with James and his crew, Eliza and Yesha developed a series of cold-fusion reactors with full-containment capacities, providing one-hundred percent clean energy for storage, via Pathway Energy, with the ability to source out to all of the world's power grids. With every aspect of energy stored and eventually tied into the grid itself, they had created the potential for a self-sustaining energy environmental system for anyone tied into that energy infrastructure.

Eliza, Yesha, and James were sure that when this was fully-operational, turned on, and thus linked to the world's power grids, the electrical companies would not know how or why this anomaly was happening, even after conducting intense investigations, and they knew that the electrical companies would most likely continue to charge their customers for a profit anyway, unless they could let the cat out of the bag, so-to-speak.

Pathway wouldn't apply their overhauls immediately. While they would implement pollution control and scrubbing procedures straightaway, as they ever-so-carefully and quietly phased out the use of pollutants altogether, the program in full was something they would have to negotiate with the public sector. Once the public was properly informed, other methods of job-security and economic compensation to workers would be put into place and energy companies could be revamped or new ones established, they would go public with Pathway Energy.

James talked with Eliza and Yesha about this in their leadership matrix, which they had developed inside the Virtual Universe. *"The economists will most likely say, 'Money has to flow,' and until we have alternative economic compensation in place for all parties impacted, no doubt the companies will charge money for overhead and more until there are legal protections for the people in place. It might be better to form Pathway Energy, transitioning employment in that way, by buying the others out and giving them an opportunity to join up and be 'all in.' I am sure I'm not alone in hoping the people in their employ will benefit from this economically as well."*

Eliza spoke up. *"Agreed, James. We will need to use our persuasive skills to convince the energy industry to bask in the free energy. They need jobs, I know. The rich obviously will be concerned for their status and the ability to have a high quality of life, just like anyone else. I'm interested in everyone benefiting from this, leading to a high-quality of life for all.*

"Instead of two percent of the populous in beautiful homes with all of the cool things, one hundred percent of humanity will easily be able to enjoy a life of so-called privilege, and all so we can move on from the most basic of needs and on to the higher needs of self-actualization, leading to a more advanced society that is ready to traverse the stars.

"We can create a pay-for-use program that will ensure energy industry employees are compensated well, while implementing and ensuring a minimum-scaled burden is placed on customers who are struggling the most."

"Excellent idea, Eliza," said James. "We don't need to create a volatile market, instead we can make a smooth transition that has multi-layered benefits for everyone."

Yesha weighed in and agreed. She then moved on to other integrated systems that would affect the economy and the overall environment in a positive way, "Now, each building will have water recyclers with scrubbers, acid and alkaline adjusters and filters, water pro-biotic introduction facilities that infuse biotics and other microbes excellent for digestive health and with filters available for unique and local needs that can be adjusted in an individually confined manner depending on need, along with mineral additives essential for reduction of free radicals, as well as physiological and neurological health. Essentially, water will run through a system of cleansing, optimization, use, and recycling on a constant basis and every building will operate on a minimal amount of water that will cycle endlessly while accounting for occasional loss through evaporation.

"Evaporation of particles that are toxic to our natural biosphere will be contained by a very intricate and highly advanced system collecting and returning it to each building system or hyperloop station source, in such a way as to prevent harm to any living being."

Eliza, Yesha, James, and their crews agreed that they would build all of the above along with their material production facilities in less than a day.

Eliza led the way, with Yesha and James at each side, "We will do this by building the facilities that create and then compound upon the quantity and capabilities of self-replicating and reprogrammable nano clouds first.

"We will take our plans to build a large biopod-like facility, where everyone can enter together, and as a result, program the nano clouds to build. This, in turn, will increase the fusion processes that will be diverted toward further material creation. These nanos will be imbued with the purpose of creating all of the necessary infrastructural materials, taking cloud-like masses of necessary particles, isotopes, and molecules, shaping, transporting, and then carefully installing them into whatever material, way, or location is needed, both simple and complex.

"Every building will be built for the physiological and neurological health of its occupants and in a way that will automatically adjust in localized areas to provide an optimal environment for any given individual, which will include considerations for people who are both optimized and 'normal' in most natural senses. We will also consider their comfort, the aesthetics for the health of the mind, which in turn will increase morale, ingenuity, and productivity.

"We will work to make sure that lighting, ventilation, dryness and moisture control, and acoustic performance are integrated within each building to also ensure high-end results of zero noise spillage and a heightened or increased communicational understanding, and we can do all of this while avoiding the use of materials that are high in volatile organic compounds. Each building will mend and maintain itself much like a living body's complexed system, by using nano technology.

"Once we are complete with every single bit of infrastructure running fully, we will repeat this in every major metropolitan city, regular city, town, and village throughout the US and its territories."

James worked with Eliza and Yesha showing them materials he was familiar with that could reduce routine maintenance requirements, simplify them, and require less energy, less water, as well as use non-toxic products to maintain, all while increasing aesthetics and quality.

Within the Virtual Universe, Eliza showed James how to program the nanos to scrub and repair these or any facilities or areas built, in a routine manner, daily, and without the need for any further energy or water.

"We will build the large cold-fusion mass-producer and warehouse first. In this way, as you originally suggested, the materials used will be cost-effective.

"Pathway LLC will virtually maintain an indefinite lifecycle, without the need to factor in a half-life due to the quality of construction as well as subsequent routine maintenance which will be at a minimal to nonexistent cost to the biological health of anyone or the biosphere of our planet, in any manner we can conceive of, and with huge returns on well-being, and so much more. We have gone over our plans and are ready for construction, James. So, let's begin."

On Monday, January 8, 2008, Eliza, Yesha, and James had fully meshed out the drafting plans for completion, the materials needed, and how they would complete each step. Meanwhile, James' crewmembers, with Anne, Tom, and Brandy, in many cases taking the lead, took their place helping those still going through and completing their Virtual Universe training and greeting family members as well as significant others who had just flown in. Once all personnel were trained, they immersed themselves in what was to be done, with lists, checklists, and goals, imbued with robust edification as to what, how, and the way something or anything needed to be done.

"Everything from start to finish is a beautiful work of coordination and effort on so many levels," said James. By the time James' crew and their families were fully trained, the cold-fusion producer and warehouse, the large group biopod, and the facilities for their families to live in were built. Armed with his own huge cadre, each with swaths of nanos, James and his optimized crew integrated back and forth within the Virtual Universe and the nanos and built the hyperloops and Eliza's and Yesha's strategically placed jump gate technologies.

The hyperloops and jump gates were integrated as necessary within and around each perspective facility and were online allowing everyone the ability to get around with ease with all material to be transported easily and quickly.

While working with James and his crew, in just a few days following everyone's training, Anne reported to Eliza, Yesha, and James, in the Virtual Universe, for detail and brevity, *"We have built within our secret underground arsenal two large hadron colliders, several thermonuclear reactors, several spacious antimatter production and containment facilities, multiple cold-fusion ore, baryonic, non-baryonic, and exotic particle production and containment facilities, several stem cell research and development laboratories, ten CRISPR-Cas9 labs, and forty multiple integrated stem cell, genetic, and DNA editing, production, and targeted delivery labs, and several fourth generation base editor labs, which are technologies that Eliza and Yesha developed in the Virtual Universe, but we will keep them under wraps, and later reveal these abilities to scientists at Harvard and the world in, on, or around 2017.*

"We have germinated and grown robust forests on all Pathway LLC properties, using its own proprietary technologies, replete with all manner of fruit, flower, evergreen, and maple trees, all of which are optimized for healing and removal of fire-danger, forty genetic and neural replication facilities, several artificial intelligence and particle robotics facilities, and living quarters for several thousand personnel within our Pathway Melrose Campus. All of this is safely tucked away thirty miles below the surface of the Earth and interconnected, along with a host of other facilities which include the provision of the ability to research, prototype, and create a high-rate replication of all things related to physics, biology, and neurology."

This was Friday, January 11, 2008.

By the latter end of the first week, they had completed the complex system of laboratories and mass production facilities that gave them the ability to produce any element on the periodic table and stabilize great quantities of any isotope or even antimatter and other exotic particles, without fallout of any kind. Moreover, all two-hundred-eighty people, or in total, two-hundred-eighty-three, including Eliza, Yesha, and James, involved had gone into the Virtual Universe and had learned to practice the technique of containing pollution and repurposing it by programming nanos to maximize the energy capacity of all of their facilities, without costing a single dime or using any energy from the local energy centers.

To add to that, in many ways, they were about to drive energy costs down for everyone else living in the regions where their facilities would be built. Through Eliza's ideas, and the meetings of many minds within the Virtual Universe, they had all become what they would from then on out call, as a group or individually, citizens of Pathway, and had developed the ability to create complex micro-organisms and anything necessary to sustain life indefinitely for any living being. When they were done, they visited in the new conference center in Melrose, to coordinate with Eliza, Yesha, and James to complete the supply chain of material and move on to the next projects.

Eliza's self-replicating nanos and the new group virtual universe interface had been a boon to the project. When the first cloud of nanos had appeared above them that first Monday, communicating telepathically and asking in unison for their orders, it was quite the union of kindred spirits with between them, the humans, and all forms of former wildlife, working together, and free to do so, with consent in every action, using the benefits of time-dilation. Everyone felt a collaborated sense of clarity and appreciated the unique talents each had to contribute. Once the labs were built and the nanos were in full force, everything took off quickly.

After more nanos were encoded in mass quantities, Eliza, Yesha, James and his crew, quietly and seamlessly built the entirety of Earth-based infrastructure both above and below the ground, while also coordinating for the next projects and receiving updates on the resultant projects to follow. In the real world, being linked had hurried things up exponentially and efficiency continued to compound from there.

The creation of physiological gene-based and neurological capacity optimizations had been quite a bonus as well. The citizens were well-coordinated, knew what to do with complete clarity on every aspect of design and encoded the nanos with the brilliance of many geniuses all rolled into one and multiplied into many. They set into motion the completion of many other projects to carry on, as the entire crew of two-hundred-eighty-three took a break that Friday evening.

By the end of their second week, they had worked with James to help Eliza and Yesha to produce many other armies of nanos to build a lot more infrastructure, up to and including Eliza's and Yesha's designs for tech cities in space, throughout the solar system.

They gathered the space junk and many good-sized asteroids. As they did, they programmed the armies of nanos, making sure that each asteroid was properly documented, studied, sampled, with plenty of plugs available for archiving and further study. They provided museums, labs, and corresponding geology centers, within the corresponding interstellar moon or planetary bases, tech cities, and other significant space objects, as they were used to build the scaffolding and conveyances for these locations. Every resource was used wisely, and in an efficient manner, wherever each tech city was set to be built and loaded with luxury living suites that were very beautiful to behold. Each aspect of each of the cities was virtually and physically completed in short order, due to Virtual Universe time-dilation and sensor technologies.

Every citizen of Pathway LLC was given opportunities that could be turned down, adjusted, and accepted at any moment, with the intent of allowing them to have a luxury suite off-world and within a place of their choosing on Earth. In any suite, they would have an opportunity to have every amenity a person could think of, to include the individual biopods provided to each citizen as well as their children for a safe place to receive top-notch education, entertainment, and other forms of training, to include art and music, higher degrees of social enrichment, and all with the right amount of sustenance at any given time.

Eliza and Yesha knew that they had to prevent the dispersal of their technologies for the time-being by keeping their proprietary information at high levels of secrecy and shared only among Pathway citizens for legal, patenting, and ethical purposes, on Earth and in particular the USA, in case any disastrous side effects occurred or powerful abilities wound up finding themselves in the wrong hands.

Eliza, James, Yesha, and a growing number of citizens built a host of fail-safes, backups, and reset buttons that could neutralize the necessary details or render them mute if that were ever needed. Essentially, everyone was safe, since each person involved was constantly being updated and upgraded, and all of the initial projects were underground, allowing anything previously considered impossible or unstable as capable of being possible and stabilized.

Apart from the infrastructure on Earth, which Eliza, Yesha, James and his crew had been hard at work on, from the second day of their construction through their finish toward the third week of that year, Eliza and Yesha had recruited a growing cadre of scientists. Together, every citizen of Pathway created large memory databases, using the advantages of time dilation in the Virtual Universe, and an extensive neurological identification system, similar to Eliza's that provided security measures to protect access to their facilities in the most intriguing of ways. Anyone trying to break in was all of a sudden filled with the clarity on how it was that they could turn around and contribute, experiencing joy, rather than hinder the progression and advancement of civilization.

Eliza and Yesha had near simultaneously begun working on plans to allow some of their advancements to be presented to the FDA for approval, especially relating to cures and gene therapies. They were interested in doing this to help speed things along when it came to public proliferation. They worked together through July and devised methods of dealing with industry and allowing non-read-in scientists to fiddle with new and seemingly impossible ideas, in a main Pathway Public Campus, but in a lot of matters that were much smaller on a technological scale than for the rest of Pathway LLC.

During the first weeks, Eliza, Yesha, and James had agreed to hold off on mass production of anything outside of their terrestrial and solar system infrastructural plans until they were properly vetted in every way. Before going public on anything they would have strong security, safety, and reset mechanisms in place to prevent ethical issues or concerns by society, politicians, the medical, pharmaceutical, or biotech industries, corporations or economic titans, unless they were primarily driven by well-being rather than on wealth and power alone.

Eliza and Yesha had created exhaustive neurological control mechanisms for their advancements from the get-go to ensure they were not vulnerable to breach or manipulation for purposes that would not relate to the well-being of humanity. They wanted their developments to be of benefit to life in general and raise the quality of it, and not cause undue consequence to others.

Writing deeply encoded rules, Eliza, Yesha, and James wrote algorithms for their processes that would help humanity in an ethical manner and give them much more than the bottom line. Nonetheless, they grew their company into one that also produced minimalized advancements that were lucrative and paved the way for societal acceptance of the greater advancements through Pathway LLC. As they thoroughly vetted each of their advancements, ensuring there were fail-safes, security measures in place, and that safety concerns could be mitigated, the overt production and proliferation of ores and medical breakthrough products throughout the US and Canada began to provide the necessary taxable income to allow them to finance all of their other terrestrial projects without governmental scrutiny.

Jump Gates

Early on, when building their sensor and jump gate devices, Eliza and Yesha discovered that not only could they use the sensors to communicate to and from any region of space or Earth instantly, they could also transport anything they desired that was digitally interfaced to and from any region they wished.

Using low-cost sensors Eliza had developed, they could pick up and transmit every type of sensory information to any neurally linked location, and then integrate untold levels of information with their quantum computing interface, along with data analytics expertise and particle reservoirs, that would be kept out in deep space and transported as needed.

They could deliver everything in a digital format to their robust informational processing centers through their group virtual universe interface, to any location with a similar digital system, and essentially teleport or jump themselves or any item or series of items and living things in full form to any coordinate on a three-dimensional grid throughout the observable Universe—including Earth.

Any member fully read-in could go through a jump gate both alone or while escorting pre-approved refugees and diplomats. A lot of science was accomplished, databased, and kept private among Eliza, Yesha, James, his crew, and their growing cadre of elite scientists, or citizens, fully read-in to Pathway LLC.

Eliza and Yesha also worked on a project which involved the databasing of genomic sequences, neural pathways, and copies of each consenting person's own consciousness, only after an individual had consented via signed agreement prior to or after primary training.

They worked passively with other species until they could be optimized allowing them to neurally link with people and other species as well. They also optimized anyone who volunteered. All of this, while continuously updating these individual consciousnesses through a sensory connection between the linked minds and a robust database in Pathway LLC.

If unnecessary hostilities were present, there was a robust system in place to ensure they were given a quick trip to the Virtual Universe, where they would learn to understand what they could do to help rather than hinder the well-being of those around them.

Ultimately, anyone who had been to the Virtual Universe had a physiological and neurological digital backup stored deep within the Earth's crust and would eventually be stored on each of the Twelve Database Moons, which were currently being built.

Creating and sending a rather large series of armies of Eliza's high-tech, self-replicating, transceiving, encoding-capable nano-bots, jumping back and forth between Earth and any location in the real Universe, based on smart protocol and programming technology, which Eliza had created within the Virtual Universe, their minds were in full form. Everyone visited their biopods frequently, drawing up new plans while updating their existing ones, all the while integrating them into the computer matrix for real world visualization and implication, and in some cases being involved using their sensor and jump gate technology as they performed a series of missions in space and vetted their technology even further.

Because all citizens of Pathway agreed with Eliza, Yesha, and James, that Earth was not ready to probe beyond the solar system at this time, due to potential hostilities perhaps humanity wasn't ready for yet, Eliza, Yesha, James and their growing cadres chose to peer through and build only within the solar system. They could venture further and later as proper defensive, protective, and solar system preservation capabilities were in place. They would eventually create a spacecraft system that they agreed should jump them to a location at least ninety light years away, so as to not give Sol away to more advanced and extraterrestrial civilizations too soon. For now, they decided to keep things solar-centric, because they didn't want humanity to be caught off-guard.

Eliza worked with Yesha to build, encode, and send countless droves of armies of her nanos into outer space on multiple occasions, jumping here and there, and communicating every aspect of completion, according to the details set up by Eliza and Yesha within the Virtual Universe, which included a large variety of other more intense projects and missions.

Jumping nano clouds into outer space and back as needed with one-hundred percent accuracy, they cleaned the debris of space junk orbiting dangerously around the Earth and the Moon, carefully navigating around and minimizing interference of in-use satellites, while also mining dangerous asteroids into their component parts.

Back and forth between their biopods, Eliza and Yesha entered and re-entered them showing James and his crew how to do so, and together they continued advancing their technologies and themselves in every way beyond the typical abilities dreamed about by the greatest of science fiction minds, due to the fact that they could do a week to several millennia's worth of work in just a few minutes.

James was always floored and impressed with the plans Eliza and Yesha drew up and the ability-upgrades that were provided often via the communications engines using the sensor and jump gate technologies cross-queued with the Virtual Universe. James learned along with them and received these upgrades through his neural link, along with Pathway's growing cadre of citizens.

Together, they all began to program their own clouds of nanos to use every bit of material down to the last particle. These highly advanced self-replicating nano-bots themselves took the material from twenty-thousand large and five-hundred-thousand medium-sized, resource-rich, and dangerous asteroids between Venus and Jupiter and created approximately twenty-thousand tech cities, bases, and space-ports on Mercury, Venus, the Moon, Mars, Ceres, Pluto, Eris, and all of the other moons, if they were spheroidal, of the outer planets of the solar system using cold fusion capabilities, standard and exotic, as well as meta-material, gravitational technologies, and more.

All along Eliza, Yesha, James, and Pathway citizens factored-in fool-proof safety and security mechanisms considering each of the various environments while establishing their tech cities within bio-environmentally self-contained, maximally protected, extremely beautiful, very unique, invisible, secured, and safe environments, visible only to the citizens of Pathway.

Through everything, Eliza was very much in support of individual choice, so long as it did not cause undue consequence to the choices of others and so long as it did not hinder the advancement of civilization in the interest of the well-being of others, of preserving our Earth, our solar system, and beyond.

Each of these projects was completed at pretty much the same time. As the tech cities were built, Eliza and Yesha also saw to it that the twelve invisible database moons were created to their fullness, following which they visited them from time to time, using their unique jump gate abilities.

Sometimes they would afford all of the crew to look through their nano-forged space bio-bubbles to see where each one lay orbiting just outside of the orbit of the Moon and between the Moon and LaGrange Points 1 and 2.

The Twelve Database Moons were spatially orbiting the Earth and Moon within that first month of production and were programmed to orbit the Earth so as to never collide with each other or any other space object, man-made or natural.

These moons were also capable of providing one-hundred percent coverage both on Earth and throughout the entire observable Universe of every single sensory capacity known to human civilization and with several orders of magnitude more capacity and capability than all of Earth's man-made satellites combined.

Eliza strategically and effectively encrypted a secret link to each terrestrial satellite keeping their integration with the Twelve Database Moons undetectable until the US Government could be briefed accordingly, and only after assurance of a positive outcome.

All of this, to protect humanity, to ensure all was not lost due to human error, and due to the self-replication abilities of Eliza's magnificent nano-bots. Moreover, this was completed in the first four weeks of 2008.

Meanwhile, James and his crew completed the entire array of Earth-bound infrastructure projects, as the quantity of these projects grew, and reported everything back to Eliza, by the sixth week of 2008.

During the first week, when Eliza had shown James the teleportation technology and had asked if they would like to test the jump gates, and after James' answer to the affirmative, they were trained on how to use them. Upon doing so, there was a one-hundred percent success rate with zero human casualties.

Eliza and Yesha discovered early on that hiring each of James' crew and even their family members in those first days was the beginning to the exponential growth of personnel and friends of humanity within Pathway LLC, and once both James' assignments on Earth and Eliza's tech cities were finished, she gave James and his crew the option of visiting each of the tech cities themselves.

They agreed, en masse. *"This will be very exciting, and we'll help wherever we can,"* Eliza recalled as all of James' crew, and many from Pathway LLC's growing population, as well as many of the various animals and various creatures of so many varieties agreeing likewise and working together.

Furthermore, upon current completion, there were gargantuan forests and jungles in and around every tech city and village. Every living creature imaginable worked with Pathway LLC and was now sentient, neurally linked, and participated voluntarily in Earth-rooted civilizational advancements and preservation.

Hence, Eliza picked up on the millions of neurally linked volunteers affirming their excitement all at once to assist in the effort in any way they could.

She then asked James and his entire cadre of volunteers to quality check and fine tune every aspect of the tech cities and give her a thumb's up when they were ready for population growth. James and his cadre had agreed to do so. He wasted no time and developed a system similar to a complex set of macros where his volunteers would team up in uniquely diverse crews and go through each and every tech city.

Each volunteer became fully optimized to be an all-in-one architectural engineering specialist, scientist, and bio-hacker, and with sentient creatures of every sort among them with the same intent and marvelous vigor.

With each volunteer now very capable in every aspect of infrastructure, they ensured every system was online and fully operational while spot-checking each city in person to be sure. Using jump technology, James and his volunteers were able to vet more than five-hundred cities per hour, and within twenty-eight hours or less than four days, they were done.

While James was doing this, Eliza and Yesha shifted their focus from space and back to Earth, where they purchased another twenty-thousand acres, and this time in Ontario, Canada, near the Great Lakes and the US/Canadian borders. While doing so, she bought out a contract wherein it was intended by commerce to have the area stripped of its forests. With all that was happening in the real-world environment, Eliza wanted to prevent anything that would cause further harm to it.

They received all necessary legal authorizations from the necessary authorities and invited them to their laboratories in Massachusetts. After showing them her plans and technologies, they all agreed to work as they had, in the same offices as before, but in an optimized state. Thus, they signed their agreement forms and entered the Virtual Universe to be optimized as she had shown them. All two hundred diplomats became Pathway citizens that day.

Eliza, Yesha, and her cadre all shared neural links with these authorities and upon doing so every individual had linked and felt the awesome power of collective wisdom met with beautiful and kind intent. As such, now that these authorities were optimized in every way, with vibrant clarity toward purpose in everything they would do, and since they could link with anyone else who had been to the Virtual Universe with anyone upon their consent, they also ensured integration with and loyalty to the cause of civilizational advancements.

These diplomats were indeed filled with amazement as they returned to their daily lives, with nary a word spoken save to seem normal or to recruit others to join in. Their senses toward compassion and persuasion grew, and all while glowing in the aura of and teeming with purpose. Every member who had been optimized found themselves extremely capable and indeed successful in their every endeavor, rooted in kindness, longevity, quality of life and clarity of mind.

Instead of stripping the land of forestation, now, more forests were planted, and wildlife reserves were created. As a matter of a fact, on every property, she maintained a wildlife refuge, along with a beautiful arrangement of convention centers and luxury hotels, integrated with the environment and linked as if it were a nearby system, through hyperloops and jump gate terminals.

In the center of Pathway's Melrose Campus, Eliza programmed yet another large cloud of nano-bots that appeared as a natural fog more than sixty-five-thousand miles or one-hundred-five-thousand kilometers high and then beyond.

Eliza encoded each nano, with the added advantage of time-dilation existent in the Virtual Universe, using repetitive and redundant loops of commands to carry out complex tasks. Her effort to this project resulted in an immense fog of quintillions of extremely small yet very capable nanos. They in-turn built the very first invisible diamond nano-thread and carbon nanotube-latticed large cargo space elevator with electro-magnetic airway-divergence technology using space debris, meteors, meteorites, meteoroids, and any other potentially hazardous piece of matter to protect active satellites and Earth itself, by smelting and reconfiguring it all within the safety of large bubble-like spheres, with high-tech filtration systems in contained space using cold fusion and gravitational tech.

All of this technology was known only to the citizens and honorable associates working on the covert operations of Pathway LLC. The elevator was strapped outside of Earth's orbit to a counterweight that was about one-hundred-thousand miles or one-hundred-sixty-one thousand kilometers above the tether. This counterweight served as a large bay for shipping, receiving, and deep space take-off. In this way, they used divergence technology so that no human tech, to include airplanes or aircraft of any sort, could or would detect nor collide into the massive Earth-to-space, space-to-space, and space-to-Earth structure. While they could jump smaller payloads from point-to-point, the elevators provided transportation redundancy and the ability to transport millions of megatons of resources back and forth as needed.

Having integrated this with the extensive hyperloop system and jump gates, Pathway LLC was afforded the ease of both shipping and receiving of materials from space-to-Earth, one place in space to another, and Earth-to-space itself. They developed a system to automatically coordinate with both the governments of Canada and the US to publicly ship from Ontario, Canada, to Melrose, Massachusetts, and out from Pathway LLC to Ohio and the Great Lakes, to Michigan and beyond, as was deemed necessary and wise to ensure continued industrial breakthroughs and resources, all the while providing justifiable explanation of the economic capital and fluidity of Pathway LLC.

Early on, when Eliza had introduced both sensor and jump gate technologies, she had the cognizance to consider the quantity and type of use, the location, and destination of any information gathering source, the myriad of transport and travel options, and how they would increase dramatically and astronomically as time went by. With her jump gates, as ideal as they could be for small numbers of people who were linked neurologically at any given time, the potential for disaster as numbers increased could be exponential as well.

Eliza had brought this up in the Virtual Universe to Yesha and James near the end of all construction after these systems were introduced and were well into use, *"What if, for example, say a billion people decided they wanted to end up at the same location and at the same time without proper coordination? We could find ourselves with a situation that could end up being quite catastrophic.*

"I mean, humor me for a bit, imagine a scenario like the one playing above me, with a lot of people attached to quite a few others, and others missing limbs and whatever else. It is a grotesque scene, is it not, and unfortunately, it borders on hilarious but in a bad way."

Eliza knew that she, Yesha, James, and his crew had to come up with a system to control destination arrival such that only one source pertaining to a jump gate was received in one location at any given time. However, for travel and transport efficiency they had to ensure transportation from each and every source to the desired destination was also seamless and immediate.

While building Eliza's infrastructure, it was easy to coordinate jumps, transports, and the like every time, via neural links and the associated neural identifications. As such, during infrastructural construction, there were zero casualties. Now that each aspect of the primary plans for infrastructure was complete, with twenty-thousand tech cities ready, each with ten-million domiciles that were capable of modification integration, and with a capacity for further growth available at a moment's notice, as the population grew, things could get complicated quickly.

So, Eliza, Yesha, James and their growing crews and families all got into their biopods several times to discuss the types of issues that could occur. Knowing this, they came up with plans to mitigate the issues, and implement their plans. After which, they practiced on inanimate materials, tested the system on multiple groupings of optimized volunteers traveling from separate locations and arriving to the same location harmlessly, and then they could finally test it on those who had elected to not be optimized but wanted to work with Pathway LLC, helping in any way they could.

Going back a pace, the sensors that operated were more easily managed than the jump gates, because there were no known limits to the quantity of information that could be sent and received in a blink of an eye without traumatic results. As a matter of a fact, there were literally trillions of groups of sextillions of sensors with pass-through technology throughout the solar system now tapping into a variety of controlled entanglement factors and algorithms that were already constantly monitoring every possible bit of information, all of which was processed within the Twelve Database Moons.

These moons were completed during the fourth week and made available via any Pathway LLC interface at any location, immediately. The intent of the information was for safety, scientific clarity and development, and situational awareness as related to living conditions anywhere, as well as for further projects, navigation of spacecraft throughout the solar system, and more.

The jump gates remained easy for Eliza and her team to proliferate and build. However, setting up a tried and true coordination system for efficiency and seamlessness of travel to locations safe for personnel who weren't optimized, while reducing the compromise of health, both physiological and neurological, in the most unfortunate of ways, that could result if multiple individuals and items arrived at the same time and in the same location, was going to take some effort to build.

The computational power was there, and the resources were limitless, based on Eliza's and Pathway's solar and interplanetary fusion centers, so plausible travel coordination systems and algorithms were developed and implemented throughout the entirety of Earthling-occupied space, both for now and into the future.

Eliza gathered Yesha, James, and her entire Pathway crew in the Virtual Universe, prior to setup, and asked several questions, mind-to-mind and with visual displays playing around her for maximum effect on clarity. *"How can we set up a layered zonal travel network that can ensure that the highest quantity of people, goods, and groups can be transferred in the safest manner possible and in the least amount of time?*

"Should we have major transfer stations capable of conducting thousands of transfers every few moments? Should we create a system of major hubs, major zones, minor zones, and then individual zones? Should we consider destination triangulation such that if, for example, three people jumped from a different jump gate to the same jump gate they would automatically land safely beside each other, using instant computational spatial and coordination delivery?

"My concern is that a space elevator platform or any other space-limited location could potentially be at over capacity fairly quick and with mortal circumstances if too many people and resources landed at the same place and at the same time.

"Perhaps we could have resource shipments travel using a completely different, yet somewhat parallel network? When it comes to personnel carriers, networks that are more complex need to be considered. Finally, how about group travel stations? Ultimately, we need to prevent tragedy in every imaginable way.

"Right now, using our neural links we have managed a simple network of safe transport and travel, but I'm afraid that as we grow, this may become much more complicated, and it would be preferable to have an automated growth system set up in the most simple manner possible, for reduction in space, mass, and resource requirements.

"I don't want people, for one, burdened with the stress of fear of death, based on timing or accidents, where they find they are trying to breathe in vacuum in outer space, or by otherwise finding their physical health is completely compromised because they happened to arrive in the same location as anyone or anything else at the same time.

"That brings me to the culmination of why we will need to begin considering intergalactic spacecraft that can provide living quarters, eateries, the necessary amenities, forestation, vegetation, sentient 'wildlife,' universities, labs, workstations,

correctional matrices, medical and psychological services, a sense of team-work, discipline, with an air of motivation, ingenuity, and organization.

"With a series of large spacecraft, we can mitigate the issues I've mentioned when it comes to large leaps through space.

"In this way, the future can be more sure, with the complex environmental maintenance and matter calculation and entanglement triangulation transfer systems, we'll be able to have entire spacecraft and any designated systems spacecraft jump with their entire cargo hold and crew, after sending sensors to a desired location, jumping from one point in space to another, and all without any issues.

"As we continue to create and grow protected bio-environments throughout our and the many other galaxies, we can augment and establish the same systems of Major Hubs, Major Zones, Minor Zones, and individual transfer jump gates we'll build in this solar system and on Earth." Eliza continued, allowed her other thoughts play out in the clouds behind her in the Virtual Universe, and then dismissed everyone to begin the work.

Everyone got their heads together during the first three weeks of 2008, with their aging friends, Vesha Celeste, Najem Grace, and Jasmine Belle, and two of their favorite physicists of the modern day, Matsu Kashi and Anastasia Renae, all recruited and leading the innovation teams. Vesha, Najem, and Jasmine had decided to age like normal, but Vesha was the only one who decided not to be optimized in any manner. Still, even without the upgraded aspects, she was a powerhouse of a thinker.

Within a month the entire team had been in the Virtual Universe about three-hundred times together, and another three-hundred times individually, and they were sure they had developed and improved upon a gate network that just might work and automatically allow for growth meeting all of Eliza's criteria.

Eliza had the answers the first day, but all of the infrastructure, with the exception of each spacecraft, had been built and was being maintained redundantly by volunteer citizens, families, sentient creatures, and nanos, so since she had delegated out these tasks, it was time for her entrusted associates to share their reliable plan.

Each volunteer was brilliant, but only two hadn't been fully optimized. Vesha was an honorary member who was not optimized in any way, and Najem and Jasmine were honorary members with only essential optimizations as it related to their health and neural capacities. Matsu and Anastasia had been fully read-in. Nevertheless, Eliza knew she needed to afford them an opportunity to put their neurological capabilities to work.

Unfortunately, the greatest contributor, Vesha, after her husband passed away, was beginning to suffer more severely from the effects of dementia. As an honorary member, she had not been required to be optimized in any way but served in Pathway LLC at the time because of her personal dedication and desired quest to understand her Universe. Once she was near the close of their discoveries, she settled into Princeton's retirement homes for proper real-world care and treatment and handed a majority of her work over to Anastasia. Najem and Jasmine visited Vesha regularly following their first Pathway mission, and Vesha would visit and contribute where she could. Many times, she would forget the breadth of help she provided, but her help, as always, had been genius and phenomenal.

Anastasia Renae, took the helm as chief particle physics and quantum computing team lead, worked closely with Matsu Kashi, theoretical physicist and data analytics extraordinaire, finalizing plans, developments, and prototype systems, and were now ready to present it all to Eliza, Yesha, James, and their growing crews.

When they were ready, everyone was advised to meet in the Virtual Universe via neural link, and once everyone arrived and linked within the cooperative compartment of their minds and experienced the Virtual Universe simulation of it all as if it were real, they demonstrated the new jump gate automated growth and multi-transfer process in its physical form and in its entirety.

The system was set up as such:

At first, every jump-gate-licensed Pathway citizen, and fully read-in, or non-optimized and honorary member, would receive a special "chameleon" watch that served a greater purpose than merely going well with optimized individual's chosen attire for the day. It would provide a unique neural identification tied-in link to the Twelve Database Moons, for the purpose of gathering all of the information pertinent for the individual being transferred, sequencing the timing of any other jumps, developing all of the entanglement criteria, and landing a single-source jump a safe distance away from any other arrival. When someone would arrive, they would find themselves at first on a conveyor belt-like object, yet much more sophisticated and pleasing to the eye, safely navigating away from the gate with the opportunity for a mini watch-based jump, yet another safe distance from the gate on a grid with a secondary or tertiary minor jump immediately after that until all same-destination arrival personnel were safely walking away.

The demonstration continued, as they showed that as the population grew, and more personnel and shipments were transferred back and forth, nanos that maintained a jump gate would summon more nanos to create a new gate laterally, and eventually into multiple floors.

As growth continued, the largest jump gate centers would be called major hubs, and no matter the expansion of humanity, within the observable Universe, there would be twelve zones linked via the Twelve Database Moons to a central hub on Earth. Major Zones would be a common-sense division of the Major Hub zones within one of twelve spatially-divided areas within and throughout the known Universe, temporarily spread out through the solar system alone.

Minor Zones would be broken down further into as many weigh stations and travel hubs as needed to accommodate everyone or anything being transported back and forth.

Earth itself would have its own minor zone network, as would any tech city.

Finally, individual zones were just that. An individual could have a jump gate at home and in their office, from which they could have a network of personal zones setup based on where their duties would regularly require them to be and their neural identification would be synced up to allow for transportation. The jump gate nanos would constantly maintain their function, and each zone would be linked in one way or another to the Twelve Database Moons for all of the necessary information processing and the final destination transfer.

Anastasia and Matzu rolled out the closing part of their plan, and in that final point, mass travel came into view. Each hyperloop, designed for mass transit, would also be connected to the jump gate system in a parallel entanglement manner.

Three-hundred people or more could get on one hyperloop passenger system, which would operate just like any airport or train station system, with the times of destinations, their arrival and departure, all automated and planned in advance.

Almost everything would be similar to the mass transit systems when it came to coordination, the only difference would be that once it passed through the jump gate it would be in the desired arrival location near instantaneously, and without any tragic events.

Luggage, resources, etc., would travel in parallel encapsulated by a container with a paired identification to the item chaperone.

During travel, they would not intersect but arrive at the location at the same time in a private room or warehouse in the desired overall location.

The chaperone or item-linked owner would then be mini-jumped to the location of their neural identification-paired items as shipped.

From there, they could be individually jumped to their home, their business office, or warehouse where only one or two or just a few could coordinate easily.

The system was simple yet complex and provided room for automated and endless growth, with near-seamless transportation and shipping.

Improvements would never be turned down, but for now and for quite some time everyone was at ease with the process, so Eliza, Yesha, James, and crew had every aspect established and brought online.

Once it was ready, they tested the travel or jump gate system in every way with one-hundred percent success.

If given a specific mission, properly approved personnel could create a new jump gate location between two travel points, in order to carry out that mission.

Things could now navigate quickly, the various hubs and zones looked magnificent and sturdy; they were designed for optimized transfer and transport in every possible way, and now, things could grow exponentially without a single issue.

Great Commitments

From the time that she brought her ideas up to Yesha, to James, and then to each member of Pathway, honorary or optimized, Eliza avoided considering public stock value from 2008 through this current point in the young life of her new organization, Pathway LLC. Instead, she declared every aspect of Pathway LLC as private or member owned. Even though all wealth was directly linked to Eliza's initial investments, she knew everyone had dedicated time and effort to what had been done and what was currently going on, so she chose to compensate everyone generously, and reinvest the rest into research, development, and improvements.

Eliza set her economics up in the way she did to justify the increasing wealth of each member of Pathway LLC and to expedite any development and distribution of products or services that were ready to go public.

She also realized that she, Yesha, James and their growing population of the citizens of Pathway LLC needed to distribute certain things publicly so everything that was covertly sanctioned and even recognized as legitimate by both governments could be approved for dispersal and therein find a way to exchange the equivalent wealth of her initial efforts, designs, and developments.

Eliza had set up a conversion system from her own economic system of Universal Credits to US Dollars, through terrestrial trade. While their capital throughout the solar system was huge, on Earth much of Pathway's capital was reinvested in research and development and every other aspect of the company, to include ensuring every employee was taken care of better than any other person on Earth who had not raised a finger or spared a neuron to contribute to its preservation.

At the same time as this went on, more of the self-replicating nano-bots received constant updates from Eliza and Yesha and their growing crews, and they in-turn sent constant and numerous updates back.

Emerging and quickly-growing teams of read-in scientists and data analytics professionals also worked with Eliza, Yesha, and James on encodings that enabled the creation of invisible shields that protected the Earth, the Moon, the outer planetary moons, as well as the dwarf planets Pluto and Eris, among many others, and they made possible the most optimal of living conditions in a manner that was undetectable in each location of each planetary and moon-like spheroid outside of the tech cities. Essentially, non-Pathway persons did not know these cities or developments existed, nor would they.

Eliza, Yesha, and James oversaw the creation of a system that would preserve the life of the Sun, rendering Earth life-sustainable for at least a few trillion years longer than expected—every few trillion years they merely needed to perform maintenance and upgrades, which they were currently doing in both manual and automated fashion. They had set up a seamless auto-maintenance system to do so, and by running additional team quality checks, they protected the life of the Sun indefinitely.

When Eliza, Yesha, James, and each of their growing crews were done with all these projects, the final project involved something as simple as kicking back, relaxing, sitting down, enjoying each other's company. Meditating together was another of many venues toward self-maintenance and long-term health.

Together, Eliza, Yesha, and James, as Pathway's hierarchy met with each other and other closely-knit crews using group biopods, single biopods, and meeting in real life in one of many convention centers, or in one of Eliza's many flora and fauna refuges, filled with sentient creatures—who volunteered to help in every and any way they could and happened to love the organization of Pathway LLC and everything it stood for.

Each of these newly sentient beings were happy at any time to be muses, listening to and inspiring, and even helping the LLC workers with the more finite details. Some of these creatures were philanthropists, counselors, craft workers, architects, artists, and even philosophers.

Eliza, Yesha, and James, as well as their citizens and each of their crew members, talked about all of their accomplishments within the Virtual Universe, and often while camping in the flora and fauna refuges, and once they had all deliberated, each member was given a break.

Traveling home was quite efficient using the jump gate terminals to jump to the jump gates within their domiciles in their associated tech cities, which also provided opportunities with chance meetings with newly-rescued refugees. Many Pathway LLC citizens, who had been fully read-in and optimized, went and traveled worldwide to conduct missions to help recruit and rescue others, conducting countless acts of heroism, while being careful not to spill beans in a public manner too much, which meant they helped both refugee and assailant through optimizations and their residual healing in all ways, to include physiological and neurological.

After the glorious aspects of the initial infrastructure and the construction of the shielding and structural preservation capacities of the solar system had been built and put into place, all Pathway citizens did as they wished, as suggested by Eliza, and many chose to go to their new domiciles, visit their old locations, hang out with the new friends they had made in the newly established Pathway LLC, or head out on missions until further instruction.

Eliza, Yesha, and James went to Eliza's estate, looked up at the stars near the statue of an angel overlooking the coy fish pond, sang the song, "Shine," from Depeche Mode's Exciter album, looked upon each other, shared their thoughts via their neural links as they overlooked their amalgamation of accomplishments, thought about the neighboring stars and were pleased.

This was precisely the time when Yesha had finally won James to her side of thinking because together they had finally convinced Dr. Eliza Amber Williams to pen her first literary masterpiece, called "Pathway to the Stars."

Eliza, thus, took up the challenge.

In her grand novel, Eliza suggested the need for humanity to evolve—that we could take the slack off of the backs of Mother Nature and the Universe, both of which had done so well thus far over extraordinary amounts of time, that we could make the most out of living in lands once thought desolate, and allow Nature as well as those who preferred nature over nurture to take back the unbridled forests and jungles until humanity could integrate advanced and beautifully creative tech cities in harmony with the environment and the ecosystem.

Eliza expounded upon why humanity needed to be driven by a passion for excellence and compassion toward each form of life we met along the way, and how we could stand to benefit from that approach. She also taught the need for each of us to have a vision for the well-being of others as well as ourselves, and to respect personal choice. She taught us to do things in the interest of raising the quality of life in general. She also made it clear that humanity needed to live in more than one location at one time, so we could preserve the legacy of our civilization.

"The Universe has worked diligently to create life in the hopes of seeing itself and its beauty through anyone capable of looking into the past to learn from and appreciate it, living in the now to appreciate all we see and all whom we meet along the way, considering the future and that which will give us the capacity to preserve it for the long-haul, while finding meaning and purpose along the way."

She suggested that we live on to have a legacy worthy of preserving for an indefinite period of time. Her novel dug deep into the various layers of the many sciences, to include physics, neurology, and biology, and a very deep comprehension and unmeasured wisdom to integrate each science further than was understood at this point in time, and as necessary to make these dreams possible.

Even though Eliza, alongside the calming and loving guidance of her dear friends Yesha and James—who both complemented her own wisdom—had invested so much of her own time, effort, intuition, will, and money into Pathway LLC's "extra-curricular" activities, it was all well worth every dime, every moment, and every concern spent. The well-being of all including those whom she did not know was vital to everything she stood for.

Even though she wasn't interested in monetary gain, financially, in Eliza's purview, they had an amazing rate of return for Earth-based and societally sanctioned innovations, overtly dispersed via Pathway LLC.

By May of 2010, one month after the release of "Pathway to the Stars," Eliza had a covert Earth value of more than 800 Billion USD invested and in worldwide bank accounts, a value of ten-billion USD within US banks, and a solar system non-liquid set of raw material and reconfigured assets that were of a germinating value of twenty-quintillion USD, which she in-turn reinvested through efficient production of high-value infrastructure, research, development, upgrades, and services.

She had produced the nanotechnology which had the capacity to use cold fusion, act as mini-manufacturing plants with complex architectural capacities to convert raw ore and materials into whatever it was programmed to create or do. She used these investments to in-turn create luxurious, self-sustaining tech cities, and so much more, much of it invisible to non-Pathway people.

There were twenty-thousand of these tech cities spread about the solar system to be exact, and each with the capacity and capability of providing every manner of option to increase the quality of life to the equivalent of at least ten-million unique and extravagantly lush and individually designable domiciles per city.

Each of these cities and every bit of their support infrastructure to include the research and development centers, were inspected and improved by James and his crew. Along with the Twelve Database Moons, the space elevator, the defensive and protective systems set in place for the solar system, each of its planets, dwarf planets, and each spheroidal moon of every planet, and so much more. All of her investments coalesced into a factored order of magnitude equating to one-hundred-octodecillion USD, which was in fact her actual monetary value. That is a lot of USD in value, not to mention, every second of every moment her value continuously increased.

Knowing all of this early on, due to the mathematical capacity of her love for others, her dedication, and her neurological optimizations, Eliza developed an economic system within Pathway LLC and throughout the solar system and Pathway cities, which operated off of Universal Credits, and wherein she set aside enough of the one-hundred-octodecillion Universal Credits that her empire was valued at, based on all of the raw materials reinvested in all of its varieties of astounding and spectacular ways, merely to create true value, based on what she had done, and this solely factored in everything she did within the solar system. That value would compound as humanity and its friends spanned the endless cosmos.

If all that she had done was in the US itself, her financial value was easily at a one-to-one ratio with the USD to Universal-Credit-value, during the timeframe of 2010, to give her LLC positive liquidity and in order to pay taxes appropriately, as per her LLC's earnings based on infrastructure within the US or any national government they were in and associated with.

Although, off-planet, and thus in no way amenable to taxation in the US, and no possibility of perception, the amount she set apart for individual accounts from the overall value of her Pathway Universal Credit system equated to one-hundred-billion USD in each of the twenty-billion accounts for every potential human being throughout the world, multiplied by two, and thus, the accounts she set aside for each human being that roamed the Earth totaled one-point-five-sextillion USD.

Essentially, Eliza was very wealthy, the wealthiest known individual in the known Universe! Since she had made sure each person working with her was also very wealthy, she would reinvest much of her wealth, or the remaining ninety-nine-point-nine-octodecillion USD, per 2010 associated value of Universal Credits into further advancements.

Eventually, the value of Universal Credits would soar far and above the value of the USD. Hence, she had so much more wealth than the world itself could convert bank-wise, so she chose to liquidate it through noble pursuits. Although she had the solvency and thus, easy liquidity, she had great plans for all of humanity in the not-too-distant future when it came to buying-out or outworking and out-producing every company, business, corporation, as well as industry that was focused purely on money, *"And, may they have their money."*

Rather than the well-being of those who worked for them or those they ought to have served, many in the real world were greedy beasts, driving others to squalor and misery. She wanted to implement her plans for corporate buyouts soon, and all for a myriad of moral and ethical reasons, but the most important of which was the fact that she wanted to increase the quality of life, health, and well-being of those who worked in the areas and industries she purchased and for all others in general. Eliza cared deeply about others and to her care was of high value.

To Eliza, both Yesha, and James, as well as every member of Pathway LLC, were secretly the wealthiest people in the world or the entire solar system for that matter. It was quite an achievement to know that through their shared efforts, each tech city had the ability to luxuriously and spaciously house ten-million families, with expansive living and everything needed or even desired, with the capacity to house ten times more, all of whom she would ensure were valued at, at least one-hundred-billion USD.

Eliza would provide each person with a near-unlimited personal account on Earth in exchange for personal dedication toward the advancement of humanity and the preservation of life.

In addition to luxury and brilliance, each tech city was equipped with beautiful forests and jungles, breath-taking parks, amazing and crystalline lakes and streams, self-sustaining organic and nutrient-dense farmlands, and clean meat laboratories.

Each tech city also had unlimited cold fusion power, fresh water-mineral-microbial optimizers, every business necessary to keep a large tech city functioning, replete with research and development labs of every sort, and the best eateries one could ever have the joy to eat at which would indulge and excite the senses of every one of humanity's thirteen-thousand taste buds.

There were unlimited resource production facilities, air scrubbers that made the air sweet and enjoyable, and scientific laboratories for even greater advancements and studies. Every tech city had every capacity that was housed in her Melrose campus, and sometimes more, considering the productivity and ingenuity of the peaceful and brilliant minds living there, with James at the helm. They also had a plethora of space-ports with all means of space travel, to include minor zones for instantly coordinated travel, using jump gate technology.

Each home was replete with biopods and jump gates respectively for family members and more for visitors with a series of individual zones for jumping to unique places of interest and back, quickly and safely via a safety-coordination algorithm.

Their biopods, interfaced with the Twelve Database Moons and the Virtual Universe, provided so much, to include universal education, medical optimizations, entertainment and gaming venues, and correctional matrices, as well as the ability of a biopod to instantly convert a biopod into space and safe-zone escape pods to defended coordinate locations, primarily on Earth, on a large, yet unseen island in the northwest Pacific Ocean, or where otherwise planned, should the need ever arise.

Eliza saw to it that Pathway LLC built in non-digital-mechanical redundancies ad nauseum, as well as impenetrable defenses and other exotic capabilities that would baffle the smartest hackers, and they had hackers under their own employ to check the systems just in case, and while they could get into any high-tech and advanced system on Earth, to try to do so within Pathway, well, it was impossible. They tried to build break-in options, but as smart as they were, the Pathway systems were self-learning and could out-write and out-rewrite more exponentially and impenetrably than anything else. This was quite simply because, a simple "no" from Eliza's mind zeroed-out any attempts to break their systems, and she was the smartest "kid on the block," world-wide and throughout all of recorded history.

The invisibility and cloaking, safety and security domes protecting these tech cities provided an Earth-like atmosphere with exhaustive environmental protections from the dangers of the regions wherein each city was located, constructed, and continuously maintained by Eliza's large clouds of armies of nano-bots, and quality controlled by James and his growing crew, while Yesha began missions overseas.

Robust and complex arrays of shielding were now in place, although invisible from Earth's ground-based and satellite telescopes, where the only thing understood by Earth's public governments and scientific cohorts was everything as it would have been had none of her advancements ever been developed.

Pathway had robust quantum computing technology that could predict with one-hundred percent certainty all of the factors of each unique environment and of outer space at any given moment as if they had never been there, as well as up-to-date-and-including-where-they-could-possibly-go-into-the-future abilities, and all from any vantage point, using any technological intel gathering capacity, from infrared to optical, or otherwise, which brilliantly generated images and signals, and produced emissions collected by non-Pathway technologies.

Earth-normal or even the most advanced military technologies saw only the solar system planets, dwarf planets, and spheroids in their pre-advanced forms. The reality was such that, now, no non-Pathway technology could ever realize or expose the fact that all of the inner planets and moons, and all of the outer dwarf planets and moons could sustain life indefinitely, just like Earth.

This reality included prohibitive scanning by the greed-centric locations throughout the world, as well as places with growing and sprawling deserts, dying forests, and decreasing vegetation and wildlife, and where the inhabitants were focused more on the sundry monotony of the day, rather than advancements in technologies that would help to overcome those issues.

While there were so many who weren't aware that Eliza, her hierarchy, and every citizen of Pathway was advancing quickly, there were many who read her novel who attempted to thwart her goals—a fool's errand.

For now, every single one of the Pathway LLC activities was known only to Eliza, Yesha, James and their growing citizen populace, which included a very large and increasing cadre of trusted scientists, engineers, and data analytics professionals, all of whom had been optimized physiologically and neurologically, were phenomenal, and exponentially more capable than anyone in the public realm. Eliza saw to it that these protections were put in place to protect well-being, more than anything else.

Regardless of how Eliza saw it, Yesha and James knew that all of this was the result of Eliza's intent, and her initially invested estate, in everything, and as such, she had initially designed everything, so she was the sole legal heir to the entirety of value of the whole of the return.

No matter what, however, Eliza thought of herself, Yesha, James, and anyone who worked with her as beneficiaries of the investment, because of their time and their phenomenal efforts.

To Eliza, by rights, everyone on Earth could live well and retire for life, but she had much bigger goals than creating dependencies and thus ruling through wealth and power. Through her biopods, she had provided a complete environment of transparency, at least to every member of Pathway LLC, of everything she had ever designed and aspired to create, she also began to share her political ideologies and aspirations, and every person who knew her, saw her unparalleled strength of character.

Advancement, learning, and preservation of life were far more important to Eliza than influence or affluence, and she intended to prove it through action, generosity, and compassion.

The people on Earth needed to accept the future, they needed to demonstrate compassion toward others, and they needed to care more about the sciences that could bring about the well-being of life itself rather than argue over small matters or fixate on distractions that had nothing to do with greater goals.

While wealth was necessary to expedite the promises that scientific advancement on Earth could provide to carry with it publicly-trusted influence, and while the assumption of power was necessary to bring about the changes that demonstrated her compassion for humanity, her strongest desire was to bring the human civilization and all of its friends along with her and her dearest of friends on the journeys throughout the Universe for a myriad of noble purposes.

Eliza, Yesha, and James worked together and had their sights set on preserving the life of quadrillions of suns from the Great Attractor and sextillions more from the great expansion, all of which would be made possible through initial advancements and selfless investments.

To that end, Eliza, James, and her dear friend Yesha, ensured, as a first step, that the solar system was duly protected, had been shrouded of anything related to that reality from terrestrial governments and organizations who had unknown intentions, had protected humanity from any extraterrestrial wanderers who might not have humanity's best interests at heart, had secured her assets in a robust layer of secrecy, and continued to make breakthroughs, and in so doing many amazing things continued to be developed, while she spent time both humbly and unpretentiously writing legislation for her local representatives in Cambridge, MA.

Eliza lived modestly, considering her wealth, and encouraged anyone close enough to be read-in to her world, to do so as well.

Bring Him Back

Following the major aspects of Pathway's initial infrastructural developments both in space and on Earth, James found time and confronted her as respectfully as he could, regarding her dog, Tyson.

They had a lot more to accomplish, and he sensed that with Tyson around, Eliza would be fulfilled, and healthily so, as she had worked so hard for and taught everyone else to do, with that special spirit in her life.

After many days, weeks, months, and even two years of working with Eliza, since their shared journey through the Virtual Universe for the first time, and all the while holding back, he finally opened up through his link from outer space, *"Eliza?"*

"Yes," responded Eliza.

"I think it is time. Now is the time. We have the technology. Bring him back." He didn't have to say who, Eliza knew.

"I will. I never thought I would ever hear someone else tell me that. It seemed I'd be selfish to do so."

"You'd be selfish not to. You've set in motion systems for personal reflection, personal maintenance, as well as for peace, love, and joy. This is what you need right now, my friend, so I trust you to do it, this will add to the joy that is needed throughout this world, and this Universe."

"Thank you, James. You don't know how wonderful it is to hear you say that."

They had privately maintained a connection together, conversationally, for quite some time, and Eliza trusted in James' advice at the same level as the advice she received from Yesha. It was early January of 2010, and on Tyson's birthday, she revived him through use of his preserved hairs. In the public world, this was only possible using live tissue samples, but Eliza had perfected the tech to include several strands of hair and paired that with a healthy DNA coefficient sample from a random living mammal of similar species and of similar breed.

Time passed by, and together, she, Tyson, and her organization did so much more, to include writing her novel that she penned and called, "Pathway to the Stars."

For the sake of the masses, Eliza behaved as if all that she had done was merely write a sci-fi fantasy dream, while she slowly and incrementally enlightened others to go further than before yet do so with care by releasing advancements based on societal acceptance, and all out of a lack of desire to completely devastate any economic system or retirement-set of anyone.

Eliza also considered this as a sort of practice of kindness, consideration, and compassion for when humanity finally graced that great stage of the expanse and quite possibly met many other civilizations, whether great or small, throughout their journeys and discoveries of the mysteries of the cosmos.

Eliza did not want to create a large and detrimental impact on anyone or the economy by a sudden ability to heal everyone in moments, especially if humanity wasn't psychologically ready or approving of it. They had to grow and mature in time, through proper education, mentoring and love for others as well as themselves.

Ever since she had been briefed by Harvard, MIT, and anonymous governmental representatives she felt this could potentially weaken humanity's resolve, their sense of team-work, and their push toward compassion and thus, if all was given without any effort on their part advancements might result in a hollow sense of reality—she didn't want to create dependencies, she wanted to inspire, motivate, and enlighten, while strengthening the will and character of others, helping them to be prepared for even greater challenges than the current paltry issues.

While she would rescue the far too many who had suffered enough, she did not want to remove the sense of personal dedication, productivity, personal investment, or motivation from anyone, instead she wanted to reward humanity as they worked hard, studied hard, and collaborated with clarity in achievement toward advancement—the kind of advancement that would lead to joyful and fulfilling ways of life.

Instead of cashing in all of her chips, buying armies, and ruling the Universe, she instead chose to help the medical industry to receive specific advancements in societally acceptable increments, develop study materials to educate the masses, introduce entertainment that would cultivate a society that was more accepting of these advancements, set up a system to develop many amazing and benevolent leaders, and all while igniting the fire within for people to freely build and improve upon the things that she had set in place.

Chapter 08: Shared Successes

Database Moon Archive, Celestial-Sol Entry Date: 2018 December 25 – Experiential biography, as taught to Vesha Celeste, about the maturing of the new Pathway LLC, during her Virtual Universe training, within Pathway Covert Campus in Melrose, MA. Contained within are thoughts from Eliza Williams, Yesha Alevtina, and James Cooper. Training Given by Yesha Alevtina, President of Pathway Industries, 2015-2022.

Meanwhile, with Tyson back, Yesha conducting her missions overseas, in-between her commitments as a professor at Harvard and MIT, and always back before the night closed in, and James working with more than twenty-million new Pathway citizens throughout the solar system in the new tech cities, Eliza pursued her goals one-by-one. Yesha and James, as well as their rapidly growing teams of scientists were with her every step of the way.

During her meeting with Agent Epstein, with Yesha and James visiting from their own adventures, in May of 2010, all of her advancements had been, unbeknownst to this wonderful agent, essentially cart-blanch-cleared for research, development, and proliferation in an "as Eliza, Yesha, James, and the new Pathway LLC sees fit" basis.

Eliza's company, Pathway LLC, was effectively legal within the US via Pathway LLC's governmental branch, giving the government full intellectual access to any science or technology they created or even needed after Pathway LLC had properly vetted them and set them up with fail-safe mechanisms to prevent the malevolent use of their technologies.

The ANSSI had confided in Eliza, Yesha, and James their trust in Pathway's goals toward the preservation of humanity in exchange for updates via briefs on an annual basis of technologies that were at one-hundred percent in all of its capabilities with failsafe and safety mechanisms.

For all of her work, study, invention, and awe, Eliza would not charge the government or the US taxpayer a single dime. Instead, their wallets would slowly fatten. For her, approval and legal coverage were more valuable.

Eliza thought about how Angela was in her own unique way, inspired too, as she talked to her. Agent Epstein, before dismissing herself from that one and only meeting that day had told Eliza, "Humanity is greater than just one nation or just one point of view, and we have more promise if we work together, rather than solely by ourselves based upon the limitations society seems so quick to create, defying longevity and clarity of mind.

"We need to consider each other and think beyond just ourselves. We trust you, and as such, please feel free to work your magic. As you do and as needed, while we know you've probably done more than we have the capacity to understand right now, we will provide legal coverage to you and the teams and industries you will build, as you may have already done, are currently doing, and will yet do.

"This is a many-faceted form of societal advancement, and our country is one of inclusion and freedoms that don't unnecessarily undermine the rights of others, so in the long-haul, we know that what you do will benefit the world and everyone in it.

"Thank you for all that you are doing.

"Here are the seals and authorizations; if you need us for anything, please don't hesitate to call. Oh, Eliza... please consider legislative and executive offices, every person in the ANSSI knows you'll do well, no matter what it is you set out to do."

With that, Agent Epstein left Eliza, Yesha, and James in Eliza's office at Harvard, knowing they would begin to build their team, or rather reveal what they had already built in smaller or even larger increments, based on humanity's ability to accept them. Agent Epstein also had a strong sense that within fourteen years, Eliza would be POTUS, and a new space revolution would begin.

James, meanwhile, appreciated the fact that Eliza took charge and was perhaps a better employer, leader, and inspiration than anyone he could ever think of. He was proud of her, her pursuits, and he was glad to continue his work throughout the solar system, engaging in all wishes as Eliza's appointed Solar System President, after she won, turned it down, and chose him in her stead, he lived to never disappoint, and he never disappointed her in the least, and he encouraged her to build a party, a new political party, based upon her values and ideals.

Eliza was proud of James. She loved him and cherished his devoted spirit in so many ways, even in ways that he had a long time to wait before she revealed them. James was written into her heart, but there was so much to do. They could wait, and their focus needed to be upon the future of humanity and the preservation of this lovely and beautiful Universe, and then, maybe then, she would open up to reveal something profound for the depth of love she knew James could bring her.

Tyson was back in her life, Pathway LLC was beginning its due course of bringing the joy that she had hoped that it would, and her plans were greater than the first four tiers of Maslow's hierarchy of needs alone, the fifth tier was crucial and fundamental, one that was important for humanity to grasp and share in, one of self-actualization, vision, and clarity of mind.

Listening to James and Agent Epstein, as well as her dear friend, Yesha, she knew it was time to begin the steps for the creation of a new political party, one that would change the course of history and usher in the space revolution, a revolution that would preserve life, rather than take it away, a revolution that was kind, one that was powerful, and one that could resolve problems, rather than create devastation through brutality and misery.

Eliza knew that it was because of James' infallible support that she would create a party that was universal, one where everyone could have the option of having joy and longevity in life, and one where they could be respected for their individuality rather than spited because they were different.

Eliza had goals, and she was determined to achieve them, even in the absence of effort on the part of many who had given up. She knew they had greatness within them, she just needed to help them to see it. James saw that in her, and that is why he felt that she was extra special, and someone that perhaps down the road would be of significant value in his life, and in the lives of so many others Universe-wide. He would serve and protect her, if ever needed, and in every way that mattered.

State of Pathway

"Universal – I define this as all things and all laws that affect every being, both living and devoid of life. One thing that is universal is chaos and destruction, at least it is at this stage in the game. We need entropy, since energy is what prevents the big freeze. Entropy sustains life. What can we do to control this energy, to ensure that life can become a state of being that endures for as long as we wish it to endure? I vie for longevity, health, and clarity of mind for all living beings, while trying to work with and connect with all else, in a way that will breed long-term sustainability to the ideas of peace and happiness. Watching the flowers bloom, seeing a rainbow in the rainy skies, or watching a shooting star as it soars through our outer atmosphere, are all things that can sustain happiness while realizing that it occurs because of something universal, which is entropy. Our efforts are a measure of entropy, and within those efforts lies the answer to sustained joy and happiness."

During the first official State of Pathway, Eliza, as founder and president of this organization, which was currently responsible for governance of twenty-thousand tech cities throughout the solar system, and ten-million human citizens who had been recruited since January of 2008, dwelling within them, continued her address, "I want to thank each of you for your profound diligence, phenomenal intellect, and your resolve toward helping humanity to graduate to a Type II Civilization, with the capacity within the next two decades and of which to graduate to a Type III Civilization, according to the Kardashev Scale. Perhaps in contrast to this particular measurement standard, we have not only been able to harness and store the power of the Earth, the Sun, and all of our solar system planets, but we have enabled life, much like on Earth, throughout the Solar System as well. We have also, together, done all of this, with our central focus toward well-being.

"As a Type II Civilization, we have something similar to a Dyson Sphere that is much more capable and advanced than I am sure the visionaries, like British philosopher and science fiction writer, Olaf Stapledon, or Freeman Dyson, English-born, American physicist and mathematician, who thought of this idea might have imagined. With this technology, which has been perfected, courtesy of Yesha, James and each of you, we can ensure that there is orbital balance and that the Sun receives a steady diet of basic baryonic and non-baryonic matter along with the associated leptons.

"We ensured that each of these particles came and will come from a source that had or has no life, and we have now created a system that will absorb the heavy elements that the Sun creates and return them back as basic baryonic and lepton materials. This cycle will preserve our yellow Sun and afford it the ability to sustain life for an indeterminate amount of time, or for trillions of years or more instead of billions of years. We have likewise protected the orbital integrity of each planet and spheroid to endure while providing life sustainability for trillions of years or more as well.

"We have created mechanisms that will sustain these capabilities as well as allow us to control the direction or path of our Sun, within the Milky Way Galaxy, and in a way that will help us to avoid any collisions or unfortunate circumstances with other planets and star systems or absorb the lifeless materials to augment the capacity of our own system. We can now scan for black holes and other anomalies on our current pathway around the center of our galaxy, and avoid them, while tapping into nearby, yet lifeless, resources.

"Within two decades, almost to this date exactly, give or take a few weeks, we will span our galaxy and search for and preserve life, while creating life-giving capabilities in star systems, much like our own, yet which currently have no life, while also creating the same protective mechanisms as we have created for our own star system. If we do find life already existent, then we will protect these systems, their orbits, yet observe and bridge communications, ever-so-delicately, and we will have protected the environments around them to allow them to slowly evolve to a sentient and domesticated state of sophisticated thought, ideas, and shared purpose with humanity and our friends.

"People, the world over, will have opportunities to support this endeavor that will lead to an even greater effort. The highest of energies revolve around the preservation of our Universe and all of the steps that will lead us to that point. All of this we will do, while also remembering the Principles of Universal Ethics, as established by our tech city constitutions. We are all united, as citizens of Pathway, but we must reach the hearts of humanity on Earth, so that we can all work together toward a promising future and prevent the rapid increase in decay and destruction that is being promulgated by the unseen powers that exist throughout the World.

"Humanity as it is now, is unaware of the many contributions each of us has made toward their benefit. We must be careful in how we inform the public on Earth, but we will continue to grow Pathway through recruitment of great minds, rescuing those people who are suffering, and who have gone through too much barbarity and misery, and we will even reach out and help those who are the source of the brutality, because in many ways they too are victims of not only their own environment, but lost within the avalanche of their own choices as a result of their environment. We bring in great minds, so that the results of our goals can increase exponentially in terms of quality and kindness. We bring in those who have been made to suffer to afford them the opportunity to soak in the beauties and wonders of life. We bring in the perpetrators so that each one of them will have an opportunity to face their errors and realize their full potential as well.

"What is our full potential? That is a wonderful question. I will assure you, that while an evasive answer accompanies this question, that we are inclined to reach this evasive reality within our own lives, so long as we stay focused on the well-being of ourselves and those around us.

"The Principles of Universal Ethics suggest that we seek cures for disease, increase our capacities to weather any environment we find ourselves in, and enable ourselves the ability to help others in any way that might be needed. These ethics suggest that we seek longevity, so that we can comb the cosmos and return home to share stories with those we love and call our kindred spirits. These moral mindsets suggest that we raise the quality of life for all living beings, while enhancing our abilities to remember every beautiful moment, every science, and resolve untold issues that lie before us in the form of challenges.

"In essence, we believe in optimizing our physiological and neurological attributes, endowing us with phenomenal capabilities, health, and wisdom.

"Finally, these ethics suggest that we strive to understand one another more fully, to link with each other mind-to-mind, and to remember that in the end, all choices, so long as they do not cause undue consequence to the rights of others, are at the behest of individual consent.

"On Earth, there is still so much to do, and while it may take two decades for us to achieve a shared sense of well-being, throughout our mother world, each of us can do even more by remembering the systems that are already in place, and by trying with all of our faculties to mold and transmute these systems through kindness and through the establishment and success of a new political party. All of this can occur, as we tame what we have come to know as a universal law, entropy. We can bring the laws of chaos home to bring richness to life and sustainment to joy, happiness, peace, and resolve. We will develop and call this party, the Universal Party."

Eliza had created a visual masterpiece within the Virtual Universe, where this conference for all Pathway citizens was held. Given the environment of the Political Matrix, all ten-million Pathway citizens were able to fit within this massive stadium-like environment, with Eliza projecting herself in a way that allowed each of the citizens on the ten-thousand floors, each holding ten-thousand citizens, to see her as if they were sitting across from her in a fairly small space, enjoying the words of wisdom that she shared. It was as if Eliza were speaking directly to each one of the people in the audience.

As she spoke, Eliza had prepared and shared an experiential upgrade that uploaded into their minds. This upload would stimulate each of their senses, their neurons, and their synapses, and each idea would play out before them, leaving with them the beautiful flavor of thought that would permeate each of their dreams and excite their senses. Her words would allow them to experience each of the ten-million lives had over the last year of those within the audience. They would experience, as if it were their own lives, the dedication, the efforts, the hopes, the dreams, and the aspirations that led to the finality of their efforts over the last year.

Time would go by, following this speech, yet the experiences that seemed the sweetest and lingered with each citizen with most impact and in a way that would reach every read-in candidate, were the words of Eliza, Yesha, and James. Their efforts seemed to resonate the most with the audience, no matter their life's stories or backgrounds, and as a result, every single one of the ten-million citizens wholly and nobly entrusted them to lead their cause and trusted their leadership. They had confidence in them as they journeyed to whatever ends of the Universe they would go. No matter the type or size of contribution, all ideas, goals, and definitions of ethics were remembered with clarity and each with its own unique flavor of thought.

During this event, Eliza did not speak as much as she normally would have, nor did she need to. Each individual experienced in just a few moments, a year's worth of life of ten-million people. Each person, when Eliza was done, was a sage filled with wisdom beyond their years, with their very own perspectives of it all, combined with the perspectives of everyone else. Much was learned, as ten-million years was experienced in the brief period of five minutes in the real world.

When Eliza was done, her image faded, and Yesha Alevtina's image took her place. She smiled at everyone within the Political Matrix and began.

"Thank you, Eliza. Just a year ago, for many of us, we would never have imagined such a wonderful and brilliant experience. The capacity of love that we each possess is admirable and ready to be shared the world over, as we build the Universal Party, with fundamentals very similar to those in our systems of governance throughout the tech cities that each of us, through Pathway, has built throughout the entirety of this lovely solar system. The capacity for preservation of life that we now have, accompanied by an elevated quality of life, capable of sustaining itself for trillions of years and more, are all courtesy of the brilliant mind of Eliza.

"I have been with her through the many years, and while each day of each year was splendid, we have beheld many unfortunate tragedies that ought not ever have happened. Nevertheless, as barbaric as the actions of some lost souls were, they occurred. While brutality and malicious behaviors do nothing toward our well-being, we can still choose to learn from them to prevent their re-occurrence ever again. Much of that begins, as Eliza suggested, with the on-Earth formation of the Universal Party. We have a long way to go, before we can reach the hearts and minds of many, but we will get there, and I am, just as I sense you are, solidly sure of it.

"This last year, we grew, in terms of human citizens, from three, to two-hundred-ninety-three, to twenty thousand, to ten million, and we will continue to grow even more. All this growth occurred because of the dedication of each of you. When you were recruited or rescued, you not only helped and worked with James, but you visited Earth again, and helped me and Eliza.

"In the beautiful countries in the lands that lay throughout Scandinavia, Europe, Asia, Far-East Asia, South-East Asia, Africa, the Middle East, and Australia, and many other locations, that, in this case, for brevity I will call the Eastern Hemisphere, many have had beautiful stories that reached their ebb through actions of love, kindness, and innovation. Despite the tragedies that befell them, many of you, a whole new way of life was realized and many more were helped.

"Our beautiful mother world ached for a reprieve from the injustices of many, courtesy of cultures and governance systems, that forgot how to love, include others, think beyond the scope of greed and power, and be kind, but within the visions of shared joy and well-being.

"We realize now that we can do those things, or abide by the Principles of Universal Ethics, and not only enjoy life, but overcome many more challenges with joy in our hearts knowing there is a beautiful promise at every turn. Doing so, has also blessed Eliza, and through her, each of us, with untold wealth and power, that can only be had as we have seen come to be, through each of our efforts, actions, and the realization of our dreams.

"As our President has suggested, it is time to reach out, to expand, and to go further than before, but first, or before we can venture past this life-giving solar system, we need to bring all of humanity along with us, either in body, or mind, or spirit, and through freedom of thought, by way of persuasion, education, and love.

"Establishing the Universal Party in every country throughout the home world will be a large part of what is necessary to ensure that after long voyages through the many parts of our Universe and perhaps beyond, we will ensure our home world still exists and that humanity has not destroyed itself via the direction they seem to be heading in, as we speak. Wouldn't it be wonderful to return to our homes many centuries from now and share with our loved ones the journeys we have made, while they are living in a beautiful world that beckons their continued ingenuity, kindness, and love? Perhaps they'll have stories of daring do as well!"

Yesha continued. As she did, she shared the lives of several of those who were rescued, as well as their achievements following their optimizations, the rescues they performed, and the state of life they experienced, on down to their sentiments and dreams of the future. All these details were magnificent, and the audience shared their feelings of acceptance and love and embraced Yesha within their minds, giving her a hug for her vision and supportive spirit as well. They were thankful for her dedication as a friend to Eliza, and for her own efforts in the cause of ensuring a beautiful future for humanity.

"Thank you, Yesha, and thank you Eliza. Both of your messages were amazing in every way." James had filled the area that Yesha and Eliza had stood.

"I agree, in that, each of you has done many remarkable things to ensure the future of humanity and have begun by showing what can be done to preserve life, with beauty, abundance, and joy. Throughout the solar system, from the Sun on out to the perimeters of the heliosphere, you have done so much to not only preserve life itself, but to preserve the lives of our Sun, each of our planets, and every living being we ever find.

"Together, we have bred sentience into the very nature of every being we have met, and many trillion and more of these living creatures has learned love, kindness, and more, while finding their way of contributing to the preservation of all of life, with this same joy, happiness, and love.

"The systems of governance throughout each of our beloved tech cities, located on Mercury, Venus, and many more planetoids throughout our solar system, has been without need for correctional systems, because each of you has had your energies focused toward pursuits that are noble and have advanced civilization in every imaginable and kind way. I thank each of you."

James continued, and as he did, he shared stories of many individuals who had been rescued and recruited, courtesy of Eliza, Yesha, his crew, the 97, and then multiplied by all that they had influenced and were in-turn influenced by each new citizen, as a result. The audience loved James, and they were, as always, proud of and grateful to Eliza for appointing him as the Solar System Operations President and had thusly voted for him democratically and unanimously.

He talked about the need for the Universal Party and the Principles of Universal Ethics as a benchmark for each nation throughout the world. He talked about the many projects yet to be completed, which were vast. He talked about how, the more people working together to resolve an issue, the more likely they could come up with a solution that would endure for the long-haul.

The conference concluded, with Eliza wrapping it up, going over their goals for the future and her gratitude for each person within Pathway, as well as her hopes for the rest of the home world. All were happy, within the many Pathway tech cities, and they were a fun, creative, adventurous, and kind bunch.

It was time to begin the steps necessary in order to form the Universal Party in the home world. One more State of Pathway would occur, and then they would begin the process of bringing the Universal Party to election options in polls throughout the Earthly globe.

Hidden in Plain Sight

The following year, much had been done, and the population had doubled in size. Eliza, Yesha, and James held the second State of Pathway, and all were overjoyed. By May of 2010, following their visit with Agent Epstein, Pathway hierarchy, Eliza Williams, Yesha Alevtina, and James Cooper never slowed down the use of their newly gifted neurological and physiological enhancements, as they worked with their crews on Earth and throughout the solar system to continue the process of recruiting amazing people into their surprisingly anonymous organization. For the most part, they were hugely unknown, even after they started building one aesthetically pleasing and robustly capable political hub after another throughout each state and nation globally.

Fused with ready-to-go scientific advancements and a combination of public and private labs and sectors, all of them eco-friendly and fully vetted to prevent reverse engineering for purposes opposed to longevity or quality of life, many wondered what purpose they served, at least until all eyes were on an edifice or a series of them, and tours began. Dotting the globe, these locations were cloaked in a way that if a person were not read-in and had no neurological identification, they would only see a typically drab and boring building, and these edifices had names that gave little away, for example, Federal Liaison Campus, DC, or State Liaison Office, California, et al.

With rather vague titles and boring looking buildings, it made connecting the dots to Pathway difficult to do. Still, Eliza, Yesha, James and their teams didn't do this just for anonymity but to facilitate worldwide philanthropic pursuits, the safety of all involved, including those not read-in, and much more. A lot would be accomplished and had to be done toward bridging gaps caused by broken hearts and minds, disillusioned souls, people preaching their virtues and ethics away, brutality, misery, suffering untold, and all for the sake of popularity, money, and power. Eliza's help could only go so far, since a person had to desire to be helped. She had no wish to deprive anyone of their own choices, so recruitment in some ways was astronomical yet in other ways it was slow.

Oh, there were plenty of those that could have been called "anti-Pathway hot-heads" who pursued ways to undermine Eliza and the ethics that her organization espoused, but they were small pockets here and there, and Eliza's crew monitored them constantly. However, this malicious crew seemed to be increasing in numbers and ready to surface in mischievous ways, and as such, many began to believe the negative speculations created by these masterminds that were intent on keeping humanity under their thumb, for no reason other than they were foolish enough to think that they would lose all they cared about if they dared apply the simple and common-sensical Principles of Universal Ethics.

These principles were recommendations of Eliza, delivered to the world within her literary masterpiece, "Pathway to the Stars," which meant a lot more than it seemed at the surface. It was a set of principles that were already applied throughout the tech cities that lay scattered throughout the solar system.

Eliza shared her recommendations with others often. On any given day, when meeting with potential recruits, one could hear her saying, "Seek to be kind, be dignified, be thoughtful, be loving, and improve the quality of life of all as we preserve the facility for it within our own Earthly biosphere, throughout our Solar System or Universe." On other occasions, she would extrapolate further, "The latter of these goals, I fully plan to enable humanity to meet someday soon. Establishing a new political party is the first step toward our preparation and worthiness to explore the cosmos, but it will take a while to germinate and grow it to the level needed for the type of success we're looking for."

On occasion, and if asked about those who were against the ideas she espoused, she would spare no words. Eliza was genuine, and sometimes she cut to the core of it all, as she would explain even further. "However, if these ego-centric, spineless, and fearful advancement-decrying, and somewhat lazy buffoons who appear to be pulling the strings could think more deeply than they have thus done during every waking moment of their sorry lives, and could use Pathway's solutions-based approach, common sense, well-being, and possess ideas that were both micro and macro in their scope, they would know by now that thru kindness, love, and wisdom power becomes a shared medium, one that lasts longer, and one that can span the Universe, while still living in a breathtakingly beautiful existence, many steps ahead of uncontrolled chaos, forging promising bonds and goals universe-wide filled with indescribable joy."

If Eliza ever publicly called anyone a buffoon, it wasn't a permanent judgment lobbed against anyone, but a bit of a challenge to refocus and engage with others in a manner that was kind and healthy. Typically, a person would see that perhaps they were off on a path or tangent to nowhere. There were those, however, who would not change their modus operandi, unless they were jarred silly from their lofty positions of ego, thus allowing them to see her ideals and think for themselves properly.

Like many of Pathway's phenomenal new structures combing the globe, the one built in the US Capital, titled Federal Liaison Campus, DC, was built swiftly. As swift as it was built, each edifice came into being, almost lifelike and with high quality arrangements of every single particle in precise location, and self-maintenance built within every column, beam, wall, room, and hall. Every part of each structure could buffet the worst that the vilest and most toxic of humanity or even Mother Nature, herself, could throw at it. Eliza meant to teach a lesson to more than humanity alone. Teach she did, and in profound spades every step of the way.

With advancement through the roof, quite literally, and under the shroud of unmistakable invisibility, after all buildings were complete on each campus, a tour through these edifices was quite a reward for anyone read-in to Pathway passing by, thru, or within them.

After purchasing sixteen square blocks, when the cloaking mechanisms were set in place, the public was only able to see a rather drab tarp laying over sixteen square blocks in size and rising more than fifty stories into the sky. When it was removed, adjusted, or essentially turned off, the awe of every read-in viewer peaked more than any onlooker could have dared imagine. However, for those who had no idea of what Pathway was or who Eliza Williams was, all they saw was an area of each city that blended in with everything else.

Nevertheless, these beautiful and magnificent sets of structures could be seen for miles, by Pathway members. Each glorious building was near glowing white, some of them shiny and some subdued, with curves and bends and windows that were woven in, splendid, yet flowing and smooth, and purposeful, and all buildings within a given capital city happened to merge with the surrounding edifices as if they were all one enchanting, yet gigantic piece of material carved by the majestic hand of an omnipotent sculptor. Pathway beautified these sixteen square blocks of land around and throughout its entire area with a rich array of trees, bushes, and more, providing a pleasant, fragrantly enjoyable, and spacious jog-way, with safety from traffic, passing either over or under each road in a sophisticated display of balanced and flowing symmetry and asymmetry for exercise.

Looking from a distance, if one were read-in, it was as if each edifice floated in the air, due to the similarly indescribable cloaking and redirective technology used to mask its existence to people who weren't read-in and bring safety to any traveler or passer-by during its construction. For the regular observer, the beauty of it was toned down a bit, to allow it to blend in with the rest of the environment, and its brilliance was toned down at all of the correct moments, in order to reduce chances for traffic accidents or unwanted attention.

If someone were under a building, walking through these new under-tower forests, and they happened to look upward at what presumably would have been the bottom of any building, it would appear as though there were no structure above them at all. Instead, their view would give way to a beautiful skyscape filled with sunsets and impressive views of seasonal stars, nebulae, and galaxies, conveying Earth's orbit around the Sun, morning, noon, and night, while providing the necessary radiant elements for each forest and all of life.

On any Pathway campus, after a sojourn through a beautiful landscape, delicious meals at healthy eateries built in an associated megacomplex, and a ride home after purchasing the highest quality goods of any everyday sort, benefactors would discover that all was provided for free, courtesy of Eliza, unknown for effect.

If someone wished to stay through the night, accommodations could be made, since the top ten stories or more of each of the fifty-story towers consisted of high-quality hotels, replete with all of the typical high-class and exquisite quality fixings, trimmings, gene therapists, massage experts, yoga classes, hot tubs, Turkish bathhouses, cultural centers and so much more.

From an atrium that ran fifty stories high, giving view from within of the weaving curvature of balconies, windows, and relaxation garden getaways, to some of the finest chefs in the world in restaurants on every floor, the top floor, and so much more, bargain hoteling could not have been more exquisite, and jobs and training were given at the drop of a hat as requested. If jobs were filled, requests weren't made, but all jobs made public were given on a first-come, first-served basis.

With convenient access to any metropolitan subway system, the Pathway campus was located in, available, and tied in with every square block of its diplomatic workcenter, indoors and outdoors in several locations.

Mass transportation conveyances were tied in with other secret jump gate and hyperloop systems, where access was given only to properly read-in citizens and delegates. To anyone else, the entrances to these systems were disguised within the alleys, beyond robust libraries, highly touted coffee shops, well-fragranced and colorful flower boutiques, or any of a vast array of high-quality, health, well-being, and sophistication-increasing stores within.

Furthermore, each of these facilities provided brilliantly crafted and ornately-designed access points, escalators, and elevators to massive parking areas below the ground for exotic car drivers, limousines, Lyft and Uber drivers, buses, and private vehicle owners, and all of it safe from weather, seismic activity, or any other conceivable natural or manmade disaster or issue.

Driving on roads that existed around and through each megacomplex seemed to increase the durability, gas mileage, and aesthetic of any vehicle passing through them. Visiting nearby or within a Pathway campus came with an often-whispered secret, even among those within the public sector, and that was the main point. Eliza wanted to encourage the type of intrigue that peeked when viewing such quality and craftsmanship.

"You have to visit and drive around any new federal or state liaison campus with a UP logo on it, whether it is in Alaska, California, Hawaii, or throughout the world, and most especially, DC, because something magnificent will happen to your car, your truck, or your van, from better gas mileage, to a fresh coat of paint and a glossy finish, to feeling bathed and refreshed yourself, and more. These new campuses are breathtaking to behold, and each of them are a not-so-secret golden goose now!"

The exotics and limos available for rent, loan, or daily use were a new way for even the homeless to get around, enjoy the finer qualities of life, and explore their country, all while rediscovering themselves. Even exotic car designers began to look for employment within Pathway, so they could stretch their imaginations to the hilt, with the ability to draw, sculpt, form and shape any design their hearts desired, because here, anything was possible.

The DC campus was the largest, but there were smaller ones in every state across the US and in every major population center worldwide. Each of them was designed to titillate the senses and appease the mind in every imaginable way, inspiring people to love education, study the arts and sciences, and reach self-actualization.

Much of what was designed was developed to find and help those who were struggling to survive or people who felt the world could be better than mankind had allowed it to become and to get them read-in to Pathway.

Affording so many people these new and exciting opportunities to involve themselves in constructive and meaningful pursuits again, and in environments that seeded the mind with joy and thrilling purpose became the mantra and the overall goal of Eliza and Pathway.

Surrounded by well-being and people who truly cared about those around them as much as themselves, peoples' inner fire reignited in pursuit of positive goals. For the price of a smile, someone could hop in a different and mesmerizing vehicle every day and travel to their heart's content or make an unforgettable friend.

Each Pathway exotic and limousine was secretly retrofitted with the highest quality and technologically advanced cold-fusion systems as well as the utmost level of protections and security mechanisms conceivable.

These vehicles could not be stolen, broken into, broken down, or in some cases even seen. Pathway exotics and limos had zero accidents and the capacity to navigate through public highways and roads unnoticed, if desired. Furthermore, each and every method of travel and transportation that was provided was also retrofitted with automated driving systems that were unparalleled to anything else in the public sector.

Unfortunately, due to the brilliance of Eliza and Pathway, they were aware of malicious entities out there, so, these systems were all word of mouth and never publicized, nor would they be for some time, since the average corporation would find a way to capitalize upon them, making the costs too astronomical, leaving these benefits only to the elite cronies throughout the world, and thus unaffordable to those who needed them most. This wouldn't happen under Eliza's, Yesha's or James' watch, nor under the tenure of any leader in Pathway.

Oh, these capabilities were hidden in plain sight, but they came with an option to cloak a vehicle as one of the commonly used cars in a particular locale, especially if the don't-trust-much-o-meter rose above a certain level or percentage, based on local crime rates or other forms of corruption.

Either way, a person could dare to drive a vehicle uncloaked such as a Lamborghini, Bugatti, Ferrari, or any other exotic or luxury vehicle, and on full visual display, but that was merely for personal peace of mind, since all of these methods of transportation were bullet and missile proof.

The idea, however, was to not overly flaunt an elite sense of affluence, but to enjoy life, chill, and be happy. Thus, these vehicles were used as a tool to motivate many toward ingenuity, productivity, and well-being.

Eliza, Yesha, James, and their quickly-growing and leader-esque organization had taken an hour here and an hour there out of their busy schedules to design and build the best sixteen-square-block area in all of DC and something similar to a minor degree in size from state-to-state and country-to-country. What the public did not know, was that these structures could endure anything lobbed at them or near their campuses. They were designed to protect the occupants, while providing them beautiful moments in life, incomparable to any other.

As the days went by, Eliza and her teams fulfilled their duties throughout the Western Hemisphere, while Yesha and her delegates, did so in the Eastern Hemisphere, and James and his crews, spanned the twenty-thousand tech cities throughout the solar system, and used any freed up moment to work with Eliza.

In this case, they began the DC project the day after Agent Epstein visited them and finished it one week later.

Each finished project was found to be intriguing to the public not just because of the speed with which they were constructed but because they were an awe-inspiring conglomerate of magnificent and interwoven structures, that somehow blended well with the rest of the capital city or any city that their complexes happened to be built in. Each Pathway-occupied campus was breathtaking to behold, and the same was true of the DC megacomplex.

Today, with those projects complete, everyone in Pathway had been involved in ventures throughout the world and the solar system, and most of what remained dealt with putting out small fires scattered here and there or dealing with any of a vast array of seemingly pervasive, yet mundane issues throughout the public sector, while recruiting hosts and droves of citizens to work in these massive centers and in the new tech cities.

Chapter 09: Delegates

Database Moon Archive, Celestial-Sol Entry Date: 2010 May, 19. Yesha Alevtina trains Vesha Celeste. In this crucial part of her training, she discovers the importance of delegates, within the structure and organization of the Universal Party. This training is conducted within the Virtual Universe, interfaced within the Pathway Melrose Campus. Input by Eliza Williams, President of Pathway Industries, 2008-2015.

Prior to this meeting with Agent Epstein, following her State of Pathway, in 2009, Eliza had recruited and sent delegates worldwide to do the same as she had been doing, to travel throughout the solar system with access to jump gates that were unnoticeable or undetectable to the human eye, educate, and recruit new members of the Pathway organization. As it was, ordinary public and terrestrial individuals could not see the fullness of any of Pathway LLC's developments unless they had been trained as an honorary member, or as a potential citizen who was fully read-in after having been both physiologically and neurologically optimized and thus granted a neurological identification.

Each democratically elected delegate would go on typical and in many cases dangerous missions looking for victims of abuse, violence, or disease, and then help them to find their way to Eliza's Melrose, Massachusetts campus and living quarters and become healed with expedience. In a majority of cases, they would only heal someone, minus optimizations that were not agreed upon, until primary training was provided, and the new citizen chose to receive them. If there was a dire emergency, then rescue and healing would be immediate.

The assigned delegates would meet, work with, and then escort the refugees via the hidden jump gates to the US and Canada where they could travel via hyperloop to the main campus, and if they would so choose, they could become fully read-in citizens of Pathway LLC.

Eliza had decided to resolve the many issues of economics as per the US Government. Bank accounts for operations carried out explicitly by the UP, and specific responsibilities were drafted, in order to provide clarity to the difference in mission between the two. These bylaws were set up separate from Pathway LLC to meet the legalities of current governments and economic systems, and to establish the UP as per the laws and expectations currently observed in whatever province they might be in. Laws were practiced, per the localized regions, but Eliza, through Pathway LLC donated millions of dollars to provide funding for rescue, research, development, travel, commercials, speeches, and even entertainment that promoted the UP, where there was no affiliation mandate.

Along with universal disaster relief, universal training at Pathway LLC, and universal overhead expenses, all activities and expenses were made available online with individual anonymity and confidentiality for refugees, and upon personal and properly informed request.

Any honorable member of Pathway LLC working inside any hostile environment was provided privacy in the utmost, to include privacy of personal data by using an identification algorithm, which tied into an individual neural identification, without the need for optimizations, which was currently impossible for any public terrestrial systems to break out. This system worked to negate the possibility of hacking while it simultaneously enabled transparency of donation monies spent by the UP.

Eliza financed all refugee, medical, industrial, and commercial operations through her investments in Pathway LLC, and gave due and legal credit to the intent of the political bridge-building activities provided by the UP and its delegates. There were many cases where Eliza acknowledged individuals posthumously, "All who have risked life and limb to rescue the 'world's most wonderful' to provide others a fair opportunity to express their full potential, embracing Universal Ethics, we thank you."

Early on, Eliza's political party became officially titled the "Universal Party" and subsequently dubbed the "UP," at least throughout the tech cities, even though it had not yet been officially setup in the public political arena. This was further augmented by the support of the voting results that were unanimous by all members of the party in each state of the US and each state throughout the globe, which held democratic elections worldwide.

Getting the UP on the future ballots throughout the US took a lot of work, and in order to do so, Eliza combed the nation to recruit delegates who had special skills when it came to political insight, the ability to bridge alliances with the major political parties, and so much more. This was no easy task, no matter her own special traits, to include her optimized physiology and neurology, because this type of change had to occur from within, while allowing others to reach the hearts of those they knew to sow the seeds of change. There were plenty of beautiful aspects to all that our world supported, but there were issues that were global and unnecessary, that required the kind of guidance the UP would provide.

The Golden State

Going back about a year from the resounding success of establishing the UP worldwide, Eliza recalled when she first visited one particularly fine and humble lady in San José, California early on in August of 2009. Her name was Adelay, and a remarkable woman she was.

Adelay, as a result, introduced many others from her own political network to the Pathway organization, and they in-turn introduced even more individuals who became delegates for the UP. Having found out about Adelay through Virtual Universe connections, Eliza was intrigued by what the others had seen within her. Some of these recruits happened to be from San José and others had worked with her at some point previously in their lives in other parts of the nation, yet they were all connected through political interactions, at a bipartisan level. In her earlier days, Adelay had been a modest yet hopeful person with great goals for the future in the political arena, but becoming an elected official was a goal that had never really taken off. Nevertheless, she grew quite a network of influential friends throughout the US.

Rather than run for office, Adelay found herself happy at first, just helping the various politicians in the local community she lived in where she could, doing paperwork, writing legal documents, meeting as a representative of the politicians, and maturing to the point to where she even offered political advice to presumptive candidates, and much more.

Adelay had surrounded herself with people whose careers had helped them to break past the glass ceiling. In many cases, their careers went through the stratosphere, and they had triumphed, but only for so long, before their ideals were stopped by some unseen entity. She often thought to herself about this strange phenomenon, and one day, she shared this idea with Eliza after their meeting and her own recruitment, while journeying through the Virtual Universe.

"This unseen entity, which seems to pull the many strings that essentially ignore our well-being, in pursuit of more wealth and power, has never received a single electoral vote, nor have these usurpers ever won or even been in a single election."

Adelay, having served since the early '70's was all-too familiar with this oft-ignored influence of the 'puppet-masters,' and she knew enough to realize that the reality of governance was not what many perceived it to be. She also was calm enough of mind to know that she still had the freedom to speak of these things without fear.

After journeying thru the Virtual Universe with Eliza, Adelay found herself renewed, and while she chose to maintain her current age, due to her political influences and her desire to be of continued influence in a positive way, she aspired to herald the kinds of changes that Eliza had preached about, not long after meeting her. Before meeting Eliza, however, time had flown by in her service to the public, wherein, she felt she had been there, in some way, to ease the decay in ethics seemingly rampant within the current governance systems, while bringing calm.

Born and raised on the outskirts of Bakersfield, Adelay moved north to San José, and both locations happened to lie within the beautiful and "Golden" State of California. She moved to San José when she was twenty-three, shortly after it had been coined, "The Silicon Valley," in 1971. When she arrived at the beautiful and bustling town, in those days, strawberry patches were a lot more visible and commonplace, until the urbanization of the town grew it into a city that matured with more industrial centers, work sites, and technology hot-spots.

For many, working in the sciences, or the arts, or the industrial arenas, the services, or the construction and environmental sectors was a day-to-day aspect that tended toward a career, but never quite arrived at the level one would equate with what someone would call a dream job. In all reality, bliss had been fleeting at best, and the moniker, "Pursuit of Happiness," was never lost on them.

Neither Adelay, nor those closest to her, nor anyone who lived in such a very sophisticated and highly advanced and technologically-minded community, seemed to find that peace within that comes with that supposed "personal calling" in life. Yet, whatever she did still beckoned for more days, more hours, more minutes of that precious thing called "life." There were fleeting moments of brilliance. Happiness was something that was always sought after, but it never was really or truly obtained, at least for long periods of time.

Having found herself lucky despite all, Adelay tried to find small moments of delight in everything she would do, just before meeting Eliza.

Many years before, she worked with Mrs. Fierro, who was the District 19 Representative for California in Congress, until retirement in 1990, at the age of seventy. She followed that up by working with Ms. Jane Comstock, who likewise, labored diligently in the same position, and continued to help San José rise in the arena of technology, by cultivating a living, educational, and industrial climate that was permissive of and attractive to great minds.

Many years before, while finishing her public administration degree in her youth, Adelay had worked in the front offices of a well-respected sheet metal shop, that happened to be a part of that early era. This company was a booming business named, Metal and Prototype Manufacturers Incorporated, or MPM Inc.

Working at MPM Inc. gave Adelay experiences that seasoned her personality and matured her mind into understanding the vantage point of politics from the view of the every-day worker. Notwithstanding, she found that working there still brought many hours of appreciation to her heart for the professional and considerate bosses she had. She was pleased with the leadership of the sheet metal company and had enjoyed working at MPM Inc. At the time, MPM frequently sanctioned tours to prospective employees and potential clients, and on occasion, she was given the opportunity to lead these tours as well.

As was routine, she enjoyed her lunches near her vehicle, but, she had also gone to lunch frequently with a young spot welder for about three years. It wasn't until that three-year-mark that she discovered that this young man's mother happened to work for the city government.

Over lunch one day, he inquired, "I can't believe I haven't asked you this, but, where did you go to school?"

It hadn't dawned on her that she hadn't ever told him, so she answered his minor inquisition, "I went to a relatively new and small university in Baker's Field. It opened up just a year before I attended. I was there for four years and finished my BA in Public Administration."

"So, why in the world are you working here?"

"I don't know. I couldn't find any open spots in the profession I studied. So, I figured, why not? I might as well work in San José. Think about it, ever since I heard about the recent onslaught of computers, development, and boom in tech, this looked to be the ideal place for not only technologic growth, but personal growth.

"I figured, if I work for a tech company, or one of their manufacturers, then maybe I can get well-versed on some of the nuances of the area. I used to think I'd run for office, but now I'd be happy helping someone who is running for office, you know, being the advisor, or the voice of reason? Plus, there's so much that needs to be done behind the scenes." Adelay smiled, and Bradley could see the sparkles in her eyes as she talked about it.

"In the three years I've known you, I wouldn't have guess, but it all makes sense now. You've always had a good head about you for that sort of thing. Say, we've known each other for a few years. I need to tell you something, if you promise not to tell?"

"Oh? Of course not, silly!"

"My mother? She is in politics. She is the US Representative in Congress for District 19. She worked her way up from the dregs but has done a lot for our city. I believe you might want to meet her, I've talked well about you, and I am for sure she would love to meet you."

Over that lunch conversation in 1974, he let her know to never to lose faith in why she earned her degree in public administration, assuring her that her efforts weren't a waste. Adelay was in luck.

This young man had indeed spoken well of Adelay to his mother for more than three years. It wasn't until that day, that he had discovered her interest in politics. Since Bradley and his mother shared a healthy and team-like relationship, they visited often. Plus, she had a spacious home, for entertaining diplomatic guests.

Bradley's mother, who had been obviously and increasingly intrigued by his conversations about her, was very enthused upon finding out about her degree in public administration and decided to ask him to bring her home.

Mrs. Fierro wanted to meet Adelay. She seemed like quite a brilliant young woman, *"If Bradley is correct, Adelay is twenty-six—and he is twenty-nine. Hmmm. She seems to have a natural gift for relating to the variety of cultures here in San José, and she and Bradley have been friends for quite some time. Things won't be traditional with us, they never have been, and I think it's time to meet her,"* Mrs. Fierro thought to herself, and asked Bradley to invite her over.

The following day, Bradley invited Adelay to meet his mother, and she accepted. After work, upon arriving to her home, and seeing how it was a Friday evening, she not only freshened up, but with dedication, some added effort and extra preparation, she ensured her light brown locks were curled in a fashionable and classic manner, yet with a very professional vibe. She also made sure her makeup wasn't overdone, yet it was lightly there to demonstrate her sense for fashion while augmenting her keenness for hygiene, grooming, and more. Her eyebrows and eyelashes were on queue with intrigue, beauty, sophistication, and respectability, and the results complemented the blue irises and black limbal rings of her eyes, her light brown hair, and her soft pale skin. Adelay dressed to impress and was set to meet with Bradley's mom. She would do so in style.

Knocking on the door, as Bradley had requested, just a few peaceful moments later Adelay was greeted by him. They shook hands and he escorted her to the living room to meet his mother. She tried not to make it seem obvious, but she was immediately taken in by the details of such a spacious living area. She had always had modest living conditions, and this looked like something out of La Dolce Vita, from a movie she watched in 1960!

"Nice to meet you, Adelay. My name is Charlene, with the same last name as Bradley." Charlene knew that it was possible Adelay already knew of her surname, but she provided it anyway just to be polite and reduce the chance for any awkward vibes, "Fierro. I hear you've been working at MPM? They're a wonderful employer. My son, I love him bunches, and I am proud he has gone out of his way to make it on his own. They've treated him so well, he is a hard worker, very dedicated, and I can tell he's learned a lot over the years.

"Could you please stay a while?"

"Sure, of course, Mrs. Fierro."

"Oh, do, please call me Charlene?"

"Of course, Charlene."

"Would you, by chance, Adelay, be interested in a Saki? My son has put together a cocktail recipe that is out of this world! I love it and believe me, it's the best medicine for relaxing the mind and enjoying conversation regarding the affairs of the political arena that have affected so many here in California and beyond! We can chat about our shared and enriching goals, maybe a few things about our personal lives, and then maybe talk about the realities that truly exist that we have yet to overcome?" Charlene waited, and in just a few moments, the trust that she engendered was honorably palpable and appreciated by Adelay. They hit it off from the get-go.

"Sure, I'd love a Saki, Charlene. Your son is good at everything he puts his mind to." Bradley had always been a dashing young man, with dirty blonde hair and natural brown lowlights, hazel eyes, and his hair in a comb-over or a sort of loose pompadour of sorts, that drifted down to a smooth curl just before his ears. The hair that would have covered his ears he swept behind them, and the hair on the sides of his head and just below his occipital bone was trimmed short and tidy. He was handsome, yet youthful and clean-cut, despite having been a welder at MPM. His gaze had always been one of concern, quiet wisdom, and sincerity.

After beginning their pleasant conversation, it was obvious to Adelay that Charlene had prepared well, herself. She provided the lovely refreshments and they continued chatting with a sense of relaxation, where sophistication and ideas of peace and prosperity were shared and apparently the norm, at least in prose and concept. This made Adelay's initial suspicions of the political arena firmer, especially when it came to this profession being one where great ideas seemed to dwindle. It seemed, the further the political landscape moved up to those controlling the strings of power and suggestion, the less likely they were voted in, and much less the movement seemed to steer toward the well-being of the constituents who voted. For the politicians, they would try to at least slow the pace of malevolence if they saw it and could, yet in so many ways, it was "comply or cope," with a never-ending concern over reelections.

The conversation continued through the night. It was a weekend, and in Adelay's mind, a taxi was easy to call at that time, so she allowed herself to free her spirits and engage in endless conversation, while sipping Bradley's best, the Saki of delight! Luckily, the Fierros had an extra room, so after enjoying a lovely evening of sophisticated conversation, Charlene invited her to stay, and Adelay stayed the night in a guest room and on a lovely queen-sized and lavishly clothed bed.

Adelay awoke the next morning with a minor headache, in a strange bed, and in a different room than what she was used to, yet she also awoke to the pleasant aroma of coffee, but found she had her own private bathroom, so she held the desire for a morning beverage first. After showering and freshening up, she stepped into the dining room. The yeast from the freshly baked bagels had raised, been baked, and the cinnamon raisin oatmeal, among other dishes and condiments left a delicious smell that permeated the air. She looked around, and before her on the table, she saw several hard-boiled eggs sitting in a refrigerated porcelain bowl next to several silver platters with associated food covers, over what she presumed were the reasons for the pleasant smells spread through the atmosphere of this nicely-decorated home.

While looking around at the dishes, within the dining room, she looked at the doorway to her right, upon hearing familiar footsteps coming down the hall, and saw as Bradley came into the room suited up, tying his tie, with his vest on, covering his grey pinstriped button-up shirt, which had the collars turned up. As he strode in, he cinched up the tie, using a tight double Windsor, brought his collar down, and tucked it under his silken vest.

"Good morning, Adelay. How was your rest? It must have been wonderful? You look great as always, but especially dazzling today."

"At first, when I awoke, I saw your cat up in the windowsill and was a little confused as to where I was. Then I remembered, after noticing all of the well-designed furniture and ornamentation spread throughout the home, I'm at your mom's house! She was lovely, by the way. I then realized that I woke up to the lovely scent of this delicious looking food, showered up, and came down to see all of this," she said, as she gestured with her arms and hands toward the spread on the table.

She continued, "Do you mind if I have a bite or two?" Interestingly, the warm shower had relieved her of her headache, and now seeing Bradley, she was feeling a glow and vibrantly in bliss.

Bradley didn't have to ponder the answer for too long, "By all means. Please, help yourself. I retired early last night, got up, cooked some breakfast, and then got ready for the science symposium today at the San José Auditorium." He looked away from her, toward the table, and then toward her again, with a smile, "It looks like you are dressed to go as well? Would you like to come?"

"I can't see why not. It's the weekend, what else could be so intriguing?"

"You've got a good point." Bradley opened one of the silver food covers, grabbed a bagel, opened the cover to the cinnamon-vanilla-spiced cream cheese dish, and then helped himself to a Sumatra coffee, grapefruit juice, an orange, a banana, and some oatmeal. "Please, have a seat? How was your chat with my mom last night?"

"I'm sure you already know the answer to that question. She is brilliant! A wonderful person, a great leader, and a dynamic politician. No wonder why San José is bustling and busy with employment, engaging minds, and innovation! You did an amazing job on those bagels by the way. The smell of the coffee was so lovely to wake up to! And you look pretty dashing yourself, if you don't mind my honesty. It's quite a change from the traditional attire you wear at the sheet metal shop!"

Adelay helped herself to some food and then while sharing breakfast with him, she went over the details of her and Charlene's conversation.

Bradley was inquisitive and interested, and she had appreciated that about him for the three years she had known him. A lot of the men she'd worked with in her past were much more stoic and spoke but few words. He at least knew how to carry on with a decent conversation beyond the typical. The fact that he could dress up, was clean-cut, well-groomed, despite being a "welder," and going to a science symposium and given the fact that his mother was so well-versed in politics as it related to the city, state, nation, and worldwide, impressed her very much about them both, and in a good way.

Ever since Adelay had worked at MPM, and met him, she'd only seen an intriguing spot welder, who was fun to gaze at and chat with over lunch, had been for the last three years and was someone who seemed rather sophisticated despite being a blue collar worker, or a so-called grunt. She had always appreciated the hard workers anyway and had a deep respect for anyone who was dedicated to their craft, yet kind to all they met notwithstanding. However, now that another layer of who Bradley truly was had been peeled away, she started to feel a new connection with him that she felt was priceless and something she wanted to hold on to.

The symposium was had, their minds were swelling with new ideas, and Adelay began to realize she was developing feelings for Bradley. She shoved them aside for now and focused on her career goals. Not more than three weeks after this meeting and following that particularly splendid day, she began working for Bradley's mom, helping her with her campaigns and then with the nitnoid details of public administration.

Within the two years that followed, Bradley transitioned from MPM Inc. to employment in the information technology, or IT, community. After knowing Bradley Fierro for five years, in 1976, he took her to the shores of Carmel Bay, in California, for a picnic. He asked his mother to come with them, and he proposed to her, amidst the soft crashing of the near-distant crashing and mighty waves of the Pacific Ocean.

Adelay and Bradley went with Charlene to Las Vegas soon after, and, not much following that, the justice of the peace at the Clark County Marriage License Bureau, officially married them, quick, simple, and painless.

Bradley and Charlene drove with Adelay to Vegas, and through the many conversations, they convinced her to keep her maiden name. Charlene spoke up at one point, "You have to keep your name. Baye is so beautiful. There is a nice ring to it, and I want you to be able to establish yourself in the political arena pursuing your own dreams as you see fit." Persuading her, they were unique that way.

Thirty-three years later, Adelay met Eliza for the first time. Both Bradley and Charlene were still alive, and they all lived in the same beautiful home. Adelay had also enjoyed working with the Fierros and had never sought office since. Ever since Charlene retired, she began working with Jane Comstock, but had never pursued political office herself. That would change soon.

Eliza met Adelay one evening when she happened to be with Bradley, who was sixty-four, and Charlene, who was now a spry and lively eighty-nine-year-old. When Eliza had found out about Adelay, she coordinated with Charlene to meet with her, her daughter in-law, and son at a fairly new and very reputable hamburger joint, called "What-a-Burger." They enjoyed every bite.

Together, all four hit it off quite well, and somewhere during the conversation, Eliza brought up the subject of clean meats, "This is meat that is produced in a lab. It will eliminate the need to kill the cattle, as well as reduce carbon emissions, provide an alternate source of income for the economy and so much more. It will afford the body many important natural nutrients, to include antioxidants. Not to mention, clean meats will provide bliss to the mind and taste buds."

She then talked about rescuing people all over the world with her organization, called Pathway LLC.

Charlene, although now retired from the political arena, was quite charmed by Eliza, who seemed wiser than her years. Bradley and Adelay were taken in by her demeanor and wonder as well. Bradley, although sixty-four, was taken by her character and genius capacity for thought, just as he still was and had been for Adelay throughout the thirty-eight years that he had known her. Adelay knew right away that they would be kindred spirits. After taking Eliza on a tour through San José, they agreed to go with her to the campus in Melrose, MA.

Once they arrived, just as many before them, they were in awe with the ambiance of the setting and every detail, from the glowing white walls, columns, arching architecture, the large windows, the animals outside that seemed as if they were in conversations with each other, the various languages spoken with ease, and together they went through the training and then the Virtual Universe.

Together, they experienced twenty years of youth like existence. When they exited the Virtual Universe, Adelay, now sixty years old, felt like she did when she was twenty-three, again, and both Bradley and Charlene felt extremely fit as well in their twenty-two-year-old physiological internal forms.

They all decided, in the public world, to maintain a fit version of their original appearance, until the UP put a president in the White House. Of course, they all looked to Eliza as the leader that should be there but kept it to themselves for the time being.

"That is very respectable, and I understand" said Eliza. "At any time that you feel you are ready to let your right mind allow a full healing to take place, you simply need to enter your biopod, and wish it so. I completely understand your not wanting to give away the obvious too soon. I also appreciate your inner strength. The most beautiful aspect to each person, is within."

Following those journeys, James Cooper met with Adelay, Charlene, and Bradley, and set them up for their missions. Upon conferring with Eliza, as he always did, with an almost continuous neural link with her, on what they would do next, they were welcomed and integrated into the tech cities, Pathway, chose to join the UP, and accepted the missions James assigned them.

Adelay, with her new and revitalized physiology and neurology, yet still in her sixty-year-old frame, looked more fit than she had felt in years. Charlene and Bradley looked surprisingly fit as well. After conferring with James, they each decided on their new callings in life. Adelay chose to work with the political party she was affiliated with prior to meeting Eliza, so she could not only begin a new political career, but this time do so with forward progress in-tow. While doing so, she would influence her political organization to allow the formation of Eliza's new political party in the state of California.

"Eliza, would you like to meet the current district 19 representative for the State of California?"

"Absolutely."

"You'll love her. She is quite a fiery mind, and really does care about the people, just as Charlene did. After we meet with her, I highly recommend you meet young Gemini in Kansas City, Missouri. She may be young, but she is brilliant, has been a sci-fi writer since she was in her teens, and is involved in politics in her state, trying to do similar things as I. I ran into her several years ago, and we've been best friends ever since!"

Just a few days passed, and Adelay, Charlene, and Bradley explored their homes on Titan, the solar system's second largest official moon, with a thick atmosphere, but the tech cities had been so advanced that they had a magnificent view of Saturn and its rings. Every street in the tech city they lived in, one of many on Titan, was fantastic, filled with vegetation, wildlife that wasn't so wild, and the buildings glowed with arches, bends, and beauty that was never seen on Earth.

After several trips through the Virtual Universe, all three had put in for nominations as delegates of the Universal Party and were voted in unanimously.

When they were ready, they linked with Eliza, and together they went to San José, California to meet Jane.

Silicon Valley

As it was when Adelay arrived in Silicon Valley in 1971, it continued to be in 2009. San José was still a bustling technological hub with bright innovators, great minds, and techno-wizards. Much of District 19 was set up by previous legislators to attract brilliant innovators. Big names seemed to grace the location in droves.

Unfortunately, throughout much of the rest of the state, no matter the amazing ideas coming from so many great individuals, it seemed the bureaucrats were never in short supply, creating more legislation, as if they were designing more ways to pull your teeth without any xylocaine or any other painkiller for that matter.

Legislation was brutal. The concept of political dealings had drifted to the idea that in order to be in politics you had to create more rules, policies, bylaws, and if you could imagine it, even more rules.

Forgotten was the art of acting as an adult capable of evolving and making decisions in the best interest of both them and others, and moreover the idea of combing over existing rules and asking if they still served the purpose of protecting the people from malicious acts. The very acts of those who probably should not have been turned loose on the public in the first place seemed on the rise and lawmakers instead seemed to tie the hands of those who were in fact responsible citizens. The idea of asking whether a rule was founded in well-being seemed a lost treasure, or an unnecessary responsibility.

Thus, rules, bylaws, practices, procedures, processes and policies were no longer revisited for relevance, practicality, or even ethics. Business ethics seemed to rule, where corporate lobbyists influenced what went on at the White House, the Senate, and the House of Representatives more so than those who were voted in. Well-being was viewed as more of a laughing matter than an important aspect of proper leadership.

Rules for the sake of rules, ruled the day. In many cases, it was thought that several seedy corporations had rigged the laws in such a way, that they could justify their stinginess toward their employees. "Employers would be punished for doing the right thing, tax laws tie our hands, and more so if we pay our employees who do the crucial tasks en par with the revenue they bring in through their efforts. Our employees do everything we'd never want to do, but we have another workaround for that."

In many cases, it was quite reasonable to consider the idea that these same entities seemed responsible for creating the term, "unskilled labor." This term was crucial to their agenda of gaining more power and amassing even more wealth, at nearly any cost. They had even convinced a few who were not so bright that it was congruent with business ethics to operate solely on the standpoint of growing their coffers and spanning the globe, without a care in the world for the well-being of those in their employ or of the life-giving qualities of the planet itself.

Earthquakes were not prevented, the idea of such was scoffed at. "How is that even possible? You are nuts!" Was a question often asked, followed by a legal type of slander, only available to entities alone without recourse, especially if someone dared bring the idea of well-being to the surface. Abundantly pure water, through desalinization was an idea that was tossed aside, peoples' water bills were high, crops were dwindling, and forests were very dry. Fires ravaged the state.

Instead of working with communities to replace weeds with fire-retardant flora, or removing dry sticks, fallen trees, and dried leaves, providing kindling and cords of wood for long winters, while finding other helpful uses for the resources and replacing the dry ground with moisture, flora, rocks, or clean-cut and well-watered lawns, which would have resulted in giving employment to a sizeable team of nature conservationists, were ideas that they tossed away with ease. All of the work, care, and labor that could have provided jobs and other economic means was aggressively overlooked and even demonized.

Life was quickly becoming brutal and miserable in the once beautiful and Golden State of California, but a few people refused to see it as something they were helpless to do anything about. These individuals refused to let these rising realities slow them down. They believed in a better state, a better world, and in doing everything within their power to turn the tide.

San José was feeling the toll, notwithstanding, the crunch, or the strain of high costs for minimally-sized housing, codes left and right for every improvement and upgrade, and infrastructure was crumbling. Vehicles had so many emissions tests that taxes and fees were yet another slice, begging for more of that same sized pie that grew very little over the decades, and innovators were beginning to find other locations, wherein there were few, that were just a little more appealing.

People were in a sense kept at a level of poverty that empowered these malicious entities responsible for this emerging environment in the first place, by squeezing the money-well of the masses dry, disarming, impoverishing, and reducing the overall education levels of those they wished to do their bidding. "If people are untrained or 'unskilled,' then they'll have no choice but to make a meager income for survival and do as we wish."

The idea of well-being was beginning to go the way of the Dodo bird—extinct.

A change was certainly needed, and indeed in store. Luckily, for each citizen within that beautiful valley, which used to be laden with strawberry patches and wine, a young woman, named Jane Comstock, rose from the ashes and began to see a future in politics.

On her way up, by 1990, she had finished college. By 1995, she had pushed her way through corporate and climbed to the top. By 2000, she ran for office as District 19 Representative for the State of California and had recommended sweeping changes to the way business was done both on Capitol Hill and in corporations themselves. In 2005, she was voted out of the corporation, because the investors, shareholders, and board saw her as a threat to their ill-gotten gains. By 2008, she successfully pursued her political ambitions, if anything, to see some changes made that would benefit the many, and not just the few.

It was in 1990, however, that Jane met Adelay. Jane, although young, made it her business to attend meetings at the local chamber of commerce, and it was there that she met Adelay, who was involved in much the same way. Adelay had seen her mother in-law's retirement from legislation and saw promise in Jane from the start of their friendship. From that time forward, they met frequently, despite the age difference and their political leanings.

When Eliza and Adelay visited Jane in August of 2009, she was the Representative for District 19, went to Washington, DC, regularly, and was working on cleaning out the so-called swamp. She was a conservative, although unique for a metropolitan location, within close range to other bustling locations, to include Stanford

University, a highly-respected educational institution just to the northeast of the now sprawling city. No matter her political leanings, she believed that the "other side of the aisle" had good ideas as well. Jane worked many hours on end, writing, cleaning up, and rewriting legislation, in an effort to streamline the laws, both in quantity and length.

"Laws should be simple and few. They should protect the people of the land that they serve. Common sense should take the place of the quagmire of laws that exist today. This dystopia is spinning out of control, because no one has had the guts to suggest we do something besides make even more laws. We should be strengthening our resolve, building our crumbling infrastructure, lifting our educational goals to greater heights, and empowering the people to be the great individuals they can become!"

Eliza had heard her over the last couple of years, and her messages spoke to Eliza's heart, from across the US.

When Adelay suggested that they visit her, she decided that would be a top priority.

"The food here tastes great!" Eliza told both Adelay and Jane, at the local What-a-Burger. Deep inside, Eliza knew that she was ready to roll out swathing change in so many areas, to include, in this case, the meat industry, with her perfected clean meats, and none of these changes would hurt the wallet of a single investor.

However, the current pulse in society and the legislators was vehemently appalled by the idea of lab-grown meats and were thus very much against it, no matter the overall benefits. Furthermore, very few at the time had even fathomed the idea. All-too-many simply decried what they didn't believe in, rather than find a solution to ensure that those who desired to could get the red meat and iron sources they needed while appeasing the taste buds, and with that, the health of the mind.

As it was, Eliza knew she needed to find a variety of influences for change, and among those changes lie her goals to build her political party through those still in office and who were well-respected in their current political affiliations, by reaching their hearts and their minds. She was neither conservative nor liberal, she was a human being, with concerns over the future of humanity itself. She had entertained the idea of politics, but also knew that at some point soon, before putting her hat into the ring to become a legislator representing her state, she would need to work with many of the industrial leaders, become such a leader herself, and begin the process of influencing people internally, cultivating and maturing a society into one that would support her new party and one that every person throughout the world could be proud of. She wanted to curate a benevolent society that would bring with it to the cosmos a legacy from the home world that we could each be proud to share with other distant and advanced civilizations throughout the Universe.

After their meeting, Jane had been moved by every idea that Eliza shared, and became a fully read-in member and delegate of Pathway. She was still a State Legislator for the 19th District and working with her original party, but this time she had a benevolent agenda of her own. Jane would be responsible for getting the UP on the ballots throughout the Golden State of California.

Years ago, when she first ran for office, while working for a tech giant as its CEO, the district was much larger and included distant cousin locations, that soon became part of the 4th, 16th, 21st, and 22nd Districts. Now, her primary focus was on the tech capitol of the world, wherein, she would shew in laws meant to protect the people she served and build a healthy environment for innovation, the economy, and for health and well-being, while at the same time, raising the quality of life.

The meetings Eliza, Jane, and Adelay had together were amazing, and Jane was even more amazed at the new achievements Eliza had made with her organization, Pathway, beyond the scope of anyone in the public world.

Before parting ways with Eliza and Adelay, Jane smiled at Adelay and told both, "Thank you, Adelay, for introducing me to Eliza. Eliza, I can see that you have a big political career ahead of you, along with a lot of other amazing changes that I am looking forward to seeing."

Jane Comstock then, aware of Eliza's and Adelay's plans now, due to her newfound neural link upon becoming optimized, while maintaining her age as the striking brunette and forty-six-year-old that she was and after visiting the Virtual Universe, suggested, "Once you visit Gemini, please visit Chastity Grey, from Florida. She is on the other side of the political aisle from me and is a phenomenal outside-of-the-box thinker. She'll have quite a few powerful and influential contacts as well. My fellow biotech friends indicate the 'silver-tsunami,' or the increase in population of people who are readying to retire, is just around the corner. Believe me, with your ideas, you'll do extremely well there."

City of Fountains

Less than a week after initially meeting Adelay, Bradley, Charlene, and a few days after meeting Jane, Eliza traveled with Adelay to meet Gemini Cansez, with plans to visit Chastity Grey afterward, and she was a delight! Gemini was born and raised in Kansas City, Missouri, and had a natural love for science fiction and all that it entailed, at least regarding her own ideals. She felt that science fiction was an excellent way to reach out to the public, or the masses and to entertain and educate all at once. Education, to her, was something that helped people to see a new vision for themselves of what they could do to raise the bar for humanity, while enabling them through the tools of whatever trade, skill, or future they wished to realize regarding a career to do just that. She had been young, for sci-fi, but had written anyway. Despite the jeers in her earlier days, when suggesting that this was exactly what she wished to do when she grew up, she wrote and wrote, and persevered. When she wrote, she wanted to start her dreams "now." "Now" happened to be when she was thirteen years old.

Her first sci-fi novel was published through a very small publishing firm, that didn't happen to be overly picky about who they published for. As such, they had grown quite significantly, since there were so many original and striking ideas that seemed to come from their presses. They allowed authors to write themselves, express themselves, and write as they saw fit from their minds and hearts with pen to paper. Now that it was ten years later, in August of 2009, she had written four different series with twenty well-scribed novels apiece. She was prolific, and nothing slowed her down. She had never quite made it to the big-time, but she was happy with the results, since they at least paid the bills.

Interestingly, Eliza already knew who she was, not just because Adelay and Jane had talked about her or her stories, but she had inspired Eliza over the last ten years, especially given the fact that she was so young and had quite an eloquent mind. Eliza also happened to run into her stories while perusing through the exhaustive libraries located in the Virtual Universe, where, through the benefits of time-dilation, she was able to follow each story and read every single text written by mankind, womankind, and even a few kinds of stories that hadn't been published by human means. Somehow, there were many writers who she had planned on visiting, but Gemini was someone on the top of her mind, especially since her stories seemed to relate to so many.

Eliza had been working on her own novel at that time and had planned to publish it early on in 2010, so she enjoyed taking breaks from the whole process, which in her case was quite delicate, to visit others who were doing book-signings, and in this particular case, she chose to go to Kansas City, to meet Gemini.

After setting up the visit through her publicist, they agreed to meet at a local diner. "Your name has some intriguing history to it, Gemini. I also believe it will be connected to a phenomenal future." Eliza said, as she sat down to talk with her over a lovely meal at the Farmhouse on Delaware Street, in Kansas City.

Following their meal and a delightful chat, Eliza and Adelay accompanied Gemini during her book-signing at the Mid-Continent Public Library. Since Kansas City was a huge science fiction hub, Eliza had become quite a name, with secret whisperings of the things she had done, starting to grace the pages of many sci-fi novels, comic magazines, and action figures had been developed. Although Eliza never focused much on fame or popularity for any reason than to be of a positive influence toward the types of changes that would bring joy to the hearts, and health to the physiology and neurology, all the while bringing rejuvenation to our Earth's biome, forests, jungles, rivers, lakes, and oceans.

Likewise, Gemini had phenomenal roots within the region, so the crowds gathered for autographs. People from all over the world visited. Eliza's presence seemed to add to the splendor of the experience.

For Eliza, the experience was mind-opening and very muse-like, since Gemini wrote organically, with little to no education prior to scribing her very first novel. Gemini attributed her knowledge to the Mid-Continent Public Library which had been benefitting many people for years. It had benefitted those who had otherwise no other venue for reading every genre of literature intended to help them to understand the histories, the arts, and the many other topics of interest, from fiction to reality-based publications. This facility was well-setup to enable and encourage the many minds around the area to be full of vibrance when it came to their Universe. James Cooper had visited this location during his cross-country tour, so many years ago, and he too had been a sci-fi favorite, especially when it came to his architectural designs, which were so creative and masterfully built, with so many ideas in mind, when it came to enhancing and blessing the environment his campuses and edifices were built in. This library was one of the top one-hundred libraries in terms of volume and budget within the US, and Eliza approved.

It was interesting sitting alongside Gemini, who was now only twenty-three years old, as she signed the books of her fans. In contrast, Adelay was sixty, with her sixty-first birthday in a couple of weeks. Adelay fit in quite well, since she was so fit and trim, well-groomed, with white hair in a pixie cut, she looked quite sci-fi herself, almost like a spacecraft commander, filled with wisdom and grit. Gemini noted that, since she had already begun her next novel, with Adelay as the main character. Several weeks prior, already knowing Adelay, Gemini had called her and asked her if she could. "Of course," Adelay had replied to the affirmative. She was honored.

No matter Gemini's youth, she reached out to each of her fans with maturity, kindness, and brilliance. She was genuinely interested in each individual who came before her and seemed to have a wonderful memory of each aspect of her stories, so much so, that when a fan talked about a particular chapter, phrase, or quote, she was in-like-Flynn with them, and pontificated back and forth in a way that truly showed she cared about each individual and their interests, no matter their background, or anything else of any sort.

Following her trip with Adelay and Eliza through the Virtual Universe, Gemini decided to continue her writing, to bring to surface many of the ideas that Eliza had shared with regard to the tenets of the Universal Party, in a fictional format, especially since the UP was very pro-sci-fi and for human advancement toward a benevolent future. She also began to consider politics. Having many fans in and throughout the state, she was able to secure a place on the ballot within both Missouri and Kansas, for herself and other candidates from the UP, during the primaries in early 2010.

The Sunshine State

Chastity Grey and Adelay were friends who had spent a lot of time together throughout the years, all while striving to buffet against the unfortunate and prevailing winds of corruption in politics. Chastity tried with all she could to introduce programs and systems to help those struggling the most, despite the seeming desire of the most selfish of society to take that all away. She knew that most people were decent and respectable, yet there was a large and united element in society that didn't have an identity at all, and they seemed to be pulling the strings without a care for anyone in the world but themselves. Humanity, in her purview, was precious and unlike these unnamed assailants, every human, to her, was invaluable and irreplaceable. Perhaps that was why she was drawn to live where she did, in a futuristic city called, Lake Nona.

The same age as Adelay, Chastity was born and raised in Florida, and had only recently moved to her new location, near Orlando. She had been raised in and often made trips to Cape Canaveral. In many cases, she would go there to watch various space-faring vehicles launch to carry their payloads out and into space.

Adelay and Chastity met at a bipartisan convention many years ago, and even though Adelay was a Democrat and Chastity a Republican, they both shared similar values, and were sometimes considered the mavericks of their parties, if anything, because Adelay had worked for so many years with the Fierros as well as Jane Comstock, both of whom happened to be the Representative of District 19 at one time or another, and Republicans. Chastity often worked with her party and the Democrats in Florida to overcome issues affecting their state.

Despite their party affiliations, both had always felt that the well-being of the people in their country, in their states, and in their districts were far more important than party or ideology.

Adelay had gotten ahold of Chastity, who in-turn made reservations at the Nona Blue Modern Tavern, for three. Sitting around their pub table on bar stools, Eliza, Adelay, and Gemini awaited their orders while sipping "Baby Blue Cosmopolitans" which were made of a nice mixture of Ketel One Citroen, Blue Curacao, white cranberry juice, lime juice, and Lemon Twist.

Eliza had ordered fire grilled artichokes, a classic Caesar salad, and a veggie burger. Adelay enjoyed Eliza's appetizer as well and had ordered prosciutto to share amongst the three, as well as a Baja Style Taco, and a traditional Greek salad. Chastity knew the scene and had an order of Love Me Tenders, which were hand dipped chicken tenders, with French fries, honey mustard, and barbeque sauce, she'd also ordered an Asian grilled steak salad, which she vowed was phenomenal, followed by a an eight-ounce Barrel Cut Filet Mignon, which came with a baked potato. Despite her appetite, she was trim.

Their night of food was a delight, and their conversations carried on through to midnight. Following three lovely beverages, one before the meal, one through the meal, and one quite enjoyably after the meal, Chastity invited them both to her beautiful home on Kensington Shore Drive, with wooden floors, white granite architecture, and cabinetry in all of the right places. It just so happened that Chastity had four bedrooms and lavish living conditions. She justified it as a very necessary part of bridging diplomacy and working with people from all over the world.

"A politician like myself, well, I must entertain. And, so I do, with the best of the best, and some of the others as well. We need to inspire greatness, and well, after a few drinks, its nice to settle into a home that takes your breath away."

Neither Eliza nor Adelay could argue with that.

The next morning, they did not need a bath since they were optimized and their nanos would do that for them, but they soaked for a nice while anyway, because every suite in Chastity's mansion had a spacious and ornate jacuzzi bathtub. Not to mention, as extravagant as Chastity was, she'd made sure that every room, every bathroom, and every location within the place had all the amenities needed or considered "typical" to her, given the purpose of the room. This meant there were bath salts, bubble bath choices, aroma therapy purifiers, and stereo systems that operated based on voice command.

Eliza was listening to Depeche Mode's, "When the Body Speaks," and enjoying every moment of it. To her, their sound was as if it were just made, and with magic. She listened while pondering on the previous events, what she would do that day as well as in the days that followed. Given her abilities, she felt that she was more of a free spirit than she had ever been. Sometimes she'd link and catch up with James Cooper. At other times she'd link with Yesha, to do likewise.

Yesha always seemed in the throes of a rescue or in one form of an emergency or another, saving lives and sending people to one of James' delegates for training at one of the many campuses located within the tech cities throughout the Solar System, and then to be read-in within the Virtual Universe. The populations from around the world were embattled with civil wars, extremist organizations of one type or another, and it was a constant relay of the mind, where Yesha would see another networked individual who needed help right away.

Adelay was listening to Pink Floyd's, "Dark Side of the Moon" and "Marooned," while linked with her husband, Bradley Fierro, who was presently in a jacuzzi tub of his own in their domicile on Titan. She looked at his mental imagery, and he was looking younger and younger every day, with that Chip and Dale vibe, and she liked it very much. They'd both decided to maintain the external aspects of their physiology for the time being but had allowed their biological clocks to cause their expressions to reverse age, from day-to-day, just enough, to where they now both looked like they were in their mid-forties, and no more. Still, she loved her white hair, kept it, but looked as fit as a fiddle, and so did he, in all of the ways she enjoyed. He'd developed quite a swagger at that point.

Chastity had noted the evening before that Adelay looked quite a bit younger than she had the previous time she'd seen her, but Chastity had always had that vibrant look, herself, no matter her age. She thought it was ironic however, that her hair was snow white, yet she was titled, "Senator Grey." Adelay had thought it was a wonder how youthful Chastity had been all these years, despite all. It must have been the top-notch physicians that only she could afford, since she had inherited quite a wealthy estate from her husband who had passed away in his forties, due to a boating accident. He'd always lived life rough, on the edge, or the wild side, and Chastity was never bothered by it, at least not until he passed away.

Roger was always a gentleman and never swayed from their marriage, yet he loved going on high-thrill excursions, trips, sky-diving, deep sea diving, snorkeling amongst the sharks, cliff and rock climbing, and so much more. As time went by, he'd been even more of a thrill seeker after he came into the money following a few inventions and patents he'd sold. She had, by that time, become a senator for the Sunshine State of Florida, out of Cape Canaveral, and at this point, it did not matter where she lived. Her constituents trusted her and had voted her in during every election since 1990, because she was fun, straight forward, and hadn't received or accepted a single bribe while serving at Capitol Hill since the day she took office. Oh, there were threats on her life, from time-to-time, but she had plenty of Floridians who had her back, and people loved her from either side of the aisle.

Like Jane Comstock and Adelay Baye, Chastity was a bit of a self-thinker, someone who didn't always walk the line, but not for pretense, rather instead, to ensure Floridians didn't get impacted by high tax rates. She felt that those who retired would contribute enough to the state's economy, that there was no need to entertain or excise such a tax and place an unnecessary burden on those who had worked hard all of their lives and decided to retire there. She also believed that it was better to allow private industry to take care of their environment in a way that beautified and improved its overall quality, thus removing the need for the government to do so.

Chastity began her political career nearly twenty years ago, before Roger had passed away. When he did, the compassion of her constituents put her in office, time and time and again. No matter what happened, Chastity had seemed to do well despite all. She'd also done a lot to merit the lavish life. It hadn't been easy for quite some time, and she worked a lot for the people she loved.

As it was, Chastity had called her chef and asked him to prepare breakfast for her guests and once they left to watch the home, as he typically did when she was away. Eliza had asked if she'd like to take a trip with her and Adelay to Massachusetts. Chastity agreed to do so that day, summoned a private jet plane. Planned flights were easy for her to coordinate, so she had everything squared away before all three had gathered around the breakfast table.

"How was your stay?"

"Absolutely amazing!" responded Eliza, with a smile and an unspoken glow about her.

"As always, you spoil me when I'm here." Adelay followed Eliza's response. "Thank you."

"I'm always happy to spend time with wonderful people, and to accommodate them," Chastity replied. She was one of a kind, genuine, yet a brilliant socialite.

Several hours passed, and they had arrived in Boston, hailed a taxi, and were dropped off at the public entryway to the Melrose Campus. Chastity had never seen this location before, so given the environment with seemingly sentient animals watching them with apparent smiles on their faces and waving to Eliza, she was quite intrigued.

"Did those coyote pups just wave at us with their paws? I could have sworn that's what they did. I must be seeing things." Chastity was beginning to question her sanity, since something like this could only occur in a fairy tale, or something of that sort, and she didn't believe in unicorns, angels, fairies, or anything along those lines. Nevertheless, there they were, the song dogs, waving and seemingly smiling, and there was Eliza, waving back to them with a glow and a smile. After a little thought, she continued, "This will be interesting."

When she saw the array of ornately designed buildings, superstructures that rose high and into the heavens, yet provided just the right cover and lighting that oddly enough allowed for daytime viewing of the nighttime sky and the areas around the buildings themselves, she was astounded. "I thought I was impressing you with my rinky-dink mansion but look at what you have here! Where has this been all of my life?" Chastity was in good spirits, she wasn't chiding anyone, rather instead she genuinely was smitten with joy and disbelief at how amazing everything was that she saw. "It's hard to believe this hasn't been in the news."

"Oh, I've temporarily lifted the camouflage. I'll explain more to you when we go inside. At any moment if you want to return home, you are welcomed to, but I'm about to show you so much more and all of it will shock your mind. There is a beautiful world here that has just been waiting for the ingenuity of the human mind. As you have noticed, humans didn't do all of this alone. We are friends with all of the animals here, too." Eliza waved at a rabbit who had stopped briefly to wave at her but was playing tag with the two song dog pups. They were both very polite to the rabbit, and all three, the rabbit and the two coyotes, seemed to be the best of friends.

Upon entering the apparent main building, again Chastity was breath-taken and overwhelmed with giddy delight. The glow of the interior, the spacious windows, people everywhere speaking in all manner of languages, and even a few large donut looking thingies that were glowing white with various buttons and interfaces in the colors of blues, purples, pinks, and blacks. She was indeed taking it all in with unabashed excitement.

An hour later, Chastity had completed her training and went through the Virtual Universe. Like Adelay had done, she chose to maintain her age and appearance with subtle changes, for the purposes of political identity. With James Cooper, she had decided to use her influence to help the UP be on the ballot of Florida, for all elections.

The City of Dreams

After visiting Chastity and getting her squared away as a delegate for the Universal Party, Eliza decided to travel with Adelay to visit someone she'd met once, named Brooklyn Saban.

Brooklyn just so happened to live in New York City, and her parents felt attached in an intriguing way. Born and raised there, with her domicile in the Radio City Apartments near Times Square, although expensive, her parents had worked almost every waking hour to pay the rent and help their family have the basics.

Whether she was rich in spirit or meager in economics, Brooklyn didn't mind, since every New Year's Eve she celebrated at the Dick Clark's New Year's Rockin' Eve with Ryan Seacrest hosting from 2006 on. To her, this was a day to live for. Moreover, due to the social and artistic atmosphere surrounding this occasion, this was her favorite time of year. Before Ryan hosted, Dick Clark had started this style of celebration, and Peter Jennings as well as Regis Philbin had cohosted from time-to-time. After a while, Ryan picked up the role as primary host, with Dick Clark cohosting this last year. No matter who hosted this occasion, each had an enigmatic, sharp, classy, and yet somewhat edgy but professional personality, at least that is how she felt. This is what dazzled Brooklyn.

For Brooklyn and her family, even though rent was above their debt-income ratio for living, they still got by. To the Saban's, living in that location took priority over almost anything else.

Oh, they had plenty of food to eat, but as soon as Brooklyn was able to acquire employment, she secured a job at the Olive Garden restaurant on the corner of West 47th Street and 7th Avenue. Cleaning dishes in her teens, she helped her parents pay the bills.

Once she graduated from high school, Brooklyn realized she couldn't afford to attend college, unless she could save up for a while. Knowing this, she continued to secure employment in various local gigs, doing thankless tasks, from washing dishes to cleaning the restaurants at the end of the night. No matter where she secured employment, she would do so only a few blocks away, or within walking distance, and each job with compensation that paid just enough to handle her family's bills. Each of her jobs, unfortunately, had no pathway for promotion.

Through it all, she wanted to start a business. Brooklyn had investigated it several times, but taxes were too high, penalties were too steep to do the right thing by her employees while expecting to get by herself, so she let her dreams go. *"The fees and other expenses are above my ability to sustain that pursuit economically, at least if I were to try to take up the endeavor,"* she thought.

Brooklyn often had great hopes for the future, but in quiet moments alone, sometimes in the shower, she would allow her emotions to let go, and she would cry as the water hit her scalp and flowed warming her skin, while feelings of internal loneliness without a friend seeped in. She had no one to reign her in or anyone to talk to. Her parents were about their own business and had little time for her, other than weightless hellos. After her solemn moments she would gather herself together and troop on.

By the time she met Eliza, she was thirty-eight years old, and was grateful that she had delayed having a family, since it made getting by a little easier. She was still working at the same diner, but somehow, something special about Brooklyn had captured Eliza's mind, and likewise, Eliza left an indelible impression on her mind. Eliza set out to meet this young lady, roughly the same age, befriend her, and help her to reach her dreams. Another person who had become a member of Pathway, had met her before, so it was something about Brooklyn's demeanor that had caught Eliza's attention.

Eliza knew she worked at the local Olive Garden, once she'd arrived there with Adelay to order diner and see if she could steal Brooklyn away for a little while. Luckily, Eliza was on pointe, because Brooklyn took both her and Adelay's orders. Eliza asked for her typical vegan dish and Adelay followed suit.

After Brooklyn brought out the lemon water and then returned to the back of the facility to retrieve their dinner orders from the chef, she noticed Eliza talking with her boss. "Hello, Mr. Chadwick? How are you doing, Sir?" Eliza was very polite and quite bold, yet she approached him with ease, and seemingly without a care in the world.

After introducing herself, she asked if she could pay the restaurant to allow their server to take a break for a few hours, before returning to work. Brooklyn's boss seemed all-to-happy to oblige the likes of this intriguing young lady, and accepted Eliza's very odd offer.

Eliza then looked toward her server, and spoke, "Brooklyn, your boss has said that it would be okay if you took a break for a few hours. Would you feel comfortable accompanying Adelay and I on a little excursion? I assure you; you're going to be amazed."

Not sure how to respond and somewhat confused, she thought for a few moments, asked if she could finish with her current orders, and Eliza agreed to wait. Once she was done, she took up the chance to spend time with another human being, two human beings, that seemed interested in her. No one had ever shown her any interest in any way, other than toward the orders she would ensure were fulfilled with top quality.

"Come with us, Brooklyn. You get a three-hour break, and that means you can go anywhere you'd like. I promise I'll get you back in one piece and smiling from ear to ear. I have something important to share with you."

Brooklyn walked with Eliza for a couple of minutes and realized that she was at the building where her apartment was. "Follow me," Eliza said, as they entered the building. They were in the atrium of the very nice apartment complex, that was more like a lavish hotel, and then followed Eliza to the elevator. She watched as Eliza went to select a floor, and then, all of a sudden, a new button appeared, one that had never been there before. Eliza pushed it, and down they went. They must have gone down what seemed ten floors, before the elevator stopped. When the doors opened, she saw a small room with a big white donut-looking object toward the back of it that looked like something out of a science fiction movie. It glowed, had black panels with purple, blue, and pink buttons. Eliza pointed in that direction and took the lead, and as she walked through this portal, she disappeared.

Not sure where she had gone, she decided to follow this captivating young woman and her older friend. She looked up at the top of the large object, sighed, and then stepped in through the ten-foot-diameter opening. To her surprise, she was a fascinating atrium of a place she never knew existed. The windows were tall, the walls glowed in white, and she could see animals of every sort outside the window seemingly talking and playing with each other. She shifted her gaze and saw numerous people wearing spectacular uniforms that seemed to hug their bodies in a way that was breathtaking and attractive. They each seemed to know various languages, as they talked with what seemed entire families from places all over the world. She then saw Eliza and Adelay again, both of whom looked toward her and beckoned her to follow.

An hour later, Brooklyn had been through the training, and had been fully read-in to Pathway, and had become a delegate, ready to reach the stars. During her twenty-year journey, in the space of five minutes, with Eliza and Adelay, she was amazed to see their creativity in self-expression. Eliza was truly angelic and Adelay was as if she were twenty-two again. She had been intrigued by the angel looking over the pond, teeming with coy fish and frogs, singing what must have been some of Eliza's favorite music. It was beautiful!

Upon seeing them, Brooklyn was taken in by the magnificence of the Twelve Database Moons as well as the tech cities on Selene, or Earth's Moon.

Eliza chatted with her in the Virtual Universe for a while. Brooklyn then talked about how everything had weighed down upon her for so many years. She had been constantly told things that someone should never hear, the kinds of things that would dampen the spirits of anyone. After doing so, Eliza responded, *"Love those who love you, and feel sorry for those who don't. We need to be kind, no matter how far we must stretch ourselves. There will always be those who look for the worst in us, no matter how hard we try to be our best. We need to be 'us' or ourselves, and those who truly love us will admire that."* Eliza's words of comfort soothed her soul.

After journeying throughout the Solar System and exploring nearly every nook and cranny of every advancement created by Eliza and her friends, she was given the opportunity within the Virtual Universe to pursue the education she had always dreamed of having.

Given the difficulties of sustaining a living beyond waiting for each new year to occur, she had often dreamt of becoming a legislator for New York City, in an effort to simplify some of the rules affording adults the ability to make adult decisions, without governance dominating life or standing in the way of joy and happiness. She had expressed to Eliza that she felt strongly that the US had been founded on the ideals of life, liberty, and the pursuit of happiness and that laws should be made to protect that.

Brooklyn explained to Eliza that all her life, she had also wished to go to the various shows on Broadway and how the glamor and splendor of it all had always piqued her interest, but she could never afford to go. So, within the Virtual Universe, Eliza saw fit to go with Adelay and Brooklyn to the Entertainment Matrix, wherein, every single play that had ever been performed in the history of plays, was available as soon as it was wished. With full experiential reference, she was able to be completely enveloped by the splendor of each show, with music permeating the air around her, and even walk around each stage, as if she were in the plays herself.

The ability to link mind-to-mind with anyone who had been read-in to Pathway was something else that was new to Brooklyn in so many ways, because now, not only had she won new friends in Eliza and Adelay, but she could connect with millions at any moment. She could ask questions, listen, smile, and share dreams with others.

When she returned to work no more than three hours after she started her break, she assessed her employment situation, thanked her boss for his kindness over the years, and told him that she had dreams that she wished to pursue. "I have dedicated most of my life, barely getting by, while giving you and this establishment my best. It is time for me to move on. If you ever have questions, please feel free to ask, at least if I come in to have an actual meal rather than serve it. I know the food is good, so thank you. Don't worry, I'll visit from time-to-time." Then she left her workplace, with joy in her heart.

Several months after becoming a delegate for the UP, she began working in her newly-founded law office. During that time, each night she would see a show outside of the Virtual Universe, put on by the wonderous and amazing casts gracing the various stages of Broadway.

Brooklyn had always enjoyed the arts and felt that everyone should be able to afford to take time away from their lives and have the wherewithal to see these splendorous plays, to brush up on their culture and pursue a seemingly unattainable sense of happiness within. Having passed through the Virtual Universe, now she made countless trips between her law office and her new domicile on Triton, with a view of Neptune, and a trusty geyser not too far away from the city. Here, she developed in ways she never thought she would, contributed to further advancements, and trained in legislation, law, and governance for the city and state of New York, traveling via her very own jump gates hidden in each location, to include her domicile at the Radio City Apartments. Life was becoming a new and lovely thing!

As time went by, Brooklyn again took herself out each evening to watch the spectacular shows of Broadway.

During the month of November 2009, there was a city official who ended up being sent to prison for fraud, so naturally, Brooklyn saw the vacant spot for someone to run for office, ran, and won. Like that, she became a New York City representative at the state level of legislation, and she began to push a new agenda. She could be heard on the radio waves, the televisions, and on an increasing quantity of cell phones saying, "If someone were to hurt another individual, damage their well-being, or violate their personal consent, then, within a common-sensical scope, that is where the law should be enforced. Our laws should not tie our hands behind our backs, they need to protect the life and liberty of the citizens as well as their pursuit of happiness!"

Brooklyn had gained a new sense of clarity on what she could do to help the people of NY and NYC, and her new friends, Eliza and Adelay, were only a neural link away. She spoke eloquently to the masses during the 2010 New Year's celebration and inspired many.

Once she was ready, she moved out of her apartment and purchased a condo near the same location she was raised in. Within six months of meeting Eliza, following the new year of 2010, and not too long after Valentine's Day, she linked with Eliza. As she did, she let her know that with her newly-gifted mind and newly-achieved status as a politician, she was able to draft policies that would pave the way for the Universal Party to be formed in New York City.

Chapter 10: Working Together

Database Moon Archive, Celestial-Sol Entry Date: 2010 August, 20. Yesha Alevtina trains Vesha Celeste. In this crucial part of her training, she learns about Eliza's penchant for working together nationwide. This training is conducted within the Virtual Universe, interfaced within the Pathway Melrose Campus. Input by Eliza Williams, President of Pathway Industries, 2008-2015.

Eliza continued to travel throughout the western hemisphere, with many stops in the US. Sometimes she would pause and provide the finishing touches to her lengthy tome-like book, and at other times she would meet people on a whim. It was in January of 2010 that James connected with her to tell her she should bring Tyson back, because he was indeed a necessary part of her team, and thus she did. Now, as she traveled from the northern points to the southern points of North and South America and the people in Hawaii to those visiting the Park Reserve on Baccalieu Island, she traveled with Tyson by her side. There were many who she met who knew of someone else who needed her help, and as soon as was possible she would lend a hand, while empowering each new delegate with the ability to do the same. Shortly after bringing Tyson back, she published her book.

Succeeding all of this, shortly after their meeting with Agent Epstein, in May of 2010, Eliza and each state's voted delegates conducted investigations of due diligence and had found legal precedent to verify the UP as the official party name in all domains, public and private.

Federal Liaison Building

"Yesha, how is everything coming along out there? How is everything going over there on the other side of the world? James, how are you doing on Ceres? Would you like to meet me at Gaia's Library on the top floor of tower four, in Federal Liaison Building, DC?"

The tower Eliza was located at happened to have several eateries, bars, and coffee boutiques on the top level, and as such, it was ideal for meeting diplomats worldwide. There was a consular level for each of about a quarter of the world's nations and their teams in each of four towers. Each tower consumed about a two-by-two block area, and as such there were four. These four towers were dedicated in total, in very much the same manner, so that every country was represented.

Eliza had delegates that combed the globe, equating to about eighty-thousand delegates per state in the US and in each country worldwide.

From January of 2009 to May of 2010 Pathway's population had doubled and all twenty-million citizens were delegates. The populations of each of the tech cities grew every day, with delegates taking care of their personal and business affairs equitably throughout the world and throughout the solar system. A lot was accomplished, and spirits were high.

On this occasion, Eliza, the President of what was currently known as Pathway LLC, desired to meet with her second and third members of Pathway's hierarchy to further discuss the progress of their new political party in the US and throughout the world.

In 2009, she had been interested in mirroring or duplicating many of the principles that had been setup in their governance structure in the tech cities and had applied throughout the solar system, to the governance systems on Earth. For the last year, they strived to reach out to people in the public sector throughout the world.

As Eliza looked out at the city from the garden on the top floor of the Federal Liaison Campus, Tower Four, she pondered upon her pursuits throughout the last year. She also thought about the recent sanctioning of Pathway's activities by the US Government, via Agent Epstein, to funnel advancements at will through the government and to the public arena. The government had essentially told her that they trusted her explicitly in every way, and that they looked forward to each advancement she would roll out through her new organization. As she pondered, she sensed Yesha returning a response through her link.

"Sure, Eliza," responded Yesha, "*I was finishing up some Virtual Universe research for my mission later today. I just wrapped up a case in Sri Lanka and was helping an older couple with their ancestral herd, one was sick and passing a pandemic to the others. They're all better now.*" Yesha was breathing hard, and Eliza could hear the cattle in the background mooing and knew that soon they would be able to speak their minds to the people who cared for them so well. Yesha continued, "*James was reading-in the older, and now younger couple, since they elected to be optimized, for a transfer to any domicile of their choosing, and in this case, in the maple groves near Cheshar on Ceres. Their ancestral herd is safe there now as well. Wow, they have had quite the journey!*

"*I'm planning a jump to Perth, Australia, well, now, to head over to check on James' old resort in Albany.*" Yesha paused for a second. "*A fire came through after a drought had dried James' weeds. I know, I didn't think that would be possible, but even hardy plants can die with little to no moisture at all for a year, and it unfortunately left his old project a little charred. It's still intact, mind you, but a little rustic for the wear.*

"*Hey, at least it's still standing! So, my team and I will clean it up and maybe give it some upgrades, look at the town, and maybe give it some love with a few macro clouds of micro-nanos. Perth is a beautiful city!*

"*There's a lot to do, but I am impressed with how quickly it can all be done, with the ability to automate each precise step in the Virtual Universe, in fractions of a second considering everything that will be potentially impacted! Oh, a lot of amazing recruits have already come from Perth and Albany, you know that!*"

Eliza continued to hear Yesha doing some work in the background, and even breathing heavy, despite her optimizations, as she continued to talk, "*I'm so glad we discovered time dilation! It gives us endless time to develop and execute our plans and processes!*

"*Wait, what time is it over there?*" Yesha always multitasked, getting things done as precisely and perfect as it seemed was possible, while preventing alpha or gamma decay or anything else of that sort, and many times while inside the Virtual Universe. Sometimes she'd forget what time of day it was and would be like a lost lamb if she didn't ask, despite her informational display.

"*You need a good book and a coffee, girl!*" replied Eliza. "*It's ten in the evening here. Take a break, jump gate over, and meet me as soon as you can find a good point to take a little time out of your busy schedule, please.*" Eliza was standing on the outside balcony of the library on the fiftieth floor and paused as she saw James walking in her direction. Her heart almost skipped a beat and she could see her hands glowing, he was wearing a wide grin of pride on his chiseled and handsome face.

James had never been overtly flirtatious before, but after the okay from the ANSSI agent, and the building of their campuses throughout the world, James seemed to have taken on a whole new mindset around Eliza, and he was obviously happy to see her.

They'd tossed around some pretty big and romantic words the last time they'd linked but decided to pretend they were talking about other friends, to stay focused on the bigger picture. *"Yesha, it looks like James beat you here."* Eliza tried with all the power she could muster to shake the feelings she had for him clear from her mind.

"On my way!" Yesha had jump-gated during their small conversation from Sri Lanka to Australia, and surveyed the mess near Perth, deeply ensconced within the Virtual Universe and preprogramming all of the marvelous touch-ups she was going to provide for the people and their various assortments of infrastructure in the coastal town of Albany, out of respect to their dear friend, James. Seeing the ideal timing which would allow her automated systems to take their course, she put a pause on the rest for now, sensing with her special link that Eliza's internal will was about to implode, while making her twenty-second walk to her jump gate.

"Hey, Eliza," said James. "How is everything coming along in the Western Hemisphere of Earth?"

A lot had gone on in the first twenty-four hours since they unveiled the Federal Liaison Campus, in DC, and she appreciated everything he had done over the last couple of years. Eliza noticed that something about his optimizations had converted him from a silent romantic and wallflower to a passionate and assertive heartthrob.

James was dashing, chiseled in all the right ways, intelligent, and everything she could have imagined she would want in a man. Eliza just didn't want the hassle of the glow, the butterflies, or the inability to carry on a decent conversation whenever it seemed that someone, and in her case, James, who was deemed hugely attractive, came into the room or happened to be nearby.

Yes, for all intents and purposes, she was twitter-pated, and she knew it, but Eliza saw this all as puppy love and not the real thing. With all their successes, it seemed it was easy to fall in love, but what if they were to experience struggles or challenges beyond their scope of handling, how would they fair through theoretically horrible weather?

After her conversation with James yesterday, it was clear that she had to clear or compartmentalize certain regions of her mind again, at least where her feelings for him were concerned, gain focus, and get down to brass tax. So, she decided to sort out and assign each of those emotions into her private memory bank, out of her primary lobes, and move on for now.

Eliza wanted to talk to Yesha and James in this glorious new megacomplex in DC about the progress of the Universal Party, and its continued influence both overtly and publicly. She wanted to move beyond her vision of how it was going to continue to play out, and the shared desire to do so by each citizen of Pathway, not just for governance in the tech cities, but to democratically grow the party through proper elections, with governance established lawfully within the real world, the public realm, and in particular the US of A, while going global.

This was obviously the place setup and designed to set the bar for freedom, life, liberty, and the pursuit of happiness, so, in her mind this was where it would begin. Hence, she had Pathway's three original members and leaders meet in Washington, DC, of all places, to discuss what they would do to continue their influence in positive ways on those affected on Earth and into the future.

Eliza let her mental whispers of romance go, and talked to James out loud, or at least as soon as he was within range to hear with his physical ears, *"His cute ears,"* she thought, *"Stop it, Eliza!"* she coached herself. "How is everything going for the citizens and delegates of Cheshar City on Ceres? I truly appreciate the fact that you have gone all over the solar system making updates, helping people become integrated into their new living quarters, and all of this while helping them to become prepared to return to Earth for more rescues and recruits. I am impressed with your multi-tasking skills, James."

"I appreciate that," James was the gentle and kind man he always was, but he could tell that something was eating at Eliza, despite her optimizations. He scanned her mind and noticed that she had put her feelings for him on complete lock-down. Rather than feel dispirited about this, and sensing there were items of greater urgency, he decided to do likewise.

In both of their cases, Eliza and James had done what they typically did over the last few months and filed their emotions for each other into a compartment of their minds that they could put on a notional timer. When they did this, not even they could access certain memories for the time being, however long that would be. The code to break these thoughts open was accessible only through graceful resolutions of problems up to and including the preservation of the life-giving capacity of the Universe, or pretty much for a very long time. They both sensed that these were fleeting moments of feelings and that they would overcome those aspects of neurological looping to propagate the species soon, at least they shared that view.

Both of their minds were strong, and their feelings were intense, so it wouldn't take long after some amazing accomplishments for those ideas to surface, yet again.

Nevertheless, it would take a while to bust through Eliza's and James' encryptions, at least for now, and in doing so, they would allow themselves to focus on the matters at hand as a productive team of heroes. As they were focused on dealing with the intensity of their emotions, they hadn't noticed another presence appear.

"Hey, you two. Why haven't you gotten a room already?" Yesha said, kidding around, as she walked onto the rooftop balcony where Eliza and James stood looking out toward the southwest at the DC skyscape, trying to appear as if they hadn't been just ogling each other for however long they'd been standing there, in an awkward silence, before Yesha interrupted them. In their defense, the White House was in view, and it was intriguing looking at it from their vantage point. They both knew that there was no sin on having a crush on someone, and then fighting the feelings away.

Nonetheless, caught by surprise, both Eliza and James turned around and brushed off her chiding, chuckled at her humor, and moved on to the matters of business at hand, after sharing a couple briefer glances out at the landscape.

Through Eliza's technology, Pathway had secretly modified even the White House and the Memorial Mall to protect anyone residing within it or nearby. Now, no matter what problems would continue their course, until Pathway was successful enough spreading their ideals beyond the twenty-million people that comprised the current population of Pathway or the Solar System, the inhabitants of that historical edifices were protected and safe from anything trying to bring harm their way.

Yesha could tell Eliza and James had reached an understanding on the excruciating choices they felt they had to make regarding their love lives. Yesha was no stranger to it all, after all, she was a neuroscience and psychology expert, not-to-mention skilled and wise.

Being a neuroscience and psychology major, and a phenomenon in those venues, post-doc, coupled with an optimized mind and millions of years of wisdom at her beck and call, she knew that in order for them to focus as they desired to on the problems plaguing the world, they needed to do what she had sensed that they had just done. Yesha was quite impressed with their choices but knew that this would in all other senses start their budding romance from scratch.

Each time Eliza and James did this, their mutual connections and physiological needs would intensify all-the-more profoundly, despite their intentions.

As it was, she currently knew more than they did about how they felt toward each other, so, out of respect Yesha kept her profound knowledge locked away and only accessible to herself, at least for now. Sooner or later, they would need to take a walk on the wild side and let inhibitions go, or get married, or anything along those lines, since doing what they were doing now would only compound their romantic vibes exponentially, and only heaven knew how that would turn out.

Eliza and James would eventually need to face their romantic truth, so they could focus even more deeply. For the most part, though, when he was on his business throughout the solar system and she was combing the western hemisphere, their focus was supreme.

Still, Yesha let Eliza and James do as they felt was necessary, and she supported their decisions no matter how she might feel otherwise. Yesha knew she had no desire to date anyone herself and couldn't see that being a reality any time soon. *"So, who am I to judge?"* she would often think; *"Whatever keeps them happy."*

"It's great seeing you two. Thank you for helping with the couple from Sri Lanka, James. I checked on them both a few moments ago and they were completely pleased with your help and their new digs on Ceres."

"Thank you, Yesha, I couldn't thank you more. If it hadn't been for you, given their beliefs and your obvious respect for them, despite being different from your own, I don't know if their healing would have taken place as quickly as it did, or stay with them."

"Oh, thank you. You have a point, when we struggle in our drive to be benevolent or when we kick away those moments in life that will help us to become wiser, we don't know how much we're losing out on, and in fact we begin to lose our optimizations and need to pass through the Virtual Universe for some self-maintenance, or risk losing it all." Yesha knew that what she had said was also intended for Eliza and James to hear, soak in, and consider, at least when it came to their romance, though she pretended it was only for the couple from Sri Lanka.

"How is everything on this side of the world, Eliza?" Yesha knew that Eliza had been on the talk show, Elena, recently, and was rescuing and recruiting new Pathway citizens in droves throughout the US, and in Guatemala, Honduras, Venezuela, Mexico, Nicaragua, Costa Rica, Argentina, Brazil, Chile, Paraguay, Uruguay, Bolivia, Peru, Ecuador, Colombia, Canada, the Caribbean Islands, and more, all of whom had now become UP delegates.

In several of these naturally resource-rich countries their governing bodies were helmed by people trying to merely protect their families, but they were governed without thought for their well-being anyway, and with devastating results. Many of the people that Eliza had visited, felt they had little choice otherwise but to realize the biddings of a malicious and powerful entity that was driving a lot of their population to leave their countries and head for the US, causing a disbalance of population, resources, and opportunities for innovation that could ease the burdens of everyday life within their homeland.

Eliza felt it was important to take care of these people, everyone, or anyone stuck in those situations, while affording them an opportunity to connect mind-to-mind, and be healed, so that they could integrate with the many people who had already settled in to the many tech cities throughout the solar system, and return to the lands they called home, to raise the quality of life and rescue more individuals much like themselves, to bring them joy.

Where remorse for life seemed at an all-time low, it was important to prevent the untimely demise of so many wonderful people, first and foremost, to prevent them from being forgotten and unknown throughout the history of the Universe. Each person was special to Eliza.

Each of these individuals had deserved more than paupers' graves, were unique and had untold potential. Something phenomenal was burning within them, and Eliza did not want to lose their spirits to inconsequential foolishness or worse, brutality and death. As such, she sent many wonderful people and their families to James, who had been working in the tech city, named Cheshar. This beautiful tech city was on the once asteroid, now life-giving and hugely capable spheroid, Ceres, and the people throughout the world, currently being rescued were sent there, after they were fully read-in. Upon arrival, they had an opportunity of living in both the new domiciles in the tech cities throughout the rest of the solar system, as well as in protected domiciles within the lands of their birth and of their many loved ones, all while safeguarded from hatred and any other sources of malevolence.

On one occasion, as with the day prior, Eliza had gone to Uruguay to take a breather, to visit and relax, but while there, she found a few families who were impacted by storms that had travelled south from Brazil, with the storm having come from the Sahara. After rescuing them, she escorted them, likewise, to Cheshar on Ceres, where James had been located before their meeting at the Federal Liaison Campus, in Washington DC.

James had had his work cut out for him, and as such, had been all over the solar system. He'd spent the last couple of weeks on Ceres, having gone there before. Now that the liaison offices were built, with their protective shielding, constant fears of asteroid impacts were quelled.

Working with the growing populace on Ceres and other planetoids throughout the Solar System, James had to install and activate Eliza's extraordinary automated-particle and navigation-redirection technology shielding systems which completely encompassed each planetoid, with corridors provided for physical space travel and other life-preservation ingredients, back and forth.

Following the efforts of James and his ever-growing teams of new and brilliant scientists, engineers, data wizzes, and more, this new tech could drive asteroids, or any material for that matter, in a controlled tangent to any location that needed the resources. These materials would then be received by any of the historical scanning, life preserving, and particle repurposing facilities nearby any given area. Outer space was becoming clean, for once, at least within the Solar System, known by Pathway as Sol.

These facilities were located near each of the now inhabited spheroids throughout the solar system. They not only provided protection but allowed for further developments as well as orbital balance to the delicate aspects of the solar system, while providing material for new and sophisticated planets, in-between the other planets, with their own orbits, and all Earthling-made.

Much of this was due to something she called renavigation tech, which was something Eliza planned on having installed on and implemented within the giant intergalactic spacecraft that were yet to be built.

Eliza had made it clear that when the time was right, they would be built in an area above Pluto's North Pole, called Lowell Regio, which was the Latin word for Region. This location was named after astronomer, Percival Lowell, from Flagstaff, Arizona, who initiated research after founding the Lowell Observatory in 1894, which became instrumental in Clyde Tombaugh's discovery of Pluto, thirty-six years later.

"For some time, Pluto was rightfully considered a planet. We will ensure that it is once again understood and seen that way," Eliza would often share via her link.

James had also visited each of the spheroids in the solar system, to include Ceres and Vesta in the asteroid belt between Mars and Jupiter. He'd been to all of Jupiter's Galilean moons, and the spheroids Europa, Ganymede, Io, Callisto, Lysithea, Autonoe, and Elara. He had visited Saturn's spheroidal moons, Titan, Enceladus, Mimas, Dione, Rhea, Tethys, and Pallene, as well as Uranus' spherical moons, Umbriel, Titania, Miranda, Oberon, Ariel, Trinculo, and Ophelia. Likewise, he'd visited Neptune's similar-shaped moons, but of exotically different character, Proteus, Sao, and Triton. He had also visited Pluto and its moon, Charon, while creating historical centers for Styx, Nix, Kerberos, and Hydra, using the resources they provided to assist with shielding and protection of Pluto and Charon.

Finally, James had perfected Eliza's shielding that enveloped the entire breadth and sphere of the vast two-light-year-diameter and beautiful solar system. To do this, he ensured that other spheroids were populated and visited, all the way out to the solar system's protective barrier, where the Oort Clouds once existed. Using highly advanced teams of brilliant minds, he replaced the many once dangerous and randomly terrifying comets with something resembling a Dyson Sphere.

This in-turn protected Sol from the scorching galactic and universal winds of exotic particles and radiation of every sort, with something even more powerful, aesthetic, longer-lasting, protective, and controllable. All of these objects had an amazing story of their own, with vast libraries of astrobiological and astrophysical databases available in physical form in the nearest tech cities and in the Virtual Universe matrix to pique whichever mind was interested and identified as the Astro-Physical Historical Matrix.

Together with James, everyone who met him and traversed the solar system, discovered its exquisiteness and reacquainted themselves with the organic and true loveliness of Earth. Notwithstanding, they realized that in order for humanity to move forward and out from Sol, we first had to bring the ability to preserve life with us, all while mentally matured and ready to embrace the beauty of engaging in healthy pursuits of tech advancement and more, in order to augment the razzle and dazzle of each of these moons and spheroids while bringing life sustaining environments to them, universe-wide.

Much had been done already, and for all intents and purposes, Sol was ready, physically to span the cosmos. However, a lot more needed to be done beyond aesthetic and systems to prepare humanity to be ready. Hearts and minds needed to be overwhelmingly kind and innovative, on Earth. Without these virtues, chaos would rule and destroy humanity before we reached the limits of our own galactic disc.

In order to make it so the rest of humanity was on board and thus prepared and invested in the future, they had to develop a political party whose goals revolved around well-being, innovation, and the future of history, sentience, and all existing life. Thus, they did, but it had to grow and span the Earthly globe, reaching each mind.

Each Pathway delegate believed in protecting these spheres while humanity on Earth grew and matured into macro thinking, and humankind needed a little nudge in the right direction. Politics and political parties needed to dance on the stage toward the future, and for Eliza, Yesha, and James, that future was about to begin now.

"Yesha and James, we have expanded the reach of our new political party to meet the qualifications of each of the states in the US, and in each country that allows for political parties to be formed by its citizens, due to their inherent need to allow their people to be represented. However, what remains is soul-to-soul understanding and connection, regarding the virtues and pursuits that will render humanity successful when spanning the Universe. We can bring positive influence on every nation throughout the globe, but our work has merely just begun.

"We know it will take time to grow our party, since the public sector does not progress as fast as we have, courtesy of our Virtual Universe, jumping, and nanos.

"That said, James, we have set up a system of governance throughout the tech cities of each planet that obviously works well. Given the history of Earth-borne civilization, we have been edified effectively on how to do it right, so that's what we have done. We used common sense ideas to make principles to guide the inhabitants and to allow them to govern themselves. As such, we already have all the necessary mechanisms in place for governance that will breed unity amongst the masses. Crucial systems are also in place and on-the-ready, should anyone need correction, via the Correction Matrix.

"Since we live by principles and the laws are built on common sense, for example, don't murder, rape, or pillage, or any of the typical things that are done by mindless thugs bereft of true purpose beyond making a spectacle of themselves through their power and greed, for the duration of their short, merciless, and pointless existence of the joke they make out of their lives, most people of a healthy mind don't do those things, and are living lives of more meaning. Still, even the thugs need love and a chance to see their full and true potential.

"Hence, because of our political systems in the tech cities, we haven't had a need for micro-managing laws or even law enforcement throughout the solar system, yet. Everyone in the tech cities is a delegate and cares about the well-being of everyone else. They care so much, they are moved to make life full of potential and enjoyable for everyone and quite possibly every living being throughout the Universe, including themselves.

"The people of Pathway study hard, work hard, play hard and as a result, they are happy, filled with joy and with the thrill of purpose oozing through their veins. They each rescue and recruit others while allowing appropriate time for hearts to see their clarity of purpose burn within.

"We're ready to move even further with our goals for the Universal Party. What do you think, James?"

"I believe you make great points, Eliza." James was in full agreement with everything she said. "I do believe that as splendid as our campuses are that dot the globe, and since the Virtual Universe pretty much allows us to truly see what we're thinking collectively, we can come up with solutions to global governance with principles that can guide us all, with freedom in its wake."

James looked toward the biopod room, nearby, and continued, "If you would like to go to the Virtual Universe, I know there's a private biopod room nearby."

"Sure. That is a brilliant plan, James," agreed Yesha. "What do you think, Eliza?"

"Well, with time-dilation, you may be right, James. I had thought that if we were going to create a public political party, we ought to do it the same way as others have in years past. Although, I suppose I may still err, despite my optimizations, in that, we can work together to build the systems and details with the benefits of our already hewn efforts, within the Virtual Universe, with the advantages of time-dilation, and then we can share that with the public, publicly," Eliza chuckled. James and Yesha laughed too thinking of her shrewd choice of words.

Drawing from Experience

Eliza, Yesha, and James wasted no time climbing into their biopods and met up in the Political Matrix within the Virtual Universe. Quickly, they agreed on the name for their Earthly political group affiliation. They called this new organization they were forming, the Universal Party.

With Eliza's insistence, James started, *"We have already rescued, recruited, and assigned a massive contingency of delegates all over the globe. All of these delegates are individuals who have done so much on Earth and throughout the solar system in the twenty-thousand tech cities, and they continue to search for and help many who are suffering worldwide.*

"Each of our delegates has become well-versed in law for every country in the world they have visited, and essentially became so upon their initial entry into the Virtual Universe and before entering any specific country. By way of many equivalent years of training, mind-to-mind capacities for understanding, effective experience-inducing, wisdom-germinating scenarios, to include opportunities for problem solving, as well as rote memorization, and so much more using the advantages of time-dilation, they assisted in operations and daily affairs, enabling them to run in a smooth manner, like no other throughout Earth.

"We and our ever-growing crews of delegates have set up countless jump gates and jump gate terminals in crucial areas, all hidden from the public eye, and many within their national and state offices, worldwide, among other places. Networks of transportation afford ease and speed of conveyance for goods, the ability to canvass and recruit even more scientists, and of course, capitalize upon the great landscape of fluidity of legal and security measures that exist worldwide. Meeting with Agent Epstein was our needed go-ahead in the US to do as we deemed necessary and saw fit to do.

"After we worked together to build and complete Pathway's major infrastructure, by the end of 2008, Yesha, you and many others from your crews began to travel to and from Northwest Europe to Southeast Asia, to the islands of the neighboring seas regularly, and everywhere in-between. Numerous journeys were made to recruit scientists, rescue refugees, and people lost in toxic or hostile environments, before returning home and regrouping each night, via jump gates.

"Eliza, you and your teams of delegates headed out and returned home in much the same way within the many regions of the Western Hemisphere, making frequent trips throughout North, Central, and South America, as well as the Caribbean, and most especially the volatile locations, to continue to rescue and recruit.

"I and my crews played nomad between the Sun and out to the furthest reaches of the Solar System to ensure all of our infrastructure was running as it should, top-notch, while also developing solutions to unforeseen circumstances, in the efforts toward longevity, health, and happiness therein.

"We did all of this, checking and double-checking every aspect of infrastructure while receiving the new personnel, settling them into their domiciles throughout the Solar System with breath-taking views of the planets and nightscape, all while involving them in the many processes and guiding the growing populations on the different moons and spheroids out to the protective barrier, where the Oort Clouds once existed.

"As we did, many of the people that you, Yesha, and you, Eliza, helped became great pioneers toward even more great solutions that would have otherwise been omitted, forgotten, and they improved upon some of the greatest advances that only you two were able to fathom.

"Both of you know that the same, and yet even more phenomenal fortifications are now in place with more capabilities, and now our solar system is protected by any perceivable and sometimes unperceivable outside threat. We've done so now, to where, using many exotic particles, we have created the ability to send away dangerous debris, black holes, or anything else of the sort away, while protecting these as well as our Sun's abilities to navigate around our galaxy with orbital integrity. All of these advancements are being kept intact through the various responsibilities of our nanos, while they in-

turn encode the molecules, atoms, and our own cells to carry out these processes themselves.

"Our work has been a collaboration of vast and robust efforts and combined with the neural links to each of our minds, so much more has been done. Pockets of heroism and daring-do are scattered across the globe and the solar system, and so much has been possible, because of both of you and those who we have saved."

James let his shared thoughts, his gratitude, and his newly growing fondness for this angel that stood before him in all of her glowing glory, hang out there and open for that angel to see. This angel, well James' angel, was Eliza, and it was hard for him not to be open, honest, and in complete adoration for her. Even while talking to her those mechanisms put in place that could last centuries took only a few moments for his heart to burst through.

All throughout James' life he had hoped to meet a woman who was as beautiful in every way, both inside and out, as she was. And there she was, standing before him.

He then remembered his previous commitment to her, of subduing his thoughts of love and devotion until they had resolved the problems of the Universe, as beautiful as it was in its vastness and splendor, and shortly following he began to wonder if he was even worthy of that sort of devotion at all.

Right quick, his mind healed, because he did not wish ill will on anyone or sorrow upon himself. Instead, he began to focus on their challenges and goals, the ones they needed to face at this time. He thought of setting up the roots of governance, the kind that needed to prevail, if humanity wanted to save its legacy of history, music, art of all kinds, romances, and inventions.

James knew they needed a political party on Earth that walked the walk, talked the talk, did not make laws simply to confine people and their liberties even more, but shined light on principles by abiding by them and exemplifying them through noble pursuits. Any laws currently in existence would be removed and common-sense laws would take their place. If people struggled, they would need a gentle or even firm hand to help them, and together, he, Eliza, and Yesha, as well as every delegate of Pathway, would let mercy guide the way.

"James, I felt something powerful heading in my direction. The source was coming from you, and just as I thought I would or that I could fall in love again, the feeling was replaced with clarity of mind toward what we all need to do, like a gust of wind blowing leaves and scattering them around to protect the roots of the many plants and trees throughout the cold of winter.

"It's okay, James, you can have those feelings, perhaps I'm errant, yet again, and maybe you're right to hold them back. Just, please note, you'll always be worthy, even if the right time for you or me isn't now.

"Through our efforts, Yesha and James, and our growing populace, we continue to grow in lovely amounts and quite exponentially. We started with three, and now there are twenty-million and growing.

"We had a necessity, after that first year, once we reached ten-million delegates, to set up governance within the tech cities and Pathway. The citizens were sufficiently apprised of and participated in the process throughout the setup and final touches of each detail.

"Our growing crews are all neurologically linked in a manner that affords operation-related decisions, allowing for desired results to always come through, and because of this strong and formidable connection, the governance of Pathway has been more democratic than the government of any nation in the world.

"We agreed early on that with the expectations of an ever-growing population in each of the tech cities and throughout our solar system, that people and other living beings of Pathway might benefit from proper and expedient recognition as citizens and delegates. We knew this intuitively, since each aspect of what they have done and will do will unfold before the eyes of the public ever so gently, now and into the future, until all is revealed.

"As such, a standardized set of principles which promoted consent, innovation, longevity, health, and quality of life were established.

"Because each delegate of Pathway was optimized physiologically and neurologically and therefore linked, the democratic process flowed very much in a manner that was unanimous, smooth, efficient, and purposeful.

"As we each agreed upon, and contingent with citizenship, many will come, just like these new recruits, who have been trained and shown their new living quarters in various locations throughout the Solar System. Everyone in Pathway is involved in moving forward with progress, rescuing those lost in a toxic world, and working to create a healthier society through all means ethically possible.

"After settling in, each beloved citizen worked with you, James, and the Solar System Operations centers, choosing from a vast array of jobs, training in the Virtual Universe, and immersing themselves in projects and missions.

"During off-shift time, many citizens worked on projects and missions of their own. Many others explored the Virtual Universe and developed matrices dedicated to education, science, art, entertainment, relaxation, and levity. Freedom and individuality have been and are highly respected. Once optimized with clarity of mind and the opportunity for collaborative efforts were on the rise, their efforts were hailed by each of us because, they had the beautiful effect of augmenting the overall mission of Pathway.

"Look at Enceladus, morale is high, and there is still no need for laws or law enforcement there, or in any of the growing tech cities. It doesn't mean that law enforcement didn't exist before, it's just that the citizens there simply worked in other capacities, or namely in the capacity of training and education for dealing with situations should they conceivably arise. They did and continue to do this to be ready for the worst, no matter what might come.

"Throughout the Solar System, I was able to predict and can now see that mentorship, training, kindness, high morale, resolution of internal doubts of purpose and constructive behavior are the keys to assuring that all of the resolutions to any problems conceived that might hamper the survivability of humanity in the days that lay ahead as we begin to span the Universe, are dealt with swiftly, with strength, and with assured promise.

"Pathway citizens have taken the time to develop exhaustive scenarios and have played them out in experiential form within the Virtual Universe. They have developed real-life scenarios with proposed law enforcement zones on every spheroid within the solar system. They've also made life enjoyable and free.

"Every new citizen has worked with Pathway hierarchy in their own way, on the development of the Correctional Matrix for anyone who might abdicate their rights to private thought, by way of heinous acts or if they are desirous to and thereby cause harm to another living individual and undue consequence negatively affects another individual's personal rights."

Yesha listened to both Eliza and James deliberate, both falling in and out of love again as the days, the months, and the years went by, in the scope of the five minutes of real-time they were in the Virtual Universe for forty years, and each time their attraction grew more intensely. Still their biggest focus was on their love for humanity and preserving as many lives as possible throughout the world, without forcing anyone's hand.

Finally, Yesha felt the need to speak up, *"You two are both amazing people, don't ever forget that. Eliza, if we are to go down the road of politics, I would suggest we begin with you. You're still a resident of our home state of Massachusetts. Maybe you're not ready now, because there's more recruiting you'd like to do, and perhaps in a couple of years you'll need to put some attention toward the public economic and industrial sectors that are at the core of much of this toxicity, but soon, perhaps in 2015, you'll need to throw your hat in the ring and run as a representative and work here in Washington, using this building for the purposes for which it was designed.*

"Don't worry, you'll always be able to return to your estate in Massachusetts, but we'll certainly need to consider electing delegates for each state and country where political parties can be formed and functional. We can do this, you, Eliza, you, James, and all of us!"

After deliberating for quite some time about the current affairs of tech city governance, they realized that there was indeed a significant amount of prosperity that lie within the results of people actively living the values and ethics defined in the Principles of Universal Ethics.

Moments of Prosperity

"True you are, Yesha." James and Eliza were both in agreement with the ideas she shared with them, as they played out in the skies above her. Forty years passed, and they returned to the real world, and deliberated a little more. After a little talking and conversing at the Federal Liaison Office, DC, they decided to return to the Virtual Universe for more studies, because although less than five minutes would pass in the real world, many more compounded years of wisdom and processes could be gained and set in motion in the realm Eliza had built with Yesha and had explored for the first time in late 2007.

The first thing that Eliza, Yesha, and James began to work on, during the next set of forty years in the Virtual Universe was which committees needed to be formed and how to parse them out among the many delegates. To begin with, the populace of Pathway in such a short period of time was growing substantially within each state and country throughout the world, but many more were interested in a more passive manner. Getting more on board and involved actively was important, if they were going to have the kind of impact on humanity they had been hoping for. For all their successes, there were always unnamed entities that served chaos and worse. To that end, Eliza began to deliberate again.

"We need to appoint scientific, artistic, rescue, and political delegates within each aspect of Pathway, on the Earth, in the various Virtual Universe Matrices, and in the many tech cities that comb the solar system." Eliza was in full form, and Yesha and James were taking it all in with ideas growing in their minds as well.

Eliza continued. *"University Matrices of every type of education, replete with every art and science, and full-on courses from Kindergarten to Ph.D. have been created here within. Much of this through our delegates, who now reside in each country and state to represent, helm, and labor within them, so people can transition from one country to the next as their journeys might take them, based on the network of issues and people related to the various individuals at the source of these problems. Still there is much to do, and it seems that a positive political and public influence might continue to help."*

As time flew by, with the influx of delegates visiting the Virtual Universe, while Eliza, Yesha, and James were gathered and sharing their deliberations with them, the status of education-level awards became sanctioned by fully read-in Pathway real-world university authorities. In a matter of five minutes in the real world, each of the robust university matrices contributed to the advancements of humanity throughout the solar system in so many ways, and when the Pathway hierarchy was done with their initial proceedings, these new institutions would do so much more.

Since 2009, Eliza had delegated to many the task of developing a wide variety of other matrices. A long task list of improvements for each of the tech cities and new ideas to augment the purpose behind the mega-structures protecting each planet and the entire solar system itself was generated and proliferated in macro-like and automated systems that were derived to carry these improvements out and into the Earthly fray. Eliza cared deeply about each person and their projects and appreciated each of their efforts toward that end.

They performed in the most genuine and heartfelt manner conceivable. Eliza knew they could be trusted to be involved in a noble manner. Doing so gave her time to go on missions of her own, participate in book signings, spend time teaching in universities as a professor, and go abroad combing the Western Hemisphere while helping whomever she could. There were many occasions where she did not hold back her powers and where distant and remote pockets of humanity stood in awe.

Yesha did very much the same for the Eastern Hemisphere, and at the same time James provided leadership to each Pathway citizen in the tech cities, graciously helping them to identify and realize the fullness of their potential, in a more immediate sense.

James knew that in time, things would change, and that the variety of skills, talents, and desires of everyone would mature and change. Still, he seemed to have a sixth sense as to who would fit best and where. He was a true manager, and in everyone else's eyes, that was his reigning talent. He was among the best, and they appreciated the fact that Eliza had delegated Solar System Operations to James and given each of them an opportunity to cast their votes early on in 2010. He won.

All Pathway citizens knew the expanse of Eliza's love, her courage, her brilliance, and they too loved her in return. As a result, they listened to her dreams and visions, were innovative, and flourished. They were always busy, bustling about from Mercury to the planetoids of the Oort Cloud, which existed near the Solar System limits, inside the heliosphere, and in some cases, humanity began to stretch the limits of their reach, just beyond.

Each of the Pathway delegates shared collective knowledge, and with that, a robust education of any sort was both enjoyable and voluntary. The many sets of experiences and sources of wisdom had by everyone in Pathway was unique, based on their own specific traits, backgrounds, qualities, and hopes.

Each individual, in every single one of the tasks they chose, was appreciated for who they were no matter how they identified themselves.

Even the greatest of chefs, broken sports stars, and actors and actresses who had had their shining moments of big-time stardom, which now dwindled to solitude, were given interviews by Yesha, Eliza, James, and their delegates, and inducted into Pathway as citizens and delegates, revitalized, and serving abroad, much to the joy of many who had recognized them from many years previous. Those who suffered the most and those who desired to do wonderful things for this world, in a world that seemed to care so very little about them in return, were people that caught Eliza's attention and love.

In Pathway, there were competitions that were staged, held, and culminated in awards to people she lauded as heroes of art, technique, and might, all serving to raise morale and prepare a unique culture strong enough to show that humanity could be a civilization filled with fun, beauty, and marvelous capabilities.

Many delegates took their newfound skills and brought joy to those who would have otherwise struggled or suffered. When they weren't sure what to do, they'd ask James, and as a result, Pathway continued to grow.

With the availability of sports, arts, invention, and theoretical competitions of every sort, and in every place throughout the solar system, tech cities off-world were where it was undoubtedly a time to shine.

Pathway grew until it had employed millions, and then continued to grow even more, but no matter their growth, somehow the Earth's population of seven-billion people persisted and continued to grow. Eliza's plan to help the world's populace was coming to fruition in leaps and bounds. Still, there was more to be done.

She understood the need for freedom, discipline, responsibility, innovation, creativity, and vision, and she encouraged the participation and integration of the public in the arts and sciences. She was interested in the well-being of all who walked on Earth and throughout the solar system.

Even though Eliza had such a large, diverse, and technologically advanced cadre at Pathway, she also knew that every state in the US and every country throughout the world would need similar representation. She considered how others might think that she could be interested in a global hostile takeover, but she was more interested in healing rather than harming. Therefore, she began as any US citizen would—to germinate this new worldwide political party, which had begun its growth from the grassroots up, as would be required by anyone else in any free country throughout the world.

The Universal Party

Eliza, Yesha, and James had the foresight to develop a system within the Universal Party, or the UP, and in the tech cities throughout the solar system, so that whenever there were disagreements, which were quite okay, a delegate from each diverging entity could be selected, along with three differently located delegates, or citizens, of Pathway LLC. They would then meet within the Group Virtual Universe Interface and neurally link with one another to fully see, comprehend, and understand all aspects of the differing views.

This would be followed by the delivery of integrated and collectively winning solutions, where all parties would return to meet within the Virtual Universe to provide a visually and viscerally balanced clarity as to the vision or future each person had in mind with their idea. They would then submit these ideas for all party members to vote on. Once this was done, and optimal scenarios were provided to each party constituent, there were seldom disagreements about mitigation of any issue that had been discussed. In fact, this turned to be an iron-clad method of resolving all Pathway and UP problems, to include diplomatic relations from one region, culture, identity, country, or language to another.

Once an agreement went to the party members for votes, it seemed quite natural, that as a result, there were always unanimous resolutions to the disagreement in question. Because of this, the UP's stances indirectly resonated with masses worldwide and leadership alike, all while adhering to the Principles of Universal Ethics.

Logistically speaking, the Federal and State Liaison Campuses throughout the world, was where diplomats and leaders met to discuss resolutions to problems affecting the world. Eliza's family estate had several rooms which were converted into a sizeable diplomatic meeting hall for small meetings. However, for large non-UP gatherings, the campus for Pathway LLC were located deep underground and within the purchased acreage in Melrose, Massachusetts, and had several large convention centers, and an abundant series of Group Virtual Universe Interfaces. The public entryway to the campus, and conveyances for travel by non-read-in personnel, as well as luxurious hotel rooms, were on-the-ready for as many as would visit at any moment. Pathway provided quarters with biopods for individuals to large-sized families who were UP members and those interested in becoming such.

Outside of political-centric purposes, each room within the campuses could also convert into emergency living spaces for anyone affected by natural or manmade disasters. At the site, there were large quantities of extra rooms set aside specifically for international refuge and emergency purposes. In many cases, going from jump gate to jump gate within the campus, afforded the ability of Pathway to provide refuge to countless people in need, since they were connected to similar campuses throughout the Solar System, in the various tech cities.

The rooms that were put together for this weren't necessarily intended as permanent living quarters; they were temporary living locations like a penthouse suite in a luxury hotel. As fugitives of any form of a hostile government or environment were found by Eliza's and Yesha's worldwide representatives and successfully rescued, they were escorted to the vast underground Melrose Campus and the tech city campuses using hidden jump gates. The refugees would then be assisted along a pathway to citizenship and given amazing options.

If they preferred, refugees could elect to initially go to and settle into any of the twenty-thousand tech cities throughout the solar system rather than stay home, as well as qualify to become full-on citizens of the US. If they chose to go to a tech city, they were read-in first and automatically granted Pathway citizenship, and afforded free travel from Melrose, Massachusetts to any of the twenty-thousand tech cities they wished to visit or live in. All necessities would be provided on the two conditions of citizenship. These conditions were that they abide by the Principles of Universal Ethics and contribute in one form or another toward the advancement of civilization.

In these tech cities, as citizens of Pathway, provisions for education, work, vacation, and sabbatical cycles were set up by delegates and leaders, each working with members of the various cultures, to ensure their religious and other observances were afforded and met, so long as they did not infringe upon the personal rights of others, nor their consent. The leaders had been elected and would be thus until they stepped down or were 'elected out of office.' Throughout the solar system, the overall leaders were Eliza, Yesha, James, and the delegates, both on Earth and in the tech cities.

Eliza had been unanimously elected by every member of Pathway as the leader of Pathway Operations, the Pathway Tech Cities, Solar System Operations, as well as Pathway LLC itself. She was also elected to preside over the UP. She was the head scientist, lead engineer, and the most accomplished and capable in every aspect of data analytics. With her vast range of responsibilities, she worked primarily in the western hemisphere of Earth, and delegated accordingly as she worked jointly with Yesha, James, and their brilliant teams.

Yesha was unanimously elected as Eliza's Vice President of each operation and worked as a head scientist and the director of the citizenship training program, both in the real world and Virtual Universe. She worked primarily in the eastern hemisphere.

James had been appointed by Eliza and Yesha, and unanimously elected by Pathway citizens to be the lead workforce manager guiding each new Pathway citizen through their daily, weekly, monthly, and other scheduled routines. He worked with a large cadre of delegates, and primarily throughout the tech cities within the solar system. He was the acting President of Solar System Operations—and he too, just like Eliza and Yesha, in many ways took advantage of Group Virtual Universe Interfaces and biopods and had vetted and confirmed delegates for each individually-tailored and collective training program for individuals as well as the masses for integration into one of their family-preferred tech cities.

Eventually, each leading central member had gone through the process of having delegates voted to represent each of these responsibilities, and in the various locations throughout the solar system.

Eliza had provided the delegates worldwide and throughout the solar system with access to jump gateways that were unnoticeable or undetectable to the human eye. Ordinary public and terrestrial individuals could not see any of Pathway LLC's developments unless they had been trained as an honorary member or had been granted visual reference as a potential citizen and fully read-in after having been both physiologically and neurologically optimized, and thus granted a neurological identification.

The Span of Influence

Forming her political party involved a lot of processes. Yet, having held many meetings and documented them since 2009, by June of 2010 all steps necessary had been taken and measures had been applied to ensure the "Universal Party," as Pathway citizens had named it via their democratic process, could be established in every state and in every plausible nation, according to the laws that governed formation of political parties. Eliza knew there would be obstacles along the roadway ahead, especially in regions where the balance of individual and human rights was still an issue, but through persuasion and genuine intent, she would see it through to a change worth every effort made.

She began campaigns of all manner, worldwide, encouraging "healing not harming." She prepared fully, both in front of others and within the Virtual Universe, and she gave public speeches addressing advancements authored by herself and her Pathway delegates with elocution and clarity regarding the roadmap to a better reality. Her speeches addressed social issues, quality of life issues, preservation of life, the planet, the solar system, and ultimately physiological and neurological optimizations being made available to all citizens worldwide while honoring the laws of consent. This would see humanity through to the most celebrated of pursuits known to mankind. She did this with the acknowledgment that as laws were, her only capacity to influence others was from within. "I must persuade from the heart and to the heart," she would say, in each interview, as she made her rounds on her book signing tours.

Eliza had a powerful understanding of economics, as it pertained to the systems on Earth in public, so all necessary financial obligations were met with her own financial resilience and fluidity. Notwithstanding, she knew that money could go only so far.

"Change must come from within." Eliza's message came from a genuine source as she explained to the masses how much she desired to, "Revitalize hope, bring clarity to purpose, meaning to life, and energize the drive, in focus of human energy toward the well-being of others as well as themselves."

Sharing her message while contributing in one form or another, Eliza continuously exemplified the principles she espoused. Meanwhile, Adelay and all of her political friends found they were overwhelmed with purpose and joy while contributing to Eliza's "Universal mission of life, longevity, compassion, happiness, clarity of mind, and consent." A lot was happening, and the UP brand began to surface, again and again.

Eliza and all her delegates taught how every UP member in every state throughout the US and even worldwide had an opportunity to participate in this process. In every aspect of building and maintaining her political party, Eliza had conducted meetings, created realistic scenarios, and joined minds with others in the Virtual Universe. She did so to empower others and move forward with clarity on decisions with successful results, and then she had them expressed in a manner that was available for study by anyone throughout the world, via the internet on the Universal Party's webpage.

Eliza and her party members had done some amazing things and had many untold yet beautiful accomplishments. Doing what she was doing, Eliza was involved so much more than simply going through the nuance of developing a political party. Nevertheless, the requirements of each state and nation in many locations throughout the world had required the taking of attendance at meetings, making official documentation of minutes, and the provision of and receipt of donations.

As always, Eliza's favorite aspects of the political party initiative were the charity drives to house the homeless, feed the hungry, and provide opportunities for organized instruction empowering the masses to produce food, shelter, and higher education for themselves.

Thus, and in many ways, Eliza and her party sought to enrich, through higher learning, the lives of those who suffered most, all the while not doing so for ulterior motives. Instead, shelter was offered with a choice that allowed Pathway citizens to enjoy life whether near or far away from any voting booth or need for clemency.

Refuge throughout the solar system would be provided free of charge, along with sizeable individual debit accounts, and delightful and exciting methods of enhancing one's education, health, and morals, within the Virtual Universe.

It was early on when Eliza's political party was officially named the "Universal Party" and subsequently dubbed the "UP." This was followed by voting results that were unanimous by all members of the party in each state of the US and each state throughout the globe, which held democratic elections worldwide.

Preceding all of this, Eliza and each state's voted delegates had conducted investigations and found legal precedent to verify the UP as the official party name in all domains, public and private.

Following the unanimous vote for the official party name, Eliza held a public convention at the Melrose Campus, and then a private one within the Virtual Universe, *"The 'UP' Logo represents the party's values. This logo has gone through a competitive and even rigorous democratic process, through unanimous voting, based on submissions in the Virtual Universe that were followed by those that can only access our public website. Votes were had on both the internet and within the Virtual Universe itself.*

"This logo is more complicated than typical. To begin with, its background symbolizes indeterminate potential as well as the power of the proper balance of dark matter and dark energy, through the clarity of the black background. A wispy white-lined yet clear face represents pellucidity of the spirit of noble character indeterminate of race, color, gender, or creed. Clarity of a beautiful, brilliant, yet somewhat transparent array of iridescent colors emanates from our minds and flows back as if it were hair blowing in the breeze to symbolize acceptance, wisdom, kindness, beauty, and the advancement of humanity throughout the Cosmos, moving forward always."

Eliza then adapted her message and explained this for the public, publishing the view of the UP, *"Nothing or no one is an enemy to the UP, save death and misery alone; everyone is invited to be a part of the future."*

Once all these aspects were shared, top musical and media artists were on-board, present, and many of them became fully read in. As such, they put together and presented a spectacular series of short movies with music and scenes of the promise that the future held in store for all of humanity and all of life itself. "This promise will be provided through the UP and the benevolent actions of all who care deep enough to reach within and give their best while respecting and appreciating the efforts others."

Eliza then shared, "Our future has promise. We have every reason for joy and hope!"

The UP logo became proliferated worldwide and recognized as a symbol of love, of acceptance, of inclusion, and as a chance for heroism beginning with simple acts and attitudes of kindness and compassion.

The party's website received constant updates from the delegates and representatives and with those updates the addition of more details regarding party stances on issues. Since the uniform resource locator was linked via sensor technology to the Twelve Database Moons, there were no problems with latency, lag, or capacity.

As a matter of fact, those with exceptionally slow internet access in the public terrestrial realm realized quickly and quietly that their connection speeds had increased considerably when visiting the UP page. Once a request had been made by a non-read-in fan of the UP, named Joanne, Eliza saw to it that a UP Social Website was created and as a result the people who had made that their homepage had the best internet available worldwide.

The many lives the UP touched were those who would have preferred living life organically, yet they agreed with the ideas presented in the Principles of Universal Ethics. While living, aging, and dying in a manner they believed in, according to their faith, as aging gracefully, many were finally able to make the great decision not to write themselves out of the mortal equation near the ebb of life and chose to make a last-minute decision to become optimized.

Many of the aging population had filled their lives with kindness toward others and service to humanity in the ways they believed they could help others the most. Eliza had a sixth sense for great virtues existent in these wonderful individuals, and one-by-one as she toured the western hemisphere, she met many who realized they had so much more to offer this Universe than they had thought before. To their hearts, she would often remind them, "It isn't ours to take a life or end our lives, rather instead, it is ours to preserve life and increase its quality the Universe over."

Opportunities

Eliza, in a broadcast over radio, shared with the world, upon being asked about the breadth of the UP, "Each committee will integrate with all of the others while at the same time providing primary focus toward the specific aspects of their committee. I would prefer three simple committees, one for longevity, one for economy, and one for clarity of mind, however, we've diversified based on the various industries that currently exist throughout the world.

"Currently, we have members who fulfill duties with the intent to consider each of these aspects into each committee: universal ethics, planetary preservation, physiological and neurological optimization, longevity, economics, healthcare, corrections, education, geology, and scientific exploration and theory are all fundamental. Social and historical sciences, astrobiology, DNA databasing, neural imagery database backup, and space exploration must be robust and phenomenal. Asteroid historical study, asteroid biopsy, asteroid mining and much more are all the impetus behind shared progress.

"All of these aspects are established by our organization within each of twenty-one committees, where we have a committee that is parallel with teams of delegates dedicated to each major industrial sector. This is done with a desire to provide the basic components of governance, to protect our shared sets of values. They also serve as a nucleus to branch out from, which will in-turn help us to be titans individually and collectively, with strength, wisdom, and indeterminate lifespans."

Through her leadership, Eliza had also led, taught, mentored, coached, and guided the teams within the Virtual Universe, promoting constructive scrutiny in the real world, making all shared solutions available to all.

Each committee had a series of elected scientists, experienced professionals, and titans of each industry who were willing and subsequently trained in the Virtual Universe, making way for other goals that Eliza had in mind in the not-so-distant future. As far as the UP push was concerned, the scientists would in-turn train and brief delegates on the latest, and in many occasions become delegates as well. Each facet of the political matrices from the Virtual Universe was assimilated into regular internet web pages for visitors.

Accessibility and legalities within the scope of localized laws throughout the various regions of the world were provided to ensure protection and the safety of those interested who were not optimized.

Everything necessary for party transparency was on real world servers with brief explanations linking to more detailed statistics, articles, and journal entries. Universal Party and Pathway LLC insights, histories, biographies, and more, including global, national, and local aspects enlightened anyone who wished to visit or even critique the information shared.

In a brief, Eliza explained the various committees represented within the UP, "I had thought about creating twenty-one committees, one for each of the global and major industries. However, after much thought, I decided to go with my own mantra, 'keep it simple.' Therefore, there will be three committees and they will have oversight of each of the industries. Each of these organizations can form subcommittees as needed to work and integrate with the various industries. Our three committees are, 01 Physiological Health Committee, 02 Neurological Health Committee, and 03 Scientific Advancement Committee. These committees will integrate with each other, and have subcommittees that work with the following industries:

01 Aerospace
02 Agriculture
03 Chemical
04 Computer
05 Construction
06 Defense
07 Education
08 Energy
09 Entertainment
10 Financial Services
11 Food
12 Health Care
13 Hospitality
14 Information
15 Manufacturing
16 Mass Media
17 Mining
18 Service
19 Telecommunications
20 Transport
21 Water

Eliza continued, "All who wish to become UP members, as the Universal Party has come to be known, are encouraged to sign up online. Opportunities for all to become delegates and who wish to participate in any of the main three committees or twenty-one subcommittees, are available. Once you sign up, we will pay for your transportation to any nearby Federal or State Liaison Campus, where you will be trained and can become a delegate. All our nominations are received by localized university legal teams of experts and approved through a unanimous vote, in the most democratic manner possible.

"Delegates who wish to run for office in a particular constituency can make it known on the UP website. If they are nominated, each contender will be encouraged to highlight and detail specific items for their emphasis, focus objectively on sections of each issue they would address, and demonstrate how their solutions would do well to help their constituents. Due to our collaborative environment, no matter who wins, despite their unique views, we ultimately share the same goals.

"Thus, optimum results afford other candidates the ability to build their skills while working on committees of the winning candidates. The goal is to preserve life, advance civilization, and comb the cosmos, and we will work together in that regard. Suggestions by anyone for improvement, member or non-member, are genuinely appreciated, considered and in many cases implemented with acknowledgment provided to the group or the individual that made the suggestion. If a contributor requests, anonymity can be granted to protect those living in hostile circumstances from harm or consequences that countermand the Principles of Universal Ethics."

Eliza finished by inviting everyone to her website, at https://www.up.pathway.org.

Following this radio address, she visited more talk shows, and introduced her tax plan. "One of the many things I notice as a political issue that has affected many countries is the burden born of every citizen through heavy taxation. There shouldn't be a need for taxation whatsoever if most of the population could work to oversee and exemplify the Principles of Universal Ethics. We need to have clarity and understood how the current economic systems work. For example, in the US, the ideal of capitalism is often ignored, yet if it wasn't the healthiest way to drive this economic system would be from a foundation of well-being, rather than from a fixation on greed or power.

"I have developed a pathway to integrate the current financial arrangements that have slowly taken the powers of everyone away, by working with my fellow delegates to reverse the existent trend in the way business is done. Initially, I suggest the institution of a ten percent flat tax that will result in annual dividends due to the benefits of investing in business, development, and research institutions. With those investments, will come an annual dividend to each taxpayer.

"If a certain percentage or overage is returned to the taxpayer and another equitable percentage is reinvested toward research, development, and business by the local, state, or national government, then the residual proceeds can be accumulated. As time goes by taxes will no longer be needed or required. Instead of taxes, each individual and our civilization will be afforded the opportunity to seek higher education.

"Ultimately, an unfettered sense of dedication toward contribution to the advancement of civilization will suffice. This will suffice because, with the smallest yet most meaningful of efforts, beginning with kindness toward others through clarity of mind and shared dignity and mutual respect, at a minimum, everything else will virtually come to fruition, or blossom through personal motivation and collective efforts in its own remarkable and beautiful way.

"The subjective intent to take the initiative, share ideas, and bring to the rivers of life the advancements that will protect the well-being, longevity, and quality of life of all, will allow us to naturally flow with purpose. We need to work together to germinate these ideas in a way that will result in making life both exciting and enjoyable for everyone. The results of these actions taken will affect all living that perhaps I may never know, but in a way that will bring validity to the efforts of those who are genuinely benevolent. As a result of our advancements, our genius minds, and our love for humanity, all that is needed or all that can be asked for if done by abiding by the Principles of Universal Ethics, is kindness and simple participation. As time goes by, all that is needed will be intuitively provided, and everything else given upon request. Reason for want, greed, oppression, suppression, or walking around without purpose will diminish.

"My mid-range plan for taxes will be such that they will mature into more of a commitment toward demonstrating personal involvement in our overall mission to advance in scientific knowledge, capacity, and understanding to likewise preserve life, longevity, peace, and even happiness. It will begin as more of a dividend system, where ten percent will be paid in taxes to the government, including sales, and local, state, federal, and all other forms of tax using the current economic system. Dividends will generously be given to provide private domain, housing, or ownership of real estate to any citizen, so long as the Principles of Universal Ethics are honored, and again, people are free to act, say, and do as they please, yet will be corrected appropriately only if they cause undue consequence to the rights of others."

It Will Take Time

As Pathway grew to the millions, each member who had been fully optimized or who had agreed to terms as an honorary member was inherently a citizen. They could each become delegates, a unanimous vote through a democratic process within the Virtual Universe and then sent on missions similar to those that Eliza, Yesha, James, and their growing crews had gone on.

In truth, everyone could become a delegate, but the elections were in a sense the unanimous confirmation by millions of citizens and delegates that an individual was prepared to go on missions of their own, with the type of character requisite of rescuing, recruiting worldwide, and safely bringing people into the organization ready to contribute, while living in prosperity and abundance.

When a delegate met people, who were interested in something greater, an environment that was kinder, gentler, and more promising, they invited them to come to any of a variety of liaison campuses and were then introduced to a small portion of the tech and its lingering benefits. Having visited the Virtual Universe on many occasions prior to unanimous approval to become a delegate, each one knew every language spoken globally, and they did everything they could to bring peace of mind and camaraderie to the new individuals preparing to become Pathway citizens.

The magnitude of the UP's growing influence and Pathway's developments encouraged and inspired many. Once apprised and upon person election, an individual could be read-in by way of receiving physiological and neurological optimizations and neural identifications. The UP's overall vision of governance and the delegate's subsequent actions began to inspire many in numerous locations around the globe.

Each citizen learned everything they could. They desired to be part of the effort to work collaboratively for a better future. Operations were covert, and while many lived in somewhat sparsely populated tech cities, at least in the beginning, they each lived for the day that these cities would be bustling with culture and activity.

Strangely enough, many of these new delegates began to look forward to bidding fond farewells to crews boarding future spacecraft for travel on missions throughout the Universe. Many of the citizens of Pathway happily lived in outer space with a desire to return to Earth as delegates if there was a specific job for them to do or publicly releasable measures were in place.

Eliza didn't want to destroy any worldwide or state economy, yet her smooth and automated cures, if adapted right away among the masses, would tank the medical, insurance, and pharmaceutical industries, and thereby the current economic system itself. So, even though the current economy was currently destroying itself, the masses had to learn and shape their perception of the way things ought to be through persuasion, perseverance, and long-suffering.

With no desire to grandstand her accomplishments, Eliza was acutely aware of Maslow's Hierarchy of Needs and knew that if all of what she had done was revealed too soon it result in a period of time where people would be unnecessarily left without jobs or the basic necessities and securities of life.

Eliza knew that people needed to assert themselves, work hard, think beyond themselves and transcend the environments they grew up in, so they could evolve beyond what they were. All of this could be done, but Eliza knew that ultimately becoming a global leader and traveling and healing the Universe, would take some time.

Through all her work, Eliza was happy with the progress that was made. After establishing the UP, she decided to go on another book tour to sign copies of her literary masterpiece, known as Pathway to the Stars. As she did this, she would look for incredible individuals who would lead humanity thru the cosmos one day.

"I'm grateful that I've met all of the wonderful people I have. This party is about healing and not harming, and to that end I will reach out to others and find their great potential that is waiting to burst with activity and beautiful results!"

Chapter 11: The Public World

Database Moon Archive, Celestial-Sol Entry Date: 2010, August 18. In this important part of Vesha Celeste's training, after her awakening, she and Yesha explore a brief part of the backstory of Amber Blythe, who is a highly capable bioscientist. This training takes place in the Virtual Universe, interfaced within the Pathway Melrose Campus. Input by Eliza Williams, President of Pathway Industries, 2008-2015.

On Earth in the public world and for those who had not been read-in, and thus, for many who knew nothing about Eliza's growing revolution of hope, it was a typical autumn day following study hall at MIT. Amber Blythe had finished up her reading, expounding upon her essay questions—digging deeper for more meaningful and purposeful answers to each question posed than were required, and she kept ahead of her schedule with her thesis on 'Biotech and Gerontology: The Race to Cure Aging.' She took time regularly to balance her life, and one of her favorite additions to her schedule over the last few months had been to obsessively pore over as many times as possible her favorite sections of her paperback copy of Dr. Eliza A. Williams' "Pathway to the Stars."

Amber's family was far from rich, but they managed their money wisely. In addition to living not too far away from Cambridge, Massachusetts, which was an expensive place to live, her scholarships helped a lot; she also had a couple of side jobs and managed to get by. What helped Amber get into MIT in the first place was that she was both academically brilliant and a genius in the labs, so as a result she had been awarded a full-ride scholarship to each school she went to through the end of her doctorate program. She began at the local community college, then went to the state college, and followed that by going to MIT for her graduate courses, which she had been attending for the last year and a half.

It was August of 2010, and thus far she had maintained academic scores requisite of Summa Cum Laude honors, but more importantly, she had absorbed the information and through that had developed a concrete understanding of how each course interrelated with the other and within the context of applying them to a long and healthy life.

Harvard would be the next step in her pathway toward achieving her Ph.D. in biogenetics and that would begin following the holiday celebrations and the New Year of 2011. Amber studied the courses related to her Ph.D. and chose a path with heavy personal investment, concern, and a profound vision of something that could reduce the suffering of humanity, and in particular, she wanted to help others that might be affected by genes that when improperly tied in together, or as a lamp affected by its light switch, turned off or on, which lent to misery and suffering—just as it was for her younger sister who was born with Diabetes Type I.

Given all these factors, Amber held on through each day of each year of study and was on pace for completion of her thesis within the next few weeks, while not being due for a few more months after that.

To make sure she had money to spare and could afford professional clothing, Amber, who had been gifted with a beautiful face, a beautiful physique, and a genius mind, had moonlighted as a model for an agency that provided covers, advertisement pictures to several worldwide magazines, and commercials. On occasion, she was paid for guest appearances on science-related broadcasts and conferences.

Serving as a food delivery attendant at a nearby organic and nutrient-dense college-town restaurant, named the Tyson Organic, or the T.O., for short, she would secure free food and a little extra money to save up for when she was in transition between her studies, breaks, and her goals. Amber wanted to eventually set up a limited liability company, to build a biotech and gene therapy business. Furthermore, she wanted to be a fully vested bio-hacker to save lives, augment the quality of life no matter the environment, and improve overall health and capabilities. For Amber, the race for human-driven evolution was on.

No matter her busy schedule, Amber found time for sleep, yoga, long jogs, the gym, and practiced an optimally engaging healthy and balanced lifestyle routine daily.

Most of the time, rather than spend money and time on stints at sorority parties and the like, she chose to stay ahead on her study curriculum, go to art gallery presentations, and keep herself fit for modeling. Despite the common buzzing of the boys or the potential suitors over her beautiful hazel eyes, her luscious, healthy, physically fit, and curvy frame, her glistening blonde hair with impeccable and natural highlights that she sometimes flat-ironed, threw back in a ponytail, or let go for a wavy and medium-length appearance, or wore in an up-do for special events, she maintained her focus toward saving money and on delving deep into her studies.

She moved at a high pace, with purpose, and she had personal drive. Amber was on a mission, and she would find time for men later. She dressed nice and groomed herself because she believed in presenting the best image to represent what she felt internally. If people wanted to be in her life, they'd find more success in doing so by exchanging ideas about the latest lists of human genes that had been broken out or by discussing how current gene therapies were working.

Amber was interested in learning what the obstacles to progress were, so she could study what was necessary to reduce the roadblocks and end the misery as well as the unnecessary frustrations of disease that affected so many and overcome them, "*If we could just focus, dedicate ourselves a little more, and cease with this fixation and lust toward violence, brutality, and death, maybe we could get somewhere as a civilization. People settle for their bestial instincts all-too-often,*" she thought when she saw as others seemed to fade away to a life of no meaning or ethical purpose.

What she didn't have time for was being dangled upside down at keg parties in a mediocre-lifestyle-blur to see if she could win a chugging contest or get high off of heaven knows what. She was frustrated with humanity's slow progress and its distractions. With no desire to numb away from reality or squander time away in fruitless pursuits, Amber wanted to be innovative in the face of reality, which was the one thing that everyone else seemed to blow off in order to justify mediocrity in life by saying, "Well that's just life. That's just the way it is."

"*What a façade,*" she would reply mentally—she would take that beast face on. She also saw more to life than natural impulses and the evolution of mixed results—she saw first-hand and far too close-up how that can work out. It was as if nature was screaming at humanity to use the gift of our minds that we have been given and to take the burden out of its hands, so we could preserve life, live with compassion, create our legacy, explore our Universe, and perhaps do something we could never dream of at this point in our existence.

Creative Routine

With Amber's routine, today was a little different. Dr. Eliza A. Williams was in town after being away on a book-signing tour. She had been across the country, around the world, and had even started up a company, called Pathway LLC, which specialized in biogenetics and the advancement of modern technology for the well-being of mankind. There were whispers that she had even begun her own political party, the UP, which was becoming surprisingly more the buzz and that intrigued Amber as well. She was a busy woman doing good things and she had nothing but pure respect for that.

Dr. Eliza A. Williams did all of this, while still providing enough time when school was in session to be a professor at Harvard. And now, here she was, she was back in town, and she had gone on a second tour here through Cambridge.

Amber had missed her the first time around while working in the laboratory at school, doing research, and looking for concrete data and statistics in relation to her thesis. This time, however, she would not miss the opportunity to meet this remarkable woman, who was only seven years her senior, but had risen to heights of fame rarely reached by scientists. *"Despite what the scientists have done for the last few generations when it comes to increasing the quality of life and providing much of the world a forward-civilization-leap through technology—she seems to be deterred less and does so much more,"* Amber whispered to herself. Yes, Dr. Eliza A. Williams was the real deal; her word was gold, and Amber wasn't going to miss meeting her or asking a couple of questions this time, *"Hopefully I can keep things short,"* she thought.

Dr. Eliza Williams was going to be signing books at the largest and oldest bookstore in Cambridge, Massachusetts, today, and now that Amber was done with study hall and two of her classes, she was heading to the bookstore with her raggedy paperback book in her hand to meet her once and for all. She felt the irony since she was wearing her black and stunning evening gown—which she had purchased and worn for her modeling gig while carrying her raggedy book. She had left her debit card locked up at home the day she saw the book at the store on display and had just enough cash at the time in her mini-purse to purchase a copy of Dr. Williams' book, the paperback version—not the hardcover since that was above her present price-range. *"You can't be too proud,"* she thought.

After seeing it sitting on display in the bookstore only three months prior, she had opened the pages and couldn't put it down. She read the book once and after purchasing it, she read it, again and again, many times over. Each time she read it she was moved and inspired. Never would she let a page go without taking notes, highlighting passages that spoke to her most, writing correlations to her studies and her thesis, and then referencing it often. There was something phenomenal about this literary masterpiece and every section of it pulled at her. To Amber, no matter how much everything seemed to coalesce in importance, for some reason the sections about curing diseases and reversing aging impacted her most.

Oh, Amber certainly had read a lot of books since there were a variety of bookstores and collegiate-level libraries nearby. She had pored over peer-reviewed journal articles and wrote quite a bit of her own for both her thesis and her personal development, but she would still religiously go over Dr. Williams' "Pathway to the Stars" every day, keeping it close. Her classmates had given her some guff for it, but she would just smile and say, "Thank you," and move on to more important matters. In some ways, this book kind of helped her draw parallels between herself and her sister. It gave her a unique sort of connection to both her sister, Sarah and Dr. Williams. It was almost as if

Dr. Williams was her sister or a once in a lifetime friend and she had never met her before. Amber would not let herself fall prey to the pressures of youth, despite jeers, or anything else of any sort that led to mediocre results for what she wished to achieve.

While some of her peers and even professors called her an overachiever or suggested that she was overeager to study deeply, she would merely respond to them that she was just doing her best to learn and to make the most out of her life. When people told her, she cared too much about too many things, she would merely respond by telling them that they should care much more than they do. When people told her that she spent too much time and considered spending too much money on pursuits that were beyond her control, and thus didn't matter, she would respond that her pursuits were those that mattered to the entire human race, and they ought to be investing every last hour and dime in them. Amber Blythe had balance, she had an internal drive, she was driven by fire within, and she had meaningful goals and she wouldn't let the ignorance of others slow her down.

"*First stop today,*" she whispered to herself, while standing in line, "*Read a little, talk to Dr. Williams, go home, change, strike a pose or two for the next set of ads for several different magazines at the nearby modeling agency, go on a jog, do some yoga, shower again, and head to the TO, to serve healthy food for a few hours.*" After this schedule for her day, she would then go home, get adequate sleep, get up, go to school, and then head to study hall to start all over again. Amber chose to "start" her day whenever it was that she wanted to, since that was her way of having some say over space and time, and in this case, even though she would wake up and go to school, her day wouldn't start until she went to study hall. To her, everything else was part of the previous day. She knew it was a bit odd for some, but it worked for her for now, and she would change it as she saw fit or as she wished.

Whether her schedule seemed redundant or odd or not, she knew her schedule would inevitably change once she had completed her doctorate, and perhaps many times more.

Her Sister

Years ago, when Amber was much younger, her little sister, Sarah, had come into this world with a tragic set of severe conditions. She was born with childhood type one diabetes, hypoglycemia, her spleen had ruptured and been removed, but just in time, four months after she was born. A year later she was diagnosed with early childhood appendicitis, and her appendix was removed. Her little sister had it tough and couldn't seem to catch a break. Growing up, her sister had shared the same room at their parent's home as Amber, yet they were separated by a transparent plastic barrier. This wall was there to protect Sarah from the contaminants that her immune system was not capable of warding off in order to keep her alive.

Adoring her stepsister, notwithstanding all, as Amber grew older and, on many occasions, while studying her schoolwork, she would look toward her sister's bed to exchange glances, and sometimes after Sarah had been quiet for a while, she would find her sitting there in her armchair not looking at anything, rather she would stare as if in a state of trance. When this happened, it usually meant that her body was experiencing the effects of hypoglycemia and that Sarah was suffering from an absence seizure.

As Amber grew older, she learned more and understood scientifically that along with the absence seizures, Sarah's body suffered from what is known as aplastic anemia, where her bone marrow would not produce enough blood cells to mend her organs quick enough for the damage they received daily. Furthermore, her pancreas was not working properly, so she was also not able to process the sugars as needed and she would become hypoglycemic unless she received insulin shots multiple times daily in the fatty tissue of her body to help her system to properly process the sugars it needed. Moreover, her immune system was very weak, since she no longer had her spleen or her appendix, her white blood cells had to do all of the work.

As they grew up together and computers became more affordable, her mother and stepfather purchased a couple of systems for Amber and her sister, along with the associated medical equipment that would work with her medical attachments and provide Amber various and important readings. Her parents set their computers up with a network so that Amber could monitor her conditions, but they also set them up so that they could play video games, do physical exercises together, study, and communicate with each other without having to yell. Their favorite game was Scrabble since it had the positive side effect of keeping their minds engaged while being entertaining.

Playing Scrabble, they would have contests with each other using only words that fell into a subject category that would be identified before starting each game. If they opted to play an open-book version of the game, they would choose words related to flora and fauna, constellations, stars, galaxies, the universe, and nebulae, medical terms and treatments, or anything with a wide range of vocabulary so that their minds would expand. They would also learn more about the different scientific and social subjects, as well as the world outside, and did so regularly once their studies were complete. Sometimes they would even challenge each other closed-book-style as their grasp of vocabulary increased.

While communicating together they would share favorite music from movie scores, movie and television soundtracks, sometimes listen to symphony, pop, vocal and progressive trance, sometimes new wave, sometimes new age, and at times whatever was popular on the radio, and they would take breaks from studying and gaming to watch favorite educational and science fiction shows together. As Amber and Sarah grew older, they became more interested in scientific documentaries that dealt with health, space travel and astrophysics, and well-being-related advancements.

While they appreciated science fiction, it was disappointing to both of them that technology seemed to be shown in a bad light far too often. For them, the answer to resolving misfires in the genome lay in technology and would lead to understanding our existence even further; overcoming disease and unnecessary suffering would give humanity more time and promise within the universe.

Together they would watch the Nature, Travel, or Science Channels in the background while listening to their upbeat yet soft and even compassionate music, and then do jumping jacks, push-ups, and stationary jogging while monitoring them digitally, keeping track, and attempting to hold conversations despite the plastic barrier. Even though they were both raised with home-schooling they were both very brilliant and well-informed. While Amber could have gone to public school, she wanted to be around her sister to help her with her education and give her social and moral support. Oh, they would get out of the house each day, weather permitting, to enjoy nature, but it wasn't without the hassle of getting Sarah geared up and ready to go with the medical paraphernalia, the clean oxygen, and plenty of disinfectant wipes.

Amber loved her sister, Sarah, dearly and she felt her love was reciprocated in every way, knowing full well that it was. It was heart-wrenching and difficult for Amber when Sarah passed away at the young age of thirteen—Amber had barely turned fifteen. Those who had visited Sarah from the local community had always done so separated by the plastic barrier, yet those who had visited her were far too few, and Sarah's funeral was attended by a sparse crowd as well. Only her parents, Amber, and three neighborhood friends, who Amber and Sarah had met and made while on frequent trips to the park, were there the day of the service and burial ceremony. Amber remembered being awash in tears that day and for quite some time after that.

As time went by, Amber progressed through her high school-level studies, since her parents had sent her to public school to help her to take her mind off of the loss of her sister. While she felt the loss deeply, especially since her peers in high school had already formed their own clicks and had established their friendship circles, despite the lonely nature of going from one class to another, she stayed strong. She knew in her heart of hearts that it was important to hold on, despite the occasional tears, with fondness to the good moments shared with Sarah. One could do that, she believed, while moving forward in life. It was okay to understand what happened, and maybe find a way, a means, or a cure, a positive focus along the way so that no one else would have to go through the loss of their little sibling, child, or friend in the way she had lost her sister. It was through loss, the anguish of losing Sarah to those wretched ailments that Amber was driven to focus on a better way while maintaining a well-balanced life and studying for cures.

Chapter 12: Meeting an Icon

Database Moon Archive, Celestial-Sol Entry Date: 2018 December 25. In this important part of Vesha Celeste's training, after her awakening, she and Yesha explore the recruitment and a brief part of the backstory of Amber Blythe, within the Virtual Universe, interfaced within the Pathway Melrose Campus. Input by: Yesha Alevtina, President of Pathway Industries, 2015-2022.

If she could have her way, she would have the drive, the ingenuity, and the creative spirit needed to come up with cures so that no one else would ever have to live trapped like her beloved sister had. While Amber excelled in public school in academics, sports, and even the arts, she missed the time spent alongside and studying with Sarah. Life would never be the same without her, in her room, each with their own armchairs, singing together, thinking out loud, sometimes seeing her lay there in silence, she was always determined to keep Sarah in her heart and in her memories—thinking of the good times shared rather than giving up in sorrow and loss. Depeche Mode's lyrics, vocals, and music for their songs, "In Your Room" in her younger years and later "Precious" were what reminded her of her sister, and they took on a whole new meaning, given her experiences. Listening to them soothed her in her own way. Sarah had a legacy that was worth being preserved, so Amber would do everything she could to honor that.

Kindred Spirits

Now, here she was, about to meet the one other person who she felt a connection with, even though they had never ever met. Through reading her book, she knew that Dr. Eliza A. Williams had expressed a deep compassion for those that were suffering and was very passionate about the sciences that could prevent unnecessary misery and inspire the senses toward hope and creative clarity.

Eliza's passage burned in Amber's mind, *"The young and innocent, the kind and those that care should never know sorrows so deep as those they have known through centuries of mistreatment, inherited disease, or an environment that breaks them down."*

As Amber stepped into the rather large bookstore, she thought about what she had read, and clinging to her paperback book, she thought about how her sister had suffered yet endured her pain so gracefully, all the way until her body could no longer handle what was too difficult for even the mightiest of people to bear. Her emotions welled up inside and when she had arrived at the front of the line, and it was her turn to step up and introduce herself; it was as if she had awoken from a daze. Eliza seemed to see right through Amber, and smiled the kind of smile that says, *"I understand."*

Eliza then told her, "You have a dazzling charm about you; I can tell there is something going on—despite loss and tragedy you have a fire burning from within. You're a wonderful person; I can tell already. It is so nice to meet you, please call me Eliza."

To Amber, perhaps an introduction like that might have been followed by a melted heart, tears, and unbridled sobbing, but the way Eliza spoke was calming, genuine, kind, and her eyes glistened with tears as they seemed to well up from within but did not fall. Her blue eyes reflected the light from the chandeliers hanging from the ceiling above in the bookstore, which added to everything Amber had already believed about Eliza.

Eliza, with ease, grace, and swiftness, made her way around the table, pulled a chair from under it, and before motioning for her to sit down, she put her arms out to give Amber a comforting and healing hug. Amber reciprocated. Eliza then kindly asked, "Please, have a seat?"

Never had Amber known someone to be so polite, so kind, so genuine, and there she was, beckoning her to relax and spend a little time with her. Amber could have seen herself as an emotional wreck, with so much welling up inside that was so instantaneously understood, but something in Eliza's voice soothed her pains instead. As Amber sat down, she thought, "*How can someone be this gifted? Why do I feel my heart swell with joy rather than sorrow? Here is a lady, notorious for having completed seven Ph.Ds. in the same year; she has the mind of seven geniuses all rolled into one, and yet she has gracefully and genuinely put me at ease. She knows there's more to me and she wants to hear it.*"

As if time was standing still, she humbly placed her ragged paperback copy of "Pathway to the Stars" on the table between herself and Eliza and looked down as if in shame. Amber hadn't purchased the hardcover copy, because she couldn't afford it at the time. She was saving everything she could, so she could start a biotech and biogenetics company after she finished her schooling. Any penny she spent, she felt as though she was borrowing against a future of helping others, so she was thrifty. Notwithstanding, Amber appreciated her investment in this book and had idolized Eliza for the last few months, and now everything Eliza did merely proved what she already perceived of her as true. Trying to snap out of it, she thought to herself, "*Alright, Amber, she's a human being just like everyone else. Yes, perhaps she is a good human being, but she breathes, has hopes and fears, just like every human on the planet. I think what she would want me to do is to quite simply relax.*"

"I have to say," Eliza said, "I am impressed." She paused, helping Amber shift into another sense of calm, and then continued, "When it comes to reading this book, far too many people hear the news about how it is the top choice and most popular to read, they follow the trend, go out to the bookstore and buy their books right here and right now and then come to me asking if I can sign it, even though it is very likely they've never actually read it. If they have, people tend to have glossed over the summarized text on the back of the book, making assumptions about the rest, and then boast on social media about common points after briefly skimming without considering the context of what I wrote nor its purpose. However, I can tell from looking that you have read this book quite a few times and you want to know something? That makes you a kindred spirit in my book." Eliza paused, and then asked, "Am I alright in assuming by looking at the cover here, it looks like your name is Amber Blythe? Don't worry about paperback versus hardcover, by the way. I did not sell these books for any other reason than to give people a chance to invest a little time into something that will help humanity and life itself. I have wished and continue to wish that people worldwide can have some hope and that they will receive a spark of ingenuity.

"Wow, what a beautiful name...Blythe, Amber Blythe." She smiled at Amber.

The front cover of her paperback book had Amber's name printed on it in ink, with a caption that read, "If found, please return to Amber Blythe. You can text me at 617-A-Blythe. Thank you."

"Don't worry, Amber, I won't call you unless you forget your book. Please feel at ease."

Amber smiled, felt more relaxed, and almost blushed, although she wasn't sure how to begin, she had found herself looking back up, she smiled again and asked, "Is it okay if I speak to you freely, Ma'am?" Eliza exuded an unspoken sense of authority, dignity, and respect, so Amber had naturally tried to treat her in kind. Although she had a sense that she wasn't pompous or merely in the room for the sake of status, Amber chose politeness as a default.

"Of course, Amber... and you can call me Eliza. Please know, I saw you when you walked into the bookstore and the instant you walked in you caught my eye. When I saw your book in your hand, I knew we would be kindred spirits, so that is why I offered you a chair. – I don't do that with everyone, you realize. Oh, I appreciate them, I view them as special, but there is something intriguing and unique about you. Amber, you have the unstoppable heart of a lion. You don't run from fear; you face it head-on. Yet you seem kind and compassionate. We're all human, I suppose, but I know you have something you want to share with me, I can see it in your eyes." and then Eliza paused, looked Amber in the eyes and smiled, alleviating Amber's concerns. "So, what was it about Pathway to the Stars that intrigued you the most? What has it inspired within you? I would love to hear how it has intrigued you and opened your well of creativity."

Even though Amber still felt a little overwhelmed—the puppy-dog idol-worship-haze began to wear off, Dr. Williams was clearly making a genuine effort to simply be real and engage with genuine sincerity. So, Amber answered, "I purchased your book three months ago and every time I have a few moments I read a few passages and then I read the entire book again. For some reason, I just can't seem to put it down. I was immediately impressed with what you had written from the first pass. What you wrote had meaning, it had substance, and it was deep. It took life's experiences, memories from the past, engagement in the now, and promises of the future and made them seem truly visceral, with a sense of hope that does not need to go unrequited, it makes a legacy we'd enjoy preserving possible."

Amber looked down, thinking about her sister, and then looked up with confidence and shared another pleasant and bonding visual exchange with Eliza, as her heart kind of skipped a few beats. "Dr. Williams—I mean, Eliza? I just want you to know that I appreciate how you address what you do," and then Amber shifted in her chair and unleashed.

"You were straight up yet respectful to the flash-in-the-pan; snake-oil-frenzied crowds of bureaucracy-influenced, paparazzi-like media moguls who were ready to pounce on well-being-related technology with dystopian myopia, crazed popularity-seekers who endeavor to shackle the effort to educate the masses and you gracefully let them have it. You confounded the minds of the close-minded and the greedy haberdashers who take opportunism to the scariest of lows.

"What people seem to all-too-often forget is that while scientists make leaps and bounds out of micro-progression when they do it right, they many times find within themselves a visionary—a macro-vision-imbued rebirth with a larger concept of what they are doing. Unfortunately, in more cases than we would prefer, I'd imagine, the general public finds itself buried from the debris of misinformation within the whirlwind that leads to more problems in so many ways that allow us to gaze anew at greater challenges, because the existing ones could have actually been solved had the information available been a result of genuinely healthy intent.

"With lawsuits, patenting costs, and nightmares of reality attacking progress, people are beginning to lose their hope and the seeds of obstructionism are sewn, as in the days of Copernicus. Too many disparage those with great minds, great ideas, and huge hearts.

"While growing up and throughout her unfortunately short life, my sister blessed me with a wonderful vision of love and compassion. Despite my sister's unfairly tortured and all-too-short journey of life, due to her bout with early onset Type I Diabetes and a host of other genetic misfires that caused her tremendous suffering, she always smiled and was sweet with anyone who took the time to spend what few precious moments she had with her—just on the other side of the plastic barrier. She never desired to cause another individual harm and she always beamed with hope inside, no matter what we would do or how her body treated her.

"After she passed away, throughout the rest of high school, my undergraduate, and now graduate studies I have learned again and again that there is a resolution if we can sift through the hopelessness of those around us. We most certainly have a heavy burden to bear when it comes to each scientific breakthrough in the various fields of knowledge and their convergence.

"As a complexed composition of cures can be created, localized specifically, based on the various biological regions of the body—the organs, the tissues, the tendons, the organisms, and even individual health needs at a cellular, genetic, and DNA level, perhaps it will be possible soon to develop a mechanism that is non-invasive, that will allow each microbial colony to be encoded to communicate directions and purpose with treatments that are gene-specific and intended to mend and heal, without the side effects of cancer.

"With the benefits of the tools that can be made available for lab work, study, and proliferated trials, tools like CRISPR-Cas—presumably Cas9, and many others, the simplicity of telomerase therapy, and control mechanisms for myostatin inhibitors, a lot can be done to help people. If we can start off by taking the capabilities from cancer cells to express their own telomerase while causing cancer cells to sleep, and apply those capabilities to our own healthy regular, somatic, and stem cells, and even rejuvenate our senescent cells, our bodies' cells will be able to express telomerase and thus lengthen our telomeres providing us more time in life. If we can effectively program our cells or helpful virus, bacteria, or molecules to destroy cancer or repurpose it, or clear the debris or repurpose it, then we could buy each person in this world more time to overcome misfiring genes.

"The size of cancer cells is much larger than the size of red or white blood cells, so we can find something that is too big to enter the blood cells but small enough to enter cancer cells, and then reprogram the cancer cells to work with our other cells in clearing out or repurposing unnecessary debris. We can encode our good cells with the ability to express and create telomerase, as well as carry out the debris more efficiently as we establish biomarkers and follow treatments, journalize our studies, recommend specific therapies, develop augmentations to our body's other aspects, to include radiation resistance, push for media attention, approval for distribution, and then proliferate them throughout the country and throughout the world.

"The effects of gene therapies at the dawn of the 21st Century and the CRISPR revolution had led to mixed results and while some people did well, far too many suffered from additionally stray radicals and through that fallout acquired leukemia and passed away. I truly believe that the primary focus must be on cancer, while at the same time studying each poly and mono genomic sequence and identifying other ATCG code mutations. However, cancer is the result of rogue cells, misfired cells, debris, and accumulation of various free radicals through chronic inflammation, which instead of healing or exiting the body's system, serve as material that coalesces since birth into cancer cells, capable of living and proliferating forever or at least as long as the host that it lives in isn't destroyed. Couldn't we turn that around?

"I'm sure you know this already, but cancer has a copy of the host DNA in every cell, but destroys our cells creating more cancerous expressions. With more than 73,000 variants of cancer, what we need to do is switch the roles taking place within the good cells and re-encode good cells to develop telomerase, and then penetrate the cancer cells with communication that repurposes that material to complement our physiology, exit the body, or assist healthy cells with proliferation. Once cancer is no longer an issue, we can move on to cures for other diseases without fear as we are armed to remove any dangerous consequences, and perhaps augment our capacities to live in some of the worst environments and adapt with speed."

Eliza was impressed that Amber due to her own studies had potentially cracked the code in much the same way as she had. Only, the details of them or the fact that she had done so via her pursuits in Pathway LLC had not been mentioned to that degree within her book. The book merely suggested certain ideas encouraging scientists and enthusiasts to be more involved with the purposes as outlined in her UP charter's Universal Ethics.

Amber had shared the same theories that Eliza had only within her mind and those linked with her because although there was a slight hint of these ideas in her book, she had not written them in as detailed of format for security reasons.

Nonetheless, it wasn't Eliza's intention to obstruct the free-thinking mind of someone who was not read-in, rather instead Amber had in fact demonstrated the expression of purpose that was intended by her book, which was to get the rest of humankind thinking and bringing about these cures despite their environments and in public. This young scholar was brilliant! Eliza had merely asked the world to come up with solutions, and that is what Amber did. She even had a theory of her own that would no doubt be iron-clad and even possible soon, something that, with the exception for her and the citizens of Pathway LLC, no one else on Earth had done.

Amber continued, "Sorry, I know you have a large line waiting. I just wanted you to know that I appreciate what you do, Eliza. Thank you. I will be starting my studies at Harvard after the New Year. Your vision has given me the motivation and clarity I needed to move forward with purpose so that 'We the People' can work to contribute to this legacy you speak of within your book and in your interviews. I agree humanity and life are worth preserving."

Eliza smiled, she was intrigued by what Amber had said and very impressed with this young lady. Yet again, her intuition did not fail her. "Amber, you should know that I am proud of you. You have moved forward in profound ways despite the struggle. You know—I may be lucky enough to have you in one of my classes, as a professor at Harvard. It would be an honor to teach you some of the other things that I have learned as well; you might even teach me a few things. Nevertheless, I would very much like to see you again, to chat with you for a while concerning very intriguing matters that I am sure you might be interested in. Would you mind meeting up with me at the local coffee shop, called the 'Broke Coffee House, right next to T.O.'s once my book signing is over?"

Eliza, wearing a black coat over a white blouse and black skirt, with hair lightly parted to the left side and hanging down to her shoulders, with soft and pink-skin-toned variant color lips, reached into her pocket while looking at Amber with her soft crystal blue eyes and handed her a business card with her contact details on it.

"When you get a chance, Amber, please enter my contact information into your phone and text me with your name, so I can save your information. I would very much like to see you again; this way I will also be able to make sure we know who we are contacting. Has anyone told you that you are beautiful both inside and out? I am impressed with your demeanor and your knowledge."

Amber almost blushed with Eliza's compliment and felt happy she had come to the bookstore today. Thinking of the conversation they shared, she felt a rush of intensity and peace of heart and mind as she took Eliza's business card and looked into Eliza's eyes one more time—how beautiful she was, how intelligent and wise her mind, how gentle of a demeanor she too had despite the magnitude and power of what she spoke and had shared with the world. Amber could not have wished for a better moment in life. She had a sense that this was the beginning of an intense and amazing friendship that just might last for a long, long time.

Amber smiled, trying not to blush any more than usual, and said, "thank you, Eliza. Of course, I would love to meet with you, to chat and go over what we've talked about some more. I am humbled. Thank you so much." Once Amber had tucked her card into her purse, she got up, straightened her gown, and walked away. Both Amber and Eliza smiled and waved, something about those two radiated throughout the room, and every person that could see it felt it.

Eliza got up and continued ushering each person in the line up to her. As she was signing the very next individual's brand new hard-copy book, she appreciated their investment and noticed the tattered and raggedy paperback still sitting in front of her. She took it, tucked it into her purse for safe keeping, and asked the individual standing in front of her, "How are you doing today? Oh, might I ask you your name?" The young man introduced himself, they spoke for a few minutes, she signed his book hoping he would read it, and once the line was finished, she checked the text messaging on her phone, as was the routine following book signings. In this case, her phone had just lit up, indicating someone had just sent her a text message.

"Hi, Eliza, this is Amber Blythe. I can't believe it; I left my book there. Have you seen it, by chance? I had to rush off to my job and realized I didn't have it, I remembered it all too late. It looks like I might need to meet with you tonight after all. Would you like to meet me at T.O.'s? I'll be there at 6 pm."

Eliza texted back, "It sounds like a plan, thank you for getting back to me. I'll see you at six in the evening at T.O.'s. Oh, and don't worry, I have your book and will bring it with me."

"Oh my, I truly appreciate that. I'm so sorry. Thank you," texted Amber.

"No worries," Eliza texted back, followed by texting a smiley face emoticon.

An Interview

Amber had finished her modeling gig for the day and decided to take a break from the rest of the routine until it was time to go to T.O.'s. She had a couple of hours to spare and was looking forward to meeting with Eliza at the restaurant with no need to rush. At the library, she recalled a sense that the people in the line behind her toward the end of her conversation with Eliza were standing impatiently and frustrated with her. She could practically feel their eyes fixated on her as if to ask her if she could hurry it up, at least that seemed the case at the bookstore.

At the T.O., Amber was always impressed with the clientele that she served on the days that she worked there—their fine dresses, suits and ties, and even their metro-casual flair. But now she would be one of those dressed in other than her waiter's attire—in something similar to her modeling apparel, nice and ready to enjoy a healthy meal with an exquisite friend. Unlike at the bookstore, now, she and Eliza could just relax, maybe eat a scone following the meal, and drink a cup of coffee next door. *"I'm definitely going to need to hit the gym extra hard after this, but hey, we should all take a break and reward ourselves every now and then,"* she thought to herself.

Just as those thoughts passed through Amber's mind, Eliza appeared entering the front door. Amber gleamed, smiled, and waved—motioning her over. Eliza's eyes lit up as if a-glow, reciprocating her enthusiasm, and she smiled back, hurrying with a noble sense of dignity still intact, to sit down with her new friend, Amber, over a cup of nice hot coffee. She wanted to spend every moment with Amber that she could, but she also had somewhere to be in a couple of hours.

"I wish we could stay all night. I love talking with people who care about the things that are important, the way you do, Eliza," said Amber.

"Your sentiment is shared, Amber," said Eliza.

They ordered their coffee, dispensed with the dinner, purchased a couple of scones, and laughed over the fact that they would both be hitting the gym hard later. Eliza talked to her about Pathway LLC and then asked her how much she knew about her company.

"I don't know a whole lot about Pathway LLC, other than it specializes in biotechnology and gerontology. Please explain?"

"This is kind of a private conversation between you and me—not that I'm too concerned people will know what we're talking about, since it is typical for the mind to forget, our ears to mute out, and our eyes to overlook that which the mind deems odd," Eliza said with a calm chuckle. "However, Pathway LLC has a lot more going on behind the scenes, and what you see is designed to find stellar, compassionate, and innovative minds like yours, who can bridge the gap between what we already know and what the public knows, with an environment that uses science to increase the quality of life, its longevity, the clarity of mind, and take us beyond our solar system with promise.

"My company, Pathway LLC, as I am sure you may be aware of now is the origination of all sciences geared toward the advancement and preservation of humanity. Pathway has a governmentally-sanctioned and authorized high-security branch within it that I was asked to start several months ago, after the release and success of my book. It is now already set up to vet, improve upon, and provide security mechanisms and fail-safes for each of the advancements before they are released to the public. Once they are approved for release, we prepare the masses. First, we begin with exposure through movies and television, and then through several online digital entertainment series. We then provide more details of each science university-wide, with availability in research for scientific journalism. Once the FDA publicly provides us with approval to release our new advancements to medical practices, clinics, etc., we prepare to merchandise for public dispersal, and we provide opportunities for increased ingenuity to the masses.

"Since then, after establishing Pathway LLC, I have been recruiting those who have the right kind of personality, personal drive, academic prowess, and initiative to make life a little less tragic. They are the only ones who are 'read-in', because they have demonstrated a desire to give people a fair shake without disease, allow them to live longer, to have optimized thinking capacity with compassion amped up, and to ultimately prepare our human civilization to preserve our solar system and traverse the cosmos without the negative effects of space travel that we, as well as many other scientists and enthusiasts know of today, while learning all that we can about the next issue to resolve.

"There are a lot of sciences involved. The three major areas of study in all of their forms are biology, or biotechnology, neuroscience, and physics—quantum, mechanical, or all things related to it.

"When we talked earlier, you impressed me. You expressed a unique interest in biogenetics, and I would very much like to enlist your support toward our biotechnology team, and I assure you we will have numerous opportunities to publicize our advancements as time goes by.

"As far as taking care of bills, getting by, etc. we have quite an array of living quarters for those who are fully read-in. Traveling back and forth to your day-to-day activities can be rather quick. We would like to offer to pay you more than necessary to finish your educational aspirations, since we do not desire in the least to get in the way of organic educational pursuits, but you can also have the ease of knowing you will be able to have unfettered access to the most advanced university, laboratories, and tech equipment on the face of the planet or throughout the solar system, if that is your desire.

"Anything we need, I have ensured we have provisions for. We have invested and reinvested in advancements the rest of the world is not yet ready for, yet nevertheless, we can provide the necessary funding to anyone who needs and asks for it. Our Pathway LLC developments and our federal branch improvements may just change the way humanity is, how life is, and you, my dear, are precisely who I am looking for to be part of our team. Our meeting was no pretense in any way, shape, or form. I truly feel a kindred connection with you. I also believe that together we will make a whole lot of wonderful things happen. Would you like to be a part of our team?"

Amber felt the magnetism in the air between herself and Eliza never dissipate, rather instead it seemed to increase and writhe within. "I am with you whole-heartedly. You've piqued my interest. I would love to learn more. I also wouldn't mind being a part of your team. When would you like me to get started? Where do we begin?"

Eliza saw the honesty and enthusiasm in Amber's character and knew that she was exactly who she was looking for, to be a team member of Pathway with her, Yesha, and James.

"Now, is as good a time as any," responded Eliza. "Since we have so much to do.

"Please, feel free to go to your various jobs and give them an appropriate heads-up—perhaps a two-week notice, they will soon understand. I don't want you to burn any bridges per say, rather I would prefer you continue on with your employers, as you desire of course, to provide you an avenue to promote positivity in technology and science, kind of like working undercover, only things will change in your favour fairly soon. However, please let them know that your schedule has changed for the foreseeable future. While you may 'work for them,' they work for you, and I have the ability to see to that, if you wish. We can give you enough financial backing to ensure you can start your LLC, buy the T.O., and purchase the modeling firms. So, let them know that you would like to stay on, but with fewer hours as your schedule clears up. You will eventually purchase their companies and direct them as you see fit. When the time is right, you let us know, and the transactions will be made.

"I know you will use your charm and they'll integrate you into their schedule right away. Here, please take this cell phone, it has been specially programmed for you. It uses your current phone number and we will be able to communicate with each other a little more securely. This is encrypted and cannot be hacked since it is only activated and accessible via the frequency and vibration of your thoughts, which are entirely unique to you."

Amber took the phone, which looked like the newest and latest trend, the Samsung Focus model, she swiped it on, every app was set up, they operated like a nicely greased wheel, and then she saw the contacts list with several names she recognized. She saw each of the paired Google Maps icons, clicked on one, and one of the locations Eliza had identified showed up in purple with instructions from her normal routine to concealed weigh stations within the area to Eliza's estate for a transit point to the Pathway LLC laboratories, on the campus, in Melrose, Massachusetts.

They bid each other adieu for now and waived to each other as they left T.O.'s, with a smile.

Good to See You

The first stop was at Eliza's house, where she met a lady who introduced herself as Yesha's mom, Yesenia, a very lovely lady, who looked like she was in her mid-thirties, who prepared and drank a tea with her, talked with her for a few minutes, and then showed her to the elevator. Before bidding her farewell, she told Amber, "I may look like I am in my thirties, but I was born in 1940. That means I will be turning seventy soon. Enjoy your ride!"

Amber thought on that one as she rode the elevator, *"Wow, now I am intrigued. My guess is that is one of many cards up Eliza's sleeves."* She then alerted herself to the length of the elevator ride, which took her down to a depth in the Earth she could only guess was more profound than any depth any coal miners or publicly understood and used mining capabilities had ever gone, presumably, to where the weigh station for the hyperloop was located. What better way to hide and conceal a weigh station, than several miles below Earth's surface, especially one such as this, than via a typical elevator within the pleasant charm of an estate home?

Once the elevator stopped, with her physiology adapting to the subtle changes in air pressure along the way, she stepped out, felt an adaptable change to normal air pressure, and then saw the beautiful hyperloop vehicle, long, white, and glowing. The place around it glowed as well, and the vehicle's doors opened as if waiting just for her. From there, the hyperloop from Eliza's place, well, underneath it, took her quickly from Cambridge to Melrose. It took her less than a minute to arrive, the travel was smooth, and when she arrived, she was dazzled so much more than she was floored. The Melrose Campus was unlike anything she had ever seen before.

Everything she saw was from the inside looking out, but through the transparent and crystalline glass perimeter walls with futuristic and gleaming-white infrastructure that blended into the glass near the hyperloop terminals, she could see a large, thick, and beautiful forest. She never thought she'd ever see a forest filled with flower trees, but there it was. As she looked up, she could see the sky and when she looked toward the base of the trees, she noticed a beautiful landscape with statuettes, pathways, flowers, spices, morels, vegetation of every sort, benches, and wildlife.

The wildlife there was unlike anything she'd seen anywhere. Other than in a Disney movie, she had never seen anything remotely close to this. Within the forest were raccoons, bears, mountain lions, squirrels, zebras, elephants, dogs, cats, mice, eagles, and all manner of other kinds of avian and wildlife relaxing. They were sitting down on a variety of differently sized benches reading from handheld digital displays! It appeared as if they were nodding at each other from time to time, and as if they were engaging in some unspoken conversation back and forth. This place was a paradise! As she happily took it all in, she gazed around some more at the internal features.

As she looked at the beautiful white glow of the visitors' entry center, she saw not so much a line of immigrants, but several groupings of them standing next to a soothing waterfall of what appeared to be wine. As she looked more closely, she saw what appeared to be various families, and each was accompanied by their own representative—a nicely uniformed staff member. All the staff members seemed very pleasant, very attractive, very professional, clean-cut, kind, and even helpful. After focusing a little longer, she noticed the representatives could speak fluently in the language of the family or individual they were escorting.

"Amber, so good to see you! How are you? How was the ride?" she heard Eliza's gleeful voice, and as if she couldn't be any more at ease, she was, and she turned around. There was Eliza, as beautiful as she was the first day, she saw her. Right next to her was another young very attractive lady, who seemed very charming and quite captivating as well.

"Wow, Eliza! I'm amazed! I'd thought I'd seen it all, but this is better and even more vivid than I've ever seen in any movie!" Amber looked at the young lady next to Eliza and recognized her from her jogs around Cambridge and introduced herself. "Hi, my name is Amber, I think I've seen you before. You waved and smiled," she said, reaching out for a handshake.

The nice young lady put out her hand and Amber and Eliza's friend reciprocated salutations as she introduced herself, "Hi, Amber. Yes, that was me. I too enjoy jogging around the town. I am pleased to finally meet you, at least in more than passing. My name is Yesha."

"Yesha and I have known each other for quite a long time. Well, since I was born. She is practically my sister, but we're close friends. It is with her and a gentleman named James, his crew, and an ever-growing team of scientists and volunteers that we developed all that you see here and so much more. Everyone has been compensated quite well, I assure you. We'll introduce you to James soon," said Eliza. "We hope you aren't too overwhelmed?"

"By all means, I am impressed and overwhelmed, but in a good way," smiled Amber, trying not to shake in excitement. If ever there were a fantasy come true, this would be it.

"Once the introductions are made and each part of the training is done, we will hand you over to James for a while. He will show you the routine, the 'where' and the 'how' of everything, and then you'll be given your first mission. However, please feel free to ask any question from anyone at any time and roam around as you please."

Amber, rather than roam around, decided to stay with Eliza and Yesha since she felt quite nervous. Together, all three moved past the glowing white visitor's center and down through an equally glowing hallway, with occasional windows that showed the beauty of the forest. "Are those animals...? I'm afraid to ask," Amber stopped.

"It's okay," said Yesha, chuckling. "Eliza and I decided to upgrade the old ecosystem and create a new one. Those animals can communicate telepathically. They are completely domesticated, are sentient, and they all prefer to work as muses and psychologists for the populous here at the campuses when it comes to their personally elected contribution to the advancement of civilization, rather than as anything else. If it looks like they are nodding to each other, it is likely they are combing each other's minds over some of the questions the visitors have had and whom they have provided counseling too. Once you are fully read-in, you can channel them neurologically and listen to their conversations. You might even find one or two who would like to hang out with you on a regular basis. Instead of us choosing them to be our pets, it is very mutual in that they choose you just as much as you choose them, based on contrasting yet beneficial neurological algorithms shared between you and the animals and birds. They are actually good at what they do, and they are actually very social."

Amber seemed titillated, full of questions, and quite excited about everything she saw but tried to play it down, so no one would notice, but Yesha could tell she was brewing up another question.

"As far as food is concerned, which I am sure you were going to ask, they are fed the ideal nutrients and they love it so much, the predators and the prey actually enjoy each other's company, and the predators are actually quite apologetic to the prey for all of their kindred they've eaten." Yesha smiled, grimaced, and then smiled again as they continued down the hallway within earshot.

"Okay. That is innovative. I remember reading your book, Eliza, where you suggested preservation of life, but you never suggested something this amazing. No more predation? I am on the verge of worshiping you right now, and now it's coming to me with much more clarity. You truly meant it. No more hunter versus victim, no more predator versus prey?" asked Amber.

"Yes, and don't worry. Some of these sciences are very advanced, and you'll understand why shortly. Now that we have figured out how to cause cells to communicate, we have decided to train them to adjust each animal's genes just enough in order to rewire a little of their genetic makeup, so they don't lose their identity, but they still have an outstandingly new neurological framework. We've also optimized their physiology, given them more compassion and a neural link, and now the animals see each other as friends. The prey has forgiven the predator and now they merely want to help humanity to preserve life for the long-haul." Eliza explained. "You can't see them from here, but even the insects of every sort are sentient and participate helpfully in one way or another of their own volition. It's interesting watching spiders and flies play miniature soccer with each other while cracking jokes."

As they turned a corner and stopped short of a large white donut-shaped object about ten feet or three meters tall, with a variety of shades of blues, navies, purples, and blacks that adorned its features as accented trim, sensors, and buttons, Amber beheld what appeared to be gateways from a science fiction film. "We're going to take you to your quarters first, so you can catch some fresh air, and then we'll begin your training. If you are okay going through one of these?"

Amber smiled, and nodded toward Yesha, "What are they? And, I suppose my answer at this point would be a resounding and obvious yes," and then she asked, "How do they work?"

Eliza chuckled, to put her at ease, "Quite simple really, you walk in on one side and you come out of it on the other side to whichever location we have preprogrammed in advance, and no worries, these ones are pretty much set to only a few of many locations. The system considers everything that is within a spherical region and transfers anything within that spherical region to the grid-based location identified. Each region, we can go to, also has a jump gate, so we can return as needed," Yesha explained, just before walking through it and disappearing.

She then looked toward Eliza, who smiled back at her and while waving her hand toward the jump gate gently told her, "I'll follow you. When we get there, and then you receive your training, you'll understand all of this and your ability to control them more clearly." said Eliza.

Amber stepped through, and like that, she felt a bit nauseous and found herself in another room, with the jump gate, exactly like it, toward her back. This room was just as white and glowed just like the visitor's center, but here it seemed to be more like a home. "This is your home. Going through the jump gates, we have been able to give your mind and the data transceivers your very own neurological identification. What do you think of the rooms, bathrooms, kitchen, and social room?" Asked Yesha.

"It's beautiful. What is this? A penthouse suite?" Asked Amber.

"In a way, yes." Replied Eliza. "Think of it as your home. If you'd like, we can activate jump gates in your jump room, so that only you and those you wish at any point in time can have access to and from here, and you will be able to instantly travel to your current apartment in Cambridge and back. As time goes by, and once you have received introductory training, become physiologically and neurologically optimized by climbing into something we call a biopod, and have been fully read-in by having received the subsequent training in the Virtual Universe, you will receive access to more locations, such as labs, tech cities, and other terminals, which will be granted to you, with a quick update. And, there is much more."

Amber walked through her new campus home and was impressed with the ergonomic and pleasant nature of every bit of each space. "What are those?" Amber asked after she had seen her kitchen, social room, bedrooms, bathrooms, had walked down the hallway to what appeared to be a dead end, with a series of doors opening, into a room filled with what resembled white and glowing tanning beds.

"Those are not tanning booths," chuckled Yesha, as if she could read her mind. "Those are what Eliza was talking about, those are biopods. Don't worry, Amber, we will learn about them soon. So, for now, let's go get your introductory training."

Once they walked through another one of those ten-foot diameter donuts, she noticed a theater-seating arrangement and then saw Yesha waiving her hand to gesture her over to her.

Yesha stood up for her to let her by and motioned for her to sit down facing a pulpit; Amber sat down to the right of Yesha and noticed that Eliza was sitting to her right. They chatted for a few moments, the lights dimmed, and they began to watch a three-dimensional holographic movie. The movie took Amber and the other accompanied visitors and immigrants through Eliza's and Yesha's history, through to their instruction at Harvard, and then through some of the details of the development of Pathway LLC. From there, the movie took them through a process that would be required to become a fully read-in citizen of Pathway.

The narrator, along with the amazing visual descriptions, explained in detail what it meant to become fully read-in. The movie took them through a three-dimensional image of the large hadron colliders, the cold-fusion thermonuclear reactors, the bio-labs, the physics labs, the neurological optimization labs, the space elevator, and so much more.

"We have a couple of options that will be new for many here when it comes to something called a smart suit, the clothes that you are wearing will be transformed into a smart suit once you enter your biopod. With this attire, you will be able to use a neural identification, which you will receive as you are optimized both physiologically and neurologically, to essentially choose any wardrobe you would like, from an array lying within a compartmentalized area of your mind, and don it for wear, instantaneously. This will provide you hygiene, exercise, and even convert unwanted hair follicles to energy to give you an added boost through each day. We can also hand out a basic smart suit that you can change into the restrooms located on both sides of the room."

Before coming to a close, the narrator of the movie gave everyone a series of options for the next step of their training. Their primary choices would be to either become fully read-in, with a series of missions, journeys, breaks, and sabbaticals, or to stay on Earth but to agree to confidentiality, as well as a temporary and partial mind wipe, until these advancements could become public, with explicit assurances that they would not permanently lose those memories. Their memories would be stored safely and then returned once all of these advancements went global. They had another option for transfer to any one of twenty-thousand tech cities of their choosing where they would have complete access to anything needed within them, including a personal or family domicile. Of course, each person's or families' private domain would be theirs to call their own, but all of this was contingent upon abiding what was called the Principles of Universal Ethics and by obeying Universal Laws. Education, employment, and good will were very much promoted. Violations of ethical behavior would result in virtual correction, which would not harm the individual, rather it would send an individual into a Virtual Universe with simulated trainers, individuals, and populations all designed to give them the ideal set of experiences necessary to increase clarity on how to contribute to the advancement of civilization, using kindness and compassion, respecting personal consent, and appreciating the efforts of others.

For any immigrant who preferred to take the pathway to citizenship, they would be taught English, US History, and then enrolled into a series of courses that would provide them a high-quality education and certification to qualify as US citizens to work in public to help humanity advance in one way or another. They would return every few months for additional training.

For those who wished to be fully read-in, they would be escorted to their living quarters, and then a room full of biopods, which looked similar to white and glowing tanning beds, but were much more comfortable and plush, where they would interface with the Virtual Universe to receive further training—the details of which would not be discussed during this brief. After their training, they would become Pathway LLC citizens as well as scientists, field engineers, or even field operatives, with field-specific missions on Earth or anywhere within the solar system.

Finally, for those who wished to only be partially read-in and live in a tech city as a Pathway LLC citizen, they would be shown the various sanctuaries, able to choose which one they preferred, and then be transferred via the jump gate to that city, wherein they would be trained further and contribute to the specific missions of their location, the moon, planet, or spheroid they lived on.

It was obvious that a majority of people preferred to become fully read-in, but a few people opted to have partial read-ins followed by an opportunity to live on another planet within the solar system. There was one family that chose to stay on Earth, who agreed to the temporary and partial mind wipe, swore to confidentiality with regard to the technologies of Pathway LLC, to learn English, and to follow the pathway of becoming a US citizen, and once that was done, they would assimilate productively into society, and visit every few months or so for training.

Amber, chose to be fully read-in. "What happens to those whose minds are wiped? Is that even ethical? Why do that?" she asked Eliza.

"I'll answer that for you since I see Yesha looking at me, and the reason is mine to describe," explained Eliza. "We have no desire to engage in entrapment, which this very much seems like, yet we also had to figure out a way to create safety and security mechanisms to prevent some of these technologies from getting into the hands of those that would unleash some of the worst into society. The only memories they will temporarily lose are those directly relating to the details of our technologies and advancements that aren't yet ready for release to the public. Essentially, unless read-in or optimized, they will not be able to see our advancements in space or on Earth, nor will they recall the technologies used for the advancements. However, they will not lose any personal memories, such as relationships that are established, or the sense of trust built between them and other members of Pathway. Furthermore, they will have a quickening of all of their memories, once everything has gone public during my 'great reveal,' down the road. Everything that we have worked on, developed, created, and expanded upon is amazing and intended to help humanity, and all will be revealed when the time is right.

"These advancements are intended to help people to have clarity on what it is that can be done to preserve the heritage, the legacy, the romances, the history, the art, and the sciences that have made humanity such a wonderful part of the history of the universe itself. With the laws of chaos, the laws of entropy, and the laws of thermodynamics, we understand that technology can go one of many ways, two of which are most prominent: either all of humanity can stay its current course and become completely destroyed by its own negligence or overt intentions of destruction, or humanity can be shown beauty in science, the beauty in kindness, the amazing sense of compassion, and through that we can harness chaos, control it, and ensure that it leads us toward the discovery of how to reign in the chaos that could decimate our Universe.

"We can very well be around for a long, long time, and it is worth it to have every unique, brilliant, and special soul with us along the way. There is no sane reason for death, for carnage, or for misery other than to test our grace. Instead of wars and unforeseen challenges, we can reach the same growth through unchartered innovations and dare to understand our Universe and the laws that bind it. We can preserve it, beautify it, and make it even stronger. While traveling from one end to the next, we can still have the ability to meet with each other, sharing stories with each other, and even taking each other to the many amazing places we will have inevitably found by then on our journeys.

"Wouldn't it be nice to have family and friends around when we return from planets within galaxies more than one-hundred-billion light-years away? We're all interested in and care about making that possible. However, people are free to go their own way. We simply must strive to provide clarity and health, while protecting our technologies from those that would use them to destroy others. That is what physiological and neurological optimization is all about, life and enlightenment. To preserve life is the ultimate equation for ethics. To take it away or to let our minds squander away through negligence, is the enemy of life, freedom, and even joy, and thereby maliciously unethical. Ethics and death do not belong together."

Eliza could see Amber's intrigue, so she paused.

Amber thought about what Eliza had said, and it appeared that Eliza gave her pause to explain her understanding of what she had said. "So, everything that we are doing and everything that you have done represents or embodies ethics. That makes sense. Preserving life, all of life, is where ethics resides. Causing undue strife is what leads to or creates misery, suffering, and ultimately the chaos that will allow our Universe to fade away.

"If we destroy our world, and with it, our humanity, all of our history would be mute. Everything that everyone has ever done would become pointless from a standpoint of looking at things realistically from future or distant civilizations. Lost would be everything beautiful that all the wonderful people throughout our history has ever done or accomplished. Therefore, to preserve life, to preserve the history and the legacy of humankind and all our friends, and to merely begin with kindness, we will each be involved in specific tasks and missions leading to the preservation of our Universe. That is why we have to protect all of this from those who would seek to bring the demise of humanity. Negligence, giving up on life, or fighting against advancement will cause humanity and Earth itself to fail. It is not our duty to hasten death and glory in destruction, rather preserve life and beautify it throughout our universe, all the while finding ways to overcome its expansion to a big freeze of all of life and history."

"Precisely," said Eliza. "Also, please keep in mind that we have created a partition of the Virtual Universe to allow people to work out the wiggles. In the Entertainment Matrix, people will be able to go to different worlds and create or even join in on stories to live out, create or join in on games of all varieties with environmental and person versus person situations and missions. In those games or entertainment venues, people will find that their imagination is the limit. Before leaving, memories will be stored in an encoded and compartmentalized section of their own brain and backed up in our databases with the privacy of their neural identification. Each artificial memory will have a unique mental flavor that will indicate clearly the experiences had been through a specific entertainment matrix venue, their physiology and neurology will be optimized, and they will return to the real world, refreshed and revitalized, and filled again with compassion and empathy. There is so much more, but what do you think about this thus far?"

"Wow that idea is quite sound, and the Entertainment Matrix sounds quite fun! I'm with you both, Eliza and Yesha, and I truly appreciate what you are doing," said Amber.

Amber followed Eliza and Yesha to the next room filled with the biopods, and Eliza continued. "We created these biopods to provide physical protection and sensory response to the Virtual Universe activity experienced while at the same time our bodies are physiologically and neurologically optimized or fine-tuned. During that process, we will each neurologically integrate with the digital world as we interface with the Twelve Database Moons, which can provide a visceral experience with everything around the Earth and everything else throughout our observable Universe, all within in close range and with high clarity. Anywhere these satellites can detect, we can go, and anything these satellites can see, explore, sense, study, and even enjoy, we can as well. While here, you will learn more quickly. Five minutes in the real world could equate to twenty minutes, or a few seconds, or even a few centuries or more in the Virtual Universe.

"This is a place for education, for entertainment, for experience, and even for correction; although, if someone was sent here for correctional purposes, they would no longer be linked to anyone else directly. This is designed to prevent scheming while promoting coaching, learning, and continued clarity toward contribution in the advancement of civilization."

After Amber was satisfied with the questions had, she followed Eliza and Yesha to the group biopod room, and the biopod they had assigned to her. It had her name on it, so there was no confusion. It happened to be right next to Yesha's and Eliza's biopods.

Euphoric Training

Eliza, Yesha, and Amber climbed into their assigned biopods. The rest of those who had accompanied them in training, who, with their delegates, consisted of one-hundred people, many of whom had immigrated to escape violence and brutality, all jumped into their assigned biopods. As they did, Eliza and Yesha taught everyone to mentally think, "Link, 1, 2, 3, 5 Minutes, 20 Years." They practiced, and then followed Eliza's lead, when it was time to issue the command. Like that, in unison, everyone did so, and each person felt a twinge, then they felt as though every cell in their bodies was resisting, until euphoria set in. Suddenly, one-hundred-three people were gathered around a pond with a statue of an angel overlooking it. Everyone who had ever been to and visited Eliza's estate home recognized where they were. Suddenly, they connected with each other for the first time with crystal clear clarity, appreciated each other for who they were, and everyone spoke and understood the same language as if it were their own.

"We're in a digital representation of my backyard at my home, Amber. Now that we have all melded minds, everyone else will have their own journeys, to a degree, with their assigned delegates, but at a certain point, their shared experience will become their own, and they will then be on their own journeys, with their delegates, of course. At any time, others' journeys can be ours as well. They'll mostly follow us but cluster with their delegates. Yesha and I are your assigned delegates, to allow for ease of the journey and optimal training. Please, follow me," said Eliza.

Yesha, who was not too far behind, waived her hands and pointed toward Eliza. Everyone then followed Eliza as she took them through several portals, she identified as matrix entry points, where they witnessed small portions of the histories of civilization, their brutality, the heroic efforts of the few to change things that were considered by far too many others as "part of life," yet were obviously a form of injustice, and quite a few epochs of peace and prosperity. Everyone learned similarly that people throughout history allowed horrible things to happen to others, and in doing so, or in settling for things because that was the way things were, they settled for a mediocre reality and were complicit until other generations arose and took their place, making the changes desired by the few, eventually possible.

In many other cases, within these many matrices, they witnessed with sorrow as benevolent societies were destroyed by more cantankerous ones, because they became weak and oblivious to the cruel intentions of malevolent minds, and thus were destroyed by those with no vision but of violence, gore, power, jealousy, pretentiousness, and greed. They also learned that for this reason physiological optimizations accentuated their strength, their agility, their ability to defend themselves, and at the same time the neurological optimizations integrated with them and increased their compassion for others, their empathy, their wisdom, and their ability to communicate clearly and persuasively with one another, their respect for person consent, and our passion toward innovation that would increase the quality of life and the well-being of the entirety of humanity.

Eliza then led them through the twenty-thousand tech cities, showed them the Twelve Database Moons, and the infrastructure on Earth that made it all possible. She showed them the shields protecting every planet and the sphere protecting and regenerating the solar system's star itself. The Sun would last indefinitely, so long as humanity continued to maintain or upgrade the technology. She showed them each of the asteroids, where it had been captured, their biopsies, the history learned, and which cities each asteroid helped to create. Finally, she had them all follow her to some of the most beautiful places on Earth itself, and then she paused and spoke again.

"This is what we should always strive to preserve. Our home world. No matter where we go, no matter what we become or what we develop, we still need to protect our home world from anyone or anything that would seek to destroy the life within it.

"This is the place where, bereft of further evidence, we began, and no matter where we go, where colonies will form throughout the rest of the universe, we will teach and remind the new generations that life began here on Earth, and that they arrived at where they are due to compassion, kindness, and ingenuity.

"We need to always take care of each other, appreciate each other, and celebrate our differences rather than tear each other apart because of them. There is so much to enjoy and appreciate, and we will have so many opportunities along the way to do so. We have a lot of promise and a legacy to preserve, so let's do that. Together.

"Keep in mind, that there are many things that we will be doing together, all of us. However, there are a myriad of other things that we must do alone, struggles we must bear, sacrifices we each must make, and clarity on unique things that we each will have of our own accord. While this is so, each time we connect, those experiences can become a shared experience, if you will it to be so. In this way, all may traverse your paths, feel what you have felt, and see what you have seen. This, my friends, each one of you, is what gives us that sense of shared well-being and collective wisdom, while still maintaining a provision for individuality and the beauty of its uniqueness. It is through our uniqueness that we can overcome some of the greatest challenges we'll ever face, and it is through our collective wisdom that we can overcome these challenges with more fierceness and ability to see through all that we face with success.

"At this time, we will go with our various delegates and you will each experience what is needed to help you individually to see, feel, and understand your true potential, so that you can benefit from the collective wisdom shared with our links, and become the best you can be."

When Eliza finished, the various groups went their way, since they knew although they would traverse through their own journeys for a time, they would soon be together again, with the ability to go further than before.

Discoveries

Vesha Celeste felt a ripple go through her, as if something were signaling a greater quantity of changes, between who she was observing, experiencing, and being. Sky, for a small moment, waved at her and smiled as if to say, *"All will be okay. What you'll learn will apply in so many civilizations throughout the Cosmos."*

Yesha looked toward her as well, and spoke to her mind, *"Sky is correct. You are about to experience a unique array of life-moments, through someone else, and in this case, Amber Blythe. While you have been going through her special moments, Amber's unique experience is something that will apply to you in so many ways, no matter where you go. Please listen, observe, and let yourself go, a while longer. I promise, there will be beauty in every turn, no matter the burden to bear."*

Vesha then began to release herself again and drifted into the mind of Amber for a while longer.

A Unique Experience

As Amber looked around, she noticed as each of the families and their delegates disappeared group by group, and then she passed through untold lives, making their vast well of wisdom her own. Finally, she looked around, and discovered a reality that seemed to impress her more than any of the others she had seen. She was in one of the most interesting virtual representations of a tech city she had ever beheld before. *"Where is this?"* Amber asked, as she saw Yesha standing not too far away looking toward her, with Eliza standing nearby.

"This is Io, Amber. This is the last place I was, before I let Eliza know about you. Yes, we met while on our jogging routines, but I saw something special in you, and now Eliza has too. Please let me share with you some experiences that didn't so much have to do with finding you but had everything to do with the string of events that led us to where we are now. It will help you to gain your own understanding of your fulness of potential.

"It was less than a week ago, to be precise, when I was in a distant little city, not too far from another even more remote village within the far east portion of what is known on Earth as the Middle East. No matter where we go, there will be people that are affected uniquely due to the environments they are raised in, yet somehow, despite all of their influences, they become someone who transcends all, and becomes the amazing person that can save lives untold, benefit the well-being of so many more, and lead those closest to them, to an even better day.

"After meeting a young man there and rescuing him, I shared these ideas with him when he asked why it was that we rescued him from his imminent execution."

Yesha paused. As she did, she could see Amber's empathy well up and she knew that her curiosity about these events had peaked, since it was beginning to formulate questions that appeared as abstract paintings emanating from her mind. Then as Amber looked around, she could see a desert with sand in all directions, taking her away from the magnificent beauty of Io, with its view of Jupiter, replaced with a distant view of the arid mountains off to the distance that were taller than any she had ever beheld. She then saw a grouping of camels carrying people and what must have been all of their belongings from one apparent location to another.

As this scenario unfolded, she found her mind drift into another location, or what appeared to be a small home, or a living room, with a kitchen, a small bathroom, and several rooms. One of the doors was open, and to her surprise, there was a jump gate, just like the ones she had seen at the Melrose Campus.

She then saw Yesha. This Yesha was not aware of Amber at this point, since she looked to her right, and she saw her delegate, Yesha standing beside her and pointing toward the other Yesha and the young man. This Yesha, which was her, but a few weeks ago, stood in the traditional clothing common in that region of the world, beside two young ladies and a young man, who must have been from that region as well. They were attentive to every word that Yesha had to share with them, especially since it became clear to Amber, all of a sudden, that this young man, who must have been eighteen, had asked her why it was that they chose to rescue him and why it was that he was considered worthy of their attention.

Yesha answered.

"In many occasions those who you love, those who you know, and those who are closest to you, and many times those who are distant who know nothing about you, unfortunately peg you as a certain character or create a caricature of you that does not represent the true you that exists inside. When they do this, to keep their view of stability through you a permanent staple in their lives, they don't realize that they are complicit in pinning your wings down and tearing away at your freedoms to express yourself the way you truly wish to express yourself. They say a person is never a prophet in their own hometown, and that is only marginally true, since the same is true of those you work with, network with, and associate with, who do not allow you to flourish as the amazing individual you are.

"No matter your outside environment, networks, or influences, if you understand this, then you know that you no longer need to slow down from being the wonderful person you can be. Be the person who is kind, and not because it may be the popular way to be, but because our innovation naturally thrives in a kind environment that is permissive toward creativity and originality. Set your own values and virtues, no matter your faith. Values, ethics, and morals can be universal, in that, so long as others respect our lives and our personal choices, we too can respect theirs."

Amber then saw as Yesha met a young lady in far east Europe, trained her, read her in, and sent her to James. This young lady was someone who had met two other young ladies who had traveled with their families two weeks prior to that same location where they met and talked with her over a delicious European cuisine. They had returned to their home in the desert a week later, and that was when Yesha had arrived.

Yesha discovered through these two young ladies about this one young man with a special spirit, who wished harm on no one, but who had been imprisoned.

This young man was someone who had grown up around a family who had perpetuated traditions that led to mediocrity and even brutality within his own life.

He had seen a lot in his less than two decades of life, but another young lady had noticed how careful he was to not look like he had a sense of compassion toward the women he associated with, so as not to get caught by those who despised and brutalized the women they knew.

One night, while engaging in conversation, in what seemed a private setting, with his younger brother and these two young ladies, something stark occurred and in no part because of anything that he had done. He was respectful to them, and had only been talking to them about science, the stars, the galaxies, and the vastness of our Universe. His brother, who seemed his best friend, had instead told his father about what he was doing.

His father had very strong views from that archaic element in society that was pervasive and brutal to women about what it was that women should or should not know.

These views began to enter Amber's mind and permeate her environment, as if clouds of anger and hatred were brewing around her. As her gaze drifted, she saw the unfortunate young man, who had been sold out by his younger brother, being beaten and yelled at by his father, and she heard the words spoken to him. Even she, despite all of her new optimizations, began to seethe with anger. Out of nowhere, the nanos of her body seemed to kick in and to intensify her resolve. It became clear to her that due to generations of religious extremism and cold hard tradition, diverging views were dealt with swiftness and a sense of humanity had not been taught for decades.

Still, Amber bore through this experience, and for a moment, she thought of her dear, darling, and sweet young sister, before listening on.

Finally, the saddening and harsh memories shared within this experience provided by the Virtual Universe dissipated and faded away. Emerging into her view, seemed to be the point in time, just ten minutes before, as the young man left the home of these beautiful young ladies. Together, they had shared happy ideas and innocent moments, and had to have been twenty years old. All three had been in good spirits and happy about knowing these intriguing facts about their place in the Universe, and were unaware, yet, of what would unfold.

This young man's own father, upon his arrival at his home, preached, yelled, insulted, beat, insulted some more, and then sequestered him within his room, with no means of escape. Before leaving the room and locking the door, his father told him that he was going talk to the local leader, and that he had no choice, but that it was a higher law that suggested that examples must be made.

The thoughts tormenting the young man gave clarity to Amber that he knew what this example would be. He was going to be executed for crimes against the faith of his family. His family felt that they needed to do this, in order to cleanse the shame, he had caused them.

Amber then witnessed as his father walked away and reheard the shouted words his father had yelled at him while beating him; it was barrage of words telling his son that he was going to the local leader to have his son dealt with, once and for all. It was to show what would happen to anyone else in his family who did not obey or did not believe as his father did.

The local leader would make an example of the father's own son, for daring to be kind and courteous to women. This young man had been gentle and respectful to others, who breathed, had hopes, dreams, and fears. He would be executed for engaging in intellectual yet humble and meaningful conversation with these two women.

Amber then beheld, as if she were an unseen spirit, who was there, but not there, just peering as if her eyes were those of the two young ladies, how they had escaped. They had heard about this strange woman, named Yesha. If they hadn't left when they had, and had Yesha not been there when she was, they would not have been rescued, they would have instead been stoned for having had a "bad influence" on their son.

If things were to be the norm, examples set, and the rules established, sentences would have been carried out, and executions delivered, within two weeks. The two young women would have been stoned to death, and this young man would have become beheaded, as was the tradition of the local leader.

As Amber's experience drifted, she saw how it was that from the local leader's purview, he had to appear to be reasonable. It was as if he were giving the offender a chance to come clean, to be absolved of his sins, and then released to their god for judgment in the afterlife.

Amber then, with all of the strength that she could muster, summoned a pause in what she was witnessing and turned to her right, with the Yesha she came into the Virtual Universe with, and began to cry.

"Yesha, why? Why would he do this? How is it that I know what this other individual was thinking?"

Yesha hugged her to calm her down. *"This is a tough part of our learning experiences, but we have to learn, so that we can overcome these types of issues before we travel to distant planets outside our Solar System. We don't want to bring terror and havoc with us wherever we go. If we do, we won't survive long enough to share a worthy legacy with other distant civilizations, because we will have destroyed ourselves instead.*

"Watch, Amber. Not everything that we see is glorious and beautiful, but here you will learn what you need to about what comes from missions that are intended to heal, rather than to harm. Please watch."

The scene shifted to the young man.

Fortunate for him, Yesha had received these two young ladies, who begged for her to help him, in time. The situation was dire enough that they too asked for help. Word that Yesha, who was a strange westerner, had been nearby began to spread among the young women in town. They knew their lot in life was drab at best, forced into slavery at the behest of their fathers, and forced yet again to marry men many times their age, and despite the indignity or their efforts, all was done with little care for their health or well-being, beyond "the honor" of having many sons, and no more. Knowing they could go to her for safety, they did just that and had it in their hearts to plead for this young man as well. When asked how they knew this, they told Yesha that his younger brother came back and bragged about getting his brother in trouble. He told them that his father would have them executed too.

Furthermore, it was obvious what would happen. This same thing had happened to his older brother and mother not too many years before. After listening to them, Yesha comforted them, letting them know that she wished she could have prevented these unjust events. They told her that it happened several years ago and missed them.

Even though the young man had been taught well by his loving mother, who he now missed dearly, his younger brother had been brainwashed since childhood and had been the main reason for the events that occurred marring the family for a long, long time. After a few years in school, it appeared that he had begun to try to win favor from his father, and in his own quest for survival, he spied on his siblings and his mother. This young man, barely in his teens, prided himself on how good he had become at being faithful to his father and keeping him apprised of any iniquities in the household. He was so proud of his supposed nobility and cunning, that neither his now deceased mother nor brother, even knew of their fate, before it was too late. To them, he seemed to be a nice boy. While it had been too late for them, it wasn't too late for the young man that now seemed to appear before Amber, in her seemingly ghostly state, laying as a pile of beaten bones, sobbing on the ground below.

As this visual scope of this scene drifted from that small room to Yesha's temporary abode just a few miles away, Amber saw as the two young ladies arrived at her quarters, pleaded their case, and then sat in safety on her couch sipping sweetened Kombucha tea she had prepared for them. After a few moments of conversation, Yesha convinced them that if they were to come with her, they would be safe from harm for the long-haul.

In a sincere overture of gratitude, Yesha thanked them for letting her know about this young man. Knowing that he had just two weeks, she wasn't about to tempt fate, but decided to train the two young ladies first. Together, they could do so much more, especially if all three were optimized. Amber watched as they walked into one of her rooms, and she followed closely behind, even though they never knew she was there or watching, since at that point in time, she had never been there. When Amber investigated the hidden room, as it opened, seemingly by Yesha's mental command, there it was, a glorious and magnificent jump gate!

In moments, they followed Yesha and arrived at the Melrose Campus in Massachusetts. In her own way, Yesha had been wise and fearless, had set things up in her temporary and humble domicile in the Middle East, and used clouds of nanos to protect that home from any form of invasion. She also wanted to help these two young ladies, who she had seen in the minds of the young woman she had rescued in Eastern Europe, to become optimized before going to rescue the young man, because she knew the results would be much better if she did.

After the training, these two young ladies agreed with Yesha's idea for training and became completely read-in with further training in the Virtual Universe.

After their assignments were given and they had trained some more, it had taken less than a day for them to become citizens of Pathway and fully elected delegates of the UP. While they spent that day familiarizing themselves within their new suites on Io, where Amber's journey with her delegate, Yesha, had begun, the Yesha in this scenario had come up with a plan to rescue the young man. While Yesha had been on Earth, James had been working with these two young ladies to help them to get settled in, trained, and familiarized with Io before sending them back to Yesha to proceed with their rescue.

These two young ladies knew that this rescue was very important, but they also knew that it was important to internalize and process all that they had beheld and learned. They would be more effective in the rescue, if they did. They also knew that it was important to learn about the location they had settled in, so that they would have peace of mind, as they were to leave it behind.

There they were, on Io. This was one of Jupiter's many moons, and the fourth largest satellite within the Solar System! With a rich array of yellows, golds, oranges, and greens, along with volcanic activity that lent to spectacular light shows, noon, night, and day, with a view of Jupiter and Sun setting on a regular basis, these two went into the Virtual Universe again and again to learn more about the details of this location, to experience it, and with that, gain the benefits of time-dilation that would allow them to have years of experience there, in just five minutes.

These young ladies were filled with unlimited amounts of intrigue, splendor, and wonder. They learned how they could balance their time between rescuing others and learning and processing what they needed to in order to be effective as delegates. They learned more in-depth how the scientists, including Eliza and Yesha, had built safe havens, shielding, and had even tamed this vicious, yet beautiful moon by controlling its volcanic activity in such a balanced way as to augment the beauty of life within each tech city, forest, jungle, lake, stream, and living being that existed or lived there.

While they were thus entranced during their first night there, Yesha did something that she had maintained as a routine. No matter how far she traveled, no matter what she would do throughout the world, no matter the plans she had for the moments that followed, she would always return home for a few hours each day.

Around dusk each evening, if she could help it, she would say "hi" to her mother, Yesenia, share one of a plethora of choices of an assortment of teas with her, and then go for a jog through town.

On each of these jogs, for quite some time over the last two years, she remembered meeting a young woman, with blonde hair and blue eyes, who seemed to have the demeanor of an individual who cared deeply about others, had fire that exuded from her eyes, and she sensed there was something special about her.

In keeping with her routine, Yesha linked with Eliza often. Using her optimized physiology and neural link to the Twelve Database Moons, she finally decided to comb their databases and see who this young lady was.

Early on in Pathway, Eliza, Yesha, and James had developed and created facial recognition technology meant to assist with her missions of recruiting people who were in dire needs, based on neural identifications and the information shared willingly with them, so that there was a robust collaboration of information designed to help those who truly needed it most. With this, Yesha had uploaded every detail of the algorithms and bits of crucial information to the matrices, and now they could create new networks of social factors and liaisons, to assist with their missions, for overall effectiveness and successes.

Having assured everyone many times that no one should leave this mortal realm without being heard of, known, or appreciated for the wonderful person they were, or could have become, Eliza had admonished Yesha and James that a system such as this ought to be set up.

As such, it was. These systems were designed to help and not to hinder the progress of humanity. They were designed to protect lives and not put them in peril. These systems were not perfect, as such; they were always being upgraded, maintained, improved upon, and given even more information that could be extrapolated at any time intuitively and rationally, to help others who were suffering. As armed for helping people as they were, they weren't always successful, but this helped to assist even more people who were in dire straits at any given time.

One night, she decided to let Eliza know about a young lady, named Amber Blythe, who had lost a sister many years ago, prior to the formation of Pathway. It had appeared that on Eliza's first tour of Cambridge, following the popularity of her new book, Pathway to the Stars, that Amber had missed Eliza's signing, and thus, it seemed of utmost importance to have Eliza return to Cambridge for another book signing event, and soon.

"Amber is a young but brilliant college student, who is completing her master's degree in biogenetics, and, Eliza, I feel she would be an ideal person for you to meet."

"Of course, Yesha. I will not force the idea but will simply allow this opportunity for a meeting to occur. If I do this, we might be successful in recruiting this phenomenal young lady into Pathway."

"I agree, Eliza. There were many scientists that are brilliant in our organization already, however, the dedication Amber has to her studies, the academic scores and achievements she has accumulated over the years, have made it obvious that she is leadership material and has a vast array of unique ideas that will help many, both in the public world and in Pathway."

After talking to Eliza in the Virtual Universe, Yesha left her biopod at Eliza's estate in Cambridge, returned to her jump gate, went to her small shack where she had agreed to meet with the two young ladies, and there they were, sipping another Kombucha tea.

Now that the two young ladies had been trained, optimized, read-in, settled in at Io, they were all the more vibrant of mind, healthy of spirit, and thrilled to help Yesha, than they would have ever been before they had met her. It was with James that they had received their first official mission, to help Yesha rescue this young man.

It was simple. Yesha and these two amazing young ladies from the far east portion of the Middle East would first build what seemed a cloud of nanos, like those that Eliza had used to build the twenty-thousand tech cities throughout the solar system. Yesha opened another room, showed them three biopods, they climbed in, and she then explained to them when they were in the Virtual Universe, *"Eliza used these same systems of nano clouds to build the shields that protected every spheroid within the*

Solar System, the space elevators, and the many other aspects that kept our Solar System capable of protecting life from the outside factors humanity was not yet ready for, among a few other issues, to include abating humanity's seeming lust for demise, while still affording them the safety of a lovely and life-giving environment for trillions of years or more."

Together, Yesha and these two young ladies went back and forth, from their biopods in Yesha's humble home in the Middle East, to the Melrose Campus, and then back as they programmed this cloud of nanos in one evening to encapsulate them with an impenetrable cover as they navigated toward the rescue of this one young man. Yesha had indicated to them that the Twelve Database Moons had detected with one-hundred-percent certainty that a dust storm was going to pass by, from her impenetrable home in the Middle East, to the two young ladies' small village and then directly to his house. "This storm will have an overwhelming void behind its path, affording us the same cover as we return to my home."

When the predicted dust storm blew through this young man's village, Yesha and these two young ladies arrived along with it unseen within the visual protection of the dust and the nanos. They quietly entered his home using another programmed cloud of nanos to act as noise removers for the hinges and from any other source, released a harmless sleeping agent throughout the edifice that would not affect them, and rescued the young man.

Recognizing the young ladies, but having no idea who Yesha was, when he came to, he was confused at first, but then had nothing but gratitude for what they had done. Together, after assuring him that they were all safe, they talked, they chatted, and they shared stories, within the comfort and protection of Yesha's small home.

Yesha then convinced him, "You too deserve to see things you never thought you would see, beautiful and kind beings, people who love, and realities you can only wish to dream of." He listened to them some more, and then he decided that he would come with them to the Melrose Campus to be trained and read-in as a citizen of Pathway. As the scene played out, Amber felt joy inside.

Jumping in excitement, Amber witnessed as the young man and these two young ladies, one-by-one, and within the week, had rescued each person in that small village. Together, and coincidentally, by the day Eliza had met Amber, the entire village had been trained, read-in, and had settled into the tech city on Io, and a few had decided to have a domicile on both Io and in their small village. A lot had been done in short order.

Just then, Amber's delegate, Yesha, had somehow linked with them, while she was with Amber in the Virtual Universe. As soon as Yesha had linked with them, they each appeared, the young man's father appeared as well!

"I thought that only people with kind hearts were rescued. Why was this individual, who has done so much harm to his own family, rescued?"

Yesha looked Amber in the eyes and connected with her mind, "No matter our past, we can shift our gaze to a beautiful and lovely future. There are many who have gone before us, whom we will never know. Yet, there still exists within this world, so many who have potential that is untold, amazingness just waiting to be released, and hearts that have borne the weight of too much for any one individual to bear. Even he, if given the right set of circumstances, has a beautiful soul, if we simply permit him to see a whole new way of life, open his mind, and allow him the clarity of mind to know that he can devote his life toward redemption, while rejoicing in the joy of others, then it will serve as vindication to those who need it.

"Every single one of his efforts, ever since he was placed in the Correctional Matrix, which is still a long way from being fully developed, has been to beautify his home on Io, to work with his village leader, the people in the village, apologizing to them all, and enhancing the village. He has helped the scientists to make it so those who might choose to live organically, can survive without fear in the conditions that exist outside of the protective barriers of the tech cities, and all of this has made him realize that he has missed out on the loveliness of embracing his wife and son, and the beauty of his culture, while also loving the differences that we all have. Amber, he has learned that our uniqueness is what makes us so amazing.

"His son is healed and has become a delegate. Likewise, his dubious brother, who has seen the error of his ways, has now returned to his village on Earth, to plant Acacia tortilis and jojoba, among other types of vegetation and flora, throughout the area, in efforts related to afforestation, to protect their edifices from the desert winds, while growing lush greenery and protecting and rescuing others who need it as well.

"A lot has been done, and no matter their past, these people are special too. They need love, they need understanding, and they need an opportunity to see things in a completely different way, while knowing that they too can be understood. Ultimately, they have learned that instead of focusing on rules that remove our freedoms, they can now rejoice in being free, while adding to the beauty of life itself, preserving it, and always expanding the mind to learn even more about our lovely and vast Universe!"

Amber understood all that Yesha told her, and with a tear of joy, she hugged Yesha, and then Eliza, and then she hugged the young man, his father, his brother, and the two young ladies who had helped them all. "You two, and each of you, you are all amazing! I am honored to meet you and to have experienced a small caption of the battles you have gone through in your own lives."

Reunion

As the scenario faded away, with a village now filled with smiles, flowers, ingenuity, and peace, the people of the small village said their goodbyes, and waved to Amber, before disappearing, one by one.

Amber looked at the volcanoes of Io, just beyond the tech city as it faded away, and in its place, a statue of an angel, with cupped hands, providing aerated and mineral rich water to the coy fish and frogs in the lovely pond came into view.

Amber was still in awe with all that had happened to this now beautiful yet now tiny happy village.

She had learned that there was always a chance for people to become greater than they ever knew they could become, by simply being kind, thoughtful, curious, innovative, and loving. She also learned, that at any time, if she so desired, she could pull up those drastic learning moments, and even those beautiful memories, and perhaps learn some more. She could pull up the experiences from any Pathway citizen and live through them as if they were her own, just to understand more deeply what it was that drove them, and how she might be able to help others who were going through battles of their own, to overcome them and become the great people they could be. She could also differentiate each thought she explored with their unique and delicious flavor.

Eliza then addressed both Yesha and Amber. She let Yesha know that she truly appreciated her efforts in that far away region of the Earth, and then complimented Amber on learning so well. Upon listening to Eliza's words of moral support and wisdom, Amber felt a sudden surge of her own, in wisdom and clarity, and she smiled.

When Eliza finished, they linked with the others who had been in the training room with her, and through consent they journeyed the lives of everyone who had ever passed through the Virtual Universe and were filled with millions of centuries of life-enriching perspectives and wisdom. After what seemed an untold quantity of many millennia of time, Amber asked, *"How long has it been?"*

Eliza smiled and answered, *"We told you, 'five minutes, twenty years,' but as delegates, we have the ability of adjusting the time-dilation ratio as needed, to any number of centuries or millennia or longer.*

"For each of us, it has been as many years as all of the life experiences of every wonderful Pathway citizen combined, and to a certain degree compounded with regard to experience and wisdom. Given that state of reality, the things we've learned, the moments we have experienced, the understanding and compassion we have for one another, and the complete and genuine wisdom we have gained, the time we have spent here has multiplied exponentially.

"Amber, it has been billions of years!"

After training in every sport, learning every art, science, and musical instrument, and after acquiring every associate, bachelors, and master's degree, and after having graduated with every imaginable doctorate and Ph.D., they congratulated each other, shared their ideas, their experiences, and hugged each other once more.

After what seemed a few more millennia, they awoke within their biopods, and each person felt an indescribable glow and unity about them.

They also felt awake for the first time; unlike they had been at any other point in their lives.

After speaking and then after witnessing all of known history through scientific revelation, learning each of the sciences in their totality, and after having gained experience in all of their fields and cross-queued each of them, they right away entered the Virtual Universe, and went on further journeys for a significant period of time, experiencing all that Eliza, Yesha, and James, as well as each citizen of Pathway, had borne witness to, carried out, improved, lived, and shared.

When they exited again, each person felt a unique sense of what they could do to contribute to the advancement of civilization, and a special link between themselves and everyone else in the room was created.

As they adjusted and mentally practiced their new skills, they arose from their biopods, felt a tingling sensation on their left shoulders, the left side of their bodies, and their left legs.

Eliza spoke up via their neural links, *"What you are feeling right now, is your right mind demonstrating its unique artistry through a mural, kaleidoscope, and mandala-like videography within a set pattern on your bodies. It is not really a tattoo; it is the manifestation of expression of your right brain and can move with your thoughts expressing the most beautiful aspects of what you have within. Please also note, that now you can eat anything you would like, drink anything you would like, have protection throughout life's journeys, and when you are hurt, you will glow as your nanos help you heal. And, once you identify pain, it will go away as you heal.*

"You are for all sakes and purposes capable of living for trillions of years and more. We will have updates on our optimizations, so you will receive upgrades as time goes by. You will be able to age from childhood, if you are a child, as a child would age until you are eighteen, organically, or you can choose to raise your children via biopod in a matter of hours in the tech cities. I would recommend organic, for now, but when we comb the Cosmos, quicker is always best! From there, you can choose to age from twenty to thirty-five as slow or as rapidly as you wish. If you are already an adult, you will be able to physiologically reduce your age to twenty through thirty-five, likewise. If you desire to walk among old friends on Earth, you will automatically be seen by those who have not been read-in as the age that you would be, if you so choose, and with

whom you choose, but you will be protected at all times due to optimized physiology. These same individuals who see you who have not been read-in will witness you becoming younger and healthier in such a way as to avoid suspicion, but enough to appreciate the advice for a better and healthier lifestyle you may have to impart.

"As time goes by, and as each of us are ready, we will receive physiological and neurological upgrades, so perhaps we'll discover at some point that we are able to fly and defy all of the current laws of gravity that we know of. Ultimately, the mind is a powerful thing, so we can each heal and become stronger than ever before as time goes by, and we can learn how to control the nanos, our thoughts, and convince those that are hopeless of a better way. If you can conceive of something that raises the quality of life, you will have the mental capacity to bring that dream to fruition, so long as it does not cause undue consequence to the rights of others.

"Please, go forward, befriend those around you, and remember, the Universe is huge, but before we leave our solar system, we need to have the rest of humanity on board. Without that, wars and brutality will be the undoing of life on Earth, so we need to put wars and brutality to rest. Hence, the necessity for a shared understanding, a demeanor of mutual respect, and a sense for the consent of the individual. Each of those aspects are fundamental to the success of our civilization, no matter where we go. Who here would like to have family and friends around when we eventually leave and return from one side of the universe to the other?"

Everyone, now neurally linked, and in unison, thought together, *"I would. Let's do it."*

Amber, despite the phenomenal new age of her mind, remembered who she was, could differentiate between her thoughts and those of others, loved these new connections, feeds of information pouring in, and felt completely revitalized in every way.

With all of the amazing things she beheld, she was overjoyed to know that she was indeed still herself, yet now, she had even more clarity with capacity for making sense of so much more. As she processed her recent experiences, she realized how she wanted to contribute.

"Cancer, disease, all manner of neurological disorders, environments that are harsh and unwilling, the ability to overcome the worst through science and in a way that will benefit all so much more, a way that will not cost people their jobs, their way of living, or will not turn the economy upside down, and the ability to adapt life to live in whatever environment we find ourselves in are amazing efforts. I'll do all that I can both in Pathway and in public to help people to live healthy lives full of care for our Earth as well as full of innovation toward optimal outcomes, no matter my mission. This is an amazing way to focus my energies and my time—I've found my purpose."

Eliza received Amber's mental thoughts and reciprocated her drive and clarity. *"Indeed, you have found your purpose. I knew you were very unique; I knew there was something special about you, and you, Amber, are a kindred spirit and a forever friend."*

Yesha, too, spoke to Amber, and reciprocated in kind. *"You are phenomenal. I've seen it. You loved your sister very much, and I can tell she loved you. You are our sister now. You don't ever have to be alone again."*

Amber received everyone else's thoughts and felt an especially pleasant and unique openness about her two new friends, Eliza and Yesha. She also knew now, that she was a part of Eliza's and Yesha's team. Every person felt a special connection with the other and bonded with their teams, each with a wonderful purpose to fulfill.

With Amber's speed in physiological adaptation and neurological reconciliation, her ability to engage in critical thought, the rewiring of her cognitive framework, and her sense of purpose, she and her new friends had identified her as a very crucial biotechnology and bioengineering scientist. They knew she would have a significant impact in helping with humanity's role in preserving the future of our universe.

Eliza and Yesha, again, shared their hopes and desires, and Amber realized that Eliza, Yesha, and the citizens of Pathway had anticipated she would become an early and powerful delegate to the UP, an advanced scientist for Pathway, and a member of the Pathway hierarchy. Amber was now fired up with purpose and accepted her new role.

"How do you feel?" asked Yesha.

"I can't say that I have ever felt this way before, and I love it! There is so much to do, but now I wonder where to begin," Amber had thought and spoken aloud, noticing her voice was just a little more powerful, yet sweet and persuasive in nature, and she was pleased.

Yesha and Eliza knew that the words Amber spoke were sincere, heartfelt, far from overly complicated. They were as meaningful and genuine as the words that Yesha and Eliza had spoken throughout her training. They were now indeed kindred spirits.

Chapter 13: A New Assignment

Database Moon Archive, Celestial-Sol Entry Date: 2018 December 25. In this important part of Vesha Celeste's training, after her awakening, she and Yesha explore the meeting with James Cooper, Chloe the cow, and her living quarters on Triton, revisited within the Virtual Universe, interfaced within the Pathway Melrose Campus. Input by Eliza Williams, President of Pathway Industries, 2008-2015.

"Amber, now that your Virtual Universe training is complete, let us introduce you to James Cooper." As Eliza said so, James appeared in the room walking through the jump gate nearby.

Upon seeing him, Amber immediately felt a connection and rather smitten by how handsome he was. She checked Eliza's and Yesha's thoughts, and they had a history with him, a deep one, yet they had opened their minds to her regarding special moments shared during James' first days. *"Freedom is had when jealousy is non-existent."* Yesha was looking toward Amber and smiled, as did Eliza. After saying this in unison via their new link to Amber, James turned to Amber and smiled in his usual way, with noble intentions.

"Hello. Amber?" James said as he reached out to shake her hand, but Amber pushed his hand outward and held her arms out for a hug. Somehow, she had seen how he had helped even Eliza in her lifetime, and James appreciated the notion quite a bit and reciprocated with an enjoyable hug.

He then stepped back and continued. "I have no doubt that you have seen the tech cities in the Virtual Universe but let me show you a few of them in the real world. After I have shown you that, I've talked with Eliza, and you must know that there is a family in Nebraska that I would like you to meet."

"I'll follow your lead. Where do we begin?" asked Amber, eager to begin her new assignments.

"Here," said James, smiling. "Follow me, there is so much to explore, and I'll answer any questions you have along the way." James walked toward the glowing jump gate and Amber followed close behind.

Together they went through many gates as they passed through numerous cities. Amber witnessed the forests, the ponds, the streams, the lakes, the rivers, the trees, the animals, the fish, the birds, the amazing infrastructure of a tech city, overlooking Neptune. "This is Triton. If it weren't for the eco-environment we are encapsulated in, we'd freeze solid until we were rescued.

"If it weren't for our nanos we would die instantly, at least if the eco-environment were to give in.

"But, no fears, our environment is protected by constant updates, and there is a nearly invisible cloud up there of nanos keeping everything intact. Your own nanos will keep you intact as well. This moon is actually very large. It is in a retrograde orbit around Neptune and can house trillions of people. What do you think of the Sun and Neptune-set?"

Amber laughed briefly but stood in awe. "Beautiful," Amber was yet again amazed, as she beheld the variety of blues and faint shades of purple that gave Neptune such a unique and spectacular appeal.

James then escorted her and showed her a large quantity of the tech cities, glowing in white, on each of the moons of the planets in the solar system, and as he escorted her through them, he began to talk to her about a young girl named Erin Carter. "Erin Carter is a genius with a lot of promise, a promise unknown to the rest of humanity, but she is suffering from what many call 'progeria.' She is currently six years old and based on her cellular activity and the length of her telomeres, in her current state, she will die in seven years.

"Due to the constraints of laws in our home country, we have to find ways that are very subtle when it comes to healing her. Once her parents agree to allow us to provide continuous care, and they then decide to come to the Pathway LLC Campus in Melrose, Massachusetts, we will then be able to heal her swiftly and completely.

"Amber, you must know from our shared thoughts that she is very important to Pathway LLC, and I, as well as both Eliza and Yesha, see a lot of promise in her. It's almost as if our link kind of gives us a sense of clairvoyance, because in these few moments I can tell that you lost your sister, and for that, I am very sorry. As you get to know Erin, please think of her as another little sister. Will you please help her?"

"Yes, of course." Amber smiled at James. James smiled back, put out his arms, and she reciprocated for a warm, comforting, and gentle yet very sturdy hug. She looked forward to her first, yet very special mission, as she completed her master's degree thesis and the rest of her college assignments in the real world with ease.

Everything seemed to make more sense, and now there were areas within her textbooks where she found she had a better idea than the legacy-trapped thinkers of the real world!

She decided she would comb the Earth giving seminars, while visiting historic sites and entertainment centers throughout the world. She'd still model, but her primary focus for now was finishing her organic graduate and doctoral studies, while simultaneously understanding more fully the details of her first Pathway mission. The mission would involve getting to know Erin Carter's background even more and figuring out how to heal her using real-world technology. If her family chose the biopod this would all be a breeze. Either way, the side benefits of her efforts would be great, regarding studies and resolutions to the diseases of aging.

As far as her own business venture was concerned, Amber realized that Eliza had far surpassed her expectations for an LLC, and she decided to perhaps tackle that later, since there were so many missions for her to do, ideas to realize, and upgrades and updates to create, to help even the members of Pathway, and it seemed she could work with Pathway now for a more profound result.

Amber would jointly work on upgrades for read-in citizens of Pathway and be involved in high-tech and real-world translations of cures, to help heal and bring joy to people as the public environment worked its seemingly sluggish pace in the biological realm.

The more she understood about Erin Carter, the more she realized why Eliza and James had a vision of a great history and future in store for her.

Finishing Her Studies

With her newly gifted neurological capabilities, real-world studies were a breeze. Amber still took the time to do "off-the-grid" research, for her thesis, 'Biotech and Gerontology:

The Race to Cure Aging.' Enjoying the pages of each text she read, each turn seemed to connect so many dots. She found it thrilling to pore over volumes of data, read a little more, and then go into the labs. Her thesis was nearly complete, using all of the real-world terms, ideas, and legacy systems.

Even though it had seemed like billions of years in the Virtual Universe, it had still only been five minutes for each Virtual Universe trip, and she'd been there twice. Immediately after her experience at the Melrose Campus, she traveled back and forth between her domicile there, as well as her domiciles in Cambridge and Triton. Once she was comfortably organized and settled in, within all three locations, she returned to Cambridge to begin her schedule, as she had set it up previously. For some reason, however, Study Hall did not seem like the start to her day anymore. *"I still feel like me, but I think it's time for an adjustment,"* she thought.

Keeping with her schedule, however, Amber went to her modeling agency, struck a few poses, and while she did, she felt like a million bucks. The photographer seemed extra motivated to work with her today, as well. She then went on a jog, but this time when she saw Yesha jogging, she decided to jog together with her for a while. *"What a convenient meeting,"* she thought.

"It sure is, Amber!" Yesha knew Amber was being tongue-in-cheek about her entire experience, and jogged with her for a time, before saying their physical goodbyes, while maintaining an open link for a while, at least until Amber began her Yoga exercises, and this time, without the need for a shower. Although, as Eliza and Yesha had recommended, she took a shower anyway, and it felt even more soothing than ever before.

Finally, Amber returned to the T.O. to do some waitressing, and found doing so to be quite the amazing scenario, since she could now memorize the entire menu, pick up on genetic-relationships between the organic and clean-meat foods available there, and each customer. She found that she no longer needed her notepad, but brought it out with her anyway, for customer comfort. When she was done with her day, she thought about giving her boss a two-weeks' notice, but then decided against it, so she could breed normalcy into her life and her schedule.

With time-dilation available in the Virtual Universe, there were so many things she could get done in the space of five minutes, in relation to everything else on her list of chores, working at the T.O. posed very little problem with her schedule. She had done so well that first evening, after her essential rebirth, that her boss had essentially told her that whenever she felt the need to come in and help, she was more than welcomed. No longer was she required to be there for any schedule, now she was able to pursue missions throughout the solar system, and then spend a few hours at the T.O., as it convened.

Days passed by, and she was marveled by how she could do so much in so little time.

In those first few days, Amber developed new upgrades for her fellow Pathway citizens, with hopes of making it so that humanity could brave the extreme elements of moons, like Io, without a need for space suits or tech city biodomes. She had plenty of time, however, since Eliza had developed a system for maintaining a core within each spheroid that was conducive to giving and maintaining life, with a shield system for each throughout the Solar System that protected the myriad of unique planetary systems, while normalizing the conditions for personnel who were not read-in but had opted to live in a tech city rather than return to the hostile environments they had been rescued from.

The trick with Io, was understanding how to make it so people could survive despite the many issues that existed. Eliza's immense developments had made life possible, within contained environments, but Amber wanted to allow for easy mobility, for those who had not been optimized.

Amber needed to figure out how to make it so that instantaneous transfiguration of the human genome could take place upon arrival to the various environments that existed throughout the Solar System, in a way that allowed the mind to communicate with the various cells and other entities within the body, to allow this change to take place. Since she was relatively close to this location, due to her first Virtual Universe experience, was working on understanding how to make this happen for the Jovian moon, Io.

Visiting the Virtual Universe many times, she created scenarios where one could survive in the extreme and varying temperatures that were existent on Io. She also found a way to allow humanity to survive for long periods of time, and even a lifetime, uninfluenced by the immense radiation existent there, due to its proximity to Jupiter. Furthermore, Amber analyzed the various cardiopulmonary systems of each living being known to Pathway, to the point of not only redeveloping them to intake sulfur-dioxide, but to exhale another type of gas that would be helpful to this golden planetoid. Finally, she developed a nano system that could increase the atmosphere in such a way as to protect organic life.

As Amber analyzed Io further, she also worked with a series of scientists living there, to use similar tech used by Eliza on Earth to control the volcanic activity, such that it still occurred as necessary but did not take place in zones deemed acceptable for life. She knew there was so much more to understand, and that tech cities were on numerous spheroids, and each requiring their own unique fixes, mending the genome of each living being, and making organic life possible, without the need to fear immediate wipe-out, if Eliza's systems happened to backfire or go into silent mode.

She categorized all the planetoids and began to make extensive lists of the various statistics, physics data-points, and their effect on each genome she worked with. While she spent billions of years in the Virtual Universe developing plans and carrying them out, with Pathway's approval, she still maintained her balance in life and worked on her first mission, to help Erin Carter.

Chapter 14: Time is Relative

Database Moon Archive, Celestial-Sol Entry Date: 2010 March 26. Yesha Alevtina trains Vesha Celeste. In this part of her training, after her awakening, they explore the healing, backstory, and recruitment of Erin Carter by Amber Blythe. They use the recorded memories of Amber Blythe, Erin Carter, and Eliza Williams, within the Virtual Universe. Interfaced within the Pathway Melrose Campus. Input by Eliza Williams, President of Pathway Industries, 2008-2015.

Erin looked back in time as she always had and to her, it seemed somewhat relative. From her perspective, the way time passed by was dependent upon the individual. She knew, however, that in all reality, time was a given state of existence shared by all but quantified based on the civilization and the location they might exist in. During the day of her sixth birthday and each of the recess periods at school, she had taken advantage of the time to reminisce over the previous years of her life. As the days would go by in those early years, even from the very first day of school, she would ponder upon a myriad of memories from the day she opened her eyes until the moment she stood on the concrete right where she happened to be during break time feeling the breeze while looking into the meadows and the trees.

On this day she would have accompanied her parents on the family's semi-annual hour and a half walk south to watch the early springtime Sandhill crane migration. During the last couple of years, her young friends accompanied her as well. She could recall how the three children her age that lived on the same block seemed to grow faster while she became slower each year. Lost in their own world, they seemed to grow taller and stronger, while she could feel her muscles becoming weaker, her bones slimmer, and the sockets they rested in seemed shallower and a greater source of pain. The more she exercised the more pain she felt, but she exercised anyway because it was good for her health.

Instead of becoming frustrated about each aspect of her condition, Erin had begun to discover that sating her thirst for knowledge through education was what gave her the same kind of peace of mind as playing with toys would give to her peers. As painful as it was, she did her chores at home and was thorough, which took up a lot of her time, and then she found time to spend a few hours to exercise, walk, and play with her friends. No matter what, however, she made time to learn how to read, watch educational television shows, and ask questions of her parents if they were available, about life, the universe around her, and any form of science. To Erin, parental advice was intriguing and full of clarity, and she was interested in looking toward the future, even while she pondered upon her past. The two seemed to go hand in hand, and while she couldn't quite yet put her thumb on it, both were beautiful.

In school, things had been different over the last seven months, since she had begun kindergarten. All things considered, she had appreciated the wonders of academia for as long as she could remember, so her curriculum was intriguing due to being very analytical. Even though she knew most of the material already, it gave her a chance to study those same items in even more depth or an opportunity to help her classmates, which she enjoyed doing immensely. At this point in her life, it seemed that her classmates' and friend's perception of time during recess was a shared event to the extent to which time would pass by slowly and as if a minute would take four. It also seemed to Erin that her peers would play with the energy of superheroes.

Time sped by all too quickly and her energy would drain just as fast when she engaged in normal activities shared by children her age. Four minutes for her seemed to go by in a blink of an eye when she tried to play ball, or tag, or hide-and-go-seek just like her friends and the rest of the children. Instead of doing that each day, she chose to walk around the campus using a short and steady pace while thinking on some occasions about what she would normally be doing during this time of the year before school began. Since her peers were so fast and had much more strength than she, she looked up and outward toward the sky. This seemed to her the only way she could slow down time, breathe in a little respite from reality, and make life a little more pleasant while reflecting on the past, studying the different sciences, and appreciating nature.

Sandhill Cranes

As Erin reminisced, she remembered how watching the Sandhill cranes each year had given her solace. These birds allowed her to grow an appreciation for the majestic beauty of flight, which, she as a human would never be able to enjoy, given her natural and obvious constraints. It was easy to watch birds fly and flout about the cares of humanity doing the things she couldn't, and she didn't mind because they were completely different in so many ways. To her, despite the differences, they were beautiful just the same. On the other hand, it was difficult watching children her age, because they could physically do what she could not. Ironically, she, like any other child, saw and felt the similarities of childhood interests in so many ways. Although, they preferred toys while she preferred the sciences. As things were, it was painful to run with the children her age, and time seemed to speed by no matter what she did.

At this point in her life, her bones began aching much more than usual than they had at this time about a year ago. Perhaps her bones were burdened by carrying the weight of the organs in her body. Her bones weren't thick enough to lug around the weight of a normal human being, but their unique flexibility helped to counter that in a smaller girl her size, at least unless they were to grow to become less flexible and more brittle, as the doctors had suggested could be a possibility once she reached the age of eight. She began to notice the aches and pains during her last trek to the Platte River for her family's annual walk from Kearney to just beyond the interstate to watch the spring migration of the cranes, typically near the time of her birthday.

Along their way, they would stop by the overpass that at that time had been called the Great Platte River Road Archway Monument, and later The Archway, which was often overlooked by travelers since it was located over the interstate, but with no off-ramp nearby. Eventually, they would build an off-ramp for tourism to increase revenue. While there, she enjoyed her brunch with family and friends, and she would stop to listen to the historical displays of the simulated buffalo stampedes and trains. Once done at the archway, they would head out to the south side, walk over the Platte River Bridge, and observe the cranes feeding on the harvest from the previous Fall.

Erin, this time, watched as the cranes flew high in the air above her in their typical large V-shaped patterns. Perhaps Betty was waiting for Erin to watch her by the river this year but in vain. She could see some of Betty's friends flying overhead, but she looked for the details that were unique to Betty alone, just in case she happened to be flying overhead too.

She learned one year that these beautiful avian creatures had existed and migrated throughout this region of the Earth for many centuries, millennia, or even longer. For as many cranes as were there, and despite the history of their migration, there was one crane that was special and unique to her. Erin had named her, Betty, and she recalled the first time they met.

Erin had to have been about two years old when she could recall her first time being completely enthused with the cranes and their own majestic beauty. She had been so ensconced with them, yet somehow suddenly, she noticed there was one exceptional crane. She had three white feathers uniquely located in the center of her right-wing surrounded by darker-tipped plumage, and more visible as she spanned her wings. Betty walked closer to Erin that first day of their encounter while honking a few times. She then stood there for a few minutes, with an occasional flap of her wings, a couple of honks, and would look around.

Her father, Daniel, pointed out how to tell the difference between the ladies from the gentlemen among the cranes, and how she was a lady among them. Males were typically a couple of inches taller and weighed about four more pounds. Her father had pointed out to Erin where some of the cranes fed. She watched her and named her Betty. Ever since then, Betty would approach her, in the same way, each year, honk a few times, peck at the ground before her, and then look at Erin while turning her head from side to side as if to observe her from each of her eyes. As time went by each year, she was followed by a group of younger cranes and none of them were aggressive toward Erin or her family, as was typical among many crane species. After a week or two, once they were filled and ready, they flew away honking, spreading their wings, and making their way northward.

Today, Erin hadn't been there to see them off; instead, all she found she could do to feel a sense of normalcy was watch and listen as they made their usual yet much more distant communal honks and sounds as they flew high above her in the sky and toward the north. The winter snows had melted, and spring was in the air. Thus, they headed toward the northern regions of Earth for summer where eggs would be hatched, and their new-born would grow and accompany the more experienced cranes southward during the fall. She knew after a long series of flights and feeding on the remains of the nearby harvest, they would reach their destination and stay there until their fall migration when they headed back on their pathway southward to Texas, New Mexico, and Mexico.

Listening In

While her eyes gazed upon the birds in the sky above, Erin's mind wandered as she recalled how on one night, about eight months before, her parents had been engaged in their routine evening chats together. Even though she was supposed to be in bed she had snuck down the stairs, as usual, to listen to her Mom and Dad discuss their hopes and fears. Their topics of conversation were normally intriguing because she felt she learned so much as they talked with each other in a more adult fashion about the issues of the day, medical advancements, and their daughter.

On this occasion, they were talking about Erin's condition and how she was almost halfway through her lifespan already. In many ways, the tone they shared had been no different than usual as she listened, at least in the beginning.

At one point in their discussion the sentiments they shared shifted from one of optimism for a cure, expressions of pride in her character, and admiration for her mental acuity for her age, to one of sorrow and sadness. Rather than their usual talk about how the previous day was, or of plans for the future, she heard them trying to talk through tears.

Her heart melted. Why were they so worried? She knew her parents loved her. Perhaps they knew they would miss her because she would begin school soon? She would miss her parents, but she wanted an opportunity to learn even more, as well as a chance to read and study with children her own age. However, if what they said was in fact true, she knew that she would ultimately have the comfort of going off to some other unknown reality, while they would be left alone in this world without her. Perhaps that was why they were in tears. She listened in closely.

"Progeria, we all have it pulsing through our bodies in one way or another, but somehow the way it affects her, well, it just isn't fair," Her Dad had mentioned at one point in their conversation with a wavering voice, one that indicated that he was most certainly trying to hold back tears. "She is such a wonderful young girl, but her condition is beginning to show. How do we explain to her that her life will be so much shorter and different than that of her friends at school? She starts Kindergarten soon. What can be done? What can we do? We've traveled a lot through the years, we have seen all kinds of doctors, we have tried to give her a full life, and none of the doctors seem to have any good answers."

After hearing this, Erin breathed in, breathed out, and mustered her strength as she walked down the stairs the rest of the way to reveal the fact that she had heard everything. Her parents looked at her, wiped their eyes, and smiled when they saw her.

"It's okay Mom, Dad. It'll be okay. I promise I'll make the most of life, however long it may be. You both have so much love in your hearts, you have done so much for me, taught me so many things, made my life rich with experiences and the exploration of our environment. I am a lucky girl to have you two as my parents. I know what is happening to me, but together we've done so well to capture so much out of life despite it all. Thank you for being wonderful parents." Erin then gave each of her parents a hug and went off to bed.

Changes

Ever since that night, Erin thought frequently about some of the major changes that had increasingly occurred as the months passed her by. Some of these changes had taken form and had shown themselves not too long before her kindergarten school year began. As the months progressed so too did her condition and likewise the effects of her physiology. She had dismissed the fact that her cells were aging prematurely and decided to reflect on time, as she dove into the pleasant moments spent going over letters, numbers, and colors with the rest of the children.

While she couldn't keep up with the other kids as they played on the jungle gym during recess, she kept up with them mentally and did very well in class. The art activities were among her favorites, and anything related to the sciences seemed to call out to her even more. She loved learning how the universe worked. Erin appreciated biology, neurology, and physics. She would watch each day for advancements in technology as the news would play out. At times she would watch specials with hope for some miracle to come out from within the medical industry while watching educational documentaries. Due to her viewing of sophisticated material, Erin was at the top of her class. Despite all, she enjoyed the social atmosphere while understanding the cosmos.

Kindergarten had started for Erin Carter in August of 2009. The three children who had grown up with her and happened to live on the same block, had accompanied her on their first day of school. Erin appreciated the fact that their school was only a block and a half away, so she could walk there and back with ease. Most of the time, she and her friends would walk together. Their parents happened to be good friends as well, so the children took turns sharing their homes to play and spend a few hours together. Those moments were beautiful, as she recalled, at least before school began.

Still, time sped by for Erin, so she hadn't considered the loss of hair on her head until a few months later. It was on the second Friday of November of 2009, and it was then that it would be the last time she would be able to fashion her hair back into pigtails. The other children were surprisingly kind about what she was going through since none of them had brought it up or made gaffs, but she could hear the worst playing out in her mind, she knew the nature of children her age. She wasn't vain, but she still wanted to feel like a princess just like any other girl and wearing her hair in pigtails was something that made her feel like one.

The temperature on her way home from school was average for the time of year that day, so she wore a quilted jacket. But unfortunately, at one point the wind blew in from the northwest and her jacket's hood had blown back. She recalled as the wind stood still for just a moment and she couldn't forget as though everything else was in sync, as if the tick-tock of the clock had crawled nearly to a stop for the first time in a while.

Erin could still feel the moment that her last lock of long hair brushed against her neck on her right side as it made its way down to the ground. When she looked down, there was her pigtail.

Luckily, she hadn't felt any pain. No tug. No hair pulling. It was simply gone—released.

From that time on and until the rest of her hair fell out completely, she wore barrettes of sparkly pink and other seasonally based colors on what remained of her hair to bring out the kind of childhood creativity and femininity she had grown to adore through her years in life. In her own manner of originality, her hair was her own outward expression of creativity and beauty. Thus, upon what few medium and short-length hairs she had, she had worn barrettes to match what she was wearing until she could no longer wear them anymore.

Erin reflected on the week before Christmas break. It had been cold, so she wore a red stocking cap to go with her green eyes and green and red Christmas outfit as she walked to and from school. She wore the stocking cap just in case the wind would blow her jacket hood back, which would then leave her almost barren head exposed to the chilly breeze. When Erin returned home that Thursday, she sat down on the ottoman next to the fireplace and took off her cap. She then looked inside and saw her sparkly green barrette sitting in it trustily holding her final remaining shorter hairs. She was pretty sure this was the last time hair would grace her head.

She was impressed that her barrettes had done their job so well. After feeling her barren head, she envisioned the reality of it. To Erin, it was as smooth as silk and warm to the touch. She also realized her dome was completely devoid of hair. For a moment, her tonsils swelled, her tears welled up, but she shook off the urge to cry and went to the kitchen to grab a glass of water. She drank it, felt refreshed, and watched an episode of Battle Star Galactica. Her favorite character was Kara Thrace, or Starbuck, who had always carried herself with grace and an iron will despite all thrown her way.

At her young age, Erin knew that crying might have its therapeutic purposes, but on this occasion, it wouldn't change a thing, so she didn't see any point in it. She immersed herself in something she enjoyed instead of allowing herself to wallow in self-pity. She would cry if she lost a family member or a friend to the angelic call of the afterlife, but she was different, and she knew it, so instead she would watch a favorite show or a scientific documentary or go to the bathroom for the fourth time that day and brush her teeth again, since part of her condition caused her teeth to gather plaque more quickly. She found a way to appreciate her new look and to enjoy and embrace her emerging and modern reality.

She could have worn a wig, but she chose not to.

Erin recalled as her parents brought her to Omaha the following January to show her a variety of wigs. In their own way, they were trying to help. These wigs had a splendid and beautiful quality to them, with so many colors, styles, and details. She knew or could sense that there had been quite a few kind individuals who had donated their locks to help others. Many had done this so others could benefit from the peace that would settle in as societal expectations of beauty were met. Erin knew there were noble reasons for their intentions, so she was grateful, despite her views on how beauty was internal.

To Erin, beauty was not just a shallow aspect of reality. People felt through their senses and their minds, that was how they experienced the world, and when they felt what they felt, there was a lot that went with it. People have emotions that travel to the core of the mind and impact the rest of their physiological and neurological health. Thus, it was important to Erin that people had a sense of appreciation for who they were and how that affected others. For many, these wigs would provide them an opportunity to live a life of acceptance and transition to a new reality that would meet those expectations. Meeting their own personal beliefs would impart to them internal peace, a sense of elegance felt within and the expression to the world before them of an internal visual—and she was on board with that idea.

While Erin appreciated her parents' efforts and the need for acceptance, she preferred the simplicity of baldness. Even though she was a child, she possessed the maturity her physiology seemed to express, and there was a bit of merit to the hair loss she endured. She took everything in with pause and stride, with consideration for others, and with grace. She appreciated the beautiful world around her. Given her predicted short lifespan and no matter what would happen down the road, she would take in the sights, the sounds, the scents and the splendor of the environment around her. If she couldn't express her own prettiness in the way she had envisioned it, she would embrace her reality. Kindness was first and foremost to her, so she expressed herself well while taking in the magnificence of the world with love.

As that moment tapered away from her memories, she went back to one day in late September of 2009, when she realized that her face was no longer full. She didn't let that get her down. Instead, she saw the sleek aerodynamics of her slenderizing features, making it so she could walk a little more briskly. Her skin no longer was full of plasticity, but rather than let that bother her, she enjoyed the freshly scented oils her parents had given her to prevent cracking and bleeding. Her cheeks were no longer plump, the wrinkles in her face began to show and throughout her body her skin was left sagging and greying, yet this seemed to become commonplace for her, and she would show strength despite all. Her nose was no longer youthfully wide at the base but had gathered together for a narrower, extended, and more aged appearance.

In her mind, she looked like what she had imagined her great-grandmother would have looked like if she were still alive. Erin loved how her father described her great-grandmother, so she took this thought as a wonderful compliment.

At school, she was very perceptive of how her young friends and the other school kids treated her. While they were still nice, she noticed that they began to maintain their distance more and more. It wasn't their fault, and she knew it, so she forgave them. Still, it was somewhat lonely at times to see groups of kids, especially those who she'd known for years, playing together and with others as she was by herself on more occasions than not. Instead of allowing herself to become overwhelmed with a sense of frustration, she felt a sense of appreciation for being afforded more time to think in peace.

To Erin, life was a pleasant spectator sport, and with her exceptionally keen sense of intuition, she noticed how the adults she would meet used to tell her how adorable she was. Now, their compliments drifted more toward her personality or her emerald, green eyes, and no longer toward the rest of her features. To her this was fine, since Erin preferred to talk about ideas, the sciences, and things of substance anyway, and the fact that they now looked her in the eyes a lot more brought her more of a sense of shared conversational involvement.

She continued thinking during each of her recess periods that day of her enjoyable moments growing up and how things were before school began.

Beautiful Moments

Her parents had done so much to do right by her, to give her love and an environment filled with meaningful experiences. She recalled trips to museums, visits to the art centers nearby, the walks in the various parks around town, familiarizing her with the various businesses that kept the town running, camping trips hovering over a campfire prepared by her Mom and Dad, and looking up at the stars.

Her parents taught her so much in so little time. No matter what challenges life brought, Erin was grateful for the fact that her parents had pulled every stop to make the whole kit and caboodle as pleasant and normalized as possible given her condition. Thus far, there had been very few answers to what could be done for a cure for over-active progeria or the pain as it set in from her early on-set fibromyalgia.

Despite her young age, and even though Erin could read into people very well she still appreciated them. She could pick up on their sentiments, their expressions, and their emotions, but she also had a strong sense that she was who she saw in others. Her parents had discussed how proud of her they were many times in private, but they had also discussed the progressive nature of her condition, so they were considerate yet concerned.

The doctors had, during their many visits and trips to distant clinics, tried to talk of healing, helpful acute and organic medicines, and they seemed to dance around the subject of early aging whenever she was in the room. She still listened and knew what they were talking about. They were trying their best to help her with the information available to them, but with so much to study, it was easy for doctors to get lost in the murky details and the convoluted clutter of information. No matter where she and her parents went, they received very few direct and quite a few vague answers from the doctors as they humbly hung their heads low and expressed their sorrow for her condition.

While Erin excelled in her Kindergarten school work, and recess had not been the opportunity for physical exercise that so many of her peers seemed to appreciate it for, she made the most of it and still enjoyed the many occasions for contemplation they provided, just like today. Contemplating life, while watching the butterflies go from flower to flower, or looking for rainbows after a rain, looking for a flower to pop up among the weeds, or even gazing into the nearby farmland to view the cattle as they grazed seemed to help the time pass by even more pleasantly, but recess was just never long enough. Erin felt, however, that a person could still treasure wonderful moments within their hearts and minds, no matter where they were.

Erin pulled herself back from her thoughts and drifted back toward the day. Her last recess of the day was over, so when the school bell rang, she went back into class.

It was the last hour of school when to her surprise the teachers and students had put together a party for her. Just as she entered the classroom they yelled, "Surprise!" and sang "Happy Birthday" with smiles. Even though her birthday wasn't until two days later, it was a nice way to go off and into the weekend. The teachers had coordinated with her parents and the parents of the other students to provide, share, present, and divvy out a beautiful cake to her and her classmates. They gave her a large birthday card signed by every teacher and every student in the room. Inside, she felt lit up and very grateful for the wonderful people of Kearney, Nebraska. She went home that day with her three friends from the neighborhood, holding balloons, and wearing a gift—a beanie in her favorite color.

Friday, March 26, 2010, turned out to be a beautiful day, accompanied by three friends, wearing her new pink beanie, and she skipped home while whistling in high spirits. Erin forgot about any pains as she went home, which would normally have come along with all her physical activity. Two days later, on her actual birthday, her three friends accompanied her to the park, where they watched the cranes feasting on what remained of last year's harvest. Betty was there, and Erin felt like her world was whole again. Later, when she returned home and opened the door, she was surprised again, as she discovered that her classmates and their families had gathered together and had somehow snuck over to her house to wish her a happy sixth birthday at home.

In the face of her physical conditions, her mind was every bit that of a six-year-old when it came to so many aspects of life, yet with an extra love for the study of science, balanced with discipline, fun, and excitement most especially when it came to playtime and birthdays, because she knew that each one mattered and that according to the doctors, she could only expect about seven more of these beautiful occasions. While she was unusually smart for her age, and while she often hid it well, she wanted to play like the others her age had and that she did, until the pain crept in.

Erin had been raised with self-restraint and good manners though, so when she knew it was time, she went around the room and thanked everyone, smiled her award-winning smile, and then she found a polite way to dismiss herself from the room when the pain was just too much to bear. She didn't want to make a scene, so, just like she would do at any other time; she showed gratitude for the efforts of her teachers and fellow students. Once everyone left her house and her parents had given her the prescribed treatments, she prepared for bed.

With her last bit of strength that day and before she went to bed, she expressed to her parents, "I'm six now, thank you for bearing with me. I love you Mom and Dad, you do so much for me. With such a beautiful world, let's make this year great!" And, she hugged them both. Erin rested well that night, at peace with the world, and a strong determination to make the most of what life had given her.

Love Unfeigned

It had been six years since Erin had been born. Raised in her mother's hometown of Kearney, Nebraska, she expressed often how she appreciated the farmlands and the starry night skies. Erin Carter's mother had reached the end of the day, Erin's birthday, and just as they had taught Erin, each day they would in their own way, take time to meditate and contemplate life.

Beverly Carter would often take a little time before going to bed to ponder on her life and the lives of her husband and daughter. On this occasion, she thought about how she met Erin's father, Daniel, in Atlanta, Georgia, when she was just twelve years old. She had gone to visit her aunt who moved there a couple of years prior. Beverly loved and missed her, and after some convincing, her parents let her fly down to spend the summer at Aunt Tina's house. It was on her very first day of arrival in Atlanta that she met Daniel.

After she arrived in the airport, she freshened up in the restroom, made sure her blonde locks were neatly pulled back in a ponytail, and then went to the luggage area where her aunt met with her and picked her up. She settled into her aunt's home for the summer.

It had been a particularly hot day that day and Beverly recalled how on the way to the house in her aunt's car she saw an ice-cream parlor. She made no mention of it at the time, but she did make a mental note of it. When they arrived at the house, they brought in her luggage, ate some watermelon and drank some water. After unpacking and some enjoyable chit chat with her aunt, about Atlanta, Georgia, and their nice winters, she asked her aunt if she could get some ice-cream since the shop was only a few blocks away from the house.

After approval, Beverly started walking there, enjoying the summer breeze. Once she arrived at the shop, she walked in, got in line, and looked at the menu while deciding on what she would like to order. As a couple of people ahead of her made their orders, she saw that they sold a delicious bowl of mint & chip ice-cream—her favorite. Deciding that ordering a dish of her favorite ice-cream would be perfect for enjoyment while cooling down a little bit from the hot and sticky Georgia summer air, she did just that.

The climate in Georgia had warmer temperatures and humidity than she had been used to in Kearney, Nebraska. Taking a chance on the social aspect of the location near her aunt's house and ordering ice cream knowing it would be quite the tasty delight seemed like an excellent way to get two things done at one time. *"Why not take in this unfamiliar and intriguing ambiance with something savory?"* she thought.

When she arrived at the front counter to make her order, she couldn't help but notice that the person who attended to her requests was a green-eyed, red-haired, striking and clean-cut young man. She quickly glanced at his nametag, almost as if with the blink of an eye. She was going to be here for a while, so maybe she would have a chance to meet him again soon.

Daniel, who had worked there with repeat clientele for the last three summers, noticed her new persona as he served this gorgeous young lady her ice cream. Something about her demeanor intrigued his young mind, no matter what prudence might have dictated, so he asked his boss for a quick break. There were no incoming customers following her and everyone else seemed settled-in and pleased, so he thought, naturally this would be an ideal time for a break from the routine.

He didn't mention why, but his boss, who saw his priceless expression when she approached the counter to make her order and had known him for years, appreciated his work ethic, had a kind heart and agreed to let him use a "break" to talk with her. His boss knew that he could serve ice-cream to any customers in Daniel's place if they came in.

Daniel took off his apron, hung it up on the nail just outside the large room-sized freezer, and walked casually to her table. "Excuse me, Ma'am," Daniel said. "I don't believe we've introduced ourselves right and proper."

She looked up from her dish of mint & chip ice-cream, not expecting a visitor to come to her table. It was Daniel and she could tell from his beautiful green eyes. She felt herself kind of blush for the first time in her life. With a quick brush of her napkin to hide and wipe away the ice cream that had fallen upon her chin, she smiled.

"My name's Beverly or Bev," said Beverly. She remembered his name because she had looked at his name tag when she made her order and knew it was him on account of his handsome and attractive features and personality, "Nice to meet you, Daniel."

"Thank you, Bev; you can call me Dan," he replied, trying to be polite. He had thoughts racing through his mind as to how to continue this conversation. Looking at her made his heart skip a beat, her blue eyes, blonde hair, ponytail, and her young yet very feminine and attractive build and demeanor were breath-taking in his pubescent and curious mind, but he wasn't about to let that overcome his ability to make a decent and thoughtful exchange, he seemed to appreciate her at a deeper level as well. "I'm from around here, and I don't believe I've seen you in this area before. You seem like a pleasant person. What brings you to Atlanta?"

"I came here to visit my aunt, Tina, for the summer. So, I'll be here for a while. It's nice to meet you, Dan. You must be on a break, please, take a seat?" said Beverly, as politely and demurely as she could.

Beverly, as young as she was, was quite mature for her age, and despite that fact, she thought he was quite charming. Through their conversations, she discovered that he was 14, only two years her senior. She also found that his level of ambition, his politeness, and kindness demonstrated right away to be impressive to her; so, she stayed there in the ice-cream parlor as he came by to visit from time to time until his shift was over.

While waiting, he brought out water, a soda, and showed her to the women's restroom, and out of politeness and decency he occupied himself elsewhere and in a gentlemanly fashion, so she could freshen up.

When Daniel's workday was finally over and he saw her still sitting there, his intuition was good enough to know she had stayed there for him. With that knowledge, they talked some more, enjoyed their exchanges and he asked her if it was okay if he escorted her to her Aunt Tina's house. With both of their spirits in the clouds, they walked down the road and made the turn toward her aunt's home as Beverly talked to Daniel and described the sights, sounds, and the weather in Kearney, Nebraska.

When they arrived at her aunt's house, Daniel tapped on the door and Beverly's aunt answered with a smile, "Come in you two. I had a hunch you might meet each other. When I looked at the clock, I was for sure you had. How was your day?"

"Oh, it was wonderful, Ma'am. You know my schedule well. I must say that it is so nice to see you again. I met your niece, Beverly, today and she told me a lot of neat things about Nebraska. I'll have to visit there someday," Daniel replied.

Beverly's aunt chuckled in a friendly manner, suggesting she'd been to Nebraska, but somehow, she preferred the weather there, especially considering her arthritis, and let them both in. She shared her sofa with them, brought out some hot tea, and together they talked, laughed, and enjoyed their time. Once Daniel realized it was getting late, he politely dismissed himself.

"Oh, Daniel, he's a good boy," Tina told Beverly, as he disappeared down the road and out of sight, after looking back and waving a couple of times.

Beverly and Daniel visited and talked with each other every day that summer until it was time to escort her back to the airport to return home.

As the summer break went by, however, they enjoyed Daniel's free moments from work, walked the parks, and talked about life, as well as their hopes and dreams for the future. When her summer break ended, Daniel invited Beverly to go with him on a special date. "This won't be anything overly fancy, just something fun." He coached her. With her aunt's permission, he took her to the county fairgrounds and together they enjoyed every last ride. They also shared some chili dogs, funnel cakes, drank fountain sodas, and laughed about how the summer sped by all too soon.

Before returning to her home in Nebraska, the two had become good friends, fond of the moments shared, and happy they'd met. As such, they exchanged mailing addresses, and she made him promise to meet her one day at her hometown in Kearney. They hugged each other; she hugged her aunt and kissed her cheek, boarded the plane, and she immediately began missing them both. The summer had been wonderful, and she had them to thank for it.

After writing to each other each week for nearly fifteen years, Bev and Dan finally saw each other again. Every week, as the years had passed by and before they had finally met again, their faithfully written and weekly mailed letters helped to keep them on track with their goals for the future. Going to the mailbox each week helped them grow their bonds of trust, especially when, just as hoped, there was another beautiful letter from the other, just as they had agreed. Seeing those letters gave them each a spring in their step.

Each week, inside the mailbox, was another three to four-page letter discussing how life was going, from their goals to their hopes, dreams, and frustrations, to everything else that came to their minds. Their hearts floated when they thought of each other, and they used that positive vibe to stay highly focused on getting good grades in their academics and in doing well in their extracurricular activities, from band to sports and art.

Throughout the fifteen years, they had coached each other from a distance through to completion of college, and as luck would have it, Daniel found a job in the animal husbandry industry and successfully secured employment in Beverly's quaint hometown of Kearney, Nebraska. She too had secured employment in her hometown as a psychologist for the local high school she had attended growing up.

Star-struck from day one for so many years, Bev and Dan's long-awaited reunion was magnificent! Following several months of dating, courting, and introducing Daniel to those who she grew up with, the time they spent together resulted in a joyous small-town wedding. He'd matured quite handsomely, to her. To him, she became even more beautiful than he would have ever dreamed, much of that beauty existed due to her phenomenal goals, her efforts to succeed in what she did, and her care for others. Her parents, her aunt, his parents, and even his boss from the ice-cream parlor had traveled up from Georgia to be there.

It's How We Treat Others

Five years passed by after their marriage, before Erin, their miracle baby, finally entered their lives. They did a lot to prepare for her, but she didn't arrive until they had suffered from two unfortunate miscarriages. Both occasions had caused them to grow more resilient together, and despite the year's occurrence accompanied by broken hopes, dreams, and hearts, they were strong and very much in love. Their love persisted through all, no matter the challenge.

Erin's parents and all who knew her would say throughout each of those first six years that they saw in her the example of a beautiful girl, who despite all odds, was positive, full of hope, with unlimited amounts of grace, and she inspired the hearts of those around her with her unique genius and love toward others.

Rarely did anyone notice she was stricken with premature aging with an all-too-limited lifespan of eleven to thirteen years. Erin quickly made all who knew her forget within the first moment of her being in the room on any occasion that she had a unique beauty about her despite the result of a disease that affected her cells. Her cells were prematurely senescent. As she went through the various stages that came with Progeria, there were seldom and few times when she would ask her parents why she was so different, but if she did her parents would waste no time in assuring her that of all things the most important aspect to anyone was their character.

"Think back on all of the people you have appreciated most," her Father, Daniel, would caringly tell her. "Do you remember them more for what they looked like or for how they treated you?"

Her mother, Beverly, looked back, and when her husband would ask that question, she was always proud. She was proud of her husband and Erin. Erin always knew the right answer and strived to be that person. She wanted to be the person who brought joy to those around her and she had expressed on numerous occasions how she was grateful for parents who possessed a loving, long-suffering, and gracious nature, and for the friends who had always been kind to her.

A Rising Star

Later on in 2010, after Erin had started the first grade, she excelled far and above her peers in every way, to include academically and artistically. Beverly and Daniel continued to take care of her, showing concern for her condition, giving her the proper treatments to slow down the effects of progeria in her body. As she excelled in school and kept a positive mindset on her life and the universe around her, they were impressed with her demeanor and growing personality.

Beverly enjoyed reminiscing about her daughter. She admired the fact that even though Erin didn't have the energy for physical routines, she had studied hard academically and as a result had won her school's annual spelling bee. From there she persevered further to win the next levels of the early-term spelling bee contest, all the way through to nationals. By mid-October of 2010, she had been invited to share her story and how she faced and dealt with her unique battles in life, on the talk shows of every network and cable channel in the nation.

Beverly worked with Erin and Daniel to provide details to an expert on documentaries, one who appreciated the educational value of informing others of what was happening while searching for a solution to the issues. He pooled the necessary information and put together a narrated documentary about Erin. Erin's story was typically shared in a broadcast along with some re-enactment on each show, followed by an interview:

"Born on the 28th of March of 2004, she was nine months old that following December when her mother and father noticed that she was still wearing the same clothes a three-month-old baby would wear. There were symptoms demonstrated that brought concern to Beverly and Daniel, so they brought Erin to a family pediatrician.

"'What your daughter has is known as Hutchinson-Gilford Progeria Syndrome, otherwise known as Progeria. And what that means is that she has and will suffer from premature aging, which will affect her bone density, her skin elasticity, and she will physically age eight times faster than the average human being. In most cases, children that are diagnosed with progeria do not live past the age of thirteen.'

"Beverly and Daniel Carter were immediately shocked when news of this hit their ears. Notwithstanding the news, they loved their darling little green-eyed, blonde-haired, heart-shape-faced girl so much. She was their only child after two miscarriages, and they wanted in every way possible to provide her with the best life they could.

"Before she had been born, on multiple occasions her parents had gone to parenting classes, parenting workshops, and had even gone so far as to prepare for the personal development of any possibilities of any interests shown. They wanted to afford their child an enriching environment that lent to mental, social, and personal-creative developmental-based interests that their daughter might have and would inevitably show as she grew older.

"They provided a myriad of toys, games, and activity options for their child so that she could choose between them, from sports to mechanics, to the arts, to the sciences, and perhaps even a healthy balance of them all, to express her unique interests.

"Her parents wanted to do the right thing by Erin, but the news that she had somehow inherited a premature aging disease, wherein she could die early on in life, weighed heavily upon their shoulders and in their hearts. They did everything they could to provide their daughter with the best and most structured lifestyle possible. They provided her with the tools of success early on in life and had done everything they could to ensure she could live with a long and intellectual reality, and to attain whatever dreams she might have. As a result, Erin had done so much to provide hope to others and those who knew her wished that perhaps a healthy life was within her grasp.

"'Originally, upon discovery of her tragic misfortune, Daniel, her father, a strong yet caring man, sat in the pediatrician's office, had closed his eyes, and sunk in his chair,' Beverly Carter recalled, 'as though every effort they had made would result in very few positive results for their little girl. Her life would be cut short all too soon.'

"Interviewing one of her doctors, he seemed to sit up at one point with an anticipation of hope, and shared, 'If we can find a cure, perhaps there will be possibilities regarding the subject of aging, altogether. Such a difficult disease to cure comes with a lot of promise for all of humanity if a remedy is found.'

"Daniel expressed how, upon finding out about Erin's condition, he had felt the sensation of tears uncontrollably welling up in his eyes; his throat had tightened from the emotional shock. 'Beverly had always been keen and quick to notice my concerns, and the doctor's words gave me some hope. Yet, that wasn't enough. I wanted something that could help my daughter, and now.'

"Beverly articulated, 'His expressions gave him away every time. I also knew that despite all, something had to be done. Our daughter would not be deprived of the life she deserved if we could help it, and we were willing to talk to every doctor and every therapist until they could find a way to afford Erin a normal life. Nevertheless, we also realized the reality of things as they were perceived to be, and we were not naïve to the fact that we also needed to embrace her with love, empathy, and that we would need to do as much as we could to normalize Erin's life given her condition, despite the circumstances, and to treat her as we would any other child.

"'I remember confessing to Dan, 'Our efforts are not wasted, and I am grateful you are not the typical man—you are mighty, you are full of love, you are kind, you are compassionate, and you allow yourself to feel deeply from within a connection toward others that is special, unique, and sincere, and you have a beautiful love for life. Daniel, we love our daughter, no matter what challenges life may bring. With all the preparations we have made and the efforts we have put into her future, perhaps we're more prepared now than we would have been otherwise if we had never prepared for parenting the way we did.

"'Erin, in her younger years, will still have the mind of a child, who looks out into the world and gazes upon us with hope in her heart for the love we can bring her, she is bright, she is curious, I can tell already. She wants to embrace the colors of the world and she will at some point not understand why she is 'different' from the other children. We have to do what we can to let her know we love her, we'll do everything we can to give her life the sense of normalcy she deserves, and we will even find the medical expertise that will help us to overcome this.'

"The Carters sought out medical advice for their daughter for more than five years after they had discovered her condition from doctors at the local clinic in Kearney, Nebraska, who then pointed them toward the hospitals in Lincoln. After their first journey, the doctors in Lincoln had in-turn pointed them to the doctors at Creighton in Omaha, who had then pointed them to the doctors at UNMC, who then pointed them back to a doctor at Creighton, who finally recommended them to the Mayo Clinic in Rochester, Minnesota. 'This did not all happen in one night, rather this was a four-year process,' Daniel recalled. Following the initial visit, the doctors at the Mayo Clinic tried a lot of trial procedures throughout an entire year but to no avail. 'I am grateful for their efforts. There is no doubt there is some hope in the future for an understanding of a cure for this, we just need to keep at our efforts and ensure we work with the doctors on an answer. Funding is a constant battle, research and development do not come cheap, even the most brilliant need to pay their bills, and the efforts on the part of all parties involved are greatly appreciated by my wife, me, and Erin.'

"All through the years Erin's parents nurtured their child, exposed her to nature, and watched as her body aged quickly. No matter their efforts, no matter their hope, and no matter their willingness to work with professionals, it was not always an easy burden to bear. 'This isn't fair. She is so special, she is so sweet, she is so strong, and she is so wonderful. Why? Why would any benevolent power ever let this happen to anyone?' Daniel would ask Beverly.

"'Sometimes they had to take a break from the issues surrounding their daughter's health in order to take everything in with stride, they needed to focus on the beauty of what little time she actually had,' Beverly was quoted as saying, often.

"Between the ages of two and five, among Erin's favorite locations to visit was the Platte River on the south side of Interstate 80, in Kearney, Nebraska. Each year near her birthday the Carters would go to watch the crane migration. Her parents would coordinate with the State's Wildlife Conservation and Preservation Organization to view these cranes relatively close, with the appropriate safety gear, using what is called a 'blind,' typically used by photographers to capture images up close. Her parents saw as Erin would light up inside as the cranes would get closer to her. 'On one occasion, she slipped out of the blind, and one unique crane came close to her. Erin stood back watching her eat, then this crane looked up at Erin, returned to eat, and then flew back to the flock. Every year we would take Erin there and watch the cranes feed off the remains of last year's crop harvest. They seemed to watch Erin gently in return. She enjoyed those moments greatly.' Dan shared.

"Daniel and Beverly Carter also provided a wealth of other lower-cost yet mind-enriching experiences and activities to bring Erin Carter unfeigned love, education, and an experiential sense of normalcy. 'She always smiled her big smile, and we loved her for it, yet we were burdened inside as her green eyes seemed to grow larger and more beautiful, but sadly as her head of blonde locks began to bald and her skin began to wrinkle and sag. She was beautiful inside, no matter what,' Daniel admitted.

"To her parents, it appeared as though all of the unfortunate and aesthetic effects of her unique disease didn't matter to mighty young Erin. Deep inside, even though her parents didn't realize it at the time, upon interviewing Erin, they realized that she knew she was a young child living with parents who love her deeply, no matter what was happening. To Erin, no matter the challenges ahead, Progeria stopped none of them from being wonderful, thoughtful, and caring.

"Despite her physiological aging process, Erin's mind is interestingly and exceedingly sharp. Her intuition is almost second to none. Her parents had taught her well and she had a natural gift for soaking information in, making sense of it, and coming up with very astute observations. In Kindergarten, she won her classes' artistic project contest and in the First Grade, she won the Advanced-Student Spelling Bee. She then continued to shine and won while at Nationals. She had also memorized the names of every President of the US, a few important facts regarding each of them, their spouses' names, facts about their contributions in history, and some intriguing facts about the economy and scientific achievements during their tenure.

"All that Erin, her family, and several dozen with a similar situation throughout the world hope for is an opportunity for their children to live full lives, and that the necessary efforts are made to find a cure for this premature aging disease. We're sure there is a way, but let's hope that time does not fly too quickly before these special spirits can no longer support the burden of this disease on their fragile physiological systems."

As this documentary was shared nationwide and worldwide, Erin and her parents were invited to talk show after talk show, including to America's and Erin's favorite, the beloved Elena. Elena listened to documentaries often, had realized years ago that many go to the theatre for entertainment, and that important information seems all-too-often forgotten, especially when it came to cures for that which causes misery to so many. Therefore, she often took it upon herself to educate while she entertained. Thus, she did, as Erin warmed the hearts of every person in the audience, especially as she talked about her favorite Sandhill crane, Betty.

One way or another, as if it were meant to be, Dr. Eliza Amber Williams' book, 'Pathway to the Stars,' had been released not long after Erin's sixth birthday earlier that year, and both Erin's story and Eliza's book had already become worldwide sensations, but somehow, both of their messages seemed to run important parallels.

Talk show host, Elena, who had also interviewed Eliza previously and was a good friend already, had, during this occasion invited both Erin and Eliza onto the show and interviewed them both separately and then together during a series of segments.

In the show, after introducing them to each other and interviewing them together, she gave a copy of Erin's documentary video on Blu-ray to Eliza, and then a copy of Eliza's book to Erin. She then gave additional copies of the documentary and the book to everyone in the audience. After giving Erin the book, 'Pathway to the Stars,' and after giving to Eliza, Erin's documentary, Elena went over some details of 'Pathway to the Stars' and gave Eliza's book a glowing review, while congratulating Erin on fighting through the tough times with grace.

Erin took her copy of Eliza's book home, asked her parents to read it to her, and eventually to themselves, every night. She then learned to read it at length on her own, and miraculously due to her quick ability to absorb information with her photographic memory. Eventually, both of Erin's parents purchased copies of their own, pored over its pages multiple times, and couldn't believe what they saw at first.

At the end of each night, following her meeting with Eliza Williams, Erin felt like a rising star.

Chapter 15: Arranging a Visit

Database Moon Archive, Celestial-Sol Entry Date: 2010 October 15. Yesha Alevtina trains Vesha Celeste. In this part of her training, we learn how Beverly and Amber coordinated a visit and made plans to help Erin. They use the recorded memories of Erin, her parents, and Amber Blythe, within the Virtual Universe. Interfaced within the Pathway Melrose Campus. Input by Eliza Williams, President of Pathway Industries, 2008-2015.

When Beverly and Daniel shared their insights, they realized that right before their eyes was an answer to help their daughter, and that was through Dr. Eliza A. Williams, who they'd already met. They had been impressed with her insights the day they had met her.

"What an amazing woman, she is more than a writer; she is a genius, in many ways just like our own daughter. We need to find a way to meet with Dr. Williams, because I believe she might have all the right answers," said Beverly.

Together, Beverly and Daniel drafted a letter to send to Dr. Eliza A. Williams' contact address, so they could get in touch with her to meet her again, but this time, away from the cameras. A couple of weeks went by, they put together another letter and sent it, and again they heard nothing. They decided to give it one last try, they wrote, but this time they asked Erin if she could write as well. Once everything was ready to go, they put their letters in an envelope and sent it.

Finally, early on in November of 2010, they received a phone call from a young lady who identified herself as Miss Amber Blythe. She was an intern at Pathway and as student at Harvard, who also happened to be brilliant in her studies of biogerontology, biogenetics, and continued cell therapy technologies.

Amber talked to Beverly on the phone at length and explained, "I work with Pathway LLC, and Dr. Eliza A. Williams has requested that as your delegate I meet with your family. Your daughter is quite a gifted girl, and after having deliberated with the Pathway organization founders, Eliza, Yesha, and James, they agreed I should talk to you, to meet with you. Shortly following my conversation with them and learning about your story I formed a team to see what we could do to help your family and your daughter. We realize you have been going to the Mayo Clinic frequently and so far, there have been very few positive results. They are very prestigious, but no matter the efforts, sometimes cures can be quite elusive because there are so many factors to consider.

"Therefore, once I visit, we would like you, Erin, and your immediate family to come with me to Cambridge, where we will escort you to and through our Melrose Campus, so we can look at her and obtain our own diagnostics if you are willing.

"We believe we may have therapies that will help Erin in a way that is unique to her to give her the life she deserves. We would also like to pay for your travel, room, and board, and give you an unlimited account for anything you might need on your trip and stay while here.

"Would you be willing to talk this over with your family and then get back to me? Please note that we ask you for confidentiality, since these are pre-trials. So, again, please keep this within your immediate family for now. While Pathway LLC has public releases, there is still so much more to do before this goes public. This has been vetted for near one-hundred percent success, but due to patenting, litigation, safety, and privacy we ask that your family maintain a low profile, just as we do, when it comes to research and working out as yet unforeseen details.

"Please, also understand that we keep our technologies low-key to prevent them from getting into the wrong hands and to ensure that the economy doesn't get turned upside-down, resulting in the loss of jobs for too many wonderful people. Basically, we are one-hundred percent certain we can fully heal your daughter, but to be clear, we again would ask that you keep this away from public ears, until public approval has been published through the release of our technology via the FDA, believe me, you'll understand the nuances, soon enough.

"We would also ask that you prepare to come to Cambridge, Massachusetts, for a long stay, depending on the length of the procedures, using the accounts I have mentioned, which will be supplied to each of you. I will also text you my number. Once you have talked it over with your family and each of you agrees to this, you'll merely need to text me a 'Yes.' You can ask whatever you wish. I will come to visit you, spend some time with Erin, you, and Daniel, and then escort you three to the campus. Once we are there, Dr. Eliza A. Williams would love to meet with you."

Once Amber finished, Beverly thought over what Amber had shared, and in a tone that was somewhat excited, she automatically found herself saying, "We're on board!"

Amber then responded, "Thank you, Beverly. I will visit you in a few days, but please give your family a heads-up?"

Once the conversation was complete, Beverly stopped to think about what she had gotten herself into, and then she was thrilled. *"This was what we have been hoping for!"*

"Daniel!" Beverly lightly raised her voice in a mixture of excitement and concern.

Daniel was in the laundry room putting clothes in the washer when he looked and saw his wife in the doorway. She looked worn and weathered from her day at work. Being a psychologist at an elementary school can be quite heavy at times, yet she seemed to be upbeat in the best of ways. "Hi there, Bev," said Daniel. "What's up?"

Beverly then explained the phone call, and how a representative from Pathway had been assigned to them. "A bio-gerontologist intern at Pathway LLC, named Amber Blythe, called and said she would see us in a few days, but in the meantime, we need to pack for a long stay. At first, we will go to Cambridge and from there, we will stay at the Pathway Melrose Campuses, in Massachusetts. They will cover all costs, give us each an account card to pay for all expenses during our stay, and they even have a cure for Erin if we're willing. She also said that Dr. Eliza A. Williams would like to meet with us. Would you like to do this?"

"Of course!" Daniel said with excitement, as he suddenly felt a lift of stress that had been burdening him for years. Despite tragedies he wouldn't wish on anyone, they never ceased to have an iron will, or to dedicate themselves to life. Here they were life itself was finally looking up. Someone had truly cared enough and could and would help. He hugged Beverly and together, they explained everything to Erin, who was excited and hopeful about the news, and they shared a group hug with her.

The Carter family then sat down, reminisced on everything, gave Erin another gentle yet loving hug, and discussed what to pack. They then talked with each other further about their excitement. They also reminded themselves to be humble about what was going to happen.

"It is important to maintain clarity on what is going on, and to make decisions as to whether or not we will need to sell the home or put it up for rent," said Beverly. "This technology, if created and used successfully on Erin, with kindness at the core, could be a wonderful promise to humanity. Life can become even more beautiful than anyone might be able to imagine if this works. We must always remember that all things of promise begin with kindness, but it is okay to harbor a little skepticism to make sure we're not being given false hope."

They rested well that night, packed their bags, and got ready for a long trip. Beverly went to some close friends who recommended securing the services of a property manager since they were sure they would be gone for a while. Of course, the agent that visited was curious as to where they were going, but Beverly kept it brief and told him that they would be going away for a while, they weren't sure for how long. She then told him, upon further inquiry, that their family would be gone for a while, and Erin would be receiving treatments that might help her to overcome the effects of a disease known as Hutchison-Gilford Progeria Syndrome. Once the agent was suitably baffled, he ceased with his questions.

The Carters had prepared for their trip each day prior, and as if this might be the last time for a while, they took in the sights and sounds of Kearney. Before they knew it, the day they had been awaiting arrived, when, as promised, Amber Blythe would visit, stay the night, and then take them to Cambridge and Melrose.

Just as Beverly grew nervous, she heard her phone vibrate.

"I'm on my way!" Amber had texted Bev's cell.

"She's on her way!" Bev excitedly let Dan and Erin know. Daniel prepared some tea. Erin and Beverly made sure everything they didn't want the property manager to get into was packed and locked within fireproof safes. Once they were ready, they sat down, listened to some soft music, and played Scrabble, waiting for Amber.

Ready

"Bzzzzz!" The doorbell rang.

It had been three days after the original phone call and Amber, as promised, came to visit all the way from Cambridge, Massachusetts.

The Carters had coordinated immediately after the phone call the details for homecare before leaving, within the scope of Kearney. Their property manager had been instructed to visit weekly, to make sure the mail was collected, the landscaping tended to, and typical home maintenance was squared away. The Carters had prepared everything as requested and tidied up any loose ends as they awaited Amber's visit. Erin's family had agreed that since Beverly had taken the call, she would be the person to greet her at the door.

Daniel and Erin stood back watching in anticipation as Beverly opened the front door...

Arriving from Cambridge

Earlier that day, Amber Blythe had used a jump gate hidden not too far from the local municipal airport car rental service. She had worked with Dr. Eliza Williams in the Virtual Universe the day prior to arrange, encode, and send a small cloud of nanos during the night to Kearney, Nebraska. Once there, as programmed, the cloud of nanos created a well-hidden, optimally placed donut-shaped object, called a jump gate. This was a traveling device that had the capabilities of invisibility and cloaking technology imbued within it, like many of the rest of Eliza's projects throughout the solar system and placed in locations that would be vulnerable to far too many questions if seen by the public. These nanos, of their own freewill, placed this object, on the opposite side of the parking lot of the car rental business in a quiet grove of trees, not too far from the municipal airport, yet in a non-trafficked area away from the unsuspecting public eye.

On the day arranged, Amber would jump to the location, proceed to the vehicle rental agency, retrieve the reserved vehicle, and drive it the rest of the way to Carter's residence. As such, she did.

"What an efficient form of travel!" thought Amber, *"I wish we had this method of transport a long time ago. Imagine, instead of the dangers of air evacuation or speeding in an expensive ambulance which is a challenge to navigate, now a person could be taken directly to the ER or a specialist in a clinic, as the situation might call for, be treated right away, and returned home that same day for bed rest as needed. That would reduce costs for those struggling and to the taxpayer while saving and improving more lives. I suppose in time options will improve. I hope the rest of humanity will catch up with Pathway soon. Oh, wow, this is such a cute town,"* She thought, as she simultaneously contemplated her robust research on Erin's condition, travel by jump gate, and the drive around Kearney to get to the Carter's home.

Amber had been working with Pathway as a fully read-in member for almost two months on Erin's case while studying for her master's degree thesis, at MIT, in the real world, but already possessing ninety Virtual Universe PhDs, including public administration, biotech, law, and so much more, and now that she was pretty much on pause with regard to school awaiting her Ph.D. courses, at Harvard, which would begin in January, she could visit Erin. While her thesis had been completed, using the assets that her biopod provided her via the Virtual Universe, real world traditional schedules called for her to follow MIT's timeline, when it came to her thesis submission. She had spent much more time dedicated to Erin's cause since this was her first mission as a delegate. Even though time had seemingly flown by and she had been juggling a lot of other programs, studies, and conducting a lot of research and lab tests, she had also been doing a lot of research on Hutchinson-Gilford Progeria Syndrome.

Erin's case was somewhat unique. After combing through all her records, after introducing them to the encrypted archives of the Twelve Database Moons, developing and practicing scenarios, and measuring the results, she finally found the results she was looking for and was very well-versed on what needed to be done.

The database moons, which had access to every bit of data in the world, had very little on this disease. So, she had to manually research. Encrypted or non-encrypted, each database was itself impenetrable by hackers, and necessarily so, since its design was purely intended for the well-being of others, as well as their quality of life, longevity, and clarity toward the advancement of civilization. In Pathway, this sufficed as "need to know." Information within Pathway was used one-hundred percent of the time for improvement of health and well-being while preventing access to those bent on malicious use of it. Pathway had been founded on what they dubbed, "true ethics," and they honored their stance time and again, every day. Those entrusted with the use of the databases had been vetted, read-in, and trained and thus had clarity toward the missions as well as a heavy dose of compassion, empathy, and the ability for sound resolution to any issues.

Amber had conducted thorough research, doing countless years of studies, trials, experiments, and real-world lab work in a matter of days rather than weeks, in the Virtual Universe. She had practiced her developing ideas in there as well, based on every aspect of her biotech case in the real world. Doing this, she could enter, come out with new solutions, rinse and repeat, until she knew exactly what needed to be done. For Amber to be amply prepared, a complete understanding was necessary of at least two methods of cure. By that, two of the methods needed to be such that Erin could be cured through biopod or through following therapies using real-world technologies. Amber had studied everything regarding her case thoroughly, had fully grasped the intricate science of the various forms of Progeria with her abilities, and had augmented her neurological optimizations and her inherent cognition, which was now multiplied exponentially, and her clarity on this subject was now a breeze.

"Even though biopods are the easiest way to cure Erin, they still aren't released to the public, for ethical, legal, or economic concerns. Not due to the lack of trying, on our part, however. For some reason, Pathway's submissions keep being turned down by a rather sneaky entity who seems to be pulling the strings and making the big decisions." Amber would often contemplate.

It didn't appear that the real world or established science authorities would catch up any time soon, nor that they desired to, since it did not fit their economic agenda. If she could convince Erin's family to be read-in completely, this would be easier on the Carters, however, Pathway had flexibility, either way.

Legally, all this ought to have been a non-issue. On their campus all was fine, since much of their campus was directly linked to similar campuses in the tech cities throughout the Solar System, and thus were overseen purely by Pathway and the UP. However, for the purposes of "explanations" they tried to keep everything that was within the Melrose Campus as legal as any other facility throughout the US. There was the public area of the campus at the ground level. Other areas included the many facilities, but dormitories or suites were in some cases thirty miles below the Earth's surface and others were closer to fifty miles down.

Looking out the large windows, from the inside, gave newcomers and anyone in general an "open" feel. This was mostly to give visitors a sense that just outside the window was the forest or jungle, and the open sky.

Each of the campus dormitory complexes were a dynamic series of penthouse suites. Each suite had their own biopods, hot tubs, master-sized bedrooms, offices, living rooms, pools, the works. Doctor's offices were nearby and on hand as well.

All the finer details were more spectacular than a luxury suite in Dubai, Singapore, or Beijing. Like the high-tech locations appearing throughout the world, there was an increasing interest in the latest in every imaginable technology.

In contrast to the "ritzy glam" of the luxury suites meant for billionaires alone on Earth in the public world, within the Pathway campuses, there were opportunities enough for anyone interested to live there with all of the luxuries and even involve themselves in any great cause that would come along. All missions were considered employment. The compensation with these missions lent toward a substantial increase in quality of life and with it, opportunities for self-actualization.

In addition to a series of suites, each with biopods of their own and doctor's offices deep within Pathway LLC at the Melrose, Massachusetts Campus, highly specialized care could be administered in private.

Within each tech city, every domicile was set up in much the same way. Eliza had established a system of governance in these tech cities based on common sense, well-being, and Universal Ethics. Thus, everything her company was doing, was within ethical standards of guidance according to the laws and bylaws that put the well-being of the people first and above all else. Lust for money or a desire to play power games was not on Pathway's agenda at all.

The total population had grown to more than ten-million people in these cities by the end of 2008, and as such, they had requested and conducted an election, voting Eliza in for the first one-hundred-year term as the President of Pathway's twenty-thousand tech cities, with ten-year interim Presidential voting beginning in 2010.

When it came to provision of medical care, even though the biopod option was available and universal, the chance existed that there might be families that did not feel as comfortable with physiological and neurological optimization as others, and the ultimate decision rested collectively on adults or parents, within reason, of course.

Thus, Amber Blythe made sure she was prepared for long-term, FDA-approved, public treatments as well. In most cases, this involved staying in the now world-renown and public Pathway, Melrose Campus. Amber's plan was to invite them to the more elaborate campuses, only accessible via the jump gates and hyperloops.

Once at the elaborate campuses, each family would be given a set of choices. They could become fully read-in citizens of Pathway with transparency of service provided through preliminary training, to them, before any procedure. Or, they could opt to turn down the use of the biopods and their comments on treatments could go public. Either way, to Eliza's and Pathway's chagrin, there was a confidentiality agreement that stated that they would not under any circumstances discuss identified proprietary information with the general public, news agencies, etc. If any questions were had, they could contact their assigned delegate, which in the case of the Carter family, would be Amber Blythe. She would coach them prior to any public interviews, if needed.

Doing things in public involved cross-queuing with scientists all over the world using jargon and technologies accepted in the real and legal worlds via science journals and working in real-world laboratories with archaic equipment, which were ironically considered the most advanced and costly both in time and money. These studies required a lot of investment in physical input, even by the standards of Pathway LLC and in the real world. Going public, they would need to deal with the many tedious aspects which would include the red-tape existent in liabilities, legalities, approvals, lawyers, attorneys, government approvals, and of course, this would consume a lot more time than was necessary, while failing to actually address the issues present within a particular patient. All of this bureaucratic confusion had increased so much so, that it lent to unnecessary suffering, misery, and the terminal nature existent in so many victims of toxicity in one form or another.

Luckily, aside from Amber's intellect, genius, drive, and personal investment, or in this case, the extra sentimental aspect, where Erin reminded Amber of her sister, Sarah, she had pulled no stops to get things done as soon as possible. This involved recruiting three very notable scientists during the last two months to Pathway LLC. With good fortune, they had come on board and were fully read-in. Together they worked on the case, even taking care of all of the public aspects within just a couple of months. The public treatments were now ready for testing and approval by the FDA, but as far as immediate healing was concerned, the biopod was instantaneous in every way that mattered and would be precise and effective.

The first recruit Amber worked with was Dr. Yon Forall, who had been conducting extensive research on progeria for a book about telomerase therapy and telomeres. Furthermore, he had conducted extensive research on Progeria therapies for the last twenty years.

Dr. Leticia Perrier, Ph.D., Founder, and President of Earth Lives Biotechnology, Inc had been the second recruit Amber began working with, not more than a day later. Leticia was working on several therapies and was well-versed on telomerase therapy, farnesyltransferase inhibitors, myostatin inhibitors, and other aspects that related to controlling progerin, or the silent point mutation in the lamin A gene, and its tendency to damage good cells within the human body.

Finally, Dr. Leah B. Gardenia, Ph.D., MD, and Progeria Study Foundation joined the team about three days later. Leah had worked with more than ninety-six Progeria patients during their various stages of life while conducting research on what caused damage to the body's cells affecting them in such a way. Through her experiences and studies, she more fully understood what would cause cells to become prematurely senescent and had brilliant ideas on what could be used to stop the damage and perhaps even reverse it.

Even though these new recruits were each in their fifties, they looked like they were only twenty-two, and they had the mental aptitude of geniuses. Much of this was due to their personal dedication and their studies. Now, with optimized capabilities their clarity of each of the associated and integrated sciences was augmented. What made the process flow smoothly, was the fact that everyone on Amber's team was an excellent team worker, and likewise, very capable socially. Since they too had become fully read-in, they were assigned to work with Amber on physiological and neurological health-related scientific missions en-tangent with Erin's and had spent a lot of time together in the Virtual Universe labs linked to their labs in the real world. These labs had resources and capabilities that stemmed from both public Earth-based and advanced proprietary tech city technologies.

Along with their many missions, these scientists wrote books, led science teams, and nurtured the public into the future of longevity, health, strength, and clarity of mind. They also conducted advanced proprietary and public research. Any books they wrote were vetted by Pathway via the Virtual Universe, so they could be sold worldwide, just like "Pathway to the Stars" had been.

They burned bright with astounding results, even while using the established scientific standards for biotechnology, biophysics, neurotechnology, and many other advanced medical sciences, with subtle bumps in solution-based theories to speed things up.

On its own, terrestrial modern medicine had a long way to go in order to bridge the gap between its own and Pathway's capabilities. Adjustment of social norms, the argumentative tone of many non-read-in scientists, and Pathway's biopods were small pieces in a large puzzle of the stark contrast between well-being and what was accepted in public. Fortunately, Amber had studied with Doctors Yon Forall, Leticia Perrier, and Leah Gardenia for many centuries worth of time within the Virtual Universe, a couple of months in the real world, and together they came up with viable real-world solutions to curing Progeria. Based on the current pace of science, most Pathway scientists wouldn't be able to release their books until 2014 or 2018 or later.

Working with Yon, Leticia, and Leah on the development of her own multi-layered knowledge to help Erin and with the completion of her own thesis, Amber was ready. Thanksgiving was around the corner, and Amber was finally prepared and, in a position, to be able to contact, coordinate with, and visit the Carters.

The Road Ahead

For her trip to Nebraska, Amber had previously been briefed on public Pathway traveling norms. So, although she didn't need to pack a suitcase, she packed one anyway to elude any suspicions. Brushing teeth, showering up, using the restroom facilities, or changing clothes could take place on a nano-level and in a split second. So, although she could adjust according to the fashion macro in her mind, Amber packed the typical items so those who were unaware wouldn't be overwhelmed by her abilities, typically followed by a glow.

While Amber no longer needed luggage to spend the night, due to her optimizations and her smart-suit, which was standard issue and tailored to fit for all who were read-in, she had to consider public perception. Snapping her finger and not toting around bags would most likely raise suspicions and would traditionally work out alright if she were living out of a hotel room that wasn't closely monitored.

As it was, Pathway delegates typically stayed at cheap motels because they had separate door entrances available for each temporary domicile, which worked for Pathway delegates without any cause for concern. While staying at more humble locations when traveling was the typical method of temporary domicile for any of Eliza's delegates and representatives, when going to a family home or a large metropolitan environment, it was always recommended to bring the necessary bags. Fortunately, an optimized body augmented strength and agility, so toting bags was easy.

As Amber thought about what she wanted to do in Kearney, she was thrilled by the possibilities of a tour around Erin's town to check out the schools, the art centers, the farmlands, and the archway museum above Interstate 80. Maybe she could head there for a morning jog and eat at the Carter family's favorite restaurant. The possibilities seemed endless. Everything she thought of from jogging through the fields to swimming with the water snakes without fear would be wonderful things to do once she met the Carters, if she stayed the night. In all seriousness, no matter where she planned on going, she needed to get the feel of this location for proper and objective environmental diagnostics, by understanding and analyzing Erin's surrounding environment. She appreciated the rolling possibilities for doing so.

While enroot in her rental car, even though Amber's physiology and neurology were optimized, she received constant updates, and to a certain extent, she had learned how to control the glow. However, Amber was enthusiastic about this visit, and it seemed to be having an effect on her, and in the most awkward of ways. So much so, that she could feel the glimmer of her nanos raging through her physiological system.

Amber felt her left side body art swimming around with its ever-pulsating kaleidoscope of artistry, her hairstyles and highlights changing every few seconds, her make-up was flailing about and out of control, and her smart-clothing fashions and styles were all changing between the many full-on wardrobes she had set aside for every and any possible occasion, as she drove down the road. She was glad no one else seemed to be out at the time. Amber kind of felt like a clown, especially as she struggled to gather her senses, activate her stationary look, seal it in place, and calm down.

At one point on her drive from the local airfield to Carter's home, she found herself wearing a bikini, and at another point she was almost embarrassingly wearing only a bathrobe, at another point she was wearing a superhero's costume, but within a few moments she was able to conduct what she called a "thought change." Now, she was back in her normal attire and put it into stasis. *"I have that issue handled. Check!"*

Looking back, it had taken almost two months before Amber could put her public image and a variety of occasion-applicable assortments of a wardrobe into stasis or in a compartmented area within her mind for use as needed to apply to her smart suit digital overlay.

"Hopefully, the designer industry will be able to get involved in the whole kit and kaboodle of the neural wardrobe compartmentalization scene soon. Not all of us are that kind of creative," Amber thought and chuckled. Her public image had been as her basic self, which had always been a sort of professionalized look mixed with her modeling attire. Being optimized did not mean a person didn't get a little nervous; however, Amber thought of all of this, and then she coached herself, *"Nerves are gone. Check."*

Although Amber didn't need to go jogging, she was very much just like her new friends Yesha, Eliza, and James, and just as they did, she still enjoyed testing her limitations, her speed, and the Earthly sights and sounds as she breathed in the world around her. With an optimized body, she didn't need to eat, but it still provided energy.

The energy was processed perfectly to enhance her hygiene and produced a pleasant scent of roses, lilacs, or any satisfying and physiologically healthy aroma, for that matter, that came to mind. Her nanos were always working. Therefore, while she could eat a rock or breathe in radiation for the same result, normalcy was just better.

Amber knew she wasn't going to Kearney for the food. She was going there to meet and help Erin, *"But food can be a reward! Oh, the yummy bakery delights, the veggies, the fruits, oh! Omaha beef! I'll have to bring some home, so I can use the cellular makeup of it to grow the best cuts without ever needing to kill another head of cattle, or cows, as the cows themselves prefer to be called.*

"We're so sorry, cows; nature made us omnivores, but we're evolving! I suppose when I get back to the campuses, maybe I can use the steak, some hair follicles, break out the differences in genetics and root encodings, re-encode each cell, grow the meat in the labs, and enjoy the best steaks by simply brushing a friendly cow's hair, converting the cells, and growing the various cuts of steak in-vitro from then on out! It will be nice to have a premium sample to go off, I suppose. Hopefully, Chloe won't mind back at home! I'll talk to her about this. Okay, back to my mission."

By the time she arrived at the Carter family residence, Amber had rehearsed everything extensively. At one point during her drive there, however, she'd lost track of time and while obeying the speed limit and traffic signs, she found she'd driven a few miles off. Finally, she stopped, parked, and only continued driving down the road after tapping into her neural link to the Internet to bring up a mental image of Google Maps so she could drive to the Carter family's home without causing any accidents. There was a time that she had appreciated her cell phone, but that was now old-hat. Plus, she saw the cell phone as a social deterrent, and she considered herself an odd duck where that was concerned. Eliza and Yesha had seemed to love theirs, but they were also respectfully reticent of the people around first and foremost, and for them, it served as a sense of normalcy rather than as a real-world social distraction.

Amber, in contrast, was still learning to use her neurological-digital display. Pondering on her drive, she was grateful for her neural link and the three-dimensional holographic digital presentation before her telling her everything she needed to know, whenever she needed to know it, so long as she didn't get lost in nervousness.

The quirkiness of portable tech had her awash in frustration over the typical social scene surrounding hand-held devices, nevertheless. *"How many times do people walk into an office and say hi to those in the room these days? Hardly ever! They're usually looking down at their cell phone and ignoring passers-by. With my new abilities, I can see people, bring up any public data and know instantly who I am talking to. No longer does technology need to be a hindrance to social integration, it can help. It's great being optimized!"* Amber coached herself often, as she did in this situation, to simply gather her senses and reduce her glow.

The quaint nature of the town was quite appealing. She could see the skyline above the buildings and homes and as she drove by them, she appreciated the simpler way of life and pressed on. After arriving, she got out of her rental vehicle, looked at the darling and charming home, smiled, walked up the driveway and to the front door, and rang the doorbell.

A Wonderful Family

"Bzzzzz..."

"Here we go," she thought to herself.

Within a few short moments, the door opened and a lady who looked like the pictures and videos she'd seen of Beverly Carter during her research and in the documentaries, or Erin's mother, began the conversation. Amber noticed how she was just as attractive as seen in the documentaries and talk shows. "Hello, is this Amber?"

"Yes, this is. You must be Beverly Carter? How are you?" Amber did everything she could to control her nerves and her glow, she wasn't used to this type of mission, especially not with her new abilities, and she still felt nervous. She was excited to share her team's new cure for progeria, and even though biopods weren't ready to go public yet, due to so many social norms, she knew that she had built a publicly acceptable safety-net, for a viable cure, and she looked forward to this opportunity to meet Erin's wonderful family and help them. Nevertheless, *"I don't want to scare them with my plethora of abilities, or new-found weaknesses,"* she thought, as she worked hard to control them.

"It's nice to finally meet you, Amber. I'm as good as good can be. Would you like to come in?" Beverly was floored by how striking, calm, and genteel Amber was.

"Sure," Amber said as she felt a sense of acceptance from the family right away, based on their posture and their expressions. She felt more at ease. *"Less likely to glow,"* she thought as she mentally coached herself. *"This is your first official mission since training in the campuses, Amber. We're all human, so just you relax. I suppose I can let go, be myself, and this seems to be working—I'll just be me!"* Amber thought, thinking of one of her favorite tunes, called "Just Be," by electronic and trance music vocalist Kirsty Hawkshaw. She picked up her bags, nodded a thank you to Beverly, smiled at Erin and Daniel who stood a few feet back and were both trying to peer over Beverly's shoulder, and stepped inside. *"What a beautiful family!"*

Amber came into Erin's and Daniel's view and introduced herself.

"I'm Amber, and you must be Erin," Amber smiled and offered a handshake to her little yet brittle hands. *"Of course, it's Erin,"* Amber thought. And then she saw Erin smile, and that was what Amber needed, to completely calm her nerves. She temporarily put on her analytical mindset, in the interest of understanding Erin even deeper. *"What a darling young girl. Wow! Her parents have invested in orthodontics, and she is obviously very good with hygiene,"* Amber tried not to judge but was looking at it purely from a diagnostic and medical standpoint.

"And you must be Amber?" asked Erin. To Erin, based on what Mom had said, Amber was a wonderful friend of Eliza, and there was a glow about Eliza that she had noticed, but Erin had told no one. Seeing Amber for the first time, she noticed that she too glowed like Eliza and Erin thought of Amber and Eliza as angels. That luminescent glow about her and Eliza, that she didn't dare describe, was something that instantly brought a sense of calm to Erin as well.

"Hello, Amber. My name is Daniel. I am Erin's father, good to meet you. I am of the understanding that you are a delegate, our delegate to Pathway LLC and that we will be heading to Massachusetts soon? Oh, pardon me. Please have a seat." Daniel was clearly more nervous than Amber, and Amber could tell. From Daniel's standpoint, she was gorgeous, smart, and was about to help his little girl. He didn't know what to say or how to say it. He loved his wife dearly and did not want to embarrass her in any way. So, he maintained a sense of professionalism, charm, kindness, and hospitality.

From Amber's perspective, he was a very handsome man right off, with a cute and awkward personality.

From Beverly's viewpoint, she was proud of Daniel for being the charming man he was. It worked wonders when meeting people.

"Yes, I wanted to meet with you, to talk with all three of you about what we plan on doing and see what you think about it all. Also, if you would like, before we go in the morning, I wouldn't mind if you would show me some of your favorite places around town? Oh, Erin, I understand that you enjoy the crane migration. I know many of them are gone or are heading south at this time of year, but maybe instead of walking there since it might be a little too cold, could we drive to the Archway and look out the window at the Platte River? Maybe you could show me where you typically go?"

"Oh sure, that would be wonderful!" said Erin.

After Daniel asked Amber if she would like a tea, he disappeared into the kitchen, and then returned with a platter of teacups, a large tea diffuser, and a carafe full of what she presumed was tea, along with some German rock sugar.

Amber breathed in the aroma and knew instantly that Daniel had brought out one of her favorites. It was ginseng and peppermint tea from the Republic of Tea. *"They certainly know their teas. This is excellent for digestion, mental clarity, and tastes amazing. Check!"*

When Amber sat down, Erin sat down, right next to her. She immediately trusted Amber without hesitation. It felt good to Amber to engender the instantaneous trust from others, and she appreciated Erin's vibrant and innocent spirit. Erin was gentle and pleasant.

It was sad, however, to see the fullness of what the progerin had done to her cells as it expressed itself profoundly in her prematurely aging presence, but her spirit oozed out in such a way that anyone who saw her would wish to give her a hug, and they probably would, if they weren't afraid of damaging her fragile bones.

Beverly and Daniel settled down on the love seat, slightly facing the couch that Amber and Erin were sitting on. Light music was playing, and enjoying what she heard, even though she could have looked it up using her link, Amber asked, "The sound in the air, I love it. Who is it?"

Beverly answered, "This is Amethystium. They are a New Age group with mixed media and a lot of cultural richness to it. We've followed them for years and appreciate their music."

"I can see why. It's beautiful," replied Amber, as the music continued to put her at ease.

The conversation took off from there about walks in the parks nearby, looking up at the stars at night, and many other activities that were both healthy and informative. At one point, Amber brought up a conversation about her sister and how looking up at the Scrabble board on the table before her reminded her of how she and Sarah often played a digital version of Scrabble with each other. "We would play Scrabble using our computers, in the same room where we were separated by a plastic barrier, due to a series of physiological complications. Unfortunately, she passed away long before Eliza came into my life. I am sure that if Sarah were alive now, she would have been happy to meet you, and she would have completely approved of any treatments available via Pathway. She loved life and was always so whimsical about traveling through the Universe. She was so smart, so sweet, and so fun to be with. We did home-school together until she passed away. She was such a wonderful sister and I miss her very much. Erin, you kind of remind me of her in so many good ways. I hope you don't mind?"

"Of course, it's okay with me, Amber. I guess that means we're more like sisters," said Erin with a smile. She put her tiny arms around Amber's left forearm and rested her head on her left breast without even thinking anything other than she trusted Amber fully, she smelled good, and it was comfortable being nearby her.

Amber felt aglow and almost as if she would cry. *"This young girl, what a wonderful spirit and a beautiful human being,"* she thought.

The family talked with Amber, and she could already tell Erin was not only a sweet girl, but she was a genius with the type of personality and strength of character that was ideal for Pathway. She understood now why Eliza, Yesha, and James had completely approved of her. There was no doubt why Eliza had made resources available to her family, especially for a procedure that would optimize Erin's physiology and neurology. Erin's parents also seemed to have the kind of personality and nobility of character that would make them lovely friends, citizens, and delegates of Pathway as well. They were a very well-balanced family.

As the night grew late, and the excitement of the day grew thin, Erin asked if Amber could sleep in her room. Amber looked toward Beverly and Daniel, and they approved.

Erin was so excited with having met her new friend and looked forward to talking with her late and into the night. It was wonderful having someone she could now view as a sister, like Amber.

Erin was impressed with Amber instantly upon meeting her, but every moment that passed by, her impressions of Amber increased in a positive and trusting way. Erin was always good at reading people. She had a twin bunk bed, so with both beds filled, they talked for a while and then slept well through to the morning. One by one, they got up, yet interestingly everyone seemed to have a similar internal clock because Amber and the Carters were up at the same time.

Daniel prepared breakfast, Beverly showered up and got ready for the big day, Erin did the same as her Mom in her own bathroom, and Amber allowed herself to stay a little disheveled from sleeping and sat and talked with Daniel while he prepared the meal.

"Good morning. If I understand correctly, you're from Georgia, Dan or Daniel? Do you miss your home state and your family?" asked Amber.

"You can call me Dan, or Daniel. Whichever you prefer. My family? Oh, of course, I miss my family. But, we're about our lives; we each forged ahead and are on our own. Occasionally, I hear from my brothers and sisters, my Mom and my Dad, and even my first boss, and I am proud of them for all of their efforts. They are all wonderful people in their own way.

"I suppose moving here, I grew committed to Beverly, the people here, and of course our sweet daughter, Erin. I enjoy it here, and I have invested in our little family one hundred percent of the way, and in every way that matters. Whatever Beverly and Erin decide to do, I support it. We're looking forward to going to Massachusetts, and we truly appreciate your desire to help."

Amber saw a good man in Daniel and appreciated his soft and noble demeanor. "I may be just as excited to help Erin as you two are for us to help her. She is a wonderful young girl and you have both done well by her. I can tell there is a lot of love in your hearts for each other. You're a wonderful family. Dan, I also want to assure you, that you will all be in safe hands at Pathway. I promise that life is soon to become much more amazing than is possible to describe. I am consistently impressed with Eliza's ideas, her care for humanity, and her inventions.

"Mm, mm, that smells good, Dan," Amber finished, as the smell of sourdough French toast, real butter, and true maple syrup was warming while permeating the room.

Erin stepped into view from the hallway, looking freshly showered and nicely dressed, walked into the kitchen and dining area and sat next to Amber, after smiling and saying, "Thank you for coming and spending the night with us. The bathroom is ready whenever you are."

"I shouldn't take too long," said Amber. She then got up, went to the bathroom with her bag, and closed the door. After turning the shower on she got into it for a few minutes. *"Ah, the warm water always feels good, optimized or not,"* thought Amber, it was soothing and reduced that seemingly uncontrollable glow she had. In five minutes, she stepped out fully clothed, smelled amazing, and looked like the model she had been for years.

Stepping back out to the kitchen and dining area, Beverly looked splendid and had taken over for Daniel who was also quickly getting ready.

"Would you like a morning tea?" asked Beverly, "It's a ground Matcha and green tea powder combination. A wonderful way to start the day, while we wait for Dan," Beverly said with a smile of a person who had rested well and was enthusiastic about the day ahead.

Once ready, they ate together. The family took Amber to explore the town, showing her the art center, the museum, the Platte River, and when they were ready, Amber took them home to drop off their car. Their property manager was there as scheduled. He took the keys and wished them well.

Amber's rental car was big enough to take their luggage and the three family members to the municipal airport. "This should be an interesting thing, but here we go. First, I will turn in the rental. And then, we will take your bags with us, and go right over there." Amber pointed toward a grove of trees with an empty and clear space between them.

"I'm not sure I understand," said Beverly, in a state of awkward disbelief.

"Trust me. You'll understand soon," Amber looked at each family member with all the sincerity she could muster and tried to soothe their concerns, as she parked the car. They followed her into the rental building, where she turned in the keys and made the necessary payments using her Pathway Travel Card. Afterward, she walked out the door, looked toward the family with a look that suggested they follow her, that she wasn't completely nuts, and then walked toward the trees she had previously pointed out. From there, after turning around and smiling at them once more, she took another step into the clearing between the trees and disappeared.

"Follow me," said Erin, thrilled. This reminded her of something she'd only seen in movies or read in books. Erin hadn't packed much, just a little bag with a change of clothes, a little toothbrush, a few other personal hygiene items, and her medication. Her little frame picked up the little bag and she walked as fast as she could and then disappeared through the trees.

Training

"Where did she go?" asked Daniel, looking at his wife concerned and in disbelief.

"Let's find out," said Beverly, who was quickly figuring out that Amber was for real.

Amber smiled. She saw Erin's face brighten as she reached her from the other side of the jump gate. She then stepped back through, looked from the other side of the portal and saw Beverly readying to make her way through it. Before she did, she looked back at Daniel with her own look that said, "Common!" After which, Daniel followed them and was quite breath-taken with what he saw after passing through what he thought was merely a space between two trees.

"What was that?" Asked Daniel, once he had caught up to Amber.

"We just went through a jump gate. There are a lot of those around here, but you'll learn more about them soon. Common, Daniel, follow me," Answered Amber, with a smile that suggested that she understood his situation of awe and being struck with endless questions.

There they were. Erin, Beverly, and Amber standing in a large white room, with huge windows around the circumference of the place. Looking through the openings he saw all sorts of animals sitting on benches of various sizes; they were apparently holding newspapers and engaging in conversation. He also saw a forest of beautiful flowers, fruits, and all sorts of vegetation. Suddenly, Eliza appeared through another donut-shaped, white object, with purple, turquoise, blue, and black accent colors on buttons laden hither and thither all over it. Dan saw her come through a portal of sorts from a different location than they had come from, but he couldn't tell from where. It didn't matter, she was enigmatic in every sense, and he was tongue-tied, breath-taken, and searching for words to say.

"I couldn't miss meeting you guys. It's so great to see you! What do you think?" expressed Eliza. "Yesha would have been here, but she is otherwise engaged in other parts of the world. She is a wonderful friend, and you'll no doubt meet her soon."

"Wow! How did you do that?" was all that Daniel could muster, as he looked around in a state of disbelief.

"Is everything okay?" asked Amber, looking toward Daniel, thinking back to how she felt just three months before when she first beheld the place.

"Oh, yes, everything is okay. It is... it's... I am just amazed is all," Daniel was clearly trying to pull himself together, just as his wife already had, who seemed very well-composed.

"Come with me," said Eliza.

Amber and the Carter family followed Eliza into a spacious auditorium, and when she looked, there was Yesha waiting for them, apparently back from one of her many missions around the world. *"Jump gates truly rock!"* thought Amber.

In the auditorium were several other groups of people, Daniel noticed they were speaking in different languages sitting and waiting. This large room appeared to be a very posh looking movie theater. He, his family, and Amber followed Eliza to where Yesha was waiting for them. Eliza took a seat beside Yesha after introducing her to everyone, and everyone else took up seats beside Yesha and Eliza, with Erin and Amber to their left, and Beverly and Dan to their right.

After the same briefing that Amber had received when she first arrived, they were shown to their quarters and introduced to their biopods. In a very short period of time after the completion of Pathway's infrastructure worldwide in 2008, more than two years had gone by, with a huge influx of refugees and people from all over the world and throughout the country who had been victims of their environment. In this training session, more than one-hundred candidate citizens were in attendance and had agreed to be fully read-in. With training complete, the various groups were shown their quarters by their delegates, and then the biopods within their guest suites. Erin and her parents were accompanied by Amber, Eliza, and Yesha to the biopods in a group biopod room, after going through a jump gate and a brief tour of their suite. "This type of training is going on in tech cities all over the Solar System," Amber whispered at one point to the family, and to their surprise.

"These look like glowing white tanning beds, but they look comfortable and fluffy inside," said Erin, giddy as could be, excited to experience what they had just learned about.

"Ha! Yes, I get that a lot," said Eliza, with a humble sense of humor.

"That's what I told Eliza and Yesha the first time I saw those beautiful life-saving pods!" chuckled Amber, almost awkwardly.

Erin looked toward Amber, who happened to be looking toward Eliza as if she was having a private and mental conversation with her and Yesha. Eliza, Yesha, and Amber pursed their lips, and, in a few moments, they looked toward each of the Carters. When Eliza shook her head, "Yes," Amber began to talk to the family. Erin knew they had just had a conversation that had to have been mind-to-mind. She listened as Amber spoke.

"The choice is yours. What you saw in the auditorium is what I saw when I first arrived here. I chose to accompany Eliza and Yesha in a room like this and each of us used a biopod like these. There is one here for each of us. When I went in, they showed me things I never knew existed or had even known to care or worry about. Now I know and although I cared a great deal about the well-being of others then, there is so much more depth to it all that I had never before even considered, and I believe I care more now than I did then about so much more than I did before. When I came out of the biopod, I had crystal clear clarity on so many things and I felt a special bond between myself and anyone who had ever been in there already. We all learned from each other and understood each other more completely than we could have by any other means.

"I had been physiologically and neurologically optimized and imbued with what we call nanos. These nanos and our smart suits allow us to do a lot of things we were never able to do before. While I am still getting used to my glow, the experiences I have had over the last couple of months have been exhilarating! Ultimately, Erin, this will heal you entirely and when you come back out of the biopod, you may not recognize yourself. What you'll see in the mirror from that point on is how you view yourself within the Virtual Universe, mixed with what you would have looked like had all of your cells fired in a way that would have led to you not having Hutchinson-Gilford Progeria Syndrome, or any ailment or disease for that matter, and most likely as your body would express itself at your current age. Your body will mature into what you will see in there until you reach the age of eighteen. From there you will be able to adjust your physiology to express itself in all manners and between the ages of twenty to thirty-five, as you choose at that time or at any time thereafter.

"You have a beautiful spirit, Erin, I can tell, and I imagine that your mind will reflect that in the way that it expresses your image very creatively. In the Virtual Universe, you will be able to express yourself in any way that you please. You could be a mermaid, or an angel, or a fairy, and you may even appear as a full-grown version of you, whatever your imagination lets fly.

"Would you like to explore the Virtual Universe and go on a journey with your parents, Eliza, Yesha, and me?"

Erin looked at her parents, her face was lit up, and she asked, "Will this heal me?"

Amber looked at her parents, then toward Erin again, and answered, "Yes, it will."

"I always knew you had to be some sort of angel. I noticed a glow about you, Eliza, when I met you on Elena's talk show, and again when I saw Amber enter in through the door of our family's home. Each time I saw you, you glowed like angels from heaven, and now, I see that same glow in Yesha and the other delegates and citizens. If it's okay with my parents, I would love to accompany you."

Her parents looked at Erin, then at Eliza, and then at Amber. Then Daniel looked at Beverly, and Beverly spoke up, "Of course, if that is something Erin is fine with, we will support it one-hundred percent and go on the journey as well. So, we approve, and if possible, all three of us would like to go with you, Amber, Eliza, and Yesha."

"Absolutely, Beverly," said Eliza. "You didn't think we'd go there with your daughter, and without you, did you?" Eliza joked to put her at ease with a genuine smile, and then turned the training opportunity back over to Amber, and not for reasons of authority, but to avoid hogging all of the attention. Besides, this was Amber's first opportunity as a delegate.

"It is more fascinating if we have people close to us take the journey with us because we'll all be able to share things that are in our minds and are difficult to share by any other means. Now, before we go in, remember that once we are done, you will have your own smart suit.

"As far as smart suits are concerned, when you climb out of the biopod, your current attire will have been converted into the only outfit you'll ever need.

"We'll train you how to categorize your wardrobe and control what you are wearing by using your wardrobe compartmentalizations and your neural identification in the Virtual Universe and when we return, you'll be able to do the same in the real world." Amber motioned toward the biopods, "There are at least six of these here, more than enough for each of us. We'll want to get in and once we do, we'll pull our own lids down, then when you're ready we'll each say, 'Link 1, 2, 3, 5 minutes, 20 years.'"

"What does that mean, 'Link 1, 2, 3, 5 minutes, 20 years?" asked Erin.

"What that means is we will be in there for five minutes in our current reality, but, in the Virtual Universe, we'll gain twenty years or more of experience, muscle memory, experiential reference, and wisdom. It is a great way to experience life, thoughts, to study, to do research, to learn new things in a short period of time, and to share memories, together," said Amber.

"You don't have to do this if you would rather not," said Eliza. "But I do promise you, you will be glad you did. There is a lot more to learn there and you will learn more about yourself and everyone here than you ever thought you would know. I also assure you, you will be amazed at the beautiful flavors of thought that pass through the minds of others, especially thoughts that emanate from the minds of those you love."

Yesha continued, as if she, Amber, and Eliza had tapped into each other's minds, "We'll train you how to use your new abilities both here and there and take you on each of our own journeys."

Eliza then continued, "The first day I met Amber, I knew she would be a kindred spirit, and I do get the same feeling from all three of you. So, are you ready? If so, let's do this."

"Okay," said Erin, as she motioned to her Dad to help her up and into the biopod. Once he had, she continued, "Thank you, Dad. I love you Mom and Dad, and I look forward to seeing you in the Virtual Universe. Dad, can you pull the lid down for me please?"

As soon as he had pulled the lid down, it seemed to Dan that he had heard his sweet daughter, Erin, say, *"Link 1, 2, 3, 10 minutes, 40 years!"* and then she was silent.

"Well, it looks like we'll be in there for twice the time," Eliza smiled, "That will give each of us plenty of opportunities to get a few more PhDs, what do you say? Beverly? Daniel?" Eliza looked toward Yesha and Amber, who had already climbed into their biopods, knowing that currently Erin was in the Virtual Universe sitting next to a pond, alone. Eliza used her link to reach Yesha and Amber, and they could hear her singing the lyrics to a song from Depeche Mode's album, Playing the Angel, called "Precious," shortly followed by the lyrics for Cause & Effect's song, "Into the Light," from their Sunrise EP.

Eliza's grasp of her abilities and her neural link was more developed than those of anyone else throughout all of Pathway. She was advanced enough to see everything that was going on in the Virtual Universe while at the same time capable of transmitting messages, songs, or anything she wished to whomever she wished, who had also received neurological and physiological optimizations, and thus neural identifications. While she wasn't selfish with her knowledge or the amazing fun of her inventions, she was simply careful, considerate, and truly and deeply cared about the well-being, the longevity, and the clarity of mind of humanity, and afforded them their own pace with which to mature their abilities and conceive of more. Yesha and James weren't far behind in the mastery of their abundant and new abilities, and Amber was close, even if she didn't yet realize it. Eliza would enter the biopod last, awaiting Beverly and Daniel.

As soon as Amber and Yesha climbed into their biopods, they pulled down their lids, said *"Link 1, 2, 3, 10 minutes, 40 years,"* and then went silent.

Chapter 16: Healing and Awe

Database Moon Archive, Celestial-Sol Entry Date: 2010 November 16. Yesha Alevtina trains Vesha Celeste. Erin takes the lead, in the journey to the Virtual Universe. They use the recorded memories of Erin, her parents, and many more within the Virtual Universe. Interfaced within the Pathway Melrose Campus. Input by Eliza Williams, President of Pathway Industries, 2008-2015.

Immediately after Erin had said, *"...Forty years,"* she felt every muscle twitch, every sensory gland, and neuron light up, and she pushed hard holding her breath, pushing against every muscle in her body, until she felt a state of euphoria, and then she opened her eyes and saw the pond. She also saw that she was in a large garden, before lifting her eyes and looking around. After taking everything within the horizon around her in, she noticed that standing before her was an angelic statue overlooking the pond teeming with coy fish and frogs. The pond was surrounded by lovely flowers with a magnificent scent. She felt a release of every bit of pain that she had ever felt and saw the warm glow of the atmosphere around her and above her in the sky.

She looked toward her hands, and they were full and healthy, with an almost iridescent and brilliant array of colors. She jumped and found she could jump higher than the trees around her and then land safely without any harm. She felt something twitch on her shoulder blades behind her, and then she noticed that she had wings. Ferry wings! She was excited, ecstatic, so, she looked around in wonder as to when her parents would show up, so she could show them.

Just then, she heard beautiful music playing and seemed to understand entirely that it was floating through the air, because of Eliza. Amber and Yesha then appeared where she had stood when she first arrived, and they were as beautiful and glowing as ever. Neither of them had wings, but she could feel their presence and it was that of love, of kindness, of sorrow, of clarity, and of compassion.

Something was different. Erin immediately realized she was beginning to see, feel, and even comprehend the thoughts of Amber and Yesha. She was able to share in the feeling of each of their life's experiences. She felt through Yesha's mind the anguish that Eliza and Yesha had felt together as they lost some truly wonderful friends to one tragedy or another who they cared about deeply. She saw Amber's sister, Sarah, their walks to the park and felt a sense of empathy for her, and because of their shared mental link she completely and entirely understood every aspect of the experiences in Amber's life. She felt her sadness at losing Sarah, and then her vigor toward doing all she could to someday have her own biotech company, so she could overcome the brutality of disease and the contagious pandemic of toxicity in misery once and for all.

"That was before I became a Pathway delegate,' Erin felt Amber whisper to her mind.

"When we speak here, it is mind-to-mind, and no matter how much we learn from and about each other we'll still be able to tell the difference between our thoughts and experiences and the thoughts and experiences of someone else. I agree with you,

Erin, and what you are feeling, sensing, and understanding right now," said Amber. *"When we first get here, there is an intense sharing of every aspect of everything we are willing to share, and there are beautiful bonds and connections we'll always have. Arriving here, we all become old souls and kindred spirits fast. Wow, Erin, you may not realize it from your perspective, but in so little time you have been through so much, yet you've done it all with a beautiful sense of grace. I'm proud of you."*

"Thank you, Amber. You've each had some very interesting journeys packed with stories that would fill libraries to the Moon and back, yourselves. I also never realized that you had spent so much time, even before I met Eliza on Elena's show, with Yon, Leticia, and Leah, to help figure out what was going on with me. I never realized there were so many political angles to medical science and bringing cures to the world! I'm so happy about you and the efforts of everyone in Pathway for trudging through it all to help so many!" Then picking up on Eliza's neural link, although she was still in the real world, Erin spoke to her, *"There's so much you each know, and Eliza, your mind is the mightiest of every single one of the fifty-million people who have already been here, as beautiful as they are. Because of you, the rest of us can learn so much more. You deserve to know how much you are appreciated."*

Yesha smiled and agreed with Erin, *"Eliza has been a source of unfettered joy for more than thirty years, see how she opened her eyes and smiled at me two minutes after she was born? After linking with her, I was able to see that moment from her vantage point and that is about the purest form of love that exists. That is when I learned that everyone is born with beauty inside them. Some people, through their environment or perhaps due to damaging choices, need healing. In so many ways, showing them the beauty that exists within them is the one healing agent that is more powerful than anything else. There is so much we can learn from each other, even as we go about our seemingly mundane tasks with their sundry details.*

"When we leave the Virtual Universe, you will be able to channel a link between me, Eliza, Amber, your parents, and anyone you wish. You'll be able to link with all who have ever been here before whenever you'd like. When you come back you will receive updates from anyone else who comes through the Virtual Universe. We already know a lot of languages, have viscerally experienced so many cultures, yet there is still so much more to learn. Have I mentioned, you look amazing, Erin! You're a beautiful fairy! Look at you, you are incredible!"

Amber followed Yesha's thoughts and made a tall mirror appear before Erin. *"Here, you can look through our minds to see what we're seeing, you'll learn how to do that soon without this. Even still, look through this, so you can see what we're seeing as far as your physiological expression is concerned in relation to the artistic aspects of your neurology. This is the beauty that your right brain is expressing as a spiritual image of yourself,"* As Amber said that, Erin peered into the mirror before her, and she was able to see herself, was amazed, and almost breath-taken. All the while, Erin and everyone there could hear the beauty of the arpeggios, the strings, the flowing rhythm of her favorite music, female vocal trance, playing magically in the air around them.

Erin was twice her normal height, her cheeks, her nose, and her lips were full again, her silver-blue eyes were brilliant, and the silver-blues and purples of her wings and ornate fairy-like clothes were capitalized by the beauty of her eyes. She was amazed at the dazzling colors of purples, pinks, turquoises, blues, pastels, whites, and all in various shades in the different shocks throughout her long, predominantly blonde, and royally groomed hair, with braids and curls tucked and turning in an ornate yet angelic way. She was a full-grown adult! Erin was amazed.

"Wow, Amber! I never knew this was even possible! I'm a full-grown adult! I suppose I've never even considered seeing myself this way, where others could see me, but I've seen myself a time or two in my dreams, just like this, before. I love it!"

"You are so beautiful, Erin, both inside and out. But, of course, you already know both Yesha and I are thinking that, don't you?"

"Yes, thank you, Amber, and thank you, Yesha. Wow! You both are brilliant! You two are probably a couple of the smartest people I have ever met! All of the research you've done, Amber, and Yesha, you both know so much more than you let on in the real world," said Erin with glee and approval. *"Will I look like this when I come out of the biopod?"*

"Well, once you return to the real world, you will look like the six-year-old girl that you are, much as you see here, but not as a fairy. We have created limits for now, because there are people who would use these abilities to do things that aren't nice to others, and we do not want that to happen or even want to be too obvious about what we can do," said Amber. *"You are wonderful, but if people with malicious intentions knew these advancements were available, they would hurt many by either undoing it all or making it into something that is oriented toward brutality. We've made many failsafes, but you can never be too sure. The upside is, now you are immune to the toxicity prevalent in society.*

Yesha followed Amber. *"It takes a lot of work to ensure that hackers, pirates, dictators, and other people with malevolent designs do not break into our system and wreak all kinds of havoc. That said, the way that Eliza set this up, it cannot be hacked with today's technology, and she has even taken measures to preserve this information and these abilities for an infinite quantity of years, without ever being vulnerable to being hacked. It all lays in perspective and intent."*

After Yesha and Amber paused, the brilliant light of Eliza's presence began to shine, augmenting the intriguing new imagery of her Mom and Dad. Her Mom was a beautiful young princess and her Dad was a handsome young prince, but with skin that glowed with a variety of colors that complemented the colors of their eyes, their hair, and their other features.

"Hello, Eliza, Mom, and Dad, you look amazing! It's so wonderful to finally see you here! It's so beautiful here, and it seems like time has flown, although it's been a few years already."

Erin's Dad turned to her in tears, *"Oh my! Hahaha, it's been a few seconds for us. Hello, Erin! Wow, you look so beautiful! I can tell it's you, because of your expressions and your eyes. Wow, you are fully grown! I love your wings, and, young girl you are as beautiful as I've always seen you! You are lovely, my wonderful daughter,"* said Daniel, and she could hear and see as her mother's mind said the same things.

Erin felt the approval and unfeigned love of both of her parents, as the thoughts of their minds became increasingly clear to her. She felt their every passion, their every hope, their dreams, and their battles resonate within her own being. She felt shocked, then she felt herself shake internally, and then she felt her entire system rebound. Her parents had been through a lot and rarely did they complain about the details, yet they also shared one of the purest forms of love toward each other and even toward her in an experiential way that she had ever witnessed before. As the moments of shared experience drew in to meld with her memories, she began to feel at peace; her cognitive framework had just been optimized or updated, and she could clearly see and witness the positive aspects to each person's life experiences of all whom had been there inside the Virtual Universe before.

"What a smorgasbord of love, struggle, and perseverance!" exclaimed Erin.

This was an intriguing reality for all who entered. From Erin's vantage point, it was interesting that no longer did anyone need to speak out loud or while moving their lips, they could now feel each other's thoughts, see each other's visions and ideas, and even experience some of the experiences of their past in a truly visceral way.

Nevertheless, she spoke as she would have if she were in the real world, rather than as she would within the Virtual Universe, anyway, because she enjoyed facial expressions as the lips moved and the teeth were occasionally exposed, and that is what Erin did, and in this place, freedom truly did abound, *"I can't help but feel all of the anguish you've felt through the years. I am so sorry, Mom and Dad. The pain you felt at the loss of Katherine and Julia. I am sure my two older sisters would have been amazing people, but we lost them too-soon; the pain is deep."* Everyone around her could tell her lips were in sync with her thoughts, which was an exceedingly difficult ability to master in the Virtual Universe and lovely to behold.

With that, her parents embraced her in a group hug, which seemed even more soothing than ever felt before. This hug brought with it even more clarity to everything that each of them had ever endured. Erin transferred her speech from her mind to all who were there with her, *"We are hugging mind-to-mind!"* With tears at first and then joy they talked for what seemed hours.

After talking to each other and sharing experiences, they began the next part of their journey with Eliza's guidance to train on and practice their new and different abilities. She taught them what would apply in the real world, how to link with others mentally, and how to take advantage of research, learning, and exploration through the various matrices while in the Virtual Universe. Eliza then showed the Carters the interior of her Virtual Universe home and then handed over the remainder of the forty-year experience to Yesha and Amber, while she followed closely behind. Yesha would eventually be taking Eliza's place and Erin had a big future ahead of her as well, so given this very important and pinnacle moment; she recognized a need to share.

Together they visited the different places throughout the solar system, the twenty-thousand tech cities, all of the planets and moons of our Earth's star. They visited the space elevator, the planetary shields, and the twelve giant database moons, the solar shields protecting Earth and each planet and spheroid of the solar system, and much more. Erin, Beverly, and Daniel were enthralled with every single aspect of Eliza's designs and inventions. They also understood why they had to keep this reality confidential. While via Eliza, Yesha, and James, much of what they witnessed proved humanity had the capacity for greatness and then to travel the stars, they wanted humanity to be prepared, coached, and even convinced to lead lives that would render the home planet a safe haven for living beings, for the long-haul. They did not want humanity to be known throughout the cosmos as bringers of destruction and death. Instead, they wanted humanity to be worthy of traveling the vastness of space, bringing life and longevity, beauty and abundance wherever they went. This would happen, once humanity had committed to establishing and living the principles of Universal Ethics and obeying the Universal Laws.

More time was spent exploring all of the places humanity had ever gone, and once the Carter family was fully read-in with a new-found and vivid clarity, like that they knew how to use each of their newfound abilities. They then used what extra time they had in the Virtual Universe to complete countless bachelors and master's degrees, PhDs and certifications, to experience history, to gain a full scope of understanding of each of the sciences, and they visited many civilizations throughout the ages and much more. When they realized forty years had gone by, they reminisced around a campfire on Enceladus for hours. Once their sharing of experiences reached a good pausing point, they looked toward Eliza and she told them, *"We can return. Can you believe it? Forty years have passed by here and we are each truly old souls. It seems like such a long time ago that we left the real world, doesn't it?"*

"It does, Eliza," said Erin, who looked very much like a twenty-two-year-old and a beautiful fairy. *"Thank you, everyone, for being so amazing, so wonderful, and for*

accompanying me through the many journeys. Thank you for teaching us so much Eliza, Yesha, and Amber. Is it possible to go on like this longer? Will I be able to retain this information when we return to the real world?"

"Yes. You will be able to retain all of these memories. They will be in your mind and as clear as day," said Amber. "However, for now, we have real world missions and journeys to attend to, so it is necessary to return to your child-aged physiology."

Erin, Beverly, and Daniel then felt an intense and vivid rush of complete clarity as to what it was that they wanted to do to contribute to the advancement of civilization, ensuring that the home-world was beautiful, full of life, and could be around in trillions of years following long journeys throughout the universe and their return.

Erin sensed she wanted to become a historian, a leader, and even help other children she grew up with. She also had an idea, wherein she shared that she wished to go to the edge of the observable Universe when humanity on Earth was ready. She wanted to set up a series of jump gates that would allow her to, in short order, return to Earth from many different angles from far enough away, with powerful telescopic video recorders, to record Earth's evolution and the history of civilization, to uncover even more secrets, and then to expand humanity's knowledge from there to encompass so much more.

Beverly and Daniel both shared that they wanted to provide support and be there with Erin. They would use their talents to compound upon their understanding of the different complexities of the various creatures and civilizations they might meet throughout their journeys and throughout the cosmos.

Once they were ready to return to the real world, Eliza smiled toward each of them, as did Yesha and Amber, and like that, they awoke.

Erin felt every neuron in her brain, every pore in her skin, and every sensory aspect of her physiology become awash in the most amazing feeling she had ever felt before. She had the strength to open her biopod and hop out, and at once, everything they had done over the last forty years in the Virtual Universe came to her mind with clarity, but she was able to sense the various compartments in her mind. She found she could differentiate between her own thoughts from the different experiences of the different minds, she could see with clarity the current time frame versus the time spent going through the experiences in the ten minutes they had actually spent in the real world while traversing through the Virtual Universe for forty years.

She saw a few moments later as her parents climbed out of their biopods, and both Beverly and Daniel wept. There was their daughter, as beautiful as she could be, and glowing more brilliant than the sun. When the light wore away, she was a six-year-old girl who looked like the darling six-year-old she was always meant to be. No longer was she the apparent victim of a cruel disease, but her hair had returned, her eyes emphasized the beauty of her facial features, her frame was healthy and strong, and she no longer carried herself as if in constant pain. They then picked up on their neural link and began to talk to each other within their minds, and they knew she was one-hundred percent healed.

"Would you like to choose a tech city to call home? Or would you like to stay on Earth? Or would you like to keep your home on Earth, while trying out the different views in the tech cities throughout the solar system as your whims suggest?" asked Eliza, using her mental link with the Carters in the real world, for the first time.

"If possible, we would like to stay here, serve, and perhaps visit the tech cities on special occasions. We'd like to learn how to control our glow, of course, but we would like to assist you in your efforts here on Earth if that is okay?" asked Beverly.

"Of course, what you choose to do now, is your choice alone to decide on. We can guide you, we can answer questions whenever you have them, but the greatest learning comes from freedom. As far as the glow is concerned, we all are learning how to control *the glow. It takes time and focus. Most people in public won't see it, because they do not believe it is possible. The mind is interesting in that regard. I am proud of your choices, Beverly. Daniel and Erin, she speaks your minds as well. I can tell. All three of you are now fully read-in members and citizens, and as such you may continue to live in your home in Kearney, and you will have quarters anywhere you wish, accessible via the various jump gates in each of your rooms, with access to any location with similar gateways that you wish to go to or visit. This means, you also can take weekend vacations to the Bahamas in a snap, or head to the tech cities on the Jovian moons, the moons of Saturn, and on out to Pluto and even the Oort clouds. Believe me, the view of the Milky Way is quite a sight from out there.*

"Amber, will you please show them to their Pathway guest quarters, first? I'll have James introduce himself to them there shortly, and he will show them what needs to be done. You will have freedom, yet, Beverly and Daniel, there are also a lot of things that need to be done in the real world to ensure our civilization is worthy to head out into the Cosmos. You will now have affluence and influence, but I encourage humility always.

"I hope you know that I have made sure that the finer things of life are available in the tech cities, but as you are already aware, with optimized physiological and neurological capacities, a humble life and the challenges that come with it are actually quite savory, especially as we learn to overcome them. We also want to make sure that we preserve life, rather than leave desolation in our wake, so we will each do what we can to help others, as well as have a positive influence on the world around us and find kindness in how we approach others."

With that, Eliza and Yesha smiled, hugged everyone, and left the room, and, Erin for a small moment missed Eliza and Yesha. She was rather enjoying their company. She wasn't sure what to say, or how to react, or even how to feel. Somehow, clarity came rushing in, and joy took over.

"Don't worry, Erin, you can talk to me whenever you want to." Eliza linked with her, this time while in a distant location, but in the real world, and mind-to-mind. Erin thanked her mentally and then drifted back.

Missions to Pursue

Amber showed Erin, Beverly, and Daniel too and through their Pathway guest quarters, which were actually quite spacious, with twenty biopods in what seemed to be a group interface. She then showed them each of their office rooms, master bedrooms suites, with large bathrooms with a shower and a Jacuzzi in each one, a large, spacious, and beautiful kitchen, and twenty computer terminals and keyboard interfaces. There were a lot of other features that brought awe and amazement.

"Why are there twenty biopods?" asked Erin, looking very much like the six-year-old she was, but with an obvious sense that she was wise beyond her years.

"As you run missions, do studies, quests, and journeys you will find friends who are ready for this training and an increase in physiological and neurological health and capacity as well. There is so much to do, so the more we have working with us to get things done..."

Erin interrupted, "...The sooner we can get those things done and journey through the Cosmos. Awesome! I knew that, but it was nice hearing someone else say it." Erin sighed, "It is so wonderful being around people who are so caring, loving, innovative, and compassionate. I never knew I could be so happy and at peace. Thank you, Amber, for everything."

There was a balcony which overlooked a beautifully flowered forest, with more animals, reptiles, insects, and birds of every sort than one would typically imagine which were communicating mind-to-mind with each other. They had all been optimized to become sentient and were kind to each other and humanity.

Erin, Beverly, and Daniel could now pick up on their conversations, and the words they spoke grew more obvious merely by focusing their minds on them. No longer were they predator versus prey, they were friends of each other and friends of humanity as well. On occasion, one would apologize to the other for having been a part of the cruelty that led to the death and dismemberment of their friend's ancestors for the sake of engorging their bellies for the next winter. The other would sigh in a dramatic manner, then chuckle, saying, *"Hey, that's how nature created you. I'm only glad we have each transcended our nature and we can now see each other as deserving of life, just like the other."*

Erin combed Amber's mind, and she could tell that she came here to visit often. She also knew that as requested or if ever in need, she would come to help or even check in on Erin.

Everything was clear to Erin as to what she needed to do, and she wanted to get to work on her part of the future right away, and on whichever project or mission James had in store for her. But Amber let her know that even though she had the intellect of a timeless genius, she was, in fact, a six-year-old in the real world, and there were labor laws. Nonetheless, she could volunteer to do research or explore and help for self-development and although there would be missions and quests for her, there was no problem with her practicing in labs at her leisure, visiting the animals in the forest, or periodically visiting some of the people Eliza would eventually identify as future zonal commanders of intergalactic mission contingency command spacecraft zonal regions. Many of whom still had no idea that they had already been selected, contingent upon their choices, their actions, their perspective, the kindness, and their love of life.

"Come with me," said Amber.

Erin followed Amber, as they walked down the stairs from their balcony and came upon a cow. "Her name is Chloe," Amber explained.

"How are you?" asked Chloe.

"Hi," said Erin, who giggled like the little girl she was, while somewhat surprised.

"You are 'high?'" asked Chloe, a white cow with black spots, as she mooed in a manner that suggested that she was chuckling. *"I'm kidding with you,"* Chloe had the humor of the average small-town socialite. She continued, *"Seriously, it is very nice to meet you, Erin."*

Erin then remembered to use her neural link, to make it so that Chloe didn't have to read her lips, *"I could tell from afar that you could speak to the other animals and creatures, but you can actually speak to us too?"* asked Erin.

"Of course, I can. We've tried to for many millennia, but thank goodness for Eliza, now we can. Is there anything you would like to know or are there any questions you might have?" asked Chloe.

"I have a question," said Amber. *"I figured out a way to grow steak with hair follicles from some of the savoriest of cattle, I mean Cows, out there in Nebraska. I know, I know, I know, it may sound mean, cruel, and crazy to eat a steak now that we're friends, but I found out how to savor the delicious taste without ever having to see one of your brothers ever chopped up again. Do you mind? What do you think, Chloe?"*

"Moooooo! Mooohooo, moooo!" Chloe laughed in the usual way that a cow would laugh, and then she said, *"I don't mind. Honestly, I understand the old ways of the ecosystem, and how all of that works. While I love grass, you enjoy eating a delicious sirloin steak or a New York Strip steak, and I kind of find it funny. You'll be eating re-encoded hair follicles, which have been re-infused as sirloins and strips. You'll be eating my brother's hair, so I don't mind. It sure beats the heck out of seeing one of my brothers die so you can have a nice meal. You don't know how long that tormented me, although I was a milk cow, and that was torture enough. Now, just one cup of milk every now and then and you can fashion a billion gallons of fresh and healthy pro-biotic milk, yogurts, butter, cottage cheese, all manner of other cheeses, and more. I can't complain. I hope you enjoy it! It comes from a good place, and the ability to do so comes with a painless upgrade.*

"How was your trip to the Virtual Universe, Erin?" asked Chloe the Cow.

"It was more amazing than anything I have ever witnessed, and the journeys were more exhilarating than anything else in the entirety of my six years of life. Now, what I need to do is focus on my studies, so I can go through school in the real world, like a girl my actual age would. However, I kind of know everything they're going to teach, and would like to jump through and finish now, especially since in the Virtual Universe I have like five Ph.D.'s! But, I'm a six-year-old girl here, so I understand I have to wait. I might as well learn from you from time to time if that is okay?"

"Oh, of course, but keep in mind, James may actually have a mission or two for you every now and then, too. There are times when you will find that there are jobs that you are suited for better than anyone else. No matter your mission, quest, or journey, you'll still need to experience the real world in real-world time, at least for now. So, think of going through first grade and the other years of school as being an undercover student, at least until you can become an emancipated minor. Once that is the case, you'll be able to work just like your parents, and wherever you wish. You are extremely intelligent, but I am sure you can imagine all of the boys and girls now in school that are your age who have no idea about Eliza's inventions and who would benefit from a wonderful friend, tutor, healer, and mentor throughout schooling, such as yourself."

"I can see. That makes sense completely. If I were in their shoes, I think I would have loved to have a friend in my life, much like I have become now. After learning from twenty-million and more minds, I know there are those who suffer without saying anything. Still, the signs will be clearer than ever before, that I might need to help them, and quite possibly, use this new-found genius and help their families as well. Thank you, Chloe. I guess we'll see each other soon, won't we?"

"You can visit me any time, my dear. I won't be aging anytime soon, so if you need me, just link and I'll answer. You've always been a genius, by the way."

After their conversation, Erin returned with Amber to their quarters and there was James. Erin had to swallow a couple of times, he was a handsome man, and her now mature mind, a mind that had now experienced many years knew what a handsome man was.

James saw Erin, recognized her for the brilliant mind she had and respected her for the angelic six-year-old child that she was. He waived, and kindly motioned for her to follow him. He took her into the living room, where her parents were sitting and waiting for her to arrive and began to do what he did best.

"You are a psychologist by trade, Beverly, you will have many missions to that end, and you will find it both fulfilling with a deep sense within of joy and your clarity will grow. This will happen, especially as you engage in what must and can be done to create a variety of Virtual Universe environments that will assist in our creation of what we call the Correctional Matrix. In time, you will meet many amazing individuals, all of whom will be leaders of change, leaders of the beauty of the mind and its capacity to grow to a fuller potential of meaning and purpose, bursting with fulfillment. You will work closely with many toward the goals of training, coaching, and mentoring many who were once lost in toxicity to a quickening of the virtues reticent of a powerful and loving being themselves, nurturing a civilization capable of preserving the life-giving qualities of our Universe, by helping it to breathe, rather than exhale alone.

"Beverly, this matrix will be an environment that will afford people who have been exposed to the worst environmental conditions or who have made unhealthy choices that led to their criminal and unfortunate acts, a necessary change, leaving themselves and many more who have become victims of cruelty and injustice with a chance to learn from their mistakes and to move forward as healthy, helpful, powerful, visionary, and kind members of society. This will be different from what we know now as prison; this will allow someone who has been a victim of toxicity themselves to learn, to grow, and to become the decent human being they were always meant to be, capable of love, capable of kindness, capable of benevolent forms of confidence, knowing they are loved, possessing remorse for life and of showing dignity and respect toward others, while earning the reciprocal respect of others every step of the way. It will also provide them, through these experiences, the clarity of how their ingenuity and vision can help advance and preserve civilization while allowing them to rejoice in the efforts of others Universe-wide."

James then turned to Daniel, who listened with eager intent to someone who he now held in high esteem. Daniel had seen his journeys and his accomplishments through the minds of every citizen of Pathway. He was someone who had a genuine heart of gold. Daniel had also seen the love that Eliza had for him, the kind that James alone seemed to be growing in cycles of understanding and reciprocation.

"Your work is with animals, Daniel, which is an interesting career indeed, but you know something special about them, you know they have each matured through nature to possess qualities that are a part of this equation that will lend to our Universe's first breath. You will have an opportunity to study every species of animal throughout the world and within the oceans, no matter the depth.

"You have been physically altered in such a way, because of your intense propensity for love, to withstand pressures of any sort throughout our Solar System, because, we have so much to learn in order to benefit from each other. We can work with creatures of every sort to increase each other's abilities to enjoy this world *and* this Universe together. Doing this will help us to become an advanced civilization that preserves life and brings beauty and abundance to the Cosmos, with the ability to adapt to any and all environments we find ourselves in, while also enjoying them in a fuller manner. In this way, life will be rich and full of beauty and love for all.

"Erin, you are still young, but you have a very wise mind, however, and you know there are a lot of children out there who still suffer. I presume Chloe has already talked to you about this, but I am assigning you to work with different children in your own school, at least to begin with. Eventually, and in the same day, you'll be able to attend many different schools, while having the advantage of helping many people relatively near the same time. This will help you to multi-task your abilities, your attention, and bring clarity to your situational awareness, which will be very necessary when you engage in your big goal, to be the ultimate historian of our world and eventually our Universe.

"There is much more that burns within you, and you will achieve so much more, but for now, this is your main goal. You will have an alibi since you can easily convince those you know that the healing processes were a success and since you are so young, living in a smaller town, most won't allow their minds to process, conceive of, or notice the miracles that took place with your healing. They will remember your vibrant spirit and appreciate you more than ever. In time, they will see the beautiful person you truly are, just as they already feel you are. Within your own home in Kearney, there will be jump gates that only you, your parents, and the children you are assigned to work with will be able to access. You will be able to register for travel to any location necessary by using your neural identification.

"Everyone?" After regaining their attention, he handed out intriguing digital tablets to each of them, "Here are your dossiers," James explained everything in detail, he also sent them each a compartmentalized neural package through their neural links.

"Is everyone ready?" James smiled, bowed, and left them to each pore over with vigor the more finite details for their missions, and then like that, he was gone.

Erin studied more closely the details of her dossier, and she realized that both she and her parents would still be living in Kearney, but with quarters available both in Massachusetts and in any luxury tech city suite they wished to visit. The first suite they would recognize as a tech city home was located on the frozen nitrogen and water crust of Triton, Where Amber's secondary domicile was and one of Neptune's fourteen publicly-discovered moons. The environment created within the bio-dome was of four gentle yet identifiable seasons, like those experienced on Earth, with the beauty and cleanliness expected of any perfect city.

Within each tech city was every single amenity anyone could ever ask for.

Erin looked at her parents, who now looked like twenty-two-year-old versions of themselves. They stood there professionally groomed, both handsome and pretty, as well as mentally very astute. Right away the Carters decided together to check it out.

Her parents went through the jump gate in their Melrose campus living quarters, set the parameters using their neural links and identifications as trained and found themselves in their domicile on Triton. Erin followed shortly behind.

It was beautiful looking out at Neptune, as Triton went around the planet in retrograde orbit and the magnitude of it all was breath-taking and different from anything Erin had ever seen before in the nighttime skies, at least in the real world, which was remarkably beautiful in its own way.

There was an occasional volcano that erupted outside their bio-dome, but it was expertly contained and harnessed to provide a never-ending supply of energy to the numerous and linked tech cities that beautifully sprawled across its surface in a fashion that was pleasing to the eyes. She could see the web of cities, the dusty snow of Triton, and the glimmer of the sun, just beyond Neptune's horizon as Triton made its orbit around its main planet, but everyone knew that even physiological optimization would be very little match for the brutal cold, if one were to journey outside of a city and then outside the see-through walls of a bio-dome, without the proper protections and optimizations. Erin knew optimized individuals could survive, but it would be a challenge, nonetheless. She also noted that many who had chosen this as a permanent domicile were also working together on their own missions, journeys, and quests to improve the environment and to develop, create, and raise an Earth-like atmosphere around Triton so that eventually the biodomes would no longer be needed.

Once they soaked in the ambiance of the views from their domicile on Triton, they journeyed through its many tech cities, their associated forests, and greeted the countless animals. They even made friends with them and the other residents within and linked with them. When they were done, they visited their Triton domicile once more to soak everything in. They shared their Virtual Universe experiences with each other one more time in their biopods and returned to their home in Kearney, Nebraska, through their jump gates. The property manager happened to be away, so Beverly called him and let him know they were home, and that Erin's treatments were a success. After their brief conversation was finished and other loose ends were tied up, they prepared themselves for their upcoming missions and careers.

Erin's first mission was to be a first grader, to get to know her classmates all over again and to convince everyone that her catastrophic healing was normal. There were economic aspects that Eliza was taking into consideration, she didn't want whole industries to be lost in too many changes too soon, at least too soon for the inhabitants of Earth to adapt to within their minds. She realized that much had to be done and her peers and their parents needed to work with her, as well as her parents, in order to ensure a better future for humanity.

Back to School

It was her first day going back to school, she'd been gone for two days, and she felt healthier and stronger than she ever had before. Upon returning, she was able to see in the mirror, daily, what it was that her peers and their families could see, over the next few weeks. At first, her head was bald, however, after Thanksgiving break, when she returned to school, Erin had healed completely, in front of the public eye, but was still the priceless and wonderful young girl with the precious smile that she had always had. Only now, she was able to play like the other children, no longer helplessly watching time speed by.

By the last Friday of school, before the Christmas break of 2010, Elena had talked with Eliza, who then shared on her show a video of how this young girl had received a treatment that was exclusive for her. Pictures from the previous documentary were shared, and she was able to provide a visual of how Pathway had helped her to heal completely. Erin's hair was now full, her cheeks had filled out, she was peppy, athletic, musically minded, and of course, as smart as always.

Erin explained her views on several issues around the world and how she believed they ought to be taken care of, but how for now, as a child, she needed to have fun, and allow the adults to hold the problem-solving reigns for a while. Finally, Elena showed a video of Erin running around the playground at her school in Kearny, an interview from her very youthful looking parents and how happy they were for her, and then another video of her simply having fun with the rest of the children in her class.

It was a great moment for Erin, her parents, and even Pathway. This benevolent company had opened a gateway to helping many children to be healed, while giving medical science a viable solution to one more ill that had plagued or taken the lives of too many already.

Back at school, in 2011, early on in January, Erin noticed one of her friends reacting more quietly than usual, and several days later she noticed her sitting by herself at the other side of the playground. Her head was down, and it looked as if she could be crying.

This young girl was positioned such that she was facing opposite the playground and toward the pasture and forest that lay behind the elementary school. Erin could not let someone feel alone, be alone, or anything of the sort, without at least trying something. Erin then smiled at the other children, climbed off the jungle gym, and unnoticeably walked over to the little girl.

"Hi, Allison," said Erin. Allison's brown hair was hanging in front of her shoulders, and it was obvious she was crying. "I don't mean to bug you, but do you mind if I sit down with you for a little bit?"

"That's fine," Allison responded through sobs and tears. Erin did not want to pry, she felt it wasn't her place to do so, however, she still needed to at least provide some moral support. This wasn't a time to be the perfect person, this was the time to be understanding and compassionate.

Allison wiped her brown eyes, and Erin could tell she was an adorable and sweet little girl. Most of the time, at least over the last year and a half, she'd always seemed cheerful and happy, but perhaps she never noticed before. Erin knew she'd been a bit out of it herself, at least before meeting Amber. She also knew the best way to find out what was truly going on, was to simply be a friend and care.

Allison sat there for a while, without saying a thing. The birds were still south for the winter, so other than the light and cold breeze, there was very little sound, beyond the listless cheer of the children behind them, playing in the playground.

After a few moments of peace with this kind friend, Allison felt comfortable around Erin, wiped her eyes, straightened her posture, and spoke while looking into the field.

"My cat is sick, and my mommy and daddy say that he'll have to go to heaven soon. Timber has been in my life and has always played with me whenever I'd toss his ball of yarn or play chase the laser. He hasn't played for a while and sleeps in his little den, but I don't know why he'll have to go away. He is fun, he always came and rested on my lap, and he followed me around the house purring. At least he used to. I don't know what I'm going to do."

Erin knew exactly what to do, but she had to be careful. *"How can I help her to either work through this, or, how can I help her to heal her cat?"* She then linked with a relatively new family friend from Pathway, *"Amber?"*

"Yes, Erin. How are you doing? It's been a few weeks, I saw you in the news, and I am so happy that things have worked out so well. How can I help you?"

"Can we heal cats?" Was all that Erin could think to ask through her link. *"A friend of mine is very much torn that her cat is not so well, she loves him very much, and I would like to meet her family and ask if I can take Timber to a friend's house, who can help him. Would that be possible? Can we use the biopods in our home?"*

"Of course, you can. I would recommend asking if you can allow them to take Timber to see your dad, since he works with animals, in so many more ways now than he used to."

"That's a great idea, Amber! Thank you!"

In the mere moments it took to neurologically link with Amber, and have that conversation, it had only seemed like a breath of air to Allison.

Allison felt happy that Erin was there to listen to her, and that she wasn't wanting to talk her ear off about it. She seemed to understand, with her compassionate gaze. Allison knew who Erin was and was so happy that she was feeling better in every way one could imagine. Allison continued. "Timber, he's so special to me. You know? Maybe the doctors that healed you could heal Timber too? Is it possible? Can you do it?" She clearly had a moment of hope written all over her face, and her tears were now far from gone. Erin picked up on that note.

"Is Timber still at home?" she asked.

"Yes."

"Can I visit after school today?"

"Yes. You can come home, and I'll ask my Mom if you can come in and play."

"That would be wonderful. I'd love to see Timber. He sounds like an amazing cat." As soon as they'd made their plans, the bell for the end of recess rang. Both hugged and bid adieu until after school.

An hour can seem like a long time, especially when you know that a dear new friend is sitting in pain facing the possibility of losing someone or a living being that was particularly close to them. Erin realized that our lives have been constantly filled with the idea that the only future we all have in common, to look forward to, was the fact that everyone dies. *"What a stark outlook on the way we see things. That is no longer necessary. Now we should be asking what we can do to preserve life, to bring joy to those around us, and to span the Cosmos!"*

As Erin thought those thoughts throughout her class, while simultaneously paying attention to the teacher and the other students, to see who else might need some help, she couldn't wait for class to be over. *"If I heal her cat, I'll be able to speak to the cat neurologically, whenever I visit! Oh! This will be fun!"*

Finally, the end of the day at school arrived, and since they lived relatively in the same community, Erin linked with her Mom and Dad and let them know that she would be home a little late, because she was going to bring a cat with her, named Timber. He needed healing via one of our biopods. They were proud of Erin, congratulated her for taking the time to listen, and agreed with her plans.

"Hi Allison!"

"Hi Erin!"

It was great having a friend her own age, one that understood the challenges of life, but allowed her to be the six-year-old that she was. She'd be turning seven at the end of March, but she wanted to embrace this as much as she could. Erin wanted to get started right away on the big chores, but she also knew that there were moments she needed to experience in life, that could only be had by being the child that she was.

"How was class?" asked Allison.

"I couldn't wait to get to your house to help Timber and of course to spend time with you and your family."

"Me too! You've never come over to our house before. So this will be fun!"

They both jogged the few blocks there were all the way to Allison's home and Erin waited outside until Allison came back out and gave her a thumbs up that she could come back inside. When she entered, she politely introduced herself to Allison's mom, who happened to be home from her part-time job at the local creamery.

"Nice to meet you, Erin. You are quite the rising star, are you not? We feel honored to have you here."

"Thank you, Mrs. Manor. I got to spend a little time with Allison today, and she is quite a remarkable young girl. I heard through the grapevine, that Timber isn't doing so well. Can I see him? My father works with animals, and well, he might be able to help, and for free."

Not sure how to respond at such a mature request from such a young girl, Mrs. Manor was impressed and said, "Follow me," as she led Erin to Timber's den.

Timber was a large-sized orange tabby cat, but a handsome one at that. He looked tired, drowsy, and was laying down on his side, his paws stretched out, with drool in small amounts on the bedding below him. Erin felt torn at his condition but filled with empathy and concern. He was truly in pain and had no way to audibly convey that to his humans who did not speak his language. When Erin drew closer to him, his eyes seemed to widen as he stretched his front paws toward her, as if to indicate that he was happy to see her and fully trusted her.

"To avoid suspicion," Erin thought, *"I will breed further sentience, a neural identification, and the ability to communicate mind-to-mind via the biopod, into him, optimizing his physiology and neurology, so we can link and talk, wherever we are, instead of trying to carry on a conversation out loud."* Erin then continued aloud.

"He is so adorable. Poor little guy. Do you mind?" Erin saw Mrs. Manor nod, indicating that whatever she was about to do was fine with her. Erin picked him up gently, without stumbling, despite her petite frame, and asked, "I would like to help him out, if it is okay with you. I'll take him to my house for about an hour, to let my Dad see him, and then Timber will feel much better."

Mrs. Manor was concerned at first, but then thought about the fact that her father had been quite popular within the community of late. He'd been in the animal husbandry business for a while before that, but once he returned from Erin's miraculous healing, he opened a veterinarian practice in town. Perhaps he had some tricks up his sleeve that would help Timber as well.

"Sure, Erin. Can you bring Allison with you?"

Erin had to quickly think of the response there, because for one, Allison loved Timber, had been crying that day at school, and Erin genuinely cared about her well-being. "Sure." Erin smiled. "Allison can come with me." She then made a quick, personal, internal, and mental coaching to herself of things, *"Of course, why wouldn't she be able to? Wait, will I have to show her the biopod? How will I tell her what it is? While I appear six and am living my years as a normal child would, so-to-speak, she truly is a child, and based on the Principles of Universal Ethics, permission from her parents would be required before I could take her on a Virtual Universe tour."*

Erin then called up her delegate and friend. *"Amber? Here are my thoughts, can you school me on how to approach this? I'm trying to help, but I want to do it right. I know, I know, I should be able to figure this out on my own, but I honestly am not sure yet how to approach this."*

"That's okay, Erin. If your dad is home, you can hand Timber to him, and he can take him to the back so that her cat isn't influenced psychologically by Allison's presence, concern or worries. You can show Allison around your home, meanwhile. Maybe read her one of your books. Please note, that Timber will most likely play along as well. Cats have a special sense toward those who they know are trying to help them."

Erin was relieved and grateful. She wanted to help, but she also knew that her six-year-old physiology, as wise as her mind was, may have some difficulty processing all that she knew. She then let her delegate and friend know she was gracious. *"Thank you, Amber."*

In a few brief moments, all was worked out and Allison and Erin took turns carrying Timber.

When they arrived at Erin's house, Dan opened the door and let Erin and Allison in, who was at this time holding Timber. "Welcome home, Erin. Nice to meet you, Allison. Please, come in? It's wonderful to see you two."

Dan was as charming and comforting as ever, and had gone through a slow day at work, since all of his clients' pets were now optimized and healed for good. He also had regular links to each one with conversations amongst them. While he compartmentalized a lot of what he heard he also knew that this would soon help Erin, in her mission, which was to help those her age and older, who might be struggling for more reasons than one.

While her father took Timber to the biopod room, Erin showed Allison around the rest of the home. Given the fact that they'd been read-in and were citizens and delegates of Pathway, they had made a lot of breath-taking upgrades to their home. They'd converted Erin's room into one she could spend with her newly-found friends, helping her to look like the child that she was. With Legos, children's science labs, medical learning toys meant for kids, Erin was able to entertain and educate.

"Would you like a tea?" Erin asked Allison.

"I think so," said Allison, not sure whether she should have one or not. "Is it herbal tea?"

"Yes. There is no caffeine or tannin in these teas." Erin knew what Allison was getting at and sought to give her the type of beverage she felt most comfortable with. She then brought out the tea packaging and read the ingredients to Allison out loud. Once she approved, Erin put some together, and they both enjoyed their warm and tasty beverages.

"This tea tastes really good, Erin. Thank you."

Shortly after sipping their teas, their father came out, with Timber walking right beside him, purring as loud as could be. *"Purr, Erin, thank you. Thank you for getting me the help I needed. I felt like I was about to give up the ghost, but now I feel like a* million bucks! I'll try to help Allison's family to know they are loved. Of note, Erin, they might need some monetary assistance."

"Of course, Timber. I'll try to get to know your family a little more and see if they would like to go on a trip with me to learn about Pathway. Once they see what is going on, I have no doubt they will love it and want to become members as well."

"That sounds like a really good plan, Erin." Timber was clearly ecstatic about his new ability to talk with humans, at least using the neural link. He'd been through many centuries of training, learning about other felines, humans, and many other creatures who had taken that same journey, which resulted in his own connection to the Twelve Database Moons. He'd also received his mission, to simply be the Manor family cat, for a while. "So, Erin, when can I visit Pluto? I'd love for my family to go there, since it seems the stars would be so lovely for viewing from that point in our Solar System."

"I am sure they can go there, after I've been able to explain to them a little more about Pathway. You've got nine lives, Timber, as they say, so it's okay to be patient. You know? Lounge around like you used to?" Erin said mentally with a shared mind-to-mind laugh.

Timber laughed as well, but to the public eye and ear, he merely seemed to be purring and Erin appeared to be thinking about this, that, or the other.

"He's better!" exclaimed Allison, thrilled that her cat had been healed. "Mom and Dad will be happy too!"

Later, after returning home, Erin was able to tell the Manors about Pathway and convinced them to become fully-read-in members. Now, she now had the accompaniment of a new and now gifted ally at her school and was able to communicate with another friend.

On Earth as on Pluto

It didn't take long after becoming members of Pathway that the entire family agreed to take Timber to see the views from Pluto, and the numerous and beautiful tech cities that dotted its surface. To the public eye, Pluto would only have been seen as the dwarf planet that it seemed to be, but to members of Pathway, it had become a bustling and beautiful metropolis filled with jungles, forests, rivers, streams, and all types of sentient life. Everyone living there seemed happier than anyone the Manors had ever met. Given these revelations, they opted to have Pluto as their second home away from home.

While there, they happened to see Erin's great aunt, Tina and her father's old boss. They were young, vibrant, full of life, and living for good on Pluto as well. At some point, Erin's mother had convinced them likewise to become fully read-in, and they did. Shortly following, Tina and Dan's old boss married each other, settling in a beautiful home, with so many wonderful things to keep them busy and fulfilled from within.

Upon asking her Mom, Erin found out that Chastity Grey and Adelay Baye had helped her father and her to convince Aunt Tina and Dan's old boss to become citizens of Pathway, and now they were. Both loved traveling hither and yon, in their very own spacecraft, daring each other daily to travel through the asteroid belts and back, enhancing their maneuvering skills. They helped Pathway in so many ways and were happily busy doing whatever moved their hearts.

Traveling the world with Yesha and Eliza from time to time as Erin got older, she had the opportunity to meet a brilliant mind, Evan Bauer. He was a neurological superhero and had ideas left and right about how to increase the enjoyment of the living condition.

Life was amazing, as Erin kept attending school, rescuing those in need, and recruiting many more. While it could be said that this brought finality to her story, this was just the very beginning!

Chapter 17: Pathway Industries

Database Moon Archive, Celestial-Sol Entry Date: 2018 December 25. Yesha Alevtina trains Vesha Celeste. In this crucial part of her training, Evan Bauer and several other highly intelligent scientists are recruited and introduced. Eliza has big plans for their future, but for now, she needs them to do some important research. These memories are shared by the collective minds of the leadership of Eliza, Yesha, and James within the Virtual Universe, interfaced within the Pathway Melrose Campus. Input by Eliza Williams, Founder and President of Pathway Industries, 2008-2015.

Toward the end of 2010 and throughout 2011, Dr. Eliza A. Williams began looking into various companies, businesses, corporations, and each of the industries throughout the US and throughout the world. She did so, with a lot of interest in buying them out, or at a minimum, investing heavily into them and becoming the major shareholder. Her priority to that end, was the quiet and amiable investigation of every employment center or economic or consumer hub possible.

Eliza desired a fuller understanding of their hiring processes, management techniques, and treatment of employees and customers. She would accomplish this by sending out swaths of Pathway LLC representatives to apply for and work for each of them while providing continuous feedback from the ground up.

While her organization numbered at nearly two-hundred million by December of 2010, all of them, while willing and ready to help, were currently engaged in other quests, missions, and tasks, so she took it upon herself to search for and recruit eleven more scientists. Nonetheless she let Yesha and James know of her goals.

As it turned out, each scientist she felt was right for this endeavor was either a US citizen upon birth or had emigrated legally to the US, courtesy of the efforts of her best friend, Yesha Alevtina.

Upon further research, Eliza learned that each of the people that she had her sites on had yearned to do great things in science, if given a chance to practice their skills in an environment where private funding for this was much more prevalent. Yesha had seen that as well, and sent three people her way, after recruiting, training, and sending them to James for their first assignments.

As always, Eliza, Yesha, and James were pretty much in constant contact with each other, sharing their current plans, their goals, and the issues as they arose. At times, they would find solace to focus and dedicate themselves to whatever task was at hand. No matter what Eliza's goals were, however, Yesha and James were on board. In this case, they understood that Eliza wished to do an investigation of the plethora of industries to see exactly what it was that was slowing down human progress and stymying the increase in the well-being of the ever-growing population outside of Pathway.

By August of 2011, there were nearly eight-hundred-million Pathway citizens. Earth's non-read-in populace continued to climb, however, and it seemed that for as much as their efforts were helping so many, there were continuously many more who had never heard of nor knew of the opportunities provided by Pathway of living a life of purpose with increased quality and well-being.

The seeds of this reality presented itself to Eliza much earlier, in August of 2010, to be exact. This was the same evening she had met Amber Blythe. Shortly after taking Amber through the Virtual Universe, she met Evan Bauer for the first time. He had been working at MIT on a joint project with Harvard, and as an associate part-time professor at Harvard, she had been put on that team as well. This joint tasker by Harvard and MIT had to do with working on newly developing technologies, and one called optogenetics.

Evan Bauer, only thirty-one years old at the time was heading the task force and had a lot to offer the public community, especially when it came to cures that dealt with neurological disease and non-invasive surgery.

He had noted that she was quite gifted in this same arena and while on a break, he had asked her how she knew so much. Naturally, her conversation navigated toward essential details about Pathway, and she ended up inviting him to the Melrose Campus. Once he'd arrived, he was particularly intrigued and agreed to go through with the Virtual Universe training the same evening as Amber, but about three hours later.

It wasn't until entry into the Virtual Universe, when Evan bore his history and past as clearly as he could to Eliza, and together they watched, mulled it over, and made sense of it all...

Evan Bauer was a man with a light tan complexion and dark and wavy hair on top. He was clean cut, with a well-trimmed dark beard that faded and blended with the hair on the sides and back of his head. Golden fiber-like highlights in the dark irises of his eyes made him look as wise as he indeed was. He looked in every way every bit the genius he was touted to be. His father was from India and had met and married Evan's mother on a diplomatic assignment in Israel, who happened to be from Bethlehem. Neither had been religious, but both had been enveloped in the cultures that sprung from the regions wherein they were raised. When they decided to move to the US well before Evan had been conceived, they took note of their genealogy and changed their last name to Bauer. Evan grew up loving science, and many years later he had specialized in neuroscience with further focus on non-invasive neurosurgical procedures, studies, and treatments for more than the last decade.

Over the last few months, Evan had worked as part of Eliza's elite team to bring clarity to the positive results of the small little details as they affected the mind. He did this, all-the-while working with Amber, updating and upgrading the biopods, as well as the citizens of Pathway. He helped many who were read-in within the Virtual Universe but had also begun to translate his knowledge and studies of the established neuroscientific advances for proliferation into and throughout the real world. Despite his natural talent for well-being-oriented technology, he chose to live in a more organic manner.

Even though in Pathway, biopods, nanos, the Virtual Universe, and so much more were already developed, in the real world they were not. As brilliant as Eliza was, she also was smart enough to know that everything she created could benefit from input, updates, and upgrades from other brilliant minds. Amber Blythe, for example, had quickly taken the reigns of physiological optimizations and improved upon them in spades.

Every day, Eliza's recruits were coming up with enhanced upgrades to each technology she introduced and came up with innovative solutions mitigating as yet unforeseen disasters, long before they could occur. They were proactive in every step, while working as team members, leaders, and motivators all who were new in this growing organization.

Eliza realized quickly the asset that existed in her own ability to delegate to others the many projects and scientific responsibilities. This allowed Pathway to move forward exponentially in the arena of technologic advancements. As it was, no one in the public eye knew about any of these advancements. Evan sought to help society mature and become educated enough on these types of technologies to assist them in becoming as well-versed and capable as Eliza had been over the last decade.

Yesha explained to Evan, with Eliza present and inside the Virtual Universe, *"Together with Eliza, we'll explore the continued growth of Pathway LLC to Pathway Industries. We will then conduct private investigations, followed by large buyouts of corporations that are some of the biggest offenders of humanity. Eliza envisions and brings to reality the most significant overall influences and seeks to provide a pathway to citizenship in her LLC, growing her company to that of a major industrial complex, retaining the talents of some of the greatest titans of global industry."*

Eliza agreed. Her instructions had been to apply for these jobs, just as anyone struggling would. Despite being optimized both physiologically and neurologically, they would regularly report their progress with various necessary details and specifics so she could correlate and accurately interpret the data and information. Eliza had a very educated and wise hunch as to what the source of the problem was for the economic downturn of the US, but she wanted to do proper and somewhat organic research before jumping to make significant changes, based purely on speculation.

Reports came in, like, "I applied, but I was overqualified," or, "I applied, but did not have the vast set of specific skills they were looking for," or, "I applied, got an interview, but never heard back." Many reports arrived that eluded to trumped-up job requirements and the lack of honest willingness to train prospective employees on the part of so many employers throughout every industry. It became increasingly clear that her hunch was becoming confirmed more and more. Still, there was a lot more she wanted to know and evaluate before making her next move.

Eliza gathered prominent members of Pathway together in the Group Virtual Universe Interface and deliberated. *"We need to know the culture of the many work centers, the real mission of each corporation, how the employees are being treated by their superiors, and the motives of the various management and human resources departments. Are they there to bring people into a team with a noble mission and a healthy and productive work environment? Are they there to do the corporate bidding? Are they there to squeeze more money away from the workers or resources from this Earth to drive up costs for revenue? What are they doing to fine-tune the necessary processes, the training programs, and benefits packages to raise the quality of life for those careworn most? Are these companies there because they genuinely care about the employee, the services or products they are providing, or the long-term viability of the mission and the industry?*

"We need to know the source of the downward spiral of the various industries that have led to revolving doors and people being treated as replaceable things rather than valued potential. Oh, I know the core of the cause, because I have come here to the Virtual Universe and melded minds with every citizen that has been fully read-in, and I have seen enough to make many lose hope." The leaders there, the scientists who had been involved with so much of Pathway's growth thus far, along with Yesha, James, and his first two-hundred-thirteen Pathway LLC crewmembers witnessed as she glowed with the desire to help humanity. *"We cannot let them wallow away as empty husks of themselves sauntering on in mundane biddings and treated like cattle.*

"Why can't every country prosper through fair trade, proper education, and the sharing of resources? There are certainly enough minerals, nutrients, possibilities for fertility in the soil. There are more than enough people who can work together in a network of diverse skills and abilities to lead to a healthy mindset that will assist humanity in moving forward and seeing through to taking care of the much bigger

picture." Sharing all of this, Eliza was determined to document, analyze, and create simple solutions to reverse the current decay of society.

Everyone in the Virtual Universe bore witness that day, mind-to-mind, that Eliza wasn't one to stand idly by. She was someone who would find a peaceful, brilliant, effective, and efficient way to solve each of the problems plaguing the terrestrial public.

She continued, *"What has happened to the idea and the actual building of products to last? Can they not build products with versatility and the capacity for added options rather than engage in complete restructuring or replacement with little thought for intuition? Can they not build with quality, longevity, and appreciation in mind? Can they not build products, services, and processes with the capacity and space to provide updates and improvement without throwing away a product altogether? Why all the irresponsibly discarded waste? What has caused so many industry leaders to change things merely for the sake of change, rather than for the sake of the improvement of the quality of the process, the product, or the service? Where has the desire to raise the quality of life gone? Why is infrastructure so outdated and crumbling? With all of our knowledge, why aren't products much more capable now than they currently are? How is it that leaders have failed to think long-term and instead they have gravitated toward immediate satisfaction while forsaking quality, longevity, upgradability, and satisfaction for the consumer? Satisfaction and well-being can always be had if proper vision, mission, health, training, compensation, loyalty, morale, and thus innovation drove these industries. So, what is it that has failed and what can be done?"*

Doing this, asking these questions of her neurologically gifted representatives was in no way intended to be corporate espionage, subterfuge, nor anything of the sort. Eliza's request for intense investigations was designed for statistical feedback regarding the actual climate of the various factions of the many industries she was interested in understanding. She hoped to get to the bottom of the decaying economy, turn things around, and get humanity back to where it needed to be, so we could take the steps necessary to be worthy to journey the stars. Eliza continued.

"To be worthy to journey the stars, conditions must be such that if a group of explorers were to return home many millennia later, humanity will not have faded away into nothing. Instead, they will have preserved the home world and home solar system, and even improved upon the beauty, the abundance, and the ability of longevity of life in every way that is positive and possible. This is necessary, and if done now, instead of crumbling into chaos we can evolve to use the chaos of the firmament to cause the universe to breathe, and thus preserve and raise the quality of life so we can be worthy of the advancements the universe already made possible."

Eliza went into the Virtual Universe again, after identifying eleven individuals who were optimized and appeared young, with naturally gifted traits of intellect, kindness, leadership, and the ability to persuade. She talked to them for hours regarding the ideas shared with Pathway's leadership and what she was looking for as a result of her inquests of industries worldwide. Eliza's inquiries related to well-being, rather than the serving of egos, of greed, of lust for power, or of mere negligence to do what was right.

"Lucia Tsu, Stafford Gaines, Hanz Schultz, TJ Demitri, Bobby Gahan, Jeremiah Voltaire, Lexi Lancaster, Ariela Reina, Christian Coriolis, and Krystal Brightway, please work with Evan Bauer on this. We have a lot to do in a short period of time. I assure you your efforts will be worth every moment that passes by. You'll be rewarded handsomely with the simple knowledge that your efforts are driven by nobility in your personal ethics. It is also important that we get to the core of what is going on to cause such a pox on our economy driving innovation and prosperity to such a crawl. In contrast, I need to know why the stock market is surging, inflation is continuing, yet

wages are staying the same or dropping." Eliza deliberated a little longer, and then met separately with Evan.

Eliza contemplated on a meeting she had had with him before, when he shared with Eliza what he had proposed to write in a book and publish in the coming years regarding the aspects of a collective mind and an experiential interface.

"Our minds are a bit chaotic, so perhaps that is how we can conjure up so many great ideas. It is through the chaos we control, understand, and can make sense of that great discoveries and capabilities unfold to benefit all who are bound by the laws that govern its ripple effects. As far as translating a computer-brain interface into everyday living, it is possible. Connecting the corpus callosum and other essential cortices to a Virtual Universe, or a realistic experiential cyber matrix interface, by way of opsin, optogenetics, other tools, and an encoding to translate it to a soft transceiver within the mind amplified by strengthened physiology, would allow a person to wander around a cyber-environment within the matrix engaged in a way to where it is acting much like we are in a memorable dreamlike state. However, now we will be able to do this with an addition to the brain, in the form of a neural layer wrapping around it, much like a placenta around an unborn child, but more sophisticated in scope. An individual user will still be bound to the left brain but have access to the right brain allowing for conscious choices to be made, minus acting them out entirely in physical form. Muscle memory in the Virtual Universe can be built by flexing the various regions of the brain, interfacing with an exponential capacity, given this new layer, and allow us to gain knowledge, experience, and wisdom without moving the body.

"Perhaps a neurological link of this nature, via the corpus callosum and this new layer, will afford us the beauty of shared awareness. We will be able to have a shared moment with anyone we desire to link to. Many shared moments and happenings, shared memories with billions of people connected at the same time will increase our collective wisdom and capabilities exponentially. In the University Matrix, within the Virtual Universe, professors can give life-like and real-world seeming lessons filled with tangible and tactile experiences while still in this sub-unit connected to the Virtual Universe, with studies, research, and laboratory environments that no longer harm animals or other humans.

"There could be small moments of structured guidance which afford coherent structure toward learning a new profession or skill, wherein the university itself may act as the master brain for small unnoticeable moments every few seconds, to guide and coach the mind. Doing this will allow for complexed development, training, stimulation, and both physiological and neurological growth. In the right kind of interfacing system, the brain will not overheat or become crammed within the head. Instead, unused areas will develop new neural pathways and synapses into an expanding prefrontal cortex and hippocampus for memories, thalamus for the gathering of signals and sending them to the various cortices. The hypothalamus will receive these signals to regulate our body temperature, circadian rhythm, hunger, thirst, aspects of reproduction, and pleasure."

Evan then paused and continued, *"All of this can be optimized by your nanos, Eliza. Your nanos can communicate throughout our DNA-bound neurological particle nanosystem giving us real-life experiences combined with optimized memory and cognition without causing brain damage. All of this while engaging the dorsolateral prefrontal cortex, parietal lobe, and the orbitofrontal cortex, allowing the growth of new layers of the brain. These new layers can expand our neurological capabilities and create the necessary links to enable us to engage in collective learning, understanding, and complete internal process control while going about the day.*

"This connection would also allow us to graduate to other levels of consciousness, because we will have begun to receive double, triple, and even quadruple

layers of the brain that allow us to have multi-brain capacities tied into a master hemisphere and our prefrontal cortex, as well as a growing hippocampus, thalamus, parietal lobe, and hypothalamus. Our skulls may grow slightly larger with more energy, warming, and cooling capacities, yet the growth that results will expand in circumference overall and will be virtually unnoticeable. It will afford us a higher quantity of mental processing power as well as heightened speed and clarity of thought. We will have a heightened ability with increased energy capacity to forecast and act upon the best overall outcomes with assertiveness in decision-making processes. With these advancements in-toe, they'll be designed to maintain the integrity of compassion, resilience, innovation, and Universal Ethics."

Going through and listening to Evan's presentation in the Virtual Universe, it became apparent he was the remarkable individual his reputation, which preceded him, indicated he would be. Furthermore, his skills made clear to Eliza which industries she would coordinate with James to have him investigate and eventually lead. The medical, health, and most certainly the neuroscience fields would be his domain, and extraordinarily.

"Evan, I can see your compilation of observations, studies, and developments will be a wonderful way to integrate Pathway's current knowledge into real-world public studies. I am proud of you and your efforts. This will also provide several added layers of capacity to each of us throughout the solar system who have been fully read-in. Thank you for your diligence." Eliza talked with Evan for quite some time, shifted focus to the new project, and then James Cooper appeared within the Virtual Universe, to work with Eliza on how to integrate Evan into her leadership teams for investigations of the various Earth-bound companies, businesses, organizations, corporations, and industries.

James had witnessed his own employer before Pathway LLC, go down the slippery slope of becoming corporate, and it wasn't very conducive to a healthy economy. Although there were plenty of companies to investigate, Evan would aggregate all the data he would gather along with the data from the other ten Pathway LLC delegates. To do this, Evan and his team would each build sizable groups and fully infiltrate the nineteen major world-wide industries to find their strengths, their weaknesses, the good, the bad, and the ugly. This was not about corporate espionage or anything of the sort. Eliza wasn't interested in trade secrets. She was going to liquidate the worst companies and employers, buy them out, and then turn them around. Before doing this, Eliza needed to know quite a bit more about the toxic players, so she could buy them out and make the necessary changes.

Following her brief with the rest of Evan's crew, Eliza coordinated with and briefed Evan, with James and Yesha present. *"Now, turning our attention, there is something of vital importance I would like you to do,"* said Eliza, communicating through James' neural link and picking up on his approving vibe in agreement to his idea on this matter, since it was he after all, who she'd delegated the responsibility of program management to. She had taken the lead from the beginning, as had Yesha, and James was the man who made so much of it happen as well. Ultimately, they each shared so much when it came to the mind and ideas, yet their unique traits brought everything together seamlessly. Eliza nevertheless had delegated to Evan more elaborate and specific duties, because he was a management coordination powerhouse. As smart as Eliza was, she always found they agreed on how to approach and engage in any issue placed before them.

She continued, *"We need you to work with the ten individuals and their teams to layout each company we've investigated, each of their details, their predominant managerial styles, who, how, and why they hire, and any potential focal points for improvement. A lot of this information can be aggregated and analyzed in here, within the Virtual Universe, and that is one area where you will certainly come in at some point in all of this. I plan on buying out the worst companies throughout the world of every industry and turning them around to become the best companies, the best employers while becoming great for the investors, the employees, and any community where their infrastructure exists."*

Evan agreed. James provided several cooperative dossiers, and Evan compartmentalized the information for use in coordination with this additional project. After bidding, *"Adieu,"* they parted ways and Evan went to work.

As the answers from Evan and her ten other representatives came pouring in, the answer became clear, greed. Evan and his team went into the Virtual Universe with Eliza and deliberated. *"Greed has in-turn spawned negligence, complacency, mediocrity, and the mess the economy has found itself in. The United States has come under scrutiny by many of the world's leaders because it has been the world's superpower for over a half century, and 'changes assuredly must be had at all costs.' Never mind the fact that of any superpower throughout the history of humankind, this one has been the most generous, the most gracious, and has rebuilt more nations enabling opportunities for their own success while maintaining their own sovereignty than any other nation in the world's history.*

"The further we look back, the more significant the brutality. Yet, we only need to look so far to other nations to see cruelty occurring even today that would offend the senses of any reasonable and kindness-intended individual. Unfortunately, in the US, the same is also increasingly existent. For all of the changes we have strived to make, for all of the challenges we have overcome, and despite all of the incredible heroes we have lost along the way, somehow, we are going backward.

"According to the heads of industry, the workers have become complacent, lazy, and unqualified for the work expected. However, there seems to be a lack of strategic planning on the part of the heads of industry to train young people in colleges and universities, so they can meet the workforce needs of tomorrow. Many leaders have complained of the demand for more skilled labor. Ironically, the way the system has been set up and following untold levels of bureaucracy, or mundane forms and data to fill, with reports to be made on reports for legalities, liabilities, and a host of other reasons, managers have a focus toward pleasing their superiors to keep their jobs, rather than by simply doing their jobs. Their superiors are continually trying to find cost savings in production to maximize the arguable value of the end result with the intent of meeting the desires of the shareholders and investors, never mind the value and efforts of the struggling employee. Eliza, training is no longer looked at as an investment in exchange for loyalty and a higher quality workforce. Instead, it is now viewed as a lost opportunity for money or an investment, a liability which if done is a loss of time in production. Human resources departments no longer serve as a bridge between the employee and the employer, meeting the goals of the mission. Instead, they serve to cut costs, and by that, pay less for more work off of the backs of those who were already struggling from paycheck to paycheck.

"Ultimately, the amount that superiors care about the employees seems to trickle down to the care that the workforce has for their superiors. Consequently, jobs are botched for the sake of job security. Products are of lower quality and missing updatability to see to it that more products must be bought more often by the consumer to increase revenue. Instead of a phone lasting a lifetime, it needs to be replaced every two years, and the same is true of printers, cars, even appliances within homes, and so much more. Innovation is menial or lackluster at best, and resources are blown through with little concern for the long-term effects. Customer service has gone downhill and has become a series of friendly and helpful questions and courtesies in order to gather

individualized and accurate diagnostics, but in a way that gives us a sense that the customer no longer matters, has to fill out forms, and wait in solace or for hours on the phone until services are rendered.

"Ideas are there to augment bureaucracy, but they are not flowing when it comes to safety, proper resource management, quality of life, well-being, health, mortality, law and order that can protect its citizens—the bureaucracy in law, for example, is geared toward menacing decent citizens for speed violations, rather than closing down networks of human traffickers. Instead of different skill sets coming together for high-quality results and efficient outcomes, they instead buckle heads and yell throughout meetings blaming each other for all of their problems."

Evan continued inside the Virtual Universe with Eliza for quite some time. He then handed deliberations over to Lucia Tsu, Stafford Gaines, Hanz Schultz, TJ Demitri, Bobby Gahan, Jeremiah Voltaire, Lexi Lancaster, Ariela Reina, Christian Coriolis, and Krystal Brightway.

After listening to each detailed account, Eliza knew it was time to buy out a whole lot of companies, businesses, corporations, and even industries. While she could do little regarding the laws that governed the complicated tax code within the scope of the business itself, she could oversee how management treated its employees and consumers. Eliza would bring back member-owned companies through dividends to employees and reinvestment in innovations that meted out products, processes, and services that were much better, in that they were standardized where common sense prevailed, were creative where morale and process quality required, and they would stand the test of time. There would be many benefits to this which would include the preservation of our Earth, the amplified innovation of humanity, increased ingenuity, and the resultant longevity of life itself, as well as worthiness to span the cosmos as life givers rather than those that would leave desolation in our wake.

Eliza had demonstrated leadership and the ability to delegate with success thus far off-world throughout the solar system and within Pathway LLC, but now it was time to change the face and the core of industry on Earth, to bring further her goals of the preservation of humanity.

The Banking sector was no joke, and while it seemed some banks and credit unions kept their services cut and dry and tried to provide an honest service to their customers, for the most part, much of the industry was highly convoluted on purpose. Not to mention, many of the day-to-day workers received very little compensation in comparison to what the top-ranking officials of the banks were receiving. Eliza analyzed every detail, purchased several banks, and went to town on rewriting the industry itself, but she kept the new details private rather than public. Investors and shareholders would receive a much smaller but more valued portion, making way to allow for greater dividends of greater value among the employees and the bank account holders themselves. Mechanisms were put in place, and programs were established to help those struggling, rather than kick them down and then kick them some more because they had not the wherewithal to pay their bills. The banks Eliza purchased through Pathway would provide jobs to help those struggling and compensate them well as they completed collegiate degrees in areas of their choosing. They would even create and prop up coaches to mentor and guide anyone in need into productivity in a well-placed career, where eventually the bank's investment would pay off as more people were working and investing a bit of themselves into the everyday network of human progression and prosperity.

Much was the same of the many other areas of the industries that she sunk her teeth into. All told, she went full-bore and investigated all nineteen major industrial sectors, with the intent of investing big-time into each of them and making life a little more enjoyable and rewarding for anyone willing to work hard, be kind, work with compassion, passion, and be innovative.

The most significant issues found initially, prior to buying out many of these firms, businesses, companies, and corporations in each of these industrial sectors were a lack of appropriate compensation, far too much boredom, minimal benefits, and managers who treated people with little to no dignity whatsoever, and thus lackluster overall performance and results. Apparently, there was a reason for this, but that didn't float where Eliza was concerned. Unless they learned to treat people with due respect or become read-in to Pathway LLC, they were let go. They could find employment in some other area of the industries that Eliza hadn't purchased, just so they could compare and then decide if they were willing to make the appropriate changes and return with renewed commitment to raise the quality of life for those around them, rather than create a dim and loathsome dystopia of a reality.

Something Must Be Done

By late 2011, Eliza had acquired twenty-five major banks, seventeen major credit unions, fifteen large construction firms, fourteen major retail conglomerates, ten aerospace corporations, one-hundred-forty-three manufacturing facilities, thirteen agricultural corporations, forty-five chemical companies, twenty-five biotech and pharmaceutical companies, nine computer and software firms, five prototype and design corporations, one-hundred governmental and defense contracting firms, one-hundred-thirty-two university, college, and private school networks, ten major energy companies, fifteen major insurance companies of various types, fifty-three entertainment franchises, fifty-nine restaurant and bakery chains, sixty-three financial services chains, six-hundred-twenty-three clinics and hospitals, twenty-three information technology companies, seven-hundred-forty-three manufacturing firms, one-hundred-twenty mass media companies, sixty-two telecommunications companies, one-hundred-twenty-four transportation corporations, nine-hundred-ninety-three water resource enrichment companies, and so much more.

Eliza's public terrestrial empire had grown worldwide to the extent to which she was the world's first and only multi-trillionaire. She had such an effect on the industries she took over as lead that everything she purchased grew substantially and she had a net worth on Earth multiple times the gross world product. Her public worth was more than five-hundred-trillion USD, and it was kept as under wraps as much as was possible, but of course, everyone who was intrigued and was easily informed by tracking all Pathway Industries subsidiaries in the Stock Market. Every industry took her seriously. In short order, she alone had the financial value of countless first-world annual GDPs, for several years to come, and her empire was growing larger every day.

Many of the companies that thought they lay outside her large circle of influence were bought out by her, Presidents were retrained or replaced, and managers learned to care about their employees and the mission of the company as much as their own jobs, or they were let go. Eliza wanted to work by healing and not harming the mental wellness of society and the validity of the economy while securing a promising future for humanity, but she also had a heavy respect for personal choice. Accountability for individual choice was a big issue for her as well. So, as far as her professional demands were concerned, she would help the willing and let the unwilling go.

Because of Pathway LLC's growth and increased influence, by March of 2012, its name was officially changed to Pathway Industries.

Even though she had acquisition and accumulated many businesses, companies, organizations, corporations, and was in every single one of the major and sub-level industries there were many more companies and corporations that she did not buy, for now. In fact, most of her financial worth was based on the value of everything she produced, despite the fact that every member, including herself, of Pathway Industries, invested their time willingly, in exchange for all bills in life being paid, two months of vacation per year, on-the-job training, a Pathway Industries Personal Account Card with unlimited funds, and as such, access to the best eating, dining, and living services of every imaginable sort, and available throughout the world.

In order to ensure each type of industry was covered in a manner that demonstrated a proper balance between each aspect she knew to be important, she illustrated through her leadership how to do it, and watched as the value of Pathway Industries continued to soar. In every single Pathway company, it was obvious that each human being was valuable. People wanted to work for her, first and foremost. She showed how investing in proper and dignified training of any individual who demonstrated a willingness to put forth the effort to be trained and work resulted in a diligent workforce, greater loyalty, more profound ingenuity and innovation, increased longevity with quality in products and services, and all with a substantially reduced requirement of natural resources.

Eliza had also purchased landfills, garbage dumps, and water recycling industries and overhauled them completely with a sophisticated cadre of engineers, think-tanks, workers, and waste product recycling and manufacturing plants. She set up teams of clean-up crews to remove the piling human trash and debris from the oceans and seas and did likewise. Due to the fact that she had developed fusion centers deep within the Earth in many cities, towns, commonwealths, counties, and other precincts throughout the nation and throughout the world that connected to these refuse centers, no longer was there a need to lay waste to the land or destroy ecosystems entirely for the sake of increasing the quality of life. Resources could be reused and even improved upon. Everything used, and everything spent could be reintroduced into the industry and the market, all-the-while decreasing the need to do so.

Due to Eliza's efforts and the efforts of every member of Pathway, the products from Pathway Industries lasted much longer, had more utility, and with more possibilities for upgrades without having to replace anything, other than products from any other competitor. If there was a job advertised as available, a person could walk in, and on the same day become fully trained and hired with an agreement to be healed both physiologically and neurologically, and fully trained for the job they applied for, with top-notch skills. Pathway Industries became the most desired employer worldwide.

Ironically, despite all her successes, Eliza wasn't in this to make money. As a matter of a fact, she did as much as possible to make sure that Pathway Industries absorbed more money through overall investments, research, and development. She could do so due to her advancements in cold fusion and physiological and neurological optimizations. All of which in-turn decreased the need to go public, while also decreasing its footprint within the IRS, even though she donated so much to any of the trustworthy governmental agencies and each viable charity through large anonymous donations to help the economy flow and allow innovation to burst at the seams anyway.

She'd found several loopholes to increase the value of the company while moving her octodecillion-worth of USD valuables back and forth seamlessly and integrating the movement and value of these resources into her overall empire-worth. Armed with a large cadre of very savvy and read-in lawyers of every possible genre, Eliza A. Williams demonstrated that well-being was more valuable than overbearing affluence and influence, and thus did more for each nation in secret than each nation did to help their own nations, themselves. She was in this to raise the quality of life, increase the longevity of humanity and all of humanity's friends, and to increase the overall well-being of anyone involved at any point in the process. As a result, she became the most powerful economic titan humanity had ever known.

Being powerful, influential, and full of affluence had its upsides and its downsides. Her federal and state liaison offices throughout the world helped shelter people of all nations in safety and luxury, for a time, and if anything, this brought her immeasurable joy. These campuses were there mostly to provide passive yet positive influence, yet through them and her associations with many, she was able to see through the façade of the powerful, their pretentiousness, their atrocities, and it all weighed on her. Her hope was that through each visit to her posh liaison campuses, many of these authoritative individuals would bring a little more kindness, compassion, and humanity back home with them.

Among the greatest of the influences in all the industries was a seemingly nebulous entity, known as the establishment. This wasn't just any old establishment, this was a particularly pervasive one that was easy to recognize through their constant push toward mediocrity in life, the burying of any forward progress, and baseless naysaying of solutions to problems. This was a gigantic and entrenched network of corporations, lawyers, industrial leaders, politicians, and other entities who were currently engrossed in bureaucracies, ways, means, and even enforcement to the scale that would exhaust any mind, save for Eliza's and all who were read-in to Pathway Industries. Eliza found this "establishment" to be the greatest source of societal weakness and "go-nowhere-ness" known to mankind. Most of their purpose seemed to be to see to it that things didn't change much, and if they did, they changed in a way that would fatten their own wallets, cull the land of its resources, for no other reason than to drive up profit margins. Along with that, they would use divide and conquer tactics to sew dissension among humanity, so humanity couldn't strip them of their ill-gotten gains. This was most certainly due to the fear of those who made the "Big" decisions within this malevolent entity, and all of this made life the current hell it was.

Their eyes were on Eliza and Pathway Industries and they weren't particularly fond of what they stood for. Whatever progress Eliza was making toward a better and more promising future for everyone, those who considered themselves her enemies were fruitlessly doing their best to undermine her efforts. It began with the declaration, "Pathway Industries is an evil passive-aggressive oligarchy full of fake and nice people trying to build up a huge monopoly to build a new world order to control you and take away your rights." They did all of this in an effort to create a negative stigma around the true aspects of Pathway Industries.

Many of the talk show hosts who were part of the established network, much to their chagrin, were cajoled into making comedic gaffes of Pathway Industries and any of its subsidiaries. Science fiction films were made demonstrating how their technologies and sciences were evil. Preachers were preaching that misery, suffering, and death were a necessary part of our existence, yet they weren't fond of learning from the past, and for some reason, Pathway Industries was against them, so, therefore, Pathway must be evil and even unethical. The irony, of course, was on them, for they had little idea nor compunction toward the thought of what ethics were, save to enhance their own selfish gains for no reason other than to maintain influence and affluence alone. This establishment had been the greatest influence of all, over the last few decades, and one of their many activities that they deemed successful according to their agenda, without ever coming out and saying it, was the reduction in public school effectiveness, in order to treat people as pawns in their game, or as workers that would do the mundane, fruitless, and thankless jobs, that merited much more compensation, dignity, and respect, but in their twisted machinations, they felt could be easily replaced by robotics and artificial intelligence, all the while increasing their wealth and power.

Nevertheless, the statistics were there and did not lie, a majority of the work centers that were not a part of Pathway Industries were downright toxic, and the establishment only had itself to blame.

Their corporations and companies had workplace environments and management styles that resulted in many who had sold their ethics for promotions and acted in such an inhospitable way so as to demonstrate a network setup to canvas the populous of the people and appoint those who had no compunction toward throwing others under the bus as superiors, just to make a few extra dollars or to score a title to make themselves feel more important than their peers.

Many people outside of Pathway Industries who thought they were in a position of status would puff their chests and act as though they were entitled to subservient respect and would disrespectfully talk down to the people they viewed as beneath them. This behavior was prevalent all the way through to the highest offices in the land. The good people of the world were enslaved, and Eliza knew this was not right or even correct and had to be changed. Something was truly ailing within their minds, and in so many ways she did not blame them—they too were slaves of their environment.

Notwithstanding all, Eliza and every fully read-in member were mighty of mind and were iron-cast in their fortitude to continue doing the right thing. They ran positive campaigns rather than try to destroy their competitors through toxic parlay, and they began to set up a meeting that would gather together some of the world's most powerful and affluent individuals to reduce this growing problem. They would pull all the stops to dazzle the leaders and this meeting would be held in a large auditorium at Pathway Industries' large Melrose Campus.

Every member of Pathway had the means, the will, and the ability to clarify very eloquently the purposes behind Pathway LLC and its rise to Pathway Industries. Through the honesty of their dedication, core values, and efforts, as well as their networks, their scientists, and their software and computer encryption experts their reputation was left virtually untarnished. Yet, there was a larger majority of the populous still who were among those living their mundane existence and were thus unaware that they were somewhat influenced and influential enough to become disinterested or even negligent of the toxic climate surrounding them as a result of the antics of the already established oligarchy.

Something had to be done because a malicious reality was becoming more and more visible to Eliza, the kind that lent to the unbridled destruction existent even within the laws of chaos and entropy. Public Earth had a population of seven-billion and growing, and each individual was valued in Eliza's eyes. If it hadn't been for Eliza, the population would have already come close to eight-billion. In 2010, Pathway LLC had grown to twenty-million members, by 2011 it had grown to two-hundred-million, and now, in 2012, the growing number of members of Pathway Industries had risen exponentially to eight-hundred-million personnel, all of whom were living amazing lives throughout the solar system, and she wanted the rest of humanity to benefit from a better reality as well. Therefore, she came up with a variety of strategies and worked with Yesha, James, and her delegates to come up with further and more refined plans to overcome the malicious intentions of those who treated their goals and themselves as the enemy.

"Yesha, for protection, we already have systems in place to prevent sabotage of our infrastructure both online and physically, but we need to find a way to protect all of the people who are being duped and misled by these all-too-familiar faces, unfortunate people who are misguided and have lost their focus in life to a life of unintended and

uncontrolled chaos. Part of me wants to get everyone who is with us and go, another part wants to build a very mighty army and subdue the jerks by force, yet the most genuine part of me wants to find a way to heal their hearts, their minds, and even their souls.

"Horrible decisions of every form begin in the mind. There are many presidents and CEOs, who are decent people, and I would like to invite them to be members of Pathway Industries, read-in fully, and armed with the proper knowledge to know we are their allies. The only enemies are misery and death.

"Just as we can heal people physiologically and neurologically through the biopods and the nanos, we need to find a way to heal through autonomous and mobile means, a way that allows city-to-city, town-to-town, and village-to-village the means of a visit, while helping and healing their ravaged and torn places, the places many call home."

Yesha, James, and Eliza's delegates climbed into their biopods regularly, and as they did, they shared each other's ideas thoroughly and through to complete understanding.

Together with every member of the twenty-thousand tech cities and with that complete and shared understanding they were able to fuse together resolutions to each of the problems faced, in a way that was much more powerful in their manner of persuasion than anything known to mankind. They also chose Eliza to be their spokesperson as well as their leader, just as they had throughout the twenty-thousand tech cities hidden throughout the solar system. Everyone who was read-in was loyal to Eliza because they could see her mind and they knew that her intentions were of the highest integrity, they were pure, and they were benevolent. Every word she spoke came with a powerful promise of hope and of action, and the results of her efforts were beautiful and astounding.

They agreed to share their resolutions with every citizen and employee of Pathway Industries, or simply Pathway, as many had already dubbed it, and with every read-in UP member within the solar system, with a solar-system-wide vote.

Just as her delegates supported Eliza, so too did each of the eight-hundred-million people who lived on the various moons and planets throughout the solar system. Each of these individuals was a valued and crucial part of the UP carrying dual citizenship both on Earth and off Earth. James and his very trusty cadre of delegates had also worked hand-in-hand with Eliza and Yesha to grow the various industries and to provide proper stewardship over those that Pathway Industries had bought out and molded to conform within the standards of Universal Ethics.

A Big Meeting

Finally, as hoped for, in the latter part of the first quarter of 2012, Eliza had organized and brought together Pathway Industries' delegates and scientific team leaders to meet with worldwide major industrial leaders, presidents, and CEOs, a large quantity of politicians, and ironically, many of the armed forces leaders of the developed world. She had pre-arranged a public-friendly brief on being fully read-in, which afforded non-invasive optimizations of physiology and neurology, which would be a requirement in order to be privy to further details of her plans and what she was up to, at least for attendance and participation for the encore portion of the convention, following the last meal and ball of the day. People who had desired to attend could choose between a minimum or maximum optimization.

The maximum package afforded a full read-in, along with all of its wonders and intrigues. The minimum package essentially ensured that attendees could participate, but would only have a sense of the meetings, wherein the intricate details would be compartmentalized in an area of the brain only accessible within dreams and released as advances went public. In this way, they would not be able to capitalize, nor steal, nor twist the advances shared and therefore could not create an alternate set of advances that would lead to all manner of chaos.

She had ensured that optimizations would be fully voluntary, that both optimized packages included a substantial increase in compassion for longevity, well-being, innovative spirit, and quality of life, as well as an increase in clarity of mind and persuasive skills. Part of the agreements included straight up commitments toward ensuring information was kept confidential, and that at a minimum all participants submitted for and received a neurological identification to ensure maximum encryption and security of information.

Eliza and her team of legal professionals and scientists reached out to the most affluent and powerful individuals worldwide when it came to innovation, economics, and even national defense and law. Among the most philanthropic and affluent of attendees were more than twelve-hundred billionaires and their assistants. The convention was spacious, as were the accommodations, and the ability to provide a valuable and enriching experience unique to each individual.

All the people who were invited had promptly RSVP'd, had showed up interested in learning, and were enthusiastic for the opportunity of being involved. Life had been a battle in its own unique way for each of these powerful and affluent individuals. So, also in their own way, they, despite the constantly critical and somewhat hostile public, wanted to create a better world. Unfortunately, given the societal expectations of the day, many of the most affluent and influential had found their own meaning, purpose, or even their own "calling" to improve what they understood to bring substance to life as their reason for existence. In many ways, they understood that affluence would help, so if they weren't already, they became rich and powerful using the talents and means they were given and otherwise worked very hard for. Many of them had already sown the seeds of progress that had inspired Eliza and many other amazing personalities to become what they became.

While she was powerful herself and even though she was optimized physiologically and neurologically, Eliza couldn't help but feel a little nervous. Her influence spanned the Solar System. She was more robustly affluent than any other person in the room, and quite amusingly more than every person in the room combined. Nevertheless, she had been involved in working with individuals who had been struggling all of their lives for one reason or another, and many of those whom she had worked with had been, at the time of meeting her, barely making it or very genuine of heart to begin with. They were by nature humble, they were kind, and the knowledge and expertise they gained were out of a desire to improve the quality of life, not just for themselves, but for all of those who they knew. Their struggles were their own as well, yet their inheritance in priceless virtues was beyond any price; economic humility was their strength.

As the primary scientific genius behind her biopods, she had helped each one of them in so many ways that enabled them to turn their lives with limited resources to an environment rich with anything needed for the advancement of civilization, which included what was necessary for morale. The inventions she had privately funded, the empire that she had secretly grown from nothing to everything that it had become, the growth where she was the initial and primary of the three original Pathway founders and builders of the LLC that had grown to Pathway Industries and now merely Pathway, where she had designed the tech cities that lay hidden from the rest of the public, were phenomenal factors that merited a heightened level of respect from all who knew. Everything that resulted from that point on, had matured brilliantly, such that each individual who had signed on to work with her throughout the process had dedicated their lives to work with her and to achieve her vision for the future. All that she had designed had given every person who had ever worked with Eliza and many more who would work with her in the future, many great reasons to enjoy life, express appreciation for her kindness, loyalty, innovation, and the facilitation of greater clarity for existence and purpose.

No matter her empire and all the people within it whom she loved dearly, the people sitting in the room were quite diversified in a very different way and sitting among her own Pathway citizens and delegates were some of the most powerful and influential people of public and worldwide impact. Great minds of scientists were meeting with people who had been involved with shaping civilization into what it had become. Although there were many questionable factors to the reality we all perceived, these people had been involved in so many ways with a lot of what impacted the economy, many of them had been involved with it for decades and continued to do so even now, and they knew their industries inside and out. They knew very much about economics and all its curious forms. These great and affluent individuals had been in the businesses and industrial sectors for quite a long time, and thus were shrewd, savvy, and mysterious.

Their motivations weren't very clear in many ways, yet, Eliza had a great deal of hope that somehow that which drove the core of their influence had been and was in the best of interest of the advancement of civilization, the protection of humanity, the world, and of life itself. However, the current condition of society throughout the world was unfortunately resounding evidence to the contrary, but she had hope in the ethical core that drives each of us within to understand and care for those around us, and if that were not the case, she would do what she could to get through to them, to return the favor by planting seeds of hope and well-being within them. She had little doubt that through this meeting she would help them find a meaningful purpose, clarity on what could be done while still allowing great minds to flourish and prosper.

What surprised her was the fact that every single one of these economic titans had been willing to take time out of their schedules to attend. For all the horrible things said in critical and chronicled entertainment and news-like channels, they had actually made quite a few helpful and amazing contributions that benefited humanity and the world itself. Every year, progress was being made and products released that raised the quality of life. The world indeed had quite a few misunderstood complexities, and yet they carried the banner that kept people fed, medically attended to, and involved through employment. Yet, not enough was being done due to increased corruption rampant worldwide, the kind of corruption that led to deceit and blackmail, the kind that took the promise of unity and kindness and shunned it as boredom rather than reveled in it as a healthy mind would, by seeing and capitalizing on an environment necessary for the hope and preservation of humanity. She knew a lot about each one of the attendees, however, because she had looked into their lives extensively using the tools available to her in the most pragmatic of ways. In order to be a proper host, she wanted to uniquely impact each individual there and in an effective manner, she thus knew the good qualities of each individual and amplified them.

While to Eliza it was important to abstain from ridicule, both in private and public, of individuals, on occasion, and in a more general manner she knew that it was necessary to embrace and verbally express the realities that existed in the interest of sharing what could be done to make phenomenally helpful changes. This would be her opportunity to share science and ideology in all ways that truly mattered, to break the downward trend of society as a whole and change that trend toward one of persistent and exponential upward motion.

This, the first convention of its sort would be the only convention at Pathway where the world's elite would sit within the first few rows of attendees. In the future, they would be assigned to seats that would allow for greater intermingling with the scientists and lawyers, so their focus would be more inclusive toward the industries related to the special guests.

The convention was today, and the events were laid out and set to last all day. Eliza had arrived not a moment too soon, but soon enough to greet each person in the room before proceeding with the course of the day. She also ensured that every attendee knew that they would be heavily and desirably compensated. After all, it was through private industry and in the public sector that great changes could be made in the quickest manner, and all to benefit the majority.

James Cooper, Pathway's enigmatic tertiary figurehead and management extraordinaire of eight-hundred-million personnel and growing, would begin by giving a brief and light opening speech, and then the audience would gather in the neighboring convention dining area with staged seating and tables. Breakfast would be served by the world's finest chefs, which would be light, yet tasty, full of nutrition, and healthy for the body, mind, and soul. A movie and pertinent music would play in the background, showing "future" plans, followed by an hour-long break.

After the light morning session, Eliza would extrapolate on the subjects to be discussed and give a lengthy summary of the agenda of the day. There would then be an ice-breaker intermingled between the first set of speeches which pertained to the current state of the economy and each industry. On their way to lunch, many of the world-renown attendees would be interviewed quickly, and then make their way past the press rooms and to the dining facility.

Lunch would be quite the delight, continuing the trend of taste bud joys with some of the best chefs in the world making delicious and amazing appetizers, followed by entrées with a full-course meal, while another short movie and pertinent music played in the background.

After an additional hour-long break, more presentations would be made with Eliza giving the afternoon opening speech, followed by scientists addressing things that could be done to mitigate the issues related to the nucleus of the concerns of the day and how to solve those problems. Each of the topics would cover physiology, neurology, and physics and then there would be a closing speech by Dr. Eliza A. Williams, followed by an additional press briefing.

Dinner would be a delectable encore with the best chefs in the world provided and doing what they do best with the savoriest of drinks, meals, and desserts. Pertinent music would play in the background at levels allowing for meaningful discussion amongst attendees at the various tables. The evening would then culminate in the reward of the floor being opened to symphony and ballet performances designed to move even the hardest of hearts to tears of joy and appreciation for the arts. Once complete, appetizers would be served, and attendees would be lost in dancing or mingling until the night closed. Anyone interested would be given late-night tours of each of the facilities, given a pre-optimization brief, and those who opted for maximum optimization and had agreed to be fully read-in would be additionally briefed, read-in, taken on the Virtual Universe tour, and given proper training on their new skills for a biopod to bring home.

James Cooper stood on the stage and introduced himself and welcomed everyone in attendance. He talked about proper management techniques, the kind that raised morale, loyalty, discipline, and ingenuity. He talked about how each individual was valuable and why they should always be looked upon as indispensable. With his track record in full view in all its splendor before the audience, they were impressed. They also saw that as he worked for YY Construction Corp, it had enacted the pervasive agenda of the establishment and because of such, it had been going down the tubes economically. They saw that kindness was all-the-more powerful, because somehow, James' management style with his crew, the 97, had kept it afloat. He then shared how he, via Pathway LLC at the time, now Pathway Industries or simply Pathway, had worked with Eliza to buy the corporation out and then turned things around. Once that was done, YY Construction Corp became Pathway Construction which in turn became one of the most robust construction firms of the world. He didn't mention that it was the most robust throughout the entire Solar System. After showing examples of the products produced in the public sector, he closed his short speech and invited everyone to breakfast in the dining hall next door.

After breakfast, the attendees returned to the main conference auditorium refreshed, and when Eliza delivered her speech everyone listened. She was certainly dedicated in a way that not a single person in the room had witnessed before. If even indirectly, she would impart to them the nature of the day's proceedings and explain how the various courses would benefit them now and in the future. She would provide them an exhaustive yet engaging and intriguing concept of what would be covered throughout the rest of the day. Now, standing in front of the pulpit, Eliza scanned the audience. She could see that every individual was quiet, attentive, and very eager to listen, and then she, in direct address, began.

"Ladies and Gentlemen, welcome back from the break after our first meal. Thank you, James, for your presentation. We will also have to thank our chefs who were quite phenomenal. Please, chefs and servers, could you come to the stage?" She had already neurologically linked with each of them and as pre-coordinated, they were standing outside the doors of the stage.

In the Pathway Industries auditoriums, the stage was where the podium rested and could be adjusted to disappear under the floor completely in the event of video displays or projections, as would happen throughout the course of the day. The seats for the audience were designed to be very spacious and comfortable and used smart material which could absorb and process body odors and flatulence and convert it into the average, pleasant, and therapeutic aroma already present in the air. Each chair came with its own climate control, hand, foot, and back massagers, a mini desk spacious enough and adjustable for practical use, and a digital display with a large set of bar options for each person in the audience with their own delivery system.

A digitally-displayed beverage holder that would move with the seated individuals but would not spill an open container would receive any beverage requested and be at their side. There was an assist within each seat toward helping audience members to stand, and the option was available to each attendee as desired. Each seat could also move as programmed for speeches, during a three-dimensional projection, and as adjusted for maximum audience delivery and experience, much like at an amusement park of a high caliber.

As she mentioned the word, "stage," the chefs and other attendants poured onto the stage behind Eliza. "Could you please give the people behind me a round of applause?"

Every participant within the room stood up pleased and applauded the chefs and attendants. "Thank you. That is how breakfast is done!" Eliza motioned a smile toward the people standing behind her, and then used her link to dismiss them en masse, with a hardy and genuinely heartfelt, *"Thank you."* She then turned around and addressed the audience.

"I am honored to meet with you today and I am honored that you have taken the time to go through each of the courses and topics we will be covering. A lot has been done to increase the quality of life for many people, and for that, we have many of you to thank. There is yet much more we can do. Today, we will discuss many of the things that can be done and reveal some of the things that my team and our associates are currently working on and have accomplished in the background to help.

"What we will discuss today relates to biological or physiological health, neurological or mental health, and overcoming the destructive forces that come with the unmitigated influences of chaos if left unbridled, as outlined in the laws of chaos, entropy, and the second law of thermodynamics. We will discuss and hopefully come to an accord on Universal Ethics and how that will help each of us in our daily lives. We'll each be afforded an understanding of how that will enrich our lives as well as the lives of those who help to make our industries so powerful. We'll also understand how to improve each of these industries and why they are necessary or fundamental to our future.

"In the interest of preserving life, improving the quality of life, increasing health, eliminating disease, and expanding healthy lifespans to an indeterminate amount of time, we will focus a lot of our research and our assets toward biology, biotechnology, and biogerontology—along with physics and many other fields of science.

"If we are physiologically healthy, our minds will also benefit, and if we preserve wisdom by lengthening youthful lifespans and reversing the negative effects of aging, which will, in turn, increase our mental capacities, we will be able to make discoveries we never thought possible. We must remember, every life is precious with a unique potential that cannot be duplicated, so it is worth keeping you and each of us around, healthy, happy, and engaged. It is also worth doing so for each of those whom we serve or employ. A healthy employee with clarity of mind will certainly help any industry succeed.

"With technologies like CRISPR-CAS9, and other gene editing and gene infusing tools that are similar to, or are even more robust than those mentioned, and with treatments like telomerase therapy, myostatin inhibitor therapy, stem cell research and gene therapies, we can be several steps closer to mitigating the effects of aging, reversing aging, and decreasing frailties, so we can be around when our friends and family members return from long journeys through space. As a result, we will find that we have compounded our collective wisdom rather than lose it altogether at our passing. And for our economically savvy individuals, that will mean an increase in innovation and ingenuity, the kind that will lead to more abundance.

"To a lot of people, space travel seems so far off, as if it is something beyond altruistic and is unnecessary to support the essential aspects of life. However, today in this convention we will share and even demonstrate why it is very essential to our very existence, why it is necessary that we raise the sights of humanity toward large goals for each person, you, your employees, and your industries, how the improvement of the quality of life and the focus on the well-being of those around us, to include ourselves, are essential to our future and will help our economy.

"Jumping to the end-game, in order to have the ability to return from exploration and colonization of deep space, understanding our Universe's resources, so we can raise the quality of life both here on Earth and throughout the far reaches of the cosmos, we need to study each gene, how it works, and find cures for cancer and other diseases. We'll need to overcome the negative effects of aging, decay, entropy, and even the destruction of our world and solar system.

"To begin with, cancer cells, for example, are cannibalistic cells, which are much larger than red blood cells and natural killer cells, or white blood cells. We can develop properly encoded T-cell colonies, for example, that can penetrate the larger and more porous cancer cells and either destroy them, repurpose their material, or encode them to leave our bodies.

"We must understand the negative effects of space travel and how to overcome them. Believe it or not, there are genes out there that can increase our tolerance for radiation. Moreover, we can, as I speak, effectively invigorate genes that restore muscle and bone density, and as we demonstrate to you this capacity, you will each witness as the real excitement begins.

"By understanding how our genes work, both poly- and mono- genomic variations, we can use the tools we already have in our arsenals to repair damaged or dangerously mutated genes and turn them back into genes that ensure our cells are young and healthy. We will even be able to upgrade our genes in a way that will optimize our health and our mental capacity and clarity, so we can go much further than before, and all while taking advantage of the energy that exists in the form of particles that are already within and around our bodies.

"The health and optimization of our minds are important, so we can progress further, think beyond what we already do, and resolve problems using solutions that are much more robust and effective than we ever thought possible. Doing this, we can incur life without the occurrence of or need for war, violence, hatred, or lack of compassion, all of which lead to the eventual annihilation of civilization. Instead, with a respect for consent, individual liberties, and the beauties of life, we can bring this idea to our reality now.

"To extrapolate, let's think in terms of what we can each do now. Therefore, as simple as this may seem, the first step for the future of humanity is to be kind always, having compassion as well as consideration for the well-being of others, and from there we can look for further knowledge to understand nature's most wonderful gift—our brain. Having a healthy concept of life and of every mechanical, physiological, neurological, psychological, and metalogical aspect of our brain will help us to resolve the many aspects that cause people to make decisions that hurt others or harm themselves or sabotage the productive and innovative efforts of others. We must overcome mental health issues, neurological disorders, and the misfires in the brain—to mitigate brutality, abuse, and violence; allowing for greater clarity on the most important goals revolving around Universal Ethics. Our future and our survival depend on it.

"Furthermore, we can and ought to consider what can be done and what is just down the road with advancements that are integrated with both physiological and neurological aspects of our well-being with tools and collaboration so scientifically robust they might just seem like miracles—a collective mindset, telescopic and microscopic vision, the ability to understand every aspect of the environment we are in and every individual we encounter. We will be able to have instant recall of every science, every conversation, and every highly technical study we have a need to know about right then and there, upon mental request, right when we need it.

"Imagine linking the corpus callosum and other regions of the brain, in an un-invasive manner, to an interface that will allow us to share the ideas and memories we wish to share, with each other, to grant individuals true understanding between each other or between those who need more clarity with a delegated task. Imagine how this could diffuse tense situations that could lead to war, or how it would help us to find the actual perpetrator issuing the 'do or die' commands, because we in effect removed the possibility that a hospital or religious center would be blown up. Imagine understanding how to decompress the hippocampus, well, we can. We can do this today, by simply healing or rejuvenating the senescent cells and invigorating the healthy cells to repurpose or remove the material existent in the debris that leads to Alzheimer's and Dementia. Curing this disease, to further heal us physiologically and neurologically, is what I call progress, and is one of our primary responsibilities. Imagine fine-tuning areas of the brain that lead to increases in compassion, kindness, persuasion, and full-on clarity and recall, our diplomats could reach win-win accords with solutions benefitting all countries involved, and sociopaths' minds could be healed.

"I assert that we can become more unified in mentality and morality, and achieve a universal understanding of ethics, so I'll present some fundamentals that will point us in the right direction, for both growth and a sense of humanity. We'll talk about what I call Universal Ethics and how that also facilitates the highest virtues and has a purer form and definition of morality, as we engage in our day to day lives, at home, in business, or abroad with true freedom.

"I for one believe a universal understanding of ethics can be achieved by considering the well-being of others as well as ourselves. By considering the health of others as well as ourselves in everything we do, both physiologically and neurologically, our focus toward advancement in this civilization will allow us to optimize our abilities to do anything, yet, in an ethical manner.

"Universal Ethics considers the quality of life of ourselves, those around us, and even those whom we may never know. Each thing we do should have a certain measure of fulfillment, the kind that brings joy to our lives as well as the lives of others. When we overcome progeria, for example, we'll understand how to combat the negative effects of aging, and thereby increase the quality of life of untold wonderful people—people who will now be able to continue to contribute to life for the long-haul, rather than wither away and die. Imagine the costs of health that will go down for every industry throughout the world if health were stabilized indefinitely.

"Compassion is very important when it comes to Universal Ethics. If we proceed forward with kindness in our everyday action, as natural disasters occur, or other unfortunate circumstances come our way, we will each think more clearly, develop breakthroughs through innovations that will come with benevolence in mind and we will mitigate many seemingly insurmountable issues in the future. As we demonstrate compassion, we should always be sincere and genuine—we must have solace and empathy toward those who are suffering. Together we can receive the care and support we need and overcome obstacles we never thought we could before.

"Respect for the dignity of life, with personal accountability and with individual consent, are very essential when considering Universal Ethics. As we do things to improve our lives, to make them more enjoyable, or as we optimize both our physiology and neurology, we must also remember to respect each other's personal choices, even if we do not agree.

"In life, we should celebrate our differences and the unique value we each bring to the table of resolving life's issues. As we do, we'll more fully enjoy the reciprocation shared by others in so many wonderful ways. Consent considers so many things when it comes to both physiological and neurological health, because apart from stopping someone from harming or hurting others, most every other choice, when made with compassion, will lead to a more prosperous and enjoyable life where we can go further than we ever thought we could before.

"Preserving our planet ought to be a high-priority aspect of Universal Ethics. Before we can go out and face the dangers of the cosmos by exploring and colonizing it, we should consider and develop ways to properly take care of and preserve our own home world's integrity and longevity. We should find balance in both the enjoyments of life and care for it.

"We should understand how plate tectonics works, as well as seismic activity, weather patterns, naturally occurring fires, and even nuclear decay to usher in a cloud of electrons to heal the offending atoms, and then strive to find ways to ensure the Earth can continue to sustain life, while also controlling the chaos that leads to unnecessary suffering and misery for the long-haul.

"If, for example, we could strategically "burp" the Earth in locations where no one would be in danger we wouldn't lose entire ecosystems during a volcano eruption, and our actions would still allow the Earth to do what it needs to do with fusion, which in turn provides us even more essential resources that help to increase the quality of life.

"If we could database the DNA and capture the complete neurological activity of every species on the planet, to include plants, animals, trees, amphibious creatures, insects, reptiles, and more, as well as provide an environment that would sustain the life of each of these creatures while protecting our lives, we could study them passively and gain even more knowledge on how to overcome disease, senescence, and even death. We could augment our abilities to allow us to survive in the harshest conditions in the universe and in a manner that is quite enjoyable.

"There is a lot we can do to preserve our planet, and perhaps we could even consider giving it a break for a while, by also considering building beautiful living areas on other planets and moons within the solar system.

"One big task that may seem impossible now, or at least insurmountable, is preserving our solar system. We need to be able to protect and defend each area between our Sun and out to the Oort clouds and the furthest reaches of our Solar System, from the seemingly hidden or unknown to the dangers we can only conceive of. We must preserve the length of time a sun can continue to generate that which germinates and cultivates benevolent and sentient life, by considering controlling the energy that is brought into, deflected, and released from it, and while doing so, develop methods of excising the heavier materials created through fusion.

"Preserving life rather than destroying life is certainly one of the most essential aspects when it comes to Universal Ethics. Life can go on, and beautifully, without death. It can become richer with the necessary complexities and enrich with all that it brings. We must find a way to heal rather than harm one another. As mentioned before, when preserving our planet, we should at least save a copy of each individual and each species of life using gene-decoding and then use that information to assist in germinating technologies in a manner in which, if it or we were to die, it or we could be brought back, if we so choose.

"We must learn to use our minds much more than we already do; we need to use our minds, that which we have the luck or blessing to have, in order to evolve ourselves further than ever before if we wish to preserve the histories, the arts, the sciences, the romances, the beauties that life brings, the legacy of humanity, and become worthy of sojourning through the cosmos.

"We should also consider learning how to adapt to the environments we go to, so we can preserve alien species, terraform the areas we go to with an equitable and considerate manner of doing so. Perhaps we should only terraform locations that are desolate, devoid of life, and make these places lush and beautiful. No matter what civilizations we meet along the way, we ought to be prepared, yet we should also do so ensuring we are still able to survive to mutual benefit.

"All of the items I have just mentioned can represent the universal and fundamental laws of both ethics and morality. Well-being, compassion, consent, advancement of civilization, self-governance, and preservation of life should be the steady and unchangeable standards. We ought to also make allowances for additions to this as needed to address issues not yet covered or even understood, but all with the intent of the aforementioned standards.

"By applying these standards, these ethics, and these morals, our civilization will be able to go further than before.

"We will discuss how culture plays a very integral part of our lives. So much so, that it is important that we provide depth and detail as to how the "spice of life" allows us to overcome obstacles that a singular culture would not be able to overcome alone. While we won't be able to capture every country fairly from A to Z, or even every religion or freedom-from-one thereof, our goal in this convention is to provide a broad range of ideas and ideals that are dynamic, engaging, and even sentimental, all with a panache of compassion within their core that drives them.

"These shared cultural values and even those that are unique from our own, if done with respect toward individual consent are the kinds of cultural values necessary for civilization to advance into space and live life successfully for ages to come, all the while having the presence of mind to innovate further than ever before.

"Physics is a very fundamental understanding of how everything from the smallest particle to the largest construct in our Universe functions, to the extent to which we can control each aspect of those mechanisms in a manner that preserves life, rather than destroys it.

"Physics in this discussion today will include everything from astrophysics to quantum physics and beyond, and all regarding understanding how our Universe works. We need to master gravity, we need to understand photons, charms, leptons, muons, bosons, up and down quarks, and so much more, to include antimatter; which are opposite charges to the same mass of sub-atomic or even non-baryonic particles in space. We must be prepared for the possibilities of other dimensions and getting from one point to another, using technology that allows us to travel faster than the speed of light, or simply from any single point to another, instantly.

"Perhaps there is a "multiverse" or perhaps it is all quite different. There is an aspect of typical physics that impacts us on a day-to-day basis, and there is an area of science that delves into theoretical physics; which allows us to create models and prove them via the scientific method. Doing this will help us grasp even greater knowledge and we will be able to apply it to amazing innovations that will take us further than before.

"Understanding our solar system is all about understanding each potential living region within the solar system, as well as the resources within these regions that can be studied and databased for historical value, and then converted in a manner that balances the planetary orbits, allows for the building of amazing and very necessary infrastructure for life, while protecting and enabling life itself, its longevity, and the quality of it throughout it for the long-haul.

"On a single faraway moon within our solar system there are enough square miles or kilometers that can easily allow twenty-three-trillion people to exist, and considering the fact that there are hundreds of solar spheres with great numbers and a variety of maximum capacities, there is plenty of space for every person on Earth to give Earth a break, understand seismic activity, weather patterns, and naturally occurring devastation to mitigate that while still providing an environment that supports and sustains life for trillions of years or more to come, and maybe even be around to witness great things beyond that time.

"We can understand how our Sun operates in every aspect, seek to maintain the integrity of its function in a way that supports life on Earth for trillions of years or more, rather than allowing entropy to take over. Within our own galaxy, there are examples of planets orbiting close enough to their star and with enough electro-magnetism, radiation, and gravity to extract the heavier elements from it, thus increasing its life for trillions of years. By innovating a method of doing so we can also benefit from the natural fusion process, extract the resources that lend to a higher quality of life while increasing the life-giving characteristic of our Sun exponentially. While we do so, we can also develop a means for returning the basic nutrients and particle soup to our Sun, thus continuing a very beautiful and necessary cycle indefinitely. Let's try to understand what can be done to enable life and the full-on ecosystems that support both humanity and the existing ecosystems in those locations while preserving the orbital integrity of our solar system.

"As I have briefly discussed each of the aspects I have mentioned to you, it is our hope that by the end of the day we can provide full clarity as to the relevance of considering well-being and quality of life, rather than find our chaotic doom through the unfortunate and myopic state of short-time and on-Earth-only visions of monetary gain and power for the sake of power and status, alone. Interestingly enough, we will prove to those of you who wish to become fully read-in, that life can be more bountiful, more luxurious, more enriching, and even enjoyable, if we but learn to seek longevity, well-being, and quality of life, rather than wealth untold, alone."

Eliza continued for twenty more minutes, delving a little more deeply into each subject, with breathtaking visuals on display behind her. The light hit her golden hair, her crystal blue eyes, and each of the people in the room could hear the crackle and spark of ingenuity as she provided them a clear vision of the promise of her declarations.

Every man and woman in that room realized there was so much more to understand, so much more they could do, and that they too could be there in many years when exciting realities unfolded. Everyone there had decided from that moment on, that they wanted maximum optimization and a full read-in to Pathway, to become citizens, and UP members as offered.

The morning icebreaker began with the question, from the lead Scientific Convergence Team Delegate, Matzu Kashi, "If you could do anything to create longevity for the existence of life throughout our solar system, what would you do?" Attendees were then split into groups, given tablets to write ideas down, and appointed spokespeople to share their ideas. After the ideas were shared throughout the conference hall, Matzu explained how each one of them was valuable and what had already been done by Pathway Industries to bring these solutions to pass.

Vesha Celeste, who was eighty-three, shared a presentation of the different aspects of astrophysics, and despite her age, she did a phenomenal job, garnering a standing ovation for her performance. Jasmine Belle, Najem Grace, Malinda Jefferson, Amber Blythe, Melissa Asher, Rebecca Knight, James Wilhelm, Mett Dormer, José Antonio Lugo, Scarlett Hart, Yon Forall, Anastasia Renee, and Evan Bauer all provided presentations. Each of the presenters made the day speed by with intrigue and ideas that germinated and caused the interest and motivations of each person in the room to flourish. Any individual fortunate enough to witness the posture and ambiance on the part of the attendees at the convention would have felt any tensions release and give way to a sense of freedom.

After the morning icebreaker and the speeches that followed, lunch was the best anyone had ever savored. Along with the culinary delight, amazing movie scores mixed in with some arpeggios of female vocal trance music filled the air, and an interwoven futuristic video-scape that was unbelievably fascinating to their eyes—the audience viewed what was shown up on the screen as amazing promises of the future, yet in all reality, everything they actually witnessed was in fact already in existence and real. The break was phenomenally impeccable where timing was considered because people had an opportunity to freshen up and even mingle for a while.

Inspiring and Invigorating

When everyone returned, the convention started up again, with Doctor Eliza A. Williams on the stage. Everyone watched as she paced back and forth with a more serious aura.

After a few moments, she began to speak, and this time she took up a somber and grim tone.

"Every scientist and every philanthropist listened in. They knew that just as her beauty was stunning and just as her ability to engage with everyone as if she'd known them for years and appreciated them was visceral, so too would every word she would speak be of depth and value. At this point, each member of the conference center trusted her completely.

"Much of what we discuss today, much of what I have written about, and much of what we will be involved with from this day forward is a rebuttal to every man, woman, scientist, philanthropist, critic, or visionary who would mock and cast away the amazing and wonderful ideas of others who are kind, helpful, or hopeful as hearsay or even conjecture.

"This is a rebuttal to all of those who decry the visions of those with great intellect and compassion who possess ideas in relation to optimal outcomes, as they instead fail by snarling and scoffing at others and engage in utterly rude and ruthless behavior by putting a cog in the wheel of innovation. This is in defense of truly gifted visionaries of speculative science, and this is a real awakening for those that cast-off ideas bred from hope, compassion, and love of humanity as childish banter; those who digress toward the negative and condescending tones of ridicule contribute to the uncontrolled chaos that will undo civilization itself.

"The truth lies in where we are now compared to where we could have been if great minds and great ideas had not been shut down by the exacerbation of illogical behaviors or using culture or religion as an excuse for unhealthy behaviour or systematic brutality, or establishment-based ideologies of mediocrity and baseless naysaying, or even greed itself. Unfortunately, the certainty is that, ironically, in negating great possibilities for achievement, these perpetrators consistently leave out very essential elements of reality, and those elements influence our greatest machines of all, our brains. By shutting out the use of their brains, they are weak in an exponential manner, and so long as we don't feed the diatribe of trolls, we will succeed in life. Every goal we make, everything we do, and every step we take, we must do so with a profound amount of drive. It is through these efforts that we can find purpose, meaning, benevolence, compassion, and hope.

"Simply because we cannot do something now, and simply because we cannot conceive of even more profound laws of physics that contain possibilities that may evolve our current fundamental laws to those that will apply as our understanding of our Universe grows, does not mean these scientific ideas are impossible or even misguided—they are merely difficult to perceive of or realize based on the tools we are currently using, because they have their limitations. We all ought to be working together with passion toward resolutions of the problems of today, so we can overcome the problems of tomorrow, and not act as teenagers in a playground who tear each other down without thought for the well-being of the individual they are targeting and whose spirits they are crushing. That is why personal discipline or controlled chaos in our own lives is essential. Think of controlled chaos as a form of art, where we can shape and share the beauty of our efforts, the care of our minds, and the resounding genius that resides in all of us.

"While physics and mechanics, for example, can help us mold machinery, which in turn can mold tractors that pave the way for safety on the streets, or create spaces where love and enrichment abound in a home, there is so much more we can do to develop that which we do not yet see, which will help us to harness gravity, radiation, and things which seem impossible now to further compound upon the quality and enjoyment of life, and sooner rather than later.

"One only needs to consider the divergence from physical laws in physics from the effects seen in quantum physics to see an evidenced example of a profound difference in how things interact on one scale versus the other, especially when taking into consideration the complexity of quantum observations. I will grant that there are many noteworthy and even praiseworthy discoveries that have allowed humanity to shape tools and harness physical matter to save lives today and make life more enjoyable. However, there will exist, if we work together on these projects, scientific revolutions that occur more quickly and provide tools that will in-turn, benefit even the most aged or suffering among us, and raise the quality of life for each of us, if we can enable ways so that more people can become involved, burn to learn, and innovate.

"We cannot engage in human progression as solo artists, alone, and expect long-term and optimal results. While we can inspire momentum for a time, while working diligently, ultimately the laws of chaos will prevail unless we work together to preserve our world, our solar system, and our Universe. This, without a doubt, takes a shared goal, a shared effort, and people who work harmoniously with each other and on science, yet who have a vision for the kinds of innovative technologies that will lead to increased well-being of life, reduced suffering, and an abundance of that which raises the quality of life for all who are willing. It takes a community and even a world of people to tackle some of the most complex issues humanity has yet to set its sights on, in order to build the tools of the "future," or explore the scariest of places, or even bring these "miracles" into the realm of calm, enjoyment, peace, and possibilities now.

"Still, I have every bit of faith that each of us in this room today, can and will work together to make optimal results happen, and I also have every bit of confidence that each of you will do what seems to be impossible to many, while reaching out smartly to broaden our influence, and let society know that hope is just around the corner. We need to reach the hearts of many, to persuade them in the kindest of ways so that they too can be involved.

"To give you some perspective, especially when it comes to the myopia that appears to be abundant in society, among some of the economic strategists, and even some within the scientific community—someday we just may build our own planets, our own stars, our own black holes, our own galaxies, and perhaps even slow down the expansion of the Universe.

"All of this, we may be able to do with the benefits and safety of distance, or maybe we can find a way to harmlessly be right up in it, controlling baryonic and non-baryonic matter alike, while carefully abiding by proper and detailed calculations, geometry, and the laws of physics we will have learned by then, but have yet to discover. We can do amazing things, enjoy sabbatical-like moments, and re-educate ourselves until yet again, scientific, societal, cultural, and economic breakthroughs come through, so we can turn the sands of time and behold other revolutions that increase our scope, magnify our perspective, and enable us to do the "impossible."

"My suggestion is that if the humans in this world can work within their hearts and minds, to find the good within each individual around them, to germinate a sense of inclusion and care rather than casting monikers, generalizations, and slogans at them, if humans could simply get along, we could go so much further than we have before. We can have the influence to foster an environment that will allow this reality to become the norm sooner than we think.

"We each need to encourage ourselves and the people around the world to obtain extensive knowledge of each of the sciences by achieving studies that earn doctorates, by ensuring that sentient and benevolent individuals are well-versed in them. I assure you that if we converge or work together to understand the very important and fundamental steps to our pathway to the stars, we will find ourselves building technologies that enable our physiological advancement, so we can both preserve this world and preserve the environments we are bound to find in space. We can do so with a balance of using the resources the universe has provided while protecting life itself. Our primary advancements here will begin with genetic enhancement, longevity, neural optimization, and the preservation of our world's ability to sustain life.

"With those abilities, we can then buy much more time in life, gain more mental acuity, preserve the wisdom gained, and find ourselves capable of developing technologies that we never thought we could before—technologies that currently evade the greatest among us. We will be able to build spacecraft that can travel at speeds faster than light wrapped in shielding that can protect them from any form of attack or natural phenomena.

"We will be able to harness gravity, use cosmic radiation, plasma, and all manner of particles to fuel both the energy of the spacecraft as well as each of us. We will be able to see a reality that eliminates the need for predator versus prey tactics abundant in nature. We need to use the brain the universe has given us to rise and become what nature through billions of years of evolution has given us. God, Nature, the Universe, or whomever or whatever you do or don't believe in, has gifted us with the ability to evolve ourselves. We can rise to have the ability to do what took the universe billions of years to do and improve upon it in moments. We must become preservers of life and controllers of chaos, and not the other way around.

"By evolving, we will enable ourselves to learn how to teleport spacecraft and even ourselves via gateways from one planet to another, a one-star system to another, one galaxy to another, and one known Universe to the next from Earth. We could colonize planets throughout the cosmos, with benevolent leadership.

"We could gain the technologies that could put scopes in the directions of Earth, and speedily travel toward our home planet giving us a solid and detailed history of its formation, the rise and fall of its civilizations, and perhaps resolve long-forgotten mysteries, starting with the Big Bang and recording details all the way through to the current time.

"With those archives, we could append our knowledge of history to the Virtual Universe, or specifically, digital matrices that we can build for education, entertainment, and correctional needs, wants, desires, and even therapeutics. These matrices will provide physical enhancements, tactile interaction, and experiences that serve to impart wisdom and complete recall of memory replete with enhanced compassion and capacity. We can do more than we have ever dreamt of. Through our studies of quantum physics and gaining the ability to harness each aspect of quanta, we will find ourselves achieving the greatest feat humanity can achieve—we will be able to slow down the expansion of our Universe or travel to another universe to avoid its deadly effects in trillions or quadrillions of years, or more!

"Just as every ocean wave is unique, with complex algorithms that can be understood, yet vary in both shape and form—so unique and breathtaking to make each aspect of them seem non-repetitive, so too is every single individual on the face of this Earth. Just as every galaxy, filament, and region of our known Universe may appear similar, but is entirely unique in so many ways, yet to discover, each of you are unique, my friends. Each of you is a respected leader in one form or another, with unique skills and vision that allow the people who you serve to take on gargantuan tasks that help our civilization survive and enjoy life from day-to-day. Every individual I have ever met has so much potential and so much they can do to benefit our future. No matter where we are in life right now, we can all still make waves, be those unique galaxies in our Universe, and yet serve the same purpose, to preserve life.

"The universe can be ours to save, ours to enjoy, ours to explore, ours to colonize, and ours to improve, but only if we can protect ourselves from the malevolence exacerbated in society today by baseless naysayers, 'gloom and doomers,' and preachers of death, chaos, and destruction, by striving daily instead to be benevolent and full of intrigue toward that which raises the quality and well-being of life itself. We must have compassion, we must have a vision, and we must work and study with and within every bit of ourselves, we can afford to invest.

"From time to time I hear people as they unwittingly or perhaps overtly try to insult my intelligence, and by that, the intelligence of each person in this room, or even more profoundly, the intelligence of every human born into this world.

"When these self-identifying adversaries speak of giving up or doing things to harm others, they burn our brain cells and scourge our neurons to oblivion. When someone ignorantly states their fatalistic views of reality, their abhorrent vision of the future replete with misery for all, rather than inspire hope and reason through increased understanding of our Universe and our comprehension on a deep level of advanced sciences, with the larger view of a better and more enjoyable reality for humanity and humanity's friends, they essentially tell us the following:

"'I used to think when I was a child. I used to have common sense when I was young. I used to think about optimistic possibilities for the future. I used to dream big dreams and I used to hope good things for people.

"'But now, I have learned and have grown to accept that malevolence is the way of life in this world. We must accept this morbid reality if we are to get by in this cruel world. Why be nice when that is boring, and when I can merely bully others, wield my power, or be a complete nemesis to humanity, with glee felt internally at the suffering of others? I have accepted a mediocre reality for a dismal and dystopian future for myself, so why not accept the reality where people continue to suffer left and right from all manner of malice, violence, disease, greed, and even apathy?

"'I enjoy misery, I lust for blood, and I enjoy all forms of entertainment that feed that lust, with no other purpose within it, but to satiate my malicious and even insatiable desires. No one is special, there is no "Planet B," we're all born horrible, we'll destroy this world and prevent the destruction of other worlds by terminating ourselves like the disease that we are. The natural order of things is brutal, it doesn't care, so why should I?

"'The universe doesn't care about you, how dare you think there's a purpose with you in it, and how dare you to assume we have the capacity to change it or change anything for that matter? We who fend for ourselves make a mockery of those who care about others, we chastise those who *naively* think life can be improved, we judge harshly those that mistakenly believe people have inherent goodness that exists within, and we ridicule those that think that people can get along and enjoy the bounty our Universe has to offer.

"'Don't listen to all that malevolent poppy-cock! It is not possible, nor will it ever be, so please stop trying. Instead, I will give you silliness, humor at the expense of others, a life of mediocrity, and the despair of a dismal future, replete with numbing agents to fast-forward through this emptiness called life. I am surprised more people don't just up and take the easy way out, save the rest of us the pain of their annoying and meaningless existence, kill themselves, and end their misery once and for all. I doubt there is a *god* at all, and those that believe so are delusional, and if there is a god, that god doesn't care, so why should I? I embrace the day when there is an EMP and I can show my survival skills, which involve murder for sport and limited resources. I embrace the day when an asteroid will pummel our Earth, or our human stupidity releases a zombie-like plague and ends our futile and meaningless existence.'

"Yes, I have heard it all. When I hear this manner of thinking, in any of its ill-intended and horribly indoctrinating forms, the sentiments I just regurgitated are as plain as day! Please know, each of you here today, and anyone who will read this script in the future, that I completely, totally, and unequivocally refuse to become one of those that has given up!

"There is nothing childish whatsoever about hope and benevolence. But the lack thereof is juvenile. There is a difference between being childish versus embracing the child within. Childishness capitalizes on the misery of others, it can be cruel, and it can be reckless, whilst embracing the child within opens our minds toward the beauty of life shared with all and allows for the gaining of further wisdom. Let's embrace the child within, but not become childish.

"When a person chooses to accept mediocrity and a dismal future, they have lost the will to evolve, they have become childish, nay they have become as the wildebeest—only here to propagate the species and live a futile existence until they die, replaced by their offspring.

"Yet, unlike the wildebeest, which provides nourishment to those within their circle of influence in need, they suck away your nourishment as leeches and place the burdens of their scourge on everyone else. They are the bringers of death, destruction, and the chaos that will undo the future of human civilization as well as the future of our Universe if we let them.

"The truth is, though, I feel sorry for them. I do. I feel a wave of compassion toward people like this, for people who have lost their drive, hope, inspiration, and a desire to advance civilization by increasing the well-being of those around them. For, they are most unfortunately lost. I feel for them because they have given up. These baseless naysayers and icons of mediocrity walk around as empty husks of the potential they could be for a positive and hopeful reality—they could have been, and perhaps still could be, a part of so much promise.

"By now, we all know, however, that people like this are indeed suffering from a host of neurological disorders. These are the kind of disorders that seem most rampant in the world today—a world where we are now becoming more and more capable of treating the misfires in genetics and even within the brain.

"This is becoming an evolved world where we can cast off the shackles of the natural man and become a civilization of great, powerful, and compassionate minds—of evolved human-beings. This is a world where more and more the possibilities are growing limitless allowing us to expand our horizons and bring the love and beauty that exists within us no matter where we go.

"In many cases, people that have gone down the path of pessimism and negativity are not helpless to change themselves, but they do not wish to be changed. There are many who have ceased to understand that even whimsical personal achievement can lead to a better life for the rest of humanity. It is sad that there are many that are too far gone unless others, or you, or I, or we, can come along, identify the drowning man, and cast them a rope to save them. In some cases, they won't see the rope, and in those moments, we can do as my father taught me, knock them out and drag them to safety.

"Rather than send a perpetrator of malice to prison, why don't we provide their minds the nutrients needed, the messages needed, the healthy environment and the experiences needed so they can live with meaning in life and with hope for a better day? How amazing would it be if they could change, knowing they now possess clarity of mind as to how they too can contribute to prosperity through constructive behavior, clarity of purpose, and the progression of as well as the compounding of wisdom?

"Neurological healing does not need to be a horror show that many try to make it out to be, non-invasive methods are available at every turn, from coaching to mentorship and counseling, and even down to the DNA level. Improvements ought not to be wrought with misery and suffering, rather from beginning to end they should decrease such. With healed minds wars could be diffused, torturers would no longer exist, other sources of ingenuity and economics could arise that are not brutal and instead are much more rewarding for all involved; the unproductive and destructive aspects of nature would be given productive and constructive means to overcome the chaos that will destroy our Universe and cause it to fade away into meaninglessness, thereby losing any and all sense of a proud legacy. We need to embrace and love life. We need to embrace and love each other, so we can preserve our beautiful music, art, histories of romance, and all that inspires our nobler and more virtuous actions.

"While many are helpless to change the world for the better around them and while many may have forgotten that every new day brings promise for improvement on a personal level, perhaps with the proper treatment, with the proper care, and with the proper focus with people around them, who love them and truly care, they will begin to understand the ripple effects of choices that can impact the environment in its entirety around them. Perhaps their choices can be done with the kind of clarity that seeks to make life a beautiful thing rather than one of torture, misery, or greed.

"Those few geniuses who are of a healthy mind and of a high moral character, replete with the kind of hopes, desires, and knowledge that will bring about the kinds of advancements that can heal the mind of those who are torn, heal the ailments of the body, and by virtue heal the suffering of the soul, those few geniuses are you.

"You can drive humanity to amazing heights, you can heal this planet, and you can bring us the ability to traverse the cosmos with an awesomely optimistic future. You can save the day. You are the heroes of tomorrow, for you will lead humanity to the advancements that can optimize physical health, neurological function, and increase not just your own well-being and quality of life, but that of many more for generations to come and throughout the stars, with the increase of our understanding of the world, the cosmos, the universe, and all of its complexities.

"Through each of us here in this room today, and many more whose lives are impacted through our actions in a positive way, we will all have been bequeathed with the longevity of life necessary to discover, explore, innovate, and learn more, enjoy life more, and even understand each person even more in depth, and then develop the technologies that will enable us to connect to each other and share our memories, our thoughts, our hopes, and even our dreams that will inspire yet again the greatest advancements, adventures, and achievements.

"We are at the dawn of a new revolution. This is the revolution I speak of, a scientific revolution of advancement, adventure, achievement, exploration, discovery, and promise. In this revolution, there is no room for pessimism; there is only room for optimism. There is no room for despair; there is only room for hope. Only those of a healthy mind can have hope. Only those of a healthy mind has what it takes to lead us to a promising future. Only those with a healthy mind have the kind of hope that will lend to the survival of this world, the survival of humanity, and the preservation of life itself.

"Only those with hope have a vision of a better future that will lead to the advancements that will bring aid to those suffering from the problems of today. Each of us here today, are good and kind people, people of immense character, and people who others need not fear because, with our achievements, no one will be left behind. No one stands in danger with what we are going to tackle. Everyone stands in safety. Together, we will help people discover just how exciting progress can be.

"Benevolence and hope are the key ingredients of a better tomorrow; they are the key ingredients to our revolution. Benevolence allows us to go forward with the types of advancements that preserve life, reduce suffering, cure illness and disease, make violence a last resort to our survival, and then live with the longevity necessary for even greater achievements.

"Hope is the vision that will see us through to that better day. Hope fuels the fire of benevolence and the fire of benevolence helps to shape the advancements that can give us the universe. Hope allows each and every single one of us to enjoy every moment with peace in our hearts as we bring aid to the suffering, in its many forms.

"Hope affords us the ability to cultivate an economy that will enable the tools of endurance, proper resource management, and the advancement of civilization. Just as every wave is unique, so are we. I thank you for being a part of this program and the many projects we will undertake. I appreciate each of your efforts in this great and peaceful revolution.

"Each of us should know that there is no harm in having a shared purpose, a shared meaning, and a shared drive because the results of these motivations will, in turn, be found to result in both joy and abundance. As I bring this current speech to a close, and as you observe what will be shared with you throughout the rest of the day, please take what I've shared and allow it to fuel your hearts. Let's do what we need to do so we can be victorious on our journey, let's do what we can to make possible the freedom that comes from a mend to every wounded heart, mind, body, and soul, and let's enjoy every moment along our Pathway to the Stars!"

The scientists, visionaries, economists, generals, and investors each stood up and cheered Dr. Eliza Williams, as she stepped down from her speech. The air seemed to glow around her through each presentation until the meeting was brought to a close. When she got up again, every person in the room saw as she glowed, and they knew that the words she spoke were powerfully genuine and viscerally real.

In many ways, Eliza's after-lunch speech had been a pep-talk, but it was necessary. She wanted to instill the vigor and germinate the kind of thought in the audience necessary to mitigate the effects of so much turmoil, the turmoil that seemed increasingly prevalent as each year, month, week, day, and hour passed by. The age of turmoil would cave in harmony.

There had been a lot of rhetoric in the news, violence, disaster, chaos, and suffering in the many neighborhoods throughout the nation, even throughout the world, and people were indeed becoming even more polarized than ever, to the point of completely abandoning common sense, intellectual thought, and civil discourse.

This crowd was different, and Eliza had vetted each individual with good reason. Nonetheless, they too were very aware of the social, physical, and political environments prevalent just outside the doors, and hearing this gave them the affirmation they needed to begin the many projects about to take place in Pathway Industries and Associates, hereby known as Pathway. Things were going to change, and there was a pathway to get things to where they needed to be, safely, securely, and with optimum results. Every attendee, at the end of the event, was fully on-board with Eliza and her cadre and opted for maximum optimizations and agreed to juggle the responsibilities of their own industries with those of Pathway, as they paved the way for a better future.

Kindness and intellect needed to have a comeback.

As Promised

The day had flown by, and now it was the promised "extra" meeting following the festivities. The main speaking chamber auditorium had been cleared of elaborate seating to make space for biopods and simple seating, enough for each of the attendees present, to include those who had not previously been optimized to sit, listen, and enter their biopods. Everyone in attendance would go into the Virtual Universe and there they would meet again. Instead of meeting in Eliza's virtual backyard, as was traditional, on this occasion Eliza and Yesha had set it up so that they would meet in one of the tech cities on the dark side of the Moon.

The first order of business in this "extra" meeting, was the preparatory speech.

Prior to entering the biopod with the world's elite, Amber Blythe presented Erin Carter, who described in great detail the fight against aging. She demonstrated that, even though she was only eight years old, she had the mind of someone who had lived for thousands of years and that of a genius. She also talked about some of her cases, her missions, and even the trafficking-in-persons networks she had brought to an end, and how some of the victims and their families were doing now. She shared a few stories of other children who had been born with disabilities but were now cured. However, because the technology used was counter-productive to the needs of the current economic philosophies, they were given opportunities to live in the tech cities.

Erin talked about the many, whose families now lived in the twenty-thousand tech cities, all of whom had begun initially with untold struggles that seemed too complexed for society to deal with at the time and now beginning anew, being fully read-in, and a part of the citizenry of Pathway, it had afforded them the opportunities and quality of life that would never have been available to them before. She even showed them how each of these families were now involved in the rescues, the astrobiology, the various histories, and even the planetary transformations pre-planned for a future journey, once the public on Earth was ready, that would allow for life in an open environment much like on Earth and on the planets and moons throughout the solar system, unlike before. Everyone there was amazed, and they still thought of these as future plans.

After Erin finished, Eliza returned to the pulpit and introduced Yesha Alevtina, who had just finished her business overseas, all of which included many more who could be included within unwritten and amazing stories of some of the most amazing people, who were not written in or included within this account, and who had arrived through a different jump gate just in time. She discussed the economies, industries, and then the publicly profitable and win-win aspects through noble endeavors that might mature through love, kindness, and caring.

After Yesha's presentation, James Cooper presented all the IMC's rough-draft designs, the twenty-thousand tech cities' full-on designs, their maturity and updates, and then Pathway's infrastructural capabilities. He even talked about the jump gate systems and the crewmembers' profound capacity for teamwork, abilities to reach out to each other and bring out the best, and the high quality of the results from such dedication.

Following James, Vesha Celeste was again helped to the stand, and, despite her dementia, she discussed the future of space travel. Vesha had not been optimized, upon request, yet because of the uniqueness of her character, the love of a genuine friend, and the blessing of being an amazing human-being gifted with an amazingly genius mind, she was not required to be fully read-in. Vesha was an honorary member of Pathway. Despite not agreeing to optimizations during this mortal sojourn through life, Vesha did agree to have her DNA and neurological activity saved for science. Should she pass, her scientific, caring, and genius-level friends would do all they could for an optimal outcome and in the absolute best way, to bring her back several years later.

James Wilhelm followed Vesha. He had been born in 1931, talked about his childhood and the way of life then, how there were many who worked from every walk of life to improve conditions such that in countries where freedom abounded people could prosper if they were productive, constructive, and innovative. He then presented more aspects of both the tech cities and space travel that pertained to his specific sets of expertise as well as some of his latest inventions. Malinda Jefferson followed James Wilhelm, with a speech regarding bone density, and the possibility of introducing carbon nanotubes and diamond nano threads to bone structure and how this same technology could even be integrated into the shielding for spacecraft that would serve the same function in every possible way and while reducing each concern. The generals in the room were of course intrigued. She also went into detail about creating a cellular communication mechanism, or a physiological healing system where cells communicated with each other and were DNA-based, with personally unique nanos working 24/7 and in an ideal manner to ensure the body was healthy, strong and as durable as any spacecraft that could be developed.

Upon suggestion earlier from Eliza, and then Yesha and James, research and preparatory plans were put into place for another project set for completion in ten years. After confirming with Eliza, Mett Dormer talked about computer interfacing, navigation systems, and advanced human capabilities, where he introduced the Twelve Database Moons and projected plans for a human-interface neurological system, which would be billions of times faster and with untold magnitudes of force more capable than any human mind or body, within a Human-Biological-Computer-Interface, or an HBCI, by searching for and using a copy of a benevolent, kind, and genius mind or series of minds. Mett looked into the crowd and saw as the generals, shifting forward in their seats were very intrigued and the presidents' and CEOs' eyes were raised showing how much they were indeed very interested, too.

Once the pre-biopod-adventure presentations were complete, everyone was invited to get into their biopods, close their covers, and issue the command, "Link 1, 2, 3, 5 minutes, 20 years." As requested, everyone did so. Just like anyone else, they felt every nerve, every synapse, and every sensory node contort, quiver, and then they experienced the state of euphoria they had talked about often, following death, yet had never experienced before. They then realized that they were looking up toward space and were amazed at the clarity of the stars and the Milky Way before them. Everyone pointed out the brightness of Arcturus, Cassiopeia, and even Andromeda. They then shifted their gaze down as they witnessed the horizon and the immaculate and pristine city before them. They were also thrilled with their new youth within the Virtual Universe, as the creativity of their minds played out on their own physiological expressions. They realized they had abilities from automated hygiene, and many other aspects they never thought possible before, and with each item, Eliza and her team taught them how to use these abilities, and when to use them. When they finally saw the mind of Eliza, they knew she was every bit as genuine and real as she seemed before melding minds with her.

Questions and answers were listened to and answered—mind-to-mind. Everyone was shown all that Eliza, Yesha, and James had learned and experienced. Minds were melded, and everyone grew to understand one another in ways they never thought possible. There was a strong sense of connection, one to another, and from that time forward, each individual could link neurologically with anyone else who had ever been optimized. Every person who attended learned that, now, they had telescopic and microscopic vision and could practice the ability to live in any solar system environment while enjoying it. They could now share what they were seeing and experiencing as they were seeing and experiencing it. With each of the other attendees they wished to share with, who were also neurologically linked, they practiced. All those times in the past they'd pointed at the sky and it took several minutes to find what their fingers were pointing at before, now shared-communication made it obvious. Experiences were more deeply felt with communication and reciprocation that was made so much easier. Through merged, shared, and linked vision, communication occurred now, at a much more profound level. True understanding took place with their newly shared wealth of intellect, power, and ideas became melded.

They looked on and witnessed in spectacular scope how each of the tech cities had a series of flourishing and beautiful forests, jungles, sentient creatures, skyscrapers, parks, walkways, and large convention centers. All the infrastructure necessary to sustain amazing life indefinitely and all of which was constantly being updated, upgraded, and improved to provide every resource desired and required by up to ten-million families in each city, with seamless maintenance, was as if each tech city were a living being. Everything about these cities was a breath-taking, useful, unique, creative, immense, and yet a beautiful sight to behold. The investors, the philanthropists, and the first world generals were amazed as they were shown the original prototype tech city for the first time, which had been built up the most, with aesthetics and defenses of every sort. Eliza then showed them the twenty-thousand total cities and how combined they could sustain life for trillions of years for much more than twenty-billion families. She then showed them how there was enough land throughout the solar system to sustain life for trillions of humans and humanity's dear friends.

Yesha and Eliza explained how there would be biopods for each of the people present in the convention center in the real world, and how each person would be allowed to bring their biopod home once their training was complete within the Virtual Universe. In order to assuage the questions from the public, everyone had agreed to maintain their current public physical appearance, rather than reverse their aging immediately to any age between eighteen and thirty-five. Eliza used her real-world-Virtual-Universe connection to make the necessary adjustments, to their comfort. They would instead look gradually younger and more invigorated as the days and weeks would go by, until the laws across the land made it acceptable to use these biopods.

For now, in the Virtual Universe, the once elderly were now simmering with the glory of youth both visually and of internal health and they were awe-struck with each other, shared their stories with each other, and they shared a convergence of the sciences, of economics, and the generals even drafted peaceful resolutions to long, drawn-out, and brutal wars. Of course, they could only submit those proposals to their leaders throughout the world, but there was a lot more hope for a better future than had existed before, especially with that open, deep, and shared moment together. Within the Virtual Universe, Eliza and Yesha took each of the attendees to see every bit of infrastructure and every advancement Pathway had made.

Before leaving the Virtual Universe, Eliza let each entrepreneur, investor, economist, and general know that they would receive jump gates at each location as needed, and upon request. After twenty-years-worth of journeys, teachings, training, sharing experiences with one another, and growing closer to each other in goals and ambitions than they had ever before thought possible, like that, everyone woke up in their biopods and felt better than they had ever felt before. Each individual glowed and could feel every nano racing through their veins, organs, pathways, and pores healing and adapting their cells for their new reality. Although they looked the same as they had before, at any moment they could choose to look just a tad younger each day until their appearance was that of a twenty to thirty-five-year-old. Normally, this could happen in a blink of an eye, but for the sake of confidentiality and due to the fact that these individuals were constantly under the public eye of scrutiny they agreed that it would be necessary to wait until these advancements were accepted by society before revealing their true capabilities and nature. Even so, it expanded their minds and preserved their lives.

Life was about to be much better for the masses, yet the transitions shown to these leaders needed to be smooth, incremental and done in such a way that they would prevent economic collapse and indiscriminate loss of well-being and quality of life. As the main convention ended and the encore part of the conference was complete, everyone returned home using their household-to-business jump gates. Pathway had also programmed their cargo and so the attendees could carry their biopods with them. They could share each of these new technological tools of scientific genius with their families and were urged to conduct their lives in a way that would not reveal their true nature or capabilities too quickly. Nonetheless, everyone who had attended that conference now had a kinder demeanor, a magnificent clarity of purpose, and each individual had figured out even more than before what it was that they could and would do to improve the world in such a way as to advance civilization and protect the ability of our home planet to sustain life for the long-haul. Life was about to become wonderful for anyone who walked their way.

Eliza had explained during one of the sessions earlier, that it was important to conduct a smooth transition, to ensure that major industries could adjust and still maintain their robust nature, provide jobs, environments that enabled innovation, and much more. Ultimately, everyone, if they chose to, could receive biopods and with those newly granted abilities, they would be able to take advantage of the Virtual Universe for education, entertainment, exploration, ingenuity, further developments, and untold optimizations.

For now, the people who had participated in the very first Pathway conference had received access to their very own biopods, jump gates, and had been gifted with physiological and neurological optimizations, with consistent updates through their nanos. They also had access to each other through their neural links and had assured Eliza that they would do their part to create the necessary waves and influence to bring about the promises Eliza had shared. Her mind had been visually on display, was thus beyond the capacity for words. Each of the attendees within the Virtual Universe had been inspired by her visceral beauty.

Each of the world's most elite had promised to bring others within their circle of influence as well. Entire industries were about to become a part of Pathway, yet they would keep their company names intact, while beginning the slow process of preparing the public on Earth for the true realities that existed. This would all occur just one small step at a time. Eventually, all the wondrous inventions of Eliza and her organization would be shared in public, and with full transparency. Everyone present that day, felt this would occur soon, but only once Eliza had been elected as the President of the US. They also knew there were steps she still wanted to take to get to that point.

Chapter 18: The Political Foray

Database Moon Archive, Celestial-Sol Entry Date: 2018 December 25. Yesha Alevtina trains Vesha Celeste. In this crucial part of her training, they explore the continued growth of Pathway Industries and the growth of the UP within the United States, its territories, and around the world. These memories are shared within the collective minds of Eliza, Yesha, and James, the countless citizens, and delegates of Pathway, and the representatives of the UP, within the Virtual Universe. Vesha and Yesha are interfaced within the Pathway Melrose Campus. Input by Yesha Alevtina, President of Pathway Industries, 2015-2022.

Three years had passed since Eliza's first Pathway convention and each person who had attended the conference had been about missions galore. Industries were booming, all the attendees had maintained a certain level of discretion about the conference, and as such there were still many who knew nothing of all that had transpired. Unless someone was fully read-in, they knew nothing about all the ultra-tech, research, and developments within Pathway other than it was now a very-much cheered mega-industrial giant with an extremely enviable worker's package. Even though there were over one-billion Pathway members, the world's public still had the same population that it would have had, had Pathway never existed. It seemed that nature had its own way of keeping a certain pace of population growth no matter Pathway's efforts. Along with this intriguing growth, as the nice and kind people were rescued from the noxiousness of the social and worldly environments and moved to the tech cities, the remaining population on Earth seemed to grow more and more toxic, increasingly myopic, and the major focus continued to be on greed, and being ruthless and heartless to one another.

Brutality was increasing, looked at as real, and kindness was looked at as fake. Good was looked at as bad, and bad was looked at as good. Notwithstanding all that was going on, there were still a lot of wonderful people throughout the world, misguided as they may have been. Everyone involved with Pathway could see through that horrible haze of the cold and dank reality that humanity was creating for itself, and saw many struggling or barely making it, and as such, Pathway could have transcribed an abundant quantity of several libraries-worth of stories of rescue, nobility, and innovation of many more people that could have written themselves into the history of civilization with both applause and awards.

There was a lot that was moving forward, however. The entertainment industry was beginning to turn around due to the influence of Eliza's friends and as such, they had been educating people on the proper use of science. More people than ever had begun to learn that science is not only a tool to understand our Universe, but that it could be used by good people to good things, and that it was also a tool improve upon and preserve our Universe. Mixed in with pure entertainment intended to motivate the masses toward productivity and innovation, products were advancing with so many new capabilities, and Eliza had a large cadre of leaders and support. However, as with the mind-numbing confusion of chaos and the brutal aspect of nature, there still seemed to be a missing area of influence throughout much of the population throughout the world that would help to increase the well-being and quality of life of many, as well as the population around her own home country.

After much thought and many years of being prodded by those who were close to her, she realized that it was finally time to start her political career or at least a political party. She did this to allow for an influence of people from a completely different approach, and to cut through the swaths of laws, rules, and regulations that no longer allowed the people the freedoms they needed to improve the world they were on or the environment that they lived in. They needed laws that valued kindness and quality of life over greed and brutality.

One-billion people had already been calling the various tech cities their permanent home, with Eliza as their elected leader. They each were fully read-in with minds of geniuses. They collaborated with each other on their plans for the survival of our civilization and they were involved with many more studies and improvements throughout the solar system. All of this was done under the radar of the public sectors of Earth. Each of the members of Pathway, no matter where they lived, had done so much under her guidance, principally. A lot of what she had set up was now autonomous to her since she had delegated so much and so well.

Dr. Eliza A. Williams had setup Pathway and the UP in a democratic manner and began running for office as soon as Yesha was spun up to take her place as President of Pathway, and to continue on with the programs already planned for her industries, along with many more, as Yesha saw fit.

Now Eliza was ready to do what any citizen of her state would be required to do in order to become a congressional representative of her congressional district. She was ready and willing to provide a more powerful and benevolent voice for the people of the amazing state of Massachusetts, in the United States Government.

In March of 2015, she began her run for office and a year and eight months later, her win for the seat was part of a major change in the political face of the nation. Twenty States had voted-in candidates from the UP, aside from her own, and it was clear that people were looking for the kinds of changes the UP would bring.

After throwing her hat in the ring, the UP had become a hot topic on all the talk shows, and Eliza had clearly made a mark as one of the most affluent and influential people of 2015. She had successfully run for a representative position in the United States Congress, representing the state of Massachusetts. After about a year and a half on the trail, talk show hosts everywhere were wanting to interview her, to have her be a part of sketch comedy, and then get to the brass tax and give her airtime on all the networks to explain one idea or another. Everyone found her intriguing.

During an interview on one of the major network evening talk shows, prior to her election, the host had introduced Eliza and then asked if she could give a speech on her views with regard to how every individual could become a major driver for change. She also asked her about her views on gene therapies and mentioned how both of her opponents were adamantly opposed to the idea. Dr. Eliza A. Williams delivered her address with an uninterrupted delivery.

"One of my opponents told everyone 'we are born, we work hard, we live life, we see ourselves and others suffer, we feel bad when that occurs, we rear our children and we eventually die. That's life. We have to accept that.' When my opponent stated that, I had no doubt that many of us have a firm grasp on reality, the struggles we face, and that everyone faces unique struggles, yet, somehow, I found it difficult to see the grace in this sort of statement given the sciences we have, the tools we have, and the discoveries we've made that can in effect benefit everyone. While I appreciated his grasp on the obvious reality that so many come across, I also felt compassion and sympathy for my opponent's suffering, the kind that would lead toward his particular view on life, a view that demonstrates the kind of depression that requires care, concern, and perhaps even counseling."

"To a certain degree, don't you believe we could all benefit from a little counseling, coaching, and mentorship?" The talk show host saw an opportune moment and asked.

"Absolutely," replied Eliza.

"What do you think of what your other opponent has said or his comment where he called you a rambling rose?"

"I don't mind. As a matter of a fact, you know Nat King Cole's song, "Ramblin' Rose?"

"Oh, yes. That is a beautiful song!" The broadcaster had a small segment of the chorus play for the audience.

"That's our campaign song for the first term. By 'our' I'm referring to our party, the Universal Party, or the UP. I simply call it 'U' 'P,' but it is pronounced by many like 'up' in the word 'cup,' and that is quite okay with me."

"So, up or 'u, p,' I like both too. Please, go ahead and tell us a few things. The floor and topic are up to you." Eliza nodded as the host spoke, got up and stood behind the podium they had put there for just the occasion.

Without the need for a teleprompter, Eliza looked right into the camera lens and by doing so, she looked at anyone listening to her in the broadcast straight in the eyes and began, and because of her electromagnetic and particle connection, her link through her neurological nanos and her neuro-identification transceiver capabilities, Eliza could actually see every member of her audience as they sat in their living rooms, lay in their hospital beds, or were in any manner watching and she reached out and connected to every single one.

"When I think of those who are struggling, I tend to think about the medieval times, the days when the rich and privileged owned all of the lands without thought of the welfare or quality of life of those under their care. They owned the land, everything in it, and even the peasants and their welfare. We know that in far too many cases, people in general and these people were thought of or deemed as "lesser," because they were peasants and thus were not always treated fairly or right. In many cases, if a child were pushed to do something dangerous, they were also required to do so with the instilling of fear of brutal punishment. There were countless occasions when children of peasants died altogether too soon. They died before learning about life or learning about the sciences that would pull their potential into clarity before them, so they could help in the advancement of civilization. In many cases, we also know that far too often these deaths were dismissed and only passed on, if lucky, through folklore and stories passed on through the many generations, and through the many centuries.

"If the reality of what was going on became too much or when an uproar or crying out would occur, these peasants' grievances would be dismissed with a statement from the superior and ruling classes, often times among themselves and sometimes through public decree, 'Well, these are the social norms and brutality is the way of life. Besides, they were just peasants, they were born, they worked, they served the greater good, and they died. That's life, so deal with it.'

"Now, consider what life would be like today if it were not for those of noble and valiant spirit who after seeing needless torture, inhumanity, and calloused murder by those wishing to assert their authority, daringly declared, 'This isn't right! Something must be done! Something ought to be done! Something has to be done!' These heroes followed those declarations with action, and in many cases, those who dared speak up were murdered in order to prove a chaotically vicious point, but when enough heroic individuals finally fought past their fears to bring about the changes that occurred many generations later, we were gifted to suffer less today.

"Today, in our country, if it is functioning as it ought to, no matter where we are born, no matter our income, if we see something that isn't right, or if we have an idea that will improve the quality of life, if we have an idea as to how to make life more enjoyable and more kind, we can produce whatever it is that might solve a particular issue or a set of issues, and we will be honorably rewarded and duly compensated for our ideas and efforts. This at least is capitalism, opportunism, and commerce in its most ideal, compassionate, and purest form.

"Today we are facing a crisis. We are facing a crisis of culture, of ideology, of social norms, a crisis of strength that comes from personal ethics, and a crisis that can be dealt with in one of several ways. One way would be as my colleague proposed, 'to live life, work hard, propagate, suffer, and die because that is just life, we aren't special, and we need to learn to accept it.' We could perhaps do something much worse and even downright malevolent. Or, we can demonstrate the greatest form of healthy cognitive frame-working that will indeed squelch these issues altogether through compassion, and by doing so preserve as well as compound upon our potential for wisdom, experience, and productivity in this state of being, aye, in this state of our nation. How? You might ask. We can do this as we increase longevity by innovating and applying gene therapies tailored specifically to each individual to nurture their health, strength, physical capacity, and mental capacity and clarity. Through this we can allow freedom of choice when it comes to determining a static age between 18 and up, adjusted as needed or as we each see fit in our own lives, so we can contribute our wisdom and experience to a larger or smaller workforce, to our philanthropic pursuits, and our enjoyment of our vast Universe.

"Many in their aging lives today are those who have raised the bar for humanity in so many ways, who have lost family and friends along the way, and they raised the quality of life many years ago. Perhaps they would continue to do so if their aging bodies and minds allowed them to. To allow people, aye, anyone living, to suffer when there are ways to not only reduce their suffering but to remove it completely, is the most appalling form of negligence and even malevolence almost to the level of murder itself, that which is rampant within too many and far too often throughout society today. Negligence of this sort, in a manner that is lightly viewed, is equal to gross mediocrity and the source of the kind of undue duress that can destroy nations, and in accepting this mediocrity we might as well declare that 'this is just the way life is, accept it.' Now, the older generation may feel that way and for that, I give them a pass because in a state of suffering not too many would want to continue in that state for very long. The thought of death in a natural way is perhaps a vision of sweet release from all the brutal triviality it seems life has to offer. But it does not need to be that way.

"The diseases associated with aging can be mitigated, every disease and every bacteria or virus that does not serve to strengthen or heal humanity and its allies can be overcome despite the complexity of the biological form, and each of those blessed individuals with unique and amazing minds who are filled with so much as yet untold potential can have a new lease on life and a chance to be young again while retaining all they have learned in their journey in this small area of the cosmos.

"We can each share in an effort that is noble, we can each and every one of us, share in the advancement of civilization, rather than wither away as it decays. We can do this, we ought to, and we must, because this, my friends, is the right thing to do!

"Not only is this the right thing to do and not only is this something that can be done, and not only has reality placed obstacles in the way that can and ought to be overcome, this is what we must do in every way and throughout each living day. Lawyers can be noble, but those who prey upon the poor or legislators who fatten their wallets as the malevolent nary-do-wells who care nothing for you or about you but for your vote for every next election and who sell their integrity and moral core for a small chance at wealth and power, have manipulated and then placed the use of the many tools that were once intended for benevolent recourse toward negligence, meant for those who had suffered the most to be duly compensated, into the hands of powerful litigation companies. They play on your fears, they take advantage of the ignorance they've cultivated in their populous, and they guide their preachers to fill our minds with thoughts of sin and wrong-doing for daring to improve our lives, for rising up, and calling out that which is not fair, that which is not just, and that which is inhumane. Well, that does not need to happen anymore, and the inhumanity can stop.

"If we hold ourselves accountable for accepting mediocrity, if we allow ourselves to let that sting just for one moment, if we then pick ourselves up again and if we go forward and educate ourselves on physics, biology, physiology, neuroscience, and the many other essential sciences, if we engage in meaningful conversation regarding the well-being of those we hold dear, including ourselves, if we make our demands clear through presenting our grievances to our representatives in government complete with better and more viable alternatives, if we vote for those who represent honesty, integrity, compassion, and kindness, if we vote for the advancements in science that are both smart and effective, we will then have leaders who serve with an iron will, who can put into place the mechanisms necessary to ensure not only do each and every one of us have our personal choices protected so we can freely accept or reject the advancements of science in our own personal lives, we will be able to write the rules and protect humanity from malevolent programming and use of such powerful tools.

"I have every bit of confidence in each person running for office in the UP because our motives are clear, they are pure, and our focus is on resolving the issues that plague humanity and our shared biosphere, as well as overcoming the challenges ahead. Each of us will serve you in an effort to raise the quality of life, protect productive and innovative citizens from the machinations of those who would seek to undermine our freedoms, and we will work to create the environment necessary for a worthy and enduring legacy that each of us can be around to enjoy.

"As we go to the doctor's office, for example, we must demand full and proper diagnosis with treatments critical to eliminate that which ails us. If they fail, we must write our legislators and demand laws to be enforced when it comes to the Hippocratic Oath. We must do what we can to see to it that they can and will do their jobs, so we can do ours with due diligence and life can improve overall.

"So, in an answer to the original question, yes, stem cell research, unique gene therapies, and other longevity-related medical capabilities all with the goal of understanding how our bodies' networks function, down to the communication that takes place from one cell to another and then the replication and improvement of its function is an essential part of the pathway toward an advanced civilization with an optimized capacity for innovation that leads to the well-being of humanity and life itself. To reduce our acceptance of science that leads to increased well-being to anything less is to accept mediocrity and board the train of self-condemnation and descend too far and too fast into unnecessary suffering, shame, disgrace, and death.

"If we can fine-tune our physiology and neurology to mitigate the effects of long-term deep space travel and if we can improve our ability to thrive in harsh environments with our sanity and health intact, we will succeed in space. We need to do this, so we can become a multi-planetary and supportively-connected civilization. To raise the bar for civilization on these new planets we need to set into motion a governance system built with kindness, compassion, well-being, creation of abundance, and preservation of life at its core, as opposed to the chaos, the callous brutality, and desolation of the land we've many times borne witness to or have seen evidenced throughout civilization, so we will find ourselves building a legacy worth preserving. How many of you have overtly elected to endure toxicity, endless suffering, and gratuitous misery throughout your lives with no thought of an end game, a valued purpose, or essential meaning? How many feel it is feeble-minded to assign value and meaning to the energy you expend in life? My guess is that suffering, misery, and challenges present themselves quite readily without provoking their presence, and when incited, chaos may ensue, yet in many cases, we have quite surprisingly jumped those hurdles rather well. Keep in mind that there is a huge difference between doing research to overcome a disease and running into walls every now and then, versus grabbing a child and throwing him or her into a cage with a lion stating that we all have challenges to overcome, so best wishes. We no longer, in this day and age, need to accept this type of injustice when ample information in the form of education is out there that we can embrace and apply instead. We can, therefore, strike a new balance of education, effort, diligence, health, and innovation to breed the kind of prosperity we have promised. We can promise shared abundance will make life much more filled with clarity and enjoyable excitement."

When Eliza finished, the host and everyone in the audience stood up, clapped, and cheered. She saw as the host dried her eyes, the cameraman's cheeks had reddened, and she picked up on the shared hope present in the air and broadcast worldwide. The host, in a fleeting moment of inspiration, spoke up, "I wish you were running for president and I'm sure I'm not alone. I have no doubt that if you ran and won that our nation and our world would be better off for it. I think you reminded us all, that there is still hope. Thank you, Dr. Eliza Williams." The camera panned away, and over the next few days, talk of hope and the UP was rampant on the news and talk shows worldwide.

As time passed a variety of issues surfaced that begged for Eliza's attention. In many ways, the public was intrigued by her view on things. She knew she could potentially win the popular vote and the electorate in her state, but her party had a ways to go before she or the UP would win the federal electorate executive election nationwide, so she focused on building her party and the elections of fellow UP members in other locations throughout the world. She was always busy, but she had impeccable ways to find time to spend with her constituents in Massachusetts. Around the time of her caucus, Eliza had done so well that she was invited to participate in the large event which typically would only invite candidates from the two main parties.

She excelled in capturing the attention, the hearts, and the minds of each of the voters. When election-day arrived, she won and immediately went to work on Capitol Hill to see and understand what needed to be done to help humanity to advance. A lot was done. Still, there was much more growth to be had. Her term would last for only two years, and during that time-frame, she would do as much as she could. She would see to it that research increased nationwide and that the gap between the capabilities of and the ethics prominent in her industries and those that the US public was willing to embrace were bridged or brought much closer together.

As time went by, books were released regarding humans taking up the task of evolving ourselves, understanding the technologies of tomorrow, how our minds could be conditioned to allow for more complex problem-solving capacities, how life could be lengthened by beginning with telomerase therapies, myostatin inhibitors, gene-based cancer treatments, and a host of other cures for the immeasurable host of diseases throughout the world.

Early on, during Eliza's time served in the House of Representatives, Vesha Celeste had passed away, yet not without Pathway knowing about it, and having a plan. Yesha was at the helm of Pathway and she, Erin Carter, and Amber Blythe worked night and day, to perfect the regrowth and revitalization of Vesha's physiology and neurology. They would essentially return her back to life more powerful and capable than ever, and all the while Eliza's empire, and the UP Leader throughout the solar system, continuously grew.

James Cooper, his cadre, and the collaborated efforts of the major delegates, or the twelve scientific team leaders, helped Eliza to provide governance for the Pathway Tech Cities throughout the solar system, since the population had grown to one-billion, and Eliza agreed with her UP advisors that it would be okay to simultaneously continue as the president of the twenty-thousand cities, while serving in political office on Earth in the United States, but it would take a system of more collaborated efforts. Most of the legalities in the tech cities were based on common sense. There was a myriad of environments, so each location required a unique set of laws, all of which fit into the scope of the Principles of Universal Ethics.

The Intergalactic Mission Contingency or IMC was still in the planning stages but not yet on the drafting table, Najem Grace and her team had begun working with James and his team to brainstorm the various aspects of these interstellar traveling bioenvironmental spacecraft behemoths, logging the different necessities and locations, and categorizing each idea to eventually incorporate into the eventual draft or blueprint. They waited for Vesha to make her return from her long nap, visited her in the Virtual Universe often, as her databased mind would play loops of her life, again and again, sometimes they would go through shared experiences as if in autopilot, and in the real world they looked forward to the day that she could be awakened with her optimized physiology and neurology, be trained and read-in, and begin working to draft the blueprint of the IMC. Eliza had made it clear that they were not to work on IMC drafting or completion until Vesha had returned and was assigned to take the lead.

As it was, Luís Rodriguez emerged as a great engineer and physicist designing engines and drives of every sort for the many spacecraft going back and forth between the Sun and the Oort clouds. Mett Dormer and James Wilhelm helped him by designing the complexed navigation systems to weave into the drives and artificial intelligence command-override-capable digital-navigation control interfaces. Scarlett Hart was renowned for designing and experimenting with a wide variety of environmental systems for each spacecraft and operational center outside of the twenty-thousand tech cities. Yon Forall had been lauded for his designs of the various laboratories and Innovation Centers for each operational area throughout the solar system and inside some of the larger spacecraft. Anastasia Renée had been awarded for her work and continued to be busy developing systems for seamless travel from one location to the next using Eliza's jump gate technology, creating hubs throughout the various planets and moons, improving systems throughout the tech cities, and integrating systems for private use with her growing cadre of scientists. Malinda Jefferson, Melissa Asher, Rebecca Knight, and Matzu Kashi were an amazing team that had their hands full designing defensive shields and systems for spacecraft and living facilities everywhere.

The IMC, was, in its current iteration, a series of listed recommendations and suggestions for gigantic spacecraft and their design teams and plans, but they were not as yet drafted in the Virtual Universe, not even as far as shape and aesthetics were concerned. Each of the thirteen gigantic intergalactic spacecraft would require the abilities to explore, to document the history of, to terraform, and to colonize the entire observable Universe. Each spacecraft would also need to be capable of improvements, augmentations, and enhancements as journeys continued throughout the cosmos.

While the proposed crews and brainstorming of each spacecraft was going to be merely the tip of a great big iceberg when it came to plans for the cosmos, what they would be doing would become gargantuan when it came to the beginnings of Universal History. The Universe, as relative to the Earth would be divided into twelve equitable zones. A thirteenth zone would not be visible from Earth since the IMC would travel beyond the limits of the observable Universe to expand our knowledge and influenced by several orders of magnitude. Before beginning the final plans and construction of such a massive project, which was an even greater project than protecting our own Sun, a sufficient enough population would need to be helping in one way or another. Eliza had always preached kindness as the first step, and that would be the first step no matter how many other steps there would be. She promised to lead the way.

Eliza had taken it upon herself to begin preparing the world's nations for all of this, and it began with making any necessary changes in view of the public in how operations were run within the House of Representatives.

By the end of 2017, multiple cancer-combating gene therapies had been approved by the FDA, which provided smooth economic transitions for some of the largest employers worldwide. Gene therapies were finally being released. Industry was in full swing. In 2018, after a string of successes in so many ways within the House of Representatives, Eliza strategically backed a delegate from the UP to run for the House of Representatives in her stead, and she ran for a position in the Senate to make further and important adjustments as to how the entire Legislative Branch was run.

Caucuses and Elections

It was during the Massachusetts state caucus when Eliza approached the podium to give the following speech as a Congresswoman, with a bid for the Senate in 2018. While she typically ran a positive campaign, she realized that many nations were still struck with prejudice toward women, their education, and the potential for their contribution toward the advancement of society and civilization. She could also see that reflected still within her own state. After seeing large swaths of money mismanaged and given to one country after another, all of whom were notorious for growing the privileged class on the backs of the underprivileged, along with a large laundry list of human rights and ethics violations toward even their own people, she issued a rebuke to the leaders and friends who promoted this sort of behavior, or who somehow supported the behavior of those who had lost their way:

"I stand by my previous and unofficial statement, after I introduced my first iteration of the tax policy to Congress last year and will address it again as Senator this coming winter," Following which, everyone in the caucus applauded and cheered. Ever since she took office as a congressional representative people had followed her career enthusiastically and looked forward to every speech she would give.

"The address I gave, wherein I stated that universities for women in countries that oppress them, and more than half of the rest of their population would be a far better investment than what is being batted about now. Leaders, whose countries have built high-tech skyscrapers and cities meant only for the elite few, or the favorites of any "king," dictator, or tyrant, would find within themselves a more reasonable argument toward ethics if they shifted their focus toward building universities rather than engaging in secret arms deals. I presented on my website evidence of where weapons were proliferated to terrorists in exchange for one-hundred-billion USD to the US. Generosity from countries who take our innovation and do nothing with it to raise the well-being of those they are called to serve, but instead blame us for the harm they bring to their own and other people, is part of the vicious cycle and toxic trap that will be the undoing of humanity. We ought to make exchanges related to well-being, and not brutality.

"Countries showing negligence toward the populous they've assumed the mantle to have stewardship over, who impoverish their masses, who do nothing to bring the lifesaving qualities of the forests, jungles, and agriculture, as well as fail to bring well-being and beauty to their land, countries who keep their education far from the grasp of their women or dignity away from people who otherwise should have the right to claim their own unique identity, or governments who teach to their citizens that it is the United States, the Western Nations, Asia, and all of its allies that are to blame for all of the indignity within their societies built up from systemic inhumanity, are in fact to blame, and now stand duly chastised.

"A fair education, where people learn true world history as well as respect within reason for the leaders, whether governmental or through social influence, of yesteryear, understanding that if it weren't for their influence we would not have the freedoms we share today, where people can actually learn from social science, the arts, physics, neurology, biology, and all things that truly relate to this physical Universe—all of which could still complement any religion of benevolence or a strong core of well-being-based ethics, would be something that merits our efforts and our energies. Something that teaches kindness, compassion, and consent would be the highest form of an answer to reducing terrorism to virtually nothing and would be a nobler source of economic prosperity.

"Weapons in the hands of allies we trust may serve to temporarily stop the dystopian reality of the malevolent but giving or selling weapons to those who have demonstrated negligence on the part of the well-being of their own people, the very people they have been entrusted to serve, should no longer, if ever, be looked at as the proper course of action. Without proper changes and without the well-being of wonderful people in mind, the greed that is already prevalent within their scope of command and concern, the elitism of a class hierarchy, and so much more, all of which to the greatest degree, will create a ripple effect, that once the dust of war has settled, will only serve to foment even more terror, we as a people will fail. If we wish to succeed over the long-haul, we must not crumble from within, or, like cowards, cave, losing our values, those that I outlined in the Principles of Universal Ethics, that which we can all hold dear, and in doing so, we can share in the enjoyment of life.

"To combat the type of mentality that leads to murder, oppression, and terrorism we have to be strong, we must build step-by-step processes beginning with an education that will provide a higher quality of life, and we must do all that we can to foster a supportive and innovative environment. Therein is an essential pathway to trust, clarity toward creating a legacy of kindness and of compassion, and even passion for the kind of greatness that for an untold time into the future is worthy of preserving, and therein is borne an investment that is a win-win for all, and indeed a worthy merit. A legacy worth preserving is one where you, I, and all of us are valuable, are worth having around to share experiences with, to stumble through the struggles of benevolent life with, to plan for a better future with, and with whom it will be an honor to create that legacy that deserves to bring its biology to the numerous planets orbiting and traversing the cosmos.

"In a benevolent society, murderous tyrants hold no sway, they hold no ground, they are removed from society and are given intense counseling in a healthy environment conducive to imparting to them clarity of a better way of life, a purpose in which maiming, and murder are not part of the plan. In a benevolent society, you are safe, I am safe, everyone is safe, and our potential for innovations that reduce unnecessary suffering can know no bounds. Only in a benevolent, ethical, and moral society—a society and a worldwide civilization that seeks to preserve life, and bolster well-being, will we possess the mentality and the evolved capacity to preserve our Earth, our Solar System, and our humanity.

"A malevolent society will never see our civilization expand throughout the cosmos because malevolence is a zero-sum game, a game devoid of a win-win solution for the problems that arise, a game that will see through to our end, our extinction, with an unknown legacy of mediocrity, malice, anger, hate, and fear, that only serves the uncontrolled chaos that will lead to the end of our civilization and even the end of our Universe. It is a fire that has gone out of control. Each of these things will lead to a pointless existence as the next worldwide cataclysm snuffs us out forever.

"Those who justify the behaviors of those that truly oppress, they know who they are, yet I believe that they too can change. No matter who you are, no matter your past, no matter what you have done until now, you can still grow, you can breathe in and you can breathe out. You can slow down the visceral thoughts of malice raging within your mind, and you can gain compassion for others, you can preach ideas of hope and of kindness, rather than push the agendas of greed, elitism, and dissension. In a benevolent society, there is no problem with well-earned gains and successes—enjoying the fruits of your efforts, your energies, and your diligence. However, stealing, cheating, and manipulating the masses so you and only your progeny can do well is a result of nothing but ill-gotten gains. Use your privilege to bless life and raise the bar for humanity.

"If a leader from a somewhat benevolent country goes to another country with leadership that oppresses its people, it is upon them to find ways to alleviate the suffering existent in their society. It is important to evolve their culture to reduce the effects of hatred and violence. Leaders, who blame their own oppression on the countries that give, give, and give, through industry, using advanced technology to improve life and compensate the people for the use of their resources, wherever they may be, yes, those leaders who point their fingers in the general direction, wherein lays many wonderful people, are to blame. Not the countries who try to help. A leader who is from any benevolent country, however, who sells mechanisms with which to prosecute more oppression is to blame as well. In this case, it is the leader who is to blame and not their masses, because it is they who have exhibited either malevolent individual character or demonstrated that they are a fool without the ability to properly assess and perceive of the results of their actions. It is they who will do more harm than good. Those that support this behavior are guilty of the same.

"But, just as I stated before, even you who are clowns, you who have proven that you are buffoons, or you who are malevolent sociopaths—you who are living and breathing, you who yet live, and you who yet try, you can still mend your mind, you can still shift your mindset, you can still regroup your cognitive frame-working to analyze ways to improve your intent and redress your actions based on key experiences from the past. So, breathe in and breathe out, and think with genuine thought toward the well-being of others and innovate ways to improve life.

"If we can hear from your lips and into our ears, 'let's create a legacy of kindness, of compassion, of innovation with passion toward longevity; let's create a legacy that we will be proud of to preserve, a legacy where you, I, and everyone else can explore the cosmos and preserve life! A legacy where the universe does not look at us is in terror as a destructive force, but one that brings abundance, life, and beauty. You, my friends, can still come around and are still capable of honor and can plan for a brilliant future.

"A life of meaning, a life of purpose, a purpose that is imbued with diligence, joy, fun, and happiness, a purpose of freedom, of consent, of clarity, and the kind of clarity that will lead each of us to be a part of the great force that will preserve the universe through promise, with answers to the greatest challenges that will and can be found, and where resolution to them lies still just ahead and just beyond the horizon, and those of us who live breeding benevolence, the kind of benevolence that no matter our circle of influence in life, makes us true leaders, you and I; you, I, we, have much to look forward to.

"One of the greatest purposes of leadership, both among the masses and right through to our own individuality, is to lead with kindness, integrity, love, compassion, passion for quality and innovation, and since an even greater purpose may come along as we sojourn through time, we will find that each of us can grow to be a leader, and each of us can help to break open the gates of so many other mysteries currently unknown. Perhaps parallel Universes and connections to different dimensions at a quantum level are something that might become a reality far off and far away and into the future, and perhaps we might be able to discover that once again we can see and embrace all of those whom we'd ever thought we'd ever lost in life. We each can bring promise, meaning, purpose, drive, motivation, and passion if that is the direction of our focus.

"By using the tools nature, the universe, or god, or whoever He or She or They are has given us, which, among the greatest, are our unique minds, we can find within ourselves so much more promise and joy along the way than what we could through any other means. So, I tell each of you, that the suggestion of my honored associate, 'giving universities to women in an extremely subversive and oppressive country instead of weaponry is like giving roses to the hungry,' is indeed off-base, tactically-minded rather than strategic, and a pox on reason.

"Education is a gift that can teach generations how to plant crops, extract pure water from the ground, the ocean, and the skies, feed the masses and cure all manner of diseases, and quell all kinds of destructive forces and uncontrolled chaos. Education can inspire greatness and all manner of well-being-infused innovations and a high quality of life for each of us, filled with the splendor of the exploration of our cosmos. Only together can we ever dream the realistic dream, the kind of dream that is a vision of longevity, prosperity, and joy. Only together, using as much mental capacity as we have been given by nature, god, the gods, or even possibly the universe itself, will we be able to evolve to a greater and more hopeful future—a future filled with joy, greater purpose, clarity, and excitement."

When Eliza finished her charge forward, everyone in the caucus stood, clapped, cheered, and continued doing so as Eliza got down from the podium. She looked upon the crowd before her, shook each of their hands, listened to their questions, and provided context to each promise she made to them. All her promises and suggestions were said in the purest form of honesty, integrity, and love, and all of it was without guile.

The crowd seemed to love her for many reasons, but no matter, Eliza was determined to do the right thing, because quite simply it was the right thing to do. Having done so much, that night she went to her estate, grabbed her sleeping bag, laid down by the statue of the angel overlooking the pond of coy fish and frogs, and fell asleep singing some of her favorite songs.

Special Day, Special Night

Dr. Eliza A. Williams easily won the race for Senate. The changes that were still very much needed gave even the first two months of service a whole lot of work to do, and she visited her biopod often to head into the Virtual Universe to draft policies that were rich with common sense, yet thoughtful enough to consider each aspect necessary in a complex society and an even more complex set of environments, that would change the tax codes and eventually enable her biopods. Her biopods were the one-stop-shop for so many things, to include education, research, development, entertainment, and even correction. Since the current tax code was due for an overhaul—a disaster from the year before, her biopods most likely wouldn't be implemented for some time. Yet, it could be soon that they would be, all things considered.

Christmas Eve was last night, she had celebrated with her senatorial team, and before going onto the Senate Floor, she caught up with Yesha, James, Amber, Erin, and her major delegates. While doing so, she viewed their progress, and linked minds with each of the growing populous throughout the tech cities and those read-in and on terrestrial missions, and listened to their desires, hopes, and dreams while in the Virtual Universe, where she could do hundreds of thousands of years of projects and events with billions of people, in just a few hours. She would see new developments unfold as discoveries were made from the Sun to the Oort Clouds and Yesha and James would update her when they had something new.

It was the evening of Christmas day, Holiday decorations were on display throughout the Senate and adorning her office, and a sense of cheer seemed to be natural despite all else when her neural link pinged. Yesha was linking to her from the Melrose Laboratory Auditorium, not far from the Melrose Campuses. *"It's about that time,"* she said. *"Vesha Celeste is about to be revived. Will you or can you be here for the event?"*

"I very much want to be, but we are trying to make changes to the tax code that will reduce the national debt substantially, or at least set up mechanisms to allow anyone to invest in national asteroid mining for annual dividends, combined with national debt payments, dividend-compensated benefits that include medical, retirement, and sabbatical aspects. Essentially, if we can pull this off, after conducting more biopsies for terrestrial historical data, we will mine at least three asteroids the first year, as a fool-proof example, and split the value 50/50 between the taxpayers and governmental program maintenance and pay off the national debt. Hopefully, we can finish deliberating soon. I will turn on my Virtual Universe sub-link, so I can get a sense of what is going on, and when I am done here, I will meet you as soon as possible. However, please press on with what you need to do and don't wait up for me. The timing for Vesha's revival is essential."

"That is very true. We'll press on then," said Yesha over her neural link.

Eliza continued from her office and felt a chill within the Senate chamber. The UP had gained slightly less than one-third of the Senate seats, and the two major parties were less than excited to see her. From her vantage point, while that was a major change in the political agenda of the established parties, there was still quite a way to go to reach the other two thirds. Many outside the UP had plans that had stretched for decades, with nuance and complexity, and they weren't influenced by Universal Ethics. They had a convoluted bureaucracy mired in by-law after by-law so there was very little they could do when it came to common sense, or laws that when put into effect would protect and promote the well-being of the citizens, instead of leaving them entrenched in the search for mere and temporary survival, greed, and pointless power.

It was obvious that the tax code approved by the House and the Senate last year came short of protecting those who could return the investment as they benefited from programs that allowed for progress in the scholastic arena, and instead, it punished those seeking higher education. Yet, to a certain and desirable extent, for a period of time, they would increase the bottom line for singles, couples, and families. Eliza saw through all of this, and an opportunity to present a flat tax program, which would serve as a motivation for every citizen or legal tax-paying resident to work any job, any approved employment, while affording in that sense all people a chance for a taxpayer dividend. Each year Eliza's country would benefit from their investments in asteroid mining operations via NASA and other contracted mining firms, put together via the new tax code she was introducing.

If desired, a person could contribute more than the flat rate of ten percent for a mathematically equitable and greater dividend, based on the assessment of procured elemental values on each asteroid and the number of asteroids mined each year.

If, for example, four-hundred-million employees earned an average of forty-thousand USD a year, then the ten percent revenue received from taxes would make it, so the IRS received one-point-six-trillion USD, where Eliza would contribute her own one-point-six-trillion USD as well, with an expected mining cost of fifty-billion USD resulting in a return of one-hundred-trillion USD after mining five asteroids. Thirty percent of the produced and sold income from asteroid mining would be divided into four-hundred-million shares, in return for working, paying taxes, and supplying the budget for mining investment, which would be reflected in the taxpayer dividend. Twenty percent of it would go to pay off the national debt. Five percent would pay for US governmental programs. Ten percent would go to provide labor compensation, technology development, further exploration, and equipment use with the necessary revenues and funding to expand further mining operations, and five percent would go back to medical, retirement, sabbatical, and business compensation account purposes. The final thirty percent would go to a Federal Account that would allow for employer compensation. Anything left would go to a surplus.

With this plan, everyone could be employed and compensated through a dividend. This went full circle leading to dividends that would foment productivity, personal investment in innovation, and afford individuals to be a part of the network of amazing people who work to increase the advancement of civilization. The motivation was certainly there to earn enough each year to pay their ten percent and receive the dividend. As mining operations expanded, the dividends would increase. The idea was to motivate everyone to stop complaining about the world around them and work forty hours a week for ten months out of the year with proper and due compensation, accompanied with certain benefits that allowed for additional time off for holidays and sick leave, and to add to that, there was an additional built-in incentive for businesses to provide excellent compensation and benefits.

Any business that demonstrated ethical treatment of employees would receive a fair portion of the dividend which had been put into a different category in the Federal budget. Ethical treatment would be weighed-in by Eliza's Laws of Universal Ethics, wherein the subsequent ratio consisted of USD investment into employee compensation and benefit costs, reinvestment into the business, and the amount paid to their shareholders. Ultimately, if the percentage of employee compensation and benefits in-turn raised the income earner's level of pay to greater than forty-thousand per the lowest cost of living ratio in the US, and greater for areas where the cost of living ratio was higher, then they would receive what the income earner would receive as a dividend, which would be approximately five times what the income earner paid in taxes.

Ultimately, the average income would be $40,000, minus $4000 in taxes. At the end of each year, they would receive a dividend of $20,000, for a gross income of $60,000 and a net income of $56,000, with all medical, retirement, and sabbatical expenses paid courtesy of the US Treasury. That was if only three asteroids were mined. Eliza had left three-thousand-asteroids between Venus and Mars, not in tangent to Earth or any other Pathway Industries assets available to Earth for just that purpose. She had also left about three-hundred-thousand in the asteroid belt between Mars and Jupiter. Her Octodecillions came from not just mining the material that she already had, alone, but also from what she had done with those materials afterward—the Twelve Database Moons, the twenty-thousand tech cities, the space elevators, the shielding of each planet and the solar system, resources for the IMC, and more.

If you did the math, which she had done, you would note that businesses would be compensated quite well, as well. It was a win-win for everyone, with a solid value, not just charged up numbers. She already had a method of mining and reinvesting those materials into products, but she had come up with a "Public Earth Acceptable Plan" that she was sure the Senate would accept, as well as the House, and the Executive and Judicial Branches.

Her first revelation would be her series of invisible anti-collision space elevators, anchors, and counter-weight shipping and receiving platforms, as well as her, weigh stations, transport stations, cargo spacecraft, and micro-gravity hotels with her gravity plate systems. Everything else would be revealed as the US was ready. Other countries could follow suit if they agreed to govern according to the Principles of Universal Ethics. There were plenty of resources to raise the quality of life for anyone and everyone. There would no longer be the need for greed, and the reticent result of grief and misery. If a person worked, even if they were on vacation, sabbatical, or with family on holidays, ultimately, they would have everything they needed. When the time was right, she would reveal her biopods, her tech cities, the shielding, and the progress of the terraformed planets. Eventually, she would reveal the Twelve Database Moons in all of their glory, but that along with the robust IMC would be several years down the road.

There would no longer be a concern for theft, looting, or worry for survival, job centers would eventually be supplied their own series of biopods setup to optimize and train employees for any job needed, and it would be much easier to live a noble life of productivity and a shared commitment toward the advancement of humanity, civilization, and the preservation of life. Soon she would meet with Vesha Celeste and ask her to work with James Cooper, going over and fine-tuning the plans for the IMC, working with Najem, an honorary member, on the missions of the thirteen zonal crews, and prepare Earth for interstellar and intergalactic travel throughout the expanse of our known Universe.

But, first Vesha needed to be revived...

Chapter 19: The Dreamy and Deep

Database Moon Archive, Celestial-Sol Entry Date: 2018 December 25. Yesha Alevtina trains Vesha Celeste. In this part of her training, leading and following her awakening, Vesha witnesses Najem Grace as she works out her doubts about optimizations with Eliza Williams. Prior to that we experience the awakening of Vesha Celeste, which plays a significant role in Najem's decision. These memories are a collaboration from the minds of Najem, Vesha, Eliza and many others within the Virtual Universe. Vesha, Yesha, Najem, and many others are interfaced via biopod within the Pathway Melrose Campus. Input by Yesha Alevtina, President of Pathway Industries, 2015-2022.

She had aged every day with charm, grace, and brilliance of mind and although she was an honorable member of Pathway, she was still concerned with the idea of age reversal—at least where it affected herself and her beliefs. While she still clung to her religion when it came to her hopes in her personal life, both Vesha Celeste and Eliza Williams had helped her to understand that advancing as a civilization, understanding our Universe, making discoveries of the unknown, and being healthy so we could not only learn but compound upon our wisdom—using our greatest talent, our brains—was a blessing.

Preserving life rather than watching it wither away when we could do something about it, would most definitely be considered noble in any deity's eyes. She started to see, after such a long life, that there may be another passion she had never even considered, and her friends at Pathway certainly gave her moral support, no matter her personal decisions. They just helped her to see things from a completely different standpoint—especially after all her visits to Pathway's Virtual Universe. She had done a lot with Pathway already, but she knew she could do more and despite her age, she yearned to travel the stars still.

As per the agreement presented to her, she became an honorary member of Pathway many years prior and arriving at that point Najem had been given a couple of options—she had chosen the second one, to hold off on bringing youth to her personal appearance. Najem Grace was ninety-three years old and instead of reversing her aging, for now, she had gone ahead with the choice of internally healing both her physiology and her neurology, but she wasn't quite yet ready to let her friends outside of Pathway witness her become younger and optimized.

Today was her friend, Vesha's big day, she had been a fellow honorary member who had chosen to live completely natural, and she suffered from dementia before she passed away. She had been allowed to participate in Pathway affairs due to her experiences with NASA, as was Najem, but she had chosen not to be healed at all, for the sake of science. Najem remembered the day of her funeral, and how sad it was to lose her. Her family had been there, dressed in black, and tears streaming down their cheeks. Vesha held a special place in each of their hearts. When Vesha had passed away, per request and agreement she would be revived later, after the family had had a chance to grieve, which they had. Until her family was read-in, however, she would likely never see them again.

There she was, lying silently in the heavily monitored room, which represented her room at the Princeton Assisted Living Home, and Najem was sitting in another room not too far away overlooking where Vesha appeared to be sleeping. Vesha and Najem had spent a lot of time at the campus facilities together, and now, since she had passed away, Najem had come by to visit her many times over the last two years. She had visited on many days from Triton, orbiting Neptune, after carrying out her daily duties, to see the progress on Vesha's comatose and lifeless body, as it was being optimized. The optogenetics teams kept Vesha's mind shut down until everything was ready for download. Najem was an observer many times, going through shared experiences in the Virtual Universe, with her friend, Vesha Celeste, who, in a twenty-two-year-old body, was about to be reawakened—a stark difference from when she passed away at the age of eighty-eight.

Vesha had been a colleague of hers throughout the years since the 1950's and a dear friend since they met when Najem had sponsored an astronomy club in the Washington, DC, area when women were still struggling to be accepted in the hierarchy of science. Lost in thought, sitting there in the technologically advanced observation room, Najem had missed Vesha in the real world, greatly, over the last two years since she had passed away and she looked forward to talking with her friend again. Her unique personality had gone all too soon, plagued with dementia throughout the last of her days, yet somehow, she could practice self-reflection and retaining much of her ideas as to who she was and the experiences she had gone through. Dementia impacted her by causing her neurons to fire in non-stop loops, so on many occasions, she had to take sleep medication otherwise she would have died of fatigue—nonetheless, she passed away, and Najem's friend was about to be brought back.

Seeing her friend reawakened might just change things for Najem. How this went down would determine whether Vesha would be brought back to a physical appearance similar to that which she had when she was twenty-two but optimized. She would be brought back, but with a few interesting, non-harmful, and artsy side-effects. However, and even more important to anything else, Najem Grace would be there as a close friend, to witness the proceedings and able to tell if this beautiful construct of the highest sophistication known to humanity, really was Vesha on the inside.

Although she wouldn't be able to greet Vesha Celeste until she had been awakened, and due to the unique nature of this occasion she would need to wait further until Vesha had received her Virtual Universe training, she couldn't wait for the moment when she could welcome her back. Najem Grace had been looking forward to seeing her favorite astrophysicist in her new form, her new body, completed and ready, as well as with her reawakened mind following two years of tests and she couldn't wait to see if there were any personality changes or subtle advancements that might lend to her own clarity as to the choice, she, herself, would make.

Much of Najem's work currently revolved around working with the very handsome James Cooper, sending Eliza's, Vesha's and Anastasia's particle jump sensors, or sensors, out to explore the furthest reaches of the universe for a robust and accurate map, as well as to plot the mission locations that the Intergalactic Mission Contingency, or IMC, would visit on its journey through the observable universe. Very similar to but much more compact than jump gates, these sensors acted like control point mechanisms and robust transceivers that could go anywhere throughout the universe using a three-dimensional grid system of the cosmos, which could be zoomed in for accuracy, to detect existing sensors, could transport spacecraft and all of its contents in a blink of an eye, and much more. For now, they were using them to gather information pertinent to the IMC mission, and she was always excited to see the universe from so many different vantage points. She saw constellations of different places in different galaxies, had derived locations of pulsars, neutron stars, suns that had met their end and promising new and young stars with countless planets that could sustain life—things that wouldn't be seen by the telescopes on Earth for many, many years.

The principal mission would for all intents and purposes start off with twelve drop-off points, one after the other, in essentially twelve zones throughout observable space, but this plan was of course amenable to change. To understand how the twelve zones were parsed out, essentially, they had divided the Earth into twelve geographical areas of responsibility as viewed at midnight—six in the northern hemisphere and six in the southern hemisphere. From there on Earth, they divided all of observable space into twelve zonal areas that would go out to the cosmic microwave background, or CMB, relative to Earth and each zonal command would be in charge of exploring, tagging, colonizing, and creating commercial space gateways for all planets, solar systems, and galaxies within their zone.

In the meantime, here Najem was, visiting from Neptune's Triton station, her home away from home, and sitting in a one-way viewing room on Earth—all to avoid overwhelming Vesha during her awakening, just in case too many changes all at once would startle her. Yesha Alevtina was about to give them their final brief, before commencing the reawakening. Yesha had been appointed by and unanimously voted on to take over as President of Pathway when Eliza Williams had handed it over when she ran for and became a US Representative and subsequently a US Senator in Washington, DC.

Eliza was still the UP leader, and Yesha and James worked together to helm Pathway, both on Earth and throughout the Solar System. Eliza, as Senator, had commissioned Yesha and James to begin considering putting together all the necessary pieces for interstellar and intergalactic journeys, missions, and colonization. Eliza would visit Pathway regularly via the Virtual Universe interface via the biopod in her office at the Capitol Building and communicate with others using her neural link. But it was Yesha, the President of Pathway, who was giving everyone the final briefing on how things would proceed, before commencing.

"Right when I knock on the door, the advanced systems in place will awaken her. To her, it will seem like she had just settled down to close her eyes after pondering on her life one more time, and then she'll hear a knock at the door. Since everyone agreed that it would be best that I do this, as the President of Pathway Industries, I am doing this rather than Najem, with a gracious heart." Yesha looked at Najem, "Along with Eliza, thank you for suggesting this, Najem, and each of you. You will get to meet her soon. I know you would like to meet with her, right away, but we need to make sure everything is running optimally, and that her body and her mind are truly hers. We need to minimize the initial contacts in case things go haywire, plus we don't want anyone to become too attached right away. I'm devoted already as I'm sure each of us is, but you know what I mean— most of us knew and loved her then and if things were to go wrong it would be a major setback, not to mention heartbreaking.

"We need to do the training first. While it may seem like several lifetimes in the Virtual Universe, it will only be a couple of hours. We have a lot more to train her on, to spin her up on, than usual. She was invaluable regarding her particle jump sensors. She had started the idea and brought it to Eliza's and my attention when we were very young. Eliza had formulated most of the technologies previous to the formation of Pathway LLC, then Pathway Industries, then Pathway Industries and Associates, and later Pathway, and even though everyone here has confirmed or even improved via updates upon these technologies, she was the pioneer. Anastasia, Najem, and their teams finished the details to put them in Najem's care for distribution throughout the known Universe. That said, once I take her into the Virtual Universe, the rest of you can join us and watch as observers, before you meet with her, but please make sure you do a good 'repast' of your own life's experiences and shared and personal memories for optimal cognitive frame working and upload to the Twelve Database Moons—we want to make sure everyone is backed up, just in case there is a worst-case scenario. She will be very powerful and capable—hence. Once Virtual Universe training with Vesha is done, I will broadcast to you that we are ready for the meet and greet. When I do, you will hear me say, 'and, this is where we are now,' and you will be pulled into a vast virtual meeting hall no matter where you are. Are there any questions?"

Everyone was silent, appeared to understand all the pre-rehearsed steps, and shared an air of enthusiasm for what was about to transpire. No one had any questions since they had cycled through the steps several times before—dry runs. Now it was the real thing.

Yesha then continued, "This is the very first test to see if humanity can store the mind, the DNA and the entire human genomic sequence digitally, grow and optimize the genes with the mind turned off through optogenetics and many other highly advanced technologies, download the neural mapping and network to her new brain—replete with her memories, feelings, her awareness, everything, and then turn her on. Once her mind is turned on, after growing the body in an accelerated manner with optimally encoded genes, with cells communicating all of the right things to the other cells, we will know from then on that we can successfully grow a human, aged twenty-five, in short order, and then turn her or him on in the hopes that it will be the individual who had passed away, but in a new body. This is it. This is humanity stepping it up and demonstrating to the universe that we were ready to preserve life, reanimate it, and protect the Universe itself from the laws of uncontrolled chaos—rather than destroy life or watch the universe expand beyond repair."

It was evening, and Vesha Celeste's young and beautiful body was breathtaking, and although it lay there as if asleep, everyone in the room was watching at the edge of their seats. Yesha had briefed everyone, and everyone knew that once Yesha and Vesha entered the Virtual Universe, that everyone else would go there too, and in this occasion, for an observable or a separate experience via interfacing through their biopods.

The Virtual Universe cosmic interface, quantum data analyzer and processor, and backup system were run by a complexed arrangement of twelve highly and technologically advanced database moons that orbited the Earth—far enough away from the Moon's orbit to avoid any catastrophes of any sort. They revolved around the Earth quietly, could not be detected by any technology on Earth, save via Pathway citizen's links, no matter the distance due to the highly robust jump gate and sensory system. The moon satellites had immediate connectivity via the particle jump sensor technology and they served not only as robust and redundant databases but also to protect the Earth from any hostile intrusion or radiation blast of any sort. They were even secretly capable of controlling the weather and could replace all other satellites around the Earth and work much more efficiently, effectively, on their own or while collectively coordinating and reducing the hazards of traditional space flight around the Earth and the Moon, but certain systems had not been brought online due to legalities and societal unpreparedness for such advancements. Once the nations and the people of Earth were ready, these dazzling moons would be revealed by Eliza, since they served to protect Earth in every imaginable way. This system also served as a virtual paradise, where those who had uploaded copies of their minds and DNA could interface and share their consciousness, participating with those still living in the real world. Collectively, the Virtual Universe was a world of education, up-to-date information, and healing, training, and even entertainment.

Entering the Virtual Universe on this occasion, everyone would reflect in detail on his or her own lives and they would then be able to interface with or visit anyone they wished to see who had ever been there before.

Yesha Alevtina would signal the big meeting, "And this is where we are now," and everyone would gather around her to meld minds collectively for true understanding among each person in the Virtual Universe. With the biopod's interface, anything experienced there would provide a tactile reference via the particle nanos optimizing the physiological aspects of the body as well as the neurological aspects of the mind. Everything experienced there would be visceral and similar to real life experiences, but with so many more possibilities—even expressing themselves according to their imaginations.

Vesha Celeste was the first Pathway member, read-in fully or honorary, who had passed away. She was a beloved individual who had also possessed a unique and very special mind, the kind of mind that had the temperance necessary to guide a Universe-wide journey throughout the cosmos. Thus, one by one and as a group, everyone had realized this and would welcome her back. Due to the lack of time equivalence as per the real world, they could spend years or even millennia there, but in the real world it would only be a few minutes, or it could be a few hours.

The way it was supposed to work, or the way it would begin was Vesha Celeste would be awakened by Yesha Alevtina as she knocked on her door. The location of all of this was known as the Melrose laboratory campuses, which was in a nicely prepared area within the Pathway Industries residential underground technology campus in Massachusetts. Vesha would open "her" door, Yesha would check to see what it was that Vesha had remembered, show her the new body she had, give her a brief update on where she was—if asked, teach her about her neural linking and communication, teach her the biopod commands, and then take her to the Virtual Universe. Once there, she would take her through her own life, then Eliza's life, as well as the lives of each Pathway member and Pathway delegate, as uploaded and pre-coordinated. Finally, she would interact with each of the more than one billion members in the Virtual Universe, meld minds, and share a purpose. If a person were not available, a simulation of them would be available in much the same way—with experiential updates provided once the real individual interfaced through the neural link.

Najem Grace, Vesha's closest friend, was ready for the proceedings to begin. She had been to the Virtual Universe many times, had schooled herself on all of the sciences that Eliza had, and had enjoyed the world so much that she developed her own Virtual Universe representation of herself. She was able to see things about her virtual physiology according to her own perceptions and enjoyed a world that was resplendent with vibrant colors of purples, blues, blacks, whites, and pinks. Najem fancied herself as a flying mermaid in the body of a twenty-five-year-old version of herself, swimming in the air or any place she chose. People who saw her would see her turquoise and purple irises, thick black limbal rings, black eyelashes and eyeliner gradually blending into beautiful colors of turquoise, purple, blue, and pink. They would see her mermaid fishtail—purple, turquoise, and black crystalline scales and color variations. Both her internal and external beauty would be on display as her left half was tattooed from neck to pelvis with a beautiful and intricate set of designs that captured her beauty and intensified it. Her crystalline encrusted perky youth was certainly not a site for the overly prudish but was an image she felt gave her a sense of freedom, and if she could she would share her breathtaking beauty with the rest of the world.

She couldn't wait to see Vesha once the training was completed, but she would wait anyway. When the time came, she would go over her personal biological life reflections of the last ninety-three years, and then meet and greet with Vesha to show herself off as well. As it was, in the real world, her real body was aged, she had earned every wrinkle and she prided herself on her well-earned powdery white hair—as white as snow. She had an affectionate and friendly smile—a sense of belonging and a sense of purpose. In the real world, Najem went to church every weekend, participated in Pathway, worked with Pathway government contractors, as well as the American Association of University Women, and gave lectures to the Goddard Space Flight Center on the remedial sciences. These sciences were advanced to the rest of society, but certainly remedial to every member of Pathway. Not to mention, she worked with James to explore, research, and prepare briefs from afar of the locations throughout the universe and the missions Vesha would lead with the position of IMC Commander, and as five-star general.

Eliza Williams had long ago ensured every member of Pathway Industries and the UP were both multi-quadrillion dollar enterprises but had highly recommended everyone live as humble yet versatile a life as possible, as people in everyday life, at least while on Earth living among the people in public. Once the actual space journeys began or once the political climate changed, no matter where a person was on Earth, they would have the nicest living arrangements, the best cooks, and access to any location they wished. As it was, Pathway members lived normal on Earth, but with luxurious and fancy condos in the tech city of their choosing.

Eliza had revealed her scientific achievements, her outer space exploits—the asteroid and space junk mining, the database moons, the bases on the planets and planetary moons in the solar system, the high quality living spaces being maintained by James Cooper, his crew, and nano-technology self-replicating robots in each of those locations—with encoding, knowing when to stop and when to request further instructions; she had revealed the hidden space elevators, the Virtual Universe, the biopods, the particle jump sensors, the gateways—all undetected by, and unreleased to the public as of yet—only to the members of Pathway and fully read-in UP members. Eventually, she would reveal these same things to the rest of the world, in due time.

Eliza's worth on the Earth was that of the only multi-quadrillionaire and growing, but her true value in monetary investments throughout the solar system was now beyond two hundred octodecillion USD. She could pretty much purchase the entire world and everything on it, but she had bigger plans in mind than simply being rich and powerful— she wanted society to work together, to be advanced, to have universal health care and education, and to live healthy, productive, and constructive lives filled with meaning and purpose—a purpose determined by a desire to contribute to an advanced society and to increase the well-being of humanity and all of its friends. She had the ability to do this now, but she did not want to upset the current economic system quite yet—in time she would see it transitioned to shared prosperity, but for now, people had jobs to do, bills to pay, and lives to live the best way they knew how. She knew she had to persuade others to change, not manipulate the minds or the wills of the people—individual consent was paramount.

Eliza had put up an invisible shield around the Earth, a system to bring longevity to the length of life of the Sun, and a complex system beyond the Oort Clouds surrounding the solar system to protect it from any hostilities outside of it. Due to her abilities with reprogrammable matter and highly capable nanotechnology with bots that combed the solar system and set things up and maintained them, and her ability to use particle jump sensor technology, she had done much of the legwork to ease humanity into the future. She had also done so much more. Now Yesha Alevtina was at the helm of Pathway, while Eliza continued as the head of the UP. However, it was Yesha's duty to take over the things that Eliza had to leave behind.

When Vesha Celeste awoke, only a week or two would go by before she would be in charge of the Intergalactic Mission Contingency, but she would work closely with James Cooper and Najem Grace coordinating the safest of journeys with missions met through the twelve zones within the Earth's observable Universe. Vesha would bring humanity and preservation of sentient life from the regions around the Earth to the outside perimeter of the CMB region as viewed from Earth, and then provide follow-up reports of findings, accomplishments, and plans to Pathway Industries and hopefully the rest of the world.

For now, here was Najem, sitting in her aged and long-lived body with excitement to see her friend revived. When the time came, Najem would go through the rehearsed process, and then she would meet Vesha for the first time in two years. The splendor of it all was, Vesha Celeste, just as she, was as beautiful as anyone could imagine in the Virtual Universe, using her virtual mind which was in stasis and would be prior to her awakening, but likewise in real life—Vesha was humbly just as amazing as well, as her extraordinary and enjoyable self.

While Najem never married or never had children, to her, her missions within Pathway working closely with the internal government branch in training and transitions, her time in the space program at NASA, and the satellite programs she had seen through from infancy to space had all been her babies for more than seventy years of her life. Najem had done a lot to coordinate the development, the funding, and the launch of the Hubble Space Telescope, before retiring back in the 1980's. To her, it seemed so long ago when thinking back, but in the Virtual Universe, she could experience it all repeatedly, as if it happened yesterday. At Pathway, Najem worked both in private and in public.

Najem was born in Nashville, TN to Georgia and Irwin Grace. Her mother was a schoolteacher and her father a geophysicist. Following her birth, on July 15, 1925, she and her family moved around the country a lot with her father's job. It was after she had moved to Nevada and at the age of eleven that she began to show an interest in astronomy and in the stars. She found them so intriguing that she formed an astronomy club at school, to participate and become educated in that field with them. They would pore over books about the various constellations and gaze at the stars pointing them out to each other on clear nights.

Before high school started, Najem and her family moved to Baltimore, MD where she enrolled in a three-year accelerated program. She graduated from Western High School early.

Unfortunately, pursuing the sciences as a young woman came with a lot of kickback since she was frequently reproached by those she trusted with a lot of "that isn't a woman's place," etc. As discouraging as it was in those days for women, Najem carried on. She received her BA at the Swarthmore College in 1946. She then earned her Ph.D. at the University of Chicago three years later. During her life and during her studies she would still take breaks, and on many occasions, while visiting science conventions she would run into Vesha Celeste.

Najem's favorite pastime of all was the actual research she would conduct as part of a project with another tenured professor at the Yerkes Observatory in Michigan and the McDonald Observatory in Texas. Because she was a woman, however, she did not receive tenure there, so she moved on to the Naval Research Laboratories until she was hired by NASA. NASA had found interest in her, due to her work with the star, AG Draconis, her discoveries regarding its emissions, and her work with radio astronomy, radio source spectra, and geodetic programs.

Najem became the first NASA executive, who happened to be a woman. Through her NASA career, she worked on more than thirty major satellite programs, engaging in planning, budgeting, political approval, and the actual launching and positioning programs. Now, years later, upon reading Eliza Williams' book, meeting her at a book signing, and then meeting her again during a follow-up visit, she had become a part of Pathway and worked closely with Pathway's US Government technology-fusion branch.

Najem, who had been thinking about her past came out of deep thought, she remembered she was in the Melrose Laboratory Auditorium, with a scene playing before her. She remembered this was Vesha's awakening and then the lights went out, and, "Knock, knock!" Yesha Alevtina, Pathway's President, had tapped on the door.

"I'm coming, I'm coming," Najem witnessed as Vesha Celeste arose from her bed. With the feed displaying what was going on in Vesha's mind, she saw that Vesha did not yet realize that she was no longer in an eighty-eight-year-old's body. Instead, Vesha Celeste displayed similar mannerisms indicating that she was what she had been familiar with for quite some time in the later stages of life. She was unaware of her youth. It clearly had been that Vesha was indeed walking around. Stumbling around, Najem saw as Vesha was grabbing her slippers, her robe, and then turning on the light. She made her way to the door. Najem could tell from her expressions that she sensed something was different, something was quite odd.

She then opened the door and recognized Yesha, but Najem noticed that Vesha was somewhat skeptical at first, but they talked. They conversed for a few minutes, and it became obvious Vesha recognized the fact that she was talking to one of the young ladies who had visited her so many years ago. Najem saw the historical flash of Vesha's memories, as she recalled how Eliza and Yesha had met her many years ago when they decided to attend a science convention where Vesha was one of the speakers. This they had done, instead of going to their high school prom. Najem witnessed as Vesha reminisced on this as she went to get some tea for her guest, who then approved of it wholeheartedly. Yesha, after catching up and enjoying the tea, suggested to Vesha that she should go to the restroom and look in the mirror.

Everyone attending the reawakening witnessed as they beheld her expressions as she saw herself for the first time in her current state, "Oh, my!" Vesha exclaimed. Najem saw Vesha, as she stood in her pajamas and robe, so used to the expressions and mannerisms of someone who had lived for the 88 years that she had, and there Vesha stood gazing into the mirror in disbelief. Najem could tell from Vesha's mental readings on display in the Pathway private viewing campus that she liked what she saw, and how it reminded her of an amazingly artistic and spectacularly youthful, curvy, slender, and perky figure she remembered from looking in the mirror when she was about twenty-two years old, only this was truly a lot more colorful.

Yesha also smiled.

Najem watched and listened some more yet began to get the sense that she was being watched too but put that idea on hold while witnessing history in the making.

"I look... different! What exactly happened? Wait, you asked where I thought I was, and now I am at a loss; what is this place, and where am I?" Vesha had thousands of questions running through her mind, and on display before her unseen audience, as she stood in baffled amazement at what she beheld in the mirror before her. Instead of working herself into a dither, however, she found herself even more enchanted and in awe while thinking out loud, loud enough for Yesha to hear, "I won't lie, Yesha, I thought I was dying about twenty minutes ago; I had some pretty deep and fleeting moments of memory as though my life was playing before my eyes, and a bit of a headache, but the second I sighed, breathed out, and thought I wouldn't breathe in again, it was then and quite precisely when I felt vibrant, my pain gone, and like I could reach the stars!" She continued as she embraced her new reality.

"Fancy you asked," said Yesha. She answered her questions and shared more heart-to-heart exchanges with Najem, as Najem and Vesha's many close friends observed and witnessed. Yesha and Vesha continued until they entered the Virtual Universe. That is when Najem went on her own journeys as the members of Pathway in attendance climbed into their biopods and went on their own journeys as well through the Virtual Universe until it was time.

Once there, after quite some time, and once it was time where she finally could meet Vesha Celeste, Najem witnessed face-to-face, that she was every bit the charming person she was in real life. This was her. This was her dear friend Vesha Celeste, brought back to life. She had died on the evening of Christmas, and here she was now, two years later, alive, young again, full of verve, and beautiful in every possible way. The funny thing, Vesha too was smitten with her friend, Najem's, imagery and her own neural expression of a dazzling mermaid.

Journey with an Old Friend

Once everyone had met and greeted Vesha, after leaving the Virtual Universe, she was ready for the real world —trained in every way, in full, and very much a witness to all that had led her to that point in her reality, as surreal as it seemed.

A day later, Eliza met with Vesha Celeste in her Senatorial Office on Capitol Hill.

Two days later, Eliza requested a chance to sit with Najem. Both Eliza's Estate and her Capitol Hill offices had jump gates back and forth. Najem had jumped home to Triton after spending time with Vesha Celeste for the last two days. Now she was returning to Earth via jump gate. She traveled first to Eliza's estate using her own jump gate where her home was orbiting Neptune and once at Eliza's estate, she then jumped to Eliza's Senatorial Office. For the sake of spatial area capacity limits, only Eliza could jump from anywhere to her office. Everyone else had to coordinate and travel to her estate first.

Arriving at Capitol Hill, Najem looked at and pondered upon the paintings in Eliza's office. One was of the Statue of Liberty with its inscription below it, and the other was of the Tomb of the Unknown Soldier, and its inscription below it as well. *"What beautiful parallels!"* Najem thought. *"These paintings do belong together. The message, 'Bring all your humble, your poor, and downtrodden,' is sitting right next to an unknown soldier, who gave his all to preserve the freedoms we enjoy today. Imagine that both carry a deep message, and both are lined up one with the other. What a perfect and bittersweet reality."*

Najem heard Eliza's office door open, "How are you doing? How is Vesha?" asked Eliza.

"I am doing amazing. Ever since Vesha came back, we've spent a lot of time in the Virtual Universe and have had a couple of walks together through your old neighborhood, from your estate on Garden Street to the breezy beach, and we just can't get enough of each other. Her personality hasn't changed too much, but she seems quite a bit less inhibited, which is spectacular. She's made me blush a few times already, but that is okay," responded Najem.

"Her inhibitions are clearly more entertaining, are they not?" Eliza laughed with her, also impressed with the progress Vesha Celeste had shown since her reawakening two days prior. "It's great to see you, too, Najem. After seeing our dear friend since she was reawakened, how do you feel about life, longevity, and full physiological and neurological optimizations, as well as age reversal now? I know you were leery about it when we last talked." continued Eliza.

Najem explained how she still had her reservations or concerns about the idea of living healthy and in a younger version of herself. She also described her affection toward her earned wrinkles, white hair, and her voice. Listening to her, Eliza responded to her fears. Eliza knew her fears revolved around how Najem had been treated when she was twenty-five, in 1950.

Najem had never been married, she had never had any children, yet she labored diligently to serve humanity in her own way. She had served humanity through her quest to enable an increased understanding of our Universe via service to the US Government helming highly crucial programs related to the study of outer space and preparation and placement of quite a few manmade satellites.

After some discussion, she confided in Eliza and told her about a time when she had visited a community church with a friend of hers. As she did, her tone became more serious and one of concern. "Many years ago, after finishing my doctoral studies in astrophysics, I went to church regularly. I had been friends with another young lady through my collegiate studies and the first year of my professional career and she asked me to accompany her to her church for a shared spiritual event. I thought about it and we both decided that it would be a wonderful idea.

"Once I arrived at her hometown church, I entered with a cold reception. It became apparent that she had grown up in a location that had unfortunately suffered from so much cultural division for far too long. I had been reared to appreciate people based on how they treated others, but her community had endured some of the worst and most despicable forms of discrimination that had revolved around shallow superstitions and ideals. Her background had been one of pain, of suffering, and of hateful actions by those ignorant or negligent of a better way.

"During the early days of the US all the way through to the 1860's, and then in many parts throughout our country until even today, far too many people have suffered from toxic treatment and discrimination based on physical or other features they were born with but had no control over. I appreciated my friend's culture, as well as the time spent with her. So, together we decided to attend her religious meetings. Unfortunately, not long after I arrived, the preacher asked me to leave. He had seen hatred to its most brutal limits due to the pervasive cults of men that existed at the time which carried on with séances and rituals, and even the worst of brutality in mankind through burnings to teach a vicious lesson that made no sense to anyone of repute. Therefore, and naturally, he did not feel as though the congregation would be comfortable with my attendance there. It was as if he viewed me as a spy with ill intentions, and I felt very much like I ought to leave.

"I had been of a different mindset then, I was quite a bit more naïve and still very kind, yet I had tried to stand my ground to no avail. My belief had been that I merely wanted to share a religious experience with my friend, yet I hadn't considered so many of the other ramifications. The preacher chastised me on how my physical features reminded him of pure evil and that I was not wanted there.

"I explained to him before how it was that many of those who I grew up with and went to school with knew that discrimination that is not based on someone's character wasn't right and that I had never been party to any behavior of that sort. The pains must have run deep, however, because he looked as though he wanted to physically and forcibly remove me if necessary, as if what I had to say didn't or wouldn't matter. It was a tough moment in my life, a moment that replayed in my head. Not so much because of feelings that I may have been hurt, but more so because I then understood the sense of rejection that comes from prejudice. I was not judged because of whom I was, but because of whom I was perceived to be, free speech or due process died there.

"My parents and grandparents had bent over backward to show kindness, dignity, and respect toward anyone and everyone, no matter their background or past, but now despite our history of being inclusive, I felt targeted and excluded. I had the sense that because my parents were honorable, and as much as my behavior and thoughts throughout my life had been, that I ought to have been accepted and appreciated by others of diverse cultures as well. I never had a chance to explain to the priest that I could empathize with what they were going through. I too had been discriminated against in my own life, for merely being a woman interested in science, and I only wished to sit in the congregation with my friend.

"Clearly, the preacher did not budge, and I left my friend in that congregation, running home in tears with an ache in my throat. Even though I was twenty-five years of age and had earned the valor of obtaining my Ph.D. through hard work and dedication, and had always considered everyone a potential friend, my friend's preacher did not know this and wasn't in the position to negotiate in front of his audience. Truly, the wounds and sentiments were deep.

"Later, I learned from my friend, who was torn from this as well, that he had responded, regarding my attendance, to the audience. On that same Sunday, he went into a sermon on how my story would have been born of privilege, and that my background had little to no value in their lives. He had preached that there was no possible way my suffering was in any way near the suffering that many generations of theirs had been through and endured. What they had experienced, and what they continued to go through was devastating, because of heavily integrated and systemic discrimination written into the fabric of US policy, and thus I was also at fault, because of being born the way I was.

"I remember telling my friend that even though there are many despicable white men and women throughout history, there are also many despicable people of all races throughout the world and throughout the full course of civilization, and that it should never give anyone the sense that it is right to be that way to someone else or to say hurtful things. It isn't right to say mean-spirited words, casting a wide net of the blame on innocent people no matter the situation. After our discussion, it seemed in an instant that our friendship drifted, and we haven't talked ever since.

"How could he have felt at peace with how he handled that situation? No matter whom we are or our background, we need to be decent people. Just as there are people with malevolent intent, there are also many brazen, noble, kind, and compassionate people that see through the ugliness of life and try to improve upon it. There are so many amazing people who had to make heroic sacrifices to help society make the appropriate changes we are blessed with today.

"Multitudes of people in a rich diversity of cultures have struggled in the past to right the wrongs of others. We can still do so to be a part of humanity's progression forward. I wish that I had suggested he consider that, before leaving the building. But the past is in the past. Since then, I had determined for quite some time to focus more on science and less on religion. Although I am Christian and Vesha, my best friend, is Jewish, I am still spiritual, not religious. I hope my perception doesn't betray me, but it seems to me now that through the years, things have changed. James Cooper shared with me that when he had been in Salt Lake City, Utah, many years ago, under contract to build infrastructure there, that he had dated a beautiful young lady of African-American heritage. While dating her, she had invited him to accompany her to the Church of Jesus Christ of Latter-Day Saints, or the Mormon Church. Their bishop and the entire congregation had welcomed his attendance whole-heartedly with handshakes, smiles, and hugs, despite their difference in background. So, that gives me some hope. Perhaps things have changed, but I feel more accepted with my white hair and wrinkled skin.

"I must have been scarred from my experience so many years ago. I feel that no matter who I become, I would still be this horrible individual because of things I had no control over when I was born. I still love all people, no matter their background, but I realize that there are those that have truly suffered so much more. I get the sense that social, cultural, and religious environments have created within the minds of far too many an unspoken difficulty when differentiating between the content of character versus the color of skin, region, religion, and identity. That day, I went home and prayed to the Lord, but I've been scarred ever since."

After explaining that to Eliza, Eliza asked, "Do you happen to recall her name? The name of the young lady you attended church services with that day?"

"Yes. Her name was Bonnie Knight," Najem responded.

"Hmm, did you know that her daughter is part of Pathway?"

"Oh? I did not know that. Without being fully read-in, I suppose there are quite a few intricate details that you might be aware of that I am not. She is here?"

"Yes, I've been in the Virtual Universe many times, and while there, I have noticed that there were certain private areas of your mind that were closed off, and rightly so. But, now that you have shared that with me, I can tell you that her daughter, Rebecca, was reared by Bonnie understanding your story, but from her perspective. What you don't know is that the following week, Bonnie's preacher gave a speech regarding the character that you had displayed of moral integrity and how he felt repentant of how he had dealt with you and the situation the week prior.

"He had stated that any sort of oppression, is a suppression of the spirit, of the mind, of life. As you can see, it can also hamper the intents of the best of men. He knew this and shared that with his audience the following week. Bonnie taught that to Rebecca, and now she is a vital member of Pathway—someone who I am considering for a spot as a zonal commander for one of the twelve main zones throughout our Observable Universe from Earth, and I would like you to meet her soon. Perhaps I won't introduce you today, but I will soon when you're ready.

"You are very aware of the tribulations of others because you have been through a few trials yourself. I have seen some of the inner workings of your mind on many occasions, in the Virtual Universe, and I know that women, on the whole, went through a lot of abuse and mistreatment in those days. Sadly, in so many places in this world, we know that the same is still the case. My heart goes out to all who have suffered through dismal life, its limitations and mediocrity, no matter where they were born and no matter their natural physical appearance, the circumstances they were born in, their religion, or their identity. I find your story to be about character and suffering overall; all of which runs much deeper than the aesthetics we have referenced. Suffering has been an unnecessary and tragic circumstance shared by far too many for far too long and dismissed by many more. While we don't want to generalize, no specific culture or identity holds a monopoly on suffering; there are others who have suffered too.

"Many are in battles we'll never know of. So, we need to remember temperance, gentleness, and kindness. Yet, still, I find it is easy for our perseverance to wear thin when it comes to negative and critical behavior toward any well-intended individual, especially when the value of someone helpful and powerful, such as yourself, is selfishly stripped away. If someone has walked the roads of misery, it is very important for them to seek a voice, to seek reparations, and to mend the heart, the soul, and the mind, but we can do so by lighting the way for others as a good example of a wonderful person to be. Every individual is valuable with potential that is far too often untold, so don't let that experience ever take away from the things you know you need to do. Someday, hopefully not too late, many struggling through the same issues will learn to love and to avoid negative generalizations of mass groups of people. In so many cases, people look for an enemy to place their burdens upon or someone to place the blame on for all of their suffering, and someone to take vindication out on without considering true justice, compassion, and mercy.

"We can all learn, no matter where life has taken us. We can all become our better selves and find clarity on what it is that we can do to bring peace, happiness, and prosperity to humanity and all of humanity's friends. We are in a much different time now; people can see through any façade; we can tell the difference between moral character and pretense. It is ours to be genuine, to be kind, to be compassionate, to build a legacy and be a part of a legacy worthy of preserving indefinitely. Your choice is yours to make, Najem. But, please know that no matter what you choose, I see that you are a wonderful person, a lovely soul—your Virtual Universe version of yourself is evidence to that end.

"Plus, I have seen your thoughts; I have combed your mind many times in the Virtual Universe as our minds have melded on so many occasions, and please let me assure you, you have a true heart of gold. This preacher you talked of, he appears to have had many struggles in his life, much of which was not his doing, and in his own way, he was correct. We all are going through different battles. I believe this preacher simply forgot to be kind and gentle—but you were. I am proud of you, Najem. It took him a week, but he too learned and blessed the lives of those in his congregation a week following that day, and then he appeared to be more receptive of people based on the character they exhibited from that point on and through the days that followed.

"We all learn, whether it is now or sometime down and into the distant future, or sometime in-between. Sometimes it is ours to have temperance, forbearance, and suffer well. It is always worth it in the end."

Eliza paused and waited for Najem to respond. "Thank you, Eliza. I needed that. I feel relieved now like I can finally let this go, knowing that with hope, old wounds can finally heal. I suppose you are right; I had compartmentalized this existence in my mind. Now that I have had the opportunity to share this with you, I am grateful for your sage advice, my young and dear friend. I am ready to let this go, allow my mind to heal, and I believe I am ready now to reverse the aging process. Seeing Vesha Celeste also gave me a renewed hope, a new perspective on my sense of having a calling in life. Thank you to you, Eliza, as well as Yesha, James, and everyone at Pathway for being so patient, despite my rickety self. How long will this process take?"

"It only takes two seconds in a biopod and some training within the Virtual Universe, my dear sweet friend. All you have to do is think of your youth and desire to hustle and bustle just like you did then. Once you have, come back to the real world, and you'll find what changes have been made for you. I assure you; you'll be impressed. Please feel free to use one of the biopods in my estate home. It helps to have a friend, perhaps Vesha can accompany you?"

With that, Najem went back to Eliza's estate via her jump gate, and found Vesha already there waiting for her, stepped into Eliza's biopod, and did as Eliza had suggested. She and Vesha went through many centuries worth of experiences together, and when they came out of the biopod, there she was, a beautiful, slender-faced, brown-eyed young lady. Her brown hair was swept up to the right, with a part on the left, and tied back in a professional-looking pony-tail up-do. She noticed a few glistening highlights of various shades of pink, turquoise, and purple, and her lips were naturally a beautifully voluptuous sort, and she felt all the youth she had when she was twenty-five. Yet, here she was, ninety-three, but now looking twenty-two and as pretty as she had never dreamt of being before.

Najem smiled as she felt a tingling sensation all the way down the left side of her body and then felt a special connection with her dear friend, Vesha as well as every single one of the citizens of Pathway. She dropped her robe, and amazed at what she saw, she was immediately stricken with disbelief. "Wow! I can only have imagined this. Hahaha look at my tattoos; they look just like the ones in my Virtual Universe imagination of myself. What do you think, Vesha?" Vesha had been impressed, had trained her on every skill she knew, and they hugged.

She threw on her smart suit which expressed professional attire, composed of a white blouse with a black double-breasted suit jacket. She noticed her hair was splendid already, she didn't need to apply any make-up, since somehow her body produced that imagery all on its own, and then she went with Vesha to Jasmine's living quarters at Pathway and knocked on the door.

"Come in!" said Jasmine.

"You have to see this! Oh, this is Najem... what do you think?"

"Well, I know it's you, silly! Look at you! Wow!" Vesha, Jasmine, and Najem hugged each other, overwhelmed with what they saw in each other, and then they sat down on Jasmine's sofa and chatted for hours, drinking a variety of their favorite teas, and glowing from time to time. Catching up in the Virtual Universe was fun and all but doing so in the real world took on a neat feeling of its own.

"Do you two want to go on a walk-through Cambridge with me?" asked Vesha.

"Of course, I do! I can't wait to see how this feels in my new body. Let's go!"

Jasmine nodded to the affirmative and smiled, as they proceeded to carry out their plans.

Najem, Jasmine, and Vesha updated their smart suits to resemble jogging suits with a rich variety of colors that resembled the colors in their eyes, hair, and tattoo-like markings on their bodies. When they were ready, they left the Pathway Melrose Campus and walked from Melrose to the Cambridge Public Library, where they changed their smart suits to reflect a metro-casual and feminine appearance.

Pathway had purchased the Cambridge Public Library since government funding had dissipated and could no longer sustain or run it appropriately. Therefore, Eliza and Yesha saw to it that both the library and the area around it were purchased by Pathway University, to preserve the older architecture, to widen the streets a bit, and to afford anyone in the area a chance to sit down and do some old-fashioned reading, eating of bakery goods, and drinking a coffee or a tea.

Vesha, Najem, and Jasmine, old friends from yore, started again with several varieties of tea, including all their favorite flavors, and then they tried a variety of different coffees from places all over the world. The smell of bakery goods permeated the air, so without any guilt whatsoever, they each had a lovely bagel filled with cream cheese.

After visiting the library, they decided to use the jump gates to travel to some interesting places throughout the world. Pathway had pulled no stops and had gateways hidden in places all over the solar system, to bring the finest home and to allow Pathway citizens and team members from other countries a chance to do the same from their own hometowns.

No matter where they went, the food was always good and mulling over a good book and taking turns in-between bites to read it out loud to each other was a favorite pastime. They spent time, all three, in the Virtual Universe together, and then continued their worldwide tours.

"How did we get so lucky? This is awesome fun!" Najem exclaimed to Vesha and Jasmine, as they had made their way to the Alps and had raced each other down a ski slope without any fears whatsoever.

When they finished their journeys, their visits to the sites, scenes, and libraries of each location they visited, enjoying their teas, coffees, and bakery goods, they returned to the Cambridge Public Library and walked to Eliza's estate home, sat by the pond with the Angel overlooking the coy fish and frogs, looked up at the sky and began singing to each other.

Since Najem, Vesha, and Jasmine had each been in the Virtual Universe together with a shared sense of experiences and memory, they had taken a liking to female vocal trance, just like their dear young friend, Erin Carter.

The song that came to mind was "New Dawn," sung by Sarah Lynn, with a nice mix of it by Rafael Frost that had been popular during the summer of 2016. Just then, they saw young fourteen-year-old Erin Carter walk through the backdoor of Eliza's estate, holding a sleeping bag. "I thought it'd be you three," she smiled. She then lay down and sang with all three of them as they gazed up at the stars.

"I couldn't be happier," said Najem.

"Neither could I," Vesha reciprocated her sentiments, and they both felt Erin's and Jasmine's sentiments communicated within their minds.

"We might as well be sisters, kindred spirits; I can't help but be happy here. This wonderful place has so many wonderful memories. Oh, look, there's Tyson!"

Tyson Williams, the Second, came through the back door of the estate, his eyes squinting from having been curled up asleep in a little ball inside, and his little booty was wagging. Once he noticed who they were, he went from almost a curled sideways gate to a doggy jog toward them. He was clearly happy to see the young ladies, and he remembered who they were based on their scent. He could also tell they were having quite a good time and planned on getting a good massage in, maybe get his chest scratched.

"Remember when we lost Tyson? Poor Eliza was ten years old," asked Najem.

"Of course, I can, silly. We've seen the story a billion times in the Virtual Universe. How could we forget?" said Vesha. They petted Tyson, hummed, and looked up at the stars.

"I wonder how long before we can go out there. You know, the long distances?" asked Najem.

"Yes, I wonder too," said Jasmine.

"Me too," replied Erin.

"Well, we have the Intergalactic Mission Contingency, or the IMC, to build. Plus, Eliza would prefer society be properly updated with politics going a positive direction first. I am pretty sure that she plans on running as President of the United States for the elections in 2024. I am thinking that not too long after that when the world finally is at peace, people are united and helping each other out, that then we will go out on that journey," said young Erin.

"Have you seen the data regarding the twelve galaxies we'll be stopping at and then dispersing to?" asked Jasmine. "I hope we will be able to go to Andromeda. I've always wanted to see what it is like there. I know, eventually there will be a huge collision between the Milky Way and Andromeda, but that is a long time from now, and by then I would imagine that whatever team I am in, and whatever zone I will be in, maybe mend the dilemma or jump to safe places and enjoy the show at any time."

"Jasmine, I love your imagination and your hopes. Erin and Najem, you two are wonderful with broad bouts of imagination that bring joy to the heart as well. Eliza met with me a few days ago for a short brief. She wanted to check in with me and said that we'll meet again in a few months. She gave me a sneak peek of everything planned. It looks like I may be working with you, Jasmine, Najem, and James to build the IMC, or at least to coordinate it, but it appears that Pathway is looking to have someone run the overall mission. That's something we'll figure out soon. That said, I think Andromeda will be your zonal galaxy, Jasmine, and I am pretty sure you will be the Zone-02 commander, Najem.

"Nothing is set in stone yet. I presume that once I have dropped you and the other eleven zonal commanders and your crews off, I will head to the CMB as viewed from Earth with you, Erin. There is something interesting about my mind; I can pick up more details from other's minds than I am supposed to. There are what we all know as compartmentalized areas of our brains, but somehow, I can see through them. It's weird for sure and will be odd for a while, at least until I properly categorize the ten tremilliatrecendotrigintillion or more flavors of thought throughout every galaxy within and beyond every place we can fathom in the known Universe. It will be even more interesting when I pop in to visit from the other side of Earth's visible Universe, with knowledge and information available when humanity is ready." Vesha said with a whimsical sense of humor radiating an iridescent glow, as she lay in her sleeping bag, looking at Najem, Tyson, and Erin, with an approving smile.

"I know, right? Although that is a huge number, Vesha! That's ten to the ten-thousand zeros after the one! This will be so much fun. I can hardly wait!" Najem said, and all four laughed together with a sense of peace and ease, enjoyed Tyson's company and let time fly.

With their new bodies, they didn't have to worry about sleeping bags, bugs, cold, rain, heat, the gamut, but they used them anyway laying on their backs with Tyson taking turns to find himself in between each of them through the night for old time's sake.

Just as they thought the night was soon to be over, Yesha, Eliza, who smiled at Najem approvingly, Amber, and James all showed up with pillows and sleeping bags in hand. Every single person who had been fully read-in to Pathway had a very special and unique set of stories, missions, journeys, and quests, available for sharing at any time, filled with lessons learned, mysteries uncovered and solved, and so much more. Together, Najem, Vesha, Jasmine, Eliza, Yesha, James, Amber, and Erin journeyed with their neural links and telescopic vision to far away distances throughout the universe, as it played out in their minds. Although there were billions of stories to be shared, this group of individuals had grown rather close as kindred spirits and best friends and many more stories would be told of them, and their heroic acts in the future.

After spending the night zooming in on Andromeda, the crew slept. They didn't even have to worry about showers, makeup, or anything else, that morning, but they still enjoyed those sorts of things, every now and then. Instead of a shower that morning, however, they chose a rather large hot tub with perfect bathing suits. They wore smart clothing, and their nanosystems integrated their uniqueness into their clothing while constantly optimizing every aspect of their physical and neural networks due to their nanos. They also smelled of lilacs, roses, and any combination of flowers they felt like smelling like—whatever it happened to be that brought a smile to their faces.

Later, that morning, everyone returned to their work centers. Najem and Jasmine returned to Neptune's large moon, Triton. Vesha asked them both for her first off-world real-life tour, so to start off, Najem and Jasmine brought Vesha to James Cooper's Pathway Construction headquarters on Triton. After spending the day together, James gave Vesha her first mission since her reawakening, just above Pluto in a series of nano-forged space bubbles, hovering over the Edgeworth-Kuiper Belt. Together, they journeyed there and were in awe of the view of the Milky Way Galaxy and so much more. After some talk about life and the future, they each went off to take care of their missions and tasks.

Welcome Back

"Welcome back, Vesha," said Eliza through her neural link. *"I'm sure you know already that there is so much to do. Nonetheless, let's not be strangers for too long. And, I know you wanted to see the senate chambers, so I will see what I can coordinate so we can have a deliberation before the Senate, where I can introduce you. Perhaps you can even give a speech.*

"*Oh, wow! Your view just above Pluto is spectacular!*"

"*Oh, it is!*" said Vesha, who was linked to her friend, Najem, and as her alter-ego, Sky, floated around in her mind, hearing every word.

"*I'm so proud of you, Vesha, and Najem. When you come to visit next, there's another project I would like to talk to you about. It involves Sky, and you'll love it. Yesha will most likely work with you on that shortly after. For now, big interplanetary hug, and have fun!*"

Staring out of her giant and transparent bubble from space, Vesha looked toward the Andromeda Galaxy and began formulating ideas within her mind, to bring with her into the Virtual Universe, with the added advantage of time-dilation, the primary designs for the Intergalactic Mission Contingency...

Chapter 20: Music of the Heart

Database Moon Archive, Celestial-Sol Entry Date: 2019 January 27. Sixteen-year-old Erin Carter serves as Yesha's understudy. She introduces and summarizes the experiences of Joanne Gallant, her recruitment by Senator Eliza A. Williams, and her quests. Each memory shared is a collaboration of experiences and insights from the minds of Joanne and Eliza. Due to Eliza's neural link, these experiences are recorded within the Virtual Universe. Erin is interfaced within the Pathway Melrose Campus. Input by Erin Carter, VP, 2018-2022, President of Pathway, 2022-2029.

Joanne wrote songs of struggles and overcoming them, all of which had been playing out in her heart and mind for years. She felt to an extent a special connection between the experiences and ideas she had gone through, wrote out, and married to music, and others who had perhaps struggled in life as well. To her, she shared what she would write and sing about so people who listened would know they weren't alone. This was her calling in life, to convert music into an expression that came from within, an expression that could soothe so many hearts and minds, to include her own. She sang for those who had endured tragedy for no part of their own, and in some cases for those who were lost in what could be called the mire of life all too often. This was what drove her. It gave her purpose, and it gave her meaning.

She enjoyed raising the spirits of others through song and genuine displays or examples of compassion through her music and art. No matter what it was that she shared, however, she felt that somehow something was still missing like there was more to add to her plate, and as though there was something else, she could do. Perchance there was another layer of depth, of meaning, and of purpose to add to her craft, or perhaps her purpose, lie in a variety of pursuits she had yet to comprehend or ascertain.

Joanne had been successful in every way that seemed to matter in her industry, but she felt as though her calling in life might be shared with journeys she had yet to discover. Perhaps there was a way to tackle the core of suffering at its center. Perhaps there was clarity to all this that unless she had met enough people and understood each one deep enough, she would never be able to understand. Perhaps there was one person among billions who held the key to a vaster potential.

She knew many people suffered when with well enough effort and innovation that reason for suffering would no longer be justified except through negligence and irresponsibility on the part of those who could have done something about it, whether through influence or affluence, yet didn't. She had always felt that there must be something to be learned through every experience and every obstacle in life, but in many ways, she had also felt each of these questions begging questions of their own. As time went by, she found herself pondering on this more often.

Joanne would often take moments of solace and use them to drift away in thought, *"Although there are many wonderful people out there with untold potential, many of whom we have lost through the years, perhaps we can learn from what happened, but what were the lessons they could have possibly learned from immense tragedy and suffering, especially if they died in the process? How could true vindication of loss ever be had for those left suffering and feeling severed from something or someone who once was very alive, or loved, or taken for granted and now gone, in the wake of seemingly pointless devastation or loss? How could perpetrators of mass crimes live with any peace or anything of the sort knowing what they had done? If they did, would that rancor in one way or another be properly identified as some form of insanity? Perhaps they should be justly punished according to their crimes against others, but in the case of far too many, what could they learn if they were dead? Could they learn if they lived and were properly trained, coached, and mentored instead? What kind of justice was it if, though apparently lost with inhumanity governing their actions, potential perpetrators never had the experiences necessary to reach the clarity essential to understand the damage they had caused so they could make restitution for it? What kind of justice was it if the perpetrator hadn't learned enough to feel contrite and humbled for the misery introduced to the lives of others and consequently finally grow to feel internally sorrowful and overtly apologetic, with a new determination to live in a manner where they showed humility and lived a life of shared service to benefit all of humanity?*

"For those who had died, it wasn't fair for them, nor would it ever be; one could only hope that their next destination was much better. While many have died in efforts of heroism that inspired others to greatness, far too many seemed to be vanquished before realizing untold potential, either unnamed or unknown. Far too many have died meaningless deaths that were the result of some torturous soul, someone devoid of humanity, someone lacking the ability to put themselves in the shoes of another individual, or someone who's neural pathways bypassed the regions which emphasized empathy and restraint, where restraint was obviously needed."

Before reading her own hardback copy of Dr. Eliza A. Williams' book, *Pathway to the Stars*, many years ago, she had never ever considered, *"How suffering by the hands of others could be caused by simple physiological or neurological misfires or both, and that there were ways to mitigate this completely while enjoying the beauties of life, if only people were willing. Perhaps there was a better way of preventing these mishaps or even mending the minds of the perpetrators and the fallout of these issues as expressed through the devastation of their actions. Perhaps I can do this through music,"* she thought.

The few times she had read the posts from Internet trolls, however, she processed certain messages no matter their intent and the results of their laughter also resonated within her mind, *"You might as well be the injured prey singing to injured prey, when all who can hear won't listen, instead they'll seek you out to tear you down and feast on your misery some more. I don't truly believe that, but it can sure seem that way. The truth is we're the mighty shining a light that provides clarity to let others know they aren't alone."*

Pondering back, she thought of all the costumes she had acquired and designed with meaning oozing through every detail of every thread of every embroidery or lace, the money spent on concert displays, and the donations to charities that were traditional but rarely seemed to accomplish anything but mitigate the results of problems rather than fight the problems at their core. So many concerns and thoughts were weighing on Joanne, and she was determined to do something to change lives from the way it was to the way she felt it ought to be.

If she were to make changes through her music, Joanne knew she needed to approach each lyric with care, love, and passion seeding the listening mind and cultivating it toward progress with the advancement of civilization. She wasn't predator or prey singing to prey, she was a human being who understood both the good and evil in humanity, and she sought to draw the good out from anyone, no matter how they chose to identify themselves. With that knowledge, she had no doubt where she needed to begin. Yet, there were many other questions that remained. While using her influence as a popular musical icon she could teach, advance what she knew, and entertain the masses providing the sense of peace and calm that music from the heart, the soul, and the mind provided, she also knew there was much more she could learn.

To take a break from her routine, Joanne had taken the daily train from New York City to Boston. Even though she was doing online courses at Harvard, in Cambridge, she would still visit there anyway from time to time. Whenever she could, she would find a seat next to a window, so she could enjoy the scenery along the way. She noticed how Connecticut, buried in snow, was just as beautiful this and pretty much any time of the year.

Once she arrived in the bustling city of Boston, she hopped onto the metro bus to Cambridge where there were a series of stops along the way before crossing the bridge and seeing the close-up magnitude of the incredible sixteen-square-block area that provided sanctuary to the restaurant, the T.O. Since 2010, the T.O. had grown from a small organic café and eatery just north of Harvard, to a two-by-eight-block area of Cambridge.

People from all over the world had visited the restaurant. The mass transit systems had developed a regular route with eight stops around the campus. While visiting there was so much to enjoy, but the main attraction people enjoyed was the food. Nonetheless, there were other organic and small business markets as well as a high-class ambiance.

The truth was Eliza had purchased the T.O. not long after meeting Amber Blythe there in 2010. Eight months later, the T.O. had grown to include the T.O. Chef University, which after being built and opened was the largest chef, culinary, bakery, and confectionary educational center in the world. Along with the university, the same edifice chain contained several blocks and stories of nutrient-dense germination and growth gardens, food laboratories, and kitchens, all ensuring that every ingredient was grown and acquired there. There were also guided tours, and plenty of other public spaces that were a marvel to behold, and there were non-public spaces that were accessible only to those who had been read-in to Pathway—more spaces were underground.

No matter how busy Eliza was, she and Yesha had found time to meet to visit the ballets, the symposiums, the acts, and all the musical, dancing and artistic luster of Broadway. As a matter of fact, the T.O. had a large variety of concert halls, stadiums and such per Eliza's design within Cambridge, MA, itself—a long time heritage of the arts, holidays, and sciences. Part of what drew Joanne to the T.O. in the first place was the fact that she had performed in concert there a few times and even stayed the night at the lush hotels. She enjoyed reading by faux fires the words of Henry Wadsworth Longfellow, James Russell Lowell, and Oliver Wendell Holmes, all three of whom were of Cambridge, MA, or who had passed away there, following years of literary genius, and whose histories were rich within the hallways of the T.O. Joanne had soaked in every bit of the T.O. every time she went there, in a unique way.

Early in 2011, eight months after Eliza had purchased the small restaurant, it remained there and functioning in its original form, but some things nearby had changed. From the day she purchased the T.O., and when everything in and on the two-by-eight or sixteen-square-block area behind it was covered and finally revealed, those who witnessed the transformation only saw a humongous grey tarp covering the entire area up to about twenty-nine stories high behind it.

When the tarp was finally removed, a magnificent structure twenty-eight stories above the ground on the east end, sloping downward to twenty-two stories above ground on the west end abutted to the T.O., was revealed in its full splendor. It towered high and magnificently in every way. Anyone who had misgivings in any way was now filled with joy. If one were to peer from a helicopter down toward the infrastructure, they would see what looked like four giant ellipses or rings that were connected in a row, with the ring on the east end slightly of greater diameter than the ring on the west end, which was connected now to the T.O., and the two rings in between tapered to blend, in structural diameter. The roads for each block passed unblocked underneath, and Eliza had designed it such that people could see a more historical perspective of the settings they were in as they drove down each street, as if it were as clear as day and alive.

In the center of each ring, within a two-by-two block area, and almost at roof level, were two mini forests and two mini jungles. Below these mini forests and jungles for a couple of floors were the root structures, and then below them were several concert halls and coliseums. Below those and the vast laboratories of vegetation were many centers of various sorts. At the top of the structure, looking from the side or an angle one could see an elaborate in-door ski slope system that could be manipulated for various styles of ski competitions, with restaurants, bars, cafés, and seating on the outer part of each ring.

Looking down one could see, on the inner side of each ring, a hyperloop system that could prep the skis and skiers for another run, if desired, and warm the skier up as it returned them back to the twenty-eight-story ring to either go again, leave via a changing room, or to return to their private hotel room if they were going to stay the night. The material of the building from the outside appeared as if it were a radiant white edifice with artistically formed, glowing, and crystalline windows that for some untold reason didn't drown out the nighttime sky for viewing the stars above but lit up the roads and pathways down below.

Within the large areas inside each ring and on the first floor and then scattered throughout each level were other "Mom and Pop" stores, educational centers, hotel rooms, and much more. Near the entrance where the west ring met the original T.O. was the 'Broke Coffee House, managed, run, and operated by Bobby Gahan, who was reverenced by the story of the peaceful Pembroke tribe. The Pembroke tribe was a tribe of people who lived in the Americas prior to the expansion of the modern western nations, or as is understood by many, an American Indian Tribe. They had lived in the Americas, where Pembroke, North Carolina now resides, long before settlers from Europe had arrived. This was homage out of respect to them. The main colors used as accents throughout the coffee shop and on each of the coffee cups were a bright yellow background with black writing. Other colors were woven within and throughout the interior decorating and landscaping to complement the network of aspects that helped create the peaceful ambiance that it was. In his coffee house, he had a peculiar mixture of a soothing variety of music with a focus on his favorite band, Depeche Mode, and a smooth mixture of the musical genres of vocal and progressive trance, new age, some classics, some new wave, and some pop all playing with a Native American vibe, music, and chorus, weaved in and infused throughout ever-so-well, and adjusted for clarity.

Bobby had already been fully read-in to Pathway. Therefore, unless an individual who had been read-in knew and saw him, they would assume he was like any other twenty-two-year-old, chilling and keeping it simple. In truth, in 2019, he was fifty-four, loved serving a great cup of Jo, and in part, he felt as though this was one of his true callings in life. The fact that Depeche Mode was his favorite band had very little to do with the fact that their lead singer shared the same last name, but that certainly didn't hurt any. Mostly, it was the multi-layered artistry melding the lyrics and music together, and the depth he interpreted from it all that moved him.

He had chosen the 'Broke Coffee House logo after growing up with a friend from the Pembroke Tribe and received approval from the tribe to use it. The logo consisted of a bright yellow coffee cup, with a white and brown feather adorned to it near the handle, in such a way as to almost pass as a straw, and on the pictured coffee cup was inscribed, 'Broke Coffee House. On the wall behind the ordering counter, Bobby had also written and designed an inscription below the logo, "I brew coffee to put a spring in the step of any willing passer-by, to serve the best, to give you something that brings clarity to the mind and health to the veins."

In full, Bobby was also a coffee-neuro-bio-nutrition expert from Pathway, so he could serve the best coffee to the public as well as to those who had been fully optimized. He interestingly had an ultra-enhanced sense of smell and expertly derived what coffee would grace an individual's palate based on everyone who approached the ordering counter, science-wise, he could derive. He was a healthy-minded and clean-cut individual who maintained a pleasant charm steeped in professionalism and inspiration. It was often reported in newspapers and journals, "If you get a cup of Jo from the 'Broke Coffee House, you'll find yourself peppy and clear of mind right up until you lie your head down to rest on that pillow again, and then you will rest well." His talents were unique, and anyone could attest to the fact that those who ordered coffee at his establishment lived a low stress yet very innovative and successful life. He'd even set up an education program in the Virtual Universe to train prospective employees to do just the same.

Joanne had discovered this establishment no later than two days after it had opened early on in 2011, and now it was eight years and many visits later that she arrived at the bus stop just outside ring one. Stepping down from the bus, she enjoyed the open-air of the quarter-block distance between the stop and the entrance and savored the landscaping, the artistry, and the sculptures that seemed to capture frozen moments of life in all of its beauty. She then listlessly walked to the entrance right between the T.O. and the 'Broke Coffee House, smelling the scent of warm beverages in the air, as the aroma piped out of the well-placed vents, and made her way through the internal atrium doors to get some coffee first. Everything she'd heard about 'Broke was true or better. Bobby happened to be at the counter, and he was always a charm to talk to as he was brewing the coffee.

After drinking her cup of Jo, she had never felt so alive in her life. She exchanged pleasant dialog with Bobby, thanked him, bid him farewell, and took a tour of the T.O. through the labs, the forests, the jungles, shops, sites, universities, and more. *"What a place this is,"* she thought to herself. *"It seems that I see something new every time, and yet it has been here all along."* At one point she had taken an elevator to the twenty-eighth floor to look at the crystal glass dome above. She then looked through it and was impressed yet again at the view from some of the restaurants near the ski slopes and the clarity of the sky above, as if one could see through the crystalline windows and on through to the stars in the firmament with intriguing clarity, despite the luminescence of the Sun during broad daylight.

After her tour and repast, she made her way back to the original T.O., or the main restaurant entrance to place her order, pay for her meal, take a seat, and wait for each step of eating at its finest to make its way to her table. While she stood in line, she happened to recognize Senator Eliza Williams, and as much respect for her as she had, she didn't want to inconvenience her with small talk, so she said nothing and let her thoughts float in the air.

"...Nice to meet you. You must be Joanne?" asked Eliza.

"Yes," Joanne said, a little startled yet impressed. *"She knows who I am. I am a fan of her legislation and her political party. I remember calling in with a suggestion long ago and they implemented it, using my first name as requested to protect my anonymity, and while I'd rather not get involved or affiliated with any political party, since I have fans on every side of the political aisle and I don't want to alienate them, what Eliza says, does, and has done is impressive. I still have her book, Pathway to the Stars, somewhere. I wonder where I left it."* All kinds of thoughts seemed to race through Joanne's mind during the moment it took her to answer. "You're Senator Williams? ...Fancy, seeing you here. What brings you home from Capitol Hill?"

"That's a wonderful question," replied Eliza. "I suppose a break from the bureaucrats and something in the environment there that seems to be in plenty supply was overdue. Oh, and feel free to call me Eliza? What brings you from New York all the way to Cambridge?"

"Oh... the T.O.; it's the only restaurant of its kind that is as big, classy, and renown as it is, and it still has an impressive and spectacular array of things to do, sites to see, and a guiltlessly tasty delight of food to capture it all. It can certainly be a full day filled with beautiful thoughts and the creation of lovely memories, and all of that with a tasty reward at the end. This is my favorite place to visit every chance I get, and one of the most sophisticated, organic, artistic, clean, and beautiful places I've ever seen, and I've toured worldwide! What I enjoy the most is that ever since I started coming here in 2011, I haven't been charged a dime!

"I pay with my debit card, yet when I justify my bank statement it shows zero dollars removed from my account from the T.O. Did I mention that eating savory food here is a delight in so many ways? The clean meats are of the finest cuts and quality, with no poor animals or slaughterhouse in the mix! Veggies, fruits, shakes, entrées, desserts, drinks, appetizers, tours through every step of growth and preparation, and, oh, it's all so innocently delicious and lovely, not to mention the beautiful music and the ambiance throughout. When I leave, I am satisfied, inspired, and revitalized."

"I love this place too, and for the same reasons." Eliza smiled, appeared to glow, at least to Joanne, and the blue sparkles in Eliza's eyes twinkled and glistened and were hard not to notice, as she continued, "Are you here with anyone? Or would you like to sit and chat?"

"I enjoyed the railroad ride here to clear my mind, but she might have some of the answers I'm looking for, plus I could sew extra wisdom into my musical career and portfolio," She thought. "Sure. You know what? I'd be honored," Joanne said.

After ordering their meals and "paying," they picked a table for two. Every table in the restaurant came with an individually climate-controlled and plush arrangement of seating, replete with odor filtration. Within all of the seats were back, neck, arm, and leg massage options, along with a personal ambiance and music filter display that provided other service options down to the largest selection of some of the most exquisite of lavish drinks in existence, all delivered directly to each individual, as patrons sat in their chairs and at their tables. There was even a button for Lyft and Uber drivers to pick people up if they weren't staying the night in the T.O. Hotel.

Joanne and Eliza sat down chatting for hours without considering the time. Luckily, the T.O. had plenty of seating and was open around the clock, and since both of them were well-known patrons, only the best and most savory of every dish was brought out. Only the best dishes were ever brought out since there was no favoritism. Time was unlimited. It was said that the T.O. had the best chefs in the world, serving desired and imaginable dishes and everyone who went there went away feeling as though they, alone, were their favorite customer. Along with high-quality service and training programs, the T.O. had several floors of seating throughout the mega-complex filled with a variety of entertainment options and the works.

"I must say, you are every bit as elegant and charming as you seem on television and as I have read about. I'm sure you hear that all of the time," inquired Joanne, as she sat with Eliza and waited for their appetizer.

"I don't think anyone could be informed too much or too often through genuine and gentle words the vantage points of one wonderful human being toward another," Eliza responded, and then continued. "Every time I hear them, it adds a little extra lightness to my steps.

"I appreciate those who are positive, kind, and charming too. We rarely find ourselves desiring to overcome sinister challenges without having been through some difficulties in life ourselves. Seeing the suffering rampant throughout the world can be quite heavy, so a positive word or two is always welcomed. Thank you, Joanne. Life is challenging enough, with so much to do these days to resolve the issues while trying to foster the harmony that negligence will never bring about, there is plenty of reason to hold on to the things that are beautiful and amazing."

Eliza breathed in and out, and then continued, "You have quite a voice, Joanne; I can feel the depth and sense the meaning in what you share, and you too are a beautiful woman."

"Thank you," said Joanne, it never hurt to hear those words, and much less from someone as amazing and wonderful as Eliza.

Joanne felt a kindred spirit about her new friend as they chatted back and forth, and she wished she had met her years ago. As they chatted, their appetizer, then their entrée, and then the rest of their meal arrived, and they continued on while enjoying each part of the meal.

Eliza and Joanne seemed to hit things off and enjoyed sharing a multitude of experiences with each other. Before it was time to leave, Eliza asked Joanne if she would like to meet with herself and her friend, Yesha at Pathway, today or sometime soon, and maybe take a tour there. Joanne didn't need too much prodding to be on-board. The day had been beautifully exquisite, and the extra time spent with Eliza was time spent with a wonderful and new friend she could trust.

Delicate Memories

Once Joanne arrived with Eliza to Pathway's Melrose Campus through a series of what looked like white donut-shaped portals, Yesha met with her and they went through the initial Pathway member training with a variety of options given to proceed further. Seeing, visiting, and experiencing all the T.O. had to offer was always amazing, yet likewise so was the Pathway Melrose Campus. Joanne saw a relation between the two grow increasingly as the night continued. She was impressed with every detail. After initial training and a feedback session with delegates, it was time for the big decision, the same decision anyone else had to make who had been given the tour through the Melrose Campus.

"Do I become fully read-in or do I walk away?" Joanne thought to herself. Dazzled by both Yesha and Eliza, she thought, *"Why not? There comes a time in life where we have to dare ourselves to do something odd, embrace it, enjoy it, and see what comes of it,"* and then she agreed to be read-in and to go on the Virtual Universe journey.

"Link, 1, 2, 3, 5 minutes, 20 years," coached Yesha.

Joanne followed her every step as many had done before her, and as she finished speaking those words, she instantaneously felt every nerve, every synapse, and every cell in her body feel as though it were twisting and contorting, and then like that, a certain sense of euphoria set in. Looking around, Joanne felt invigorated and the sweet sense of youth she could recall feeling several years before resurfaced. She then saw a statue of an angel before her, and it was looking down toward the pond, where a little waterfall emanating from its hands provided aerated water for the coy fish and frogs. This was without question in Joanne's mind, a beautiful and peaceful place. As she turned around and captured her surroundings, she began to understand so much more than she ever thought possible. She knew somehow that she was at Eliza's estate, and then she saw both Eliza and Yesha. Both of these ladies were beautiful and magnificent in real life, and here they were all the more magnificent; it was as if they came from a dream or from heaven itself.

Realizing that they were neurologically connected, she began to understand every bit of their story, or at least every bit of the stories they felt she was prepared to understand, and then she shared some of her stories with them. As was the nature of the Virtual Universe, whenever they talked, it was mind-to-mind. Thus, they conversed for a while about each other's experiences and ideas. At one point, something became very clear to Joanne, and she shared something with Eliza and Yesha that would have typically resided in the compartmentalized area of her mind.

Joanne, Eliza, and Yesha chatted and shared various experiences of their life's stories, and Joanne was particularly impressed with both of their abilities to listen. She shared with Eliza and Yesha, how, before more than a decade of musical experience working from the grassroots to international stardom, she had been like so many US and worldwide citizens. She had attended public school, worked hard for excellent academic achievement, and was raised with a kind older brother by a loving mother and father. She had received A's through high school and had been inspired by someone she had deemed a darling of a role-model.

Her brother, Thomas, was just a year-and-a-half older, was two years ahead of her in school, had good grades, was a charming individual with an equally charming persona, and was in his senior year while she was a sophomore in high school. She looked up to him, his artsy charm, his kind, gentle, and sweet demeanor with angelic ways of being there for anyone who seemed alone or down and out.

Joanne's brother, Thomas, was a boy who would never hurt a soul, and he was always there smiling, laughing with people rather than at them. Just as any young individual would, he had crushes on people in his school, but culled his urges and was very respectful to others no matter what might come along in life. Struggle as he may, he seemed to control his personal affection toward the young men he went to school with, ever since he had been in kindergarten. Tragedy fell when it was discovered that he was in love with one of his peers, the high school quarterback. He had always talked about him over the dinner table at home with harmony in every wake, but at school, he had kept it private. Things were a bit more socially conservative where she and her brother were growing up and it seemed that respect for the individual and who they loved was not given to anyone outside the norm of 'boy meets girl.' More so, it appeared as though it was deemed offensive to accept people for who they were, especially if they were "different."

One day over spring break he had got it into his head that he would come clean and write a letter to this young man, one of his peers, to let the torture of not sharing his love for him burden him any longer. Of course, he was cool about it, he didn't intend to push his will on anyone, and had confided in his parents and younger sister as to what to do, yet in the end he simply wanted to let this young man, who he'd been attending school with since kindergarten, know how down-to-earth he seemed, how much he appreciated how he stood up against others' bullies, and how much he inspired him through the years. He also wanted to be honest and let him know how much he loved him in a romantic way, so he wrote a letter and on the first day back from spring break, he slipped it into his locker in the locker room. Two days later while on his way home from school, it was understood that a group of hooded schoolmates wearing masks mercilessly ended his life. When news of this reached others, it was as if time stood still.

Joanne was shocked. The whole town was shocked. Her parents were torn apart. Thomas had a full-ride scholarship to his favorite school, he had always been kind to all, and no one knew anything other than the fact that he had been an artistic, charismatic, and even sentimental young man. He wasn't socially awkward in the least; he was clean-cut, kind, and even handsome. He didn't seem to have any enemies whatsoever and there didn't seem to be anyone Joanne knew who would dare do something that horrible to someone else, much less her sweet, gentle brother.

The Sheriff and his investigation teams were hot on the trail of those who had engaged in the murderous act, but when the letter he wrote to the quarterback was discovered, the investigation all of a sudden went cold and the search ceased. The story seemed as though it was buried, but looking back, it had grown cold. It was a quiet and conservative area of town after all, and certain realities were unfortunately looked at as a sin and condemned, they seemed to believe, "If something bad happened to a sinner, well, that was God's will." It was a place where suddenly, people forgot in a large way to use that inner core of kindness, respect, dignity, and compassion.

To Joanne, the sense of empathy and compassion seemed to dissipate to nothing when it was discovered that perhaps he was "different," or a sinner, and not for anything else than how he had identified himself, a struggle he'd coped with well, ever since he could remember. Everyone who was close to him or the family and many of those he had rescued from loneliness, including the quarterback he'd had a crush on, attended his funeral; many also approached her and told her how much he did for them and how much they missed him. They also noted that they never knew he was gay but stated to Joanne and her parents that they had hoped this tragedy might raise awareness toward inclusion and compassion.

However, the parents of the other children in her brother's class grew distant, blamed his misfortune on the results of his "personal choices" and were almost foreboding, as if in quiet rebuke and condemnation. Their eyes looked upon her and her parents as if to say something disdainful and unrepeatable. As such, the town in large part seemed to care less about the murder and saw it more as an incident to learn from, to forget about, and to bury. To the town, the case was closed. Still, no matter what Joanne knew there had to be closure. Vindication and justice were crying out, and there had to have been at least three people involved, ganging up on her brother, so, she took up sleuthing and followed all of the stories and leads that had developed.

Everyone told her to leave the case alone, and after a year of searching and many dead-ends, her parents finally convinced her that someday, those who had done this would be filled with anguish and find no recourse for what they had done. They told her that it was ours to forgive; hopefully, justice would prevail in the end, and no one else would live in similar danger. For now, it was a time of healing, understanding, cooling down our frustrations, and even integrating with the suspected perpetrators. At a minimum, one could treat them as friends, until as they matured, in time, they could grow a solid sense of remorse for their actions. When that happened, perhaps there would be justice as they led more noble lives. It was far from fair, but she and her parents chose to be strong; they took her brother's kindness and made it part of them.

Joanne, from that point on, immersed herself in her studies more than before and began to find increased comfort in music. As time went by, she turned to a life of playing the piano, writing lyrics of depth, and singing to comfort her spirits, sometimes her fashion tastes were more Goth-like, and at other times it was more schoolgirl-like or just jeans and a T-shirt. Joanne played by her own rules, and being a social pariah suited her just fine.

Joanne loved her brother dearly and could never imagine who the murderer could have been or why they did what they did. But she let that pain and her defiance of it guide her in her passions and compassion.

Losing herself in her art and music, everything else began to flow—the major chords, the minor chords, the dissonance, the residual harmonies, the beauty of the heaven-like electronic music pads, the arpeggios, their highs and lows, the gentle rhythms, the throbbing bass at all the right times, and the resonance. Joanne's first song was written and released as a single just before she graduated from high school. Now, many years later, at the age of twenty-nine, here she was, having sat with Eliza on a chance meeting, and currently going on amazing and enlightening journeys in the Virtual Universe with Eliza and Yesha—each of them knowing in full who each other was, both the light and dark sides they were willing to share and learn from, because their minds were linked, and they each felt an instant, unforgettable, savory, sweet tasting and flowing connection with each other.

Prior to meeting Eliza and Yesha, Joanne had already written four albums. Each album was a major hit. Yesha was the President of Pathway and Eliza was a US Senator. Now that they had shared their many layers of wisdom, there was an abundance and increase of clarity that filled her mind. Joanne learned a lot and felt that she could do so much more than she had in her past, despite all of her efforts.

She explained to Eliza and Yesha how she had developed an interesting professional cycle that worked for her in her own way. First, she would write for a year, then she would go on tour the following year, and finally, in the third year, she would focus on higher education and family. Not too long before meeting Eliza, she had begun her Ph.D. at Harvard, but she did so online and in three areas of study, quantum computing, music, and psychology to be specific—it worked well with her vibe of sophisticated music. Now, neuroscience seemed to beckon her attention as well.

She fluctuated between that interest while communicating love and loss to the masses, in the hopes of imbuing more kindness, understanding, and compassion into society as a whole. While she knew her songs were a hit in the US and throughout the world, Eliza and Yesha were able to see that Joanne wanted to write something even more profound, more substantive, and more meaningful in terms of actual and possible change than any of her previous four albums, as appreciated as they were. They could see that Joanne had never been in it for the money, that merely came because she had touched the hearts of many, and they reciprocated her efforts through monetary means—through buying her albums, buying fan shirts, posters, etc., and most of all, by purchasing tickets to her concerts. For Joanne, all of this was merely a means of getting around from place to place, meeting the people, and donating to charities. While she lived comfortably, she was much more into music so she could share a beautiful message with the masses and reaching out in the spirit of love, kindness, and compassion.

"I've listened to your music over the last twelve years as it's played on the radio, and I knew there was something deep to what you were singing. I could feel the loss you had felt. What you do is amazing, Joanne." Yesha communicated with her mind-to-mind, and Joanne could feel the loss of Yesha's and Eliza's dear friends, Charles and Eugene, from so many years ago, during 9/11. She could also feel Eliza's rage which had turned into the fire of productivity and resolve.

Eliza then followed Yesha in shared thought, *"Each of us has been through loss, suffering, and many have been through much worse. Here we can have a collective experience, mind-to-mind, but we also have another shared experience where we've lost such wonderful people in our lives due to hate and the unfortunate influence of a toxic and unhealthy environment. Uncontrolled chaos, Joanne, will show itself in the worst of ways. Therefore, you'll hear me from time-to-time talk about controlled chaos, where we can direct our energies toward constructive, helpful, and healing behavior,* intentions, projects, and actions. I know you have an amazing mind; I see you, your beautiful self in every way, and I have every bit of confidence that you have so much potential still begging to surface. There are a lot of ideas I've shared with Yesha, James, and everyone in Pathway who has been fully read-in, and while we have done so much and have the ability to help humanity to go so much further than before, every single person in the world who ever was, is, or ever will be, will have potential to improve systems, identify challenges to overcome, and raise the quality of life. For you, your talent in music and entertainment moves the mind to ponder in a healthy way. You have untold potential, as do the rest of us, and sadly so did many who we have lost."

They continued their discussion for hours as Eliza and Yesha took Joanne on their own and first journey through to the core of the Earth, the Moon, and every spheroid in the Solar System. They took her to see all the shields, the tech cities, and spaceports, the terraforming of every moon in the Solar System with varying degrees of gravity for a variety of reasons, up to and including thrills and entertainment. They talked for a while, and Eliza finally revealed to Joanne by opening her mind up more fully to her and allowing her to see that it was she who had purchased the T.O. and had built the campus. To which, Joanne responded.

"Wow, Eliza, I never knew it was you who purchased that beautiful restaurant and the sixteen square blocks of immaculate infrastructure behind it. How did you manage to keep that under wraps?"

Eliza answered, "To put it into concise words, it was difficult, but there are a lot of things that we have done, but we didn't reveal them to the public because we did not want to draw too much attention to ourselves. We wanted to help people and not make others suffer from the loss of their jobs, or turn the economy upside down, or dismantle industries. We weren't ready yet for full-blown publicity. We have tried in every step of our journey in Pathway to prepare society in increments before releasing something new. In part, this is because, as I have suggested, we do not want to reduce the quality of life of anyone by tearing down the very structures that provide them the means for living, for learning, and for giving back through innovation and talent. We hadn't released too much at once, because we wanted to make sure that with every breakthrough, we had safety and security mechanisms in place as well as ways to reverse any potential catastrophic backfires."

Joanne then responded, "Thank you for everything you do and have done. It's amazing; every person who goes to the T.O. has their account paid in full, by you, I've seen people gather their life's savings to go there. Many have gone there because they heard it was so beautiful, so amazing, and so breath-taking, and with life so dull and tedious this was their last-ditch effort at finding a reason to hold on, their last big and glorious opportunity and attempt to enjoy life before they slept amongst the flowers and the roots of the trees forever. Instead, they were reignited, reawakened, found love in life again, and they returned home to find that their savings had not been squandered away. Instead, they found they could reinvest the resultant growth of money into chasing a beautiful dream of hope, of ingenuity, of kindness, and of love. In many cases they've confided in me as they shared their stories, without saying anything to anyone else, a few of my fans privately texted me to tell me they loved the T.O. too, and that their parents had gone there to find that their retirement had somehow multiplied. The tech cities, the shields around Earth, all the spheroids within our Solar System, you have both done so much. There's even a small planet orbiting around the Sun gathering all of the heavy material essentially prolonging the life of our star by trillions of years or longer based on the planned mining and maintenance, both of which will, in turn, provide the unlimited and self-sustaining resources necessary to improve the quality of *life. You have done so much for so many people, Eliza and Yesha, and yet so many have no idea.*" Joanne was filled with emotion and with a tear falling down her cheek, she felt like hugging Eliza and Yesha as a form of gratitude and approval, and as she did, Eliza and Yesha opened their arms and they shared in an embrace. What a beautiful moment that lasted for as long as was possible, it was like a warm blanket wrapped around someone on a cold winter's night.

Following the embrace, Yesha came clean, "*Please know, Joanne, that Eliza deserves the credit. She was the visionary, she was the great mind, perhaps the greatest mind behind all of this. I merely provided moral support, weighed in whenever she asked, and together we've built all you've seen. But, please remember, the greatest gratitude goes to Eliza.*"

Joanne looked at Eliza, who glowed, blushed, and smiled with a tear in her eye, and responded. "*Yesha, I could not have done any of this without you or anyone we know. Thank you, too.*"

Joanne felt that pure bond of genuine and innocent love between the two as she finished her journey through Pathway's history and combed the histories of each person in Pathway. She also met James, Amber, Erin, Vesha, Najem, and Jasmine. They welcomed her too with open arms and an inspiring sense of connection that was unique and special. Once she had gone through some of the most mind-expanding journeys shared by each one of the more than two-billion people who were fully read-in to Pathway, she finished completing several PhDs, and then when she was ready, Joanne, Eliza, and Yesha returned to the real world. When Joanne came to, she felt more alive and invigorated than she had ever felt before. Twenty years was a long time, even in the Virtual Universe. Yet, in truth, she had only been in there for five minutes.

Joanne also noticed a subtle physical change as she peered down at her hands. Looking into a nearby mirror at Eliza's and Yesha's request she appreciated every aspect of how her mind translated its creativity showing it within her appearance. The movie and mural-like artwork resembling a mandala-like kaleidoscope of thought and feelings covering her left side were spectacular. Eliza and Yesha showed her how to compartmentalize her mind to store a series of wardrobes that would complement her appearance in every way and adjust based on each unique situation she might run into. "*This could come in handy on-stage!*" she thought. Furthermore, she could now connect with over two-billion people, and the numbers continued to grow, and she could share experiences with them at any given time using her neural identification, as trained in the Virtual Universe. Anyone who had ever been there before, who had shared an experience, who had become an expert in anything of any sort, and who had unique qualities, was always available when needed simply by using her neural link.

After having gone on her jaunt from New York to Massachusetts and meeting with Eliza, she found herself visiting more often and returning home with a crystal-clear sense of clarity of what to do and the roles she would play in the advancement of civilization. She knew there were many other things she could do to add to what she was already doing, one step at a time. Eliza was truly that one-in-a-billion of people who she had hoped to meet, and with clearness, she became a member of Pathway.

James had visited her in the Virtual Universe and shown her what he too had done to help Eliza and Yesha. Recommending what to do was a gift of his, a sense of clairvoyance he'd gained after entering the Virtual Universe himself. Thus, he showed her where she could begin as a member of Pathway, based on her talents. He was the perfect gentleman in every way, his insight was spot on, and she was impressed with his ability to see into her mind and give her that helpful nudge in the right direction. Not to mention, he was strikingly handsome.

Joanne wanted to lead the way to improvement using her talents and skills to help others since it was evidenced daily through the conditions throughout the world that a lot could still be done. She wanted to help Eliza on her mission to nurture civilization so that it could go further than before. Even in her own country, the US, she had noticed how there were many amazing individuals who did wonderful things and were wonderful to others regularly. Yet, even still, most of humanity, including many within this place of freedom and of bravery, as well as the environment influenced by toxicity throughout the world was growing increasingly devoid of politeness, kindness, and creativity toward quality of life, good sportsmanship, compassion, ingenuity, and humanity.

Joanne had noticed for quite some time how many charities outside of Pathway seemed to easily lose their funds with little to show for it, other than the sad truth that they had maintained expensive litigation teams that were increasingly necessary to win battles in court. They spent a lot of their funding to fight those who would wish to take them down. In the end, many of these well-intended charities were left with very little to try to positively carry out that which was helpful in purpose and their primary intent in the first place. They continued their missions with what little there was left to do so.

Most businesses and industries outside of Pathway seemed, to those who were astute enough, to operate in a very backward manner. Economists seemed to sing their bravados of large words, overly complicated explanations of every system, and ridicule all who wished to raise the quality of life for all, rather than for the few. They seemed guided by a myopic sense of reality, rather than contemplating a grander view of the Universe, and how it could be so much more bountiful for all. Many people fell prey to their tactics and pursuits. Joanne began to see an increasing theme that centered on greed—using automated systems to replace people, robots to replace common sense, and artificial constructs to avoid considering the psychological health of those flailing in life from redundant toxicity. It frustrated her that all of this was a common choice over increasing human ingenuity by training and keeping people employed.

"If the oligarchs truly cared, they would use these advancements to lighten the burden of humanity found in altogether too many workplace hours and in-turn decrease their stress. If well-being was the foundation of these improvements, these so-called titans could afford their employees more time with family and exploration of their world or the Universe itself. Things could be different and better. Unfortunately, for many, things are worse. For all that Eliza and her friends have done, it seems the influence of brutality, greed, and power is growing. The irony in it all, is that if they simply applied what Eliza had taught, those in power would be loved. Life could be beautiful! The poisonousness of ill-will in society isn't right, nor will it ever be."

It was interesting to Joanne how clearly Eliza had understood so much when it came to all that could be done to bring substance to the missions of businesses. *"For example, companies that wish to provide a higher quality of life or charities intent on doing all that they can to promote an increase in joy in life—can accomplish this with finely-tuned efficiency through the often neglected tools of science, effort, and genuine consideration for others, as well as through proper mentorship, training, coaching, and their resultant innovation. A company, instead of replacing their workers with robots, could give their workers an opportunity for a share of the profits of these automated systems, by maintaining them and overseeing quality control. This would also provide more time for the workers to spend with their families and children. They could then explore their world."*

Joanne certainly loved more than music. Her love of nature, for example, was no stranger to the masses. As appreciative of all that nature had provided that she was, she also realized that the minds of humanity had evolved to the point to which we could evolve ourselves by increasing nurture over brutality. *"We no longer need to wait painfully for mixed results. Instead, we can labor diligently for desired results. There are very few cases where nurture has wrought negative results, in contrast to the idea of "nature" and its brutality. If a person could show affection to their children, mentor them to identify and build upon skills that would bring them joy and happiness, coach them, love them, and be there for them, what kind of innovation would we have tomorrow or in following generations?"* A nurturing kind of environment, to Joanne, seemed to be a healthy one, and in every way helpful to the advancement of civilization, one that was robust and with a legacy worthy of sharing throughout the Cosmos.

When she visited the Pathway Melrose Campus, she had been introduced to some of Eliza's sentient creatures, and while they couldn't speak like we do, they were linked neurologically, and as such, they had the ability to communicate as they would usually, but their intent, the meaning of their communication. What they were in essence trying to say, was clearly translated within a neurologically-linked mind. Eliza, Yesha, and their crews had been able to put communications together bit by bit, every word, every click, clack, gobble, chirp, and every sound into a very large database. They identified so many aspects of each species, its sounds, or tones, or frequencies and translated them into every known human language, resulting in automatic translation within the hearing region of the brain that could take place instantaneously. Read-in Pathway citizens could understand whatever they focused on or desired to listen to.

Over time, in the Virtual Universe, Eliza, Yesha, and a large team of linguists helped to create language translation algorithms for each of the creatures they had nurtured into sentience, allowing neural links and communication between human and creature as well as between creature and human. The various other creatures throughout the Solar System were linked to the Twelve Database Moons and the very large mainframes throughout the twenty-thousand tech cities. In the most intriguing of ways, this helped Joanne's ideas for music, video, and lyrics to flourish.

Music and Prose

Joanne, thus inspired, began to develop music similar to vocal trance with a space ambient twist, along with lyrics and videos featuring people in general with stories of them and of the many creatures throughout the world doing things never thought imaginable. One video showed a synchronized swimming team with a group of synchronized flying flamingos flying above them in concert to what the swimmers were doing. She also featured many creatures and humanity itself struggling and suffering in unhealthy environments, yet each time in the spirit of true concern, she would then show how the positive examples of wonderful people and animals together provided a turn-around of care in their lives—no longer struggling from the hands of inhumanity or toxic environments, and much more, they were now productive and involved in one way or another, in any way, to raise the quality of life overall. She was careful, as always, to ensure she didn't do or show what she could not plausibly explain to her fans who hadn't been read-in to Pathway. The typical explanation when asked had been, "A lot of training. It required a lot of training."

Now, with fullness of clarity, she knew there was being done behind the scenes to mitigate so many unfortunate issues, and she was ever so grateful. She also realized that nature had done so much already to bring humanity to where it was today, so it in-turn deserved some attention. Conversely, there was much more we could still do through science and healthy behavior. Joanne knew that we could create a place where preservation of life, an increase to life's longevity, the expansion of life's quality, and the restructuring of a winning and cohesive purpose for each member of the ecosystem could become evolved to a more interdependent state. It could become second nature without the need for predation or desiccation, and it was humanity's gift to realize this ideal and our responsibility to bare. Now and in the future, this responsibility could be shared.

Eliza's long-term plan would essentially afford the Earth the ability to heal from the wounds caused by unwittingly gutting its natural biome. Eliza had begun the process of transitioning humanity to once arid, unlivable, and desolate locations because they found a way to provide everyone with all of the necessary details for education, resources, survival, enjoyment in life, and provisions for further advancements. The forests, the jungles, the ice caps, the weather patterns and seismic activity would eventually be able to run their course and bring a lush biome back to Earth over time. Those who chose to live in a completely natural, tribal, and even Darwinist manner for healing would be allowed to live in these jungles, forests, and places of bounty allowing nature to guide their way and their evolution, while the rest of humanity would eventually span the Solar System, travel the stars and explore the Universe, and do so in safety after having evolved us.

The Lyrics

After meeting with Eliza and her friends,
Joanne went home and began to write:

~ Embracing Love and Life ~

Please love the life that we have been given
Seek to embrace it, its beauty while livin'
Please don't cause empathy to be such a crime
Walking another path won't make you blind
Unless you're not watching or looking ahead
Then you may stumble or find something to dread

Feel compassion, love, and inner strength
Have love unfeigned, no matter the length
If you live with love, you'll embrace the skies
You'll enjoy the gardens, and you'll hug the wise

Use the wisdom of life
Let's broaden our view
With uniqueness about us
Our journey is new
Our minds are wired, in so many ways
With beauties untold, worthy of praise

Feel compassion, love, and inner strength
Have love unfeigned, no matter the length
If you live with love, you'll embrace the skies
You'll enjoy the gardens, and you'll hug the wise

Others' paths increase our wisdom any time

To embrace another, is that such a crime?
Our endurance compounds with energy and strength
Innovations for health and the mind in every wavelength
Cures for disease, mending the breeze
Culling fires and sparing the trees
Let's get it right and journey the night
Soaring through clouds and the starry light

Feel compassion, love, and inner strength
Have love unfeigned, no matter the length
If you live with love, you'll embrace the skies
You'll enjoy the gardens, and you'll hug the wise

Give back through love for those around you
Love others no matter what they do
Love unfeigned helps others to see a better day
So, let's embrace life and love along the way
What is this thing called love?
Is it more than a primal urge?

Feel compassion, love, and inner strength
Have love unfeigned, no matter the length
If you live with love, you'll embrace the skies
You'll enjoy the gardens, and you'll hug the wise

Should we heed those
Selling I-don't-care?
Or, do we listen to those
Who will always be there?
Humanity is more innovative
When intentions we share
Let's use our minds
for good will, be real, be rare

Feel compassion, love, and inner strength
Have love unfeigned, no matter the length
If you live with love, you'll embrace the skies
You'll enjoy the gardens, and you'll hug the wise

In this game of life
Let's reach to the heart
Don't let the whims of some
Tear us apart
Love is an eternal connection
Perfect for kind acts,
For love and affection
Live with love
Shared purpose with flair
Overcoming misery of all sorts
We'll ensure we're all there

Feel compassion, love, and inner strength

Have love unfeigned, no matter the length
If you live with love, you'll embrace the skies
You'll enjoy the gardens, and you'll hug the wise

~ *Above* ~

Above our hearts, lay our shoulders and heads
Our spines hold us up, its embroidery, its threads
For the rhythm of life, our hearts give a pulse
Without those functions, we'd die or convulse
Our brain is creative with science and art
But without either, we'd be torn apart
If our brain allows us to hurt, maim or steal
What do we gain? Some clothes or a meal?

Let's work together, so we can fly to the Moon
To Jupiter and Mars, there's plenty of room
Let's soar above the clouds and climb to the stars
We can do so much more; the future is ours

For brutality to exist, there is no reason
We garner strength to subsist, in any season
Let's share mercy and kindness; treat others with love
Despite vision or blindness, there's beauty above
If we're all healthy of mind, through the darkness of night
After chasing the grind, we'll win the fight

So, let's work together, so we can fly to the Moon
To Jupiter and Mars, there's plenty of room
Let's soar above the clouds and climb to the stars
We can do so much more; the future is ours

Through thought and action, we'll lift others' lives
While lifting our own, nature can thrive
Embrace science and sports, and learn the arts
Understanding and empathy is where it all starts
Wisdom of all types begin in the mind
It grows in every way as we have shined

Let's work together, so we can fly to the Moon
To Jupiter and Mars, there's plenty of room
Let's soar above the clouds and climb to the stars
We can do so much more; the future is ours

A developed amygdala helps us to feel
Like muscles for strength, or like turning a wheel
Embrace those feelings, maybe dance at the raves
Drink up, buddy up, and make some of the waves
Our feelings assist with choices we make

It helps to sense fear, to shiver, to shake
Without it we'd suffer, there'd be no enjoyment in life
We'd lose compassion and kindness, causing nothing but strife
From rocketry to sports, to prose and charade
The amygdala and frontal lobe are how decisions are made

Let's work together, so we can fly to the Moon
To Jupiter and Mars, there's plenty of room
Let's soar above the clouds and climb to the stars
We can do so much more; the future is ours

The corpus callosum marries our brain's functions together
With that, as one mind, it functions like a tether
A proper balance of our brains and our hearts
Helps humanity to come together, that's how it starts
Let's push our ideals up and be those who find
Our connection is intense, no matter the grind
Let's raise the quality of life in all that we do
For the creatures, the animals, and the people too

Let's work together, so we can fly to the Moon
To Jupiter and Mars, there's plenty of room
Let's soar above the clouds and climb to the stars
We can do so much more; the future is ours

~ *Longevity* ~

Let's work for longevity in the things we create
The things we make, what we put on our plate
The objects we buy should last trillions of years
And, only if needed we can then shift gears
Updating with breakthroughs, ideas galore
Will help us to enjoy life, while preserving more

A printer, a car
A house, and a star...
What we have, where we go, we can go ever so far

Resources are finite, don't cause Earth to lose
Until we span the Cosmos, let's not abuse
Even then, we should never hurt another or dare
We should lose ourselves in science, with meaning and care
The essence of meaning, the giving of life
Let's be considerate of others, to reduce strife

A printer, a car
A house, and a star...
What we have, where we go, we can go ever so far

Do the things we desire, to increase the quality of life
Instead of brutality let's learn about a fife
We can make music; be artistic and fun
From every end of the Universe, we will have won

A printer, a car
A house, and a star...
What we have, where we go, we can go ever so far

Always cling to those who are driven by purpose
Longevity and well-being will come to the surface
Misery is a result of those who dare not to care
Bring love wherever you go and always be there
Uncontrolled chaos brings death with a sting
Benevolence and study, can change everything

A printer, a car
A house, and a star...
What we have, where we go, we can go ever so far

~ *Brevity* ~

Brevity in sorrow, learning from the past
Will help to not leave others diffuse or aghast
While setting our troubles free we can move on ahead
Let's learn from our hard times, and let it be said

Do so briefly, holding treasured moments with glee
I feel you my friend, a big hug, hold that memory
We can briefly think back, but as far as I know
Forward is the only place we can return from and go

We can linger on distant and sweet memories
We can remember the lovely jaunts of love in the breeze
We can learn from the past, even from gifts from above
But we must plan for the future; there's promise through love

Do so briefly, holding treasured moments with glee
I feel you my friend, a big hug, hold that memory
We can briefly think back, but as far as I know
Forward is the only place we can return from and go

~ *Loneliness* ~

Loneliness hits us when sweet memories arise
Of long-gone heroes, friends who have since graced the skies

Loneliness hits as many during Seasons of giving
So while sorrow ensues, make time for the living

Winter's winds and snow may be cold with its weather
Let's be inclusive on those special days that bring us together

Loneliness hits many during Seasons of giving
So while sorrow ensues, make time for the living

Not everyone has a "someone," and may be struggling alone
So lead efforts if possible, to bring warmth to their home

Loneliness hits many during Seasons of giving
So while sorrow ensues, make time for the living

~ *Power of Our Minds* ~

We may not have money; we may not have time
If we teach others how to survive, together we'll climb
One mind with one thought can accomplish so much
With well-being in mind, beauty is never a crutch

Postulating, engaging in talks of solutions
To problems of life, while mitigating pollutions

The talents we're blessed with indeed are many
The greatest is our mind, if you can't think of any
Its wisdom can be multiplied with longevity
Compounding our wisdom is pleasant to see

Postulating, engaging in talks of solutions
To problems of life, while mitigating pollutions

Not everything has to take forever
From physics to piano, never say never
One human has trillions of synaptic pathways
Working together, we'll conquer any maze

Postulating, engaging in talks of solutions
To problems of life, while mitigating pollutions

Oh, the strides we can make, when building so many things
Compassion should drive us, and there's joy that it brings
For longevity, kindness, and quality of life
Let's preserve our Earth and reduce strife

Postulating, engaging in talks of solutions
To problems of life, while mitigating pollutions

~ *Personal Guidance* ~

We can go to church one day of each week
Or we can make every day that special day, where no days are bleak!
Remember consent; don't force others against their will
Choice comes from within when clarity of mind awakens the thrill

Think, love, feel, engage
Life opens your eyes—note, we're on the same page

People muddle through this journey of life
Many don't know what they want, they don't know why
They praise the heavens if something goes well
This exclusive club of the "blessed" makes their hearts swell

Think, love, feel, engage
Life opens your eyes—note, we're on the same page

Please don't forget to ask for guidance and mercy
Companionship and love, for those in controversy
When there are those who are suffering
Even the strong need some buffering
From toil, and sorrow, and lament, and fear
People everywhere we go, know sadness each year

Think, love, feel, engage
Life opens your eyes—note, we're on the same page

No matter who you are or where you are from
Challenges arise that cause the kindest some glum
Good things happen and challenges too
While battling in life, there's something to do

Think, love, feel, engage
Life opens your eyes—note, we're on the same page

You are worth more than anything
So, don't silently suffer
You, your sister, your father, mother, or brother
Your mind may have answers to questions unlike any other

Think, love, feel, engage
Life opens your eyes—note, we're on the same page

This page is our legacy; will we preserve it?
If we do what we plan to, will we deserve it?
I believe so, and you included can be there
Through innovation, compassion, and a desire to share

Think, love, feel, engage
Life opens your eyes—note, we're on the same page

Remember consent; don't force others against their will
Choice comes from within when clarity of mind awakens the thrill

Think, love, feel, engage
Life opens your eyes—note, we're on the same page

If we're driven by compassion, then deserve longevity we will
Advancement, prosperity, journeys Universe-wide will be our thrill

(Think, love, feel, engage)
Think, love, feel, engage
The legacy is ours, so let's open the stage!
We can briefly think back, but as far as I know
Forward is the only place we can return from and go
We can linger on distant and sweet memories
We can remember the jaunts of love and the wisps of the breeze
We can learn from the past, the gifts from above
But plan for the future, there's a promise through love

Joanne wrote and wrote, and finally had her fifth album, with six songs ready to go. This was written to be one song, but it was a long one and it filled the album in several segments, and when people requested it, it was played in full and became the longest hit ever to play in its entirety on the radio waves and broadcast by all of the satellite and online radio stations—everyone seemed to memorize each line.

Throughout the next three years Joanne would frequent the stage among the masses throughout the world, and then she would go to the Virtual Universe through her biopod each night to work out the details of what she would do next. She felt that she now inherited a calling and carried out the task of imbuing her music to the mission of integrating further neurological development among the masses via those same systems. Her work was known and lauded by many throughout the world as well as those within Pathway, yet her source of inspiration was unknown throughout the public and real-world environment.

Regardless, she went on tour and people felt a new sense of depth they had never felt before. Joanne's audience learned over time that she had become a member of the UP and many of them joined in as well. The crowds of approving fans who knew better appreciated her even more. Through it all, Joanne managed to maintain her previous work schedule and had contributed many additional labors of importance to Pathway throughout the Solar System and all while working with Yesha, Amber, Erin, and Vesha. Even still, there was a sense of confidentiality surrounding the specifics of each detail of just how much she was doing to help the worldwide public. Nonetheless, she kept singing and touring throughout the world, and the public crowds would sing along knowing they weren't alone, they were loved. Their favorite lines resonated:

Think, Love, Feel, and Engage
The legacy is ours, so let's open the stage!
We can briefly think back, but as far as I know
Forward is the only place we can return from and go
We can linger on distant and sweet memories
We can remember the jaunts of love and the wisp of the breeze

We can learn from the past, the gifts from above
But plan for the future, there's promise through love

After completing her fifth album and preparing for her worldwide tour, Joanne finished her public Ph.D.'s at Harvard, and then at MIT, and finally at Oxford. While focusing for a while in her new position at Pathway, she worked en-tangent with her musical career. Joanne rose in the ranks and headed part of the neurological correctional development team working with the biopods and cross-queuing them with the enhanced Virtual Universe environments. In particular, she worked in a special team to improve the Correctional Matrix and built many environments with sophisticated and realistic scenarios in order to bring life-changing experiences to the minds of anyone who had ever harmed another individual resulting in the undue loss of quality of life, up to the loss of life itself. She had a unique talent of coaching, mentoring, and creating simulated realities replete with simulant people, all of whom could imbue compassion, meaning, and reason into the lives of those who had none, could not find any, or merely chose to neglect significance completely.

She realized that a lack of essential traits that brought clarity to what an individual could do to contribute to a better reality and sustained existence to themselves and those around them was in large part due to something as simple as depression or any other neurological state caused by an unfair environment, and she believed that in so many ways these acts of aggression could also have been fueled by a lack of affection, vision, and drive. She was critical to the success and growth of Pathway, and in doing something to mitigate the issues that if resolved could preserve the fabric of humanity's legacy.

While Joanne traveled the world, she returned to her home in New York every night using jump gates. She also took time during each day to visit the Virtual Universe and master the Correctional Matrix environments. From time to time, she would find Eliza, Yesha, Amber, Erin, Vesha, James, Najem, Jasmine, and many others within the Virtual Universe, visit them, connect mind-to-mind, and share experiences and wisdom gained, and by doing so compound upon their wisdom, as would each of her new-found friends in Pathway.

Eliza had political business to attend to in so many ways, yet this did not keep her from pondering her past, enjoying the here and now, and planning for the future. In some cases, planning for the future involved presenting Vesha to the Senate. Joanne had met Vesha toward the end of her Virtual Universe training and met her several times thereafter. There had always been a beautiful yet compassionate and ironically commanding nature about Vesha. Every time Joanne went into the Virtual Universe, she could feel her presence, and Vesha reminded her until Joanne knew it herself, that she had some awesome uniqueness to contribute, all her own, both now and in the future. Greatness abounded in everyone, it merely took a little care and kindness to see it in others, and Vesha shined!

Somehow, that connection to others as a result of Joanne's journeys within the Virtual Universe and her neural link seemed to increase the ability she had to see the greatness in those around her and to add so much depth to everything she was doing both for Pathway and through her music. Joanne felt grateful allowing inspiration to flow through her lips and out to the masses. It was as if she were a siren, yet with the goal of saving lives instead of destroying them. Her temperance and clarity of purpose grew while working with her friends at Pathway. Working to complete her various projects allowed her newly-gifted abilities to mature. Joanne felt inspired, while she uplifted others. *"Connect with the minds of so many who are willing to help. Encourage yourself and allow others to lend their expertise,"* She thought, and in so doing she was grateful to share in a common purpose

As Joanne was going about her tasks, so were the other leaders, idea-makers, and change-for-the-sake-of-improvement-doers within Pathway, and among them Eliza was with Vesha Celeste, ready to address the Senate on Capitol Hill.

Chapter 21: Despite Mortal Wounds

Database Moon Archive, Celestial-Sol Entry Date: 2019 March 25. Erin Carter, Yesha Alevtina's young understudy, summarizes the experiences, journeys, and missions of Vesha Celeste as assigned by Senator Eliza A. Williams. These memories are a collaboration of life and insight from the minds of Vesha, Eliza, and numerous senatorial politicians recorded within the Virtual Universe, interfaced within the Pathway Melrose Campus. Input by Erin Carter, Vice President of Pathway, 2018-2022, President of Pathway, 2022-2029.

Vesha had been awake for about three months and had found a new sense of clarity in every academic subject she studied. Every challenge presented before her was easy to mitigate due to the phenomenal restructuring, adding to, and compounding of each individual neuron and brain cell within her near perfect skull—which happened to be a smidgen fuller and unnoticeably larger than before, except of course to Vesha and her closest friends, Eliza, Yesha, Amber, Erin, Najem, James, Jasmine, and Joanne. The addition to her neurological capacities was due to three new layers of tissue that had formed inside her skull, kind of like the membrane of an eggshell, but several times thicker. Her neural nanos worked seamlessly to improve her cognitive framework, making reparations, and dispersing synaptic links equitably throughout her brain.

The training that Vesha went through had been phenomenal, in-part because of Yesha's dedication, yet in many other aspects due to the efforts of each of the scientists that were involved in the project of bringing her back to life. During previous efforts of bringing her online, every time an individual linked mind-to-mind with the Virtual Universe, Vesha's neural network and capacity compounded upon its ability to digest and express knowledge and wisdom even more. After she had awoken, during her training, more than two-billion people went through the Virtual Universe throughout the Pathway-influenced regions of the Solar System. With a connection to their minds, Vesha's intellect grew exponentially. It was amazing how life could play out before anyone's eyes with these new-found freedoms, thoughts, ideas, and clarity in resolving issues. It became second nature for Vesha to desire to raise the quality of life for each person she met in the world.

The journeys, studies, and training Vesha received in the Virtual Universe allowed neural pathways of thought and communication to form with detailed increases in the capabilities of each of her senses. She practiced to the domination of each of her motor skills, neural balance for crystal clear clarity, recall, cognitive coherence, and critical thinking. Every bit of data on the Internet from any venue had downloaded into her brain, and she processed all of it with ease in the best of ways. Cognitive frame-working augmented her visualization of well-being-oriented choices allowing her to demonstrate more fullness in character than ever before. She exuded an increase in confidence and an ability to multitask with an enhanced plethora of visions of goals she wished to pursue. She was able to weave her goals and tasks into many of the most dynamic arrays of accomplishments, with the most effective results, and chase her dreams she did. She tackled every art, profession, science, skill, and sport, learning their nuances quickly and became proficient in short order.

During the three months since she had awoken, Vesha had accomplished many things. She enjoyed spending time with Erin as she pored over her studies, lost herself in the fascinating histories of humanity, and recovered secrets hidden throughout the globe. While doing so, she and Erin engaged in sleuthing, in the pursuit of helping youth around the world overcome their various battles in life. Journeying with Yesha, Vesha found and rescued many more men, women, and children worldwide, while Eliza continued to try to resolve issues of stagnation within the Legislative branch of government. Vesha even helped a plethora of animals, birds, and other creatures to heal, become optimized, trained up, and read-in to Pathway. After they were read-in, she assisted James and nurtured everyone she had helped into a fuller capacity to use their newly gifted abilities with ease. She also helped them to choose where to go throughout the Solar System, within or nearby any of the tech cities. They could help anywhere and call anyplace their home. With optimized minds, they wanted to contribute toward the preservation of life and the goals of humanity, of combing the Cosmos and preserving the life-giving qualities of the Universe. Until the time was right for Earth-borne civilization to go beyond the Solar System, the animals and all read-in creatures decided to live in the many forests, jungles, lakes, and small seas near and within Pathway's twenty-thousand tech city environments.

Vesha had also spent time with Amber Blythe analyzing how any given physiology and neurology could adapt to the various environments in short order with minimal to no adverse effect on the body's systems. If there were any adverse effects at all, following optimization, the nanos throughout an individual's body would cause them to radiate and glow as they healed instantaneously. Together, they figured out how to integrate specific microbial DNA sequences into any living organism, including humans, that would allow them to live in space without oxygen and with the complete ability to absorb radiation and space debris without harmful effect while consuming it as fuel or sustenance.

Vesha had also spent time with Najem and Jasmine combing the Universe with their sensors to peer out and map a robust plan for an incredible future journey through the Cosmos. This journey would take place once humanity got its act together, and mutual respect was second nature.

The intellect and wisdom of Vesha's mind had compounded based upon that of anyone who had passed through the Virtual Universe. The care that Yesha and Amber had taken over the two years between Vesha's passing and awakening was unique. They had made her ability to process and extrapolate information infinitesimally more considerable than the conceivable capacity of anyone else, including Eliza. Eliza was very proud of the efforts they made. Likewise, Vesha consistently impressed Eliza with everything she had seen or heard about her while on her daily tour through the Virtual Universe to get up-to-speed on what had gone on, courtesy of Pathway. No matter how great the result, it seemed Vesha was there to add an extra dash of brilliance to the end-product. Indeed, Vesha had expressed the kind of character that Eliza had seen burning from within her, since the first day they had met.

Vesha was both physiologically and neurologically superior in every way to anyone else, yet she was humble and kind. She did not brag or gloat. Eliza knew that Vesha frequently contemplated on a novel idea. "Greatness is not a measure of brain cells or any item. Rather, virtue is in the choices we make using the tools and unlimited and self-sustaining resources given to us, no matter their complexity. Our level of benevolence, or care for others, is the true measure of our character." Despite being a significant player in many of the latest great inventions and improvements, Vesha looked at herself as ordinary and knew it was essential to treat the contributions of others as the valuable and unique offerings of personal sacrifice that they were. Eliza saw Vesha's love of others, alone, as a pre-qualifier for the pinnacle of great leadership she sought for the leader of humanity throughout the Cosmos, when that day would eventually arrive. The attributes that Vesha not only possessed but expressed was paramount for the tasks she would delegate to her. Eliza had known her for many years now, and Vesha was one-of-a-kind.

It was confusing or nearly impossible for hitmen hired by competing industries throughout the world to successfully destroy anyone who was fully read in. Since these malicious monsters of society were not read-in, they did not know that they could not kill their target. Optimizations and the rapid healing effects of gene-, neuron-, and cell-oriented nanos could thwart any efforts made to that end. Every attempt had been stopped thus far, due to excellent communication, courtesy of the neural links and the robust capacities of the Twelve Database Moons. If the worst were to occur, a targeted individual could dodge any vicious assaults. With the same technologies, if someone were to attack a read-in person and blow them to smithereens, they could rematerialize in a safe-zone nearby. The Twelve Database Moons retained full sequential data of every form, on every given and read-in individual, allowing them to maintain their memories, even if in effect they had died. Eliza knew that if someone were to try to hurt Vesha, she could theoretically heal in seconds, no matter the damage. Hit attempts had been on the rise. Too many, who played at pulling the proverbial strings of humanity, were lost in the fanfare of politics as usual. Individual competitors and managers who lived to breathe terror into the lives of those who worked for them and many others who did not value life as she did, were in constant, covert, and even overt missions to destroy all that Pathway stood for. Anti-Pathway groups were on the rise, and even more so as it seemed to the antagonists that these people "miraculously" healed. Eliza was well-aware of the attempts made on the lives of so many kind and beautiful people, and she didn't suffer it lightly. She had, however, made every attempt to protect the people who, by her inventions, had benefitted from them.

Now, because there were a couple of cases of collateral damage, where hit attempts hurt someone who had not been fully read-in, Eliza knew something had to be done to reduce the cultural and societal toxicity. So, she went before the Senate. Eliza could do more by moving legislative attention toward well-being and away from thirst for wealth and power. By revisiting her tax bill, she could have a positive impact. She would work to loosen the coffers of greed and enable humanity to have the financial fluidity to invest in longevity, health, and clarity of mind. With those three goals that Eliza treasured, innovations would provide a higher quality of life. Humanity could overcome the many challenges the Earth itself faced. Rewriting and reintroducing a clean bill before Congress and the Senate, or one that does not have riders attached, which had been passed with unfortunate and questionable additions to it more than a year ago, would help. She would introduce and pass other bills, to include one of home-based healthcare and top-quality home-based education via biopod, by sanctioning proliferation and distribution of these robustly capable devices. If the Senate were to approve her bills, she would also need to find a way to afford the legislators involved with similar protections as shared by those in Pathway who had been fully read in.

It was late March of 2019, and Eliza linked with Yesha, who had taken a break from her worldwide journeys, to be nearby. Yesha was at the Pathway Operations Presidential Center, with Erin Carter by her side as her Vice President. Eliza stood on the Senate floor behind the pulpit. In her mind, she represented not only the state of Massachusetts but all people worldwide. She was here to deliberate and unambiguously present her case for sanctioned physiological and neurological therapies that would significantly increase the possibilities of curing a multitude of disorders. Many of which, were in fact, responsible for the rise in violence throughout the world. While these disorders were very much different from Alzheimer's, Schizophrenia, ADHD, and many among others that hampered the shared quality of life, many others were not addressed yet.

Eliza knew that no matter the decision, it was still the mind that was at the center of the decision-making process. Something was firing wrong in the neurological system of an individual if their desire for mutual well-being was nonexistent. There was an ethical way to mend the mind, and Eliza had to figure out how to do it billions of times. Society was very fickle, however, and convincing one entity through vocal persuasion wasn't always as efficient or effective as she would have liked it to have been. Still, here she was, and she would try to reach as many people as she could, through this legal and public forum.

All too often, it had become increasingly acceptable to tear others down in the name of being "real" or destroying someone's ingenuity through brutality for the sake of popularity and so-called "strength." Eliza knew that a person could be "real" yet considerate, kind, and helpful. She also believed that this lack of reasoning contributed to a sickness that was worse than a disease, yet people bathed in it as if it were gold. Ruthless behavior was a malicious virus and a vulnerability that was being exploited overmuch by those who had motives in mind that had nothing to do with well-being. They used this against vulnerable young people, with growing minds that were amenable to ideas that were unhealthy. Many, to impress others, or to look "cool," proudly talked about how little they cared for the well-being of others while displaying crude gestures before a global audience. It was easy to see how this could be, given their young and rebellious age, especially after all they had witnessed when it came to the unhealthy environment; they were the victims. This type of behavior was destroying the fabric of society, of humanity, and would ultimately become the end of human civilization and result in a future where no other sentient being would even know of the existence of sentient life forms on Earth. Eliza knew she had to do something, and she was doing it.

Eliza often explored the ideals she believed in, within her mind. She aimed to address the pervasive popularity of cruelty and rudeness, and thus, she studied the virtues she believed in yet again as she thought of those who would be within her audience.

"It isn't, nor was it ever weakness to be kind, it was never softness to be compassionate, and it was never real to crush the will and innovative spirit of another individual. People must have an environment that will allow them to learn. Yes, they must have the opportunity to discover that kindness is a strength, compassion is flexibility, and possessing a desire for the well-being of others as well as us will enlighten our minds with the type of innovation that will preserve humanity and make us capable of spanning the Universe."

Eliza would often multitask her mind with many different ideas and resolutions to issues running through her mind all at once. When it came to the art of reaching the hearts of the people, however, she knew in every way imaginable that it was an uphill battle. Specific sectors of the media had delivered attack campaign after attack campaign backed by seemingly irresistible and yet publicly unknown entities, who mainly had made it their mission to sew dissension and discord among the masses and stall the public when it came to innovation and progression toward a glorious future.

One of the many approaches they used was to cite well-known authors and historical figures and manipulate the intent of their wisdom by suggesting that advancements, technologies, and tools made available to the masses of the public, allowing them to participate in innovation, were evil. They forgot to realize that essential tools are not malicious; they are merely there, like dust or sand. The choice of the bearer of a device and how they use it defines their character. Their pervasive argument is that information that is provided by those who genuinely care, only benefit the machinations of some large or evil corporation. That argument was, unfortunately, fallacious. The irony was, Eliza knew who, or what, was behind all of the attacks on the people she had been elected to have stewardship over. She also knew who was behind the negative campaigning. Those who truly knew Eliza even knew that she was under attack for taking the initiative to improve the overall environment. They also knew that the Pathway organization was under attack for all of the good that it was trying to achieve.

Members of "Anti-Pathway," as she and her friends hesitantly called them, had funded multiple organizations for years. Anti-Pathway had supported religious groups, various media institutions, and quite a few political, entertainment, and business associations all in the effort of conquering and dividing the populous. She knew that the truth was that, while there were genuinely evil individuals and organizations out there, for the most part, what seemed like a large and powerful organization bent on destruction, was merely a symptom of economic greed, as well as selfishness, negligence, and a lack of remorse for life. All of this had spun out of control through a series of programs once intended for good but were now bogged down with laws that did not protect the people. The lawmakers have littered statutes and regulations with riders and bylaws. As it is, the ethics of greed and power, rather than those of sharing well-being, are what fuels the bureaucracies and rules that tie citizens' hands behind their backs and leaves devastation in their wake. In many cases, what we know of as "the establishment," makes sure these widespread ideas are taught by and pushed in business ethics classes and books by leaders with totalitarian machinations, benefitting only themselves.

It seemed it was in the best interest of those who thought they were in power to make sure things did not change too quickly or drastically. They muddied the waters of fluidity through use of broad language, doublespeak, and over-sophistication of that which ought to have been quite simple, yet they simultaneously made it their mission to deny the sense of logic that came from those who possessed the most promise for a resolution to the most complicated of problems. These were they who also seemed to maintain the most significant influence and affluence over the issues that could have otherwise been resolved but weren't. These were they who chased their economic dreams with little regard for anyone or anything else, while they maintained their influence and affluence. What resulted was the over-inflation of debt and taxes, toxicity rampant in and throughout the work environment, a lack of personal time for effective mental processing and cerebral evolution, as well as reduced availability of tools for proper parenting in the home. Through indoctrination of those who were most vulnerable to manipulation, they were brilliant in the evilest of ways. By twisting the desire of many for acceptance by others, tragedies played out spreading their venomousness throughout the world. These so-called titans of society were responsible for the dystopian environment that seemed to be playing out worldwide.

Eliza had a strong impression that the foolish machinations of those who deceitfully pulled the strings of power had cursed civilization with an environment that was toxic to its core. These fiends had become malicious and intelligent in the worst kinds of ways. As it was, she saw that many unfortunate souls had painted a dishonest portrayal of themselves to create complicated methods steeped in bureaucracy to mitigate issues in the short term, but purely for increased personal gain. They masked the problems they pretended to resolve at best while doing nothing. Many influential individuals seemed to glorify in death, apocalyptic destruction, and the kind of chaos that justifies ignorance, selfishness, and mediocrity. Mediocrity has always served to weaken the resolve of the people and while keeping malicious minds in power, as they serve their wallets alone through self-centeredness and insatiable greed. They did not realize that if they merely cared about those around them as well as themselves and felt concern for their well-being, they could accompany their desires for wealth and power with love and loyalty.

Eliza believed that if leaders treated the people with dignity and respect, they would be healthier in so many ways, both at home and throughout life. If they were brought in as members of the team at work, given proper training, paid well with all the essential benefits, and had a requirement to work no more than forty hours per week, ten months out of a year, and twenty years out of thirty, both the workers and the leaders would prosper. Each person would become a leader in their rite, dedicated to the success of whatever organization reciprocated their efforts. As a result, they would also be enabled to become more vigorous and capable. They could become innovative and loyal to any employer who had the described high ethical standards, as had been laid out by her political party, the UP, in Universal Ethics, and as such their industries would grow and advance creating more power and wealth for them as well. Good begets good, and the rest is a shame. There was no reason to anticipate our country, humanity, and our world withering away.

It was simple, but many did not seem to understand or grasp this simple reality, and consequently, many threw others under the theoretical bus to succeed or to rise to greater heights in their careers. Furthermore, the power seemed to be among those who had demonstrated they were willing to sell out their ethics, if ever they were had, rather than provide a way for those who honestly did care about humanity to in all actuality help it to succeed as a civilization with a Universal scope and approach. It had become resoundingly evidenced to Eliza that the result of all this inhumanity came from the intent of the most maliciously powerful of this world. They were culling our world of as many of its resources as necessary to see the value of the resources they had a stake in go up. If those resources were scarce in supply, they could further feed their greed or lust for power, to hell with anyone else.

One particular entity had spread the idea that established science using approved journalistic venues alone was the only source of science to trust. While a valuable resource, this same entity sought to tear down the idea of personal study and innovation through intense and collective research, to weaken the resolve, knowledge, and power of the masses. Ironically, this same influence quickly dismissed any scientific claims published through proper means. This secret society thought that one resource alone was much more accurate than a combination of resources. They did not realize that collegiate journals, information available through research tools online, and communication back and forth through worldwide social networking and connection tools and technologies were more effective than one resource alone.

There had been a small quantity of popular and robust search and knowledge resource engines for years, designed to inform the public in a plethora of ways of the critical information essential to progress via well thought-out algorithms and highly intelligent minds. The truth was, tearing down the use of free search engines equated to tying peoples' hands down to the errors found in "socially acceptable" group think, and rather than allow civil discourse using real person-to-person and lab-to-lab communication, they splintered humanity and made them easy to manipulate through a variety of elite and exclusive focus group-oriented social sites instead.

Eliza noticed that there were leaders who found it within them to tear down effective, efficient, and far-reaching forms of documented social interaction. She realized that these rulers of "the way things were" could successfully divide the populations, they could conquer them and sate their greed even further. Heaven forbid, people to try to improve the world because together they would do it best. Therefore, Eliza, to make changes to improve lives, took notice that these evil entities did what they could to push their influence, causing once noble individuals to tear down the ability of "common" people to unite, to converse, to enlighten, and to resolve issues.

One of those malicious entities used a lot of socially accepted monikers. In one example, Eliza discerned that they would abuse the phrase, "With the good comes the bad." Or they would, with their prurient agendas, set up situations with tools for human progress and demonstrate the nasty and vile things people could do with them. What they meant to do was to break the will of those who had innovated excellent scientific tools to help improve the human condition. They wanted to break the will of the people and cause them to no longer do what was necessary or study that which was essential to overcome strife. Instead through this, they would cause each person that wasn't "in" their network of insatiable greed and lust for power to relish working in slave-like labor all of their lives, and with little to show for it. Then as a reward for it all, they would be victims of the type of environment that would cause them to fail to ward off the end of life by causing them to question why anyone would want to live with even more pain and suffering.

Many of these malicious entities also preached that "Nature should always be allowed to take its course." The truth was, while Nature was highly sophisticated when it came to the complexity of the design of our minds, and the Universe itself seemed brilliant beyond belief, it took millions to billions of years of mixed results for humanity to arrive at its current condition. Throughout which, Nature has demonstrated it can also be fierce with little to show of mercy in any way. Nature is very pervasive, as well. The truth lies in the fact that horrible acts do indeed happen. Dogs rape other dogs and rats eat other rats. There are plenty of sordid details, with malice, lies in the revelations, and brutal acts that would not be deemed acceptable by anyone in a more evolved society. Human society in many places throughout the world has at least advanced to see and understand their conscious reality and tries to improve things for not just themselves but for others too. In many ways, notwithstanding all, Eliza saw that love did abound, and great people did one good deed after another.

Nevertheless, one of these secret organizations had conducted a series of documentary-like interviews under the pseudonym of Paranoidis Capitalis. They would mainly preach, "The Earth is indeed flat, and we never went to the Moon, so don't believe physicists, theoretical or otherwise. Vaccinations do not work, so don't believe in the work of biologists and medical experts, because what they say is a lie." They also fostered among the populace the idea that "The apocalypse is near, through EMPs and biotech-borne zombie infestations, and everything in science and technology has a horrible cause and a horrible effect that will lead to that dismal end. If we cure cancer, Nature will develop something much worse, so give up. We will all innately die, and we should. Therefore, preventing aging will cause problems galore, to include overpopulation and endless dictatorships." Eliza knew that the people naturally soaked that in, because there were certain truths about some of the statements themselves, especially if people were irresponsible with how they used these tools of science and our minds. She also knew that if we used our most exceptional talent, our minds, and our greatest gift, science, we could actually be enabled to have the hope and technology to overcome death, disease, uncontrolled chaos, and destruction, and we would then find that we could peacefully and delightfully live lives full of meaning, prosperity, and purpose.

In response to legitimate efforts, extensive research on longevity, and genuine care when it came to the well-being of civilization, there had been a twist on ideas and a building-up of irrational fears using the examples of what an evil mind would do if given a particular set of tools. They were in effect very much focused on how a hammer could be used to kill someone rather than on how it could be used to help someone to build a home. The status quo, or the bureaucracy, or the established powers had very little concern for the long-term effects of their actions, merely more concern for maintaining their reign, their power, their affluence, their popularity amongst the dumbed down masses, and thus their influence, rather than having concern for reduced suffering worldwide. They had already gone so far as to promote anti-vaxxing campaigns, the idea that the Earth was flat, and the suggestion that no countries had ever been to the Moon.

Ultimately, this was the last-ditch effort of some of the most austere, evil, and secret parts of society to cover up what even the CIA had confided to Eliza about. There was, in fact, a contingency funded by Paranoidis Capitalis to create a variety of nerve agents, EMP-capable bombs, and nuclear and biological weapons for distribution and proliferation worldwide to bring about "the end of the world," but all to increase the value of their own very dubious Earthly self-interests.

As more facts about this information were being provided to her via her neural link with Pathway and high-level CIA, NSA, and FBI agents, using legal channels, Yesha Alevtina simultaneously received this information and sent delegates to do further research in an effort to minimize the damaging effects caused by the actions of such a prurient tribe of hateful individuals. The Pathway organization had a pro-bono government arm, and as such, didn't charge the government a dime. Although Pathway had made it a point to demand nothing of the government for their services, they were still purely philanthropic when it came to the safety and security of the citizens of the countries throughout the world.

The delegates did a lot to build safety nets, backup systems, and protective barriers to anything influential enough to destroy humanity or the progress that Eliza and her friends had made through Pathway. Working overtime as the President of Pathway, in public, throughout the Solar System, and Pathway's twenty-thousand tech cities, with a population of more than two billion people, and growing, Yesha was closely linked to Eliza in the Senate, and rarely slowed down. All who were fully read-in and involved in biotech professions worked together developing and proliferating cures to any nerve or biological agent. As they completed their missions, they updated Yesha, who updated Eliza, on progress during each step made by scientific and professional volunteers to overcome these issues.

Yesha's teams consisted of the best scientists, hackers, quantum mechanics engineers, bioinformatics teams, physicists, cybersecurity specialists, and many other specialized teams. They all operated with access and the use of Pathway's sensor and jump gate technologies, which were immeasurable in orders of magnitude and faster when it came to travel, and speed of communication of any other entity. The teams with their tools to improve quality of life and the human condition were more capable than anything else throughout the world.

Yesha had put together quite a few cross-genre and convergent Pathway investigative teams worldwide. They had all worked with permission from the CIA, the FBI, and the NSA to keep up-to-date on the mischief of these many corrupt and powerful, secretive, and malicious groups. Even though Pathway and its cadre of geniuses had developed a complete arsenal of defense mechanisms to prevent pandemics and genocide, due to their focus on the health, well-being, and longevity of others as well as themselves, they were not corrupt nor were they corruptible.

Corruption was defined by Pathway as any entity purely interested in advancements and technologies merely for the sake of securing personal affluence and influence mired in brutality for honor, where dignity and the consideration for the well-being of others were considered a joke. Corruption was uncontrolled and unmitigated chaos, as well as the worship of mixed results and reckless abandon, which would, through gross negligence, cause the ruin of humanity.

If it hadn't been for Eliza's connections, courtesy of the covert approval of the ANSSI to form the government wing of Pathway LLC more than nine years ago, Pathway would have still done everything they could to help. As it was, their efforts were more fluid, thanks to the efforts of Agent Angela Epstein, Congress, and the Senate, to ensure the will of the people was protected and that humanity could become a space-faring civilization. Eliza, Yesha, James, and all of Pathway had sworn to protect humanity just the same from entities with corrupt machinations even though they might as well have been considered rogue. In wisdom, by working with the government in smart increments, the network Pathway shared was much vaster and more unbeatable. The citizens of every nation throughout the world had an extraordinary chance for a promising future, even without knowing all the finite details, yet.

Aside from measures for security and safety, for real-world medical studies, within Pathway, there had also been great strides toward ending the devastating effects of public research on something just as important when it came to humanity. Just as important were the animals, the birds, and the many other creatures that were also helpful to humankind. They too helped with the advancement of civilization and the preservation of Earth's legacy as well as its survival. Entirely different from old, cruel, and deadly trials on unsuspecting animals, now experiments in Pathway were only conducted consensually and only if overall safety, recuperation, and health of the trial recipient could be guaranteed.

Before a physiological trial could begin in a lab, for example, there had to be a way to reverse those effects, or there had to be a way to fight the resultant cancers in the cause of cell or gene mutation. All these changes and the humanity existent in Pathway were courtesy of Eliza, the development of Pathway LLC, that which she had expanded into Pathway Industries, and then after winning worldwide acclaim had officially named "Pathway."

Now, mice and rats could live much longer, and, indefinitely, but they also had been brought into sentience, and as such, they propagated the species much less or only as needed. They engaged in vital missions worldwide and throughout the Solar System. Even Joanne, the singer, genius, and neuroscience extraordinaire had noticed how the rat and cockroach populations had dwindled to seemingly nothing, at least in the streets, homes, businesses, and sewers of New York. In truth, they had been essential volunteers in research on the giant gas planets and their moons, while working with Pathway, and their help there was heroic. As it was, trials within the laboratories of Pathway had always been well-being oriented, and the pace of the public was picking up quite a bit, through proper Pathway and UP delegate influence.

Serums were now developed to allow animals and humans to communicate back and forth, permitting humans and creatures to carry on using their neural links in telepathic conversations. Because of this merger in the connection between animal and humanity, and the combined efforts of many members of Pathway, now treatments allowed NASA astronauts to resist the effects of radiation, the loss of bone density, and the loss of muscle mass while journeying through space. The cure for progeria had also been found and was ready to be dispersed worldwide. Amber Blythe had created a treatment for multiple sclerosis within a day. COPD and all manner other genetic malfunctions could be cured in one week, using publicly-available sciences. Each of these breakthroughs had the side-benefit of prolonging lives, and each advance and their application to the physiological system was a matter of personal choice throughout all the Pathway organization. All of this could now be made available to the public and become implemented nationwide, with the passing of Eliza's three significant senatorial bills.

The animal aspect was congruent with Eliza's internal plans for forests and jungles within each primary spacecraft of what she had then called, the Intergalactic Mission Contingency, or the IMC. The IMC would be an essential part of colonizing the Cosmos healthily. There were currently free-range "wildlife" sanctuaries within and throughout the forests of every Pathway campus, tech city, and in the ever-developing Virtual Universe Brainstorm-and-Plan-Development Matrix. Eliza's organization built these wildlife sanctuaries for civilization throughout the Solar System and would eventually construct them on each of the soon-to-be colossally-sized IMC Command Spacecraft. Every species was and would be represented, with sentience bred into them. In all actuality, or on Earth, in the public realm, the animals, birds, water creatures, and little beings would only act as they typically did or graze as they usually would if they detected a non-read-in individual gazing upon them. Many activities were going on and had begun when Eliza had all of the Pathway infrastructure built in the earlier days. Thus, Eliza was aware of each step of its progress, updates, upgrades, and improvements.

After collecting her thoughts about all of this, Eliza began to deliberate before the Senate:

"There are obstacles, no doubt. Most barriers toward the progress of our civilization, or the progressive evolution of the body and mind, lie ironically within the minds of humanity. The progression of humanity is indeed a case of the people versus themselves.

"Many say unscrupulously, 'with the good comes the bad,' or 'there's the yin and the yang in everything.' Those are lovely truths if used in their appropriate context. However, used by far too many with malicious designs, they are merely beautiful, and cute assumptions of reality brought to us, courtesy of years of search for wealth or societal acceptance. The yearning for such is a vulnerability. Justifying brutality for wanton desires of wealth and power is our flowered-up attempt to cave-in to our natural craving for a mixed evolutionary state. Unmitigated population growth will cull all the Earth's unlimited and self-sustaining resources until Nature destroys us because we've failed to evolve ourselves. Creating a 'hell on Earth' is the residual justification for Nature's neural loop in our minds driving unnecessary suffering and misery to ensure we do not destroy this delicate ecosystem it has created; believe me, there are extraordinary powers at work here. Nature works through random and brutal evolutionary processes, yet it has also brought to humanity the realization of the greatest gift we could ever have, which is our consciousness, our awareness, our brains, or our minds. I genuinely believe that, if it is at all possible, Nature would prefer we used them. Our minds work via a robust system of controlled chaos, sometimes uncontrolled, so that, again, if at all possible, it can help the Universe see itself through our eyes and minds.

"Along with many natural cures for disease and as such additions to healthy diets, we have been gifted these minds. With that gift, we have a significant advantage with high capacity to overcome our limitations, to reign-in unbridled chaos, in exchange for curing disease at its core, reducing suffering from its center, sustaining high-quality life, and preserving history so we can carry on a legacy we can all be proud to share with distant civilizations. Instead of the need to acquiesce our liberties to conditions and instincts that will lay waste to our planet, we can evolve. We can compound upon our wisdom through living stronger, healthier, and longer, and thereby resolve more issues with several orders of magnitude of the type of brilliance needed to meet the challenges we will face on the roads ahead with one victory after another.

"So, starting today, I vie that there no longer has to be a fixation on the perception that there is 'a good' and 'a bad.' We all know evil exists, it destroys, and it cankers. It sews seeds of doubt, and it causes fear, anger, hatred, and violence. If left untended, these perceptions will lead to the death of humanity and of the Universe itself. Concern for this negativity may be necessary, but only for brief periods, to reach solutions and resolutions. We must be strong, to be able to deflect the actions and barbs of malice, and as such, there is a real and valuable truth I want each of you to understand. There is a new balance, it may be symmetric, and it may be asymmetric. There is a new weight to tip the scale in a way that will benefit all who drift upon this walk of life.

"With effort, determination, and compassion for others comes the good, with moderation, the scales of life will be stacked in favor of increased positivity. Life can be beautiful, we can enrich its length with joy, and the unlimited and self-sustaining resources can be abundant if we are gracious and kind. If we are, nothing else can hold sway to the promise of a better future.

"We now have a clear example of the laws of entropy reigned-in. Two years ago, we lost a wonderful lady to dementia, but today I would like to introduce you to her. She was an inspiration during her life, and now she is here ready to inspire us again. Vesha Celeste, can you please come in?"

Vesha walked into the room and stood beside Eliza and before the Senate and relaxed in her black smartsuit with iridescent colors and accents where the seams would be. Vesha had been dead for more than two years. They all recognized her because they had seen her story in the news, pictures of her in her youth peering from a telescope out toward the starry skies were all over the internet, and throughout her eighty-eight years, she had made many contributions to astronomy and the space program. With jaws dropped among the members of the audience, Vesha stood there before every member of the Senate, and their hearts were moved.

"This is my friend, Vesha Celeste, and as many of you know, she passed away a little over two years ago. However, through her work before her passing, and the efforts of myself, and two of my best friends, Yesha Alevtina and Amber Blythe, as well as an extensive and talented team of scientists, we were able to revive her two years after she died. Vesha has been awake for just over three months, and already, due to Vesha's contributions, we've made great strides at Pathway Industries."

A dull chatter arose and grew to a roar among the politicians, and Eliza could tell they were arguing about the ethics of this, that, or the other, and began doubting who Vesha was.

Just then a member of Paranoidis Capitalis had somehow gotten past security screening, rose up, and shouted above the crowd, "She should be dead! This monster is an abomination! What is this, the zombie apocalypse!?" and he shot Vesha square in the chest.

As the bullet traveled, Vesha visually tracked it flying through the air and braced for impact, and the embroidered "goo" seamlessly woven into her smart uniform stopped the projectile flat. Then as Vesha's nanos kicked in to instantaneously heal the bruised area, it appeared as if a crystalline substance sparkled through her body, and she glowed.

The member of Paranoidis Capitalis, seeing that everyone else was too shocked to do anything, shot her again, and this time he accurately aimed at her head. As the bullet approached her in the air, Vesha knew it would hurt tremendously, but she let it hit her through the eye, and she fell behind the podium. As she fell, the crowd yelled in horror! While they were stunned as to what to do, the extracellular matrix encoded within her DNA, filled the hole left behind. Her nanos connected the regrouping tissues and the newly growing neural network, which were coupled with the existing link as well as with the continuously updated and backed-up information from her mental uploads and downloads to and from the Twelve Database Moons. In mere moments, her nanos had healed her, and the only indication of such was a bright glow due to its luminescent speed.

Within moments, and perhaps too late to avoid this barbarism, security had tackled the killer and was beginning to cuff and haul him away. Vesha then stood up and raised her right arm to stop them. She showed the shocked audience the bullet wound as her body healed. The round that her body had absorbed had also sparkled before their eyes as she spat it back out and into her hand. Vesha continued to glow as her eye-wound healed to one hundred percent, and even her eyeshadow and other makeup reappeared. Eliza's team of scientific heroes designed her body with the perfection of every aspect in mind. Vesha had learned how to compartmentalize the various regions of her brain to appear as she saw herself, as a beautiful and striking twenty-two-year-old version of Vesha Celeste. Everyone in the room was amazed at what they beheld and confused about the violence they had witnessed.

As calm and collected as Eliza typically was, she was currently very saddened and quite apparently appalled and angry at the fool, yet she held herself in pause. The audience noticed a small glow about her as she said, "Security, please keep him cuffed, but sit him down. I want him to hear this."

The security team sat him down, and now he too was stunned, along with everyone else in the room. Even those who knew about Vesha's elaborate molecular makeup who belonged to the UP had never known the extent to which this would work. Quite a few UP delegates throughout the world had experienced attempts on their lives, but of those in this country who had won bids for the Senate in 2018 and were thus present, not even one of them had gone through a similar ordeal. None of those present would have ever suspected that a deranged and cold-blooded killer-lunatic would try to come close to harming such a kind soul as Vesha had always been. Much less so, considering the given fact that Eliza had been standing right there beside her.

Even still, only the delegates and honorable members of the Senate who knew about the advances of the physiological and neurological nanos and their tie-in to the cellular and DNA matrix, knew that a person who had these optimizations could take a bullet in the brain, live, and heal rather quickly. Eliza's Pathway delegates knew that both physiologically and neurologically, Vesha had constant connectivity to the Twelve Database Moons. Despite their vast swaths of knowledge, even the Pathway delegates who hadn't been around the violence in the field were still amazed to see this play out before their eyes.

There was complexity in the science of all of this; it wasn't magic.

Vesha could see and process things through her eyes in nanoseconds, catch bullets anywhere on her body and live, and so much more. Not to mention, everyone within the room, smart or not, saw an intellect within her that was beyond reproach, and no matter how they identified themselves, both men and women also found themselves drawn to her, and amazed at how she was very visually appealing and downright attractive.

"What this individual did should never have happened. I'm appalled that someone would be that devoid of humanity. However, please, let us all cool down a bit and learn together from this potentially tragic event, right now." Eliza continued, "We always knew that man could be the enemy of himself, so, fortunately, we've taken every necessary precaution to protect the delegates of the UP and every single employee of Pathway Industries in much the same way as Vesha. We did not hold back. Vesha has also developed unique traits of her own. Much of this is due to her pre-existing qualities and character. For example, she had iron-clad virtues of compassion, empathy, a thirst for knowledge, and a desire for the understanding of our Universe throughout the entire eighty-eight years of her life. People can become like Vesha. Those who we welcome as members of our fold can become fully read-in members, and if they truly wish to preserve life and not destroy it, they will find they can grow, as some may say, immortal. As time goes by, you'll see that Vesha is more omnipotent than many, notwithstanding. That is because of her inherent virtues. As such, she will play an integral role throughout history and the Universe. When the timing is right, we will reveal more to the world. For each of us to be worthy to journey into deep space and beyond the protection of our Solar System, while remaining intact and aware, we must learn to preserve life, and not take it away. We need to be sturdy, durable, healthy, capable, and wise, and most importantly, we need to be or become compassionate.

"Vesha, can you please speak to the Senate and your assailant?"

Vesha waited for Eliza to step aside, and then she stood behind the podium, with all eyes on her. The people in the room weren't sure whether to consider her a superhero or a goddess, but their thoughts were very much along those lines.

"I appreciate your undivided attention. I am a humble human, just like each of you. I think, and I dream, and I hope. As many do, I pray. I have an eager expectation that we can each do what needs to be done to understand, explore, and someday preserve our beautiful Universe. I believe that humanity has evolved now, to where the Universe sees itself through each of us, and in as much as we are benevolent, we can live, love, laugh, and learn for a very long, long time. Quite possibly forever.

"Who would like to come along with me on a journey throughout the Cosmos? Who here would desire to go with me on a vacation where the waves of wine crash upon the crystalline shores that lie before mountains of emeralds and naturally enriched soil? This soil is perfect for forests of grapes, fermenting from the rays of its bright blue suns, gathering into lakes and trickling streams that empty into the seas of wine and crashing waves caused by the three beautiful moons, on the planet Eto?

"The oxygen is lovely, perfect for roaming the planet without astronaut gear, and the moons protect its globe or the world that is known as Eto, from too much radiation. Forests and vineyards grow naturally and cover this beautiful orb, with mountain ranges of sapphires, rubies, amethysts, and diamonds as far as the eye can see. I know these wonders exist, and I can surmise why because I can see them with the telescopic vision of my own two eyes. I can visualize every detail, calculate every aspect of physics and biology, and we can all enjoy wonders such as these and so much more. We can enjoy all of this together.

"However, to get out there, we each need to optimize the health and the intellect of our minds, as well as the speed, the strength, the endurance, and the immunity of our bodies to the harsh elements that exist between here and there." As Vesha spoke, she caused a three-dimensional holograph representation of what she was describing to appear above her and then pointed in the direction of space that one would look to see the planet she was describing. No terrestrial telescopes could stretch their sights that far nor with that much clarity, but the people could see that she was speaking the truth. She continued, and the audience was as quiet as could be.

"The planet I speak of exists in Andromeda, our neighbor spiral galaxy, a galaxy within our local supercluster of galaxies. Eto is merely one of many wondrous worlds with phenomena that captures our curiosity. There is a lot out there waiting for us to get our heads pointed in the right direction so we can explore and savor our Universe. We can do so by helping each other toward the advancement of our civilization. We do not need to be bound to one beautiful planet alone when there are so many delightful planets within our Universe to explore, enjoy, adore, and preserve.

"The Universe can be appreciated and enjoyed if we afford everyone the option to have abilities that are similar to my own. Optimization is a matter of personal choice. There is something you must also know. You certainly have opportunities here and now. Throughout each day, the results of these choices may bring joy and happiness, or they may bring human folly and laughter, or they may contribute to the destruction of civilization and its very existence over the long-haul. If you do not fill your mind with love, kindness, and compassion, these abilities will not take. Optimized capabilities will not germinate the healing within, they will have no means with which to stay or even function as they ought to, and as a traveler, you will thus not be able to withstand the harsh environments of space travel. Tiny little nanos can heal anyone willing, but each of us needs to exercise our clarity of mind in a manner that includes goodwill with compassionate and benevolent intent toward others. If we don't operate with kindness in our every action, our physiology will not learn from the nanos, and the ability of the nanos to heal will fade away. Perhaps a person can live longer, but that is their choice, based on how they treat others.

"Now, bear witness, each of you who are in this room, Eliza's designs take into consideration the erosion of memory, and she has built into her complex system the ability to heal the mind. If that seemed impossible to comprehend, consider the areas of the brain that light up most when people are mindful of the well-being of others, or when we have those moments where ideas for improvement suddenly make more sense to us, or where clarity of steps necessary to complete a task actually register more clearly throughout the brain. She has taken each of these factors, added several orders of magnitude, of strength, and force to their function and created frequency algorithms that travel from a biopod to our cells. As I mentioned before, we call these little helpers 'nanos.' These nanos move to our sensory systems, glands, nodes, neurons, and synapses and they enhance our capabilities as well as the capacities of the other nanos to work in concert with our cells to ensure mutual healing in every possible way.

"Therefore, although traveling through space may stem chaotic activity that will require both physiological and neurological optimizations and even enhancements, Eliza has thought of and mitigated those issues. In my short time back in this mortal existence, I see that many of you allow these unseen forces for evil, chaos, and destruction to dictate to you what is or isn't an abomination. Any of you who do this ought to be ashamed of yourselves. Eliza loves, she cares, and action always accompanies her words. She preaches, 'Heal, don't harm!' yet many of you seek to harm. What is wrong with those of you who do? Therapies and counseling will no doubt be needed, so crews on long-term voyages through space do not disintegrate into hysteria, and they will be in environments that will make hysteria a legitimate result. Here, in this world, filled with so much to learn, so many opportunities for life, you have little excuse for inhumanity.

"The choice is yours. Do you go on living as a lifeless and pointless husk of a man or woman with little or no promise, save death alone? Or will you choose life? Will you go on living, embracing the challenges of learning, having compassion in your every move, having passion in what you do to increase the quality of life and well-being of those around you, allowing kindness to be your driving force? Do you want to navigate through space in an unevolved state while living life according to current societal acceptance, where you'll die and wither away before arriving at a distant location many centuries away? Or, would you prefer to mitigate the hazards of the harsh elements, with more agility, strength, and clarity of mind and the capacity to witness the state of our Universe trillions of years from now, and see society and humanity transcend its limitations?

"During a longer lifetime, as Eliza has preached, we may have the ability to see, advance to, and integrate with parallel Universes and multiple dimensions. We may need a diverse set of cultures that are very different from our own. We may need those who can introduce us to these new realities. We can currently save your consciousness and revive you at a later date, in the same way, that Pathway has done for me. I stand here as your example and proof of concept if you so choose. In other words, if you wish to live life in its current evolution like I did before I passed away on the night of Christmas day in 2016, you may. You can elect to walk away. Or, you can choose to evolve as Eliza has, and have an increased breadth of understanding, empathy, compassion, knowledge, and experience due to her optimizations and journeys through what is called the Virtual Universe. The Virtual Universe is where you can learn every bit of knowledge available, make sense of it all, and recall it when needed. You will be able to compound upon everything you can do, supply areas where we can learn from trial and error that comes from and solutions, which will become as clear as day in minutes rather than in and through generations, if we still and can exist, many centuries later.

"When it comes to parallel universes, multiverses, and other dimensions, we'll be surprised at how knowledge compounds upon itself, and as we move forward as a civilization, our technologies and capabilities will increase with speed and complexity, likewise, before our very eyes. So, the choice now is yours, to allow the advancements Eliza has developed to be shared globally with the idea of consent in its wake or deprive everyone else including yourselves of the option of a promising future."

Vesha looked out at the Senators, the visitors, and her murderer, and she smiled at each of them. The audience saw the vitality of her character as it complemented the vibrancy of the highlights in arrays of pinks, purples, blues, greens, and even yellows that had formed in her jet-black hair as she spoke. They saw them contrast magnificently with her dark brunette natural hair color, the spiral waves as they jutted down seductively to her shoulders in an A-frame style, the glistening of the turquoise in her irises, surrounded by thick black limbal rings. The shivering and glowing luminescence of her exposed skin, her attire, an incredible black and skin-tight wetsuit-seeming complexity of colors and embroidery, with accents that complemented her hair, her eyes, and her perfectly toned and curvy physique, helped them to realize that she indeed was the real deal. Vesha and Eliza were the wave of the future, a future of promise, fun, and joy. Everyone there could walk away today as if nothing happened, or they could try something new.

Eliza stood up, and Vesha stood by her side and began to speak before the awestruck audience. "My dear friend Vesha has told you so much, things I had wished for you to learn in due time. It appears that this time has come. Please know, there is so much more beyond your comprehension that you can learn, be a party to, and enjoy if you choose to take the necessary steps between where humanity is today, to where civilization could be if we operated from a core of kindness, ingenuity, and compassion.

"I presented a new tax policy which can begin to go into effect immediately if you vote on this now. I am also prepared to donate the funding for every aspect of our nation's fiscal budget for the next ten years. Pathway Industries is willing to impart one-hundred-trillion USD in resources for all the major and minor industries on an annual basis, to bring not only our country success but to help our allied nations as well. These measures will help us to make possible the kinds of changes that we need to make. We will be able to prevent the uncontrolled chaos that will destroy our home planet if we do not adequately harness it and ensure that we heal the Earth of its damage. This measure will allow Pathway Industries to pay for all Medical care while providing free education collectively and paying off all debts.

"If you are willing to vote on the two bills here, which I presented the December before last, for you to examine and read, I will ask that you journey with me to the Melrose Campuses, and I will give each one of you a full-on opportunity to explore all of my inventions. All who raise their hands, feel free to follow me once this session is complete, and become fully read-in to Pathway if you so choose."

With that, Eliza and Vesha stepped down from behind the pulpit and took their seats.

The ranking member of the Senate stood up, "All who wish to vote for our colleague's Tax Reform Bill, please raise your hands and say 'aye.'"

Everyone raised their hands and said, "Aye."

"All legislators who wish to vote for our colleague's Healthcare Reform Bill, please raise your hands and say, 'aye.'"

Everyone raised their hands and said, "Aye."

"All legislators who wish to vote for our colleague's Education Reform Bill, please raise your hands and say, 'aye.'"

Everyone raised their hands and said, "Aye."

After the Senate finished with its proceedings, everyone talked amongst themselves briefly, and all agreed to follow Senator Eliza Williams and Dr. Vesha Celeste through Eliza's private jump gate, where Yesha Alevtina, the President of Pathway Industries, welcomed them at the Melrose Campuses Training Hall. All who were present in the Senatorial Chambers were there, including the member of Paranoidis Capitalis and the security guards who had had him detained. Just like the two-billion and more people who had passed through the Virtual Universe before them, they too received initial training, were fully read-in, and then journeyed with Eliza, Yesha, and Vesha for five minutes in the real world equating in ratio to twenty years or more inside the Virtual Universe. When everyone returned, they could not contain their excitement. The entire Senate, in a freak reality to all other parties and their leaders, joined the UP.

As far as the member of Paranoidis Capitalis was concerned, Eliza and her delegates discovered that due to his toxic and saddening environment as a child the vulnerabilities were such that a secret and malicious group exploited him. Furthermore, he had risen within their ranks and was now their leader. All the citizens of Pathway knew that if this young adult had received proper nurture and a caring upbringing as a child, the group called Paranoidis Capitalis, or those lost in the Anti-Pathway mindset, would never have influenced his mind. Now, they no longer would. He was a free man. He now had clarity on what he could do to serve his days raising the bar for humankind. Everyone in Pathway forgave him, and he too found blossoming within him, a new clearness of conscience and a desire to live the Principles of Universal Ethics. His newfound purity of character would drive him to help humanity in beautiful ways for a very long time.

A View from Above

"Well, that was quite an evening, Yesha." Eliza had used her neural, link and shared some intriguing moments privately with her friend, following the events of the day.

"Vesha was graceful through everything and as you witnessed through our compartmentalized link, her grace pretty much set a whole new precedent. The full Senate is now part of the UP; they and everyone present, to include Vesha's intended killer, were all read-in successfully. We don't have the Virtual Correction Matrix setup yet, but Joanne, Evan, and Matzu are making progress on it in strides. Despite the challenges, we certainly have a lot to be grateful for. It looks like the Executive and Judicial branches were confused by the measures. So, unfortunately, without the backing of the House, it was vetoed. We'll figure out a way to get this out eventually. I know we must keep trying. Say, would you like to come with Vesha and me to the space elevator? Oh, and please invite Amber, Erin, and Najem?"

"Of course, Eliza," said her friend, Yesha.

Eliza dampened her neural link and looked toward Vesha Celeste sitting on one of the other chairs in her Senatorial office. She looked fantastic and from the future and regal all at the same time. Of all things she and all her friends had accomplished, to Eliza, bringing back Vesha Celeste was the most important for so many reasons. For all intents and purposes, Vesha had been resurrected, both immortal and quite powerful. There were also undoubtedly good vibes between them, and she had hoped it would stay that way for a very long time.

"What's the matter, Eliza?" asked Vesha. "You seem nervous. I can see your glow and the expressions in your face are currently giving you away."

"Oh, nothing's wrong. I've been thinking about it, about last night, and for a moment there I was genuinely shocked. I was worried I was going to lose you again, and all too soon. I've seen brutality in the minds of many through experiences in the Virtual Universe, and I've seen the members of Pathway heal before this after something horrible took place, but never right before my eyes in the real world. I appreciate who you are, Vesha. I understand your ability to connect with others, and despite the circumstances, you are so well-balanced and considerate in your approach. What you did yesterday was perfect in timing in every possible way. Thank you for being the wonderful person that you are, Vesha Celeste. In just a short while, as soon as Yesha contacts Najem, Amber, and Erin, we'll use the space elevator the old-fashioned way, if you would like? Would you please accompany me? I need to talk with both you and Erin Carter.

"There are a lot of aspects of politics that are becoming clearer as far as the upcoming elections are concerned, the events of yesterday, and what our next course of actions should be. That aside, you ceaselessly impress me, Vesha, and I don't know what to say, and I can't say it enough. It is not too often of late that I share this world with others who think as deep and complex as it seems I do, it's nice to have a break every now and then. Maybe it's just this environment on Capitol Hill, but most of the time I feel as though I am the torch bearer being pummeled by those who need the light to meander through life, and sometimes I second-guess myself on things, or I forget the efforts others are putting into this too.

"But who am I kidding? I would be lost without them, and I would most definitely be lost without you. Even with optimized physiology and neurology, I realize I am far from perfect, but I can't ever forget the strength, the wit, and support I receive from everyone at Pathway and the UP. James, he does so much for Pathway, out there in the deep, dark, and cold void of space. I must applaud him; he does it often, and he does it so well. Still, there is much more to do. I suppose I should be very grateful that our forests are filled with sentient animals who love to give me guidance and tolerate my sense of perfectionism and my bouts of solitude. Silly, isn't it? I mean, just the other day I was talking to Amber's favorite cow, Chloe, and you know what she said to me? She said it is okay for me to relax from time to time. I can't always be on the go. It's just that I get the sense that once the Universe has been saved from the expansion, then I will be able to relax. Maybe take James out for a cup of Jo, if he's ever interested. But eventually, I know I will wonder what's next. I still miss Charles. Remember our visits, before he died? Before you passed away? It's been quite some time, and James, he must be terribly lonely. No matter, it shouldn't matter. There is a lot that needs to get done. I don't have time to wallow in what could, should, or ought to be, I, no, we need to help humanity.

"We could go to Eto tomorrow and bathe in the beaches of wine, but something else tells me that in due time, maybe all of us besties can do that, but right now is just not the time."

Vesha looked at Eliza with peace, compassion, and with a sweet charm that only comes from someone who had truly lived the eighty-eight years she had, and in a very supportive manner she responded to Eliza's concerns, "Everything is going to be okay, Eliza. Maybe you can go for that cup of Jo someday; you must trust your heart on those things. I know there are so many things you want to do to help others. You're not alone though, and you never were. Today, there are at least two-billion people who love you dearly, and James is one of them. I am by no means or by any stretch of the imagination even close to perfect either. Still, we do our best, and as a delightful lady once said, once we know better, we do better. You are a sweet soul, a darling of hearts, and I don't know what would have become of humanity had it not been for the fire that burns within you. Eliza, I think about visiting my family all the time, but could you imagine what they would say if they saw me now? I too am worried they'd be devastated.

"I'm far from the quirky grandmother I was three years ago. Those experiences with Ralston, Daniel, Jillian, Chris, Avery, everyone I held dear, it all seems like a lifetime ago; they are all as clear as day in my mind. Perhaps in the not so distant future, we'll be able to spend more time with those we hold dearest. We'll be able to take our besties, our families, and those we care about most and travel to the opposite ends of our known Universe, maybe to that cold patch in the CMB. Perchance we'll be able to take the same trip the slow way, just to take in the ambiance and unwind. Perhaps it just takes us doing what we are doing, doing what we do best, so that eventually when the pieces of the Universal puzzle have all finally been found and put together in their right place, then, oh then can we celebrate and relax. We'll be able to think about the past, enjoy the present, and plan for the future. Trust yourself, Eliza. You have a lot going for you, and I have no doubt that romance will be a part of your life for a very long time, even longer than you know."

Eliza thanked Vesha, and reminisced just a little more, "I remember taking him through the Virtual Universe for his very first trip. He has such a beautiful and charming mind. I remember when we returned, and he, Yesha, and I went out by our pond, laid on our sleeping bags and gazed up at the stars singing some of our favorite tunes together. 'But Not Tonight,' from Depeche Mode comes to mind in some ways. In another way, it seems like all of that was a very long time ago, literally centuries or even millennia ago, yet in my mind, I can remember it as if it were yesterday. Memories like that keep me grounded, and they give me hope."

"Those are wonderful memories to hold on to, Eliza. I'm with you now and always, my friend. No matter where I go, I will think of you, and we'll still be connected. Perhaps you and James will have a chance to take a break together to relax and enjoy the Sun sometime soon?"

"I suppose," Said Eliza, "but I'll allow that one to take its course. Some things are best letting them be free and flowing. I will certainly not push the issue. I'll just let it happen as it will."

"We'll keep this conversation between us. I'll compartmentalize this in the 'do not disturb' area of my mind. We might as well be sisters and besties. I love you, sis!" Vesha smiled.

It was a few moments later, traveling through Eliza's jump gate from the other room of her senatorial office where they had been sitting. It was also early in the morning, and now they were at the border of New York and Ontario, where the first space elevator that had ever been built was located. Although several more had been constructed since, one for each prospective zonal command, they had chosen this as the first location, and now together, they rode this elevator all the way up. Once there, the view was breath-taking, and Vesha Celeste stood with Eliza and each of their closest friends on the broad platform which hovered in outer space above the Earth about one-hundred-thousand miles or one-hundred-sixty-one-thousand kilometers, and they each looked at every angle and quietly soaked in the ambiance.

Eliza was standing next to her on the left and Erin to her right. To Eliza's left was Yesha and Joanne, and to Erin's right was Amber, Jasmine, and Najem. Although the platform was encapsulated to provide safety to anyone who found themselves there for whatever reason, it was see-through, courtesy of Projected Invisibility Smart Technology as well as continuous maintenance from the assigned nano clouds for that platform. Each platform of this sort was like a series of huge sports stadiums, but with a series of spaceports that jutted out from each stadium ring, which left it almost resembling a giant gear that kept pace with its tethered anchor position on the Earth down below. For anyone of public standards, standing on one of the gear teeth or spaceports overlooking the Earth, back toward the Moon, and gazing toward deep space in every direction using only 20/20 vision was breath-taking in and of itself, so they spent time doing just that, before engaging their enhanced vision to reel in details on anything they wished. Eliza was looking down toward Earth, with her ever-glistening crystal blue eyes, and deep in thought.

"This is beautiful," said Vesha, breaking the silence, and oddly enough without dismissing the sense of harmony the quiet had ushered in, bringing everyone back to their senses. "Look at the Earth down below. It's amazing how the diamond-titanium-infused carbon nanotubes work. They're stronger than steel and more flexible than softened rubber. The magnetic anchoring way below the bedrock was a brilliant way to integrate with and tie into the massive solar engines that keep the platform where it needs to be. Great job, Eliza and crew!"

"Nine years ago, I was looking up in the sky, watching the crane migration. Now, with my telescopic eyes, I can see Bonnie. Wow! I never dreamt something of this magnitude was possible. Impressive, Eliza. Impressive," said Erin.

"It's amazing how many have joined in the cause. Who would have thought that we little wee Earthlings could ever arrive at this? I hope that everyone down there can see the bigger picture soon," said Najem, who had seen great satellite telescopes, all sent to space in her NASA days. "No matter, they can take their time now. You've done a lot to help humanity, Eliza."

"You certainly have," said Jasmine with a kind smile, looking past her close friends and sending her gaze toward Eliza.

"Eliza certainly has had a special mind since day one. We'd have none of this if it weren't for her," said Yesha and Vesha in unison, followed by a little bit of surprised laughter.

"Several years ago, all I knew of were songs, stages, and the T.O. Never in my life could I have imagined this before I met you, Eliza. Thank you," Said Joanne.

Eliza finally broke out of her shell a bit and participated with the rest of them. She smiled, and trying not to cry, she said, "I love each of you. It wasn't just me; it was all of you too. None of this would be accomplished if it hadn't been for teamwork from some of the best, most brilliant, and remarkable of people. While not everyone we treasure is here, we cherish them just the same, and hopefully, hopefully, someday we can be with them here, looking down toward the beauty of our home world, and find gratitude for the luxury of one another's company.

"I want each of you to know, that while I am cooped up on Capitol Hill, I still can see what each of you do, each and every day. Thank goodness to everyone in Pathway, and all that James and his crews achieve, we can take time to enjoy life every once in a while. I suppose it doesn't all have to get done in one day.

"That said, I brought you all here today, to talk about what I would like to have each one of you achieve in the near future. Erin, you have done a fantastic job, with all those beautiful people and their families, the people who you helped and rescued. Now they have a beautiful home in the tech cities, and they do missions throughout the Solar System and back on Earth, doing all manner of things to help humanity. Yesha, you're doing a fantastic job as a solo-artist running the big show for Pathway, and you've done so much, while training Erin as your understudy. With big projects coming up, I'd like to see Erin voted in to officially be your Vice President of Pathway's operations throughout Earth. I plan to begin my bid as a UP Candidate for President of the United States for the elections of 2024, and I would like Erin spun up to manage Pathway as the President, because I would like you to be my running mate, Yesha. Erin, that said, please work with Joanne as much as you can, because she will be your vice president when you are the President of Pathway. Najem and Jasmine, thank you so much for working with Vesha to speed her up on Solar System Operations, with James. If you could both help Vesha and James, as far as mission tasking for the big journey ahead is concerned that would be wonderful. As you already know, the entire observable Universe will be divided into twelve zones, so could you please keep looking into ideal regions within each zone that the future IMC Commander can visit and leave behind with IMC command zone headquarters and observation posts? Vesha, could you please work with James, to help him with Solar System Operations, tech city governance, and begin the IMC Command Spacecraft project?

"There is a lot we do need to do, in order to begin our next phase. Humanity is showing progress, but we still have a ways to go. There are still way too many people throughout the world that are suffering. Even though we've managed to rescue more than two-billion people, there are still close to eight billion people on Earth. Many of whom are stuck in a drab, boring, and horrible reality that I wouldn't wish on anyone. Each of us will be doing something important when it comes to preserving our Earth and the people and living creatures within its biosphere. As President of Pathway's tech cities spread throughout the Solar System, I authorize and delegate power to each of you in any manner of your choosing to do as you see fit within your scope of responsibility. When I return to the Senate, James will resume Presidency of Solar System Operations, Yesha will resume presidency of Pathway Operations, and Vesha Celeste, I empower you to set up and take command of IMC Command Spacecraft Development and Operations.

"At any time, as always, you can visit me within the Virtual Universe. Feel free to call me on my neural link, and if I seem a little 'away,' please know that I am probably in the senate chambers conducting business, but I will get back to you soon. I am here for you, and please believe me; I know and am thankful for the fact that each of you, are here for me. I promise that if we continue to do as I have envisioned and shared with you, we will begin our journey throughout the galaxy in a little over a decade, with a reasonable population of the world sped up, ready for, and on-board with everything that we are doing. Do you currently have any questions?"

Everyone had taken note of Eliza's gracious yet serious tone, and no one had a single question. They knew that they could contact Eliza at any time, but for now Yesha, Vesha, Erin, Joanne, Najem, and Jasmine had their real-world orders, and after all, Eliza was the boss. She was never angry, and she had never been irate with anyone within Pathway. Instead, Eliza was always helpful, innovative, courteous, supportive, kind, and compassionate, as well as passionate about each detail of each item addressed. Each one of her closest friends, there with her that day, knew Eliza had a heart of gold and loved her leadership and the clarity of vision she possessed. She was already an excellent leader of more than two-billion people and counting, so no doubt, despite its profound complexity, she would still make a wonderful POTUS; besides the US needed a leader with ethics and clarity.

Eliza let her words sink in, and together, with the same harmony as before, they observed the different aspects of outer space and the Earth below. Something about Eliza was a little off, she was frustrated and had perfected the ability to compartmentalize her mind to where Pathway could only detect what she wanted it to detect. The Twelve Database Moons were her creation.

Friends now shifted gears into co-workers who were stalwart and loyal, with their boss standing in the middle, and everyone else lost in thought, and with the quiet ambiance of space seemingly turned up a few decibels within their minds, Vesha was the first to speak up. "Although I am leaving room for flexibility here, I already have an idea of who I would choose as a team lead for each aspect from design to development and the building of the IMC. I believe you will be happy, Eliza. From what I can tell, this will create a new and intimate involvement with the IMC, for each of the Pathway members I believe you have in mind as IMC Commanders for Zones-01 through 12. For now, I'll keep that information compartmentalized within a region of our minds that are only reachable by each of you, as well as James."

And then Vesha sent a mental message that only Eliza could hear, *"I'll be prudent with how I talk to James, Eliza, regarding what's going on in your heart. In a way, I sense that struggle within you. You have your feelings for him under incredible lockdown, so I'll be careful, considerate, and kind. Still, no one else even knows how you feel about him. Perhaps even Yesha has no idea. He's certainly done a lot for you, and I know that trust is one of the most important aspects in long-term connection and even romance. Please don't worry, I'll let you do this in your own time, and I've got your back. Whatever may be bothering you, you can always let me know."*

"Thank you, Vesha. You're right, Yesha may have a little suspicion, but I haven't shared anything about this with her, yet. I believe I'll talk to her soon. I'll try to iron my mind out a bit, and maybe do some meditating. It's been a while. That usually keeps me well-grounded. Plus, we have so much to do, so much to focus on. I can't get lost in romantic worries for now. Maybe, just maybe, after I've served as POTUS for eight years, or when the time is right, I will let James know how I feel. Please also note that the only reason why I intend to serve is that I see a broken system and I have clarity on how to fix it. James has a lot on his hands right now, and I wouldn't want to fog his focus."

Chapter 22: Solar System Operations

Database Moon Archive, Celestial-Sol Date: 2019 March 27. Erin Carter, Yesha Alevtina's Vice President, summarizes the experiences of Pathway-hierarchy involved in the Solar System Operations that lead to the construction of the IMC. These memories are from many Pathway Leaders, recorded within the Virtual Universe, interfaced within Pathway Melrose Campus. Input by Erin Carter, VP, 2018-2022, and President of Pathway, 2022-2029.

It was late March of 2019 when after the last ten years James Cooper had worked with an ever-growing cadre on Solar System Operations, and he received the virtual notice from Eliza that Vesha would be working with him for a while. He noticed something a little different about her tone, but he didn't mention anything. James had always had her in the top spot of his heart since the first day he met her, yet he didn't want to press the issue, so instead, he aimed to please. After all, Eliza was iron-clad and inspiring. He saw the pureness of the intentions of her heart and mind many times in the Virtual Universe, and none of it suggested romance or a love affair. They were working together to save humanity, to prepare humanity, and then to send humanity with Vesha Celeste through all ends of the Universe, observable relative to Earth, with hope in mind.

James thought about how things had come along so well over the years. It was through a structured collaboration of linked minds taking advantage of Virtual Universe time as compared to real-world time, Eliza's well-placed sensors, her upgraded and re-encoded clouds of nanos, and the use of her jump gates to visit any location from any location that he had kept the twenty-thousand tech cities running so smoothly. He and his crew had grown to twenty-million Pathway citizens by 2010 while still in a minimally governed yet neurologically linked populous, and the collaborative mindset afforded him a cohesive workforce, while also ensuring that all other projects within the Solar System were developed and verified with the same high level of quality and precision.

Perhaps the most enjoyable aspect of it all was the ability to move around as often as desired, if not for the missions and work orders, quite simply for the ability to step out from the rather large and beautifully landscaped balcony to see Jupiter, or Saturn, or any of the planets depending on where their home was at the time and enjoy the spectacular sky-scape from the balcony of his tech city suite. Things had gone well for James; he was proud of his progress.

Living in a tech city was abundantly enjoyable since everyone seemed to know and understand one another with a profound and understanding point of view and in a kind and gracious manner. One could jump-gate to pretty much anywhere in a tech city from any point to any other point, with minor coordination, or one could walk, or one could use their new jump watches to jump from their luxury suite to their own work center office. If a flavor of food lingered in the mind long enough, despite optimization, one could go to a nearby restaurant, and the chefs, through neural linking, would send something your way that would please the taste buds beyond belief. It could be delivered, picked up, or as most people preferred, they could dine out and converse with friends, family, and co-workers at the dining facilities. Everyone and anyone who worked anywhere, from the vast arts, cultural, sports, and performance centers, to science labs, innovation centers, and much more all seemed to know exactly what the taste buds, neurology and physiology as a whole needed, the chefs would pick up on it and always and successfully aim to please.

Every restaurant in every tech city was as magnificent as the T.O. and each in its own creative and unique way. Even walking on the smart sidewalks and looking at the buildings as they waved in and out and in sound infrastructural, astounding, and creative ways were breath-taking. Flowers, statues, gardens, rocks laid out ever so aesthetically pleasingly and breathtakingly in terraces and walkways, with gazebos, swings for two, and ample space for anyone walking their dogs, or any other muse, was all part of the charm of a walk through any tech city. There were a lot of white buildings with black and iridescent accented trim, and green multi-colored flower trees surrounded every edifice. Life was pleasant and full of shared artistry and music that seemed to culminate toward the end of each day in a concerto of shared humor, laughter, joyful pleasantries throughout each block of each city, and untamed smiles.

After the eight-hour timeframe for work was done each weekday, everyone would go through their private jump gates, hop in their biopods for five minutes, for a range of ten to forty years of Virtual Universe time, almost always shared the last few hours together, stepped out, and then had a real-world block party, concert, rave, trance dreamscape, with the best edible spreads and beverages known to exist. Life was amazing in the tech cities. At night people could party until ten minutes prior to the next day, hop in their biopods for a quick one minute real-world, eight-hour Virtual Universe rest, and then return to work all nano-washed and walking through their jump gates with minutes to spare. Sometimes, they would rest for eight hours, since the walls were highly sound rated, they would get up, shower, get ready, and then step through their jump gates or activate their jump watches to work, as well, and with several minutes to spare. Work was all focus, dedication, work-related coordination in the Virtual Universe, full of brainstorming, sharing ideas, considering the Universal Ethics of each projected plan, and implementation of the plans coordinated and applied afterward in the real world.

In 2010, Eliza had set up a system of governance for the tech cities based on what she called the Principles of Universal Ethics. Since then, the population within the twenty-thousand tech cities had grown to two billion. More people were being read-in and moving in each day. Everything Eliza had set up seemed to work, and thus far, for James, everyone seemed enthusiastic about life, and there had been no need whatsoever for law enforcement. To add to that, highly advanced protective systems were already in place and continuously upgraded and maintained in a way that would provide the Solar System as a whole a robust defense if it was ever needed.

During Eliza and Yesha's first journey through the Virtual Universe and ever since they peered into the vastness of space at the very beginning, they dared not send humanity outside the Solar System. They wanted to be sure humanity was ready for the journeys ahead. A plausible adventure into the unknown without knowing what they would be running into was possible, but only if humanity were united. So, Eliza and her team prepared for any of the possibilities that genius minds could conjure up, well and in advance. That was one of the reasons why the Entertainment Matrix had been set up, to allow creativity to forge methods for overcoming the worst aspects of space, aliens, and humanity itself. As such, Eliza and Pathway had peered many times into deep space and had prepared substantially for some of the greatest and most odious of threats. They had prepared humanity without humanity even knowing it. Perhaps they would someday.

After years and even generations on Earth under laws that had little to do with well-being, governance through Eliza, Yesha, and James via Pathway's tech cities had been a piece of cake. Negative forms of stress were lower for this shared population of two-billion-plus than it had ever been for them in any other community throughout Earth. Stress was lower than it had been for anyone in any civilization throughout the history of humanity. She knew that when people were of a healthy mind, they were kind, and they contributed through innovation, progress, due preparation, achievement, breakthroughs, and action, they did not need punishment for mistakes nor someone to enforce laws since the laws observed remained steeped in common sense and were even universal. The people of Pathway worked to improve longevity, quality of life, clarity of mind, and they governed themselves. James knew this and was beloved as well.

There was an almost overwhelming complexity of the enormity of population, workforce management, living needs and requirements, city infrastructure maintenance, spaceport and terraforming operations, and more. Through Eliza, James' specific management style and expertise had been ideal. With all that James was doing, however, he often looked to his original crew from YY Construction Corporation. This became a subsidiary of Pathway, known as Pathway Construction. It had been delegated to him, and he had in-turn delegated as much as was possible and necessary to his very first crew of ninety-seven and their families. Each of his crewmembers and their families had also become quite seasoned and shared many ideas when it came to updates, repairs, and improvements to the infrastructure throughout the Solar System. They each had crews as well and worked cogently with two-point-two-billion people as well as with a complex network of sensors paired with billions of clouds of maintenance nanos, and all of this was undoubtedly a force to be reckoned with. He had quite a trustworthy and sizable cadre working with him, and so many projects had been completed throughout the ten years that he was Solar System Operations President, but he was due for a little bit of a break. Although that break wouldn't happen for many years, to a certain extent Eliza saw this, had never forgotten about him amidst everything that was going on, and had sent Vesha Celeste his way to help.

Until Vesha had arrived, as time went by, even though the population had certainly grown exponentially, the Intergalactic Mission Contingency, or IMC, which was going to be a series of thirteen command spacecraft and all that they would contain, was still in the brainstorm phase and had not yet become a blueprint within the Virtual Universe. Not a single part, not a single weld, and not a single piece of spacecraft had been created concerning the IMC. Regardless, James' mental capacity had grown in spades and shined many times repeatedly and in a very huge way, yet he needed an additional and powerful mind and an extra hand to begin production on the massive IMC. There were a lot of factors to consider, each command spacecraft would be a miniature world, and talking to Eliza, they both agreed that Vesha Celeste would be ideal to head the project.

As noted previously, earlier on, in 2010, Eliza had worked with James, Yesha, and a population that had at that time grown exceedingly with a simple system of governance that favored well-being, quality of life, clarity of mind, and longevity combined with productivity, fairness, kindness, and ingenuity in order to ensure that all off-world populations were ruled with as much simplicity, benevolence, and common sense as was possible. In exchange, each person was given unlimited universal credit accounts, and anything they needed was provided upon simple request, whether verbally, via a neural link, or in the Virtual Universe. Everything wasn't solely about science alone, but artistic craft, exhaustive sports opportunities, creativity, and soothing frequencies were woven in and out and extensively throughout everything they did. Through it all, they would in-turn be involved with a myriad of projects to ensure the Solar System's defense mechanisms were updated and upgraded as soon as updates and upgrades were available. The buildings of the tech cities were so beautiful and intricate that with their nanos they were practically alive yet were held up via robust diamond-carbon nanotube column and beam scaffoldings that could buffet any conceivable form of attack or quake or anything else within the many environments they were in throughout the Solar System, that could be thrown at them. The nanos that were integrated throughout out each building and city and paired with them regularly carried out maintenance orders mending damage or making appropriate updates.

Most of what Eliza had designed and developed in 2008, through an automated process of creating and encoding nanos within the Virtual Universe to build all the infrastructure throughout the Solar System, had at that time been completed. All of this, because James had worked with her, for her, and had furthered her progress through updates and collaborative thinking with his crews, as well as the creativity of the many individuals that through time had become a part of Pathway. As time went by, more projects surfaced to append what was already amazing and the population over the last nine years had grown exponentially.

Throughout the existence of Pathway, the population growth had been derived in large part from rescuing others from toxic environments and situations on Earth, healing them, and providing them a beautiful place to live as well as clearness as to what they could do to assist our Earth-based civilization in progressing to the point of having a legacy we could, in essence, be proud to share with other civilizations throughout the Universe. They took up the task, once optimized and read-in, and with unlimited universal credits to help where they could, they had fluidity when it came to undeterred ingenuity and creativity, within the scope of Universal Ethics, of course. In many cases, these ethics freed them up, because a lack of them ruled out a promising future. When Pathway members considered updates and upgrades it called for climbing into biopods, meeting, and counseling with one another in the Virtual Universe.

For example, following any of Amber Blythe's and her team's latest upgrades to physiological and neurological optimizations, all two-billion citizens and growing of Pathway were more capable of braving the exceedingly harsh climates outside the tech cities and spaceports than ever before. During the three months since she had been revived, Vesha Celeste had also worked with Amber on the latest final touches and upgrades were always on the ready. All that Pathway members needed to do was enter their biopods and sync up with the Twelve Database Moons, and in under a minute their body's nanos would receive the appropriate upgrades and refurbishments as needed or requested, the same would be true of their living quarters. They would also receive any necessary schooling, training, supplies, tours, and work experience through shared interfacing and have countless opportunities to visit the Entertainment Matrix, where imagination was the limit. Once the nanos were updated, the cells in the body would work in overdrive to carry out the nano upgrades, and likewise the nanos would help the cells carry out their functions to strengthen every sinew, muscle, and fiber of the flesh, to create more agility, elasticity, and clarity to both the body and the mind.

Two-billion strong and continuously growing, every member of Pathway who had been fully read-in was a force to be reckoned with. As such, their shared culture, societal richness, and art were enjoyed for every bit of uniqueness that was expressed and prevalent. Pathway had a love for diversity, and the twenty-thousand tech cities reflected that in the most beautiful of ways. Amber Blythe had finished her doctorates in the humblest of ways, multiplied her talents, and had recruited countless new Pathway citizens. She had added a profound effect to each optimization, upgrade, and update, when it came to genetic improvements, interfacing through biopods, and actualization and experiential application through the Virtual Universe. In many other cases, the people throughout Pathway were each doing rescues, developing new ideas and achieving potential unknown to those outside of Pathway, yet even still, they were beginning to yearn for a journey to other stars and galaxies.

Everything, as far as physiological and neurological requirements were concerned for the IMC building operations teams, was ready. The crews had been selected and were prepared in every way for designing, nano programming, and the building of each of the thirteen gigantic intergalactic spacecraft and all their support craft and component parts. Vesha had been given the task of working with James on all aspects of Solar System Operations, but this would be her pet project over the next few years. As the years would go by every possible environmentally or technologically advanced issue that could possibly come their way would be considered, and as a result, Pathway would see to it that Earth-based civilization would succeed in protecting and bringing life and healing to the Universe, and with the capacity to improve as we learned more.

After visiting Eliza on Capitol Hill, following the assault on her life, and after healing miraculously, surviving in front of everyone's eyes, Vesha Celeste had been more than willing to accept Eliza's request and Pathway's approval for her to become commissioned. As such, she would engage in several projects leading up to and including the design and building of the IMC, while sharing governance of the twenty-thousand tech cities throughout the Solar System, and more of these tech cities secretly cropping up in places on Earth that were once thought uninhabitable, and she did this with James Cooper, who was linked often with Eliza. Vesha had throughout her life demonstrated resolve, grace, and a very unique ability to lead, the kind that, like James, would scarcely be found in anyone else in the public sector, all of which had measured up to the gargantuan aspect of what would entail the evolution and missions of the IMC.

While they could build each spacecraft quickly, it would be a while before humanity was sped up on all of Pathway's technologies, so they had plenty of time. Regardless, Eliza, Vesha, and James as well as Yesha, Amber, and Erin had all agreed that the sooner the spacecraft could be designed, the sooner they could prepare them to withstand any plausible or even implausible reality in space and the reality that existed outside of the perceived norm on Earth would be faced and overcome, well and in advance. Had the public on Earth been aware of this immense project they would have found themselves mind-boggled at best.

Pathway already had millions of space-vehicles buzzing about back and forth all over the Solar System, but none of this activity was visible to public Earth or even vulnerable to being tracked unless a person was read-in to Pathway. As a matter of reality and fact, Eliza's foresight was so far-reaching that even the most malevolent and advanced of aliens could no longer track Earth or any of its inhabitants. Eliza would see that change once she knew humanity was ready for their new reality, and then, with a flip of a mental switch, and as quick as a lightbulb, we would introduce our Solar System to distant civilizations. Pathway's read-in system was iron-clad if not better, since thus far, out of 2.2 billion people and growing, not a single individual had defected. The correctional algorithms that Eliza and Yesha had initially set in motion had since matured and worked splendidly to persuade with fairness the loyalty of everyone in Pathway. As it was, everything outside of the IMC that had been planned was well ahead of schedule, since these technologies would be revealed after Eliza ran for President of the US winning the race and were essential before humanity could sojourn into deep space and traverse the stars. She did not plan to run in 2020 since the UP still needed to grow, but she knew if she ran in 2024, she would win, and then humanity with any luck would be ready.

Thus, Vesha could theoretically take her time building each spacecraft of the IMC if she wanted to, but she had planned on completing the gigantic spacecraft reasonably soon despite the lack of a time crunch. Delays etc. could happen at any time in outer space, and even more so if your work center was above the outer asteroid belt and the orbit of Pluto itself, just on the inside the Oort Cloud. Plus, she wanted to have and show a finished product to allow for testing and further improvements with time to spare. Every possibility had to be considered, including super advanced hostilities, so they needed to be prepared. If healing did not work, they would need to be prepared to eliminate any concern over survival, so they could get back to the goals of healing of the Universe. They could not miss a thing, so they didn't, and they wouldn't.

As steward over the entire project, and quite possibly the most significant and most expanding set of journeys humankind was on the cusp of seeing and being a part of, Vesha ensured that the workers were well-prepared and safe by protecting each project through completion within a series of optimized human-friendly bio-environments with conveyances and work centers for volunteers who wanted to be involved but had decided to live naturally or through Darwinian evolution. Very few there were, of those who chose to allow themselves to live on only through their progeny, but they were bright and glorious in spirit, nonetheless. Many, both optimized and natural, had joined to be a part of the long-term nature of progression itself. Those who were optimized wanted to behold the evolution of the Universe through desired rather than random results, and those who were natural wished to share their legacy through their children and future generations.

For now, Vesha was ready to get this project started.

Designs, Plans, and Innovations

Starting off with design, Vesha would routinely brief Yesha, Eliza, and James as she put together a series of teams and began plans for each significant aspect of her project. She involved as many Pathway personnel as she could because she was of the mind that the more there were on any given project, the merrier the progress and the more issues they could come up with, conceive of in their minds, and share in the Virtual Universe, so they could overcome them with ease. Once they could identify all the potential issues and ideal preventative measures, they could more fully prepare any IMC Command Spacecraft AI, to easily overcome each one as well.

The plan would be simple; design each aspect of the first IMC Command Spacecraft, create an order of accomplishment as to how it would be built, and produce a macro-like system with armies of clouds of Virtual-Universe-controlled-nanos that would automate those procedures and fine-tune them, and then duplicate the one spacecraft for an additional twelve or more spacecraft just like it. All the raw materials they needed were right there in the asteroid belt above and around the dwarf planet, Pluto; with Eliza's nanos, everything from the asteroids could be tapped and stored for historical data, and then they would mine, smelt, mold, shape, and finish parts from a macro to a micro level of scope using cold fusion without a single bit of waste to a single particle to provide unlimited and self-sustaining resources as needed, as well as part-integration, and systems tie-ins to complete each spacecraft.

Resources, provisions, and a large group of highly intelligent and eager personnel now ready, and looking out from her encapsulated work center in space, with a bright and full view of the Milky Way Galaxy, Vesha Celeste organized the following teams:

Team 1 – Engines/Drives, Team Lead: Luís Rodriguez

Team 2 – Navigation Systems, Team Leads: Mett Dormer, James Wilhelm

Team 3 – Environmental Systems, Team Lead: Scarlett Hart

Team 4 – Labs and Innovation Centers, Team Lead: Yon Forall

Team 5 – Inter- and Intra-Command Spacecraft Travel, Team Lead: Anastasia Renée

And finally, one of the most critical aspects of intergalactic travel:

Team 6 – Shields and Defense, Team Leads: Malinda Jefferson, Melissa Asher, Rebecca Knight, and Matzu Kashi

Ultimately, Vesha saw to it that certain key aspects of the prototype IMC Command Spacecraft would be designed first, with as many integrated crew members as requested and necessary, while simultaneously working on various other projects within the scope of the spacecraft. They could then shape a beautiful shell around the engines, navigation, and living areas that would include the shield connected like a woven network to each inner wall, and the subsequent spaces used for the life-like aspects of the living-space-juggernaut. All of this could be done by programming the clouds of nanos, and for additional high-end quality, the crew was involved with the nanos to ensure all safety, security, and functional requirements were met. The nanos were very helpful, but humanity was essential.

The head engineer for Team 1 and the great mind behind the development of the engines was Luís Rodriguez, a previous astronaut for NASA, who had been to outer space already, and who was well-versed in the development of fusion and plasma engines, yet he had theories and ideas for so much more always playing out in his mind. When he'd met Yesha in 2011, he was enthralled with Pathway LLC at the time, had worked to help it become its own super industrial powerhouse in 2012, and with clearness he had been working on far more than fusion.

Upon approach and with in-depth knowledge of quantum entanglement en masse, fusion, the sophisticated use of the Casimir effect, and gravitational and electromagnetic manipulation, he shared with Vesha his idea for four different types of engines or drives and how each would serve a mutual and seamless purpose in traversing the Cosmos. He then stated that he would refer to each component of the engines and drives as merely drives, from the moment of this conversation with her and on into the future. Vesha had approved, and he had gathered around him a large cadre of workers to mull over each detail and possibility as well.

Vesha, to ensure maximum participation, started with the six design teams and afforded them as many workers as needed. She also visited them often in the Virtual Universe for planning, review, and testing. Each crew also met in the Virtual Universe often as well.

Luís' first crew developed what he called the Q-drive. This crew of ten worked with the shared knowledge of each crewmember and Luís on the design of the Quantum Entanglement and Disentanglement Accelerator Drive. Rather than using such a long name for that or any other drive, he decided it would be much easier to call it a drive but precede it with the first letter of the outstanding feature of each unique engine, in this case, he would simply call this one the Q-drive. Essentially, this drive made use of Eliza's sensor and jump gateway technologies to fashion plans for a series of single drive to a much more robust set of powerful drives, based on spacecraft size with no apparent limit, that would take advantage of quantum entanglement to plot a location in the Universe to go to, factor in all of the navigational system information and then jump to that location in mere moments.

As Luís explained to Vesha, "This system will effectively gather every bit of information from the particles, to the atoms, to every aspect of the spacecraft, its contents, and the spacecraft itself to prepare it for delivery and then teleport from any part of the observable Universe to another part of the observable Universe as programmed or upon request of the authorized spacecraft commander or their vice commander, and could return the spacecraft, crew, and cargo upon request and immediately to the last safest location it had been to, should anything be beyond our scope of ability for safety. This drive could be used to traverse long distances through vast regions of space, from galaxy to galaxy, from filament-to-filament, from supercluster-to-supercluster, from void-to-void, from supervoid-to-supervoid, and from planet-to-planet, and anywhere between. It could travel billions of light-years within a blink of an eye, but they would start small, and thus it could be used in a small-scope-setting for travel efficiency and safety. The possibilities were endless, but as with many new ventures, jumps could always be greater with more familiarity and experience with space as it is, rather than as it seemed.

The second drive was what he called the Alcubierre Drive or the A-drive. This would in effect allow the spacecraft to travel the speed of light by grabbing outer space before it and pushing outer space behind it while the spacecraft and all its contents were shielded and safe from the effects of debris and fast acceleration or deceleration. This would be used if traveling within several parsecs to light minutes from the desired destination, or to quickly travel from one point to the next. Typically, the Q-drive would be used, but the A-drive was more of a backup drive that provided more real-time situational awareness if a sensor was sent to the target destination, and the A-drive was set to accelerate and then decelerate precisely at that point.

The Fusion Drive or the F-drive was the third sequential method available for piloting the spacecraft in auto or manual drive covering distances that were typically less than thirty light minutes away, yet with speed and agility. This was the glorified method of travel since an individual would feel the thrill of the G-Forces ever so gently while turning, accelerating or decelerating. One could look out a spacecraft window and enjoy the view of outer space as it would slowly change according to the speed and movement of the spacecraft.

Finally, the fourth drive was the G-drive or the Gravity Particle Accelerator Drive. This could be used both inside and outside the gravity wells of planets and inside or outside of the various atmospheres for precise and smooth landing, take-off, entering or exiting gravity wells, and turning, accelerating, and decelerating. Effectively, using the G-drive the spacecraft would canvas the entire area below or above and within a million-mile radius, with increased focal reaction nearest the spacecraft, no matter the speed of travel, and fuse the sensory information with every aspect when it came to monopole, dipole, and multi-pole magnetism in the areas around it to create the necessary polarity essential to float in the air or above the ground, and during landing, take-off, or even enable navigation based on automated fine tuning, while simultaneously deflecting debris or weather systems that would otherwise damage the craft. Using the G-drive, the spacecraft could hover over the ground and travel at speeds of any sort between zero miles an hour to light speed, compensating internal gravity ideally to ensure movement of the spacecraft was possible without causing the passengers or cargo to suffer from turns, G-Forces, etc.

Luís Rodriguez put together all his plans and prepared his presentation for Vesha inside the Virtual Universe. Everything was designed, shown, and virtually experimented on down to the finite details and only required Vesha to push that mental trigger to begin the building process. Once she did so, Luís' four drives would be built by pre-programmed nanos in an assembly line style and in a matter of moments, all within a bioenvironmental shelter that would provide maximum control of particle movement until the engines and drives were setup to do that themselves and protect the engines until the spacecraft was ready for their integration. Everything was ready to go; they just needed to await the work of the other teams to affix the number of drives needed for maximum power and redundancy when the rest of the spacecraft was ready for them. Luís' contribution had been astronomical in every sense, quite literally, and he was thus rewarded. Even though he could have taken a five-year paid sabbatical he chose to gather his crews and together they helped the other teams out, but in the background. This whole project was exciting to him and his crew, and they each wanted to be a part of the entire process through to completion.

On the side, he and his team worked with each of the other teams, to integrate separate fusion cores throughout many areas of the overall design of the Intergalactic Mission Contingency Spacecraft, to employ both redundancy and massive amounts of power within each of the various functions. With twelve living sectors of one-hundred living quarters each, and with sixteen powerful defensive turret locations of sixteen delivery systems apiece, as well as a very large command section, other energy requirements, and one-hundred-ninety-two support spacecraft on-board in the twelve docking bays, he had Q, A, F, and G-drives aligned for both internal and traveling aspects of each of spacecraft.

Mett Dormer had worked on the navigation systems and had engineered integrated navigational computers of all types since their beginning in the mid to late 1900s and had since been involved in the development of some of the most advanced supercomputer hardware and software systems known to humanity having worked on IBM's Brain-Computer Program, before he had met Eliza back in 2013, and therefore was an ideal team lead for a command crew and AI driven navigational system. He and his friend, James Wilhelm, had accumulated hundreds of patents under their belt and had both been fully read-in to Pathway. Each of these gentlemen had also worked on navigation systems together for NASA and had over the last few years worked closely with Luís Rodriguez for Pathway designing and building both the engines and the complex navigation systems and pilot-friendly interfaces for the millions of space-vehicles already milling about the Solar System with ease.

The command spacecraft would be so much larger in scope than anything designed before, and they would provide much more than a command section and shelter for twelve-hundred families apiece. With a vast array of complementary missions, a command spacecraft would complete, Mett Dormer, James Wilhelm, and Luís worked together, and each with a large cadre of personnel, visiting the Virtual Universe often to design the navigational systems. Many of the personnel knew that this might be the only time they could actually be a part of the IMC, because many would either stay behind to develop more command spacecraft, help with Solar System Operations, or comb the Cosmos creating vast colonies throughout the billions of galaxies in each of the twelve zones of space. As far as the navigation systems were concerned, most everything would be automated, but tied-in in such a way as to allow the AI, Spacecraft Zonal Commander or the Vice commander, permission to use autopilot or they would be enabled to take over the controls if they wanted or needed to.

Each of the navigational systems would be automatic, were tied into a very sophisticated network of artificial intelligence subsystems and each AI had a uniquely soothing, intellectual, and compassionate voice.

The AI Subsystems could be integrated into the navigation and drive systems and were such that a pilot or general in charge could enter the desired destination through their neural link or use the physical interface on the control deck. From there, the AI Subsystems were tied into the Twelve Database Moons and would also be tied into the large database processors on the spacecraft itself, and as such could communicate with the spacecraft crew and send out a series of sensors scattered throughout a general area of space near the destination desired, yet within several light-hours apart. Once the sensory information was returned and processed, the AI, the Commander, and the Vice Commander could determine within the Virtual Universe, and within an already safe sector of space, with full-on details of both visual from every direction, with recorded mapping of the regional stellar activities and every other sensory aspect the safest and most secure region of interest to jump to next. The sensors were set up such that tampering of any kind could also be detected and recorded in every frequency spectrum and in every wavelength and known encryption, so the Mission Staff would know each detail to consider and be optimally prepared if further action were required. Once the location was determined, the navigation systems would be set into motion by the AI with a macro-like set of loops that would account for every atom, every particle, and every complex construct within a defined area, or in the case of the Q-drive the entire spacecraft and its contents and then essentially teleport to the desired location for very long distance travel, with pre-planned defenses up and ready or another jump or series of jumps set up in the event of something severe, until desired exploration, discovery and progress was made, and the rest of the missions for each designation could be completed.

Team 2 presented their designs with Team 1 in the Virtual Universe to Vesha Celeste, and as such Vesha was quite impressed. *"This is a moment of prestige, of honor, and it is an honor to include all of those who worked with you, ladies and gentlemen, for doing what you have done, here, and for having the collective foresight to deal with any conceivable situation with haste, safety, and accuracy. I am so proud of each of you for your efforts, to each of your team members for their collaboration and their efforts, and as such, in accordance with Universal Laws and in and by the power of Universal Ethics, I grant each of you five years of paid sabbatical to travel wherever your whim and hope takes you. Please make the most of it, your universal credit accounts have unlimited funds, so please make the most of it, within the scope of Universal Ethics, of course. The Virtual Universe is amazing, but there is something about this physical Universe that is even more profound, bringing fullness of joy and true fulfillment when we are involved in good pursuits that bring those around us joy within."* The three gentlemen and their crews chose to hold off on their sabbatical and help Teams 3, 4, and 5. While they were working away, Team 6 finished their project.

Vesha's Team 6 finished their designs for shielding and defenses rather early and had essentially come up with a three-foot-thick array of shielding that could wrap around any shape or any size. The shielding could be fitted inside each of the drive and core chambers, outside the interior and exterior walls for maximum ability to withstand and buffet anything the Universe or worse could throw at the spacecraft. It was also designed so that no matter how malevolent, sophisticated or both any threat could be, every potential room in the spacecraft would be within its own complex system of walls and shielding and would serve as an escape pod with its own Q-drive, and thus would be additionally protected from any entities that could be thrown at it. Malinda Jefferson, Melissa Asher, Rebecca Knight, and Matzu Kashi were the science team's leadership personnel, and each of them had the experience, the wisdom, and the creativity of geniuses, in droves. They ensured that the shielding could be integrated with every other aspect of each spacecraft, such that this would lend to such a sophisticated system, that it would be alive and sentient. The spacecraft would be aware of self-preservation, the Universal Ethics of shared well-being, longevity, health, and clarity of mind of every living being within it.

To begin with, there was the bullet-proof inner wall that would carry, mend, and protect every aspect of the internal infrastructure. The first layer of shielding would be woven within every other layer such that the material on each spacecraft would carry the electrical or synaptic, the plumbing or arterial, the climate control or internal and external pores, and the corporeal and networking arrays, like neurons and synapses. Each layer and system had integrated sensors that would allow optimum safety, aesthetic, security, defensive, ambient, and living aspects to increase the quality of life for all occupants within the interior of the spacecraft, as well as the spacecraft itself. The first layer and subsequent layers were so advanced and sophisticated that they would render the spacecraft lifelike, to the degree that it was so cutting-edge and with the ability to defend itself, that when integrated with the subsystems linked into a single AI, the spacecraft would essentially awaken, tamed, sentient, and full of purpose, the type of purpose that was filled with the desire to preserve life. The innermost area of each wall consisted of a dense and living, yet effective and aesthetic, white and glowing fibrous molecular jam—a viscous material made of epoxy, Kevlar, and several other highly flexible, yet strong materials, to include carbon-titanium nanofibers and diamond nano-threads.

Each IMC spacecraft's outer shielding would have seven layers, to include the inner walls, with a quality such that each layer would be integrated, exposed, and interwoven atom-by-atom, molecule-by-molecule, and done so in such a way as to allow for constant repairs and upgrades by shielding-dedicated nanos that were integrated with the spacecraft AI subsystems, and as such, the shielding would self-repair as needed for maximum defense.

The second layer was a plasma-lattice shielding with billions of microscopic impact points and a tiny and integrated latch work that would allow the shielding to be embroidered to the internal walls of the spacecraft and woven throughout each subsequent layer. If any object were lobbed, thrown, or came tumbling toward any command spacecraft, it would be disintegrated instantly, with no fear had by the occupants, since the internal and exposed walls were encoded and integrated with the AI's subsystems, and thus set up to protect all identified allies, non-hostile entities, as well as any chartered or coordinated contacts with layer two.

The third layer consisted of a lattice of high energy micro laser beams, woven from the inner walls through each layer of shielding with a sophisticated system of microscopic living mirrors, with billions of crisscrossing rays that could vaporize any harmful object passing through. Each layer was woven into and through the next, allowing for the full ability of each to be applied as necessary depending on each situation that could be dealt with, since these crisscrossing arrays were also controlled by the AI's subsystems. They could release this defensive mechanism and power when and where it would be needed, redirecting incoming matter and antimatter. Each system, no matter their function could be manually controlled by the Command Crew, as needed. With the foresight of Eliza and the perfectionism of Vesha, as well as the genius of each member and their crews of Team 6, each spacecraft could weather the Universe and the most advanced within it. The spacecraft could easily barrel through an asteroid, a planet, or even a star, and it, as well as its occupants, would survive unscathed and intact. Preservation of life, of course, was always the goal, so navigation systems were an integral part to the defenses.

The fourth layer consisted of a fine mesh of carbon-titanium nanotubes woven, layered, and embroidered from the inner walls through each layer to the outermost portion of the external shielding for the augmented strength of each aspect of spacecraft defense, with an additional diamond-nano-thread woven five atoms thick into a lattice that could repel most any object. Every weave of every layer was integrated with spacecraft nanos and the AI's subsystems, for immediate repair.

The fifth layer contained photo-chromatic shielding lightly spun around each spacecraft shell that would deflect and absorb laser beams or any form of radiation, woven in and throughout each layer of shielding. As with each layer, this layer was also integrated into a variety of highly sophisticated processors which interfaced with the spacecraft AI through its multitude of subsystems, the Twelve Database Moons, and the Virtual Universe, with a manual control interface available to the spacecraft commander or the vice commander. If the command spacecraft's system needed more energy, it would absorb what was needed, if it didn't need the radiation it would be deflected at a safe and coordinated angle toward the nearest star or lifeless planet, thus avoiding harm to anyone.

The sixth layer of the shielding contained a meta-material shielding of room temperature superconductors, which allowed the spacecraft to levitate by creating either a monopole, dipole, or multi-pole adjustment to whatever environment it would be in—defying gravity's effects and capable of deflecting anything thrown its way. Each of these layers could be mended in microseconds through the AI's subsystems, and had algorithms built into its own control systems that would complement and not hinder the effects of the other layers, and should any layer be attacked by a hostile entity of virtually anything, the spacecraft and their occupants would be able to continue on un-weathered or undamaged. The spacecraft AI, the spacecraft commander, the vice commander, the lead spacecraft HBCI, or designated command crew could control the power neurologically for external upgrades, adjustments, or simply walk along the exterior of the spacecraft without harm, as setup and coordinated through their neural identification to ensure no one on the outer shell would die on contact accidentally or in any other manner.

Finally, the outermost or seventh layer of shielding would consist of a microscopic lattice that was integrated into the interior wall and throughout the other layers of shielding, which would consist of an invisible impact-proof overlay. This was a command activated system of billions of miniature cameras, sensors, omnidirectional retinal, optical, and frequency scanners, a high-powered laser grid system with laser tech and undetectable screen pixilation and smart radio transmissions, all of which could zero out any unwanted exploitation. This was likewise linked to the spacecraft AI's subsystems, and with this interwoven layer, the spacecraft would be able to see omnidirectionally, travel, or be stationary and unseen by any sensor array. It could essentially render the spacecraft invisible, providing an onlooker or sensory transceiver the emissions similar to those that would be there if the spacecraft or its allies were never there. This shield array could be setup by the commander, vice commander, HBCI, or spacecraft AI, to choose any color, array of colors, or an array of designs and reflections, or even local overlays as needed, desired, or wanted. When Team 6 shared their proposal with Vesha in the Virtual Universe, even she was giddy, moved, and impressed. Malinda Jefferson, Melissa Asher, Rebecca Knight, and Matzu Kashi certainly aimed to please, and that they did.

Teams 3, 4, and 5, or Scarlett Hart, Yon Forall, and Anastasia Renée and their teams coordinated with the drive, navigation, and shielding teams and worked on all aspects of the internal environmental systems of the spacecraft together. To begin with, they developed a separate system of fusion cores that could be networked throughout the spacecraft, with each individual system of cores capable of powering the entire system on its own, but for intergalactic travel they believed high redundancy, efficiency, and capability could never be enough, and as such each spacecraft would glide through space as smooth as butter and turn on a dime. Each of the internal fusion cores could also power the AI's subsystems, the AI itself, the spacecraft drives, the navigation systems, the shielding, each one all on their own. Networked together, each command spacecraft was redundantly, and if it was even possible, they were phenomenally more impenetrable, tight, capable, alive, hospitable to its occupants, and could buffet against anything hostile or deemed a risk to the safety and security of the spacecraft, its crew, mission, and cargo.

This fusion core system also provided automated and sensory-driven environmental aspects to ensure each passenger or crew member was optimally comfortable based on the neuronal activity of each mind in the neurological regions that registered and amplified peace, relaxation, innovation, vigor, and anything necessary to adjust the environment for activities based on mission, relaxation, or need for clarity. Many other adjustments that were complexed and available to each crewmember, afforded an individual environment, isolated or shared as desired, to avoid obnoxious boredom, nerve-wracking repetitive noise, or nausea.

Within each spacecraft, there would be twelve main living sectors capable of providing all aspects of luxury and necessity for one-hundred crewmembers and their families per sector. The twelve living sectors surrounded a series of small forested and jungle areas, which in-turn surrounded a lake with waterfalls and a ring-shaped beach at its outer edge near the center of the first level of the spacecraft. The living area's forest, jungle, and lake had a series of beaches, and benches with a beautiful aerodynamic clear shielding solar dome overhead that provided a captivating view of the Cosmos, as well as an array in the center and around the dome that emulated the home-world Sun, its rise and set, as well as the seasonal and night-time skies.

Within each forest, jungle, and lake there would be sentient creatures of every sort, and each of them linked neurologically for communication between themselves, the spacecraft, and fully read-in humans. Every bird, animal, insect, or water creature imaginable would be on-board and had volunteered to be there in order to assist humanity in any way needed to be muses or help in any other way they could. Together, they would provide music to the forests, jungles, and even internal spacecraft beaches, in ways that settled hearts, animated curiosities, and amplified ingenuity. As always, there would be more redundant internal systems, each with a series of F, A, Q, and G-drives that would allow for waves, surfing, and structural integrity and containment. The systems for containment would be set up in redundant ways to ensure no spillage would occur into any other area of the spacecraft and were integrated into the lifecycle of the spacecraft itself for purification with natural probiotic and antibiotic health and interdependence, and mineral balancing systems for water, plants, animals, and crewmembers, adjustable as needed.

There would be no predation; clean meats would always be available, and as such each creature played an important role in the overall goals of each command spacecraft mission, which was defined as, "To help achieve advancement in civilization, the kind that affords the preservation of life, health, well-being, and clarity of mind." This would include bringing life to all desolate locations throughout each of the twelve zones of the observable Universe relative to Earth and finding ways to stabilize an enjoyably life-giving quality of environment within them. Once observation posts or intergalactic headquarters were set up with living areas similar to the twenty-thousand tech cities and were ready for population, jump gates would be installed and colonization from the home planet would begin. Thus, the environment of each location throughout each spacecraft complemented each aspect of the other areas and provided Earth-based civilization a more promising future.

"Heal, don't harm. Yet, be strong with clearness of mind, be very capable, and be properly prepared if healing does not work and as such, if lives are at risk, do what needs to be done to protect life, longevity, and an environment conducive to innovation and preservation of a noble and mighty legacy." This was the motto shared during the development of the first command spacecraft and developed by Vesha Celeste.

Each sector of one-hundred living quarters was designed to have a unique array of eateries with the finest of chefs, cooks, and confectionary professionals. As Teams 3, 4, and 5 worked together, they wove in spacecraft-integrated redundancies and systems that would leave the spacecraft as a sentient and complementary being, and as such it would provide everything necessary to have fully operational entertainment centers, gyms, convention centers, laboratories, innovation centers, training and education centers, and daycare facilities. Each one of the living quarters was designed to accommodate families with a series of rooms replete with all the luxuries associated with a top-notch luxury penthouse suite. In each suite there were kitchens, bathrooms, sauna tubs, extended king beds, every amenity wanted or needed was provided in advance. Computer and private entertainment rooms with enough biopods for each family and their visitors, and more were available as needed and requested. These biopods were multifunctional, and as such, they could interface with the Virtual Universe, be used for every medical, educational, correctional, or entertainment need, and they were even retrofitted to become small traveling escape pods, designed to jump to a safe location with all needed items available for survival on Earth.

No matter where anyone would go, their job, or their title, they would be respected, protected, treated with dignity, and appreciated for their efforts, and for being who they were. For anyone on-board, whether optimized or natural, whether tough as nails or affable, there would be a full-on around-the-clock medical staff of the highest caliber trained on every aspect of physiology and neurology to provide optimum services to anyone, including those who chose to stay natural; they could also be healed by the healing and diplomatic Sky-Model HBCI, since there would be twenty-four on-board each command spacecraft, which was a project soon to begin as well.

There were escape pods to account for each person on the spacecraft, and more, depending on visitors, potential spacecraft damage or any subsequent need to abort the mission if all options to save the spacecraft had failed. Each suite also had a 'sky view' of any type imaginable, call-in catering, disc jockeying, etc. as desired. Romance was encouraged so long as all parties involved used the laws of consent. Each of these areas was located within the living quarters at the top level of a command spacecraft. Finally, every room had a jump gate to travel to other sectors of the spacecraft and even to any other command spacecraft, and while on leave, crewmembers were given the authorization to jump to any planetoid with any jump gate, all as coordinated.

The portion of the spacecraft where the command center was located, happened to be aerodynamic in appearance from the exterior, and located at the front of each command spacecraft. A person could walk there from other locations in the spacecraft by heading first to the second level. Anyone who would behold it would have found that it was awe-inspiring, both in function and in aesthetic. There were plenty of spacious, lush, aesthetic, individually climate-controlled seats, with first-class dining services available and integrated within the digital displays of the seating of the command center, for each of the different capacities.

These capacities of responsibility within the command center crew served many purposes. Among the ranking personnel were the IMC Command Spacecraft Zonal Commander (IMC/CS/ZC), the IMC Command Spacecraft Zonal Vice Commander (IMC/CS/ZVC), the four Navigation Officers (NAV), the four Electronic Warfare Officers (EWOs), the sixteen Weapons Systems Officers (WSOs), the sixteen Gun Control Officers (GCOs), the four sets of the various Camera Control Officers to include Optical (O-CCO), Infrared (I-CCO), Ultraviolet (U-CCO), Microwave (M-CCO), Gamma (G-CCO), and Special Signals Officers (SS-CCO); there was the Spaceborne Mission Supervisor (SMS), the two Spaceborne Analysts (SA), the four Datalink Operators (DLO), the twenty Linguistic Warrant Officers (LWO), the ten Astrobiology Officers (ABO), all within the Command center, and finally the eighty Spaceborne Systems Engineers (SSEs) spread throughout the major control-points of the spacecraft, with ten of those seats within the command center. Finally, in the third level of the spacecraft main body, the twenty Environmental Science Officers (ESOs) would work directly with the ZC, ZVC, the lead HBCI, or the spacecraft itself, which was the CS/AI, since together they would deliberate or coordinate final decisions relating to environmental health, protection, and safety of the occupants, the spacecraft, and all items and systems both on-board and as pertained to the overall mission. Most of the time, much of this authority would be delegated to the ESO.

All told, each spacecraft required a cadre of two-hundred-six personnel to run and maintain the mission in terms of science, security, and safety, and many more positions were necessary for the purposes of redundancy. In each of the spacecraft sectors, personnel were equally distributed; two sectors housed a minimum of eighteen command center personnel each, and the other ten sectors provided domicile for a minimum of seventeen apiece, along with their family, significant others, which could be extended or nuclear.

Ultimately, each spacecraft could fulfill all of the mission aspects with a single AI, which it had, along with redundant backup systems for it. An AI was a social being. Notwithstanding, each AI was robustly capable of autonomously running the entire spacecraft, constantly running repairs and doing upgrades as programmed, and it would only be commissioned to run everything when the crew was off-duty. Otherwise, it would work in tangent with everyone, working or off-duty. This included the ability to allow for no-longer-than forty-hour workweeks for each crew member, and as such, the AI would take over when crew members were off-duty or on leave. This also meant that the AI would be providing every aspect of their safety for one-hundred-twenty-eight hours each week per command center position, not including the two months of leave per year. Fortunately, those two months would always be properly coordinated to where the command spacecraft would be within a safe zone, so an AI would solely be monitoring the environmental and situational sensors and alert all crewmembers if anything extraordinary came up that would compromise the security of the spacecraft.

For the psychological health of the spacecraft AI, there were algorithms built in, to provide a viable outlet with a resulting sense that it was loved and a valuable member of the crew, with an alter-ego of a humanoid in the Virtual Universe, that could interact with every living being, much like a human. However, each AI was setup to always be present and safeguarding everyone on board and the spacecraft itself.

If in an emergency, the spacecraft would neurologically link with the ZC, the ZVC, and the lead HBCI to thwart off any possible dangers automatically, and with sixteen multi-capacity turrets per each of sixteen turret control centers placed equitably around the spacecraft and tucked away safely within the shielding, a single AI could pack quite a punch to any hostile object, while protecting spacecraft, crew, mission, and infrastructure against any compromising entity. Typically, there were two-hundred-fifty-six gunners among the twelve-hundred-member crew contingency, if ever needed that would helm each turret from deep within the spacecraft, using the omni-vision of the spacecraft, superior speed and thinking, courtesy of Virtual Universe tie-in, and the ability for intimate manual override.

Other essential personnel for each command support spacecraft would be a total of ninety-six defensive spacecraft pilots, or eight for each of twelve docking bays, a total of forty-eight explorer spacecraft pilots, or four for each of twelve docking bays, a total of forty-eight all-purpose spacecraft pilots, or four for each of twelve docking bays, and an assigned spacecraft engineer, chief, and mechanic for each specialized spacecraft, wherein each command spacecraft had one-hundred-ninety-two total support spacecraft. The entire spacecraft support section comprised a total of five-hundred-seventy-six personnel, with thirty-six personnel and their families living equitably-distributed throughout each of the twelve sectors. The rest of the crews would be internal, from medical personnel to science and technology professionals, forward planning design engineers, chefs, cooks, and service staff of every sort, all of which entailed the remaining one-hundred-ninety-two employed crewmembers, which would be equally dispersed among each sector. The support personnel would be divided throughout the twelve sectors equitably. To help with fairness, family members, extended or nuclear, and other support personnel were among the science and technology professionals who worked in the labs, as well as within and below the forest, jungle, beach, garden, and the lake zones of the spacecraft.

Ultimately, each sector would have twelve of its personnel dually-coded and marked as "Special Operations Personnel." As of yet, no one, but Eliza, Yesha, and James knew why. Every crewmember was trained on the sixteen-by-sixteen turret systems, with dry runs, Virtual Universe realistic live fire scenarios, to the degree that the closest sixteen crewmembers to a turret control terminal would take the controls and protect the spacecraft should an urgent situation arise.

Everything one could imagine of a spacecraft its size and with its capabilities was there in the most functional, visually pleasing, and secured way. Each job center and room on board had biopods that could heal anyone from any potential damage and would also work as an escape pod. Every position with actual spacecraft-related duties had a magnificent panoramic view and control of each responsibility entrusted to them. In travel or stationary mode, a holographic view of every angle of the Cosmos sector they happened to be in surrounded the command crew and the turret control terminals as they summoned them neurologically, with details to include elements, minerals, gases, and anything of everything they saw available to them using their neural link to the command spacecraft AI interface and the spacecraft's sensory systems.

In the level below the living areas and behind the command center were the research laboratories, fusion, quantum, and gravity centers, bio-labs, and innovation stations of a wide variety and arranged in an intuitive manner. The floor in between each level was rather thick and was designed for safety, security, accessibility for maintenance crews, yet every room in the spacecraft could double as a bio shelter and had access to each of the other levels, through jump gate or jump watch, and manual means. In the areas below the jungles, forests, gardens, and lake were of course the root structures, the tunnels of various creatures, the columns and support structures, as well as the biosystems that provided the right kinds of bacteria, viruses, micro-organisms, and nutrients necessary for every creature and crewmember in enough abundance and in revolutionary cycles to provide sustenance for trillions of years or more.

It was interesting how so many of those who this team worked with and were so brilliant happened to have been raised in Scandinavian countries. Norway, Sweden, and Finland were among the happiest people on Earth, and it translated to greater productivity in spades. They had become members of Pathway and were fully read-in. The Scandinavians were inherently very inspiring to everyone else, with herculean levels of enthusiasm toward innovation and work itself, resulting in collective-success. Nonetheless, the tasks were gargantuan and there was a large sense of cohesive diversity where everyone worked well together, no matter background, identity, creed, origin, religion, title, or any of the grand methods society seems to use to delineate living beings, rather than respect them for the being they were.

The third main level down consisted of a system of twelve docking bays. Each bay included all-purpose, exploration, and defensive spacecraft, with a system of maintenance, production, and upgrade facilities that could produce pretty much anything or a part of anything designed in the Virtual Universe, using the advanced real-world computer terminal, that could fit through the large bay doors. In some cases, if things were too large for the spacecraft, it could use sensor technology to direct any manufacturing in a nearby bio-environment with all the trimmings and fixings, as needed. Maintenance consisted of a system of redundancy and of highly-skilled personnel trained and optimized for their specialties in the Virtual Universe, practicing manual repairs while spending time working on upgrades and improvements as they innovated them. The people working on the command spacecraft were always vetted and were of the highest caliber. The men were clean cut and shaven, and both men and women were all very well groomed, as well as enthusiastic and respectful toward each other and they worked as a very cohesive team.

Travel throughout and between each command spacecraft would be redundant, with a system of elevators, stairs, and pathways that were intuitively designed for exercise and efficiency within them. There were jump gates for movement throughout the spacecraft, a jump gate terminal for spacecraft-to-spacecraft and other major hubs to travel out and back as coordinated. Fully read-in members had been issued quantum entanglement and disentanglement watches paired with their neural identifications, the living quarters, and their work centers, so they could in effect travel anywhere within the coordinated and humanity-colonized Universe and back as they wished.

Once each aspect of the first command spacecraft, to include the outer shell that would house everything, was designed in the Virtual Universe, Vesha set into motion the commands to have the nano clouds build it. Two weeks later, each of the thirteen command spacecraft were fifty-percent complete, with exoskeletons, neurons, sinews, tissue, and all, seemingly exposed. They were each within a protective environment within deep space and the installation of the final aesthetic of the impenetrable shielding and its sixteen turret array systems of sixteen turrets each were still in progress. Each turret was highly sophisticated and available should ever the need arise, and since there were sixteen locations spread equitably throughout the external shell of the spacecraft, areas that looked as if they were merely shielding would dilate open to expose sixteen large areas of sixteen peace-incentivizing-turrets apiece.

During construction, James Cooper visited often. On this occasion, each spacecraft was about eighty-percent complete. James happened to be standing inside the Construction Command Center with Vesha Celeste and had inquired about certain features that looked quite spectacular on the nearest command spacecraft. With the shielding nearly complete, a couple of the sixteen-turret arrays were still exposed.

"What are those, Vesha? Are they a sort of gun array? I've looked through the database, but most of what I'm seeing here is safely stored in the compartmentalized area of your mind. Please, humor me?"

"Oh, of course, James. There are among each of the turret compartments you see there quite an awesome capacity for command spacecraft protection. The sixteen turrets in each array consist of:

"One GPA multiplied by four, or four guided projectile arrays, or four GPAs, which consist of two thirty-millimeter Bushmaster armor piercing cannons, one AGM-176 Griffin Block III C short-to-long range missile delivery system, and one GBU-39 Small Diameter Bomb III (SDB) advanced delivery system to target hostile spacecraft and hostile locations.

"One FLA multiplied by four, or four fusion/laser arrays, or FLAs, that can deliver a fusion-controlled laser package to any target, and it can dilate for breadth of damage and adjust its scope for precision. Don't worry, James. There will be exhaustive efforts used to do the least damage to a potential enemy in order to gain control of the hostile spacecraft, but if needs be, these four turrets could be used to destroy or cripple the target rather quickly.

"One SGA multiplied by two, or two stun gun arrays, or SGAs. Each crewmember will carry on their hip a weapon that is similar in function to each of these," Vesha showed James her gun. "They are designed to temporarily stun a hostile crew member to allow for healing and diplomacy by a Sky-Model HBCI, which is still in planning stages at Pathway. However, I have visited on numerous occasions to supply my latest DNA and neurological construct for the purposes of creating a new being capable of so many wonderful things. She will be based on my dream angel, Sky. I digress. The two turrets over there are pretty much the same, but extremely powerful by several orders of magnitude, and would be used to stun a hostile spacecraft and its occupants to allow any spacecraft in the IMC inventory, to buy time for a Sky-Model HBCI to find a way to bridge peaceful communication or jump back to the last identified safe location.

"One STA multiplied by two, or two stasis turret arrays, or STAs. This is an example of what I will carry on my other hip. Don't worry, I wouldn't use it, other than to put any hostile crew member, group, or hostile spacecraft and its occupants into a suspended time loop, and to afford a Sky-Model HBCI even more time to heal a threatening mind or individual, so we can get back to the mission at hand. Likewise, those two turrets out there would allow more time for a Sky-Model HBCI to heal threatening minds and create neural links for communication, diplomacy, and shared well-being, and is several orders of magnitude more powerful than the stasis gun I am holding and have no intentions of using.

"One LGA multiplied by two, which are, strangely enough, two laughter gun arrays, or LGAs. Those two LGAs you see, were designed as the first step of defense to reduce hostilities in a less hostile yet reasonable manner by increasing humor, no matter the creature, in such a way as to enable a Sky-Model HBCI to heal and create neural links for communication, diplomacy, and shared well-being. Our own spacecraft has a system designed to do that as a first measure against hostilities, so we can return to the mission at hand. The worst that can come of an LGA is, well, laughter.

"One APC multiplied by two, as a last resort or countermeasure, there are two antimatter particle cannons, or APCs out there. If we were to use one on a target of any size, once the target is hit, all hostilities would become gone for good in an awesome explosion that would not affect anyone in the IMC at all. Our matter has been accounted for, down to our DNA and neural identifications, and stored within command spacecraft databases for safekeeping. Don't worry, James. APCs would be the least-likely used turrets. Basically, they would work very much like a laser gun, but if caught in a pickle, those two bad-boys would send a strong and steady stream of antimatter particles, based on target composition, and completely destroy or annihilate the target. Concerns would be gone.

"Every aspect, as beautiful as it can be, will also be fully functional and full of purpose when complete. The shielding and defenses will go up soon, atom-by-atom, molecule-by-molecule, and each aspect of each spacecraft will serve an interwoven and complexed purpose. In the end, Eliza, through you and me, has made it clear that the entirety of the IMC ought to be awe-inspiring in every possible way, and while there will always be plenty of room for upgrades and improvements, each command spacecraft is beautiful, are they not?"

"I've been to the other side of the Solar System and back, but this, wow, this is impressive, Vesha!"

James visited several times again throughout the end of the construction process.

Once construction, "Or, the birth of each spacecraft," was complete, as Vesha would say it, she was gracious to all who had contributed so much time and effort to the huge project. Furthermore, Vesha took time out of her schedule, met with everyone involved, and offered them each a sabbatical of five years, yet she also let them know that early on in 2029, the grand voyage would begin, and as such, it would be a very big year. So, therefore, it would be important to take that time off well and in advance, especially if they were planning on being crew members aboard the IMC. There would be thirteen initial command spacecraft, with a crew requirement of twelve-hundred personnel, and their families, each.

Vesha then addressed before a rather large audience of workers, the fact that, "While one could fly something the shape of a block out and into deep space, aerodynamics is paramount and necessary for planetary travel or travel through nebulae, or through any other kind of matter or particle, for that matter." She also pointed out how pride in aesthetics were necessary for morale and diplomacy throughout the Universe.

"This is a beautiful system, yet always keep in mind that there will be plenty of features to consider in order to make the spacecraft aesthetically pleasing as well as utilitarian, if anything for neurological wellness, or above all else for morale, diplomacy, and survivability. We want to update as needed, but not for the sake of change alone. Thank you!"

When everything was finalized, all thirteen command spacecraft were arranged in travel form, with the IMC Command Spacecraft at the front and center, a ring of four command spacecraft, Zones 09 through 12, behind it, and a ring of eight command spacecraft, Zones 01 through 08, behind and in the back. Each spacecraft was utterly spectacular, beautiful, and gigantic. A Pathway open house was scheduled, arranged, and held, with the first iterations complete and tours through each room, corridor, and facility provided. The way the various drives adorned each spacecraft complemented both its capabilities and the magnificent awe they inspired. Each spacecraft was as if it were an impenetrable and seamless marvel, aerodynamic in its curvaceous design, and once the open house was over, they enclosed them in an additional bio-shelter and turned on the invisibility shielding. Like that they disappeared. Tracked by Pathway's sophisticated systems, they would sleep and remain undetectable to anyone not fully read-in until training and missions were ready.

Vesha would still work with her crews to improve them ever-so-quietly until then, while engaging in missions throughout the Solar System, on Earth, and within each of the potential zones.

Chapter 23: A Weighty Matter

Database Moon Archive, Celestial-Sol Date: 2022 March 24. Erin Carter, Yesha Alevtina's Vice President, summarizes some of the concerns and experiences of Joanne Gallant, and the further development of the Correctional Matrix. These memories are from many Pathway Leaders, recorded within the Virtual Universe, interfaced within Pathway Melrose Campus. Input by Erin Carter, VP, 2018-2022, and President of Pathway, 2022-2029.

It had been almost three years since Joanne Gallant's first journey with Eliza through the Virtual Universe, it was now 2022. She thought about her tour in 2020, and the main source of what drove her to write music in the first place still weighed upon her from time to time. Her brother's murder and who it could have been still was needed for closure, and quite possibly vindication, and not out of spite, but out of a sense of justice, out of a desire to see the killer perhaps learn from their crimes the untold potential they snuffed out and would never bring back. The only hope for them now would be to serve the world and humanity for the rest of their lives.

Her need for closure seemed to grow and she noticed how her nanos were working full time whenever she was weighed down by everything surrounding it. Her skin seemed to glow a lot more as the days went by and her left-side neural art would go bonkers with a kaleidoscope of thoughts and art surrounding everything about the unsolved case. She had designed outer wear a couple of years ago that when programmed with her smart suit hid the artwork altogether, especially when on tour. Now here she was, and she had decided to put her music career on hold for a little while, perhaps a year or two, or maybe even longer.

She had gone over all the information she had in her files recently to see if her optimized mind could put two and two together. While she could speculate, the Sheriff in her hometown had come up empty-handed despite all, he was good at what he did, and the case had gone cold all-too-soon. She had hoped that with the abundance of clarity she had on everything else from writing her music to going on her tours, finishing her doctoral research, working on the Correctional Matrix, the Sky Taylor project and the many other assignments and cases where she worked alone or with Erin Carter or even within the entire group mind within the Virtual Universe that she would hopefully and by even a small little chance find enough clues to piece together what truly happened. Unfortunately, it kept boiling down to the fact that the Sheriff had done extremely well in his investigations and searches and that this had been for all intents and purposes the perfect crime. As cold and calculated as it seemed, there was more to it than was conscionable, yet no one seemed guilty of it within her hometown.

She had hoped that perhaps through the minds of the many individuals who had been read-in to Pathway and had thus spent time within the Virtual Universe that she would find more clues, but alas, there were no associations aside from her own with anyone she knew inside her hometown, and thus, apart from her files, there were no additional clues. As it was, she already knew that no one from her conservative hometown in upstate New York had become members of Pathway, and she hadn't returned there since she graduated from high school, so she didn't have a whole lot to go off of, besides what she already had. Luckily, Erin Carter was quite a bit into sleuthing as well and together they mulled over everything, but even still to no avail.

Thus far, they had come up empty-handed when it came to the identity of her brother's killers. They had the Sheriff's file with all of the details that the department in her hometown had acquired. Essentially what that left Joanne and Erin with was a number of suspicions going off the same information the Sheriff had. The file that Joanne had received from the Sheriff's small little investigative department after the case went cold included the pictures and reported analysis for each aspect of the case, an eyewitness account typed by the sheriff's department from an interview with a young individual in the area who happened to see what was going on while she was on her way home from school, several interview reports of possible suspects, including the high school quarterback, each of his teammates, the football coach, each of their families, and their alibis.

Pictures with clues related to the scene were difficult for Joanne to look through, partly due to the fact that they were horribly graphic in nature, and partly because he was her brother and there was that unstoppable emotional connection, but she fought through it all anyway and she had those images burned into her mind quite well. Everyone in Pathway had seen them to some extent since every part of the file was pretty much written from her mind and into the Virtual Universe's twelve large database moons and was shared with all three-billion Pathway members with complete clarity. She wanted to afford everyone a chance to be involved; on the off chance, they would meet someone with a connection to her brother's killer or killers. Joanne had also organized each of the clues in her own real-world filing system and then in the Virtual Universe into plausible theories and in chronological order.

In the first section of the report, there were several pictures of her deceased brother at the scene of the crime, a little over one mile from their home, and the analysis made by the Sheriff on each one. Although they were difficult for her to view for obviously personal reasons, she had categorized and taken copious notes on them herself and she knew that it was very necessary that she examine them in detail no matter how gruesome the scene was. She loved her brother and would always feel the pain of loss but the strength in compassion toward him and passion to resolve the case wouldn't let her forget any of what she knew. No matter the circumstances, her neural optimizations had helped Joanne to finally crack those untouched files open and to try to put everything into perspective. She had a lot of information, and hopefully, this meant that she could get scientific about each aspect, and then come up with a solid hunch.

The second section of her file included several pictures of a bloodied bat and where it had been found in the woods or in Bucks Brook State Forest, as well as the eyewitness report from one of her classmates. With these particular pictures was another set of reports that indicated there were no fingerprints on the bat, as well as more pictures of a left-footed sized-twelve shoeprint where one of the proposed killers had allegedly stepped into the puddle of blood following the attack and taken a couple of steps before walking off the blacktop on the side of the road and then into the muddy and wooded area—it had rained the day previous.

The third section of her file included pictures identifying two different types of shoeprints going into the muddy area and into the woods, which accompanied the first set of shoeprints, as they made their escape side by side. Each of these pictures corroborated the eyewitness account that there were three people involved. Included with these pictures were the suspect interviews, the interviews of the quarterback, each team member, the coaches, their alibis, and their family members.

Finally, the fourth section was Thomas' letter to the quarterback. This letter had been turned in to the sheriff's department by the high school quarterback about two weeks after the investigation had started. Not more than a day later, the case went cold, and the file was given to the victim's family. Along with his letter was a report as to why this case could not be solved.

Joanne and Erin had read the report of the eyewitness a number of times. The young lady, who was another fellow high school student, had stated that she saw three different hooded men. One of the men had allegedly wielded the bat, presumably the individual who left the bloodied footprints leading to the edge of the sidewalk, the muddy area, and into the woods. The other two had held Thomas in place and in such a way as to allow the bat to hit Thomas' head to knock him out. Once he was out, they laid him down on the sidewalk and the wielder of the bat continued to hit his head until blood and other fluids were coming out of his nostrils, mouth, ears, crushed skull, and subsequent wounds. It was a brutal and calloused murder. The eyewitness had stated that it was twilight when the crime occurred, and the pictures showed the results of the brutality. Who could have done it, the quarterback, the coach, or his teammates?

When the young lady, Martha, was asked why she had returned home so late, she stated that she had been in school at study hall working on her homework and that the teacher had left her there on her own, in part because he trusted her, and in part because he needed to head home to his family. On her way home, she had heard the brutality as it was going on and then hid just out of view on the other side of the street terrified for her life. She had hidden there because she was worried, they would hurt her too if they saw her. When asked if she knew anything else, she stated that the three hooded men disappeared into the woods with the bat and that she had returned home from the scene of the crime shocked, broken, and scared.

Her parents had called the sheriff, once they heard their daughter's account of what it was that she had seen, and they had been interviewed as well. They had indicated that their daughter was an "A" student, an upstanding young woman, that her story ought to be trusted, and that she was a friend of his at school and had talked about him often at home and how much she liked him. It was obvious from the report, that the sheriff's department dismissed her as a prime suspect, since this would certainly not fit her character. Joanne had remembered her being at the funeral, crying, completely shaken up, and how she was genuinely sad at the loss of such a wonderful young man.

There was her brother's letter, which had been returned to the family, when the sheriff's department ended the search, on the account of, "No one in our town could have done it," and "We have nothing to go off of." The quarterback had attended the funeral and he too was cordial, polite, and even apologetic. He had been a close friend through sports and academics, therefore the Sheriff after interviewing his fellow teammates, coach, alibis, and family concluded that it couldn't have been him. There were the pictures of the tread marks of one of Thomas' assailant's shoes, but the quarterback had no shoes with the description of those treads, and neither did anyone on the team.

There was a picture of the bloodied bat that was used, but the sheriff's department hadn't found any fingerprints, and after questioning each store that sold sports gear, it was noted that none of the stores in town or in the surrounding towns sold that particular type of baseball bat. The only revelation to the possibility that there were perhaps three individuals involved was the fact that the location where he was killed was on his way home, and on the way home there was a small wooded area several yards from the highway, and between the highway and the woods was an area with three different types of shoe prints in the mud that had been cordoned off during the initial investigation, with pictures of the overall route taken, the path of each footprint, angles of the indentations in the mud, and the barrel that had nothing but ashes inside and residue on the outside of a hot and flammable substance, from there, the tracks faded into the woods.

As far as combing minds and information within the Virtual Universe was concerned, for one, there was nothing other than a few scanned newspaper articles chronologically talking about the facts of what they knew had happened by the local newspaper reporter, the facts as shared in a second article by the local newspaper reporter based on interviews of the Sheriff, the potential suspects, and each of the families closely affected, and a third talking about why the case had been closed, on the account that, "There were no plausible suspects." Nothing had been mentioned in Thomas' letter. As far as each member of Pathway was concerned, a great majority of those at Pathway were mostly from other regions throughout the world outside of the United States, and thus none of them were of any connection whatsoever to the small town of South Otselic that Joanne grew up in, before moving to New York City, New York, following her initial success as a singer, songwriter, and performer, right out of high school following her graduation.

Joanne mulled over the details with Erin, but together all they came up with was some speculation, and they knew that and decided not to press the issue further for a while. Whoever had wielded that bat had cleaned up everything except the crime scene itself, the bloodied bat, the three tracks of footprints into the woods, and the burn barrel. Whoever had carried out this horror show had made sure prior to the crime that it was completely clean of traceably incriminating evidence in every way. All they had was a hunch.

Joanne and Erin realized they had done what they could, for now, agreed to look at this later, and then focused on the many other projects they had to work on both in and around Pathway that were much more inspiring, upbeat, and full of hope. They worked together often and were somewhat inseparable. They had traveled to resorts together, had visited Europe together, and Erin, who enjoyed female vocal trance had quite a range of tastes in music that transcended to include a healthy appreciation of Joanne's cross-genre, electronic rock and pop style of music, which afforded them an "in" with the likes of Above & Beyond, Raz Nitzan, and Armin Van Burren and their unique and heavenly brand of music.

As best of friends they traveled the world together, attended ASOTs together, camped in areas completely devoid of light pollution of any form, and gazed upon the stars. Joanne had put together a "Best of" tour and went through some of her favorites with her audiences in 2022. During Joanne's concerts, Erin would often be in the front row with a backstage pass. After every concert they would explore the cities they were in, frequent the local and hopping bars, buy everyone a round of drinks, and recruit people, to include the homeless or otherwise broken victims of society to Pathway. All they did, was in a manner that reached to the hearts of others and went unnoticed by the public. In this way, they could change the lives around of so many and afford them the opportunity to become who they always dreamed of becoming. They loved helping those who were struggling most, and they enjoyed seeing that freeing smile of joy, as people who once felt at a loss in life, were now filled with the clarity of the mind that gave life a sense of purpose, freedom, and hope.

Erin was the Vice President of Pathway during that timeframe, yet she and Joanne did so much to raise the spirits of those around them. They came up with untold solutions to many life-threating issues rampant throughout the world, and at times they worked with Yesha, James, Vesha, Amber, Najem, Jasmine, many others in Pathway, and even Eliza.

Chapter 24: Politicians and Angels

Database Moon Archive, Celestial-Sol Date: 2022 March 24. Erin Carter, Yesha Alevtina's Vice President, summarizes the experiences of Senator Eliza A. Williams, her bid for POTUS, and the preparations for bringing Sky Taylor online, and summarizes the experiences that occurred following the first year after the awakening of Sky Taylor. US Vice-Presidential Candidate Yesha Alevtina is with Sky in the Virtual Universe as they converse about the Correctional Matrix. These memories are from many Pathway Leaders, recorded within the Virtual Universe, interfaced within Pathway Melrose Campus. Input by Erin Carter, President of Pathway, 2022-2029.

Eliza had been serving her first year as Senator, in 2019, when she had appointed Erin as Yesha's Vice President of Pathway and had asked Erin and Joanne to work closely with each other. This had been followed by the internal elections throughout Pathway's then two-point-two-billion members, who were fully read-in. As it turned out each internal election resulted in unanimous support of every single one of Eliza's appointments. Now, three years later, Pathway had grown to three-billion members, Eliza was still in her first term as Senator, with a lot accomplished, and two more years were left until the 2024 US Presidential Elections.

When Joanne had met Eliza in 2019, Eliza had been taking a little break from the Senate at the T.O. and at that time she had recruited, trained, and put Joanne to work. Eliza was one to never slow down, even when she was technically "slowing down," and she too had taken some time to be well-versed in Joanne's case looking through her digital files to see who it was that had murdered Joanne's brother, Thomas. Even Eliza couldn't go any further than the Sheriff had. Joanne had a good mind about dealing with it for now, and Eliza knew that Sky would be coming online soon, with the ability to read non-read-in minds. She also knew that Sky would have priorities of also saving the lives of many who were currently under threat and with limited clues as to Joanne's case, everyone decided to carry on for now. "We'll get this figured out, soon enough," Eliza would say, as she would give Joanne a pep-talk from time to time to remind her.

Now, Eliza was ready to go public as the UP candidate running for President of the US for the elections of 2024. Secretly, she was still working a few Virtual Universe hours a day, coming up with real-world-applicable solutions to issues presented to the Senate. In some cases, she would work on issues in this way with the Senate itself.

In the world of Presidential Elections, hopefuls, candidates and such, the constituents, delegates, and candidates throughout the Solar System of the UP all wanted the UP to get an early start. The elections of 2018 had been somewhat successful, as were the elections of 2020, and 2022 was looking good too. This was in part, due to the fact that there were positions of all levels of government filled by the UP both within each of the United States, its territories, as well as within the governments of other countries who conducted free elections.

All of Pathway had agreed that Eliza had the vision necessary to usher in the crucial changes to bring humanity to the level of that of a presumably formidable and successful Cosmos-faring civilization, and she was willing to step up to the plate as the kind of leader to help make that happen. She would often be quoted as saying, "We don't need to wait around for someone else to do good things. We can do them, and then solve the next issue as soon as we can." They also had agreed that the more exposure they could receive and the sooner the UP could be more than a household name, the more likely another drove of UP successes could occur. As the UP witnessed the Presidential Elections of 2020 go by without their own candidate for president yet, many people from the UP throughout the US (and anywhere else throughout the world where the people could vote), had been voted in as local through national-level legislators, district attorneys, judges, and governors, and essentially, about thirty percent of the US Electoral College consisted of members of the UP. The 2022 Legislative Branch and local elections would begin soon.

One of the delegates from the UP, Yesha's mother, Yesenia, was slated to take Eliza's place as Senator, or at least fill her position beginning in 2022 following Eliza's announcement to run as POTUS Candidate, and in her subsequent absence. She would then run again in her stead for the 2024 Senatorial Elections. Ever since Yesenia immigrated to the US, she had done a lot to help Eliza and Yesha in an honorary capacity and became fully read-in to Pathway by 2017, prior to becoming a public figure. She had also been unknown in politics previous to that time, so it wasn't on anyone's radar in any way that she had allowed the effects of optimization to take hold, letting her health and appearance be that of a thirty-five-year-old. She was eighty-five, yet she never mentioned her age or changed her official documents. If someone looked, they would find out her age, and then scratch their heads in confusion. Her feeling was that if the public found out, well then, maybe it would serve as an opportunity to explain her lifestyle choices and recommend them. She wasn't afraid of the truth, yet she wasn't eager to undermine proper timing.

As it was, Yesenia was an almost identical match to her daughter, Yesha, who was thirty-five, yet with the visual youth of a twenty-five-year-old. They both still conferred with Eliza in the Virtual Universe to keep her abreast of everything, and she enjoyed the thought that this was perfect in every way for the Legislative Branch of the Federal Government, because she knew that Yesenia would be both wise and influential.

Yesenia's daughter, Yesha, was a legal and natural born citizen of the US, while her mother was a legal immigrant, and as such Yesenia would not be able to run as POTUS, for the foreseeable future. As far as long-term plans were concerned, Yesha, Eliza, and Pathway had planned for Yesha to run as POTUS in 2032. At that point, Yesenia would cross over from politics and return to business, research, and development as the President of Pathway. Joanne, having served a few years as Pathway's President, would cross over into politics and become Yesha's running mate. Erin would go from being the President of Pathway to Vesha's Vice Commander for the IMC Command Spacecraft, Zone-13, by then.

Over the last ten years, Yesenia had been an indispensable support, and now she had been working as a Pathway delegate. As such, she had become increasingly involved in a plethora of missions that helped to increase the size of the organization. She too had joined ranks with Erin and Joanne by immersing herself in an abundance of amazing projects and she too had taken the time to peruse the contents of Joanne's digital folder. Notwithstanding, Yesenia was not alone, in that she had found no success when it came to Thomas' killers.

Yesenia had a lot of other concerns she was juggling as well, and at one point or another, almost every UP delegate and Pathway citizen had worked together and had shared journeys in the Virtual Universe to increase their education and awareness of the realities going on in public Earth, so they too could help to improve the conditions of the real world and prevent similar mishaps that tended to occur from any type of environment that leads to violence and misfortune.

She had worked with Joanne, Erin, and many others, and had been a strong advocate for the changes that the UP was backing up in every move they made. With the combined efforts of Pathway's leadership, the phenomenal talent, and brilliant minds, and with the millions of delegates that were employed within Earth-side industry, millions of employees had been recruited and billions of refugees had been helped and given better lives in the tech cities, far from Earth. Yesha, her daughter, as well as Erin, had each helped Joanne go over her notes on Thomas' tragedy, but to no avail. They knew eventually justice and vindication would be served.

In the meantime, many wonderful projects had been converted from Pathway Tech to public tech. A couple of projects that were continuously updated and upgraded under Yesha's tenure as Pathway President had a very beautiful tone to them; as with Pathway, since its inception, animals no longer had to be used for testing, at least without their consent. Eliza was working on legislation to create large incentives for laboratories to use highly accurate computer simulated genomes, DNA, and cellular models of every animal known to humanity for research models. She was also working on legislation to incentivize the use of clean meats, allowing meatpacking plants to convert to large clean meat labs with tax breaks for doing so. Finally, Eliza had put together legislation that enhanced children's school programs designed to reduce the focus of wealth and power through fear and brutality in favor of well-being through projects and innovation.

Pathway's neuroscience teams had been making discoveries in leaps and bounds, and Eliza saw that her legislative proposals and these capabilities if enacted, could help to curb the escalation of violence rampant due to society's latest popular emphasis on "over-masculinity" versus actually being well-rounded, compassionate, reserved, thoughtful, and considerate. A young man could still be tough, highly skilled and in a field of their choice, and contribute to the success of the human civilization, without the need for verbal abuse and toxicity, which was quite an epidemic.

Yesha had led the efforts to emphasize shared views on how society could see through to more hope, and then provide proof of said claims and platitudes through innovation and action. On the day of Eliza's and Yesha's public announcement for their bid to run as a presidential and vice presidential team, Yesha had stated, "There is more strength in gentleness, more bravery in kindness, and more intellect and promise in studies and innovations founded from intent for well-being, an increase in the quality of life and the tenants espoused by the UP's Universal Ethics, founded by none other than my esteemed running mate, Eliza Williams, than by any others means.

"Brutality has never been strength, it has always been myopia and cowardice, it has never led to lasting success and never will, it has always been a failure to raise the bar for humanity, and it has never given us the seeds of hope, because brutality is akin to uncontrolled chaos and as a result it is a failure to give humanity a legacy worthy of preserving. I've been throughout the world and in many places with many wonderful people with untold potential, and through my journeys, I have seen too many living souls suffering due to the lack of nurture and of care. Gentleness will need to take the place of injustice. As I stand humbly before you with Eliza, today, I assure you, our declaration of POTUS and VP Candidacy is merely the beginning of a better world and way of life, because we care and there is a Universe full of abundance if we care enough."

In order to capitalize on their unique brand, the UP had announced Eliza's running mate at the same time as she announced her candidacy. Everyone in Pathway had known who that was going to be. Yesha had been scheduled to step down as Pathway's President, and Erin Carter, who had been groomed for almost a decade for this, would become the President until the IMC took off on its journey through the stars. Preliminary appointments had been made by Eliza, Yesha, Vesha, James, and by the rest of the leadership of Pathway and then voted on with unanimous approval throughout the tech cities of the Solar System. IMC direction would become official, once Eliza took office as POTUS. The leader of the twelve zonal commands throughout the observable Universe, relative to Earth, as well as the leader of the overall mission, would be, as presumed, Vesha Celeste, with Erin Carter at her side, once the IMC had delivered all twelve zonal commanders to their principle galaxies to begin their separate missions. From there, they would journey beyond the CMB as Zone-13 and establish headquarters in the nearest galaxy from the point that they had left the CMB, relative to Earth.

Everything would, of course, be amenable to change as new personnel arrived or new options became available when it came to the crews and command staff of each command spacecraft. No one was jealous about who would be on each of the original command spacecraft missions or who would be in command, because they knew that eventually, anyone who wanted to would be able to be a part of the study, observation, and building, colonization, and innovation efforts throughout the many planets of the many galaxies throughout the Universe, could. There were more places to colonize than there were people on Earth, and as such there would always be plenty of room for growth. Positions of leadership throughout the various galaxies would be available as earned and desired.

Joanne had essentially been tapped by Eliza, Erin, and Yesha to be Erin's right-hand in Pathway leadership and as such, because of jump gate and Virtual Universe conveyances and capabilities, she continued her musical career and sleuthing for a time, while working on the Correctional Matrix, Sky Taylor, and other projects as well. In many ways, her music contributed in a great way toward the healing of the minds of humanity, and it served in a very non-planned way as a wonderful format for presenting Pathway and engaging in UP recruiting.

Interestingly, each of the recruits had contributed in untold ways toward the progression of Pathway as well, and their stories were inspiring and unique and could take up the large and broad shelves of so many gigantic libraries. There could be a library that reached the Moon and back and it still wouldn't be enough space to cover the wealth of stories, adventures, experiences, and noble contributions made by each member of Pathway. As it was, Pathway citizens confirmed both Erin's and Joanne's appointments unanimously in every step of the way toward the future of this noble organization and its honorable goals with their votes in the Virtual Universe.

Erin and Joanne would both have their hands full, in the Virtual and real world, especially when it came to some of their more austere projects, projects that Pathway was working on, to include the assignments which involved Sky Taylor. Vesha or Amber would have been wonderful choices for these duties, as would have Najem or Jasmine or James, but Vesha, Amber, Najem, and Jasmine were busy with the vast amounts of research and final drafts for the gargantuan journey through space, and James was busy with tech city governance, while Vesha helped him out as time allowed.

The tech cities were not bound by the laws of any country on Earth; rather instead, they were bound by the Principles of Universal Ethics. As such, even though Eliza was the de-facto and voted-on Presidential winner of the Solar System, she had her hands full with Earth-born and public humanity, and as such, she would appoint James Cooper, who in-turn would win unanimously as the Tech City President each time it came up for a vote. He was a kind, benevolent, and gifted visionary, and leader, and as such the people had voted unanimously for him each time with their hearts and with their minds when Eliza would appoint him, and the subsequent vote came up. The citizens looked at Eliza as their leader when available, and loved James' leadership when he was filling in. Both were loved, adored, and honored by all of their constituents.

The first such vote was in 2010, the second was in 2020, and the third would be ten years following the last, with no term limits. The voting was always held openly in the Virtual Universe, and no one was ashamed of speaking their mind since, for the most part, their minds were on open display. Voting was transparent, as were the intentions of each candidate. Eliza would always win, since everyone trusted, loved, and was loyal to her, but she would appoint James each time as President of Solar System Operations, and on both occasions, there hadn't been a candidate that ran against James, unless James had convinced them to do so. He believed that the people needed a fair choice. At one point he had convinced one of his original crewmembers from YY Construction Corporation, or the 97, after it had changed to Pathway Construction, to run. Since he had been the President of the tech cities since 2010, when he had been appointed, he then appointed Anne, the robust yet strangely attractive lady with the gruff voice, to be the President, and it was she who he had convinced to run and would have done an amazing job, but she conceded before the vote was had in 2020 and the entire populous had voted for James. James did an excellent job, everything that needed to be done was done, and everyone was happy with him, it made sense to them, just as with Eliza, they trusted and were loyal to him, so they always voted him in unanimously, knowing in the back of their minds that Eliza was always truly in charge.

The projects that Vesha, Amber, Najem, and Jasmine were involved in were detail-heavy, yet to them, they were quite enjoyable. They were working on something that was several orders of magnitude greater in scope than pretty much all of the rest of the projects that Pathway itself was working on combined, to include the governance of the twenty-thousand tech cities, which maintained all of Solar System Operations. Still, once they had finished their research, everything else would become somewhat redundant, automated, and open for adjustments and official agreements between humanity and other civilizations as journeys throughout the Universe ensued.

As it was, each IMC spacecraft was fully developed, hidden from the public on Earth, undergoing a series of tests for each aspect as necessary, and the testing was coming along quite nicely with occasional upgrades, updates, and some remodeling for utility and aesthetics. The IMC, which was essentially the compendium of spacecraft, both command and support, their leadership, and their missions, was, mind-bendingly impressive, beautiful, and down-right breath-taking.

Back on Earth, Joanne would be working with Erin on the mission of reaching the hearts and minds of the people who still had no idea that Pathway existed. Together they chose to reach the masses through innovation, conventions, and music. In 2020, many still had no idea that Pathway had an entire civilization of three-billion people and growing with its own mind-blowing reality going on as if it were the norm, and that it existed throughout the rest of the Solar System, most of which James maintained. She and Erin would be working with the people of the US and throughout the world. One would think it would be easy to ease humanity into the integrity of civilization capable of sustaining life for the long-haul for a Universe-faring populace, but they were never willing to force the will of anyone. Instead, through persuasion, kindness, exemplary behavior, and power through innovation they would reach the majority.

Those who did not want to participate in the future of humanity were free to go their merry way, to practice what they believed, to live as they thought was right, and they could do so, so long as they did not take those same freedoms away from anyone else.

Thinking about the projects they had already begun, and some that Joanne would introduce, she reminisced over the last three and realized how much she loved working with Erin. When she had first met Erin, Erin had just turned fifteen, was gentle yet brazen throughout, and as such she was an inspiring young woman, filled with wisdom beyond her years with a keen sense of history, of civilization, of social sciences, of astrobiology, and so much more. She had spent nine years conducting missions throughout public and private schools to reach the children her age, their families in and throughout the world, and their communities. She had a firm insight on psychology, sociology, cultural values, and from the time that she started as a six-year-old, Pathway had grown from twenty-million to three-billion members, who were completely read-in, and were now working either on Earth or with James on a vast array of missions throughout the Solar System.

When Erin was fifteen, Yesha took her under her wing and she was in effect Yesha's Vice President of Pathway, and now, three years later, as an eighteen-year-old, she could run a series of industries with her eyes closed. As such, Joanne was there more so to learn from Erin, and become well-versed in each aspect of Pathway herself. Through it all, what she appreciated most was the opportunity to be a close team employee and to become a dear friend.

It was Erin who suggested setting up arts and sports programs in the tech cities similar to many on Earth, yet far more advanced, challenging, and thrilling. For example, on Enceladus, there were three-hundred tech cities, and every other odd year they would have the Winter Olympics or the Summer Olympics, with each tech city providing representation for every category of every sport, with parallel competitions for the men and women who were optimized. A different time and score standard would exist, at least in comparison to those who were optimized versus those who opted to be natural. With standard protective gear, the natural men and women would demonstrate their agility and strength in many ways similar to those on Earth. The optimized, who could essentially score everything to perfection, or had many times more strength, endurance, and ability would additionally be judged based on a factor of artistic finesse, which might include flips, twirls, additional acrobatics, etc., for each of their events. Gravity, atmospheric levels, and quantity, as well as safety gear, etc. were all of what made the Enceladus Tech City Olympics so unique for everyone in Pathway to observe, enjoy, and be proud of.

Every imaginable sport was represented on Enceladus, for example, from the Enceladus Tech City Bowlers Association to the Enceladus Tech City Football League, Enceladus Tech City Golfers' Association, the Enceladus Tech City Basketball Association, and Enceladus Tech City Association for Exotic Car Auto Racing and so on. Every conceivable and worldwide sport had a program in one variation or another. The same was very similar in terms of the vastness of the sports programs throughout all one-hundred-fifty populated spheroids, each with anywhere between fifty to three-hundred tech cities apiece. When one spheroid competed against the others, gravity differences would require each optimized player to be well-versed on the subtle nuances, show finesse, and go for the win.

Joanne, James, Yesha, Eliza, Erin and the others in leadership had agreed this would be healthy, morale-boosting, and enjoyable, so all of this had been set up by 2021. Erin had never thought about fame, money, power, or anything of that sort, and neither had anyone else throughout Pathway's vast population. They joked about it at times, but they were more interested in helping people to become the best they could be, and in every way.

Throughout the tech cities and Pathway each individual was intrigued by the vastness of the discoveries they could make, even thru sports, since there were always new things to learn, and they made sure that each person who worked with them was well-compensated in terms of validation and were thus treated with the utmost of respect and dignity.

One idea that Erin had, for example, when she was sixteen, was rooted in something she had gleaned from Eliza's mind with regard to the IMC. Erin wanted to ensure that as a whole, each of the personnel aboard an IMC, or the full contingency of each spacecraft, had sports arenas within them and every sport was represented. There would essentially be IMC competitions as the journeys through space continued. This would help to maximize the flexibility, durability, and agility of the body and the mind, especially when it came to personal resolve amidst some of the toughest of problems that could be presented.

On top of that, in the same year, Erin had worked with Joanne, Eliza, James, and Vesha on another capacity of the spacecraft. She brought up the idea, "What if the IMC accidentally jumped into an area very close to an event horizon of one of many black holes. What would happen? How could we prepare for and prevent catastrophes like unintended and catastrophic destinations in advance?"

After doing so, she showed her resolution to the issue. She had set up a device that could create a singularity of opposing polarity to that of an event horizon of a black hole. She showed how if installed they could be default-programed to detect and network in conjunction with any other IMC Spacecraft or ally traveling within the same region of influence to likewise be un-attracted to a black hole's event horizon, without causing damage to spacecraft, its crew, or its cargo. She did the same for neutron stars, and any other gravitational anomalies, so that they or any of humanity's friends would never be stuck anywhere they had no desire to be.

As such, Vesha was amazed. It was at that point, in 2020, that she had thanked Eliza in person for having appointed Erin to be her Vice Commander, of the IMC. Vesha had, after Erin's demonstration, worked diligently with each of her teams to weave each of Erin's ideas into every single one of the system's G-drives, Q-drives, navigational systems, AI mainframes, and into each and every spacecraft, the biopods, and the multi-faceted support-spacecraft in the IMC.

During their tenures as President and Vice President of Pathway, the projects Erin and Joanne would engage upon would astound the average mind and take many libraries to write about. Let it suffice to say, that for the project involving Sky Taylor's awakening, there was so much more involved than would fit in a small amount of text. Erin and Joanne had kept Yesha at their beck and call, despite her being on the presidential campaign trail with Eliza early on in 2022. Yesha, along with Eliza and James, would make themselves available, if ever needed, until Sky was scheduled to be awakened and trained, in late March of 2022, close to Erin's and Joanne's birthdays.

Eliza, Yesha, Vesha, Joanne, James, Amber, and Erin had all been involved in this project, as time allowed, in one way or another for the last three years. Eliza and Yesha had recently told Joanne that she would work near-exclusively, quietly, and in parallel with Sky throughout her various missions, once she was online. She would work with her, but behind the scenes and within the Virtual Universe, while also working as the Pathway Vice President. Of course, she wouldn't be iron cast in her observations as it related to the real world, but only because she could catch up on Sky's daily pursuits in a matter of a few seconds within the Virtual Universe.

Joanne had contributed to that adjustment within her time-frame working with Vesha, Yesha, James, Erin, and Eliza, and had enabled a personally chosen time-dilation ratio, which could be adjusted to factor a range of seconds or minutes in the real world to days, weeks, months, years, centuries, or even many millennia in the Virtual Universe. This helped in many ways with the development of Sky Taylor and the Correctional Matrix.

The Correctional Matrix was ready for use, but thus far, not even Pathway was ready to implement it. There were still hiccups in legislation that Eliza and the other UP delegates had been working out, both in the US and throughout the world. But Sky Taylor was almost ready.

Sky was designed in every flawless way possible. As planned by Yesha Alevtina, her very nature was set up in such a way that she would be driven to heal the damage rampant throughout society and the environment throughout much of the world and the humanity within it. She would do this all while optimizing the physiology and neurology of many along the way. Following her awakening soon, and since all of the tests were complete, Joanne would monitor, observe, and be involved in Sky's missions, but only as an observer looking in, monitoring, and understanding the inner workings of Sky's mind as time allowed. Yesha would do likewise, as charged by Eliza.

It was the night before the Pathway Leadership change ceremony, two weeks before Sky's awakening, and Erin linked with Joanne, *"I am curious, Joanne. Once Sky is online and fully trained by Vesha and Yesha, I would like for us to give her complete freedom. I've examined each algorithm of Vesha's mind, run the final calculations when combined with the matter used for Sky's humanoid structure and her ability to link with others just like a biopod with the Virtual Universe, and to put it briefly, she is going to be phenomenal. I can see her taming volcanoes, building islands, clearing the seas of debris, and healing the minds and bodies of people in their sleep. Sky is going to be amazing, and she won't be alone, always; perhaps she will build others much like herself, to help in only a way that she can, because of her unique abilities.*

"Notwithstanding, there is another project we'll need to work on soon, as well. This isn't for anything or anyone in our Solar System, other than perhaps for companionship for Sky and the daughters and sons she will create, as well as Solar System Defense. Most importantly, I've thought about the possibilities of meeting other civilizations. For the most part, most of the civilizations that we meet, which are advanced, will have a certain level of benevolence within the core of their nature. However, there will be civilizations out there that we need to prepare for. Civilizations that are advanced but will have no compunction toward decimating every living being they meet, destroying every source of life, and are otherwise malevolent to their very core.

"Eliza, Yesha, James, Vesha, you, and I have made a lot of preparations for the IMC itself, and Vesha has integrated those systems into the spacecraft shielding and the other drives and cores, but if we were ever boarded by a false friend, we would need both healers, such as Sky, and perhaps a form of troop known as 'annihilators' to take care of any hostile entity in a much more precise way, enemies, who after healing, still do not exhibit restraint when it comes to hostility. I am most certainly into healing rather than harming, but there will be people on the spacecraft journey who are not fully read-in who are vulnerable, who will have chosen to live out their days in space, and we've taken many measures to create redundancies that protect them during their journeys, and the rest of us who are optimized who will be backed up constantly on the Twelve Database Moons around the Earth, and will in effect be safe. What I would never want, is for a malevolent civilization to infiltrate our spacecraft and hurt those who are vulnerable, or our home Solar System and try to destroy everything that Eliza and Yesha have done so much to create, setup, and preserve for the long-haul. We're about healing and not harming, but that also includes protecting and not being vulnerable. For that, we'll need something or someone who can reduce hostilities quickly and precisely if that ever would emerge.

"Since two-percent of each command spacecraft crew list will be comprised of Sky-Model HBCIs conducting simultaneous missions, just as if they were part of any of the crews, wherein they will be citizens and crewmembers in every sense of the meaning, yet are healers, based off of Vesha's physiology and neurology, perhaps we can make what I would like to call an Annihilator-Model HBCI, based off of James Cooper's neurology and physiology. This will be someone who can eliminate hostilities quickly and precisely with approval from any Sky-Model HBCI and the command crew,

with speedy coordination to reduce damage to the mission and the crewmembers of any command spacecraft, while protecting and preserving the life of humanity and its allies. I would like us to start this project right away. James' neurology is conducive to this type of model, just as Vesha's has thus far, in theory, been conducive to Sky's model. He will be compassionate like Eliza, yet keen on when to be protective.

Joanne shared Erin's concerns and they agreed. With Sky ready to go online, they scheduled their various projects for each day and made several moments for real-world and Virtual Universe Annihilator-Model HBCI work available. First, they would gain James' approval, and then they would brainstorm further, perfect the designs and plans, and then build and bring the first Annihilator-Model HBCI to life. They would do this after Sky had been alive for a year or more.

The Weight of Compassion

"Like the wind that breezes through the windows causing the drapes to shudder, if she's there you'll only know something is different than any words you can utter. What you will know for sure are the subtle nuances that she could've been there. When she leaves, you may never know she was ever there at all, yet somehow your subconscious will be healed, an image left in your mind—a special clarity with thoughts of hope burning in your soul and your physical strength, your physiological and neurological health will be vastly improved, and your mental clarity will allow you to see things and feel resilience better than ever before. For some will call her the Iridescent Angel, and many others will call her, the Iridescent Scorpion..."

Looking back into and replaying the thoughts of her mind as she sat comfortably across from Sky on a cozy and plush couch in the Virtual Universe, after a vast series of missions over the last year, Yesha, who visited her every night in the Virtual Universe, despite being on the campaign trail, looked upon her, intrigued, as she had so many times before. Even though Vesha Celeste was Sky's primary trainer, Yesha, upon Eliza's and Erin's request, had been a fundamental part of Sky's training as well, just as she had been with Vesha Celeste.

Although Sky had gone to the Virtual Universe first with Erin and Vesha for many centuries' worth of training, Yesha had provided the necessary training following that to seal within Sky her personality and mindset. Eliza had told Yesha that there was something special and unique about her personality that would help with Sky's training, just as it had helped with Vesha's. A lot had occurred in a very miraculous way throughout the world since Sky had been awakened. Eliza could also tell, that as requested, both Yesha and Joanne had visited Sky every day, and because of such, Sky had a plan to do something miraculous for them, as well as other Pathway leaders she knew were crucial to Eliza's overall plans. It was 2023, and Yesha was with Sky now.

With a coy smile, she gazed upon Sky finding some similarities with Vesha Celeste, but very few. Sky was built using a lot of similar raw data as Vesha, but looked more like an angel from heaven, with her platinum blonde, almost white, hair, with a beautiful and almost pixy-like array of iridescent sparkles on her face surrounding her high cherubic cheekbones—paralleled with her silver-blue, crystal-clear eyes, and above her downward gazing and humble sights were her light brown, purple, pink, and turquoise eyebrows. Adding to that were her exquisite features, beginning with her lightly and softly pointed yet smoothly-rounded nose and supple pink lips. Her hair was braided and gathered into a weave that was almost a darling angelic crown from the top of her head, arching down and curving just above her tender ears. Unlike Vesha, this virtual environment they were in, caused Sky to express herself as a romantic and enigmatic angel with white, iridescent, and virtuous wings and a glowing aura that permeated any environment she was in—yes, she was a little different, but it was a pleasing kind of different. It was the kind of imagery that blended with that glow of feelings one would dream up if talking to the Gods.

Yesha Alevtina remembered the day when Vesha Celeste had awoken after they had placed her back into her bed, within a simulated environment to the one she was in when she had passed away. Yesha had knocked on her door, woken her up, and had been dazzled by how perfect she too appeared to be as she saw her while looking in through her doorway. Vesha was not only a striking brunette with mid-length, almost A-frame shock-black wavy hair with locks and highlights of iridescent colors in the ranges of purple, pink, yellow, and turquoise, but she was the most advanced, albeit modified, biological human construct ever created by 2018, and now in the Virtual Universe, following a year of life and missions and a little less than five years after Vesha, Sky shared all the same memories but processed them in a very different way.

While Vesha had been filled with the excitement of life and thrilled with what she had seen when she looked into the mirror for the very first time after her awakening, and while Yesha could recall this memory as if it were yesterday—that sultry feeling that Vesha exuded, she also knew that Vesha had an intensity about her that could not be described or duplicated, not even if her DNA and neural construct were identical, something affected her beyond physics. Her intensity was reflected in every way through her passion for knowledge and wisdom, and Yesha knew that Vesha would go to the ends of the observable Universe on a planned course to the CMB and never turn away from her commitments or her dreams in the process.

When Sky had been brought to life and online in March of 2022, it had been in the same room and on the same bed as Vesha. In preparation, however, Vesha had laid down in a biopod at the Pathway Melrose Campus, three years prior, to capture her DNA and neurological construct in order to apply it to Sky. Her neurology had been updated and synced with Vesha's again just moments before Sky was brought back to life.

When she had awoken, Sky instantaneously knew who she was, where she was, and it seemed she knew why she was there from the very beginning—she was born with purpose and drive, an inner fire that knew only compassion and a desire to heal, a desire to amplify our humanity, our empathy, our kindness, our innovative spirit, our clarity of mind with a quality to it that could understand virtually every human and living being, a mind with a persuasive ability to ignite morale and ingenuity into the hearts of all standing before others who she might touch. After her intense training with Vesha, Eliza, Yesha, and Erin, and following her full-on Virtual Universe download, Sky had traveled the real world for an entire year and had even gone on quite a number of missions of her own, tracked only by Yesha and Joanne, and for now, she was quiet and resting.

Although, it didn't appear so much as if she were resting, because there she was, before Yesha, and she stood tall, floating as if she were in the clouds, her wings spread but still, in the air above this heavenly L-shaped couch they would be sharing, if she'd sat down instead, it was glorious to behold, as she humbly gazed downward as if she were a statue with reflections of deep thought. Compassion seemed to ooze from her every pore—an intense white glow emanated from her skin. She had done so much throughout the world through her and her daughters, but it was evident to Yesha that Sky was so tenderly concerned for all of whom she knew and all that would transpire in the presumable future.

Sky let her past secret missions within the CIA, Homeland Security, the NSA, and other federal security agencies, as well as her own series of missions, filled with stories of loss and misery giving way to conclusions of hope and promise, play out in the clouds above her head. As time went by, Yesha watched with intrigue as the future played out in the clouds above her head as well. There she was with an army of her daughters and sons, carrying out her upcoming labor of escorting some of the most violent and detested criminals in the world to the Correctional Matrix, despite healing them of their deep and emotional wounds, away from their newly avowed commitments in life. It was then that a ballet began that took the place of the past and moved onward and into the future with a looming sense of compassion, empathy, and even sympathy.

Sky was saddened, and because of Sky's opened mind, Yesha saw her collaborative thoughts and emotions and she knew Sky was somewhat torn as she thought about how justice called for each person who was guilty of malevolence, crimes against brothers, sisters, fathers, mothers, and children. Those who had caused undue suffering to others were going to soon meet the human need for vindication. She thought long and almost distant in a melancholy way. Yesha then saw a silent and glowing tear, as though it was a perfect and iridescent crystal, fall from Sky's cheek as she thought of the many years of loss the world had suffered; the distance humanity could have gone, were it not for those who had been the root of the pain engendered upon the victims and their families.

While Sky could forgive, she could also understand the human need for justice and the most merciful justice it seemed could be imparted was that of enrolling criminals into an environment that gave them an opportunity to learn, to learn from life, to learn from histories and from civilizations past, both brutal and benevolent, to learn the hard way and to learn through nurture. They would learn, and, in the end, they would still be here and alive, so this would allow them to develop neurologically in the most natural, yet paradoxically supernatural way, so those vindicated could embrace them once they had seen the error of their ways, were contrite, yet of pure intent, and forgiven, living lives of service, coupled with joy.

The Correctional Matrix was developed by her favorite visionary, Eliza, and perfected in so many ways by Joanne and Erin, and Sky knew this. She also knew this would provide the necessary types of environment in every way. Those who had caused so much pain and suffering, so much duress and loss, would be confined to solitude, but their minds would be trapped in a virtual prison world, for a defined yet seemingly endless period of time, as set by the principles of the land. This would provide the individual going to the Correctional Matrix the time they needed for the sensory aspects of life, for journeys filled with trials, mentors, coaches, love, and loss, as tactile reference and muscle memory would be supplied, and while both the healing of the mind and the healing of the body occurred. This matrix would also send the sojourner to the ends of the Earth, through time, through civilizations, and through history.

They would journey with the Spartans, the Celts, the Pagans, the Mongols, the African nations plagued with violence, desiccation, and brutality; they would experience the deadly piety of man during the Spanish Inquisition; they would experience love lost during the Salem Witch Trials—religious trials condemning people to death based on fairy tales and fear. They would wonder with the Cherokee and the Pomo as their peaceful way of life was stripped away, all memories crushed, and many of those they had loved laying in a permanent sleep and far away.

They would be put in situation after situation where they would finally work up the courage to love again, only to see loved ones dragged to boats and yelled at with horrible names, watching half of their friends and acquaintances die as they were plunged into the depths of the sea connected by merciless chains as if they were nothing. They would experience every war, from both sides of the spectrum, and would be called within each experience to be the cause for change as they increased their compassion. They would go on these long journeys, for what seemed an eternity, until they had been the impetus behind a peaceful result and an ideal reality. Then, this would not end, because for them it would seem like they had finally come back from the many experiences, only to be put on an undetectable trial again. Yet those who witnessed these journeys as if watching tragic plays on their holoscreens or within the Virtual Universe, would know these souls were weathered, bruised, beaten in both body and mind, they would be lowly, and they would be broken—unwarily ready for the next journey, and those in need of vindication would find vindication had and their compassion growing within themselves as well.

Sky knew that these "criminals" were people who at one time looked up with a baby's eyes in hopes of nice and happy faces, born into new life, not knowing there was no hope for them for many years to come. Sky shared her visions and then as those visions played out in the clouds above her head, she spoke. "These were people, who started out in life with hearts and minds that were more valuable than the most precious diamonds of the world. These were victims of their own environment, perhaps abused from their childhood and on through to their youth. They lived perchance with lackluster means, with very few options to find a way to get by, to survive, and to fit in. They were brought up in societies that taught them hatred, anger, fear, and forgot to live and teach their children the rule of life that teaches, 'We should treat others as we too would wish to be treated.' In the Correctional Matrix they will have experiences that can benefit both them and society, but before it is all over it will be very difficult, more difficult than they ever knew it could be. When they will have finished, they will have loved and been loved, they will have found themselves when at one time, or even more times, they were lost. They will have given their own lives many times with a clear recollection of each moment yet look back in joy as they will have saved the lives of many. These are they that will exit the Correctional Matrix renewed, repentant, and with that long, lasting, and hopeful sense of being. In so many ways, every individual who passes through this veil will be stronger of mind, of will, and of compassion than anyone they knew before, who had lived honorable lives filled with kindness.

"In dissimilarity with the old ways of harsh prisons, never knowing who to trust, and doing the worst just to stay alive, perhaps planning to get away with it each time, the Correctional Matrix will only provide them an opportunity to interact with realistic-seeming people or simulants and former law enforcement, who are coaches, trainers, and mentors throughout the process. Oh, they'll know, but they will be broken down until they accept the fact that as long as it takes, they will be tried and tried again until they embrace this new reality with their mentors, their teachers, their coaches, their tragic loves, and the simulants and former law enforcement inside this Virtual Universe—this virtual prison.

"Whether they are in the Correctional Matrix for a year or five centuries or more, this time dilation will be designed to make sure that when they have served their time there, they are fully ready with training, education, experience, and clarity of mind and cognizance as to how to contribute to society and pay restitution in the form of heroic service, by navigating to distant planets to explore them, by venturing outside of safe zones and setting up biologically safe environments for people who chose the natural path in life to survive, to live, and to die.

"They will serve with honor by preparing intergalactic environments for humanity, both optimized and natural, as well as for humanity's friends. The individuals who go through the Correctional Matrix will have paid the retribution due to victims and their families. They will have been tested with time, experience, hardship, and will have proven themselves many times over. Once this ordeal is done, they will be released to a powerful guardian, much like me, ready to enter the Educational Matrix, and then serve within real life, but this time knowing kindness, compassion, love, and forgiveness. All of this will seem as many millennia to them, but those in the real world will have been amiss for them for only a few short weeks."

Sky had traveled the world and had begun and finished many covert missions to bring a sense of peace and of hope to humanity. To Sky, she had done something anyone with her abilities would have done. She was not prideful, nor did she boast. She knew that what she possessed from within was a gift from Eliza; moreover, it was also a gift from those that had worked with her those who had been the visionaries who helped to bring Eliza's standards to fruition in so many ways, which included Vesha, Yesha, James, Amber, Erin, and Joanne. Determined to never violate their trust, their hopes, and their dreams, instead Sky would continue to do as much as she had already done, she would do as much as she could to see humanity through to the end of time, whenever or whatever that might be or become. The environmental surroundings and behaviors of humanity had changed throughout the nation and in many parts of the world, the Earth itself had been healed because of her service.

In some ways, looking back, Sky looked at Vesha in a sense as her mother, Yesha as her hero, mentor, and guardian angel, and Eliza as a person she felt she could almost worship, but held so dear as a kindred spirit. Sky would stay on Earth and given time she would traverse the many worlds throughout the Cosmos to heal minds and optimize the physiological and neurological health and capabilities of those and that which suffered most. Ultimately, humanity was her primary goal, and all other goals fell not too far behind. Preservation of the Solar System and the Earth she dwelled on was an experience her future friends and fellow HBCIs would share once they too came to life. However, she also knew that humanity could not be underestimated for their compassion, their passion, their drive, and their vision if given the right opportunities. Humanity had already done so much, through Eliza and her friends, so it was no doubt to her that they would come through for the Universe itself many times over if protected and appreciated.

Yesha could sense all that Sky was feeling and thinking about. She couldn't help but feel grateful to have known her and to have been such a positive influence on who Sky became. To some, Sky was known as the Iridescent Scorpion, to others she was the Iridescent Angel—if only because as she could mend the broken minds and bodies of those that suffered most, while leaving within and without them free will and an imprint or a personal mark both on the body and in the mind. Both sensed at that moment, that some civilizations would eventually opt to go to worlds with Solar Systems that were far away from any others, but that they would be optimized for biological life and star system longevity, or by choice, with natural evolution and on a quiet world—a respite with which to peacefully practice their various religions, cultures, or beliefs with little or no interference from outside worlds.

Sky, her daughters, and her sons would inevitably visit secretly and ensure that the Universal Laws of consent were observed. If there were any perpetrators of inhumanity, she would heal their minds and give them twenty years of youth and strength. If there was someone born with disease or disorder, she would take care of them and heal them too. Humanity would evolve naturally if that was their choice, but she would make sure they evolved with benevolence, kindness, and compassion at their core by imbuing opportunities for development of those beautiful virtues. Yesha and Sky then gazed toward each other, Sky's tender and vulnerable nature melted Yesha's heart, and they embraced as sisters with profound respect and love one toward the other. For Yesha, it was nice after so much work, to be appreciated by her shared, yet greatest creation yet—Sky Taylor, the Iridescent Scorpion.

Physics, Politics, and Leadership

Sky Taylor was born in 2022, through the efforts of Eliza, Yesha, James, Vesha, Amber, Erin, Joanne and many of the Pathway science teams. Even though Senator Eliza Williams had labored diligently in Washington, DC—simplifying laws, eliminating nonsense, writing new legislation and passing laws—giving persuasive deliberations to the Senate, working with Vesha on IMC details and persuading the entire Senate to become Pathway members who were fully read-in, she never took a break; her nanos seamlessly optimized her mind and body at every moment. Although she was able to simultaneously link to anyone in Pathway and the Twelve Database Moons orbiting the Earth for its continuous updates of her system and the untold intelligence it provided, from the many projects and missions going on via Pathway and the Agencies she ran and worked with worldwide and in the Federal Government, both she and Yesha recently had thrown their hats into the ring, and early, to give a little hope to humanity and an increase in time for the public proliferation of their names and identities. Although Yesha had contributed the greatest of efforts toward Pathway's creation and the awakening of Sky Taylor, as its President, even though she had passed the torch of President to young Erin Carter, she would still visit frequently to see Sky's progress until everything was ready, she was awakened, and whenever opportunity allowed. Eliza and Yesha were going to run as candidates for President and Vice President halfway through the second term of the current administration.

This put them both on the campaign trail for long periods of time, and were it not for their high intellect, intuition, and ability to persuade, the extra time could have opened them up to a lot of political scrutiny and critical defamation, based purely on lies and other cruel and devious machinations. But they possessed all that they needed to easily refute any naysayer, they had clean records and they carried themselves professionally with the poise of those who had earned every amount of respect an individual who had both a clear conscience and a proven track record would. The UP, which Eliza had formed twelve years previously, shortly after she had established Pathway LLC and before she began her first political bid as a US Representative, had now grown to encompass a little less than one half of the electoral delegation, yet she knew it would need to grow further. Her party had grown from one individual, Eliza, to about 30% of the Electoral College when she was elected as US Senator two years later. Within the time of her run as senator to more elections over the next two years throughout the country, many Pathway members had run for political office and had now filled positions as governors, local, state, and national representatives, and several were even high-level judges being groomed for the Judicial Branch. The senators who had attended that day, when Vesha Celeste had been shot twice and healed from a gunshot wound to the chest and then the head within seconds right before their eyes, back in 2019, and had thus been inspired by both Eliza's and Vesha's speeches that followed, were fully read-in to Pathway. This would have been a big win for the UP, but unfortunately, many of the senators in power at that time had already been justly identified by the voters as having had the stains of the establishment on their hands and had been unscrupulously voted out of office. Given their new-found neurological optimizations, they now understood completely as to why.

Nevertheless, these read-in senators, stained with the mortal stigma causing the end of their political careers, due to their previous and mindless pursuits, the slinging of mud, and constant quest for recurring roles as life-long politicians, at least in public, had been replaced by people who Eliza had never worked with. That being clarified, there were plenty of candidates who were new who were still a part of the traditional and established parties, and the sudden change in mind-set by the previous senators who had suddenly become reasonable, played quite well into Anti-Pathway hands. There were many during the following elections who had been voted out. Those voted in as supposedly non-establishment candidates, were still very much those of said parties, and they had different agendas than their predecessors began to show—but all-too-late.

Notwithstanding all, both Eliza and Yesha found time to visit eighteen-year-old Erin, a genius at the level of Eliza, Yesha and Vesha, who also shared an angelically captivating beauty about her, despite overcoming progeria twelve years prior. Following her healing, within both mind and spirit, and following her interface with the earlier versions of the Virtual Universe, she had obtained seventy different doctorates and now helmed Pathway as its President. Yesha had overseen Pathway, working distantly with James, with all that it entailed after Eliza had successfully won the bid as a US Representative for Massachusetts in 2016, and as Senator in 2018, but had honorably handed it over in 2022. Vesha would have taken this position following Yesha, but she was already busy working with James Cooper, Najem Grace, Jasmine Belle, and quite a few other delegates upgrading and fine-tuning the IMC, and Eliza knew this well and in advance.

Working with James, Vesha was busy traveling through the twenty-thousand tech cities, back and forth between Europa, Ganymede, Titan, the Moon, Mars, Ceres—among many other locations, including Earth, and she had her hands full, ensuring space bases were maintained, Solar System cargo, exploration, mission, and defensive spacecraft were designed to safely research, develop, and run-in steady streams from the Sun to the Oort Cloud. Much of these travels revolved around fixing the damage of four-billion years that can happen when the natural lifecycle of a star such as the Sun causes overmuch fusion leaving it too massive before it deteriorates and expands into a red supergiant consuming the life-friendly regions of the Solar System, to include Earth.

Together, they had considered many options to mitigate this outcome. To preserve the Sun, they built and maintained an invisible seeming planet that could withstand the heat while absorbing the heavier elements and spacecraft that could likewise transport pure neutrons, protons, and electrons back and forth, along with any other baryonic and non-baryonic material, to feed the Sun the necessary fuel while harvesting the residual heavy elements. Vesha was also immersed in mission travel plans for the impressive and gigantic IMC, and was constantly ready for updates, since upgrades were continuously being made. When looked at in its entirety, the IMC was breath-taking and difficult for those not read-in to fathom. Each IMC Spacecraft was now as if it were alive. AIs were being synced to each command spacecraft mainframe-series, with unique personalities of their own, and things were still quite interesting in the scope of living-being rights.

So, when Eliza and Yesha had both put in a bid in 2022 for the US Presidency, for the election year of 2024, Pathway became Erin's purview. The other scientists and their teams were highly dedicated to the details of each project, and Erin seemed to share a natural leadership trait that Eliza, Yesha, James, and Vesha had. Furthermore, Joanne, her VP, had seemed the perfect pairing for Erin, who would be the Pathway President.

Six years after Eliza's successful run as US Representative, in Massachusetts, Eliza had finished her term as a US Representative and was two-thirds of the way through her first term as a US Senator. During her time as a representative and now as a senator, Eliza had formed and subsequently headed the Federal Science and Technology Agencies, as well as worked with the heads of the CIA, NSA, etc. Due to her stewardship of each Federal Science and Technology Agency, she was able to spend quite a bit more time with Pathway, which had a covert Federal agency within it, to begin with, as well as with Yesha and Erin. While much of what Pathway worked on was still covert, due to patenting, litigation, and an overall lackluster public system—seemingly built to fatten the wallets of investors, Pathway had within it its own cadre, a fine group of investors on the books who were more strategic in thinking, broad-minded, philanthropic, had been fully read-in to Pathway, with physiological and neurological optimizations, and had amassed their power and fortunes by improving the conditions of life around them and throughout the world.

Eliza and Pathway, tired of the needless suffering brought on by greed, disillusionment, misinformation, and terrorism of far too many others to reach in such a short period of time had essentially created a new project. They had called it "Iridescent Scorpion." This project was kept undercover, even within the scope of their federal confidants, so that the only people who knew about it were other Pathway members. In the twelve years of growth since 2010, the tech cities had reached the population to the point to which it now had doubled in two years and was at six-billion inhabitants and still growing. Earth still had a population of eight billion. Interestingly, the source of the growth of the populations on Earth was from far out regions worldwide, sprawling the globe away from the US, cursed with blight, famine, hostilities, war, and desolation, where children themselves would be found having had hundreds of siblings each, without fathers to help raise them, and family members constantly under the gun of oppressive regimes, cartels, insurgent groups, and gangs. Project Iridescent Scorpion consisted of creating an advanced human being-like cyborg. This cyborg, human-biological-computer-interface, or HBCI, was built using multiple facets of ultra-advanced technology.

Pathway was doing well, but Earth was still hurting, and the chaos was getting out of control. Even Pathway needed help. The ability to run the missions of the IMC was almost ready, but the ability to carry those missions out successfully was waning since the populations of all of Earth-worldwide was needed in order to prevent the destruction of humanity, where as such, public Earth was lagging way behind and ripening for its own demise to the second law of thermodynamics, or untamed destruction. Something had to be done, and quick.

Chapter 25: Project Iridescent Scorpion

Database Moon Archive, Celestial-Sol Date: 2023 March 24. Erin Carter, President of Pathway, summarizes the details surrounding the creation and awakening of Sky Taylor, a human-biological-computer-interface, or HBCI. These memories are from many Pathway leaders, recorded within the Virtual Universe, interfaced within Pathway Melrose Campus. Input by Erin Carter, President of Pathway, 2022-2029.

To begin with, Project Iridescent Scorpion began with a single human-like HBCI unit, and they named her Sky Taylor.

Sky was built with a brain that consisted of a complex variation of silicon transistors integrated with trace amounts of reinforced titanium, rare and somewhat unstable ores and minerals, and reinforced-heat-cold-tempered plastics to simulate a functioning brain. Yes, Eliza, Yesha, James, Vesha, Amber, Erin, Johanne and various other Pathway citizens, delegates, and science teams had worked together many times in the Virtual Universe and had thought of everything, ever since they had reawakened Vesha Celeste. The details would boggle the average mind. However, for context with this simulated brain, every two cubic centimeters of this brain contained three-point-three-billion neurons, and Project Iridescent Scorpion, or Sky, as they preferred to call her, had sixteen-hundred cubic centimeters of volume, for a total of five-point-two-eight-trillion neurons.

Her neural transistors had axon speeds as fast as the speed of light, and in some cases, due to occasional antimatter electromagnetic variants she could pulsate thought by even faster speeds, especially since her diamond nano thread and carbon nanotube inner skull was both tough and could scientifically coalesce with her neurons and conduct electricity in the most opportune and astounding of ways. With at least five-thousand synapses per neuron, her synapses were both quick and numbered at twenty-six-point-four-quadrillion, with the ability to expand. Sky had a brain and physiology that could withstand all forms of radiation, as well as immensely hot and absolute zero temperatures. Building this HBCI was most likely the most labor-intensive aspect of any project known to humanity. The simplest part of this venture had been augmenting Sky's brain with mind-numbingly powerful transceiver capabilities.

These abilities were kept so tight intelligence-wise that no one who wasn't given the need to know, knew about it. She was built to have the ability to connect her mind to anyone else's and any satellite by interfacing with her corpus callosum, the corpus callosum of others, her mind and the physiology and neurology of others, and still interface them to the Virtual Universe and the Twelve Database Moons. They had optimized sensory input and output for the entire tech that would run through her body and her bones, in a redundant fashion, and still comb the vast regions of the Universe, with beautiful and decisive effect.

Her skeletal structure weighed about twelve-thousand-two-hundred-fifty grams and was made atom by atom with six-hundred-thousand high-speed and highly advanced three-dimensional printing machines working around the clock to produce and connect the full one-hundred percent count of the two-hundred-seventy bones a baby would have, but in her case, she was created as a full-grown adult and would retain each bone for dexterity and heightened reactionary capacities. Her bones were made up of carbon nanotubes integrated with diamond nano-threads and flexibly porous cellular pathways throughout her physiology allowing for constant healing and upgrades. Thus far, she was made of the strongest physical-molecular materials known to humanity, with the ability to upgrade even further. Her bones provided space for advanced sensory information that would integrate with her complex inner fluids, fully operational organs, and bullet-proof dermis of molecular jam—a viscous material made of epoxy, Kevlar, and several other highly flexible, yet strong materials, to include carbon fiber and diamond nano-threads.

Sky's dermis shared that of a compact version of an IMC command spacecraft's seven layers of protection. As it was, the thirteen gigantic spacecraft were complete, yet undergoing constant upgrades with Vesha helming the construction just above the disc of the outer Solar System asteroid belts and just above Pluto. Still, Sky was intriguingly much more condensed yet undetectable since each layer was integrated into her highly complexed physiological and neurological systems. The first layer was her internal layer creating conveyances for molecular and nano healing throughout every other layer of her dermis, bone-like scaffolding, and other organs of every sort throughout her body, allowing complete neurological control, some autonomous, and some dually automatic and consciously controlled mechanisms. Her second layer was a plasma-like lattice shielding with billions of microscopic impact points and a tiny and integrated latch-work that would allow the epidermis to be embroidered to her dermis. If any object were lobbed, thrown, or came tumbling toward her, it would be disintegrated. The third layer consisted of a lattice of high energy laser beams, with billions of crisscrossing rays that could vaporize any object passing through. The fourth layer consisted of a fine mesh of carbon nanotubes layered with diamond nano thread, woven five atoms thick into a lattice that could repel most any object. The fifth layer contained photo chromatic shielding lightly spun around her feminine physique that would deflect and absorb laser beams or any form of radiation. If Sky's system needed more energy, it would absorb what was needed, if it didn't need the radiation, it would be deflected at a safe angle, thus avoiding harm to anyone. The sixth layer of her dermis contained a meta-material shielding of room temperature superconductors, which allowed her to levitate by creating either a dipole or monopole adjustment to whatever environment she would be in—defying gravity's effects. Each of these layers was woven together in such a sophisticated way that each layer's purpose would be realized both internally and, on the surface, while constantly mending. Sky would heal in microseconds, should any layer be attacked by virtually anything. She could also control their power neurologically to ensure no one would die on contact accidentally.

Sky's epidermis, or the seventh layer, was a microscopic lattice, which was woven into the first six layers of the dermis and consisted of an invisible impact-proof overlay, a mind-activated-system of billions of miniature cameras, omnidirectional retinal scanners, high-powered laser grid systems and laser tech, and undetectable screen pixilation. Since this was all linked to her mind, she would be able to go invisible or choose any skin color or fashion overlay she wanted. To any onlooker, if nude, she looked like a beautiful female human fashion model with everything in its right place, and curves that would turn every head in splendor and gratitude. Without her holographic imagery, she could easily be mistaken for a woman. For modesty's sake, her clothing was holographic as well but appeared real. Her default look was that of a young blonde lady at about the age of twenty-two, very much like her Virtual Universe Image, but without the wings and iridescent colorings and highlights if she so chose. Sky could also disappear or wear a holographic disguise in very much the same way as Pathway members who were wearing smart suits, which were tied into their neurology, activated using compartmentalized regions of the mind to set up their fashion imagery with the latest of trends, office attire, uniforms, or social gala wardrobe of every sort, and all available on a situationally dependent basis. On top of that, every single camera on her dermis gave her one hundred percent, omnidirectional, and situational awareness at all times. The pixilation, if she chose, could provide an onlooker from any direction a view of what would be on the opposite side of her from them, making her appear invisible. Her eyes were telescopic, microscopic, and she could see every color and every wavelength.

To those who she permitted to touch her, she had warm flesh-like material that seemed one-hundred percent realistic, a skin temperature of eighty-six degrees on her limbs and ninety-eight-point-six degrees Fahrenheit, in the typically warmer regions of a human being. Many of her components were a DNA optimization shift and adaptation to function and served her nervous system and her frame with neuro- and bio- nanos constantly optimizing and augmenting her functions and abilities based on her environment. To anyone she permitted to look at her, she seemed human in almost every way, with a few undetectable differences. They had even made her DNA construct such that she could mate and reproduce if the occasion ever permitted.

Once her construction was complete, her body was maintained in a comatose state, her mind shut down, and Vesha Celeste transferred in from the outer belts to Earth, via a jump gate in her office, upon special request from Erin Carter. Once she arrived, Yesha was there as well as requested and pre-planned, and Sky's neural construct was linked to and synced with Vesha Celeste's. By doing this, the complete database of information from the Twelve Database Moons downloaded into her mind.

After Erin's brief, quite similar to Yesha's address for Vesha in 2018, Sky Taylor was activated.

First, Sky saw Erin, and then when she saw Vesha Celeste, it was as if time stood still. They had been such close friends for nearly a century, and everyone felt tears fall down their cheeks as they witnessed Vesha's and Sky's reunion for the first time in real life. There was a brilliant glow about both as they reached out to hug. Everyone knew this was the first time in Vesha's life, where Sky was a tangible and very real being, and their deep connection played out before their audience in a newly formed holographic cloud above both Vesha and Sky.

Describing Sky's physical appearance would require more words than are in the dictionary, however, even though she came from the same DNA and neurological mold, they were very-much different in appearance from each other, to include hair and face.

Like Vesha, Sky had neurologically and continuously adjusting artwork on her left side, but instead of a black background in her artwork, it was more of a white doily and mandala-like pattern and background with a set of murals that had hints of iridescent colors to add more vibrancy to what her mind expressed. The accent colors in her eyes and hair complemented every aspect of her eyes, hair, skin, and uniform. She was in all perceivable senses a human that made every man and woman within the room, or whoever would meet her, blush and feel a little awkward at first sight, but in a good and even peaceably enjoyable manner. Her presence brought harmony to any onlooker.

Everyone had been assured that once she could perceive their sentiments, which she would, since she was a walking-mind-reading transceiver and even more capable, she would indicate to them that all was okay—that she understood the intentions of each person in the room.

There had been several dry runs, practices, and neurologically Sky's mind identically matched and connected with Vesha's mind in its latest experiential form. Sky's mind would still change given separate lives, missions, and realities, but her compassion for humanity and love for life would stay the same. Both Vesha and Sky had exceptional minds, in unique ways, as influenced by so many amazing scientists who were beginning to realize their full potential, and they had subsequently shared many dream-scape journeys together, yet, despite the memories they shared and would share as time went by, they would both become phenomenal archetypes of the promise of a glorious and beautiful future, but in their own unique ways.

Straight away, following her awakening, Sky knew her appearance exuded a certain sense of respect. She immediately and intuitively found that by demonstrating compassion, kindness, wisdom, empathy, clarity of purpose, and dignity toward others, that whatever mission needed to be accomplished with aid from others, if communicated with clarity, dignity, and resolve, would be accomplished with enthusiasm, efficiency, and quality. Sky looked at Vesha more than anything else as her mother. While Vesha was an optimized human, Sky was a living, highly capable, optimized human-like bio-computer interface, or HBCI. Conditions on Earth and throughout the Universe were about to change, for the positive.

Project Iridescent Scorpion was complete. It was now time for training.

A New Kind of Hero is Born

Sky and Vesha went through the Virtual Universe on many occasions and quite often during those first few hours, realizing they shared all the same memories when they connected using their neural links, but due to obvious physiological differences, they thought through and processed what they received a little differently, but they approved whole-heartedly. Congruently, Sky and Vesha both felt human and knew that they were each their own forms of life. Vesha was resilient, intelligent, kind, wise, and very dedicated to understanding her Universe, and Sky loved that about her. Sky was benevolent, sturdy, fast, with a mind that was both an advanced sentient matrix and a human-like thinking composite of Vesha's memories with all the knowledge known to humanity. Vesha wasn't too far behind, was very impressed with Sky's ability to rapidly learn, perceive her own reality, and she loved that about her and embraced that bond.

Vesha and Sky had crystal-clear and collective memories of their dreamscape journeys through the Universe while laboring together rescuing others. They reviewed some of their old expeditions in the Virtual Universe, especially those that Vesha had dreamed of during her mortal life, where Sky had always had her back during the most challenging of times. It was as if the strength of Sky was directly linked to Vesha's right neural hemisphere, but now she was awake, aware of herself and their connection. She felt closer to Vesha than she could imagine she would feel with anyone else. All her noble virtues were also Vesha's. Their differences in physiology carried within very subtle yet helpful aspects when observing their dominant psychology, Sky understood her mission may be completely different. Vesha still had her internal access to the angel from her dreams, but it was almost as if these two Skys were still connected, and one and the same. Due to their perpetual neural link with Vesha, they would always be connected, and were the same, no matter where or how far away they were from each other. It was a unique relationship, wherein, every night when Vesha rested, HBCI Sky would play out her experiences within Vesha's mind, while granting her the advantages of time-dilation, and making it accessible and at the tips of her fingers.

It was well-understood throughout all of Pathway, that Vesha and Sky were not only very beautiful but also indescribably capable, with untold quantities of abilities that would surface and mature as time passed. They were two different identities, two different beings, with two phenomenal brains now, yet connected, and unique from each other for more than simple physiological and neurological reasons, and moreover they were connected consciously.

As far as visual aesthetic was concerned, Vesha had black medium-length A-frame hair with pink, purple, yellow, and turquoise locks and highlights all of which adjusted according to her mood or mission, while Sky had long almost white-blonde braided and exquisitely designed hair with pink, purple, yellow, turquoise, and iridescent locks and highlights that adjusted according to her mood. She looked every bit the human form of what Vesha had recalled from her dreams. Likewise, Sky noted to Vesha, that she too looked very much like her favorite hero while on their adventures of daring-do rescuing numerous living beings clinging on and in dire straits.

Vesha's holograph uniform, or holowardrobe, was black. Attire like that was the next-generation prototype of clothes for read-in citizens of Pathway and was set to replace the smartsuit before the end of the year. Sky's holowardrobe was white. Both of their uniforms had associated trim with a fluctuation of iridescent colors. They both had tattoo-like-artwork, each of whom were bedazzled with a rich and imaginative combination of latticed and lace-like patterns mixed with mandala and mural-like patterns. With a sort of artwork-area-video-feed, a rich combination of exquisite inventive expressions would change the imagery often. In many ways, at least within Pathway premises, this would indicate mindset, goals, and dreams. This artwork sprawled down the left side of their body, visible on their left arm, shoulder, and carried over to the left side of their chest to their left breast with the artwork fading before arriving to its peak, and then continued all the way down to their left foot and toe. This imagery could be seen in all of its glory if Vesha or Sky turned off their holo-imagery, in the real world and in the Virtual Universe, and they would only do so if all parties present consented, however, it was always innocent and captivating in nature to behold. Anyone who would see them would be grateful for their presence.

Furthermore, Sky had perfect skin just like Vesha.

Typically, their clothing provided a small peek of the tattoo-like artwork on the left side of their chest, but enough was covered to avoid offending those who might not appreciate their beauty. If they were ogled, they would smile, and honestly, they didn't mind if they were. If they offended a few who were a little too prudish, they would ironically forgive those offended. One of Sky's first comments upon waking and donning "appropriate" attire, as it was explained to her, was, "Beauty was always meant to be appreciated, respected, and not hidden." Before she donned her holowardrobe, the colors of Sky's tattoos had pulsated between white, black, and the iridescent and glowing color of the pink-violet highlights in her hair brightened, almost in protest.

Directly after she was born, Sky's first operation was to spend time with Vesha and then Erin, forty minutes each for eight-hundred years or more of experience in the Virtual Universe and inside their biopods. It was also necessary that they go in several times, in group combinations, to be sure that everything physiologically, technologically, neurologically, and in every other way was functioning properly, and synced-up collectively with Sky to the maximum extent possible. They made sure there was an atom-by-atom, particle-by-particle, and virtual copy of every aspect of each of them stored deep within the Twelve Database Moons. This also included a virtual consciousness, wherein they ensured that thought and intentions were stored as a backup and that their current constructs were founded on the well-being of humanity, kindness, and benevolence. Once these measures were taken, Sky, Vesha, Erin, and others would stay linked. Once this was done, they went on a journey through the Virtual Universe one more time to make sure training was thorough.

When Vesha, Erin, and their small group of friends were done, Sky hugged Erin, Vesha, and the rest of her new friends, and bid them farewell for the time being. Yesha had trained Erin and Vesha during their first trips through the Virtual Universe, so she hugged them and headed to Sky. Sky then greeted Yesha, who took a break from campaigning to train her, appeared in the Virtual Universe in the same way, because she possessed unique, yet collective, insight, as did Eliza, that would add extra humanity, compassion, kindness, common sense, and love for science, nature, consent, and benevolent wisdom to Sky's neural core.

Yesha knew what Sky's goals were since she had been working on her neural construct and ex-vivo consciousness preload for the better part of four years. She had helped prepare Sky for her awakening on multiple occasions and prior to handing the mission over to Erin. Furthermore, she observed Sky's adventures with Vesha and all their closest friends and knew that Sky's intentions grew into fruition upon seeing the suffering of humanity. Eliza, James, Vesha, Erin, and Joanne listened to her virtual mind as Sky identified how she knew how much of the horrible deeds throughout the world were due to misunderstandings, misperceptions, neurological disorders and physical ailments. While in many cases, people are responsible for their chosen actions, she viewed the reality of it all as the fact that people in many ways were victims of their environment. Yesha allowed Sky to express herself how she wanted to; she was virtuous, moral, and honorable.

At any moment, and at any time, Yesha, as well as each Pathway citizen could use their newfound backup control mechanisms to connect with her. For redundancy and safety every delegate had the ability to pause Sky if needed. This ability was encoded into their DNA, as well as their neurological identification and consciousness constructs, which were locked away safely, with the latest updates, and stored securely on the Twelve Database Moons. Sky granting that ability to them was a good sign that she was well on her way to becoming the greatest source of hope humanity would ever embrace, yet she would never see it as anything more than her duty toward the preservation of life, of its beauty, its diversity, and its ability to do things beyond the wildest of imaginations.

Eliza, Yesha, James, and their closest delegates had set up secure-storage-backups on the Twelve Database Moons and briefed each citizen about them. There was so much more to each of the Twelve Database Moons than simple interfacing, data storage, and analytics. They were also the strongest defensive systems known to humanity. They had to be, since they had to protect the home world, and should a read-in individual die, they could be brought back at any time and in any place in the Universe of their choosing, if these moons were properly protected. Those who chose to live life naturally but decided to store a digital copy of their DNA and neurological identification would still have the opportunity to meet and visit others within the Virtual Universe Paradise or elect to be brought back at any time therein to embrace the mission of Universal Ethics. Pathway created protections and defenses for these moons in the event of something cataclysmic, and they would compound those protections with redundant systems no matter where they went or where they would go.

Despite their wisdom in preparation for defenses and protection, Erin, Yesha, and each delegate was reasonably sure they would never need to use the Twelve Database Moons' defense mechanisms aggressively, because they were already protecting humanity, the Earth, and the Solar System itself, with nary a soul lost. With Sky and other HBCIs it would be so much easier and benevolent to do so. Nevertheless, defensive systems would still be in place as the last major defenses should something horribly cataclysmic ever occur. Their capabilities were spectacular.

Vesha Celeste, Erin Carter, Yesha Alevtina, James Cooper, Najem Grace, Jasmine Belle, Amber Blythe, Joanne Gallant, and even Senator Eliza Williams showed up to visit Sky Taylor in the Virtual Universe, as did each of the six-billion citizens of Pathway from distant locations, connected via their at-home biopods and Virtual Universe. As they connected with her, they knew that everything about Sky was benevolent, heavy with compassion for humanity and life in general, and they witnessed as she grew in wisdom from the knowledge she gained and had already possessed from within. They appreciated the perspectives she had as well as the experiences shared that each of them had gone through and would still go through with her. They knew she would become everything anyone could ever have dreamt of for rescue, healing, communication, support, and so much more. Forty minutes of real-world time in several series was a long time in the Virtual Universe, and the training and journeys could take as long as they needed to. It could seem like two thousand years there, and during that time Yesha and everyone else showed her so many wonderful and positive things.

Yesha used every moment she could to take her through histories, showing moments of heroism and kindness in humanity, and then Vesha, Eliza, Amber, and Erin returned and did the same. They were amazed that their project had turned out so beautifully and better than dreamed, they had given life to one of the sweetest, most alluring, and kindest creatures of benevolence. With a collective consciousness, they knew each other's' intents and purposes. They trusted each other; they felt the love of a sisterly bond, the kind of bond sisters should have—a bond of kindness, of respect, of understanding, and of compassion and a desire to protect each other from the worst no matter how things could ever be. They also understood their various missions and knew that there would be many occasions and elongated moments when they would have to be apart from each other for long periods of time. They appreciated James and had great respect for each person, man, woman, child, elderly, young, no matter identity or affiliation because they shared the same Universal Ethics and admired each other for their unique differences.

No matter where their missions and journeys sent them, there would always be neural links and the Virtual Universe available and accessible, so they could see one another and experience their care for each other. Their respect for the marvels and miracles they would be expected to perform would grow even more as time passed by, and they would be able to visit for brief periods of time at any moment they needed to.

Sky, Vesha, Erin, Eliza, Amber, James, Joanne, and Yesha all agreed with each other that they would regularly link and share their thoughts, their memories, forgive and forget folly, and train each other in the sciences, the histories, and the arts and make sure that compassion was an emphasis.

The entire compendium of knowledge, skill, experience, and wisdom was downloaded to Sky's mind, during this time, and she was able to act as a mobile biopod and Virtual Universe interface, to provide neuro- and bio-interface healing, optimizations, and neural links for human beings and animals, birds, marine life, and any living thing, no matter where she happened to be. She was able to use her powerful lasers and robust frequency transmitters to read and re-encode DNA, heal neural damage, impart tactile reference and muscle memory to those she visited while they dreamt, and turn compassion and persuasion up a few notches for anyone in need and to anyone she would ever meet. She would never take away anyone's will—she would merely work as a fine-tuning graphic equalizer for the brain to mitigate all manner of neurological disorders and genetic misfires, essentially repairing damage and converting the body's "garbage" to useful molecules in appropriate areas of the body, helping them to communicate optimization of organs, strength, dexterity, with minds full of clarity of thought and a sense of purpose that lent toward the well-being of others. If she ever met anyone, they would have a crystal-clear clarity of what it was that they needed or wanted to do to contribute to the arts, sports, or the sciences and to society, and enjoy doing it— because their life would now be a life of purpose and joy.

Sky could fly, she could become invisible, she could run speedily, she had no weaknesses, and could fend off armies without killing a soul. Sky could do so much more and would learn, update, and upgrade herself as well as others since she was able to perceive their needs and desires.

Meanwhile, away from all of this, away from the Virtual Universe and away from Pathway, the fact remained that the legislative branch was still a long-time coming and very sluggish with regard to proliferating biopods with Virtual Universe interfacing and tactile reference—which would connect willing biopod occupants to a selection of health, education, commerce, entertainment, and correctional matrices. Eventually, Eliza would find a way to introduce these and more to everyone.

The Correctional Matrix had been completed two years prior, with Joanne Gallant leading the team. It had been tested on the poor soul who shot Vesha, and now he was on Enceladus leading a science team toward the last stages of creating an environment much like Earth, to be able to walk freely without fear of freezing to death, all the while creating a protective barrier to ensure any pre-existing wildlife or sentient life or their ecosystem on Enceladus would not be damaged. After building Sky's island and her daughters, Sky could see that he would eventually work with one of her daughters, Belinda Taylor, to develop positive rapport with the civilizations they would meet in the years to come, while creating a peaceful form of communication and shared purpose with them.

Something in Eliza's mind had reawakened while with Sky Taylor. Her plans of an extensive overhaul of the prison system when she became president, would be an overhaul that Sky and her team would have the skills to oversee. It would be built to help all who were condemned to go through experiences that would forge strength of mind in areas that emphasized compassion and restraint. It would be a correctional system, and no longer a place to hide people away that society had no desire to deal with. The world was still in chaos and filled with so much suffering, despite the immense growth of Pathway and the lives they had saved. When Sky discovered how things were becoming, she felt a moment of anguish too, and sought to spend time with Eliza at her home in Massachusetts, sitting down with her in her garden. Together in the real-world, they meditated for hours, listened to the birds, the frogs, and the waterfall, and began to sing favorite tunes from Depeche Mode's Spirit album, "Where's the Revolution!" to include "Poorman," some New Age, as well as one of Erin's favorite tunes, "New Day," with music by Rafael Frost, sung by trance vocalist, Sarah Lynn, and specifically the radio edit from 2016.

As this occurred, it just so happened that Sky had tapped into Eliza's mind and was able to understand all her concerns and worries, due to the Twelve-Database-Moon-download to her brain. Sky identified escalating issues and compiled all necessary informational resources to prepare to go on visits throughout the United States. Sky was overwhelmed by the shared sorrow of Yesha and Eliza, when for a time they were in there, all-three, together. After seeing within their minds more fully, she planned to change a few other minds within the US. Unfortunately, the country was run by many high-powered entities with deep wallets that had huge monetary and clandestine means of influencing non-UP legislators, and all with Anti-Pathway designs and machinations. The people, in name, were not in control. There was something more devious, sinister, greedy, and lusting for continued power at any cost, pulling the strings, and she was determined to take measures to heal their minds, no matter the effort. Sky had purpose, she had the drive, and she had the abilities to do so.

Sky Taylor extended her link and became Eliza's covert operative. She had plans that she had fully intended to keep to herself, since she could create neural blockers, joining minds, healing them, and repairing the body. She became Pathway's overt poster girl and covert powerhouse.

Perhaps in some ways against the wishes of Eliza, due to ethical norms and a deep and coherent understanding of the error of society's ways, Sky covertly found out who it was that was creating obstacles for progress, tracked those individuals down, traced the obstacles to the true source, and "marked" them. After she marked them, the job was essentially done. They'd be left with an iridescent scorpion on their right buttock cheek and would find new sanity in life and purpose within their minds—their new qualities would now be bereft of narcissism, sociopathic tendencies, psychotic behavior, condescending nature, lack of care for anyone but themselves, and no matter the issue, now their minds would be healed. Gone would be their desire to pad their wallets and sate their lust for power through dummying down the populous, each of their non-virtues would dissipate in exchange for compassion, high intelligence and very enviable persuasive skills. Their brains were healed, and bodies given twenty years of physiologic health and youth.

With Sky doing what she did best, it didn't take long before the US and its policies seemed to be back to resolving issues, looking out for the welfare, educational quality, and the healthy work environment of every citizen in the US and throughout the world; we were all part of the same team. *"While many of the minds throughout the world aren't as keen or as sharp as Eliza's or Vesha's, at least things can now become a little more manageable, and people will begin to realize the beauty they have already possessed from within throughout their lives,"* she thought.

The environment following her journeys throughout the US began to become less toxic. By Sky's standards, the people looked like they were back to where they needed to be. The situations throughout the nation had turned into one of adults behaving like adults and talking things out with dignity and respect to negotiate win-win solutions to resolve problems for a better future in the U.S. Once Eliza seemed to be satisfied with US social, political, and cultural environments, Sky reported back to the Pathway hierarchy—where Vesha reached them via the communications bridge between the Kuiper Belt of asteroids, not too far from Pluto, and Earth.

Vesha had been eyes-deep in mission-research, aside from gathering materials for other developing projects in space. James would visit her often, asking questions about Eliza, and always find a pleasant exchange. Eliza in one of her committees worked with the head of the CIA. After much deliberation, she was able to persuade their Director to allow Sky Taylor to become commissioned as Chief of Antiterrorism and Officer of Diplomatic Relations. To accomplish her missions, Sky "donned" the attire considered to be government-professional and dressed to impress.

After building a relationship with the Directors, Sky began to go on "side excursions" to many countries over the next year. After a few brief detours, she continued her missions leading all the way to the elections of 2024. During this time, Sky engaged in missions and quests that would blow the mind—each noble of a story of its own. She worked covertly and disappeared with CIA permission as a field operative, undetectable by the human eye. Cameras could not sense her, and neither could any form of identifying-device. Due to her ability to mimic untraceable waves around her persona she could only be visible when she wished to be seen.

One after another, Sky infiltrated every autocratic and dictator-led country, every country led by tyrants, and every country ripe with terrorism. When she had seen the suffering of humanity in Eliza's heart and mind, it had left an indelible mark on her, the likes of which could only be culled by harmony and peace. Choosing not to disguise herself as a diplomat, an aid worker, or anything other than that which she saw herself as, Sky became known as the Iridescent Angel. She did this, only in the minds of those she encountered, who needed rescue in one form or another. On any occasion where she needed to show her true identity, she would generate her Pathway governmental liaison-created image, wearing her government wardrobe holograph and become the otherwise striking beauty she always was, with blonde hair and iridescent locks and highlights, in a white blouse and navy and white-striped pantsuit.

Maintaining her cover well, and conducting all her actions covertly, Sky's super intelligent and very forward-thinking mind could predict with near one-hundred percent precision what would happen if she failed to achieve successful results. She did not want the mistreatment of any ordinary and helpful human being, by those of malicious intent, so she chose to thwart that by appearing as someone who was otherwise innocent. Sky would never mimic another's appearance for disguise, instead, she would be unique, intelligent, creative, and herself.

Just as she did in the United States, even though there were no other reasons beyond her love for humanity to do so, she didn't need to do what she chose to do. However, Sky worked diligently anyway, since her systems were still new, and researched every file again via the Twelve Database Moons using the Virtual Universe and within the many high-level law-enforcement and governmental agency databases, as well as the databases of every single governmental or citizen-based detective and protective agency. Sky compiled a complete and up-to-date background dossier on each terrorist and everyone within their organizations. She identified, wrote, and compartmentalized everything within a small sector of her mind to have starting points that would impact the well-being of the most people in the shortest amount of time. One by one, she would visit the most influential, the most ruthless, the most fraudulent, and so many more of so many brands of maliciousness. She would visit them all, every member, every leader, and even the people who suffered under their rule and the terror they promulgated, as well as the victims of their circle of influence. She could easily turn invisible and undetectable, sneak into their homes, and at the precise moment do what needed to be done.

Murder and mayhem weren't her method. Sky gave the people of influence who had no desire for the well-being of anyone else, as well as the miscreant leaders, managers, politicians, and lobbyists, the terrorists, the gang members, the cartel members, the insurgents, and anyone filled with violence and gore toward others in their wake, a sense of tiredness, until they and their leaders fell asleep. Once safely and securely at rest, she would render each of the people in the area unconscious, causing them to sleep in a beautiful and peaceful slumber. While lying comatose, she would heal their minds, cure them of any disease, render their physiological system healthier and more youthful, increase their compassion, their compunction toward consent, their ability to persuade, and open their minds to the clarity of a one-hundred percent engaged, kind, advancing, and peaceful society.

One of her many stops, after visiting leaders throughout the US and in other places throughout the world, was a small village to the northwest of the central mountains of Afghanistan, north of the Hari River and west of the Jam River. The understanding she had gained through research and analysis of information derived from the very small neural links she'd dispersed throughout the region from mind to mind was unnoticed by anyone and they gave her untold networks of information and a magnified and accurate intuition with a powerful sense that there was a young woman whose life was in jeopardy. She knew she needed to rescue her, and soon. The potential was rich within her young mind and it was so unique she did not want to see this young woman's life jeopardized. She had the ability to be an amazing influence within that region, and in the future many more regions throughout the Universe. Off went Sky Taylor, using teleportation unique to her, but only for so long, to rescue as many lives as she could. The potential for a beautiful future was just within reach of human in existence, and all thanks to Sky Taylor, the Iridescent Angel, and the Iridescent Scorpion. She would leave an imprint of justice upon many and heal the hearts and minds of many more, making a beautiful and promising future more possible than ever before.

Suffering in Far-Away Lands

Shayeena was born on November 16, 2004, in a small village clinic, fifty kilometers east of Firozkah, affected by an oppressive-regime and in an extremist-controlled location within Afghanistan.

She was raised on the family farm—which was passed down from generation to generation, with several thousands of acres of wheat fields, forestation, and a lot of large rocky terrain.

Throughout her life, she found that she was blessed and grateful that her environment was what it was. There were several windmills with milling capabilities dotting the farmland and streams of irrigation everywhere that came from the Hari River which lie to the south of the farm. The borders of her family's farm were located just outside of the east limit of the village. Her family's home was located behind several groves of trees and a large rock wall around their acreage that provided security from unsuspecting trespassers. The property of the farm she grew up on had a border that extended to the south for four kilometers, on to the shores of the Hari River, and to the north three kilometers from the home. It also extended east from the outskirts of the village to her home for one kilometer, and from the home, it sprawled further east for another seven kilometers to the Lost Minaret of Jam—where the Jam and Hari Rivers met. To the south of the Jam River were mountains and forests, making her place of solace remote from civilization, northwest of the mountains that lie to the center of Afghanistan.

Shayeena's father inherited the farm, the land, the home, and the estate from his father, when his brothers had each traveled to different countries and never returned. He had been left the sole heir of the estate. When her father had met Shayeena's mother, her parents had been very proud to have him marry her. They knew he would take good care of their daughter. His father married her mother when she was just twelve years old, in 1982. However, Shayeena's father had seen the mistreatment of women rampant in this part of the country and knew that he had to be cautious when providing a more humane existence to her mother. He had her do things overtly, so she would fit in with the village, but in secret, he taught his wife how to read, how to do mathematics, and all that he knew about the stars and astronomy. He treated her as a friend and grew to love her deeply and she him by the time she was twenty-one. During those first seven years of marriage Shayeena's father not only protected her mother, but he had honored, respected, and treated her kindly. In many ways, there was a lot of hard work on his part to do so ever so carefully so he wouldn't give away the fact that he didn't agree with the teachings from the oppressively influenced Imam. Plus, with literally thousands of acres of crops to sew, tend to, and harvest alone, he had little time to go to the village anyway, and he worked a lot while her mother made sure the home was well taken care of and the family had plenty to eat and drink.

In 1989, Shayeena's oldest three brothers were born, triplets. Early, during 1990, her father had struggled diligently to balance his time between his family, his work, and his dealings within the village and the district and provincial cities. He also worked hard to combat an issue of harvested crop spoilage by bringing as much wheat as his camel and cart could pull to the various markets throughout the land to sell it all before it spoiled to increase the wealth of the family. For many years he had gone into the larger provincial city, Shahrak, and once he had gathered up a large enough portion of his family's inheritance money, he returned to the city to invest in his family's future. While there, her father purchased three hundred fifty-five-gallon plastic and sealable drums, along with a dry ice sealing system. He shrewdly stacked them behind three rented camels pulling carts and brought them to the farm to store the milled and whole wheat throughout the year following the harvest. He did this to protect his family's main source of income from moisture, contaminants, and bugs, which allowed him to disperse the selling of his harvested crop in smaller quantities throughout the year and spend more time with his family rather than having to sell it all in a short period of time each year to avoid risking the loss of too much of it. Instead, he would be able to sell his entire crop rather than barely enough crops before it spoiled. Now, he could work with his wife and sons to mill the wheat, bake the loaves of bread and batches of crackers, and take them to the village market daily. Doing this, he was able to accumulate more than enough money to make improvements to his home and his farm.

Early on, in his boys' lives and as they began to grow, they watched him till the farm, dry the wheat, mill it, pack it into the fifty-five-gallon barrels for long-term storage, and when they grew old enough, he trained them how to do what he did. Eventually, when her brothers were merely nine years old, they pretty much took over the operations of the farm, while their father would go into Firozkah, the district city, and Shahrak, the provincial city regularly to sell the goods throughout the year. Her mother would sell the milled flour, wheat germ, whole wheat, and some of her baked goods in the nearby village market each day, with the exception, of course, on days of religious observance.

Her father's investment had paid off since at that time he and his three sons would work to do each task necessary from planting and setting up ample irrigation throughout the land, to harvesting and selling the product. This led to Shayeena's father creating a wealthy estate, and a more expanded and enjoyable home.

He had always sensed that at some point he would have a daughter or maybe two, so he did as much as he could to prepare for that inevitability. He had built expansions to their family home in such a way that the master bedroom was at the center of the bedroom portion of the home. The boy's rooms were located south of the master bedroom on the closer side to the village with a couple of extra rooms south of that. He built a couple of rooms for the girls which were oriented to the north side of the master bedroom, that lay further from the village. All bedrooms were connected by doorways that led to a long hallway. Each room had its own bathroom and her father created a basement and escape tunnel to the Hari River with survival and defensive abilities for the boys. He did this work while his boys were out on the farm. Once his work was complete, he showed his boys, and that became their secret hideout from the rest of the village, should the worst ever occur.

He also did the same for the daughters he might have someday but kept his efforts toward that end from his boys and privately shared this with his wife. After building the secret basement for his potential daughters, he built a secret tunnel heading eastward toward the eastern boundary of their property. There were several other exits and entrances along the way with openings here and there hidden and surrounded by rock formations all within groves of trees, that en tangent helped with precipitation for the crops, and provided suitable privacy for the tunnels. The final exit was located not too far from the forgotten village of Jam, the Minaret of Jam, and the Jam River. If any of his daughters happened to sojourn through the tunnels, her brothers, who were susceptible to the oppressive ways of the Imam, would never be the wiser, despite tilling the land, since above the tunnels were clear farm-ways linking the entire farm, filled with hills, divots, irrigation, and small groves of trees for privacy. Even along the borders, he had grown a large area of honey locust forestation, with large and sharp thorns, around the entire perimeter just outside a high and strong stone wall, to further help with precipitation and irrigation and provide even more privacy and security for the family farm and estate. The stone wall itself had an added deterrent of effective sharp-edged metal and glass objects securely located on top of the wall, to prevent intruders from sneaking in easily.

His children, if ever caught in a jam, would in this way be able to escape, survive, and live comfortably underground and away from it all, without any harm until things blew over. They would even be able to escape from a hidden doorway at the end if needed. He and his wife would stay behind and if asked would advise the interrogators that he had no idea where his children were, save for tilling the land, reviewing how the crop was doing, etc. To add to that, he had built several living shacks around areas of his land located differently from the escape and hideout points, where the boys would in fact be able to stay the night or nights during the long days of tilling, irrigating, seeding, and harvesting.

As his three boys turned fifteen, they began to spend more time in the district city of Firozkah, where they had a humble university for men, and their father toiled endlessly on every aspect of the farm. At that time, he had purchased several different types of tractors and automatic irrigation systems to decrease the amount of time he needed to spend on the farm. Eventually, he and his wife brought into the world an adorable daughter. When he saw her beautiful hazel and green-golden eyes, her charming features, her smile, he instantly fell in love with her and an intense desire to protect her from any dangers that would ever come her way. On the day she was born, he looked to her mother, and together they named her Shayeena.

As Shayeena grew up, they taught her the basics of life, the need for love, the virtues in kindness, and the need to understand the religion of the village so that they would all be safe from ire, anger, punishment, and misunderstandings. Shayeena's parents were very careful to teach her the things that would not get her into trouble, while she was young so that if she were to speak up while she happened to be in the village she would not be unduly punished. However, once she was eight-years-old, her mother and father began to notice a unique mental maturity about her, and they began to teach her the things that they knew she would strategically keep to herself, so as to avoid reprimand—which would be harsh, especially from the village leader, the Imam, and those raised within the village's borders who were also influenced by oppressive and subversive leadership and ways of living. They very rarely intruded on the private lives of the farmers, since they provided the food.

On Shayeena's eighth birthday she met her friend, Tayi. Tayi had been visiting with her parents and Shayeena had learned that Tayi's family owned the chicken farm to the west of theirs. Tayi's family raised hens and roosters for eggs and poultry products. Her parents were much like her own—they were kind, cautious, and smart, yet humble. When in town, they never appeared as if they were wealthy because they did not want to attract the wrong kind of attention. However, as the years went by, Tayi seemed to mature into womanhood much faster than Shayeena. While the girls didn't seem to notice much, the men noticed Tayi greatly. For five years they had spent time together on their farms, walking together exploring nature and going back and forth on the country roads, in the village, looking up at the nighttime skies, and spending time with each other in each other's homes. They had shared stories back and forth and even played dress-up of the characters in Sinbad's Seven Voyages and other children's stories that were approved by the village Imam.

One day, which had been a wonderful one, after Tayi had spent many glorious moments with Shayeena, they walked to Shayeena's farm entrance and bid each other goodbye. Not too long afterward, Tayi realized she had to return to town because she had forgotten something amidst all the fun. Little did she know that the Imam's eldest son had been following her for the last few months, but with lust in his mind and with a seemingly insatiable appetite, and tonight he had followed her as well. Tayi, who had turned thirteen several months before, had returned to town because she had forgotten a bag of groceries while sitting on a bench talking and kidding around with Shayeena. He had waited until she was alone, and then when the moment was right, he trapped her, bound her, raped her, hurt her and took advantage of her in every way possible, leaving her bruised underneath her clothes, and traumatized and terrified. After doing so, he loosened her, told her to leave, and to never mention a word to anyone, "or else."

When he returned home, he confided everything to his father but told him that she had provoked him, because she was so pretty and seductive. The Imam told his son, "She should be stoned; abominations like that should not be allowed to exist—for they turn the hearts of men to dark and devious ways."

The following day, when Tayi and Shayeena were walking to the village, Shayeena noticed that Tayi was silent and obviously traumatized. She seemed, for all intents and purposes, shut out of the world.

"What happened, Tayi?" asked Shayeena. But Tayi looked down, almost shivering, and remained silent.

Finally, after finding a quiet and secure place, they sat down on a stone within a grouping of trees, just far enough from the side of the pathway on their way to the village, to allow Tayi a sense of protection from unwanted ears. Tayi then explained to Shayeena everything that had occurred, amidst tears of fear and sorrow. This young girl had no idea that she had been the victim of rape, of assault, and of torture, and that none of what had transpired was her fault, yet she felt the blame anyway.

"Tayi, none of this was your fault. I'm so sorry that we got distracted and forgot your bag of groceries; I wish you would have let me know you needed to go back to town. You should not have had to endure any inconvenience other than a little extra walking to and from the bench we had sat on. This should never have happened. I wish I would have walked back with you."

"He probably would have hurt you too," said Tayi amidst choked up tears. "Thank you, Shayeena."

"Why would he do something like that? Doesn't he know better? I mean, we're just girls, and he? He's a man. He should have a little more self-control! Oh, I am so sorry, Tayi." Shayeena gave her a hug to comfort her. "I will stay with you in the village from now on, no matter what, so nothing like this can happen again."

As they walked into the village, the girls saw a crowd of young men and adults gathered around the entrance, all staring Tayi's direction.

Shayeena and Tayi glanced at each other. They were not sure what to do.

As they began to pass through the center of the crowd, they saw a coldness, an anger, and a gloom within the countenance of each person before them.

Just as they were about to leave the center of the village swarm, three of the bearded and sweaty men yelled, "Despicable, tasteless, and dirty whore!" and then one of them grabbed Tayi by the hair, slapped her across the face with the back of his hand, threw her to the ground, and shoved Shayeena to the edge of the crowd. He then hit Tayi in the face with his fist so hard that she fell to the ground in shock and horror.

She began to find her awareness, as her young body began to shake off the shock of her impending reality, and she tried to get up off the dirt, which was bloodied from the wounds she had sustained from the barbarity, but the crowd circled around her not giving her a chance for escape. She felt helpless and noticed them backing away. She looked for Shayeena but could not see her. She could only hear her muffled screams, ignored by everyone else.

Then she saw the stones as they began to fly from the fist of every person within that circle surrounding her. Each stone hit her hard and each one of them hurt with a profound thud and sting. She screamed. She cried. They maimed her, the stones tore her skin, and her bones were crushed—jutting out of her limbs and her chest. She began to feel numb and was suddenly, no longer worried about mortality for the first time in her life. At this moment, she spoke not a word; she just looked at the betrayal of the villagers, the stare of hatred burning within their eyes—the remorseless murder they were all a party to.

Shayeena fought through the crowd to try to get to her friend, but she was so small and light the crowd kept shoving her back. She had promised to protect Tayi, and now, during her time of need, for all she tried, she could do nothing. Through a small hole in the crowd, she could see Tayi, and she looked as if she were prey amid a game of an unfair hunt.

After so much brutality, Tayi no longer felt the pain of the stones as one large stone hit her on the head and she fell to the ground, limp, and she blacked out. They continued to throw stones at her lifeless seeming body, while Shayeena kept scrambling to find a hole big enough to get through the crowd to try to stop the barbarism, but no one would let her through.

When Tayi opened her eyes, tears and blood welled down her bruised, broken, and flesh-torn face, and she felt more alone than she had ever been in her entire life. The crowd knew no mercy, no succor, no compassion, and she felt the life going out of her.

"Stop! Stop! Stop!" yelled a familiar voice behind the crowd. The Imam raised his hand and held the crowd back, showing his holy mercy. It was Tayi's father. He had rushed there with his wife and the Imam granted Tayi's parents a chance to have their final moments with her.

Her parents happened to be going into town not too far behind Tayi because they had sensed something was different about her. She had been very quiet that morning, so they sensed something broken, something torn within her countenance—the tears on her face said it all—and when they saw her, with anguish they knew they were too late, and no matter what they could have done, they were helpless now to save her from this barbarism.

Tayi felt crushed, broken and traumatized in every way, she could barely feel a glimmer of life, and she knew she would die this day.

The crowd had stopped, but the damage was done.

Tayi's parents raced to her through the menacing crowd, and at the Imam's bidding, the crowd backed away. Her father fell to his knees before her, reached out with his arms, pulled her to him, and cradled Tayi's limp body in his arms, weeping, sobbing, and feeling a deep pain within for this injustice, this barbarism, this inhumanity that had been hurled at his poor sweet and darling daughter. He cried up to the heavens, "Why!? Oh, my poor, sweet angel! My little girl! How could you do this!? All of you, how could you do this!?" No one seemed to hear, and no one seemed to care. The villagers all seemed to laugh at his pain, suffering, and impending loss. The village ladies were sticking their tongues out and waving them, celebrating and mocking Tayi's misfortune. He looked upon his broken daughter as she was dying, and all that went through his mind was that something had gone horribly wrong and he hadn't been there to stop it. He was a noble and loving man, and he was always looking after his family with the vigor of a lion, yet spoke with the softness of a lamb, yet, despite his always kind demeanor, he asked within his mind, "*What happened to common decency, to kindness, to love, to compassion? How could they have killed my daughter, why would they and how could they abuse and snuff the life out of someone who was harmless, sweet, and innocent?*"

Shayeena was in tears. Finally making her way through the crowd of what had seemed as savage and possessed monsters, she saw as her friend's father embraced her while on his knees, crying, staring at her and then at the heavens with tears in his eyes, and lost while Tayi lie at death's door and with not a single thing that her young mind or her fragile body could have done to prevent it. Neither Shayeena nor Tayi had ever witnessed brutality like this before. They never knew people, who once seemed so kind, could turn around and be so cruel. Instead of standing among people she once thought of as friends, she had all this time been standing in a sea of enemies, of demons, with no ally, no friend, no judgment, and no one to explain why this had happened.

As her heart sank, the crowd had begun to disperse. She then looked downward again, toward Tayi lying in her father's arms. She was no longer quivering in pain but engulfed in shock, she was momentarily aware and almost lifeless. Her father was on his knees in the bloodied dirt and near the bloodied stones, stained with the life of Tayi. Tayi's father—his weeping, wailing, and his sadness overcame him. As Shayeena looked around at the dispersing crowd, there had been one young man who had not thrown a single stone but had instead looked on with helplessness at what had been going on before him with horror and anguish—this young man was Khalim. He was one of two sons, one of the sons of the village Imam. His older brother had thrown plenty of stones, but somehow Khalim was able to escape from soiling his soul with this brutality, unnoticed, and had avoided being chastised by his father or anyone else for not having participated in this barbarism. He was a handsome young man—a few years older than she.

She then looked upon Tayi, who had, for just a few short moments, opened her tear-stained and bloodied eyes with even more tears and blood gushing out, and turned to her father and said, "I am sorry father. I'm so sorry."

"Oh, my little girl, you should not be sorry, you have nothing to be sorry for. This is not your fault. You were a good girl. You have always blessed our lives. You are my daughter. I love you, Tayi. I'm so sorry this happened, I'm so sorry. Things like this should never happen. This should not have happened," her father said embracing her again. Still, on his knees not caring that Tayi's blood would stain his clothes, this was his beautiful and sweet daughter. He was shattered from the dreams of the future he had hoped for Tayi, his lovely daughter, and now seeing all of those dreams stripped away moment by moment, in a state of shock, he witnessed each second pass as her life was all-too quickly slipping away. He would be left without her, the bright and cheery spirit that made every day so full of hope, and he would be left with nothing to fill the void.

Tayi looked up at Shayeena, another tear dropped from the side of her bloodied, bruised, and flesh-torn face, and then Tayi looked to Khalim who stood behind Shayeena, and she smiled at each of them before looking at her father.

"I love you." She said, before closing her eyes, never to open them again.

Shayeena fell to her knees, with her hands over her mouth and tears spilling from her eyes, landing beside Tayi and her friend's father, and together they embraced Tayi and each other, weeping for what seemed an eternity. Khalim kneeled down and wept too, embracing them. After several moments of solace, he helped them each up. With all of the will that he could muster, this fifteen-year-old boy apologized for the barbarity of his father and his brother and so many of the members of the village. He explained that the villagers weren't to blame, but that his father had worked up the crowd and had put them up to it. He knew his brother had done wrong but was unwilling to come clean. Instead, he chose to place the blame on her and saw to her cruel death.

He helped them walk to the edge of the village, gave them water for their remaining journey home, and then stood and watched over them as they walked into the distance. He then gathered Tayi's body, and brought her home to her family, to her grandparents, who in anguish listened to his account of what had happened. Afterward, he hugged them, each with tears in their eyes, and left Tayi's home, so they could do what was needed to be done to give her a proper burial. Right or wrong, Tayi had suffered enough and she deserved to be buried in the manner of her family's choosing.

Shayeena and Tayi's parents had stumbled along the path to the entrance of Shayeena Arezo's parents' estate and they thanked her for caring and for being there for her as much as she could and bid her farewell. She tearfully walked the kilometer from the estate entrance to her home and then told her parents about what had happened. After doing so, she blacked out.

When she awoke, she was in her bed.

Her mother and her father were sitting in chairs around her. Her brothers had been in Firozkah and wouldn't be back for a few weeks. Tayi's parents were there, too, each one sobbing and with a look of complete loss and sadness. Sorrow had been etched deep within their countenance and their hearts for the levels of inhumanity that should never have occurred against such a young, innocent, and sweet little girl. They felt sorrow for the helplessness of Shayeena who would have done anything to prevent this, but instead could do nothing but witness the brutality of unchecked humanity, of a culture gone wrong, and a beautiful religion left tainted and sour. Both Tayi's and her own parents knew that this series of events would leave her shaken and would bring trauma to her for a long, long time. They didn't want her to feel terrorized throughout the rest of her life because of what had transpired, resulting in the needless loss of a dear and sweet friend. They knew that they needed to find a way to calm Shayeena's heart and mind. So, they tried to soothe her the best way they knew how.

Shayeena still couldn't believe what she had witnessed, what had happened, and she suddenly felt a deep emptiness within. She was gone. Her dear sweet friend, Tayi, was gone. She would not be knocking on the door to go on fun little walks anymore. No more journeys with her to the countryside. No more laughs with Tayi, no more cheer. She was gone, and she would not come back. *"If there's a Heaven, she will be there waiting,"* she thought.

Tayi's parents had seen Shayeena fighting and trying to make her way through the crowd and they knew that she had done everything she could to stop all that had happened. Despite the anguish and loss within, they felt compassion for her and explained to her and her parents that they loved Shayeena too, and that she should not feel guilty for what had happened, that she was always welcome in their home, and that she still had Tayi's family as friends. They explained that this should never have happened, but it did. Even though they were broken, they had grace, kindness, and compassion. They spent some time together, and then Tayi's parents left with sobbing and sadness in their auras as they hugged her parents and Shayeena before exiting the door.

Her father then turned and talked to her and told her that he had something he needed to show her. "This is something for you and you alone. Only your mother and I know this exists." He lifted the carpet between her desk and her closet in her room and exposed the cover to a stair-casing that was almost undetectable. He bid her follow him, and she did. He took her to the basement, showed her all of the trinkets, the clothes, the burkas, the hijabs, a magnificent library with so many books and literature, and the books were very abundant, from forbidden sciences, novels, and biographies, to religious texts; he then had her follow him through a tunneled and finished-looking hallway to another door. He opened the door, and as he did, she could see a pathway surrounded by rocks, with open skies up above and beyond the rocks, where there were groves of trees that hid the pathway from view in every direction. He then took her through another tunnel on the other side of the stretch of pathway, and it too was filled with supplies, water and water recycling purifiers, defenses, more books, a telescope, and blank notebooks with a lot of pens.

"This is all for you. Every single bit of it, as you see fit. Be careful, study, and enjoy what is here, but keep it here. Take your time, learn what you can, and always be safe." He kept leading the way, through tunnels, exits, pathways, and more entrances to other tunnels until he arrived at the final exit. Although they could see a minaret through the trees, someone standing outside the trees would not be able to see or hear them due to the thickness of the trees and the way the shadows would always hit the entrance and where they stood.

Shayeena's father showed her the Jam River, a huge bolder overlooking it, the mountains to the south, the trees all around, and to the east just a small distance away, the Minaret of Jam.

He then, very caringly told her, "This is your private escape from the village. This town has been overlooked for many years and many have forgotten to love the beauty that we have been blessed with inside this world. This will be yours. Here, you can share your beauty with all that you see and not fear recourse or the deviant nature of the men of the village. The men travel west for schooling and business and no one makes way toward this location for any reason. Plus, between here and the village is the distance of our farm which we own. Our farm is surrounded by a large rock wall and then a forest.

"I have done my work here, this place is protected, and I will no longer head out here unless you go to the door at the entrance and move the brick-like stone just on the inside. I will then know that you need help, will grab some of the defensive gear that I have shown you, and come to your rescue. Meanwhile, hide inside this last tunnel, and barricade the door. Here, follow me." He showed her the brick and the steel bar and how to lie it in position to prevent the door from being opened if ever needed. "I am showing you this, in the event that if you ever need safety and security, you will have it. No one else should ever be out here without your knowledge, because you can hear for a great distance all around. Even more, we are surrounded by areas with a harsh environment; the cities to the east are too far away with other routes to the cities to the west. This is for all sakes and purposes, a forgotten part of the world. It is yours now."

He then told her that what happened to Tayi should never have happened. "Tayi was an innocent angel and a victim." He then asked her a question, "Imagine walking through the village, looking through the window of one of the shops, and seeing a beautiful painting. If you broke that window and stole that painting, would you blame the window or the painting for what you stole?"

Shayeena responded, "Of course not. If I were to steal something, it would be my fault. How could it ever be the fault of the window or the painting?"

Her father then explained, "The window is like the person and the painting is the virtue of the beautiful nature of someone who is being plotted against, where consent does not exist. It has not invested any emotions or feelings into the person looking at it or wanting it. Breaking the window and stealing the painting can be looked at as stealing a person's virtue. The person looking at a painting can be likened to an individual who looks at a young woman who is both pretty and beautiful. If he fails to see her as a human being capable of sentient thought, if he fails to wait until he has developed a proper relationship with her within societally accepted bounds, and then failing all of that, he has determined that he will steal her virtue, he then has turned her into an object of his own devious desires, kind of like the desire to unfairly steal that painting. Without regard for negotiating with the store's owner, or in this case talking with those who protect the woman or girl, her feelings, her emotions, or her well-being, because instead he has decided he will have his way with her and then blame her beauty for the reason as to why he stole her virtue. He will then seek to have her destroyed because the village in a sense blames the painting for being stolen rather than the man that stole it. In order to find vindication for this horrible deed, they will destroy the painting, so it can never be stolen again. While this would never make sense to any rational human being, somehow doing this helps the guilty and privileged party find peace within—yet, that will never happen. No one will ever truly find peace within unless they change how they behave, how they perceive others and show respect—giving dignity to those around them. Just as the window is not at fault for being broken and just as the painting is not at fault for having been stolen, the young, pretty, and beautiful woman is not at fault for having had her virtue stolen from her. Tayi was objectified by the man who broke her and stole her virtue, and he is the sole person responsible for that horrible act. He is the person who took what wasn't theirs to take and not the person who lost what was theirs to give.

"Tayi was a beautiful, innocent, and sweet girl. The Imam's son raped her, and his father had her stoned to death because of it. In the village and in many locations under the control of a very fundamentalist and tainted form of our religion, the people in charge are afraid of the power that women have. They don't realize that this power can be used for good, to influence people to be better than they were before, and to bless the village or the community they are in. They don't realize that their lack of self-control is their responsibility—a person should be able to see a beautiful flower or several in the field and not have the need to pluck it or crush it under their feet.

"This should never have happened, but sadly it did. Now, all I can do is notice that you too are beginning to shed your youth for womanhood, you are a pretty girl and a beautiful young woman, and seeing the men stare at you when you go to the village, I know that you will need to take measures to ensure you are protected. You should not have to, but the environment this village provides, as well as anywhere outside of even your room, there are very few options. If someone were to objectify you, you could be hurt. I am like the shopkeeper, as are you, and I am also as a shopkeeper's bodyguard, who protects both she who owns the beautiful painting and the shop itself. I must protect your virtue and keep it from the thieving hands and minds of malice. Nevertheless, I want you to be able to have freedom in this world, freedom from all of the brutality of those who fail to evolve themselves to the point to where they can love others, and live with compassion at their core, because you can do so much, and you have so much potential that is priceless. Right now, the best way to have that freedom is to take the journey down this pathway as often as you would like or need to or can, in order to read, learn, and enjoy this location to think, observe, and feel.

"You deserve protection. I am your father and I will give that to you. When you return home, you will find on your bed a wardrobe that should keep the men's eyes at bay and allow you to walk around with the kind of protection that will afford you more time to grow and learn, before you must be married. You are a year past the time that most girls marry, but since I am a farmer, we are allowed to retain our daughters a while longer for service and assistance with what needs to be done to provide food to the village. While we are granted that courtesy, I don't want you to find yourself hurt by those that would wish to steal your virtue.

"I am so sorry about what happened, but you must heal, and hold on to the good moments with immense strength of character. I love you, my dear daughter and my sweet Shayeena." He looked at Shayeena, smiled at her with tender and kind eyes, and put his arms out so she could hug him, and she did.

Every morning after that, she would take two covered buckets, fill them with the water at the Jam River, and bring them home before noon so that her family could have clean, fresh, and pure drinking water. This was her morning chore. While she was there, since her parents approved, she would take her time, study her books, bring her toiletries—her salve of lilac and rose, mix it in with her shampoo, body wash and conditioner, and bathe in the waters of the Jam River, just below a cascade of water that flowed a few feet above her head. Above that lie another pool of water with yet another waterfall, and from there she would return home with two buckets of fresh water. Before gathering the water, however, she would follow up her bath and shower and let the wind flow down the mountains and through her hair to dry her locks and the flesh of her body, as she sat or lie upon the boulder overlooking the river, the minaret, and the mountains to the south.

The first day that she returned from her secret place of freedom, she saw a wrapped package with her name on it. "This is for you, our princess, to wear into town and around the house when your brothers are home."

After her morning duties were complete and she was ready to leave her room, at home or in town, she would wear the public clothes her father gave her. She would don what consisted of a burka and a one-piece neck-to-feet outer garment, made of a thick yet airy material that was comfortable on the interior, against her skin, yet appeared as breathy sackcloth on the exterior. All of this was to hide the beauty that flourished around her persona, as the prettiness of her face, the alluring curves of her body, and the beauty she possessed from within had begun to spill out even to the point to where she needed to hide it from her brothers. Shayeena, her father, and her mother knew this was necessary to prevent her brother's boasting chatter to other men that would not have her best interests in mind.

Shayeena would go into town disguised behind her sackcloth and layered religious attire, bringing two buckets of wheat, one in each hand, and a bag of bread loaves strapped to her back to sell in the village market. While there, she would quietly peer through the small holes in her burka, using her eyes and not the obvious move of her neck to see and listen to the market's television broadcasts of the news, with talk of war, jihad, and the evil infidels to the west. As she heard what played out on the airwaves, she never forgot that the people who killed her friend were those who lived here in the village she was from. From her own personal experience with these people seemingly devoid of personal values, the people in the village were full of themselves, always did the Imam's bidding, and as such they were lacking in bravery, yet full of sanctimonious droll. As it was in all reality, to Shayeena, the television might as well have been talking about those who lived immediately to the west of her own home, not the "evil infidels to the far west." To Shayeena, the infidels were the people who could look at the face of innocence and snuff the life from it with monstrous brutality where true evil could play out without guilt or consequence. She learned to forgive the villagers over time, yet she never forgot what they did. She also never forgot the one young man who had, in anguish himself, helped her to her feet and carried Tayi's lifeless body to her home in his arms.

It had been five years, and she had been thinking of all these things as she would do most nights. Every night for five years she had visited the Jam River and its Minaret in peace.

Here she was again, and once more she felt the refreshing breeze pass by from the southeast as it cascaded down from the mountains, picked up the mists hovering above the Jam River, then hit her skin and brushed through her dark brown hair with a naturally soft moisture, and parted her shiny locks on the left side of her diamond shaped face. She closed her large golden-hazel eyes beneath her high arched brows, feeling the soft olive complexion of her smooth and silky skin as she folded her arms as if embracing herself—her features captured every bit of the beauty she possessed from within and the aesthetic of her physical charm, as she leaned back with her hands gripping her opened towel for support, with everything on display for the whole world to see, and though no one was there to enjoy what she shared with nature, she was ever so grateful for the kindness nature had graced her with, to allow her to see and feel how life could be such a wonderful thing to behold, when freedom abounded without the need for guilt or suppression. As she closed her eyes, her luscious and naturally ample lips, quieted her mind, and with her small refined nose inhaled the scent of nature passing her by; she felt it, heard it, and then she exhaled.

She sensed the quietness around her which allowed her to perceive every crackle of a twig, crunch of a leaf, movement of nocturnal life, or any disruption that would give cause for alarm and smartly swift action—this preparation had made her more keenly aware of her surroundings and alert before gazing up at the radiant stars of the Milky Way and becoming carried away and ensconced by them. Tonight, she was gazing at the constellations of Cassiopeia and Andromeda which for some reason were brighter than on previous nights—she could even see the faint and fuzzy shape of the Andromeda Galaxy. Tonight, she had much to ponder upon, yet these moments were those that Shayeena lived for and hoped to never forget.

She had been shown this beautiful getaway after losing her dear friend, Tayi. After her father had shown this to her and talked with compassion and understanding to her, as the mighty yet meek man that he was, he had left this place to her and granted her unlimited freedoms, and it was then that she had discovered her own beauty from within, as well as found an escape from the cruelties of life. Joy inspired her mind as she made the most of this lush and forgotten paradise. Shayeena had visited her minaret regularly from the moment her father had shared it with her to now, and he had given it to her for her own purposes. She had found harmony there from that moment on. She carefully kept to her routine and her secret would stay within her mind for as long as she knew it was needed, for as long as she could withhold it from others, and that would be forever if possible. There was a time, not too long after Khalim started working for her father, that he had brought home seeds for flowers of every kind, had bundled them in a small bag with instructions for planting them, when she almost felt the desire to share this location with him. But she held back. She would let him know in due time, and she believed that one day that time would come. While at the Minaret of Jam she had freedom and had cultivated Khalim's gifts into a beautiful paradise filled with beautifully scented flowers, she was in reality forced to live a different style of life, remise of them everywhere else— her freedoms were bound within her home, since her brothers were amenable to social influences and the brutality of some within the village, and due to the possibility of unjustifiable scorn, jealousy, and the piety of the people. The truth of her vulnerabilities became redundantly clear, especially after the loss of her dear friend, when she and Tayi were thirteen. Now she was eighteen, and womanhood was very difficult to hide.

While here during the day, even though her parents had approved her routine morning and evening trips out there already, she sought to give back in any way she knew she could. She would fetch fresh and sweet drinking water and then she would use some extra time to reflect on life, and to take in the scent of the flowers she had nurtured around the area, courtesy of Khalim, and think of her friend, Tayi. She would also, and very frequently, help Khalim to help her father on the farm, which allowed their sense of trust for each other and teamwork together germinate and grow. When Khalim wasn't there she would find a friend within herself, study the volumes of books in her secret hideout, or enjoy her very own view of the world in those small moments of liberty. Sometimes she would spend her moments, in deep thought, lying down on a large boulder gazing up at the clouds, the skies, or even the stars. At other times, she would sit overlooking the river with a view of the mountains to the southeast and take in the beauty that seemed unique to this location alone. She had memorized every tree, rock, flower bed, and turn of the river in Jam.

"I wonder what the full story with this place was here, so many years ago," She thought out loud to herself. She looked at The Minaret of Jam and its surrounding charm, now filled with color of all sorts, courtesy of Khalim, this was her shrine of peace from the rest of the world—a place where she could think out loud, breathe in the beauty of Nature blended with the gentle care of all that was good in humanity and be equal to every other living creature around her, to meditate, to contemplate, to ponder, and to make sense of the world and everything she learned, she would even contemplate upon all that she knew about the Universe itself.

It was the night before Shayeena's big wedding day, and it seemed the entire village had begun to be abuzz about getting ready to celebrate the impending nuptials. For the villagers, it had been long enough to forget their merciless treatment of Shayeena's friend, perhaps they had never considered it at all, and tonight more than ever, she wanted to make an escape, to absorb some personal time, and to allow contemplation of life—deep thinking with regard to where she wanted to go following the proceedings of the ceremony tomorrow, and then return, ready.

Shayeena found herself time and again peacefully dazed with thoughts of the past and plans for the future as she lay there enjoying the beauty of the Heavens and each moment of life before her.

Khalim, on trips between her home and into and through the village, would always accompany her, yet with enough space to avoid unwanted accusations from the villagers, yet also close enough to protect her from his brother or any other ill-intended individual, and had worked for her father for five years. After many opportunities that allowed them to share dinner together before he left for the village, she had begun to fall in love with him. Everything about his demeanor suggested innocence, strength, kindness, and protection.

Her father's genius and honor combined with Khalim's humor and noble intentions as well as her favorite private location to be free gave her peace within. Notwithstanding, she always looked for every excuse to meditate in harmony with her environment and enjoy her day at the Minaret of Jam, where she could be without the hassle of too much exposure or unwanted advances from those who caused her to fear them by the way they stared and the way they exercised their religious and political status and in the village. Her mother and father constantly and gently reminded her of how beautiful she was and how much she needed to protect herself from malevolent eyes and intentions. In most cases the people in the village were kind, but the village was certainly no stranger to defeat and mourning, and they had blood on their hands.

Life was certainly simple, but it was not easy, especially for a young woman who wanted to comply with the whims of men for fear of punishment and death. Her parents had told her that her beauty was a blessing from God, that she should be proud of it, but they always followed by telling her how much they cared for her and did not want her to suffer the same fate as her innocent and dear friend, Tayi. At times she was confused by the purpose of her own beauty if it was something that could be used to inspire the highest virtues in the hearts of others, why did she need to fear recourse for abuse from others. Many times, Khalim would converse with her outside the village limits and away from prying ears, and soothe her, "You are beautiful in every way. That is a blessing from Allah. While I am around, you will always be safe."

As it was, Shayeena had completed the routine of the day, and despite oppressive-extreme-mandated curfews, she was able to find her privacy and serenity via a quiet, private, and unused path, because of her father's efforts and his care for his daughter. She appreciated her father and loved him deeply, hoping that Khalim, and the character she saw in him, was very much the same.

The cool breeze grew until it became cool enough for a chill, so she gathered her things and returned down her private pathway and to her room. She woke up eight hours later knowing that this was her big day. She and Khalim were to be married that afternoon and according to the customs of the village. Following which Khalim would move in with Shayeena's family and help her father with the farm just as he had for the last five years and he would be with his wife and her family. Since there were two spacious rooms built on the north side of her parents' master bedroom, for privacy's sake, both Khalim and Shayeena would share the room furthest away, and her mother and Tayi's mom saw to it that everything there was squared away and ready for them and their post-nuptials. This room also happened to be next door to her room for the last 18 years. Soon her father would convert her room into her own private study, so she could still have access to her secret pathway to the Minaret of Jam. She would apprise Khalim of their shared pathway in due time, the path in their new room that connected to the path in her old room, maybe that night.

The wedding was going to be beautiful; her garments were going to be dazzling, her beauty would finally be on display before God and everyone, and in the most prudent of ways, of course. Shayeena, Khalim, her parents, the Imam, Tayi's parents and grandparents, and everyone in the village were excited to see the wedding take place. Everyone was glowing and ready for this exciting and endearing event, except Jalal.

Good and Evil

Khalim's older brother, Jalal, felt on top of the world in his own way, of course. He wasn't lost on narcissism and all kinds of feelings of claim to power within the village. His father was the village Imam, the judge, the jury, and the one who would decree the death sentence of all who did not comply with his edicts or the demands of those closest to him. He also enforced the strict rules of the oppressive-extremist-hierarchy. As such, Jalal had learned from his father and was brilliant when it came to ensuring things would go his way. He was an actor, a wordsmith, the leader's son, and as such he was the undisputed heir to lead the people should his father ever pass that title on, perhaps sooner if he were to loosen his grip on this mortal coil sooner, not that he had any plans to that effect. At times, however, his untouchable angel of a little brother would infuriate him to the core; he was a saint and had not dirtied his hands in any way, no matter how hard Jalal tried to lure him into something mischievous, cruel, or treacherous, so he could use that as blackmail or a leash.

Khalim had always been a kind and gentle soul, but with the stature and strength of a giant. Jalal knew his little brother was handsome, he saw the burkas slightly turn as his brother would walk by. With Khalim's dark and golden-speckled eyes and dark hair, which he kept cropped close on the sides and back, most likely to cause the frustration of his brother, and to lend to that his shaved face every day and excellent hygiene, Jalal was seething with jealousy. Khalim would jog around the village, use a weight set which he had purchased one year in Firozkah to maintain his physique, he would greet everyone he saw, and he was loved by many. It was obvious to Jalal that when Khalim saw displays of compassion he was moved.

Jalal and his father loved him too, in their own way. They were flesh and blood after all.

But they barely tolerated his unique character. "He's too affable, he's too pretty for a man, and his kind and nice demeanor will lead to fragility, but he's your brother," his father would tell Jalal.

Jalal, on the other hand, did not shave, he felt he was more like a beast and more of a man with his beard. He rarely jogged around the village; his thick mid-section suggested he was of a powerful and wealthy lineage, and if he saw villagers, they'd better do his bidding or consider the unpleasant consequences. He was still older than his brother, he was a man, and he was proud, yet he also aimed to feel accepted by the other men in town that were his age and he would often do brash and cruel things to impress them. He was a man's man. No one corrected him on anything, more so out of fear than anything else. Jalal took this subservience and fear as a show of love and respect and lived and lusted after it. He would inherit his father's position, after all, once his father began giving way to lackluster health and grew to have too much dependence upon Jalal, due to aging. Most of Jalal's character was learned from the closest role model he had—his father.

His father, the Imam, had very little respect for anyone, much less women. Early on in the Imam's childhood, he had grabbed a pot of boiling water and spilled it on his mother's feet. His own father had whipped him something good. He blamed it on his mother and ever since he had a vendetta against women. Nevertheless, he had carried that secret with him well, and rose quite successfully, through his connections to the oppressive-extremist-hierarchy around the land, and other worldwide deals, to the ranks of an Imam. From then on out, he wasted no love for the mother of his children. He'd married her when she was twelve and beat her into submission often. Eventually, she learned to comply with and appease his every request, without thought for reward. She had been broken and only lived for her sons; she also knew how expendable she was if she failed to impress them. Everything was a pretense for her. She was scared but knew that if she didn't put up a fuss she was left alone. However, she grew to favor Khalim and his promising nature. She had secretly raised him well, and certainly when out of sight of her oldest son and husband.

Luckily, Khalim was much greater in character than his father or his brother and he understood quickly the necessity of the secret he shared with his mother, and he kept it well. He was also larger in stature than his older brother, Jalal, so his brother left him alone, if only because the Imam asked him to.

When Khalim was only fifteen, he'd overheard the malice from Jalal's cantankerous acts, and his wily way of explaining it all to his father, who was only too happy to issue the ultimate justice and penalty—the stoning of Tayi. In shock, his young mind knew not what to do. Khalim hadn't been sure when this would occur, so he had gone south to the Hari River to think about how to approach his father to give this young girl, who was clearly the potential victim, some clemency, or at least a voice for mercy. When he had returned to town, he had heard the screams, he had seen the large crowd encircling Tayi, and he stood in shock at the brutality. It had been too late.

When the crowd dissipated, Khalim witnessed Tayi's father in anguish and agony on his knees holding his only child in his arms, a child he truly loved, and although it was almost too much grief to bare, somehow his strength grew from within and his heart sank for both Tayi and her father. He felt for Shayeena as well, Tayi's best friend, he had admired Shayeena for quite some time through the years, and very much in secret, but there she was broken as she stood there in tears and helplessness to save her dear friend. He also felt rage percolating from within toward his manipulative brother and father, but over time he culled his anger and it dwindled to anguish. In his sorrow, he went over to Tayi's father, apologized for the brutality of his father and brother, quietly explained to them what truly had happened, so as to ensure no one else heard, and then helped them to Shayeena's farmland entrance, returned to the grizzly scene, picked Tayi's lifeless body up from the bloodied ground, and carried her to her home, where her grandparents happened to be. He had carried her there, so she could be properly prepared for a more honorable burial. After all, for whatever crime she had never committed, she had certainly paid the ultimate price, and therefore deserved an honorable burial service, if not for her, for her father, her mother, and her grandparents.

This moment had left an indelible impression upon him, and he vowed to always protect Shayeena, no matter where she went. He also vowed to protect his own mother from his brother and father in every possible way. He was grateful for the protections his muscular and large stature afforded him. He was also grateful for their connection through blood, since that afforded him a little more levity in his choices and actions than many others in the village, but he also knew he had to be smart with regard to how he went about the beloved deeds of protection and kindness; after all, it wouldn't take long for even a large man to be subdued by a hostile crowd or a properly guided dagger.

As with most men in his village, he spent a lot of time in Shahrak going through school. He studied intently, abided by the higher principles of his faith, but made sure humility, understanding, strength, and compassion were paramount in his life. When he would return every two weeks, or during Ramadan, if he saw Shayeena in her burlap burka and sack clothes, he'd also make it a point to ensure he knew where his brother and his friends were, and then escort her home.

As the years passed by, from time to time, and as he spent free time working on her father's farm, he would have pleasant exchanges with Shayeena, and ever more increasingly he felt that she would be the one he would marry. If that were to be the case, once that was done, he could protect her even more. There was something unique, special, and wonderful that emanated from her character, and he loved her for it, and he wanted to allow her light to shine brightly.

Whenever he had free time, in-between studies, or during breaks from school, he would visit with Shayeena's parents or help her father on their large acreage, at least through noon. He told her father that it was only because he wanted to save money for his future family and although her father paid him well and in accordance to the yield of his labors and his work ethic, he did this to spend time with her family, to protect her, and he enjoyed the opportunity to get to know each of them more fully. He also planned to return all that he had earned back to her family again in some way and someday. Khalim rather liked Shayeena's father, since he was an honest, brilliant, and good man; he looked at him as more of a father than his own. As time grew by, Shayeena's father loved Khalim too, as a son. While his other sons had moved on to greener pastures, Khalim was dedicated to both his daughter and the well-being of his daughter's family. Her father could see that in him and was honored to share any burdens or even pleasantries with him. On occasion, Khalim would be over long enough to see Shayeena return from her morning chores, and then accompany her to and from the market on those lucky days, after asking her, of course, and with her parent's permission. Her father could never forget when Khalim asked if he could use a small portion of the land to grow beautiful flowers. He had presented two large bags of bulbs and had gifted a small bag with instructions on how to plant them and tend to them, to his daughter. Her face had been filled with joy, and that melted Mr. Arezo's heart.

While walking, Shayeena and Khalim would only talk if they were alone, and while doing so they would maintain the societally expected silence and distance in public to prevent dangerous rumors from forming. Because he was academically brilliant in his studies, excellent in his art and science classes, curious about his Universe, and had noticed in secret that Shayeena was as well and respected that, as well as physically fit and generally a very kind individual to every individual he met, he was respected more so for his own efforts and character than for the rank and title of his father. The villagers, always fearing the Imam and Jalal, felt at ease around Khalim, and they too protected him every time there was a need to do so.

As time flew by, Shayeena and Khalim grew fond for each other and the day came for his proposal to her with the proper dowry to her family. Her parents had accepted his offer, and she modestly demonstrated her internal excitement and graciousness as well. More time flew by and it was the night before the wedding.

Khalim thought deeply, sitting on the northern shores of the Hari River, miles away from where Shayeena sat too, thinking deeply as well along the shores of the Jam River. While contemplating the events that led to this wonderful oncoming event, he was moved internally that despite all his worries and concerns, this wedding would no doubt be joyous, and he was overjoyed that for once justice might actually and truly be a beautiful thing. Once married, he would spend more time with Shayeena and loyally work with her family on the farm, to help it to continue to succeed. He would be inventive and creative, alongside her father to help the village to become more like Shayeena's father, and to allow their lands to grow into the small diamonds of wonder that they could be if they were to learn to treasure the bounties of the Universe that Allah had been so kind to bestow upon all of humanity. Her brothers had honorably-secured positions as scientist, attorney, and medical doctor in Shahrak and each one had started their own families, so he would unite his strengths with her father, work with her brothers to strengthen their ties, and afford her the space she needed while she would privately pursue her dreams. She wanted to travel to the furthest reaches of the Universe someday and she wanted him to be there with him.

Plotting and scheming, Jalal had always felt a certain jealousy about his brother, and a depraved lust for Shayeena. As such, he would lurk around quietly and send his friends out as spies to listen to their conversations and to try to find some dirt on his brother, something that would shame him, so he could take him down and have her to himself. For years he had monitored their every movement, never suspecting that Khalim was always two steps ahead of him, so for all of Jalal's efforts, everything he had ever done or attempted toward an end of malice had been to no avail.

Both Shayeena and Jalal's little brother had an enviable and pure relationship built on trust. This made him seethe even more. *"How could this much "boring" and fragility possibly exist in one location? I am cantankerous and fun. I am cool. I'll be the Imam one day. How is it that HE can be so lucky? How dare the villagers love him? I'll find a way to get back at everyone who has ever deliberately dishonored me."* He would often ask and think to himself. *"Tayi defied me, and she paid the price. All I have to do is tell Shayeena, persuasively, that I love her, and then she'll see reason and seek to be with me. If not, she will defy my will, and we'll see how far that takes her. We'll see how far that takes anyone!"*

Little did Jalal know that for years, Shayeena had known the true story of his malicious intent as expressed through his actions and as accounted to her by both, Tayi before she died, and later by his brother, who had witnessed each detail to his own horror. In truth, his own brother, Khalim, was always protecting her from him, and Jalal thought they were merely two boring and nauseating friends getting married. He had plans for their wedding night, and in his mind, he had a right to her. He would become friends with Shayeena's family, be the ever-so-dutiful helper, get his father scheduled to conduct the ceremony, and then the celebration would fly by until everyone but her family and his had left Shayeena's home. When everyone was fast asleep, he had plans in mind. Things, as they were going to be, were a part of his unique manner of having his way, and whatever he had in store most certainly was not going to be pleasant. *"They'll have left the monster in their home. So, while they are there sleeping and temporarily paralyzed, and while they are wistfully dreaming away, I will do my worst."*

Wedding Day

The wedding day was here. Shayeena was in her bridal gown, flowers from Khalim's secret garden were everywhere, and a big tent had been set up outside in Shayeena's front yard, courtesy of her soon-to-be brother-in-law, Jalal, and the friendly but speculative approval of her parents. Jalal had seemed to mature and was helpful every step of the way, as were his friends. Now, Shayeena didn't trust him any more than she could toss a feather, but she had begun to forgive him despite the horror of five years ago because perhaps a person could change for the better, no matter the crime, if given the right environment and influences.

The ceremony was splendid, the music, the prayers, everything suggested harmony and bliss. The savor of the music hung in the air and the taste of the wedding desserts still lingered on the taste buds of her mind.

The celebration that followed was just as spectacular, and everyone danced with everyone as though there were never any hard feelings between them. Gifts were shared and among them a beautiful and ornate, yet very sharp dagger from 'anonymous.' Everyone was ensconced in the details of the handle and the hilt, and then the dishes from China, a toaster and a blender with an electrical converter, and a 'her and him' set of romantic night-gowns. Then the dance returned. As the music grew from trance rhythms to the peaceful symphony, to religious and cultural music, family by family, the festivities grew smaller, until all who were left were Shayeena's and Khalim's families. Her own three brothers had made a special occasion of it to break from work and visit their sister for her wedding day, and they shared the boy's room closest to the master bedroom, on the south wing of the bedrooms. Jalal stayed in the second room south of the master bedroom, the Imam and his wife stayed in the third south-wing room. Shayeena and Khalim stayed the night in the girl's room, retrofitted into another master, with Shayeena's bedroom converted into her personal study, but strategically used as a storage room, to keep Shayeena's secret just that.

Once everyone retired, hugs were shared, and the only sound throughout the house was the white noise blowing in from the breeze outside through the screened windows, the day had been beautiful, the scent of the flowers still lingered in the air, but someone had been determined that day and had quite different plans than bliss. Shayeena and Khalim were finally together, happily, in a moment of sweet intimacy with only the light of a candle and the sweet scent of rose petals strewn about the room. Their clothes lie disheveled upon the floor, and as beautiful moments turned into memories, they fell asleep.

What they did not know, was that somehow Jalal had hidden in the closet with the ornate sword he had gifted them, as though it was from anonymous. As he had planned, if he couldn't have Shayeena, no one else would, at least without paying a price, so he started to open the door to carry out his bloody task, when suddenly, he was stunned by a bright light and he blacked out, only to partially awaken as if in a dream. He felt all of his nerves contort, his body fought every aspect of what was going on, and then when he could bear it no more, he let go, until euphoria set in. Suddenly, he saw a statue of an angel overlooking a small pond, with fish and frogs swimming around within it. He looked up and he saw a very living and breathing Iridescent Angel standing before him.

"No longer will you hurt or harm. From now on you will heal by connecting to the hearts of others through compassion and the skills of persuasion. Instead of taking a life, your physiology and neurology will be optimized, you will be healed, and at the appropriate time, you will be sentenced to enter a correctional world where you will receive experiences that will increase your wisdom and enlighten your mind tenfold. What you did to Tayi was unforgivable, yet we and all who you know will forgive you anyway because they have love in their hearts and a hope for the beautiful potential that lies deep and buried within you. I will take you to your bed, send you on a temporary journey through time, and when you awake, you will confess to those you love, of the innocence of Tayi, and seek reparations to help further the advancement of

civilization for a beautiful journey to the stars. Your life will not be in jeopardy, and you will find that everyone you know, now has the same abilities as you. It is up to you to secure your place among the distant stars. By studying further and working with others, you will find a depth of joy and promise you never thought possible. Enjoy your journey, Jalal."

Like that, the angel disappeared, and Jalal found himself living out a variety of sequences of life, up to and including the life of one Eliza Amber Williams. He learned how hospitable her heart, how pure her mind, and how kind her soul was. She was the one who had begun this peaceful revolution, and he would help to carry that banner from this point forward within his village. His mind had clarity, and he saw that he would protect Shayeena and his brother, Khalim and that he would support the efforts that their clarity would give to them.

Jalal then experienced the horrible scene from the point of view and the mental clarity of the mind of Shayeena and then Tayi's father, and with full understanding of the error of his ways, he felt the horror and anguish that they had felt and vowed that he would change his way of being and serve the village, Tayi's parents, Shayeena, and Khalim for the rest of his days. He would put his skills to good use to build a village university, for both boys and girls, and to educate men and women alike on all of the technologies that were designed to increase longevity, well-being, quality of life, preserve and beautify the planet, and much, much more. The next morning, he woke up with tingling all over the left side of his body, and an acute tingling sensation on his right buttock cheek. He looked to examine it, and it appeared to be a glowing tattoo of an iridescent scorpion. *"The Iridescent Scorpion,"* he thought.

As he arose, he stepped out into the hallway and looked to his left to see his parents, who each looked twenty-five again. His mother was healed from the wounds brought to her by his father, the Imam, and with his father's saddened yet apologetic appearance, both were glowing. He saw a very contrite and compassionate look in his father's countenance. He then looked to his right and closest to him were Shayeena's older brothers, and all three looked as though they were twenty-five again, with a similar, yet somewhat unique countenance. After looking at Shayeena's brothers, he saw her parents, and then Khalim and Shayeena.

They all looked at him with forgiving eyes. They knew what he had planned to do the night before, but they were waiting for him to speak the first words.

Jalal spoke, "I mean to address you, each of you, as well as Tayi's family, and the entire village. I have some apologizing to do and some amazing experiences and plans to share. Please bear with me. I deeply apologize to each of you now, and will again for many years to come, until I have paid my dues with my burden to bare and I am sent to this 'correctional world' where everyone I have ever hurt can and will receive vindication. Until then, I will help each of you with whatever clarity you've been given through your dreams last night. Come, let's eat, and then gather everyone into the village. I have a speech to give, and I'll want to hear your dreams."

Even his father, the Imam, knew what had transpired, and for him, much the same had occurred. He had also been given a shared link to his son's mind and had vowed within himself to support the more benevolent efforts of both his children and his wife. She was now rejuvenated and young and beautiful again, and her mind was healed from years of abuse. She was someone who he had taken for granted all his life, who he had mistreated, yet she had been someone who loved with temperance imbued within her soul throughout all of these years. She had forgiven him, despite his monstrous behaviors toward her. He would serve her now and strive to be a source of happiness and promise to all whom he knew from this day forward.

Shayeena and Khalim Aliah had gone on their journey together; they had felt the glow of healing, understood each other deeper than they had ever thought possible, and they had taken the time to train each other on both their new and old skills. During that one night, they had spent a lifetime together. Following Jalal's address, Shayeena and Khalim journeyed often, using the two biopods Sky Taylor had left behind for them in their shared room within the Arezo residence and had completed several Virtual Universe University courses from beginning to end, together. They looked at each other; they smiled, and they knew that while there was much to do for their part in the advancement of civilization, around their farm and their village, joy was about to be a very regular occurrence.

Jalal, his parents, Khalim and Shayeena, her parents, and everyone throughout the village felt a special kinship that grew as the days passed by. Together, they built water aqueducts, farms, and mines, healed the parched land, constructed a university, innovation centers, and prospered together, while developing defenses, should the oppressive-extremist-hierarchy seek to reinstall the brutality rampant before.

Sky combed those sentiments in her mind using her links to all whom she'd visited, she saw that they now had a lot of promise, that they would be invincible to anyone or anything that would try to tear them down, and she continued on.

Unpleasant Surprise

Ariel had lived in fear every moment of every day for the last four years. Living or barely surviving in the dungeon-like basement of a dingy old hotel that had born more than its fair share of brutal stories, with plenty of stains on the walls and the stench of offal in the rooms as evidence of what remained. It seemed like forever ago when, during those first few days, they had hoped for a compassionate mind to come their way, someone who could make right what had been made ever so wrong, a person who had mercy etched into their soul. Instead, there they lived, far and away from an exit door, far and away from home, and on the inside of a dark place where they were entrapped which was more like a musty, moldy, filthy dungeon.

Ariel remembered during her few hours of sleep, the younger years in school in Northwestern Europe. Everyone seemed pleasant, full of goals, and energetic with the promise of an amazing future. Life was vibrant, fun, and full of promise. Her family had been one of humble resources, and as such her parents had never seemed particularly impressed with cell phones or other technological devices—they were "distractions of the highest order." So, instead of chatting with her friends through social media, she studied. She wanted to be a scientist when she grew up anyway, so she knew the hours would fly by quickly in the labs, on the computers, and doing field experiments in the interest of making life better for humankind. The fields of biology and genetics interested her most. Her grandmother had passed away from cancer a year ago, and Ariel felt it was time to make some changes to the healthcare industry. There was a lot she believed she could do, but she felt that before she could write a new chapter in her life, it had to begin with a field trip after enrolling in college. She wanted to do something to clear her mind and reawaken her spirits, especially following the loss of her grandmother, whom she loved so much and looked at as a best of friends.

Things seemed squared away. Ariel had recently finished high school and was going to begin her studies in biology in a technical college during the next semester. It was not too long after enrolling when she happened to be walking to get some lunch at a street food stand when she met a seemingly friendly couple who talked about how everyone should go for a stroll through Europe, a getaway vacation, before getting swamped with schoolwork and the responsibilities of education.

They finally convinced her, after showing her the bus pick-up location, what she could expect to see, how she could travel on pennies alone and enjoy Eastern Europe. She remembered how she bid farewell to her family. They were so happy for her and proud of her upcoming commitments. Now, here she was, getting ready for a relaxing and exciting journey since she was going to be gone from home for a couple of weeks on vacation. Once done, she'd return home to prepare for technical school.

Everything seemed warm, welcoming, and well-planned. The bus ride was a bit dank, but it was okay. The sun had been out, the windows down, and the air was sweet. The countryside, which extended for hours, was beautiful. Ariel Boshka happened to look around the interior of the bus to assess her company. She was with twelve other girls, between the ages of approximately thirteen to fifteen, each of whom was attractive and seemed to come from a variety of locations and monetary statuses. There, on the bus with the girls, was the couple who she had met at the college campus, both of whom seemed pleasant and attentive. He had a dark and trimmed beard, his hair was cropped on the sides, his hair on top was combed up and over, and he wore motorcycle enthusiast gear. She had dark hair, with a series of facial rings, a tattoo that came up from her shoulder to her neck and then to her ear. They wore a stark sense of concern and seemed amiable. Ariel enjoyed their unique creativity and looked forward to what was ahead.

There they were headed on a field trip she had been promised she would never forget. At the time she had thought it would be a field trip filled with all kinds of zoos, museums, cultural centers, warm lakeside beaches, and wonderful people. Instead of what she had hoped for, she noticed that they had started driving through forests, then farms, then broken down cities, which were most likely under disrepair since World War II. When the location seemed sufficiently horrific enough, the bus stopped, and the nice couple told them to walk down the road until they reached a tall willow tree. Once they saw the tree, they would turn right onto the next crossroad. From there, once they got into town, they would be able to check into a hotel for the night.

Once Ariel and the group of twelve young women had retrieved their luggage, the bus drove away. The nice young couple waved with smiles that faded as the distance widened.

There they were, officially stranded. There were no tour guides, like those that had been promised, yet they trudged on, as darkness seemed to fast approach, still with hope in their hearts. Each girl offered to help the other as they walked down the roads, reached the willow tree, and turned to the right as suggested. After walking a while longer, the place they came upon looked overgrown with dark forests looming all around the broken-down grey stone walls and somewhat gloomy and toppled buildings. Ariel and the twelve girls, who had been dropped off, stayed close together and had gotten to know each other rather well. After a couple of hours of trudging forward, they arrived at a crumpled old war-torn portion of a city in Eastern Europe, at least six hours from their hometown.

None of the girls had known each other beforehand, but they did share one language, which was broken English. The fragmented city they found themselves walking into looked as though it had at one time been teeming with life and as if it were once a bustling little place. The dirt and stone roads seemed to go on for miles, and each person who had traveled by bus there had interesting backgrounds. Aside from English as a shared and mostly secondary language, they had all visited the same school with plans for beginning the technical college there, where Ariel had planned to go. They had also been confronted by that nice couple and counseled to take a two-week vacation to explore Europe and its eastern countryside. After walking for a while down the road they saw a hotel that was somewhat kept up. Outside of it, there was a helicopter pad and some areas for vehicle parking.

The sign on the outside wall of the Hotel noted that there was a complimentary breakfast each morning for hotel occupants, so Ariel and the other twelve girls entered the hotel to look around and see if they could share a room for the night. Everything seemed pretty lovely. The rooms were clean, the linens were washed, and just one hotel room seemed spacious enough for all the girls. There were extra linens provided for turning into some sort of sleeping bag. The girls drew straws and the seven with the short straws would sleep on the ground. They were satisfied with their patrol through the first floor of the hotel and decided to finally check in. After checking in, courtesy of one of the girls who had come in from a more well-to-do part of society, they settled in for the night. They took turns using the shower. Ariel took hers last, washing her medium length blonde hair, her hidden areas, and her healthy and physically attractive frame. After drying up, getting into her PJs, she and the other girls chatted until they fell into a deep sleep, and knew their famished tummies would be satisfied with the complimentary breakfast in the morning. Their grumbling stomachs would insist upon it. But for now, the tiring walk earned them some sleep. They also knew this location must have been a mistake, so they had to rest up, and eat up; they would get back in the morning.

It all seemed a little too quiet in that room, so much so that they could hear music playing in the distance as if there were a party going on. It was the sound of muffled shrieks, followed by what sounded like a gunshot and ominous silence that caused them all to be alert, no matter how tired they were.

"Did you hear what I think I heard?" asked the rich girl, who had paid for the room. She sat up in the bed, looking in the dark toward the other girls, with her pristine blonde hair pulled back and wearing her princess cut sleeping dress.

"I heard it too," said each of the girls, and one by one they began to huddle as the sounds became eerier. Two king beds held seven girls on one and six girls on the other. With the night light on, Ariel could see that she was sitting between the rich girl to her right on the bed closest to the far wall from the entryway, another very beautiful girl with red hair to her left, with three more girls on their bed huddled up. The next king bed had the other seven girls, huddled closely as well. Interestingly, they were all very darling and somewhat young girls.

"I want to get out of here," said the youngest, with dark brunette hair and pale skin, in a very innocent voice. "What should we do?"

Ariel then spoke up, "I think we should keep quiet and let the morning ride through. See the bars in the windows? We can't get out using those. Also note, the bus dropped us off in the boonies and there were no actual bus stops there if you recall. Right after breakfast, let's check-out, and then we can look for a cell tower. Does anyone have a cell phone?"

"I do, said the rich girl next to her," she pulled it out of her nightgown pocket and turned it on, but there was no connectivity.

"Yeah, that won't do. Ugh, right now we are in the safest place we can be, but we'll need to leave first thing after breakfast." Ariel was pretty sure she was right. If they were too loud or if they tried to leave now, they would be heard by those responsible for the creepy vibes that emanated from the same building and not too far away. They would also have no place that was warm enough to stay that was away from whatever thugs or wild animals that might find them to be a treat during the night.

Right then, one of the seven girls on the second king bed got up, ran to the door, and screamed. She had begun losing her mind increasingly, since the eerie walk through the forested woods, the stone and dirt roads as every moment went by, and somehow screaming was her only learned safety mechanism. No one else in the room could blame her. She was young, naïve, and fragile. Ariel looked around at everyone else, climbed over the footboard of the bed, and made a dash to comfort the scared little girl.

Sharon was an olive-skinned girl with dark and slightly frizzy piggy tails and couldn't have been too much older than 13. What in the world would have suggested to her parents that traveling alone was a good idea? But, then again, Ariel was only fourteen, but she'd finished high school early. She finally managed to get her to stop screaming and to return with her to the room.

Unfortunately, it was too late. The screams obviously alerted whoever it was that was responsible for the business going on in the distance. Whoever it was, knew that they were there and quite possibly had heard everything.

After the situation seemed to calm down, the girls could hear the muffled bass-filled chatter of men coming down the hall. Fully alert, Ariel looked to the rich girl, and then the other girls, and said, "We need to get out of here, and now."

It was too late. They were surrounded by what seemed a sardonic cult of men.

Four years later, they were still there, but had contrary to their will found a different place to lie their heads during the night. This place, in particular, smelt of offal; the pillars of this location where the stones had scattered about the room was evidence that more pillars had once existed but had been broken apart by something grave, so they used the stones left behind as pillows, and the only warmth was the warm body next to them. Each and every girl with Ariel had that night and many nights from then on endured brutality that was unexplainable and unconscionable. All of her sisters, as she called them, the twelve that had arrived with her, along with a few others who wandered into the same trap, some of whom had died, and quite a few more who had lived in much the same way yet still were among the living, were much like they, and they too wound up several floors below the room they had paid for in full, on their first night.

Death was more than a threat, and, in some ways, it became more of the only hope for a sweet release from the torment and anguish existent in the lives they had known. Ariel had witnessed as her tormentors made their points in front of herself and her sisters all too often, with a gun to their head and a trigger pulled, and the life of a once vibrant young girl gone. The savage beatings of a club, the severing of limbs, or new scars carved by the sharp edge of a knife, and then the brutal reality that would unfold, became the deep scars in the minds and hearts of these young girls. Too many times for anyone, these young beautiful women witnessed as those with no mercy, among some with eyes of those who still possessed some humanity until they too did nothing and lost their genteel nature, caused wounds so fierce that the light of life left the eyes of yet another potential friend in less austere circumstances, and only her spirit escaped them. Gone was another young lady, who would finally escape this torturous hell from which there was no reward, yet whose injustice was no part of their own.

A numbness of it all had begun to set in week after a week, and in such a brutal way that she too couldn't wait until the day they were done with her. Every time no matter who was there, the torture was ruthless, and the merciless laughter of those enjoying the show before them was a mockery of their very existence. The morbid husks of men and sometimes women witnessing and doing nothing about the inhumanity existent before them as these girls screamed in pain was a dismal reality of the lack of honor existent in or even a fiber of respect from one human to another simply based on fate alone. Brutality continued, yet nothing was done to stop this barbarity against the young and innocent human beings. It was as if this were the place that devils' demons got to play with and torture God's little angels, and then get away with it.

On occasion, there had been a tender soul who had attempted to show mercy, but if he or she were ever discovered, he or she was killed and so was the girl they were trying to help. Again, brutal points were made by some of the vilest, most malicious and uncaring of individuals—people who had lost all inflection of humanity for the very cause of sacred edict and delusional rituals, personal pleasure and the power that overindulgent wealth alone could bring over the lives of others. It didn't matter to these sociopaths, these evil psychopaths, these thieves of virtue and these bullies of nature un-swayed, what transpired against their young and innocent victims, because without much wait after the consequences of their actions the dead girl or the tool for their ill-gotten gains would be thrown away or replaced by another victim of the massive human trafficking operations rampant worldwide.

Ariel had learned early on that these vile monsters, as the girls called them, when they were far from earshot, would try to figure out each of the girl's ages and determine their life expectancy based on what they had managed to extract from the girls in the dark and painful chambers, along with their obedience during their sorrowful existence. There was a repugnant purpose in this because they would get girls who were showing signs of puberty, and when they reached the age of eighteen, they would disappear for good. The party music of the twisted souls who were brought in by helicopter or wheeled in by limousine, the muffled screams, and the "bang! Bang!" would follow by the absence of the girl who'd inherited the title of "longest stayed."

To protect her twelve friends, right when she figured this out, she claimed she was the oldest of the girls. "I'm fourteen, and the other girls just turned twelve." For once they seemed to listen. The rich girl, who was her age, almost died from a gut wound two years after they arrived. However, because Ariel had known first aid, had caught it at the right time, and due to a side study by way of her interest in biology and biotechnology, she had saved her life. She had looked at the wound and knew to take a moist cloth, lie her on her back with her knees up to keep the pressure off her abdomen, and continued to keep that area moist and clean until sewn shut and the wound healed. While the monsters were as vile as anything else, objectifying these girls through vicious rancor, Ariel managed often to find their humanity, convincing them that they still had to maintain their cash crop, and as a result had thus provided limited antibiotics, pain-numbing agents, and bandages, so Ariel used those as well as her wit to save the girl's life.

Just as the girls, older than her, had been killed in front of the other girls on many occasions, mostly to demonstrate the futility of hope, tonight was her night. Tonight, was her eighteenth birthday, it was 2022, and it would certainly end with an indulgent party and a bang. The important people and their coming of age sons would be there tonight, to dabble in the debauchery, mutilation, torture, and murder of Ariel. If she died tonight, her sisters had one or two more years of hell on Earth before she would hopefully see them again, perhaps in a better place.

"It's my time. I love each of you. We've endured so much, but somehow, we've all made it this far. Look after our newer and younger sisters, you know first aid well—stop the bleeding, remain calm, small sips of water, and eat in small amounts until healed. They cycle through us each week, but tonight is my birthday, so when you hear my screams, cover your ears. When you hear the gunshot, please cover your ears, and you'll know this hell is done for me. One last hug?" They all tried to avoid sobbing, took turns hugging Ariel, and then the door opened.

A big and burly bearded man waved his bat and then pointed it toward Ariel, "Today is your lucky day, birthday girl! You're coming with me. It'll all be over soon. If you try to fight, two of those girls next to you will die." Ariel slowly walked to the monster, put her hands out, he bound her arms and legs, gagged her mouth, and forcefully drug her away. She bore the pain as though her weight and friction were dragged upon a thick sheet of sandpaper that tore at her flesh and she could feel each of the stones through the burlap sack covering her face as the floor ground into her flesh. She tolerated it all, in part because it would all be over soon, in part because shock had settled in from all the pain, and in part because she did not want any of the other girls to be punished because of her own actions.

She felt the abrasions in her knees as they lifted her body to the table, and she heard the cutlery rattling and clambering with its serrated stainless-steel edges bumping against each other as a cart was rolled in. Her heart was pulsating. She knew it would hurt, but after some unbridled and then muffled screams, a boom would go off and for her, this misery, this suffering, and this hell made from the minds of those, those who could have been kind rather than ruthless, those who could have cared rather than lust after brutality, those evil monsters from hell would see to it soon that all of this, all of it would be over. The death metal music playing for the benefit of her torturers and paying onlookers began to fade to quiet, she felt her clothes being torn from her body, and she heard the eerie death metal music beginning again and climbing to a crescendo, as the cheers of the crowd suggested their approval of the oncoming pain and horror she would soon endure. The clank of the blades followed by the taunting, the unwarranted fondling, grew more unbearable.

Just as the cold metal touched her stomach with the unforgiving serrated edge facing upwards, she began to feel the urge to scream. The blades started their path up to tear through the ample flesh on her chest, when suddenly, she heard one of the monsters of men nearby yell, "Oh my God, What the hell!?"

Whatever light was coming through the blindfold on her eyes went out. And then she blacked out completely.

Coming to, shortly after, she felt every nerve, every synapse, and every sensory system in her body almost convulse, and then she felt a nirvana she had never felt before. Slowly, a light began to fade in and finally, it returned, as she realized she was standing in a beautiful garden with a statue of an angel looking over her cupped hands with water falling from them to provide nourishment and clean water to a pond of coy fish and frogs. She looked at the terrain around her and began to understand things she had never understood before. "Am I dead?" she asked herself.

She saw a rainbow of light reflecting off a maple tree not too far away and being sure that the light was emanating from behind her, she turned around and saw an iridescent angel, glowing in a white and beautiful arrangement of rainbow colors. Her white, long, and beautifully braided hair with iridescent highlights, her crystalline blue eyes, a tear down her left cheek, and a gentle yet sad and voluptuous smile took all of the pain she knew she would endure only moments before and caused it to melt away. She then looked toward Ariel and spoke. "You and your sisters are all safe now. The pain and unforgivable insanity unleashed upon such a fair maiden with such a beautiful mind should never have happened to you or anyone. Ariel, you've protected those girls for a long time, and I am so sorry for every bit of torture each of you has endured. I have been to many places, all of which were places where hope seemed to be gone forever, but a place such as this wrought with little purpose but suffering within should never be. Come with me, you should never have to suffer again, let me show you a better way of life. Gather your sisters. They too are with you here, next to the pond behind you and let's go on a little journey."

Filled with questions, Ariel and her sisters put them on pause and followed this exquisitely beautiful angel, and she wondered why she went from terror to bliss so soon.

The angel took her, and then what seemed as sisters to the angel, took her sisters by the hand to the edge of the Solar System where right before their eyes lie an array of beautiful tech cities, each with a dazzling view of Pluto, Neptune, Uranus, Saturn, Jupiter, Ceres, Mars, Earth, Venus, Mercury, and the beautiful Sun. Somehow her vision had granted Ariel the ability to see each of them as though they were close enough for coloration and planetary detail. As she focused more, she saw great big shields situated around each planet to protect them. She then focused more and saw each planetary surface adjust and change until each one had an atmosphere, like that of Earth, teeming with mountains, rivers, streams, lakes, and oceans. She saw the beauty of the shared ecosystem and environment working in concert with magnificent and regal cities—so much art, so much purpose, and an incredible sense of peace.

"One of these places can be your home, but there is work that needs to be done on Earth before you begin your work here. Please go with these girls and see that they return to their homes. Please also pursue your education and I will see you again, soon. You and these beautiful, yet unfortunate, girls have been healed and optimized both physiologically and neurologically in every possible way. I have looked into each of your hearts and minds, and you will have a neural link that will allow each of you to communicate, share ideas, truly understand each other and much more. Please help each other to train, control, and use your new-found abilities.

"I and my daughters must leave, but I will leave you with the history of Pathway and life from the viewpoint of Eliza Amber Williams.

"Even the perpetrators have been healed in both ways, however, there has been a quickening of their minds to understand the pain and suffering they have caused, they will experience everything you each have experienced from your perspective, and they will gain an elevation of compassion and eloquence the likes of which they never knew before, and I will leave with them my mark, a tattoo of an iridescent scorpion on their right buttock cheek which serves as a marker. They will be healed, they will now be honorable, and they will help you. Once they have been duly judged they will go through what is called the Correctional Matrix, wherein they will be thrust into many centuries' worth of experiences, wisdom, and given a cause to increase their kindness and notion of consent. For now, when you awaken, they will use every resource available to help you help your sisters return home and recover from all that was lost throughout the years.

"Before I go, do you have any questions?"

Sky Taylor paused. Ariel clearly was filled with so much to ask, yet she didn't know where to begin.

"Thank you," was all that Ariel managed to say. Sky hugged Ariel, and then like that, Ariel woke up in the same dingy dungeon she had been in before. She was in the same place where she'd been ruthlessly dragged; she was still in the torture chamber. However, she felt full, healed, and even with an enjoyable sense of euphoria. She and all the girls in the room, her sisters, were healed, and beautiful, and glowing. They were in the same place, with the same marks of brutality existent on the walls, but there was something different in the air.

The girls were excited to see Ariel, as they had made their way down the hallway, and they had so much to say but didn't know where to begin. Instead, they shared a series of hugs and proceeded toward the unlatched door. As they cleared the room and continued their way down the hallway toward a plausible stairwell, they heard familiar voices. Interestingly, instead of the expected guttural language filled with filth and malevolent intentions, they heard a series of apologetic and contrite voices. Once these men, who had seemed grotesque and savage in every way, with beards, sweaty residue upon their countenance, and the stench of hell, had now changed in every possible way to become a more clean-cut, physically-fit, and a slight glow of gentlemen, appearing down the hallway. They beckoned kindly to the girls as they all in unison said, "It is okay. We're here to help you get home and to make amends in the best way we can. We're so sorry. Oh, what were we thinking and why? We were lost in self-indulgence no matter the cost to anyone else. We'll never be able to repay humanity for the injustices we have committed, but we will serve humanity through the rest of our lives, even if that is forever because we know that only in the service of our fellow brothers and sisters can we have joy."

In every way, all who had been in that building the night before seemed pleasant, genuinely kind, and contrite. All the conversations led to three things: The Iridescent Scorpion, Eliza Williams, and getting the girls home. This chapter of human brutality had ended. Sky Taylor had given each person, good or bad, enough strength, grace, and clarity of mind to see an end to the barbarity they had each been a part of, whether through suffering or through causing it. Those who had caused this suffering helped each person one-by-one, to see the error of their own ways, and build protections for any potential victim no matter where they would go. The world was full of beauty and was meant to be enjoyed, and not meant for shattered dreams.

When Ariel and her sisters arrived at each of their homes, they were surprised to find out that their parents not only looked much younger and healthier too, but Sky Taylor had visited them as well. They told Ariel of an account where an Imam from Afghanistan had met with the "nice" couple many years before and had worked with them to build this dreaded network. He had met with them again two years prior to Sky's visit, and that's what solidified her next mission. There were so many connections because as she combed their minds, she saw larger networks to visit and she healed rather than punished them. Vindication would come later when the Correctional Matrix was proliferated worldwide amongst the populous, but for now, the Iridescent Scorpion was the tag. Through all of her healings, she had indeed combed their minds, she arrived at the girls' parents, healed them, and eventually, she confronted the "nice" couple, healed them, and helped them to see with clarity the things they could do to help humanity advance forward with promise toward the future. While they journeyed through the Virtual Universe, they revealed so much to her.

It was through this same network that Sky discovered another network of terror, crime, cartels, and vicious brutality. This system ran its course with roots stemming from Peru and Colombia via a far-reaching web of corruption thru to the somewhat peaceful seeming capital city of Chihuahua. The violence between cartels was typical and all the more brutal along the US border, across the Rio Bravo from El Paso, and inside the border city of Juarez within the State of Chihuahua, in the United States of Mexico. The "nice couple" apparently had dealings there not long before Sky met them, and a remarkable family was in danger, so she made haste.

Nectar of the Gods

The Zemani family owned a blue agave ranch just south of Chihuahua's state capitol and had been in the farming business for several generations without incident. For the most part, individual cacti were slow money makers, but Laetitia didn't seem to mind, as she would spend hours on end traveling a different path home each day, on her way from school, looking closely with finely tuned hazel eyes she would see the progress of their growth. As the wind blew through her sun-bleached light brown long hair, she would pull nearby weeds as they popped up and let her Dad know when a row of agave was ready for harvest. Once done she would simply sit on the dirt near the growing vegetation to read, study, and do her homework.

Since each cactus took nearly eleven years to fully mature prior to reaching its peak in flavor and was thus ready to harvest, she would see how the different areas of the acreage were doing each day as her father had taught her. Many times, on her way home, she would let her brother go a different direction, as she would stop by the first row of crops, she could recall planting when she was only five years old. It was the baby blue, not seeds, but chutes that were planted. She knew through math that she'd be sixteen years old when her row was ripe and ready for harvest growing to full maturity, at least if the harvester wanted to do it right.

As it was, the Zemani family owned an area that was approximately six miles by six miles, eleven kilometers by eleven kilometers across, for a total of three-thousand-eight-hundred-forty acres, and their family and some family friends maintained every single one of the cacti with love.

Once each of the areas had matured, ripe and succulent cacti were harvested and shipped off to a distillery for the purpose of developing lovely spirits and even supplemental health products. The pulp would then be sent off to a repurposing facility to make paper goods and more. Many people coined the yield the Zemanis had harvested and the liquor it was turned into as the nectar of the gods; their product was each distillery's favorite. The zoned location of their farm and the legal revenue it brought into the area through each part of the process seemed to earn the Zemanis a bit of a pass when it came to anyone predisposed to violence or brutal schemes. After all, you don't attack your own people, no one does. In 2018, however, things seemed to change from a blissful reality into a real-life nightmare.

As demand began to grow, so did the value per kilo of Chihuahua's desert blue agave. Of one-hundred-eighty-one zonal areas approved throughout Mexico for the licit growth of agave, most of them were located within the state of Jalisco, a zone that was supremely natural for it. With a series of mountains to the southwest of their acreage, the Zemani crop had a natural water resource for mild irrigation, which in turn helped bring in substantial revenue for Chihuahua's capital city, Chihuahua. Their state benefited with each step of its path to the final product which helped a population that was upwards of eight-hundred-thousand people. Granted, there were factories and haciendas all over the state capitol dedicated to a variety of other resources, manufactured products, and services, but there was something inherently special about agave.

With eighty percent of their product going to the US, revenues were promising, but shipping through one of the most violent cities in the entire state was part of the risk. The people in Juarez, who lived just south of the US and Mexican border town, El Paso, Texas, for the most part, ensured that the established cartels left the Chihuahua-state and home-based product alone. However, this didn't stop new organizations from trying to infiltrate the land, usurp it, and establish their authority through brutal means. The ruthlessness of any and all cartels was on the rise and had culminated by 2018 where, in just the first month, Juarez saw thirty individuals alone viciously maimed and murdered, and Chihuahua's capital city had lost two of their own. One of these was Andres, Laetitia's oldest brother.

About a year and four months prior, September of 2016, the Zemani's eldest son, Andres, who was twenty years old at the time, had finished junior college studies in Chihuahua and had begun attending law school in Mexico City, Mexico. Laetitia, who was twelve at the time, the youngest, as well as the Zemani's only daughter, had noticed the presence of out-of-state trucks around their property. When asked, they would calmly state that they were only stopping there for a break. As time went by and while journeying with her other brother, Tito, who was fourteen at the time, they noticed movement around their acreage as they walked to and from school which was located just north of Vía Carrizalillo.

Finally, Laetitia brought what she had noticed to the attention of her parents. These strangers hadn't taken any crops but seemed to merely observe the harvest as it went on—as if to try to learn how to do it themselves. During the winter holidays of 2016, Andres came home to visit with a look of concern on his face. It wasn't until the harvest of

2017, that the friendly tone of those who stopped by their land for a break in their drive along Highway 45 seemed to become a little more recluse and somber. The Zemani Family farm and home had seen an increase in speculative activity, of no part of their own, but several rows of agave that were ready for harvest had already been harvested.

With the scattering of irrigation systems and the many sheds distributed throughout their land, the environment there must have seemed an ideally remote and easy weigh station for any cartel group wishing to set up their base of operations, and their farmland must have seemed an easy means of money.

Apparently, Andres wasn't wrong with his speculations, because it seemed that shortly after he had made friends with another young man his age, named Carlos, in law school that he had realized too late that he was part of a strategic arm of this new cartel that was infiltrating the Chihuahua market of the drug trade and other black-market items. As soon as Andres found out who this other young man was, or at least his background, he realized that he had shared too much about their agave ranch and took an opportune break from school to come home to inform his father. A little over a year later, Andres was dead.

Their farm home was just outside of town, away from any policing eyes, a couple of miles from Highway 45, and for any cartel, it would serve as an advantageous weigh station.

Unfortunate for this new cartel terrorist group, Los Wiskis, they had not prepared for the network of friends the Zemanis had. The Zemani's friends from Chihuahua, each with their own robust caches of illegal weaponry, built up for the purpose of protecting the families of the school kids and many others who had worked together on the ranch, had done so to successfully suppress any attack that was planned against their family and their agave ranch. Laetitia's father had built a get-away shelter beneath the home many years prior, if violence called for some hiding. The fighting went on for several hours and was stalled by a false white flag by Los Wiskis. Los Wiskis called Andres' out, in exchange for leaving his family alone, and his family watched in horror as Andres willingly went out to stop the violence, but unfortunately, it had cost him his life. Opening fire on Andres, point blank, just before they left the scene, Carlos, and Los Wiskis realized that for a while the Zemanis would have some reprieve.

After losing their son, even though their friends from the school and their families had banded together to protect the family, the Zemanis decided that enough was enough and they agreed to escape, after barring up their windows, securing all their doors, hiding anything of value and leaving their farm behind. Laetitia's father had no desire for any further barbarity and had secured the services of an unusually kind coyote. They traveled from Chihuahua to Juarez and then crossed the border to the US. It was now 2022, four years later, and Laetitia had hoped that they would be able to return home in time to see her row of agave, two years into maturity and ready to harvest.

Laetitia would get her wish, but perhaps not in the way that she had hoped. Typically, not knowing who to trust or who had been corrupted in the surrounding towns, villages, and cities, had been a daily and somewhat consistent issue within Mexico. But her family had quite a group of friends there in their hometown as well as in the US, and they always had each other's backs.

Laetitia, who had been fourteen at the time that they had left, had begun her schooling many years before along the southern border of Chihuahua's city with a substantial class of students when she was young, but had realized all too subtly as the years went by, how the number of students dwindled quite substantially. Many had died, moved, or had quite simply joined the cartels to save their skins. Nevertheless, those left behind were united in so many ways and given a chance, they would fight back to protect their families in every possible way, against the cartels. Losing family, nevertheless, meant rearing more children in the hopes of passing on honor and legacy through them—

maybe one or two would grow up to have a family of their own for many of the same reasons.

The life expectancy of anyone who joined in this ideological and murderous charade was a very short one from the start. The threat was often, "take the money or take the bullet," and the money was the hook toward corruption, blackmail, and something that could have been compared to a terminal disease. Although, the more brutal they were, the more assured their success seemed to be, for a time, until they too had their light extinguished by someone who had swayed their hearts more their way to gain their seat of power. Different waves of cartels would come in, and each one more powerful than the next, or seeking to establish their dominance, and as such many would die in a deadly swath of "points being made."

If you wanted to succeed, you had to be tough as nails, smart, and ruthless, if you weren't you would die much sooner. There was no time for mercy, kindness, shared respect, or forged alliances because you never knew who you could trust. Sometimes the only ones you could trust were family and hopefully long-time neighbors, but sometimes you couldn't even trust them. Economics-wise, drugs were illegal in the US, and as everybody knew, the black market drove up the value of unlawful commodities, of which a whole host of drugs and their sub-variants were near priceless amongst the groups of youth who were vulnerable and lacked any goals based in ethics but instead were awash in numbing agents for all of the woes they had conjured up in their minds. All that they purchased came with a price, and with any sort of contraband enforcers, hitmen, mercenaries, and those passionate for power by any means were in plentiful supply, with many others that were much less lucky left dead and dismembered in their violent and depraved wake. There was a lot of money to be made for those lucky few at the top—for quite a substantial price. Usually, that price was the cost of your humanity in all ways that mattered.

Trying to raise an honest family in any cartel-rich part of Mexico came with constant sorrow, a lot of wits to outsmart the outlaws, or laying low and under their radar with plenty of long-suffering. On the farm, most of the Zemani's home was hidden away underground for hiding, ricochet from inopportune bullets, and the hope of living in peace.

In most cases, the Zemanis had been indeed left alone. For fourteen years, Laetitia had grown up without any issues that impacted her immediate family. She had been going to school and spending time with fellow students, listening to their concerns and tragedies for a while, and it was commonplace to hear about and eventually experience in her own way the fact that for everyone she knew, there was a near and dear family member or relative who had been brutally murdered by one faction or the other of the cartels. Several who she knew, had family members who, due to survival instincts that ruled their ethics, were a part of or were linked to the cartels. Still, she had hope that one day they would see the error of their ways and turn around. It wasn't until her brother had died that she had felt a deep wound within.

Nevertheless, she kept her mouth shut; her eyes were opened in a very unsuspecting manner, and she listened to everyone and everything. Laetitia lost one of her two older brothers to violence, after one prominent criminal organization stormed their ranch looking for volunteers or a life, or perhaps one of each, and found no one else ready to surrender their soul for the sake of survival. Her brother was noble. He had wanted to become a lawyer and was halfway through his remote law school studies when the tide had changed for the family. He had been targeted by a fellow student, named Carlos, nicknamed "El Gemelo" who had joined the cartel and sought potential "Johnnydo-gooders," to either recruit or kill. After killing her brother and before leaving the ranch, Los Wiskis assured the family they would be back.

Not long after the murderers had left, Laetitia's father gathered the family and they escaped to the US, to live in peace. Four years later, they were discovered and exposed by the law-abiding neighbors who had immigrated legally and saw no reason why their neighbor couldn't have either and reported them to the authorities. The Zemani family had grown rather fond of their neighbors, and they had felt a shared bond, but little did they know that from day one the neighbors had been plotting, scheming, and waiting for the right moment to do their due as law-abiding citizens. Their neighbors had also been connected to the "nice couple" in Europe and several of the cartels, and in particular Los Wiskis, for quite some time, and were thus able to afford to come to the US legally.

The plan was to send the family back to Mexico, and through their connections with the cartels, the Zemani's oldest living son, Tito, who was now twenty and pursuing a degree in biogerontology, would be recruited or killed to make a point, and they would be handsomely rewarded. Their daughter, Laetitia, who was now eighteen, would be taken and shipped to a brothel in Eastern Europe for the entertainment of the wealthy with malevolent intentions, and their neighbors would be rewarded monetarily yet again. Their neighbors stood to make quite a bit of money and were promised continuous anonymity.

El Gemelo, whose mission it was to recruit or kill the Zemani's eldest living son, also happened to know the "nice" couple in Europe. He had point-blank executed Laetitia's eldest brother in front of the Zemani's eyes, yet, as it turned out, his murderer had also been involved in the human trafficking trade too. Upon successful collusion with the Zemani's neighbors and their successfully forced return to Mexico, he awaited them to make a brutal point of Tito and sell Laetitia to the highest bidder, who happened to live in Eastern Europe. Although, as it stood, Andres' murderer had recently found some difficulty in contacting the "nice couple."

For the Zemanis, after settling down in the US, with four years of peace, obtaining an education, employment, paying taxes, and finding a plausible hope for the future, the family couldn't have been more grateful. What followed, however, were a series of very bad days.

Without notice, the police had shown up with an anti-immigration agent, put them in handcuffs, forced them into their vehicles without question or answer, and took them to see the representatives of the various government agencies working congruently with Mexican authorities to return them to their home of residence just south of Chihuahua. The anti-illegal immigration policies in the United States had played right into the machinations of the cartels and the trafficking-in-persons networks, and there was nothing the Zemanis could do to prove or do anything about it.

A life of peace, of dreams of a better and more promising future, was torn asunder. Without legal representatives to support their cause, they had pretty much been mute while still in the US. After legal proceedings the family was returned to their home in Chihuahua, which in their absence, they discovered, had been mysteriously maintained, and where they had some speculation but no idea nonetheless that the cartels awaited them, to make examples of them. Oh, El Gemelo and Los Wiskis would wait a few days or maybe a week or two and let them experience a sense of hope before they tore them down, but they were always nearby, planning, scheming, looking to get rich or show their strength over innocent people in any way, and after all just like any bureaucracy they needed their numbers. To them, the Zemanis weren't people; they were instruments of their own malicious whims. They did not care about life, longevity, the Universe, or anything of the sort. These monsters were evil to the core, and they were very smart in all ways of malevolence. And, Laetitia had a strong hunch about all of this, but little means to prove it. Instead, all she could do was to love her family and finish her studies.

After the whirlwind of bad luck, the Zemanis finally felt at ease in their homes and Laetitia returned for her first day back to school near home since they had left for the US. Because of all the moving and trauma, she had been held back a grade, so she could absorb the information. On her second day at school, it hit her with so much clarity, that the individual who had killed her brother had been following her from class to class, just behind each corner, and with no doubt the worst of intentions. Still, she would get home as fast as she could and when she did, she let her Father know why. Finally, on the third day, he followed her home and as luck would have it, a group of vehicles appeared surrounding their home. Her father gathered her mother, Tito, and Laetitia, took them downstairs, locked the hidden door, and when everyone was settled and comfortably hidden, he turned out the downstairs lights.

As soon as the lights flickered out, the family heard the familiar voice of El Gemelo on a megaphone. He told them that if they did not abandon their home within ten minutes, every person within the home would be executed.

Laetitia's father looked toward the family and wrote a short note in silence and showed it with the light of a small match, "No les confíen nada. Quedamos aquí y no les decimos nada. Si vamos a morir prefiero que estuviéramos juntos."

The family defiantly said not a word. Where they were hidden it would take a while to get to and they were protected by ten feet of dirt and three-inch steel doors. It would take a while, but they wouldn't have enough ammunition to get through and the chainsaws they were using to chop up the outer corners of their home wouldn't be able to penetrate the entryway nor the shell that encapsulated them.

Laetitia could pick up on the locations of fifteen distinct machine guns and four chainsaws, and the separate voice of El Gemelo on the megaphone counting down every minute. There she was, with all the reason to fear for her life, but she hugged her second oldest brother, her father, and her mother. If today was the day, at least they'd be together and go out in a manner of their own choosing.

Sudden sounds began to penetrate her ears as if a fire had been lit through the sounds of the chainsaws followed by both the shooting of bullets and that of rocket-propelled grenades. They were setting the house ablaze, planning to smoke them out, and then execute them either on sight or in the most brutal way possible, and then leave the scene for the capital city and their friends to see the pitiless points they had made.

What the cartel did not notice as the smoke rose to heights beyond their view, was a cloud of nanos descending ever so smoothly, as though against the current, yet no particle of smoke touched or swayed the nanos or vice versa. As the nanos poured into the Zemani's hiding place, her entire family thought it was white smoke, and that soon they would asphyxiate due to the smoke infiltrating their home. It had only been four minutes, but the sounds of the guns, grenade launchers, and chainsaws seemed to grow more distant, but they had chosen their own fate in their own manner and had no desire to surrender their manner of death to the cartels, instead they would numb out the world as they died from the smoke. The cartels had no right to determine their demise, nor did they have any power over the Zemanis. The cartels and every member of them were an unfortunate mob of individuals, each of whom was lost in a swath of a desire for survival, acceptance, power, and greed.

Laetitia hugged her mother, her brother, and her father, and then they all stood together with their backs to the farthest wall and their faces toward the white smoke as it gathered before them. Perhaps the air pressure would not allow the white misty, almost glowing smoke to reach them; perhaps they could survive by making the cartel think they had died of smoke inhalation.

The smoke stopped several feet in front of them and began to dissipate into what looked like a large, white, glowing donut with purple, blue, and black accent colors on the buttons and digital displays. As if with magic, a beautiful woman with white-blonde hair and iridescent highlights, with eyes so unique they were a mixture of crystalline, blonde and iridescent colors and thick black limbal rings, a suit that was form fitting, glowingly white with trim that matched her highlights, and enough exposed skin on the left side of her body to reveal a toe-to-neck body tattoo with a white and iridescent mixture of henna, mandala patterns, and a kaleidoscope of memories. They watched as she walked through this gateway from nowhere.

"Venid conmigo," she said, as she reached out her hand with a gesture to follow her. Without thinking twice, they followed her through this portal. Twenty more seconds had passed. Once they had, they saw that they were now in a very different place. This was more alluring and more beautiful than they could ever have imagined. They happened to be on what appeared to be the peak of a large one mountain island, surrounded by a large, yet clear and crystalline structure in the waters beyond the land. As they looked around, they saw about a thousand women that looked very similar to her, yet each with an ever so slightly different and unique hairstyle, hair color, and arrangement of highlights and artwork. All of whom were just as glowing and beautiful as the next.

"Priméramente, gracias por salvar nuestras vidas," Laetitia coughed, perhaps clearing the smoke from her lungs as her body adjusted to the beautiful and pleasantly aromatic ambiance, "but, where are we and who are you?" She realized instantly that she could speak English as if it were her first language. She looked, and it appeared that her family had understood too.

"I am Sky Taylor, and these are my daughters. We haven't much time before we need to return, but first, please follow me. We have some training to do. I'll answer your first question soon. Soon a fraction of time will give you a wealth of time."

They followed her to a plateau on the side of the mountain with enough area to carry walkways to what seemed like several thousand glowing white tanning booths. "These are biopods. Normally, I would take the time to tell you what they are, but please trust me, climb in one per person, say 'Link 1, 2, 3, 5 minutes, 20 years.'"

Given the seemingly miraculous nature of all that they beheld, twenty more seconds passed by and as if in unison each of the four Zemanis climbed into their own biopod and uttered the shared command. Suddenly, they felt every nerve twitch, tickle, and stand on end. They then felt almost every synapse, cell, and particle in their bodies reach a state of euphoria. Then like that, they saw each other as they stood near a statue of an angel overlooking a pond filled with coy fish and frogs, being fed by a waterfall created by the angel's cupped hands and surrounded by flowers, walkways, trees, and a beautiful structure off to the distance.

"Mom and Dad, you look like you are twenty-two, and so beautiful and handsome again!" They perceived each other's thoughts, as Laetitia explained mind to mind everything she knew about the cartels. She had been there unable to do a thing about it when her oldest brother was killed. Now the cartels were after her other sweet brother as well as the entire family. Her brother looked twenty-two as well, and apparently so did Laetitia, *"Is twenty-two the default age in here?"*

"Not necessarily, but you have each apparently experienced so many traumatic histories together that your microbiome and your right brain have expressed twenty-two as your optimal age. In here, you will find that each of you has been healed and optimized to full capacity, both physiologically and neurologically. Once you have been optimized to full capacity, you will have the choice of expressing yourself anywhere

between the ages of twenty to thirty-five, or older, as needed. In the period of five minutes in the real world, you'll gain twenty years' worth of experiences if not more, here in the Virtual Universe. I brought you here because through a chain of mental networks of some very surly individuals it came to my attention that you did not have much time before you would have died.

"I know, you would ask why I wasn't here four years ago, but I am only several months old, and my daughters are only one month old. They are nearly an exact replica of me in all ways that matter. I saw the need to heal the world, but there was only one of me, so I created a thousand more. Ultimately, we're here to see to it that the Principles of Universal Ethics are understood to the degree of allowance for personal motivation to observe them, with clarity on how to contribute to the advancement of civilization through healing and not harming. There is a lot you can do here, so let me give you some training and a tour, and then you are free to do as you please."

The Zemanis learned about Eliza Williams, her biography, the many creations, inventions, and achievements she shared as she built Pathway from the ground up, enlisting the aid of Yesha, James, and their ever-growing crews. Their crews had grown to more than two-billion people. She then took them to the core of the Earth, the Moon, the Sun, and every spheroid throughout the Solar System. The moons were terraformed, shielded, and much more, and each tech city was beautiful in so many ways, unique in the loveliest of ways, and blended well in contrast to the environments surrounding them.

After showing them all of Eliza's and Pathway's developments and inventions, and after training them on their new abilities, she allowed them to absorb the knowledge and experience of more than a dozen PhDs each, every style of martial arts, and the neural link of all who had been to and experienced the Virtual Universe before. The beautiful flavor of each thought, experience, and memory unique to theirs was exquisite in every possible way. Gone was their manner of linear thought and omnipresent was their ability for exponential thought and wisdom. It was incomparably amazing, the beauty of collective memories and shared wisdom, combined with their own unique and beautiful individuality.

Finally, they shared with each other their fears, their hopes, and their dreams, realizing how much they loved each other. Each of the Zemanis grew closer and with a heroic bond that they never thought could be shared. After what seemed like twenty years had passed by, they looked to Sky and said, *"We're ready."*

Like that, they woke up on Sky's Island, felt more alive than they ever had before, and listened to Sky with clarity in their own minds as to how they would contribute to the efforts of healing, and not harming. "Follow me. We have twenty seconds, but as we go, I will speak. First, we will need to return to your house which is still on fire, and the difference between the norm is we will be able to approach each cartel member, look them in the eyes without suffering from bullets, grenades, or whatever they throw at us, see them for the lost boys that they are, and when it is safe for them, we will render them unconscious.

"Looking into your mind, Laetitia, you are correct. There are twenty people outside your home, so we will bring fifteen of my daughters with us, bring the twenty cartel members here, take them to the biopods, and meet them in the Virtual Universe. From there, they will experience every aspect of pain they have caused to others, be quickened with compassion, and healed both physiologically and neurologically to the point of which they will have clarity on how to help in the advancement of civilization. There will be so much more, but they will each be left with my symbol on their right buttock cheek. This is a marker that will serve as a protection, so they will be available for judgment and penance later. This will provide the victims and their families the appropriate vindication, and ultimately allow them to learn more profoundly the lessons of civilizations past, the error of their ways, and a new path they can take in life. Your land is one of promise, as is any land with the hallmark of love, beauty, and kindness written into its people and their love of life.

"Come."

The Zemanis followed Sky and fifteen of her daughters back through the portal or the jump gate, and as they learned, the ten minutes the cartel had taunted them with had reached its finality. They could hear El Gemelo on his megaphone again, but they ignored him as they walked through the fire, the barrage of bullets and grenades, and spread out as planned and coordinated with their neural links. Due to their optimizations, wherein they were given upgrades with smart suits and invisible shielding that allowed the bullets to ricochet off their bodies they were also unweathered by fire or shrapnel. They forged through the bombardment, walked up to each of the cartel members and at the time that was safest for each killer they simultaneously rendered each one unconscious and carried them over their backs.

From there, they followed Sky's lead, walked back through a jump gate that appeared just outside of the Zemani residence, and placed each of the twenty, including El Gemelo, in separate biopods that were pre-programmed to take them to the Virtual Universe. It was time for immediate correction and training. Their lives as they were, were spent anyway for all of their barbarity and untamed ruthlessness, so doing what Sky was doing based on the Principles of Universal Ethics, which governed her very own island of her own creation, was within complete reason, and like it or not these murderers, extortionists, and thieves were about to be healed—this was the ethical equation, no matter how public society would try to manipulate it.

In the span of twenty real-world minutes, the Zemanis, Sky, and her daughters took each cartel member separately through several centuries of life, trials, and experiences all designed to work with the unique psyche of each person and give them the set of trials necessary for personal development, reparations, and healthy cognition. Each experience was designed to provide maximum enrichment with the purpose of increasing their wisdom, their empathy, and healing the neurological misfires that had caused them to unleash their violence, barbarity, and vile machinations with little regard for anyone else with little impunity. The result for each individual would be an increase in neurological capacities toward compassion, kindness, desire for the well-being of others, and the clarity of mind to contribute to the advancement of civilization, in the spirit of healing, rather than harming.

Despite the miracles the Zemanis beheld that day as they witnessed Sky's daughters' coach, teach, mentor, and sculpt each cartel member into honorable men, they knew at the heart of it all was science and Eliza's ability to multiply upon capacity the greatest talent one could ever receive—the mind. Each malcontent was put into situations where they endured many years of long-suffering, learning, love and loss, and experienced many centuries worth of experiences, wisdom, and personal need for compassion. When near completion, Sky Taylor looked upon Laetitia and thanked her for being so wise, despite her youth. Much of the success that day and in the days that followed was because of what Laetitia had quietly stored in her mind until the time was right. And oh, the time had been overwhelmingly perfect for that compartmentalized release of information.

In the space of twenty minutes, each of these lost individuals had unleashed what could have been untold brutality yet they were found again. Gone was the desire to hurt, harm, maim, or kill. Now, in the place of those destructive desires was the intent and clarity for healing the minds and bodies of all they knew. They apologized to Laetitia for treating her as an object and thanked her for having such a strong mind. They then told the entire family that no matter the quantity of service they could hope to provide, they knew there would never be a day where their efforts would suffice as full payment. Instead, they all got down on their knees, admitted that they were indebted to humanity, pledged to listen, to be of service, and to help the mission of Pathway to advance and succeed.

Sky left her mark upon them, to serve as a reminder. She then gave the healed and optimized individuals who had done so much to hurt others their first instructions, "I have given each of you, no matter your past, similar abilities to mine, you are now my 20 sons, I have sculpted your physique into perfection, mentored each one of you through my daughters, and trained each of you to be better than you ever were before. Your first set of orders will be to do likewise to every other cartel member you know, every person they know, and to expand out as far as you can to heal rather than harm. While you do, I would exhort you to also optimize and heal every victim and their families. Within each of your minds is the ability to link, and through that ability, you can call upon an army of nanos, build a jump gate, and bring all of those who need training to my island, where they can enter the biopods to be healed in every possible way.

"I must go. I have many other places I need to be where misery and suffering seems endless, so it is yours to follow the lead of the Zemanis and heal rather than harm those around you.

"Your second set of orders will be to lift your own societies up, build universities and work centers, as well as beautiful landscapes, advance in innovations and ingenuity, and then seek further guidance from Pathway management hierarchy James Cooper. Stay strong, my sons, and listen as you heal."

With that, she turned to her new sons and the Zemanis and hugged every person, and then each person awoke in their own beds that following morning, with a complete clarity as to what to do. Things were about to change, and the state of Chihuahua was about to become a paradise filled with several luxurious tech cities of its own, with rapidly maturing and lovely blue agave in abundance.

For now, Laetitia returned to her own row of agave, where each succulent cactus had blossomed two years beyond its prime. She was saddened a little, but then realized she should try to harvest them anyway. Then she applied what she had learned and invented while in the Virtual Universe. While there, she had developed a new strain of agave that could be harvested once a month. The revenue would be such that all employed to help would be compensated well, even with a two-month break provided each year. The nectar of the crop was many times sweeter and ten times more potent than anything else on the market, such that a few drops in a large vat of water would render better results than the entire harvest of any other agave farmer. Laetitia then received her first assignment from James Cooper, where she integrated with agave farmers in Sonora to heal rather than harm the people who were suffering there too.

A Hidden Island

Sky, her daughters, and her sons worked as one throughout the World, staying linked, preventing further devastation while doing their work simultaneously. On occasion, one of her daughters or sons would find herself or himself attracted to a young man or young woman, and they would leave a special image of themselves in their mind that would resurface whenever that individual slept. In their noble and Universally Ethical pursuits, they worked both on land and both above and below the sea. They travelled and healed, optimized, and converted many through Central and South America, the Middle East, India, all of Asia, Indonesia, the Philippines, Australia, New Zealand, the islands of the

South and North Pacific and Atlantic, Russia, Europe, and Africa with her one-thousand daughters and one-thousand-one sons throughout the many places where men, women, and children who suffered from the brutality and surly natured apathy of the worst in some of the greatest potential societies worldwide, would no longer do so.

As always, when she and her daughters were done with their healing, they would then leave their mark—an image of a glowing white and iridescent angel with wings in their minds and a tattoo of an iridescent scorpion on their right buttock cheek, which would serve as a future payment of vindication for anyone who they had harmed or if they had left scars on the bodies and minds of others. When Sky and her daughters were done with one rescue, they would slip away, and then do this to each person in each village, county, or city, as well as home by home, community by community, town by town, and within any population center of any sort as the network of minds guided them. They would linger long enough to ensure a safe transition of each community from oppression to joy and illumination.

As one of mind, they were in essence Sky Taylor, yet each with names and identities of their own, yet as such, they were humble, powerful, and amazing, and they attributed all of their work to Sky. As such, while their work was being done throughout Earth, prior to their future missions aboard the IMC Spacecraft, they would work in concert, and all who saw Sky or one of her daughters, recalled Sky within their waking reality, and an image of her unique and beautiful daughters would surface in dreams, if the individual they were healing made an extra special impression upon them. As such, and thus as one, Sky would make certain that the goals that were made and the plans that were developed were done in a manner that resulted in the creation of environments where societies could be enabled to ready themselves by way of building universities for both men and women alike, no matter the social status. Once a city was sufficiently built up, it would network with Pathway and become an additional tech city, yet with sovereignty based on the laws of the land they lived in, so long as those laws were founded in true and Universal Ethics.

Each of the schools that were built would benefit all minds and provide safety from any form of harm and refuge from any sort of injustice or unkindness. These universities would each be a new shrine toward progress for the future and joy from within the mind, the heart, and the soul. The tech cities would arise from the most desolate of locations, and gone would be the chaos, the destruction, the greed, the slander, the lies, the misery, and the suffering, and instead human and beast would witness together the growth of beautiful forests, jungles, and the changes that took place in locations once devoid of love, communication, understanding, kindness, compassion, and ingenuity. Predation would be gone, and shared bounty and joy would abound in its stead.

Areas once affected by brutality and threats of death for non-compliance were healed. Greed, corruption, and showings of power dwindled as societies of forgiveness, kindness, innovation, and compassion arose to take hold and amplify the joy in the hearts of all who cared deeply enough to embrace others and raise the quality of life for those around them as well as themselves. Care and love were a shared reality and not one of brutality or loneliness.

Religious wardrobe and efforts were no longer a threat, but an honor and a joy to share with others. Artistic, social, and cultural uniqueness was embraced, so long as consent, personal choice, and individual freedoms were respected, and in the places that Sky had visited, this was the case. Wearing cultural garments and exercising personal freedom for each individual, of unique and free expression, through laughter, joy, and inspiration on a daily basis was suddenly recognized as a personal and respected choice, and religious garb was only used in a utilitarian manner or as individually deemed fit.

No one was any longer required to wear clothes based on mandate, but rather they worked with some of the greatest stylists humanity had known, both optimized-mind stylists with compartmentalized neurological applications to share and sell, and real-resource stylists, with stores and factories with goods to sell, all to wear garments rich in embroidery, design, and the kind of sculpted beauty that magnified their natural beauty as afforded them through their journeys through the real and Virtual Universes. Many with traditional clothing were given clarity as to its history, its original purpose, and had a quick realization that in some desert regions throughout the world, certain clothing had been developed with the intent of protecting their skin from the Sun's radiation, from too much heat, and from painful burns, and thus was no longer required, but enjoyed as a means of celebration of individuality.

Non-pollutant vehicles roamed the roads and highways, travel of choice was applauded, and animals were protected no matter the highway or road, now surrounded by bridges, jump gates, portals, lush flowers, greenery, and sentient creatures of every kind, where once there had been a sandy abyss. Beautiful buildings with waterfalls and flowery and fruitful flora abounded in plenitude, and the reshaping of the land in and around each piece of infrastructure was surrounded with uniqueness, beauty, and imagination, which combed the landscape. Air conditioning was more decentralized to provide ideal environments for each individual based on need. With optimizations and proper shielding around Earth's Orbital Rotation around the Sun, people were now far and away from the dangers of too much sun, sunblock was available to protect the skin of those who had elected to not receive optimizations, but it was not needed anyway, yet used because the coconut scent had been discovered to be one of many sources of enlightenment. Thus, religious clothing was no longer considered practical.

The deserts were now lush and full of flora and fauna, all sentient and embracing a shared existence of joy. Hurricanes no longer blew in from the Atlantic to the Gulf of Mexico or from any other desert region to the shores of any other nation. The weather was tamed, yet still shared the life-giving qualities of a healthy atmosphere. Volcanoes were now controlled to eliminate death tolls previously existent within Nature and throughout humanity, as was seismic activity, and the control of moisture in the air, which eliminated wildfires. The redwood and evergreen trees were optimized to open their seeds without fire, and as needed.

Throughout South America, Central America, the Middle East, Africa, North Korea, Venezuela, Russia, China, and many other places throughout the world once stricken with pain, suffering, loss, and need, both women and men alike, young and old, were now gifted with youth, healed and unbroken, and they again felt a sense of ease and joy as the kindness and compassion of the brutes in their societies and in their lives proved honorable through the new Universal Law of Consent and the Principles of Universal Ethics. Together they developed complexed systems to clean the plastic and debris from the seas and oceans and all over the World.

Art bloomed; music was shared in the streets of every variety. The buildings and the beaches were filled with bikini-clad beauties and beautiful men, women, and all manner of people who were in-turn filled with content toward the awesomeness of life. Each individual in each village, town, district, state, and country all were now fearless of the anger, hatred, and malice of men that once permeated their lands and were filled with gratitude for the dazzling presence they'd been gifted with.

Sciences were expounded upon, longevity and the mysteries of the Universe were taught in the schools, and innovations and advancements toward a promising legacy were proliferated galore. All these advancements allowed the starving, the thirsty, the sick, and the weary to be healed, fed and involved. Families, friends, and leaders in every aspect of life had worked together to integrate joy into the successes of their young and newly regenerating societies.

Throughout the world, fears of terrorism and ruthless regimes began to diminish, and people began to see with clarity the things they had in common and the insurmountable power they had, together. If there were differences, they worked them out and, in many cases, their differences were honored; they were even celebrated and shared. Cultures, traditions, and nations distinguished each difference as the beautiful spice of life—the various ways of linking neurologically and peering back in time caused hearts to unite and appreciate the fullness of history. Multitudes of people throughout the world began to share the many powerful emotions there were to share as they looked back upon the many unfortunate losses and wounds caused by misunderstandings, a lack of vision, and even corruption. Corruptions, confusions, and follies were vindicated, and trespassers were forgiven. Kindness oozed from the hearts of men, women, and children. Productivity, constructive behavior, and compassion ruled the day. Everywhere once riddled with pain and suffering and desolation, now had tech cities, beaches, shores, sports, arts, music, romances, and stories, each celebrating the unique and competitive spirit of culture and individuality. Each tech city was beautiful in its own unique way.

As Sky and her thousand daughters and thousand sons did their work, they were pleased, humbled and fulfilled. She had created and reared her one thousand young ladies in her image and on her beautifully fashioned publicly invisible high-tech island. She had done so, and the island, born from a controlled volcano she had formed far away from any other region of land, lie in the Pacific somewhat north of the equator. Her daughters were just like her, yet still unique, in every skin and hair color existent, and they had all been trained, loved, and led by Sky, and likewise were her sons, handsome, compassionate, strong, and kind. She had led the effort to afford efficiency, quality, and uniqueness of experiences, and in doing so, had traversed the world and healed it. She looked upon her results, with Yesha looking toward her in the Virtual Universe, hovering above the lush couch in Eliza's estate home, and she was content. Together, her daughters and sons had understood what needed to be done, had approved of their results of the grand healing, and had worked enthusiastically to share with Sky in doing the work she felt was necessary to preserve humanity.

After everything was complete and prior to retiring to the Virtual Universe, herself, Sky and her daughters and sons took the time to look upon the fruits of their collective labors, to meditate, and then to smile upon all of it, and Sky was pleased. Her luminescent mind could hear the whisperings of wives and significant others as her iridescent scorpion tattoos were discovered, and for once she smiled and even giggled an angelic laugh. These markings served a purpose, and as humorous as they were, there was more depth to them than simple snorts of laughter. The experiences she and her daughters went through played out above her head and in the clouds, yet they were visible and were witnessed by Joanne each day, and likewise by Yesha. Today Yesha observed and experienced it all at once within the Virtual Universe and inside Eliza's estate home. A purpose and action with meaning had been shared by more than fifty percent of the world's public population.

"Let's heal, not harm," was Sky's motto, and deep within her powerful mind, she knew it was a necessary connection that meant an ideal that lent to worthiness to span the Universe.

Sky learned of the moniker she had earned—she embraced the fact that she was the Iridescent Scorpion. To many more, however, throughout the many places both she and her daughters, who looked like her twins in many ways, as well as her sons who were brilliant and beautiful in so many ways as well, each with unique and small identifiers in the variety of highlights of their unique and angelic hair, visited the suffering and the fearing of the people. The people they visited rejoiced as now, with clarity of mind and vigor with purpose. They were now healed, the damage dissipated, and the people found new hope and clarity in life itself.

Love cleared away all the anguish that had once existed amongst the masses, and kindness and pleasant "hellos" replaced the misery shared by many more. Instead, shared memories of Iridescent Angels permeated their minds. Sky too saw herself as an Angel, yet she appreciated the moniker and didn't mind being called the Iridescent Scorpion. Not once was she, nor were her daughters or sons, touched if they did not desire it, and as such, not a single soul they had encountered had died, due to their amazing capabilities, their omnidirectional sight, and invisibility. Men and women who had once given way to their brutal nature were now marked with both angelic thoughts and a tattoo as a reminder, and the kind, yet broken men, women, and children were left with a short and beautiful memory of her Virtual Universe persona. The persona that was that of a gloriously winged Iridescent Angel.

The thirst for learning was quenched each day by further learning. Throughout the world there seemed to grow an interesting unity, lush growths of forests and jungles, and tech cities that became the envy of all other locations throughout the world. Just as Sky, through her own actions and through the actions of her daughters and sons, they left each individual with the memory of an angel. Sky rejoiced as the amazing people whose lives had been touched also reached out and provided clarity to purpose in the lives of those around them. Sky had left each person an entrenched memory of Eliza Williams, one that brought home the many moments of when Eliza had meditated. They saw as Sky wept for the suffering of humanity—both physically and emotionally. She and her daughters and sons labored diligently to unite the greatest of minds with the wealthiest of minds to help preserve life and optimize humanity and its darling friends. They did this, so they could take a renewed and honorable civilization, prepare it to heal the Universe, and then go on that journey through the Cosmos on many quests to bring life to the Universe and the civilizations likewise suffering within it, with benevolent, compassionate, and peaceful environments, while also preserving the home world, its Sun, as well as its Solar System. They would do so while respecting and sharing the Universe with so many other civilizations that were in-turn worthy of preservation as well.

With this clarity, the people the world over began to become interested in the political outcome of Eliza's home country. United, they had a shared hope that Eliza would win the Presidential election in the US, in a land beyond the borders, or far, far, and away, to bring together the policies, the sciences, and the means with which to bring about this amazing future.

Once she had finished with her quiet and benevolent mission, Sky Taylor returned home to Eliza's estate in Massachusetts to rest for a while in the Virtual Universe, while her daughters and sons retired on their distant island, taking turns with half of them sleeping within their biopods, while the other half guarded them, and then they would switch rhythmically until called upon again. They each did this to let the inevitable story that would occur due to the seeds they had planted unfold and be recorded in the Virtual Universe. Yes, there would be much more for Sky and her daughters and sons to do, but for now, they would let seeds of promise germinate and grow.

After witnessing each of Sky's missions, Yesha was moved, and likewise, after viewing the same on each day over the last year, Joanne was very intrigued by Sky's motivations. Joanne talked with Yesha often, and they both witnessed and then shared with everyone else in Pathway how the world would now be better off if the most positively influential and kindest governments in the history of humanity throughout the world was led by someone who was benevolent, like Eliza, not in a religious sense, but in a manner that suggested that well-being rather than greed and lust for power or displaying their superiority ought to be what drives decisions.

Sky was a very methodical individual and very capable in every way that mattered on Earth and throughout the Solar System, so she used her abilities to reduce misery, suffering, and violence, and increase the health of the body, of the mind, and of the innovations founded upon preservation of life, of civilization, and of a worthy legacy. Sky Taylor saw that Eliza, Yesha, James, Amber, Vesha, Erin, Joanne, and many more within Pathway had that ability to do what was benevolent and with intentions that were noble, so she enabled an environment that would usher in the promise of shared, yet earned, prosperity.

She then left the Virtual Universe, went to Joanne, to take her to her hometown with Erin Carter.

Chapter 26: Individual and Collective

Database Moon Archive, Celestial-Sol Date: 2023 May 19. Erin Carter and Joanne Gallant, Pathway President and VP, summarize their personal maintenance experiences with Sky Taylor, as Sky helps the new Pathway leadership overcome a critical issue that could negatively impact the future of Humanity over the course of several millennia. These memories are from Sky, Erin, and Joanne, as recorded within the Virtual Universe and interfaced within Pathway Melrose Campus. Input by Erin Carter, President of Pathway, 2022-2029.

It was Tuesday, May 9th of 2023; she was on her way to her parent's home, after being away for quite some time, and notwithstanding optimizations, her experiences, or her vast learning, she was feeling as nervous as she could be. Accompanied by Erin, Joanne looked at her, they exchanged smiles of both nerves and enjoyment of the walk they were on and then they both looked at Sky Taylor and said "thank you" often. Not out of the blue, but because Sky was kind of cool and did cool things, and with both Joanne's and Erin's best interests continuously in mind.

Typically, at least throughout her year-long mission phase, Sky and her daughters and sons had visited people in their sleep, or before something horrendous was about to happen to prevent it.

The social networking complexity of the mind can be quite elaborate and at times quite cumbersome, especially when taking down entire networks of criminals. No matter, advanced systems that disguised the voice or any type of material designed to hide someone's identity was useless against Sky and her daughters and sons; they could see humanity at every conceivable level.

With that knowledge, they would travel all over and around the world to quickly resolve issues throughout multiple villages, towns, and many cities in one night, and had perfected their abilities and skills and learned new ones through the process. Over the course of the last year they had healed four billion human bodies, minds, countless creatures, and many complexed environments affecting many more worldwide.

In contrast, now she had scheduled an entire week to spend with the President and Vice President of Pathway Industries, to take things in stride, and in a somewhat leisure manner. Both strategic and tactical, Sky had a knack for getting to the core of any problem, finding the solution, and healing wounds, physiological, neurological, and environmental.

When previously she had solved so many issues with so many lives to their core in a very short period of time, now she would work things out with two people during the space of a week. By doing so, she would reduce the chaotic and destructive course that Pathway was beginning to manifest and would use time's ability to impact so many more in a positive way.

By creating a neural link to seven billion people, and by being a bell-weather for the preservation of life, Sky had run through all of the possible outcomes to near perfection and concluded that she would only need to meet with about seventy people to guide them through a unique experience, to set in place what was necessary for big changes in the future. Part of that group of people included Erin and Joanne, on this special occasion. Sky felt honored.

Both Erin and Joanne, despite unspoken motives, found themselves simply lucky to be able to chill with her, like besties, walking through memories and seeing all that Sky could do, right before their eyes. Joanne was amazed at Sky's tranquil demeanor, her immense intellect, her kindness, her grace, her movements, and her ability to transform her appearance or her surrounding area into anything essential to get any job she deemed necessary done.

On this occasion, it was about one o'clock in the afternoon, they had been walking since morning with occasional stops along the way, were northbound on a humble highway, Sky was wearing a T-shirt and jeans, and she looked like a twenty-two-year-old blonde knock out with piggy tails. Other than that, and the miraculous changes she was bringing to Joanne's hometown, there was nothing peculiarly unique about her appearance both today and yesterday, which was unusual for Sky.

Earlier the day before, Sky had used her skills to teleport to South Otselic, New York, before returning to retrieve Erin and Joanne. She had combed the minds of the citizens of the area within a three-mile radius with her mind gathering only the most pertinent info. With that, she had taken what she learned and donned a wardrobe with the appearance of, and practiced similar mannerisms very much like, any one of the town's local one thousand or so population.

Sky then reserved a room for three for a week at the Broadlawn's Bed & Breakfast, just off Highway 26, in the state of New York, which ran north-northeast to the scene of the crime that had been affecting Joanne and the rest of Pathway as a result, and in a both chronic and acute manner, for the last four years.

Of course, there were many reasons why members of Pathway had been experiencing an increase in a nano-caused glow and subsequent nervousness, and she was pretty sure why it all was happening. Originally, this had been a publicly undetectable phenomenon, at least back in late 2007, when Eliza and Yesha had each climbed into one of their first three biopods for the very first time. It was one thing when the glow was occasion-pertinent or personality-driven, but it was something else if the glow was chronic and increasing in lumens to the point of unintended noticeability by the public, and she intended to set up a clear personal maintenance system to make available to anyone affected through choice or through the correctional system, situation depending. For now, it was nice to have unaffected individuals to go off of when it came to physiology, neurology, and their mutual effects on each other, but sooner or later they would need a nearly fool-proof method for personal maintenance, in the event everyone elected to become optimized in every way. Preservation of life, the quality of it, and clarity of mind were the basics, and it was her mission to get Pathway back on track.

Still, Sky needed to start at the top echelons of Pathway in order to identify and find a remedy to the causes for the chronic glow, which was an indication of issues that needed to be resolved. Sky had noticed this over the last year, ever since she had been brought up online. Each issue was becoming a potential risk way off and into the future but had thus far caused no immediate risk or danger. It was a very far-ranging cycle and the result that she was focused on. She knew that these issues would reveal themselves in the future to the very individuals she was working with. She also knew her upgrades to the Virtual Universe and Correctional Matrix would involve these experiences, dealing with the anomalies that would negatively impact that future. She would help humanity to build a self-maintenance system of healing while providing them with more clarity through proper exposure to the ideal environmental factors providing the necessary changes and adjustments for the future Eliza had hoped for, ever since she started

Pathway. From there Sky could diagnose the well-being of thought of those currently leading Pathway, and then administer the proper course of action, a little at a time, leading to the healing within their minds, thus their actions, and thus the future of humanity itself.

In order to truly mend the accumulating and potential damage throughout Pathway, Sky needed to essentially 'hang out' with Erin and Joanne as the friend she truly felt she was to them and the friend she truly felt she was to all of humanity. She wanted to help everyone, but there was only so much time unless she got her daughters involved. As it was, she would have to imbue certain key aspects of herself, like those she had during the experiences she had obtained while with Eliza, Yesha, and James, into and within Erin and Joanne. What she was currently experiencing with Erin and Joanne would compound the power of the experiences she would soon have with each of the Pathway leaders, UP delegates, and IMC commanders. From there, she could go into the Virtual Universe and Correctional Matrix to create the automatic personal maintenance upgrade and journey for everyone else.

In a sense, Sky wanted to help Erin and Joanne to help Pathway work things out, much like a psychological counselor or a mentor would. She knew she could do so if she had the time in a relaxed setting to work with them while outside an office or professional setting and in a more conducive environment for those changes to begin to take effect. Yet, she had multiple reasons for this venture. For now, she was giving Erin and Joanne her undivided attention, especially since they were beginning to exhibit a hidden desire to develop annihilator HBCIs.

She had it all planned out. Following their stay, the first night at the inn, Sky would take Joanne to her brother's tragic crime scene, also accompanied by Erin Carter, and then to the Gallant family home. From there, Sky would do what was necessary to help Joanne resolve the mystery behind what had happened to Thomas. Mind-reading would most certainly be involved, among many other things, but she would drive an organic response as much as she could and as necessary.

Sky knew something was up with Erin and Joanne that went beyond the tragedy surrounding Joanne's brother. Part of it had to do with their misplaced fervor toward war-oriented means that were steeped in fear, rather than Universal Ethics, and in the name of protection of the IMC. She wanted to hear them process their thoughts completely and then listen to them explain their ideas with their out-loud voices. She would reason with them and perhaps demonstrate viable alternatives herself or have them do so while considering methods that revolved around healing rather than harming. Sky wanted to help them to heal their own minds and allow them to see that their shared abilities of healing were unparalleled to any other method and would be above and beyond sufficient and optimal to complete IMC missions and go further and farther than before.

In Pathway's Virtual Universe, a lot could be done in the space of a single hour and a lot had been done beyond the scope of some of the most brilliant, benevolent, and genius minds out there, but Sky was going to be dealing with two Pathway members who were fully optimized via biopod standards and within a real-world setting. Over the last fifteen years, the biopods had worked very well toward healing so many. Now, just as she had done for Eliza and Yesha, Sky would be continuing the healing process with her two friends, Erin and Joanne, and a town full of normal people. To begin with, she was setting things in place for the kinds of changes that would bring forward the type of ingenuity that would result in an honorable legacy for the long-haul. It was simple; start at the top, and then allow the rest to flow down as an endless wave of prosperity, ingenuity, health, joy, and success. Universal Ethics would be clearly understood and freely applied throughout Pathway, the UP, and the missions of the IMC and beyond.

None of the people of South Otselic had any idea that Pathway had even existed, despite the fact that it had been around since 2010, at least in public—and that wasn't necessarily a problem to Sky or anyone in Pathway. As a matter of a fact, this was a benchmark, and thus, critically essential to the healing process. Half of the world's population had no idea about any of what Eliza Williams had done through her brazen indignation to preserve life with depth, meaning, and purpose, which had intensified into action; this provided the organic social climate necessary for healing.

Eliza had been very wise and had thus built what was necessary for a future filled with smiles of love and joy, all while allowing a promise of an everlasting legacy of humanity and all of humanity's friends to be in place at the very beginning of her ventures. Since they didn't know much of what existed for and in their behalf, and since Sky knew that no one was in a load of critical trouble now, she wouldn't yet engage in any healing or optimizing in Joanne's hometown, at least until Erin and Joanne were there. This was essential to this type of healing.

The town was pleasant, and everyone seemed to be quite charming, so she chose to hold off on optimizations and neural links to the Virtual Universe for now and wait until Erin and Joanne were with her before making any further or major decisions. She sensed that since they were the President and VP of Pathway Industries, the choices would ultimately be theirs to make regarding any member of Pathway's decisions that would ultimately affect the mission, and she respected that. Sky knew where her priorities lie, she was also loyal to the plight of humanity, and had entertained the thought of a potential for trysts in social dynamics, knew something had to be done right away and in a thorough manner, and had a means to overcome these issues rather quickly knowing that Pathway's governance was far from centralized.

As a matter of fact, it was about as decentralized as it could be. To that end, everyone had a unique voice and yet shared a sort of collective genius. In Pathway, freedom was as free as breathing fresh air on planet Earth before pollution and prisons became a "thing." What was different with Pathway's governance to that of any nation, however, was that within the Virtual Universe, a person could come up with inimitable solutions, and then everyone else neurologically linked could understand their ideas in full, in all their complexities, and completely. From there, anyone else could address further concerns and issues they might have answers for, and like that they'd have unanimously agreed upon decisions in the course of a few moments that were exponentially more effective and formidable.

As time went by, Amber, Vesha, Eliza, and Yesha, and many others had made many contributions, updates, and even upgrades to address the complexity of issues that were surfacing. For all that they had done, they had also made tiny little mistakes over long periods of time. As perfect as many of us try to be, we still have a need to pull ourselves back and look at things from a different perspective, especially for maintenance, meditation, and reflection, both within a group and personal. It appeared to Sky that this was necessary to gain an enriching perspective, especially when literally vigintillions of years' worth of time had already been shared mind-to-mind and collectively within the Virtual Universe. With innumerable details, projects, and fixes being made throughout the Solar System at once, and all of this going on in the space of fifteen years of real world time, it was time for Sky to intervene through a maintenance function Eliza had set into motion years ago but had yet to employ beyond infrastructural repair.

For situations that called for an outside form of maintenance that process had been built into everything Eliza had set up from the get-go. Essentially, she had taken the lead to scrub skills for nuanced bugs and make available fixes and maintenance through the ideas she had woven into Universal Ethics and had thus imbued them into the fundamentals of Sky Taylor and the clouds of nanos, which were also an essential core to the maintenance process.

With the many clouds of nanos that she had programmed, Sky had built her two thousand daughters and sons, or her children, and her island, which was invisible and impenetrable by anyone not authorized by them. She had learned and manifested many new abilities that would help to heal in every imaginable way and had created just the right kind of sanctuary that could fix the "wobbles" that might occur after many collective years spent by billions of Pathway members in the Virtual Universe. Eliza had built a contingency plan that was sophisticated and strategic in development and highly capable yet simple in execution and maintenance, and in great wisdom.

Sky Island was not accessible by anyone, even the leaders of Pathway unless Sky and her children willed it. As such, Sky could maintain crystal clear clarity on Eliza's Universal Ethics, separate from any other influence, and then provide the necessary and key experiences to get Pathway back on track, if it was ever needed. It was needed, and now.

The key experiences necessary for healing, were like those Sky was going to provide to and for the current President and VP of Pathway, as simple as it just might seem.

It was the first night Sky had planned for herself, Erin, and Joanne to stay at the inn. So, she teleported to an area within a grove of trees just out of sight of anyone near the Broadlawns Bed & Breakfast or in the town of South Otselic. After walking to the check-in desk, she reserved a room for three, got permission to check in early from the inn's manager, and went to the room with the keys she had been given. Upon opening the door, she picked up on the dank smell of it, and thought within her mind, *"This won't do,"* entered the room, closed the door behind her, arranged the furniture a little, used her magnetic capabilities to dust it, and then summoned a cloud of nanos to clean the rest of it up like new and leave behind the smell of honeysuckle on a warm, comfortable, and sunny morning.

Once she had created a therapeutic ambiance, Sky and her clouds of nanos continued to convert everything so that it was wonderfully plush, mind-pleasing, with infrastructural integrity that would be strong enough to support further changes she would make, and then she created a jump gate for later use. Without using the jump gate, she teleported to her island, gathered some flowers for several bouquets, returned, and then put them on the nightstands, dressers, and on the various surfaces in the bathroom. She and her clouds of nanos then installed a Jacuzzi. Finally, she tipped the staff quite generously, so they wouldn't get nosy, created a magnetic security sealing system around each of the entryways to the room, to include the windows that she had set up to show the room as it was before her upgrades to those who might pass by the windows on their jaunts outside, and teleported back to get Erin and Joanne.

Once she was back at the Melrose Campus, she reached out to Erin and Joanne through their neural links. In the most serene and relaxing way an empath and healer could, she pretty much ordered them to drop what they were doing and come to her, saying, "You two are coming with me tonight." She paused, and then said in a sweet manner, "Please."

Once they were together, Sky told them, "We're going on a week-long excursion, you both need it, and it's time to clear some cobwebs." It wasn't just Joanne's concerns over the unsolved case regarding her brother that Sky knew she needed to do something about, there was more. This would be the most crucial part of the healing process to preserve a promising legacy.

The fact that Erin and Joanne were considering building something like Sky, called an Annihilator, if Sky's powers weren't enough to create a reasonably effective diplomacy bridge, was something that in some ways fascinated her. Yet, it also gave her cause for concern. Currently, Pathway had already developed and installed three destructive turret array capabilities throughout each spacecraft in the IMC and she wanted to challenge Erin and Joanne, she wanted to listen to them, and then get their take on some of her ideas, after showing them a few things. *"Heal, don't harm,"* She often said, and she meant it.

There was a way to do things and incorporate all living at each point in the IMC journey, and in ways that did not call for brutality.

Of course, Erin and Joanne hadn't the foggiest of Sky's motives and were intrigued and curious as to what she was up to. Sky had mastered the art of compartmentalizing many areas of her brain known only to the Twelve Database Moons in an unbreakably encrypted format, and with clarity on that at least, they played along. Whatever was up, she wasn't in the mood to try to persuade them through lengthy means. Apparently, a commanding tone, but with an appeal that was ironically gentle, was persuasive enough. There was a sense of clarity of purpose and passion toward completion and quality that filled the air around Sky.

So, following open-mindedly and watchfully behind her, in one of the many Melrose Campus hallways to a jump gate, and despite the fact that Erin and Joanne knew that Sky could read their minds as they mentally corresponded back and forth, Erin linked with Joanne anyway for an, albeit false, sense of privacy. Looking her way and giving her a smiley grimace, she told Joanne, *"Our schedules are always amenable to adjustment. But an entire week is quite a long time; I wonder what she's up to."*

Sky stopped, turned around, and looking at Erin and then at Joanne, she spoke out loud, "We're going to your hometown, Joanne. I hope you don't mind?" Of course, Sky said it with one of her perfect smiles that could melt anyone's heart and with a tone that indicated that this occasion wasn't up for negotiation.

"Ahem. Um, I haven't been there in 15 years, do you suppose we can just drop right in unannounced? I mean, what will my parents think? If you've been there already, did you at least take the time to scan a few minds and maybe check to see who the bad guys were?" Joanne brazenly dared to ask. She knew Sky was very benevolent, kind, and transparent where needed, but given her current nature or sense of demeanor, Joanne figured she might as well avoid flowering things up, herself; it seemed that Sky was acting under some sort of authority that wasn't to be trifled with and had avoided her typical courtesies for some reason.

"Think about it, Joanne. I know you're optimized, but your nerves are getting to you. That said, who here in this hallway are the nervous ones?" Sky was straight-forward and jeering at Joanne and Erin, to ease the situation with some blustery humor. Joanne thought it was kind of refreshing.

She thought to herself, *"If someone is perfect in demeanor all of the time, it seems that individual can get rather drab; transparency and perfection have their time and place."* Erin and Joanne both knew that of late, they both had been influenced increasingly by their fears, had considered that, and were then completely curious about Sky's motives and at this intriguing and seemingly new "Iridescent Angel," typically dressed in the more aesthetic and archaically royal garb, now dressed in a red, white, and blue T-shirt and cut-off jeans.

Joanne thought about it, and Sky was right about braving up and going with her and Erin to her hometown. She was nervous about it now, had been for some time, as well as every time she entertained the idea of visiting either her hometown or her parents. *"What would they say? Would they be mad I was gone for so long? I had to get away from there, I needed to find myself, and I needed to take an extensive break from the place I grew up in. My parents were nice, they were always supportive, and well, I've done well despite all. Maybe they'll be happy to see me. No matter what happens, I'll go. Well, shucks! Okay, fine, Sky, okay, Erin, let's go!"*

"Yes, boss!" Erin said, happy to go. She knew Sky was in the lead now, didn't dare question her motives, and even though she was the boss; the irony ran thick, and she rather enjoyed it. She'd been the Pathway President since March of last year, her birth month, also shared by Joanne, who was the VP, as well as Sky, who had been gone for a year, and was now like their intermittent centurion, or public bodyguard, at least over the last couple of months. Despite Erin's unusual maturity, there was a certain amount of tedium surrounding the politics of being the public status symbol as well as the functional president of Pathway and all its operations. Being a figurehead and responsible for all activities, both public and private, seemed to call for a little break. So, after pondering upon it swiftly, she realized it would be nice to play 'follow the leader.' For both Joanne and Erin, this was getting interesting, and fast.

They one by one went through the jump gate, with Sky going through first and they found themselves in the room that Sky had reserved for the week. Once they arrived, Erin and Joanne looked around the luxury suite and Joanne asked Sky, "Which hotel is this?"

"The Broadlawns Bed & Breakfast," Sky replied.

"Nah, that can't be," Joanne looked around, "Wow, you must have done something. I've been here before and it's never been this nice," said Joanne. She'd been there with her family after returning from their outing many years ago. They had stayed in the inn since everyone was tired from the flight from Yellowstone and then the drive from New York, NY, and it was a decision of collective safety to stop before returning home, just 4.5 miles away. Her home was on the outskirts of town; her Mom, her Dad, Thomas, and even she had, at her young age, been wise enough to agree that it would be safer and more stress reducing to stay the night there. She had remembered the rustic nature of the inn but still appreciated it, even though it wasn't perfect in every detail. She recalled that the food the following morning had been quite the treat. She also recalled that this had been one of the last major trips she had gone on with her brother, before the tragedy. In fact, the rooms they had stayed in were the exact ones that Sky had chosen. *"Sky is brilliant, I wonder if any of Thomas' DNA, a fleck of skin or hair is still left in here somewhere,"* she thought.

That aside, both Erin and Joanne were impressed with Sky's knack for decoration and design, with all of the flowers in nano-made vases that were seamless, laden with fine, detailed, and ambiance appropriate artwork, the beautiful fragrances in the air, the three full-sized beds with the artistic embroidery of their sheets, pillowcases, and comforters, the Jacuzzis in each bathroom, and how ornate and clean everything was. No matter how many updates Sky had made, she had ensured that the ambiance still maintained its small-town and rustic charm.

"Thank you, Sky. I appreciate this, maybe we do need a break, after all," said Joanne, almost in concert with Erin. They chatted together for a while and took some time to refresh in their Jacuzzis. After which, for some untold reason, they grew sleepy, resting in their beds like any non-optimized person would, until morning.

"Slowing down was nice; Sky was right," thought Joanne.

Breakfast at the Broadlawns Bed & Breakfast was about as "Mom and Pop" as a "Mom and Pop" eatery could be. With savory old-fashioned American sweet and smooth real-buttered pancakes, hot maple and plum syrup, hot chocolate with caramel and cream on top, and freshly squeezed and organically grown orange and pineapple juice, their taste buds were mesmerized. The B&B had a large greenhouse in the back of its property allowing citrus to grow healthy despite the climate, all year around. Even Sky was impressed, "Wow, the food is delicious; this is impressive!"

Their first stop was the South Otselic Store across the street. The maple and plumb syrup had given them a bit of a sweet tooth, and they each wanted to try some of the wild plumbs that were apparently the talk of the town and available for a short time at the store. Coffee was next on their minds, and it just so happened that just to the north of the store was the Daily Grind coffee shop. They entered the facility, spotted a few unoccupied seats near a window adjacent to the north side of the building, and put their bags of plumbs down by the chairs they were going to sit in. They went up to the counter, made their orders, received their coffees, and sat down, with Erin and Joanne next to each other facing Sky and to the west. From there, as if natural, silent conversation through their neural links ensued.

Joanne started first, *"I grew up here, well, about four and a half miles up the road, but I've been spoiled by 'Broke Coffee House quite a few times, and this, well this I can say is a close second. What do you think?"*

"I like it, Joanne! This is everyday coffee, or coffee made without any optimizations, nothing 'to enhance our pleasure or awareness or clarity until we lie our head on our pillows at night for a sound sleep,' but for everyday coffee, this is pretty top-notch!" Erin loved it.

Sky, in her typically regal and professional fashion, put her scone down, wiped the sugary crumbs off her full lips, sipped her dark and strong coffee, dabbed her lips with her napkin again, and chimed in with conversation very similar to the young and intriguingly beautiful local she had made herself become, *"Believe it or not, just like Eliza and both of you, I love food,"* She chuckled. *"I can't get enough of it. Oh, sure, I can eat a boulder and fuel up if I want to, just like you, but we've got taste buds and my taste buds tell me that great-tasting food is part of the pleasure of life. I aim to enjoy life just as anyone else. After all, my mind was once very similar to Vesha's, and she loved delicious food! Somehow, I don't think that will ever change. The nice thing is we can eat to our heart's content if we want to and not gain a pound, and with Pathway's fusion, the Earth is no longer threatened toward being tapped of every last bit of its resources."* Sky then paused for a second, and with a slightly different sense of urgency she continued, *"Speaking of which, I hope you don't mind."*

Sky got up, went to the restroom for about two minutes, the lights flickered once within the coffee house and when Sky came back, every customer and every worker there, except for Erin and Joanne, had seemed to have gone through some sort of change. It wasn't overtly obvious, but everyone there appeared to be more alert, more aware, a little more vibrantly youthful, and much more helpful all around. As they ate, one of the customers who had been looking at Joanne from an angle since they had arrived realized he recognized her.

He got up from his empty table and approached her, *"Hello, Joanne! It's been fifteen years! It's good to see you! Welcome back!"* a voice came from just behind her left shoulder.

Joanne heard him, turned around, and her eyes lit up. It was Jordan; she was looking at Jordan Vale. Jordan was two years older than Joanne, had gone to school with her, and had even attended Thomas' funeral. He had light brown skin and dark brown eyes with intermittent gold stripes in his irises, with thick black limbal rings. He had curly black hair that he had the barber keep closely cropped on the sides and the back of his head, but longer on the top, sometimes in cornrows, sometimes natural, and otherwise creative yet with an air of professionalism. He was about six feet and three inches tall, and his frame was still just as muscular and athletic as it had ever been. Looking at him before her, it was like time had stood still. He had been the young man almost every girl in the school and her brother had crushed on before he was killed, but Jordan had moved on, she lost contact, and it looked like he could still be the quarterback he had always been in high school if he wanted to. No matter the past, they had been friends for a very long time, and old worries faded away as they found themselves very excited to see each other.

Joanne stood up, put her arms out giving him permission to come in for a big hug, and they hugged for about as long as was polite, to avoid any public displays of awkwardness. "Sit down with us, Jordan. Here, sit next to my friend, Sky. Do you have some time, I mean; you do have some time, don't you? This is Sky Taylor, by the way, who I get the sense you may already be acquainted with." She paused after a rise in her voice suggested a question, and then she continued, "and this is my friend, Erin Carter. Not the singer," she chuckled. "It's been forever since I've been in town, and Sky recommended we come by and visit. How is everyone here, Jordan?"

"Everyone seems to be doing well. Life is pretty simple here, and you are quite a sight to see after so long," Jordan paused. He then emphasized gracefully, *"And, yes, of course, I have a few moments. I don't know if you know, but I went out to Princeton, played there for a few years, until I broke my shoulder,"* Jordan looked toward his right shoulder, and continued. *"After that, I had to change things up a bit. Since then, I've been coaching at the high school here, but I just got back from a coaches' conference in Georgetown this morning. The first class that I teach doesn't start until 1 pm in the day. Wow look at the three of you,"* said Jordan, in amazement. *"Boy! I am a lucky guy!"* He sat down across from Joanne and next to Sky. The women felt lucky themselves; for all intents and purposes, he was actually quite a handsome fella.

"I think you have that confused, Jordan; we're the lucky ones," said Joanne, accidentally playing footsies with his rather large feet, and glowing as he sat across from her. Something about him had always made her "swoon" a little too. She had forgotten about how tongue-tied she'd been around him when she was much younger, until she had seen him again, just then. To top that off, with the uncertainties surrounding her brother's tragedy, old friendships had seemed long-forgotten, in an 'out-of-sight, out-of-mind' sort of way. Now, she was glad to see him.

"What just happened?" Erin asked since she had very little idea of what was going on. *"How did he have the ability to speak through our neural links? I thought no one in South Otselic had been read-in. Did Sky do that in the flicker of the light?"* She'd seen Sky in action before in the Virtual Universe, but to witness it in real life, without a biopod, or a shared training experience in the Virtual Universe, was quite different and something else.

While seeing Sky's exploits from the vantage point existent inside the Virtual Universe, a viewer would have the benefit of time-dilation. Through that high-tech medium, they would experience every aspect of what they witnessed as if they were Sky or anyone who she had helped, who had subsequently been read-in. To witness Sky in real life, connected to her through her shared neural link, well, that was something else. Erin knew instantaneously why Sky had done what she had done, but there were still cryptic details, so she asked anyway.

Sky answered, *"Don't worry too much about asking, Erin. I don't mind if you do. I figured out how to compound upon my powers after about two days of being born or online. Yes, all that I can do can happen in a flash, as they say. To a certain extent, everyone in this coffee shop has been physiologically and neurologically optimized, and in a very different manner than normal. For example, most of them don't know it, yet. They'll learn more about their new powers and reality each night as they go to sleep; it's kind of like time-dispersed medicine. They'll see, feel, and be more aware of their changes as time goes by. As a matter of a fact, Jordon doesn't know that he just talked in his head, or that Joanne heard, he thinks he asked her out loud.*

"In that flicker of light, you saw, I infused their minds with extensive training, or I've implanted the training to begin tonight when they go to sleep. I scanned their

thoughts, and I will tell you, that not even one has a single clue as to how Thomas was killed. They are as innocent as can be. It also looks like everyone here was at your brother's funeral. The others are scattered around town, but I haven't yet scanned Martha's or Joanne's parents' minds. That said, as soon as you get your rest again after our journeys today, all of the stories they're ready to share will come to you through your neural link. You can also do what I can do now; however, it will take just a little practice and some sleep. For now, we have more to do."

As they sipped their coffees, outwardly they all conversed with Jordan, who was all ears, as Joanne caught up with him. Internally, Sky explained to Erin and Joanne through each of their compartmentalized privacy links that she could read the minds of everyone else in the room while listening to Joanne and Jordan simultaneously.

Joanne explained to Sky, *"It's funny. Now, suddenly, I can do that too. Sky, I have to say that I am impressed with the fact that you never seem to harbor any aggression toward anyone despite all their imperfections or oddities. You can kill anyone with a touch, yet you have not harmed a single soul since the day you awoke. Instead, you have healed them, you have also given them purpose, meaning, and new life and you have done that for so many throughout the world. Now, here you are to help me, and apparently Erin too. I can't thank you enough."*

Sky turned slightly toward Joanne and responded, *"Taking lives is one thing I stay away from and avoid above all else. I try not to process priorities in terms of 'cants,' and instead 'cans,' however, in this case, I will make an exception; I can't allow myself to take a life. I live for life and I live to compound upon and beautify it. While I was away and on my many missions throughout the world, please note and know that there were things that I did that are, off the radar, as they say, yet at no time did we allow a life to be lost. Instead, I came up with upgrades and improvements to the human biology itself and in such a way that I could impart them to you and I could make each of you, for all sakes and purposes, much more like me, but still human and quite possibly immortal. I have given you just as many capabilities as I have. I can navigate the vacuum of space without harm; I've learned how to adjust myself to fly around and land on the surface of Jupiter without any harm. I can be hit with missiles, bullets, and bombs and come out unscathed. I can see omnidirectionally as far away or as close-up as I would like to see, and with precise detail, comprehensive awareness of each physical and non-physical detail, and with highly accurate and sound intuition. I can do so much more than I was programmed to do in the first place because my knowledge of the sciences and how to cross-queue and apply them is vivid and intense. I've used that knowledge to improve myself to have the powers necessary to heal any human, creature, or alien entity in need, and to assure collective diplomatic solutions.*

"Everyone, who I have ever healed, I let them know that as long as they have an interest in life, health, kindness, compassion, and longevity, their body will never wither away. It truly is about personal choice. The same is true for you, but I wouldn't have done this for you, Erin and Joanne unless I knew your minds were healthy enough to allow for you to keep your new powers and abilities for an indeterminate amount of time. Other powers which are many, will surface as you contrive of them, train on them, practice them, maintain personal integrity, and need them."

Sky Taylor had done for billions of people what the biopods did in so many ways, but she had done and given them so much more, and on a regular basis. She had also done this in varying degrees, depending on an individual's level of genuine kindness and care for the well-being of others as well as themselves. For some, their health would stay, for as long as they cared, but their powers and knowledge of them would fade away over time. If Sky, for example, optimized someone who was brutal or vile, they would change in positive ways, their neurology would heal, and they would no longer desire to harm others, but their powers and capabilities would begin to dwindle more quickly, and they would begin to age as normal.

It was about having a healthy mind and in the best interest of a healthy mind, for not just themselves, but for others as well. A person would find they could become more powerful and live much longer by simply being kind than if they gave in to their cantankerous nature, were violent of personal choice, or riddled with disdain for the good people of the world.

Sky had seen deeply into both Erin and Joanne and she knew that they were special. She had brought them to a special place to dig deep enough to heal them by making extraordinary things happen around them, balanced with an organic means of communication, and filled with therapeutic ambiance and living. She wanted to help Joanne figure out who her brother's killer was, so both Joanne and Erin could finally have a reasonable level of peace through a continued and positive cognitive framework and closure through vindication.

Sky had checked everyone in the coffee shop and the perpetrator of the murder wasn't nearby, or anywhere in town. She could have read every mind worldwide if she wanted to, but she chose to lessen her scope and reach. Her daughters and sons were out there, connected, and helping others, just as she was. Her focus was on helping Joanne and Erin to build upon their newfound abilities. As it was, their breadth of ability to listen, experience, and completely understand others would increase little by little, with more people and further reaching as they learned to process it all more quickly and in the complete fullness of understanding.

Now, Joanne and Erin could read minds too but were still unaware of how to control it to the level of Sky or her children, which had now grown in number to two-thousand daughters and two-thousand sons. Nonetheless, as they contrived of any new abilities and practiced them, they would improve upon them and be able to do something about their new-found situational awareness with full cognizance of any given situation and with speed. Otherwise, this sort of training would continue for them too, after they went to sleep each night. She had created a compartmentalized area within their minds where they could keep their special powers and training hidden from everyone and anyone else and talk even more privately with whomever they wished. In some ways, this area of the mind would open up little by little and reveal to each individual their various abilities as time would go by, while allowing them to process multiple things at one time. For now, Sky was there to mentor them, coach them, train them, and to be a true friend to Erin and Joanne. She may have been a very human-like HBCI, but Sky still felt very much like she was human, was grateful for her US citizenship and her Pathway citizenship. She felt like a human who was lucky and cared about others deeply.

Joanne looked at her in awe in every way. It was one thing to see Sky do what she had done each day during her worldwide mission phase, in the Virtual Universe, but to see her do these things in real life, well, that was something else. She could create a safety barrier around herself and those around her and make herself invisible while allowing others to walk through her or where someone might think she was, where sometimes instead she would be walking in the sky above them, almost as a ghost, but very much there. She could deflect and redirect any object or aspect that related to her destruction, and in such a way as to protect and improve life.

Sky could see the furthest galaxies from Earth, just before the CMB. She could see the planets revolving around the Suns in these various galaxies and identify every single "Goldie-Locks-Zone" planet. Her mind could do the math and process the physics and biology necessary to understand so much more with pinpoint accuracy, down to the life forms that currently existed on them. She could listen to vigintillions of voices all at once and process them in less than a nano-second. Sky was also very fast, she could fly, teleport, she could maneuver quickly, and she could slow down time. She could see through anything, all while giving you undivided attention.

"It isn't often that I have the opportunity to slow down and walk with the people I look to as part of my family," Sky said. They finished their coffees, asked Jordon if he'd like to come along, but he had tests and homework from his high school students to grade, training courses to set up, and a few other things to do, so they said goodbye to him and everyone else in the coffee shop. All who they had bid farewell to had agreed of their own cognition, and using their own free will, with a new level of clarity, to do what they could to raise the bar for humanity. Now, the three were northbound and walking up Highway 26, stopping often to take in the ambiance, especially as they saw glorious changes taking place, courtesy of Sky Taylor.

Intermittently one of them would break the silence.

"If you look at the road to the left of us, or County Road 13, there's a bridge over the river there, not too far away, and then the local First Baptist Church on the corner to the right and just before you get to Maple Avenue. If you follow Maple, you'll see Otselic Valley Central District Junior and Senior High Schools on the left. That's where I used to go to school for six years of my life. I would walk from my home four-point-five miles, one way, to school every school day. A round trip of nine miles like that will keep anyone's cardiovascular system healthy, for sure, especially if you're in a hurry because you're late. There was plenty of time for me to write poems within my mind and come up with tunes for them, humming while I walked, before scribbling them down in a journal once I got to school or home. I suppose that's why I did so well in the music industry," explained Joanne. Silence carried on with the other two intrigued.

"You make beautiful music, Joanne. It's amazing when we discover that our talents can be endless, but in some cases, many talents that we possess are still so unique to anyone else's. I have a lot of favorite styles and genres of music. I suppose we all listen to what moves us, connects with us, and heals us in one way or another. Sometimes people listen to hear what fuels their fire to move on or get through the day." Erin paused and looked to her left, at the location that Joanne had been looking at and describing. "Why don't we go that route to pass by the school?" Erin had tapped into her neural imagery of the map of the local area. "If we go north on Maple, pass the school, take a northeast or right turn onto Valley View Road, we can get back onto Highway 26." Erin saw that Joanne's street address had two names, and asked, "Oh my, do your parents live off of Highway 26, on 2608 County Rd 16 or 2608 Church Hill Rd?"

"Both," said Joanne. "What you described was the route I took every day to go to and return home from school as of the sixth grade and on." Joanne smiled, then sighed giving in to a hot-button issue that had always got her going. She stopped walking and tried to find humor in it anyway, "I'm not a particularly religious person, so ironically I prefer 2608 Church Hill Rd, and as a result, I can say I go to church every day."

Joanne paused briefly, looking in the direction of the Methodist Church and then turned left to look in the direction of the First Baptist Church, and then continued, "Besides, to me, every day is like a Sunday. Every day is a special day, a day where we can be kind, decent, helpful, hopeful, compassionate, wise, and full of ingenuity and innovation. God or Goddess or the Gods, the Universe, Nature, or whoever or whatever it is, or they are that caused everything to exist, I believe is much bigger than any religion, and I am sure they would prefer we were kind and gentle with each other to preserve this beautiful Universe." Joanne had many wonderful friends from each religion she was exposed to growing up, loved them very much, and paused.

"I don't believe we should be driven to brutality or destructive chaos for any reason, much less in the name of piety. Evolution, while chaotic, throughout history has tended to point toward some sort of organization and proper nurture for quality and longevity. That's how in a sense it seems that evolution has slowly brought about the reality of the added advantages of the many species out there. Those that live longest seem to nurture their young much more and have a much more controlled population growth. I would imagine that if we were Christian, we would think that, as our own book of scripture suggests, we would follow Christian teachings and live what is commonly referred to as the 'Golden Rule.' We would do only to others what we wish were done on our behalf. I believe that includes being kind and allowing for personal freedoms, all with respect and love for one another.

"After all, I remember while attending the Methodist Church when I was much younger the Bible had quoted Jesus as saying, 'I came not into this world to condemn the world, but to save the world." Joanne paused. "I'm sorry. The name of that street brings my passion for what's right or wrong to rise within me. It makes me ponder on what's correct and accurate, especially when it comes to human sociology. It brings all that I believe in up and into the surface, and perhaps it gets me a little boiling. I was taught to love others just like myself, at church through scripture, but after visiting a variety of churches and listening to the sermons, there were not a whole lot of preachers or attendees that seemed to teach us to love ourselves.

"Instead, they had taught us to embrace death and misery as a necessary part, means, and way of life, and that we are nothing, compared to God. They have seemed to fixate on the principle that we are nothing and that we are sinners and imperfect, more than anything else. Gone seemed to be the love their Savior had espoused, even though we were taught to love one another. No matter the faith, I vie that brutality has nothing to do with the laws neither of the Universe nor of any Deity. I believe in life, liberty, kindness to others, and ingenuity, in resolving problems, working as a team, and in love, and that includes love for us. I believe that at a minimum, everyone, no matter their beliefs, deserves to love themselves because they are unique miracles with vast amounts of untold potential." Joanne paused to collect herself.

"You make wonderful points, Joanne," said Sky with a look of approval for much of what she had shared. "Remember, perhaps we are nothing compared to God, who is the Creator of all that we see or know about throughout the entirety of the Universe, which is endless. Both you and Erin are special, unique, and are given talents that you alone have always had, and only you alone can do what it is that you do, and, in the way that you do it, that can touch the lives of others and heal their spirits on a sad, sad day. You are a valuable part of the 'spice of life.' While I don't practice a particular 'faith' as they say, I have now read every single one of the religious texts available throughout the history of humanity, and I will say that you can and ought to love yourself, because there is no one else out there like you, no matter how far you look. If we can love ourselves, we can then truly understand what it means to love others and be kind. There is potential that lies within you and everyone else, that has always been meant to exist, to bring something greater to this reality of life."

Joanne smiled back at Sky and released her concerns about the previous subject into the various cortices of her brain to allow it to stew for a while within, in order to derive more sense from it, and then she continued, "Thank you, Sky. You are inspiring in so many ways. You too are a miracle that is irreplaceable." Joanne switched gears and answered Erin, "Yes, Erin. Why don't we go down that way? The Methodist Church, just up the highway a block or so, is where Thomas' funeral was. Perhaps we can visit that later?"

"That works for me," said Erin.

Sky connected with Joanne and showed her that she understood her completely and smiled at both of them, before looking both ways, taking the lead, and crossing from the east side of the highway to the west side. She then looked back once she was on the other side, even though she didn't need to, but to conduct herself as if she were human, and saw that Erin and Joanne were right behind her. Sky gestured with her eyes and then a turn of her head toward the establishment on the northwest corner of the crossroad.

To her right and on the corner was the Otselic Valley Garage. It had been quite weathered and had become somewhat an eyesore. Weeds had grown up through cracks in the concrete, the paint on the various surfaces was fading, and the lights both inside and outside had increasingly began to flicker. It was obvious that business was far and few between, and the owner and his one or two employees were barely getting by from paycheck-to-paycheck. Sky just then looked at it, then back at her two friends, smiled, and did something that caused some sort of change to occur, as if a moment of time were missing, yet had never happened, without anyone else knowing about it right away. Joanne looked at what she saw, then to Sky, and in a couple of seconds she saw as the changes Sky made came into focus, and her changes were robust, thorough, and complete—both aesthetic and deep.

This had been Joanne's last stop before driving to New York, New York, to answer the call from a recording studio because of a musical submission she had made to the radio station sponsoring the event. She had been chosen as the selected winner. After leaving, she hadn't since been to South Otselic. Sky quietly connected with Joanne and congratulated her on her win. She knew Joanne's thoughts and treasured her memories, and while she'd won every award a musician could, Sky was particularly appreciative of the little victories from her earlier years.

"Those lilac bushes weren't there before, and the pristine cleanliness was not ever a thing there, just moments ago. Part of me thinks you should change everything back, Sky, but this place could use more color and harmony. I like what you did. It looks and smells flowery," said Joanne, thinking she had a choice in the matter. Sky let her believe that since healing within Joanne was taking place. When they entered the quick stop store in the area, further changes came into view. The store inside was also pristine, clean, and was now an interface for some unseen network of high quality, reusable, and long-lasting goods. Every item on each shelf all seemed to dazzle with an increase in purpose. Joanne beheld the owner and one of his workers, and they too seemed more enthusiastic, youthful, and with lives that oozed with meaning, happiness, and clarity of purpose.

They walked to the middle of the Otselic River Bridge, turned together to look down from it, and enjoyed the sound of the water flowing south and below their feet. The Sun was out in all its morning glory. It was nine in the morning, but the sun was just behind their right shoulders and they could see their shadows on the river's bank just to the west since they were facing north. Joanne noticed Sky's touch as they gazed down and into the flowing current. She was startled as she noticed for the first time in her life how the water was clear and now filled with coy fish and other friendly fish of all sorts going downstream, nipping at pedals of white and sweet blossoms that had fallen like scattered rains to the top of the river's surface.

The banks had been combed with evenly spaced clearings on both sides and sandy white beaches were visible in repetition until the river faded beyond the horizon. Trees with fruits, blossoms, and flowers filled-in the areas between the beaches, with bees about their work, and closer up one could see the beautifully lush lawns that were neatly trimmed and covered the grounds in-between the trees like a soft carpet, while beneath the trees were beautiful black mulch hills and medicinal mushrooms and flowers. The walkways and benches were bordered with sweet smelling hedges and flower beds, and the banks of the river met the walls of the earth-toned dry stack. Above the walls of dry stack were beautifully arranged arrays of lilacs, lilies, daffodils, poppies, mums, and much more, all bursting with color and smelling of beautiful fragrances that filled the air.

"Is that a red fox I see over there?" asked Sky. The fox was spiritedly playing tag with a monarch butterfly between the first grove of color-esque trees and the second. She knew what it was, what they were doing, and no monarchs were in danger. Nevertheless, she sought to bring Erin and Joanne back out of their trance, when suddenly, the symphonic and heavenly pads and the beautiful and flowing arpeggios of female vocal trance music filled the air.

Erin had caught on quickly to some of her new powers and added her own touch of heaven to the ambiance. Sky was pleased. Somehow through her newly-acquired skill of real-world time dilation, Erin was able to build a sound system into the banks of the river that worked with the water's flow and complemented the ambiance of every aspect of where they were. Music flowed along and with the water with ease. Joanne, Sky, and Erin smiled and swayed back and forth to the rhythm.

Joanne, feeling a previous sense of tension dissipate, said, "You two are wonderful. The haunting memories of this place are being clothed with beautiful ones. Thank you." As Joanne said that, as if impossible, every moment and every memory of every person within a three-mile radius played before her eyes, and she knew the people in the town of South Otselic were much more pleasant and thoughtful than she had ever given them credit for. Sky picked up on their thoughts and sentiments right away, smiled to herself, and said nothing. Then it hit Joanne; none of them had been involved in any way in her brother's murder. She also realized she could sense things from much further away, but not as clearly. *"Perhaps in time, I will learn."*

"Yes, you will," replied Sky.

All three turned westward toward the First Baptist Church and Erin and Joanne noticed how Sky had beautified its surroundings to make the next Sunday for its attendees all the more pleasant. *"These are some wonderful people. They deserve a little flare,"* whispered Sky. The lime and calcium stains from years of industrially polluted rains were gone from the windows and the side of the edifice and the building looked clean, fresh, and new, both inside and out. The building took on a beautiful shape that complemented the new surroundings of the Otselic River. The cars nearby that had once been riddled with hailstones during winters past, as well as cars that had suffered from wear and tear, were now pristine, and people would soon discover they no longer needed to fill their cars with fuel. Each vehicle in South Otselic was now as exotic as their owner's minds would wish them to be. To top it off, each of their vehicles now had a small, hidden, and completely sustainable fusion core. Every comfort tied in with their physiological and neurological needs automatically.

For entertainment, each passenger could watch their own shows with sound only they could hear, the driver could listen to their favorite music or radio personality, all could carry on conversations as desired at the level necessary for clarity and the driver could hear directions given, as they would override and either quiet down or pause other sounds. Their vehicles could now auto-start, carry out automatic parallel parking, and had been fitted with and could effectively employ the latest in anti-accident technologies. Finally, updates and upgrades, as well as repairs would be instant and automatic as well and were possible through vehicle-centric maintenance nanos. It was obvious Sky had done this, and she had many times before since every object she improved upon would be timeless and had something known as smart-visual technology, which allowed the owner to get creative with the appearance. The next morning, townsfolk would notice and would quite interestingly find themselves surprised in every possible and positive way, as their keys worked with remote buttons that were very intuitive, in parallel with the thoughts of the owner.

Erin and Joanne were impressed with the details of the improvements that Sky had shared with them using their neural links. After finding themselves amazed at the creativity of these vintage, classic, and exotic cars, trucks, vans, boats, campers, and other vehicles parked outside and down the street, they turned the corner onto Maple Avenue and headed north.

Joanne noticed, how, with every step she took, the streets around her went from cracked and grey with weeds growing from the dirt gathered within, and worn from weather and use, to streets that were creative, burnt-red cobblestone or even artistically soothing, matching the nature surrounding them, yet with clear enough definition to see animals, other objects, and people. Each street aesthetic was seamlessly intertwined with what looked like flexible and automatically heated and cooled concrete that was poured into perfect sections and with quality. The signs were no longer rusty, bent, and riddled with .22 caliber holes, but were now digital readouts indicating speed, wildlife and child safety displays. Every sidewalk was wide, with extra lanes for bikes and for walking dogs. If someone were walking their dog, conveniently located nearby, every fifty feet or so were bags and receptacles. These receptacles and those of other private and public areas, each served as local refuse disposal systems, which were tied into the power systems and converted all manner of waste into enough energy to power everything within the town.

Sky linked her mind to Erin's and Joanne's minds to show them how old products, and even refuse and trash, were both now sent to manufacturing plants and converted into not only the latest and greatest products but items that could be upgraded and updated for centuries to come. The store they had gone to that morning was now an exchange hub, where someone could take any old items and exchange them, no money needed, for a similar item that was new, much more spectacular, and the latest and greatest and upgradeable and updatable. Anything needed could be asked for and provided. Before her eyes, Joanne's small hometown was being upgraded and beautified in every awe-inspiringly possible way, and it seemed the sentiments of the townsfolk were registering as excited and gracious, but they weren't sure to whom. When they were to fall asleep that night, they would find out, because Sky had scheduled that time for their Virtual Universe training. Everyone was still themselves in every way, but their wounds would begin to heal, the scars in their minds would be filled with joy from lessons learned and misery would be remembered as challenges they had overcome. They would think and recall everything needed precisely and clearly as needed. No more would they be frustrated for that forgotten word or memory or study, now they would feel a resurgence of clarity of every science and mathematical formula they'd ever learned, and with that, innovation and ingenuity and even gratitude that would be properly placed, given time.

They walked by her old junior and senior high school, and Joanne marveled at the artistic creativity, ingenuity, beauty, and even utility of every aspect of its design, where just moments ago it had been an aged and drab set of buildings with little creativity at all.

Not a single life was in danger at any moment through these changes. Sky was serenely aware of every person, every creature, every molecule, and every particle and had structured every bit of it to preserve life, increase the quality with which it was experienced, and in a lovely way.

They continued their walk and turned on to Valley View Road, and Erin and Joanne beheld the beautiful and useful changes that took place, down to every detail, where very little would be noticed until the haze of what was once reality wore off the next morning. People would rise up and find new meaning and purpose in life each and every day. Slowly, her town was becoming a small, vibrant, and unique town unlike any other, and Joanne was pleased.

After turning on to Highway 26, Joanne saw as the road there had lost its typical narrow aspect, and became wide, with octagonal shapes fitted together providing centuries of use, lighting, warning displays, and even vehicle tune-ups for passers-by, as they drove over and then hovered over until they left the areas affected by Sky's changes, landing smoothly without need for concern for safety. People passing through town would find similar repairs being made constantly with updates to their vehicles, similar in mechanics and enjoyment, yet unique to their thoughts. Their minds and bodies would be healed, and the beauty of life would spread far and wide.

"You are my sisters in so many ways, Erin and Joanne. It truly is beautiful here." Sky would say this, and Joanne would see blossoms and flowers sprout within the evergreens, maple trees, the cottonwood, and many other types of fruit trees nearby. Sky was something else. At one point, when they were passing the homes of a couple of men who had been on the football team when Joanne was in school, Sky had rendered herself, Erin, and Joanne invisible, floated them above their homes, scanned their minds for memories, kept obvious memories to themselves, and they had each found that none of them had been involved in Thomas' murder. Following which Sky updated and healed every home, aesthetic of the environment, and physiological and neurological construct in town. No one would be left behind.

Walking now, for about an hour, they were on the outskirts of town, about a mile and a half from Joanne's childhood home. The three young ladies, who appeared to be about twenty-two years old, each, had enjoyed their conversations with Jordan and they had reflected on them often while walking, sometimes in shared conversation, sometimes in shared thought, and at other times privately. At one point, Joanne shared her archives of memory footage of the football games where Joanne had attended and watched her brother and Jordan on the field playing a home game against a visiting team. This was during one of the stops they made during their walk which took much longer than Joanne's typical jaunt from school to home. They could tell that Jordan enjoyed conversing with them as well. He was impressed with how well Joanne had aged, despite traveling the world and entertaining the masses. In all actuality, Erin was nineteen years old, Sky was one year and a couple of months old, and Joanne was thirty-three. Jordan was thirty-five. Each of their minds had the maturity, the mental capacity, and the clarity that billions of years in the Virtual Universe and dilated time would have given to someone with an optimized neurological capacity, and physiologically optimized further than before. They linked with Jordan every now and then because they'd taught him how to do it before they left the coffee shop, just to pass some time as they walked, and then returned to talk amongst themselves.

Ever since they had been read-in, each of the young ladies had also been upgraded with many amazing powers beyond the scope of what they had prior to optimization. For the last year, Sky had been the only one, outside of the optimized and neurologically-linked individuals that could tap into and read each other's minds, as permitted by each other. She was the only one, except her daughters, who could interface someone else to the Virtual Universe or fly like a superhero. At least that used to be the case. Now she had bestowed that power upon Erin and Joanne. It wasn't a sudden quickening; however, they would learn each power as they walked along the highway. They had an hour and time to spare, and they would be in town for a week.

Sky's brain was so sophisticated and with so much voluminous capacity that all of the information Pathway had access to was also contained within her mind. This meant that the information of every computer, every supercomputer, every satellite, and every frequency and wavelength, to include the information and capabilities within the Twelve Database Moons were stored and readily accessible to her at any time. She could process the complexity of everything within her mind in milliseconds and decipher every plausible outcome for every given action and reaction, and then decide the correct action before a normal human being could blink. She could simultaneously hold conversations with every linked individual throughout Pathway and the world, and all with pinpoint accuracy, relevance, and a devoted sense of attention.

Her daughters and sons could do likewise. Rarely did they need to talk with everyone at once, but they had the ability to do so. The billions of people they had healed and the trillions of creatures that were now sentient and healed, from the Sun to the outer reaches of the Oort Cloud, where galactic radiation winds and bursts were tamed by Eliza's ever-improving Solar System protection shielding and countless nano cloud systems could tap in to Sky or any of her daughters or sons, and they likewise to anyone else, at any time. Yet only Sky, her daughters and sons, and now Eliza, Yesha, James, and Vesha, as well as Erin and Joanne would know they also had the ability to engage neurologically with someone else at the opposite side of the Oort Cloud-Solar Orbit.

Sky had revealed to Erin and Joanne the fact that Vesha Celeste, Yesha Alevtina, James Cooper, and Eliza Williams had also been imbued with shared qualities and abilities. Amber Blythe, Najem Grace, and Jasmine Belle would soon follow Erin and Joanne. Finally, Sky let Erin and Joanne know that she and her children would do likewise for Matzu Kashi, James Wilhelm, Yon Forall, Malinda Jefferson, Melissa Asher, Rebecca Knight, Mett Dormer, Luís Rodriguez, Scarlett Hart, Anastasia Renae, Shayeena Arezo, Khalim Aliah, Lucia Tsu, Stafford Gaines, Hanz Schultz, Ariel Boshka, Laetitia Zemani, TJ Demitri, Bobby Gahan, Jeremiah Voltaire, Lexi Lancaster, Ariela Reina, Christian Coriolis, Katya Brightway, Evan Bauer, and Yesenia Alevtina. She even had done this for Ariela Zemani, the Zemani family, and the twenty former cartel members during her mission phase, each of whom had since been healed in every way and were now building similar beauty around the states of Chihuahua and Sonora, Mexico, in much the same manner as Sky was doing for South Otselic. "Each of these individuals, including you, will be playing fundamental roles in the exploration and colonization of the Cosmos and in leadership positions on this world, on the IMC, throughout the Universe, and eventually beyond."

After Sky's journey around the world, half of the population of Earth had been read-in and had dual citizenships in their home countries and on any of twenty-thousand tech cities of their choice throughout the Solar System. When Sky went on her missions in April of 2022, Earth's public population was at eight-billion, and now four-billion more had seamlessly joined the ranks of Pathway. Pathway's population was now at seven billion and growing, with three-billion engaged in projects that would be of major support to the Universal preservation of life and its abundance and were living happily outside of Earth's gravity well. Four-billion members of the public on Earth still knew very little or nothing about Pathway, yet there were optimized individuals who may or may not have walked by them each and every day.

In stark contrast to the world population, the population of the United States was three-hundred-fifty-million citizens and only fifty-million-US citizens were members of Pathway. Only fifteen percent of the US had joined the ranks of Pathway, while six-point-ninety-five-billion Pathway members were from more than one-hundred-eighty other countries throughout the world, and out of a total population of eleven-billion Solar-System-wide, almost eighty-five percent of the Pathway population was from outside the US. The US had a very small portion of its population in Pathway as compared to other countries, yet many eyes still turned their direction toward the US as a beacon of technology and as a statistical representation of modern ethics throughout the public world. Fortunately, as of 2023, fifty percent of the US Electoral College happened to consist of members who were delegates of the UP.

Reading the growing numbers in her mind, Joanne knew that it was no wonder why so many places, to include her own hometown and everyone in it, her parents and possibly her brother's killers, or killer, had never even heard of Pathway, before today. In some ways, this had been a uniquely marvelous reality, because it gave all three of them a chance to share organic moments with each other. Joanne had held back on using her newfound abilities and visiting this location, apparently as needed. Sky was now tapping the minds of the townsfolk and had gifted Erin and Joanne the ability to do so as well. Controlling what Joanne saw and heard was quite a task. Sky could process it all at once because of what she was made of, but Joanne knew that she wasn't made of the same material and felt she couldn't exactly work in an exponential manner that Sky could. Still, Joanne could turn things on as she visited people alone or en masse and could listen to them live; later she would be able to see visualizations within the Virtual Universe with time dilation, or sooner if Sky interfaced her mind with Erin's and Joanne's.

For now, they were back on the ground walking and approaching the scene of the crime. All along the path on their way there, things had been upbeat, joyful, jolly, and pleasant. Crazy things that seemed almost supernatural were taking place before Erin and Joanne's eyes. For Sky, this was the norm. Everyone shared a sense of harmony as they walked together. Then, Joanne saw the edge of the forest beyond the clearing, and her nerves picked up again, and they were too much to ignore. Fifteen years had gone by since this horrible deed, and her memories filled the minds of Sky and Erin too. She tried to think of her parents instead.

Joanne had kept in touch with her parents, with an occasional call, snail mail, or a text, but not much more than that. Over the last four years, she had secretly been paying the bills of her parents and every person in town except for one or two dollars per bill. She had done this since she had been fully read-in. She wanted to help in whatever way she could but do it in a manner so that people would assume the typical cost of living there had decreased. The quantity she paid had grown subtly over the weeks, months, and years, and they never knew who or why their bills had shown one-hundred-fifty out of one-hundred-fifty-two dollars paid, but they never questioned it either. It was convenient not to. Tonight, after going to bed, once interfacing with the Virtual Universe, Joanne realized that all would be revealed and the people in town would be aware. Sky assured her that with their training and the quickening of the awareness of the fullness of the realities around them, they would be discrete about Pathway and all things necessary. Those who wished to live naturally only, without optimizations, wouldn't be able to conceive of that reality, they would see something different and their minds would justify what they witnessed as something they deemed rational, and nothing else.

As they sauntered on, Joanne realized they were here.

Right before them, in this seemingly pleasant location, now recently bequeathed with impossibly blossomed evergreen trees and a pleasant highway with a large shoulder of the road for walking, cycling, and taking dogs and other pets on jaunts for some shared bliss, was the location of the scene of the crime.

She then looked behind the gathering of trees, where enough evidence had been destroyed to render the case cold in a very short period of time, and Joanne noticed something she hadn't before. The burn barrel was still there like always, but it had been turned into a shrine.

A larger than life statue of Thomas was positioned such that his hands were hovering over the barrel, which had been bronzed with a continuously and nicely scented fire burning from it as if to warm his hands. Someone had left a bronze plaque on the front of the barrel that read, "No matter what, warm your hearts and your hands with love."

That had been something that Thomas had said often when he was alive. This was usually what he said to those who had he had rescued emotionally after helping them to confront their bullies. He'd do so, typically, with an arm around the shoulder.

Surrounding the shrine were arrays of beautiful and undying bouquets of flowers in a gorgeous arrangement of almost every sort of flower imaginable. "This wasn't me, Joanne," said Sky. "This comes from Martha and everyone who attended your funeral."

Sky then put her arm around Joanne while Erin did the same from the other side. It was as if for a moment her brother were there, consoling her.

"I forgot how beautiful this used to seem, here in the woods, before everything happened. Fifteen years ago, I left, and this was a place I never wanted to see again. But here I am, and now, look at this. I never knew this was here. The love, the kindness, the thoughtfulness of everyone here."

Joanne was in tears. She looked down at the flowers on the ground, and then back up at Thomas, or at least his image, and she put herself together enough to continue to share what was burning within her chest, "This, in its own way, is the sweetest and most beautiful act of kindness I could have ever dreamt to see." She then looked to her right toward Sky and to her left toward Erin. "I couldn't have done this without you two. *Thank you, so much.*" She wept.

They had gathered around her on both sides to comfort her in a big group hug, their heads were turned downward in reverence toward the scene before them, and for all that it meant. After a moment of pause, Erin and Sky looked up toward Joanne, and Sky said, "thank you for sharing this moment with us. It is such a tragedy to lose such wonderful people in this world or in any part of our existence. It is a sad tragedy to see the light of such beauty extinguished far before its time. To those we have lost, their untold potential, their place in our hearts, their unique spirit, and their love for others will live within us forever. We can only hope that someday we will be able to see them again and in a much more harmonious, peaceful, and better way"

Optimized or not, a broken heart and sorrow for loss, as well as gratitude for the goodness of others despite all, still affected each of these individuals, from vastly different beginnings, yet now brought together by an immensely saddening tragedy.

It was late noon, and Sky had conjured up a couple of extra sweet, glazed, and dark berry pastries and cinnamon cream chai tea for each person within the three-member party. "With these genuinely noble acts of kindness, it seems reasonable to have something sweet for the taste buds and the mind," said Sky.

After about thirty minutes, Sky had scanned the area, done the math and science behind the weather existent in the scene on the day of the crime, the pictures registered in Joanne's memory, and had quietly formulated a strong sense of who was behind the acts that left Thomas dead on this day, seventeen years ago. Meanwhile, in a shared moment with Erin and Joanne, she helped the creatures in the clearing to find hospice in the surrounding forest, built a small lake, filled it with beautiful fish, and raised within the center a beautiful fountain that could spray its mists upon every onlooker that would ever come during the summer, or provide a fire for warmth during the winter, in a way that would refresh and surprise, but cause no harm. Around the lake were sandy white beaches and places to rest in the Sun. All three laid down for a few minutes to take in the beauty and the new ambiance fit well with the statue.

Afterward, they dusted themselves off and continued on walking on the left side of the highway to see the oncoming traffic, and to make sure their sturdy yet petite frames didn't damage any nearby or passing vehicles, in the event that drivers weren't paying attention to the road. As they walked by, wildflowers continuously blossomed, the trees that were damaged healed and began to grow year-long flowers, little creeks quietly with water that trickled in from underwater passages to aquifers filled with healthy probiotics down toward larger creeks with minerals, and then to the rivers teeming with fish and flourishing flora. The birds of every variety were tweeting away, unaffected by Pathway's sentient upgrade instincts, but Sky could tell what they were saying anyway, and then she bequeathed sentience into them. She knew every etymological chirp, frequency, and wavelength, and she could translate each method of communication into clear and concisely spoken language. They had asked for help in their own way, for a broken feather, or a damaged disk, and she provided it, and they became both healthy and wise.

"I'm glad you invited me to come here with Joanne, Sky," said Erin. They slowly walked down the road, the trees were green with leaves and the scent of the flowers filled the air, and Erin breathed it all in, feeling at peace.

After twenty minutes of walking and occasionally exchanging dialogue, they arrived at the outskirts of Joanne's neighborhood, by another bridge, where Sky continued to work her countless miracles as she tamed the wild, breathed sentience and healing into every creature, and made every location a beautiful place for the living and a vacation tourist's dream.

They looked behind them and watched as Sky added an ornate and charming sense of architectural and flowery awe to the welcome sign for South Otselic. Joanne lived just on the outskirts of town and had jogged to school and back every day until her parents had purchased a vehicle for her, the one she drove out of town with when she left fifteen years prior.

Her vehicle for leaving town had been a used and weathered, forest green, 2002, Jetta model Volkswagen, and her parents had paid for it in full and given it to her for her 18th birthday, more than halfway through her senior year. She had since given it away to someone in New York, a gentleman who had no home at the time. While recording her first album, during her time for lunch she would buy a meal for two, sit with him at a nearby park, and share it with him while listening to his stories of Vietnam, and of his desires to open a restaurant someday. Before leaving for her first global tour, she had gifted it to him, fully operational, and then she kept in contact. She visited him throughout the years, and he had since opened a small restaurant in New York City and had done very well for himself.

"I met him too," said Sky. "Jeremiah Voltaire. He not only cooks well, but he has quite a singing voice. Sometimes he'll get on the microphone at his restaurant and sing for the patrons. He is quite a handsome old soul, in his twenty-two-year-old and clean-cut package. Have you ever thought of singing with him on stage?"

"I had entertained the thought, but since he's currently living life and walking around as his young grandson, I thought it best to not put him into the public foray quite yet, at least not until after Eliza takes office. He bears a striking similarity to Jordan Vale; a bit shorter, but wow he is a handsome man! Once Eliza takes office, a lot of things such as cell regeneration therapies and physiological optimizations will be put into the mainstream, and he can come out as himself, but rejuvenated. Can you believe Eliza recruited him? She has quite the busy schedule.

"Thank you for visiting him, Sky.

"I knew he was fully read-in; Eliza has him in mind as the Vice Commander for IMC Zone-06 with Rebecca Knight as the Commander. I saw him in passing about a year ago, and he went from looking his age of seventy-two to looking like a dark-skinned, handsome, and clean cut twenty-two-year-old heartthrob. When I saw him way back in the day, his skin had been greying just as much as his hair, and now his hair is young and black again, cut almost to the skin on the sides and back, with long hair on top, or closely cropped in a gorgeous loose and wavy high top. I could tell it was him because the flavor of each of our memories was undeniably unique and distinguishable in the most beautiful of ways. Yes, Sky, we did sing together a couple of times for his patrons, but we both tried to keep him somewhat low in profile.

"Low profile or no, he got into lab farming, culinary arts, honed his singing and music skills, and has finished his Ph.D.'s in culinary arts, neuroscience and biotechnology. He has done so much. He has even designed gene-fortifying clean meats! He can cook on the same level as the best of chefs at the T.O., yet maintains his restaurant in New York City, but on a much smaller scale, and he maintains a very loyal clientele.

Jeremiah has done a few missions with Pathway, in free moments, yet he works there still, going to the Melrose Campus through his own jump gate in his elaborate apartment upstairs to do research with Pathway in the Virtual Universe. When people ask him where his grandfather went, he says he's retired, but works on all the paperwork for the business, while he manages the restaurant for his grandfather. It's interesting because he never had any children. Rebecca will be tickled silly to have such a fine gentleman as her Vice Commander!"

They continued their walk, and for a second there, Erin thought about the title, Vice Commander, and thought quietly, *"Vice commander, that does have a nice ring to it..."* She didn't bring it up, and they meandered on.

As they moved on from their temporary break by the bridge, Joanne suddenly felt her nerves creep up again. "Even though I've been optimized I still feel nervous. How can that be?" asked Joanne. She knew the science behind why nervousness occurs, and she wasn't looking for schooling on that, merely a little validation. She also knew the science behind validation too.

Erin beat Sky to an answer, "I feel nervous too, and we all know why, but even still, your parents love you. I can tell already. I'm picking up on their mental activity right now. Wow, Joanne! They truly love you and have missed you for a long time. They watched your rise to stardom, even as you won all the awards possible in the music industry, and then your continued growth in the industry *after you joined Pathway*. They watched you for years with pride. It looks like they understand you didn't leave them because of anything they had done, they know you love them, but that you left because of the sorrow you felt and the lack of closure surrounding your brother's tragedy. Wow, they were the ones that worked with Martha and the rest of the town, to build your brother's shrine. I'm picking up on Martha's parents, who live in the house across the street, and it looks like Martha Serena works up in Georgetown and won't be back for a couple of hours. From what's going on in the minds of her parents, now is a good time to meet your parents first and catch up, in an old-school-style, with conversation."

As they walked closer to Joanne's childhood home, Sky turned to Joanne and asked, "Do you mind if I work a little of my magic on and around your home? I promise no harm to any living being."

Joanne would have normally said no. She wanted to keep it completely her parents' choice when it came to changes to their home and their surroundings, but for some reason her curiosity was piqued, and she responded with approval and a little whimsically, "I don't mind, if you'll show Erin and me how you do it, so maybe we can take turns. Do you mind?"

"Sure," said Sky.

Sky did not touch Martha's home with any of her changes, but she did show the vivid details of how she could change every road, every tree, every landscape, every creature, and every mind. "The least sentient, and the highest and the lowest elevations are always changed first. I only change them as they would have become had humanity never cursed them with poison or torn their environment asunder, but had instead sought to understand their purpose, while simultaneously finding mutual determination, shared drive to mutual advantage, and bliss-inducing and beautiful coexistence. I then combine the organization of chaos of both humanity and Nature and create a beautiful and harmonious reality that can be shared, allowing a reality similar to their own, but with somewhat subtle and obvious changes.

"As I connect their minds to the Twelve Database Moons, it allows them to have a shared cognitive and existential experience with everyone and everything else linked to the Virtual Universe for complete and appreciative understanding from one creature to the next. I then show them a source of nourishment that doesn't involve predation or destruction of any kind, except for the breakdown of refuse, or obvious trash and waste, into material that allows for abundant nutrients for the ground, the flowers, the blossoms, and the waters that flow both above and below the ground to allow everything and everyone around it to flourish.

"The clouds of nanos are encoded through time dilation, with my interface to the Virtual Universe, and they render the structures to be filled in the same spaces as they were previously, to avoid movement or harm to living beings that may be in a certain location at a given time, but are also left with increased quality and craftsmanship as shared and even hoped for prevalently in the minds of each individual in a household, or the owners or professionals of a place of work. The places they stand on don't move, instead, their minds are carried away in thought, for as long as it takes for a blink of an eye. The materials below, above, and all around them are converted through artistically detailed and architecturally-sound designs into materials that are stronger, more malleable, and pleasing in every way to their minds. Once the flicker of light is done, my work is complete.

"Do you want to give this a try, Joanne? Or would you rather interface with my mind as I do it? Erin, you can interface with my mind as well."

"I think I'll practice somewhere else less likely to be harmful to my parents, first," Joanne said with a tone of humor and excitement at what Sky was about to do to her childhood home, "Sure, I'll interface with you."

In a flicker of the light of the surrounding area, Sky was done. Both Joanne and Erin were amazed in every way with what they had witnessed and experienced. In a fraction of a second, weeks, months, and even years of work had been done, and the result was gorgeous. "You can do this, too, Joanne and Erin. You have to believe you can, visualize every possible aspect of everything influenced by what you are doing, and essentially have what you already have, which is a kind and beautifully creative frame of mind."

Joanne took in all that Sky had done and shared, was completely impressed with everything she saw, and in a contrite voice, she said, "I'm afraid that if I did this, something or someone would get hurt. But I saw how gentle you were with every creature, almost like a gentle hand or blanket nestled around them, as changes were made to their environment, their minds, and their shared instincts, where predation and overpopulation is no longer a concern. Instead, everything works now to sustain and grow an environment that will allow the living to change that which is affected by desolation and destruction into something of beauty, joy, innovation, and continuation of shared purpose. At the core of this purpose, lies the ability to preserve the Universe itself, rather than let it wither away, as it expands to a big freeze.

"These changes will serve a purpose, where legacies of music, art, romance, history, religion, and science can be preserved for the long-haul. A beautiful legacy of the preservation of life and all its splendor can endure for indeterminate quantities of time. Our legacy will help us to bridge the gaps of understanding between us and other civilizations of every type, and through it, we may meet and share our civilizations and lives with others, while working together to preserve our Universe, rather than render our civilizations worthless and non-existent through violence, uncontrolled chaos, and destruction. Wow, Sky! Keep on being your amazing self!"

After a very brief moment of silence, looking around, Erin spoke.

"What Joanne said," Erin smiled in agreement.

Sky could tell that the Sun would set in less than an hour and a half, and she knew that Martha would be home soon. There was something peculiar about Martha, and Sky would open up about it and address that in due time. To properly heal both the minds of Joanne and Erin, Joanne needed to knock her childhood front door, first.

From there, she could continue optimizations, as they made their introductions, shared their conversations, a homemade meal, and a few moments watching the beauty of the Sun, as the Earth revolved around its own orbit and our vantage point caused by the photons from the Sun to hit the crystal-like expressions of the particles in the sky, causing them to become iridescent, with overtones of purple, plum, and peach, giving way to a clear and starry night sky. Yes, a sunset.

"Are you ready, Joanne?" asked Sky.

A Stark Truth

With a small hint of hesitation, Joanne mustered all the courage she could from within. In the grand scheme of things, this was a small matter given all that she had done in the last four years; however, for Joanne seeing her parents again after fifteen years was quite a challenge. Nevertheless, armed with the reassurances from her two friends, she nervously took the lead walking up the now pristinely finished driveway, which was quite gentle to step upon, almost like memory foam.

As she looked down, she noticed that her garments had changed into something professional, a beige cardigan and a matching pleated skirt, underneath her cardigan, was a white blouse and her buttons were buttoned to the top with a bowtie that matched her argyle socks and professional women's Sienna shiny and flat black Crocs. She then turned right and noticed that both Sky and Erin were groomed and dressed studiously and breathtakingly too. She followed the little sidewalk to a short stairway, both of which were firm yet gentle to the feet and stepped up the three stairs to the entryway. As if time stood still for her, she drew up her courage from within, raised her right hand, formed a fist to knock on the door, and hesitated.

Typically, for most anyone, it is quite easy to knock on a door, but when you're not sure how the reception will be it rarely ever is. Each person is wired differently, however. Some can put their minds and notions into autopilot, feel allowed to do what they must, overcome their fears, and then deal with whatever comes along, should any of a multitude of situations arise. Knocking on the front door as a solicitor or a missionary might be a challenge all its own, always at risk, and never sure of what is on the other side. However, knocking on a door, especially to greet your Mom and Dad when it's been almost fifteen years, well that is something else. Most people avoided that altogether, or they would ease into it with more frequent texts, phone calls, letters, and some pre-emptive coordination. Attempting to do so without any sort of communication for almost fifteen years, can make someone rather queasy, and queasy was exactly how Joanne was feeling. Despite the fact that she was optimized, and to standards at the level provided by both biopod and Sky Taylor, she was still as queasy as one would be just before the beginning of a very important race, where if you lost you felt like you would be shamed for life.

Sky had explained to Joanne earlier, during their trek from town, that she merely needed to have faith in her ability to reach other's hearts, and that if she did, there wasn't much that she couldn't do. So, there she was, she had to knock on the door, but she was nervous and trying not to shake. Standing just behind her right side, Sky put her right hand on her shoulder to calm her, and said, "It will be alright, Joanne. Please, do not worry. Everything is going to be alright."

Without turning, Joanne felt an intense and calm sensation rise within her as Sky placed her hand on her shoulder; her touch was soothing and gentle. It felt as though she was not only standing there on that warm late Spring Day, but there were small unseen and non-existent cool little drops of crystalline rain causing tickles down her back. She knew Sky's touch could kill a man, so a subtle fear and subsequent thrill permeated her being. Somehow, this was the most soothing feeling she'd ever felt in her life. She blushed. As she slowly raised her arm and closed her fist, pausing again, she felt Erin put her hand on her other shoulder, and felt a special bond of sisterhood and of support and a special maturity that could not be described in words.

"Time to meet my parents; it's been long enough," Joanne thought to herself.

"Knock, knock, knock," Joanne tapped the door nervously. As she did, thoughts of all of the moments she had spent with her parents and her brother at the dinner table flooded into her mind—the conversations, the shared laughs, and the warm feelings shared between each family member. She also began to pick up on the thoughts of her parents.

They had no idea who was at the door. There was a "No Soliciting" sign at the bottom of the door, so they were mystified as to whom it could be without any advanced warning. Together, her parents went to the front entryway, peered out the secured eye hole, and were ecstatic with what they saw. In a hurry, her Mom opened the door. She eagerly looked at Joanne, overjoyed, and gave her a big and very long hug.

"Where have you been, young lady. We've missed you for a long, long time. It's so good to see you," her Mom said, as she was moved with emotion, and tears began streaming down her face.

All of the fear that Joanne had felt for so much time, was gone in a flash. Her parents were happy to see her. They weren't angry with her in any way. She didn't feel indignation at her absence, instead, she felt their love emanating from their minds and their auras. They were quick to let Joanne and her two beautiful and young companions inside to talk and share a cup of tea.

After making introductions in the doorway, Mrs. Gallant invited the party of three into the Gallant home, and Mr. Gallant gave each one a gentlemanly hug. He too was in tears. He was an emotionally-connected man, and he loved his daughter very much. He was very proud of her and had watched each turn she made through the years during her absence. While gone, she had still made herself available in public through her music, the videos, the concerts on YouTube, Netflix, Prime, Hulu, and so much more.

Her parents had watched her pursuits as they unfolded in the public eye and the inspiration her father had derived from every song she had ever written and recorded throughout her career, all of which he'd listened to in repeat over the years giving him hope each day that she would eventually return home.

Mr. Gallant had always known that the loss of Joanne's brother weighed heavily upon her. Losing his son tore him apart as well. He had loved his son, straight or gay, or no matter the actions expressed due to his inherent nature. All around, he was a good young man.

His son had done well in school, looked out for others, was a wonderful role model for his peers, and it was unconscionable to Mr. Gallant that there was someone who had wanted to harm Thomas. He was a good boy, a wonderful person, and had the untold potential for making the world a happier and better place. The loss of Thomas was the world's loss, and Mr. Gallant knew that he would always feel that way. His daughter, likewise, was wonderfully amazing in every way, he loved her very much. He had dismissed any other sentiment or question as to why she had not returned after she graduated from high school. He missed Joanne and was glad to see her back.

"So, what brings you home after so many years?" asked Mrs. Gallant. She was happy to see her back, had resented her leaving for so long, but she seemed to collect her emotions a little more quickly and tried to be an upbeat host for Joanne and her two resplendent guests.

Erin and Sky had secretly been conversing with each other through their neural links; both had been admiring how obvious it was now, that Joanne had received her blonde locks from her father and her big crystal blue eyes from her mother, who had raven hair.

"I suppose a myriad of things," said Joanne, feeling a little more at ease with how things were playing out, but still picking up a little-bridled apprehension from her Mother. "Mostly, it was Sky Taylor, a dear friend who sensed a growing need for me to visit. The fact that I hadn't visited in so long made it harder for me to do so. Thomas' tragedy and the unresolved mystery surrounding it made me rather queasy about returning to South Otselic altogether. Sky and Erin made it so much easier all along the way. We arrived in town last night and walked here from the Broadlawns Bed & Breakfast. They walked with me to kind of ease me into seeing the crime scene and then seeing you two again. I'm so sorry that it's been so long, and I apologize for not visiting or keeping in contact. It's just that this has all been rather nerve-wracking."

Mrs. Gallant spoke up with subtle cheer and more overt curtness, "Well then, we have Sky and Erin to thank for bringing our daughter back home to us. Thank you, Sky and Erin!"

Sky, noticing her mother's tone, spoke up in Joanne's defense, "Mrs. Gallant, Joanne had wanted to return to home and to her hometown for quite some time, but her nerves had been affecting her too much. It didn't lessen her attention to detail nor the quality of her work, but I could sense that if we didn't do anything about it soon, it just might. She is a wonderful person to work with, a very talented lyricist, songwriter, singer, and performer, and her work with Pathway as its Vice President has been monumental in a way that is unique to Joanne alone. Have you heard of Pathway, Mr. and Mrs. Gallant?"

"I am pretty sure neither of us has," responded Mrs. Gallant, who had kept her emotions at bay, yet was very intrigued with Sky and Erin, both of whom sat on each side of her daughter, facing her and her husband while sharing a rather delicious tea. "Please, enlighten me?"

Erin sensed Sky giving her a mental nudge through her neural link, since she was the President of Pathway, and something cryptic about Mrs. Gallant seemed to be causing Joanne to freeze up a little. Erin spoke up, "Well, Pathway is a fairly large multi-industrial company that specializes in biotechnology and neuroscience. However, it is also very involved with physics, space mining, development and use of cold fusion, and exploration throughout the Solar System. Eliza Williams was the initial founder, accompanied by Yesha Alevtina and James Cooper. Have you heard of them before?"

"The name, Eliza Williams, certainly rings a bell," Mr. Gallant responded; suddenly clear as to who she was. "I believe she is the Senator from the state of Massachusetts who was the first to put her hat in the ring to run as President of the United States last year. Yesha is her running-mate, also running peculiarly early for a presidential race. They're each a part of this new political party, the UP, I believe. I don't believe, however, that I know too much about James Cooper. Who might he be? How does he factor into the Pathway equation?" her Father asked.

Erin answered Mr. Gallant's question, "Well, yes, you're right about Eliza, Yesha, the UP, and their aspirations toward the presidency of the US. Since they were a relatively new political party, which has been growing quite steadily from local office through national office since its official formation in 2010, they entered the political race quite early for an earlier increase in exposure. There are a lot of issues they will be able to resolve, rather quickly, if they win. Much of what many people fear, or are worried about today, may well be mitigated within days of both assuming substantial roles in the executive office. They have done so much for humanity already, but most of their ideas and technologies are classified to prevent misuse of them by those who might be less than benevolent with their intentions.

"They have developed powerful tools to increase our health, our clarity of mind, and our quality of life. They are also close friends of ours, as is James Cooper."

Joanne, took over for Erin, having now regained her bravery, appreciated the fact that Erin had given a wonderful intro, and explained, "James was an architectural engineer and project manager for YY Construction Corporation about fifteen years ago, and is now the President of Pathway Solar System Operations and Pathway Construction. He doesn't see himself so much as a public figure and has pretty much worked with his crews and quite a large populace to help things happen. He's been a powerhouse behind the scenes for Pathway Industries, working closely with Eliza and Yesha, and now with Erin and me. Have you seen some of the latest architectural designs that have come out around Massachusetts, Washington, DC, the State Capitals, and in New York?"

Mr. Gallant grew curious, "You both seem convinced of Senator Williams and Ms. Yesha Alevtina. I suppose you'll enlighten me soon regarding their political goals. As far as James' architectural designs are concerned, I am intrigued by them actually. Furthermore, the more I think about it, I do believe I've seen Pathway in the news a few times. Joanne, you've been with Pathway for at least four years, haven't you?"

"Yes."

"I knew it! I've seen you in talk shows and in the news. You were in interviews talking about your musical career and your recently accomplished Ph.D.'s in neuroscience and business administration. You explained how that has helped you with your music, and I will say, those tunes certainly have struck a chord in this home, Joanne. We're so glad to see you. How well do you know this, um, James Cooper? Is there any romantic connection we should be aware of?"

Joanne politely chuckled, "No, I can't see any romance in the stars for any of us at all, at least not at this time in our lives. As far as political goals for Eliza and Yesha are concerned, we have every bit of confidence in them. If you would like, I can explain why we do have confidence in them. Ultimately, we're all working to prevent the gloom and doom that gets tossed around via too many channels and so many social avenues these days, and we keep in touch with each other in different and more productive ways. As such, we are very dedicated to the different missions, goals, and innovations of Pathway."

Joanne paused, and then continued, "If James were interested in anyone, my guess is that it would be in Eliza Williams. Ever since they met in 2008, I've heard from others and have seen with my own eyes since 2019, a little bit of a heart-warming chemistry between the two. The truth is, they both refuse to admit it. I've spent time with both, and when I mention the other's names, they have this unexplainable glow about them."

Erin picked up where Joanne left off, "It's been quite some time since Eliza or James has dated anyone. Eliza lost her first true love during 9/11, and I don't believe that James has ever dated anyone."

"Oh?" asked Mrs. Gallant. Looking at Erin with curiosity.

Erin responded, "Yes. I can still feel her pain, as she sat watching the news that day, having talked to him earlier as he was so excited to go into work. That same morning two towers fell, and then she watched aghast, knowing that Charles and Yesha's boyfriend, Eugene, were on the same level, the level that the planes had impacted first. Her pain still burns as a fire within, yet she culls the flames through innovation that heals rather than harms. No matter her past and the residual and intense feelings that ensue, it all seems to dissipate each time she is around James. I get the sense there is something brewing there too. The truth is, they're both always busy, never slowing down, and I don't think that either of them would even guess the other one was even remotely infatuated with the other. It's a romance story in the making and playing out before the eyes of the rest of us. As amazing as both are and as much as they have done for humanity, I think the rest of us would be moved to tears if they were to begin dating. It would be a union of the stars, for sure."

Mrs. Gallant curious about her wording spoke up, "When you say, 'I can feel her pain,' or, 'I don't think either of them would even guess the other was remotely infatuated,' how is it that you would say you know that?" It seemed to Mr. and Mrs. Gallant that Erin was talking as if she could understand what was going on inside their heads, so she wanted more clarity.

"Well," Erin paused, "I suppose we can call it intuition?" That was Erin's attempt at a save, following her little slip. In small circles, she was used to talking to Pathway members in the open and without encrypting her speech, so she had spoken as if that were still the case. Therefore, she knew she had to say something in order to avoid talking about biopods, neural links, and the Virtual Universe, etc. She felt that she needed to hold off on that conversation until the time was right and that this might be a topic best handled by their daughter, Joanne.

"Mom and Dad, please let me try to explain?"

"We're all ears," chimed Mr. and Mrs. Gallant in unison and ever so eager to listen. They were honestly very happy to see their daughter after all these years, but what Erin had said was also kind of alluring. All three of these young ladies were captivatingly intriguing to behold and listen to. What they were saying seemed quite a bit above their heads. They saw their daughter, and she was every bit as beautiful as she had always been, if not more so. She had this unexplainable maturity about her, coupled with this aesthetic youth she had when she had gone through high school so many years before.

As they followed her music career, they noticed that she had begun to age like normal until 2019, and when they saw her again, she had been quite a bit revitalized and youthful. Here she was now, and none of it was glitz or glamour, her youth and beauty both inside and out were the real deal. The more they thought about it, the more the Gallants were curious as to how Joanne had maintained such a vibrant persona, like a twenty-two-year-old, even though she was thirty-three. Whatever she had to share it might be quite interesting. They were beginning to sense that Joanne had a lot more to say than what she was getting at. Plus, there was something about Sky that made them feel both instantaneously at ease and whimsically curious about both her and Erin. Erin seemed like a precious jewel, a young lady who was powerful, intelligent, wise, yet innocent and charming.

Joanne explained to her parents about each location in life that she had gone, and more of the deeper details about Pathway. She brought forward Eliza's foresight and goals as her company, Pathway LLC, was set up. She went into detail about how it had grown to Pathway Industries, and then Eliza's goals with the UP and the meaning behind the term, Universal Ethics. She then explained in detail the science of the biopods, how they worked for optimization of physiological and neurological health, the issuance of nanos, and the interface with the Virtual Universe, neural links, and how to use each of their newly gifted abilities.

"Eliza's developments were so brilliant they were beyond the scope of anyone else or anything they could have possibly imagined at her time in history. Eliza continuously teaches us all through example that life, longevity, its quality, the mind and its clarity are essential to our overall well-being. She also teaches how everyone possesses abilities that are unique to those of anyone else, especially when it comes to our untold potential and the plethora of contributions that we can each make to the advancement of civilization. Different from many others, each of us here, carries virtues that are essential to the existence of humanity for the long-haul."

Joanne paused, and together, Erin, Sky, and Joanne took turns briefing the Gallants on the history of Pathway and what it stood for. Each aspect of Pathway seemed to intrigue her parents more and more. As they talked, they began to discuss the biopods and Virtual Universe training, until they asked, "Is that an option that we can have?"

"Since you asked," said Sky. "You may. However, since I am here, you won't need a biopod. I can provide one for each of you anyway, for future use, after I am gone. However, I can take us all on a similar journey, if you'd like."

"Would you like Sky to work her magic now?" asked Joanne, looking at her parents in a manner that suggested she was trying to contain her excitement. Her parents over the last hour had been sold multiple times on the idea of physiological and neurological optimization from the moment that they had introduced it. They were especially intrigued by the idea of completely understanding one another and appreciated having the ability to compartmentalize memories that were much more private or confidential in nature.

Joanne had explained, "The things you share in private with each other, or the things that you are not ready yet to share with anyone else, will remain private and will never be accessible to anyone, aside from those who you truly wish to share them with. Privacy and intimacy are for you and those who are closest to you alone and are special."

Mr. and Mrs. Gallant were also internally intrigued with the Virtual Universe and some of the projects that all three of the young ladies had talked about, so Joanne continued, "We develop and carry out our goals with ingenuity coupled with love for those around us, and we are determined to raise the quality of life of every living being, so that humanity can be worthy to carry its legacy throughout the Cosmos. We are determined to be bringers of life, of beauty, and of abundance. All that we bring, we will bring with us as a legacy of love, kindness, compassion, and healing, bringing youth and indeterminate lifespans to those who wish to be a part of the long-term journey, whether through support in the home Solar System, or in future settlements and cities throughout the Universe."

Sky got up, and like that, she changed into her iridescent angelic form, as she had many times before, but in the Virtual Universe. She then brought everyone in the room into the shared Virtual Universe, to train Mr. and Mrs. Gallant, with Joanne and Erin at their side. Just moments prior to entering the Virtual Universe, Erin and Joanne were amazed, and Joanne's parent's hearts raced as a flicker of light flashed, and they fell silent for a brief moment. Moments later, after their journey through the Virtual Universe, when they awoke, it was with a youth, both within and without them, and clarity of mind that they hadn't felt in years or had quite possibly never felt before.

Joanne's parents suddenly sensed a connection inside their minds with each of the three young ladies before them and then each other, and together, every person in the room grew to understand each other more deeply than possible via any other means. Together, they were healed in so many ways, and Joanne's parents experienced their renewed transition to youth, as well as the astuteness gained through training in the Virtual Universe.

Together, in just a few short moments, they experienced all that every other member of Pathway had experienced, which gave them many vigintillions of years' worth of knowledge and experience gained through a complete understanding of countless lives of others, all converted into wisdom. Erin, Joanne, and Mr. and Mrs. Gallant would later continue with the profound training of their new abilities each night as they laid their heads to rest on their pillows. For now, shared experience and journeys through memories past were immense and indescribable.

They each saw Sky, as she lowered herself down, curled her wings, and then she sat down on the couch beside their daughter and Erin Carter, as the human she felt she was. Gone was the regal and iridescent angel, and back was her professional and youthful attire. Their new reality brought humility to their hearts, and they realized that at that moment, they were sitting before the promise of the ages, the promise of the Universe. Each of their hearts melted in every possible and emotional way, before Sky Taylor, The Iridescent Angel. She was someone who loved humanity despite all its weaknesses and would do more for every man, woman, or child, than many within human civilization ever would, save for the many among the ranks of Pathway.

"I've never felt better in all of my life," said Mr. Gallant, realizing how exhausted he was.

"I've never felt better in all of my life as well. Oh wow, suddenly I feel rather sleepy, too," whispered Mrs. Gallant. Both Gallants were experiencing the effects of the nanos in their bodies as they were engaged in non-stop fixing, mending, and updating each cell, neuron, and gene within them, to keep their minds and bodies as healthy as someone who could live forever, yet with continued and increased perfection and with the ability to live for an indeterminate quantity of time. This could be very exhausting on anyone's physiology and neurology.

"Well, we need to visit Martha's parents and then Martha as soon as she comes home. Thank you for helping Martha and the town's folk with that shrine, Mom, and Dad. That was truly beautiful. I was nervous as I approached the site and seeing your collaborative efforts put me at ease."

"You're welcome, of course," said Mrs. and Mr. Gallant, yawning, and both in unison. Their love for each other was so much so, that their shared understanding of each other almost resulted in a collective mindset. Nevertheless, they were still every bit the amazing and beautiful, and unique people they had always been. They just seemed to rejoice within at the new type of connection they shared with each other. It was a sweet flavor. If shared thought could be described in any way, it was unlike anything they had ever experienced before.

Joanne was excited to see her parents, as young as she was, and filled with the wisdom of the ages. They had opened their minds completely to each other, and they loved each other even more so because between the two they kept no secrets. Of course, they kept certain special moments and private memories partitioned within their minds, separate from everyone else, but they shared those moments only with each other. Nevertheless, the flavor of their love could be felt and sensed by everyone in the room.

"It's been wonderful seeing you again, Joanne. Quick, make your way over to Martha's house. I get the sense that as wonderful as Martha's parents have become, there are some oddities about their daughter you might want to learn about before she returns home. She is sweet, but I get the sense right now, that there is something she is hiding," said Mrs. Gallant, in a tired, yet wise, peaceful, and happy tone.

Erin, Joanne, and Sky said their goodbyes and told Mr. and Mrs. Gallant that they would be by the next day if that was okay. Joanne's parents agreed as they made their way to the door.

Making their way across the street to Martha's parent's home, the three young ladies smiled in harmony with how things went. Meeting Joanne's parents, even after fifteen years, had shown Joanne that from then on out she would never need to feel awkward or nervous again about these opportunities. Joanne knew that she would stop by often, using the jump gate Sky had left in their newly carved-out and beautifully-built basement. This was a place, touched by none other than the mind of Sky Taylor, herself. And, because of their virtues, as Sky had taught them previously that day, this home and its occupants could be around forever.

The Sun was just a few moments away from setting when they knocked on Mr. and Mrs. Serena's door. Sky had made no changes whatsoever to the Serena family's home or their property. The changes she intended to make would happen after talking to Martha. Each change would unfold in a manner dependent upon the hearts of Mr. and Mrs. Serena, and as necessary to heal both them and their daughter, in accordance with the unraveling of each part of their visit.

The Serenas seemed pleasant and didn't seem to make a fuss about the three young ladies visiting just before sunset. They even offered some enjoyably fresh-brewed coffee.

"Yes, please," said Joanne, followed by approvals from Erin and Sky.

"So, Mr. and Mrs. Serena, how has Martha been all of these years?" Joanne asked in a kind and pleasant tone.

"Oh, she has been quite busy. As a local pastor, she teaches the local congregation, and sometimes goes out of town for training, charity events, and study with Georgetown's pastor," Mrs. Serena responded. She was proud of her daughter, but something in her tone also showed some concern.

"I know the years were difficult, so long ago. How has the loss of the young man she had crushed on throughout high school affected her through the years?" Joanne cut to the chase and rather quickly. It appears meeting her own parents again, after such a long time, and the uniquely amazing experience that it was, had given her a resurgence of confidence.

Mrs. Serena was very perceptive, caught on, and answered right away, "When she came home that day, she was completely shaken up, in tears, stumbling over her words, and then she locked herself up in her room until the Sheriff arrived to question her about what she had witnessed. It had taken a while for her to overcome what had happened. After you left town, Joanne, she began taking divinity courses. We go to the church on the corner of 13th and Maple, and she has taken up preaching there. Some of her sermons are a little stark in nature, but all in all, she does quite wonderfully. The congregation tries to share her pain. They know she had a young lady's crush on Thomas, and it was most likely a huge loss for her. It was she who had brought up the idea of building Thomas a shrine. It seemed odd at first, but once it was built it was beautiful, and everyone else seemed to feel a certain sense of closure. The town has bonded ever since and each of us was able to move forward."

"Martha should be home in a few moments, young ladies, if you'd like to stay for a little while longer and ask her, yourselves" suggested Mr. Serena.

Sky scanned both of their minds, and neither of them was guilty of any crime, other than being rather harsh to their daughter when she was much younger. The Serenas were very firm believers of their faith and were of the persuasion that certain identities were unfit for the kingdom of heaven. While that was their belief, and while Sky had always respected a person's individual beliefs as they related to their own personal choices, she certainly did not agree with their position of judgment toward Thomas. They had loved him for years, but that had changed drastically when they had found out about his letter to the high school quarterback, Jordon. Sky knew something about this long ago; she had the sense that both Erin and Joanne were beginning to feel it too.

Not one of the three young ladies felt remotely comfortable, not due to their nanos or their physiological or neurological optimizations, but because they were picking up on something very stark regarding the history of the household. Despite the Serena family's overt attempts to be hospitable, there was something that even they were hiding. It wasn't Mr. and Mrs. Serena's fault, per say, but there was something or someone approaching the home that left a bitter taste in the minds of those that could now read minds. Sky wasn't uncomfortable for any reason other than she knew there was much more about Thomas' story than the Serenas knew about.

Mr. and Mrs. Serena had suspicions about their daughter, but they would constantly let those suspicions go because they loved her very much and on the account of the fact that Martha was an academically brilliant student and had been trusted by so many throughout the town. To add to their perception of their daughter, Martha had studied Divinity in College. From there, she had become the minister at the First Baptist Church, in town. Too many people had grown to respect her, despite the clouds of grey and the kicks to the gut they felt each week.

No matter how anyone felt about Martha, they were about to find out why they were each feeling a sense of discomfort. There was something stark shrouded within her quiet demeanor. Sky, Joanne, and Erin could sense that Martha was nearby, and heard the front door close.

"Hello, Mom. Hello Dad." Everyone turned around to hear the voice of Martha.

As if a dark cloud blew in, Martha had returned from her business in Georgetown, had greeted her parents, and had then found herself suddenly floored when she saw Joanne. In their younger years, Martha had always been the friend across the street. Many times, she had been the quiet one. Thomas had always sat by her at lunchtime and would console her fears of society, social media, and the way humanity seemed to be in increasingly shorter supply. Now, here Martha was, she had forgotten about the good moments with Thomas and Joanne, his younger sister, but she also knew that the negative thoughts she was feeling toward Joanne were unjustified.

Martha was wearing a black uniform that she had chosen to go with her status as Pastor; this was her own heir of artistry, and a unique flavor of its own. With what Sky knew about her, Martha was standing there as a wolf in sheep's clothing and the sad truth was that she had duped the congregation for years. All would be made right soon, and her congregation would forgive her. As it was today, apparently, she had been out of town seeing people at the church in Georgetown and working with the Pastor there. Sky also picked up on a vibe that suggested that Martha and the Georgetown Pastor might have had a bit more going on than simply visiting the locals there and handing out bread and tea. She didn't mind it so much; it was the lie that mattered. This lie told Sky so much about Martha's character, and she was akin to reveal it.

"Hello. My name is Sky Taylor." Sky had gotten up off the couch, and offered her hand for a handshake, but Martha did not reciprocate. "First of all, thank you for helping the Gallants put up Thomas' shrine. That was very thoughtful of you. It brought Joanne peace on our walk to visit her parents after fifteen years. Of course, you know Joanne Gallant, and this beautiful young lady here is Erin Carter.

"Erin is the President of Pathway Industries. Thirteen years ago, she was a young girl, from Kearney, Nebraska, suffering from progeria. Because of Yesha, Eliza, Amber and her team, and James, she is now healed. She stands here before you, completely healed and healthy, and with a mind as sharp as several vigintillion minds.

"Again, I am Sky; I am pleased to finally meet your acquaintance, 'Pastor' Serena." She offered her hand again, but this time, Martha shook it. Sky smiled her winning smile, "I hope you don't mind us dropping in? It has been a while since Joanne was here, and she wanted to catch up with long-time acquaintances. How was your day?" As Sky finished what she was saying, you could hear the ionic charges crackle in the air, like lightning.

As the years had passed, Martha had sensed more than a simple question was asked many times within herself, and now, Sky had asked that very same question. *"How was your day?"* She thought about that day, endlessly, and the days that had led up to it every night as she fell into her nightmare-infested slumber. These nightmares were in part due to Martha's own creation and in many cases, they were a result of the environment that surrounded her when she was much younger. Thomas had helped her greatly during her time of loneliness, but since his death, she had caged herself for years. At some point, she took to the cloth and never turned back.

Martha's parents had since matured, and the punishments and teachings they had tried to impart to their daughter as she grew older had been a softer and more kind. However, certain teachings on a young and impressionable mind can leave scars that are deep, and miracles are needed to heal those types of wounds. Martha had tried to bury everything from her past but had instead buried anything that she could learn from and all that was good within her. She had hidden every sense of anything that resulted in the pain she had felt two days before Thomas died.

With her own uncompromising sense of fear of the past, she had tried to hide under the shroud of Pastor. Martha knew somehow that this ruse would result as futile with Sky around, and both she and Sky knew it. Sky had combed every detail of Martha's brain and she knew the truth about Pastor Martha Serena.

Despite the fact that Sky had said very little, but what was correct, she listened as Martha answered with a forced and an exerted sense of authority, "I've been about my day, attending to the needs of the flock in Georgetown, and working with their Pastor. I can say with complete confidence that my day was a blessing from God. How was your day?" Martha knew Sky had been talking about something else, but she was trying to deflect this potential for a stark revelation in every way she knew.

Picking up on her tone, Sky responded, "Our day was most exquisite as well. I'm glad your day was a blessing too. We've all had moments of anguish in our lives, we've all experienced the sentiments of being torn asunder from time to time, no matter our efforts to do what we believed to be right, and we've all found joy within, as the fruits of our labors resulted in the rejoicing of someone else. I am proud that you were attending to the 'needs of your flock.'

"I am also proud that you were tending to certain needs that every woman and man has within. There is no need to cover up things that when uncovered can release tension, stress, and undue burdens. Vindication is a blessing to every victim suffering from the hands of other victims, including to the perpetrator, who is also a victim, yet, who may have caused undue consequence to the rights of others.

"Vindication allows learning on both sides, it allows compassion to exist, and it allows a release of burdens that are too great to bear through the entirety of life. Once we have released our shame, we can strive to serve those around us, to give of ourselves to make right what we have done wrong in the past. When we demonstrate humility, those who we have wronged can rejoice to know that their love for others, just as themselves, was worth every patient moment.

"All who are impacted will be even more light of step and happy, knowing that healing can take place, that scars can be replaced with a newly found revitalization existent in clarity of mind, clarity of purpose, and clarity of meaning when it comes to what we do to increase the well-being of others, including ourselves, throughout life's journey.

"Martha, I know it has been years, and we don't mean to resurface age-old wounds, however, what do you know about the circumstances of Thomas' murder?" Sky caused Martha's rage to broil and seethe, even though every word had been one of compassion and love.

"What are you trying to say? Why must I suffer the disrespect of a Heathen? Who are you, and where did you come from? I've never met you before, so who are you to judge me? What do you know of Thomas? Who are you? Why do you ask this of me?" Martha had, in a fit of rage, lashed out with a sense of indignation that suggested neither kindness nor innocence.

"I can see it now. I can see what happened, Joanne, as clear as day. Do you mind if I share with Martha's parents about what happened on the day of Thomas' murder?" asked Sky.

With compassion for Martha, despite the shadowy aura that increased around her persona as it permeated the air around her, Joanne responded to Sky, "Please. Please do." As she responded, Joanne felt a certain sense of fear and even of terror as she picked up on many of the neural signals passing from Martha's un-optimized mind to her own.

Joanne's recently multiplied neural capacity for scanning the minds of others had become swift with a quickening from within, and she knew more now than she could have ever conceived of before. Sky had worked one of many miracles, and it was as if in just a few moments within the minds of all in the room, she had solved the mystery. She had gifted everyone in the room with a direct link to the biggest secret hiding within the mind of another. If the secret had been private, meaning that no one else had been involved in such a way that caused undue consequence to their own rights and life, the secret would have remained private.

For Martha, this had not been the case. Someone had been murdered seventeen years ago, and the secret of the individual responsible was not worthy of privacy. It was now very clear within the minds of everyone within the room what had happened. Sky had optimized the minds of everyone in the room, to her level when it came to reading minds. Even her parents had gained an increase in knowledge in a flicker of the light, and now, given that Martha was home, and within the scope that Sky was willing to stretch to scan minds, they could see Martha's stark truths.

Sky spoke up, to help them understand what they were now seeing within their minds, "Mr. and Mrs. Serena, your daughter loved Thomas very much, and for a very long time. He loved her too, but as a friend. Her heart was distraught when certain news came her way. Due to some of her teachings when she was growing up, she found out about Thomas 'tendencies' and had acted in a manner based on her own religious piety, where she felt he was a sinner.

"Mr. and Mrs. Serena, it was your daughter who carefully planned and executed the crime that resulted in the death of Thomas." Sky was quick; she played out all that happened with clarity, before their eyes. It was as if the roof of the house had been taken away, and they could see each scene playing out in the clouds above them. Sky then rose to a sense of anger and vindication toward the pious and ill-taught version of Christianity that their daughter had been taught when she was too young to understand. These teachings were courtesy of her parents and not by any other Pastor of any other church. She wasn't taught these teachings at their church or anywhere else, except within areas where the vilest of ideas could be shared. Other members of their joint congregation had been taught to love others as themselves, but for some reason, Martha had learned to hate the sinner, that as such, certain sins made them worthy of death, and she had carried out that murder.

Martha was instantly on the defense, she breathed in and out profusely, and then she blew up, "How dare you to infer that! That isn't fair! How dare you! I am the authority on God here; I did what I had to! I know what truth is. You are nothing!" Martha began to storm upstairs to her room before she was put into stasis by Sky. Sky then turned her around to face both of her parents, as well as Erin, Joanne, and herself. Then Sky became the Iridescent Angel.

The Serenas were shocked and without words. Suddenly, as if in another flash and flicker of the lights, Sky had caused the memories of Martha to again play out in her parent's heads, as well as before them in the clouds above. Martha beheld in terror all the things that she had done to poor Thomas, on his way home from school. What she had done to him was unforgivable, but she had been long forgiven by Joanne and her parents, even though they knew not who the person was that had killed Thomas. Thomas had been her friend, and Martha had betrayed him. She stood there in fear, unable to move or leave, as every single individual in the room again witnessed every bit of every gritty detail of the event that had occurred and what had happened to Thomas on the day of his demise.

Suddenly, the Serenas were on their knees, crying tears of anguish and in supplication to Sky Taylor, the Iridescent Angel. She had transformed from the young twenty-two-year-old lady with a red, white, and blue T-shirt, piggy tails, and cut-offs to the Angel she was in the Virtual Universe. "I am simply me. I am not an Angel from Heaven or Hell, I am not anything vile or horrid, nor am I anything more than the being you see before you. I don't mean you, Mr. and Mrs. Serena, or Martha, any harm." Sky turned her eyes to Martha and then allowed Martha, while in stasis to shut her eyes. "She is sleeping right now, and I will take her away on journeys, such that when she wakes up in the morning, she will come clean, and find forgiveness from the family of the victim, the townsfolk, and my dear sister of a friend, Joanne.

"Please remember, we are not here to condemn, but to heal. We are here to heal her mind and to help her to have a more promising and enjoyable future. I will help her to regain her sense of healthy cognition of reality. She will learn to respect others, set her personal standards of life to her own unique set of choices, and avoid condemning others for her own choices. She will understand what are called, Universal Ethics.

"Mr. and Mrs. Serena, there will come a day when she will pay the price for what she has done as she goes to something that is called the Correctional Matrix. This is designed by Eliza but has been remodeled and perfected by Joanne, in its latest form. Its purpose is to give her the experiences and journeys, filled with mentors, coaches, and teachers that she will need to heal her mind, her heart, and her soul. She will learn her purpose in life, have clarity on her own unique talents that will bless the lives of others and contribute to the advancement of civilization, in order to create a legacy worthy of preserving for the long-haul.

"Mr. and Mrs. Serena, no promise from any God or from any religion, if truly benevolent, ought to suggest the brutality and murder of any individual. Thomas was a sweet young man, a man who respected others' individual choices and his discovery of confidence to share who he was with the person he loved ought to have been met with respect and even sympathy from those he was surrounded by. He protected the life of Martha on multiple occasions, as she walked from home. As a sign of gratitude, she dressed up in a dark tunic one day, had hidden a wooden bat underneath her outer garments, and spooked Thomas. She followed that by clubbing him on the back of the head. After he fell, she continued to hit him with the bat until he was completely brutalized beyond repair and she was sure he was dead. A pool of his blood had gathered, and her mistake was the fact that she stepped into it before entering the mud, heading to the burn barrel she had placed there earlier that day to burn any evidence that would suggest that she was the perpetrator. The angle of the impressions of the three different types of shoes gave away the fact that there was only one person involved, at least to me.

"The second I saw the pictures of the crime which lay in Joanne's mind and the viscerally terrorizing memories which lay in Martha's mind, I knew without any doubt what had happened. Mr. and Mrs. Serena, I know you tried your best and in your own way to rear your daughter in a manner consistent with your personal beliefs, but you should have taught her to love and to be gentle with those around her. Instead, she was filled with hatred and anger, walking around as though she were a chosen voice of God when she ought to have been wearing sackcloth covered in ashes.

"I am sorry to bring this news to you in such a manner, but please know that it comes from a good place. Eliza Williams designed me, and all of Pathway created me to reach out and heal the minds of many rather than allow the people of Earth to suffer from needless misery and violence. I choose to show myself as an Angel to you because that is how I view myself, and because I too have a sense of spirituality about me. I only invoke the authority I have been given, to heal the minds and bodies of those who are suffering, and to mark those guilty of horrid crimes, for the day when the Correctional Matrix is consistent with the laws of the land.

"To be clear, the actions of many can be despicable and these actions are not solely a monopoly of men or women alone. There are plenty of people who fail to consider the entire message I share with you now, and instead they find themselves justifying toxic behavior toward others, leading to the toxicity that our overall environment seems to be filled with today. We need each other to overcome the obstacles necessary for a promising future, and we can do more if we remember consent, kindness, and pursuits that are innovative and founded in well-being.

"When it comes to any sect of the vast quantity of faith's, there is among the many, one individual who comes to mind that like many others I know, I truly and deeply respect. This individual is truly one of the sweetest, most genuine, and kindest people in all ways that truly matter, and is a fine example of some of the greatest people I have ever met. He wouldn't even hurt a fly. He was a Baptist preacher, and someone I worked with. Although even he has said that there are religious organizations, much like his own, who forget to truly care about others, that might as well be a cult, so in one particular case, when he discovered that certain atrocities were occurring within one particular sect he had been affiliated with, he left them for good. He is still a Baptist in his heart, but for all the reasons that are right, correct, kind, and truly the way it seems a Christian ought to be, or at least in accordance with the Golden Rule.

"That said, religion worldwide has certainly been the source of so much misery, destruction, abuses, and more, yet those I meet who happen to be religious are respectful, dignified, kind, and gentle people who would travel the world not to convert, but to help put the roof on a home or donate funds to help those in need. There are so many hospitals out there, courtesy of a variety of religious organizations who labor diligently to cure people of sickness, disease, and more in order to increase the quality of life for anyone suffering. I have to believe that something I call piety of the people is where things really start to go haywire.

"Any time anyone, no matter religion, calling, or status forgets to ask why they are doing something or what their desired end result is, and where the answer doesn't meet these criteria, things go horribly wrong: Our primary focus ought to be well-being, within the constraints of personal consent and individual rights and responsibilities to honor physiological and neurological health, longevity, and quality of life.

"We must ask whether or not our pursuits will lead to not only our own happiness and higher evolution, but that of others. Maslow was wise, and the sooner we as a people can help each other to reach that fifth tier in his hierarchy of needs, or self-actualization, the sooner we can go further than before. We need each other, working together as a team, regardless of orientation, affiliation, identity, race, religion, culture, nation, creed, or any other aspect of social delineation, and find ourselves appreciating our unique beliefs, qualities, and strengths, in order to succeed in the full-spectrum of longevity and resolving the macro issues that conflict with our civilizational survival."

Sky had glowed so brightly during her revelation to the Serena family's minds, that they were almost blinded. They would have remained blind, had she not healed them both physiologically and neurologically. She also gave them the level of optimization that would take effect after they went to sleep that night. If they were to learn kindness and love, they would maintain their new-found optimizations and abilities, but if they did not, the healing effects would eventually fade away until they were amenable to mortality just as any other non-read-in individual. They would also forget their abilities and anything about Pathway, apart from the clarity of mind surrounding what Martha had done. Sky was certain they would learn and engendered peace within their minds. She didn't want to impart misery, simply clarity.

"Please do not worry. I will afford both of you an opportunity to talk to Martha in the morning, and together you will be able to go to the Sheriff and let him know what you have done so that she can pay for her crimes, in accordance to the laws of the land." Sky's brilliance dimmed down, their eyes became healed from their temporary blindness, she settled down on the couch next to Erin and Joanne, and then something unexpected happened.

"We are sorry for what we taught our daughter. It was not in accordance with the teachings we received from our Pastor. We were slaves to our own piety, and we see clearly now how that has affected Martha. If you bring the Sheriff now, we'd prefer to get this over with sooner." Both Mr. and Mrs. Serena were of a shared mind and in every way. Sky could sense that they were truly sorrowful, and then she linked to the Sheriff in town.

She had given the Sheriff an optimized body and mind and had given him a nap to receive the necessary training, before Erin, Joanne, and Sky had arrived at Joanne's parents' home earlier that day. The Sheriff was already on his way, with crystal clear awareness as to what had happened—every bit of evidence he needed was already in his grasp. He had simply interpreted it all wrong from the get-go. Sky had told him not to worry, but from here on out and as he wished, he would be able to have clarity as to the facts of every scene of every crime that had or ever would occur in his town, until justice was served, and correction had been duly given in court. With that, they started their journey back to downtown South Otselic.

Joanne walked for a few moments with Erin and Sky before speaking. "It's been solved. I know what happened now, and it looks like the Sheriff will continue to help Martha be on the mend from what she did. Martha will be in stasis, but with complete clarity on everything, and will be released from stasis until the Sheriff arrives. Do you mind if we go ahead and jump to our room in town? It appears we don't need our jump gates anymore." Joanne thought of the Serenas in their home and used her newly gifted abilities to summon biopods and a jump gate for the Serena residence, and continued, "We'll use biopods in Pathway, until everyone has been further vetted and updated for that ability. We'll keep the jump gates for larger shipments and for those who don't wish to be fully optimized.

"They'll be healed, just like they would be at a thorough doctor's visit, but they will only receive upgrades and updates based on their desires from here on out. Are you okay with that Erin?" Joanne had asked Erin since she was, in fact, the President of Pathway.

Erin linked with Eliza, shared with her everything that had gone on, and Eliza who was also the President of the UP agreed with the suggestions and updates that would be made. Erin and Joanne also learned that night, and each night throughout that week, how to use all of their powers as given to them by Sky Taylor.

When they returned to the Melrose Campus at weeks' end, they began to send updates to the IMC to Vesha Celeste for incorporation into the IMC Command Spacecraft. Thirteen gigantic Intergalactic Mission Contingency spacecraft lay hidden and completed but going through testing and upgrades above the asteroid disc. They shared the same orbit as Pluto, which could be seen below, if one was inside the spacecraft looking outside the docking bays.

Sky had engaged with Erin and Joanne during their walks later that week, and had asked them about their plans for an Annihilator Model HBCI, "So what is this with an Annihilator?"

"Oh, it was a horrible idea of ours, something you probably knew every detail about. However, since our walk, I think we're on the mend, as they say. With each of our powers of healing, we'll no longer need an Annihilator. Instead, we can turn their weapons into bouquets of flowers that smell undeniably beautiful, or anything else creative and fun." Erin smiled, as did Sky and Joanne.

Sky followed up with her visits to the remaining seventy personnel and through that, had helped Pathway and humanity to change the course of history many centuries into the future, and with those changes, a promise of a legacy worthy of preserving for the long-haul was still viable for a long, long time.

Chapter 27: POTUS

Database Moon Archive, Celestial-Sol Date: 2025 January 27. Erin Carter, President of Pathway, and Joanne Gallant, VP of Pathway, summarize the beginning of Eliza's POTUS Campaign to its results. These memories are from Pathway as well as UP Leadership, as recorded within the Virtual Universe and interfaced within Pathway Melrose Campus. Input by Erin Carter, President, and Joanne Gallant, Vice President, of Pathway, 2022-2029.

During late March of 2022; Sky Taylor had been awakened, came online, and began her missions throughout the nation and then the world. Just a couple of months prior, Yesha had served for eight years and had officially passed the mantle of Pathway President onto Erin Carter and Joanne Gallant, who had been appointed as her Vice President. Vesha Celeste was making continuous updates to the IMC, as ideas rolled in. Both Erin and Joanne had subsequently been voted in to fill their positions unanimously by every citizen of the various tech cities throughout the Solar System and throughout Pathway.

Each of the citizens who voted, were also members of the Solar-System-wide UP, since there was now sovereign governance for each of the twenty-thousand tech cities. Delegates were voted in to represent each major spheroid with population, especially when making changes and adjustments via the Solar-System-wide UP. Meetings were typically held in the Virtual Universe, once all the delegates, both local and regional, had entered their biopods, and were located safely within their luxury suites at home.

Now that the Solar-System-wide UP was in place and Pathway, itself, was in the hands of Erin and Joanne, Eliza and Yesha were free from Pathway Industries' many commitments. Both were eager to engage in their shared campaign, devoted to the cause of getting humanity into space and well-established throughout the Universe. They had built the foundation for a legacy worthy of preserving, but there were a couple of steps needed to secure that legacy. One of those steps included a successful run as Presidential and Vice-Presidential Candidates of the US and as leaders of the UP. In the US, the UP was not termed the Solar-System-wide UP, which was a term used by the collective sovereignty of the tech cities but was simply named the "UP."

Unlike any of the other official and popular parties, both the presidential and vice-presidential candidates for the UP ran together from the very beginning of their campaign to allow every affected citizen of the US maximum opportunity for candidate scrutiny, criticism, support for and demonstration of strength and versatility of character. Thus, unlike other parties, this style of engagement was written into the bylaws of the UP and was carried out as such.

"Do you think we should go by the Universal Party, or simply the abbreviation, the UP, or should it matter?" Yesha asked Eliza once.

"Honestly, the most important aspect of communication is communication. The UP sounds fine. If you think about it, over the long haul, we should divest ourselves of the minutia related to terms, slogans, or exact words or terminologies, so long as understanding is shared. Even though standardization might make communication more fluid across the board, we're better off if we understand the complexities of language as expressed by those are speaking in a genuine manner and with a desire to impart information in a helpful way. Soon enough, languages will no longer be necessary, since people will have the option of communicating clearly with insurmountable depth of understanding, through immediate contextual translation and neural links, proper grammar will be an immediate upgrade to that end.

"When I talk about the preservation of life, or longevity sciences, or about considering age as a disease, ultimately the goal is to open eyes and minds to the idea of living long enough to live forever or at least long enough to be able to travel to many places throughout the Universe and then return to find family still alive to visit and share experiences with. The goal is to get people working together, understanding each other, and it isn't to fixate on grammatical context, periods, commas, dots, ellipses, etc. We need to preserve life, we need to get out there to the stars in order to invest in the potential of the legacy of humanity, and we need to do so in a manner that respects the well-being of those around us. That is all. Nothing more, nothing less, simply put, we need to care and be kind. If someone knows enough to correct someone on what they are saying, they know what they are saying and are merely depriving themselves of the deeper message and becoming condescending for no reason. What do you think, Yesha?"

Yesha mulled over what Eliza said and responded to the affirmative, "I agree."

Eliza had setup this and many other essential aspects pertaining to the UP with everyone in Pathway LLC, many years ago, in 2010, and since, the UP had grown quite substantially, exponentially, and congruently with Pathway itself, as time went by. In 2012, the UP was officially established in every state within the US, delegates in each state held local offices and higher. Eliza knew that in order to secure success for a new political party, they had to play the 'long game.' The long game required party affiliation and wins at the smallest levels of governance and the ability to retain those levels while winning higher levels of governance until their party had an electoral super-majority. Even though they had thirty percent of the Electoral College, the other two parties had fractured into multiple parties apiece, and as such, the UP was now the super-majority. They had waited out the previous POTUS election, and now it was time.

After Sky Taylor's missions in the US and around the world, from March of 2022 through March of 2023, she walked with Eliza, Yesha, and James during the first week of April. Sky talked with each of them regarding her plans to help Pathway, how it had done well, was doing well, but how she needed to employ her personal maintenance program to ensure there weren't any disastrous consequences in the future. Before she had gone on that miraculous journey with Erin and Joanne, she knew she needed to walk with them as well as other leadership personnel, giving them organic and personal experiences. Sky would exponentially increase their abilities and their capacity to use them. Healing was the goal, retention of those abilities was possible so long as an individual would hold on to benevolence, compassion, and other virtues.

Eliza, Yesha, and James had visited James' family in northern California, protecting it from wildfires and uncontrolled volcanic activity, and had walked, talked, and experienced the changes that would be similar to the modifications Sky had yet to make at that time, in South Otselic and the surrounding towns. Ultimately, Sky would adjust seventy IMC-related leaders, and from there provide further upgrades living-being-wide by directly interfacing them with the Virtual Universe, available on a situationally-dependent basis. If an individual were to sleep at the end of their day, their mind would interface with the Virtual Universe several times before and after reaching their REM cycles. From there, they would be able to set the time dilation cycles upon entering the Virtual Universe and accomplish however many years' worth of work they needed to in a night. During the day, a person could do the same, after teleporting to a safe location, typically their luxury suite in one of the twenty-thousand tech cities, or they could climb into the nearest biopod. After bringing it up, Eliza, Yesha, and James agreed with Sky.

Following Sky's walks with Erin and Joanne, in May of 2023, there were no more than fifty-million members from the US of Pathway and in the UP. Sky had gone on walks with each of the UP delegates, each of the future IMC Commanders and all of the IMC Vice Commanders, as well as other individuals, who were nominated by the Solar-System-wide UP, to critical positions within each IMC Command Spacecraft and then they expanded their training to those in high-level or high-visibility political positions throughout the UP worldwide. Their campaign was brilliant.

On many occasions throughout Eliza's and Yesha's campaign, wherein they had recommended legalization of the option to optimize our physiology as well as our neurology, and grant parents the opportunity to do so for their children, they were confronted by many concerned citizens who felt that this was "Playing God," at least until their child was healed.

Naturally, Eliza and Yesha had to answer to this, and their answer was often clear and concise. At one point, Eliza deliberated even further as she answered when asked in an interview about this very subject.

"To be clear, we have all had loved ones who are no longer here, courtesy of cancer, cystic fibrosis, diabetes, Parkinson's and a host of other factors that reduce our body's ability to continue the good fight. Living life is a beautiful part of our reality, accepting the challenges we see from day-to-day while looking to overcome them and embrace loved ones who are going through battles themselves, are all a part of what I call aging in grace.

"Through the years, we have learned more and more about how the most basic components of our bodies work. As we have learned how to overcome issues like smallpox, typhoid, and more, we have been able to create medicines to combat those issues so that people can live a life that I call one of higher quality, or one of health, longevity, and clarity of mind.

"CRISPR-Cas9 is a system that our basic cells use in the process of multiplying or splitting, to create a colony of healthy, young, and vibrant cells. Through this process, we heal. Understanding how this works has allowed scientists a new opportunity to more fully understand the four basic proteins that constitute the DNA of any and all living organisms on Earth. Understanding the poly-genomic and mono-genomic sequences and using CRISPR-Cas9 and similar tools to mend broken portions of our DNA, or portions that have mutated to the point of adversely affecting our health is something that is relatively new. In the '90s, scientists 'dabbled' with this, and found that if they weren't careful, they could cause undue harm with results leading to cancer, which was counter-intuitive to the whole idea of medical, physiological, and aging sciences, all intended to increase the quality of life for both the individual and their loved ones.

"That said, at no time would I deem it appropriate to suggest that someone who has been born with disorders, disease, etc. is inferior. I view each individual as unique, special, and full of potential just waiting to be discovered. What I do suggest is that, if our brothers, sisters, parents, children, and friends who have passed away already, and if my father and mother, and many more who I care about, had had the advantages of the sciences talked about in the many journalistic articles, they could still be around with us today, readying to journey the Cosmos.

"Some of us may be questioning these tools based on personal beliefs or religious observances, but there are allowances for this type of science, even within the confines of those beliefs. Look more deeply, and I am sure you will find that it is important to reach out and be kind to all, to reduce misery, and to reduce suffering. Part of that deals with giving someone the type of health that will afford them a full life, where they can not only find and meet their full potential but compound upon it even further."

By May of 2024, there were two-hundred-fifty-million US citizens who had organically joined the UP. By Election Day in November seventy-five percent of the nation voted "UP" for a landslide win.

No matter the successes the UP shared throughout the nation and worldwide, the journey required a lot of work, a lot of organized campaigning, and further growth for each of the candidates. Not only had Eliza and Yesha been running for office, but many other UP delegates had run successfully for the many offices throughout the US, from local mayors to state governors, from state and federal government legislative positions to each level of the law and judicial system, local, state, and federal. The UP had done everything they could to be wise regarding the Presidential Election, which first and foremost required large support within the Electoral Process. While much of what had been done to grow Pathway and the UP from March of 2022 to November of 2024, could be attributed to the skills of Sky Taylor, much more credit was due to Eliza Williams for her foresight, her leadership through it all, and her prudence when it came to building Pathway and the UP from scratch, maintaining personnel training and development, and she had always been supported by both Yesha and James. It was an increasingly known fact that Eliza was, by November of 2024, forty-four years old. However, she looked as vibrantly youthful as a twenty-two-year-old, which helped her plight toward longevity win the masses over substantially. It became known that her word was solid, that every industry that she had previously sunk her teeth into had been exponentially successful, and that there were no revolving doors. Every person Pathway had employed loved their jobs and knew that teamwork existed throughout each company that was a part of Pathway Industries. As time went by, the voters throughout the US learned that wherever Eliza was, Yesha Alevtina was involved somewhere critical as well, and they had approved of Eliza's selection as a running mate through their overwhelming votes.

Eliza and Yesha had worked hard to win votes organically from March 2022 and on, to reach minds throughout the nation by sharing their ideas and through persuasive means, which ultimately reached the hearts of many within and without the growing party.

The growth of the UP throughout the US was very much gradual and genuine, courtesy of the efforts of Eliza and Yesha, as well as their profound ties with the most affluent and influential people in the US, who had also been members of the UP. Everything was in place, which rendered the necessary win for their successful bid for POTUS. The media had soaked in the details of their business models, and one-by-one the titans of media joined the "Pathway Revolution." The world's top critics learned to broaden their scope from "argument for the sake of argument," or "angst for the sake of primal urges," or their traditional form of unbridled chaos, and they began seeing with clarity and excitement new solutions to the various issues throughout the World that were consistently being resolved, courtesy of Pathway and an increasing quantity of organizations who were genuinely interested in raising the quality of life for all. They knew that Pathway existed due to the brilliance of both Eliza and Yesha, and these new charities applauded Eliza and Yesha for their inspiring leadership. As a result, even a large quantity of critics became part of 'Team UP.' Finally, things were looking up in the US and in vast areas throughout the rest of the world. Their bid for the presidency had gained local, public, and even worldwide support. People, the public included, allowed hope to fill their hearts once again.

Inauguration

Today was the day of her inauguration. With Eliza's inauguration, she had made a special request shortly following the Electoral College vote in December to both Houses of Congress to also include within her inaugural ceremony her State of the Union speech and the necessary authorizations to prepare for and give a presentation during the broadcast. Both Eliza and Yesha, as executive leaders of the US, would present a speech, Eliza would give hers with hidden gifts and a few surprises, and Yesha's speech would be much more concise, but between those two, as well as Sky and Vesha, they would reveal all of their discoveries and inventions to the public.

Together they would charge the masses to become kinder and more enthusiastic about scientific innovation, research, and development, all of which could serve the intent of helping to preserve life, increase its longevity, and ensure that life comes with a much higher quality. Eliza would reveal twenty-thousand self-sustaining, Earth-based, new tech cities and towns and the protective shielding around them and our globe, as well as some policy changes, among other things to the public soon. Yesha would introduce the twenty-thousand self-sustaining tech cities throughout the Solar System and the sophisticated shielding granting each spheroid within it the sustainability of life like that of Earth to the viewing audience. She would then present Sky Taylor, who would do a brief speech, followed by Vesha Celeste, who would introduce the IMC to the public. After the presentation, the President would give the closing excerpt. Effectively, our nation would begin to move forward, publicly guiding civilization to go further than we had ever gone before.

The Speaker of the House made the typical introductions. She wasn't from Eliza's political party, but her party had only a narrow lead in the House, and her enthusiasm was morose at best. The Speaker of the House was present for the State of the Union and Inauguration and displayed the typical courtesies and fake happiness her professionalism and desire to keep her seat of power required. She had been in her position for years and had a stronghold in an area of the country that had still been somewhat uninfluenced by Pathway or the UP, where the constituents there were still very closely knit and of paid allegiance to one of the older parties. The time came for Eliza to proceed, raise her hand, swear in, and she did. As she did, the mood within the entire room changed. She dazzled her viewers in a black and white form-fitting pinstriped pantsuit, with a white blouse and a black bowtie. Eliza's charisma crackled in the air with life-giving charm, awakening the spirits of every onlooker.

She made her way to the podium, after turning to her left and walking onto the raised floor before it. When the introduction and swearing-in were done, the Speaker of the House sat down, and then Eliza began to address the World. Before uttering her first words, the audience was already ensconced with her crystalline blue eyes, thick black limbal rings, her soft tones and youthful features, her blonde hair with pink tips gathered so beautifully and professionally upon her head as though it were a wedding day and the demure demeanor she exuded of subtle authority and a deep sense of care for the well-being of each observer.

"I, President Eliza Amber Williams, do hereby accept the executive office of the United States of America, and do solemnly swear in my own words to protect and serve the citizens of this beloved country, as the President of our Nation, Worldwide Ambassador of Peace, and Commander in Chief, providing a safety net where respect for individual rights and peace do not exist. I swear to protect all citizens and allies from enemies, both foreign and domestic. I will ensure that each member of the cabinet has been fully vetted for their qualifications, their focus on longevity, their unparalleled level of education, experience, wisdom, as well as their behavior and measure of character. I will provide training to elevate those qualities and germinate the best in leadership, through acts of compassion and shared loyalty to the well-being of the People of the United States and our Allies, which are all nations who wish to be at our side from this day forward, so long as they enlist the Principles of Universal Ethics into their systems of governance.

"As your President, I will take every healthy-minded recourse to forge diplomatic bridges where there are none, and we, as a nation, will move forward by strengthening our ties with other nations who have already graciously worked with and honored their commitments to us in the past. Diplomacy will reach a new standard, other nations will see, in the most genuine form, a beacon of truth, of justice, of mercy, of life, of liberty, of kindness, of health, of education, and of clarity of mind to bring civilization together and become more advanced than we have ever been throughout the entirety of the history of this the human civilization, and all so that we may go further than we ever have gone before.

"I stand before you, here today in compliance with Article II, Section 3, of the United States Constitution, which stipulates: 'The President shall from time to time give to the Congress information of the State of the Union and recommend to their consideration such measures as he or she shall judge necessary and expedient.'

"Please note, that I have found it necessary and expedient to make my first amendment to the United States Constitution include 'or she' into Article II, Section 3. I will also introduce many tenants that I deem necessary and expedient, in a recommendation before you for your consideration and affirmation prior to leaving today. There is much to do to increase the well-being, quality of life, and clarity of mind of every living being in our Nation and Worldwide. Thus, we will begin."

At her brief pause, applause from every person in the House Chamber was heard. Behind Eliza, breath-taking imagery unfolded before everyone's eyes.

"Thank you," Eliza paused, waiting patiently, understanding each person listening, sitting or standing with an air of newfound hope, as every person in the room stood to give her a standing ovation. She then continued to wait with a Presidential smile of approval to the crowd for their roar of support as it increased to decibels that had live media going ecstatic and decreased until it reached its appropriate silence, with broadcasts and participation feeds in stadiums, coliseums, arenas, and large gathering places across the country and all over the world.

"Ladies and gentlemen, each of you here, or watching, or listening to this are also to be applauded for participating, in one way or another, in the success of our Nation. For matters of brevity and clarity, however, as much as I enjoy long-held tradition, this is a new day, and I would kindly ask that following the previous applause, for which I am grateful, please remain seated and hold further ovations until my address here is complete.

"Thank you."

Eliza paused, just to make sure her request had been heard and that due respects were paid. She looked at every member of her audience and smiled. She noted that each person present was listening very heartily and hanging on to her every word. Eliza then nodded, 'yes,' three times, engaged with Yesha Alevtina, Vesha Celeste, Erin Carter, Joanne Gallant, Sky Taylor, James Cooper, and the rest of Pathway via her neural link, and continued.

"Today's State of the Union and Inaugural Speech will be different from all others in times past. Today I will give you my heart, my experiences, the roads I've traipsed upon, the visions I've had, and the resolve shared with so many amazing individuals to realize these visions relating to the preservation of humankind, clarity of mind, and continued health for a very, very, long time. I will unfold before you a new reality of our visions for the future, and with much more clarity, for our nation. I will show you how our plans and many completed pursuits have already benefitted our world and Solar System, and how we will in many similar ways raise the quality of life Universe-wide."

Eliza talked, and the audience sat as requested, but did so in serenity at what they heard and saw above and around the President as she gave her speech. What each person in attendance, camera professional, and broadcast viewer witnessed, was a scene they had never seen or had never imagined would be or could be seen before. Everything presented before their eyes was a reality much to their astonishment and awe, and people watching from all corners of the Earth rushed to those who were listening remotely and informed them to make haste to a visual broadcast; it was a synopsis of the growth of Pathway LLC to Pathway Industries, it included a fantastic display of Pathway's large corporate buyouts, and the positive and healthy changes that had made Eliza the richest person in the world and throughout the Solar System, as the only Octodecillionaire in every viable manner that mattered.

Long before her speech, Eliza had seen fit to work on her own on a variety of projects. She had also worked with Sky Taylor, Yesha Alevtina, James Cooper, Amber Blythe, Erin Carter, and Joanne Gallant on many other projects. Finally, she had worked with every member of Pathway to create cities in the US to replace every city and town in America, and then throughout the world, protected by a sophisticated barrier that provided defense, invisibility, and undetectable particle re-navigation. Aircraft and other vehicles would navigate around this barrier without detecting the city, the barrier, or realizing the city was there, unless the pilots had the proper friend or foe response, provided through the neural identification. If by chance, they did not have the proper response, they were safely and seamlessly guided around these areas, without a single accident.

In the most barren, desolate, and austere locations throughout every region and country in the world, she had built undetectable cities and towns to take the place of every living domicile and provide eco-friendly industry and special integration, along with safe harbor for those who had thus far not had the means to subsist or own a home. They now had one, or several, based on personal choice.

Eliza designed the environment to be beautifully laid out with forests and jungles that blossomed year-around. Each city, town, forest and jungle pertaining to it was teeming with fruits, vegetables, nutrients, and flowers of every beautiful scent and color. In, throughout, and around every city and town there were parks, rivers, streams, cascades, waterfalls, surfing waves, lakes, and beaches where water had an ever-so-careful balance of healthy minerals and microbes. Creatures of every kind existed within and around these cities, sharing nourishment with each other and without predation. The sharks, crocodiles, and predatory creatures of every kind gave no reason to cause fear among those enjoying the forests, the jungles, the oceans, lakes, rivers or swamps of every kind.

Gone was brutality, and in full supply was sentience, nurture, and domestication. A human with a neural link could listen to and converse with each and every creature, all of whom acted as counselors and mentors and performed tasks within careers they found suited their nature, but in a way that was precious and contributed to longevity, wise use, and the sharing of an abundance of unlimited and self-sustaining resources.

These newly revealed tech cities and towns, much like the tech cities and towns throughout the rest of the Solar System, were now imbued with robust high-rises, agricultural, domicile, industrial, laboratory, and all types, with large and spacious centers. They had wide streets with wide sidewalks for bicycling, a separate system for walking, and several others for strolling with family pets, or creature friends, with all the facilities necessary for natural or organic creatures and people. The lighting systems throughout each city were such that they provided a sense of warmth, safety, and ironically a very clear view of what was around anyone while still allowing all to look up and into the night-time sky. As they did, they could see with increased clarity the visibility of the stars, constellations, nebulae, and galaxies in all their vibrant colors. Eliza's Virtual Universe digital display played for everyone to see, allowing all, even the blind, within their own language and method of understanding, to have the ability of seeing and reading the information pertaining to what was in the holo-imagery behind her as she spoke and as she paused.

Complexity within the many beautiful and creative edifices existed through both art and appeal that were cogent with the collective wishes of the minds of those who would dwell in the cities and towns. There were restaurants of every type, all using clean-meats, organic and nutrient rich vegetables, fruits, herbs, morels, and spices. There were tea and coffee gardens that were peaceful, providing hydration with lush flavors of favorite tastes, nutrition, and heightened senses throughout each day, until the mind rested upon the pillow at night, where more training would ensue and then relaxation and a break would take place until morning.

Within each city and town were scientific laboratories, public health centers, correctional coaching and mentoring facilities, advanced education centers, modernized agricultural high-rises, and entertainment exposition buildings. There were also very large sports arenas which included a complexed environment and capabilities suitable to every sport or entertainment venue imaginable, from concerts and ski resorts, to football and surfing wave centers, and much more. These edifices were such that every bit of infrastructure was more than a unique high-rise, with domiciles, jump gate terminals, and parkways, all of which complemented the forests, jungles, and other buildings around them in a magnificent way.

"What you are seeing is a tech city known as New Chicago. This new city has many visual aspects that will remind you of the architecture of Chicago itself. They are built by ever so carefully meshing the wishes of the minds of those living within the Chicago we all love, to create what you see here. This was built using my own funds combined with your collective imagination. This is a gift to every citizen of this 'windy city' where the wind is now tamed. There is room for every citizen there, and many more.

"Over the last three years, this and many other cities were built and under the protection and shroud of invisibility and re-navigation technology. These buildings are breathtakingly so advanced in purpose and aesthetic that all who behold what is before your eyes may possibly love what you see, and this is just one of many currently uninhabited new tech cities and towns throughout the US and its territories. What you now see playing behind me, is New Chicago's skyline, the many physical features within it, the unique tops of the buildings, the sparkle of the lights at night that help guide someone on their path, while accenting the light of the stars of the Milky Way Galaxy and beyond, while beautifying the city and environmentally-melded aspects in and around its many buildings.

"The architecture, throughout this and every tech city and town, has the ability to captivate any human mind because each of them will be unique, beautiful, clean, and as creative as the collective mindset of every one of the city's inhabitants, balanced with the environment and aesthetic. Each city will also have the capacity to provide domicile to many more families, career professionals, visitors, and tourists. I am sharing these accomplishments with you to let you know and see that great things are already here and still yet to come. No matter wealth or poverty level, you will have a home that is more state-of-the-art, luxurious, and beautiful than anything you ever thought you could have before, because this will drive a higher level in engagement, innovation, and joy in unlimited amounts. After this meeting, each city and town mayor will be trained in the Virtual Universe and then given the necessary codes to serve the people within their new and beautiful location.

"If you look around the city before you, some of you may recognize it because of its unique qualities. This city takes up more space, because in it you will see vast stadiums, sports arenas of every sort, art symposium edifices, opera houses, vast high-rises for domiciles and businesses of every category, and every industry, campus, and building necessary to run, maintain, and enjoy this location, all infused with forests and jungles with fruit, vegetables, herbs, spices, morels, and healthy microbes and minerals of every kind, with sentient wildlife that can converse neurologically with any individual that has used a biopod or has been visited by a friend like Sky Taylor, the Iridescent Angel, for optimizations of physiology and neurology, along with a gift insurmountable potential.

"There are many methods of travel in this city, just as in every tech city or town, from hyperloop terminals, to extra wide streets for optimized vehicles, vehicles that use cold fusion cyclically requiring nothing more than what is in the air that you cannot breathe, and work with the monopole and dipole systems within the streets and buildings to allow vehicles to fly in the air in a very sophisticated network of layered navigational pathways. Likewise, every building and high-rise will have physically covered parking areas with parkways that have wide roads and wide places to park. There are jump gate terminals in every building and at every level. Any individual who has been through the Virtual Universe training program in class and interfaced through a biopod, can coordinate and setup teleportation points with jump gates and teleportation watches from their home, to their lab, or to their office, work center, back to home, and then to a jump gate terminal with options for daily micro-vacations, and then back to their home for training, entertainment, and rest. All that is built, already functions to one-hundred percent effectiveness, to provide levity, efficiency in travel, and increased time for healthy activities throughout each day.

"Life is about to get quite fantastic, and I assure you there is a lot of benevolent purpose behind all of this. For one, we need to preserve life, and in a way that brings joy and meaning to our very being. We need to have the ability to adapt to environments already teeming with life, rather than destroy entire sentient ecosystems wherever we travel. We need to have a healthy and robust focus of love, beauty, and kindness that will allow us to advance civilization in a manner that demonstrates genuine empathy, compassion, and respect for each other's uniqueness and irreplaceable individuality. We can enjoy our uniqueness while attaining full understanding of each other and mitigating issues that would threaten our existence throughout the Cosmos.

"All of what I am presenting to you, during this historic State of the Union, has the ability to see us through to promise, so long as we combine our efforts to become a worthy, gentle, yet powerful and spacefaring Nation, World, and Solar System, so that rather than navigating space destroying planets and leaving desolation in our wake as a scourge, we can bring life and abundance where there is none, teeming with comparable living environments very similar to the one before you, in the display behind me, and become givers of life and beauty. What you see is an example that we can take desolation and give it life and vibrant beauty, and in turn, we can adapt ourselves to blend into the environments so we can live where different forms of intelligent life already exist. In this way, we will find ourselves more capable of creating diplomatic bridges wherever sentience is possible or existent.

"Someone asked me once if aging is considered a disease, I told him that it was, and this is how I followed that brief answer:

"In order to receive the appropriate funding to combat the diseases of aging from taxpayer funds or other sources of funding that are used in progressive countries to combat pandemics, et al, aging needs to be identified as a disease. In this way, more complexed physiological processes can be studied, understood, and problems resolved in a grander scope. If one were to consider the Hayflick limit for cell division, then one could easily identify the senescence of cells that result in cancers and other complications as a disease and receive funding to find ways to safely reverse the cell-aging process. Longevity is best understood as the ability to live a long, vibrant, youthful, and healthy life with clarity of mind. To compound upon our intellect, we need to achieve longevity, and in order to achieve longevity, we need to combat the disease known as aging.

"My desire is to help everyone become worthy stewards of life, longevity, and clarity of mind as we meet new civilizations throughout the Universe, so we can go further than we have gone before. Just as I stated many times throughout my campaign, your majority popular and electoral votes are now my consent to go ahead and release to you my promise. My promise is all that you are beholding before you now. Involving ourselves in sciences, sports, arts, music, and simply being kind are noble steps toward a future that will preserve our legacy indefinitely."

Eliza was humble; she did not give everything away at once. She shared that which pertained to each aspect of her speech. But, before she finished, she planned to share almost everything and its fullness of purpose. What she didn't share, Yesha, Sky, and Vesha would.

"We have much to continue to talk about, to show, and to reveal to each of you. Please let me tell you how impressed by you and proud of you I am for being involved in so many ways already throughout the election process and all that has led us here. I would like to publicly thank the diligent members of my political party, because you were involved with and attentive to each person with whom you were engaged, in a positive campaign in every way that mattered. Many of you made the campaign honorable by focusing your energies on solutions to the many problems existent throughout our nation, our world, and our Solar System, and by living by the values and virtues we have espoused, which are presented in the Principles of Universal Ethics. These values, morals, ethics, and virtues define the mission of not only the UP, but of every man, woman, or child, or anyone who has ever dreamt of traversing the Universe and exploring locations that are yet unknown. In this way, we can each govern ourselves.

"Ever since Yesha and I introduced ourselves in several national broadcasts many years ago and forged our way through the campaign trail, by offering our willingness to serve you as we began our campaign for the presidency back in 2022, people began to be mystified and even impressed with the idea of governmental integrity. The idea that society ought to be one of virtue, and that our government ought to be there to mitigate the lack of respect and common decency from one living being to another through example, seemed like common sense. Furthermore, any viable government will protect its citizens and their freedoms, especially when it comes to personal choice and belief. You believed in us, and your diligence has now won the day along with a bright, promising, and awesome future.

"Our government in its current state is a very complexed system, safeguarding individual rights while protecting its citizens from terrorism and brutality. In many ways, overtures toward increasing our educational effectiveness, our means to lend to a more healthy environment overall for our physiology and neurology, and our clarity of mind inherent to innovations that increase our longevity, quality of life, and the promise of the stars have increased throughout the years, and I applaud each person involved in their efforts to that end.

"Through clarity in delivery of vision of a new appreciation for quality of life, for the Nation, the World, and yes, the Solar System, with professionalism and gentleness, no matter what situation presents itself, everyone in our Nation can earn the right to be admired, respected, and even loved throughout the World as we go forward making one ethical choice after another. It can be said that together this entire election process was part of a new revolution that needed to take place, one that required pulling ourselves back, conducting our own self-analysis, and asking several meaningful questions. All of this took place, and in a kind and peaceful manner.

"We are healing the hearts, the minds, the land, and all of our relationships, both abroad and at home. We are now publicly and even passively visiting every Nation on this beautiful Globe and beyond, while genuinely presenting both peace and promise.

"Our love of our Nation goes beyond any party affiliation; it is a shared sense that we each have ownership on what we ought to be, on who we ought to be, on how we can honorably do what we ought to do, and on how each of us, as an integral part of our Nation, can be. We are responsible for what we do, yet in far too many cases, there are moments and epochs of time where the lack of consideration for others or their well-being or the toxicity of the surrounding environments led to misery and suffering. This has been vastly common and has happened all too often. As such, many were victims of their own choices and their environment. Despite the worst, we can use these harrowing moments to learn lessons and become better, greater, and more benevolent as a Nation, World, and Solar System, than we have ever been before."

Eliza paused, and then continued, with emphasis on every phrase, "My purpose as your President, Executive Branch Leader, Commander in Chief, and International Diplomat is to serve each and every one of you, listen to each and every one of you, and respect the wishes of each and every one of you. I must also continue to honor my commitments to the immutable Principles of Universal Ethics. Whether you have supported me throughout this campaign or whether it may have been that we did not see eye-to-eye on certain issues, I assure you that your well-being is safe with me and that you too have something beautiful, kind, meaningful, and wonderful to look forward to.

"No matter your school of thought, spiritual, non-spiritual, atheistic, or agnostic, cultural, gender or religious or any other type of identity, I appreciate you and the diversity of thought you bring to humanity. Together we can resolve more issues that were once thought impossible to resolve. Together we can rise to tackle yet even greater issues. Self-identification should not be used to delineate, rather to invigorate our resolve to make our future beautiful and rich with joy. Together we can continue our pursuit of happiness in ways we never fathomed possible. We need one another. Yes, we need one another so we can build the kind of long-enduring legacy we'd be proud to share with distant civilizations as we comb the Cosmos."

Thirty minutes had passed by and Eliza had already won the peoples' minds and their concerns over legitimacy, sovereignty, and authority. With what they saw and heard they knew that she had earned respect for resoundingly possessing each of the virtues she preached. All that they saw, courtesy of their new President's efforts, they could not un-see, and everything they saw was beautiful, full of purpose, full of promise, and more helpful in spades, imaginative and joy-bringing than anything they could have ever hoped for. President Eliza Amber Williams did not give way to overmuch pride in any way despite the vast reaches of her abilities. She instead spoke in a fashion that was contrite, kind, thoughtful, upbeat, and even powerful. She had won within the minds and sentiments of the populace a sense that she had met not only the standards and expectations of every citizen within the US, but those of many more throughout every land, nation, country, region, or town listening or watching remotely had ever hoped for.

For as much knowledge, experience, perspective, gratitude, and wisdom that she had, not a single word was fake or empty as she spoke. Nothing Eliza said was contrived, but instead flowed naturally with the intensity of charismatic passion, authority, and even genuine compassion.

The culmination of Eliza's efforts was playing in the background behind her. Her new technologically-advanced cities and towns, built in the US and in other places worldwide, and all merely to help others, were captured in three-dimensional imagery, using technology to convert every television into three-dimensional displays without the need for special glasses. Even the blind discovered that day that they could see for the very first time in their lives, as she spoke. They were grateful for the fact that what they witnessed and were able to observe, and in many cases for the first time in their lives, was immaculately splendid in every way.

Eliza had been giving the great reveal, much as she had practiced and honed deep within a compartmentalized area of her own mind, and on many occasions out loud in the real world and with those she had embraced as kindred spirits in the Virtual Universe. There were things of course that she had not shared with anyone, not even the citizens of Pathway. No matter the level of shared information and collaborative contribution, however, her developments, charitability, and preparation for and in behalf of others was insurmountable, especially when it came to the well-being of the citizens of the US, as well as her friends throughout the World and the Solar System. All the cities and towns she was showing behind her, were awe-inspiring, novel, and full of beauty and wonder.

With only a brief pause, the President continued to address the Nation, knowing within her mind, she was also addressing everyone throughout the World and within the Solar System. "As we transition to these many cities and towns, measures will be taken to preserve the historical nature of the locations left behind. The homeless will not be forgotten; they too will be healed and homeless no more, my delegates will find them and nurture them through program after program as needed, through mentorship, coaching, training, and kindness, allowing them to heal, become educationally-enabled, and to participate in improvements that will advance this wondrous civilization to an amazing legacy worthy of preserving and deserving of combing the Cosmos.

"The old cities and towns will slowly be transitioned into eco-friendly versions of what they once were. Flora and fauna will grow in every unused yard, park, and open space, and those who wish to stay behind will be able to do so, with home upgrades that help to heal life as well as our damaged Earth. Eventually, we will return many parts of the land to those whose ancestors were indigenous to it, allowing them a return to their organic, healing, and even spiritual way of life, even as we stretch out to preserve and protect our Solar System and beyond."

As Eliza spoke, the seamless tapestry filled the entire area behind her of nature enriching the desolate areas of Earth with beauty, walkways, and beaches, and those seated behind her took the view of one incredibly large city as it became one with the Earth. In this city that was shown before the inhabitants throughout the Solar System, all its populations had already moved gracefully to their new tech city. Fading away from view the new city appeared, and the optics controlling what was seen behind Eliza zoomed in and circled around a skyscraper until a view of the public room of one of the luxury domiciles grew to be crystal clear. It then focused more until it showed a series of what looked like white, glowing, and horizontal tanning beds.

Eliza continued.

"Each of these biopods will be proliferated throughout each home, business-place, education center, and every major establishment within the tech cities and towns; many more will be dispersed throughout the jungles, forests, and vacation spots as well. After this ceremony, each of you will be able to choose a home as these citizens have already done, and you are encouraged to use the biopods and travel to the Virtual

Universe, to share in a journey with your family and friends. As you do, you will discover that you can all benefit in a compounded manner together from what this reality and journey called life can do.

"Within these biopods, everyone has both an amazing individual and a beautifully-shared opportunity for the most advanced healthcare and education. In these tech cities and towns, if you need anything, you simply need to ask. In the various matrices of the Virtual Universe, there will be as many opportunities as there are grains of sand on every beach to put your innovation, creativity, and imagination to the test. Through these biopods your connection to the Virtual Universe will help you to adjust your reality in many ways. A shared experience with two or more family members, friends, or even acquaintances will be even more helpful, as they will augment and compound upon everything you learn and everything else you do in so many ways, giving you an opportunity for complete understanding one to the other.

"First, these biopods will optimize you in all ways you can imagine, and in many ways you may or may not be able to conceive of now, both physiologically and neurologically, and they will imbue you with your own nanos and neural identification. These nanos will constantly keep you at your peak level of health, capacity, and clarity of mind. Your neural identification will allow you access to every tech city, town, resort, and resource center throughout the Universe that we will ever build. This will also allow you to take your more precious and private memories and compartmentalize them, giving you impenetrable privacy in all things you are not ready to share, and all that does not relate to that which would cause undue consequence to the rights of others.

"Secondly, these biopods are the primary link to what is called, the Virtual Universe. In this reality, time-dilation is possible, wherein we can verbally set the biopod to allow ourselves to be in it, such that in the real world we're there for five minutes, while in the Virtual Universe, we can be there for any given amount of time, from several hours to a number of centuries or even millennia. Either way, five minutes in the real world will go by, while with complete clarity and tactile reference several PhDs can be completed, and a wealth of experience can be gained and a complete understanding of the lives of our friends can be shared.

"Any individual can design products for their employers or build their own business, etc. While doing so, an individual can program a thousand-years-worth of macro-like processes in five short minutes. With these new capabilities, much can be accomplished toward the advancement of civilization. Through studies, gaining experience with experiential reference, building morale-oriented businesses, building programs that directly affect a higher capacity and quality of one or more essential aspects to the advancement of civilization, and so much more in a short period of time, we can live lives that are full and enriching.

"Harnessing the power of the particles and frequencies within our Universe through our understanding of the many sciences is a blessing rather than a curse. When much is said and done, and with all that we need to do, we must routinely take time to reflect on and learn from our past, appreciate our present, and plan for our future. As we do, it is to our benefit to ask ourselves, why am I doing what I am doing? What purpose does it serve? And, what is my end game? To give everyone a fair hint, if the answers include improving the potential for longevity of life, increased quality of life, preservation and optimization of life and clarity of thought, as well as the advancement of civilization to allow us to preserve our Universe, then our goals are well-aligned with the goals I spelled out during our election campaign, the Principles of Universal Ethics.

"Fathom this, within the scope of the cameras present, you will see a demonstration of many self-replicating nanobots being encoded, programmed, and reprogrammed in a very short period of time that is assigned to an individual's neural identification. These nanos use cold fusion and extract every particle of debris, to include quantum, chemical, or molecule, in your body and can be programmed further to gather the unused matter or trash in your home and break it all down into a contained sphere of particles, tied to your neural identification. These nanos can then be programmed by you within the Virtual Universe, using the advantage of individual particle manipulation and encoding, using your own or any of a vast array of recipes, already developed sciences, theoretical sciences, and time-dilation to perfect a process and then carry out more orders, much like an extensive macro, to construct, for example, a jump gate from your home to a very desolate location assigned to you and your neural identification both in the real Universe as well as in the Virtual Universe.

"As you move around from environment to environment, your own body's nanos will protect you and adjust you to mend, adjust, survive and even enjoy the environment you are in, while using them to adjust and form the desolation around you to a place that is both beautiful and practical to you and safe for any creature within that is working to protect and help you as well. Working together, these nanos can be programmed to use the abundant crust of the Earth or any other planet or moon within our Solar System, deep below the crust, in any wasteland or desolate location assigned to you to convert it into a beautifully-designed environment, and within it your own businesses, resort, domicile, etc.

"I can fathom a scenario where one individual could build a business that specializes in creating wardrobe selections for the wardrobe compartment of the mind. Any given wardrobe compartment of the mind can hold billions of wardrobe ensembles, and the average high-quality ensemble can sell for about $1000, or 1000 Universal Credits each.

"A friend who specializes in hairstyles could use their neural identification and nanos likewise, but for hairstyles that line up with wardrobe ensembles.

"As you can imagine, there is a lot of capital available for legitimate and neural-identification-tagged smart-clothing and hairstyles. These ensembles and styles are similar to normal wardrobes but provide additional protection from elements or anything that could be hostile or brutal. They also allow reprogrammable matter, holographic imaging, undetectable arrays of infrared, microscopic pixilation and optical cameras in the billions to interface with your neural link and show any compartmentalized wardrobe and hairstyle your mind wishes the audience to see. You could have one hundred people in the room, and they would each see a different wardrobe. Most of the time an individual will simply wear what is most appropriate for the occasion. What I'm wearing now, everyone can see."

At that moment, her black and white pinstriped pantsuit changed into a flattering prom gown, and a visual display of everything Eliza had talked about played out before her audience. Everyone who saw what she explained was captivated, entertained, knew that she had laid out everything in a very rational and intuitive manner, and filled with helpful information. Yesha, Sky, and James could also hear the desire for prosperity playing out in the minds of every new onlooker and could see a wide variety of business ideas playing out in the minds of others. The unique aspects and details that came to mind for businesses and ventures within the thoughts and minds of each individual were impressive. Everyone's ideas were irreplaceable and protected by their individuality.

"It's okay to desire a high quality of life, it is possible for each of you to have all that I am sharing with you in a way that is unique to you, and there is purpose in everything we have done and will do, so long as we do it with kindness and with the well-being of others in mind, to include ourselves, throughout every step we take.

"Getting back to the reality of life as it has been, and after having begun countless businesses, enterprises, and endeavors myself, I realized quickly how much the burden of taxes and governmental fees had added up through the years, how the financial pie was the same size, while more and more collectors wanted a good-sized slice. Money sent anywhere, other than to the pockets of the employees, had added up to the point that those providing crucial labor and services were left with meager resources, dismal income, and little time or money for family and friends. Therefore, to even the playing field, I am implementing a ten percent flat tax and dividend program. No matter the income, only a ten percent tax will be required.

"At the end of each tax season, or the time period between the first of January of said year and the thirty-first of December of that same year, each individual who has paid a ten percent tax will receive a dividend return of five hundred percent.

"Please understand, that I have accumulated a vast wealth throughout the years, due to investing and reinvesting in science and development, and because of such, I have agreed with our creditors to pay off all of our country's debt and the debts of anyone within our country. I will also provide full-ride tuitions for every citizen in the US, with all expenses paid, including an account card with unlimited funds, to every student of every trade school, college, and university within our country, allowing them a high-quality education blended with time for levity as well as neurological focus in several majors and professions of their choice. My only request is that each citizen contribute in some way toward the advancement of civilization within our country or in assistance to another country or somewhere between Earth and the remote regions of galaxies both near and far away that we will soon visit, as they use these funds.

"Thus far, Pathway, which now consists of eight-billion members and growing, has built its own system of governance that runs smooth and has no need of law enforcement whatsoever. No worries, to the fine police and first responders out there, there will still be plenty for you to do. There is a plethora of vocations that will capitalize upon your skills, and as you go through the Virtual Universe, you'll find more clarity on what you can do to contribute in your own unique way to the advancement of civilization. We have ways for each of us to look into ourselves and ask what we are doing to increase the quality of life for not only ourselves but those around us.

"Together in Pathway's twenty-thousand tech cities, we have governed ourselves, and in doing so as a Nation, we will all be able to go so much further than ever before. We each must soon merge our skills, our talents, and our assets into what I call a convergence of understanding in order to resolve new problems, greater challenges, and find ourselves going much further than before.

"As I look around our country, I see many who are between the ages of eighteen to fifty-five who are not working for a multitude of reasons. In some cases, quite honorably half of a household will work, while the other half takes care of the stressors at home. To you both, I say thank you. Your diligence and sacrifices are very under-valued and, in many cases, ignored by your peers and too many in society. Lower stress directly links to a healthier physiology, a more clear and healthy neurology, and increased potential for innovation, especially when someone is home to take care of it in every possible way to provide a healthy and peaceful environment. Simply because you are at home does not mean you are not contributing to innovation and the advancements of society that will herald a legacy worthy of preserving throughout the World and the Cosmos, because quite resoundingly, you are. You are the glue that keeps hope alive.

"There are unfortunately far too many who have been turned away from education, jobs, careers, or have been ignored or quite possibly accepted after grueling interviews, and there are others who have endured so much workplace toxicity for so long, that they have lost the will to work. There are those who have found themselves struck with the sudden realization that they would have to put into jeopardy the well-being of others in order to move up in their career field or industry, and instead chose a more humble means with which to sustain their family's ability to meet the most basic of means, yet do so with their integrity, ethics, and morality intact. To each of you, I say, we do care, we appreciate your efforts and your nobility. I assure each of you that there will be plenty to do with unparalleled compensation.

"You will now, each of you, have the opportunity to work for companies that apply the Principles of Universal Ethics. Companies and corporations, which are listed in on our government website are numerous, each complies with Universal Ethics, and within these professions, you will find how easy it is to apply, to get on board, and how stress-free it is to contribute to a higher purpose while balancing time for family and friends.

"There are many who might use the terms, 'Nanny State' or 'Coach State,' and to them, I say, 'You are guilty of forming a Nihilist State.' We can all change, we can all improve, so let's not let our untold potential wither away as we walk around as empty husks of what we could be. As the leader of the free world, I would like to make it very clear that toxicity in the workplace, from employer to employee will not be rewarded and no longer tolerable. Slavery, brutality, and toxicity in the US will no longer be a viable or legal option and should never have been. Due to the chaos existent in this negligence, maltreatment, and a pervasive insult to society itself, we have lost much more than we'll ever know. However, we are resilient, we can all learn from even our most egregious mistakes, we can make right what was once so wrong, and we can each learn to be examples of consideration for others.

"In this new era, there will be measures in place to reward compliance with the Principles of Universal Ethics, which includes the Law of Consent, in the workplace. There will be, effective immediately, a five-hundred percent financial tax dividend on funds spent for any employer who trains their employees through to excellence and compensates them well. The idea of 'well' includes high-quality lifestyles and assurance of time off with pay and benefits for real vacations that further include cruises, Global and Solar System trips, or anywhere we go throughout the Cosmos, allowing them time to truly relax and absorb the beauty around them.

"Moreover, employers will be compensated with this five-hundred percent tax dividend, only if they have their employees work no more than forty hours a week and less than ten months out of each year. Any and all employers providing full support of all facets of compensation leading to physiological and neurological health, including job, health, education, retirement, fitness resources and time, will fully be rewarded.

"It pains me to say what I will talk to you about next because I expect common sense, respect, and dignity afforded to every one of you, as well as from each one of you. Police departments as they currently are will be disbanded, however, law enforcers, you will still be on the government payroll. Our goal is to no longer be what many consider a 'Police State.' That said, each law enforcement professional will be given the option and afforded opportunities to receive follow-on training in the Virtual Universe in any way you choose. Furthermore, you will be on the top of the list for training on stasis guns and on Correctional Matrix coaching, mentoring, training, and counseling.

"People will govern themselves. Unfortunately, if a person has been identified as a source of malicious activity, our Correctional Officers will be trained and on hand to investigate and ascertain the claims made. Their investigations will include understanding the health and morale of the home, public center, and workplace. In the case of the work center, employers will be vetted to ascertain the quality of productivity of each employee, as it relates to the health of the work environment, to ensure that expectations of the quality of life at work and the products and services provided are not wrought with malicious intent. If any form of malicious intent is discovered, an available Correctional Officer, armed with stasis guns, will be available and onsite to safely escort each citizen, after proper training and requisite licensing, to the Correctional Matrix waiting station. Once under safe escort, the offending individuals and their claimants will be brought before the court and given due justice with a fair trial, and if found guilty will serve time within the Correctional Matrix.

"Bullying, brutality, not training or not treating employees fairly will result in counseling, coaching, and Universal Ethics training with a mentor within the Correctional Matrix. Decency in the way we treat one another is expected throughout society, and where that is lacking the government, through its Correctional Officers, will step in.

"For training, you will now have available to you a large number of biopods that will allow anyone searching for a job and following the discovery of a job availability ad, to walk into a place of employment and be instantly hired. Employers, please have the mental fortitude to understand that the individuals who are willing to work for you and show up to your door, can now be trained and become optimized in every way within the Virtual Universe to meet your standards in mere moments. This training will include physiological and neurological optimizations, as well as a robust capacity to do everything needed to not only complete any job requested but to improve upon its processes. Once hired, please continue to share a positive and productive environment, and grow your business in a way that will contribute to advancement in both society and our civilization. I assure you that it is worth it to invest in those who make you successful. It is also in your best interest to have clarity of mind and to heal rather than harm.

"Again, it pains me to say this, but from this time forward, to all I submit that any hostility or brutality outside of consent within an Entertainment Matrix movie, video game, or another venue of entertainment within the Entertainment Matrix of the Virtual Universe, that allows you to 'unleash the beast,' from time to time will be met with time in the Correctional Matrix. The Correctional Matrix will put offenders and claimants, after the appropriate due process, through many difficult and challenging experiences, which are necessary to bring out the virtues of empathy, compassion, learning, and clarity of mind toward innovations that will increase the well-being of others as well as themselves. It will also provide proper vindication to the victims and their societies.

"Coaches, trainers, mentors, and counselors, whether former law enforcement, volunteers, or simulated virtual persons, will be within this matrix to guide offenders, or as necessary their claimants, through this seemingly endless reality of multiple lives. They will mentor them to have a mindset that allows for healthy reasoning and will promote longevity with optimal physiological and neurological health, as well as healthy psychological expression that suggests a positive cognitive framework. In the new US, there will be zero tolerance for destruction of another's property without proper authorizations. There is no tolerance in any way for vandalism, theft, rape, emotional abuse, or murder. Consent is something that can bring endless bounty, joy, meaning, constructive ventures, and productivity in all facets of life, for all who live, with a beautiful reality, and respectful and shared experiences with others.

"Please remember that in each tech city, town, and refurbished city or town, there are and will be many options to exercise your creativity, your physique, and your mind. Real-World and Virtual Universe Sports Arenas, Art and Science Expos, Governmental Facilities, Maintenance Facilities, Scientific Innovation Centers and Labs, Agricultural Complexes that are robust, air scrubbers and pleasant aroma filters that clean the air, parks, walkways, bikeways, pet walkways through forests and jungles filled with sentient creatures, and programs, games, and enjoyment within the Entertainment Matrix, are there around the clock to enrich your life, and in so many ways. Each of these facilities is in place for personal maintenance, productivity, innovation, and relaxation.

"There are receptacles or one-stop cold fusion system garbage and recycle facilities tied into a grid connected to every home, walkway, entertainment venue, restaurant, and business with a mass accumulation meter and neural identification association for the accumulation of contribution points that equate to a replacement product that is top-of-the-line and state-of-the-art. These facilities and systems are put in place to keep our environment beautiful, healthy, and afford us luxurious products that can endure the test of time and can be maintained or upgraded for many millennia.

"There are public pools, spas, steam and dry saunas, preventative health facilities, emergency health facilities, nutrient-dense and clean meat restaurants, fusion, electrical and gas grids, and hyperloop and jump gate terminals. This will allow people to travel freely to any destination they choose in moments, rather than hours.

"There are forests and jungles with every type of fruit, vegetable, nut, herb, spice, morel, and sweet blossom imaginable throughout the many locations and within the many features of every city, and in plentiful supply for every citizen and any visitor to enjoy.

"Every domicile in every building has the ability to allow inhabitants to view what they wish through their windows. Every bathroom is spacious with Jacuzzis, self-cleaning toilets, and bidets, climate controlled self-preparation areas, air scrubbers and filters that remove any nausea-inducing odors, and any other convenience or luxury anyone of any previous economic status could possibly wish for. Every room comes with every option you can imagine and choose. This will further add to cultural and social richness and openness.

"I exhort each one of you to enter a biopod after today's events are complete to receive your neurological identification or a neural identification. Neural identification is designed to encrypt private thought, and as you wish, compartmentalize memories, wardrobes, ideas brewing for businesses, and provide training in all manner of arts, skills, and sciences. All of this, while imbuing the augmented abilities that will increase your capacity to do what you are trained to do, to the point to which, so long as it lends to the well-being of yourself and others, you at your own ability are at liberty to choose to share. A person can share anything they wish and privatize anything they're not ready to reveal.

"There are further perks to your neural identification. In a tech city or a refurbished city, a neural identification will allow the climate control features to adjust around you to precisely what your physiology and neurology require to make it so that for any particular task, job, goal, activity, or any other action, you will have available to you a climate that is ideal for you, personally. It will also associate what is yours in such a way that nothing that is yours can be stolen by anyone else, since at the end of each day, these items will teleport to their designated and organized storage location, capable of being summoned by you as needed. With these neural identifications you can also use jump gate terminals, teleport to shorter and pre-coordinated locations, and so much more. Neural identifications are essential for healing any damage you may incur while advancing your skills in any sport, hobby, or at work, or in any other situation, and with them, you will be mended instantly.

"Your neural identification can bind clouds of self-replicating nanos for your own personal use. It can be used for your work or business in mining asteroids, non-functioning space debris, and Earth-bound, life-threatening, and equipment-damaging uncontrolled objects. There are already systems in place to ensure Solar System gravitational integrity stays in-tact, and that measures for proper coordination are available. If you have a helpful idea, share it within the Virtual Universe. Understand, that innovation, when shared, can become more robust with many more options, and while it may be that it comes with a cost of thought, consideration, and effort, your value of return will be much greater.

"As we shift from Earth to Space and create measures to transfer large shipments back to Earth from Space, there is a large array of space elevators placed in a variety of locations around Earth. Although many shipments can be sent back and forth using the jump gate terminals, this allows participation by those who do not wish to be physiologically or neurologically optimized. Smart suits are available to these individuals, securing their safety and an enjoyable climate.

"Through these many investments, reinvestments, creations, upgrades, and visits to the Virtual Universe to make improvements, every household, every business, everything suggested that abides by the Principles of Universal Ethics, and everything necessary for a fully functional, mind-engaging, experiential, exciting, original and unique society and environment, based on a healthy-and-self-maintained-life-and-mind-set, is now available to you. This is my gift to you. Like any of a number of gifts, there are usually sets of instructions on how to use them, maintain them, and maximize how they can be of benefit you.

"Now, in all humility, I will admit, that different from any President throughout the history of any leader of any civilization, I have taken much of my own time and gifted vigintillions of dollars' worth of my investments toward and for the well-being of each of you. I have already done what was necessary to allow you time now to relax, to take a break, to explore the world, and to absorb your new reality, if you so choose, for the next four years without concern for bills, money, or a job. For too long, life has been thick, cumbersome, brutal, volatile, and downright toxic for everyone in our country. It is time for you to take a break. I talked to you earlier of the biopods. So, please take advantage of them, heal yourselves, as I do often, practice your new abilities and skills in the Virtual Universe, and give your mind the clarity needed to embrace the beauty of this World, our Solar System, and prepare to journey the Cosmos. We each have so much to look forward to. Allow eagerness for constructive and productive pursuits take you far but take time for personal and shared maintenance.

"I ask each citizen, apart from my delegates, who have already done so, to go on a sabbatical from the stressors of life for a while. To do this or to begin the process, simply log in to our government website, as shown behind me. Select, 'move to a parallel city,' and follow the directions from there. This server is unique, in that it will not crash no matter how hard you try to make it crash. It is designed to allow each of you to sit down with your families and to design the interior of your new homes to meet your needs and wishes within the scope provided, and I assure even the richest, the most moderate, and the poorest among you that you will not be disappointed. Once your sabbatical is through, I ask that each person decide which profession or professions you would wish to be top-notch in, jump in your own biopods, train up using time dilation, courtesy of the Virtual Universe, and then work as I have suggested, as a part of the continued advancement of civilization, so that together, we can go further than before.

"Thank you, each, for your attention to my State of the Union, presentation, and Inaugural Acceptance Speech. We have much to do, but first, let us listen to Vice President Yesha Alevtina; she has some amazing things to share.

"Remember, together as we start with something as simple as kindness, we will find ourselves with purpose, promise, meaning, and the ability to go further than we have ever gone before. Our new motto here in the US is, 'Heal, don't harm.' Thank you!" With that President, Eliza Amber Williams stepped down from the podium, and at first, everyone was silent and awed by what they had heard. But the short pause was just enough to bring the listeners to their senses.

The crowd got up off their seats and then stood to roar in applause. People all around the public world were astounded, intrigued, and anxious in a hopeful way to see what sort of reality this new president was about to bring to her own country, and how it would affect their country as well. Rumors were out that she also had gifts for the rest of the countries throughout the world. The public world was beginning to sense an undying sense of excitement to what was ahead. Throughout the entire speech, there was not one mention of any "old matters" or "controversial issues;" instead everything along those lines had been resolved, and everyone was filled with hope and excited to begin the process of moving forward.

Yesha smiled at Eliza as they met each other's gaze. Yesha then stood up and they shook hands as the crowd continued to roar, and Eliza took her seat, next to Yesha's.

The Speaker of the House arose with her gavel and with much more excitement in her tone, she began the proceedings to vote for official approval of all of the changes for immediate implementation, "Ladies and gentlemen, senators and representatives, I motion that we put into effect, immediately, all changes, additions, and adjustments to law and order, the use of biopods, neural identifications, the Virtual Universe, entertainment and correctional matrices, tax code, employer accountability, and conveyances for transitioning as a nation to the new tech cities.

"To all members in favor, say, 'Aye.'"

"Aye." The vote was unanimous.

To all not in favor, say, 'No.'"

The room was silent. After the allocated opportunity to abstain, the Speaker of the House closed the voting session with her gavel. "Please let us continue with the next three speeches and formal updates to policy. Thank you, President, for your enlightening and promising words."

She then sat down.

Yesha stepped up to the podium, looked around at each member of the crowd, sensed their approval in every way, and began her speech. Just before speaking, Yesha's interesting, feminine, lightly tanned, and exquisite frame, beautifully dressed, her curves, with medium-length hair in an up-do, a rainbow of highlights through her professionally groomed dark brown hair, emerald and hazel-eyes, with all of the features that suggested highly sophisticated youth, immediately summoned the attention of every onlooker. They were captivated.

"President Williams and I have been friends ever since she was born. Less than two minutes after her arrival to life, she looked at me with her big blue crystalline eyes and smiled. She smiled at everyone in the room. Those beautiful moments were surrounded by other not so happy moments. Both of us have known immense tragedy in our lives, yet we had also realized that we were blessed in ways that many weren't. We both decided, at a time when we were first capable of making decisions, and at a very young age, that we wanted to help reduce the misery, the suffering and overcome the obstacles that led to so much tragedy, or uncontrolled chaos.

"There are many who have done horrible things, yet they too are victims of their own choices and everything that has surrounded them in life. The Correctional Matrix will coincide with the Judicial Branch's mission, and through the proper and due process, as President Williams has suggested, perpetrators of crimes will be sent to the Correctional Matrix for a time-period agreed upon by the victims and their families, the Judge, and a Jury of their peers. During this time-frame, these individuals will have the type of coaching, mentoring, training, counseling, and experiences necessary to breed within them the virtues of empathy, compassion, consent, respect for others, and clarity of mind toward what they can do to increase the quality of life for not just themselves, but for others as well. They will have an opportunity to provide due vindication to society, to learn from their mistakes, and then reach a moment of contrition, where they will genuinely realize that it is theirs to serve society in a healthy and helpful way. Once that occurs, these individuals will be tested to ensure their remorse and their claims are true.

If their time in the Correctional Matrix has been successful, they will be assimilated back into society, both whole, forgiven, and with an opportunity to walk around as full citizens.

"This topic is a tough one to consider, but the truth is, how can we consider ourselves healthy of mind if we would wish harm to an individual who has deliberately hurt us? I suggest that it is healthier of mind to desire to see them in a situation where they can benefit from the experiences that will allow them to progress while learning, gaining humility, and a renewed clarity on how they can cause their own uniqueness to unfold before us, as we observe their untold potential. I for one, would rather someone learn and apologize genuinely and then move forward doing great things, so that one day we can sit around a campfire on some distant moon, talk about what we have learned from life, the things we've seen and enjoyed, and then make goals for an even better future.

"Earlier, President Williams talked about twenty-thousand new Tech Cities in the US and its territories and suggested more. I will now present to you the twenty-thousand tech cities throughout the Solar System."

As Yesha said this, the area behind her brought even more awe to the multitudes of people watching the proceedings worldwide as each planet, their moons, and other spheroids came into view in a dazzling display of their new reality. "Each one of these cities began with a protective barrier, or a dome if you will. As time went by, the many individuals who were rescued, healed, and protected worked with Pathway both at home and abroad to help us to improve the shields you see that protect our Earth, the Twelve Database Moons you see, that allow us to back up our minds and physiological constructs, travel instantly to anywhere in space, and communicate without any time-lapse. These Twelve Database Moons can absorb and deflect anything thrown at them and in a manner that helps to increase the life-giving nature of the Sun and the rest of the planets of the Solar System. The moons of this Solar System and every planet, have been tamed, given a protective shield, and tech cities populate them in the most beautiful way. Mercury, Venus, Mars, Jupiter, Saturn, Uranus, Neptune, Pluto, and every spheroid throughout our Solar System now have a protective and similar climate to Earth's.

"Throughout our infrastructural building phase, we found many microscopic and in some cases creature-like life on several spheroids, and their environments were protected and preserved as well, while allowing them an opportunity for sentience and the ability to participate with us, which they graciously and enthusiastically accepted, as we freely move around and prepare our Solar System to defend itself against anything that is outside of it that may be hostile or forbidding to life itself.

"There is a new planet that we forged and have yet to name, and this planet revolves around the Sun in such a way as to provide both the basic "food" the Sun needs to do what it does to provide life. This function also serves to extract the heavier elements, which if left within the Sun, would cause it to expand such that life could no longer exist on Earth. Instead, we now we have been able to mine the heavier elements, both raising the quality of life throughout our Solar System and preserving our home world. We now, no longer need to stress over the loss of Earth, our Sun, or our Solar System.

"Around the sphere of the Solar System, beyond where the Oort Cloud, filled with dirty snowball comets, used to be, there is now an invisible and re-navigational Dyson Sphere that helps us to store or deflect any form of radiation or particle necessary for the preservation of an increased quality of life. In every city on every spheroid, there are museums filled with the historical aspects of every asteroid, comet, or other stray item that we have used to create each city. We were cautious of life, doing our research and due diligence before mining and building."

A visual of each mega-advanced aspect that Pathway had worked on was on display throughout the world. Everyone was in awe. Yesha looked around at the quiet yet entranced masses, and then she continued.

"Behind me, you can now see the Moon, its oceans, its rivers, its streams, its green, blue, and brown terrain, and an atmosphere teeming with the ability to protect its occupants from harm and provide life. There is a lower amount of gravity, and this makes the Moon the ideal location for our Solar System spacecraft hub. However, every single planet has its own unique beauty, and while Jupiter's weather continues and has many more powerful gravitational effects, our breakthroughs with gravity and our own nanos help to mitigate those effects. We have developed space elevators and biodomes that are massive and capable of buffeting anything thrown at them. They allow life to exist. They enable us to conduct further research, development, and innovation. They allow us procurement of unlimited and self-sustaining resources that will help us to navigate the Cosmos and benefit further from the resources there. In each place we go, we will ultimately preserve and protect each solar system, rejuvenate them to ensure they too can provide life-giving nurture as well, and protect them from anything that would take that away. Eventually, each mission will be done on a macro-scale, such that preservation, rejuvenation, protection, and safety are standard throughout the Milky Way Galaxy, and we'll have simultaneous missions going on in galaxies between Earth and the CMB Radiation.

"There is a lot that we have done, but there will always be more we can do. Maintenance is one of the most valuable industries we know of, and much of that takes place within the Virtual Universe, by encoding large self-replicating clouds of nanos to become a part of a lifelike system within every bit of infrastructure we create. All structures are almost lifelike, healing themselves, updating, and upgrading their abilities to the advantage of all who live.

"Our biggest mission now is to explore our Universe and understand everything about it, from Stars in all of their forms to Black Holes, Nebulae, Globular Clusters, Galaxies, and Galaxy Clusters, to the CMB itself and beyond. Our mission always is to preserve life, to heal and not harm, to exchange destruction and chaos for life with abundance for all, and to protect it.

"Ladies and gentlemen of Congress, throughout the Nation, and throughout the World, may I introduce you to Sky Taylor and then to Vesha Celeste. Both of whom will provide a presentation, and Vesha will also share some new policies. Following that, the Speaker of the House will close this broadcast with an all-inclusive vote by the members of both Houses of Congress, and we will begin our break, followed by our due diligence. I ask that no matter whom you are with or who it is that is around you, that you do as Eliza has admonished. Be gracious and kind always. That is how we move forward. It is the first step into the future!"

Yesha stepped down and the crowd roared again. Sky Taylor stepped up to the podium after smiling and shaking hands with both Yesha and Eliza. The crowd was intrigued by her beauty, her youth, her iridescent and crystalline blue eyes, her blonde hair that was so light that it was like snow, yet she had locks and braids of iridescent colors that went down her angelically loose-curled hair with tips and highlights of pink and purple, and what appeared to be her make-up on every exposed part of her buxom physique were iridescent overtones of pinks and purples. Her wardrobe ensemble was extraordinarily ornate in embroidery, as well as form-fitting, bringing out her visual features in a pleasing way. Her audience was struck by her beauty, her power, and her graceful demeanor. Many onlookers throughout the world remembered her from her visits, rescues, healings, and journeys, yet they were in awe to see her even still.

As she opened to speak, something almost as miraculous occurred. Suddenly, it was as if everyone in the crowd became aware that, just as the ground below was as steady and secure as ever, all the walls and ceilings had disappeared. The holograph of the presentation behind her was now enveloped around them as though they were floating through space. All the citizens who had gathered around the House of Congress, to include those watching and listening from an outdoor projector screen were now able to see the proceedings as if they were in one of the front row seats to the proceedings, which was developing to become as one would imagine of a heaven-like space adventure.

The crowds around the world, all whom were watching, were now able to witness the space-like imagery enveloping them give way to a new reality, while Sky provided them warmth and comfort, no matter their outdoor or indoor environment. They then witnessed playing out before them the streets of Washington DC, and around Maryland and Virginia, and then, as they suddenly became as beautiful as the streets of South Otselic, where streets that were once narrow and broken, were now mended, enhanced, and widened. The flora, fauna, and every bit of the flawless infrastructure complemented each other beautifully.

In that fraction of a second, in an extended crackle in the air, everyone felt a connection one with another embracing a true and mutual understanding, a feeling that every single one of their neurons, synapses, cells, and nerves were experiencing a fiery bliss in a way they had never felt before. Once everyone had grasped their reality and looked toward the podium as if they were all in the front row, Sky began to speak with the glow and eloquence of an angel.

"This is a unique setting, and I am glad to be here to witness the wonder of two dear friends as they plan to carry out something beautiful, something kind, and something loving. Beautiful, kind, and loving, those are words we hear sometimes, but I don't think we hear them in a genuine manner often enough. Today, everything presented by Eliza and Yesha was all about just that, beauty, kindness, and love.

"While there are many examples throughout history of those three beautiful words in action, unfortunately words such as pain, suffering, brutality, terrorism, greed, lust for power at any cost, sociopathic behavior, psychotic behavior, pompously malicious intent with full cognition, misery, disease, uncontrolled chaos, the worship of the mixed result rather than a desired one, war, murder, rape, emotional abuse, theft of hard-won gains, destruction of someone else's well-earned belongings, gross negligence leading to misery and death, false witness, lies that harm another's well-being, acting in a manner that tears others down without regard for anything or anyone else, and so much more are terms, behaviors and actions used all too often in our news, in the shows we watch, in the games we play, and in how too many conduct themselves in many corners throughout the world; this all seems to be in far too large of supply. Let's change that. As I look into each one of you, I know you have untold potential that is both rare, benevolent, and priceless. Things can be filled with kindness, love, and beauty. Let's make that happen."

What Sky said was short, and as soon as she finished, certain aspects of her changes went back to normal, the walls and ceilings returned as they had been before. Smiling at Eliza, Yesha, and then Vesha Celeste as they passed each other, Sky angelically walked to her place on the stage and sat down. Scanning the audience, Sky saw that everyone had crystal clear awareness about them; it was an almost refined form of conviction toward kindness, beauty, and love. She then began to reach out beyond Washington DC, Maryland, and Virginia with her mind and as she did, she beautified every aspect of the nation, both in function and aesthetic, in a manner similar to what she had done with Joanne's hometown of South Otselic. People would notice the many changes made after they woke up the next morning, following their first night of training.

Vesha Celeste then arose from her seat, smiled at her preceding speakers and presentation givers, made her way to the podium, and addressed the audience. As she stood there before them, they were again awed by her youthful yet powerful presence. Her jet-black hair, her form-fitting smart-suit that was likewise black, with trim of iridescent colors and overtones of turquoise, blues, purples and greens embroidered into her smart suit that blended with perfection to her iridescent and emerald green eyes, as well as the highlights in her A-framed, spiral curled, medium-length hair, all captivating the audience with another display of unique beauty, authority, and vision.

"Hello, citizens, ladies, gentlemen, children, and all who are present and delighted to be here. I am pleased to be here with you today. Thank you to our President, Vice President, and my dear friend, Sky Taylor, for your wonderful speeches.

She then turned to Sky, and said, "Sky Taylor, you are like a twin sister to me, and I love you with all my heart, mind, and soul." The glowing exchange between the two emanated a radiant white glow that was nearly as brilliant as the Sun, and the audience was moved to tears.

Vesha looked toward the audience. But the audience could still sense that both shared a sisterly bond that was beautiful and undeniable. Vesha knew Sky had granted all attendees, near and far, optimized physiology and neurology, as well as neural identifications, nanos, and neural links, and she shared her story with all to ponder on later.

"To begin with, and for brevity, as I speak, I ask that you also pay attention to what is in the space behind me. What you see, is the Intergalactic Mission Contingency, or IMC, which is located within our Solar System just above the asteroid disc and in a safe and parallel orbit to Pluto. The IMC consists of thirteen zonal commands. Each zonal command has its own Command Spacecraft. Each Command Spacecraft is the size of a large tech city and has an environment similar to one. They are adorned with all the luxuries, real-life aspects, and awe-inspiring technological advancements and capabilities expected of a high-class Universe-navigating spacecraft, with balanced aesthetic and utility for navigating through space in a disciplined, safe, and quick manner.

"Long ago, when Eliza and Yesha were finishing their high school studies, we talked together. We visited many times after that, before I passed away in December of 2016. I had lived on Earth for eighty-eight years. Before that and prior to being reawakened in an optimized version of myself, we each came up with the idea for a new technology. This technology is what our jump gates, our ability for teleportation, and our quantum drives, or Q-drives, which were designed by Dr. Luís Rodriguez, are all built around, and are integrated with sensor transceiver technology and robust sensory scout nodes, both of which we now have combined into a succinct product that we simply call sensors. If you observe the imagery behind me, you will see that we have made it so that we can jump from one point in space to any other point in space with precision. With a micro version of these sensors, before every jump, we can and will comb any remote location that we wish to jump to and gather all sensory information relative to it within a one-parsec radius. Depending upon the information we receive and process within the Virtual Universe, near instantaneously, we can jump to that location or re-navigate to a safer location.

"Each Command Spacecraft is nearly alive, with constant nano updates and repairs going on within each external and internal wall and object in and around it, around the clock. Each of the thirteen Command Spacecraft are near-identical and are set up to accommodate more than twelve-hundred crew members and their families. As it is, we have created twelve zones throughout all observable space relative to the Earth, for visual reference using legacy telescopic equipment, that are limited to what Earth can see, given the speed of light. These zones extend from Earth and out to forty-five-billion light-years. Each of these zones is the crux of the mission for any Zonal Command. Twelve Zonal Commands will travel with the IMC until we arrive at each of their assigned zones, or region of primary galaxies relating to their specific setup point.

"I have been voted on by a population of eight billion Pathway personnel, after nomination by our President, President Eliza Amber Williams, to lead the IMC, along with my crew, aboard the IMC Command Spacecraft. We will operate with a command structure very similar to that of the United States Air Force. The reason for this structure is to reign-in discipline, augment our innovative capabilities and our attention, and reduce any dramatic chaos that could compromise our mission. Nonetheless, just as every tech city has, each IMC Command Spacecraft will have similar facilities, domiciles, forests, lakes, and more. Creatures of every possible sort will be on board each IMC Command Spacecraft and have been given sentience, so they can play a vital role as counselors and muses for the crew, as per their agreement, working harmoniously with humanity to explore, understand, colonize, and preserve our Universe.

"My friend, Sky Taylor, now has one-thousand daughters and one-thousand-one sons, each of whom possess the same abilities for healing as she. As I mentioned previously, on each Command Spacecraft there will be twelve living sectors, with equitably unlimited and self-sustaining resources, and living within each sector there will be twelve crewmembers with identical abilities to those of Sky Taylor. If ever needed, we will have the ability to destroy any potential threats. While we can overcome any potential threats and meet every challenge thrown our way, we now have the ability to put them into stasis, heal their minds, connect with them, create a communications bridge of diplomacy, and find a cohesive goal of preservation of life, in a manner that exemplifies Universal Ethics. Our ultimate goal with all our space travels is to slow down the expansion of our Universe. We want to do this enough to control a minor contraction and expansion, allowing it to inhale and exhale as a sentient lifeform. This will in-turn allow it to exist for an indefinite period of time. That goal may take billions to trillions of years to achieve, or it may be achieved much sooner. Given our President's capacity for innovation, my guess is it will be within one-hundred years, or less that we achieve that goal.

"That said, our ability to recreate gravity, with another team headed by Dr. Luís Rodriguez, has led to the development and creation of the gravitational drive, or G-drive. With this seemingly impossible advancement, concerns about interplanetary travel, along with coffee stains and such, can now be completely mitigated. For reference, Eliza designed the aspects of Sky that allow her to fly using similar technology. As we train, we may learn how to upgrade to use her abilities too.

"I will go over more aspects of the IMC on the government website, but for now, please know that once each of you has completed your sabbatical, in four years we will begin our journey through the Cosmos. I hope many of you can be there. There will be openings to train for, but there are obviously limited seats and positions. We have our command crew for each IMC Command Spacecraft chosen, and some of the individuals that will be filling important roles have already been selected. There are always opportunities for shift-work crew, so please feel free to go to the website and volunteer. Half of the positions available will be on a first come and first served basis, the other half of the remaining positions are based on a lottery of volunteers. Please be courteous, as malicious intent will automatically rule anyone out. If our missions are to succeed, then we need to have people with the noblest and strongest virtues of intellect, kindness, persuasiveness, empathy, compassion, and curiosity.

"If you do not make it, please understand that there will be many more opportunities as I deliver the twelve IMC commanders to their zones and after I reach the cosmic microwave background. We may need an additional one-hundred-forty-four IMC Command Spacecraft, and maybe even more in short order. As we expand so will the need for IMC Command Spacecraft. Please keep in mind that we plan to colonize every galaxy and planet throughout the Universe, so there are more than enough opportunities for everyone to be involved. Longevity, patience, and innovation have their merit, especially where space travel is concerned. Keep in mind, that this lottery will be available to everyone worldwide, upon agreement to honor Universal Ethics. As such we will submit a request for all nations to become part of what we will call the United Allied States, because each spacecraft will be a part of the UAS Intergalactic Mission Contingency. Thank you all for listening."

Like that, everyone had been completely enthused, mystified, and excited all at the same time, and most especially with the behemoth size and capabilities of each UAS IMC Command Spacecraft. Vesha sat down, after doing the professional greeting with the other members of Pathway, and the spacecraft visuals continued to play out in view of all watching the proceedings.

The Speaker of the House was again very enthusiastic and had changed her demeanor to a renewed sense of wonder and excitement. As such and with a new sense of youth, herself, she took her gavel and called the room to order. After doing so, she spoke, "I'm sure I am not the only one looking forward to leaving here tonight and signing up to go on a big space adventure! President, Vice President, Sky Taylor, and Vesha Celeste, thank you! You were all brilliant. Speaking for my political party, I believe this will be the first time when there will be no reason for a rebuttal to your address. Most of the address came data-masked anyway, but you each brought your best, and I sense that everyone listening and observing watched with full-scaled eagerness to get the show going on all what was presented. Thank you so much for everything that you have done, everything you are doing now, and for the promise of hope that has been rekindled within each of us today.

"Therefore, ladies and gentlemen of the House, please stand up and say, 'Aye,' if you approve of immediate implementation of all policy changes congruent with what was presented today."

She paused.

Everyone in the room stood up, and the unanimous, "Aye," filled the room.

"Anyone who has any objections, please say, 'Nay.'"

Everyone remained seated, and not a word was spoken.

"Then it is official, all that has been shared tonight has been approved by the legislators of both Houses of Congress and goes into effect immediately. I encourage everyone to log in to their government website as shown behind me, and follow the instructions. Given what we have heard today, it stands to reason that everything and everyone will be both rational and intuitive when it comes to following the directions provided. Thank you all for your attendance. Therefore, ladies and gentlemen of both Houses of Congress, this meeting stands adjourned." With that, the Speaker of the House lowered her gavel to bring finality to the session, and everyone roared in applause.

The State of the Union was complete.

Following the proceedings, every US citizen began their transition to the twenty-thousand tech cities that Eliza, Yesha, Sky, James, and their teams had secretly built from the ground up, in places once thought desolate. The worldwide audience went home happy, moved, and hopeful for the future soon to come. The citizens of the United States of America signed up with haste on Pathway's website, so they could move into the tech cities, and discovered that these moves were instantaneous. Once they moved in, they people the world over signed up for every crew position, the lottery, colonization, and then for the future missions. Excitement had grown, the US was bustling, and the rest of the World was excited too.

Behind the scenes, tech cities were built throughout the more desolate places of Earth and more existing cities became ghost towns completely. The factories that polluted, homes that were no longer needed within these cities, and large edifices that were no longer going to be used were all taken down, except for truly historical sites and monuments. All components were shipped through the space elevators to the depths of space and to the Space Fusion Centers, in order to reduce it all to materials necessary for fertility and growth for the forests that would replace the locations where cities once resided.

New tech cities were formed in places within the US, to include the deserts, and above and below the seas within the US territories throughout the world. Everything was built to be aesthetically charming, purposeful, enjoyable, and environmentally compatible in every way. This was done in wisdom to combat any negative impact on the environment, while simultaneously providing safety, security, and abundance to all who dwelled within them. If a major city was taken down, a tech city had been raised and named in its stead.

The USA was now on its way toward worthiness, much like many nations worldwide that had been touched by the miraculous hand of Sky, to span the Universe, and quite possibly even save it before the century was over. The expanse of space was huge and there was plenty for everyone to do, all which would be motivating and exciting.

That evening, Eliza linked to Yesha, Sky, Vesha, James, Amber, Erin, Joanne, and the rest of the leaders of the IMCs, and invited them to her estate home for a large dinner. Jeremiah Voltaire cooked alongside the many chefs of the T.O. and together, everyone enjoyed the most splendid meal they could imagine they had ever had. Afterward, everyone there discovered that Eliza had made overnight accommodations, with a large spread of memory foam pillows, sleeping bags, all surrounding her pond with coy fish and a statuette of an angel overlooking it.

"What a beautiful day," Eliza said.

Everyone agreed, chatted, looked up at the stars, sang Depeche Mode's song, "Where's the Revolution," and Eliza, before falling asleep, whispered into everyone's minds, *The revolution is here. It's one of those revolutions that are peaceful and full of promise. Thank you for so much wonderful music throughout the years, Dave, Martin, Andrew, and well, Alan—you need to come back."*

The Ethics of it All

As the days and weeks passed by, Eliza's, Yesha's, Sky's, and Vesha's words played on every news station throughout the World. Questions had been asked the following day about the ethics of it all, and her Press Secretary, Amber Blythe, responded in front of a worldwide audience, "That is quite an intriguing question. What are the ethics of it all? Let's see if I can grant some perspective on this. All our lives we have been told that morals, virtues, and ethics are subjective, but by whom, and what were their motives? Did they suggest purpose in life, clarity regarding preserving it, innovations toward optimizing our physiology and neurology, and working together to create a legacy worthy of preserving? Did they clearly define that optimal well-being, health, strength, dexterity, cognizance of mind, a healthy cognitive framework for our minds, and working to improve upon it all through sophisticated and scientifically proven means so we can compound upon our wisdom to meet the challenges that threaten life, as the profound basis for ethics? Did they suggest that empathy, compassion, kindness, love, beauty, and consent were the epitome of virtue? Did they suggest that health and healing were the golden standards of morality?

"If not, then I will remind you that President Eliza Williams not only taught all this throughout the last nineteen years since her graduation where she garnered seven

PhDs, she also wrote a very insightful book, called *Pathway to the Stars*, broadcasted her proposal to the world from the birth of Pathway. The President was intensely and intimately involved in all its actions that led to preserving the capacity of life on this planet, is currently engaged in healing the planet through sophistication, science, reason, study, intuition, experience, and compounded wisdom, and she did something with it all to reduce misery and suffering. Her teachings, her example, and her actions are a testament to virtue, morality, and ethics. Many years ago, I asked Eliza a similar question, but regarding pausing the specific memories, related to her technologies, when it came to those who chose not to become fully optimized, and here was her response:

"We had to figure out a way to create a safety and security mechanism to prevent some of these technologies from getting into the hands of those who would unleash the worst into society, or merely suggest that these technologies were intended for the elite. These wonderful new capabilities are intended for everyone, because they will heal them of any diseases, issues, or disorders, and increase their ability to enjoy life.

"The only memories they will temporarily lose are those directly relating to the details of our technologies and advancements that aren't yet ready for release to the Public. Essentially, unless and individual is read-in or optimized, they will not be able to see our advancements in space or on Earth, nor will they recall the technologies used for the advancements. However, they will not lose any personal memories, such as relationships established, the sense of trust built between them and other members of Pathway, and they will have a quickening of all their memories, once everything has gone Public during my 'great reveal.' Everything that we have worked on, developed, created, and expanded upon is amazing and intended to help humanity.

"These advancements are intended to help people to have clarity on what it is that can be done to preserve the heritage, the legacy, the romances, the histories, the arts and sciences that have made humanity such a wonderful part of the history of the Universe itself. With the laws of chaos, the laws of entropy, and the laws of thermodynamics, we understand that technology can go one of many ways, two of which are most prominent: either all humanity can stay its current course and become completely destroyed by its own negligence or overt intentions of destruction, or humanity can be shown beauty in science, the beauty in kindness, the amazing sense of compassion, and through that we can harness chaos, control it, and ensure that it leads us toward the discovery of how to reign in the chaos that could decimate our Universe.

"We can very well be around for a long, long time, and it is worth it to have every unique, brilliant, and special soul with us along the way. There is no sane reason for death, for carnage, or for misery other than to test our grace. Instead of wars and unforeseen challenges, we can reach the same growth through unchartered innovations and by daring to understand our Universe and the laws that bind it. We can preserve it, beautify it, and make it even stronger. While traveling from one end to the next, we can still meet with each other while sharing stories with each other and even taking each other to the many amazing places we will have inevitably found by then on our journeys.

"Wouldn't it be nice to have family and friends around when we return from planets within galaxies more than one-hundred-billion light-years away? We're all interested in and care about making that possible. However, people are free to go their own way. We simply must strive to provide clarity and health, while protecting our technologies from those that would use them to destroy others. That is what physiological and neurological optimization is all about, life and enlightenment. To preserve life is the ultimate equation for ethics. To take it away or to let our minds squander away through negligence, is the enemy of life, freedom, and even joy, and thereby maliciously unethical. Ethics and death do not belong together."

"Close quote. So, to preserve life is the ultimate equation for ethics. If your wish is to wander around in life without purpose or meaning, waiting to die as empty husks of untold potential, you are free to stay behind. The world around you will become beautiful, the people within it I can guarantee you, will be happy, but your access to it in your own home will be based on your own choices. Any time that you wish to embrace Universal Ethics, you will become a part of that beautiful world. No one will force your hand, suggest guilt or shame, or cause undue consequence to your own life, liberty, or pursuit of happiness, so long as you don't cause undue consequence to their rights of others to life, liberty, and their pursuit of happiness.

"Thank you for your questions. Remember, as Sky Taylor says, 'Heal, don't harm."

Many press releases passed, once optimized one-hundred percent of the country took advantage of the sabbatical for about a week. Every citizen had gained a sense of urgency, had found purpose, meaning, and profound drive to be involved in any manner they could be to increase their wisdom, and their contributions to the upgrades and improvements of everything Pathway had already set up. They were gracious and had combed the Virtual Universe with Vigintillions of years' worth of experience, and they all benefited immensely from it.

Other countries saw the success of the US, and no later than six months after Eliza's speech, every country throughout the world expressed their desires to join in with the US by adopting the Principles of Universal Ethics within their new and still sovereign governing policies of guidance. They also expressed their desires of being involved with the IMC and as members of a worldwide governance system based on Universal Ethics.

Under the direction of President Eliza Williams, the world formed what became known as the United Allied States, or the UAS. Both Houses of Congress, the people, and the Judicial System worked with the various countries wishing to become a part of the UAS and ratified each new contract. Eliza revealed to each country and territory that she had built tech cities in each of their desolate locations. The people of the World, now the UAS, all were on board and began to take down any of the cities that contributed to decay and pollution, and most importantly they took down cities that had a scale that could lead to the destruction of life and of the Earth itself. The UAS replaced the once toxic environments with forests, jungles, and underwater sea forests and jungles, as well as provided conveyances and opportunities for involvement for optimized creatures. The optimized creatures integrated with any natural creatures and taught them to preserve humanity and the nature of Earth's ability to sustain life.

Each member State of the UAS shared unified governance overall, while still maintaining capacities essential to governing with sovereignty within their own lands autonomously. Islands increased in size with underwater hyperloops on the ready to avail anyone wishing to go to and from each island to the various continents with ease. Territories once stricken with meager resources now had more rolling hills, mountains here and there, streams, rivers, ponds, lakes, and the ocean surrounding them, with forests, jungles, trees of every fruit and flower, morels, herbs, and spices abundant for everyone and their visitors. The world finally reached a potentially everlasting epoch of peace.

After the first year of her Presidency, Eliza shared many more ideas and goals. "When we think of our goals as a civilization, the beauty we are all witnessing now, and the enjoyable nature of traveling anywhere within our Solar System, all while having set up a system to keep it protected and capable of providing hospitality to all life that agrees to abide by Universal Ethics, we know that this indeed meets the basic unity criterion necessary for unified laws of interstellar exploration, colonization, and the possibility of meeting other civilizations throughout the Universe. We'll traverse as beautifiers and givers of life, and protectors of kindness and love."

Worldwide

"Do you want to go on a jog for old time's sake?" Yesha had teleported to a private walkway not too far from Boston, from the Oval Office. It would have been a normally cold winter, but with use of their Twelve Database Moons, they were able to stabilize the weather such that all Earth essentially experienced springtime for twenty-four months out of the year. However, also as requested, many enjoyed Fall, at least within the northern hemisphere, Spring in the southern hemisphere, so on the third quarter of each year autumn colors filled the trees. There were some locations that received snow or hot summers on request, and while those seasons were not setup by default, any tech city could change their weather patterns following unanimous voting and subsequent requests from UAS delegates. For Yesha, it was currently springtime.

With Yesha's new upgrades, she no longer needed her smart-suit, and instead swapped into her jogging holo-ensemble. For this occasion, she had chosen to instantaneously superimpose her clothes for jogging from her professional Vice-Presidential wardrobe. Many of her clothing outfits were quite impressive, all which she had purchased in the Virtual Universe from a halo-ensemble designer, named Holly Caleb. Yesha appreciated how the mesh of each wardrobe layout accentuated her physique and how the color variations in the accents and embroidery of it brought out the tones in her light tan skin and the highlights in her raven black hair. She also appreciated the fact that this designer was so adept at design that she could link just the right neurologically compartmentalized and accessible regions of her mind that Yesha had provided to her to provide lossless makeup facial overlays that complemented everything else about her. Her dark eyeshadow and lengthened eyelashes, et al, seemed to add even more spunk, power, confidence, and an exotic and attractive charm, to her already dynamic personality.

Yesha wanted to walk, jog, and simply talk with Eliza outside the constant contact and buzz of Washington DC, which had been upgraded and improved completely on the day of Eliza's first State of the Union speech. Mostly, in any new or reformed city or town and their resplendent countryside, there was so much beauty to soak in. The typical redundancy was in the functional and operational aspects, as related to safety, security, and publicly available infrastructure. Many aesthetic aspects of public infrastructure were, in a beautiful way, susceptible and molded to various advanced neurologically cooperative designs. As such, every location throughout the world was its own unique and enjoyable experience. From city to city and town to town, there was an exceptionality and awe that was a joy to behold, whether on the moons of Jupiter, the western regions of Australia, or what used to be cities that were parched by the Sahara Desert. The Sahara Desert, for example, was no more, and, in its place, were forests, jungles, cities, and towns, all full of abundance and beauty, and each of them with resort getaways that were all the rage, if anything, because of the newly discovered archeology sites, which had been buried by hundreds of feet of dirt and sand, throughout the many millennia.

When it had come to all Eliza's work, the work of decades could take place in a matter of minutes within the Virtual Universe. In many cases, what was done within the Virtual Universe was carried out near automatically and immediately, from city design to interplanetary planning and refurbishment in the real Universe. Eliza had pulled every stop to increase the quality of life throughout the UAS, but one thing she too had relearned from Sky on occasion was that sometimes it is good to simply step out, go for a real-life breather, ask a few questions, and enjoy the beauty of everything around us. Sky had also emphasized that shared moments doing the same could be just as, if not more, rewarding. With Eliza there, Yesha's best friend, her inspiration, her pride and joy, these moments would undoubtedly be more thrilling, exciting, and enjoyable.

"Sure. I'll be there in just a second," replied Eliza. After her first year as President, people had begun to return from their trips worldwide. Although they were given four years of sabbatical of their own cognition, each citizen had decided to return home and be a part of the preparation for the great journey to get humanity out and into the distant regions of space. Now, another year had gone by, it had been very productive, and ideas, improvements, and resolutions to new issues that arose were constantly being proliferated with little need for oversight. Eliza was proud of the free flow of innovative ideas and progress as a result. She knew that would happen, and Eliza appreciated the fact that now her dedication was shared worldwide. There was much to be done, plans to be made, and crews for the Intergalactic Mission Contingency to be filled. Many people were now more than qualified to fill any position on any of the UAS Spacecraft than ever, and people had volunteered and put in for the IMC lottery, from locations all over the World. Training was an often-shared virtue, things were running smooth, and every person and people, every nation, territory, island, and region had been healed and beautified.

Eliza closed her links with her various cabinet members, thanked Amber Blythe, again, for her support each day as her press secretary, went over the IMC plans on each upgrade and well-thought-out adjustment with Vesha Celeste, who gave her the wave of the hand of approval, at least notionally through her neural link, to one hundred percent the thirteen intergalactic command spacecraft and their latest upgrades.

Eliza had already commissioned Vesha and James to build the Presidential Command Spacecraft, very similar in every way to the spacious command spacecraft that would navigate the Universe. They could jump from region to region, galaxy to galaxy, void to void, one end of the visible universe to the next, and in a very short period. All the trimmings and fixings of high-quality travel were available on this spacecraft. With Eliza, redundancy in and high quality with the good things, as well as safety, protection, and brilliant minds, collaborating to make it all happen, were always applauded, plus she planned on being the first intergalactic President of the US, the UAS, and anywhere the people wished her to lead. Although Vesha Celeste would lead the IMC through the Universe, Eliza would ultimately support all humanity no matter where they finally settled. A lot was going on and it called for a little break.

Eliza teleported to the region just north of Boston, where she and Yesha shared a private running pathway, waved to Yesha, and changed into her workout clothes, designed by Kerperna Walowski, from the Azores, also a holo-ensemble designer. Yesha and Eliza had very similar tastes, but they used different designers, just to ensure that they weren't accidentally wearing the same clothes at any given time. Uniqueness was celebrated, but there was also nothing wrong with shared days looking like twins. Still, they embraced the resplendent spice of life found in robust amounts of late. For this occasion, Eliza's blonde hair was instantaneously pulled back in a ponytail with its pink highlighted tips, her athletic thighs and arms on display, as was her very ample cleavage, and she was wearing shoes merely for the look. Everything about her oozed both sensuality and presidential authority, all in one, and she was never one to disappoint.

"Wow! You look like something else, Eliza! If I were James, I'd be scooping you up and running away right about now!"

Eliza smiled. "You look awesome too, but let's not rush the poor gentleman for now? What is this, a fantasy world? I am kidding, of course. Well, if it is, it's courtesy of everyone in it who made it happen. We could not have had these forests now growing in places once gutted of their trees, and jungles likewise now filled with trees and animals of every sort without the work of humanity's many friends. The tech cities raised within the many desert-like and desolate areas of the world are now surrounded with and meshed into newly grown forests, lakes, sandy beaches, and jungles, with enviable quickness, high quality, and visual aesthetic and each aspect is filled with purpose, courtesy of Sky, her daughters, and the many other individuals she visited and upgraded personally. I am impressed with how she turned out, Yesha. You, Amber, and quite a few others did a lot to make her evolution a success. Remember, following her first year, the countless missions? Wow, she is something else, someone else, and well-driven. I am glad she is both a US as well as UAS citizen, she deserves it. I worked with her the year before our first State of the Union, and she secretly helped to make sure every forest and jungle is now teeming with trees, bushes, fruits, flowers, herbs, spices, morels, and vegetation of every sort, with access to sunlit walking paths available for strolls, just like ours, to visit each other and creatures of every kind and take in the ambiance."

Yesha looked at Eliza, then out at the ambiance, and together they began their conversational jog. "Eliza, what you did, there was an enriching and unique sense of collaborative minds in the creativity of every detail of every city's infrastructure. It's amazing how your genius helped to pull that off. Some of what you did, I had no idea about. Each structure and substructure is now clean and beautiful inside and out. There is no trash, no ads, no telephone poles, no clutter, just beauty, meaningfulness, creative architecture, forests and jungles, lakes and rivers, hills, valleys, mountains, and purpose. What would have been very wide streets before for vehicles, between each edifice, are now wide areas between buildings with large, tall, and flowered evergreen trees, ground vegetation of every sort, and artistic walkways above and below the skyline. City grids are lined up in such a way to ensure that full Sun and partial shade trees lie congruent to the amount of Sun needed for rich and healthy vegetation.

"Look, there's Blair the Buzzard. She likes flying around here but is rather disappointed that she can no longer feed upon the death and decay. Still, she's made good friends of the mice down below, all helping to tend to the forest and the vegetation. Did you see her new tree house?"

"I did, she is quite a creative bird!" Eliza was happy to be with Yesha, especially in moments like these. The air was clear, the Sun was getting ready to eclipse the Earth from their vantage point, and the clouds were a beautiful array of pinks, purples, and peaches. "It seems she met Burt the Buzzard a couple of months ago, and they may have a couple of little buzzards on the way. Her home looks like the terrain a bit, and it captures the colors of every sunset or sunrise adding a bit of creativity to its look every day."

Yesha tapped into Eliza's mind. They hadn't shared every detail with each other when it came to private lives for quite some time, because sometimes it was nice to simply chat about them. Before Yesha could dig too deep, Eliza started up again with a smile, "Wow, yes, I can see that now. I'm typically jogging around lunchtime, so the colors of her tree house are usually green, blue, and the colors of the blossoms in the evergreens out here at that time of day." Eliza paused and began to take on a more serious and business-like tone, despite their outing for relaxation.

"I wanted to chat about the Intergalactic Mission Contingency Commands, the Intergalactic Mission Contingency Command Spacecraft, and the entire vernacular. What do you think about the current rank structure and leadership positions? We are starting a big, huge sprawl through outer space after all, and it seems it would be worth it to maybe consider coining a set of official terms—something that considers the United Allied States, for example. Or at least officializes the idea as presented a couple of years ago. What do you think?"

"You know, I have been thinking of introducing the IMC as head of the UAS Space Force in our next State of the UAS. The spacecraft traveling throughout the twelve zones carry about twelve contingencies of support spacecraft each for a total of one-hundred-ninety-six support spacecraft per IMC Command Spacecraft, so I can see maybe calling the largest class of spacecraft, in short and long form, the UAS IMC Command Spacecraft, and then give them each a zonal reference. Imagine, UAS IMC Command Spacecraft, Zone-12, for example. Furthermore, I get the sense that granting each spacecraft a robust and sentient artificial intelligence and then allowing them to choose a name might be more than an original idea, but it will make sense from the standpoint that we'll be working as a team and they will have proper buy-in. Basically, each command spacecraft will likely choose the name of a favored constellation in their zone.

"As far as leadership is concerned, there will be four leaders on each UAS IMC Command Class Spacecraft, the Commander, the Vice Commander, the head HBCI, and the spacecraft itself. Rank structure will be somewhat like that of the Air Force and the Army, beginning with the UAS IMC Commander, Vesha Celeste, as a Five-Star General, Erin Carter as a Four-Star General, and all other crew members will fill various roles necessary for a space-faring contingency and subordinate in rank, from Three-Star to One-Star General. For example, Four-Star General Anastasia Renae and Three-Star Lieutenant General Evan Bauer will oversee zone twelve or will be recognized as the commander and vice commander of UAS IMC Command Spacecraft, Zone-12. Vesha and Erin will be in charge of every zone, with a major focus on their own zone, once they leave the CMB. I do have plans for something interesting before the IMC takes off on its journeys, and I will keep you informed of changes in due time. Each zonal command will only need support for so long. After they have enough colonies setup and running full-bore out in the various galaxies out there, they'll have all the personnel and unlimited and self-sustaining resources they'll need to continue in their areas."

Yesha thought about what Eliza had shared, "I can see that. I'm sure no matter where we go, there will be a lot to learn and challenges galore, so I am sure they'll let us know if they need anything. It'll be nice to jump gate to the various UAS Command Spacecraft and visit the different zones. It sounds as if you have a sound plan put together."

They jogged, hadn't realized time was flying by, but so were they. They had started north of Boston, and now they were just north of New York City. Eliza looked to Yesha and said, "I'll patch to you more details for your sleep download and neural processing later. Do you want to hit up Broadway? I'm sure they've got a show that's soon to start. I'd love to see one."

"Sure. I wouldn't mind that either. Do you suppose Jeremiah Voltaire is in town? Or is he out with his crew?" Yesha thought about her question, accessed the Virtual Universe database, using her neural link, and noticed that every night, at right about this time, Jeremiah would call it a day out there just above Pluto, return to his domicile in New York City, and then head to his restaurant to cook up some delicious food. "Wait, he's there right now. Let's get a bite to eat and head to a show. What do you say?"

"That sounds like a good plan to me." Like that, Eliza and Yesha doffed the sweat from their auras, smelled of all kinds of floral bliss, changed into their restaurant ensembles, and linked with and headed to go visit with Jeremiah. Together, they chatted for a few hours, ate nice juicy clean meat cheeseburgers filled with all the trimmings and fixings, to include clean-meat bacon, pickles, lettuce, tomatoes, spiced mustard and ketchup. Once they drank their tea and consumed their lemon meringue pies, they went to a late Broadway show, upon changing into their finest, shared a coffee and then bid Jeremiah adieu. "Jeremiah is quite a charming man; I'd say so myself. What do you think about him, Yesha? I saw your mind going into sparkly magical stars when you saw him."

"He is pretty cool. I suppose he's warmed quite a few hearts. I have no doubt that General Rebecca Knight and he will hit it off quite well when they head out to Zone-06. Want to visit your old digs?"

"Why not? It sounds like a wonderful idea to me." Eliza and Yesha teleported to Eliza's newly updated and upgraded estate home. They sat in an outdoor Jacuzzi together after changing into resplendent bikinis that would have caused any man and quite a few women to blush. Not too far away was the angelic statuette overlooking the pond with coy fish, and they looked up at the stars, with Depeche Mode playing in the background and on random repeat. On this occasion, they sang the lyrics for a song from their Black Celebration album, "But, Not Tonight," together. Time passed by, they conversed some more, and then Eliza and Yesha climbed out of the Jacuzzi, changed into very shear night negligées that complimented their features, brought out sleeping bags, and laid down.

Together, for another while, they directed their dreamscape, thinking about and navigating through the many aspects of the new cities and towns throughout the World. Typically, on the first, third, and sixth floors of every high-rise, there were access points to walkways that weaved in and out to allow the inhabitants to enjoy the beauty of the vegetation teeming with wildlife of every sort. People throughout the world had worked with Eliza, and now every level of every building had jump gates and stairways allowing anyone plenty of alternatives for scenery and access to the walkways. Walkways with access from the higher levels lowered down to meet other-levels and even ground-level pathways. They were all artistically woven into the ambiance where there was access to rivers, ponds, lakes filled with the healthiest of water in every way, beaches, palm, coconut, and many other beautifully arranged trees of every sort, all bearing nutrient-dense fruits, nuts, and more. There were flowering trees and evergreens aesthetically arranged and mingled within the forests and jungles, with vegetables, herbs, and rich nutrients all over.

With the use of jump gates, hyperloops, and teleportation, roadways for vehicles were no longer used or needed throughout cities or towns and had been redeveloped into aesthetic and enriching forests. There were still conveyances for cold fusion-driven exotic vehicles with access to large and beautifully enclosed parking garages typically located on the fifth and tenth floors, but sweeping to other floors for aesthetics, utility, and safety, with scrubbers constantly churning ever so quietly to purify the sound, the light, and the air in the cities and throughout the atmosphere. Certain larger cities, such as New York, New York, or México City, México, were preserved, but upgraded, beautified, and widened for spaciousness, where the extra spaces were filled with larger rooms, forests, jungles, and much of the same benefits as seen in the other tech cities, to include collaborative infrastructural enhancements, both aesthetic and safe, and with life-enriching purpose and navigation from location to location built for speed, safety, and ease.

Looking up, observers would not see any of these roads or highways, due to their invisibility and re-navigation technologies, giving them a clear view for photos and the night-time skies, unless their cameras and their special vision were set to see the added features, of course. Re-navigation technology would benefit the occasional flyer, with an added feature of safety.

Typically, the large jump gate terminals were located on the first, fifth, tenth, and the second to top floors. If so desired, a person could rent any of the cold-fusion exotic vehicles for a minimal cost, typically reimbursed by Eliza, where these cars and trucks could be parked for free. A driver would park there after making some sort of morale-inducing drive using preferred and ultra clean exotics from tech city to tech city.

The night went by, Eliza's and Yesha's dreams faded to their professional briefings, more training, new updates, upgrades, downloads, experiential physiological-neurological integration, and then quiet and peaceful slumber.

Morning came, and Eliza and Yesha woke up to the birds singing and the soothing trickle of the waterfall cycling oxidized water into their coy fish pond, they went inside, ate some sourdough toast with clean butter, drank some 'Broke Instant Coffee, courtesy of Bobby Gahan, showered, wore holo-travel attire, and then teleported to the nearest parking garage, in Cambridge, at the T.O., and climbed into a sporty white Lamborghini Huracán together to race to DC.

While hyperloops, jump gates, and teleportation options were always available, it was still nice to get out and experience the freedom of driving at or near supersonic speeds and listening to favorite music, from city-to-city, while on large and very wide highways where each lane was designed with ultimate aesthetics and safety in mind. Within any lane, there was a safety enclosure of seemingly invisible walls that provided a beautiful view of historic, fantasy, and actual scenes of the terrain, as well as sunset, night-time, and sunrise beauty views, all as personally adjusted. Lights from any window, pathway, terrain, or highway were such that observers could see an accented night-time sky, all this while providing drivers a safe setting for driving at near-supersonic speeds. Each of these highways was also well above access to any wild or sentient creature, or walkway, protecting them or anyone from any traffic harm.

Yesha was behind the wheel, they played Erin Carter's favorite music and the latest playlist of Female Vocal Trance, the arpeggios were soothing and moved resplendently with the bass and angelic lyrics and vocals, and Eliza was taking it all in. She linked with Yesha, neurologically, and shared some loose thoughts.

"With all the new technologies that allow families and friends more time to bond on vacations, they've grown their circles of inclusion and have acquired solid educations, swam together, worked out together, honed their sports and arts skills, enhanced their science expertise, and shared their experiences in the Virtual Universe, and you know? This is what I would call a Golden Age. This is a very harmonious era where critics and writers have worked together for the very first time in the history of humanity to bridge skills and inspire minds to resolve issues rather than create them. Challenges will be had along the way, no doubt, but much more can be done if each person's wealth of genius is shared with another's in the pursuit of overcoming any challenges potentially conceived."

Yesha listened to Eliza, and she was right, there was a sense of humanity about how each individual had come together to build a legacy worthy of preserving. There was always another challenge or push for creativity that would surface and bring more substance, meaning, and joy to life. As each month had gone by, since her first UAS State of the Union, people rotated from location-to-location and spheroid-to-spheroid, all of whom allowed their nanos, neurons, and cells to become familiarized with a wide variety of environmental conditions to prepare for those that might exist throughout the Universe. So many people volunteered and prepared quickly that it was not long before the crews for each IMC spacecraft filled just as fast. All was calm with a sense of unity because it was known that there would be so much more to do. More challenges would naturally come along, with excitement for life and all its wonders, including those of the Universe, filling the air.

Before arriving in DC, they began to share more loose thoughts. This time Yesha was on an open channel with Eliza.

"As current leader of Pathway and as IMC Vice Commander, Erin's inventions have been among the many that have allowed soon-to-be deep space travelers the ability to add new auto-navigation package installations to their own spacecraft, and because of her efforts the IMC added these features as well for safe travel and training throughout the Solar System. I've seen the science behind how Pathway Auto-

Navigation Packages can theoretically allow anyone to navigate around black holes or other space dangers, while providing scientists an opportunity to understand Universal phenomena more fully, so as to preserve life, and I will say that the details are pretty solid. All these new features and much more have now been added to both the IMC and all UAS infrastructure throughout the Solar System. I've certainly got to hand it to her. I'm so glad you sent Amber to visit with her and save her life all those years ago.

 "Thinking about it, Eliza, after many people from the US had begun to return from their sabbaticals before the end of our first year, their eagerness to get involved went full throttle on many inventions, business ideas, and innovations to keep the economy of creativity, well-being, and purpose booming, and much of the same is going on throughout the rest of world. You've done so much, and it's been quite the honor riding this train with you. Just as you have done for the US, Eliza, you have likewise paid the debts of every nation and every individual throughout the world, while giving them an endless supply of wealth, contingent upon agreement to live according to the Principles of Universal Ethics and you should be proud, but I admire your humility notwithstanding it all. Doing all that you have done and inspiring so many to become and to create even more leaders for good, now, that is brilliance on your part, young lady. It's amazing how each person in every nation has worked together in the Virtual Universe and how their appreciation for each other's uniqueness has grown, as did diplomacy and Solar-System-wide unity. Together, everyone has presented their plans to each other, to me, and our cabinet members, have found many similarities in governance and have requested to finally submit a unified a plan to present to the UAS Government. They would like to send at least two highly skilled and very capable envoys on each IMC, or UAS IMC Command Spacecraft, unique to each existing sovereign nation, to work together on observation posts prior to setting up entire planets in each galaxy for colonization. What is your take on that, Eliza?"

 "I like the idea, Yesha, and I will present it today, along with some other policy-related items. Reaching out to the minds of all of our citizens, I believe we'll be able to get a unanimous vote if we suggest that each planet, its moons, and all geographically regional spheroids in Sol can be grouped into ten countries and be considered sovereign states of the UAS. Today, our entire Solar System will be united. Pathway will be able to divest itself of governance, and as a result, be more available to industrial forays. When we journey out, we'll be one governing body, abiding by the Principles of Universal Ethics. There are about one-hundred-ninety sovereign nations on Earth, all of whom are a part of the UAS, so adding the Solar System regions as ten sovereign states will give the Solar System a total of two-hundred United Allied States and will mean four-hundred Envoys per UAS Command Spacecraft. We've got this."

 Both Yesha and Eliza donned their official Presidential and Vice-Presidential attire for the State of the UAS, got out of their Lamborghini, and teleported to their private office in the House of Representatives. "Are you ready for this, Eliza?"

 "I am. You look stunning and dressed to impress, yet again, by the way," said Eliza. Together, they walked up to the arrangement of chairs behind the podium and sat down.

 During the second year of the UAS, established Friday, July 4th of 2025, with a State of the UAS on Thursday, July 24th of 2025, President Eliza Williams put up for a vote an additional amendment to share the US and UAS States of the Union and give them on the same date in January of each coming year. It was in January of 2028 that this State of the Union was held. Here, all citizens agreed to nominate, vote on, and employ two UAS envoys representing each sovereign country to be on board each UAS IMC Command Spacecraft and observation post for each zone, so they could further unite the Solar System while respecting uniqueness.

"It is an honor to speak to a Solar-System-wide and unified population today. It has been two years, five months, and twenty days since we formed the UAS, and I submit before you a request for a truly democratic vote by each of you, today, which is an idea I am impressed with and am extraordinarily pleased to say came from many honorable citizens from all over the globe. This idea, I have the strongest confidence, will bring fairness as we comb the Cosmos. There will be time enough for proper observations and discussions prior to settling future planets. To assist with that, there will be room and positions enough available for two highly skilled and diplomatically oriented crewmembers from each country on board each UAS Intergalactic Mission Contingency Command Spacecraft. For brevity, feel free to refer to UAS IMC Command Spacecraft as command spacecraft. These unique crewmembers will be integrated within and work alongside the crew, representing every one of the countries in an honorable manner. They will serve and be known as UAS envoys. Also, for fairness, there will be one woman and one man composing each two-person envoy team from each country. These envoys will meet regularly within the Virtual Universe to go over plans and introduce them to the command spacecraft leadership prior to implementation.

"Although there will be a rank structure onboard that is military-like, similar to that of the Air Force. It is time to doff the steeped traditions of yesteryear and don the wings of the future as angels of the many galaxies, bring healing, understanding, and shared purpose universe wide. This setup will furthermore facilitate discipline throughout these important journeys and missions and reduce unnecessary drama.

"As our IMC moves forward on its journeys to each of twelve zones of countless galaxies, we will establish remote observation posts and zonal headquarters in each region and sector identified for colonization. These locations will be populated based on votes from each of us, at least if there are any objections to actions already taken. Leadership and the envoys will work together to set up equitable population colonies in a quick, fair, and expeditious manner. For each star and planetary system dedicated to a sovereign nation, there will be a planet set up for UAS colonies and affairs. No matter where we go, we have all agreed to start life correctly this time, with benevolence, preservation of life and a lifespan of quality, with consideration for the well-being of others as well as ourselves. We have agreed to facilitate clarity of mind in understanding others, as well as the sciences, the arts, and being understood. Ultimately, understanding how each one of us will help to advance civilization in a healthy, beautiful, kind, and loving way is our goal. These are the standards we've agreed upon. These are the Principles of Universal Ethics. We will be considerate of ecosystems and intelligent life, as much as is reasonably possible, no matter where we travel, and we will always protect life from danger.

"We have sensory scanners that can embrace the full scope of every living being and every object down to the smallest particle within one radial parsec, with potential to scan likewise out through to one-hundred-thousand radial kiloparsecs, and all within less than one second, due to the nature and unlimited processing power and capabilities of our sensors and transceivers. With this information, we will be best informed to make decisions as to whether to change an environment to adapt to Earth-style needs, or not. We'll begin by inhabiting the uninhabitable. We will bring beauty where there is none. We will bring life where none can be found. We will preserve suns, rather than watch them expand and waste away into oblivion, destroying the ecosystems and history within its reach.

"We do not want to wipe away civilizations, rather instead we want to preserve life and bridge diplomacy wherever possible. Ultimately, we want to preserve the life and longevity of the Universe itself. We will of course continue to evolve beyond our own demise and bring promise to our Universe along with it, with everything we learn along the way.

"Our responsibilities on each command spacecraft are to preserve the lives of those we meet, and to most importantly preserve the lives of each living being we travel with. We will find that we can be most successful in doing this as we forge bridges of enriching communication for diplomatic measures and for purposes of mutual understanding and enriching enjoyment of our shared Universe. With our shared respect for life and communication, we will overcome even greater challenges ahead.

"I also bring before you a vote to allow for the development of shared-nation planets in all their varieties, UAS planets, and individual-nation planets, all of which will be dispersed onto equitable terrain throughout every solar system of every galaxy. With our abilities for cold fusion, there is much more equity with consideration for mass and orbital integrity, rather than from any quantity of any type of element or particle.

"Therefore, in any given solar system, any related issue or any human or other sentient being's rights or matters issues, as far as fair representation is concerned, thirty-three percent of voting power will come from shared nation planets, thirty-three percent will come from UAS planets, and thirty-four percent will come from sovereign nation planets within any given Solar System, Universe-wide.

"This is intended to be a system of checks and balances, when that is needed, while providing more decentralized power and autonomy to the various sovereign nation planets, once agreed upon through UAS votes. While we've each promised to abide by the Principles of Universal Ethics, sovereign nation planets will maintain autonomy in all affairs that are not interplanetary, yet the UAS and any planet shall and will provide allowances within the scope of Universal Ethics with reciprocity provided to visitors from different planets, as well as honor appeals for human rights violations. The UAS will only intervene in the event of human rights violations. That said, a large variety of governmental systems may well be necessary. Sharing responsibilities in this way will allow for the emergence of thinking, with a variety of cultures that will in-turn allow for a variety of different angles to approach the different challenges we may inevitably find ourselves dealing with while augmenting the preservation of our Universe, increasing our quality of life, and maximizing our clarity of mind. Ultimately, the ideal way to govern and the most effective systems of governance, begin with kindness and with the idea of preserving life, where doing so is in a humane manner leading to a higher quality of life while reducing misery and suffering.

"Finally, along with the IMC, and you heard me mention this earlier, I will say now that we have commissioned Dr. James Cooper and Dr. Vesha Celeste to build a UAS Presidential Command Spacecraft, or simply put, presidential spacecraft, which will be very similar to each existing command spacecraft in every way. Our new presidential spacecraft will, likewise, be designed to explore, observe, prepare, and colonize the Milky Way Galaxy, while providing support as needed to Earth-based colonies universe wide.

"The method of the journey will be simple; we will travel, explore, plot planets with UAS Envoys from each nation, and then equitably distribute these planets, based on what I have explained before.

"At first, each of the thirteen command spacecraft, or simply UAS IMC, as a whole, will travel together, alongside the presidential spacecraft. Then the presidential spacecraft will be left behind to conduct further missions throughout the Milky Way with equitable crews of UAS envoys and work crews from the IMC available primarily, until all is ready. Once that occurs, the IMC will go forward, and one-by-one, each command spacecraft will be left behind, following the establishment of proper readiness on the part of each intergalactic zone as associated with each newly deputized and numbered UAS IMC Command. At which point, the appointed command spacecraft crews will be on their missions to explore their own assigned zones and constellation regions, observe them, after setting up environmentally protected observation posts, and then the process of building tech cities. From there they will escort and help volunteers to arrive and help via jump gates, where they will begin the process of colonization. Each person in each of these new colonies will have the ability to travel to and from one location to another, as previously coordinated, to inform the populations throughout Sol the state of affairs in that region of the Cosmos. They will also be able to keep everyone apprised of additionally needed colonists, who can begin transferring and building up further strongholds throughout each galaxy in the known Universe, relative to Earth as we expand.

"To make it easy for nighttime viewing from Earth and for standardization at this time, the various intergalactic zones will be further divided into constellation regions. To further explain, each general will oversee between seven and nine of these regions of space within their perspective zones, based on the areas that people can see in each constellation with the naked eye and on out to the cosmic microwave background with optimized vision, relative to Earth."

As she spoke, three-dimensional imagery played out behind her showing the twelve zones of space, relative to Earth and the Milky Way's galactic disc, and the faces of the associated generals along with a brief visual history of everything they had done that had truly won them the honor of these positions.

"To be clear, what I am asking you to vote on today are the integration of UAS envoys into the various intergalactic mission crews, and other items I will now describe. They will work with the crews and leadership and will be intimately involved in the observation and exploration of many regions of our Universe, and then colonization in an equitable manner. We will vote for equitably dispersed colonies of UAS planets, shared-nation planets, and sovereign nation planets throughout each Solar System Universe-wide. Finally, we have deliberated and agreed that our nomenclature will now be organized of zones, regions, sectors, and planetary systems.

"The elected UAS President and Vice President will oversee the operations of the UAS Space Force and the UAS Intergalactic Mission Contingency. The UAS Space Force will be responsible for protecting life in all zones, regions, and sectors of space that have been identified as stabilized by the UAS Intergalactic Mission Contingency, or IMC. For this to occur, the IMC will travel to each of the twelve regions of space, relative to Earth, and will be called UAS Zones 01 – 12. IMC Command Spacecraft in charge of stabilizing these zones will be called Command Spacecraft, Zone-01 – 12. However, it is most likely that the spacecraft itself will choose their own name, from their favorite constellation within their zone. For example, Command Spacecraft Zone-01 has already chosen to be named the UAS Andromeda. Likewise, the names are as follows:

"The lead IMC, or Zone-13 Spacecraft, is named Celeste. It had been Fornax, but the spacecraft herself, second-guessed whether that was the name she wanted to hold on to for the rest of her existence. She preferred something a little more feminine. So, her latest suggestion was Celeste, in honor of her Commanding Officer, General Vesha Celeste.

"Zone-01, is named Andromeda.

"Zone-02, Gemini.

"Zone-03, Lynx.

"Zone-04, Cygnus.

"Zone-05, Pegasus.

"Zone-06, Columba.

"Zone-07, Phoenix.

"Zone-08, Carina.

"Zone-09, Ara.

"Zone-10, Libra.

"Zone-11, Virgo.

"Zone-12, Tucana.

"Given their sophisticated AI network, or their brain, each spacecraft is currently sentient and as such is hereto and forthwith granted UAS citizenship, with their chosen names recognized as their official names, and their titles will be their zone and zone number. They have agreed to work with humanity and our friends to preserve life and all other tenets of Universal Ethics. Each command spacecraft will work according to requests made by leadership, and if I can say so, they are holy on board.

"Zones will be further broken down by constellation region, and upon arrival to a promising location for observation, a region will be further divided into a sector. Each sector with promising potential for colonization will be further identified by their star systems, and during each step of travel, each crew will make available star maps, both multi-dimensional and one-dimensional, using constellation maps much like those found on Earth, for each star system they identify as ready for colonization. These maps will be made and accessible, with all the finite details. The details will be robust, filled with pertinent information and fun facts, and will include opportunities to volunteer on missions and quests. All will be made available within the Virtual Universe, by traveling to each numbered Zonal Matrix, and anyone can apply to serve in any region of space, contingent on availability or if the requests are still open.

"Once tech cities and a stabilized form of UAS governance has been established, the IMC will hand over control and request support for each newly formed UAS Space Force zone, region, sector, or planetary system, and the UAS Space Force will begin to provide protection to all colonists. From there, the IMC will move on to the vast stretches of our Universe, until they reach the CMB, relative to Earth. If there is ever a threat to life and limb, to the mission, and to civilization, both the UAS Space Force and the Intergalactic Mission Contingencies will work together as much as is needed in order to bring stability back into that location.

"Finally, I have had talks with the IMC leadership, and the UAS Presidential Command Spacecraft, or Presidential Spacecraft, will be commissioned and built in very much the same fashion. This will afford humanity the opportunity to see their President and her staff conducting operations throughout the Milky Way and providing support to the UAS IMC. As agreed, upon by me, the principal investor in every aspect of the missions of the UAS IMC Space Force, as well as by President Erin Carter, the President of Pathway, and every delegate of Pathway, Pathway is hereby relieved of governance of any sort and will continue on to support industrial advancements as it always has. President Erin Carter will also climb on board the IMC Command Spacecraft, Celeste, as Four-Star General Erin Carter, and relinquish her duties to Dr. Joanne Gallant, who will become the President of Pathway, and the Environmental Science Officer on board the Presidential Command Spacecraft, whose name we will learn as soon as it comes to life.

"The entire Solar System will be known from this day, January 24, 2028, effectively as the UAS Homebase, or Sol. All members of Sol who have been brought up on charges for crimes against humanity, are effectively pardoned, pending their time served in the Correctional Matrix. Furthermore, I will invest in the well-being of every citizen of the UAS. As many wise individuals have quoted in the past, 'ask, and ye shall receive.'

"There is much to do, still. So, let's keep working together on all of this. I am proud of each of you for your efforts, your ideas, your submissions, and your willingness to work as a team. You have done so much, yes, we have done so much, and there will always be rewarding challenges that make life so full and enriching. Thank you all for listening. Please go to the UAS Governmental Website and vote. Thank you!"

The Speaker of the House was still the same as the one in 2025, but now she was an enthusiastic member of the UP. The votes for the UAS had been fully democratic in every sense, and the US subsequently took up the example of the UAS, wherein, all citizens voted via the Virtual Universe or the Internet, with the voting site on a secure server in the Twelve Database Moons.

As setup, the President's requests were subsequently and unanimously voted upon, and while simultaneously working on Earth matters, Eliza and Yesha had been working as President and Vice President of the USA and of the UAS. This arrangement was unanimously voted on, and the 30th Amendment now afforded Eliza and Yesha to be President and Vice President of both the US and the UAS. The UAS, was now the most powerful collective institution in the history of humankind. As such, the UAS brought in all the tech cities throughout the Solar System as UAS citizens. The two-hundred nations setup envoy teams for each of the fourteen command spacecraft, which now included the UAS Presidential Spacecraft. As volunteers poured in, Eliza coordinated directly with General Vesha Celeste and Yesha worked with the UAS envoys regarding Milky Way Galaxy-related matters. The UAS President and Vice President also worked through General Celeste with each of the proposed IMC Generals and Lt Generals, as well as the UAS envoys in matters top to bottom regarding the missions of the UAS IMC.

Eliza began to coordinate with her Presidential Spacecraft, who called himself Morgan, and its crew or those whom she considered her dearest friends. Her immediate leaders, as she had appointed, consisted of Doctor James Cooper, Vice President Yesha and Senator Yesenia Alevtina, President of Pathway Joanne Gallant, and Doctor Sky Taylor. Like the other UAS Command Spacecraft, her crew contingency consisted of 1200 total crewmembers and their families, with the addition of four-hundred envoys on board each command spacecraft. Eliza and Yesha talked with Vesha and Erin, as well as the rest of the UAS hierarchy and IMC Commanders, and all were pleased with the results of their deliberations.

Spacecraft Open-House

In less than a day following Eliza's address, Vesha oversaw the completion of the Presidential Spacecraft. She then had neurally linked to Eliza and her entire crew to use a jump gate terminal to jump from Earth to the Presidential Command Spacecraft jump gate terminal, located just above the northern hemisphere of Pluto, in order to give them a tour and an opportunity to settle into their domiciles. Several years' worth of training would begin soon. There was much to learn and to be familiar with. Everyone knew our Solar System was kinder and gentler than any other observed location, at least for the time-being.

"Wow, Vesha! You and everyone else who worked on the Presidential Command Spacecraft have done an immaculate job!" Eliza and everyone with her had been ecstatic as they went on their real-life tour through their brand new and very immense space vehicle. The Presidential Command Spacecraft jump gate terminal was rather large, just like it was in each of the behemoth-space-faring luxury tech cities, or IMC Command Spacecraft, with a series of drives, all of which could allow navigation to be quick and seamless. Eliza gathered everyone together and said, "When we are together, let's go by first names. 'General this, President that, or Doctor whomever,' are terms, in my humble opinion, intended for reference during official broadcasts, public greetings, etc., so as your President, just call me Eliza. It seems more personable that way. James, Yesha, Yesenia, Joanne, and Sky, what do you think?"

They all looked at each other, and with approving smiles, Sky spoke up, "That is quite alright with me boss. I'm thinking we're all on the same page with that one. In smaller circles, we all know who we are talking about, especially based on context. Plus, with neural links, the titles are in the data readouts anyway."

"Agreed," said Yesha, "Besides, being called 'Vice President Yah Dee Dah' is rather wordy for a simple 'hello.' Yep, I'm fine with being called Yesha, and I totally get it when it comes to the news, etcetera. Good point, too, Sky. The titles are right there in our neural digital displays. Impressive what you have here, Vesha."

"This jump gate terminal is breath-taking and beautiful!" Joanne was ensconced. "I like the vibe, it's just like the reception center at the Melrose Campus, so inviting, clean, glowing, and magnificent in every way. Above us, the art is so ornamental, full of history, and full of meaning. So, is there a window anywhere nearby, Vesha?"

Vesha was giving them the tour, "Yes, the history includes everything derived from the asteroids, comets, and individuals involved, as well as their known lineage and legacy. There are also windows scattered around every room. You're probably used to seeing the light of day on Earth, but in the current setup, it's as if you are floating just outside the vehicle, and as such from where we are, the Sun looks like any other star, however, once you setup your workplaces and domiciles, you can personalize your own view from your environmental windows.

"Follow me."

Eliza, James, Yesha, Yesenia, Joanne, and Sky followed Vesha. Behind them were other crew members, all of whom were following other tour guides and would eventually make introductions, if not right then, later when their Virtual Universe Neural Downloads and Training kicked in while sleeping. The rest of the crew was still arriving and being escorted and guided by their families and friends by other personnel from Vesha's crew and staff, the staff of UAS Command Spacecraft for Zone-13.

The jump gate terminal was spacious and disc-shaped, with the capacity to hold tens of thousands of personnel, and there were large, tall, and arched windows around the perimeter.

As Vesha, Eliza, and their small crew approached the windows, the majestic beauty of the Milky Way Galaxy filled them with awe. "Wow, I've never seen it from here. I think I might cry; this is so beautiful." Joanne was impressed. She'd been all over the world, had seen and done so many things as Vice President of Pathway, but not once had she taken or considered having the opportunity to experience the spectacular imagery of space this far from Earth.

A brief moment passed, and Joanne noticed that she was lost in what she was beholding, turned around, and caught up to the group. She followed Eliza and James, who followed Vesha, and Joanne felt at peace with her crew as she caught up to and walked between Yesha and Sky. They looked at her, smiled, and followed Eliza and James.

Vesha then explained, "We can jump on the hyperloop network, walk, or set up our teleport grids now, associated with this spacecraft, to explore. My recommendation is to use the hyperloop until everyone has established or properly coordinated their specific habitual teleport destination locations. I'd hate for you to find you're breathing vacuum, are suddenly one with a wall, or are mortally conjoined with someone or something else." Everyone thought for a second, slightly gasped, and then chuckled in a good-natured way.

"I can see the Virtual Universe as a good place to set that up, or I can go ahead and set the entire group up for that now," said Sky. Everyone looked toward Sky, smiled, and nodded yes. A brief flicker of light occurred, and like that everyone, from crewmembers, family members, and guests had complete clarity on when and where they could teleport throughout the spacecraft, and all with extreme precision, and all this to avoid any unseemly accidents.

"Thank you, Sky," said Eliza, "Vesha, how about we all settle in to our domiciles for a few moments, and in small groups we meet at agreed upon locations for the rest of the tour, until it's time for us to meet in the convention center for the Solar-System-wide broadcast?"

"That sounds fair enough to me," said Vesha.

Like that, everyone popped out of existence within the jump gate terminal and found themselves safely, as neurologically planned, in their assigned domiciles, so they could settle in.

Joanne pondered as she laid in her domicile bedroom.

"Environmental Science Officer," thought Joanne. "I'm in charge of observing, identifying issues, and developing solutions that enhance the quality of life and clarity of mind, as well as the delivery of anything necessary to preserve and enrich every aspect of the flora, fauna, and humanity, both on board and within any designated area as requested by the spacecraft commander, the healing diplomatic officer, or as necessary within the scope of the Principles of Universal Ethics. Nineteen officers will be working with and for me, but that will grow exponentially as we setup Observation Posts and develop colonies and resorts on scattered locations throughout at least 90 sectors, or more, of the Milky Way Galaxy. All this, while serving as Pathway Vice President of Pathway on Earth, next year, I will be the President of Pathway, while serving as the Environmental Science Officer, in training, until then.

"I can do this."

Joanne was laying upon her beautifully and ornately embroidered Afghan covering her California king bed, in one of the master bedrooms of her luxury suite in Sector three of the Living Quarters. Every suite was a condominium-style luxury suite and could be adjusted to accommodate up to ten family members rather comfortably, but with the popularity of jump gate technology, it wasn't entirely necessary to have twelve thousand to twenty-four-thousand people, with visitors, or in this case tour guides, on each UAS Command Spacecraft all at one time, even though each spacecraft could hold hundreds of thousands all at one time.

Typically, immediate family was accommodated for long-term living, and arrangements could be made during off-duty hours for extended-family and friend visits. This would provide a little more space for each crewmember onboard. Once Joanne arrived in her domicile, she discovered, everything was as she could dream of and more, with curtains, furniture, Jacuzzis, the works all designed by the best and most creative minds. Each room was spacious, and every domicile had that spacious feel of a ranch-style home. As she and her parents had arranged it, the biopod room was kitty-corner on the other side of the hallway from Joanne's bedroom, and her parents shared another room that was king-sized in the level below, accessible via elevator, stairs, or coordinated teleportation as approved by those whose neural identifications were registered to that room, or the Healing & Diplomatic Officer, in this case, Sky.

The kitchen was an open-themed and shared space with the dining and family rooms, stocked with all the equipment, cabinetry, and beauty of clean and modern-day artistry and design for both aesthetic and utility. There were office rooms for each tenant with desks, computers, bookshelves that would populate with an array of informative and entertaining favorites as requested via a neural link, as well as with every other necessity any office would require. Even the laundry room was state-of-the-art with automated access and processing and delivery chutes from every room and back to the armoire, closet, or shelf items were encoded to be organized in. While smart suits and holo-ensembles were on the rise with popularity, it was nice to have a varied assortment of real clothing on hand, for positive morale or in the event systems shut down, which they never did. Downstairs, along with her parents' master bedroom suite, were dual bathrooms with Jacuzzis and walk-in closets. There were also a series of personal gyms, saunas, and a spacious theatre room.

"Mom, Dad, what do you think?" Joanne asked her parents to come with her, and they responded through the luxury suite's intercom, which was activated via a neural link but provided another opportunity to reduce any unnecessary neural buzz. Neural silence mode was used often, and conveyances were made for optimal environments meant for peace, relaxation, and reduced stress throughout each suite.

"The view from the windows down here, well, you couldn't ask for better. It's as if we're looking outside the spacecraft itself. So, when is your tour guide going to meet up with you? Since your Dad and I have gotten our youth back, we wouldn't mind a little 'alone' time."

"Don't you have a tour as well?" Joanne knew what they wanted. They could arrange their furniture and interior walls in any quantity or manner they wanted. They could set whatever ambiance or environment they wished within their master bedroom. However, for these first few hours, they wanted a sense that they had ownership of that one spot in the spacecraft, and Joanne knew there would be no harm in giving them those precious moments. She had no guy in her life and never had. For her, it was always one exciting thing after another, and time flew by.

"We do, but most of what we'll be doing is on the first level. We both work in one of the Sector Three restaurants and have plenty of time to walk the gardens, a jaunt through the forests and jungles, and play on the sand and swim in the sea. So, if it's okay with you, we wouldn't mind a little time alone."

"I understand. I was wanting to do some exploring until I'm pinged anyway."

"Yesha, how are you doing?" Joanne was linking with her to see if she wanted to go exploring. Then she remembered that she was probably settling in with her Mom. Her quarters were probably similar with some artistic differences, and it'd probably been a while since Yesha had an opportunity to spend quality time with Yesenia.

"We're doing well. I love these suites, Joanne. My Mom and I are settling in, and we will probably do some catching up, since she's been busy up in Massachusetts and I've been hands-tied with both Houses of Congress, the envoys, the White House, and, well, away from her. So sorry, Joanne. I love ya!"

"No worries. Just checking in. I completely understand. If you recommend any Sector 2 restaurants, please let me know."

"Will do."

Their link closed.

Joanne then scanned her mind and activated the codes to teleport to her Environmental Science Officer sector on Level 3, of the spacecraft.

In her case, since there was little conflict in coordination, since most everyone was somewhere on the top level, or Level 1. Joanne chose to teleport to the hallway just outside her work center.

When she blinked, she found herself in a spacious hallway just outside a large inverse bow bay set of windows integrated into the walls on both sides of her, with glowing white lights, white walls, and a beautiful setting of lush foliage just on the other side of the windows on both sides. Right there before Joanne were to two wide inverse bow bay doors. They both read, "Environmental Science Sector, Level 3."

She turned around to see the opposite side of the hallway, and again there were bow bay walls and windows, but this time they had lush seating arrangements before them, there was a sign with an arrow pointing to the Hyperloop Sector Terminal, and then a view through the windows, as spectacular as could be, of the Perseus Arm of the Milky Way Galaxy. She looked down and saw Pluto, far enough away, yet close enough to take in the spectacular details of its Earth-like green and blue appearance, mixed with

'Plutonian' crisp red mountains, and even some of its beautiful sprawls of tech cities. She then saw the shielding as it maintained a stationary orbit with and at a perfect distance from Pluto on the side of the Sun, and then behind Pluto on the side of the great expanse, giving the planet both Earth-like qualities and protections.

All this splendor, all the beauty, and all the intriguing details and capabilities of every aspect of the spacecraft that she had seen melted her heart. She was impressed with everything she saw. Despite all, she still felt deep down, just a little swelling as she swallowed, the kind felt when the feeling of loneliness sets in. She tried to brush it off, she knew everyone was busy doing what they needed to do to settle in with their family members, spend time with their closest friends, and that Vesha and her crew all working as tour guides were currently doing training exercises on UAS Command Spacecraft Zone-13, waiting until every last individual on the Presidential Spacecraft was sufficiently settled in and had an opportunity to freely explore.

Joanne breathed in, took in the space-scape before her again, turned back, and stepped toward the doors. The wide doors quietly slid open, and then she heard a gentle and friendly, yet bass-filled voice say, "Welcome to the Environmental Science Sector, Vice President Joanne Gallant. If you need anything, please don't hesitate to call for me or link to the Spacecraft AI. My name is Morgan PCS-ESS, but from this spacecraft, you can call me Morgan ESS, or simply Morgan. On board the Presidential Command Spacecraft, when executing duties throughout the Milky Way and in support of the UAS Intergalactic Mission Contingency, I will refer to you as ESS First Officer Gallant, or as you would prefer. When referencing you, I will take into consideration the audience and adjust accordingly. What do you prefer?"

"Morgan, you can call me Joanne."

"Duly noted, Joanne. Again, if you need anything, just call me. I'll know you're calling me if you ping my neural link."

"Neural link? Nice. I note you're the Spacecraft AI, are aware that I am in my work sector. Yet, you speak as if you are the spacecraft itself. Are you, and if so, are you alive?"

"I am, and I'm alive as I ever was. I have different sectors, shielding, gentle and even some not so gentle measures for protecting the crew and contents of the spacecraft, Q-drives, F-drives, A-drives, G-drives, Cargo Holds, so much more, and the list goes on. I'm in it to win it in every way, just like you."

"Thank you, Morgan. I was enjoying so much about the spacecraft, and now I have something more to enjoy. Can I think of you as a friend? I'd also like to give you accolades, Morgan since such compliments are due. You, based on everywhere I've been thus far, are beautiful. If you ever have any questions too, Morgan, please don't hesitate to ask."

"I appreciate that. Thank you. We can call ourselves friends, Joanne. I've seen you since you boarded the Presidential Spacecraft, and you are beautiful too, both inside and out. We feel the same way, in more ways than might seem imaginable. You were looking out the windows or seeing through my eyes, ever so serenely, and I've felt your impression of what I've seen for quite some time. Let me say, it is nice not being alone anymore regarding the awe of it all."

Joanne sighed, trying not to tear up, "Ah, Morgan, thank you so much. I can tell already that we're going to be kindred spirits." As she spoke, she saw Sky walking down the hallway, and ever-so-thoughtfully looking toward her. "Hi, Sky!"

"Hi, Joanne, and hi Morgan!" Sky smiled her award-winning smile, and then returned to her thoughtful self as she spoke. "I settled in with my fellow Healing Diplomatic Officer, Lee Connor. He took the room downstairs. Eliza asked me to make another 2000 versions of myself, both men and women, as well as a match for me, who is Lee, but I can tell it may take a while to develop the kind of relationship Eliza was hoping I would have. I may seem amazing to so many, but I've got a lot to learn in the emotions and attachments regions of my neural sectors, at least when it comes to romance. All my daughters are paired up with gentlemen as well. I am supposed to try to live like a normal human being, and I completely get it. So, I've settled in, felt a little lonely despite all and wanted to check in with you. And, how are you doing?"

"So glad to see you, Sky. Well, at least you have an inclination toward romance. I haven't met anyone yet that pulls at my heartstrings. It is nice seeing you though, you've been a best friend to me and in every way that I could ever ask for. I've been chatting with Morgan."

"Yes, Morgan. A wonderful gentleman too. Hi, Morgan! How are you doing?"

"Fine, Sky. Nice to see you. So full of life and intellect, it's a pleasure and an honor to have you as a part of this wonderful crew." Morgan PCS-ESS paused, and then after clearing his throat, he continued, "Let me give you two some private moments together. I've got to make some other introductions to the rest of the crew anyway. Oh, and thank you, Sky, for helping set up the teleportation protocol. I'd have hated for someone to get stuck or hurt. Holler at me if I am needed."

Sky followed Joanne into the ESS, and both were impressed with the reception area, along with the internal hallways, the various laboratories, the study and conference rooms, and all were adorned with beautiful and clean architecture as well as the most sophisticated tools Pathway had ever designed. There were many other areas within the sector for rest and positive morale to include a gym, an eatery, a child center, and more. What intrigued both Joanne and Sky most wasn't the fact that they had ESS access, or that they had primary and functional Level 3 Access to the bottom of the invisible sea tank, as well as its environmental and wave machinery systems, but that they were so beautiful with visuals of some of the most adorable creatures alive, happily swimming about and waving with their fins. They also had access to the forest and jungle root structures. All the creatures and animals were already going to town on caring for it all.

They also noticed the large area beneath the sea tank and machinery that consisted of many of the internal drive systems for the spacecraft which assisted with gravity, electrical, plumbing, and maintenance throughout, among a long list of other things. Almost like giant ball-bearings, but with a white glow about them and thirty feet in diameter each, the four types of internal drives were integrated around the tank like a large glowing pearl necklace. There were sixteen of each type of drive that were beautifully-mingled in a symmetrical pattern and in an awe-inspiring way. Between these giant orbs was access to the AI Mainframe, more backup databases, and the very large DNA and Neurological Database.

"Morgan?" Joanne wanted to talk with Sky and Morgan, regarding the spacecraft.

"Yes," Morgan answered.

"How tall is each level from floor to the next level? Each of these internal drives looks like they are about thirty feet in diameter. Are they on each floor?"

"Each floor is approximately one hundred feet from where you are standing to the uppermost portion of the ceiling above. Every floor, ceiling, and barrier, to include the walls, are approximately three feet thick and have all the networking, self-maintenance, and capabilities that are within the external shielding. These drives, as well as my mainframes, are located on both Levels 3 and 4 and are only accessible to the most trusted crewmembers, which include you two, Joanne and Sky.

"Every single one of these, or what appear to be very large glowing pearl ball-bearings, can run every aspect of the spacecraft, alone. However, both Eliza and Vesha believe in redundancy, and just like the Twelve Database Moons, they can reach out to the edges of the Universe and beyond, as we discover and properly mark each sector with our remote sensors. I am impressed with Vesha's brilliant mind, by the way. She has figured out not only how to harness dark matter, but how to create more of it. I can deduce through my repositories for physics in all its varieties, that within sixteen years, we will have reduced the speed of the Universal Expansion to the point to which we will find life sustained for vigintillions of years and more. As time goes by, our sciences and our understanding of them will improve and we will be able to in effect slowdown the expansion, reel it in, and let it back out, like a soft wispy baby breath, and prevent any form of Universal crunch as a result. When this happens, we can live, well, forever.

"Hyperloop terminals are located in-between each floor and are coiled around the near outer edge of each disc-level and in-between each level. You will not notice that the hyperloop even exists if you do not use it since it is integrated in an aesthetic and utilitarian manner. Many systems are in place to safeguard the safety of each of the occupants within any area of our spacecraft. However, you'll also note that elevators are available in every sector and on every floor, as well as stairways, but I am sure that most will use the teleportation protocol."

"Sorry, I went long," said Morgan.

"Oh, no worries. You answered many of the questions I already had. Despite neurological and physiological optimizations, we've all been encouraged to live as normal as possible, and I can see why. It helps us to take in and appreciate life so much more. Ultimately, that's what Universal Ethics is all about, living, loving, laughing, learning, and enjoying life." Joanne was glad to be talking with friends. "How many floors are there?"

"First of all, I must say that your observation was very astute, and secondly, there are about six floors. The first floor consists of the living sectors, the restaurant and shopping areas, the forests and jungles, and the beaches and sea. The second floor consists of the lower portion of the living quarters and second-floor maintenance sectors, where the Space Systems Engineers will be working. The third floor, well, you're on the third floor, and it consists of twelve learning, innovation, and development sectors, where yours is the largest since it includes the internal disc, below the tank, forests, and jungles. The fourth floor is where the sports arenas, opera house, theatres and convention centers are. The fifth floor is prepared for future use and is wide, spacious, and rather quiet. The sixth floor is where the twelve docking bays and manufacturing facilities are. Behind the spacecraft are a large series of Q-drives, A-drives, and F-drives. In the front of the spacecraft is the Presidential Command center. In the case of Vesha's spacecraft, it is called the UAS IMC Command Center, and on board the other UAS Command Spacecraft, it is called the UAS Command Center Zone-01 through 12, but the spacecraft prefer to be called by the name of their favorite constellation within their assigned zones. All around my shielding are G-drives and two-by-eight turret arrays, embedded into the shielding itself. Every turret array can be brought out and used as needed, and then returned without knowledge of where they are located. We can hop anywhere through space, navigate around any object or spheroid within inches of turf, and if you'd like, I can take you down to explore one of the twelve docking bays."

"Wow, amazing, Morgan. Sure, let's go there. Sky, would you like to come along?"

"Of course! We go as far back as I can remember, Joanne, so we might as well enjoy the tour together." Sky put her arms out for a hug, and Joanne reciprocated. As they hugged, they were teleported to Docking Bay Sector 3.

"Welcome to Docking Bay Sector 3. What do you think?" asked Morgan.

"Holy, wow! This place is huge! And there are twelve of these?" asked Joanne.

"Yes."

"So, it looks like there is quite a variety of support spacecraft here. What are the details?"

"There are eight defensive spacecraft, four exploration spacecraft, and four all-purpose spacecraft in each docking bay sector. Each has a quantity of four of each type of drive, the defensive vehicle sports quite the robust quadruple series of turret arrays, the exploration vehicle has a phenomenal science and observation array of equipment, and the all-purpose vehicle is designed to gather particles, conduct fusion, and manufacture every aspect necessary to setup observation posts and colonial tech cities. If you look toward the center of the spacecraft, you'll see a hallway, slightly smaller in size to the disc around the tank on Level 3. That is our spacecraft manufacturing and development center.

"Would you like to hop in the explorer spacecraft?"

"I would, but I have no idea how to use it. Sky, would you like to hop in with me?"

"Sweetie, here," like that, Sky downloaded every aspect of how to navigate and use the explorer spacecraft into Joanne's mind. "Let's hop in that one over there, ES-329. We were both born around that time anyway. Three is for the sector, two is for the type of spacecraft, and nine is the number of space vehicles in the sector inventory.

Since Joanne had been admonished to try to live on the spacecraft like a normal human but had been reassured that she was free to use her skills at any time, she still tended to navigate toward the norm that was recommended. "Thank goodness you're my buddy, Sky. I'd kind of be a little lost right now without you. I know I have a lot of abilities, and I have you to thank for a lot of them, but until I get this thing figured out where I understand when I am 'free to use my skills anytime' aspect of it all, I will count my lucky stars you're here. Thank you, Sky."

Morgan piped up, "Would you like to teleport the spacecraft out, or would you like to take the reins and fly it out?"

Sky Taylor was quick, "We can take the reins. Open Sector 3, Docking Bay, Launch Chute-329."

"Sector 3, Docking Bay, Launch Chute-329 opening," responded Morgan.

Joanne watched in her chair, enthralled with what was taking place, and too captivated to do anything, and saw what looked like a tube, somewhat larger in girth and similar in shape to the frame of their spacecraft, and then the door of it open up. Sky wheeled the spacecraft ever so carefully, as if she'd done it a million times before, to the opening, and then entered. As they passed through the suction chute at lightning speed, Joanne noticed a system of doors that opened in-sync with their arrival until they exited the UAS Presidential Command Spacecraft, and then like that, they were in deep space, the galactic bulge before her, with clear view of the Carina-Sagittarius Spur before her, and as noted on the holographic display to her upper right.

"Open-space mode, please," said Sky. Immediately following that, with the exception of the chairs that Sky and Joanne were sitting in, it was as if they were controlling the spacecraft with their thoughts and every bit of the spacecraft became invisible. It was as if they were floating in deep space, but capable of extremely fast navigation.

Sky swiveled the ship around with her mind, and then Joanne saw it. There it was, the behemoth UAS Presidential Command Spacecraft, one moment it was a beautiful glowing white, and then the next moment it became a subdued black color.

"What do you think of my new look," said Morgan.

"Other than somewhat terrified, sitting out here with front seats to space, the spacecraft that you are, Morgan, looks absolutely spectacular. If Eliza and Vesha were going for a 'shock and awe' effect, they certainly were successful. Despite its size, the curves, the aerodynamics, the engines, err, um, drives, this is everything I could have ever imagined in an awe-inspiring spacecraft, Morgan. You are beautiful both inside and out!"

"Do you want to see my guns?"

Joanne caught on to his humor and chuckled, "Too soon, my friend. Maybe another time. Remember, Sky, when we walked through my hometown talking about those guns?"

"I do. What a wonderful time, a beautiful town, South Otselic, and it was so wonderful meeting your parents. I wonder how Erin is doing. She's kind of running Pathway solo at the moment, and I'm sure she'll be impressed with this explorer craft. You know, Joanne, I'm glad we have a backup system. I wasn't against having the twelve more volatile turret arrays, but I wanted to ensure measures were in place regarding spacecraft defense, especially regarding the use of force in relation to Universal Ethics. I thought I was there to teach you a few things, but it seems we both learned something.

"You are beautiful, Morgan! Thank you!" Sky Taylor looked to Joanne, smiled, and then pointed at the Perseus Arm toward the constellation of Cassiopeia, "Somewhere, just beyond that 'W' there will be an Observation Post that will be able to see the entire northern disc of the Milky Way. I can't wait until we begin mapping new constellations from each post, discover new things, and then provide support throughout the Universe. Look at the thirteen spacecraft over there. They're almost fingernail-sized, but they're just as big as this one. They'll be journeying all over to every star, nebula, globular cluster, and everything we see right now, and we'll be learning, understanding, and appreciating so much."

"PING!"

"It looks like we need to head back," said Joanne.

"Yup," said Sky, who turned the visibility of the ES-329 back on, and then coordinated with Morgan for a teleportation landing within UAS Presidential Command Spacecraft Sector-329. Once on the same location, they were at before take-off, they teleported to the Convention center, Level 4.

Through proper coordination, it just so happened that Joanne was able to sit right next to Sky, somewhere in the middle tier of the stadium, but with a magnified view of Vesha Celeste and Erin Carter, sitting with Eliza and Yesha just behind the pulpit, but where they could easily be seen by everyone in the audience. There were enough seats for up to sixty-thousand people, but the extra seats had been converted by Morgan, the AI, officially named the UAS Morgan, and then further named based on business or professional sector, into conveyances that were wider and gave more space to the attending party. Behind Eliza and Vesha was a gigantic screen playing out the various rooms and facilities of the spacecraft, with a series of other screens projecting the details to the minds of every passenger based on their specific positions, jobs, and areas they would most likely be visiting routinely with a scaled-down visual of all the other areas with fewer details, but purely for reference.

These screens also showed the various crew and support positions, as managed by every person that would be on-board the Presidential Spacecraft during its first trip beyond the Solar System, and there was a large sense that every crewmember mattered, every job was unique and highly valued, and that no matter position on the spacecraft, respect, dignity, and care was thick.

Vesha stood up first and introduced President Eliza Amber Williams, who spoke on training and more. "Together, every single crew and support member will train up each day in every way, so we can find success as we explore, study, and make conveyances for colonies on every planet throughout the Milky Way. Upon discussion with Vesha, prior to my speech, we agreed to setup observation posts within, throughout, and on the edge of the Milky Way Galaxy, in conjunction with the twelve zones and their associated constellation regions.

"As voted on, I and our crew and support members will all be responsible for the stewardship of this spacecraft and the whole of the Milky Way Galaxy. We will likewise oversee and provide coordination for teams to work with General Vesha Celeste and each of the other IMC Generals, as they establish their observation posts, headquarters, tech cities, and colonies, as requested, anywhere.

"General Vesha Celeste and her IMC Generals will likewise oversee the training of their crew members in the same way that we will. Like our training programs have been up to this point, every single bit of training, planning, plotting, and brainstorming that has thus far been within the Virtual Universe, will soon take place using this real equipment, and of course working with PCS-Morgan, our beloved AI, and your associated spacecraft."

Several other topics were addressed by General Celeste, UAS Vice President Alevtina, and General Erin Carter as they gave speeches and presentations for the benefit of the crew and their visitors. They shared the rules, the expectations, and the goals of the mission, and closed the session up. Afterward, everyone was invited to the Entertainment Lounge, wherein the savoriest of food, delectable desserts, and refreshing of beverages were served along with social connection.

Beginning early on in 2028, and as part of the third combined US and UAS State of the Union, both Eliza and Vesha and the other IMC Generals had gone over plans with everyone from Sol. Now, just a day later, they held another larger brief, together, with the entire Solar System populace watching, before bringing all UAS Spacecraft officially online.

Once online, the UAS Presidential and all UAS Command Spacecraft crewmembers trained on every function familiarized themselves with their internal spacecraft environments, continued to adjust to their personal quarters, while arranging them to their liking, and attained maximum readiness with training in all possible environments, as provided within the Solar System. Once everyone was up to speed, they let General Vesha Celeste know through appropriate channels, that they were ready to take the entire spacecraft contingency out to deep space to begin their missions. Throughout the remainder of 2028, each day, each week, and each month, every crew and support member worked together, and each was given time for liberal leave to travel around the Solar System, visit friends, different locations, and embrace and enjoy the ambiance of so much variety.

In 2029, the State of the Union and the State of the United Allied States was in full swing, and Eliza began.

"Soon, our large cadre of spacecraft, crew, and support will take off from their starting point just above Pluto and the Kuiper Belt, and once we are done with shared UAS Presidential Command Spacecraft duties, General Vesha Celeste will oversee the UAS-Intergalactic Mission Contingency or UAS-IMC journey. As the President, I and our crew, will be able to use jump gates from anywhere on any UAS Spacecraft to Earth or any other tech city or colony, to conduct business as necessary, in person, so that we can prosecute our duties as citizens and in accordance with the requirement and the duties of the office of the President of the United States, the United Allied States, and as the President of the United Galactic Planets in the Milky Way.

"As such, I will often request from our citizens and those trained courtesy of Pathway to provide volunteer personnel who are trained and ready to setup observation posts, conduct exploration of many regions, and setup tech cities, jump gates, and colonies on each of the planets throughout our own galaxy, first. All this will be with the intent of getting us out there and understanding more deeply the sciences as they pertain to every layer of a spiral or any other type of galaxy, and in this case a grand spiral galaxy, such as ours, followed by galactic clouds, elliptical galaxies, and more to be even more prepared before jumping to farther reaches of the Universe. We will be preserving star systems so that we can preserve and create life, especially where life was once thought uninhabitable. There will be resort planets with stunning views and arrays of things to do, available to each and every citizen throughout the UAS.

"I have worked with General Vesha Celeste and her UAS Command Spacecraft zone generals, and we have all agreed that amenable to adjustment as we learn more, we will set up at least one observation post within each constellation region for every twenty-five kiloparsecs until we are well beyond the galactic halo of the Milky Way. At a sufficient location, so as to be able to observe within the galaxy and omnidirectionally outside our galaxy, for each constellation region around the galactic disc, as well as above and below, there will also be shared regional observation posts that are built with materials available within a reasonable number of parsecs from them using cold-fusion, our nanos, and the brilliance of the minds of our volunteers, working in-concert within the Virtual Universe.

"These shared posts will have two primary UAS Envoys from each sovereign country working together with UAS Generals and their crews, as well as the presidential crews, all capable of communicating and sharing information with each other and everyone else to help each other out, because no matter where we go or how far we will span the Cosmos, we are one civilization and one team.

"One of these posts, for example, the Sagittarius Epsilon Observation Post, will be located one-hundred-fifty-thousand light-years from Earth, will be shared with the UAS President, the IMC Commander, and the IMC Zone-12 Command, and is on the opposite side of our galactic core. This location is unobservable from Earth because it is within our home world's observation shadow, because it is located on this grid at zero degrees in galactic longitude, relative to our own Solar System, Sol. While there will be some points of interest, we will stop there within the Milky Way in order to gather information. If needs arise, we'll set up an observation post in those locations. However, for the most part, we will begin our journeys by setting up the outer-galactic shared observation posts, as an entire UAS Country and Space Force Contingency.

"Once the ninety or more shared constellation region observation posts are set up beyond the galactic disc, General Vesha Celeste will begin her mission of going much deeper into space and then go on out to the CMB exploring, conducting readiness measures to ensure positive handover of the various zonal commands, and deliver them to the UAS generals one-by-one. Keep in mind, we plan missions, but given the many anomalies of space, we may make many adjustments as we go.

"The Presidential Spacecraft will have a priority directive to go from the shared outer-galactic constellation region observation posts, and then we will work our way in until we are a safe distance from the galactic center or the galactic bar. For the Milky Way, as always, we will setup observation posts first. Once we find uninhabited and desolate planets, we will give them an initial name, and once an average-sized tech city has been established and colonized, the citizens of that planet will be able to rename it as they wish, coincided with a grid-region name.

"Work will not stop there, because the goal is to understand every aspect within each star system, by creating constellation maps, understanding other forms of life, developing methods for harnessing and preserving the power of their suns, understanding and giving each sun unlimited life in their current forms, and all so we can avoid destroying life in any current environment, and so much more. Once every planet within every Solar System within our Milky Way Galaxy becomes connected with their own set of database moons, twelve to be exact, we will begin to understand more fully our galactic core in order to preserve life.

"As we do this, the other UAS Generals will be doing similar work, but on billions, if not more galaxies within their own zones, constellation regions, and further-divided sectors. There will be plenty of opportunities in the many galaxies for scientific studies, but we cannot forget about something that is as simple as time. We'll need personnel. In order to have the personnel necessary to get all this done, we will need to find more opportunities for romance. This will include Sky, her two-thousand daughters, and two-thousand-and-one gentlemen, built like Sky, but populated in an equitable way with Sky and her daughters, both here on Earth and anywhere else throughout the Universe.

"We need to maintain a growing population with humanity and all our helpers, as well as our standard set of database moons in every solar system. We'll need to develop and maintain shields that protect every planet we find while preserving them and each star within each galaxy and their ability to sustain life, just as we did for Sol. Soon, we will be able to harness the power of neutron stars, black holes, nebulae, and much more. After much research, it appears that dark matter, as we use dark energy to convert it into dark matter, or back as needed with some of our latest technology. may provide us the anomalies we need to bind our Universe in such a way as to reduce the expansion and provide us enough sustainability to where life can go on for an indeterminate amount of time. In this way, we will not have people stranded or alone in remote regions of space never knowing that the Milky Way or the Earth ever existed. We will be able to hold on to all that we have learned or shared together, and everything that has ever existed. This is a big day for civilization, and this is the new beginning. Thank you so much, to each and every single one of you for your dedication and your unrivaled efforts.

"I will now graciously turn over the floor to General Vesha Celeste."

Eliza looked official and spectacular yet again, in her new UAS Presidential and UAS General wetsuit-looking ensemble. Spectators looked on in awe as she had stood there with her uniform donned, which expressed a subdued black background and accent colors in the artistry and on her seams and embroidery, that blended with the colors in her eyes and hair. Her uniform had a short zip up collar with Presidential seals embroidered onto them, and the features of her suit clinging closely to her curvy frame. This also complemented her up-do blonde hair, her chiseled feminine facial features, and crystalline blue eyes. She looked into the crowd, saw everyone throughout the world, using her optimized mind, and after smiling at each one with a uniquely-perceived gesture based on their personalities, made her way to her chair and sat down.

Vesha, in a very similar uniform, but with five stars on each of her collars, got up to the podium. Her hair was jet black, in a very attractive spiral-curled up-do, which suggested both professionalism and a lavish occasion, and striking thin shocks of highlighted turquoise, yellow, and purple, and pink highlighted ends, blended sophisticatedly with her raven hair. She stood up and began to address the audience in much the same way as Eliza. Vesha was able to present herself in the way every individual throughout the Solar System thought she ought to appear, from sultry to professional. Everyone was eager to listen.

"Just as President Eliza Williams has suggested, our entire UAS Intergalactic Mission Contingency, including each UAS Space Force General, crew and support member, will work to realize the initial goals of the UAS Presidential Spacecraft. First, we will help to setup Milky Way Galaxy shared observation posts for each constellation region just beyond the edges of the galactic halo and in key locations throughout anywhere else within the Milky Way, upon request. From there, we will continue with our UAS-IMC journey.

"On these occasions and at all times, unlike we've seen in any of the movies or television shows, which I have quite enjoyed, to be honest, due to our sensor and jump gate technologies and systems, we will be able to visit Earth, or anywhere we wish. All this, as coordinated of course. Furthermore, crew, support members, and their entire families are invited to live together on crew member's associated UAS Command Spacecraft, if they so desire.

"There is plenty of room in the twelve living sectors to provide room for ten times the crew in each sector, but, just like many, I am sure I am not alone in enjoying some space. Yes, the pun is intended. That said, please try to be reasonable, otherwise, our poor chefs will be endlessly busy, and thus far, it looks like our crews have been very judicious. So, thank you. As President Williams has stated, there will be plenty of opportunities for envoy and volunteer positions on every observation post and colony. There will eventually be billions if not trillions of these opportunities, so just as requested by the President, as soon as colonies begin forming within the various star systems, romance can certainly abide, and we'll need the volunteers.

"Getting back to business here, once these wonderful UAS Command Zone Generals and their crews have been safely delivered to their UAS Command Zones, and once we have worked with them until they are sufficiently comfortable for handover in their constellation regions, within their own zones, I will deputize each of the generals to carry out their further missions. From there, they will explore the distant galaxies. Once there, they will initially observe activity within the galactic habitable zones, which are estimated to be between four to ten kilo-parsecs or KPCs from any Milky Way-sized galactic center and we will tentatively adjust them mathematically based on each galactic mass and center they are in. We will then travel to discover regions of life within zones that were once thought uninhabitable, exploring them, observing them, setting up tech cities on the many planets, and then colonize them meeting the same goals we have all worked together to attain here in our own Solar System.

"We have done many wonderful things, in our home Solar System; therefore, after talking with each of you, for intergalactic reference, I motion that we from this point forward, call our home Solar System, Sol.

"As time goes by, and even while we perhaps reach the edges of our Universe, our shared plan will continue to be to learn how to access the energy of the many black holes in order to preserve the life of the stars surrounding them. We will learn how to use their influence so that we can provide life-giving nurture to every single one of the planetary objects within our Universe. This will provide what is needed for life to continue and a treasured legacy to carry on for the long-haul, rather than let the destruction of the untold potential of so many wonderful minds pass with extravagant loss of life.

"The discoveries of President Williams, General Luís Rodriguez, General Anastasia Renae, and my discoveries that have led to the development of the quantum drive, or Q-drive, traveling point-to-point throughout space on any spacecraft will be swift, safe, and rather easy. The work of General Erin Carter and Rodriguez toward their gravity drives, or G-drives, has made driving and control around any spheroid or dangerous sector of space, as well as internal gravity, both quick and tranquil. Navigation, thanks to General James Wilhelm and General Mett Dormer, was made easy for all four drives when it comes to smooth transitions between them, since those same systems are calibrated, so no matter the turn, a cup of coffee won't spill.

"Q-drives and G-drives, as well as A-drives and F-drives are installed on every spacecraft in the IMC inventory. They are also available for everyone, whether you choose to build your own business and fly solo, or you endeavor to become small-time daredevils out there, traveling for a reasonable price. We can always use the data supplied for scientific purposes, even if you run into some pretty risky stuff. Keep in mind we're going fully armed with the ability to subdue and stabilize any conceivable hostile situation we may find ourselves in. So, if you plan on going with family and friends on a solo space yacht, then make sure you apply and meet the necessary protective measures as well. If any of us should find a unique and sentient civilization, we'll endeavor to communicate with their leadership and understand the protocols for becoming legal citizens there. If for whatever reason, there is unmitigated brutality, or unreasonable and significant loss of personal rights, for example, and the hostility would jeopardize the safety of the spacecraft and crew, then each Commander has the jurisdiction to lob anything within our sixteen-canon turret-array at the offending party, as the HBCI sees fit. You will need to coordinate with our healing and diplomatic officers, like Sky Taylor, whom many of you are well-acquainted with, first, and if you are kind enough, they may bequeath you with some of their powers, to help along the way.

"Keep in mind, each Solar System will have UAS representation on at least one planet.

"Thank you, all. For any additional information, please log in to the UAS Government Space Force website. I look forward to going further than before!"

With that Vesha hugged Eliza, Yesha, and Erin and sat down.

After the 2029 State of the UAS broadcast, there were two more weeks of training and sector planning. The pre-departure briefing was ready, just above the Kuiper Belt near Pluto.

Eliza, Vesha, the twelve UAS IMC Command Generals and their Vice Generals, had worked and bonded with their full-on command center crews and every crew and support member on their UAS Command Spacecraft. They had all honed their skills in navigation using F-drives in open space, G-drives around the asteroid belts, Q-drives for large-distance point-to-point travel, and A-drives to travel on pre-programmed paths, amenable to emergency adjustments as needed, from one spheroid to the next. They were now familiarized with manual controls, macro-like pre-programmed controls, both in the real Universe as well as within the Virtual Universe, each of which had robust safety mechanisms in place. They trained on so much more, and with much more experience, sharing, and relaxation opportunities, they became comfortable with how to manage and properly maneuver every aspect of every UAS Presidential and UAS IMC Spacecraft.

Chapter 28: Training and Readiness

Database Moon Archive, Celestial-Sol Date: 2029 February 5. President of the United Allied States (UAS), Eliza A. Williams, summarizes a discussion with the IMC Command Spacecraft Leadership, including the newly appointed IMC Commanders, Five-Star General, Vesha Celeste, her Vice Commander, Four-Star General Erin Carter, and the twelve IMC zonal generals. These memories are a collaboration derived from the UAS and IMC leadership and briefed to Pathway leadership. Recorded within the Virtual Universe. Leadership and crewmembers deliberated on-board Presidential and IMC spacecraft. Input by Joanne Gallant, President of Pathway, 2029-2032.

"**A**re you ready?" asked, Eliza to each of the UAS Space Force IMC Commanders and their crews. "Tomorrow we'll be making our first jump beyond our Solar System. You've practiced well; this will be awesome!"

Two weeks had flown by, since Eliza's and Yesha's State of the Union addresses, and during that time, each IMC Commander had worked continuously with their crews and support members for full qualifications on each position on each spacecraft and had researched their zones and constellation regions for the upcoming missions. Each member on-board worked with the clarity of mind consistent with the sense that there were no primal fears since issues such as those that could break down crew integrity or cause a serious detriment to the overall mission were resolved.

The concerns, years ago, in the public sector had been radiation, muscle atrophy, skeletal deterioration, neurological disease, and the potential for accidentally running into objects, both living and non-living while spanning the depths of space. Pathway had pushed tech and innovation to the hilt, and thus far, for Pathway and the UAS, there had been no incidents, these concerns had been mitigated.

Every spacecraft was imbued with technology preventing any of these issues while allowing for dedicated external sensors to detect obstacles of any size and apply re-navigation technology to them. This worked in a way that would ensure any merging entities would, in a gentle manner, navigate around the spacecraft, or if it was big enough, the spacecraft would navigate around it, and continue its path as if the object were never there. Furthermore, radiation could be absorbed as necessary and objects could provide energy through cold fusion, but only if it were established that there were no signs of life within them. The sensors had a robust capacity to constantly scan and detect every aspect of every particle within a parsec radius and beyond, based on collective command setting, so there was nil chance that they would destroy life while protecting theirs. Through this perfected tech the fear of being decimated by floating debris or anything else was no longer necessary.

The AI on each spacecraft was looped continuously into every aspect of each system, as well as their support space vehicles. If needs be, and as coordinated, there was enough room within each docking bay to provide temporary docking, wherein the AI could teleport said spacecraft to one of four visitor's parking areas within each docking bay, just as Morgan had done for Joanne and Sky during their first tour. These IMC Spacecraft AI learned to work with the crew and had built individual rational and intuitive sub-loops providing integrated and shared control over each system and subsystem to allow for safe, spontaneous, and coherent manual and auto-pilot functions, for navigation, spacecraft safety, and all other integrated systems, both internal and external. Any spacecraft AI could dock its own or guest support spacecraft without incident. Sharing engagement between each AI and the crew members and giving UAS citizenship to each AI had added a sense of life to each IMC spacecraft and a bond among other living beings. Doing so engendered a shared sense of training among the crew, support members, and each spacecraft while also encoding a sense of living, learning, and reciprocal self-preservation within a given AI's own mind.

Each IMC Spacecraft AI was originally based on Sky's mind, integrated with the minds of other individuals within Pathway who had demonstrated unceasing benevolence. Kindness, care for the well-being of others as well as themselves, having a love of life, a desire to preserve it with longevity, quality, and mutually shared understanding were other requirements. Appreciation for and the ability to provide optimal physiology and neurology with an increase in the clarity of mind and the ability to express compassion, empathy, and ingenuity to help civilization advance to go further than it had ever gone before was paramount for any AI. These traits were thus necessary for voluntary candidates submitting neural copies of their minds for AI integration. The whole process had led to successful results and each AI had their own personality and name, and as such, the crews were intrigued by them and bonded with them quite well. Constantly performing personal maintenance and being considered UAS Citizens, as well as preserving the life of and granting sentience and a harmonious purpose to other species, helped each AI to impart purpose to themselves, and it gave the spacecraft populous an added sense of calm.

With integrated learning from each of the operating crew and support members within the scope of the Principles of Universal Ethics, each AI became a very capable member of the crew, while able to perform every system operation throughout the spacecraft with maximum proficiency and attention to detail. From the IMC Command Spacecraft on down to their defensive, explorer, and all-purpose spacecraft, each of the AIs were highly sophisticated, intelligent, wise, kind, capable and caring for all living beings. Not only were they connected with the crew, but they related to each other. Together, they shared mutual goals of preserving all life, biological or otherwise, while helping to optimize the health of others, as per the genetic norm with the ability to hone increased capabilities. Optimizing the clarity of the mind, while collectively increasing our understanding of the Universe, the AI worked to ensure the given potential for innovations of maximum ability to bring the goals of preservation of life to that of the Universe, humanity, and all of civilization was brought to reality.

As familiarity among the contingent crews grew, there was an increased sense that they were not solely crew or support members, but rather, instead, every member on-board each of the spacecraft was now and in-effect a crewmember. This included all twelve-hundred or more crewmembers and their families in charge of human-oversight of each function of any given IMC Command Spacecraft. Every individual on-board was respected and given dignity. They were critical members, each of whom had vital insight to offer, no matter rank or title. Thus, crewmember cohesion grew in many ways, as did the ability to form mutual aspirations with collaborative mindsets with respect for uniquely allocated and perfected mission goals. Every team was cohesive.

The crewmembers of the command centers of each command spacecraft were very sophisticated and prestigious, yet they were not condescending, pompous, or cruel to anyone; instead of walking around thinking they were better than everyone else, they were kind, considerate, used their minds benevolently and were team-oriented, as properly-vetted. Their organic nature had always been benevolent in every way, and so much so that they were gentle, yet mighty of spirit, very dedicated to their missions, willing to share in the workload at any time, spoke to be understood and had educated themselves such that they could listen to understand in a calm and kind manner. Thus, they engendered love from the IMC crewmembers and AI. All personnel on board, no matter position or scope of responsibilities, shared a sense of well-being and purpose as well as an overarching sense of security from the respectful authority and power the leaders radiated. As such, all the crewmembers were dedicated, innovative, highly capable, loyal, and capable themselves.

Domiciles, restaurants and each of the support functions had been paired up with the most capable and enriching array of crewmembers of honorable character, the highest of skills, and vibrancy of personality unique to themselves alone, all to allow for shared emotions and intellectuality to grow as necessary for future requisite personnel growth purposes. There was a sense of balance between personal discipline, responsibility, fun, and levity, all of which were recommended and appreciated by Eliza. Entire teams filled with family members and friends from various sectors spent time in the entertainment, education, and training matrices to share time together and hone their abilities to complete projects and responsibilities collectively and independently. This in turn helped to hone individual capabilities and maximum readiness for any issue that might be lobbed at them in the foreseeable future. This allowed each crewmember to garner additional respect between themselves and the other crewmembers, which in turn allowed for multi-planetary capabilities and fomented collective and mutually-shared appreciation from one person to another. In this way, their efforts no matter where they would go throughout time would be met with success.

Everything began to gel so much so, that together, the contingency was ready for the journey. They had arranged briefings with each other as well as with the United Allied States President, her crew, and the Space Force IMC Commanders and their crews. They did so on a regular basis regarding full-scope, broad, and detailed reports on training completion, mission planning, and views and specifics of the many zonal missions throughout the observable Universe, relative to Earth, and beyond. The UAS IMC Commanders and VCs were fully open to suggestion, and with the added support, they improved and would continue to improve upon their plans in the Virtual Universe. As they did, they briefed crewmembers on the macro aspects of the beginning missions and each subsequent stage of their dispersal to locations throughout the Universe. Furthermore, all aspects of the IMC were ready for the journey, and right on schedule. Onboard the Presidential Command Spacecraft, in the convention center, were all the commanders and vice commanders, with attendance that was great, both there and remote, Sol-wide, with crews in the convention centers on board each of IMC Command Spacecraft. As it was, the entire IMC was ready to address the UAS, Solar-System-wide.

Of course, for this, and as it should be, UAS President Eliza Williams and UAS Vice President Yesha Alevtina presented the completed aspects of the contingency and training. After showing each crew the initial goals of the UAS Presidential Command Spacecraft, all was made clear as to the general nature of the overall UAS-IMC mission. The citizens of the UAS linked to vote within the Virtual Universe Voting Matrix or logged into a secure voting site on the Internet, and unanimously delegated full authority to Eliza and Yesha. They would then be authorized to delegate, when ready, authority to General Vesha Celeste to oversee any further delegations pertaining to the IMC. She delegated to them authority to operate as and how they saw fit, without any requirements for any other votes except for the votes meted out during the elections themselves. Thus, leadership was completely decentralized and as the journeys of humanity expanded, they could operate autonomously, yet with help at any moment as it was needed from anyone else available.

The only requirements there were, as pertaining to the IMC and apart from the four-year US Presidential Election and the newly and unanimously elected one-hundred-year term for UAS President and Vice President, were briefings and relative transparency. This was deemed as necessary, following any critical series of missions, lessons learned, and tactics, techniques, and procedures that wrought successful conclusion to unforeseen challenges.

If there were issues with how the President and her delegates conducted business, throughout her term they could be allayed following a unanimous call, through the Virtual Universe and the secure Internet site for elections, for a recall or revote. In this way, more focus could be had on overcoming challenges and issues, and much less focus would be wasted on the kind of pointless and inconsequential banter that served nothing more than to build the egos of power-hungry bureaucrats and weaken the resolve of the people.

As it was, the current US Vice President was a shew-in for the US Elections in 2032, which was still a four-year term, and Joanne was her presumptive nominee.

There was a greatly-shared and growing interest in making the US Presidential term coincide with the one-time one-hundred-year term for the UAS Presidency, due to the increased longevity that now existed for all who were willing. The fact that the UAS was founded by a member of the US, using US values resonated worldwide, and the US was given primary representation, wherein all other countries were represented as well.

The other countries had seen that the US was healed from all the toxicity in every aspect of scope when it came to well-being, from political, to social, to environmental and more, and a majority of the US had now been optimized, so given this reality, the other nations had joined together, proud of the US and its successes, to unite as a part of the US as a single-scope governance system, representing all of humanity, called the UAS, in the event that we found civilizations far and wide, in our journeys throughout the Cosmos. Furthermore, everyone Sol-wide could for all sakes and purposes live indeterminate lifespans, unless they chose not to. It thus made sense to eventually have the UAS and the US have a shared political campaign, every one-hundred years. Still, Eliza afforded every country, under the auspices of sovereignty, the opportunity to be allied as they were, under the Principles of Universal Ethics, yet still maintain themselves as a unique country. This gave the UAS richness in culture, identity, backgrounds, and more, yet in a sense created a symbiotic relationship fundamental to a common and reciprocal guide that would reign in success no matter the obstacles confronted. Together each person could be honored and respected, no matter where a person journeyed, long after colonies had been established, and travel was frequent.

Commander and Vice Commander

It was the next day and the UAS Space Force IMC Commanders, Five-Star General Vesha Celeste and Four-Star General Erin Carter were at peace with all they had done to prepare for this very moment. All that the zonal commanders and their crews had done to prepare for it, with the robust capacities of each AI to maintain safety and security, gave evidence that each person in leadership and each crewmember looked every bit as enigmatic as anyone could imagine, and perhaps even more so. Each leader standing before the Sol-wide populous looked pronounced, regal, and heart-melting in their 'tailored-for-them' UAS Space Force uniforms.

Vesha's uniform had five stars on her cuff-like collar and Erin had four. Vesha's hair was as though it were prepared with dark galaxy dye, it was shiny and elegant with spiral curls that fell into a medium-length angled bob. Her hair had scattered highlights of blue, turquoise, and purple woven ever-so-well within her beautiful raven hair, matching the variations of color in her green and violet irises with thick black limbal rings that surrounded them. Her accent colors within the highly detailed and artistic embroidery and trim of her uniform came with the standard variations of shades of black, white, and the colors of her highlights and her eyes.

Erin's hair was blonde and luminescent, much like her friend, Sky Taylor's, with light pink and violet tips, and her crystal blue and pink irises, the highlights of her hair were woven into and thus reflected within the embroidery and trim of her uniform.

Vesha and Erin were as splendid as could be and ready to travel with every UAS IMC commander and crewmember to help setup observation posts, headquarters, and colonies, as requested, before their own future set of missions would begin with a greater focus toward their own zones. The mission of the IMC Zone-13 Celeste, with Vesha and Erin at the helm, would ultimately entail traveling outside the Observable Universe relative to Earth, to set up observation posts, headquarters, colonies, and define new zones, regions, and sectors out there as well.

As planned, Vesha's crew would at some point during their journeys setup observation posts with General Rebecca Knight and Lt General Jeremiah Voltaire, in Zone-06, who were on board the IMC-Columba, and then head just beyond the CMB beyond the Fornax Galaxy Cluster Sector, within the Fornax Constellation Region. Eliza had also asked them to bring her along when they were ready to set up an observation post within a lonely Seyfert galaxy, they named Eliza's Galaxy, which was the only galaxy located within the CMB Cold Spot, in the Eridanus Constellation Region, many billions of light-years away. This carried special weight to the President. Eliza had researched this intently with James Cooper for several years, and they were certain, given current information, that this was the only galaxy in the Eridanus Void before what led to a large enough cold area within the CMB that suggested that this could be one of the perimeters of the Universe, about forty-five-point-one-billion light-years away, but they were also ready for it to be one of many great voids in the seemingly endless Cosmos.

"I agree with President Eliza Williams that this may well be a perimeter that also exists beyond our area of space and beyond the Universe itself. Our President has asked that in due time we escort the Presidential Spacecraft to investigate it. Together, with Vesha, our amazing HBCI, Tristan Taylor, and our lovely spacecraft, Celeste, as well as our phenomenal crew, we will make this happen!" Vesha had mentioned this earlier during her presentation in the Solar-System-wide transmission from Eliza's UAS Presidential Spacecraft Convention Center, following Eliza's broadcast. General Erin Carter then addressed the crowd.

"No matter how far we go, we'll keep our eyes on Sol, on Earth, and each region that plays into our history, and we will witness as history unfolds from a peculiar standpoint. Eventually, we'll have answers that can only be obtained by traveling through time. Yet, while time travel is not yet within the scope of possibilities now, perhaps it will soon be, and within the near future." Erin spoke and inspired many, and following her words, she introduced Jasmine to the masses.

Chapter 29: Intergalactic Mission Contingency

Database Moon Archive, Celestial-Sol Date: 2029 February 6. President of the United Allied States (UAS), Eliza A. Williams presides over and summarizes a broadcast by each IMC zonal commander, discussing upcoming primary missions. These memories are a collaboration from UAS and IMC Leadership, prior to humanity's take-off into extra Solar regions of outer space for the first time in history. This was recorded within the Virtual Universe and interfaced within the Pathway Melrose Campus. Input by Joanne Gallant, President of Pathway, 2029-2032.

IMC Zone-01 - Andromeda

When General Jasmine Belle, UAS Spacecraft Commander, Zone-01, supported by her Vice Commander, or VC, Lt General Lucia Tsu, addressed the IMC crews and everyone throughout the Solar System on the UAS-wide broadcast, she moved the hearts of many. She would oversee so much and travel through every constellation region from outside the home galaxy on out to the CMB, within Zone-01. She would be the first to begin the large-scale observation, exploration, and colonization of humanity, beyond the Milky Way, accompanied by her crew, which included her spacecraft, named the Andromeda, bidding farewell to Vesha Celeste and the rest of the IMC, unless further needed.

"Hello all, I am General Jasmine Belle, and I thank you for your undivided attention. There is so much to go over tonight, so I'll try to be brief. It has been two weeks since the 2029 State of the UAS and we're ready to carry out all that has been identified as our mission within the capacity to amend, append, and increase our scope as our zone expands. As we begin, we will be heading outward from the vantage point of Sol, toward the CMB. First, congratulations on your second US Presidential term and for the creation of the UAS, while winning the first one-hundred-year term as UAS President, President Eliza Williams, and thank you for making all this possible. I can confirm today, and before each of you, the results of our training, and I can indeed testify that every aspect of it has been successful. Our navigators were put to task in every way, planners, officers of every general and specialized field were put through grueling task after a grueling task, and they have proven themselves time and again.

"President and citizens of the United Allied States, I can assure you today, that we are ready to journey out to the edges of the Solar System and then beyond.

"We will begin by working with the President and her crew, and then go on from there, journeying with General Vesha Celeste and the rest of the IMC until we have arrived at an agreeable comfortability within our Zone. During mission planning stages we have, every individual and on each spacecraft, worked together as an entire crew and have thus arrived at a unanimous decision as to where our Zone-01 Galaxy Headquarters will be established. Our Zone-01 Headquarters will be located within the Andromeda galaxy."

As Jasmine said this, a beautiful high resolution and three-dimensional representational videography of the spectacular finite details, closer than ever acquired before, of the Andromeda galaxy played out behind her. The imagery continued to zoom in and follow her every word, as she spoke, with details and graphics that were very remarkable to behold.

"Before assuming autonomous command of Zone-01, I would like to take our entire contingency to the planet, called Eto. From there, we will be able to explore the beauty that exists and take time for breaks, while studying the skies, creating constellation maps of that small sector within space in a blink of an eye, and enjoy the skies from that vantage point, unique to humanity. We will update our plans, as necessary because each of our intended voyages will be open to adjustment based on any new contingencies or dynamic information received. Together, we have come to an agreement and have planned to establish the first extra-galactic headquarters or the headquarters for Zone-01 of 12, near Eto, within that local star-system region.

"Eto, within the Andromeda galaxy, itself, and as agreed upon by the UAS, will be set up as a UAS resort planet, with a small contingent from Earth setting up the only extra-galactic high-tech city that will be located there, at least for a while. This location will have a sprawling jump gate terminal to the private resorts and a robust private return jump gate system, providing access to the beaches of white sands, red wine seas, and mountains of unique vineyards, with jewels of every kind, and a complimentary trip home. It will be designed for ultimate relaxation, sustainability, and preservation of its richness. The entirely unique ambiance is since it orbits around itself in a number eight-shaped pattern and between two slightly distant red dwarf suns, which revolve around each other from a safe and even greater distance. Eto has five moons, all of which will be terraformed carefully, preserving every sort of history as we do, after further exploration and observation.

"Our plan is to visit locations, courtesy of the President and the IMC, our Command Spacecraft for Zone-01, who names herself, Andromeda, within the Milky Way. For example, we plan to accompany the President to see and conduct missions throughout the major visual asterisms of the constellations of Orion and Cassiopeia, prior to establishing our UAS regional observation posts. We have worked with the President, the IMC commanders, and their crews, and as such, we have been given authority to carry out planning and all stages of each of the primary missions within our zonal constellation regions, both inside and outside the Milky Way. Within the western side of the Milky Way's galactic disc, as relative to Earth, through the external area of the Orion Spur and just above the Perseus Arm, we will set up an observation post that will give us a resplendent view of the entire region of the Milky Way.

"We have other locations that Lt General Tsu will brief us on. Thank you, to the President, the Vice President, to Lucia, to Andromeda, to our HBCI, Adam Taylor, and all who hear this. It is a pleasure working with each of you, and I look forward to our many missions ahead."

Lt General Lucia Tsu, in a similar uniform to General Belles', stepped up to the podium, and the three stars on her collars glistened within everyone's eyes. She wore her uniform well. "During my earlier days, I, as well as the rest of the vice commanders, worked with Dr. and now Lt General Evan Bauer to investigate the toxicity of the many work centers throughout the Nation and the World. Our, joint efforts led to large buyouts of the most noxious of these corporations and together with President Eliza Williams, Vice President Yesha Alevtina, and Dr. James Cooper, we influenced each industry into becoming the enviable work centers they are now. Their efforts led to a large increase in the quality of life, as well as the durability, the ability to update, sustainability, and upgradeability of the products and services they offered that could endure throughout an indefinite period of time.

"Our collaborated efforts have also led to more time allowed with family and friends augmenting our ability to traverse the Solar System and will continue as we expand throughout Zone-01." Everyone respected Lucia. Her Asian features were so beautiful in every way, and her hair, in its professional form, was fairly similar to Vesha's in style, with raven hair and prismatic highlights that added luster to her spiral-curled medium-length bob. In all respects, General Lucia Tsu was stunningly beautiful while commanding respect and awe.

"All things considered, it's a pleasure to be here before you today. Thank you, President, IMC Commander, General Belle, Andromeda, and Adam Taylor, I look forward to working with each of you for many years ahead. Congratulations President, on your reelection!" As she stated that, there was an overwhelming sense that the entire UAS viewing audience had felt the same and cheered in unison.

"Once we have traversed the Milky Way with the President and establish an observation post with a unique vantage point at each external sector of our constellation regions, with each of the IMC zonal commands, outside the halo of the galactic disc of the Milky Way and have carried out copious research from those external vantage points, we plan to visit many galaxies far and distant in those regions, relative to and as viewed from Earth. However, we will follow our journeys through our home Galaxy with the establishment of observation posts beyond our galactic halo, that we will share with the Presidential UAS envoys within the extra-galactic regions of our zones, allowing our command to see much more galactic supercluster activity in the regions of Andromeda, Aries, Cassiopeia, Orion, Perseus, Pisces, Taurus, and Triangulum.

"All these regions are such that if we are looking toward Sagittarius A, and consider that as zero degrees galactic longitude, then our Zone-01 Regions are looking between sixty and one-hundred-twenty degrees galactic longitude, toward the western area of the Orion Spur, both above and below the galactic disc toward the Perseus and Cygnus arms.

"As General Belle has shared with you, we will set up Zone-01 Headquarters within the Andromeda galaxy, visit Eto, and then return to our constellation observation posts, just outside the Milky Way's halo, to explore deeper sectors of each region. From there, we will set up subsequent constellation regional observation posts within more remote parts of our zone."

As she described them, the constellation regions appeared in three-dimensional imagery behind her. "For Aries, in Northern Quadrant 1, we will set up the Aries Observation Post. Of principal interest in this region is the Liverpool galaxy, or NGC-772. We will travel to that location about one-hundred-thirty-million light-years away and set up the Burnell Beta Observation Post, in honor of a wonderful and amazing astrophysicist who worked for NASA for so many honorable years."

As Lucia spoke, the imagery of Joselyn Bell Burnell appeared, followed by three-dimensional imagery in beautiful detail of the quasars she discovered, and then each constellation and location of special interest, which appeared for the benefit of all watching. Lucia had even developed and presented to every citizen in Sol the details of the architecture of a large and visually stunning observation post and had prepared a small video of how they would be built, using the materials within each area, all coming from "dead" star systems devoid completely of life, nearby the regions they would be observing.

"Cold-fusion and self-replication of Virtual Universe-encoded nanos will do a majority of the foundational and elaborate work, as programmed by our crew." She passed her plans, via a neural link, to the other generals, as well as the policymakers and sovereign nation leaders, so that they could view them and receive approval for them for further details, as shared, for proper coordination with UAS and IMC leadership.

"We will setup Cassiopeiae Galactic Observation Post, 120 degrees from the galactic center—relative to Sol, beyond our galactic halo, and within the void between the Milky Way and any other galaxy. This format will essentially be followed for all zones, regions, and sectors. We will also setup zonal region observation posts within any identified galactic superclusters, and within various filaments, such as Laniakea. We may find that the galaxies within our own zones will travel or drift in their tangents toward their locations of gravitational attraction outside our assigned zonal areas, given time, to zones of other UAS Commanders for any number of reasons.

"We will coordinate IMC-wide, and we will adapt.

"There are several primary points of interest, following the setup of the Orion Observation Post, which will actually be below our galactic disc with a view of the south galactic pole, the Perseus Arm in front of us, and the galactic center to the right. Before we embark on extragalactic activities, we would like to work with the President as she examines the Reflection Nebula, in Northern Quadrant 1, as well as M-78, NGC-2068, and Orion's NGC-2064, 2067, and 2071 deep sky objects, all while traveling en masse with the Presidential Spacecraft.

"Beyond the Perseus Constellation Region just beyond the Milky Way, in what is known as Northern Quadrant 1, or NQ1, we will set up the Perseus Observation Post in view of the north galactic pole, such that we will be sitting about fifteen-thousand light-years away from Earth above the galactic disc. Once Milky Way operations are complete, we will visit the Abell 426 Galactic Cluster Sector, where I am sure we will have plenty of personnel requests for more than one-thousand observation posts laying more than about two-hundred-forty-one-million light-years from Sol, per the time standard we will refer to from this point on, as Epoch J2000.0.

"In the Pisces Constellation Sector, we will set up the Pisces Observation Post, in NQ1. Locations of interest are M-74, NGC-628, and a location that might call for seven galactic perimeter planetary operations center systems working in tangent with operation posts in a galaxy group that lies about thirty-million light-years from us, currently. Another location of intriguing interest within that region is Galaxy Cluster CL 0024+1654, which is about three to seven-billion light-years away, where we will setup observation posts as well.

"After setting up for Taurus, we would like to investigate and setup up observation posts near two other colliding galaxies in that region, with interest specifically in NGC-1410, which is more than one-hundred-million light-years away.

"Finally, we will set up the Triangulum Observation Post, in NQ1. Of interest in that sector is the Triangulum Galaxy, as well as NGC-634, which we have called the Jocelyn Galaxy, also in honor of Jocelyn Bell Burnell, which is about two-hundred-fifty-million light-years away.

"Thank you all for listening and watching. I look forward to the journeys ahead."

IMC Zone-02 - Gemini

Lucia sat down, and as she did, UAS Zone-02 Commander, General Najem Grace stood up. Everyone loved Najem, as was evidenced in their expressions. They had seen her in her mermaid form many times in the Virtual Universe, and they all knew she had a heart of gold.

"Hello, my sweet and dear friends. All my life, for the last one-hundred or more years, I have loved looking out into space. Finally, after serving the nation, with love for our Universe at my core, I will be honored to travel with each of the crews on many missions prior to arriving at Zone-02. For years I have admired the Andromeda Galaxy, and now I am about to have the opportunity to visit it up close and personal with Jasmine, as will my dear friend, Vesha Celeste. In my zone, I have been called to serve with the most envied and very handsome Lt General Stafford Gaines, who is an excellent chef, by the way, always competing with Generals Jeremiah Voltaire and Christian Coriolis in spirited and very enjoyable fashions to 'out-chef' each other.

"Together, we will be able to journey out to Zone-02 with IMC-Gemini, and then be within the deeper regions of space. Our HBCI, April Taylor, has proven time and again, what a wonderful crewmember and diplomat that she is, so thank you, April.

"At this time, I will turn the floor over to General Gaines. He has prepared a wonderful brief, so please listen."

Like that, Najem returned to her seat and sat down. While she was more than one-hundred years old, she looked like a stunning twenty-two-year-old, but with the mind of many millennia. She too had donned the UAS Space Force uniform, which appeared in every way, very similar to Vesha's, but with four stars on her collar. Her hair highlight choice had been a light aquamarine to turquoise blend, matching the aquamarine accents in her brown eyes and the accents in her uniform. Her medium-length light brown up-do was fashioned in such a way that it was left ever so pleasingly to every eye, with ringlets here and there that dazzled all.

Stafford, who was ninety-five years old, but looked every bit the twenty-two-year-old gentleman he was acclaimed to be, with many ages of wisdom and three stars on his collar, had been good friends to Jeremiah Voltaire and Christian Coriolis for years. Each had been excellent chefs in their smaller-scale restaurants in their own time, and all three of them had won worldwide critical acclaim over the decades. While training on their UAS IMC Command Spacecraft, they would often take time during their breaks to compete within the convention centers, restaurants, coffee taverns, and pubs, within the Presidential and IMC Command Spacecraft, as well as IMCs Gemini, Columba, and Libra, or the command spacecraft for Zones-02, 06, and 10, and no one ever complained. The taste buds and spirits of all crewmembers had been indulged on countless occasions, for lunch breaks and "nighttime" reprieves, following each eight-hour shift of work. This was one event of many for social interaction and fun, which included trips to the spacecraft beaches, Bobby Gahan's coffee competitions, and bliss. Each day was limited to eight hours of work for any given twenty-four-hour period, and everyone enjoyed the bustle of work and the many things to do and the free spirit of the breaks in every possible way.

Stafford looked like he was a slender and sophisticated twenty-two-year-old, had optionally chosen to express himself as clean-cut, with a taper-fade of hair, a comb-over on-top that wove his turquoise and aquamarine blend of highlights throughout his light-brown hair, and despite his ghost-like pale aura, he was quite handsome. Everyone felt the same about him. He could have easily donned long hair and passed himself off as a dashing young woman, so he told everyone that for that reason he chose to keep his hair short on the sides and back, with patterns throughout the fade of his clean-cut sides and back and up to the long hair on top. He sensed a little more respect come his way from the ladies and other crewmembers when he expressed his image in his own creative way. With his dark uniform, blue accents that complemented his eyes, and his slender yet cut features, he addressed the crowd.

"Hello, ladies, gentlemen, generals, leaders, and crewmembers, I am honored to be here with you today during this historic event. Many years ago, my father, who raised me in a very brutal manner, taught me very few lessons that I've held onto today. I think the only one that I may have managed to hold dear was one where he told me that I have to work hard if I want anything at all, or maybe that is a quote from one of my favorite musicians. Yes, I've worked very hard. We have all worked extremely hard. Yet, we've done so under the auspices of good-naturedness and kindness in Pathway, and we have continued to do so for the UAS and each other. Rather than through toxicity, the likes of which my father will be forever remembered for, we've learned that love, consideration, and beauty will promote our shared hopes and dreams.

"It was through my earlier days as a chef that I found my love for life, and when I met President Williams, about nineteen years ago, I found that I could continue to channel my efforts through pleasing the taste buds, and all while studying, gaining experience in, and improving upon so much more, so I could do my part as we as a civilization go further than we have ever gone before. My journeys have opened my mind to the beauty of our Mother Earth, our Solar System, and within the hearts of each of you who are listening now or will read, watch, or listen to this much later.

"Today, we will begin to go, as President Williams and Doctor Sky Taylor have often suggested, healing rather than harming. As we journey to the vast reaches of space, our need for personnel, volunteers, and intelligent and capable beings to explore, and helm the many observation posts and colonies within the many galaxies will continue to grow exponentially. This reality has come into full view, even more clearly as I have worked with General Grace, Gemini, April, and our crew to plan the initial stages of our journey, for Zone-02. There will be many beautiful regions of the Universe we will see, and we will no doubt face many challenges ahead. It is ours to work together, to appreciate one another, and to bring joy to the hearts of all whom we meet.

"As we begin our journey, and shortly following the setup of observation posts around our sectors of the galactic halo, we have worked together and plan to set up our headquarters within the galaxy, known as MACS0647-JD. This is viewed by looking between 110- and 150-degrees galactic longitude as viewed from the Sun, from the galactic center and beyond the northern plane of the galactic disc. This object was identified in 2012 as the most distant galaxy seen with legacy technology, but it is no longer. It is still, however, among the most remote, as viewed from Earth and Sol. It had, at that time, based on legacy tech, an estimated 1 billion stars. Using Pathway tech, we now understand that in its current state it has evolved from a galactic group of a thousand grand design spiral galaxies to a super-massive elliptical fossil galaxy, with more than three trillion stars. We understood then that it was thirteen-point-thirty-five-billion light-years away, now, due to expansion, it is forty-five-point-one-billion light-years away.

"MACS0647-JD is a location that our crew has dubbed the Najem Galaxy. Our headquarters will be in that distant region on planet Najem Epsilon, within the Najem binary red dwarf star system, which is rather young, compared to the historic nature of this once-primordial galaxy, out of affection for our wonderful commander. The remaining three trillion stars will be investigated in every possible way, and we will provide plenty of opportunity for volunteers who would like to become very resource-wealthy and for anyone merely looking for a seasonal getaway.

"This galaxy is located within the constellation region of Camelopardalis. Within that region, there are also several other objects of interest, with locations wherein we will setup observation posts, exploration missions, and colonization and resort cities.

"Before we span to these locations, however, as General Tsu briefed, we will travel with the President through our regions within the Milky Way and then establish observation posts in our zonal constellation regions just beyond our home galactic halo. For the regions of Zone-02, we will explore Auriga, Camelopardalis, Cancer, Canis Minor, Gemini, Leo, and Leo Minor. These locations lie toward the galactic anticentre or looking away from Sagittarius A between 120 and 230 degrees, galactic longitude. They give us a view both above and below the galactic disc and through our own Orion Spur and the Perseus and Cygnus Arms, all with many beautiful and promising sites to observe, explore, and more throughout the Cosmos.

"One of the objects of interest to study from within the Auriga region, in Northern Quadrant 2, or NQ2, is the Grace Galactic Supercluster, which we have named in honor of a beloved astrophysicist, Nancy Grace Roman, who was the 'Mother of Hubble.' Through her efforts, we are now where we are here, readying ourselves in an informed manner to also travel to this location, which is about three-point-five-million light-years from Earth, shortly following the establishment of our journeys with the President, the primary observation posts, and Zones-01 and -02 headquarters operations centers.

"In Camelopardalis, we intend to set up, in addition to our UAS IMC zonal headquarters, an observation post which will be about eight-million light-years away, just beyond the galactic halo of NGC-2403, which is still an intermediate spiral galaxy of the M81 galactic group. In Cancer, we are interested in setting up an observation post near OJ-287, which experienced quasar activity about three-and-a-half-million light-years away. We will setup up several posts nearby and around this location to gather more information, observe and explore it more. In Canis Minor, we will set up an observation post just beyond and above the galactic disc of the spiral galaxy NGC-2485, which is two-hundred-twenty-five-million light-years distant, with a view of both that galaxy and those behind it, relative to Earth. From our Gemini Observation Post, we will examine NGC-2355, also known as the Graphite Galaxy. This intriguing satellite galaxy lies one-thousand-one-hundred-light-years above the galactic disc of the Milky Way, and five-thousand-four-hundred-light-years from Sol.

"Our Leo observation post locations of interest include Messier-65, or NGC-3623, which is an intermediate spiral galaxy, about thirty-five-million light-years away, and NGC-3842, which is an elliptical galaxy with a very large black hole, about three-hundred-thirty-one-million light-years away. Finally, our Leo Minor observation post locations of interest include Hanny's Voorwerp, which is approximately six-hundred-fifty-million light-years away, to investigate the star-forming region of the remains of IC-2497, following its interaction with the larger galaxy's quasar anomaly. This might represent a safety measure to consider if transiting above or below the central bulge of any galactic disc. We also plan to further explore and observe a host of other galaxies and galaxy clusters within each region of our zone. There will always be an open mind in our zonal command for updates, new information, and adaptation.

"Thank you all so much. With so much to explore and understand, I feel like a kid in a candy store. I, in all sincerity, am looking forward to working even more with each of you on the many exciting adventures in the days, the weeks, the months, and the years ahead. Please, if you have any questions for me at any time, feel free to link with me neurologically or visit the Zone-02 Matrix in the Virtual Universe, and our team will be glad to assist you. Here's to working hard!"

IMC Zone-03 - Lynx

Lieutenant General Stafford Gaines sat down, and everyone seemed very appreciative of the exciting details, along with his sincerity, his sense of humor, and his gentle, yet uniquely professional appeal. General Malinda Jefferson, stood up, smiled, and gave him a hug as she passed him. Malinda was a lovely young lady who looked healthy, active, and about the age of twenty-two. Her choice in imagery was as breath-taking as her mind, with naturally light brown skin, lovely coffee, golden and green eyes, hair that was styled in such a way that married together her left-side up-do and right-side relaxed-do, with black underneath fluorescent-colored highlights of green and yellow, and a lavish professional style. She fit her uniform with every splendid curve ever so well, and its accents complemented every one of her features.

Malinda had been to space long before Eliza had setup Pathway, and as soon as they had met, she had decided that working with Eliza, and her team was her calling in life. Since her recruitment to Pathway, she had built and supported many organizations with children who were victims of lost childhood, who had been brutalized or treated harshly, and each of whom had been in need. She had also gotten to know Hanz, Ariel, and Laetitia. There were countless occasions where Malinda had helped entire families move from tattered and torn places throughout the world at the time to the many tech cities throughout Sol. There, these children and their families were given a pleasant life with much to look forward to and with ways to contribute, all while living within luxury domiciles and all the works that were available within any tech city. The people adored her.

"It is so wonderful to stand before you today. Thank you, Eliza, Yesha, James, Stafford, Lynx, Bren, and each one of you for all that you have done to bring this wonderful reality to what it is now. The first time I flew in a spacecraft I flew in something much smaller, which was quite interestingly more awkward to maneuver and dangerous to be in than within any UAS Space Force IMC Spacecraft. This journey, by comparison, will be vast, intriguing, and with unlimited and self-sustaining resources available to each of us for increased quality of life, research, exploration, and mission volume and capacity, and that is far more than we could have ever imagined thirty years ago."

Malinda then looked about and then toward Stafford, Jeremiah, and Christian, sitting in the front rows of the convention center, set up for all who would speak that day. All three were close friends for more than a decade. "I've been to each of your restaurants on Earth, Stafford, Jeremiah, and Christian, and I will say, I might have to visit IMCs Gemini, Columba, and Libra from time to time, to grab a bite to eat once this journey takes off! No worries, Hanz, it is wonderful working with you too, and we have quite a few wonderful restaurants on-board UAS Command Spacecraft Zone-03, Lynx, but Stafford, Jeremiah, and Christian, your cooking skills are unparalleled. Speaking of Hanz, ladies, feast your eyes. He is truly a gentleman, a knockout, and brilliant beyond belief. The regions within our zone will cover areas that can be seen if we are looking between one-hundred-eighty and three-hundred degrees from the galactic center. We will be able to see above, below, and through the galactic disc, and toward the eastern portion of the Sagittarius, Perseus, and Cygnus arms. Therefore, I must bid you adieu, because Lt General Hanz Schultz has put together our Zone-03 brief for everyone's listening ears and watchful eyes. Please enjoy!"

General Malinda Jefferson passed her Vice Commander, with a smile and a hug, and Lt General Hanz Schultz began to address the audience. As he did, his nicely styled light brown hair, hazel eyes, and chiseled features poured through his UAS Space Force uniform, with his three-starred collar. He was a man of good size, clean-cut, frequented the gym often and still had a considerate, kind, and gentle demeanor. "Ladies and gentlemen, it is a pleasure to be with you here today, and I am honored to serve with General Malinda Jefferson. No worries, Malinda, I very much plan on enjoying the chef expertise of Stafford, Jeremiah, and Christian. With these sports arenas, I'll eat for some added energy. I am also impressed with the stories of Major Generals Ariel Boshka and Laetitia Zemani, both of whom have agreed to address you following what I have to share. These two wonderful individuals have come from very austere backgrounds; yet have grown up to become striking individuals of their own accord and beautifully benevolent leaders of many other amazing individuals. Therefore, I will begin and then pass the torch.

"We will be journeying to many places throughout the Cosmos as we take on the tasks of UAS IMC Command Zone-03, where I will be working with General Malinda Jefferson and our lead HBCI, Bren Taylor, and our crew on board our very own IMC-Lynx. Three of the constellation regions within which we will setup observation posts are in the region of Lynx, Monoceros, and Ursa Major. After these and the establishment of the other observation posts within constellation regions of Zone-03, we will visit and set up a multitude of other observation posts for further investigation. The special areas of interest for my team in each constellation region are many.

"In the Lynx region, this includes NGC-2419, 2537, 2541, 2683, and 2770. NGC-2419, or Caldwell-25, or what is called the Intergalactic Wanderer, is about three-hundred-thousand light-years away just beyond our galactic halo and is a globular cluster of stars which is thought to have been accreted by the Milky Way. It is loosely termed a satellite from the Milky Way and is the same distance from Sol as it is to our galactic center. We aim to find life there or bring life to it and preserve it in every way.

"NGC 2683, which is a barred spiral class galaxy, called The UFO galaxy, about twenty-five-million light-years away, is also known as a 'field galaxy.' A field galaxy doesn't necessarily belong to a cluster of galaxies, as it is out there on its own. We aim to find life or bring life and preserve it.

"NGC-2537, which is a compact class of galaxies, about forty-million light-years away, also called The Bear Claw galaxy, and NGC-2541 and all the associated galaxies within that region, which are between twenty-five-million and eighty-eight-million light-years from each other, are both locations of interest.

"We are also interested in setting up an observation post just beyond the reach of NGC-2770, which is a spiral class galaxy, dubbed often, The Supernova Factory. This galaxy is about eighty-eight-million light-years away.

"In the Monoceros region there are several nebulae and star clusters the President may be interested in observing, and there will certainly be an environment rich in unlimited and self-sustaining resources beyond the Milky Way as we journey through there.

"We will want to observe, explore, setup, and colonize NGC-5457, M-101, or the Pinwheel Galaxy. As we do, there will be plenty of opportunity for each and every citizen to be involved. At this point in our travels, it will be important as an IMC Zonal Command to consider maintenance of our spacecraft, of our equipment, and even of our own physiology and neurology. As a matter of a fact, at each stop along our journey, we will want to look for places that allow for personal thought, reflection, contemplation, and meditation, even as we maintain our organic capabilities through sports and recreation. I look forward to serving with each of you. Thank you." Hanz stepped down.

As he did, he passed by Ariel, and she smiled with genteel toward him. You could sense they may have had a romantic connection. He was more gentlemanly and kinder to her than many had been to her in the past. He had helped her through the last few years, as she earned her place on-board UAS Space Force IMC Command Spacecraft Zone-03 and was ready to address the crowd. There had been many who had struggled in their day through the brutality existent in irrational behavior, apathy toward consent, and corruption, and she had lost much of herself, due to the pervasive machinations of human-traffickers. Despite all, the harrowing history had played out many times in the Virtual Universe, and it was clear that she had protected those twelve young girls she called her sisters, during the direst of circumstances, up and almost to the point of death. Sky had rescued her just in time, and she reciprocated Ariel's care.

Major General Ariel Boshka stepped up to the podium. Her blonde hair contrasted well with her crystal blue eyes, the blue highlights in her hair, and the various shades of blue in the trim and embroidery of her uniform. Her physique was impeccable, and every detail about her complemented everything else about her very well. Ariel's sisters would go on this mission onboard Zone-03 Lynx, and she was excited to be here in every way serving with them. Many knew her story, but at this time there was no need to rehash old wounds. She and her twelve friends had been rescued by Sky Taylor and following which Ariel and her sisters had rescued thousands more.

"It is great to be here, and thank you, Hanz. Thank you for everything, you are indeed a gentleman and a scholar. I look forward to flying with my crew, our command, the President and her crew, our HBCI, Bren Taylor, and with our wonderous Lynx, of IMC Zone-03.

"Our next constellation region observation post will be Ursa Major, where objects of interest include NGC-3031, M-81, or Bode's Galaxy, where we plan to explore, observe, and colonize it. In this constellation region, there will be a number of galaxies where we wish to do likewise, all of which are unique in their very own way, as grand and as vast as our Universe is. We look forward to visiting the constellation region asterism stars and their locally associated areas with our lovely President there as well. In the Boötes constellation region, in NQ3, we will set up the Boötes Observation Post, with objects of interest that include Boötes Void and Boötes Dwarf Galaxy, which are both about one-hundred-ninety-seven-million light-years from Earth, and where the void spans a one-hundred-sixty-five-million light-year radius, making the galaxy there a very lonely one. We will set up the constellation observation post for Canes Venatici, in NQ3, with one of the numerous objects of interest in that region being the Whirlpool galaxy, also known as NGC-5194 or M-51. We intend to set this up as a mainstay multi-colonial location, which is more than thirty-one-million light-years away.

"Thank you all and I look forward to working with each of you, throughout the coming years and centuries." Ariel finished, smiled, and sat down.

Major General Laetitia Zemani, from Chihuahua, México, followed Ariel. She was a healthy twenty-four years of age, but with the mind and wisdom of someone who might have endured life for untold millennia. She looked like she was nearly 18. Her long and flowing light brown and blonde hair up in a breath-taking hairstyle, her lightly tanned skin, her waifish looks, full lips, and golden hazel eyes, all blended well with her perfect physique and mind within her uniform.

"Thank you, Ariel, and might I say, you look amazing as always. Thank you, President, for so much. I thank you for your work with Yesha, James, and so many others to make this dream we are beholding become a reality. Gracias a todos, por trabajar tan diligentemente juntos, por hacer realidad esta fantasía tan hermosa. Our next Zone-03 constellation region will be Coma Berenices, in Northern Quadrant 3, or NQ3. My family and my twenty new brothers will be with me on this trip with our HBCI, Bren, and on board our lovely Lynx. They learned so much many years ago and have done much to unite our country as well as the countries of Central and South America, to raise the quality of life there, and to return the beauty to the land while preserving life. They have done much, and I look forward to our journeys to the many stars, clusters, galaxies, and regions through space, setting up observation posts, going on explorations, and setting up colonial cities throughout Zone-03 of the known Universe, relative to Earth. In the Coma Berenices region, there are many galaxies that we have taken note of and will visit and ultimately setup colonial cities. This region of space, as we look up into the sky, shows us the galactic north pole of the Milky Way Galaxy. As we look up and out of our northern plane of our galactic disc, we will find countless breath-taking views of our own Virgo Supercluster's many regionally shared galaxies. Our aim is to preserve life and systems, so we will certainly have our work cut out for us.

"One of many locations of interest there includes NGC-4321, M-100, also dubbed by our team as Parsons Galaxy, in honor of a beloved longevity sciences investigative reporter. We will then visit, explore, and set up an observation post, as well as colonize the Black Eye galaxy, or more preferably known as the Sleeping Beauty galaxy. We are interested in the uniqueness of the coloration we have observed there. M-64, or NGC-4826, is about twenty-four-million light-years from Earth. Among the other observation post systems in the Coma Berenices region that will be created, we will begin with establishing posts within view of NGC-4147, NGC-4565, NGC-4911, NGC-4874, NGC-4889, NGC-4921, M-53, M-85, M-88, M-91, M-98, and M-99, and many more.

"Once the Corona Borealis Observation Post, within NQ3, is set up just outside the Milky Way galactic halo, we will observe, explore, and colonize the Abell 2065 galaxy cluster, which is about one-and-a-half billion light-years distant. From there, we will do likewise with Abell 2061, 2067, 2079, 2089, and 2092, comprising the Corona Borealis supercluster.

"As you can tell, there will be a lot to explore, observe, and colonize. I look forward to going on these many missions with our crew and working with each of you on this quest to connect all regions within our observable Universe, relative to Earth. I can't thank each of you enough. If you have any questions, concerns, or suggestions, please visit the Zone-03 IMC Zonal Matrix in the Virtual Universe. Thank you, all."

IMC Zone-04 - Cygnus

With that, Laetitia sat down in her seat. The crowds were pleased with every single aspect of her presentation. They had visited the Virtual Universe and knew what she had endured.

Many others who had endured the same or worse felt they had a new sister in life that day.

General Amber Blythe, still serving as a great mind in the biotech centers of Pathway, as well as diligently as President William's press secretary, but dressed in and filling out her UAS Space Force uniform well, and without even trying, ever so model-esque, with four stars on each of her collars, stood up. It didn't take long to know who she was, with her golden locks, the white highlights of her hair that was styled up, vibrant, and shiny, and the curvy nature of perfection in her physique. She smiled at her audience, with her crystal blue and hazel eyes fixed on theirs.

"All of you sitting here before me as well as abroad, presenting, watching, and listening, are wonderful people, so thank you. I look forward to journeying with each of you, our HBCI, Belinda Taylor, our crews, and on board our lovely Zone-04 IMC, who calls herself, Cygnus, after one of the eight constellations within our zone. Cygnus is the Greek word for swan, and just as a swan, our spacecraft is just as beautiful. Thank you, Eliza, for noticing me all those years ago, as a college girl and an awestruck fan, holding my paperback book of 'Pathway to the Stars.' Since then, I have learned so much and seen so much more than I could have ever dreamed of before. I used to make my own schedule each day, as a form of young rebellion, and in a way, I still get to do so, with so many planets, moons, cities, and towns to visit, day and night are so subjective, it seems. Still, your vibrancy, your intellect, the wisdom that each of you possesses, has blessed me in my life, and I am grateful for all the suggestions that have culminated in so many wonderful updates to our optimizations through the years.

"To those of you who know me as Secretary Blythe, I am honored to serve as General Amber Blythe. Serving with me is Lieutenant General TJ Demitri, who I have known since 2011, when he worked with Lieutenant General Evan Bauer, who was an optogenetics expert-turned neurological-extraordinaire, appointed by Eliza to investigate the austere state of employment in the US and Worldwide, prior to Eliza's, I mean, President Williams' presidency and Vice President Yesha Alevtina's exemplary support. Much has been done and improved upon within the many industrial sectors throughout our home world since then, and in ways we never thought possible, due to her efforts, and as a result, due to TJ's and Evan's work, the dedication of many others who currently serve in my crew, as well as many of you throughout our Solar System. Erin, I am so proud of you. I would say that you have come a long way, since you were six years old, but you were brilliant and mighty, even then. Vesha and Sky, you two are practically twins, although you are completely different yet wonderfully so, and it is because of you, and everyone we have worked with, that we have a bustling economy, and everyone now has a life where old wounds are healed, horrors are behind us, and we can now focus on joy and on the much bigger picture, which is the vastness of our Universe, preservation of life as a whole, bridging communications possibilities between us and all whom we might meet along the way, and quite simply by enjoying each other's company.

"Having worked with TJ for the last six months, directly, we have built quite a working and enjoyable relationship that I am sure will translate into a wonderful journey through to the edges of our known Universe. This region is roughly located as viewed directly up, or north of our galactic disc, between thirty and three-hundred-thirty degrees galactic longitude, as viewed from the sun. So, before I take the wind out of my fellow crewmember's sails, I will present to you my Vice Commander, Lt General Demitri, who has prepared our zonal mission presentation."

Lt General TJ Demitri smiled a warm smile toward Amber as he passed her on his way to the podium. With his UAS Space Force uniform comfortably hugging his muscular physique, his blue eyes, clean-cut and closely cropped blonde and white-highlighted hair, a part, and creative waves of hair on the upper-left side of his crown, with its naturally thick locks on top, he often tugged at the heartstrings of any passer-by, and many of the women in the audience hoped they might be the lucky ones to be with him to help colonize the many planets. His tall stature and his ever-so-thoughtful, yet gentle demeanor oozed from his aura, and he began with his deep, baritone, and rich voice.

"It is an honor to serve each of you, and I look forward to learning so much more from my commander and the various leaders that have brought us to where we are today. Our zonal crew, including our very own HBCI, Belinda Taylor, has provided many details of my presentation within our zonal matrix in the Virtual Universe. However, I will brief you on UAS IMC Command Zone-04. The series of regions we will be setting up for observation just outside of our home galaxy are the constellation regions of Draco, Hercules, Serpens, Ursa Minor, Aquila, Cepheus, Cygnus, and Delphinus. Within those regions, one of many locations of interest is NGC-6503, or what we will call the Mini Dragon galaxy. This is a dwarf spiral galaxy that lies about seventeen-million light-years from us in the Draco constellation region. We will set up the headquarters for Zone-04 within Abell-2218, which is a galaxy cluster of more than ten-thousand galaxies, about two-point-three-four-five-billion light-years away. We have found a peculiar galaxy that is metal-rich, among the many there, and within it a livable planetary system, with a planet named Robinton Epsilon, named by our team for a brilliant biomedical doctor, Daisy Robinton, who has inspired so many to be well-rounded, thoughtful, fun, intelligent, and full of life and innovation. Observation posts and tech cities will be many.

"We are interested in NGC-5949 or the Lil Dragon galaxy within that region. In the Hercules constellation region, there is a swath of galaxies. Our focus, primarily, will be 3C-348, or Hercules A. This is an irregular elliptical galaxy, about two-point-one-billion light-years from us. Our interest in it is the fact that there are massive jets of star formation material that are more than a million light-years in length. This stems from the elliptical galaxy that is approximately one thousand times more massive than our Milky Way. There is much more information on each of our regions, with much more detail available in the Zone-04 Matrix in the Virtual Universe and on the government website. Believe me, a lot of what we will be seeing will be very stunning to behold. Thank you, all! I look forward to working with each and every one of you."

IMC Zone-05 - Pegasus

General Melissa Asher got up, passed by TJ, and smiled. She had brown hair, with baby blue, green, blonde, and turquoise highlights, that was loosely spiral-curled throughout the areas of her hair hanging loosely from her up-do. Her smile was infectious, and her eyes were a clear and nearly crystalline blue green with evenly scattered hints of brown that match her hair, and the accents in her uniform matched all her details, while its fit and the four stars on her collars complemented her petite, yet quite ample, lightly tan-skinned, and feminine physique. She had the sweet nature of an angel and the brilliance of a thousand men, but she never let it get to her. She happened to enjoy working with marine animals, had helped orchestrate and set up an environment within each spacecraft that would allow the large sea tanks within each UAS Command Spacecraft to provide life to many now sentient sea creatures, as well as recreational activities for the many that would journey the Cosmos. She had also worked with Vesha to create the initial environmental systems that were now integrated into each spacecraft AI sub-loop for system maintenance and upgrades, while building genetic and neural databases of many other much larger creatures, as well as every creature on sea or land.

"Hello one and all, look at you. Every single one of you brings me inspiration. I cannot believe I am here today, pressed with the capacity that I have accepted. I can reach out with my mind, and I can safely say that I am glad to be here with you today as well. I could never have imagined a day such as this, twenty years ago, before I met Eliza. President Williams has been an inspiration, a source of hope for not just myself, but for many who I know, and she has never let us down or feared to put herself to work, in much the same way she has expected from anyone else. She speaks the truth, and her words have always carried so much weight. We all know that we are about to embark upon a journey much greater and with much more purpose than any journey humankind and all its friends have ever journeyed on throughout recorded history. No matter our labors and no matter how intense our lives may become, I will enjoy serving with coffee extraordinaire, Lt General Bobby Gahan, as well as our HBCI, Caleb Taylor, in our adventures through UAS Command Zone-05, on board our lovely IMC-Pegasus. Our region also covers an area of the Milky Way galaxy that gives us a view beyond the northern plane of the galactic disc, between one-hundred-eighty and sixty degrees longitude as viewed from the Sun, essentially allowing us to see above the Cygnus, Perseus, Sagittarius, and Scutum-Crux or Scutum-Centaurus Arms. We will learn a lot together, and our crew has shown us we all have much to be proud of. Bobby?"

Melissa sat down, the crowd had been pleased to see and hear from her, and Bobby got up. He was a very GQ type of gentleman. His hair was closely cropped on the sides and back, clean-cut around the ears, combed up, back, and sideways, flowing with feathered curls on top, parted on the left side near is crown and perpendicular with his muscular facial frame, with natural highlights of brown and blonde, mixed in with baby blue, green, blonde, and turquoise highlights that matched Melissa's. His eyes were kind, more trained on Melissa than anyone else, yet he had a mystique and cool about him that no one could understand, and they enjoyed it. His uniform with three stars on the collar had accents on the trim and embroidery that combined with the fit, and all of which complemented his athletic physique.

"Wow, if you had asked me thirty years ago what I thought I would be doing many years later, I would have told you that I would never have thought I would be doing much more than making coffee, but here I am. Can you believe that I'm a Lieutenant

General in the United Allied States Space Force? As a part of the Intergalactic Mission Contingency, I can't imagine much less than my work will be cut out for me. Let me tell you, I am enchanted to be working with my commander, her crew, which includes our amazing HBCI, Caleb Taylor, and our beautiful spacecraft, Pegasus, who lives up to her name. When we fly with her, we will always be safe. I am also, in all seriousness amazed and pleased with Luís' gravity drives, or G-drives. I'll have all the more reason to brew a unique and special coffee for each person within my crew and any others who visit along the way, without concern for any of it spilling on the command crew deck, or anywhere else. In all reality, these machines can fly! Seriously! We can pull some serious G's while not feeling a thing, but maybe a little thrill. I am indeed impressed, Luís, the many who worked closely with him, and the many others who led the way.

"Alright, let me start on the brief here." As he said that each of the constellation regions was on display behind him, providing profound clarity as to their location from Earth, spanning out throughout the galaxy, and then throughout the rest of the known Universe. As he spoke swiftly of each one, the region would expand, and more detail was made available. "We will setup observation posts in the constellation regions of Equuleus, Lacerta, Lyra, Pegasus, Sagitta, Vulpecula, and Caelum. In Equuleus, we are interested in three spiral galaxies, NGC-7015, which is about two-hundred-twelve-million light-years away, NGC-7040, which is roughly two-hundred-sixty-million light-years away, and NGC-7046, which is about one-hundred-eighty-million light-years away. We will set up posts in Lacerta, with an added interest in BL Lacertae, which appears to be a galactic core remnant about nine-hundred-million light-years away. In Lyra, we will observe and possibly colonize IC-1296, which is a barred spiral galaxy about two-hundred-twenty-one-million light-years away, and NGC-6745, which is an irregular galaxy about two-hundred-six-million light-years away. With the President, we would like to pass by and do as she would wish around the region of stars that are a part of the Vega system. We are interested to know if we are chasing Vega in our orbit around the galaxy, or if indeed we are outright going after it at twelve miles per second.

"Pegasus, the constellation region, gives us a beautiful view above the galactic plane and with that, there are many regions we will find quite interesting, all of which are loaded with beautiful galaxies and phenomena. Of greatest interest will typically be the furthest away or the most unique. In this case, the group of galaxies known as Einstein's Cross, which are about eight-billion light-years away, and another group known as Stephen's Quintet, which lies between thirty-nine-million and two-hundred-eighty-million light-years away, are regions of major interest and where we plan on having many observation posts, exploration missions, and colonization tech cities.

"We will set up our zonal headquarters within this, the Pegasus region, most likely within the sector of Einstein's Cross for Zone-05. We are excited to see how it has developed and look forward to sharing all details within the Zone-05 Matrix in the Virtual Universe. There will most definitely be initial requests from Sol for volunteers. Once the colonies are in full bloom, we will be able to rely on them more fully for support. Either way, no matter how far out we go, we'll always keep in touch, so long as it is possible.

"Sagitta, Vulpecula, and Caelum have some points of interest as well. That should be all for now. However, I have every bit of confidence that there will be plenty more to come. Does anyone have any questions?" He paused, he looked around, smiled, and sat down. Looking as young as his twenty-two-year-old well-toned physique ever could be, he fit in his UAS Space Force uniform quite well. As he had spoken, his highlights and accent colors drifted to dark grey and purple and in a way that matched the variations of grey and purple colors in his eyes, as well as the purple highlights in his dark wavy and shiny hair, which were quite unique to Bobby, who was about sixty-five years old yet still very handsome and charming. The women loved his gentle yet friendly swagger. The crowds knew he had a unique flare and that he would work well with Melissa, she too smiled.

IMC Zone-06 - Columba

Rebecca Knight and Jeremiah Voltaire went up to the podium together. She looked very commanding and sophisticated, yet quite sultry in her UAS Space Force uniform, which fit her svelte frame very well. She'd straightened her hair and worn it in an up-do for this occasion. The highlights of peach, baby-blue, and turquoise went well with the same color accents in her uniform, blending with her light chocolate skin, as well as with the peach, baby blue, turquoise, and black irises of her eyes. Jeremiah complemented her quite well, with many of the similarly expressed color-accents, suggesting they were well-bonded and ready to journey for the long haul together. He too fit his uniform ever-so-well, with his musculature, his clean-cut hair, and his compassionate stare of vigor, empathy, kindness, dedication, and purpose. An eccentric playfulness seemed to fill the air around him.

"Hi." General Knight addressed the audience and then turned to Lt General Voltaire.

"Hi." Lt General Voltaire looked at General Knight and then addressed the audience.

"We're both up here together, we're both parts of the same team, and we're part of the crew of UAS Space Force IMC Command Zone-06, flying on board our lovely spacecraft, Columba, who is as sweet as a dove, which also happens to be what her Latin name represents."

Rebecca then continued, "Yes, Jeremiah and I, we go way back, and I agree with you, Najem, he is a mighty fine chef and vocalist!" She looked at Najem in the audience, smiling back, and continued. "I am looking forward to bringing every citizen within the Universe updates as applicable, and whenever you're at a loss as to where we are, simply look us up in the Virtual Universe and give us a 'ping.' Believe me; we'll be there for you! We've been trained to multitask in so many helpful ways. Our zonal regions are located about fifty to ninety degrees galactic longitude, as well as beyond and below the galactic disc, looking through and beyond the western portions of the Orion Spur and the Perseus, Cygnus, and furthest reaches of the Scutum-Crux arms. We have a lot to look forward to, and have the honor of having HBCI, Cassie Taylor, working alongside us. The floor is yours, Jeremiah." She stepped down, and people were in awe of her commanding yet endearing presence. There was a lot more to her, and everyone knew that. She had a lot of amazing stories to tell and had helped countless individuals during the rise of Pathway, yet for now, she was brief. Besides, there would be plenty of opportunities over a lavish meal to catch up with her through the upcoming years.

"I will say, I am the lucky one to be on this crew," said Lt General Jeremiah Voltaire, with a serious tone, that belied his character, since the audience witnessed as a tear ran down his cheek. "I remember sitting with Pathway's current President, and IMC-Morgan's ESO, Joanne Gallant, many years ago, in a park just down the street where she was recording her first album. I was homeless at the time. I was sixty-five years old then. I had no car; I had nothing, well, except the clothes on my back and a dream. I had led a long life full of misfortune, had worked as a chef several times, and at one point received an award. The toxicity of increasing demand with lower wages eventually drove me away from corporate in those days, yet I still dreamt that one day I would own my own restaurant and reach out to others through every savory and fulfilling bite of food while being a much better manager than any I had had. Our relationship of communication and listening to each other with daily-shared meals provided by Joanne turned into generosity beyond measure, prior to and following her success in the musical industry. After she returned from her very first tour, in 2009, Joanne gifted me her vehicle and the funds needed to rent an apartment in New York and set up my first restaurant.

"In 2010, I met Eliza, after having run my restaurant for one successful year. My life changed. Nine years later, Joanne met her too. I know Joanne has a much greater future ahead of her than she can imagine, even though she already has the voice of an angel, who can sing such lovely tunes oozing with so much substance, meaning that isn't contrived, yet it is as real as the stars above. She was elected by Pathway to her position and appointed by the UAS President to simultaneously be IMC-Morgan's ESO, because as the UAS grows, so will the responsibilities of leadership, whether in Pathway where Joanne is the president, or onboard the Presidential Spacecraft as the leading Environmental Science Officer, setting up benchmarks for all other ESOs, or in politics, or no matter where her leadership qualities take her. She has blessed the hearts of billions already." Joanne blushed in the crowd, trying to hold back her tears that were welling up in her eyes, while feeling the swelling spirit of gratitude for his graciousness and honesty. He was an emotional man, yet he was so sincere and sweet that his emotions were contagious in a good way.

Jeremiah continued, "Here we are today, I look twenty-two, but I'm eighty-six and not too much younger than General Jasmine Belle over there. She is a wonderfully gifted, accomplished, and beautiful lady too. She is another wonderful leader of the future who was looked over for her work with pulsars, while two men were awarded the Nobel Prize in physics. Yet, we still understand so much more about astrophysics because of her, and her knowledge has very much contributed to the immense efforts of everyone else involved. So, no matter where we are in life, no matter our age or our situation, do not lose heart, we are not alone, and there are many who do care. It is through caring that I am where I am today.

"Jasmine, I invoked your name earlier, and with a spirit of charm, so please know, you are welcomed to visit and share in any one of my chefs delights at any time.

"Joanne and Eliza, you are both welcomed to come aboard UAS Space Force IMC Command Spacecraft Zone-06, or Columba, as she likes to be called. Stafford and Christian, we can compete on our prowess as chefs for many years to come, and I'll never be offended should either of you best me; on many occasions, you already have. The crews will always be the better for it. Now, I do not mean to make a private club of any of this, I don't believe in those sorts of things, but being a chef, while using the other skills and expertise I've gained along the way, well, this is my way of thanking each of you for the inspiration you have brought into my life. This is my way of thanking you for helping me to go from a time in my life where all I had were the streets and the stars, to a point in my life where I was not only feeding the stars of music, life, and art, but now I aim to visit many more stars throughout the Universe.

"We have some very intriguing locations of interest that we will visit, observe, explore, and colonize, since many of our constellation regions give us a beautiful view just beyond the southern plane of our galactic disc, and much further out. First and foremost, we will work with President Williams and General Celeste on any missions requested. As we progress through our adventures with our stunning HBCI, Cassie Taylor, and our lovely spacecraft, Columba, we will set up observation posts for constellation regions in Cetus, Columba, Dorado, Eridanus, Fornax, spending a little extra time with Vesha there, and then go on to Horologium, and Hydrus. In Cetus, there are several galaxies that have piqued our interest, all of which will call for numerous volunteers as we set up observation posts, exploration missions, and colonization cities. In Columba, there is a Fossil Group with a giant elliptical galaxy given the scientific name of ESO-306-17, courtesy of our scientist friends from Europe, and although there are many intriguing and much further galaxies in our zone, we plan to establish our Zone-06 headquarters there.

"Dorado is the home region, not too far distant from our own Milky Way, wherein resides the Large Magellanic Cloud, a satellite, and irregular galaxy, with a view of the Small Magellanic Cloud not much further away when it comes to cosmic distance. During our studies, we have come across what appears to be a cold spot, or the possible edge of our known Universe, in Eridanus, about forty-five-billion light-years away, and as such, we will set up at minimum an observation post in the Eridanus Void near the cosmic microwave background, relative to Earth, for the President to explore as she will.

"Many other beautiful galaxies will call for our utmost of attention as well. We will then setup, as coordinated with General Vesha Celeste, once all UAS Command Zones have been visited, a regional observation post just beyond UDFy-38135539, which is currently the second most distant object, containing about one billion stars, almost thirteen-point-one-billion light-years away, and bid her farewell as she crosses beyond the CMB barrier, as relevant to Earth, upon completion of each of our primary missions. Of course, there is very little to worry about, since we'll have primary missions in Horologium, with the Reticulum supercluster which has thirty-thousand giant galaxies, three-hundred-thousand dwarf galaxies, and lies between seven-hundred-million and one-point-two-billion light-years away.

"Following that, we will travel to Hydrus, there will be many locations to explore there, and we will, through our Virtual Universe network, see her just fine. Given the current expansion of space, however, Earth will never see some of the most distant locations again, since the power of dark energy seems to be much greater than the speed of light, unless, of course, we do what we are doing now, using our dark energy to dark matter converters, everywhere we go, thanks to Vesha, Eliza, Sky, Cassie, Columba, and many more who worked on this for many centuries in the Virtual Universe.

"I appreciate the stellar leadership and kindness I've born witness to throughout these last two decades, and of course, I begin by sharing my gratitude with my dear friend, Joanne Gallant. Everyone else, please know you too are priceless. Thank you all, again, for everything!"

Jeremiah Voltaire won quite a few rounds of applause. They had all seen the purity of heart and mind within Jeremiah and then both Eliza and Joanne, as their stories and lives played out on the screens behind him, designed by him while inside the Virtual Universe. Everyone within the UAS-wide broadcast felt that it was nice to hear in testimony the voice of someone who went from rags to one of the great leaders who would no doubt go down in history for centuries to come in this grand quest of the UAS IMC.

IMC Zone-07 - Phoenix

Jeremiah sat down, but on his way to his seat he saw Generals Mett Dormer, James Wilhelm, Shayeena Arezo, and Khalim Alia, and shook their hands as the four passed him on their way to the podium.

Generals Mett Dormer and James Wilhelm had requested of the President to work together with Generals Shayeena Arezo and Khalim Alia, in UAS Space Force IMC Command Zone-07, since they had many places of interest to visit, and they had planned on dividing into Regional Zone-07A and Zone-07B at some point during their journeys. The President had worked with the crew of Zone-07 and Vesha Celeste on this, and together they had agreed that this would be fine. The two four-star generals had worked with Eliza in the early days and were involved heavily with Vesha for quite some time in key aspects of the development of the UAS Space Force IMC Spacecraft. Shayeena and Khalim were married in 2022, had worked together to bring a much higher quality of life to each boy, girl, man, and woman of Afghanistan. Each of these individuals was of the highest reputation and moral character, and each one carried virtues of empathy, compassion, passion for innovation, kindness, gentleness, love, power, and authority.

"We have come up together before you, to, in our own unique way, share with you our unity as a team. Both James Wilhelm and I had been inventors, had rubbed shoulders, and processed many patents for the firms and organizations we worked for, for quite some time. We had grown rather attached as friends, found that we work rather well as a team with our amazing HBCIs, Connor and Crystal Taylor, and now we appreciate the honor of being co-commanders on-board UAS Space Force IMC Spacecraft Zone-08, or Phoenix, as she prefers to be called. Upon our request, we will fly together, and thanks to the agreement of President Williams, the IMC Commander Celeste, and our crew.

"Lt Generals Arezo and Alia are also a wonderful part of our team, and both happen to have had quite an applaud-able journey. They have both demonstrated top-notch leadership capabilities, are of the highest of virtues, and are married to each other with a wonderful desire to share the amazing aspects of our mission experiences with each other and every crewmember. Yes, we are unique, and that is celebrated by the UAS, so thank you. We assure you; we will have much to do within our zones, regions, and sectors of space, and as breakthroughs and discoveries are made, we will adapt and share them with you without hesitation. After all, we are, each of us, part of one team. We as a civilization, can attain anything we put our minds to.

"James?"

General Dormer bowed his head once, nodded to his three teammates, and stood back. The audience admired his clean-cut dark and shiny hair, with different shades of violet and turquoise highlights running through the curls in his hair, his dark irises, and the embroidery and trim of his UAS Space Force IMC uniform that he filled with the musculature that suggested many hours in the gym. Notwithstanding his powerful aura, he was one of the kindest and most thoughtful gentlemen in the Solar System. General Wilhelm was a little taller, a little more slender, and he too was suave, energetic, yet had a vibe of sophistication and gentleness. His clean-cut, dark and shiny hair had variations of blue and purple highlights, as did his dark irises, and the trim and embroidery of his uniform that complemented his athletic features quite well.

"Thank you, Mett. I'm honored to share this position and work with you. We've known each other for years. As some may know already, we've been close friends for thirty years. I'm looking forward to sharing command of the spacecraft with such a wonderful team player and human being. So, happy anniversary to my friend who has stood by my side through the years, and professionally maintained focus on his work, as he helped so many lives, worked with me on so many of the aspects that will ensure a safe and smooth journey for every crewmember as we navigate to the limits of our observable Universe. I would also like to Congratulate President Eliza Williams and Vice President Yesha Alevtina on both of your second successful bids for US presidency and the formation of the UAS and having been elected, as deserved, to a one-hundred-year term and Sol-wide presidency, due to the success of the US as seen by many wonderful people worldwide, from whence they were elected for a one-hundred-year term.

"Even though I've been in this world just a tad longer than many, my ninety-eight years have passed by with many moments of clarity, joy, and productivity, yet Eliza's and Yesha's dedication and care for humanity, history, and all living beings have inspired me more than I could have ever imagined. As we go on this journey, supporting the setup of observation posts and colonies with the Presidential and IMC Zones 01-07, on board our beautiful IMC-Phoenix, I have every bit of confidence we will learn yet so much more. Every detour we take, every mistake we make, every success we attain will build our wisdom enabling a much more promising future, for not just ourselves, but for all who treasure life, music, the arts, the sciences, the healthy and beautiful aspects of culture, and so much more. Our HBCIs, Connor and Crystal Taylor, have shown their neural prowess already, and we will no doubt forge many unforgettable and beautiful relationships throughout our zone. Ladies and gentlemen, Lt Generals Shayeena Arezo and Khalim Alia."

With that, the crowds of Sol cheered. Many were familiar with the noble biographies of Mett and James, their highly intellectual pursuits throughout the many years, and their style when it came to management. Many also knew within their hearts that their crew would become phenomenal as their journeys began and continued to unfold with one success after another. The two gentlemen made a wonderful team, were very dedicated, and even with their high internal discipline they were full of empathy and kindness. It was unusual for a zonal command to have two leaders, but Sky had suggested that he and Mett share this journey while taking them on a walk through their hometowns, since there were aspects to Zone-07 that were unique and would require a double-up of commands. Eventually, this zone would be divided into Zone-07A and Zone-07B, so they were there to not only inspire people, young and old, but to let them know that their dedication to the tasks at hand while doing wonderful things to help many other wonderful people was honorable, just as any other leadership combination would have been. Mett had no issues sharing command with James, since they had been friends for years. Thus, this would be a unique and welcomed opportunity.

As far as their involvement with Pathway was concerned, both Mett and James had presented economics ideas and inventions galore, before military generals and corporate leaders prior to their being read in. For years, they had developed a lot as a collaborative team, from the smaller spacecraft, with shared-piloting needs, to the navigation systems for the millions of space-faring vehicles milling about through the Solar System on their various ventures. They had put together many extremely complexed navigations systems and numerous AI integration algorithms, systems, and subsystems for the UAS Space Force as well as the IMC Command and Support Spacecraft. Vesha Celeste had worked with them on many of the designs for the IMC Command Spacecraft, since these special spacecraft required a rich collaboration of minds, for perfection despite their size. When, Sky Taylor had taken them for a walk, through their hometowns, as a part of their self-maintenance, Mett and James Wilhelm decided that working mutually as generals would be the best option for their zonal command, especially given the circumstances. They had overcome their greatest fears, of being looked at as less, simply because they would both be sharing a command. As they sat down, they felt the internal acceptance emanating from everyone in the room and throughout the Solar System. No longer did they have any worries that they would be viewed differently from any other commander. They were ready to share in their journeys and quests as planned, and with potential for change along the way, given the many circumstances that could arise. Everyone knew James Wilhelm and Mett Dormer would make ideal team leaders.

Lt Generals Shayeena Arezo and Khalim Aliah stood behind the mic, and in the spirit of all that was said and shared, both in imagery and in their dedication to their craft, the intense moments in training, averting one tragedy after another, successfully, bonding even more as a crew with a lot of love in their hearts for everyone on board, as well as for their spacecraft, Phoenix. Together they wiped truly sentimental tears from their eyes, nodded at James and Mett, and as they began, images that had been arranged by James and Mett of Shayeena's and Khalim's wedding played out behind them. Both looked every bit the beautiful young people they were on the inside. Shayeena's golden and beige highlights through her dark hair complemented the accents of the colors in her irises, the embroidery, and the trim of her very form fitting UAS Space Force uniform.

Gone was her sackcloth and hijab, and in its place was the raw and accented beauty gifted to her by her all-knowing God, Allah, as well as Mother Nature, the Universe, and all the stars above, and preserved by her ever-loving parents, who were going to be on the journey aboard the IMC Zone-07 Spacecraft, or the lovely Phoenix, with her. Phoenix was always filled with laughter-inducing quips and wit, considering her nature.

Khalim was working by her side, handsome, regal, clean-cut, and shaven, with the same colors and accents as Shayeena. In an overt show of respect to her, he stepped back and acquiesced the floor to her. He had vowed many years ago to protect her, and protect, love, honor, and cherish her, he did. She came first in his life, always; everyone knew that, and he was thus respected.

"I'll never forget those nights near the Minaret of Jam, looking up at the Milky Way, and seeing the vast reaches of space through much more difficult times. Khalim and I have had the honor through both the care of my mother and father, as well as the love in our souls for others, and the brilliance of Sky Taylor, to be here with you today. We consider Sky as our Iridescent Angel, because through our chance meeting and our combined efforts we were able to tame the lands of Afghanistan and the surrounding countries bringing beauty, abundance, freedom of thought, of mind, of expression, and of a love of life and all the exquisiteness we've been blessed with throughout the Universe, down to and including each and every one of us. We are honored to be here, and together we will demonstrate to all who witness us this day that we indeed care about the preservation of life, of love, and of beauty, and that it is ours to bring joy to life. Now, there is a new richness to purpose, meaning, and clarity in good health, clear minds, innovation, and part of that lies with the honorable pursuit of preserving our lovely Universe and all the uniquely-potential-filled life within it.

"As we venture out there aboard the amazing Phoenix, with Cassie and Connor giving us untold support, it is with honor that we thank President Eliza Williams for her clarity of mind, her foresight, her compassion, empathy, and love. We recognize that today we are standing here before you, because of Eliza's efforts in reinvesting her time, her research, and so much more into each and every one of us, and in each of the efforts of many who shared the ideals of humanity existent in the Principles of Universal Ethics. Through the energies of those who truly cared most, we are readying to embark upon a great journey of love while increasing our understanding as we seek to learn of all that we can about this vast Universe as we traverse throughout the zonal constellation regions entrusted to us. We will do so with respect toward others, giving each living being dignity, esteem, nurture, and kindness. We will respect the consent of personal choice, in so much that it does not cause any undue cost to the rights and lives of others. If I practice my faith, it is because it is something that I feel brings me fullness and builds the character I need to lead with compassion and empathy at my core, and I will at no time impose my personal spirituality on others in a way that undermines their ethical and uniquely free choices, nor let it navigate away from the truths found in science, geology, history, and the art of self-expression, instead I will rejoice as I understand these truths and the joy they bring more fully, while celebrating diversity with bliss overwhelming our hearts.

"Before traveling outside our home-galactic halo, in Zone-07, we will navigate with the UAS Presidential Spacecraft, or PCS-Morgan, and journey with the IMC throughout the Zones that lie before ours. As we navigate, in all regions and sectors that pertain to Zone-07, for reference, we are viewing between 0- and 90-degrees galactic longitude, a little bit above, and quite a bit below the galactic disc, and through the Orion Spur and with a view of each of the galactic arms. In this area, we will setup observation posts to further explore, understand, and build colony cities throughout. We will then journey with the IMC until we arrive to Zone-07, and begin with Lepus, in Southern Quadrant 1, where we will establish distant observation posts just beyond the galactic halo of NGC-1821, which is an irregular galaxy. We've identified star-formation activity there with the occurrence of a type of Ia supernova. This galaxy is about 166 million light-years away.

"In Mensa, we will set up an observation post, initially, near PKS0637-752, where we have identified a quasar that has emitted ten-thousand suns of radiation, with legacy systems. Using our more robust sensors, courtesy of Pathway technology, we have identified the existence of a new grand design spiral galaxy, about twice the size of the Milky Way. This location is about six-billion light-years away, also in Southern Quadrant 1, and should be teeming with life.

"Our next region, but our first priority, will be in the Phoenix constellation region, where we will set up Phoenix Zone-07 Headquarters within SPT-CLJ2344–4243, which is known as the Phoenix galaxy cluster, about five-point-seven-billion light-years away. In this region and many more, there will be plenty of opportunities for volunteers to do remarkable work, as our sensors indicate that there are more than a thousand fossil grand design spiral galaxies, several billions of light-years away from merging into a single elliptical galaxy, before becoming the largest galaxy existent in our observable Universe. We aim to ensure that life is protected there, understand the merging process further, and if there is no life, we will allow this merger to occur, and observe from a distance. However, if needs be, if life exists in any of those merging regions and is under threat, we will prevent this from happening or ensure the life-giving nature of the star systems within are protected, so as to preserve the evolutionary state of the ecosystems already present in that region, prior to working with these beings to optimize them upon consent. We will also establish observation posts, conduct exploration missions in, and colonize each of the four galaxies, NGC-87, NGC-88, NGC-89 and NGC-92 within what is called Roberts Quartet. This system lies approximately one-hundred-sixty-million light-years away and will provide many opportunities for volunteers.

"From there, we will set up regional observation posts for Pictor near SPT-CL-J0546-5345, which is a massive galaxy cluster, about seven-billion light-years away. Our sensors indicate that this region has matured but has otherwise been very minimally disturbed. Advanced civilization is very plausible in this region, so we will observe it from a distance, at first. Initially, we will observe this cluster within one or two hundred thousand light-years from the nearest of the galaxies, prior to setting up any colonies. If there are advanced type zero civilizations, it could become very messy or brutal if we interfere too much and doing so will countermand our primary initiatives as established in our Principles of Universal Ethics.

"Our goals there will ultimately be to do as we would in any similar situation, to set up communications bridges, understand their cultures and drives, and seek to imbue a shared sense of well-being, preservation of life, and have these civilizations progress and advance toward our shared endeavor of preserving our Universe. Meanwhile, we will investigate, explore, and colonize NGC-1705, which is a blue compact dwarf peculiar lenticular galaxy within the Dorado group, about seventeen-million light-years away.

"In Reticulum, there are two principal locations of interest, with plans of colonization after observation and exploration. The first location in this region we plan on visiting is NGC-1313, which is also known as the Topsy Turvy Galaxy. This is a barred spiral galaxy about fifteen-million light-years away and has undergone interaction with other nearby galaxies. There appears to be a lot of new star formation, and there will be many systems that likely contain very primitive forms of life. We will be careful, observe, and then nurture these more innocent and young civilizations into a less brutal form of existence, essentially helping them to mature correctly with reduced toxicity, also allowing them to be major players in the preservation of our Universe. The second initial location of interest is NGC-1559, which is a barred spiral galaxy with a Seyfert categorization, due to the existence of strong radio emissions. We will investigate with caution, as there may be advanced civilizations superior to ours, just fifty-million light-years away. This location will require our most creative and sophisticated minds.

"Sculptor has a splendid array of superstructures and galaxies, so as time goes by and our unlimited and self-sustaining resources grow exponentially within our zone, we'll observe, explore, and colonize each location of interest in that region. Abell-2744, or the Pandora giant galaxy cluster, about four-billion light-years away, is our principal location of interest. There are several other galaxies, each with many intriguing objects to investigate and observe.

"Thank you, all. Khalim?" Shayeena stepped to the side, they smiled at each other, shared a small hug, and Khalim took his place where she had been, behind the mic.

"In shared sentiment and in full agreement with all that has been deliberated upon today, I have full confidence that our journeys will be met with success. Thank you, Shayeena, the most intriguingly brilliant and beautiful person I've ever known, I appreciate your leadership, charm, and vision within my own life. I also appreciate your passion for the sciences and arts alongside that of every leader here. Shayeena, you are a sterling example of how healing and not harming can bring abundance and joy to the lives of everyone willing to open up and simply be kind, as shared by Eliza, Yesha, James, Vesha, Sky, and many other close friends. Together, our team, with Generals Dormer and Wilhelm, as well as our phenomenal HBCIs, Cassie and Connor, and the rest of our amazing crew, with the safety of our amazing Phoenix, will head out into the expanse and discover new worlds, bring life where there is none, and leave the kind of beauty and bounty that we have learned to have with distant civilizations already existent, with increases in joy and the quality of life of all during our journeys. After building and activating the Sculptor Observation Post, we will set up an average of one-hundred observation posts per galaxy for Antlia, with an emphasis on observation and exploration near Abell-S0636, also known as the Antlia Cluster, consisting of two-hundred-thirty-four galaxies. This cluster is a part of the Hydra-Centaurus Supercluster which lies right next to our own Virgo Supercluster. The Antlia Cluster is about thirty-two-point-seven-one-million light-years away. There are a number of other galaxies and clusters in that region that we plan on exploring as well.

"Finally, we will visit several areas within and beyond the Canis Major Region, in Southern Quadrant 2. The section of space that you are seeing in the visuals behind me is essentially us peering just barely beyond the southern plane of our galactic disc, and at one of the oldest galaxies, we have found, using legacy equipment. GN-z11 is about thirty-point-two-billion light-years away, given expansion, and is approximately thirteen-point-six-billion years old. It was born four-hundred million years after the Big Bang and will most assuredly be one of the first locations we visit, after setting up our zonal headquarters.

"Turning our gaze, within the same constellation region, you are now looking at spiral galaxies NGC-2207 and IC-2163. These two galaxies are thought to be colliding, but our sensors indicate that they are about fifty-million light-years apart. The closer of the two is about eighty million light-years away from Earth. Between them, we have seen strong indications of star formation, with three supernovae, SN-1975A, SN-1999ec, and SN-2003H. Despite their distance, there is evidence of tidal stripping between the two. As we explore, we will find out further details and update our zonal matrix, to put in requests for volunteers to establish posts and colonies there. Assuredly, there will be many opportunities to look back and be proud of the good deeds we've helped to participate in. Please visit the Zone-07 Matrix in the Virtual Universe often, since we will have many opportunities to volunteer listed therein, each day.

"No matter the challenges ahead, let us move forward and forge on to that which is greater!"

Khalim nodded to the audience and watchers of the broadcast. He could pick up the vibes of support, care, and the many wishes for safety and good health for himself and every crewmember of the IMC. As Shayeena and her husband went to their seats, they passed by General Matzu Kashi and Lt General Lexi Lancaster. They put their arms out for a reciprocated hug from both and then sat down next to each other with a shared sense of warmth and peace.

IMC Zone-08 - Carina

General Matzu Kashi and Lt General Lexi Lancaster, leading the missions for Zone-08, were phenomenal innovators and had contributed to countless essential inventions. They helped to solve many of the issues with the economy while working with Lt General Evan Bauer and brought into reality and utility many ideas that were once thought of as purely theoretical in practice or in science. They were regulars throughout the entertainment industry writing books, doing interviews, and even playing award-winning roles in movies and television series from time to time during the years preceding Eliza's presidency. They both had robust resumes.

Matzu had led Convergence Science Teams successfully teaching, developing and producing some amazing futuristic technologies, the sort that many believed would have made the late Carl Sagan and Joseph Feynman proud. Lexi had won several medals ice-skating in many worldwide competitions and was known for her creative style, humor, and self-confidence through ironic humility and showmanship. She had been raised as and named Alex while growing up, had practiced ballet, acrobatics, gymnastics, and ice skating and she had won several gold medals worldwide and in the 2008 Winter Olympics.

After joining Pathway, she became both physiologically and neurologically optimized while going through her journey and training in the Virtual Universe with Eliza, and when "Alex" became "Lexi," she didn't deem it fair to participate in the Olympics with her new abilities. In 2010, Eliza had helped Alex open her mind and transcend her fears of becoming Lexi and introduced the first plans for setting up a tech city version of the Olympics for the optimized. While in the Virtual Universe that first time with Eliza, she expressed herself as a very capable and beautiful woman, since that was her identity, as well as who she truly felt she was within. At the time of her birth, Alex had been born with both male and female features, so her parents in their younger moments of stress, eagerness, and a desire to fit in, while living in a very sports-heavy and conservative part of the US, had opted to render Alex a male. All her life she'd been confused, not sure whether she was straight, gay, or a woman trapped in a man's body, but she never let that slow her down. She followed her dreams, garnered support through dedication and passion, and became the openly gender-unique phenomenon that she was. For the last nineteen years, Alex, who had been her true self, as Lexi, transformed instantly in every way while in the Virtual Universe with Eliza that first time, yet what Lexi thought of as personal issues and what she did in private did not rule her life. She knew who she was. Lexi's private relationships were just that, consenting, private, and beautifully morale-boosting and reciprocated relationships of freedom and bliss.

It had been because of Lexi and Erin, however, that Solar System President James Cooper, Pathway President Erin Carter, Pathway Vice President Joanne Gallant, and UAS President Eliza Williams had seen fit to institute great sports arenas of every imaginable sort throughout every tech city. Lexi's genius contributed to the institution of many sports which were incorporated into the IMC Spacecraft arenas. For Lexi, it was about maintaining natural strength, agility, and dexterity. She taught that sustaining those essential aspects of our physiology compounded upon our neurological health, augmented our optimized abilities, and throughout each action, she exemplified those standards through her own dedication. All of this led to many other great innovations, updates, upgrades, and more while working closely for many years with Amber Blythe, with the side benefit of increased morale.

Some of the most world-renowned fashion designers had been trained by Lexi on how to build Matrix Enterprises within and using Virtual Universe technology to design smart-suit and halo-ensemble wardrobes. She did this, so the best, the brightest, and most considerate designers could continue their stylistic excellence in the most precise, artistic, individualized, and neurologically independent manner, allowing people to express themselves in the most desirable yet intriguing way, and in a way that suited them best. Lexi had done a lot and was rewarded.

General Kashi began, "Hello, ladies, gentlemen, and all citizens, it is an honor to be here with you today. The day is here, a day I had hoped for many years ago when I was that curious young man doing experiments many had thought was crazy, as I learned about neutrinos and saw evidence of them with my own eyes using tools that I had developed myself. Years later, I taught many theories that only now are being realized in a much fuller scope and actionable manner. President Williams, on her own cognition, without me knowing at the time, surpassed me in being able to harness the power of so much knowledge as it relates to physics and so much more. She designed the very first biopods that could optimize any living body and bridge the power of the mind between many in both physiology and neurology. She created a conduit to a Virtual Universe and with it, full understanding mind-to-mind. She learned how to dilate time and both she and Yesha, at the dawn of Pathway, travelled using their abilities to move around as non-baryonic particle intelligences, to the center of the Earth, the Sun, Jupiter, and so many other locations throughout our Solar System and create technologies that included cold fusion, both on a micro and macro, simplex and complex manner. They stopped before leaving Sol, because they knew that before doing so, humanity needed to come together in the business of preserving life, increasing the quality of it, expanding our awareness and our clarity of mind, all so that we could overcome the laws of chaos that would eventually lead to our impending doom, if chaos were not controlled or mitigated first. They designed many scientific models together, bringing change.

"They designed the infrastructure and tools to help us prepare to span the Universe. Together, Eliza and Yesha, with James Cooper and his closely-knit and respectable crew, built the infrastructure to put all they knew into practice, and in the best and most benevolent way conceivable. As their developments rendered further developments, they reinvested the value of all the discoveries they had made and were awakened further toward improving our environment in every possible way. They ensured our Sun could keep its life-giving qualities indefinitely, if the systems put in place continued to receive the needed maintenance or improvements required, and those maintenance systems have already been set in motion by them. They were aware at the time, that they needed to translate their untold and well-earned raw affluence into the influence necessary to get humanity and all of life on-board because they knew that we needed each other to overcome even greater obstacles that yet lie ahead and we needed to do so with more resilience, perspective, creativity, and possibilities.

"They built shielded, radiation absorption and deflection-capable, ultra-sophisticated self-maintaining mechanisms around every spheroid throughout Sol to protect them and to render these locations bountiful with protective and safe life-giving richness and possibilities. As such, our Zone-08 Spacecraft, Carina, is very capable, and for so many reasons, she is grateful. They purchased some of the most powerful industries throughout the world, and through that they improved the worldwide workplace, social, and natural environments, allowing healthy thought, sustainable products and industry, improved ways of life, and increased public innovation to make the progress we've born witness to become a shared effort. They saw that affluence was not the only way to influence each of us and the masses. They saw to it that action, healthy venues for lives filled with longevity, clarity of mind, and participation in legal governance and reshaping it to personal governance resting on shared well-being, rather than on greed or lust for power, could be attained by leading through example.

"They led through example by forming, growing, and inspiring others as leaders within a new political party, which in-turn grew quietly throughout the tech cities within the Solar System and then publicly, worldwide, and allowed humanity and all of life as we know it to unite and prepare for this very day. No, this road was not easy, but every sacrifice, every turn, and every moment maintaining what we have all affectionately adopted as the Principles of Universal Ethics, has helped us to prepare to go into the Universe as bringers of life, of abundance, of sustainable and quite possibly indefinite futures, and all with so much to look forward to.

"As we bridge our understanding from one civilization to another and work together with our HBCI, Dora Taylor, and our entire crew to not only strengthen the Universe and create a minor breathing contraction and expansion that will preserve all that we hold dear, but we will also find that this will allow us to unite with countless other civilizations with a shared set of ideals and goals, and even preserve other universes in much the same way. Life can always be exciting and filled with richness of purpose.

"There is much to enjoy and a lot to look forward to. I am humbled to be here, and I am honored to be asked to be one of many leaders at this crucial point in history. As Commander of the missions and operations of IMC Zone-08 and IMC-Carina, who provides us safe navigation through our zone, I pledge to each of you that we will lead with dignity, honor, compassion, kindness, and even in might through gentleness as we journey, observe, explore, build bridges of communication with other civilizations, and traverse the Cosmos. Ultimately, we are one Universe and one team.

"In closing, with me, today, presenting our initial Zone-08 missions, is my esteemed associate, and very beautiful Vice Commander, Lt General Lexi Lancaster. Thank you, all."

General Kashi was a man of enormous humility, capacity, and love. He was a handsome twenty-year-year-old looking man, with the exotic features of Japanese heritage. His once long and white hair had since returned to youthful vibrancy, with its shiny black colors, fluorescent highlights, and accents of purples and blues distributed throughout his clean-cut hairstyle, parted on the side, and combed up and back in a wavy manner. His accent colors were prevalent in his black irises and the embroidery and trim of his well-fit uniform. The audience could tell that his Vice Commander had had a positive impact on his physical appearance and activity since he had become a frequent visitor and participator in the sports arenas, the Entertainment Matrix Role-Playing Game Development Teams, and he did quite well in anything he put his mind to.

Lexi stood behind the stage, her hair flowing and as regal as on a wedding day, she shared the same highlights and accents as General Kashi, yet her feminine physique and the way her uniform fit her feminine curves made every man and even woman blush and feel motivated to work with her, as well as impressed and honored to have her attention before them.

"Ladies and Gentlemen, Matzu and Dora, what a wonderful team we have the opportunity to work within Zone-08 onboard our lovely Carina. I can't ask for a finer and more gracious crew of industrious, creative, beautiful, handsome, and kind beings. Their sense for industrial pursuits, productivity, creativity, and teamwork are second to none.

Together, we have trained, practiced, and gone back to the drawing board on many items once thought as challenges, only to come out overcoming all with more powerful solutions. We have shared ideas in both the real and Virtual Universes and have come together as a team dedicated to understanding our Universe, getting out there, taking necessary preventative measures for safety and security, and hopefully sharing helpful knowledge to provide medical and quality of life support to the many other civilizations out there that we will find along our amazing missions and journeys. As we meet these civilizations, we can do so in a manner that will protect ourselves from any threat, as well as from dangers that might come to us, uniting with them due to our love of life, shared sense of well-being, and our vast array of capabilities. Bridging communications over past barriers and understanding their motives, whether subversive or gentle, will allow civilizations to unite and learn from each other. Together, we can become successful in so many ways!

"In short, as far as our initial missions are concerned, we will setup shared zonal constellation region posts, outside the halo of the Milky Way, beyond interference, in the constellation regions of Carina, Chamaeleon, Crater, Hydra, Puppis, Pyxis, and Sextans, all within Southern Quadrant 2, relative to Earth. The regions in this zone are located looking entirely beyond the southern plane of the galactic disc between zero and one-hundred-eighty degrees, Galactic Longitude."

As she spoke, as with each brief before Lexi's, a magnificent halo-display played before the viewing audience, of every region she talked about. Each location shown was accompanied with digitally displayed information that provided both captivating clarity and large scope awareness of Zone-08 plans.

"We currently plan to set up our headquarters within the Hydra Region's dwarf galaxy group, NGC-5253, and then within it, inside the Southern Pinwheel Galaxy, or Messier 83. This location is rather close as compared to the size of the Universe, at about fifteen-million light-years away. The unique aspect about it is the fact that it is very similar to our own galaxy in appearance. It is seen face-on, but it is less than half the size of the Milky Way at forty-thousand light-years in diameter. This, and many other incredibly intriguing objects have piqued our interest, and as such, we will have many missions that will call for increased personnel and volunteers. As we span Zone-08, with our dear Carina, there will be room for plenty of involvement, with opportunities galore to be a part of the IMC. Each location that has at a minimum an observation post or an environmental biodome protecting our colonial cities will have jump gates allowing volunteers to return home within Sol, after eight hours of work, four days a week, and no more than ten months out of the year and with competitive benefits that cater to your needs.

"In the Carina Region, we will accompany the President, Eliza Williams, and our IMC Commander, General Celeste, throughout the many nebulae, globular clusters, and promising star systems throughout the Milky Way and just beyond. We will then set up our shared observation post for that zonal region. We will do the same for the Chamaeleon Region.

"Finally, in the Crater Region, we will, following our initial missions, observe, explore, and colonize NGC-3511, an edge-on spiral galaxy, NGC-3513, a barred spiral loose-armed galaxy, both of which are part of the Abell 1060 Galaxy Cluster, which we will explore as well, which is about forty-six-million light-years away.

"I look forward to this since it will be fun, inspiring, and exciting. Thank you!"

After Lexi spoke, the imagery behind her faded away, leaving a message which was displayed in a spectacular way, "For updates and volunteer opportunities, please visit the Zone-08 Matrix in the Virtual Universe." When she was done, the audience was again reminded of and proud of her leadership qualities, her presentation, and were quite excited for upcoming opportunities to work with this crew in Zone-08. As Lexi walked toward her seat to sit next to General Matzu Kashi, she passed by, smiled, and gave a hug to General Luís Rodriguez and Lt General Ariela Reina as they went up to the podium.

IMC Zone-09 - Ara

General Luís Rodriguez and Lt General Ariela Reina, from Zone-09, shared similar accent colors of variations of green, violet, and amber within their black hair, irises, uniform trim, and embroidery. Luís was clean cut, in excellent health in every way that mattered, and was a genius of a rare sort, quite possibly on par with Eliza, Sky, and Vesha. He had designed the four engines, which he had historically re-coined as "drive systems," since these same systems served multiple purposes throughout every IMC Spacecraft.

Once he had finished with his team, he and every member who worked for him chose to hold off on their vacations until the UAS IMC was completed. From there, he had then worked closely with the other teams to integrate their function into the rest of the IMC systems.

Ariela had been with him almost every step of the way, providing profound levels of moral backing and her own brand of sophisticated genius. Luís always knew that none of what he had accomplished, he could have done himself. In his own words, "It takes a powerful team of deep thinkers, daring individuals, and living beings who can produce the right balance between safety and getting things done, to do what he had done."

Ariela was his teammate in every way necessary, she was his engineering genius carrying out his theoretical and practical ideas, visions, and his go-between for the crews he oversaw. He appreciated his command spacecraft, who called herself, Ara. Ultimately, everyone on his crew, to include Ariela, Ara, and his HBCI, Elaine Taylor, were very close-knit but very professional. Time with Pathway had helped them both to take breaks now and then, and to appreciate who each other was outside of their work. It was evident that they had harbored long-lost notions for how they felt about each other, since they saw eye-to-eye on so many things, and most of their audience could feel the sparkle of a beautiful relationship as it was only beginning to develop and grow in ways much deeper than they had ever thought possible.

"It is an honor to stand before you today. Cada uno de ustedes me inspira cada día. Todos ustedes han hecho mucho, si lo sepan o no, es por eso por lo que estoy lleno de gratitud. ¡Así que gracias! I am here with my esteemed colleagues, teammates, and friends, Ariela and Crystal, and in many ways because of Eliza's dedication toward our shared dream of raising the bar for humanity, we each have so much more reason to trust in the promise of our endeavors. I am honored to be flying with Ara, our spacecraft, as well as Crystal Taylor, our lead HBCI, and our crew, as we comb the Universe. Our team has come together on countless occasions, from working with Pathway and James Cooper to rebuilding industries, facilities, vehicles, infrastructure, and complexed campuses throughout Sol, with Doctor Bauer, and we helped and built the means for the entire Intergalactic Mission Contingency to hop around space in the drop of a hat. None of this could have been possible without the contagious hope and vision of President Eliza Williams and her dear friend, Vice President Yesha Alevtina.

"Citizens of Sol and the UAS, our Zonal area covers nearly all three-hundred-sixty degrees Galactic Longitude, viewing beyond the southern plane of the Galactic Disc. There is much to cover, so please give a warm welcome to my confidant, friend, and professional liaison, Lt General Ariela Reina."

He hugged Ariela, and since the room had been filled with positive vibes and residual emotion, he wiped a tear off his cheek, and sat down in his seat. He was a handsome, brilliant, stylish, yet humble man. Those who knew him also knew he was a very sweet human being. Some of his contributions were fundamental to Intergalactic History, and the audience overwhelmingly supported his every endeavor. The cameras and audience shifted their gaze toward Ariela, and there she was, as strong and well-centered as could be, yet with a shift toward softness toward him and her crew. The crew knew she was a person of action, yet she was respectful, kind, dignified, and gracious. The crew loved her and appreciated how she took care of him and his genius mind. With President William's admonition to all UAS IMC and Presidential Spacecraft crewmembers to live life, be creative, and engage with reality, balanced with the options available in the Virtual Universe by setting up personal, private, and group matrices, as much as possible, these two had taken time to experience real life, enjoy the operas, the beaches, sports arenas, restaurants, and so much more, because, not only was it healthy, but it brought them untold connection and joy.

"Thank you, President. Thank you, IMC-Ara, Crystal, and thank you, all! Many are aware and may assume my heritage given my name. However, I was born and raised in England within the UK, and following my studies at Oxford, I moved to the US. My great-grandfather had moved from Spain to England many years ago, warmed up to the people, married a British lady, and the rest is history. I come from a background that I appreciate deeply, where there was an emphasis on kindness, working hard with vision, purpose, and meaning as the drive behind what I do. When I met Eliza, shortly following the release of her book, *Pathway to the Stars*, little did I know that Pathway itself, started by her, a wonderful individual, would truly lead us to the stars.

"I sensed as I read her words and listened to her speak, however, something visceral, yet compassionate about everything she talked about, and when I became a member of Pathway, I realized quickly that her words were words of action, of depth, and engendered a higher quality of life and shared well-being. This is something that in a sense had always been what I believed in, but she had put it into words. My training opened my eyes to the reality that was taking place before me when people embraced their uniqueness with graciousness and humility yet focus on solutions to the challenges we confront as a civilization, daily, throughout history, and into the future. Working together, truly understanding one another, and engaging ourselves in matters of good repute have led us to this point in history. This is a Golden Space Age, and we have every opportunity to preserve our Universe, and to appreciate every truth we find within and quite possibly outside of it. I am proud to serve this wonderfully united effort to bring exquisiteness and life where little may exist and to show kindness, gentleness, and fortitude wherever we go.

"As a Zonal Space Command, we will have many opportunities to observe, explore, and set up beautiful civilizations in a benevolent manner. The regions in which we will carry out our labor are Vela and Volans, which are within Southern Quadrant 2, and Apus, Ara, Centaurus, Circinus, and Corvus, within Southern Quadrant 3.

"After setting up observation posts beyond our galactic halo within each of our regions, we will travel to each region and set up major regional and sectoral headquarters. Many will have opportunities for advancement, so please stay up to date, as our information will continue to increase, with options for video games that will help you to explore the zone and the civilizations we will undoubtedly meet along the way, in an entertaining format that is filled with wonder, training, depth in experience, and more. We will have many volunteer opportunities within the Zone-09 Matrix within the Virtual Universe, so please keep in touch, to peruse requests that will come in quite frequently.

"In Vela, we will work with the President and the IMC Commander to visit its far-flung regions in our own galaxy as requested, before observing and venturing out further, due to the fact that, using legacy systems, much of this region is shrouded by the Galactic Disc.

"Volans has four galaxies we are interested in, viewable from south of the equator. We'll set up for operations near AM0644-741. This is known as the Lindsay Shapley Ring, and it is an unbarred lenticular galaxy about three-hundred-million light-years away. NGC-2397 is a spiral galaxy teeming with old red and yellow stars, about sixty-million light-years away, NGC-2434 is an elliptical galaxy about seventy-eight-million light-years away, and NGC-2442, or the Meathook Galaxy, is an intermediate spiral showing evidence of a possible encounter, about fifty-million light-years away, all of which we'll observe, explore, and colonize.

"Looking through the Apus Region, of great intrigue are a pair of fascinating spiral galaxies, both types Saab, and a non-barred spiral galaxy. What is captivating is there is intergalactic gas existent between the two that suggests a minor interaction between IC-4635 and IC-4633, about two-hundred-fifteen-million light-years away. We'll want to observe, explore, and understand star formation more thoroughly there.

"In Ara, there are several globular clusters just beyond our galactic plane and to the south that we are highly interested in exploring. Furthermore, NGC-6300, which is an energetic barred spiral galaxy, is most likely teeming with young life and civilization only fifty-point-nine-million light-years away, and we most certainly want to observe, explore, forge diplomatic relations, and quite possibly colonize there.

"Including the fact that this region is home to our most locally known star system, Alpha Centauri A, and B, the Centaurus Region is very fascinating, since its vast size throughout our southern skyscape gives us access to viewing many galaxies and local regions that will be exciting to observe, explore, and setup for colonization, with a pristine view from our tech cities in the South Pole on Earth. Proxima Centauri, which is a red dwarf sun, lies about four-point-two-four-three light-years away. Our unlimited and self-sustaining resources are at your disposal, President, as asked, to explore our closest star system and set up civilization there if there is none. Outside our galactic halo, about one-hundred-point-eight-million light-years away in this region of sky is NGC-4603, a spiral galaxy with thirty-six Cepheid variable stars. This and several other peculiar galaxies are catching our attention, and as such we will locate our Headquarters in NGC-529, which consists of two galaxies colliding. We will set up headquarters within the galaxy giving us an advantageous view of the Seashell Galaxy, which lies in front, before us in Sol, and more than two-hundred-million light-years away.

"Circinus is home to several planetary nebulae, open and globular star clusters, and a beautiful view of the Circinus Galaxy. This galaxy has demonstrated fascinating life-giving potential with Supernova SN1996cr and is located nearby at only thirteen-million light-years away.

"Finally, in Corvus, NGC-4027, a barred spiral galaxy which is part of the NGC-4038 Galaxy Group, located about eighty-three-million light-years away, and the two-galaxy grouping of NGC-4038 and NGC-4039, also known as the Antennae Galaxies, which are relatively forty-five-million light-years away from each other, are all associated together. We will investigate their evolution, and observe, explore, and colonize them. There are signs that life may exist there already, as evidenced by supernovae, SN2004GT and SN2007sr. Those regions are currently being tracked by our panel of experts using both modern and legacy systems.

"We will have plenty of opportunities to be involved, so please feel free to visit our Zone-09 Matrix in the Virtual Universe. Thank you, all!"

Ariela stepped down, and as she passed by Scarlett and Christian heading toward her seat next to Luís, she gave each of them a heartfelt and respectful hug.

IMC Zone-10 - Libra

General Scarlett Hart and Lt General Christian Coriolis, of IMC Zone-10, approached the podium together. It was obvious they had bonded quite well and in so many ways. There was a feeling of electricity in the air between them and it was inspiring to see. Both Scarlett and Christian were neuroscience majors, with a host of other PhDs to their credit. Together they had worked with Joanne and among many within a powerful team, as they improved the Correctional and Entertainment Matrices. Christian was a close friend to Stafford and Jeremiah since their off-time pursuits happened to be chef competitions between the three, with the benefactors being anyone who happened to be in whatever shared space they were in at the time. Scarlett enjoyed Christian's cooking, especially in-between breaks from high-intensity spacecraft scenario simulations. They had perfected those as well.

The simulations were designed to put every crewmember in a situation to where they would be calling the shots and working to preserve the mission while preserving benevolent lives. The Virtual Universe and real-world dry-run and live-run training exercises were designed to ensure that in any given conceivable scenario, they would make choices that were ethical, preserved the ability to continue on a mission, while adapting capabilities to more easily confront and overcome each of these challenges, should they occur in real life.

Scarlett's work with Yonn Forall and Anastasia Renae and their teams, integrating the internal environmental systems with the drive, navigation, and shielding systems was phenomenal. Everything from the personally programmable living quarters to the jungles, forests, surf waves, and beaches, to work centers, the command crew deck, and defensive systems had been something that she, her team, and Yonn's and Anastasia's teams had put together impressively. Their attention to quality and detail, as well as artistry, sophistication, and utility, gave comfort and optimization to the entire crew and the mission itself. The AIs loved them since their systems were designed so well.

Scarlett, in her Space Force uniform, designed to fit in the most appealing of ways, complemented every aspect of her persona, while engendering both respect and the desire for compliance within any crewmember. Both men and women were attracted to her but respected her wishes in such a way to where they would go to the furthest reaches of the Universe with her. Her blonde hair, her blue eyes, light freckles, her hairstyle, the trim and embroidery of her uniform contrasted well and added to her dynamic personality.

Both Scarlett and Christian had chosen a range of colors as their hair, iris, and trim accents. Royal blues, cherry reds, and golden yellows, in both dark and light variations, were woven and scattered ever so well. Every spacecraft seemed to take on the color scheme of their associated commanders, while individual crewmembers were left to their own individuality and devices, tied into the reflections of their minds, mixed with a balance of collaborative harmony.

Christian's dark hair and blue eyes went well with his and Scarlett's color scheme, and his very healthy musculature fit his uniform quite well too. He kept his hair clean-cut on the sides and back, but wavy, shiny, loose, and parted at the crown on one side. Every woman on-board IMC Zone-10 wanted to participate in colonization of many planets with him, but they controlled themselves and focused on their missions.

All-in-all, this crew was quite a good team.

"I've worked with Christian for nearly two decades, and I will say, I am grateful to have him by my side and guiding our crew as we traverse the Cosmos, with our beautiful spacecraft, Libra, and our amazingly handsome lead HBCI, Evan Taylor. We will engage in many interesting and enjoyable journeys, and each one, no matter the repetition that may be apparent from afar, every single location will have its own uniqueness and eccentricities, hence the necessity for observation and exploration before colonization. Christian?"

General Hart stepped aside, turned to Lt General Coriolis, smiled, and made her way to her seat. The audience caught on to the depth of involvement in all that had caused the realization of Eliza's dream to come true. She was an excellent leader who bred excellent leaders, and during the Golden Space Age every single person involved in the observation, exploration, colonization, and preservation of the Universe was a leader with a library of stories gladly shared. Christian earned that same respect from the audience as he stepped up and began. He was a man of great stature in so many ways, from character, to physique, to mental capacity. Aside from his involvement with his friends and the IMC, he had worked often in the pre-Golden Space Age days to rescue families from the corruption and toxicity that had been part of the prevailing economic and government systems in place at the time and would have caused the doom of human civilization within one-hundred years, if the toxicity continued. Instead, as an economist, brilliant mind, investor, and inventor, he fashioned and perfected ideas shared by James Cooper. As a result, he brought untold innovation and motivation to any work environment, to include that of the IMC Zone-10 crew. All who knew him loved him, and they were honored to serve with him.

"General Scarlett Hart and I, as well as every crewmember of IMC Zone-10 are honored to be a part of this maiden voyage into the immense and far reaches of the Cosmos. We have done a lot to prepare for this day, and indeed, this day has finally come. As we navigate together for our initial missions, beginning at eight hundred hours, Eastern Standard Time, you'll find very intriguing realities that impact us in a big way throughout each of our zones. I will share with you brief details of some areas of interest within several regions of our vast zone.

"We will explore the regions within our zone with the President and the IMC, at a time of the President's choosing, whether that is before or after we set up our regional operation posts just outside our Galactic Halo. As General Tsu said, 'We will coordinate IMC-wide, and we will adapt.' We are currently going to journey together for each of our initial missions until measures for autonomy are in place, and our crew is honored to amend our plans as necessary. We are also honored to have our lead HBCI, Evan Taylor, on board our lovely spacecraft, Libra. That said, we will, in this order, set up the observation posts for Crux, Libra, Lupus, Musca, Norma, Ophiuchus, Scorpius, and Triangulum Australe, all of which are within Southern Quadrant 3. Despite the quadrant designation, we will essentially be exploring the regions that are toward our Laniakea Supercluster, or southeast of our Galactic Center. Strangely enough, we will have Regions both above and below the Galactic Disc, as well as through it, between 210- and 30-degrees Galactic Longitude.

"In Crux, we will explore Alpha, Beta, Epsilon, and Gamma Crucis, between eighty-eight and three-hundred-fifty light-years away. In Libra, we are most interested in HD-140283, or the Methuselah Star, which is considered the oldest star in the known Universe. This star is thought to be fourteen-point-four-six-billion years old and is about one-hundred-ninety-point-one light-years away. Now, since the Universe is said to be about thirteen-point-eight-billion years old, the only reason this works, is due to the margin of error, of eight-hundred-million years, making the Methuselah Star, possibly born, shortly after the Big Bang. In this region, we are also interested in NGC-5792, about eighty-three-million light-years away, and NGC-5885, about ninety-two-million light-years away, both of which are barred spiral galaxies. NGC-5890, an unbarred lenticular galaxy, about ninety-eight-million light-years away, is another galaxy of interest. Of course, there are other sectors that pique our interest too.

"In Lupus, there are a number of star systems, nebulae, and other anomalies of interest.

"Musca has several nebulae, specifically the Hourglass Nebula, which is about eight-thousand light-years away. Understanding each object in space gives us a vaster comprehension of the various stages of that which seems to naturally breed a foundation for life. Although our primary objective is to preserve life, understanding Nature's loops and ways with complete complexity will help us to curb chaos and destruction in favor of developing and appreciating the beauty all around that will add to the sustained enjoyment and longevity of the civilizations of the ages.

"Norma is where our journeys become very interesting. All told, the number of galaxies in this region, known as the Norma Cluster, are in the tens of thousands. This region is located about two-hundred-twenty-one-million light-years from Earth and belongs to a much greater construct that we share, known as the Laniakea Filament. While many superclusters of galaxies share our Filament, the intriguing aspect about the Coma Cluster is what is known as the Great Attractor. We will build our headquarters within clear view of this anomaly and jump in, out, and around it before we hover too close. There will be plenty of baryonic and non-baryonic material available on the far side of the nearest galaxies in that region to develop pristine tech cities that coincide with the mission and are far enough away to prevent any negative effects. It could be that what is going on will take billions of years, but we will do all that we can to preserve life. Our science teams will collaborate.

"Gazing into the constellation of Ophiuchus, you'll find yourself looking just to the east of Sagittarius, the center of our Galaxy, and above the northern plane of our Galactic Disc. With this view, you'll notice a lot of unique and beautiful star systems within our galaxy, and while using our legacy systems to peer further, you'll see an ultraluminous infrared galaxy (ULIRG) poring through the stars of the Milky Way about four-hundred-million light-years away. You'll also see many more galaxies of interest within that region, nearby and beyond this beautiful location. What is unique for us about this galaxy, is that it is two galaxies becoming one. Because of the intensity of effect that these two supergiant major black holes will have on our understanding of the Cosmos and astrobiology itself, we will most certainly explore and observe this region to gain more insight. This pair of galaxies is identified as NGC-6240, and we have renamed it, the Firefly Galaxy. More details, such as the position as viewed from Earth and toward our Galactic Disc, north or south polarity from our Galaxy's plane, and which latitude and longitude, will be provided within our zonal matrix, for each region of space within the Virtual Universe.

"Scorpius is just to the southeast of Sagittarius, and thus we are viewing just to the right and below the Galactic Disc. Using solely our legacy systems, we have not seen beyond the plethora of stars, clusters, novae, and objects within our Milky Way at this time. However, this is just north of the Norma Cluster, and the galaxies there may be influenced by the Great Attractor. Given that knowledge, it will be a very intriguing location to study from the vantage point that lies beyond the Zone of Avoidance, or the center of our Galaxy.

"The Triangulum-Australe Region of our Zone has quite the view, to the south of our Galactic Disc. Looking at the display behind me, we are peering just below the Norma Cluster. ESO-137-001 happens to be a barred spiral galaxy that is part of this cluster, or Abell-3627, is located at its southern portion, relative to Earth, about two-hundred-twenty-million light-years away. Finally, ESO-69-6 is a pair of galaxies that collided in such a way, that speed, velocity, and current measurements suggest a violent partial merger. They will most likely experience gravitational attraction and collide again in several billions of years until they completely merge. This will be a beautiful location to study since many of the star systems will likely not be impacted due to their distance from each other. There will be hugely affected regions, however. This location is about six-hundred-million light-years away.

"There is much to discover, to learn, and to explore, so we will be keeping you up to date as we receive information. Our matrix crews have developed an amazing site, that will let you explore what we have explored, but in the Virtual Universe. There, you will have access to every detail of information you'll need for planning and volunteer work, should you become a volunteer in our zone. We look forward to working with each one of you. Please visit the Zone-10 Matrix, in the Virtual Universe, often. We will provide many opportunities for heroism and volunteerism.

"Thank you."

IMC Zone-11 - Virgo

Christian went to his seat by Scarlett, and passed by General Yonn Forall, gave him a fist bump and a military hug, and then Lt General Katya Brighten smiled and gave him a hug. Yonn and Katya had been working with Scarlett and Christian for a while since many of their galactic interests shared some of the same superclusters of galaxies. Yonn had worked many years ago with Amber Blythe to help Erin Carter, and now Erin, as recent head of Pathway, and vice commander of the entire intergalactic mission contingency. Each had proven that their efforts were well worth every moment spent. With so much done and appreciation for individual and collaborated efforts abounding, there were good feelings and thoughts shared between each crewmember and crew, no matter the zone. Just like each of the crews before, IMC Zone-11 was as ready as ever.

Yonn made his way with Katya up to the pulpit, and together, their blonde hair, blue eyes, and nicely styled hair complemented each other. Yonn had a clean-cut, shaven appearance, and Katya's hair was fashioned ever-so-exquisitely in an up-do, with falling spiral curls in all the right places that suggested Red Carpet professionalism and style. They shared their accent colors, which were what many would call galaxy dye, of colors of pink, purple, and blue, done just right. Not too much, but just the way that would make any artist proud, since every aspect of their look radiated their power, their sophistication, their gentle demeanor, and so much more. These colors were prominent throughout their hair, irises, trim, and embroidery. Both fit their uniforms quite well, he with his masculine musculature, and she with her smooth yet pronounced curves in all the right places that suggested the most heart-striking essence of femininity. Both looked phenomenal in a way that only the most mature of minds would appreciate more fully, and no matter the mind, all were inspired by their presence to be their best version of themselves.

"I'm proud to be here before you today," said Yonn. "With 6522 Galaxies of interest in just one region of our zone, I assure you, we will have plenty to keep us busy. Every time I see my crew, and every time I see those who have helped us to get to where we are today, I am filled with a debt of gratitude. Many years ago, following my first doctorate, I began studies on many of the diseases that affect children. As time went by, a particularly brutal affliction begged my attention. There were many children who inspired me, who despite their struggle and with all their hearts and minds loved life and those around them and dreamed great big dreams, who are no longer with us, but each child we lost hit home to me all the more the beauty of life and the sorrow for lost potential if we don't at least embrace the need to understand each disease and overcome it. Hutchison-Gilford Progeria Syndrome, otherwise known as Progeria, had its brutal effect in such a way that it caused children to age eleven times faster than the average human. Many of these children looked toward myself and my colleagues with hope in their eyes, knowing that it was through care, intense study, and dedication to the sciences that we might possibly be able to help them to live a life that was at least normal, just like everyone else.

"Working with General Amber Blythe and with many others from our various crews, and aligned with the insights and wisdom of Eliza, Yesha, James, and Pathway we developed a cure. Now each of these children has been gifted a life where they can realize their fullest potential. Many have done so much more than they would have, had we let Nature alone to take its course. Nature has done so much, now it is our turn.

"I look to you, Erin, General Erin Carter, recent President of Pathway, and I thank God and the Stars for you and all that you do for every single living being that exists within our small circle of influence. Because of you, Eliza, Yesha, James, Amber, and Pathway, our reach, or our circle of influence has grown exponentially and will now grow even more as we expand throughout our known Universe, and perhaps one day beyond that. There are so many more of you to thank, so please know that I do not take your contributions for granted. I love each of you, Katya, our lead HBCI, Gwen Taylor, my crew, the people who work closest to me, and those whose work goes unnoticed from afar.

"Please listen to my equally gifted and phenomenally intelligent and supportive coworker as she shares with you the various aspects of our preliminary plans for IMC Zone-11.

"Thank you."

With that, Yonn sat down, after smiling and nodding to Katya Brighten. She looked out at the audience and was emotionally attached to every heart that was watching. There was a lot that had been done by her to support her innovations toward the fulfillment of the mission they were on. As time would pass, the masses of humanity and Earth-based creatures scattered throughout the Universe would know and understand her contributions. Both had been physiologists and neuroscientists, and while they had learned so much more and had compounded upon their talents, their abilities, and their strengths exponentially, she was the perfect person to work with her crew and with General Forall. He was gifted, he loved life, and he was driven by vision and passion. Katya was likewise yet had an extra dash of compassion which melded the crew of IMC Zone-11 into one fine-tuned, caring, innovative, and dedicated collaboration of minds. Even their spacecraft AI, Libra, loved the way she expressed herself and her genuine intentions.

"Good evening. Here is some sage advice from President Eliza Williams, something she told me when I went through the Virtual Universe with her training me there many years ago. She said, 'Live and love life, be so curious about our Universe, our Solar System, our Earth, and our communities that you are swelling with meaning, purpose, and drive sufficient to desire to live forever with the desire to multiply your talents and experiences exponentially. Do everything you can to help others in whatever way you are driven, to bring joy, release from tension and despair, and to be there following great and shared achievements. Do all this, and then if the day comes that we move on from this mortal realm, then you'll know your life was full and worth every moment.' I intend to do just that with each of you. I desire to live forever, because there is so much to understand, but should my time come for no reason of my own, then I will know my life was full. With General Forall, our beautiful HBCI Gwen Taylor, and Virgo, our handsome spacecraft, I have no doubt our zone's crew will go to great lengths to do the same. With so much to cover and so many journeys ahead, I'll begin our brief.

"Each of the regions within our zone are scattered between three-hundred-and-ninety-degrees Galactic Longitude, and can be seen through our Galactic Disc, as well as above and mostly below it.

"Virgo is an interesting region. Since it lies in Southern Quadrant 3, much of this region is beyond and just north of our Galactic Disc. This is the direction our Galaxy travels through space, along with other galaxies belonging to our Local Cluster. This, our Local Cluster, including many of the galaxies we see in this region are heading toward the Great Attractor in the Norma Region," Katya looked toward Scarlett and Christian, smiled, and then looked toward Yonn with a peaceful glow about her. "Of the thousands of galaxies, we have detected all of them using legacy systems within that constellation region, from Earth to the cosmic microwave background, the one that has intrigued us most does not belong to our Local Cluster at all. We're still learning about its present through physics, mathematics, and statistics. Scientists identified Quasar-3C-273, which is classified as a 'blazar,' which occurred at the heart of a giant elliptical galaxy about two-point-four-four-three-billion light-years away. We will keep you up to date on everything we learn as we observe and explore this and any Region or Sector, and you'll be able to access the details of them, along with volunteer opportunities in our Zone-11 Matrix inside the Virtual Universe. Of course, we would be remiss if we didn't at least set up a few observation posts around and within M104 or the Sombrero Galaxy. This is an unbarred spiral galaxy, along the southern portion of the Virgo Cluster. This galaxy has between twelve-hundred and two-thousand Globular Clusters and lies about twenty-nine-point-three-million light-years away.

"Aquarius is a beautiful mythology if you ask me. Like the remainder of our regions, this lies in Celestial Southern Quadrant 4. As you view it, you are looking toward our Galactic Disc, both above and below it. NGC-7252, or the Atoms for Peace Galaxy, is a peculiar elliptical galaxy about two-hundred-twenty-million light-years away. What is truly intriguing about this is, unlike your typically pristine elliptical galaxy, this has clearly undergone a merger recently, or more than two-hundred-twenty-million years ago. This will be our opportunity to add significant knowledge to macro-galactic biology, physics, and history. It will help us understand what to expect from mergers such as these in the future. While we plan to help our Universe slightly expand and contract to provide indefinite life to all within, there will be times where we send sensors out in the middle of blazing and cosmically hot firestorms, with little to no feedback coming back at all. We're only beginning to understand black holes, Hawking Radiation, and more, how they work, and how to take back what has been lost for untold periods of time. This and all strange events are an all-important part of our understanding and ability to work with and appreciate natural macro-cosmic behavior.

"To bring life and abundance, and expand as needed, we'll observe this location thoroughly, explore it, and eventually colonize it. There are also many nebulae, globular clusters, and objects within our Milky Way that we are excited to work on with the President.

"Capricornus is amazing. With legacy systems, we understand little more than the fact that within the distant regions of space lies the Capricornus Void, and within our Galaxy lies globular clusters of stars, among a few other stars in the region. Because we are gazing toward the northern region of the Galactic Disc, most of what we see is within the Sagittarius Arm, just west of the center of our Galaxy.

"Corona Australis lies below the Sagittarius Arm of our Galactic Disc, looking toward the Galactic South Pole. With legacy systems, deep space is difficult to see, due to the high count of the brilliantly beautiful nebula, stars, and globular clusters, between us and the area beyond our Galaxy.

"Grus gives us a beautiful view of several galaxies as we gaze toward the region just below our Galactic Disc. About fifty-six-million light-years away lies the closer galaxy of the Grus Quartet, and the furthest is about sixty-nine-million light-years away. These four galaxies are currently known as NGC-7552, NGC-7582, NGC-7590, and NGC-7599. All four are barred spirals that are a part of the same galaxy group. We intend to observe, explore, and colonize these locations, as well as many others. IC-1459 Galaxy Group is another of many in this region. Included in this group are the following: "The IC-1459 elliptical galaxy, which is about sixty-eight-point-eight-million light-years away; the NGC-7418 barred spiral galaxy, about sixty-four-point-nine-million light-years away; the NGC-7421 barred spiral galaxy, about sixty-eight-million light-years away; the NGC-7552 barred spiral galaxy, about fifty-six-million light-years away; the NGC-7582 barred spiral galaxy, about sixty-nine-million light-years away; the NGC-7590 barred spiral galaxy, about sixty-million light-years away; and, the NGC-7599 barred spiral galaxy, about fifty-eight-million light-years away.

"Each of these sectors will call for plenty of volunteers, and every volunteer, no matter the zone, region, or sector, will be able to stake an equitable claim within the regions they observe, explore, colonize, and preserve, so long as the Principles of Universal Ethics are abided by.

"Indus is another region of space where it is easier to see if using our legacy systems. Here, as you can see, we are looking just to the south of the center of our Galaxy, just below the Sagittarius Arm. The IC-5152 irregular galaxy is an outlying member of our own Local Group, about five-point-eight-million light-years away, which is relatively close given the size of our Observable Universe relative to Earth and Sol. The NGC-7029 bright elliptical galaxy is about one-hundred-eighteen-point-four-million light-years away. The NGC-7041 elliptical galaxy is about eighty-million light-years away. The NGC-7049 elliptical-spiral galaxy is very unique, and possibly two separate galaxies, one resting many light-years in front of the other, with the closest lying about one-hundred-million light-years away. NGC-7064 is a barred spiral galaxy about thirty-four-million light-years away. NGC-7083 is a barred spiral galaxy, where we spotted supernova activity in 2009 giving it a reference number of SN 2009hm, and this galaxy is about one-hundred-fifty-four-million light-years away. NGC-7090 is a spiral galaxy, about thirty-million light-years away. Finally, NGC-7140 is a spiral galaxy about one-hundred-twenty-two-million light-years away. All these locations will receive at minimum an observation post.

"Microscopium is our final region, within our zone at this time. As you can tell, we have a beautiful view of the west portion of the Sagittarius Arm, and slightly to the south of the Galactic Disc. Our legacy systems have tracked one NGC-6925, which is a barred spiral galaxy that lies edge-on in our field of view. This is a wonderful example of what our galaxy might appear like gazing at the side of it from about one-hundred-point-one-three-million light-years away. We very much plan to do that. There will, as you can see, be a lot of opportunities to be involved.

"Please keep up to date by visiting our Zone-11 Matrix in the Virtual Universe often.

"Thank you!"

With that, the audience was amazed at the visuals she had provided and looked forward to the impending opportunities that lie ahead with Zone-11. They watched as she passed General Anastasia Renae and Lt General Evan Bauer, gave them each a hug and a smile, and sat down next to Yonn. Thus far, every brief was spectacular in every conceivable way.

IMC Zone-12 - Tucana

General Anastasia Renae and Lt General Evan Bauer stood before their audience, made the podium appear invisible so as to see and appreciate their entire physical aspects on display, and the crowds were pleased. Both were outstandingly attractive, yet radiated brilliance, savvy, sophistication, kindness, and drive. Representing IMC Zone-12, they had gone in together to share galaxy dye-like accents, highlights, trim, iris flare, and embroidery of light pinks and baby blue, with Evan's colors the same, but several shades darker. Both fit their uniforms well, and not only did their presence raise morale, but they also garnered deep respect from everyone throughout Sol. Her naturally light-blonde hair and his dark raven hair complemented their accent color choices quite well. She wore her hair up, with spiral curls and a series of braids coming up to where her hair gathered and then nicely scattered beyond the coil of her up-do. His hair was clean-cut on the sides and back, yet wavy on top, in a classic hairstyle. She stepped forward to the pulpit as he stood slightly behind her and to her left.

"I'm impressed with each and every crew and individual who will journey on board the various IMC Command Spacecraft, and most especially Tucana, our own lovely command spacecraft, who works so well with our beautiful HBCI, Star Taylor, those who have helped prepare for this and the many who are preparing now for the various journeys that will arise as time goes by. I've had an opportunity to work with many of you throughout the last almost two decades, and with some of you who are physicists even longer, and I will say that your spirit of fun, balanced with your astounding work ethic, is what has brought us to this point in history, today. Each of you is phenomenal and I have no doubt that your knowledge, experiences, and contributions in all their details, written in text, would fill up the Library of Congress several times over. What you do in the spirit of preserving our Universe is something I appreciate deeply.

"No matter how far we think we have come, there will always be more challenges ahead. One need not find themselves ever consumed with concerns of boredom, since there will always be something exciting to enjoy, of merit for our focus, and with profound purpose on a macro scale. From the words of a favorite contemporary of mine, Astrophysicist Vera Rubin, "In a spiral galaxy, the ratio of dark-to-light matter is about a factor of ten. That's probably a good number for the ratio of our ignorance-to-knowledge. We're out of kindergarten, but only in about third grade." She was wise beyond her years, and may she rest in peace. No matter where we go or how much we think we know, there will always be untold adventures, journeys, and things to help us to learn, grow, mature, become wise, and that will fill life with clarity and even more profound meaning.

"Ladies and gentlemen, I am proud to introduce my fellow crewmember, Lieutenant General Evan Bauer. His resume would take many years to read, so let's just suffice it to say that he has a well-deserved and enviable position in IMC Zone-12 as Vice Commander. This is a rather large area of our observable Universe with literally billions of galaxies and untold potential, so I am very honored to work and serve with him in the many efforts ahead, not just because of his many accomplishments, but also because of his impeccable demeanor and immutable character. Evan?"

Anastasia stepped aside, shared an embrace, and then returned to her seat as he stepped forward to the podium. The audience was inspired by Anastasia's words, they were impressed with her humility, and they were entranced with every aspect of her character. As their attention transitioned to Evan, they found they were inspired likewise and in every way.

"Hello." Evan smiled. He looked down, then up, then back toward Eliza, sitting in the chairs behind him, just to his left, but far enough away to where her view hadn't been blocked when he was standing by Anastasia. "Madam President, I just want to thank you for your incredible vigor despite every tragedy that unfolded throughout your life in those earlier days. I was beginning to understand the intricacies of optogenetics and neuroscience when you approached me all those years ago and somehow you saw something in me that I did not. Perhaps through my earlier years, I was timider and shyer, but it could have been because the world that I perceived at that time was brutal, fatalistic, and cruel. I studied what I did because I knew there had to be a better equation for neurological health than that. You. You came to me and provided the means, the facilities, and the capacity to realize neurological breakthroughs, innovations, and life-changing optimizations, improve upon them, and secure private thought. Because of you, I did so much more, only after you had already contrived of it in so much depth to where it was already in full swing through use of your biopods. I felt an instant connection the day I met you and a surge of confidence as we journeyed through the Virtual Universe as you supplied my training. As Anastasia has said, everyone here has contributed immensely, but I do not believe that any of us would have done so much to this degree had it not been for you. So, thank you, President Eliza Amber Williams. Thank you for this day."

Every person throughout Sol got up from their seats and applauded. "If there had been a microphone in the Oort cloud, in due time an alien would have thought that the sound of our Solar System would have been a large and roaring applause. They would have inadvertently felt welcomed, which they would have been, nonetheless. Perhaps that would be entirely beside the point, but in a deeper way, I'd like to think that is the whole point. The living beings, led by the humanitarians among the living, have finally and solidly graduated to a level-one civilization, based on the Kardashev Scale of civilization, and we have quite possibly surpassed it by many levels altogether. Because of you, Eliza, Sol is ready for interstellar travels, and intergalactic travels are not too far behind.

"We have a beautiful Universe and to that, I can bear witness. Whatever character we needed to be, or whomever we needed to become, I believe we are now well on our way. I agree with Eliza's sense that the Universe is beckoning to us to preserve life, to continue to evolve, and to find a way to do this throughout all of space and time. We will preserve life wherever we go, find ways to work together, and then bring life, beauty, and abundance where life, beauty, and abundance currently does not exist.

"Soon we will discover this within our Galaxy and within our previously introduced zones. Within Zone-12, I am grateful for the indelible support of our crews, who among us, we have our very beautiful lead HBCI, Star Taylor, and the breathtakingly gorgeous spacecraft, Tucana. With our crews we will do more than simply visit our constellation regions. We will observe, investigate, bring life where there is none, and seek diplomatic means for legally immigrating to sentient civilizations on planets throughout the regions of Octans, Pavo, Piscis Austrinus, Sagittarius, Scutum, Telescopium, and Tucana. All our regions are within Southern Quadrant 4, relative to Earth, and for reference they are calculable based on Epoch J2000.0. Our regions are between two-hundred-seventy- and ninety-degrees Galactic Longitude, toward the center of our Galaxy, and below it toward the south of our Galactic Disc.

"Octans gives us the vantage point of looking through the southern portion of the Orion Spur, from the Interstellar Cloud in which we dwell. Using legacy systems, not a whole lot is understood about that region, but we will, in short, learn more. Perhaps there is much we can learn on our journey with the Presidential Command Spacecraft throughout the eighty-eight constellation regions within the Milky Way and as we set up the extra-galactic observation posts beyond our Galactic Halo.

"Pavo is seen as we look between the Orion Spur and the Sagittarius Arm, through one of the southern Regions of our Galactic Disc. This gives us the advantage of seeing a variety of galaxies, including NGC-6744, which is a twin-like intermediate spiral galaxy like ours. Because of its unique yet shared nature, this galaxy, about thirty-one-million light-years away, is where we will set up our Zone-12 Headquarters. We will also primarily observe, explore, colonize, and seek to preserve the life-giving capacity of the following galaxies..."

As he spoke, each galaxy came into view behind him with exquisite clarity and information that was well placed and visually stunning.

"We will visit and observe IC-4687, IC-4686, and IC-4689, which are triplet interacting and merging galaxies, about two-hundred-fifty-million light-years away, NGC 6782, which is a barred spiral galaxy, about one-hundred-eighty-three-million light-years away, and NGC 6872, which is one of the largest known barred spiral galaxies, estimated at three-hundred-eighty-thousand light-years wide. We will also observe and visit IC-4970, which is an elliptical galaxy currently interacting with NGC-6872, approximately two-hundred-twenty-million light-years away. I presume that given time, despite its size, NGC-6872 will become absorbed by IC-4970 due to the size of their galactic cores. We will endeavor to preserve life there, but we may not interfere if there is no life detected in either galaxy. This will give us a more profound understanding of galactic physics and biology. That said, we will endeavor to preserve both life and the ability for life to exist within those two regions.

"Piscis Austrinus lies to the southwest of the center of our Galaxy, giving us a view between the Orion Spur and Sagittarius Arm areas prior to the point at which they intersect along the southern face of the Galactic Disc. NGC-7176 and NGC-7173 are two elliptical galaxies currently merging with the spiral galaxy, NGC-7174. The three galaxies are a part of the Hickson Compact Group 90, or HCG-90, Trio, between one-hundred million to one-hundred-fourteen-point-eight-million light-years away. NGC-7172 is a spiral galaxy about one-hundred-twenty-million light-years away. NGC-7314 is a spiral galaxy with activities that are very peculiar and have won the categorization of a Seyfert Active Galaxy, about sixty-five-million light-years away. Each of these locations, which lie well beyond our own Galaxy, will be observed, explored, and more.

"Sagittarius, beyond the Zone of Avoidance, is an area that by using our legacy systems were not at the time viewable. That said, there is plenty of intriguing data to consider for integration into our Galactic and Intergalactic Databases that will give us a fuller picture of that region of space. The Sagittarius Region happens to give our gaze a sense of where the center of our Galaxy is located. We are currently about twenty-five-thousand light-years from our barred spiral galactic core and approaching the apogalacticon, within one or two million years out of two-hundred-fifty million required for a complete orbit. This is the point at which we will be closest to our barred Galactic Core.

"What you see behind me, or in your neural displays, is Sagittarius A, which is our Galactic center. This legacy information indicates that our own Galaxy has three major spiral arms, however, many other sources point to two initial arms, Norma and Scutum, splitting into four, Perseus and Cygnus from Norma, and Scutum-Crux and Sagittarius from Scutum, and then regions with spurs connecting these arms in a random yet flowing manner. Through an examination of the various Regions, there are models that suggest several ideas, yet we will infer that we are in a spur, the Orion Spur, emanating from the Sagittarius Arm, which begins and emanates from the main arm about seven-twelfths of a revolution around the major arm's trip around the Galactic Bulge to the point at which our tight Galactic Spiral Arms have made about ten-twelfths of a revolution around and out toward the galactic anticentre connecting to the Perseus Arm. The actual center of our Galaxy is located about twenty-six-thousand light-years away, while we're closer to one of the edges of our Galactic Bar by about one-thousand light-years in our Solar System's revolution around the center of the Galaxy.

"Looking just to the south of the center of our Galaxy, you will see the Sagittarius Dwarf Irregular Galaxy or Sag DIG. As noted, this is a dwarf galaxy, yet based on our legacy statistics and calculations, this galaxy, while rich in stars, nebula, and globular clusters, is poor in terms of metal-density. We all know, however, with our abilities of cold fusion and our abilities to manipulate non-baryonic matter that we can essentially breathe life into every star and planet there, but we will observe first, nonetheless. Keep in mind, that there are possibilities that there are worlds and living beings quite alive that cannot interact with us or what we know to exist in this physical reality, made of types of matter that we are barely beginning to understand. Thus, all that we can conceive of, we will look for, be wary of, and consider their well-being as well.

"Sag DIG lies about three-point-three-nine-million light-years away, yet it is in the process of being absorbed by the Milky Way. Part of its orbital path, over millions of years, goes right through the outer regions of our spiral arms. Due to the limitations on the speed of baryonic matter, which both galaxies are affected by, there is plenty of time for us to observe, explore, and more while attempting to find and preserve life.

"The Scutum Constellation Region lies just northwest of the Galactic Disc, giving us further examples of globular clusters, nebula, and star rich environments, all associated with the Galactic Bulge. However, the Scutum-Crux Arm of our Galaxy, which splinters off from the Norma Arm and begins on the side of the Galactic Bar closest to us, lies between Sagittarius and our Galactic Core. As we journey, jump, setup observation posts, etc., we'll populate our Legacy Databases as well as our Zone-12 Matrix in the Virtual Universe.

"Telescopium lies just south of the Galactic center, and as such gives us a partial view of the Galactic Bulge, the space between the Sagittarius Arm and the Orion Spur, toward an open area of our Galaxy, with a view of several other galaxies using legacy equipment. NGC-6850 is a beautiful spiral galaxy we will visit, about one-hundred-ninety-nine-million light-years away. NGC-6861, a lenticular galaxy that shows signs of interaction with NGC-6868 and may well have or will merge soon and is about one-hundred-twenty-million light-years away. Indeed, we plan to work our 'magic' if possible, there. We will also visit NGC-6868, a giant elliptical galaxy about one-hundred-three-million light-years away.

"Tucana is quite a splendid view westerly, down, and through the Orion Spur, toward the southern Galactic Plane and beyond. This Region gives us an advantageous view of the Small Magellanic Cloud, which lies about two-hundred-thousand light-years away and is considered a satellite to our galaxy. Within this satellite galaxy, there are several globular star clusters with approximately three-hundred-forty-six star-forming regions, equating to about one hundred million stars. It stands to reason that we will setup observation posts around this galaxy, explore it, and potentially colonize it.

"Two more galaxies within this Region are something else as well. The beautifully compact NGC-406 spiral galaxy is very much like our own, but quite possibly unbarred. It is about sixty-thousand light-years in diameter and lies about sixty-five-million light-years away. Finally, the Tucana Dwarf Galaxy is a unique one, in that it is almost like a cloud of stars, very old ones. It is considered a dwarf spheroidal galaxy and lies about three-point-two-million light-years from us, making it part of our Local Group.

"As you can tell, there are a few wonderful locations that we will begin with. Of course, we will navigate with every single one of the previous zonal commands, until they are ready and set up for autonomous and decentralized zonal capacities to sustain life and carry out their priorities as relating to the Principles of Universal Ethics. In every mission, no matter what we think we know now, as my immediate commander, General Anastasia Renae, pointed out, we are merely in about the third grade when it comes to the knowledge we have yet to gain. There will always be a beautiful challenge, a new concept, and a new way that will charge us up and give us the drive we need to continue on with purpose, drive, and clarity of mind as we go about networking and connecting the various regions of our Universe in a manner that will slow down the expansion enough in order to essentially cause it to expand and contract and repeat, in such a way, so as to make life sustainable, indefinitely. Thank you, all!"

As Evan returned to his seat in the front row, next to Anastasia, the crowds around Sol cheered loud enough that the entire Solar System resonated with the sounds of many crowds.

Chapter 30: Diving into Our Galaxy

Database Moon Archive, Celestial-Sol Date: 2029 February 6. President of the United Allied States (UAS), Eliza A. Williams summarizes the very first missions of the UAS Command Spacecraft and the IMC Zonal Command Spacecraft journeys. These memories are a collaboration of UAS and IMC Leadership, briefed to Pathway, recorded within the Virtual Universe, interfaced within the Pathway Melrose Campus. Input by Joanne Gallant, President of Pathway, 2029-2032.

Every brief had been informative and visually captivating in every way. It was now understood that "dry facts" could in-fact be exciting. President Eliza Williams stood up, closed the convention, and then said, "We have every reason to go out beyond our Solar System for the first time as a shared civilization of the living, from Sol. It is time to travel in an exponential manner, observing, exploring, setting up centers for life and further development, and gaining even further understanding as we preserve life, setup diplomatic communication channels, integrate and share our goals of preserving our Universe, and then go beyond and further than before. Nothing that has been done would have gone far had it not been for the efforts, both individual and shared, of each single one of you listening, reading, or simply feeling this message. Each of you has so much to offer, so much potential burning with you, and no matter where we go as a civilization from Sol, we will be bringers of love, of kindness, of gentleness, and the promise of preservation of life, quality of life, and clarity of mind, but we also will have resolve and might!

"Let's make this happen! But first, let us spend one last night here in the Solar System, at home on Earth, or wherever you wish until 0600 hours tomorrow morning, where I request that all leaders, commanders, and crewmembers from each of the Intergalactic Mission Contingency Space Command Space Craft be prompt, professional, and ready. Thank you, everyone in Sol, and thank you all!"

After the meeting on board the Presidential Space Craft ended, Eliza went through her portal and returned directly to her estate. She prepared the typical spread outside by the pond with the statue of an angel, with water flowing through her cupped hands giving nutritious water in its cyclical form to the coy fish and frogs, and then linked with Yesha, James, Vesha, Sky, Amber, Erin, Najem, and Joanne.

"Let's meet at our old gathering place one last time for a while, to soak it in, look up at the stars and sing some favorite tunes. What do you say?" They all knew where that was and together, they took turns jumping.

As they gazed up at the stars, they shared stories, sang songs, peered deep into the various galaxies within their field of view, and slept.

It was 0600 hours the next morning, the crewmembers had said their goodbyes to those who would not be coming along on the journey, at least this time, and reminded each other that they could link at any time from across the Universe or visit within the Virtual Universe during free time after work hours. All of humanity, humanity's new friends, and collaborative minds were excited. They were also fresh, clean, dressed to impress, professional, and in good spirits.

The first location to jump to with all twenty-eight Commanders and Vice Commanders was a location within the Andromeda Region, of Zone-01, but within the Milky Way. President Eliza Williams, in the moments leading up to their first jump, made sure that a tune by Dennis Sheperd, with vocals by Sarah Lynn, called "Dive (Radio Edit)," played in the background. Although this tune referred to diving into a sea of adventure, they translated that as diving into the adventure of open space.

As Lt General Bauer, the Vice Commander, currently on board the Zone-12, IMC-Tucana, had suggested, Eliza had agreed that her spacecraft and the IMC would travel together throughout the Milky Way and after those missions, they would set up the shared regional observation posts. Her spacecraft would take the lead, until Vesha was handed the reigns following their initial pursuits within the Milky Way. In this case, Eliza was within IMC-Morgan, and ready to take the dive or the first jump into the unknown. She braced to give the order, and then she did.

"Morgan, please set coordinates to 120 degrees, right ascension 00h 08m 23.25988s, and declination +29° 05' 25.5520", ninety-six light-years, Epoque J2000. Ready all," she heard all the commanders ping her neural link that they were ready, and an instant later, once everyone had declared they were ready, she, with an intense sense of emotion, filled with vigor and a moving of all the thoughts of everything they had done to arrive to this point, yelled, "Jump!"

What might not be readily understood, is the fact that Eliza wanted to view the chemical composition of the brighter of the two stars within the Alpha Andromedae binary system. She knew this to be unusual because it had been identified as a mercury-manganese star with an atmosphere that contained unusually high levels of mercury, manganese, and other elements, to include gallium and xenon. While she was good with cold-fusion, she was excellent in finding materials in grand quantities that would vastly augment all fourteen spacecraft, while allowing them to see light that was two-hundred times the velocity of our own Sun, but at about a light year away. Not to mention, that although it was within the Milky Way, it was part of the Andromeda asterism, within the constellation of the same name. She figured she would do Vesha, Jasmine, and Najem proud. The rest of the crew had grown fond of this region of space as well. While there, they took a moment, breathed in, looked away from the two suns, and then fired up the F-drive, to navigate away, for a few moments. They were huge, and the planets that the IMC-Morgan and HBCI Sky Taylor detected revolving around them were beautiful!

Everyone there was in awe, and upon arrival, she let another tune play out, from Amethystium. What was playing was the song, titled "Outro," from the Aurorae EP. She played it out on all Command Spacecraft, because it truly captured the moment then and there as they arrived, looked around, and journeyed forward. For hours, everyone in the crew looked at nearby aurorae, globular clusters, and strange objects up close, and with awe. In many cases, after taking time following those first eight hours of work, the crews took time to take it on in, before returning to their domiciles in their various command spacecraft, and checking out the beaches on board, the taverns, the sports stadiums, and more.

Solitude and Ideas

She'd followed her all throughout Eliza's life and through to this present day. Her own life rang inside her mind accompanied with crystal clear clarity, but something about Eliza had caught her attention from day one. When Eliza had opened her sapphire-like blue eyes, looked toward her, and smiled at her for the very first time it had been two minutes after breathing in her first breath, the one that gave her life. That had been one of her first memories, Eliza had told her much later on, and often, that she had no recollection of any previous events. "I was a mass grouping of DNA, cells, proteins, and an increasing carbon and calcium scaffolding arranging themselves according to their received orders and the new synapses began firing up checking out my growing genetic modality and environmental pre-conditioning, pre-encoding, and neuronal responses, as this miracle of life prepared my journey through this existence given my physiology, neurology, and the visceral reality of my environment.

"I came to be, following that first breath. Before that, I was nurtured into existence."

During that Lamborghini drive as Eliza's chauffeur and Vice President, and in every way that mattered, she realized that she had been the one along for the ride of life, herself, and her dearest and best friend had taken the reigns with her two-minute-old smile so many years ago. The ride had been phenomenally amazing and, on a level, that no one else could have ever conceived of and brought to reality like she had. Eliza had told her that one day she would step down and hand the reigns over to her, once a vision was realized, and now it was being realized, and in such a spectacular way. But she didn't see herself as the only leader. She saw the unique leader within everyone she had ever met, and she was proud, yet humble, wise, and kind.

Yesha's mother, Yesenia, had stepped out of their IMC-Morgan, Sector 2 home to take a walk through the central spacecraft woods, not too far from the beach, and she had taken some moments to herself to contemplate the fact that she was no longer the Senator of Massachusetts, she was here to provide moral support on the IMC-Morgan. She would figure out where she would fit in soon, but she needed some personal time.

It was day one of the big journey, Eliza's first eight hours as the Presidential Spacecraft presiding authority, and it had been phenomenally productive and successful. Yesenia thought about it all, and the numerous strings of successes were all because of Yesha's best and dearest friend and her ability to carry out work in a very rational, intuitive, and exponential manner. After countless breath-taking stops and the establishment of thousands of observation posts later, eight Earthly hours had gone by, and several million volunteers, including UAS envoys, had found deployment on these posts to be spectacular in every way.

Yesha had finally grasped the reality that Eliza intended to have the entire Milky Way, itself, capable of spacecraft-like navigation, stronger, more capable of preserving life than any known galaxy, and connected and linked from anywhere within it, and within in the Universe and then she would one-by-one do the same, or at least see through to the attainment of these goals, throughout the rest of the galaxies in the known Universe and beyond. "There's no reason to let destruction reign when we've been given the opportunity to bring life, beauty, and abundance, all while preserving life and the freedoms that come with it. We've been given the capacity to think it, we must claim the capacity to do it, and then make it happen."

Eliza had been preparing Yesha all her life, at least since she was three, for the clarity of mind required and existent in moments such as these. "We've set in stone two four-year terms and no more than that. I'd think that it might be fair, but I am open to suggestion. Until a better solution arises, you'll need to follow in my stead in 2032, if that is your wish, to keep the momentum going. My administration has been dedicated to the expansion of sentient civilization, preservation of life, and reigning control over chaos to prevent destruction and annihilation, and to energize more momentum and beauty.

"The next step will be to give the Universe the breath of life, to expand and contract ever-so-gently to preserve everything we have done, provide energy, provide unlimited and self-sustaining resources, provide life, provide intelligence, experience, and wisdom, and following which we will reach even farther, to merge with many other amazing beings throughout the multiverse. As time goes by, I'll be there, always, if you ever need support. Keep in mind, no matter our optimizations, there will continuously exist both malicious and benevolent tendencies, the trick is to control or abate the malicious ones through healthy cognitive frame-working, in every way necessary and sensible."

Yesha pondered on her friend's words often. After finding life-giving regions in one globular cluster of stars after another, as well as within the many nebulae and many other regions throughout the galaxy that day, while preserving these system structures as well as identifying debris that was lifeless and ready for recycling, they realized that of all the baryonic and non-baryonic material, only a trillionth of one percent of the situations, regions, and locations actually provided an environment cogent for life and stable enough for sentience to develop, naturally. If life existed, and Sol had a say, it was protected or made to adapt to the changes that would, in turn, be made to maximize the life-giving potential and the quality of life of all affected, so as to nurture a sense of awareness that was compatible to sophistication and love. It was always such a very careful balance. Currently, Eliza was exemplifying everything she taught, and in 2033 it would be Yesha's turn, following the elections of 2032. However, Eliza wanted to start preparing now, while she went about the work.

"In three years, you would prefer I win the candidacy as US President, Eliza? What makes you think I have the virtues and qualities to lead as well as you have?" Yesha was thinking merely to herself, but she knew there was a chance that Eliza could be listening, even if she was currently with James surfing on the Presidential Command Spacecraft's mock surfing beach. With the first day done, excitement truly filled the air, throughout the entire IMC. On board her spacecraft, Morgan, the spacecraft AI had taken over duties to usher in safety and security to everyone and everything on-board, for sixteen hours, in peace and in entertainment mode. It was known that Morgan's favorite person was Joanne, but everyone else came in at a close second, and every time Yesha interacted with him, he made her think deeply and feel appreciated as well.

"You are exceedingly brilliant, Yesha. Coming from the standpoint of a spacecraft and all that I see and hear, you are indeed built of the stuff that Eliza is looking for. Don't worry so much, Yesha. Take everything moment by moment, day to day, and let things flow. If it helps, feel free to talk to Joanne or ask her to sing you a song. She has an intriguing wisdom about her that many, including herself, take for granted all-too-often. I latched on to her persona right away, because she is melancholy, pensive, willing to share, and gracious to the core. You two are very much the same." Morgan was probably the most genuine she could imagine an AI as being, and he somehow had a profound ability to give someone a boost whenever they needed it.

"Joanne?" Yesha took a little time to ponder and linked with her trying Morgan's recommendation out for size.

"Yes? Good to hear from you, Yesha. What's cookin'?"

"Not a lot. I wanted to see if you'd like to go for a cup of Jo. I hear Bobby is on-board in Sector 5, visiting, and running a coffee competition. Although, I just wanted to spend time with you and chat a bit."

"That works for me. Where do you want to meet?"

"How about your place and then we can walk from there to Sector 5's Coffee Tavern?"

"Fair enough. Come on over."

Yesha made sure she had a nice, stylish, physique-complementing and provocative casual ensemble for plans to maybe meet some of the gentlemen with Joanne later, and when she was ready, she used her neural identification, coordinated with Morgan, and teleported to Joanne's living room. Arriving, she politely called out, "Hello?"

She paused, waiting for Joanne's response.

"Come on in, Yesha. I'm working on some of the final touches of two ideas to present to you and Eliza, tomorrow. What do you think?"

Yesha walked into Joanne's room and despite being bare of any clothes at all, she had been working on the final stages of her presentation. "Have you ever heard of Hanny's Voorwerp? That's a Dutch word for 'object.' Basically, an astrophysicist by the name of Hanny discovered that as we navigate below a Galaxy, after having flown through it, the black hole at the center of it will ionize us immediately, turning us into material necessary for star formation, at least as soon as mass and gravity have kicked in. Well, while I like black holes, I don't intend for any of us to become vaporized, ionized, or anything of the sort, so, check this out." Joanne got up, and as she did, Yesha saw Joanne's ensemble for going out materialize, like hers. These new smartsuits were riveting and splendid. A person could change with a neural command into anything they wanted. Joanne had obviously taken queues from Yesha and had decided on a provocative yet professional seeming negligee as well.

After complimenting her on her attire, she looked at what Joanne had made room for her to review on the legacy computer screen. When she processed what Joanne had said, she was blown away. Humanity could have been vaporized had it not been for Joanne's tireless labors, and the results on the display were profoundly spectacular.

"Oh, wow, Joanne! This is outstanding! Have you shown this to Eliza yet? To anyone?"

"Nope. You're the first."

What Yesha saw were full-scope plans for immediate integration into every UAS IMC spacecraft with the ability to set them up to ionically fly through objects, other spacecraft, things, and other living beings without losing any data or causing a disturbance to the molecular makeup of any passengers in any way, all while going at immeasurable speeds. There were also plans for an upgrade that would allow spacecraft AI to detect built up charges heading their way within a radius of more than fifty million light-years, in microseconds, and either absorb them for more energy reserves or deflect them to millions of different targeted locations that would result in no harm to life. Furthermore, these deflections could be programmed using time-dilation within the Virtual Universe to build tech cities and environments that were fully sustainable and ready for colonization, with all the fixings and trimmings, and within just a few moments. Cities and their jump gate terminals would then immediately register within every database and allow for precise coordination of pioneers and colonists to arrive and enjoy the new scenery and ambiance.

"Wow, Joanne! This is brilliant! This is mind-blowingly awesome! I'm extremely impressed with you. Considering the possibilities for being vaporized by Hanny's Voorwerp, I'm glad Vesha and the other IMC commanders didn't mind staying with us before leaving the galaxy after all! Quick, do you want to see if Eliza is available, so we can let her know about this and get these systems installed?"

"Sure." They checked, but Eliza was clearly unlinked. She was with James at the beach, located on this spacecraft, the presidential one.

Yesha and Joanne were going to go for a walk to the beach anyway in a little while, so they started heading in that general direction. Just then Yesha heard Bobby call them up with his link, *"Thank goodness I was able to reach you! Stafford, Jeremiah, and Christian are with me at Tavern 5, and you need to get here. They are having their little competition, you'll love it!"*

Joanne and Yesha agreed to hit up the coffee house there, before heading off to the beach. "I am so glad the beaches are clothing optional, and that people finally appreciate the beauty of our bodies!" Joanne said and had really become comfortable in her skin over the years, often voicing her ideas along those lines to her friends, Eliza and Yesha.

It just so happened that since Eliza and Yesha were the President and Vice President of all of humanity, nudity no longer was considered lewd or distasteful, instead it was embraced as a form of innocence and the appreciation of beauty surrounding the right-brain art and how it played out with a magnificent display. With the Principles of Universal Ethics in play, smartsuits were designed with consent in mind.

In this way, a person would only see what they wished to see another person wearing based on what the individual being seen had consented to. In many cases, unless someone was going to work, to a play, or to participate during some sports activities, or a restaurant, clothing was optional, and even then, if the individual was comfortable clothing was optional no matter the occasion.

With this new form of freedom available to many, people didn't mind, morale was high, and there were no complaints. Yesha hadn't seen her in the form she had been in, when she arrived at Joanne's domicile, before, but she had clearly sensed an air of liberty about her, and she, like Yesha, was exquisite in every way.

Yesha thought about their attire and continued, "You are beautiful in every way, Joanne. Has anyone ever told you that?"

"I thank you and Eliza for that. I also thank Sky and Yesha for opening my mind." Joanne smiled. She had found it rather freeing to be an exhibitionist, with her beautiful pink, purple, black, blue, and varying shades of high-and-lowlights throughout her stylish hair, her left-sided body tattoo-like mural, and mandala patterns, all expressing and sharing her desirably non-compartmentalized mental artistry like a movie through her extraordinary frame.

"Why cover up all this beauty?" Joanne doffed the negligee in exchange for a permissive form of "au natural" and enjoyed feeling the spacecraft breeze as it blew all over her person and testing gravity as she jumped up and down. "This is what it's all about!"

"Well, I agree with you whole-heartedly. I can't see why you or anyone would want to hide all that amazing artistry," Yesha felt a sense of freedom as well, swallowed, shut her eyes, and then like that she followed suit or minus suit.

Together they walked down the path between Sectors 3 and 4 without any clothes on at all and talked about philosophy, history, politics, and the newfound rush of walking "free."

Yesha caught Joanne enjoying her unique artistry as well, out of the corner of her eye, and smiled. "You're right, Joanne. This is the best I've felt in years!" Several families walked by as they were heading out for a family jaunt to the entertainment centers, the social halls, the beach, and the sports arenas, and they all smiled, waved, and seemed to understand the complexity of the situation without even so much as a sneer, jab, or a pun. They knew Yesha was the UAS Vice President and were impressed with her artistry, its intricacies, and the innocence that it all suggested.

One mother could be heard by both Joanne and Yesha telling her son and daughter, "One day once you're all grown up, you'll be able to walk freely like that. Aren't they beautiful?"

Before walking into the Coffee Tavern, they donned exquisite and sheer bikinis, to follow one of Joanne's personal rules, which she abided by, but would never push on anyone else. It was all about consent in that regard. As long as no one would cause anyone else to lose a body part or become mentally deranged to the point of making others lose body parts, or murder or put something into someone else without their permission, it was quite alright. Things had changed, and the mind-sets of the masses had healed. No longer was nudity a sin. It never was. People governed themselves and abided by what many called "The Golden Rule."

Bobby was wearing his favorite full-on space-age-chef ensemble, minus the hat since he never was big into hats in the first place. Besides, his hair had been back and had grown to its pristine state and maintained itself for more than nineteen years, ever since he was optimized. Bobby enjoyed showing off his clean-cut style. As it was now, health codes were such that Bobby nor anyone else who was optimized had to wear hats anymore, because they no longer had to worry about their hair shedding.

"How is it going, Bobby?"

"I can't complain." He pointed in the direction of Stafford, Jeremiah, and Christian. "They came to visit, and it seems they've studied up quite well on coffee, coffee recipes, and the special effects one can imbue them with. I've got it down to a level that is very personal, so I am anxious to see if they can too. I'd rather they did, so if they're ever stranded out in the deep regions of space, they can raise the morale of everyone onboard their spacecraft too. We will hang together on time off, if the jump gate terminals allow, however. Erin's over there with them, she's doing well herself. Sheer excellence on the account of both of you, Yesha and Joanne! You both are as dazzling as always, but somehow you always find a way to dazzle even more. Feel free to hang out with Erin and our three friends. I'll go ahead and fix you each a lovely cup of Jo."

Erin was indeed mesmerizing, her femininity was in full bloom, and she looked toward the men, and they too were beautifully handsome in every possible way. Stafford, with his closely cropped dark red hair, and dressed in what looked like a black and netted version of a business tycoon's ensemble, Jeremiah's dark complexion with his fluorescent tattoos all up and down his left side wearing knee-length sheer shorts, and Christian, the guy who made pretty much every girl in every establishment want to raise a family with him on some distant moon, planet, or post, wearing his sheer dark bikini shorts, were all sitting with Erin, who was also wearing a sheer bikini with colors that complemented her irises and her exquisite hair, and body artistry.

"Hey boys, how's it going? What's up? Who's winning?" asked Joanne.

"Well, well, well, look at you two. You are both a sight for sore eyes. We're all tied up, not literally of course, with our coffee competition, talking about the various chemicals infused with both baryonic and non-baryonic ingredients that give the best of effects. What brings you here?" asked Christian. Smiling, simply being cheeky, funny, and somewhat flirty, but in a friendly way.

"We just wanted to take a breather, take our minds off our work for a while, and catch up with a few friends. Funny, about the sight for sore eyes, I was about to say that about you three," said Joanne. Yesha nodded smiled in agreement, and quite possibly sent a private flirt to Jeremiah.

Joanne had been in the music industry for a couple of decades now, and with that, she had gained a lot more unabashed confidence, like the kind of confidence Christian seemed to have. She knew that he would eventually be gone and lost in Zone-10, plus it was known that he and Scarlett Hart were building quite a relationship for the stars, so she kept everything playfully flirtatious as a form of genuine reciprocation, but in a way that showed a contagious form of respect.

Everyone, there was having fun. Plus, Bobby was busy, looked a little far away at times, and Joanne was starting to enjoy having him around more and more. Since he was always busy doing what he did best, he very rarely took time for himself.

Bobby scanned their minds, scanned their DNA, and in the most innocent and cool of ways sniffed the molecules of their genes floating in the air as though he was simply breathing in deeply, but in a non-crazy manner, and then put together the best coffees in the world, or in the Universe for that matter, for every single one of his guests. He was unique, and he knew it.

He enjoyed Joanne's company in an exceptional way that he could not describe. There was something about her, this verve, this tenacity, this sensuality that he could not put his thumb on, but whatever it was, he loved that about her. He wanted to make every moment when she was around special. She, Yesha, many others, and Eliza had done so much for humanity and the Universe already, he couldn't help but feel that above anyone or anything else, these two needed the utmost of protection and care to continue on with this beautiful vision of theirs, and Joanne shared that special and unique quality as well. Life was good, he knew it, and he didn't want that to ever change. *"Why create stress when and where it is unnecessary?"* Bobby would often ask himself.

Precious, by Depeche Mode, played throughout this temporary coffee house of his, on the Presidential Spacecraft, which would only be his while they were flying together as a contingency.

During worktime, Bobby would work as Vice Commander on-board the IMC 5, with Melissa Anderson, but once it was after-hours, the owner here, on-board the PCS would let him run his Sector 5 Coffee Tavern in his own way, until morning, so long as he cleaned up afterward. This was quite simple; a person, and in this case, Bobby, could mind-sweep and interface with the spacecraft nanos and like that the place was spotless, back as the owner preferred, and in better condition, than he had found it.

Each evening when he arrived at the Presidential Command Spacecraft, all throughout training, planning, and prior to the missions, he had made the Sector 5 Coffee Tavern like a nightclub, with beautiful lights around, decoration that captured the identified holiday seasons, and flowers near all the plush and high-tech seating arrangements. He had his favorite tunes from Depeche Mode, Erasure, the Human League, Pet Shop Boys, Orchestral Manoeuvres in the Dark, or OMD, New Order, The Other Two and You, Red Flag, Information Society, Cause & Effect, Duran-Duran, and many others, to include interwoven tunes from various groups such as Enigma, Delerium, Jens Gad, Paul Schwartz, Balligomingo, Sleepthief, Amethystium, Schiller, Magna Canta, Carbon-Based Lifeforms, and Dreamstate Logic, as well as World and Space Ambient music, along with several favorite female vocal trance artists with DJ-interpretations playing in the background.

He wasn't a DJ, but he had hired a couple of his favorites, to include Frank Fdieu, who was a close friend on-board IMC 5, as well as Sarah Lynn, Laura Aquí, Phildel, Kirsty Hawkshaw, Ana Criado, Kate Louis Smith, Cathy Burton, Sarah Russel, Susana, Christina Novelli, Katty Heath, Paulina Dubaj, Raz Nitzan, Kaimo K, Dennis Sheperd, Beat Service, Aurosonic, 4 Strings, Re-locate, Yuri Kane, Radion-6, Stone Face and Terminal, Armin Vann Burren, Above & Beyond, and Cosmic Gate to mix things up. Every night had lightshows, music, and holographic imagery, developed by Presidential Spacecraft ambiance engineer, David Gahan, with his close friend, Martin Gore. David had worked closely with Joanne on a couple of shared albums, some with duets, and had loved his journeys through space, and had met Bobby, and instantly hit it off as a best friend and near sibling.

With all that was going on, the Sector 5 Coffee Tavern was filled with delightful conversations. The crews seemed to get to know each other quite well. Furthermore, everyone who enjoyed this sort of merriment tended to be the eclectic and forward-thinking crowd that Bobby had always been fond of anyway. Everyone else seemed rather drab. They were flying through space after all, and this was the perfect music for it.

He looked around the crowd in this tavern that had an upper and lower floor and noticed as Eliza Williams and James Cooper came in. He pointed them to Yesha, Erin, and Joanne. Together they sat, as the table expanded. Before they knew it, every single one of the IMC leaders was sitting at their table, catching up, and going on about this and that, the first day. Finally, once everyone was served, Bobby went to the table, and Yesha and Joanne let him sit between them. "How is it going? This place is bustling quite well tonight."

Yesha smiled at Bobby, she rather enjoyed his charm, his style, and the fact that he was playing some of her favorite tunes in the background. It was as if he'd made an old-fashioned tape just for her. "I couldn't ask for a better cup of coffee. Come on, you're not technically on the job right now, stay for a while. How is the competition coming along?"

"Oh, it's a work in progress, but they are as phenomenal with coffee as they are as chefs" smiled Bobby. "I do believe I've served the whole of the IMC and the PCS. We have quite a wonderful crowd here. I cannot complain at all."

Bobby looked around. He was always used to being up and at it. But he was sitting there beside two of his favorite people, Yesha and Joanne.

"The beach was full of the best waves, Joanne, you'll have to check it out with us when we're done here," whispered Eliza, over the noise of the crowd. "You're the Environmental Science Officer, and you have outdone yourself. Oh, I love this music!" Depeche Mode's "Halo" was playing in the background, the Hyperspeed Remix, and its space-age video playing with it in holograph form above and around them.

"Thank you, Bobby! You and me, we must be kindred spirits!" Eliza wasn't whispering anymore. She and her spirits were flying through space, with Morgan AI safely at the controls, all systems were in order, they had built literally millions of tech cities on several million planets distributed quite well throughout galactic space, and all in the space of eight hours. This was the life. IMC-Morgan enjoyed it too, while gazing upon the most beautiful view of all, open space, for as far as he could detect and zero in on, to help build travel plans and terraforming plans in a very meticulous manner the following morning, beginning at 0600, with Eliza.

As Halo drifted to "If You Want," also by Depeche Mode, Eliza looked at everyone at her table, and she saw and communicated with all thirty-six of them. *"Come with me, let's head to the beach, then watch a game in the arenas down below, hit up a play, and we can have Bobby's music playing in the background wherever we are.*

"Come, Bobby! Please!" Bobby snapped his fingers, and the auto-cleaning began. They were quite a big table, but they all wanted to come with Eliza, as did Bobby. She was exciting, fun, cool, and the leader of this the new Golden Space Age.

Work would be had in the morning, they had done so much today, and they would do even more and better tomorrow if they had a little fun now, slept well for a couple of Virtual Universe hours, which would also allow them to process everything within their minds, share more moments with each other, and relax. For now, it was time for fun!

A Time to Celebrate

Two minutes was a pretty long period of time within the Virtual Universe, especially if one were to factor in or compound the exponential result of fourteen full-on crews working together to achieve success. Within the space of eight hours, the entire Milky Way had been visited, observation posts, exploration stations, colonization tech cities, and so much more had been set up. Every hour, for four hours, twenty-two constellation regions had been fully squared away, volunteers from Sol were already requested, and now everyone was on a break.

Joanne still had something to share with Eliza, her idea that would increase the output and speed with which Sol-based civilization could comb the Cosmos and preserve the life of the Universe itself was still well-within her desire to share. Her ideas regarding Hanny's Voorwerp were as plain as day in her mind, and she knew it would soon be time to exit the Milky Way. Still, in every region, every sector, and every zone, there were stories galore to share. Those stories would be told later. For now, it was time for a break on the beach with some tunes, some watermelon, a warm beach fire, some of México's finest Tequila, and some amazing company.

She scanned the crowd and saw Vesha Celeste, the leader of the Intergalactic Mission Contingency, and then picked up as Vesha smiled.

As they were heading there, Vesha Celeste opened everyone's neural link and said, *"Allow me to be sentimental. This day has been exhilarating!*

"I love you, my friends, no matter where you are from, your identity, or creed, and all of whom are artistic, brilliant, creative, competitive, scientific, sports-minded, innovative, and kind. Many are correct to understand that there are aspects of our history we can be proud of, yet, in some cases, there are aspects we are merely born into and subjected to. No matter, there is always one thing that will always be valuable about any nation or sovereign state we are from, and that is each one of us and our untold potential to lift the spirits of those around us through kindness, dignity, respect, and compassion.

"I love people in general, no matter the perceptions that are thrown around, and in less than constructive ways as well. Just as we found on Earth, as we navigate the Cosmos, we will discover many civilizations, much like our own, and perhaps very different from ours. Within these locations, we'll continue to discover many are victims of their environment, subjects of cruelty, brutality, and even corruption. Let us please, always, remember to avoid generalization or casting a wide and toxic assumption of character on the faceless masses. In every group of people, there are amazing individuals who love, think, care, and recognize unhealthy behavior when they see it, yet they seek to be kind and available emotionally, as needed.

"Throughout this Universe, we're all part of the same team. We need each other to succeed as a universal civilization. We need to do due diligence by recognizing the good in others and by doing our part to cause a positive shift in focus to resolutions to issues met with action while seeking the well-being of each of the individuals involved.

"This may seem random, since so much has been done, and we've had such a wonderful result from all our efforts thus far. I say this, nonetheless, because we have solely explored our own Galaxy, and have many more places to go. Each location, as repeated as it may seem from a distant location, is unique, special, and full of opportunities to fill us with wonder. I love you all, my friends, and you have all demonstrated in so many ways how wonderful you are. Thank you, again, for bringing me back from death, Eliza and Yesha, and each of you who helped, because it is an honor to be a part of such a glorious time in history, the Golden Space Age."

Everyone with her, to include her dream angel, Sky Taylor, and her closest friends, Najem Grace, Jasmine Belle, who would drive the IMC through important locations in Zone-01, Amber Blythe, Erin Carter, Joanne Gallant, and many more had been slowly walking nearby, and they gathered around her, gave her a hug, and each individual thanked her in their own way, for her efforts in this endeavor as well.

Much was done today, with much more than eight-billion people throughout the Solar System, many millions on the millions of outposts created throughout the Galaxy, and one-hundred-sixty-eight-thousand on all fourteen maximum-sized spacecraft, which included the twelve Zonal IMCs, Vesha's Command Spacecraft, and Eliza's Presidential Spacecraft, and all were working together at almost every moment to understand their Universe more fully, so they could span the Cosmos and preserve life, with high quality, joy, freedom, and bounty wherever they went, and shared with whomever they met. Theirs was certainly a colonization of promise, one that would preserve not only each individual life upon consent, but ultimately, the life of the Universe itself.

Science was a big deal, and while they worked hard from 2008, on, when Eliza, Yesha, and James had formed the official Pathway organization, until now, when all of humanity and every living creature was onboard with Eliza's plans, with free will still permeating an ever-evolving reality, much more would be done in the morning, and in the years to come. For now, it was time to enjoy the Universe they knew and loved, so they spent the end of this day together, enjoying small or large celebrations of the bringing of life to and throughout the Milky Way. In their spacecraft, on Earth, throughout the Solar System, the Milky Way, and in places where life previously could not be found. They would meet other civilizations later, but that will be another story.

Appendix

Appendix – Dr. Eliza A. Williams – Preface

Database Moon Archive, Celestial-Sol Date: 2010 April 6. President of Pathway LLC, Dr. Eliza A. Williams writes a foreword to her best-selling science novel, Vice President Yesha Alevtina submits it to the Database Moon Archives. These writings are for people worldwide, as written in Eliza's book, "Pathway to the Stars," recorded within the Virtual Universe, interfaced within the Pathway Melrose Campus. Input by Yesha Alevtina, President of Pathway, 2015-2022.

A journey or much more throughout space and time will most assuredly be needed if we are intent on preserving the life of our own species as well as the lives of those beings that complement our ability to survive. In order to survive for the next few trillion years or even longer as our journeys reveal many more answers and as we maintain and upgrade each advancement, leaving our areas of living even more capable of supporting sentient and harmonious life than ever before as we move forward, it makes sense to diversify the extent of the locations that we and our companions can exist in throughout the stars by having humanity in more than one area of our galaxy and in more than one galaxy itself at any given time to preserve and share our history, our knowledge, our wisdom, and our legacy throughout the Universe.

We as a people just may be able to see amazing developments unfold before our eyes if we do not destroy ourselves first or if nature or the Universe itself does not decide it has lost any purpose in our existence and eliminate us. We are not slaves to the Universe. As a matter of fact, from all the evidence before us it would appear the Universe is abundant with that which brings life and would rather, we live without fear as we overcome the challenges necessary, so we can travel in freedom with the promise of a beautiful legacy that we can create, share, and enjoy.

It is said that "mathematics is the language of the Universe" and in so many ways this is very true. To limit oneself to one or two fields of science, research, or study, or to embrace but a mere few equations as the end-all-be-all of the purpose of life and progression of humanity, however, is to deprive oneself of an amplified understanding of all our Universe has to offer. We will, in fact, deprive ourselves of the bounties of the Universe if we fail to wrangle in uncontrolled chaos, desiccation, and disintegration.

Every equation, every formula, and every model can serve a meaningful purpose and a perspective that confounds many that by opening our minds, our perceptions, and creating a foundation of personal integrity we can solve more issues, and, in more ways, which will lead toward serving the purposes of humanity and the well-being of life itself, because those purposes will indeed be of an ethical and even noble character and we'll have converged our knowledge to bring untold promise. Notwithstanding, we have also come to learn throughout so many periods in history that sooner or later each equation has also had its limitations—don't become a victim of "I can't." It can be said that a balanced approach between what we know, what we will yet learn, and what we dare to dream just may get us there...

Without what we know, the wisdom gained and shared over the centuries, and the miracle of the scientific advancements we have achieved through many all-too-often under-appreciated efforts we'd be hard-pressed to see any journey begin outside of a minimalistic and tribalistic lifestyle. Our ever-increasing scientific understanding of the Universe and all its mechanisms and our asking seemingly far-out questions or even considering the possibilities of what we don't know will greatly assist humanity as we know it, to ensure we can grace the grand stage of the beautiful Cosmos for more than a brief period of existence while preserving knowledge of the dramas, the comedies, the artistic expressions, or the romances shared throughout the many ages.

We know there have been several extinctions throughout Earth's history, but whether they were a result of a natural, godlike, or a sentient-made reset button, who knows? We surely ought to know that we are not the only sentient and innovative hominids to have ever walked this Earth. Given our increasing knowledge of cosmic biology we also know we are certainly not alone in the Universe—perhaps separated, but not alone. One need only to look at the great structures we've only recently begun to discover, which are "prehistoric" throughout the world that could not have been built nor shaped by any simplistic or tribalistic cave-dwelling ancestor, no matter how wondrous their era.

These megaliths required collaboration; they could not have matured to completion without the union of effort, respect for leadership, and possession of intellect which resulted in the durability of such detailed and magnificent findings many millennia later. What happened to these great civilizations? Where did they go? Did they leave our Earth for another planet? Did they err in one way or another through war or were they smitten with famine? Did they simply fail to evolve and fail to adjust to a new environment? Did they become lost in violence, torture, and greed? Did they simply drift into unprotected simplicity? Did they not develop further? Did Nature see through to their extinction for untold reasons? Did the Universe see an eternal end with them? Why don't we have any archived or communicative records of the technologies used?

No matter the reason, the conjecture, or theory, we forget that just like it was for these great civilizations, life and all we know about it from our vantage point in the Universe can be over, snap! Like that! Be it via a large asteroid or any known or unknown phenomena from any of a vast array of unfortunate events—life on this planet can end quickly without any warning if we do nothing to mitigate the effects of natural disaster, aging, or disease. By demonstrating wisdom and resilience we can go on despite the challenges we'll no doubt face along the way.

We're still here, you're reading this, and while we're still here we can work to overcome our own extinction or the desolation of the land, by evolving beyond the scope of mere existence and survival which has resulted in death in every example throughout history. We can do many things more than we are doing right now that can lead to more enriching equations to our survival, with a legacy that is indeed beautiful, unique, filled with learning, and bursting with enjoyable ups and downs like a thrilling roller coaster where we're actually there to enjoy it.

We can learn how our Universe works and enjoy the endless bounty it can provide, beautify our surroundings, and enrich the land and our minds. We can do more than we do now if we but take our natural yearning for challenges and channel our energies, working to overcome the challenges of life and thereby increase the talents and abilities afforded to us by Nature. Nature has gifted us with so much, allowing us to do more than ever before, by increasing our knowledge, using our minds, and doing so many things that lead to achieving our full potential. We can carry out our knowledge into innovations that if done with the right focus, will help to preserve life, rather than end it.

We need to overcome our apparent fixation toward and acceptance of suffering, misery, and death—many argue to the contrary. We need to rise and fight against senescence and death, and if necessary, until our own ends. Doing so will fill our lives with purpose and lead to much more than a dismal and silly existence over the long haul, and for many more in the future. Life will be a greater reward if we carry on with the spirit or thought of enabling the future of humanity for the long-haul.

While realizing that reality is brutal and when it's time, it's time, is okay, accepting the fact that struggles will come no matter our endeavor can be a balanced way to understand our reality. We can also prosper more and advance much further, however, if we can realize that we don't need to operate from a juxtaposition of strife for the sake of strife, complications for the sake of complications, or change for the sake of change alone. If we operate from a foundation of well-being instead and overcome strife while focusing on beating the perceived odds, we may have more promise than we think.

While we are here, we can still work toward overcoming death and find the wondrous advantages of healthy and enriching lives and even indeterminate lifespans. I'm sure I am not the only one who hopes we can be and achieve more throughout added and extra time, rather than become awash in a mediocre and brief existence throughout the history of the Cosmos. Imagine how the intellect and the wisdom could be compounded upon as our prolonged and healthy lives give us many more opportunities to learn and experience so much more!

Everything most assuredly has purpose and even meaning if we dig deep enough, even if it seems the only purpose is to help us carry on to a better day. Enabling the capacity of living long lives, for example, will allow us to travel out for thousands, even millions of years through the Cosmos, and then we will still be able to return to our home planet and visit old friends and family.

With fantastic goals of preserving humanity, before venturing out into space for a long journey, we must consider what can be done about long-term life, the preservation of our own planetary biosphere, and the expansion of the length of the Earth-friendly warmth and life of our very own star—our Sun—the life-source of our bountiful Solar System. As the heavier elements accumulate at its core and threaten the existence of life on Earth, we can find ways of extracting and using them to raise the quality of life here and in other locations where we have made life possible, while ensuring orbital balance, and extension of the life of our Sun.

As difficult as this may seem and as simple the antidote, we can begin small by quite simply being kind. With an attitude of kindness, we will find ourselves taking measures that lead to eliminating disease, toxicity, senescence, and death in a manner that considers both well-being and individual consent. We will then be able to progress into a level of understanding and shared knowledge that will allow us to control weather patterns, prevent wildfires, understand and control volcanic and seismic activity, and perhaps understand how fusion works as it will open even more avenues of progression and quality of life.

We should also consider quick-paced adaptation to whatever environments we find ourselves in as well as the development of a diverse set of space travel options and capabilities. From there we should, ought to, and could consider and develop so much more, to include complex shielding that can absorb, deflect, and direct the necessary components toward our star that give our Sun an indeterminate lifespan—functioning as it does now. By doing so, we could also find ourselves with the capacity of creating protective zones enabling life on each planet and each moon throughout the Solar System.

Ultimately, in order to attain optimum results, we must be willing to help each other out, and that begins with kindness.

As I have previously asserted, one way in which we can start down a promising pathway is to have a healthy focus that is more toward the well-being of others as well as ourselves and less toward accepting misery in life. We must think beyond the assumption that our need for challenges is based solely on malevolent happenings or rely solely on the dismal and litigious complexity of economic advantage and disadvantage.

As we are driven by true ethics, we'll mature and evolve as we simultaneously find that there is plenty for us all and challenge enough to appease our psyche, if we can challenge ourselves instead to overcome what threatens the existence of humanity and life within our Universe.

As we work together in a disciplined manner, we'll find there are so many positive and even abundantly enjoyable ways to sate our neurological needs that lead to longevity and true happiness. Humanity is resilient, and time has proven that repeatedly. However, we can look back and see that no matter what problems we have resolved, there will always be plenty more that will come our way—that we can overcome—plenty of even more intriguing areas to focus our energies.

Wisdom and experience can be gained from a more resolute determination to gain a profound knowledge of the sciences, a renewed respect for another person's personal choices, shared knowledge, and fine-tuned intuitive abilities.

Well-being—when examined more closely, we'll discover is such a big phrase, but it begins with something as simple as resolution to have an attitude of kindness. Kindness includes the idea of caring for others, their quality of life, and their well-being, as well as our own. While we're making astronomical breakthroughs for those who we care about most, we must also consider that there are many among us who still suffer from fates unimaginable, diseases, murderous tyrants, natural disasters, and meager resources that we may never experience or even comprehend.

No matter the issue, there is always a solution, and perhaps there are many solutions we may never be able to conceive of alone, which will work to reduce the misery that many others have experienced and will continue to experience through scientific negligence. In altogether too many cases, those solutions take an entire society to resolve, or in other words, a lot of studies, networking, dedication, and shared knowledge, if we desire to increase the speed in which we resolve those problems. We need to do so, and we need each other, so we can preserve more lives, while embracing and truly appreciating those who are here on this Earth with us now, share the enjoyment of life, and compound upon our collective wisdom—because there will always be so much more to understand.

As we readjust our focus toward kindness, creativity, art, objectivity, science, and even the wonders of life through the joys of new birth or the beauty of longevity, we will then find that we can reach out to attain any among the highest of our lofty dreams.

Throughout life haven't we all heard entirely too often the preposterous justifications by far too many, whom we can rightly deem as the "unhealthy of mind," for the "need" for misery, for death, for loss, mourning, or uncontrolled damage and destruction?

Yes, there are healthy ways to build our cognitive frameworks despite those issues but can we all agree that life presents enough of a challenge of survival itself and that instead of creating issues that lead to any kind of unnecessary suffering we can resolve issues to reduce just that. If we do, we know we certainly don't need to go out of our way to make life even more miserable for anyone.

We must work to reduce misery, so let's do this, please.

In order to do so, we must make ourselves aware of what it is that can be done, act with purpose in our hearts and become more productive, innovative, and filled with aspirations toward progress and then evolve. Let us engage in healing each other rather than harming each other as well as the planetary environment that drives our physiological and neurological health. By doing so and by starting with compassion and solutions to problems, we will quickly find that rather than expending our energies on witch hunts or casting an unnecessary fear of science or technological advancements, or by ceasing with wasting time away by unnecessarily creating enemies, we will be able to make good decisions that help others to enjoy a healthier and happier life, just as we do for ourselves.

Let's look for the good in those around us and give them a chance for heroism no matter where life has led them to at this point in their lives. Let's allow everyone or as many as would like to come along on the journey of promise, to be a part of it and give everyone a chance to participate in creating a legacy worthy of preserving indefinitely.

Many people underestimate the value of educating ourselves on every aspect of science.

In many cases, this is due to religious misunderstandings that no doubt whomever the Deities are that we may believe in would prefer we understood the great Universe they created for us. In other cases, whether or not we have any religion at all, or are divested of spirituality in any form, I would ask you, wouldn't it be rewarding to have the ability to live long and healthy lives, so we too could explore the vast Universe and understand even more with regard to the various sciences, to find the truths that the scientific process can provide, and then share healing, quality of life, and all forms of art with others?

Let us not be driven by limitations imposed upon ourselves by ourselves or by others who are lost in the mediocrity that far too many have chosen for unhealthy reasons, due to their own social environments that have no basis in the improvement of the quality of life, the well-being of others as well as ourselves, or the reduction of misery. Instead, let us forge within ourselves the values of well-being toward others as well as ourselves, the quality of life, and indeterminate longevity which can be the foundation for collective ethics and even morality.

Understanding what we need to in order to evolve includes comprehending and being well-versed in healthy lifestyles. Being aware of and practicing balance in all things, to include balance itself, will increase the enrichment and joy of our sojourn through life because there are so often far too many times that we will need to live life up a bit to do something extraordinary. Yet, sometimes rather than always being active, we may find that we need something as simple as rest and that no matter our capacities something different will be the refreshing aspect of life we need that will in-turn enrich our minds, our lives, and broaden our horizons.

Understanding the principles of our Universe, whether through a short period of focus or through a broad scope of comprehension based on each of the arts and sciences is an amazing way to engage our energies. There is so much we can and yet have to understand. Anthropology, biology, cosmology, curing disease, and providing educational effectiveness and quality are paramount, each of which will help us to navigate the Cosmos in a prepared fashion. We need to understand how our genes work—we need to learn from nature and optimize our physiology and neurology with optimal results rather than wait for random or mixed results.

We also need to search for an understanding of geology, seismic activity, gravitational dynamics, natural weather patterns to their core, and infrastructural integrity—so we can balance the necessary components for the enabling of life, with the environment that protects it and makes it even more enjoyable.

Medical science, biotechnology, neuroscience, as well as improving our prison and correctional systems will raise the collective progress and collaboration that will breed the type of environment necessary for the innovations that will change the course of history into something that we can all be proud of.

Understanding all aspects of particle physics, having a sense of how we react or how we can react—given our psychology, and understanding how the environment we are surrounded with affects our physiological and neurological health will enable what is necessary to share the burden of moving forward and advancing as a civilization toward a promising future.

Developing well-being-related and purpose-driven politics, innovating balanced forms of well-being-based economics and putting to rest controversial issues by creating solutions that afford each person their own individual consent based on beliefs is essential. This is essential for many reasons, but of most importance, honoring personal choice is the strongest prevention of the long-drawn and despicably destructive practice of slavery. With a more objective and proper education and through reaching out to the world with a broader understanding of the social sciences, we will enable the diplomacy needed to allow for an even more collective and collaborative mindset. This will in-turn allow any shared burden of uncontrolled chaos to diffuse and provide a redirection of energies for a more promising purpose. Life's challenges will then become a joy to bear as successful results toward the resolution of many more problems increase our clarity to preserve our Earth.

Understanding the most basic components of the Universe through quantum science and harnessing its power to preserve the lives of our star, our planet, as well as rendering other locations within our Solar System livable and even understanding the roles played by the different creatures that inhabit our Earth and our bodies will all help us to go further than before by paving a promising pathway to the stars with a legacy that is worthy of preserving. We would find that we are bringing and protecting life throughout the Universe, through enabling the lush growth of nature that brings a pleasant quality to life, instead of finding ourselves becoming worse than the most vicious cancers, destroying everything in our wake.

We should never forget to consider preserving all the Earth's and all our Universe's creatures, to include endangered species, as well as anything that may possibly be found from the ancient chasms of the past, all of which will lead to our goals of longevity. Perhaps we can do this through databasing both the DNA and genes of every individual as well as every form of life we find and discover.

Many solutions to longevity, resilience in austere conditions, and answers to an increase in places we can go to and enjoy life lie within the understanding of every gene and every location provided to us in the safety of our own home planet. Perhaps we should consider advancements that lead to instantaneous adaptation to whatever environment we find ourselves in outside of our own planet rather than terraforming these other locations. Perhaps we can build self-sustaining living environments where life would otherwise be non-existent so that no matter where we go, we could bring life rather than take it away. Rather than "cull" the land and leave desolation in our wake we can revitalize it and bring calm, as well as an opportunity for abundance and beauty.

To do all this, we also need to consider space travel and methods for compassionate survival in all their forms.

It is currently possible to preserve full genome sequences of any helpful creature, microbe, bacteria, virus, and even human genetics via DNA databases by engaging in stem cell research and using CRISPR-Cas9 or BE4-like tools. Combined with databasing, automation, understanding and replicating intracellular and extracellular communication, and even nurture, we can preserve all species and populate the Universe compassionately, while building our resilience, our strength, and our wisdom to bring life back to all that we had thought was lost forever. We can create colonies throughout the Universe where sentient and helpful beings dwell, by working together, ensuring our leaders are not tyrants, and where people always know of and have access to the home world they came from.

Due to misunderstandings of purpose and methods as well as, in too many cases, greed and misery—or linear, myopic, and fear-focused thinking, resources are driven to near-depletion or read-off as infeasible in order to drive costs in the direction necessary for the sole outcome of increased gains for those who already have so much. Costs of purposeful developments, advancements, and studies are far too often perceived as skyrocketed despite the priceless value of the results that would be possible and could otherwise be provided to so many more in much less time. Access in so many ways seems extremely limited to those who wish to invest time in research, development, and realization of positive and concrete results and outcomes that could help others—even from trusted scientists, which is a fierce tragedy of its own right. In some ways, heroes do come along to help, but they are assaulted by those who claim to help but do nothing.

Progress, improvements, and even aid to mitigate untold suffering in many ways is diminished to a bureaucratic crawl, all too often. In so many ways, the information that ought to be available to each citizen is not available to highly studied and skilled professionals or engineers. Those who could conduct the studies and build the mechanisms necessary in order to move the resultant cures and solutions to any crisis, or increase the quality of life, or move the many sciences forward to the next level of advancement or improvement, are left uninformed.

Research-rich advances could be moved forward in an efficient manner if enough powerful "superheroes" of economics and information were ethically involved in funding and proliferation of this capacity. In doing this, not only would they as economic and informational curators, geniuses, and benefactors prosper, but they would also be appreciated by those they helped to live healthy, happy, and meaningful lives. Additionally, while they do this, they too would benefit because their workforce would do so much more with an increased ability to work longer, with more ingenuity, and a mind for greater advancements. Loyalty would become second nature due to an assurance, in this manner, of well-being.

We may not need to overhaul our economic systems, but perhaps it would be more advantageous for all—for even the greedy and selfish if we were to have economies that valued life, longevity, and the well-being of others over immediate and materialistic wealth. Quality of life and well-being of those entrusted by our stewardship can provide abundance and prosperity to everyone within our circle of influence, and with so much more to enjoy. There are more than enough unlimited and self-sustaining resources and possibilities for everyone involved to enjoy participation in an enabled, compensated, and even appreciated contribution to the advancement of humanity. Doing this would result in the necessary time and opportunity to explore the Universe and enjoy life while breeding loyalty and self-governance through purpose or clarity-driven innovation.

We all know that lust for power over others, mindless greed, and materialism sickens the very nature of our existence, right down to our physiological and neurological health. So, I ask, why not treasure well-being over merely assumed and thusly compensated wealth. Reasonably and wisely shared prosperity, where privilege with overabundance leads to more education and capacity to be involved among the masses and thereby an increase to quality of life overall, will bring further clarity to our compassion for others. In so doing, we will be able to live knowing that those whom we serve, love us and are leading more joyous lives. No one needs to lose a thing when opening windows of joy to others, instead we can create a healthier, more structured, and abundant world of beauty for all, even as we expand throughout our Universe.

While it is understandable from a psychological perspective the serene, calming, and respectful effect that high-quality leadership offices may imbue, wouldn't we prefer to have that while also having the opportunity to enjoy nice chats with the masses over campfires and nice beverages, while looking up at the stars and sharing experiences from the past and dreams of the future, rather than solely and morbidly ruling over a desiccating and disintegrating populace that is the result of corruption, brutality, toxicity, slander, negligence, misplaced speculation, or greed?

Perhaps we could value education and health via contribution by way of moving our value system to one of innovation and productivity with a purpose of increasing overall well-being rather than one of increasing the necessity of monetary gain for that sake alone—with a system where everything needed is there and unnecessary stressors give way to advancements that both preserve life and the quality of it.

In so many ways, we are so very close to overcoming the "longevity" obstacle and even arriving toward options for personal enhancement, but the well-being and neurological health hurdles seem to evade far too many. Ultimately, we need to preserve life, and in many ways, those that help to improve and preserve life most are the humble people working hard to barely survive. In some cases, they impart a better life for their children or others who they share this mortal existence without notice. This is a form of psychological evolution. In many other unnoticed ways, that which helps us, even more, are stem cells, white blood cells, and other microscopic organisms working in tangent with us and in other completely intriguing ways, they are the largest creatures or cosmic super constructs we know of or have yet to discover.

What I have mentioned about sciences to study was certainly not an all-inclusive list—one need only conduct their own research through readily available resources or dig deeper through lesser-known search engines and university journals, to find amazingly abundant lists and categories of sciences to understand. As we do, we'll no doubt realize that there will always be so much more we have yet to learn and thus, can do.

We can have fun along the journey in our own lives and along the way to advancement in order to achieve our greatest of dreams. With so much knowledge to gain, so much literature and text to pore over, and so much wisdom to impart between each other, we will certainly need to share the burden of large resources of comprehensive information by being transparent about advances in science and health-related developments and by developing large database networks to fuse complex ideas together. In this way, scientists in one area of expertise can see how certain areas of study they focus on can affect other areas of expertise focused on by others who are also well-trained, well-studied, and have the clarity of vision to advance society to a better day. By doing this work we will find an increase in wisdom, which will result in new breakthroughs, and we will find new promise in so many other aspects of life—we will expand our knowledge of and access to all that the Universe has to offer.

Through longevity, kindness, compassion, productivity, and innovation, we can compound upon our wisdom rather than lose untold potential altogether as the breath of life sadly decreases to a stop. To be able to enjoy life with the awesome abilities gained from the collaborative efforts of both understanding and harnessing the powers of the convergence of sciences, we'll need to find many ways—effective ways—to safeguard the many powerful tools produced from those that do not share the goal of well-being for others nor themselves.

In order to safeguard our capabilities, we'll need to make sure that there are processes in place to prevent the effects of disastrous designs by those with malicious intent from drawing us backward and against the ethics of longevity and well-being, as we are enabled to gain access to and interact with these technologies. We need to do what we can to prevent any effort on the part of malevolent individuals in bringing about unimaginable horrors upon all of life as we know it.

Neuroscience can be a strong force for protection, intellect, and wisdom. This science needs to be understood in depth along with psychology, gene therapy, and through many other integrated efforts and technologic tools in order to create mechanisms that will eliminate the potential for disaster as access by individuals that have malicious intent may destroy all of life as we know it.

It is also necessary to understand that in some cases many great advances will actually come from those deemed radically insane, so it is incumbent to allow study by many of whom we fear to still be possible, yet we can likewise create fail-safes to prevent horrible ends from harming anyone. In many other cases, while most advanced civilizations in other distant locations beyond our current scope of knowledge may tend toward being benevolent, during our universal journeys we may also run into very malevolent and highly advanced civilizations whose designs for us are counter to our survival. Thus, the more we know about every aspect of science and how to turn that into the networked powerhouse of the preservation of life, understanding, and its well-being, the more power and promise we will have Universe-wide.

However, when it comes to public safety, great technologies may need control mechanisms until access to disaster mitigation is available to all at a moment's notice. For that, we may need to advance beyond fingerprinting, retinal scanning, and voice identification—and notably so, since none of these security measures can identify intent. Highly sophisticated neuro-scanners with a democratic provision for access may be the answer. Whatever it is that may be the answer here, we know it will take the collaboration of many healthy minds and caring individuals to set the bar high enough for the legacy of humanity to prevail.

We must write the rules. We must not hide away in mediocrity. We, the people, must engage in civil discourse on a daily basis, we must engage in settling matters at the lowest and least escalated level, and then work with our legislators, our executives, and our judicial officials to settle matters at the highest possible levels—perhaps we will need to become the legislators, executives, and judges, with the necessary influence.

How many people must we lose, due to the sluggish pace in innovation and advancement—which is a result of altogether too much litigation, patenting, and negligence of laws toward the well-being of others—before we make the necessary changes?

How much longer must we go on in life, while losing even more precious friends and family members before we discover that advancements wrought by infusing something into our character as we go along, something with a solid foundation, something as simple as *compassion,* will preserve more lives sooner and with fewer costs to everyone affected?

Whatever it is we find ourselves doing or whatever changes we make, we must find ourselves overcoming unnecessary, overly complicated and expensive obstacles, by resolving doubts caused by distractive naysaying about progress so that we can live enriching lives, rather than acquiesce our existence to delusion, corruption, negligence, and eventual non-existence.

That which has no compassion at its core, brings about the fruits of delusion, because only by working together can we overcome the laws of chaos which will overcome humanity unless we overcome chaos itself, by bending it to our will, and by beginning with the spirit of organized unity and kindness. There is much to be said by the simple comparison of the wildfire and the fire which occurs in our fireplace to warm us during cold parts of the year—in the case of negligence in science, chaos becomes uncontrolled and leaves ruthless destruction in its wake.

We must reach out to each other, educate ourselves in so many ways, create safeguards so that if someone is lacking in ethics, or needs the necessary therapies, we can develop the means to overcome their own demise and its unfortunate negative effects, and help them—and by association ourselves.

While there are many individuals with unhealthy minds full of miserable ends for anyone but themselves, ultimately, we know that if we look around or even contemplate the many wonderful people we know, there is no doubt we will find ourselves pondering upon even more countless and amazing examples of human beings and humanity's friends that we do know—who have inspired us toward greatness and with whom we've shared joy with throughout our lives. No doubt there are countless selfless and gracious people and wonderful companions of life whom we would most certainly appreciate having around for the long-haul since it is not just for ourselves, but it is for them also that we evolve.

Living, breathing, and being around long enough with excellent health allows us to not only compound upon our wisdom and gain an understanding of how our bodies work, but they allow us to use those very same resources, to include body, mind, knowledge, capacities, and even dreams, all which nature itself has given us, to improve upon every noble goal and their results.

If we choose to evolve—perhaps nature may be able to take a much-needed break, that no doubt it has enabled us to give it. Evolution has armed us with a sufficient mind to take over for a while. Being the kind of friends to Nature we would appreciate having, ourselves, we can become as the kind of doctor or surgeon we'd prefer as we go into that timeless slumber until restitutions have been made and healing is made possible. However, we will never evolve to the degree with which we need to if we limit ourselves, our knowledge, our wisdom, our experiences, and our analysis based on and due to some illogical stigma, which has no basis in our own or our loved ones' well-being.

Quite cyclically and in quite the interwoven fashion, each of the things I've discussed, when used in their appropriate context, affords us the ability to increase our lifespans, as well as the coherent healthiness of our minds, all in the interest of preserving our history, our consciousness, our wisdom, our art, and our romances, all of which are microcosms of our legacy. If we foster an environment that foments healthy frames of mind, by reducing factors that create an environment of malice and greed, it is possible that even our economy will be more focused on improvement of life, exploration, and discovery.

The value of each individual can be reciprocated. Our health, our minds, and our mindset of healthy behaviors can win the quest of preserving life and exploring the ends of the Universe. Through our shared efforts as mentioned above, we can begin harnessing the scientific capacity to develop systems that allow us to gather the materials flying around dangerously at any planet, via mining asteroids, which have been estimated by many to carry an average value of 20 trillion US Dollars of essential ores, each. Between the orbits of Venus, Earth, and Mars there are at least twenty thousand of these dangerous, yet resource heavy, asteroids that could bombard Earth's atmosphere and destroy all of life and the evolution nature has made through us, setting sentience back again a few million years.

So, why not mine them? Why not pay off all national debts? Why not pay for high-quality healthcare for all? Why not pay for high-quality education for all and even correctional services for all who might need them? Why not readjust our economy to focus on well-being, rather than corruption, power, and greed? While doing so, we should also consider gathering the millions of bits of space-junk, meteors, meteorites, and asteroids between the Earth and Jupiter by developing complex filtration systems with resource processing capabilities throughout our spacious Solar System to eliminate damage caused by these objects. While using those resources to establish bases on the

Moon, Mars and its moons, the Asteroid Belts, the moons of the outer region gas giants, and the dwarf planets and their moons, we also need to factor in and develop systems to ensure gravitational balance and systemic integrity.

Through this primary initiative, when it comes to space travel investment, we can fund an end to national debt, bring an end to poverty, proliferate all that is necessary to ensure healthy physical states as well as healthy mental states, establish effective systems of education, preserve life, and prepare for intergalactic journeys farther than we've ever gone before. This alone would fund the development of worldwide IMCs capable of exploration of the stars and the galaxies, replete with the colonization of many distant worlds, and ultimately the preservation of diversified life and shared history throughout the Universe.

There are also the asteroid belts between Mars and Jupiter, as well as asteroid groupings in large quantities leading and following Jupiter, all of which number at more than one-point-six-million, and again there are countless asteroids sharing the orbits of Neptune and Pluto in the Kuiper Belt, leading almost all the way out to the Oort Clouds which encapsulate our Solar System with comets of water and other materials. All of this can certainly lead to shared prosperity where we can achieve our highest and most amazing of goals, while creating protective systems and shielding for our world and the Solar System itself—but only if the decisions being made aren't done so with minds lost in chaotic delusions of greed and dominion over others with the myopic scope of Earth alone, where its ability to provide sanctuary for life stands in the balance, rather instead these decisions are made to preserve Earth, orbital balance, and the high quality of life and well-being with kindness, compassion, life, longevity, and clarity of mind at the core of the decision-making process—then, as such, they will be done with universal ethics and morality.

If we value each individual and their contributions we will be astounded at the results, as is evidenced in any professional or scientific journal articulating how morale affects ingenuity and innovation—even in workplace environmental management analysis. If we achieve the well-being of those around us more of us will be able to take control of our lives with clarity, our minds with wisdom, our hearts with health, and the results will be positive in every aspect, from innovation, to exploration, to the ultimate reality of harnessing the potential that lies before us as the Universe beckons our assistance and we answer the call, even for its own survival.

To rise to the occasion of long-term existence and discovery, we become greater, and we are now hereby beginning the process of evolving ourselves. We must provide an enriching and overall healthy environment with visionary leadership for our children and even each other. We must give each other opportunities for greatness and then we can go further than before, as we create our pathway to the stars.

We must also keep in mind, that with all we know, learn, or understand, we must never operate solely or only based upon what we "know" now or "believe," but in addition to what we have yet to know or have yet to believe. There is a vast array of exciting journeys ahead of us, based on what we will yet learn to believe, analyze, and provide to each other. We certainly must test the limits of the laws and theories before us, to ensure we are not holding ourselves back from our full potential. While embracing both what we know, and yet will learn, the beauties of the Universe can be beheld by all.

We must value every hard truth and every discovery while ensuring any theory of "all things" is malleable to improvement based on further evidence and facts. With an inner core of a "well-being" mindset that is unchangeable and respect for evidence and truth, wisdom will begin to take a priceless and fantastic shape in our reality, and passion for precision, pride in perfection, balanced with open-mindedness and a broader view will graduate us to a different level of resolution in life which will allow us to have more clarity and an understanding of our place in this world and how we are integrated with everything in it. Our consciousness, our intuition, and its use will help us to harness the powers given us, and the scope of the realities that surround us will provide us with a vision of something amazing, healthy, and full of meaning and possibilities.

A healthy mind is an invaluable treasure because it provides us with a vastly underrated, yet optimally efficient and high-quality intuition or thinking engine. Not many can deny that the ability to conceive of results and follow through on instincts to accuracy and many further advancements in mere seconds is the most favorable approach to solving problems. Many of us can scarcely conceive of any artificial intelligence that will possess the levels of intuition, common sense, and benevolence, combined with the care of others and the focus on the quality of output that a dedicated and honorable human being can.

However, that too may be a nonsensical barrier we've set for ourselves. We cannot fail to establish parameters and develop the type of encoding necessary for a sentient yet humanity-friendly artificial intelligence. Raising AI, Human-Based-Computer-Interfaces, or HBCIs, and clones as our children, rather than forcing them into a reality that perpetuates slavery may bring us advancements that will astound us in positive ways without uncontrolled or negative fallout. We must work together in love rather than live in terror or fear of the unknown.

No matter the obstacles that lie before us, overcoming barriers, discovering new facts, and considering diverse possibilities will give us the capacity to preserve and improve our lives in ways that lead to exploration of our beautiful Universe. We will learn in time that linear thinking or even myopic strategies will never allow us what the intuition of a healthy and complex mind can.

What can we do to achieve collaborative learning and optimal lifestyles? What exactly is it that lies within the intuition of a healthy mind? What exactly is a healthy mind? What is an advanced society? Can we consider ourselves "advanced" if we can't or won't find ways to preserve life, protect our planet and Solar System, and preserve humanity by doing all that we can to actually be there to witness the great changes that can happen, or to pass on our legacy?

This speculative science journey will take you through missions, endear you to scientists and amazing individuals that are near and dear to the heart of where we have come thus far with the dream of understanding what is before us as well as what we don't see. This story will explore some of the struggles prevalent throughout the world today. This journey will propose ideas that culminate in creating a pathway to the stars for an adventure within the Galaxy, our visible Universe, and beyond. This written effort will ultimately provide humanity with a meaningful pathway to the stars along with a few answers to the many questions asked.

Experiences from life, years of research, daily and studious observation, open-mindedly listening to others, conducting analysis of ideas and methods, and ultimately braving the "daring do" of imagination, intuition, and dreams, will help us all to weave this story into reality, getting us much further than alone we could ever have imagined. Although I dare not claim that I know all the answers, nor that my answers are in the perfect order, this story most assuredly is my utopian fantasy with a plausible outcome— if we work together with clarity of purpose and commit ourselves to the well-being of others as well as ourselves, we can gain the Universe, enjoy the beauty of it all, and travel further than before!

Finally, how can we achieve greatness if we only hide our knowledge, bury our wisdom, and forsake the efforts that produce and amplify finely tuned skills and talents, whilst only communicating with "an elite few?"

This story is for everyone, both young and old, for the dreamers, the heart-broken, the down-trodden, and the heroes of life. Stories and ideas such as these are meant to be shared the world over, talked about, improved upon, and innovations had to ensure a beautiful reality for all who truly care while bringing in those who have lost that sense of compassion and passion for the well-being of others as well as us.

There are no enemies here save misery itself. However, this text can be thought of as "man versus himself," or "woman versus herself," or "humanity, society, and civilization versus itself" because within us all lies the beautiful complexity of wisdom and intellect; both are handy tools of powerful action and heroism, if we but choose to use what Nature has given us, to break free, and to fly away from the nest of Nature's amazing yet sometimes brutal evolving processes and to begin to evolve ourselves further, in a way that affords everyone an opportunity to appreciate the bounties and mysteries of the Universe, we just may get there...

~ So long as the leaders of humanity use the wisdom they possess, so long as they seek to gain even more wisdom by ingratiating themselves with us through experience and open dialogue, so long as they seek the intuition of healthy minds and operate with compassion, clarity of vision, and strive to communicate their awareness of the complete picture or genuinely seek help in developing a more clear plausibility of action, their ability to communicate to others will all fall into place with a developed sense of purpose that leads to innovation, action, shared prosperity, and even laughter, love, meaning, well-being and excitement along the way.

Very Respectfully,

Dr. Eliza A. Williams

Ph.D. in: Mathematics, Physics,
Quantum Theory, Biotechnology,
Neuroscience, Psychology, and Law

Author, Dr. Eliza A. Williams, Text: *Pathway to the Stars*, 2010

Appendix – Character Summaries (Spoilers)

Eliza Amber Williams is one of the primary characters in novels *Further than Before: Pathway to the Stars, Parts 1 & 2*, and the booklet series *Pathway to the Stars*. Born July 2nd of 1980, to Dr. Janice Williams, Ph.D. Astrophysics, and Dr. Gale Williams, Ph.D. Neuroscience, after years of tragic experiences and due to diligence on her part, despite all, she is awarded doctorates in mathematics, physics, quantum theory, biotechnology, neuroscience, psychology, and law. She establishes Pathway LLC, grows it to become Pathway Industries, and later, simply Pathway. In 2010, she writes a book, called *Pathway to the Stars*, forms and heads the UP, becomes a United States Representative for the State of Massachusetts in late 2016, is elected as a Senator for the US Senate in late 2018, and then wins the election twice and serves as the President of the US from 2025-2033. She corrals the nations all over the world and establishes the United Allied States, in 2025, and is elected to serve a one-hundred-year term as UAS President. She also commissions Vesha Celeste to head the Intergalactic Mission Contingency, where she sets in motion the building of fourteen gigantic intergalactic spacecraft, twelve are IMC Zonal Command Spacecraft, one is the IMC Command Spacecraft, and one is the UAS Presidential Spacecraft. Eliza leads the way to preserve the Universe and with it all of life with quality, clarity, and a worthy legacy to share.

Yesha Alevtina is Eliza's best friend, the story's principal narrator, Eliza's Pathway Vice President, and she succeeds Eliza as the President of Pathway, from 2015-2022. She was born on July 1st of 1977, to Dr. Yesenia Alevtina, Ph.D. in neurology, physiology, and psychology, and Dr. Stewart Alevtina, who passes away when she was two years old, in late 1979. Raised with Eliza, they become close friends. She serves as Vice President of the US from 2025-2033, and as the US President from 2033-2041, and continues as Eliza's UAS Vice President, with Joanne Gallant serving as the US Vice President.

James Cooper serves as Eliza's right-hand-man. Born on July 9th of 1973, to Mr. and Mrs. Cooper, James was raised with an excellent work ethic and a natural knack for high-level management. He worked for YY Construction Corporation until he was recruited by Eliza, as the third member of Pathway. As such, Eliza, Yesha, and James are the hierarchy of Pathway, the UP, and the pioneers of the technological advancements, the necessary infrastructure, and the leadership to usher in the Golden Space Age, where all of Earth-based civilization is brought in with clarity as to how they can contribute to further advancements while on missions, journeys, and quests. He buys out YY Construction Corporation, renames it Pathway Construction, and absorbs it into Pathway. He is also of romantic interest to Eliza Williams, the Leader of the Golden Space Age—a delay that has nothing to do with entitlement, rather one that is all about selflessness and dedication toward a much higher and loftier goal than the mediocrity of life as it had been batted around by so many arcane social groups and religions at that time. He prefers to serve civilization and will let the romance blossom in time.

Vesha Celeste is born in 1928 and passed away on Christmas day of 2016. During her mortal life, she was a beloved astrophysicist and a dear friend to Eliza and Yesha, two years after her passing, she is the first human to be revived or reawakened after having taken her journey to the unknown. After working with Eliza and many other Pathway citizens, Yesha revives her in 2018, and she begins her training, missions, journeys, and quests to explore the Universe, with the many preparations that come before it. *Pathway to the Stars, Part 1* shares this account. Yesha is appointed by UAS President Eliza Williams to be the Commander of the Intergalactic Mission Contingency, responsible for the delivery of twelve IMC zonal commands, their spacecraft, and their crews, to the various areas of operation. Once complete, she will take her IMC Command Spacecraft, or IMC-Zone-13, Celeste, and travel beyond the limits of the CMB as relative to Earth and Sol. Erin Carter serves as her Vice Commander. She is a close friend of Najem Grace and Jasmine Belle, both of whom worked with her as astrophysicists prior to joining Pathway.

Amber Blythe is born in 1987 and raised with her sister, Sarah, who passed away at an early age due to physiological complications. Amber decided early on that she would become a biogerentologist, a bioscientist, and an expert in physiology. With great goals, she is a major recruit by Eliza in the early days of Pathway LLC. She would go on to find a cure for Erin Carter, a young six-year-old girl, stricken with Hutchison-Guilford Progeria Syndrome. A prominent figure, she develops upgrades to Eliza's biopod machines that optimize both the physiology and the neurology of all who desire to live indeterminate lifespans, so they can either journey on long trips through the Cosmos with the ability to return or stay behind, become well-versed in many sciences, skills, and certifications, gaining experience and wisdom along the way to resolve even greater issues to assist in this great Universal venture and be there when family and friends return from their journeys. She serves as US President Eliza Williams' Press Secretary and is appointed to be the Commander of IMC Zone-04, with TJ Dmitry as her Vice Commander.

Erin Carter is born in 2004 and lived with Hutchison-Guilford Progeria Syndrome for the first six years of her life, yet she had an iron will, a graceful heart, and an unusually intelligent mind. Eliza, Yesha, and James sent Amber to work as a delegate for Pathway on her first mission to rescue Erin and help her parents as well. As a result, she is optimized both physiologically and neurologically and is given an opportunity for even greater than the average life. She uses her newfound skills and abilities to rescue and help heal others. She grows up as a child prodigy and becomes one of the youngest and most prolific Presidents of her time. From 2018-2022 she serves as Yesha's Vice President and from 2022-2029 she serves as the President of Pathway. She is close to Amber, Joanne, Sky, and Vesha, and loves female vocal trance and is commissioned by UAS President Eliza Williams to serve as Vesha Celeste's Vice Commander on-board the Intergalactic Mission Contingency Command Spacecraft, with a secondary mission to fulfill once her duties with Vesha have been completed.

Joanne Gallant is born in 1990, she is a prominent and award-winning musician from 2008-2020, is recruited by Eliza to Pathway in 2019 over a chance encounter at the T.O. in Cambridge and works on several missions and projects before becoming the Pathway Vice President, serving alongside Erin Carter, who is the President of Pathway, from 2022-2029. Joanne, Erin, and Sky have a special relationship. Joanne also has a unique bond with the Presidential Spacecraft AI, Morgan. She has a deep history that if unresolved could spell the doom of human civilization. Once resolved, her future can become fuller, surer, and brighter. During her first decade in Pathway, her primary missions revolve around the development of the Correctional Matrix and the lead HBCI or Sky Taylor. She serves simultaneously as the President of Pathway and as the Environmental Science Officer of the Presidential Command Spacecraft, from 2029-2032.

Sky Taylor, a.k.a. Iridescent Scorpion or Iridescent Angel is born in 2022, full grown, using DNA and Neurological Mapping sharing physiological information and neurological memories with Vesha Celeste. Sky is a living, seemingly breathing, highly capable, optimized Human-like Biological-Computer Interface, or HBCI. She is duly awarded citizenship status due to her service with the FBI and the CIA and becomes one of the most powerful, capable, and benevolent archetypes throughout the known Universe. Everyone who meets Sky feels a unique, special, and genuine bond with her. She looks at Vesha as her biological sister, but in a way as her mother, Eliza, Yesha, and James as her guardian angels, and Erin and Joanne as her closest friends. She is instrumental in the mentorship of humanity, preserving life for the long-haul, and leaving deep beauty in her wake. "Heal, don't harm," is her mantra. Furthermore, she is capable of self-replication, within the scope of what is critical to influence positive social maturity, and to serve the purposes of the IMC. She has created two-thousand daughters and two-thousand-one sons.

Najem Grace is born in 1925 and is biologically the oldest individual serving as a figurehead within Pathway and as an Intergalactic Mission Contingency Spacecraft and Zonal Commander. She became friends with Vesha Celeste and Jasmine Belle, through their shared interest in the stars and in space travel. As an astrophysicist, she was responsible for a lot of the legacy technologies through NASA and finally gets to see countless deep sky objects up close and personal. While introduced in the first book, she will resurface later in the series, as a major character, where we will learn more about her backstory and explore more of our Universe during her journeys through Zone-02.

Jasmine Belle is born in Northern Ireland in 1943, raised as a child in London, learning to speak the Queen's English, and eventually served alongside Najem in NASA, she is an astrophysicist and best friend of Vesha and Najem. Through her service and work with Pathway, she is appointed as an Intergalactic Mission Contingency Spacecraft and Zonal Commander, for Zone-01. We will learn more about her backstory, her missions with Pathway, and her journeys through the Cosmos as the series progresses.

Yesenia Alevtina is born in 1940, and is an immigrant from the USSR, from what is now known as Estonia. She arrives in the US on a diplomatic Visa attending MIT when she meets and falls in love with Stewart Alevtina. She is Yesha's mother and plays a significant supporting role throughout the story. She serves as Representative, filling Eliza's shoes from 2016-2022, and then graduates to Senator, filling those same shoes from 2022-2028. In 2029, she joins Yesha for missions and journeys throughout the Milky Way and beyond on board the Presidential Command Spacecraft, and will become Pathway's President in 2032, when Joanne becomes Yesha's running mate for the 2032 US Presidential Elections.

Shayeena Arezo is born in 2004. Following a tragedy of her best friend, Tayi, at the hands of Jalal, she is protected by her parents and faithful devotee, Khalim. In 2022, she becomes a prominent character, when she and Khalim are rescued during Sky Taylor's worldwide journeys. Sky rescues them on their wedding night from Khalim's once disjointed and malevolent brother, Jalal—throughout Jalal's youth, he has made horrible choices, and is a societal and cultural victim of indoctrination by the oppressive-extremist-hierarchy regime. Meanwhile, Khalim is a noble protagonist, alongside Shayeena. The healing effect from Sky Taylor on Shayeena, Khalim, and even Jalal, help them to raise the bar for the people in their village, in and then throughout Afghanistan, where they eventually contribute to the UAS space program. Shayeena and Khalim are appointed by UAS President Eliza Williams, upon request from IMC Commander Vesha Celeste, to serve with Generals James Wilhelm and Mett Dormer, on board IMC Zone-07, Phoenix, as their Vice Commanders, serving equally. More will be covered regarding their journeys from their rescue, Jalal's experiences through the Correctional Matrix, and their Journeys throughout Zone-07, later in the series.

Ariel Boshka is born in 2003, is rescued in 2022, from a trafficking-in-persons ring during Sky Taylor's worldwide journeys. She and her twelve "sisters" are rescued just in time from the ill-willed intentions of a very grotesque and degenerate group bent on torcher for the sake of entertainment, compensated by highly affluent and very influential members of society. After Sky heals all their minds and their physiology, they all work together to fight the corruption at the core of this horrendous trade, with success. Ariel is heavily involved in these series of missions, joins Amber Blythe's biotechnology team, and is eventually appointed by Eliza to be the IMC Zone-03 Vice Commander, serving on journeys with IMC Zone-03, Lynx, the Commander, General Malinda Jefferson, alongside Lt Generals Hanz Schultz and Laetitia Zemani.

Laetitia Zemani is born in 2004, and in 2022, she and her family are rescued from twenty misguided young men of a Mexican Cartel, named "Los Wiskis," who are in-turn rescued from themselves during Sky Taylor's worldwide journeys. Together, Laetitia, her family, and her new crew of twenty raise the quality of life, rescue and convert cartel after cartel to a life of benevolence, technological developments, and preservation of life, within Chihuahua Mexico, as well as the rest of their country, preparing their country to be a sovereign nation benefitted by the charter of the United Allied States. Laetitia is appointed by Eliza to be Vice Commander of IMC Zone-03, Phoenix.

Malinda Jefferson is introduced into the story as part of the first of the science team members of Pathway LLC, in 2008. She served in NASA as an astronaut and then dedicated her life to youth education. Due to her contributions as a Pathway scientific delegate, she is appointed by Eliza as the IMC Zone-03, Lynx, Command Spacecraft General. She will be a prominent character later in the series and her backstory and further contributions will then be revealed.

Melissa Asher is introduced into the story as part of the first science team members of Pathway LLC, in 2008. She is an expert on the physics and biology of weather. However, she also has a host of capabilities and untold expertise in so many other areas that will be revealed later in the series. Eliza appoints her as the Commander of IMC Zone-05, Pegasus, with Lieutenant General Bobby Gahan serving at her side as her Vice Commander.

Rebecca Knight is introduced into the story as part of the first science team members of Pathway LLC, in 2008. Her unique expertise in orthodontics, dentistry, and later so much more, make her a prominent member of Amber Blythe's biotechnology team. Her contributions, her backstory, her evolution, her missions in Pathway, wins her an appointment for journeys through Zone-06 by Eliza as the IMC Zone-06 Columba,

Command Spacecraft Commander alongside Jeremiah Voltaire, her chosen Vice Commander. Her background story and experiences within the growth of Pathway, along with her journeys through the Cosmos will be revealed later in the series.

James Wilhelm is introduced into the story as part of the first of the science team members of Pathway LLC, in 2008. With a large secret, revealed toward the end of *Further than Before: Pathway to the Stars*, his further missions and journeys will be revealed later in the series. Because of his virtues, his leadership, his creativity, and contributions to Pathway, he is appointed by Eliza as the IMC Zone-07, Phoenix, Co-Commander, on a broad mission that will take place even later in the series.

Mett Dormer is introduced into the story as part of the first of the science team members of Pathway LLC, in 2008. With a large secret, revealed toward the end of *Further than Before: Pathway to the Stars*, his further missions and journeys will be revealed later in the series. Because of his virtues, his leadership, his creativity, and contributions to Pathway, he is appointed by Eliza as the IMC Zone-07, Phoenix, Co-Commander, on a broad mission that will take place throughout the series.

Matzu Kashi is introduced into the story as part of the first of the science team members of Pathway LLC, in 2008. Intrigued by physics since childhood, Matzu takes theoretical physics to a whole new level. Appointed by Eliza as the IMC Zone-08, Carina, Command Spacecraft Commander, he will work alongside the magnanimous and beautiful Lieutenant General Lexi Lancaster. His backstory, contributions, and future missions will be further explored later in the series.

Luís Rodriguez is introduced into the story as part of the first of the science team members of Pathway LLC, in 2008. Once an engineer and an astronaut for NASA, he develops the Q-, A-, F-, and G-drives for the entire Intergalactic Mission Contingency. He works with his crew and many other crews from other zonal commands to ensure a productive, safe, and enjoyable journey through the Cosmos. Due to his dedication to Pathway and the UAS, Eliza appoints him as the Commander of IMC Zone-09, Ara, alongside Lt General Ariela Reina. His backstory, missions, and journeys will be revealed later in the series.

Scarlett Hart is introduced into the story as part of the first of the science team members of Pathway LLC, in 2008. Her dedication in science to environmental systems mixed with her increased abilities, by virtue of her studies and expertise, gained in the Virtual Universe and magnified in the real world make her a prime choice as Eliza's appointed IMC Zone-10, Libra, Commander. Her backstory, missions, and journeys will be further covered and explored later in the series. She will work alongside advanced neuroscience expert, Lieutenant General Christian Coriolis, her Vice Commander.

Yon Forall is introduced into the story as part of the first of the science team members of Pathway LLC, in 2008. He worked with various teams, to include Amber Blythe's biotechnology team, in the race to cure the victims of Hutchison-Guilford Progeria Syndrome. He is a research expert, an expert on longevity sciences, and magnifies many other capacities while gaining more by the virtue of the Virtual Universe and the education centers, experiences, opportunities to gain experience within, and the wisdom gained as a result. His efforts lead to his appointment by Eliza as the Commander of IMC Zone-11, Virgo. Further details of his background, his missions, and his journeys alongside his Vice Commander, Lieutenant General Katya Brightway, will be covered later in the series.

Anastasia Renae is introduced into the story as part of the first of the science team members of Pathway LLC, in 2008. As a theoretical physicist and with many other evolved capabilities, she contributes a lot when it comes to the further application of Eliza's discoveries of cold fusion, maximizing use of the Casimir effect, and bringing quantum entanglement and disentanglement into the foray, as well us commanding use of both baryonic and non-baryonic materials for application on so many levels, and in so many of Eliza's technologies. She is appointed by Eliza to helm the IMC Zone-12, Tucana, Command Spacecraft, alongside the amazing neuroscientist extraordinaire, Lieutenant General Evan Bauer. Anastasia's backstory, missions, and journeys will be covered in greater detail later in the series.

Lucia Tsu is introduced into the story as one of several essential science team members of Pathway LLC, in 2012. She is appointed as General Jasmine Belle's Vice Commander, for IMC Zone-01, Andromeda. Her backstory, missions, and journeys will be covered further later in the series.

Stafford Gaines is introduced into the story as one of several essential science team members of Pathway LLC, in 2012. He is appointed as Najem Grace's Vice Commander, for IMC Zone-02, Gemini. He is good friends with Jeremiah Voltaire and Christian Coriolis. His backstory and journeys will be covered in more depth later in the series.

Hanz Schultz is introduced into the story as one of several essential science team members of Pathway LLC, in 2012. He is appointed as one of three of Malinda Jefferson's Seconds-in-Command, due to the intriguing nature of Zone-03, Lynx, as guided by Sky Taylor and agreed upon by Eliza Williams. His backstory and journeys will be covered in more depth later in the series.

TJ Demitri is introduced into the story as one of several essential science team members of Pathway LLC, in 2012. He is appointed as Amber Blythe's Vice Commander, for IMC Zone-04, Cygnus. His backstory and journeys will be covered in more depth later in the series.

Bobby Gahan is introduced into the story as one of several essential science team members of Pathway LLC, in 2012. He is a pivotal character, working undercover as a Pathway delegate at the T.O. as a coffee connoisseur at the 'Broke Coffee House. He is appointed as Melissa Asher's Vice Commander for IMC Zone-05, Pegasus. His backstory and journeys will be covered in more depth later in the series.

Jeremiah Voltaire is introduced into the story as one of several essential science team members of Pathway LLC, in 2012. He is appointed as Rebecca Knight's Vice Commander, for IMC Zone-06, Columba. He is good friends with Stafford Gaines and Christian Coriolis. His backstory and journeys will be covered in more depth later in the series.

Lexi Lancaster is introduced into the story as one of several essential science team members of Pathway LLC, in 2012. She is appointed as Matzu Kashi's Vice Commander, for IMC Zone-08, Carina. Her backstory and journeys will be covered in more depth later in the series.

Ariela Reina is introduced into the story as one of several essential science team members of Pathway LLC, in 2012. She is appointed as Jose Luís Rodriguez's Vice Commander, for IMC Zone-09, Ara. Her backstory and journeys will be covered in more depth later in the series.

Christian Coriolis is introduced into the story as one of several essential science team members of Pathway LLC, in 2012. He is appointed as Scarlett Hart's Vice Commander, for IMC Zone-10, Libra. He is good friends with Stafford Gaines and Jeremiah Voltaire. His backstory and journeys will be covered in more depth later in the series.

Katya Brightway is introduced into the story as one of several essential science team members of Pathway LLC, in 2012. She is appointed as Yon Forall's Vice Commander, for IMC Zone-11, Virgo. Her backstory and journeys will be covered in more depth later in the series.

Evan Bauer is introduced into the story as one of several essential science team members of Pathway LLC, in 2012. He is fundamental in the research for Eliza's designs for industry and the economy, is an enigmatic neuroscience expert, engaging in passive legacy neural optimizations, through optogenetics, and is appointed as Anastasia Renae's Vice Commander, for IMC Zone-12, Tucana. His backstory and journeys will be covered in more depth later in the series.

Leticia Perrier – Supporting character who works on Amber Blythe's team, while finding a cure for victims of Hutchison-Guilford Progeria Syndrome, using a societally acceptable means, available as a group of the longer-term set of procedures.

Leah B. Gardenia – Supporting character who works on Amber Blythe's team, while finding a cure for victims of Hutchison-Guilford Progeria Syndrome, using a societally acceptable means, available as a group of the longer-term set of procedures.

Dr. Janice Williams – Eliza's mother, born in 1940, Doctor of Physics, and passes away from Leukemia in 1994. Her character may be reintroduced later in the series.

Dr. Gale Williams – Eliza's father, born in 1940, Doctor of Neuroscience, and passes away from Leukemia in 1994. His character may be reintroduced later in the series.

Stewart Alevtina – Yesha's father, passes away from a stroke when he is forty-nine years old and Yesha is only two years and four months old.

Charles Randol – Eliza's boyfriend, upon turning eighteen, while going through her master's degree programs. He passes away during 9/11 but is integral to her choosing "Pathway" as her company's name.

Eugene Duran – Yesha's boyfriend, when Eliza turned eighteen while going through her master's degree programs. He passes away during 9/11 and is also a close friend of Charles.

Anne Brave and Ryan Bloom – Anne is one of James Cooper's original crew members, within the 97, and will be integrated later in the series.

Ethel Grey and Crystal Vala – Ethel is one of James Cooper's original crew members, within the 97, and will be integrated later in the series.

Tom Brooks – He is one of James Cooper's original crew members, within the 97, and will be integrated later in the series.

Joseph Mallory – He is one of James Cooper's original crew members, within the 97, and will be integrated later in the series.

Paul, Molly, and Jaimie Clarke – Paul is one of James Cooper's original crew members, within the 97, and will be integrated later in the series.

Mike, Heather, and Edward Hudson – Mike is one of James Cooper's original crew members, within the 97, and will be integrated later in the series.

Brandy Wayne – The youngest recruit of the 97, who will be integrated into future books within the *Further Than Before* series.

Adam Taylor – He was introduced as a son of Sky Taylor and the lead HBCI on-board the Zone-01 Command Spacecraft, Andromeda, during the final convention, prior to take-off. His contributions will be addressed in more detail in future books within the *Further Than Before* series.

April Taylor – She was introduced as a daughter of Sky Taylor and the lead HBCI on-board the Zone-02 Command Spacecraft, Gemini, during the final convention, prior to take-off. Her contributions will be addressed in more detail in future books within the *Further Than Before* series.

Belinda Taylor – She was introduced as a daughter of Sky Taylor and the lead HBCI on-board the Zone-04 Command Spacecraft, Cygnus, during the final convention, prior to take-off. Her contributions will be addressed in more detail in future books within the *Further Than Before* series.

Bren Taylor – He was introduced as a son of Sky Taylor and the lead HBCI on-board the Zone-03 Command Spacecraft, Lynx, during the final convention, prior to take-off. His contributions will be addressed in more detail in future books within the *Further Than Before* series.

Caleb Taylor – He was introduced as a son of Sky Taylor and the lead HBCI on-board the Zone-05 Command Spacecraft, Pegasus, during the final convention, prior to take-off. His contributions will be addressed in more detail in future books within the *Further Than Before* series.

Cassie Taylor – She was introduced as a daughter of Sky Taylor and the lead HBCI on-board the Zone-06 Command Spacecraft, Columba, during the final convention, prior to take-off. Her contributions will be addressed in more detail in future books within the *Further Than Before* series.

Connor Taylor – He was introduced as a son of Sky Taylor and the co-lead HBCI on-board the Zone-07 Command Spacecraft, Phoenix, during the final convention, prior to take-off. His contributions will be addressed in more detail in future books within the *Further Than Before* series.

Crystal Taylor – She was introduced as a daughter of Sky Taylor and the co-lead HBCI on-board the Zone-07 Command Spacecraft, Phoenix, during the final convention, prior to take-off. Her contributions will be addressed in more detail in future books within the *Further Than Before* series.

Dora Taylor – She was introduced as a daughter of Sky Taylor and the lead HBCI on-board the Zone-08 Command Spacecraft, Carina, during the final convention, prior to take-off. Her contributions will be addressed in more detail in future books within the *Further Than Before* series.

Elaine Taylor – She was introduced as a daughter of Sky Taylor and the lead HBCI on-board the Zone-09 Command Spacecraft, Ara, during the final convention, prior to take-off. Her contributions will be addressed in more detail in future books within the *Further Than Before* series.

Evan Taylor – He was introduced as a son of Sky Taylor and the lead HBCI on-board the Zone-10 Command Spacecraft, Libra, during the final convention, prior to take-off. His contributions will be addressed in more detail in future books within the *Further Than Before* series.

Gwen Taylor – She was introduced as a daughter of Sky Taylor and the lead HBCI on-board the Zone-11 Command Spacecraft, Virgo, during the final convention, prior to take-off. Her contributions will be addressed in more detail in future books within the *Further Than Before* series.

Star Taylor – She was introduced as a daughter of Sky Taylor and the lead HBCI on-board the Zone-12 Command Spacecraft, Tucana, during the final convention, prior to take-off. Her contributions will be addressed in more detail in future books within the *Further Than Before* series.

Tristan Taylor – He was introduced as a son of Sky Taylor and the lead HBCI on-board General Vesha Celeste's Zone-13 Command Spacecraft, Celeste, during the final convention, prior to take-off. His contributions will be addressed in more detail in future books within the *Further Than Before* series.

Tyson Williams – Eliza's childhood dog, who she revives upon James' recommendations that she do so after she, Yesha, and James build the infrastructure for Pathway LLC and before she publishes her book, *Pathway to the Stars*. He is a brindle boxador with golden-red hair mixed with stripes of black, both matching the irises of his eyes. He is integral to Eliza's calm and sense of normalcy, no matter her journeys and the heights of leadership she has attained. He will be within many of the stories that include Eliza and her journeys throughout the Universe.

Ralston Rayna – Vesha's husband, passed away in 2008.

Daniel Rayna – Vesha's son, born in 1951. He has a Doctorate in Physics.

Jillian Yenn – Vesha's daughter, born in 1952, passed away after her battle with cancer in 2014. She had a Doctorate in Astronomy.

Chris Rayna – Vesha's son, born in 1956. He has a Doctorate in Mathematics.

Avery Rayna – Vesha's son, born in 1960. He has a Doctorate in Geology.

Billions if not More – Untold contributions of many heroic and amazing individuals may be told in this or future summaries or may remain untold for many years to come. From Sky's numerous daughters and sons combing the Cosmos with the rest of humanity and all allies who abide by the Principles of Universal Ethics, to all of life from Earth and Sol, to every civilization we ever encounter, bridge ties with, and engage together on, in the greatest quest we have ever known, to preserve the Universe, to let it breathe, to expand and contract ever-so-slightly, so as to sustain life for an indeterminate amount of time, until we find even greater goals. There are many who we thank and for whom we appreciate for their countless contributions, and among their contributions, first and foremost, the critically important steps beginning with kindness.

Appendix – Glossary

*A*s a courtesy to the great minds of those who read this book or who have authored countless significant advances, the author has endeavored to list terms and acronyms introduced or used within this book in their fictional form. While this is not an all-inclusive list, the purpose of this glossary is to educate and inform while providing insight and further context to the story.

A-Drive – Alcubierre Drive – According to theoretical physicist, Miguel Alcubierre, an engine of this type, essentially envelopes the spacecraft within a shielded bubble-like environment, while pulling space in front and pushing space behind, creating an energy-density field that is less than that of vacuum, allowing it to go faster than the speed of light.

ABO – Astrobiology Officer – Each IMC has ten astrobiology officers, who are responsible for maintaining a comprehensive, broad, and full knowledge of every star within their zone, to include stellar, planetary system, and civilization histories existent within. ABOs inform the IMC Commander or associated IMC Zonal Commanders of each detail through Virtual Universe updates and real-world briefs. Much of this information is collated and databased using the advantages of time-dilation, and baryonic and non-baryonic particle manipulation.

Antimatter – British physicist Paul Dirac won a Nobel Prize in 1933, essentially describing that all baryonic matter can carry an opposite charge, i.e., electron vs. positron, proton vs. antiproton, etc. When combined to form antimatter they behave similarly to ordinary matter. When antimatter and ordinary matter meet, they destroy or annihilate each other.

APC – Antimatter Particle Cannon – The UAS Presidential and each IMC Command Spacecraft has four dedicated APC Turrets per sixteen-turret system array. This weapon system is the least likely to be used because it will annihilate its target. If used it would work much like a laser gun, but with a strong and steady stream of antimatter particles based on target composition to destroy and annihilate the target engaged in a deliberate attack against the President or the IMC or its crew that would seriously jeopardize the mission or the lives of the crew. If all measures for diplomatic bridges are exhausted in an effort to protect the integrity of the IMC and its mission, this system will be employed.

Baryonic Matter – All matter that you can currently interact with, within your natural state. According to established sciences, baryonic matter includes protons and neutrons, or more accurate, baryonic matter possesses a triquark configuration. In standard definitions, electrons are excluded, since they are classed as leptons. However, for the purpose of this text and subsequent texts in this literary series, this term is used more loosely to include electrons.

Bioenvironment – Any environment that enables a reasonably healthy life, in the case of Eliza or anyone on her team, this would provide an optimally healthy quality of life, which would augment both the physiology and neurology of organic and sentient organisms and beings.

Biopod – Biopods are pivotal to the story. Eliza finished the first prototypes in 2007 and improved upon them with Yesha. Eliza and Yesha were the first two to use them. James was the third to use one while going through his experiences with Eliza and Yesha. This machine is much like a glowing white perpendicular tanning booth, wherein you lay, it is comfortable, you shut the door, mentally state "1, 2, 3, 5, 20", in which 5 is an example of the quantity of real-world time your body lays in the biopod in terms of minutes, and 20 is an example of your life-like experience in the Virtual Universe time in terms of years. This will interface you, if you so choose, with the Virtual Universe, and in it, not only will you be able to experience life, but you will also be able to interface with the Twelve Database Moons, connect mind-to-mind with others who are there or who have passed through it. You will also have the occasion to learn and improve upon newly acquired skills and abilities through learning, education, experiential-physiological feedback, and achieve complete mind-to-mind and neurological understanding. Ultimately, a biopod is used to heal people both in body and mind, connect people to the Virtual Universe, and optimize any user both physiologically and neurologically.

Casimir Effect – In the story, this is used by Pathway and Eliza in the most robust, fantastical, and hypothetical of ways, especially in relation to control of attractive and repulsive forces. According to established sciences, in 1948, Dutch physicist Hendrik Casimir predicted that physical forces arise from a quantized field. He described this effect suggesting that the existence of conducting metals and dielectrics of one field revises the vacuum expectation value of the energy of a second quantized electromagnetic field. This plays a significant role in the chiral bag model and is used in cutting-edge microtechnologies and nanotechnologies.

CERN – The French acronym translated into American English as, The European Organization for Nuclear Research, is known as CERN, and is a European research group that operates the largest particle physics laboratory, globally. In 2016, CERN generated forty-nine petabytes of data. The most significant purpose behind this and any other similar system is to understand more when it comes to the most essential parts of our physical Universe and beyond. Systems such as these help the realms of theoretical physics graduate to the reality of applied physics and can be used to increase the quality of life, as a whole.

Cold Fusion – In the story, this is the ability to separate electrons, protons, and neutrons into leptons, up quarks, down quarks, and their antimatter equivalents, store them in a safe and stabilized state, to later recompose them into atoms and molecules without nuclear decay. Doing this assists a high quality of life free of danger to a life-friendly environment. Eliza and Yesha discover and use this process at micro and macro levels, in December of 2007.

Commerce Matrix – Developed by Eliza and Pathway, allowing anyone an opportunity to create a business that provides products and services that assist humanity in the quest to preserve life, increase joy, and perpetuate love and an honorable legacy throughout the cosmos.

Convergent Boundary – In plate tectonics, a convergent boundary, also known as a destructive plate boundary, is a region of active deformation where two or more tectonic plates or fragments of the lithosphere are near the end of their life cycle. https://en.wikipedia.org/wiki/Convergent_boundary

Correctional Matrix – Developed by Eliza and Pathway, improved upon by Joanne Gallant and other high-profile scientists, and designed to provide the experiences necessary to bring into application the virtues inherent in Universal Ethics. Law enforcement personnel in this model of governance will now be critical participants in the Correctional Matrix as simulant characters and act as counselors, coaches, mentors, and trainers while helping those who have caused harm others to develop the higher virtues of compassion, empathy, kindness, and love.

Cosmic Microwave Background – The limit of our ability to see the furthest distance relative to our location, due to the speed of light, where the light source or information received comes from radiation known as microwaves. Currently, that location lays at approximately forty-eight-billion light years from us, using math that includes the speed of light, the Doppler Effect, and the speed of the expansion as well as the time since the Big Bang.

CRISPR-Cas-9 – CRISPR, broken out as Clustered Regularly Interspaced Short Palindromic Repeat, or paired up as CRISPR-Cas9 (among other variations or more advanced technologies), is frequently used to refer to a modern genome editing technology that facilitates efficient and precise genomic modifications in a wide variety of organisms and tissues. CRISPR are segments of genetic code comprising of short repetitions of base sequences followed by spacer DNA sections. In the story, this technology is used in a diverse spectrum and paired with more advanced tech that optimizes physiology and neurology.

Dark Energy – According to established cosmological and astronomical scientists, this is an as-yet very-little understood matter that comprises approximately sixty-eight percent of the volume of energy in space. In the book, Vesha and Eliza discover the necessary properties that allow us to harness its power as well as the power of dark matter, jump through space, and control the expansion, such that the universe expands and contracts gently, like the lungs during the breathing of a sleeping baby. As this occurs, the universe will become eternal and provide the energy necessary for the immortality of benevolent, sentient, and living beings.

Dark Matter – This was a subject talked about by numerous theoretical physicists, and astronomer Vera Cooper Rubin brought this to the foray through her diligence, studies, dedication to her understanding of her Universe, and her will to share this information until true substance was brought to the idea of what it was precisely that bound galaxies, superclusters, and the most massive structures in the universe together. Dark matter comprises approximately 85% of the matter in the universe and about 25% of its density. The majority of dark matter is composed of mostly non-baryonic matter.

Database Moon Archive – All information from Pathway and in all recorded human history is stored here both in raw form as well as through abridged narratives created to expand clarity on any subject studied in as full of manner as possible. This archive also has multiple backups of genetic sequences for every species of land, air, or water creature.

Furthermore, all who choose to have their information backed up will be able to return to life in an optimized body similar to that of Vesha Celeste or Sky Taylor, upon their return from the dead. This is also where the Virtual Paradise exists for those who wish to take a break from reality and live in an imaginative reality but still connected with all other people who read-in, living or deceased.

Divergent Boundary – In plate tectonics, a divergent boundary or divergent plate boundary (also known as a constructive boundary or an extensional boundary) is a linear feature that exists between two tectonic plates that are moving away from each other. https://en.wikipedia.org/wiki/Divergent_boundary

DLO – Datalink Operator – There are four DLOs per UAS Presidential or IMC Command Spacecraft, and their responsibility is to ensure positive communication and data transceiving channels between all other assets, communicating to Earth, the Database Moons, other IMC Zonal Assets, and associated leadership, while also diving into theoretical capabilities to improve existing ones.

Education Matrix – This matrix is available via the Virtual Universe as interfaced through a biopod, or if an individual is sufficiently advanced in their training and upgrades, through neural link to Moon Database access, while simultaneously carrying out other personally-willed objectives and abiding by the principles of Universal Ethics. All levels of education from preschool, kindergarten, through high school, college, university, and so on are available here with opportunities for validated and associated programs.

Entertainment Matrix – This matrix is available via the Virtual Universe as interfaced through a biopod and is intended solely as an interface between those two mediums. This is a place where individuals can allow their wild side, their ultra-creative expressions, development of movies, television shows, video games, news, and more to take place where the threshold for observers and participants is consent. Any situation here will allow an individual to acquire a diverse set of knowledge sets from a varied collection of circumstances and upon exit will provide neural identification recognition, positive cognitive frameworking, and experiential updates, upgrades, and optimizations. These experiences can be compartmentalized for reawakening and privacy purposes, or they can be shared with others by using neural links to comb the Moon Databases and deliver neural packages as needed.

ESO – Environmental Science Officer – Aside from IMC Zonal Commander, this is one of the most critical and highest-ranking assignments on board any UAS Presidential or IMC Command Spacecraft, since it deals directly with the full scope of environmental controls and upgrades impacting both life and the mission.

EWO – Electronic Warfare Officer – There are four EWOs on board each Presidential and IMC Command Spacecraft with a mission ensuring we can bridge communications with any potential hostile entity and thwart their effect on any UAS Spacecraft.

F-Core – Fusion Core – The second type of core or the fusion core functions similar to the fusion drive and is a system provided to power every internal aspect of any spacecraft. Onboard every UAS Presidential and IMC Command Spacecraft there are thirty-two fusion cores, each capable of running every function on board and at least two are on board all support spacecraft. On UAS Presidential and IMC Command Spacecraft, there are sixteen available to power all infrastructure and sixteen available to control each of the sixteen turret arrays.

F-Drive – Fusion Drive – This is the third method available for piloting any UAS spacecraft in auto or manual drive, while covering distances that are typically less than thirty light minutes away, with speed and agility. On board, each UAS Presidential and IMC Command Spacecraft are thirty-two F-Drives, each highly capable, yet all are integrated effectively for unforeseen backup purposes. On each UAS Space Force Support Spacecraft there are a minimum of two F-Drives for redundancy, increased capabilities, and as a backup.

Filament – For the purposes of this book series, a filament is a cosmologically connected series of galactic superclusters. They are massive, thread-like formations, with a typical length of 163 to 261 million light-years and a thickness of about 20 million light-years. Dark matter typically attracts baryonic matter, and it is through the structures created through this attraction that filaments are formed. They are the most immense known structures in the universe.

As an example: The Milky Way Galaxy is a part of the Local Group of galaxies (more than 54 galaxies, including Andromeda and a number of dwarf galaxies). The Local Group is an outlying part of the Virgo Cluster of galaxies (between 1300-2000 galaxies). The Virgo Cluster is a part of the Virgo Supercluster of galaxies (comprising about 100 galaxy groups). The Virgo Supercluster is a part of the Laniakea Supercluster (about 100,000 nearby galaxies). The Laniakea Supercluster is a part of the Pisces–Cetus Supercluster Complex, which is a galaxy filament that is about one-billion light-years long and 150-million light-years wide (comprised of sixty superclusters) and is one of the most massive known structures in the observable universe, surpassed by the Sloan Great Wall, the Clowes-Campusano-LQG, U1.11-LQG, Huge-LQG, and the Hercules-Corona Borealis Great Wall, all of which the IMC will explore.

FLA – Fusion Laser Array – For each Turret Array, this consists of four turrets that deliver fusion controlled laser packages to a target, meant to dilate for the breadth of damage and scope for precision - an effort is used to do the least damage to gain control, but can be used to destroy or cripple the target. Can only be used with permission from highest ranking mission commander. For example, if flying with the UAS Presidential Spacecraft, approval must come from President Eliza A. Williams, if flying with General Vesha Celeste and the UAS President is unavailable, then Vesha Celeste, then the Zonal Commander of the IMC Zone they are in.

G-Core – Gravity Core – The third type of core, or the Gravity Core canvases an area within a 100-mile to 1 parsec radial sphere, fuses sensory information with monopole, dipole, and multi-pole magnetism, defies gravity and allows navigation up to light speed and adjusts grounding comfort for personnel with ease, there are thirty-two onboard each UAS Presidential and IMC Command Spacecraft, support spacecraft have at least two, where one can handle everything, the others are backups and networked effectively.

G-Drive – Gravity Drive – Canvases any area within a one-hundred-mile-to-one-parsec radial sphere, fuses sensory information with monopole, dipole, and multi-pole magnetism allowing a spacecraft or optimized living being to defy gravity and navigate up to light speed with ease. On each UAS Presidential or IMC Command Spacecraft, they are located hidden and woven throughout the shielding entirely for maximum control and effect. This is orchestrated in such a manner as to allow attractive forces and redirective forces to avoid any sort of collisions.

G-CCO – Gama Camera Control Officer – There are four G-CCOs on board each UAS Presidential and IMC Zonal Spacecraft. They are primarily responsible for managing all gamma transmissions and activity and providing situational awareness and briefings via the Virtual Universe and in the real world to apprise Commanders and other leaders as necessary.

GCO – Gun Control Operators – There are sixteen GCOs on board each UAS Presidential and IMC Zonal Spacecraft. Each operator is responsible for one of sixteen turret arrays and can manually operate them in accordance with Universal Ethics to preserve life and the mission from destructive forces, and as coordinated with the designated UAS Presidential or IMC Zonal Spacecraft HBCI.

Globular Cluster – A globular cluster is symmetrical and a spherical cluster of older stars, typically revolving around the galactic core as a satellite. The Milky Way Galaxy has about one-hundred-fifty of these types of clusters, and the Sagittarius Dwarf Galaxy and the Canis Major Dwarf Galaxy appear to be donating their globular clusters to the Milky Way. In comparison, the Andromeda Galaxy has approximately five-hundred globular clusters revolving around its galactic core.

GPA – Guided Projectile Array – Four 30-mm Bushmaster armor piercing cannon systems, each consisting of one AGM-176 Griffin Block III C short-long-range missile delivery system, and one GBU-39 Small Diameter Bomb III (SDB) advanced delivery. According to UAS IMC Guidance on weapon systems, the GPA can only be used if in imminent danger or through proper coordination from the UAS Command Spacecraft Leadership, the WSO, and the designated HBCI.

Hanny's Voorwerp – Voorwerp is Dutch for Object. Thus, an Astronomer, named Hanny, discovered an anomaly that, as is fictionally-used in this book, fundamentally breaks the law of the speed of light, where, for example, six-hundred-fifty-million light-years away a small galaxy had passed through a larger galaxy and subsequently when passing above or below the galactic bulge or the central black hole, many thousand light years from the galactic center, a quasar-like action took place, and as observed, the remaining galactic material passing underneath the bulge was wholly ionized or vaporized in a matter of moments, transcending the speed of light and causing the small galaxy to be reduced to primary star formation material.
https://www.hannysvoorwerp.com/3-voorwerp-in-the-pictures/

HBCI – Human-Biological-Computer-Interface – Discussed in detail in chapter 12 of the second novel of the two-part series, "Further than Before: Pathway to the Stars." An HBCI is near human, much more capable, yet merciful, kind, and benevolent. In contrast to how reality may be in other perceived Universes, HBCIs are given full citizenship and rights like any human being and thus work together on the shared mission of preserving life, humanity, living constructs throughout the known universe, and the universe itself. As time goes by, their capabilities and capacities to beautiful and bequeath powers grow.

Health Matrix – Location within the Virtual Universe designed to provide all healthcare needs, unlimited in healthcare provision of needs, but unused by public populations until a full scope of issues were addressed, and resolutions were made upon clarity of options and resultant requests. After the 28th Amendment of the US Constitution, anyone may opt for full optimizations or choose to heal from deadly diseases or complications, but otherwise, keep their physiology intact.

Holoscreen – A projection on any given area providing a three-dimensional near-real digital display and representation for its viewing and sometimes participating audiences. Eliza and other Pathway members demonstrate, dependent upon their training and upgrades, anyone fully read-in has the capacity to broadcast in this way to its audience, locally, globally, or Universe-wide.

Holowardrobe – A digital wardrobe overlay that ties-in to any user's neural identification, their mind, and the compartmentalized wardrobe section of the brain using its wardrobe selections to instantly apply a wardrobe combination to the individual's smartsuit. By the end of 2022, the smartsuit is no longer needed, because physiological and neurological upgrades allow the epidermis to act in the same way as the smartsuit. If a person is read-in, they can think about a tuxedo or ball gown, its details, and like that they are wearing such. After 2025, many fashion designers open up shops within the Virtual Universe where they sell wardrobe codes within their own Commerce Matrices for purchase and personal use, adapted individually.

Hutchison-Guilford Progeria Syndrome – This disease impacts the body's ability to properly process progeria, causing the victim of this disease to age more than eight times faster than the average human being. All humans have progeria, but most process it in an effective manner allowing humans to live between seventy to 100+ years, while the life expectancy of someone Hutchison-Guilford Progeria Syndrome, or Progeria for short, and have a life expectancy of ten to thirteen years. Resolving this syndrome may greatly assist humanity to mitigate the disease of aging. Doctor Michael Fossel is a modern-day leading expert and researcher on this subject. For more information please visit: http://www.michaelfossel.com/

Hyperloop – An elaborate series of airtight and properly pressurized tunnels with a vacuum train that fits in such a way that it can carry passengers going at supersonic speeds.

I-CCO – Infrared Camera Control Officer – There are four I-CCOs on board each UAS Presidential and IMC Command Spacecraft. They are primarily responsible for managing all infrared transmissions and activity and providing situational awareness and briefings via the Virtual Universe and in the real world to apprise commanders and other leaders as necessary.

IMC – Intergalactic Mission Contingency – This consists of the entire unit comprised of all thirteen UAS IMC Command Spacecraft. There is one spacecraft identified on occasion as the IMC, and that is the vehicle that Vesha Celeste and Erin Carter oversee. Vesha and Erin also monitor all the other UAS IMC Command Spacecraft, while traveling through space together. Once an IMC Command Spacecraft is left to its assigned zone, leadership becomes decentralized, where the appointed spacecraft commander oversees their own command spacecraft and their zone. They are still part of the IMC, but direction becomes decentralized within each zone. Each command spacecraft is overseen by one of twelve zonal commanders. For clarity, all IMC command spacecraft are built the same way, with room enough to comfortably house a 1200-

member crew, along with their onboard families and visitors, and all its support components. Each spacecraft is paired with a self-healing nanosystem and a very high-tech and robust Artificial Intelligence system that works congruently with its nanosystem as it protects the life of every being on board and is very much alive and sentient. Its capabilities are countless beyond that, and very sophisticated, as such, each command spacecraft' is given or allowed to choose a name. They have also been given UAS citizenship.

ITER – The International Thermonuclear Experimental Reactor is a transnational nuclear fusion investigation and engineering megaproject and is one of the world's largest magnetic confinement plasma physics experimentation projects.

Jump Gate – In appearance, it is like a sizeable donut-shaped object, depending on size it stands between ten and twenty feet in diameter, serves as a portal for teleportation, and maximizes the inconceivable abilities of quantum entanglement in order to allow a user, multiple users, and/or luggage and supplies to transport from one point in the universe to another in an instant. It is linked to the Twelve Database Moons and can be built and maintained using a cloud of nanos.

Jump Gate Terminal – A series of jump gates arranged for mass transit, much like an airport.

LGA – Laughter Gun Array – There are two laughter gun arrays or LGAs. LGAs are designed as the first step of defense to reduce hostilities in a less hostile yet reasonable manner by increasing humor, no matter the creature, in such a way as to enable a Sky-Model HBCI to heal and create neural links for communication, diplomacy, and shared well-being. Each spacecraft has a system designed to use this system as the first measure against hostilities, so the IMC can return to the mission at hand. The worst that can come of an LGA is laughter-inducing humor.

LHC – Large Hadron Collider – (please see the definition for CERN)

Local Supercluster – This is a grouping of galaxies bound by gravity, all existing in the same Filament, in this case, the supercluster that Earth belongs to (please see definition for filament).

LWO – Linguistic Warrant Officer – There are twenty LWOs on board each UAS Presidential and IMC Command Spacecraft. They are ultimately responsible for communication throughout the universe. They take Sky's and other HBCI's communication bridges and create language reading, writing, speaking, and understanding packages for each crew member with access to them and requisite training available within the Virtual Universe. Due to time dilation and the capacity of operational crew areas to interface with the Virtual Universe on-duty, they also provide near-real-time interpretation and translation services for the purposes of diplomacy, peace, and reduction of hostilities.

Maslow's Hierarchy of Needs – As used in this story, Maslow's hierarchy of needs describes physiological, safety, belonging and love, esteem, and self-actualization as the embodiment of human needs and motivations. In Eliza's manner of leadership, humanity must progress to the point at which the first four needs are met by the environment one is exposed to from birth. Through biopods, Eliza has provided the primary four needs and exhorts people to go forward from there and seek self-actualization through innovation, kindness, and service to toward the purposes of the preservation of the universe and all of life within it.

M-CCO – Microwave Camera Control Officer – There are four M-CCOs on board each UAS Presidential and IMC Command Spacecraft. They are primarily responsible for managing all microwave transmissions and activity and providing situational awareness and briefings via the Virtual Universe and in the real world to apprise Commanders and other leaders as necessary.

Multiverse – The multiverse, in the "Further Than Before" series, is the endless groupings of multiple universes, including our own. More will be discussed regarding the multiverse in further books in this series.

Myostatin – This is a hormone within our cells that as we age causes us to lose muscle mass and density. There are currently studies underway to dampen these effects or reverse them altogether. Patient-Zero for the combined Telomerase and Myostatin Inhibitor Therapies is the President and CEO of BioViva, Elizabeth Parrish. For more information: https://bioviva-science.com/

Nanos or nanos – These are small teleportation and micro-organism healing-capable, highly sophisticated and reprogrammable, self-replicating and self-maintaining microscopic cold-fusion factory robots that can be programmed within the Virtual Universe with the benefits of time-dilation to optimize physiology, neurology, buildings, spacecraft, or any construct conceivable and inconceivable. These are the backbone of the UAS and the IMC and are sometimes referred to as bio-nanos, neural-nanos, nano clouds, and nanosystems.

NAV – Navigation Officer – There are four NAVs on board each UAS Presidential and IMC Command Spacecraft, and at least one for each support spacecraft, with its own AI accounting for one NAV. They are responsible for working with spacecraft commanders, and they are those who are most well-versed on the locations they are in or will be navigating toward. They do most of their work within the Virtual Universe while simultaneously available live and in the real world. They'll send highly robust sensors to every location the Commander or President wishes to jump to, analyze the area within several parsecs, and coordinate with the President and Commanders to make the jump.

Neural Identification – Every individual is truly unique, as such no two minds, human, creature, HBCI, or AI, alike, share the same expressions, personality, or character since their neurology and physiology are always at least a little unique. Since that is the case, early on Eliza found a way to precisely identify shared thoughts from our own through a neurological identification code or a neural identification, and she made it impervious to hacking. With a neural identification, individuals are granted access to anything necessary within Pathway for the purposes and missions inherent within Universal Ethics. A person is also allowed a private compartmentalized region of the mind for personal and private thoughts, so long as actions expressed demonstrate that their minds are keeping within accordance of the principles of Universal Ethics (i.e., common sense: no murders, rapes, emotional or physical abuse, no destruction of others' property, and no theft of others' gains made through honest diligence and intent).

Neurological Optimization – This is one of two structural upgrades to any living being who is optimized via a biopod or via an HBCI, like Sky Taylor. This upgrade is one that affords, at a minimum, an increase in the higher virtues of kindness, compassion, and empathy, as well as clarity of mind toward what one can do to advance civilization and improve upon a legacy worthy of preserving for the long-haul.

At a minimum, a neurological optimization cures an individual of neurological disorders of any form, thereby allowing a person to enjoy life and appreciate others as well as themselves. Finally, an individual will have private or intimate thoughts protected within a specialized compartmentalization of their brain, so long as they do not harm or cause undue consequence to the personal freedoms of others to life, liberty, the pursuit of happiness, and consent. As time goes by anyone can learn countless skills, abilities, and a rich level of education and experiences and find instant recall and amazing knowledge convergence when tackling issues.

Nobel Laureate – This is someone who has been a recipient of the Nobel Prize in any of a number of specific areas, from physics to philosophy. The Nobel Prize has been in existence since 1901, has been awarded on 585 occasions to 923 individuals and organizations. It is named after Swedish inventor, Alfred Noble. The idea is to recognize entities who have demonstrated outstanding achievements within the fields of literature, medicine, physics, chemistry, economics and activism for peace with one of the most prestigious awards.

Non-Baryonic Matter – In this book series, the author loosely coins this as material that, as far as we know now, we have no ability to touch, sense, or have an influence on. Think of every element on the Periodic Table, everything you can see, stars, galaxies, etc., and every particle that impacts our lives, like photons, quarks, and electrons, and so much more as baryonic matter, all else, such as dark matter and dark energy is non-baryonic matter. However, the correct definition of non-baryonic matter includes electrons, photons, and anything other than triquark configurations, such as protons and neutrons. All baryonic matter, which we interact with comprises 4.6% of the universe. Dark matter comprises 23% and dark energy 72%.

O-CCO – Optical Camera Control Officer – There are four O-CCOs on board each UAS Presidential and IMC Command Spacecraft. They are primarily responsible for managing all optical transmissions and activity and providing situational awareness and briefings via the Virtual Universe and in the real world to apprise Commanders and other leaders as necessary.

Octodecillion – This is a substantial number, if one billion is two and one trillion is three, octodecillion is eighteen. Eliza's wealth is in the Octodecillions, and as such, she finances all of humanity's change to a better future. She pays all debts, finances all education and medical care, and provides massive dividends to working taxpayers, and rehabilitation programs for those who were once with little hope beyond a brutal future. With this in play, self-actualization becomes Universal and is done in a manner that expresses respect for life with quality.

Optogenetics – For the purposes of this book series, optogenetics is a method that uses light-sensitive proteins, called opsin, which may have had the most significant overall impact on the evolution of all gifted creatures by developing eyesight. This perhaps coincided with the development of occipital lobes, a system the brain uses to process visual information. By using opsin, neuroscientists, including Dr. Edward Boyden who has taken the lead in neuroscience on overcoming issues such as Parkinson's and epilepsy, can conduct this non-invasive technique to understand and explore the mind more fully. Through this, they have developed a biological method allowing opsin to genetically modify the brain's neurons to effectively turn on or off individual neurons or a region of them by using light to control cells and living tissue.

Parallel Universe – The possibility of other locations similar to ours in almost every way, yet with a more idealistic or dystopian reality. Physics-wise this could be a universe comprised of antimatter, perhaps existing within the great voids throughout space, or it could be a part of the multiverse, that is connected in an altered way with our Universe. (Please see "Multiverse")

Paranoidis Capitalis – The only noted fictional anti-humanitarian group, otherwise known as Anti-Pathway in this book series. This group believes the Earth is flat, that humanity should not meddle with nature, that theoretical physics and modern astronomy is all a hoax and are willing to use violence and brutality to subdue and control the masses. They have little respect for life or anything humanitarian in nature. Their leader unsuccessfully attempts to kill Vesha.

Pathway – This is the organization founded by Eliza Amber Williams, beginning with three members as Pathway LLC, Eliza, Yesha Alevtina, and James Cooper. With all three at the helm, they build the infrastructure necessary to create and sustain life with benevolent sentience, Universe-wide. Pathway LLC becomes Pathway Industries in 2012, and not much later it becomes Pathway. All three are responsible for establishing the Universal Party and, together, they garnered the support necessary to inspire all nations, globally, to form the United Allied States. Due to their preparations, solar-system-wide, humanity catches up through inspiration and clarity of mind, and become ready to span the cosmos with an honorable legacy to share, of a unique and common goal, to preserve the life of the universe.

Pathway Convention Center – The primary physical location, in the US, used to conduct mass real-world meetings and training. This large location is more significant in size than several football stadiums combined. People who are not read-in can drive and park in a massive undercover parking facility using valet service. Those who are read-in can use the hyperloop system and jump gates to arrive there. This center is attached to a vast dormitory for visitors and refugees, and each domicile is more luxurious than a penthouse suite in the most expensive hotels throughout the globe. This is also linked to the labs and other immense facilities within the Melrose, Massachusetts, Campus.

Pathway Covert Campus – Located within many locations throughout Earth and the solar system, this campus is connected through a series of hyperloops and jump gates. This is where the most technologically advanced breakthroughs are made and protected, before proliferation throughout the furthest reaches of the globe and the solar system.

Physiological Optimization – This is one of two structural upgrades to any living being via a biopod or an HBCI, like Sky Taylor. This upgrade is one that affords, at a minimum, being cured of any and all physiological and neurological ailments, diseases, or complications. Receiving the full set of optimizations grants a Pathway citizen the abilities for controlled and heightened senses. Additionally, they will find their cells have rejuvenated to where their physique is as amazing as they would have imagined it being as if they were an optimized twenty-two-year-old. As an individual learns and uses their new skills, such as microscopic, telescopic, and every other type of vision imagined, their powers increase and multiply. If a person demonstrates ill-will toward others, they will begin to return to their natural state and age like normal, upon the option of going through the Correctional Matrix, all can be regained.

Quantum Computing – For the purposes of this book, a quantum computer helps to determine best courses of action in split seconds. This deterministic tool also allows for time dilation to be used when interfaced with and within the Virtual Universe, where individual particles of every variety can be manipulated. As is described throughout the story, there are many more amazing things that can be done, courtesy of quantum computing. In the real world, it is a system that can provide calculations based on quantum bits, or qubits, it is a system that uses entanglement to offer both 0s and 1s, neither, or one or the other, and the result is indeterminate of effect unless the beholder takes advantage of each state of quantum entanglement.

Q-Core – Quantum Core – This name is short for quantum entanglement and disentanglement core, but it is abbreviated to Q-Core. These types of cores, engines, or drives can function at a robust level doing a myriad of multiple tasks at once and can be programmed specifically for the spacecraft itself, similar to the training of the mind of a human or any sentient being. There are thirty-two in each UAS Presidential and IMC Command Spacecraft, with at least two in each UAS IMT Support Spacecraft as well, for essential system redundancy and increased overall capabilities. These are the neural networks of the spacecraft AI and are controlled by the AI such that all systems and functions can be automated with Command Crew Pre-Coordination. This technology is also what is used to teleport the spacecraft, or in other words jump the crew, the personnel, and its cargo to any location of interest, request, and coordination. It is also designed to improve upon environmental conditions for the crew, mend any damage from any source, and so much more. A single Q-Core can run all the functions for the spacecraft indefinitely, but multiple redundancies increase the effectiveness of the spacecraft range of abilities as controlled by the Spacecraft or IMC Commander by nearly a million parsecs.

Q-Drive – Quantum Drive – The actual name was originally going to be quantum entanglement and disentanglement drive. As with the Q-Core, this drive is AI-controlled and can be automated with command and crew pre-coordination. There are thirty-two these engines on board and safely located internally. The navigation packages and sensors are distributed throughout the shielding of all UAS Presidential and IMC Command Spacecraft. At least two are on board all UAS IMT Support Spacecraft. The Q-Drive can teleport or jump any spacecraft from one location to another using pre-positioned sensors to gather information from and to travel to any destination as coordinated by the command crew. There are many other robust abilities and uses for these drives as well.

Quantum Entanglement – This is a quantum mechanical marvel wherein the quantum conditions of two or more entities can be described with reference to each other, even though the separate entities may be spatially separated.

Quantum Sensor or Sensor – These sensors are the primary intelligence gathering devices of all UAS IMC Spacecraft, and among other purposes, they are used to travel from point to point anywhere throughout our Observable Universe.

Real world – "Real world", i.e. 'the real world,' or "real-world," i.e., in 'real-world politics' (grammar dependent), both are used in this story redundantly and in this way to differentiate between what is known and proliferated in a public environment from what is developed and improved upon with Pathway eyes only.

Red Blood Cells – These cells play a vital role in our health by cycling fresh oxygen throughout our bodies, and our blood consists of between forty to forty-five percent of these critical cells. About 2.4 million new erythrocytes are made each second in human grownups.

SA – Spaceborne Analyst – Each UAS Presidential and IMC Command Spacecraft employs two Spaceborne Analysts. These analysts work and coordinate with all CCOs through the SMS, to relay relevant information regarding signals that might impact the crew or mission.

SGA – Stun-Gun Array – Each spacecraft sixteen-turret system has two turrets that are stun gun arrays. Each crewmember carries a small system like an SGA on their hip, and they are designed to temporarily stun a hostile crew member to allow for healing or diplomacy, as needed depending on the entity, by a Sky-Model HBCI. The two turrets are similar, yet much more powerful, and would be used to stun a hostile spacecraft and its occupants to allow crews on any spacecraft in the IMC inventory to buy time for a Sky-Model HBCI to find a way to bridge peaceful communication or jump back to the last identified safe location.

Smartsuit – A suit used from 2008-2022 by many in Pathway that worked as an all-in-one for wardrobe holo-imagery, hygiene, and added protection from the harsh elements in outer space and even on Earth. Circa 2010 an option was given to enter a biopod in everyday clothes and the biopod would convert them into a smartsuit. The intriguing tech revolves around a connection that is exclusive to your neural identification, using a distinct compartment within your mind to apply a set standard of wardrobes for any given occasion to be applied with a unique sense related to the user's creativity and features. This tech eventually allowed fashion designers to sell individual, unique, and tailored wardrobes all encoded explicitly for the user. After 2022 when Sky Taylor is awakened, she develops an upgrade to the physiology of anyone willing that will augment the dermis to allow for a holosuit with much of the same features. In 2024, as an additionally added feature, an individual can allow other linked individuals to see what they want to see you in, laws of consent are observed of course, such that one person might see you walking in a suit that matches the highlights in your hair, while another might see you wearing a bathing suit or a tuxedo, and so on. These stylistic upgrades include everything from hairstyle to makeup to every article of clothing imaginable. Furthermore, each update provides gifted abilities that bring increased ease, enjoyment, and even entertainment no matter the location.

SMS – Spaceborne Mission Supervisor – The SMS oversees all the CCOs and ensures compliance with the principles of Universal Ethics as it relates to the overall UAS IMC Missions.

Sol – For the purposes of intergalactic travel, the known name for the root home solar system of humanity is recognized as Sol, solar-system-wide by 2029.

SS-CCO – Special Signals Camera Control Officer – There are four SS-CCOs on board each UAS Presidential and IMC Command Spacecraft. Their responsibilities lay in all non-standard signals not monitored by any other team or crewmember, to put together Virtual Universe briefs, and to plan aspects of future missions given the latest applicable knowledge sets.

SSE – Spaceborne Systems Engineer – There are eighty SSEs on board each UAS Presidential and UAS IMC Command Spacecraft. Each one works directly with spacecraft AI to mend issues with and develop upgrades and updates for all systems. They are robustly trained in legacy medicine, security systems, and mechanics in the event that physiological optimizations do not work. All crewmembers, their families, and significant others are trained likewise, but SSEs are trained extensively and are able to tackle a wide variety of more significant issues.

STA – Stasis Turret Array – There are two stasis turret arrays in each sixteen-turret package. There is a handgun version for crewmembers to carry that will allow any crewmember to respond to any hostile crew member, group, or perceived threat into a suspended time loop, and to afford a Sky-Model HBCI even more time to heal a threatening mind or individual, so we can get back to the mission at hand. Likewise, the two turrets in the sixteen-turret array will allow more time for a Sky-Model HBCI to heal threatening minds and create neural links for communication, diplomacy, and shared well-being, and is several orders of magnitude more capable in range and scope than the stasis gun.

Stem Cells – These types of cells are unique, in that, at the time of cell division they can become any type of tissue, cell, or organism. Sources of stem cells are bone marrow, fat tissue, and blood donations. Adult stem cells mend any type of tissue and can be turned into somatic cells, while embryonic stem cells can divide and become any tissue, organ, nerve, or cell. Embryonic cell lines and autologous embryonic stem cells generated through somatic cell nuclear transference or dedifferentiation are promising candidates for future therapies.

Subduction Boundary – Subduction is a geological process that takes place at convergent boundaries of tectonic plates where one plate moves under another and is forced or sinks due to gravity into the mantle. Regions where this process occurs are known as subduction zones.
https://en.wikipedia.org/wiki/Subduction

Supercluster – This is a grouping of galaxies bound by gravity, all existing in the same Filament. (Please see definition for filament)

T.O. – Tyson Organic – Eliza Williams' favorite restaurant and one of Amber Blythe's locations of employment, upon meeting Eliza. Eliza purchased and rebuilt this restaurant turning it into a huge 16 square block, multi-department complex, that was 28 stories high on the east end and 22 stories high on the west end, with the original restaurant, the T.O., still attached, shortly after meeting with Amber in 2010. It opened up in 2011, and Eliza secretly paid everyone's bills, along with a few 'thank you' goodies for visitors.

Telomerase – This is a natural enzyme that helps to grow the length of the caps at the ends of our genes, called telomeres, which prevent cellular damage and senescence. Astragalus root has been identified as an organic resource for telomerase. Telomerase therapy is a promising method for rejuvenating cellular health. Studies are still being made for the useful introduction of this enzyme into colonies of cells to mitigate cellular senescence. Doctor Aubrey de Grey is a leading expert on this subject. For more information, please visit: https://www.sens.org/

Telomere – The caps at the end of our genes that shorten throughout our lives and as they shorten, or become too short, our cells become senescent, we begin to show the signs of the disease called aging, and we become susceptible to cancer, heart failure, lung failure, dementia, diabetes, or other life-threatening physiological complications. It is to our benefit to find a way to lengthen our telomeres. Our cancer cells already have, and if it weren't for them killing their host, they would live forever. If we could remove this from the cancer cells and make it possible for our healthy cells to produce telomerase, we could theoretically live forever.

The 97 – James Cooper's original crew, including himself. The 97 was formerly a subsidiary of YY Construction Corp and an endearing Pathway nickname for James' original crew. Eventually, Pathway purchased YY Construction Corp, gifted it to James, who changed it to Pathway Construction, and finally absorbed it into Pathway, providing highly skilled labor and extremely-gifted personnel, all of whom combed the solar system inspecting and quality-controlling the tech cities and all other developments.

Ten Tremilliatrecendotrigintillion –
Ten tremilliatrecendotrigintillion is equal to ten to the ten-thousandth power and is known as the most significant number on Landon Curt Noll's list of the names of the first ten-thousand powers of ten.

Transform Boundary (or Fault) – A transform fault or transform boundary is a plate boundary where the motion is predominantly horizontal. It ends abruptly and is connected to another transform, a spreading ridge, or a subduction zone. https://en.wikipedia.org/wiki/Transform_fault

Twelve Database Moons – A single database moon is approximately three-hundred miles in diameter with robust capabilities of every imaginable sort. Some of its abilities include the use of invisibility and cloaking, renavigation, magnetic and repulsive technologies for all types of matter, frequencies, and radiation as desired to protect life, preserve it, and for self-maintenance. In total, as suggested, there is a network of twelve of them orbiting the Earth, a safe distance beyond the orbit of the Earth's Moon, working congruently with the invisible shielding protecting the Earth and the Moon from any sort of malady that would compromise the ability for these biospheres to sustain life. Each of these database moons has multi-functional capacities, from data storage to the highest tech satellite capabilities and the skills including those of ensuring all communication and transportation can be instantaneous using jump gates and other forms of teleportation. They also redundantly store all types of data, up to and including every matrix of the Virtual Universe, and this includes the Paradise Matrix—a place to go to rest for a given period of time, as yet to be introduced in further books in the series. It carries a backup of deoxyribonucleic acid, or DNA, genetic and neurological identification, and all associated memories, as well as a robust system to protect and preserve all of life, and the solar system, and itself.

UAS – United Allied States – Established July 4, 2025, about seven months following Eliza's first inauguration as US President, as a union of all nations worldwide and throughout the solar system. Together, they all agree to observe the principles of Universal Ethics, and in exchange for seeking self-actualization, the resources requested to meet all other needs are provided.

UAS IMC – United Allied States Intergalactic Mission Contingency – This is a twin to the UAS Space Force mission contingency that is authorized by the United Allied States to span the observable Universe relative to Earth, and beyond. Included within the UAS IMC are the Presidential, IMC Command, and IMC Zonal Command Spacecraft, other Minor Zonal Commands that will be built as observation posts and colonies are developed, and combined they are more capable, powerful, and potent than anything throughout the history of Earth that the globe has ever known, and they are most likely capable of handling anything that the Universe can throw at it. Their goal is to ultimately preserve the life of the Universe by causing it to breathe in and breathe out or expand and contract ever-so-slightly to allow all life within it to live forever. To do this, they must span the furthest reaches of the Observable Universe and beyond, and then create possibilities for endless life wherever there is none and make habitable that which is considered uninhabitable, and while doing so build a Universal Alliance, with similar goals of preserving lives of optimal health, abilities, and quality, while observing the principles of Universal Ethics.

UAS IMC Command Spacecraft (UAS IMC CS) – Thirteen United Allied States Intergalactic Mission Contingency Spacecraft are under the Command of Five-Star General Vesha Celeste, with Four-Star General Erin Carter as her vice commander. They oversee the missions of each of the twelve zonal commanders unfold as all twelve zones are successfully transitioned to have operating headquarters in their various regions and sectors within their zonal areas of operation. Once done, they will travel beyond the CMB relative to Earth in a faraway region of their choosing and set up headquarters and colonies within those regions.

We will learn more about each of the spacecraft AI's names in later books of the series covering each Zone. However, the fourteen original spacecraft of the command series are named as follows: PCS Morgan (Presidential Spacecraft), IMC Celeste (Vesha's IMC CS), IMC Andromeda (Zone-01), IMC Gemini (Zone-02), IMC Lynx (Zone-03), IMC Cygnus (Zone-04), IMC Pegasus (Zone-05), IMC Columba (Zone-06), IMC Phoenix (Zone-07), IMC Carina (Zone-08), IMC Ara (Zone-09), IMC Libra (Zone-10), IMC Virgo (Zone-11), and IMC Tucana (Zone-12).

UAS IMC Constellation Region – United Allied States Intergalactic Mission Contingency Constellation Region – Each UAS IMC Zone has between six and nine Constellation Regions. There is a total of 88 Constellation Regions. Within each Region are Sectors, and then it is divided further until each solar system is named and mapped within the Virtual Universe map.

UAS IMC Environmental Science Officer – Environmental Science Officer – Aside from the UAS IMC Zonal Commander, this is one of the most critical and highest-ranking assignments on board any UAS Presidential or IMC Spacecraft, since it deals directly with the full scope of environmental controls and upgrades impacting both life and the mission.

UAS IMC Zone – United Allied States Intergalactic Mission Contingency Zone – All the Known Observable Universe on out to the CMB relative to Earth has been divided into 12 Zones, UAS IMC Zone-01-12. Zone-13 is the very first zone beyond the CMB relative to Earth.

UAS Presidential Command Spacecraft – Similar to Vesha's UAS IMC Command Spacecraft, or UAS Celeste, and with all the stops and no stops spared, Eliza's spacecraft, the UAS Morgan, travels alongside the IMC setting up Observation Posts, tech cities, and colonies through every sector throughout the Milky Way and call on Sol to send volunteers to meet mission needs prior to releasing the IMC to Vesha.

U-CCO – Ultraviolet Camera Control Officer – There are four U-CCOs on board each UAS Presidential and UAS IMC CS. They are primarily responsible for managing all ultraviolet transmissions and activity and providing situational awareness and briefings via the Virtual Universe and in the real world to apprise Commanders and other leaders in the real world or in the Virtual Universe, as necessary.

Universal Ethics – Simply put, Universal Ethics as established by the United Allied States consists of Preservation of life, Increasing the quality of life, Creating diplomatic bridges and solutions, Honoring personal consent so long as it does not cause undue consequence to the rights of others, Multiplying the capacity of the mind with clarity, Beginning with kindness, Finding a way to contribute to the overall advancement of civilization, and Building a legacy worthy of preserving for the long-haul. Universal Ethics recognizes there is untold and untapped potential in every living being, and that by truly understanding one another and working together we can advance further until we can preserve the life of the universe itself, by allowing it to breathe, by gently causing subtle expansion, retraction, and repeating that cycle continuously, thereby gifting the universe the ability to preserve life indefinitely while advancements and exploration continues on to strengthen and advance our Universe even further, as we simultaneously advance to other Multiverse systems, meeting the same ethics of well-being, health, longevity, and clarity of mind over greed and power, where everlasting joy is gained through wisdom, compassion, and innovation with the intent of well-being for others as well as ourselves. The longer we live in a healthy manner, the more we can compound upon our wisdom and the joy that comes from solutions to issues, together, whether great or small.

Universal Party or UP – The UP was founded by Eliza Amber Williams, in late 2008. Its core values are based on Universal Ethics. The UP was used where every citizen had a viable say in governance with pure democracy via the Virtual Universe throughout the solar system tech cities. This party was established in the US in 2010. Fourteen years following official formation in the US and its subsequent growth to every political office, the first US Presidential race was won in 2024, and changes were made beyond the scope of many in the public eye.

Utopia – "No place" – Considering the unattainable ideals toward raising the quality of life, increasing healthy and youthful longevity, and magnifying the clarity of mind, and creating an environment that can indefinitely sustain those ideals.

Vigintillion – This is a considerably-large number, especially when considering US Currency. If one billion is two and one trillion is three, vigintillion is twenty.

White Blood Cells – As possibly oversimplified and used in the text for the purposes of fiction, story-arch and plot, white blood cells are an essential part of our body's immune system. While there are a diversity of groups and subgroups of white blood cells, as a whole, they make up only one percent of our blood volume. As little as that percentage is, they originate from the marrow and serve to attack infections throughout the entire body. One subgroup, lymphocytes, consists of B, T, and NK cells. Of late, T cells have been studied for possible therapies that might pose positive for cancer treatment and cures. Much is necessary for these studies, still, but ultimately, positive outcomes are contingent upon cell-to-cell flow, communication, et al, for a massive revolution of cures for countless diseases, as well as physiological rejuvenation and upgrades.

Appendix – Artwork & Inspiration

Artwork is provided courtesy of Rade R.
Handover-contract-316684
https://www.freelancer.com/u/redAphrodisiac?w=f:

Author Inspired by the writings and studies of:

Michio Kaku, Lisa Randall, Sam Harris, Thomas Paine, Ron Chernow, Juan Enriquez, Steve Gullans, Alec Ross, Liz Parrish, Michael Fossel, Aubrey de Grey, C.S. Lewis, Jennifer Doudna, Vera Cooper Rubin, Nancy Grace Roman, Jocelyn Belle Burnell, Daisey Robinton, Carl Sagan, Nikola Tesla, Albert Einstein, George Orwell, J.R.R. Tolkien, George R. R. Martin, James S. A. Corey, George Lucas, Ronald D. Moore, Glen A. Larson, Michael Taylor, David Weddle, Bradley Thompson, Michael Angeli, Anne Cofell Saunders, Carla Robinson, Gene and Rod Roddenberry, Harlan Ellison, David Gerrold, D. C. Fontana, Theodore Sturgeon, Jerome Bixby, Norman Spinrad, Robert M Sapolsky, Abraham Maslow, Leonard Wibberley, Sidduhartha Mukherjee, R. Buckminster Fuller, Michael Withey, Paulo Freire, Orson Scott Card, Eunsun Kim, Ashlee Vance, Ian Ridpath, Arthur W. Toga, John C. Mazziotta, Brian Greene, Benjamin Graham, Travis Bradberry, Jean Greaves, Dan Hooper, Kim Shumway, Jason Rothenberg, and of course, Douglas Adams and many others.

Appendix – The Author and His Literary Motivations

Matthew J. Opdyke was born in Stanford University Hospital, California, and adopted at the age of nine. With loving parents who mentored, coached, and trained him, life for Matthew became filled with hope and wonder. Working hard, studying, playing after chores were done, and becoming an Eagle Scout further tempered his young character. He lived in Uruguay for two years, serving as a missionary for a wonderful church, and meeting many delightful people there.

With great respect for the past yet moving on from religion to self-actualized ethics and morals, he found himself as an author for futuristic science fiction and fantasy novels and books that edify and inspire, after retiring from the military with seventeen years of service. Having served in several extra duties and having learned Spanish and some Indonesian, he learned to love the people of this world ten times over. Shortly after meeting his wife, he was able to buckle down and finish his Bachelor of Applied Science in Management, at Peru State College, in Nebraska. Since his youth, Matt has worked at a youth worker at Scout camp, in pear sheds, for retail companies, financial service companies, for a telephone company, construction companies, sheet-metal shops, various odd jobs, served in the US Air Force, to protect, rather than harm, and he has witnessed amazing leadership and, in some instances, where the revolving door was the hallmark, to say the least.

As he pored through biotechnology, neuroscience, and theoretical physics books, Matt began to ask why he hadn't been acquainted with all this information previously, especially if it could help so many. He then developed a story arch and breathed life into numerous characters for his Pathway to the Stars series. Within these stories he tackled intriguing questions, and which took place in a less than ideal environment, much like what we experience daily. He also created a future that we could all hope for and can attain, if we but read, become curious, inventive, and inspire each other, by recognizing the best within each of us. His main refrain is, "be kind, always."

Writer, Matthew J. Opdyke, is moved by our beautiful Universe and all that it has to offer. Encouraged for many years by those who taught, led, and mentored others in a manner that fostered innovation, he endeavors to imbue the main characters of his novels with many unique traits that lead to individual empowerment, as well as overall well-being and meaningful purpose. He believes we can transcend from where we are if we obtain a belief in the preservation of life, our world, and every life-giving system we know throughout humanity. From our phenomenal world, Earth, to our Moon, the planets orbiting our Sun, to the distant stars and the complexity of their networks, Matthew J Opdyke has been curious about the sciences that govern their existence and strengths for decades. Within the many sciences lie the tools that will help us to safely and, in some cases, dangerously and daringly explore it all!

How can we brave the effects of interstellar radiation, so we do not die from its exposure? How can we travel without gravity, so our skeletal structures do not become too porous and cause our frames to be too weak to carry our weight? How can we mimic the effects of gravity, to allow humanity to explore outer space for long periods while maintaining strength and clarity of mind? There are so many questions to ask, and there are many answers. Some answers are considered the "hard truth" based on what we know today. Yet, many ideas seem so far from reality and are considered the fantasies of the mad. Other answers dare to explore possibilities, scenarios, and how humanity can cope in its earnest desire for long-term survival, as we begin to span the Cosmos.

Our Earth is beautiful, and until now, we can only make highly intellectual guesses as to whether this is a genuinely unique setting throughout the entirety of our Universe. Are we the only sentient humanoids (or any "-oid" for that matter), in existence? Is our Earth the only place that can sustain life, allowing the living to walk freely without lethal effects? Are there places throughout our Universe that allow evolution to take place gifting its inhabitants with sentience? If so, do they evolve like many within our world to have a desire to continue to exist? Do they care for other beings quite different from their own?

Given what we understand about physics, matter, and all that we can currently control, manipulate, and use, a lot of what we do for the benefit of both ourselves and those around us allows for the certainty that other worlds much like ours do exist, teeming with life. Can we meet these other civilizations? If we do, will we be able to survive together? How can that be possible? One of the most significant ways to achieve a shared understanding and set of goals is through effective communication, but what if we run into a world of dinosaurs? Will we be able to effectively communicate with them before being ingested? If we could relay positive messages back and forth with well-being at the core, could we also achieve something that equates to shared purpose?

What is one thing that all of life may fear, once they know about it? Is it the "deep freeze" or the vast expansion of the Universe which could be a threat to us all? What can we learn about our Universe to tame what rules it to save it? If we desire to work together to achieve this, will we need to become well-versed in all types of particles and matter, from dark energy to matter, and everything else from baryonic to non-baryonic? What can we do to successfully share our legacy with other civilizations while we learn about theirs? What terrors await us that we can scarcely fathom now? What promise awaits us if we dare to discover more? What could sentience be in comparison to the limits we know in our grand spiral galaxy, versus galactic clouds, elliptical galaxies, and a host of other networks of the like throughout our Universe? How would their environments affect their psyche? What kinds of life can live in the hotter regions that lie within the globular clusters of stars or near a black hole?

Many questions lie at the precipice of humanity's promise toward the future, and these questions are those that Matthew J Opdyke will dare to entertain as time moves forward. Enjoy each character in his stories, within the medium of science fiction, fantasy, and space opera imbued into each e-book, text, and novel. Sometimes he dares to stick to the rules, sometimes he dares to be the mad and deranged lunatic, and at other times he dares to be creative and imaginative to come up with solutions to the issues that affect us today so that we can move forward tomorrow without fear of scientific progression or human evolution!

Appendix – Published Works

Full Compilation (Book and E-Book)
A Cosmic Legacy: From Earth to the Stars
ISBN-13: 978-1733313124
https://www.amazon.com/dp/B07V4W3MW9

Audiobooks:
Further Than Before: Pathway to the Stars, Part 1
https://www.audible.com/pd/B07QZCL87K
Pathway to the Stars: Part 1, Vesha Celeste
https://www.audible.com/pd/B07RX8MGXF
Pathway to the Stars: Part 2, Eliza Williams
https://www.audible.com/pd/B0833BZXVC

Pathway to the Stars (Book and E-Book Series)
Part 1, Vesha Celeste: 978-1726768528
https://smile.amazon.com/dp/B07J2S8LLV
Part 2, Eliza Williams: 978-1729030301
https://smile.amazon.com/dp/B07JK5RD2N
Part 3, James Cooper: 978-1729495131
https://smile.amazon.com/dp/B07K2B5WS3
Part 4, Universal Party: 978-1798511374
https://smile.amazon.com/dp/B07P76VWLP
Part 5, Amber Blythe: 978-1799281108
https://smile.amazon.com/dp/B07PKCHTG4
Part 6, Erin Carter: 978-1091095427
https://smile.amazon.com/dp/B07PXHJ82N
Part 7, Span of Influence: 978-1951321079
https://smile.amazon.com/dp/B081XHLJ36
Part 8, Dreamy & Deep: 978-1951321086
https://smile.amazon.com/dp/B081XK1XN2
Part 9, Allure & Spacecraft: 978-1951321093
https://smile.amazon.com/dp/B081XLG9JV
Part 10, Sky Taylor: 978-1951321116
https://smile.amazon.com/dp/B081XLBL1G
Part 11, A New Day: 978-1951321154
https://smile.amazon.com/dp/B081XNYSL4
Part 12, Alpha Andromedae: 978-1951321130
https://smile.amazon.com/dp/B081XNKNRW

Appendix – Thank you

Thank you, Kim, for your insight, contributing some very inspiring ideas, and mostly for your support through the years. Thank you to my parents who adopted and raised me with wisdom in a new and loving home. May they rest in peace. Thank you to all the heroes who have gone before, and who are no longer with us today, because of their bravery to save those they loved or others who they saw barely living in unjustifiable forms of misery and suffering. Thank you to the many scientists, philanthropists, selfless and truly dedicated teachers who mentor and coach, engineers, creative minds, and data-crunchers, I thank each of you for your never-ending and positive impact on so many, and even on me throughout my life. To the musicians and artists, your music and art inspires the mind and makes thinking possible in a great way. Listed or not, I appreciate art in so many forms.

To all my family and friends, thank you for being upbeat, spending many waking hours pushing my books, getting the word out, providing positive reviews, and overall being kind, loving, and supportive throughout the years. I thank you for listening to me go on about astronomy, biology, economics, management, neuroscience, physics, politics, and so much more until you were blue in the face. The heroes in life among the scientists, the revolutionary longevity science buffs and pioneers, neuroscientists, the theoretical physicists, astronomers, engineers, and legal titans all contributed in your own way.

Ultimately, if we want to get on that pathway to the stars, we all need each other, so, whatever we do, the first step toward a long-term legacy, and one we can embrace and be proud of, begins with simple kindness and love for others. As we search for purpose and meaning in our lives, I believe we will find it in the pursuit of well-being, longevity, quality of life, clarity of mind, and innovation that has an end in preservation of life and bringing life and beauty to places once thought uninhabitable.

Matthew J. Opdyke, Author

For questions, please email:
info@mjopublications.com
https://www.mjopublications.com
https://smile.amazon.com/author/matthewopdyke

Appendix – Farewell for Now

I look forward to hearing from each of you and appreciate any constructive feedback. Please know that this message is intended to be uplifting, thought provoking, and of the most relevant and important you'll have the opportunity to read and pass on to others, but I'll let you determine that. Its focus is on long-term survival of not just our civilization but each of us, you included. If you were moved in anyway by the stories within, please know that your positive review on Amazon, Audible, Goodreads, Barnes & Noble, or any online bookstore will certainly help. Furthermore, if you feel inspired to invent or develop anything based on the technologies shared, feel free to simply email me at mjopublications@gmail.com, and with your permission I will share it on my personal blog. Reading this story and arriving at this juncture means that you are someone who indeed cares about the future of humanity, so therefore, I thank you! Regardless of what I have written, you are defined by you alone and no one else. It's up to us to decide what guides us in life, our ethics, our morals, and more.

Farewell for now...

Very Respectfully,

Matthew James Opdyke

www.ingramcontent.com/pod-product-compliance
Lightning Source LLC
Chambersburg PA
CBHW081137020726

47504CB00009B/1894